Archaeologist and anthropologist Steven Erikson is a graduate of the Iowa Writers' Workshop. His first fantasy novel, *Gardens of the Moon*, marked the opening chapter in his epic 'Malazan Book of the Fallen' sequence and was shortlisted for a World Fantasy Award. The equally acclaimed subsequent volumes are *Deadhouse Gates*, *Memories of Ice*, *House of Chains*, *Midnight Tides* and most recently, *The Bonehunters*. He lives in Victoria, British Columbia.

www.**booksattransworld**.co.uk

REAPER'S GALE

Steven Erikson

BANTAM PRESS

LONDON • TORONTO • SYDNEY • AUCKLAND • JOHANNESBURG

TRANSWORLD PUBLISHERS
61–63 Uxbridge Road, London W5 5SA
a division of The Random House Group Ltd
www.booksattransworld.co.uk

First published in Great Britain
in 2007 by Bantam Press
a division of Transworld Publishers

A CIP catalogue record for this book
is available from the British Library.

ISBNs 9780593046319 (cased)
9780593046326 (tpb)

Addresses for Random House Group Ltd companies outside the UK
can be found at: www.randomhouse.co.uk
The Random House Group Ltd Reg. No. 954009

The Random House Group Ltd makes every effort to ensure that the papers used in its
books are made from trees that have been legally sourced from well-managed and credibly
certified forests. Our paper procurement policy can be found at:
www.randomhouse.co.uk/paper.htm

Typeset in 10.5/12pt Sabon by
Falcon Oast Graphic Art Ltd.

Printed and bound in Great Britain by
Clays Ltd, Bungay, Suffolk

2 4 6 8 10 9 7 5 3 1

To Glen Cook

Acknowledgements

Thank you to my advance readers: Rick, Chris, Mark, Bill, Hazel and Bowen. Thanks also to the folks at Black Stilt Cafe, Ambiente Cafe and Cafe Teatro in Victoria for the table, the coffees and AC access. And for all the other support that keeps me afloat, thanks to Clare, Simon at Transworld, Howard and Patrick, the scary mob at Malazanempire.com, David and Anne, Peter and Nicky Crowther.

Contents

The EMPIRE of LETHER
and its neighbours...

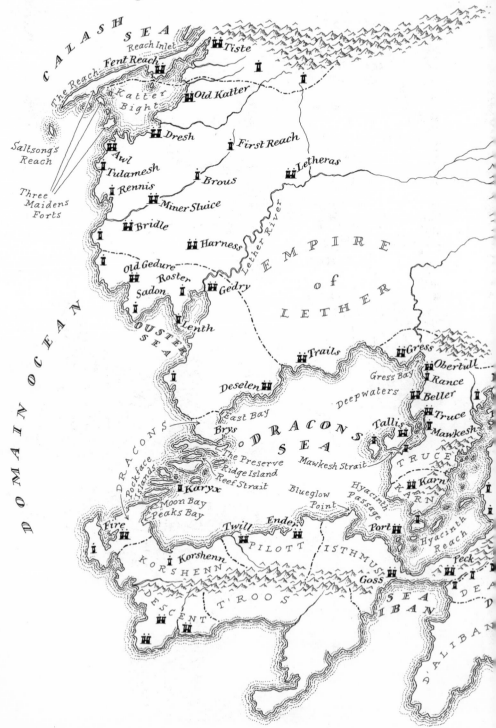

CALASH SEA

Reach Inlet

The Reach · Fent Reach

Tiste

Katter Bight

Old Katter

Saltsong's Reach

Dresh

First Reach

Awl

Tulamesh

Brous

Letheras

Three Maidens Forts

Rennis

Miner Sluice

Bridle

Harness

Lether River

EMPIRE

of

LETHER

Old Gedure

Roster

Sadon

Gedry

Lenth

DOMAIN OCEAN

OUSTER SEA

Trails

Gress

Obertull

Gress Bay

Rance

Deselen

Deepwaters

Beller

East Bay

Brys

ODRACONS

SEA

Tallis

Truce

Mawkesh

DRACONS

Mawkesh Strait

TRUCE

The Preserve

Ridge Island

Reef Strait

Karn

Pockface Islands

Karyx

Blueglow Point

Hyacinth Passage

KARN

Moon Bay

Peaks Bay

Fire

Twill

Ender

Port

Hyacinth Reach

PILOTT

ISTHMUS

Peck

Korshenn

Goss

SEA IBAN

DEA

KORSHENN

DESCENT

T'ROOS

D'ALIBAN

DRAMATIS PERSONAE

THE LETHERII
Tehol Beddict, a destitute resident
Bugg, Tehol's manservant
Shurq Elalle, an itinerant pirate
Skorgen Kaban, Shurq's First Mate
Ublala Pung, an unemployed Tarthenal half-blood
Ormly, a member of the Rat Catchers' Guild
Rucket, Chief Investigator of the Rat Catchers' Guild
Karos Invictad, Invigilator of the Patriotists
Tanal Yathvanar, Karos' personal assistant
Rautos Havanar, Master of the Liberty Consign of Merchants
Venitt Sathad, Rautos' principal field agent
Triban Gnol, Chancellor of the New Empire
Nisall, First Concubine of the old emperor
Janall, deposed empress
Turudal Brizad, ex-consort
Janath Anar, a political prisoner
Sirryn Kanar, a palace guard
Brullyg (Shake), nominal Ruler of Second Maiden Fort
Yedan Derryg (The Watch)
Orbyn 'Truthfinder', Section Commander of the Patriotists
Letur Anict, Factor in Drene
Bivatt, Atri-Preda of the Eastern Army
Feather Witch, Letherii slave to Uruth

THE TISTE EDUR
Rhulad, ruler of the New Empire
Hannan Mosag, Imperial Ceda
Uruth, Matriarch of the Emperor and wife to Tomad Sengar
K'risnan, warlocks of the Emperor
Bruthen Trana, Edur in palace
Brohl Handar, Overseer of the East in Drene

ARRIVING WITH THE EDUR FLEET
Yan Tovis (Twilight), Atri-Preda of the Letherii Army
Varat Taun, her lieutenant
Taralack Veed, a Gral agent of the Nameless Ones
Icarium, Taralack's weapon
Hanradi Khalag, a warlock of the Tiste Edur
Tomad Sengar, Patriarch of the Emperor
Samar Dev, a scholar and witch from Seven Cities
Karsa Orlong, a Toblakai warrior
Taxilian, an interpreter

THE AWL'DAN
Redmask, an exile who returned
Masarch, a warrior of the Renfayar Clan
Hadralt, Warleader of Ganetok Clan
Sag'Churok, a bodyguard to Redmask
Gunth Mach, a bodyguard to Redmask
Torrent, a Copperface
Natarkas, a Copperface

THE HUNTED
Seren Pedac, a Letherii Acquitor
Fear Sengar, a Tiste Edur
Kettle, a Letherii orphan
Udinaas, a Letherii runaway slave
Wither, a shadow wraith
Silchas Ruin, a Tiste Andii Ascendant

THE REFUGIUM
Ulshun Pral, an Imass
Rud Elalle, an adopted foundling
Hostille Rator, a T'lan Imass
Til'Aras Benok, a T'lan Imass
Gr'istanas Ish'Ilm, a T'lan Imass

THE MALAZANS

Bonehunters

Tavore Paran, Commander of the Bonehunters
Lostara Yil, Second to Tavore
Keneb, Fist in the Bonehunters
Blistig, Fist in the Bonehunters
Faradan Sort, Captain
Madan'tul Rada, Faradan Sort's lieutenant
Grub, adopted son of Keneb
Beak, mage seconded to Captain Faradan Sort

8th Legion, 9th Company

4th Squad
Fiddler, sergeant
Tarr, corporal
Koryk, half-blood Seti, marine
Smiles, Kanese, marine
Cuttle, sapper
Bottle, squad mage
Corabb Bhilan Thenu'alas, soldier

5th Squad
Gesler, sergeant
Stormy, corporal
Sands, marine
Shortnose, heavy infantry
Flashwit, heavy infantry
Uru Hela, heavy infantry
Mayfly, heavy infantry

7th Squad
Cord, sergeant
Shard, corporal
Limp, marine
Ebron, squad mage
Crump (Jamber Bole), sapper
Sinn, mage

8th Squad
Hellian, sergeant
Touchy, corporal #1
Brethless, corporal #2
Balgrid, squad mage
Tavos Pond, marine
Maybe, sapper
Lutes, squad healer

9th Squad
Balm, sergeant
Deadsmell, corporal
Throatslitter, marine
Galt, marine
Lobe, marine
Widdershins, squad mage

12th Squad
Thom Tissy, sergeant
Tulip, corporal
Ramp, heavy infantry
Jibb, medium infantry
Gullstream, medium infantry
Mudslinger, medium infantry
Bellig Harn, heavy infantry

13th Squad
Urb, sergeant
Reem, corporal
Masan Gilani, marine
Bowl, heavy infantry

Hanno, heavy infantry
Saltlick, heavy infantry
Scant, heavy infantry

8th Legion, 3rd Company

4th Squad
Pravalak Rim, corporal
Honey, sapper
Strap Mull, sapper
Shoaly, heavy infantry
Lookback, heavy infantry

5th Squad
Badan Gruk, sergeant
Ruffle, marine
Skim, marine
Nep Furrow, mage
Reliko, heavy infantry
Vastly Blank, heavy infantry

10th Squad
Primly, sergeant
Hunt, corporal
Mulvan Dreader, mage
Neller, sapper
Skulldeath, marine
Drawfirst, heavy infantry

OTHERS
Banaschar, the Last Priest of D'rek
Withal, a Meckros Swordsmith
Sandalath Drukorlat, a Tiste Andii, Withal's wife
Nimander Golit, a Tiste Andii, offspring of Anomander Rake
Phaed, a Tiste Andii, offspring of Anomander Rake
Curdle, a possessed skeletal reptile
Telorast, a possessed skeletal reptile
Onrack, a T'lan Imass, unbound
Trull Sengar, a Tiste Edur renegade

Ben Adaephon Delat, a wizard
Menandore, a Soletaken (Sister of Dawn)
Sheltatha Lore, a Soletaken (Sister of Dusk)
Sukul Ankhadu, a Soletaken (Sister Dapple)
Kilmandaros, an Elder Goddess
Clip, a Tiste Andii
Cotillion, The Rope, Patron God of Assassins
Imroth, a broken T'lan Imass
Hedge, a ghost
Old Hunch Arbat, Tarthenal
Pithy, an ex-con
Brevity, an ex-con
Pully, a Shake witch
Skwish, a Shake witch

PROLOGUE

The Elder Warren of Kurald Emurlahn
The Age of Sundering

IN A LANDSCAPE TORN WITH GRIEF, THE CARCASSES OF SIX DRAGONS LAY strewn in a ragged row reaching a thousand or more paces across the plain, flesh split apart, broken bones jutting, jaws gaping and eyes brittle-dry. Where their blood had spilled out onto the ground wraiths had gathered like flies to sap and were now ensnared, the ghosts writhing and voicing hollow cries of despair, as the blood darkened, fusing with the lifeless soil; and, when at last the substance grew indurate, hardening into glassy stone, those ghosts were doomed to an eternity trapped within that murky prison.

The naked creature that traversed the rough path formed by the fallen dragons was a match to their mass, yet bound to the earth, and it walked on two bowed legs, the thighs thick as thousand-year-old trees. The width of its shoulders was equal to the length of a Tartheno Toblakai's height; from a thick neck hidden beneath a mane of glossy black hair, the frontal portion of the head was thrust forward – brow, cheekbones and jaw, and its deep-set eyes revealing black pupils surrounded in opalescent white. The huge arms were disproportionately long, the enormous hands almost scraping the ground. Its breasts were large, pendulous and pale. As it strode past the battered, rotting carcasses, the motion of its gait was strangely fluid, not at all lumbering, and each limb was revealed to possess extra joints.

Skin the hue of sun-bleached bone, darkening to veined red at the ends of the creature's arms, bruises surrounding the knuckles, a latticework of cracked flesh exposing the bone here and there. The hands had seen damage, the result of delivering devastating blows.

It paused to tilt its head, upward, and watched as three dragons sailed the air high amidst the roiling clouds, appearing then disappearing in the smoke of the dying realm.

1

The earthbound creature's hands twitched, and a low growl emerged from deep in its throat.

After a long moment, it resumed its journey.

Beyond the last of the dead dragons, to a place where rose a ridge of hills, the largest of these cleft through as if a giant claw had gouged out the heart of the rise, and in that crevasse raged a rent, a tear in space that bled power in nacreous streams. The malice of that energy was evident in the manner in which it devoured the sides of the fissure, eating like acid into the rocks and boulders of the ancient berm.

The rent would soon close, and the one who had last passed through had sought to seal the gate behind him. But such healing could never be done in haste, and this wound bled anew.

Ignoring the virulence pouring from the rent, the creature strode closer. At the threshold it paused again and turned to look back the way it had come.

Draconean blood hardening into stone, horizontal sheets of the substance, already beginning to separate from the surrounding earth, to lift up on edge, forming strange, disarticulated walls. Some then began sinking, vanishing from this realm. Falling through world after world. To reappear, finally, solid and impermeable, in other realms, depending on the blood's aspect, and these were laws that could not be challenged. Starvald Demelain, the blood of dragons and the death of blood.

In the distance behind the creature, Kurald Emurlahn, the Realm of Shadows, the first realm born of the conjoining of Dark and Light, convulsed in its death-throes. Far away, the civil wars still raged on, whilst in other areas the fragmenting had already begun, vast sections of this world's fabric torn away, disconnected and lost and abandoned – to either heal round themselves, or die. Yet interlopers still arrived here, like scavengers gathered round a fallen leviathan, eagerly tearing free their own private pieces of the realm. Destroying each other in fierce battles over the scraps.

It had not been imagined – by anyone – that an entire realm could die in such a manner. That the vicious acts of its inhabitants could destroy . . . everything. Worlds live on, had been the belief – the assumption – regardless of the activities of those who dwelt upon them. Torn flesh heals, the sky clears, and something new crawls from the briny muck.

But not this time.

Too many powers, too many betrayals, too vast and all-consuming the crimes.

The creature faced the gate once more.

Then Kilmandaros, the Elder Goddess, strode through.

2

The ruined K'Chain Che'Malle demesne
after the fall of Silchas Ruin

Trees were exploding in the bitter cold that descended like a shroud, invisible yet palpable, upon this racked, devastated forest.

Gothos had no difficulty following the path of the battle, the successive clashes of two Elder Gods warring with the Soletaken dragon, and as the Jaghut traversed its mangled length he brought with him the brutal chill of Omtose Phellack, the Warren of Ice. *Sealing the deal, as you asked of me, Mael. Locking the truth in place, to make it more than memory. Until the day that witnesses the shattering of Omtose Phellack itself.* Gothos wondered, idly, if there had ever been a time when he believed that such a shattering would *not* come to pass. That the Jaghut, in all their perfected brilliance, were unique, triumphant in eternal domination. A civilization immortal, when all others were doomed.

Well, it was possible. He had once believed that all of existence was under the benign control of a caring omnipotence, after all. *And crickets exist to sing us to sleep, too.* There was no telling what other foolishness might have crept into his young, naive brain all those millennia ago.

No longer, of course. Things end. Species die out. Faith in anything else was a conceit, the product of unchained ego, the curse of supreme self-importance.

So what do I now believe?

He would not permit himself a melodramatic laugh in answer to that question. What was the point? There was no-one nearby who might appreciate it. Including himself. *Yes, I am cursed to live with my own company.*

It's a private curse.

The best kind.

He ascended a broken, fractured rise, some violent uplift of bedrock, where a vast fissure had opened, its vertical sides already glistening with frost when Gothos came to the edge and looked down. Somewhere in the darkness below, two voices were raised in argument.

Gothos smiled.

He opened his warren, made use of a sliver of power to fashion a slow, controlled descent towards the gloomy base of the crevasse.

As Gothos neared, the two voices ceased, leaving only a rasping, hissing sound, pulsating – the drawing of breath on waves of pain – and the Jaghut heard the slithering of scales on stone, slightly off to one side.

He alighted atop broken shards of rock, a few paces from where stood Mael, and, ten paces beyond him, the huge form of Kilmandaros, her skin vaguely luminescent – in a sickly sort of way –

3

standing with hands closed into fists, a belligerent cast to her brutal mein.

Scabandari, the Soletaken dragon, had been driven into a hollow in the cliff-side and now crouched, splintered ribs no doubt making every breath an ordeal of agony. One wing was shattered, half torn away. A hind limb was clearly broken, bones punched through flesh. Its flight was at an end.

The two Elders were now eyeing Gothos, who strode forward, then spoke. 'I am always delighted,' he said, 'when a betrayer is in turn betrayed. In this instance, betrayed by his own stupidity. Which is even more delightful.'

Mael, Elder God of the Seas, asked, 'The Ritual . . . are you done, Gothos?'

'More or less.' The Jaghut fixed his gaze on Kilmandaros. 'Elder Goddess. Your children in this realm have lost their way.'

The huge bestial woman shrugged, and said in a faint, melodic voice, 'They're always losing their way, Jaghut.'

'Well, why don't you do something about it?'

'Why don't you?'

One thin brow lifted, then Gothos bared his tusks in a smile. 'Is that an invitation, Kilmandaros?'

She looked over at the dragon. 'I have no time for this. I need to return to Kurald Emurlahn. I will kill him now—' and she stepped closer.

'You must not,' Mael said.

Kilmandaros faced him, huge hands opening then closing again into fists. 'So you keep saying, you boiled crab.'

Shrugging, Mael turned to Gothos. 'Explain it to her, please.'

'How many debts do you wish to owe me?' the Jaghut asked him.

'Oh now really, Gothos!'

'Very well. Kilmandaros. Within the Ritual that now descends upon this land, upon the battlefields and these ugly forests, death itself is denied. Should you kill the Tiste Edur here, his soul will be unleashed from his flesh, but it will remain, only marginally reduced in power.'

'I mean to kill him,' Kilmandaros said in her soft voice.

'Then,' Gothos's smile broadened, 'you will need me.'

Mael snorted.

'Why do I need you?' Kilmandaros asked the Jaghut.

He shrugged. 'A Finnest must be prepared. To house, to imprison, this Soletaken's soul.'

'Very well, then make one.'

'As a favour to you both? I think not, Elder Goddess. No, alas, as with Mael here, you must acknowledge a debt. To me.'

'I have a better idea,' Kilmandaros said. 'I crush your skull between

4

a finger and thumb, then I push your carcass down Scabandari's throat, so that he suffocates on your pompous self. This seems a fitting demise for the both of you.'

'Goddess, you have grown bitter and crabby in your old age,' Gothos said.

'It is no surprise,' she replied. 'I made the mistake of trying to save Kurald Emurlahn.'

'Why bother?' Mael asked her.

Kilmandaros bared jagged teeth. 'The precedent is . . . unwelcome. You go bury your head in the sands again, Mael, but I warn you, the death of one realm is a promise to every other realm.'

'As you say,' the Elder God said after a moment. 'And I do concede that possibility. In any case, Gothos demands recompense.'

The fists unclenched, then clenched again. 'Very well. Now, Jaghut, fashion a Finnest.'

'This will do,' Gothos said, drawing an object into view from a tear in his ragged shirt.

The two Elders stared at it for a time, then Mael grunted. 'Yes, I see, now. Rather curious choice, Gothos.'

'The only kind I make,' the Jaghut replied. 'Go on, then, Kilmandaros, proceed with your subtle conclusion to the Soletaken's pathetic existence.'

The dragon hissed, screamed in rage and fear as the Elder Goddess advanced.

When she drove a fist into Scabandari's skull, centred on the ridge between and above the draconic eyes, the crack of the thick bone rang like a dirge down the length of the crevasse, and with the impact blood spurted from the Goddess's knuckles.

The dragon's broken head thumped heavily onto the broken bedrock, fluids spilling out from beneath the sagging body.

Kilmandaros wheeled to face Gothos.

He nodded. 'I have the poor bastard.'

Mael stepped towards the Jaghut, holding out a hand. 'I will take the Finnest then—'

'No.'

Both Elders now faced Gothos, who smiled once more. 'Repayment of the debt. For each of you. I claim the Finnest, the soul of Scabandari, for myself. Nothing remains between us, now. Are you not pleased?'

'What do you intend to do with it?' Mael demanded.

'I have not yet decided, but I assure you, it will be most curiously unpleasant.'

Kilmandaros made fists again with her hands and half raised them. 'I am tempted, Jaghut, to send my children after you.'

'Too bad they've lost their way, then.'

Neither Elder said another word as Gothos departed from the fissure. It always pleased him, outwitting doddering old wrecks and all their hoary, brutal power. Well, a momentary pleasure, in any case.

The best kind.

Upon her return to the rent, Kilmandaros found another figure standing before it. Black-cloaked, white-haired. An expression of arched contemplation, fixed upon the torn fissure.

About to enter the gate, or waiting for her? The Elder Goddess scowled. 'You are not welcome in Kurald Emurlahn,' she said.

Anomandaris Purake settled cool eyes upon the monstrous creature. 'Do you imagine I contemplate claiming the throne for myself?'

'You would not be the first.'

He faced the rent again. 'You are besieged, Kilmandaros, and Edgewalker is committed elsewhere. I offer you my help.'

'With you, Tiste Andii, my trust is not easily earned.'

'Unjustified,' he replied. 'Unlike many others of my kind, I accept that the rewards of betrayal are never sufficient to overwhelm the cost. There are Soletaken now, in addition to feral dragons, warring in Kurald Emurlahn.'

'Where is Osserc?' the Elder Goddess asked. 'Mael informed me that he—'

'Was planning to get in my way again? Osserc imagined I would take part in slaying Scabandari. Why should I? You and Mael were more than enough.' He grunted then. 'I can picture Osserc, circling round and round. Looking for me. Idiot.'

'And Scabandari's betrayal of your brother? You have no desire to avenge that?'

Anomandaris glanced at her, then gave her a faint smile. 'The rewards of betrayal. The cost to Scabandari proved high, didn't it? As for Silchas, well, even the Azath do not last for ever. I almost envy him his new-found isolation from all that will afflict us in the millennia to come.'

'Indeed. Do you wish to join him in a similar barrow?'

'I think not.'

'Then I imagine that Silchas Ruin will not be inclined to forgive you your indifference, the day he is freed.'

'You might be surprised, Kilmandaros.'

'You and your kind are mysteries to me, Anomandaris Purake.'

'I know. So, Goddess, have we a pact?'

She cocked her head. 'I mean to drive the pretenders from the realm – if Kurald Emurlahn must die, then let it do so on its own.'

'In other words, you want to leave the Throne of Shadow unoccupied.'

'Yes.'

He thought for a time, then he nodded. 'Agreed.'

'Do not wrong me, Soletaken.'

'I shall not. Are you ready, Kilmandaros?'

'They will forge alliances,' she said. 'They will all war against us.'

Anomandaris shrugged. 'I have nothing better to do today.'

The two Ascendants then walked through the gate, and, together, they closed the rent behind them. There were other paths, after all, to this realm. Paths that were not wounds.

Arriving within Kurald Emurlahn, they looked upon a ravaged world.

Then set about cleansing what was left of it.

The Awl'dan, in the last days of King Diskanar

Preda Bivatt, a captain in the Drene Garrison, was far from home. Twenty-one days by wagon, commanding an expedition of two hundred soldiers of the Tattered Banner Army, a troop of thirty Bluerose light cavalry, and four hundred support staff, including civilians, she had, after delivering orders for the setting of camp, slid down from the back of her horse to walk the fifty-odd paces to the edge of the bluff.

When she reached the rise the wind struck her a hammer blow to her chest, as if eager to fling her back, to scrape her from this battered lip of land. The ocean beyond the ridge was a vision from an artist's nightmare, a seascape torn, churning, with heavy twisting clouds shredding apart overhead. The water was more white than blue-green, foam boiling, spume flying out from between rocks as the waves pounded the shore.

Yet, she saw with a chill rushing in to bludgeon her bones, this was the place.

A fisher boat, blown well off course, into the deadly maelstrom that was this stretch of ocean, a stretch that no trader ship, no matter how large, would willingly venture into. A stretch that had, eighty years ago, caught a Meckros City and had torn it to pieces, pulling into the depths twenty thousand or more dwellers of that floating settlement.

The fisher crew had survived, long enough to draw their beleaguered craft safely aground in hip-deep water thirty or so paces from the bedrock strand. Catch lost, their boat punched into kindling by relentless waves, the four Letherii managed to reach dry land.

To find . . . this.

Tightening the strap of her helm, lest the wind tear it and her head from her shoulders, Preda Bivatt continued scanning the wreckage

7

lining this shoreline. The promontory she stood on was undercut, dropping away three man-heights to a bank of white sand heaped with elongated rows of dead kelp, uprooted trees, and remnants of eighty-year-old Meckros City. And something else. Something more unexpected.

War canoes. The seagoing kind, each as long as a coral-face whale, high-prowed, longer and broader of beam than Tiste Edur craft. Not flung ashore as wreckage – no, not one she could see displayed anything like damage. They were drawn up in rows high along the beach, although it was clear that that had happened some time past – months at least, perhaps years.

A presence at her side. The merchant from Drene who had been contracted to supply this expedition. Pale-skinned, his hair pallid blond, so fair as to be nearly white. The wind was blasting red the man's round face, but she could see his light blue eyes fixed on the array of war canoes, tracking, first westward along the beach, then eastward. 'I have some talent,' he said to her, loudly so as to be heard over the gale.

Bivatt said nothing. The merchant no doubt had skill with numbers – his claim to talent. And she was an officer in the Letherii Army, and could well gauge the likely complement of each enormous craft without his help. A hundred, give or take twenty.

'Preda?'

'What?'

The merchant gestured helplessly. 'These canoes.' He waved up the beach, then down. 'There must be . . .' And then he was at a loss for words.

She well understood him.

Yes. Rows upon rows, all drawn up to this forbidding shore. Drene, the nearest city of the kingdom, was three weeks away, to the south-west. Directly south of here was the land of the Awl'dan, and of the tribes' seasonal rounds with their huge herds virtually all was known. The Letherii were in the process of conquering them, after all. There had been no report of anything like this.

Thus. Not long ago, a fleet arrived upon this shore. Whereupon everyone had disembarked, taking all they had with them, and then, presumably, set off inland.

There should have been signs, rumours, a reverberation among the Awl at the very least. *We should have heard about it.*

But they hadn't. The foreign invaders had simply . . . disappeared.

Not possible. How can it be? She scanned the rows once again, as if hoping that some fundamental detail would reveal itself, would ease the hammering of her heart and the leaden chill of her limbs.

'Preda . . .'

Yes. One hundred per craft. And here before us . . . stacked four, five deep – what? Four, maybe five thousand?

8

The north shoreline was a mass of grey-wooded war canoes, for almost as far as she could see to the west and to the east. Drawn up. Abandoned. Filling the shore like a toppled forest.

'Upwards of a half-million,' the merchant said. 'That is my estimate. Preda, where in the Errant's name did they all go?'

She scowled. 'Kick that mage nest of yours, Letur Anict. Make them earn their exorbitant fees. The king needs to know. Every detail. *Everything.*'

'At once,' the man said.

While she would do the same with the Ceda's squad of acolytes. The redundancy was necessary. Without the presence of Kuru Qan's chosen students, she would never learn all that Letur Anict held back on his final report, would never be able to distil the truths from the half-truths, the outright lies. A perennial problem with hiring private contractors – they had their own interests, after all, and loyalty to the crown was, for creatures like Letur Anict, the new Factor of Drene, always secondary.

She began looking for a way down onto the beach. Bivatt wanted a closer look at these canoes, especially since it seemed that sections of their prows had been dismantled. *Which is an odd thing to do.* Yet, a manageable mystery, *one I can deal with and so not think about all the rest.*

'*Upwards of a half-million.*'

Errant's blessing, who is now among us?

The Awl'dan, following the Edur conquest

The wolves had come, then gone, and where corpses had been dragged out from the solid press atop the hilltop – where the unknown soldiers had made their last stand – the signs of their feeding were evident, and this detail remained with the lone rider as he walked his horse amidst the motionless, sprawled bodies. Such pillaging of the dead was . . . unusual. The dun-furred wolves of this plain were as opportunistic as any other predator on the Awl'dan, of course. Even so, long experience with humans should have sent the beasts fleeing at the first sour scent, even if it was commingled with that of spilled blood. What, then, had drawn them to this silent battlefield?

The lone rider, face hidden behind a crimson scaled mask, drew rein near the base of the low hill. His horse was dying, racked with shivers; before the day's end the man would be walking. As he was breaking camp this dawn, a horn-nosed snake had nipped the horse as it fed on a tuft of sliver-stem grasses at the edge of a gully. The poison was slow but inevitable, and could not be neutralized by any of the herbs and

9

medicines the man carried. The loss was regrettable but not disastrous, since he had not been travelling in haste.

Ravens circled overhead, yet none descended – nor had his arrival stirred them from this feast; indeed, it had been the sight of them, wheeling above this hill, that had guided him to this place. Their cries were infrequent, strangely muted, almost plaintive.

The Drene legions had taken away their dead, leaving naught but their victims to feed the grasses of the plain. The morning's frost still mapped glistening patterns on death-dark skin, but the melt had already begun, and it seemed to him that these dead soldiers now wept, from stilled faces, from open eyes, from mortal wounds.

Rising on his stirrups, he scanned the horizon – as much of it as he could see – seeking sight of his two companions, but the dread creatures had yet to return from their hunt, and he wondered if they had found a new, more inviting trail somewhere to the west – the Letherii soldiers of Drene, marching triumphant and glutted back to their city. If so, then there would be slaughter on this day. The notion of vengeance, however, was incidental. His companions were indifferent to such sentiments. They killed for pleasure, as far as he could tell. Thus, the annihilation of the Drene, and any vengeance that could be ascribed to the deed existed only in his own mind. The distinction was important.

Even so, a satisfying conceit.

Yet, these victims here were strangers, these soldiers in their grey and black uniforms. Stripped now of weapons and armour, standards taken as trophies, their presence here in the Awl'dan – in the heart of the rider's homeland – was perturbing.

He knew the invading Letherii, after all. The numerous legions with their peculiar names and fierce rivalries; he knew as well the fearless cavalry of the Bluerose. And the still-free kingdoms and territories bordering the Awl'dan, the rival D'rhasilhani, the Keryn, the Bolkando Kingdom and the Saphinand State – he had treated with or crossed blades with them all, years ago, and none were as these soldiers here.

Pale-skinned, hair the colour of straw or red as rust. Eyes of blue or grey. And . . . *so many women.*

His gaze settled upon one such soldier, a woman near the hill's summit. Mangled by sorcery, her armour melded with the twisted flesh – there were sigils visible on that armour . . .

Dismounting, he ascended the slope, picking his way round bodies, moccasins skidding on blood-soaked mud, until he crouched down at her side.

Paint on the blackened bronze hauberk. Wolf heads, a pair. One was white-furred and one-eyed, the other furred silver and black. A sigil he had not seen before.

Strangers indeed.

10

Foreigners. Here, in the land of his heart.

Behind the mask, he scowled. *Gone. Too long. Am I now the stranger?*

Heavy drumbeats reverberated through the ground beneath his feet. He straightened. His companions were returning.

So, no vengeance after all.

Well, there was time yet.

The mournful howl of wolves had awakened him this morning, their calls the first to draw him here, to this place, as if they sought a witness, as if indeed they had summoned him. While their cries had urged him on, he had not caught sight of the beasts, not once.

The wolves had fed, however, some time this morning. Dragging bodies from the press.

His steps slowed as he made his way down the slope, slowed until he stood, his breath drawn in and held as he looked more closely at the dead soldiers on all sides.

The wolves have fed. But not as wolves do . . . not like . . . like this.

Chests torn open, ribs jutting . . . they had devoured hearts. Nothing else. Just the hearts.

The drumbeats were louder now, closer, the rake of talons hissing through grass. Overhead, the ravens, screaming, fled in all directions.

BOOK ONE

THE EMPEROR IN GOLD

The lie stands alone, the solitary deceit
with its back turned no matter the direction
of your reluctant approach, and with each step
your goal is driven on, your stride carried astray,
the path enfolding upon itself, round and round
you walk and what stood alone before you,
errant as mischance, an accidental utterance,
now reveals its legion of children, this mass
seething in threads and knots and surrounded,
you cannot draw breath, cannot move.

The world is of your making and one day,
my friend, you will stand alone amidst
a sea of dead, the purchasing of your words
all about you and the wind will laugh you
a new path into unending torment –
the solitary deceit is its solitude, the lie is
the lie standing alone, the threads and knots
of the multitude tighten in righteous judgement
with which you once so freely strangled
every truthsayer, every voice of dissent.

So now ease your thirst on my sympathy
and die parched in the wasteland.

Fragment found on the day
the poetess Tesora Veddict
was arrested by the Patriotists
(six days before her Drowning)

CHAPTER ONE

Two forces, once in vicious opposition, now found
themselves virtual bedmates, although neither could
decide which of them had their legs pried open first.
The simple facts are these: the original hierarchical
structure of the Tiste Edur tribes proved well-suited
to the Letherii system of power through wealth. The
Edur became the crown, settling easy upon the
bloated gluttony of Lether, but does a crown possess
will? Does the wearer buckle beneath its burden?
Another truth is now, in hindsight, self-evident. As
seamless as this merging seemed to be, a more subtle,
far deadlier conjoining occurred below the surface:
that of the specific flaws within each system, and
this blending was to prove a most volatile brew.

The Hiroth Dynasty (Volume XVII)
The Colony, a History of Lether
Dinith Arnara

'WHERE IS THIS ONE FROM?'
Tanal Yathvanar watched the Invigilator slowly rotating the strange object in his pudgy hands, the onyx stones in the many rings on the short fingers glimmering in the shafts of sunlight that reached in through the opened window. The object Karos Invictad manipulated was a misshapen collection of bronze pins, the ends bent into loops that were twisted about one another to form a stiff cage. 'Bluerose, I believe, sir,' Tanal replied. 'One of Senorbo's. The average duration for solving it is three days, although the record is just under two—'

'Who?' Karos demanded, glancing up from where he sat behind his desk.

'A Tarthenal half-blood, if you can believe that, sir. Here in Letheras.

15

The man is reputedly a simpleton, yet possesses a natural talent for solving puzzles.'

'And the challenge is to slide the pins into a configuration to create a sudden collapse.'

'Yes sir. It flattens out. From what I have heard the precise number of manipulations is—'

'No, Tanal, do not tell me. You should know better.' The Invigilator, commander of the Patriotists, set the object down. 'Thank you for the gift. Now,' a brief smile, 'have we inconvenienced Bruthen Trana long enough, do you think?' Karos rose, paused to adjust his crimson silks – the only colour and the only material he ever wore – then collected the short sceptre he had made his official symbol of office, black blood-wood from the Edur homeland with silver caps studded in polished onyx stones, and gestured with it in the direction of the door.

Tanal bowed then led the way out into the corridor, to the broad stairs where they descended to the main floor, then strode through the double doors and out into the compound.

The row of prisoners had been positioned in full sunlight, near the west wall of the enclosure. They had been taken from their cells a bell before dawn and it was now shortly past midday. Lack of water and food, and this morning's searing heat, combined with brutal sessions of questioning over the past week, had resulted in more than half of the eighteen detainees losing consciousness.

Tanal saw the Invigilator's frown upon seeing the motionless bodies collapsed in their chains.

The Tiste Edur liaison, Bruthen Trana of the Den-Ratha tribe, was standing in the shade, more or less across from the prisoners, and the tall, silent figure slowly turned as Tanal and Karos approached.

'Bruthen Trana, most welcome,' said Karos Invictad. 'You are well?'

'Let us proceed, Invigilator,' the grey-skinned warrior said.

'At once. If you will accompany me, we can survey each prisoner assembled here. The specific cases—'

'I have no interest in approaching them any closer than I am now,' Bruthen said. 'They are fouled in their own wastes and there is scant breeze in this enclosure.'

Karos smiled. 'I understand, Bruthen.' He leaned his sceptre against a shoulder then faced the row of detainees. 'We need not approach, as you say. I will begin with the one to the far left, then—'

'Unconscious or dead?'

'Well, at this distance, who can say?'

Noting the Edur's scowl, Tanal bowed to Bruthen and Karos and walked the fifteen paces to the line. He crouched to examine the prone figure, then straightened. 'He lives.'

'Then awaken him!' Karos commanded. His voice, when raised,

16

became shrill, enough to make a foolish listener wince – foolish, that is, if the Invigilator was witness to that instinctive reaction. Such careless errors happened but once.

Tanal kicked at the prisoner until the man managed a dry, rasping sob. 'On your feet, traitor,' Tanal said in a quiet tone. 'The Invigilator demands it. Stand, or I will begin breaking bones in that pathetic sack you call a body.'

He watched as the prisoner struggled upright.

'Water, please—'

'Not another word from you. Straighten up, face your crimes. You are Letherii, aren't you? Show our Edur guest the meaning of that.'

Tanal then made his way back to Karos and Bruthen. The Invigilator had begun speaking. '. . . known associations with dissenting elements in the Physicians' College – he has admitted as much. Although no specific crimes can be laid at this man's feet, it is clear that—'

'The next one,' Bruthen Trana cut in.

Karos closed his mouth, then smiled without showing his teeth. 'Of course. The next is a poet, who wrote and distributed a call for revolution. He denies nothing and indeed, you can see his stoic defiance even from here.'

'And the one beside him?'

'The proprietor of an inn, the tavern of which was frequented by undesirable elements – disenchanted soldiers, in fact – and two of them are among these detainees. We were informed of the sedition by an honourable whore—'

'Honourable whore, Invigilator?' The Edur half smiled.

Karos blinked. 'Why, yes, Bruthen Trana.'

'Because she informed on an innkeeper.'

'An innkeeper engaged in treason—'

'Demanding too high a cut of her earnings, more likely. Go on, and please, keep your descriptions of the crimes brief.'

'Of course,' Karos Invictad said, the sceptre gently tapping on his soft shoulder, like a baton measuring a slow march.

Tanal, standing at his commander's side, remained at attention whilst the Invigilator resumed his report of the specific transgressions of these Letherii. The eighteen prisoners were fair representations of the more than three hundred chained in cells belowground. A decent number of arrests for this week, Tanal reflected. And for the most egregious traitors among them waited the Drownings. Of the three hundred and twenty or so, a third were destined to walk the canal bottom, burdened beneath crushing weights. Bookmakers were complaining these days, since no-one ever survived the ordeal any more. Of course, they did not complain too loudly, since the true agitators among them risked their own Drowning – it had taken

17

but a few of those early on to mute the protestations among the rest.

This was a detail Tanal had come to appreciate, one of Karos Invictad's perfect laws of compulsion and control, emphasized again and again in the vast treatise the Invigilator was penning on the subject most dear to his heart. *Take any segment of population, impose strict yet clear definitions on their particular characteristics, then target them for compliance. Bribe the weak to expose the strong. Kill the strong, and the rest are yours. Move on to the next segment.*

Bookmakers had been easy targets, since few people liked them – especially inveterate gamblers, and of those there were more and more with every day that passed.

Karos Invictad concluded his litany. Bruthen Trana nodded, then turned and left the compound.

As soon as he was gone from sight, the Invigilator faced Tanal. 'An embarrassment,' he said. 'Those unconscious ones.'

'Yes sir.'

'A change of heads on the outer wall.'

'At once, sir.'

'Now, Tanal Yathvanar, before anything else, you must come with me. It will take but a moment, then you can return to the tasks at hand.'

They walked back into the building, the Invigilator's short steps forcing Tanal to slow up again and again as they made their way to Karos's office.

The most powerful man next to the Emperor himself took his place once more behind the desk. He picked up the cage of bronze pins, shifted a dozen or so in a flurry of precise moves, and the puzzle collapsed flat. Karos Invictad smiled across at Tanal, then flung the object onto the desk. 'Despatch a missive to Senorbo in Bluerose. Inform him of the time required for me to find a solution, then add, from me to him, that I fear he is losing his touch.'

'Yes, sir.'

Karos Invictad reached out for a scroll. 'Now, what was our agreed percentage on my interest in the Inn of the Belly-up Snake?'

'I believe Rautos indicated forty-five, sir.'

'Good. Even so, I believe a meeting is in order with the Master of the Liberty Consign. Later this week will do. For all our takings of late, we still possess a strange paucity in actual coin, and I want to know why.'

'Sir, you know Rautos Hivanar's suspicions on that matter.'

'Vaguely. He will be pleased to learn I am now prepared to listen more closely to said suspicions. Thus, two issues on the agenda. Schedule the meeting for a bell's duration. Oh, and one last thing, Tanal.'

'Sir?'

'Bruthen Trana. These weekly visits. I want to know, is he compelled? Is this some Edur form of royal disaffection or punishment? Or are the bastards truly interested in what we're up to? Bruthen makes no comment, ever. He does not even ask what punishments follow our judgements. Furthermore, his rude impatience tires me. It may be worth our while to investigate him.'

Tanal's brows rose. 'Investigate a Tiste Edur?'

'Quietly, of course. Granted, they ever give us the appearance of unquestioning loyalty, but I cannot help but wonder if they truly are immune to sedition among their own kind.'

'Even if they aren't, sir, respectfully, are the Patriotists the right organization—'

'The Patriotists, Tanal Yathvanar,' said Karos sharply, 'possess the imperial charter to police the empire. In that charter no distinction is made between Edur and Letherii, only between the loyal and the disloyal.'

'Yes sir.'

'Now, I believe you have tasks awaiting you.'

Tanal Yathvanar bowed, then strode from the office.

The estate dominated a shelf of land on the north bank of Lether River, four streets west of Quillas Canal. Stepped walls marking its boundaries made their way down the bank, extending out into the water – on posts to ease the current's tug – more than two boat-lengths. Just beyond rose two mooring poles. There had been flooding this season. An infrequent occurrence in the past century, Rautos Hivanar noted as he leafed through the Estate Compendium – a family tome of notes and maps recording the full eight hundred years of Hivanar blood on this land. He settled back in the plush chair and, with contemplative languor, finished his balat tea.

The house steward and principal agent, Venitt Sathad, quietly stepped forward to return the Compendium to the wood and iron chest sunk in the floor beneath the map table, then replaced the floorboards and unfurled the rug over the spot. His tasks completed, he stepped back to resume his position beside the door.

Rautos Hivanar was a large man, his complexion florid, his features robust. His presence tended to dominate a room, no matter how spacious. He sat in the estate's library now, the walls shelved to the ceiling. Scrolls, clay tablets and bound books filled every available space, the gathered learning of a thousand scholars, many of whom bore the Hivanar name.

As head of the family and overseer of its vast financial holdings, Rautos Hivanar was a busy man, and such demands on his intellect had redoubled since the Tiste Edur conquest – which had triggered the official formation and recognition of the Liberty Consign, an association of the wealthiest families in the Lether Empire – in ways he could never have imagined before. He would be hard-pressed to explain how he found all such activities tedious or enervating. Yet that was what they had become, even as his suspicions slowly, incrementally, resolved into certainties; even as he began to perceive that, somewhere out there, there was an enemy – or enemies – bent on the singular task of economic sabotage. Not mere embezzlement, an activity with which he was personally very familiar, but something more profound, all-encompassing. *An enemy.* To all that sustained Rautos Hivanar, and the Liberty Consign of which he was Master; indeed, to all that sustained the empire itself, regardless of who sat upon the throne, regardless even of those savage, miserable barbarians who were now preening at the very pinnacle of Letherii society, like grey-feathered jackdaws atop a hoard of baubles.

Such comprehension, on Rautos Hivanar's part, would once have triggered a most zealous response within him. The threat alone should have sufficed to elicit a vigorous hunt, and the notion of an agency of such diabolical purpose – one, he was forced to admit, guided by the most subtle genius – should have enlivened the game until its pursuit acquired the power of obsession.

Instead, Rautos Hivanar found himself seeking notations among the dusty ledgers for evidence of past floodings, pursuing an altogether more mundane mystery that would interest but a handful of muttering academics. And that, he admitted often to himself, was odd. Nonetheless, the compulsion gathered strength, and at night he would lie beside the recumbent, sweat-sheathed mass that was his wife of thirty-three years and find his thoughts working ceaselessly, struggling against the currents of time's cyclical flow, seeking to clamber his way back, with all his sensibilities, into past ages. Looking. Looking for something . . .

Sighing, Rautos set down the empty cup, then rose.

As he walked to the door, Venitt Sathad – whose family line had been Indebted to the Hivanars for six generations now – stepped forward to retrieve the fragile cup, then set off in his master's wake.

Out onto the waterfront enclosure, across the mosaic portraying the investiture of Skoval Hivanar as Imperial Ceda three centuries past, then down the shallow stone stairs to what, in drier times, was the lower terrace garden. But the river's currents had swirled in here, stealing away soil and plants, exposing a most peculiar arrangement of boulders set like a cobbled street, framed in wooden posts arranged in a rectangle, the posts little more than rotted stumps now, rising from the flood's remnant pools.

At the edge of the upper level, workers, under Rautos's direction, had used wood bulwarks to keep it from collapsing, and to one side sat a wheelbarrow filled with the multitude of curious objects that had been exposed by the floodwaters. These items had littered the cobbled floor.

In all, Rautos mused, a mystery. There was no record whatsoever of the lower terrace garden's being anything but what it was, and the notations from the garden's designer – from shortly after the completion of the estate's main buildings – indicated the bank at that level was nothing more than ancient flood silts.

The clay had preserved the wood, at least until recently, so there was no telling how long ago the strange construct had been built. The only indication of its antiquity rested with the objects, all of which were either bronze or copper. Not weapons, as one might find associated with a barrow, and if tools, then they were for activities long forgotten, since not a single worker Rautos had brought to this place was able to fathom the function of these items – they resembled no known tools, not for stone working, nor wood, nor the processing of foodstuffs.

Rautos collected one and examined it, for at least the hundredth time. Bronze, clay-cast – the flange was clearly visible – the item was long, roundish, yet bent at almost right angles. Incisions formed a cross-hatched pattern about the elbow. Neither end displayed any means of attachment – not intended, therefore, as part of some larger mechanism. He hefted its considerable weight in his hand. There was something imbalanced about it, despite the centrally placed bend. He set it down and drew out a circular sheet of copper, thinner than the wax layer on a scrier's tablet. Blackened by contact with the clays, yet only now the edges showing signs of verdigris. Countless holes had been punched through the sheet, in no particular pattern, yet each hole was perfectly uniform, perfectly round, with no lip to indicate from which side it had been punched.

'Venitt,' he said, 'have we a map recording the precise locations of these objects when they were originally found?'

'Indeed, Master, with but a few exceptions. You examined it a week past.'

'I did? Very well. Set it out once more on the table in the library, this afternoon.'

Both men turned as the gate watcher appeared from the narrow side passage along the left side of the house. The woman halted ten paces from Rautos and bowed. 'Master, a message from Invigilator Karos Invictad.'

'Very good,' Rautos replied distractedly. 'I will attend to it in a moment. Does the messenger await a response?'

'Yes, Master. He is in the courtyard.'

'See that refreshments are provided.'

The watcher bowed then departed.

'Venitt, I believe you must prepare to undertake a journey on my behalf.'

'Master?'

'The Invigilator at last perceives the magnitude of the threat.'

21

Venitt Sathad said nothing.

'You must travel to Drene City,' Rautos said, his eyes once more on the mysterious construct dominating the lower terrace. 'The Consign requires a most specific report of the preparations there. Alas, the Factor's own missives are proving unsatisfactory. I require confidence in those matters, if I am to apply fullest concentration to the threat closer to hand.'

Again, Venitt did not speak.

Rautos looked out onto the river. Fisher boats gathered in the bay opposite, two merchant traders drawing in towards the main docks. One of them, bearing the flag of the Esterrict family, looked damaged, possibly by fire. Rautos brushed the dirt from his hands and turned about, making his way back into the building, his servant falling into step behind him.

'I wonder, what lies beneath those stones?'

'Master?'

'Never mind, Venitt. I was but thinking out loud.'

The Awl'dan camp had been attacked at dawn by two troops of Atri-Preda Bivatt's Bluerose cavalry. Two hundred skilled lancers riding into a maelstrom of panic, as figures struggled out from the hide huts, as the Drene-bred wardogs, arriving moments before the horse-soldiers, closed on the pack of Awl herder and dray dogs, and in moments the three breeds of beast were locked in a vicious battle.

The Awl warriors were unprepared, and few had time to even so much as find their weapons before the lancers burst into their midst. In moments, the slaughter extended out to encompass elders and children. Most of the women fought alongside their male kin – wife and husband, sister and brother, dying together in a last blending of blood.

The engagement between the Letherii and the Awl took all of two hundred heartbeats. The war among the dogs was far more protracted, for the herder dogs – while smaller and more compact than their attackers – were quick and no less vicious, while the drays, bred to pull carts in summer and sleds in winter, were comparable with the Drene breed. Trained to kill wolves, the drays proved more than a match for the wardogs, and if not for the lancers then making sport of killing the mottle-skinned beasts, the battle would have turned. As it was, the Awl pack finally broke away, the survivors fleeing onto the plain, eastward, a few Drene wardogs giving chase before being recalled by their handlers.

Whilst lancers dismounted to make certain there were no survivors among the Awl, others rode out to collect the herds of myrid and rodara in the next valley.

Atri-Preda Bivatt sat astride her stallion, struggling to control the beast with the smell of blood so heavy in the morning air. Beside her, sitting awkward and in discomfort on the unfamiliar saddle, Brohl Handar, the newly appointed Tiste Edur Overseer of Drene City, watched the Letherii systematically loot the encampment, stripping corpses naked and drawing their knives. The Awl bound their jewellery – mostly gold – deep in the braids of their hair, forcing the Letherii to slice away those sections of the scalp to claim their booty. Of course, there was more than just expedience in this mutilation, for it had been extended to the collecting of swaths of skin that had been decorated in tattoos, the particular style of the Awl rich in colour and often outlined in stitched gold thread. These trophies adorned the round-shields of many lancers.

The captured herds now belonged to the Factor of Drene, Letur Anict, and as Brohl Handar watched the hundreds of myrid come over the hill, their black woolly coats making them look like boulders as they poured down the hillside, it was clear that the Factor's wealth had just risen substantially. The taller rodara followed, blue-backed and long-necked, their long tails thrashing about in near-panic as wardogs on the herd's flanks plunged into feint attacks again and again.

The breath hissed from the Atri-Preda's teeth. 'Where is the Factor's man, anyway? Those damned rodara are going to stampede. Lieutenant! Get the handlers to call off their hounds! Hurry!' The woman unstrapped her helm, pulled it free and set it atop the saddle horn. She looked across at Brohl. 'There you have it, Overseer.'

'So these are the Awl.'

She grimaced, looked away. 'A small camp by their standards. Seventy-odd adults.'

'Yet, large herds.'

Her grimace became a scowl. 'They were once larger, Overseer. Much larger.'

'I take it then that this campaign of yours is succeeding in driving away these trespassers.'

'Not my campaign.' She seemed to catch something in his expression for she added, 'Yes, of course, I command the expeditionary forces, Overseer. But I receive my orders from the Factor. And, strictly speaking, the Awl are not trespassers.'

'The Factor claims otherwise.'

'Letur Anict is highly ranked in the Liberty Consign.'

Brohl Handar studied the woman for a moment, then said, 'Not all wars are fought for wealth and land, Atri-Preda.'

'I must disagree, Overseer. Did not you Tiste Edur invade pre-emptively, in response to the perceived threat of lost land and resources? Cultural assimilation, the end of your independence. There is no doubt in my mind,' she continued, 'that we Letherii sought to obliterate your civilization, as we had done already with the Tarthenal and so many others. And so, an economic war.'

'It does not surprise me, Atri-Preda, that your kind saw it that way. And I do not doubt that such concerns were present in the mind of the Warlock King. Did we conquer you in order to survive? Perhaps.' Brohl considered saying more, then he shook his head, watching as four wardogs closed on a wounded cattle dog. The lame beast fought back, but was soon down, kicking, then silent and limp as the wardogs tore open its belly.

Bivatt asked, 'Do you ever wonder, Overseer, which of us truly won that war?'

He shot her a dark look. 'No, I do not. Your scouts have found no other signs of Awl in this area, I understand. So now the Factor will consolidate the Letherii claim in the usual fashion?'

The Atri-Preda nodded. 'Outposts. Forts, raised roads. Settlers will follow.'

'And then, the Factor will extend his covetous intentions, yet further east.'

'As you say, Overseer. Of course, I am sure you recognize the acquisitions gift the Tiste Edur as well. The empire's territory expands. I am certain the Emperor will be pleased.'

This was Brohl Handar's second week as governor of Drene. There were few Tiste Edur in this remote corner of Rhulad's empire, less than a hundred, and only his three staff members were from Brohl's own tribe, the Arapay. The annexation of Awl'dan by what amounted to wholesale genocide had begun years ago – long before the Edur conquest – and the particulars of rule in far Letheras seemed to have little relevance to this military campaign. Brohl Handar, the patriarch of a clan devoted to hunting tusked seals, wondered – not for the first time – what he was doing here.

Titular command as Overseer seemed to involve little more than observation. The true power of rule was with Letur Anict, the Factor of Drene, who *'is highly ranked in the Liberty Consign'*. Some kind of guild of merchants, he had learned, although he had no idea what, precisely, was liberating about this mysterious organization. Unless, of course, it was the freedom to do as they pleased. Including the use of imperial troops to aid in the acquisition of ever more wealth.

'Atri-Preda.'

'Yes, Overseer?'

'These Awl – do they fight back? No, not as they did today. I mean, do they mount raids? Do they mass their warriors on the path to all-out war?'

She looked uncomfortable. 'Overseer, there are two . . . well, levels, to this.'

'Levels. What does that mean?'

24

'Official and . . . unofficial. It is a matter of perception.'

'Explain.'

'The belief of the common folk, as promulgated through imperial agents, is that the Awl have allied themselves with the Ak'ryn to the south, as well as the D'rhasilhani and the two kingdoms of Bolkando and Saphinand – in short, all the territories bordering the empire – creating a belligerent, warmongering and potentially overwhelming force – the Horde of the Bolkando Conspiracy – that threatens the entire eastern territories of the Lether Empire. It is only a matter of time before that horde is fully assembled, whereupon it will march. Accordingly, every attack launched by the Letherii military serves to diminish the numbers the Awl can contribute, and furthermore, the loss of valuable livestock in turns weakens the savages. Famine may well manage what swords alone cannot – the entire collapse of the Awl.'

'I see. And the unofficial version?'

She glanced across at him. 'There is no conspiracy, Overseer. No alliance. The truth is, the Awl continue to fight among themselves – their grazing land is shrinking, after all. And they despise the Ak'ryn and the D'rhasilhani, and have probably never met anyone from Bolkando or Saphinand.' She hesitated, then said, 'We did clash with a mercenary company of some sort, two months past – the disastrous battle that spurred your appointment, I suspect. They numbered per- haps seven hundred, and after a half-dozen skirmishes I led a force of six thousand Letherii in pursuit. Overseer, we lost almost three thousand soldiers in that final battle. If not for our mages . . .' She shook her head. 'And we still have no idea who they were.'

Brohl studied the woman. He had known nothing about any such clash. The reason for his appointment? Perhaps. 'The official version you spoke of earlier – the lie – justifies the slaughter of the Awl, in the eyes of the commonry. All of which well serves the Factor's desire to make himself yet richer. I see. Tell me, Atri-Preda, why does Letur Anict need all that gold? What does he do with it?'

The woman shrugged. 'Gold is power.'

'Power over whom?'

'Anyone, and everyone.'

'Excepting the Tiste Edur, who are indifferent to the Letherii idea of wealth.'

She smiled. 'Are you, Overseer? Still?'

'What do you mean?'

'There are Hiroth in Drene – yes, you have met them. Each claims kinship with the Emperor, and upon that claim they have commandeered the finest estates and land. They have hundreds of Indebted as slaves. Soon, perhaps, there will be Tiste Edur among the membership of the Liberty Consign.'

Brohl Handar frowned. On a distant ridge stood three Awl dogs, two drays and one smaller cattle dog, watching as the herds were driven through the destroyed encampment – the livestock bawling in the stench of spilled blood and wastes. He studied the three silhouettes on the ridge. Where would they go now, he wondered. 'I have seen enough.' He tugged his horse round, too tight on the reins, and the beast's head snapped up and it snorted, backing as it turned. Brohl struggled to keep his balance.

If the Atri-Preda was amused she was wise enough not to show it.

In the sky overhead, the first carrion birds had appeared.

The South Jasp River, one of the four tributaries of Lether River leading down from the Bluerose Mountains, was flanked on its south bank by a raised road that, a short distance ahead, began its long climb to the mountain pass, beyond which lay the ancient kingdom of Bluerose, now subject to the Letherii Empire. The South Jasp ran fast here, the momentum of its savage descent from the mountains not yet slowed by the vast plain it now found itself crossing. The icy water pounded over huge boulders left behind by long-extinct glaciers, flinging bitter-cold mist into the air that drifted in clouds over the road.

The lone figure awaiting the six Tiste Edur warriors and their entourage was if anything taller than any Edur, yet thin, wrapped in a black sealskin cloak, hood raised. Two baldrics criss-crossed its chest, from which hung two Letherii longswords, and the few wisps of long white hair that had pulled free in the wind were now wet, adhering to the collar of the cloak.

To the approaching Merude Edur, the face within that cowl looked pallid as death, as if a corpse had just dragged itself free of the numbing river, something long frozen in the white-veined reaches of the mountains that awaited them.

The lead warrior, a veteran of the conquest of Letheras, gestured for his comrades to halt then set out to speak to the stranger. In addition to the other five Edur, there were ten Letherii soldiers, two burdened wagons, and forty slaves shackled one to the next in a line behind the second wagon.

'Do you wish company,' the Merude asked, squinting to see more of that shadowed face, 'for the climb to the pass? It's said there remain bandits and renegades in the heights beyond.'

'I am my own company.'

The voice was rough, the accent archaic.

The Merude halted three paces away. He could see more of that face, now. Edur features, more or less, yet white as snow. The eyes were . . . unnerving. Red as blood. 'Then why do you block our path?'

'You captured two Letherii two days back. They are mine.'

26

The Merude shrugged. 'Then you should have kept them chained at night, friend. These Indebted will run at any opportunity. Fortunate for you that we captured them. Oh, yes – of course I will return them into your care. At least the girl – the man is an escaped slave from the Hiroth, or so his tattoos reveal. A Drowning awaits him, alas, but I will consider offering you a replacement. In any case, the girl, young as she is, is valuable. I trust you can manage the cost of retrieving her.'

'I will take them both. And pay you nothing.'

Frowning, the Merude said, 'You were careless in losing them. We were diligent in recapturing them. Accordingly, we expect compensation for our efforts, just as you should expect a certain cost for your carelessness.'

'Unchain them,' the stranger said.

'No. What tribe are you?' The eyes, still fixed unwavering upon his own, looked profoundly . . . *dead*. 'What has happened to your skin?' *As dead as the Emperor's.* 'What is your name?'

'Unchain them now.'

The Merude shook his head, then he laughed – a little weakly – and waved his comrades forward as he began drawing his cutlass.

Disbelief at the absurdity of the challenge slowed his effort. The weapon was halfway out of its scabbard when one of the stranger's longswords flashed clear of its sheath and opened the Edur's throat.

Shouting in rage, the other five warriors drew their blades and rushed forward, while the ten Letherii soldiers quickly followed suit.

The stranger watched the leader crumple to the ground, blood spurting wild into the river mist descending onto the road. Then he unsheathed his other longsword and stepped to meet the five Edur. A clash of iron, and all at once the two Letherii weapons in the stranger's hands were singing, a rising timbre with every blow they absorbed.

Two Edur stumbled back at the same time, both mortally wounded, one in the chest, the other with a third of his skull sliced away. This latter one turned away as the fighting continued, reaching down to collect the fragment of scalp and bone, then walked drunkenly back along the road.

Another Edur fell, his left leg cut out from beneath him. The remaining two quickly backed away, yelling at the Letherii who were now hesitating three paces behind the fight.

The stranger pressed forward. He parried a thrust from the Edur on the right with the longsword in his left hand – sliding the blade under then over, drawing it leftward before a twist of his wrist tore the weapon from the attacker's hand; then a straight-arm thrust of his own buried his point in the Edur's throat. At the same time he reached over with the longsword in his right hand, feinting high. The last Edur leaned back to avoid that probe, attempting a slash aimed at clipping the stranger's wrist. But the longsword then deftly dipped, batting the cutlass away, even as the point drove up into the warrior's right eye socket, breaking the delicate orbital bones on its way into the forebrain.

Advancing between the two falling Edur, the stranger cut down the nearest two Letherii – at which point the remaining eight broke and ran, past the wagons – where the drivers were themselves scrambling in panicked abandonment – and then alongside the row of staring prisoners. Running, flinging weapons away, down the road.

As one Letherii in particular moved opposite one of the slaves, a leg kicked out, tripping the man, and it seemed the chain-line writhed then, as the ambushing slave leapt atop the hapless Letherii, loose chain wrapping round the neck, before the slave pulled it taut. Legs kicked, arms thrashed and hands clawed, but the slave would not relent, and eventually the guard's struggles ceased.

Silchas Ruin, the swords keening in his hands, walked up to where Udinaas continued strangling the corpse. 'You can stop now,' the albino Tiste Andii said.

'I can,' Udinaas said through clenched teeth, 'but I won't. This bastard was the worst of them. The worst.'

'His soul even now drowns in the mist,' Silchas Ruin said, turning as two figures emerged from the brush lining the ditch on the south side of the road.

'Keep choking him,' said Kettle, from where she was chained farther down the line. 'He hurt me, that one.'

'I know,' Udinaas said in a grating voice. 'I know.'

Silchas Ruin approached Kettle. 'Hurt you. How?'

'The usual way,' she replied. 'With the thing between his legs.'

'And the other Letherii?'

The girl shook her head. 'They just watched. Laughing, always laughing.'

Silchas Ruin turned as Seren Pedac arrived.

Seren was chilled by the look in the Tiste Andii's uncanny eyes as Silchas Ruin said, 'I will pursue the ones who flee, Acquitor. And rejoin you all before day's end.'

She looked away, her gaze catching a momentary glimpse of Fear Sengar, standing over the corpses of the Merude Tiste Edur, then quickly on, to the rock-littered plain to the south – where still wandered the Tiste Edur who'd lost a third of his skull. But that sight as well proved too poignant. 'Very well,' she said, now squinting at the wagons and the horses standing in their yokes. 'We will continue on this road.'

Udinaas had finally expended his rage on the Letherii body beneath him, and he rose to face her. 'Seren Pedac, what of the rest of these slaves? We must free them all.'

She frowned. Exhaustion was making thinking difficult. Months and

28

months of hiding, fleeing, eluding both Edur and Letherii; of finding their efforts to head eastward blocked again and again, forcing them ever northward, and the endless terror that lived within her, had driven all accuity from her thoughts. *Free them. Yes. But then . . .*

'Just more rumours,' Udinaas said, as if reading her mind, as if finding her thoughts before she did. 'There's plenty of those, confusing our hunters. Listen, Seren, they already know where we are, more or less. And these slaves – they'll do whatever they can to avoid recapture. We need not worry overmuch about them.'

She raised her brows. 'You vouch for your fellow Indebted, Udinaas? All of whom will turn away from a chance to buy their way clear with vital information, yes?'

'The only alternative, then,' he said, eyeing her, 'is to kill them all.'

The ones listening, the ones not yet beaten down into mindless automatons, suddenly raised their voices in proclamations and promises, reaching out towards Seren, chains rattling. The others looked up in fear, like myrid catching scent of a wolf they could not see. Some cried out, cowering in the stony mud of the road.

'The first Edur he killed,' said Udinaas, 'has the keys.'

Silchas Ruin had walked down the road. Barely visible in the mist, the Tiste Andii veered into something huge, winged, then took to the air. Seren glanced over at the row of slaves – none had seen that, she was relieved to note. 'Very well,' she said in answer to Udinaas, and she walked up to where Fear Sengar still stood near the dead Edur.

'I must take the keys,' she said, crouching beside the first fallen Edur.

'Do not touch him,' Fear said.

She looked up at him. 'The keys – the chains—'

'I will find them,' he said.

Nodding, she straightened, then stepped back. Watched as he spoke a silent prayer, then settled onto his knees beside the body. He found the keys in a leather pouch tied to the warrior's belt, a pouch that also contained a handful of polished stones. Fear took the keys in his left hand and held the stones in the palm of his right. 'These,' he said, 'are from the Merude shore. Likely he collected them when but a child.'

'Children grow up,' Seren said. 'Even straight trees spawn crooked branches.'

'And what was flawed in this warrior?' Fear demanded, glaring up at her. 'He followed my brother, as did every other warrior of the tribes.'

'Some eventually turned away, Fear.' *Like you.*

'What I have turned away from lies in the shadow of what I am now turned towards, Acquitor. Does this challenge my loyalty towards the Tiste Edur? My own kind? No. That is something all of you forget, conveniently so, again and again. Understand me, Acquitor. I will hide if I must, but I will not kill my own people. We had the coin, we could have bought their freedom—'

'Not Udinaas.'

He bared his teeth, said nothing.

Yes, Udinaas, the one man you dream of killing. If not for Silchas Ruin . . . 'Fear Sengar,' she said. 'You have chosen to travel with us, and there can be no doubt – none at all – that Silchas Ruin commands this meagre party. Dislike his methods if you must, but he alone will see you through. You know this.'

The Hiroth warrior looked away, back down the road, blinking the water from his eyes. 'And with each step, the cost of my quest becomes greater – an indebtedness you should well understand, Acquitor. The Letherii way of living, the burdens you can never escape. Nor purchase your way clear.'

She reached out for the keys.

He set them into her hand, unwilling to meet her eyes.

We're no different from those slaves. She hefted the weight of the jangling iron in her hand. *Chained together. Yet . . . who holds the means of our release?*

'Where has he gone?' Fear asked.

'To hunt down the Letherii. I trust you do not object to that.'

'No, but you should, Acquitor.'

I suppose I should at that. She set off to where waited the slaves.

A prisoner near Udinaas had crawled close to him, and Seren heard his whispered question: 'That tall slayer – was that the White Crow? He was, wasn't he? I have heard—'

'You have heard nothing,' Udinaas said, raising his arms as Seren approached. 'The three-edged one,' he said to her. 'Yes, that one. Errant take us, you took your time.'

She worked the key until the first shackle clicked open. 'You two were supposed to be stealing from a farm – not getting rounded up by slave-trackers.'

'Trackers camped on the damned grounds – no-one was smiling on us that night.'

She opened the other shackle and Udinaas stepped out from the line, rubbing at the red weals round his wrists. Seren said, 'Fear sought to dissuade Silchas – you know, if those two are any indication, it's no wonder the Edur and the Andii fought ten thousand wars.'

Udinaas grunted as the two made their way to where stood Kettle. 'Fear resents his loss of command,' he said. 'That it is to a Tiste Andii just makes it worse. He's still not convinced the betrayal was the other way round all those centuries back; that it was Scabandari who first drew the knife.'

Seren Pedac said nothing. As she moved in front of Kettle she looked down at the girl's dirt-smeared face, the ancient eyes slowly lifting to meet her own.

Kettle smiled. 'I missed you.'

'How badly were you used?' Seren asked as she removed the large iron shackles.

'I can walk. And the bleeding's stopped. That's a good sign, isn't it?'

'Probably.' But this talk of rape was unwelcome – Seren had her own memories haunting her every waking moment. 'There will be scars, Kettle.'

'Being alive is hard. I'm always hungry, and my feet hurt.'

I hate children with secrets – especially ones with secrets they're not even aware of. Find the right questions; there's no other way of doing this. 'What else bothers you about being among the living again, Kettle?' *And . . . how? Why?*

'Feeling small.'

Seren's right arm was plucked by a slave, an old man who reached out for the keys with pathetic hope in his eyes. She handed them to him. 'Free the others,' she said. He nodded vigorously, scrabbling at his shackles. 'Now,' Seren said to Kettle, 'that's a feeling we all must accept. Too much of the world defies our efforts to conform to what would please us. To live is to know dissatisfaction and frustration.'

'I still want to tear out throats, Seren. Is that bad? I think it must be.'

At Kettle's words, the old man shrank away, redoubling his clumsy attempts at releasing himself. Behind him a woman cursed with impatience.

Udinaas had climbed onto the bed of the lead wagon and was busy looting it for whatever they might need. Kettle scrambled to join him.

'We need to move out of this mist,' Seren muttered. 'I'm soaked through.' She walked towards the wagon. 'Hurry up with that, you two. If more company finds us here, we could be in trouble.' *Especially now that Silchas Ruin is gone.* The Tiste Andii had been the singular reason for their survival thus far. When hiding and evading the searchers failed, his two swords found voice, the eerie song of obliteration. *The White Crow.*

It had been a week since they last caught sight of Edur and Letherii who were clearly hunters. Seeking the traitor, Fear Sengar. Seeking the betrayer, Udinaas. Yet Seren Pedac was bemused – there should have been entire armies chasing them. While the pursuit was persistent, it was dogged rather than ferocious in its execution. Silchas had mentioned, once, in passing, that the Emperor's K'risnan were working ritual sorceries, the kind that sought to lure and trap. And that snares awaited them to the east, and round Letheras itself. She could under-stand those to the east, for it was the wild lands beyond the empire that had been their destination all along, where Fear – for some reason he

31

did not care to explain – believed he would find what he sought; a belief that Silchas Ruin did not refute. But to surround the capital city itself baffled Seren. *As if Rhulad is frightened of his brother.*

Udinaas leapt down from the lead wagon and made his way to the second one. 'I found coin,' he said. 'Lots. We should take these horses, too – we can sell them once we're down the other side of the pass.'

'There is a fort at the pass,' Seren said. 'It may be ungarrisoned, but there's no guarantee of that, Udinaas. If we arrive with horses – and they recognize them . . .'

'We go round that fort,' he replied. 'At night. Unseen.'

She frowned, wiped water from her eyes. 'Easier done without horses. Besides, these beasts are old, too broken – they won't earn us much, especially in Bluerose. And when Wyval returns they'll probably die of terror.'

'Wyval's not coming back,' Udinaas said, turning away, his voice grating. 'Wyval's gone, and that's that.'

She knew she should not doubt him. The dragon-spawn's spirit had dwelt within him, after all. Yet there was no obvious explanation for the winged beast's sudden disappearance, at least none that Udinaas would share. Wyval had been gone for over a month.

Udinaas swore from where he crouched atop the bed of the wagon. 'Nothing here but weapons.'

'Weapons?'

'Swords, shields and armour.'

'Letherii?'

'Yes. Middling quality.'

'What were these slavers doing with a wagon load of weapons?'

Shrugging, he climbed back down, hurried past her and began unhitching the horses. 'These beasts would've had a hard time on the ascent.'

'Silchas Ruin is coming back,' Kettle said, pointing down the road.

'That was fast.'

Udinaas laughed harshly, then said, 'The fools should have scattered, made him hunt each one down separately. Instead, they probably regrouped, like the stupid good soldiers they were.'

From near the front wagon, Fear Sengar spoke. 'Your blood is very thin, Udinaas, isn't it?'

'Like water,' the ex-slave replied.

For Errant's sake, Fear, he did not choose to abandon your brother. You know that. Nor is he responsible for Rhulad's madness. So how much of your hatred for Udinaas comes from guilt? Who truly is to blame for Rhulad? For the Emperor of a Thousand Deaths?

The white-skinned Tiste Andii strode from the mists, an apparition, his black cloak glistening like snakeskin. Swords sheathed once more, muting their cries – iron voices reluctant to fade, they would persist for days, now.

How she hated that sound.

Tanal Yathvanar stood looking down at the naked woman on his bed. The questioners had worked hard on her, seeking the answers they wanted. She was badly broken, her skin cut and burned, her joints swollen and mottled with bruises. She had been barely conscious when he'd used her last night. This was easier than whores, and cost him nothing besides. He wasn't much interested in beating his women, just in seeing them beaten. He understood his desire was perversion, but this organization – the Patriotists – was the perfect haven for people like him. Power and immunity, a most deadly combination. He suspected that Karos Invictad was well aware of Tanal's nightly escapades, and held that knowledge like a sheathed knife.

It's not as if I've killed her. It's not as if she'll even remember this. She's destined for the Drownings in any case – what matter if I take some pleasure first? Soldiers do the same. He had dreamed of being a soldier once, years ago, when in his youth he had held to misguided, romantic notions of heroism and unconstrained freedom, as if the first justified the second. There had been many noble killers in the history of Lether. Gerun Eberict had been such a man. He'd murdered thousands – thieves, thugs and wastrels, the depraved and the destitute. He had *cleansed* the streets of Letheras, and who had not indulged in the rewards? Fewer beggars, fewer pickpockets, fewer homeless and all the other decrepit failures of the modern age. Tanal admired Gerun Eberict – he had been a great man. Murdered by a thug, his skull crushed to pulp – a tragic loss, senseless and cruel.

One day we shall find that killer.

He turned away from the unconscious woman, adjusted his light tunic so that the shoulder seams were even and straight, then closed the clasps of his weapon belt. One of the Invigilator's requirements for all officers of the Patriotists: belt, dagger and shortsword. Tanal liked the weight of them, the authority implicit in the privilege of wearing arms where all other Letherii – barring soldiers – were forbidden by proclamation of the Emperor.

As if we might rebel. The damned fool thinks he won that war. They all do. Dimwitted barbarians.

Tanal Yathvanar walked to the door, stepped out into the corridor, and made his way towards the Invigilator's office. The second bell after midday sounded a moment before he knocked on the door. A murmured invitation bade him enter.

He found Rautos Hivanar, Master of the Liberty Consign, already seated opposite Karos Invictad. The large man seemed to fill half the room, and Tanal noted that the Invigilator had pushed his own chair as far back as possible, so that it was tilted against the sill of the window. In this space on his side of the desk, Karos attempted a posture of affable comfort.

'Tanal, our guest is being most insistent with respect to his suspicions. Sufficient to convince me that we must devote considerable attention to finding the source of the threat.'

'Invigilator, is the intent sedition or treason, or are we dealing with a thief?'

'A thief, I should think,' Karos replied, glancing over at Rautos Hivanar.

The man's cheeks bulged, before he released a slow sigh. 'I am not so sure. On the surface, we appear to be facing an obsessive individual, consumed by greed and, accordingly, hoarding wealth. But only as actual coin, and this is why it is proving so difficult to find a trail. No properties, no ostentation, no flouting of privilege. Now, as subtle consequence, the shortage of coin is finally noticeable. True, no actual damage to the empire's financial structure has occurred. Yet. But, if the depletion continues,' he shook his head, 'we will begin to feel the strain.'

Tanal cleared his throat, then asked, 'Master, have you assigned agents of your own to investigate the situation?'

Rautos frowned. 'The Liberty Consign thrives precisely because its members hold to the conviction of being the most powerful players in an unassailable system. Confidence is a most fragile quality, Tanal Yathvanar. Granted, a few who deal specifically in finances have brought to me their concerns. Druz Thennict, Barrakta Ilk, for example. But there is nothing as yet formalized – no true suspicion that something is awry. Neither man is a fool, however.' He glanced out of the window behind Karos Invictad. 'The investigation must be conducted by the Patriotists, in utmost secrecy.' The heavy-lidded eyes lowered, settling on the Invigilator. 'I understand that you have been targeting academics and scholars of late.'

A modest shrug and lift of the brows from Karos Invictad. 'The many paths of treason.'

'Some are members of established and respected families in Lether.'

'No, Rautos, not the ones we have arrested.'

'True, but those unfortunate victims have friends, Invigilator, who have in turn appealed to me.'

'Well, my friend, this is delicate indeed. You tread now on the thinnest skin of ground, with naught but mud beneath.' He sat forward, folding his hands on the desk. 'But I shall look into it nonetheless. Perhaps the recent spate of arrests has succeeded in quelling the disenchantment among the learned, or at least culled the most egregious of their lot.'

'Thank you, Invigilator. Now, who will conduct your investigation?'

'Why, I will attend to this personally.'

'Venitt Sathad, my assistant who awaits in the courtyard below, can serve as liaison between your organization and myself for this week; thereafter, I will assign someone else.'

'Very good. Weekly reports should suffice, at least to start.'

'Agreed.'

Rautos Hivanar rose, and after a moment Karos Invictad followed suit.

The office was suddenly very cramped, and Tanal edged back, angry at the intimidation he felt instinctively rising within him. *I have nothing to fear from Rautos Hivanar. Nor Karos. I am their confidant, the both of them. They trust me.*

Karos Invictad was a step behind Rautos, one hand on the man's back as the Master opened the door. As soon as Rautos stepped into the hallway, Karos smiled and said a few last words to the man, who grunted in reply, and then the Invigilator closed the door and turned to face Tanal.

'One of those well-respected academics is now staining your sheets, Yathvanar.'

Tanal blinked. 'Sir, she was sentenced to the Drowning—'

'Revoke the punishment. Get her cleaned up.'

'Sir, it may well be that she will recall—'

'A certain measure of restraint,' Karos Invictad said in a cold tone, 'is required from you, Tanal Yathvanar. Arrest some daughters of those already in chains, damn you, and have your fun with them. Am I understood?'

'Y-yes sir. If she remembers—'

'Then restitution will be necessary, won't it? I trust you keep your own finances in order, Yathvanar. Now, begone from my sight.'

As Tanal closed the door behind him, he struggled to draw breath. *The bastard. There was no warning off her, was there? Whose mistake was all this? Yet, you think to make me pay for it. All of it. Blade and Axe take you, Invictad, I won't suffer alone.*

I won't.

'Depravity holds a certain fascination, don't you think?'

'No.'

'After all, the sicker the soul, the sweeter its comeuppance.'

'Assuming there is one.'

'There's a centre point, I'm sure of it. And it should be dead centre, by my calculations. Perhaps the fulcrum itself is flawed.'

'What calculations?'

'Well, the ones I asked you to do for me, of course. Where are they?'

'They're on my list.'

'And how do you calculate the order of your list?'

'That's not the calculation you asked for.'

'Good point. Anyway, if he'd just hold all his legs still, we could properly test my hypothesis.'

'He doesn't want to, and I can see why. You're trying to balance him at the mid-point of his body, but he's designed to hold that part up, with all those legs.'

'Are those formal observations? If so, make a note.'

'On what? We had the wax slab for lunch.'

'No wonder I feel I could swallow a cow with nary a hiccough. Look! Hah! He's perched! Perfectly perched!'

Both men leaned in to examine Ezgara, the insect with a head at each end. Not unique, of course, there were plenty around these days, filling some arcane niche in the complicated miasma of nature, a niche that had been vacant for countless millennia. The creature's broken-twig legs kicked out helplessly.

'You're torturing him,' said Bugg, 'with clear depravity, Tehol.'

'It only seems that way.'

'No, it is that way.'

'All right, then.' Tehol reached down and plucked the hapless insect from the fulcrum. Its heads swivelled about. 'Anyway,' he said as he peered closely at the creature, 'that wasn't the depravity I was talking about. How goes the construction business, by the way?'

'Sinking fast.'

'Ah. Is that an affirmation or decried destitution?'

'We're running out of buyers. No hard coin, and I'm done with credit, especially when it turns out the developers can't sell the properties. So I've had to lay everyone off, including myself.'

'When did all this happen?'

'Tomorrow.'

'Typical. I'm always the last to hear. Is Ezgara hungry, do you think?'

'He ate more wax than you did – where do you think all the waste goes?'

'His or mine?'

'Master, I already know where yours goes, and if Biri ever finds out—'

'Not another word, Bugg. Now, by my observations, and according to the notations you failed to make, Ezgara has consumed food equivalent in weight to a drowned cat. Yet he remains tiny, spry, fit, and thanks to our wax lunch today his heads no longer squeak when they swivel, which I take to be a good sign, since now we won't be woken up a hundred times a night.'

'Master.'

'Yes?'

'How do you know how much a drowned cat weighs?'

'Selush, of course.'

'I don't understand.'

'You must remember. Three years ago. That feral cat netted in the Rinnesict Estate, the one raping a flightless ornamental duck. It was sentenced to Drowning.'

'A terrible demise for a cat. Yes, I remember now. The yowl heard across the city.'

'That's the one. Some unnamed benefactor took pity on the sodden feline corpse, paying Selush a small fortune to dress the beast for proper burial.'

'You must be mad. Who would do that and why?'

'For ulterior motives, obviously. I wanted to know how much a drowned cat weighs, of course. Otherwise, how valid the comparison? Descriptively, I've been waiting to use it for years.'

'Three.'

'No, much longer. Hence my curiosity, and opportunism. Prior to that cat's watery end, I feared voicing the comparison, which, lacking veracity on my part, would invite ridicule.'

'You're a tender one, aren't you?'

'Don't tell anyone.'

'Master, about those vaults.'

'What about them?'

'I think extensions are required.'

Tehol used the tip of his right index finger to stroke the insect's back – or, alternatively, rub it the wrong way. 'Already? Well, how far under the river are you right now?'

'More than halfway.'

'And that is how many?'

'Vaults? Sixteen. Each one three man-heights by two.'

'All filled?'

'All.'

'Oh. So presumably it's starting to hurt.'

'Bugg's Construction will be the first major enterprise to collapse.'

'And how many will it drag down with it?'

'No telling. Three, maybe four.'

'I thought you said there was no telling.'

'So don't tell anyone.'

'Good idea. Bugg, I need you to build me a box, to very specific specifications which I'll come up with later.'

'A box, Master. Wood good enough?'

'What kind of sentence is that? Would good enough.'

'No, wood, you know, the burning kind.'

'Yes, would that wood will do.'

'Size?'

'Absolutely. But no lid.'

'Finally, you're getting specific.'

'I told you I would.'

'What's this box for, Master?'

'I can't tell you, alas. Not specifically. But I need it soon.'

'About the vaults . . .'

'Make ten more, Bugg. Double the size. As for Bugg's Construction, hold on for a while longer, amass debt, evade the creditors, keep purchasing materials and stockpiling them in storage buildings charging exorbitant rent. Oh, and embezzle all you can.'

'I'll lose my head.'

'Don't worry. Ezgara here has one to spare.'

'Why, thank you.'

'Doesn't even squeak, either.'

'That's a relief. What are you doing now, Master?'

'What's it look like?'

'You're going back to bed.'

'And you need to build a box, Bugg, a most clever box. Remember, though, no lid.'

'Can I at least ask what it's for?'

Tehol settled back on his bed, studied the blue sky overhead for a moment, then smiled over at his manservant – who just happened to be an Elder God. 'Why, comeuppance, Bugg, what else?'

CHAPTER TWO

The waking moment awaits us all
upon a threshold or where the road turns
if life is pulled, sparks like moths inward
to this single sliver of time gleaming
like sunlight on water, we will accrete
into a mass made small, veined with fears
and shot through with all that's suddenly
precious, and the now is swallowed,
the weight of self a crushing immediacy,
on this day, where the road turns,
comes the waking moment.

Winter Reflections
Corara of Drene

THE ASCENT TO THE SUMMIT BEGAN WHERE THE LETHERII-BUILT ROAD ended. With the river voicing its ceaseless roar fifteen paces to their left, the roughly shaped pavestones vanished beneath a black-stoned slide at the base of a moraine. Uprooted trees reached bent and twisted arms up through the rubble, jutting limbs from which hung root tendrils, dripping water. Swaths of forest climbed the mountainside to the north, on the other side of the river, and the ragged cliffs edging the tumbling water on that side were verdant with moss. The opposite mountain, flanking the trail, was a stark contrast, latticed with fissures, broken, gouged and mostly treeless. In the midst of this shattered façade shadows marked out odd regularities, of line and angle; and upon the trail itself, here and there, broad worn steps had been carved, eroded by flowing water and centuries of footfalls.

Seren Pedac believed that a city had once occupied the entire mountainside, a vertical fortress carved into living stone. She could make out what she thought were large gaping windows, and possibly the fragmented ledges of balconies high up, hazy in the mists. Yet something – something huge, terrible in its monstrosity – had impacted the entire side of the mountain, obliterating most of the city in a single blow. She could almost discern the outline of that collision, yet among the screes of rubble tracking down the sundered slopes the only visible stone belonged to the mountain itself.

They stood at the base of the trail. Seren watched the lifeless eyes of the Tiste Andii slowly scan upward.

'Well?' she asked.

Silchas Ruin shook his head. 'Not from my people. K'Chain Che'Malle.'

'A victim of your war?'

He glanced across at her, as if gauging the emotion behind her question, then said, 'Most of the mountains from which the K'Chain Che'Malle carved their sky keeps are now beneath the waves, inundated following the collapse of Omtose Phellack. The cities are cut into the stone, although only in the very earliest versions are they as you see here – open to the air rather than buried within shapeless rock.'

'An elaboration suggesting a sudden need for self-defence.'

He nodded.

Fear Sengar had moved past them and was beginning the ascent. After a moment Udinaas and Kettle followed. Seren had prevailed in her insistence to leave the horses behind. In a clearing off to their right sat four wagons covered with tarps. It was clear that no such contrivance could manage this climb, and all transport from here on was by foot. As for the mass of weapons and armour the slavers had been conveying, either it would have been stashed here, awaiting a hauling crew, or the slaves would have been burdened like mules.

'I have never made this particular crossing,' Seren said, 'although I have viewed this mountainside from a distance. Even then, I thought I could see evidence of reshaping. I once asked Hull Beddict about it, but he would tell me nothing. At some point, however, I think our trail takes us inside.'

'The sorcery that destroyed this city was formidable,' Silchas Ruin said.

'Perhaps some natural force—'

'No, Acquitor. Starvald Demelain. The destruction was the work of dragons. Eleint of the pure blood. At least a dozen, working in concert, a combined unleashing of their warrens. Unusual,' he added.

'Which part?'

'Such a large alliance, for one. Also, the extent of their rage. I wonder what crime the K'Chain Che'Malle committed to warrant such retaliation.'

'I know the answer to that,' came a sibilant whisper from behind them, and Seren turned, squinted down at the insubstantial wraith crouched there.

'Wither. I was wondering where you had gone to.'

'Journeys into the heart of the stone, Seren Pedac. Into the frozen blood. What was their crime, you wonder, Silchas Ruin? Why, nothing less than the assured annihilation of all existence. If extinction awaited them, then so too would all else die. Desperation, or evil spite? Perhaps neither, perhaps a terrible accident, that wounding at the centre of it all. But what do we care? We shall all be dust by then. Indifferent. Insensate.'

Silchas Ruin said, without turning, 'Beware the frozen blood, Wither. It can still take you.'

The wraith hissed a laugh. 'Like an ant to sap, yes. Oh, but it is so seductive, Master.'

'You have been warned. If you are snared, I cannot free you.'

The wraith slithered past them, flowed up the ragged steps.

Seren adjusted the leather satchel on her shoulders. 'The Fent carried supplies balanced on their heads. Would that I could do the same.'

'The vertebrae become compacted,' Silchas Ruin said, 'resulting in chronic pain.'

'Well, mine are feeling rather crunched right now, so I'm afraid I don't see much difference.' She began the climb. 'You know, as a Soletaken, you could just—'

'No,' he said as he followed, 'there is too much bloodlust in the veering. The draconean hunger within me is where lives my anger, and that anger is not easily contained.'

She snorted, unable to help herself.

'You are amused, Acquitor?'

'Scabandari is dead. Fear has seen his shattered skull. You were stabbed and then imprisoned, and now that you are free, all that consumes you is the desire for vengeance – against what? Some incorporeal soul? Something less than a wraith? What will be left of Scabandari by now? Silchas Ruin, yours is a pathetic obsession. At least Fear Sengar seeks something positive – not that he'll find it since you will probably annihilate what's left of Scabandari before he gets a chance to talk to it, assuming that's even possible.' When he said nothing, she continued, 'It seems I am now fated to guiding such quests. Just like my last journey, the one that took me to the lands of the Tiste Edur. Everyone at odds, motives hidden and in conflict. My task was singular, of course; deliver the fools, then stand well back as the knives are drawn.'

'Acquitor, my anger is more complicated than you believe.'

'What does that mean?'

'The future you set before us is too simple, too confined. I suspect

41

that when we arrive at our destination, nothing will proceed as you anticipate.'

She grunted. 'I will accept that, since it was without doubt the case in the village of the Warlock King. After all, the fallout was the conquest of the Letherii Empire.'

'Do you take responsibility for that, Acquitor?'

'I take responsibility for very little, Silchas Ruin. That much must be obvious.'

The steps were steep, the edges worn and treacherous. As they climbed, the air thinned, mists swirling in from the tumbling falls on their left, the sound a roar that clambered among the stones in a tumult of echoes. Where the ancient stairs vanished entirely, wooden trestles had been constructed, forming something between a ladder and steps against the sheer, angled rock.

They found a ledge a third of the way up where they could gather to rest. Among the scatter of rubble on the shelf were remnants of metopes, cornices and friezes bearing carvings too fragmented to be identifiable – suggesting that an entire façade had once existed directly above them. The scaffolding became a true ladder here, and off to the right, three man-heights up, gaped the mouth of a cave, rectangular, almost door-shaped.

Udinaas stood regarding that dark portal for a long time, before he turned to the others. 'I suggest we try it.'

'There is no need, slave,' replied Fear Sengar. 'This trail is straightforward, reliable—'

'And getting icier the higher we go.' The Indebted grimaced, then laughed. 'Oh, there're songs to be sung, are there, Fear? The perils and tribulations, the glories of suffering, all to win your heroic triumph. You want the elders who were once your grandchildren to gather the clan round the fire, for the telling of your tale, a lone warrior's quest for his god. I can almost hear them now, describing the formidable Fear Sengar of the Hiroth, brother to the Emperor, with his train of followers – the lost child, the inveterate Letherii guide, a ghost, a slave and of course the white-skinned nemesis. The White Crow with his silver-tongued lies. Oh, we have here the gamut of archetypes, yes?' He reached into the satchel beside him and drew out a waterskin, took a long drink, then wiped his mouth with the back of his hand. 'But imagine all of it going for naught, when you pitch from a slippery rung and plunge five hundred man-heights to your ignominious death. Not how the story goes, alas, but then, life isn't a story now, is it?' He replaced the skin and shouldered his pack. 'The embittered slave chooses a different route to the summit, the fool. But then,' he paused to grin back at Fear, 'somebody has to be the moral lesson in this epic, right?'

Seren watched the man climbing the rungs. When he came opposite the cave mouth, he reached out until one hand gripped the edge of stone, then followed with a foot, stretching until the probing tip of his moccasin settled on the ledge. Then, in a swift shifting of weight, combined with a push away from the ladder, he fluidly spun on one leg, the other swinging over empty air. Then stepping inward, pulled by the weight of the satchel on his back, into the gloom of the entrance.

'Nicely done,' Silchas Ruin commented, and there was something like amusement in his tone, as if he had enjoyed the slave's poking at Fear Sengar's sententious self-importance, thus revealing two edges to his observation. 'I am of a mind to follow him.'

'Me, too,' said Kettle.

Seren Pedac sighed. 'Very well, but I suggest we use ropes between us, and leave the showing off to Udinaas.'

The mouth of the cave revealed that it had been a corridor, probably leading out onto a balcony before the façade had sheared off. Massive sections of the walls, riven through with cracks, had shifted, settled at conflicting angles. And every crevasse, every fissure on all sides that Seren could see, seethed with the squirming furred bodies of bats, awakened now to their presence, chittering and moments from panic. As Seren set her pack down, Udinaas moved beside her.

'Here,' he said, his breath pluming, 'light this lantern, Acquitor – when the temperature drops my hands start going numb.' At her look he glanced over at Fear Sengar, then said, 'Too many years reaching down into icy water. A slave among the Edur knows little comfort.'

'You were fed,' Fear Sengar said.

'When a bloodwood tree toppled in the forest,' Udinaas said, 'we'd be sent out to drag it back to the village. Do you remember those times, Fear? Sometimes the trunk would shift unexpectedly, slide in mud or whatever, and crush a slave. One of them was from our own household – you don't recall him, do you? What's one more dead slave? You Edur would shout out when that happened, saying the bloodwood spirit was thirsty for Letherii blood.'

'Enough, Udinaas,' Seren said, finally succeeding in lighting the lantern. As the illumination burgeoned, the bats exploded from the cracks and suddenly the air was filled with frantic, beating wings. A dozen heartbeats later the creatures were gone.

She straightened, raising the lantern.

They stood on a thick mouldy paste – guano, crawling with grubs and beetles – from which rose a foul stench.

'We'd better move in,' Seren said, 'and get clear of this. There are fevers . . .'

*

43

The man was screaming as the guards dragged him by his chains, across the courtyard to the ring-wall. His crushed feet left bloody smears on the pavestones. Screams of accusation wailed from him, shrill outrage at the shaping of the world – the Letherii world.

Tanal Yathvanar snorted softly. 'Hear him. Such naivety.'

Karos Invictad, standing beside him on the balcony, gave him a sharp look. 'You foolish man, Tanal Yathvanar.'

'Invigilator?'

Karos Invictad leaned his forearms on the railing and squinted down at the prisoner. Fingers like bloated river-worms slowly entwined. From somewhere overhead a gull was laughing. 'Who poses the greatest threat to the empire, Yathvanar?'

'Fanatics,' Tanal replied after a moment. 'Like that one below.'

'Incorrect. Listen to his words. He is possessed of certainty. He holds to a secure vision of the world, a man with the correct answers – that the prerequisite questions were themselves the correct ones goes without saying. A citizen with certainty, Yathvanar, can be swayed, turned, can be made into a most diligent ally. All one needs to do is find what threatens them the most. Ignite their fear, burn to cinders the foundations of their certainty, then offer an equally certain alternate way of thinking, of seeing the world. They will reach across, no matter how wide the gulf, and grasp and hold on to you with all their strength. No, the certain are not our enemies. Presently misguided, as in the case of the man below, but always most vulnerable to fear. Take away the comfort of their convictions, then coax them with seemingly cogent and reasonable convictions of our own making. Their eventual embrace is assured.'

'I see.'

'Tanal Yathvanar, our greatest enemies are those who are without certainty. The ones with questions, the ones who regard our tidy answers with unquenchable scepticism. Those questions assail us, undermine us. They . . . agitate. Understand, these dangerous citizens understand that nothing is simple; their stance is the very opposite of naivety. They are humbled by the ambivalence to which they are witness, and they defy our simple, comforting assertions of clarity, of a black and white world. Yathvanar, when you wish to deliver the gravest insult to such a citizen, call them naive. You will leave them incensed; indeed, virtually speechless . . . until you watch their minds backtracking, revealed by a cascade of expressions, as they ask themselves: who is it that would call me naive? Well, comes the answer, clearly a person possessing certainty, with all the arrogance and pretension that position entails; a confidence, then, that permits the offhand judgement, the derisive dismissal uttered from a most lofty height. And from all this, into your victim's eyes will come the light of

44

recognition – in you he faces his enemy, his truest enemy. And he will know fear. Indeed, terror.'

'You invite the question, then, Invigilator . . .'

Karos Invictad smiled. 'Do I possess certainty? Or am I in fact plagued by questions, doubts, do I flounder in the wild currents of complexity?' He was silent for a moment, then he said, 'I hold to but one certainty. Power shapes the face of the world. In itself, it is neither benign nor malicious, it is simply the tool by which its wielder reshapes all that is around him or herself, reshapes it to suit his or her own . . . comforts. Of course, to express power is to enact tyranny, which can be most subtle and soft, or cruel and hard. Implicit in power – political, familial, as you like – is the threat of coercion. Against all who choose to resist. And know this: if coercion is available, it *will* be used.' He gestured. 'Listen to that man. He does my work for me. Down in the dungeons, his cellmates hear his ravings, and some among them join in chorus – the guards take note of who, and that is a list of names I peruse daily, for they are the ones I can win over. The ones who say nothing, or turn away, now that is the list of those who *must* die.'

'So,' said Tanal, 'we let him scream.'

'Yes. The irony is, he truly is naive, although not of course as you originally meant. It is his very certainty that reveals his blithe ignorance. It is a further irony that both extremes of the political spectrum reveal a convergence of the means and methods and indeed the very attitudes of the believers – their ferocity against naysayers, the blood they willingly spill for their cause, defending their version of reality. The hatred they reveal for those who voice doubts. Scepticism disguises contempt, after all, and to be held in contempt by one who holds to nothing is to feel the deepest, most cutting wound. And so we who hold to certainty, Yathvanar, soon find it our mission to root out and annihilate the questioners. And my, the pleasure we derive from that . . .'

Tanal Yathvanar said nothing, inundated with a storm of suspicions, none of which he could isolate, chase down.

Karos Invictad said, 'You were so quick to judge, weren't you? Ah, you revealed so much with that contemptuous utterance. And I admit to being amused at my own instinctive reponse to your words. *Naive.* Errant take me, I wanted to rip your head from your body, like decapitating a swamp-fly. I wanted to show you true contempt. Mine. For you and your kind. I wanted to take that dismissive expression on your face and push it through an offal grinder. You think you have all the answers? You must, given the ease of your voiced judgement. Well, you pathetic little creature, one day uncertainty will come to your door, will clamber down your throat, and it will be a race to see which arrives first, humility or death. Either way, I will spare you a moment's compassion, which is what sets you and me apart, isn't it? A package arrived today, yes?'

45

Tanal blinked. *See how we all possess a bloodlust.* Then he nodded. 'Yes, Invigilator. A new puzzle for you.'

'Excellent. From whom?'

'Anonymous.'

'Most curious. Is that part of the mystery, or fear of ridicule when I solve it after a mere moment's thought? Well, how can you possibly answer that question? Where is it now?'

'It should have been delivered to your office, sir.'

'Good. Permit the man below to scream for the rest of the afternoon, then have him sent below again.'

Tanal bowed as Karos left the balcony. He waited for a hundred heartbeats, then he too departed.

A short time later he descended to the lowest level of the ancient dungeons, down spiralling stone steps to corridors and cells that had not seen regular use in centuries. The recent floods had inundated both this level and the one above it, although the waters had since drained, leaving behind thick silts and the stench of stagnant, filthy water. Carrying a lantern, Tanal Yathvanar made his way down a sloping channel until he came to what had once been the primary inquisition chamber. Arcane, rust-seized mechanisms squatted on the pavestoned floor, or were affixed to walls, with one bedframe-like cage suspended from the ceiling by thick chains.

Directly opposite the entrance was a wedge-shaped contraption, replete with manacles and chains that could be drawn tight via a wall-mounted ratchet to one side. The inclined bed faced onto the chamber, and shackled to it was the woman he had been instructed to release.

She was awake, turning her face away from the sudden light.

Tanal set the lantern down on a table cluttered with instruments of torture. 'Time for a feeding,' he said.

She said nothing.

A well-respected academic. Look at her now. 'All those lofty words of yours,' Tanal said. 'In the end, they prove less substantial than dust on the wind.'

Her voice was ragged, croaking. 'May you one day choke on that dust, little man.'

Tanal smiled. ' "Little". You seek to wound me. A pathetic effort.' He walked over to a chest against the wall to his right. It had contained vise-helms, but Tanal had removed the skull-crushers, filling the chest with flasks of water and dried foodstuffs. 'I shall need to bring down buckets with soap-water,' he said, drawing out the makings of her supper. 'Unavoidable as your defecation is, the smell and the stains are most unpleasant.'

46

'Oh, I offend you, do I?'

He glanced over at her and smiled. 'Janath Anar, a senior lecturer in the Academy of Imperial Learning. Alas, you appear to have learned nothing of imperial ways. Although, one might argue, that has changed since your arrival here.'

She studied him, a strangely heavy look to her bruised eyes. 'From the First Empire until this day, little man, there have been times of outright tyranny. That the present oppressors are Tiste Edur is scarely worth noting. After all, the true oppression comes from you. Letherii against Letherii. Furthermore—'

'Furthermore,' Tanal said, mocking her, 'the Patriotists are the Letherii gift of mercy against their own. Better us than the Edur. We do not make indiscriminate arrests; we do not punish out of ignorance, we are not random.'

'A gift? Do you truly believe that?' she asked, still studying him. 'The Edur don't give a damn, one way or the other. Their leader is unkillable, and that makes their mastery absolute.'

'A high-ranking Tiste Edur liaises with us almost daily—'

'To keep you in rein. You, Tanal Yathvanar, not your prisoners. You and that madman, Karos Invictad.' She cocked her head. 'Why is it, I wonder, that organizations such as yours are invariably run by pitiful human failures? By small-minded psychotics and perverts. All bullied as children, of course. Or abused by twisted parents – I'm sure you have terrible tales to confess, of your miserable youth. And now the power is in your hands, and oh how the rest of us suffer.'

Tanal walked over with the food and the flask of water.

'For Errant's sake,' she said, 'loosen at least one of my arms, so I can feed myself.'

He came up beside her. 'No, I prefer it this way. Are you humiliated, being fed like a babe?'

'What do you want with me?' Janath asked, as he unstoppered the flask.

He set it to her cracked lips, watched her drink. 'I don't recall saying I wanted anything,' he replied.

She twisted her head away, coughing, water spilling onto her chest. 'I've confessed everything,' she said after a moment. 'You have all my notes, my treasonous lectures on personal responsibility and the necessity for compassion—'

'Yes, your moral relativism.'

'I refute any notion of relativism, little man – which you'd know had you bothered reading those notes. The structures of a culture do not circumvent nor excuse self-evident injustice or inequity. The status quo is not sacred, not an altar to paint in rivers of blood. Tradition and habit are not sound arguments—'

'White Crow, woman, you are most certainly a lecturer. I liked you better unconscious.'

'Best beat me senseless again,' she said.

'Alas, I cannot. After all, I am supposed to free you.'

Her eyes narrowed on his, then shied away again. 'Careless of me,' she muttered.

'In what way?' he asked.

'I was almost seduced. The lure of hope. If you are supposed to free me, you would never have brought me down here. No, I'm to be your private victim, and you my private nightmare. In the end, the chains upon you will be a match to mine.'

'The psychology of the human mind,' Tanal said, pushing some fat-soaked bread into her mouth. 'Your speciality. So, you can read my life as easily as you read a scroll. Is that supposed to frighten me?'

She chewed, then, with a struggle, swallowed. 'I wield a far deadlier weapon, little man.'

'And that would be?'

'I slip into your head. I see through your eyes. Swim the streams of your thought. I stand there, looking at the soiled creature chained to this rape-bed. And eventually, I begin to understand you. It's more intimate than making love, little man, because all your secrets vanish. And, in case you were wondering, yes, I am doing it even now. Listening to my own words as you listen, feeling the tightness gripping your chest, that odd chill beneath your skin despite the fresh sweat. The sudden fear, as you realize the extent of your vulnerability—'

He struck her. Hard enough to snap her head to one side. Blood gushed from her mouth. She coughed, spat, then spat again, her breath coming in ragged, liquid gasps. 'We can resume this meal later,' he said, struggling to keep his words toneless. 'I expect you'll do your share of screaming in the days and weeks to come, Janath, but I assure you, your cries will reach no-one.'

A peculiar hacking sound came from her.

After a moment, Tanal realized she was laughing.

'Impressive bravado,' he said, with sincerity. 'Eventually, I may in truth free you. For now, I remain undecided. I'm sure you understand.'

She nodded.

'You arrogant bitch,' he said.

She laughed again.

He backed away. 'Do not think I will leave the lantern,' he snarled.

Her laughter followed him out, cutting like broken glass.

The ornate carriage, trimmed in gleaming bloodwood, was motionless, drawn up to one side of the main thoroughfare of Drene, its tall wheels straddling the open sewer. The four bone-white horses stood listless in

48

the unseasonal heat, heads hanging down over their collars. Directly ahead of them the street was framed in an arching open gate, and beyond it was the sprawling maze of the High Market, a vast concourse crowded with stalls, carts, livestock and throngs of people.

The flow of wealth, the cacophony of voices and the multitude of proffering or grasping hands seemed to culminate in a force, battering at Brohl Handar's senses even from where he sat, protected within the plush confines of the carriage. The heaving sounds from the market, the chaotic back and forth flow of people beneath the gate, and the crowds on the street itself, all made the Overseer think of religious fervour, as if he was witness to a frenzied version of a Tiste Edur funeral. In place of the women voicing their rhythmic grunts of con- strained grief, drovers bullied braying beasts through the press. Instead of unblooded youths wading through blood-frothed surf pounding paddles against the waves, there was the clatter of cartwheels and the high, piping cries of hawkers. The woodsmoke of the pyres and offer- ings enwreathing an Edur village was, here, a thick, dusty river tainted with a thousand scents. Dung, horse piss, roasting meat, vegetables and fish, uncured myrid hides and tanned rodara skins; rotting wastes and the cloying smells of intoxicating drugs.

Here, among the Letherii, no precious offerings were thrown into the sea. Tusked seal ivory leaned against shelves like fang-rows from some wooden mechanisms of torture. In other stalls, that ivory reappeared, this time carved into a thousand shapes, many of them mimicking religious objects from the Edur, the Jheck and the Fent, or as playing pieces for a game. Polished amber was adornment, not the sacred tears of captured dusk, and bloodwood itself had been carved into bowls, cups and cooking utensils.

Or to trim an ostentatious carriage.

Through a slit in the shutters, the Overseer watched the surging to and fro on the street. An occasional Tiste Edur appeared in the crowds, a head taller than most Letherii, and Brohl thought he could read some- thing of bemusement behind their haughty, remote expressions; and once, in the face of an overdressed, ring-speared Elder whom Brohl knew personally, he saw the glint of avarice in the Edur's eyes.

Change was rarely chosen, and its common arrival was slow, subtle. Granted, the Letherii had experienced the shock of defeated armies, a slain king, and a new ruling class, but even then such sudden reversals had proved not nearly as catastrophic as one might have expected. The skein that held Lether together was resilient and, Brohl now knew, far stronger than it appeared. What disturbed him the most, however, was the ease with which that skein entwined all who found themselves in its midst.

Poison in that touch, yet not fatal, just intoxicating. Sweet, yet perhaps, ultimately, deadly. This is what comes of . . . comfort. Yet, he could well see, the reward of comfort was not available to all; indeed, it seemed disturbingly rare. While those who possessed wealth clearly exulted in its display, that very ostentation underscored the fact that they were a distinct minority. But that imbalance was, he now understood, entirely necessary. Not everyone could be rich – the system would not permit such equity, for the power and privilege it offered was dependent on the very opposite. *Inequity, else how can power be assessed, how can the gifts of privilege be valued? For there to be rich, there must be poor, and more of the latter than the former.*

Simple rules, easily arrived at through simple observation. Brohl Handar was not a sophisticated man, a shortcoming he was reminded of every day since his arrival as Overseer of Drene. He had no particular experience with governing, and few of the skills in his possession were proving applicable to his new responsibilities.

The Factor, Letur Anict, was conducting an unofficial war against the tribes beyond the borderlands, using imperial troops to steal land and consolidate his new-found holdings. There was no real justification for this bloodshed; the goal was personal wealth. As yet, however, Brohl Handar did not know what he was going to do about it, if indeed he was going to do anything. He had prepared a long report to the Emperor, providing well-documented details describing the situation here in Drene. That report remained in Brohl's possession, for he had begun to suspect that, should he send it off to Letheras, it would not reach the Emperor, or any of his Edur advisors. The Letherii Chancellor, Triban Gnol, appeared to be complicit and possibly even in league with Letur Anict – hinting at a vast web of power, hidden beneath the surface and seemingly thriving unaffected by Edur rule. At the moment, all Brohl Handar had were suspicions, hints of that insidious web of power. One link was certain, and that was with this Letherii association of wealthy families, the Liberty Consign. Possibly, this organization was at the very heart of the hidden power. But he could not be sure.

Brohl Handar, a minor noble among the Tiste Edur, and newly appointed Overseer to a small city in a remote corner of the empire, well knew that he could not challenge such a thing as the Liberty Consign. He was, indeed, beginning to believe that the Tiste Edur tribes, scattered as they had become across this vast land, were little more than flotsam riding the indifferent currents of a turgid, deep river.

Yet, there is the Emperor.

Who is quite probably insane.

He did not know to whom to turn; nor even if what he was witnessing was, in truth, as dangerous as it seemed.

Brohl was startled by a commotion near the gate and he leaned forward to set an eye against the slit between the shutters.

50

An arrest. People were quickly moving away from the scene as two nondescript Letherii, one to each side, pushed their victim face-first against one of the gate's uprights. There were no shouted accusations, no frightened denials. The silence shared by the Patriotist agents and their prisoner left the Overseer strangely shaken. As if the details did not matter to any of them.

One of the agents was searching for weapons, finding none, and then, as his fellow agent held the man against the ornate upright, he removed the leather hip-satchel from the man's belt and began rummaging through it. The prisoner's face was pressed sideways against the bas-relief carvings on the broad, squared column, and those carvings depicted some past glory of the Letherii Empire. Brohl Handar suspected the irony was lost on all concerned.

Sedition would be the charge. It was always the charge. But against what? Not the presence of the Tiste Edur – that would be pointless, after all, and certainly there had been virtually no attempts at reprisal, at least none that Brohl Handar had heard about. So . . . what, precisely? Against whom? The Indebted always existed, and some fled their debts, but most did not. There were sects formulated around political or social disquiet, many of them drawing membership from the disenfranchised remnants of subjugated tribes – the Fent, the Nerek, Tarthenal and others. But since the conquest, most of these sects had either dissolved or fled the empire. Sedition. A charge to silence debate. Somewhere, therefore, there must exist a list of the accepted beliefs, the host of convictions and faiths that composed the proper doctrine. Or was something more insidious at work?

There was a scratch at the carriage door, and a moment later it opened.

Brohl Handar studied the figure stepping onto the runner, the carriage tilting with his weight. 'By all means, Orbyn,' he said, 'enter.'

Muscle softened by years of inactivity, fleshy face, the jowls heavy and slack, Orbyn 'Truthfinder' seemed to sweat incessantly, regardless of ambient temperature, as if some internal pressure forced the toxins of his mind to the surface of his skin. The local head of the Patriotists was, to Brohl Handar's eye, the most despicable, malicious creature he had ever met.

'Your arrival is well timed,' the Tiste Edur said as Orbyn entered the carriage and settled down on the bench opposite, the acrid smell of his sweat wafting across. 'Although I was not aware that you personally oversee the daily activities of your agents.'

Orbyn's thin lips creased in a smile. 'We have stumbled on some information that might be of interest to you, Overseer.'

'Another one of your non-existent conspiracies?'

The smile widened momentarily, a flicker. 'If you are referring to the

51

Bolkando Conspiracy, alas, that one belongs to the Liberty Consign. The information we have acquired concerns your people.'

My people. 'Very well.' Brohl Handar waited. Outside, the two agents were dragging their prisoner away, and around them the flow of humanity resumed, furtive in their avoidance.

'A party was sighted, west of Bluerose. Two Tiste Edur, one of them white-skinned. This latter one, I believe, has become known as the White Crow – a most disturbing title for us Letherii, by the way.' He blinked, the lids heavy. 'Accompanying them were three Letherii, two female and one an escaped slave with the ownership tattoos of the Hiroth tribe.'

Brohl forced himself to remain expressionless, although a tightness gripped his chest. *This is none of your business.* 'Do you have more details as to their precise location?'

'They were heading east, to the mountains. There are three passes, only two open this early in the season.'

Brohl Handar slowly nodded. 'The Emperor's K'risnan are also capable of determining their general whereabouts. Those passes are blocked.' He paused, then said, 'It is as Hannan Mosag predicted.'

Orbyn's dark eyes studied him from between folds of fat. 'I am reminded of Edur efficiency.'

Yes.

The man known as Truthfinder went on, 'The Patriotists have questions regarding this white-skinned Tiste Edur, this White Crow. From which tribe does he hail?'

'None. He is not Tiste Edur.'

'Ah. I am surprised. The description . . .'

Brohl Handar said nothing.

'Overseer, can we assist?'

'Unnecessary at this time,' Brohl replied.

'I am most curious as to why you have not already closed in on this party and effected a capture. My sources indicate that the Tiste Edur is none other than Fear Sengar, the Emperor's brother.'

'As I said, the passes are blocked.'

'Ah, then you are tightening the net even as we speak.'

Brohl Handar smiled. 'Orbyn, you said earlier the Bolkando Conspiracy is under the purview of the Liberty Consign. By that, are you truly telling me that the Patriotists are without interest in that matter?'

'Not at all. The Consign makes use of our network on a regular basis—'

'For which you are no doubt rewarded.'

'Of course.'

'I find myself—'

Orbyn raised a hand, head cocking. 'You will have to excuse me, Overseer. I hear alarms.' He rose with a grunt, pushing open the carriage door.

Bemused, Brohl said nothing, watching as the Letherii left. Once the door was closed he reached to a small compartment and withdrew a woven ball filled with scented grasses, then held it to his face. A tug on a cord stirred the driver to collect up the traces. The carriage lurched as it rolled forward. Brohl could hear the alarms now, a frantic cacophony. Leaning forward, he spoke into the voice-tube. 'Take us to those bells, driver.' He hesitated, then added, 'No hurry.'

The Drene Garrison commanded a full dozen stone buildings situated on a low hill north of the city centre. Armoury, stables, barracks and command headquarters were all heavily fortified, although the complex was not walled. Drene had been a city-state once, centuries past, and after a protracted war with the Awl the beleaguered king had invited Letherii troops to effect victory against the nomads. Decades later, evidence had come out that the conflict itself had been the result of Letherii manipulations. In any case, the Letherii troops had never left; the king accepted the title of vizier and in a succession of tragic accidents he and his entire line were wiped out. But that was history, now, the kind that was met with indifference.

Four principal avenues extended out from the garrison's parade grounds, the one leading northward converging with the Gate Road that led to the city wall and the North Coast track – the least frequented of the three landward routes to and from the city.

In the shadows beneath the gabled balcony of a palatial estate just beyond the armoury, on the north avenue, a clear line of sight was available for the short, lithe figure standing in the cool gloom. A rough-woven hood hid the features, although had anyone bothered to pause in passing, squinting hard, they would have been startled to see the glint of crimson scales where the face should have been, and eyes hidden in black-rimmed slits. But there was something about the figure that encouraged inattention. Gazes slid past, rarely comprehending that, indeed, someone stood in those shadows.

He had positioned himself there just before dawn and it was now late afternoon. Eyes fixed on the garrison, the messengers entering and exiting the headquarters, the visitation of a half-dozen noble merchants, the purchasing of horses, scrap metal, saddles and other sundry materiel. He studied the skin hides on the round-shields of the lancers – flattened faces, the skin darkened to somewhere between purple and ochre, making the tattooing subtle and strangely beautiful.

Late afternoon, the shadows lengthening, and the figure made note of two Letherii men, passing across his field of vision for the second time. Their lack of attention seemed . . . conspicuous, and some instinct told the cowled figure that it was time to leave.

As soon as they had passed by, heading up the street, westward, the figure stepped out from the shadows, walked swiftly and silently after the two men. He sensed their sudden, heightened awareness – and perhaps something like alarm. Moments before catching up to them, he turned right, into an alley leading north.

Fifteen paces in, he found a dark recess in which he could hide. He drew back his cloak and cinched it, freeing his arms and hands.

A dozen heartbeats passed before he heard their footfalls.

He watched them walk past, cautious, both with drawn knives. One whispered something to the other and they hesitated.

The figure allowed his right foot to scrape as he stepped forward.

They spun round.

The Awl'dan cadaran whip was a whisper as it snaked out, the leather – studded with coin-sized, dagger-sharp, overlapping half-moon blades – flickering out in a gleaming arc that licked both men across their throats. Blood sprayed.

He watched them crumple. The blood flowed freely, more from the man who had been on the left, spreading across the greasy cobbles. Stepping close to the other victim, he unsheathed a knife and plunged it point-first into his throat; then, with practised familiarity, he cut off the man's face, taking skin, muscle and hair. He repeated the ghastly task with the other man.

Two fewer agents of the Patriotists to contend with.

Of course, they worked in threes, one always at a distance, following the first two.

From the garrison, the first alarms sounded, a shrill collection of bells that trilled out through the dusty air above the buildings.

Folding up his grisly trophies and pushing them beneath a fold in the loose rodara wool shirt that covered his scaled hauberk, the figure set off along the alley, making for the north gate.

A squad of the city guard appeared at the far mouth, five armoured, helmed Letherii with shortswords and shields.

Upon seeing them, the figure sprinted forward, freeing the cadaran whip in his left hand, while in his right hand he shook free the rygtha crescent axe from the over-under strips of rawhide that had held it against his hip. A thick haft, as long as a grown man's thigh bone, to which each end was affixed a three-quarter-moon iron blade, their planes perpendicular to each other. Cadaran and rygtha: ancient weapons of the Awl'dan, their mastery virtually unknown among the tribes for at least a century.

The constabulary had, accordingly, never before faced such weapons.

At ten paces from the first three guardsmen, the whip lashed out, a blurred sideways figure-eight that spawned screams and gouts of blood that spilled almost black in the alley's gloom. Two of the Letherii reeled back.

The lithe, wiry figure closed on the last man in the front row. Right hand slid along the haft to run up against a flange beneath the left-side crescent blade, the haft slapping parallel to the underside of his forearm as he brought the weapon up – blocking a desperate slash from the guard's shortsword. Then, as the Awl threw his elbow forward, the right-side blade flashed out, cutting at the man's face, connecting just below the helm's rim, chopping through the nasal ridge and frontal bone before dipping into the soft matter of his brain. The tapered, sharp crescent blade slid back out with ease, as the Awl slipped past the falling guard, whip returning from an over-the-head gather to hiss out, wrapping round the neck of the fourth Letherii – who shrieked, dropping his sword as he scrabbled at the deadly blades – as the Awl dropped into a crouch, his right hand sliding the length of the rygtha haft to abut the flanged base of the right-blade then slashing out. The fifth guard jerked his shield upward to block, but too late – the blade caught him across the eyes.

A tug on the whip decapitated the fourth guard.

The Awl released his hold on the cadaran's handle and, gripping the rygtha at both ends, stepped close to slam the haft into the last guard's throat, crushing the windpipe.

Collecting the whip, he moved on.

A street, the sound of lancers off to the right. The gate, fifty paces to the left, now knotted with guards – heads turning his way.

He raced straight for them.

Atri-Preda Bivatt took personal command of a troop of lancers. Twenty riders at her back, she led her horse at a canter, following the trail of a bloodbath.

The two Patriotist agents midway down the alley. Five city guardsmen at the far end.

Riding out onto the street, she angled her mount to the left, drawing her longsword as she neared the gate.

Bodies everywhere, twenty or more, and only two seemed to be still alive. Bivatt stared from beneath the rim of her helm, cold sweat prickling awake beneath her armour. Blood everywhere. On the cobbles, splashed high on the walls and the gate itself. Dismembered limbs. The stench of vacated bowels, spilled intestines. One of the survivors was screaming, head whipping back and forth. Both his hands had been sliced off.

Just beyond the gate, Bivatt saw as she reined in, four horses were down, their riders sprawled out on the road. Drifting dust indicated that the others from the first troop to arrive were riding in pursuit.

The other survivor stumbled up to her. He had taken a blow to the head, the helm dented on one side and blood flowing down that side of his face and neck. In his eyes as he stared up at her, a look of horror. He opened his mouth, but no words came forth.

Bivatt scanned the area once more, then turned to her Finadd. 'Take the troop through, go after them. Get your weapons out, damn you!' She glared back down at the guardsman. 'How many were there?'

He gaped.

More guardsmen were arriving. A cutter hurried to the screaming man who had lost his hands.

'Did you hear my question?' Bivatt hissed.

He nodded, then said. 'One. One man, Atri-Preda.'

One? Ridiculous. 'Describe him!'

'Scales – his face was scales. Red as blood!'

A rider from her troop returned from the road. 'The first troop of lancers are all dead, Atri-Preda,' he said, his tone high and pinched. 'Further down the road. All the horses but one – sir, should we follow?'

'Should you follow? You damned fool – of course you should follow! Stay on his trail!'

A voice spoke behind her. 'That description, Atri-Preda . . .'

She twisted round in her saddle.

Orbyn Truthfinder, sheathed in sweat, stood amidst the carnage, his small eyes fixed on her.

Bivatt bared her teeth in a half-snarl. 'Yes,' she snapped. *Redmask. None other.*

The commander of the Patriotists in Drene pursed his lips, glanced down to scan the corpses on all sides. 'It seems,' he said, 'his exile from the tribes is at an end.'

Yes.

Errant save us.

Brohl Handar stepped down from the carriage and surveyed the scene of battle. He could not imagine what sort of weapons the attackers had used, to achieve the sort of damage he saw before him. The Atri-Preda had taken charge, as more soldiery appeared, while Orbyn Truthfinder stood in the shade of the gate blockhouse entrance, silent and watching.

The Overseer approached Bivatt. 'Atri-Preda,' he said, 'I see none but your own dead here.'

She glared at him, yet it was a look containing more than simple anger. He saw fear in her eyes. 'The city was infiltrated,' she said, 'by an Awl warrior.'

'This is the work of one man?'

'It is the least of his talents.'

56

'Ah, then you know who this man is.'

'Overseer, I am rather busy—'

'Tell me of him.'

Grimacing, she gestured him to one side of the gate. They both had to step carefully over corpses sprawled on the slick cobblestones. 'I think I have sent a troop of lancers out to their deaths, Overseer. My mood is not conducive to lengthy conversation.'

'Oblige me. If a war-party of Awl'dan warriors is at the very edge of this city, there must be an organized response – one,' he added, seeing her offended look, 'involving the Tiste Edur as well as your units.'

After a moment, she nodded. 'Redmask. The only name by which we know him. Even the Awl'dan have but legends of his origins—'

'And they are?'

'Letur Anict—'

Brohl Handar hissed in anger and glared across at Orbyn, who had moved within hearing range. 'Why is it that every disaster begins with that man's name?'

Bivatt resumed. 'There was skirmishing, years ago now, between a rich Awl tribe and the Factor. Simply, Letur Anict coveted the tribe's vast herds. He despatched agents who, one night, entered an Awl camp and succeeded in kidnapping a young woman – one of the clan leader's daughters. The Awl, you see, were in the habit of stealing Letherii children. In any case, that daughter had a brother.'

'Redmask.'

She nodded. 'A younger brother. Anyway, the Factor adopted the girl into his household, and before too long she was Indebted to him—'

'No doubt without even being aware of that. Yes, I understand. And so, in order to purchase that debt, and her own freedom, Letur demanded her father's herds.'

'Yes, more or less. And the clan leader agreed. Alas, even as the Factor's forces approached the Awl camp with their precious cargo, the girl plunged a knife into her own heart. Thereafter, things got rather confused. Letur Anict's soldiers attacked the Awl camp, killing everyone—'

'The Factor decided he would take the herds anyway.'

'Yes. It turned out, however, that there was one survivor. A few years later, as the skirmishes grew fiercer, the Factor's troops found themselves losing engagement after engagement. Ambushes were turned. And the name of Redmask was first heard – a new war chief. Now, what follows is even less precise than what I have described thus far. It seems there was a gathering of the clans, and Redmask spoke – argued, that is, with the Elders. He sought to unify the clans against the Letherii threat, but the Elders could not be convinced. In his rage, Redmask spoke unwise words. The Elders demanded he retract them. He refused, and so was exiled. It is said he travelled east, into the wildlands between here and Kolanse.'

'What is the significance of the mask?'

Bivatt shook her head. 'I don't know. There is a legend that he killed a dragon, in the time immediately following the slaughter of his family. No more than a child – which makes the tale unlikely.' She shrugged.

'And so he has returned,' Brohl Handar said, 'or some other Awl warrior has adopted the mask and so seeks to drive fear into your hearts.'

'No, it was him. He uses a bladed whip and a two-headed axe. The weapons themselves are virtually mythical.'

The Overseer frowned at her. 'Mythical?'

'Awl legends hold that their people once fought a war, far to the east, when the Awl dwelt in the wildlands. The cadaran and rygtha were weapons designed to deal with that enemy. I have no more details than what I have just given you, except that it appears that whatever that enemy was, it wasn't human.'

'Every tribe has tales of past wars, an age of heroes—'

'Overseer, the Awl'dan legends are not like that.'

'Oh?'

'Yes. First of all, the Awl lost that war. That is why they fled west.'

'Have there been no Letherii expeditions into the wildlands?'

'Not in decades, Overseer. After all, we are clashing with the various territories and kingdoms along that border. The last expedition was virtually wiped out, a single survivor driven mad by what she had seen. She spoke of something called the Hissing Night. The voice of death, apparently. In any case, her madness could not be healed and so she was put to death.'

Brohl Handar considered that for a time. An officer had arrived and was waiting to speak with the Atri-Preda. 'Thank you,' he said to Bivatt, then turned away.

'Overseer.'

He faced her again. 'Yes?'

'If Redmask succeeds this time . . . with the tribes, I mean, well, we shall indeed have need of the Tiste Edur.'

His brows rose. 'Of course, Atri-Preda.' *And maybe this way, I can reach the ear of the Emperor and Hannan Mosag. Damn this Letur Anict. What has he brought down upon us now?*

He rode the Letherii horse hard, leaving the north road and cutting east, across freshly tilled fields that had once been Awl'dan grazing land. His passage drew the attention of farmers, and from the last hamlet he skirted three stationed soldiers had saddled horses and set off in pursuit.

In a dip of the valley Redmask had just left, they met their deaths in a chorus of animal and human screams, piercing but short-lived.

A bluster of rhinazan spun in a raucous cloud over the Awl warrior's head, driven away from their favoured hosts by the violence, their wings beating like tiny drums and their long serrated tails hissing in the air as they tracked Redmask. He had long since grown used to their ubiquitous presence. Residents of the wildlands, the weasel-sized flying reptiles were far from home, unless their hosts – in the valley behind him and probably preparing another ambush – could be called home.

He slowed his horse, shifting in discomfort at the awkward Letherii saddle. No-one would reach him now, he knew, and there was no point in running this beast into the ground. The enemy had been confident in their city garrison, brazen with their trophies, and Redmask had learned much in the night and the day he had spent watching them. Bluerose lancers, properly stirruped and nimble on their mounts. Far more formidable than the foot soldiers of years before.

And thus far, since his return, he had seen of his own people only abandoned camps, drover tracks from smallish herds and disused tipi rings. It was as if his home had been decimated, and all the survivors had fled. And at the only scene of battle he had come upon, there had been naught but the corpses of foreigners.

The sun was low on the horizon behind him, dusk closing in, when he came upon the first burned Awl'dan encampment. A year old, maybe more. White bones jutting from the grasses, blackened stumps from the hut frames, a dusty smell of desolation. No-one had come to retrieve the fallen, to lift the butchered bodies onto lashed platforms, freeing the souls to dance with the carrion birds. The scene raised grim memories.

He rode on. As the darkness gathered, the rhinazan slowly drifted away, and Redmask could hear the double-thump, one set to either side, as his two companions, their bloody work done, moved up into flanking positions, barely visible in the gloom.

The rhinazan settled onto the horizontal, scaled backs, to lick splashed gore and pluck ticks, to lift their heads in snapping motions, inhaling sharply to draw in the biting insects that buzzed too close.

Redmask allowed his eyes to half close – he had been awake for most of two days. With Sag'Churok, the hulking male, gliding over the ground to his right; and Gunth Mach, the young drone that was even now growing into a female, on his left, he could not be more secure.

Like the rhinazan, the two K'Chain Che'Malle seemed content, even in this strange land and so far away from their kin.

Content to follow Redmask, to protect him, to kill Letherii.

And he had no idea why.

Silchas Ruin's eyes were reptilian in the lantern light, no more appropriate a sight possible given the chamber they now found themselves in, as far as Seren Pedac was concerned. The stone walls, curving upward to a dome, were carved in overlapping scales. The unbroken pattern left her feeling disoriented, slightly nauseous. She settled onto the floor, blinked the grit from her eyes.

It must be near morning, she judged. They had been walking tunnels, ascending inclines and spiralling ramps for most of an entire night. The air was stale, despite the steady downward flow of currents, as if it was gathering ghosts with every chamber and down every corridor it traversed.

She glanced away from her regard of Silchas Ruin, irritated at her own fascination with the savage, unearthly warrior, the way he could hold himself so perfectly still, even the rise and fall of his chest barely discernible. Buried for millennia, yet he did indeed live. Blood flowed in his veins, thoughts rose grimed with the dust of disuse. When he spoke, she could hear the weight of barrowstones. It was unimaginable to her how a person could so suffer without going mad.

Then again, perhaps he was mad, something hidden deep within him, either constrained by exigencies, or simply awaiting release. As a killer – for that surely was what he was – he was both thorough and dispassionate. As if mortal lives could be reduced in meaning, reduced to surgical judgement: obstacle or ally. Nothing else mattered.

She understood the comfort of seeing the world in that manner. The ease of its simplicity was inviting. But for her, impossible. One could not will oneself blind to the complexities of the world. Yet, for Silchas Ruin, such seeming complexities were without relevance. He had found a kind of certainty, and it was unassailable.

Alas, Fear Sengar was not prepared to accept the hopelessness of his constant assaults upon Silchas Ruin. The Tiste Edur stood near the triangular portal they would soon pass through, as if impatient with this rest stop. 'You think,' he now said to Silchas Ruin, 'that I know virtually nothing of that ancient war, the invasion of this realm.'

The albino Tiste Andii's eyes shifted, fixed on Fear Sengar, but Silchas Ruin made no reply.

'The women remembered,' Fear said. 'They passed the tales to their daughters. Generation after generation. Yes, I know that Scabandari drove a knife into your back, there on that hill overlooking the field of battle. Yet, was this the first betrayal?'

If he was expecting a reaction, he was disappointed.

Udinaas loosed a low laugh from where he sat with his back to the scaled wall. 'You two are so pointless,' he said. 'Who betrayed whom. What does it matter? It's not as if we're relying on trust to keep us together. Tell me, Fear Sengar – once-master of mine – does your brother have any idea of who Ruin is? Where he came from? I would suggest not. Else he would have come after us personally, with ten thousand warriors at his back. Instead, they toy with us. Aren't you even curious why?'

No-one spoke for a half-dozen heartbeats, then Kettle giggled, drawing all eyes to her. Her blink was owlish. 'They want us to find what we're looking for first, of course.'

'Then why block our attempts to travel inland?' Seren demanded.

'Because they know it's the wrong direction.'

'How could they know that?'

Kettle's small, dust-stained hands fluttered like bats in the gloom. 'The Crippled God told them, that's how. The Crippled God said it's not yet time to travel east. He's not ready for open war, yet. He doesn't want us to go into the wildlands, where all the secrets are waiting.'

Seren Pedac stared at the child. 'Who in Errant's name is the Crippled God?'

'The one who gave Rhulad his sword, Acquitor. The true power behind the Tiste Edur.' Kettle threw up her hands. 'Scabandari's dead. The bargain was Hannan Mosag's, and the coin was Rhulad Sengar.'

Fear stood with bared teeth, staring at Kettle with something like terror in his eyes. 'How do you know this?' he demanded.

'The dead told me. They told me lots of things. So did the ones under the trees, the trapped ones. And they said something else too. They said the vast wheel is about to turn, one last time, before it closes. It closes, because it has to, because that's how he made it. To tell him all he needs to know. To tell him the truth.'

'Tell who?' Seren asked, scowling in confusion.

'Him, the one who's coming. You'll see.' She ran over to where Fear stood, took him by one hand and started tugging. 'We need to hurry, or they'll get us. And if they get us, Silchas Ruin will have to kill everyone.'

I could strangle that child. But she pushed herself to her feet once more.

Udinaas was laughing.

She was inclined to strangle him as well.

'Silchas,' she said as she moved close, 'do you have any idea what Kettle was talking about?'

'No, Acquitor. But,' he added, 'I intend to keep listening.'

CHAPTER THREE

We came upon the fiend on the eastern slope of the
Radagar Spine. It was lying in a shallow gorge formed
by flash flooding, and the stench pervading the hot
air told us of rotting flesh, and indeed upon examination,
conducted with utmost caution on this, the very day
following the ambush on our camp by unknown
attackers, we discovered that the fiend was, while
still alive, mortally wounded. How to describe such
a demonic entity? When upright, it would have balanced
on two hugely muscled hind legs, reminiscent of that
of a shaba, the flightless bird found on the isles of the
Draconean Archipelago, yet in comparison much
larger here. The hip level of the fiend, when standing,
would have been at a man's eye level. Long-tailed,
the weight of the fiend's torso evenly balanced by
its hips, thrusting the long neck and head far forward,
the spine made horizontal. Two long forelimbs, thickly
bound in muscle and hardened scales providing
natural armour, ended, not in grasping talons or hands,
but enormous swords, iron-bladed, that seemed fused,
metal to bone, with the wrists. The head was snouted,
like that of a crocodile, such as those found in the
mud of the southern shoreline of the Bluerose Sea,
yet, again, here much larger. Desiccation had peeled
the lips back to reveal jagged rows of fangs, each
one dagger-long. The eyes, clouded with approaching
death, were nonetheless uncanny and alien to our
senses.

The Atri-Preda, bold as ever, strode forward to deliver
the fiend from its suffering, with a sword thrust into the
soft tissue of its throat. With this fatal wound, the fiend
loosed a death cry that struck us with pain, for the sound

it voiced was beyond our range of hearing, yet it burst
in our skulls with such ferocity that blood was driven
from our nostrils, eyes and ears.

One other detail is worth noting, before I expound on
the extent of said injuries. The wounds visible upon
the fiend were most curious. Elongated, curving slashes,
perhaps from some form of tentacle, but a tentacle bearing
sharp teeth, whilst other wounds were shorter but deeper
in nature, invariably delivered to a region vital to locomotion
or other similar dispensation of limbs, severing tendons
and so forth . . .

Factor Breneda Anict, *Expedition into the Wildlands*
Official Annals of Pufanan Ibyris

H E WAS NOT A MAN IN BED. OH, HIS PARTS FUNCTIONED WELL
enough, but in every other way he was a child, this Emperor of
a Thousand Deaths. But worst of all, Nisall decided, was what
happened afterwards, as he fell into that half-sleep, half-something else,
limbs spasming, endless words tumbling from him in a litany of pleading, punctuated by despairing sobs that scraped the scented air of the
chamber. And before long, after she'd escaped the bed itself, drawing a
robe about her and taking position near the painted scene in the false
window, five paces distant, she would watch him crawl down onto the
floor and make his way as if crippled from some spinal injury, the ever-
present sword trailing in one hand, across the room to the corner, where
he would spend the rest of the night, curled up, locked in some eternal
nightmare.

A thousand deaths, lived through night upon night. A thousand.

An exaggeration, of course. A few hundred at most.

Emperor Rhulad's torment was not the product of a fevered
imagination, nor born of a host of anxieties. What haunted him were
the truths of his past. She was able to identify some of his mutterings,
in particular the one that dominated his nightmares, for she had
been there. In the throne room, witness to Rhulad's non-death, weeping there on the floor all slick with his spilled blood, with a corpse on
his throne and Rhulad's own slayer lying half upright against the dais –
stolen away by poison.

Hannan Mosag's pathetic slither towards that throne had been halted
by the demon that had appeared to collect the body of Brys Beddict,
and the almost indifferent sword thrust that killed Rhulad as the
apparition made its way out.

The Emperor's awakening shriek had turned her heart into a frozen lump, a cry so brutally raw that she felt its fire in her own throat.

But it was what followed, a short time after his return, that stalked Rhulad with a thousand dripping blades.

To die, only to return, is to never escape. Never escape . . . *anything*.

Wounds closing, he had lifted himself up, onto his hands and knees, still gripping the cursed sword, the weapon that would not let go. Weeping, drawing in ragged breaths, he crawled towards the throne, sagging down once more when he reached the dais.

Nisall had stepped out from where she had hidden moments earlier. Her mind was numb – the suicide of her king – her lover – and the Eunuch, Nifadas – the shocks, one upon another in this terrible throne room, the deaths, tumbling like crowded gravestones in a flooded field. Triban Gnol, ever the pragmatist, knelt before the new Emperor, pledging his service with the ease of an eel sliding under a new rock. The First Consort had been witness, as well, but she could not see Turudal Brizad now, as Rhulad, blood-wet coins gleaming, twisted round on the step and bared his teeth at Hannan Mosag.

'*Not yours*,' he said in a rasp.

'Rhulad—'

'Emperor! And you, Hannan Mosag, are my *Ceda*. Warlock King no longer. My Ceda, yes.'

'Your wife—'

'Dead. Yes.' Rhulad lifted himself onto the dais, then rose, staring now at the dead Letherii king, Ezgara Diskanar. Then he reached out with his unburdened hand, grasped the front of the king's brocaded tunic, and dragged the corpse from the throne, letting it fall to one side, head crunching on the tiled floor. A shiver seemed to rack through Rhulad. Then he sat on the throne and looked out, eyes settling once more on Hannan Mosag. 'Ceda,' he said, 'in this, our chamber, you will ever approach us on your belly, as you do now.'

From the shadows at the far end of the throne room there came a phlegmatic cackle.

Rhulad flinched, then said, 'Now you will leave us, Ceda. And take that hag Janall and her son with you.'

'Emperor, please, you must understand—'

'*Get out!*'

The shriek jarred Nisall, and she hesitated, fighting the urge to flee, to get away from this place. From the court, from the city, from everything.

Then his free hand snapped out and without turning he said to her, 'Not you, whore. You stay.'

Whore. 'That term is inappropriate,' she said, then stiffened in fear, surprised by her own temerity.

He fixed feverish eyes on her. Then, incongruously, he waved dismissively and spoke with sudden weariness. 'Of course. We apologize. Imperial Concubine . . .' His glittering face twisted in a half-smile. 'Your king should have taken you as well. He was being selfish, or perhaps his love for you was so deep that he could not bear inviting you into death.'

She said nothing, for, in truth, she had no answer to give him.

'Ah, we see the doubt in your eyes. Concubine, you have our sympathy. Know that we will not use you cruelly.' He fell silent then, as he watched Hannan Mosag drag himself back across the threshold of the chamber's grand entranceway. A half-dozen more Tiste Edur had appeared, tremulous in their furtive motions, their uncertainty at what they were witnessing. A hissed command from Hannan Mosag sent two into the room, each one drawing up the burlap over the mangled forms of Janall and Quillas, her son. The sound as they dragged the two flesh-filled sacks from the chamber was, to Nisall's ears, more grisly than anything else she had yet heard on this fell day.

'At the same time,' the Emperor went on after a moment, 'the title and its attendant privileges . . . remain, should you so desire.'

She blinked, feeling as if she was standing on shifting sand. 'You free me to choose, Emperor?'

A nod, the bleary, red-shot eyes still fixed on the chamber's entrance-way. 'Udinaas,' he whispered. 'Betrayer. You . . . you were not free to choose. Slave – my slave – I should never have trusted the darkness, never . . .' He flinched once more on the throne, eyes suddenly glittering. 'He comes.'

She had no idea whom he meant, but the raw emotion in his voice frightened her anew. What more could come on this terrible day?

Voices outside, one of them sounding bitter, then diffident.

She watched as a Tiste Edur warrior strode into the throne room. Rhulad's brother. One of them. The one who had left Rhulad lying on the tiles. Young, handsome in that way of the Edur – both alien and perfect. She tried to recall if she had heard his name—

'Trull,' said the Emperor in a rasp. 'Where is he? Where is Fear?'

'He has . . . left.'

'Left? Left us?'

'Us. Yes, Rhulad – or do you insist I call you Emperor?'

Expressions twisted across Rhulad's coin-studded face, one after another, then he grimaced and said, 'You left me, too, brother. Left me bleeding . . . on the floor. Do you think yourself different from Udinaas? Less a betrayer than my Letherii slave?'

'Rhulad, would that you were my brother of old—'

'The one you sneered down upon?'

'If it seemed I did that, then I apologize.'

'Yes, you see the need for that now, don't you?'

Trull Sengar stepped forward. 'It's the sword, Rhulad. It is cursed – please, throw it away. Destroy it. You've won the throne now, you don't need it any more—'

'You are wrong.' He bared his teeth, as if sickened by self-hatred. 'Without it I am just Rhulad, youngest son of Tomad. Without the sword, brother, I am nothing.'

Trull cocked his head. 'You have led us to conquest. I will stand beside you. So will Binadas, and our father. You have won that throne, Rhulad – you need not fear Hannan Mosag—'

'That miserable worm? You think me frightened of him?' The sword-tip made a snapping sound as its point jumped free of the tiles. Rhulad aimed the weapon at Trull's chest. 'I am the *Emperor*!'

'No, you're not,' Trull replied. 'Your sword is Emperor – your sword and the power behind it.'

'Liar!' Rhulad shrieked.

Nisall saw Trull flinch back, then steady himself. 'Prove it.'

The Emperor's eyes widened.

'Shatter the sword – Sister's blessing, just let it fall from your hand. Even that, Rhulad. Just that. Let it fall!'

'No! I know what you want, brother! You will take it – I see you tensed, ready to dive for it – I see the truth!' The weapon was shuddering between them, as if eager for blood, anyone's blood.

Trull shook his head. 'I want it shattered, Rhulad.'

'You cannot stand at my side,' the Emperor hissed. 'Too close – there is betrayal in your eyes – you left me! Crippled on the floor!' He raised his voice, 'Where are my warriors? Into the chamber! Your Emperor commands it!'

A half-dozen Edur warriors suddenly appeared, weapons out.

'Trull,' Rhulad whispered. 'I see you have no sword. Now it is for you to drop your favoured weapon, your spear. And your knives. What? Do you fear I will slay you? Show me the trust you claim in yourself. Guide me with your honour, *brother*.'

She did not know it then; she did not understand enough of the Edur way of life, but she saw something in Trull's face, a kind of surrender, but a surrender that was far more complicated, fraught, than simply disarming himself there before his brother. Levels of resignation, settling one upon another, the descent of impossible burdens – and the knowledge shared between the two brothers, of what such a surrender signified. She did not realize at the time what Trull's answer would mean, the way it was done, not in his own name, not for himself, but for Fear. Fear Sengar, more than anyone else. She did not realize, then, the immensity of his sacrifice, as he unslung his spear and let it clatter to the tiles; as he removed his knife belt and threw it to one side.

There should have been triumph in Rhulad's tortured eyes, then, but there wasn't. Instead, a kind of confusion clouded his gaze, made him shy away, as if seeking help. His attention found and focused upon the six warriors, and he gestured with the sword and said in a broken voice, 'Trull Sengar is to be Shorn. He will cease to exist, for ourself, for all Edur. Take him. Bind him. Take him away.'

Neither had she realized what that judgement, that decision, had cost Rhulad himself.

Free to choose, she had chosen to remain, for reasons she could not elucidate even in her own mind. Was there pity? Perhaps. Ambition, without question – for she had sensed, in that predatory manner demanded of life in the court, that there was a way through to him, a way to replace – without all the attendant history – those who were no longer at Rhulad's side. Not one of his warrior sycophants – they were worthless, ultimately, and she knew that Rhulad was well aware of that truth. In the end, she could see, he had no-one. Not his brother, Binadas, who, like Trull, proved too close and thus too dangerous for the Emperor to keep around – and so he had sent him away, seeking champions and scattered kin of the Edur tribes. As for his father, Tomad, again the suborning role proved far too awkward to accommodate. Of the surviving K'risnan of Hannan Mosag, fully half had been sent to accompany Tomad and Binadas, so as to keep the new Ceda weak.

And all the while, as these decisions were made, as the Shorning was conducted, in secrecy, away from Letherii eyes, and as Nisall manoeuvred herself into the Emperor's bed, the Chancellor, Triban Gnol, had watched on, with the hooded eyes of a raptor.

The consort, Turudal Brizad, had vanished, although Nisall had heard rumours among the court servants that he had not gone far; that he haunted the lesser travelled corridors and subterranean mysteries of the old palace, ghostly and rarely more than half seen. She was undecided on the veracity of such claims; even so, if he were indeed hiding still in the palace, she realized that such a thing would not surprise her in the least. It did not matter – Rhulad had no wife, after all.

The Emperor's lover, a role she was accustomed to, although it did not seem that way. Rhulad was so young, so different from Ezgara Diskanar. His spiritual wounds were too deep to be healed by her touch, and so, even as she found herself in a position of eminence, of power – close as she was to the throne – she felt helpless. And profoundly alone.

She stood, watching the Emperor of Lether writhing as he curled up ever tighter in the corner of the room. Among the whimpers, groans and gasps, he spat out fragments of his conversation with Trull, his forsaken brother. And again and again, in hoarse whispers, Rhulad begged forgiveness.

Yet a new day awaited them, she reminded herself. And she would see this broken man gather himself, collect the pieces and then take his place seated on the imperial throne, looking out with red-rimmed eyes, his fragmented armour of coins gleaming dull in the light of the traditional torches lining the chamber's walls; and where those coins were missing, there was naught but scarred tissue, crimson-ringed weals of malformed flesh. And then, this ghastly apparition would, in the course of that day, proceed to astonish her.

Eschewing the old protocols of imperial rule, the Emperor of a Thousand Deaths would sit through a presentation of petitions, an ever-growing number of citizens of the empire, poor and rich alike, who had come to accept the Imperial Invitation, feeding their courage to come face to face with their foreign ruler. For bell after bell, Rhulad would mete out justice as best he could. His struggles to understand the lives of the Letherii had touched her in unexpected ways – there was, she had come to believe, a decent soul beneath all that accursed trauma. And it was then that Nisall found herself most needed, although more often of late it was the Chancellor who dominated the advising, and she had come to realize that Triban Gnol had begun to view her as a rival. He was the principal organizer of the petitions, the filter that kept the numbers manageable, and his office had burgeoned accordingly. That his expanded staff also served as a vast and invasive web of spies in the palace was of course a given.

Thus, Nisall watched her Emperor, who had ascended the throne wading through blood, strive for benign rule, seeking a sensitivity too honest and awkward to be other than genuine. And it was breaking her heart.

For power had no interest in integrity. Even Ezgara Diskanar, so full of promise in his early years, had come to raise a wall between himself and the empire's citizens in the last decade of his rule. Integrity was too vulnerable to abuse by others, and Ezgara had suffered that betrayal again and again, and, perhaps most painfully of all, from his own wife, Janall, and then their son.

Too easy to dismiss the burden of such wounds, the depth of such scars.

And Rhulad, this youngest son of an Edur noble family, had been a victim of betrayal, of what must have been true friendship – with the slave, Udinaas – and in the threads of shared blood, from his very own brothers.

But each day, he overcame the torments of the night just gone. Nisall wondered, however, how much longer that could last. She alone was witness to his inner triumph, to that extraordinary war he waged with himself every morning. The Chancellor, for all his spies, knew nothing of it – she was certain of that. And that made him dangerous in his ignorance.

She needed to speak to Triban Gnol. She needed to mend this bridge. *But I will not be his spy.*

A most narrow bridge, then, one to be trod with caution.

Rhulad stirred in the gloom.

And then he whispered, 'I know what you want, brother . . .'

'So guide me . . . guide me with your honour . . .'

Ah, Trull Sengar, wherever your spirit now lurks, does it please you? Does this please you, to know that your Shorning failed?

So that you have now returned.

To so haunt Rhulad.

'Guide me,' Rhulad croaked.

The sword scraped on the floor, rippling over mosaic stones like cold laughter.

'It is not possible, I'm afraid.'

Bruthen Trana studied the Letherii standing before him for a long moment and said nothing.

The Chancellor's gaze flicked away, as if distracted, and seemed moments from dismissing the Edur warrior outright; then, perhaps realizing that might be unwise, he cleared his throat and spoke in a tone of sympathy. 'The Emperor insists on these petitions, as you are aware, and they consume his every waking moment. They are, if you forgive me, his obsession.' His brows lifted a fraction. 'How can a true subject question their Emperor's love of justice? The citizens have come to adore him. They have come to see him for the honourable ruler he is in truth. That transition has taken some time, I admit, and involved immense effort on our part.'

'I wish to speak to the Emperor,' Bruthen said, his tone matching precisely the previous time he had spoken those words.

Triban Gnol sighed. 'Presumably you wish to make your report regarding Invigilator Karos Invictad and his Patriotists in person. I assure you, I do forward said reports.' He frowned at the Tiste Edur, then nodded and said, 'Very well. I will convey your wishes to his highness, Bruthen Trana.'

'If need be, place me among the petitioners.'

'That will not be necessary.'

The Tiste Edur gazed at the Chancellor for a half-dozen heartbeats, then he turned about and left the office. In the larger room beyond waited a crowd of Letherii. A score of faces turned to regard Bruthen as he threaded his way through – faces nervous, struggling with fear – while others studied the Tiste Edur with eyes that gave away nothing: the Chancellor's agents, the ones who, Bruthen suspected, went out each morning to round up the day's petitioners, then coached them in what to say to their Emperor.

Ignoring the Letherii as they parted to let him pass, he made his way out into the corridor, then onward through the maze of chambers, hallways and passages that composed the palace. He saw very few other Tiste Edur, barring one of Hannan Mosag's K'risnan, bent-backed and walking with one shoulder scraping against a wall, dark eyes flickering an acknowledgement as he limped along.

Bruthen Trana made his way into the wing of the palace closest to the river, and here the air was clammy, the corridors mostly empty. While the flooding that had occurred during the early stages of construction had been rectified, via an ingenious system of subsurface pylons, it seemed nothing could dispel the damp. Holes had been knocked in outer walls to create a flow of air, to little effect apart from filling the musty gloom with the scent of river mud and decaying plants.

Bruthen walked through one such hole, emerging out onto a mostly broken-up cobble path, with felled trees rotting amidst high grasses off to his left and the foundations of a small building to his right. Abandonment lingered in the still air like suspended pollen, and Bruthen was alone as he ascended the path's uneven slope to arrive at the edge of a cleared area, the other end of which rose the ancient tower of the Azath, with the lesser structures of the Jaghut to either side. In this clearing there were grave markers, set out in no discernible order. Half-buried urns, wax-sealed at the mouth, from which emerged weapons. Swords, broken spears, axes, maces – trophies of failure, a stunted forest of iron.

The Fallen Champions, the residents of a most prestigious cemetery. All had killed Rhulad at least once, some more than once – the greatest of these, an almost full-blood Tarthenal, had slain the Emperor seven times, and Bruthen could remember, with absolute clarity, the look of growing rage and terror in that Tarthenal's bestial face each time his fallen opponent arose, renewed, stronger and deadlier than he had been only moments earlier.

He entered the bizarre necropolis, eyes drifting across the various weapons, once so lovingly cared for – many of them bearing names – but now sheathed in rust. At the far end, slightly separated from all the others, stood an empty urn. Months earlier, out of curiosity, he had reached down into it, and found a silver cup. The cup that had contained the poison that killed three Letherii in the throne room – that had killed Brys Beddict.

No ashes. Even his sword had disappeared.

Bruthen Trana suspected that if this man were to return, now, he would face Rhulad again, and do what he did before. No, it was more than suspicion. A certainty.

Unseen by Rhulad, as the new Emperor lay there, cut to shreds on the floor, Bruthen had edged into the chamber to see for himself. And in that moment's fearful glance, he had discerned the appalling precision of that butchery. Brys Beddict had been perfunctory. Like a scholar dissecting a weak argument, an effort on his part no greater than tying on his moccasins.

Would that he had seen the duel itself, that he had witnessed the artistry of this tragically slain Letherii swordsman.

He stood, looking down at the dusty, web-covered urn.

And prayed for Brys Beddict's return.

A pattern was taking shape, incrementally, inexorably. Yet the Errant, once known as Turudal Brizad, Consort to Queen Janall, could not discern its meaning. The sensation, of unease, of dread, was new to him. Indeed, he considered, one could not imagine a more awkward state of mind for a god, here in the heart of his realm.

Oh, he had known times of violence; he had walked the ashes of dead empires, but his own sense of destiny was, even then, ever untarnished, inviolate and absolute. And, to make matters worse, patterns were his personal obsession, held to with a belief in his mastery of that arcane language, a mastery beyond challenge.

Then who is it who plays with me now?

He stood in the gloom, listening to the trickle of water seeping down some unseen wall, and stared down at the Cedance, the stone tiles of the Holds, the puzzle floor that was the very foundation of his realm. The Cedance. *My tiles. Mine. I am the Errant. This is* my *game.*

While before him the pattern ground on, the rumbling of stones too low and deep to hear, yet their resonance grated in his bones. *Disparate pieces, coming together. A function hidden, until the last moment – when all is too late, when the closure denies every path of escape.*

Do you expect me to do nothing? I am not just one more of your victims. I am the Errant. By my hand, every fate is turned. All that seems random is by my design. This is an immutable truth. It has ever been. It shall ever be.

Still, the taste of fear was on his tongue, as if he'd been sucking on dirtied coins day after day, running the wealth of an empire through his mouth. *But is that bitter flow inward or out?*

The grinding whisper of motion, all resolution of the images carved into the tiles . . . *lost.* Not a single Hold would reveal itself.

The Cedance had been this way since the day Ezgara Diskanar died. The Errant would be a fool to disregard linkage, but that path of reason had yet to lead him anywhere. Perhaps it was not Ezgara's death that mattered, but the Ceda's. *He never liked me much. And I stood and watched, as the Tiste Edur edged to one side, as he flung his spear, transfixing Kuru Qan, killing the greatest Ceda since the First Empire. My game, I'd thought at the time. But now, I wonder . . .*

71

Maybe it was Kuru Qan's. *And, somehow, it still plays out. I did not warn him of that imminent danger, did I? Before his last breath rattled, he would have comprehended that . . . omission.*

Has this damned mortal cursed me? Me, a god!

Such a curse should be vulnerable. Not even Kuru Qan was capable of fashioning something that could not be dismantled by the Errant. He need only understand its structure, all that pinned it in place, the hidden spikes guiding these tiles.

What comes? The empire is reborn, reinvigorated, revealing the veracity of the ancient prophecy. All is as I foresaw.

His study of the blurred pavestones below the walkway became a glare. He hissed in frustration, and watched his breath plume away in the chill.

An unknown transformation, in which I see naught but the ice of my own exasperation. Thus, I see, but am blind, blind to it all.

The cold, too, was a new phenomenon. The heat of power had bled away from this place. Nothing was as it should be.

Perhaps, at some point, he would have to admit defeat. *And then I will have to pay a visit to a little, crabby old man. Working as a servant to a worthless fool. Humble, I will come in search of answers. I let Tehol live, didn't I? That must count for something.*

Mael, I know you interfered last time. With unconscionable disregard for the rules. My rules. But I have forgiven you, and that, too, must count for something.

Humility tasted even worse than fear. He was not yet ready for that.

He would take command of the Cedance. But to usurp the pattern, he would first have to find its maker. Kuru Qan? He was unconvinced.

There are disturbances in the pantheons, new and old. Chaos, the stink of violence. Yes, this is a god's meddling. Perhaps Mael himself is to blame – no, it feels wrong. More likely, he knows nothing, remains blissfully ignorant. Will it serve me to make him aware that something is awry?

An empire reborn. True, the Tiste Edur had their secrets, or at least they believed such truths were well hidden. They were not. An alien god had usurped them, and had made of a young Edur warrior an avatar, a champion, suitably flawed in grisly homage to the god's own pathetic dysfunctions. Power from pain, glory from degradation, themes in apposition – an empire reborn offered the promise of vigour, of expansion and longevity, none of which was, he had to admit, truly assured. *And such are promises.*

The god shivered suddenly in the bitter cold air of this vast, subterranean chamber. Shivered, on this walkway above a swirling unknown.

The pattern was taking shape.

And when it did, it would be too late.

'It's too late.'

'But there must be something we can do.'

'I'm afraid not. It's dying, Master, and unless we take advantage of its demise right now, someone else will.'

The capabara fish had used its tentacles to crawl up the canal wall, pulling itself over the edge onto the walkway, where it flattened out, strangely spreadeagled, to lie, mouth gaping, gills gasping, watching the morning get cloudy as it expired. The beast was as long as a man is tall, as fat as a mutton merchant from the Inner Isles, and, to Tehol's astonishment, even uglier. 'Yet my heart breaks.'

Bugg scratched his mostly hairless pate, then sighed. 'It's the unusually cold water,' he said. 'These like their mud warm.'

'Cold water? Can't you do something about that?'

'Bugg's Hydrogation.'

'You're branching out?'

'No, I was just trying on the title.'

'How do you hydrogate?'

'I have no idea. Well, I have, but it's not quite a legitimate craft.'

'Meaning it belongs in the realm of the gods.'

'Mostly. Although,' he said, brightening, 'with the recent spate of flooding, and given my past experience in engineering dry foundations, I begin to see some possibilities.'

'Can you soak investors?'

Bugg grimaced. 'Always seeing the destructive side, aren't you, Master?'

'It's my opportunistic nature. Most people,' he added, 'would view that as a virtue. Now, are you truly telling me you can't save this poor fish?'

'Master, it's already dead.'

'Is it? Oh. Well, I guess we now have supper.'

'More like fifteen suppers.'

'In any case, I have an appointment, so I will see you and the fish at home.'

'Why, thank you, Master.'

'Didn't I tell you this morning walk would prove beneficial?'

'Not for the capabara, alas.'

'Granted. Oh, by the way, I need you to make me a list.'

'Of what?'

'Ah, I will have to tell you that later. As I said, I am late for an appointment. It just occurred to me: is this fish too big for you to carry by yourself?'

'Well,' Bugg said, eyeing the carcass, 'it's small as far as capabara go – remember the one that tried to mate with a galley?'

'The betting on that outcome overwhelmed the Drownings. I lost everything I had that day.'

'Everything?'

'Three copper docks, yes.'

'What outcome did you anticipate?'

'Why, small rowboats that could row themselves with big flippery paddles.'

'You're late for your appointment, Master.'

'Wait! Don't look! I need to do something unseemly right now.'

'Oh, Master, really.'

Spies stood on street corners. Small squads of grey rain-caped Patriotists moved through the throngs that parted to give them wide berth as they swaggered with gloved hands resting on their belted truncheons, and on their faces the bludgeon arrogance of thugs. Tehol Beddict, wearing his blanket like a sarong, walked with the benign grace of an ascetic from some obscure but harmless cult. Or at least he hoped so. To venture onto the streets of Letheras these days involved a certain measure of risk that had not existed in King Ezgara Diskanar's days of pleasant neglect. While on the one hand this lent an air of intrigue and danger to every journey – including shopping for over-ripe root crops – there was also the taut nerves that one could not quell, no matter how many mouldy turnips one happened to be carrying.

Compounding matters, in this instance, was the fact that he was indeed intent on subversion. One of the first victims in this new regime had been the Rat Catchers' Guild. Karos Invictad, the Invigilator of the Patriotists, had acted on his first day of officialdom, despatching fully a hundred agents to Scale House, the modest Guild headquarters, whereupon they effected arrests on scores of Rat Catchers, all of whom, it later turned out, were illusions – a detail unadvertised, of course, lest the dread Patriotists announce their arrival to cries of ridicule. Which would not do.

After all, tyranny has no sense of humour. Too thin-skinned, too thoroughly full of its own self-importance. Accordingly, it presents an almost overwhelming temptation – how can I not be excused the occasional mockery? Alas, the Patriotists lacked flexibility in such matters – the deadliest weapon against them was derisive laughter, and they knew it.

He crossed Quillas Canal at a lesser bridge, made his way into the less ostentatious north district, and eventually sauntered into a twisting, shadow-filled alley that had once been a dirt street, before the invention of four-wheeled wagons and side-by-side horse collars. Instead of the usual hovels and back doors that one might expect to find in such an alley, lining this one were shops that had not changed in any substantial way in the past seven hundred or so years. There, first to the right, the Half-Axe Temple of Herbs, smelling like a swamp's sinkhole, wherein one could find a prune-faced witch who lived in a mudpit, with all her precious plants crowding the banks, or growing in the insect-flecked pool itself. It was said she had been born in that slime and was only half human; and that her mother had been born there too, and her mother and so on. That such conceptions were immaculate went without saying, since Tehol could hardly imagine any reasonable or even unreasonable man taking that particular plunge.

Opposite the Half-Axe was the narrow-fronted entrance to a shop devoted to short lengths of rope and wooden poles a man and a half high. Tehol had no idea how such a specialized enterprise could survive, especially in this unravelled, truncated market, yet its door had remained open for almost six centuries, locked up each night by a short length of rope and a wooden pole.

The assortment proceeding down the alley was similar only in its peculiarity. Wooden stakes and pegs in one, sandal thongs in another – not the sandals, just the thongs. A shop selling leaky pottery – not an indication of incompetence: rather, the pots were deliberately made to leak at various, precise rates of loss; a place selling unopenable boxes, another toxic dyes. Ceramic teeth, bottles filled with the urine of pregnant women, enormous amphorae containing dead pregnant women; the excreta of obese hogs; and miniature pets – dogs, cats, birds and rodents of all sorts, each one reduced in size through generation after generation of selective breeding – Tehol had seen guard dogs standing no higher than his ankle, and while cute and appropriately yappy, he had doubts as to their efficacy, although they were probably a terror for the thumbnail-sized mice and the cats that could ride an old woman's big toe, secured there by an ingenious loop in the sandal's thong.

Since the outlawing of the Rat Catchers' Guild, Adventure Alley had acquired a new function, to which Tehol now set about applying himself with the insouciance of the initiated. First, into the Half-Axe, clawing his way through the vines immediately beyond the entrance, then drawing up one step short of pitching head-first into the muddy pool.

Splashing, thick slopping sounds, then a dark-skinned wrinkled face appeared amidst the high grasses fringing the pit. 'It's you,' the witch said, grimacing then slithering out her overlong tongue to display all the leeches attached to it.

'And it's you,' Tehol replied.

The red protuberance with all its friends went back inside. 'Come in for a swim, you odious man.'

'Come out and let your skin recover, Munuga. I happen to know you're barely three decades old.'

'I am a map of wisdom.'

'As a warning against the perils of overbathing, perhaps. Where's the fat root this time?'

'What have you got for me first?'

'What I always have. The only thing you ever want from me, Munuga.'

'The only thing you'll never give, you mean!'

Sighing, Tehol drew out from under his makeshift sarong a small vial. He held it up for her to see.

She licked her lips, which proved alarmingly complicated. 'What kind?'

'Capabara roe.'

'But I want yours.'

'I don't produce roe.'

'You know what I mean, Tehol Beddict.'

'Alas, poverty is more than skin deep. Also, I have lost all incentive to be productive, in any sense of the word. After all, what kind of a world is this that I'd even contemplate delivering a child into?'

'Tehol Beddict, you cannot deliver a child. You're a man. Leave the delivering to me.'

'Tell you what, climb out of that soup, dry out and let me see what you're supposed to look like, and who knows? Extraordinary things might happen.'

Scowling, she held out an object. 'Here's your fat root. Give me that vial, then go away.'

'I so look forward to next time—'

'Tehol Beddict, do you know what fat root is used for?'

Her eyes had sharpened with suspicion, and Tehol realized that, were she indeed to dry out, she might be rather handsome after all, in a vaguely amphibian way. 'No, why?'

'Are you required to partake of it in some bizarre fashion?'

He shook his head.

'Are you certain? No unusual tea smelling yellow?'

'Smelling yellow? What does that mean?'

'If you smelled it, you'd know. Clearly, you haven't. Good. Get out, I'm puckering.'

A hasty departure, then, from the Half-Axe. Onward, to the entrance to Grool's Immeasurable Pots. Presumably, that description was intended to emphasize unmatched quality or something similar, since the pots themselves were sold as clocks, and for alchemical experiments and the like, and such functions were dependent on accurate rates of flow.

He stepped inside the cramped, damp shop.

'You're always frowning when you come in here, Tehol Beddict.'

'Good morning, Laudable Grool.'

'The grey one, yes, that one there.'

'A fine-looking pot—'

'It's a beaker, not a pot.'

'Of course.'

'Usual price.'

'Why do you always hide behind all those pots, Laudable Grool? All I ever see of you is your hands.'

'My hands are the only important part of me.'

'All right.' Tehol drew out a recently removed dorsal fin. 'A succession of spines, these ones from a capabara. Gradating diameters—'

'How do you know that?'

'Well, you can see it – they get smaller as they go back.'

'Yes, but how precise?'

'That's for you to decide. You demand objects with which to make holes. Here you have . . . what . . . twelve. How can you not be pleased by that?'

'Who said I wasn't pleased? Put them on the counter. Take the beaker. And get that damned fat root out of here.'

From there it was across to the small animals shop and Beastmonger Shill, an oversized woman endlessly bustling up and down the rows of tiny stacked cages, on her flattened heels a piping, scurrying swarm of little creatures. She squealed her usual delight at the gifts of beaker and fat root, the latter of which, it turned out, was most commonly used by malicious wives to effect the shrinkage of their husbands' testicles; whilst Shill had, with some delicate modifications, applied the root's diminutive properties to her broods, feeding the yellow-smelling tea out in precise increments using the holed beaker.

The meeting soured when Tehol slapped at a mosquito on his neck, only to be informed he had just killed a pygmy blood-sucking bat. His reply that the distinction was lost on him was not well received. But Shill opened the trapdoor on the floor at the back of the shop nevertheless, and Tehol descended the twenty-six narrow, steep stone steps to the crooked corridor – twenty-one paces long – that led to the ancient, empty beehive tomb, the walls of which had been dismantled in three places to fashion rough doorways into snaking, low-ceilinged tunnels, two of which ended in fatal traps. The third passageway eventually opened out into a long chamber occupied by a dozen or so dishevelled refugees, most of whom seemed to be asleep.

Fortunately, Chief Investigator Rucket was not among the somnolent. Her brows rose when she saw him, her admirable face filling with an expression of unfeigned relief as she gestured him to her table. The surface was covered in parchment sheets depicting various floor plans and structural diagrams.

'Sit, Tehol Beddict! Here, some wine! Drink. By the Errant, a new face! You have no idea how sick I am of my interminable companions in this hovel.'

'Clearly,' he replied, sitting, 'you need to get out more.'

'Alas, most of my investigations these days are archival in nature.'

'Ah, the Grand Mystery you've uncovered. Any closer to a solution?'

'Grand Mystery? More like Damned Mystery, and no, I remain baffled, even as my map grows with every day that passes. But let's not talk any more about that. My agents report that the cracks in the foundation are inexorably spreading – well done, Tehol. I always figured you were smarter than you looked.'

'Why thank you, Rucket. Have you got those lacquered tiles I asked for?'

'Onyx finished the last one this morning. Sixteen in all, correct?'

'Perfect. Bevelled edges?'

'Of course. All of your instructions were adhered to with diligence.'

'Great. Now, about that inexorable spreading—'

'You wish us to retire to my private room?'

'Uh, not now, Rucket. I need some coin. An infusion to bolster a capital investment.'

'How much?'

'Fifty thousand.'

'Will we ever see a return?'

'No, you'll lose it all.'

'Tehol, you certainly do take vengeance a long way. What is the benefit to us, then?'

'Why, none other than the return to pre-eminence of the Rat Catchers' Guild.'

Her rather dreamy eyes widened. 'The end of the Patriotists? Fifty thousand? Will seventy-five be better? A hundred?'

'No, fifty is what I need.'

'I do not anticipate any objections from my fellow Guild Masters.'

'Wonderful.' He slapped his hands together, then rose.

She frowned up at him. 'Where are you going?'

'Why, to your private room, of course.'

'Oh, how nice.'

His gaze narrowed on her. 'Aren't you joining me, Rucket?'

'What would be the point? The name "fat root" is a woman's joke, you know.'

'I haven't drunk any yellow-smelling tea!'

'In the future, I advise you to use gloves.'

'Where's your room, Rucket?'

One brow lifted. 'Got something to prove?'

'No, I just need to check on . . . things.'

'What's the point?' she asked again. 'Now that your imagination is awake, you'll convince yourself you've got smaller, Tehol Beddict. Human nature. Worse that you happen to be a man, too.' She rose. 'I, however, can be objective, albeit devastatingly so, on occasion. So, do you dare my scrutiny?'

He scowled. 'Fine, let's go. Next time, however, let us dispense entirely with the invitation to your room, all right?'

'Misery lies in the details, Tehol Beddict. As we're about to discover.'

Venitt Sathad unrolled the parchment and anchored its corners with flatstones. 'As you can see, Master, there are six separate buildings to the holdings.' He began pointing to the illustrations of each. 'Stables and livery. Icehouse. Drystore, with cellar. Servants' quarters. And, of course, the inn proper—'

'What of that square building there?' Rautos Hivanar asked.

Venitt frowned. 'As I understand it, the interior is virtually filled with an iconic object of some sort. The building predates the inn itself. Attempts to dislodge it failed. Now, what space remains is used for sundry storage.'

Rautos Hivanar leaned back in his chair. 'How solvent is this acquisition?'

'No more nor less than any other hostel, Master. It may be worth discussing investment on restoration with the other shareholders, including Karos Invictad.'

'Hmm, I will consider that.' He rose. 'In the meantime, assemble the new artifacts on the cleaning table on the terrace.'

'At once, Master.'

Fourteen leagues west of the Draconean Isles, doldrums had settled on this stretch of ocean, levelling the seas to a glassy, greasy patina beneath humid, motionless air. Through the eyeglass, the lone ship, black hull low in the water, looked lifeless. The mainmast was splintered, all rigging swept away. Someone had worked up a foresail, but the storm-rigged canvas hung limp. The steering oar was tied in place. No movement anywhere to be seen.

Skorgen Kaban, known as the Pretty, slowly lowered the eyeglass, yet continued squinting with his one good eye at the distant ship. He reached up to scratch one of the air holes – all that remained of what had once been a large, hawkish nose – then winced as a nail dug into sensitive scar tissue. The itch was non-existent, but the gaping nostrils had a tendency to weep, and the feigned scratch served to warn him of telltale wetness. This was one of his many gestures he probably imagined were subtle.

Alas, his captain was too sharp for that. She drew away her sidelong study of Skorgen, then glanced back at her waiting crew. A miserable but cocky bunch. Doldrums weighed everyone down, understandably, but the hold of the raider was packed with loot, and this run of the Errant's luck seemed without end.

Now that they'd found another victim.

Skorgen drew in a whistling breath, then said, 'It's Edur, all right. My guess is, a stray that got tossed around a bit in that storm we spied out west yesterday. Chances are, the crew's either sick or dead, or they abandoned ship in one of their Knarri lifeboats. If they did that, they'll have taken the good stuff with them. If not,' he grinned across at her, revealing blackened teeth, 'then we can finish what the storm started.'

'At the very least,' the captain said, 'we'll take a look.' She sniffed. 'At least maybe something will come of getting blown into the flats. Have 'em send out the sweeps, Skorgen, but keep that lookout's head spinning in every direction.'

Skorgen looked across at her. 'You think there might be more of 'em out here?'

She made a face. 'How many ships did the Emperor send out?'

His good eye widened, then he studied the lone derelict once more through the eyeglass. 'You think it's one of those? Errant's butt hole, Captain, if you're right . . .'

'You have your orders, and it seems I must remind you yet again, First Mate. No profanity on my ship.'

'Apologies, Captain.'

He hurried off, began relaying orders to the waiting crew.

Doldrums made for a quiet lot, a kind of superstitious furtiveness gripping the sailors, as if any sound reaching too far might crack the mirror of the sea.

She listened as the twenty-four sweeps slid out, blades settling in the water. A moment later came the muted call-out of the cox, and the *Undying Gratitude* groaned as it lurched forward. Clouds of sleeper flies rose around the ship as the nearby sea's pellucid surface was disturbed. The damned things had a tendency to seek out dark cover once driven to flight. Sailors coughed and spat – all very well for them, the captain observed, as a whining cloud spun round her head and countless insects crawled up her nose, into her ears, and across her eyes. Sun and sea were bad enough, combining to assail her dignity and whatever vanity a woman who was dead could muster, but for Shurq Elalle, these flies made for profoundly acute misery.

Pirate, divine undead, strumpet of insatiability, witch of the deep waters – the times had been good ever since she first sailed out of the Letheras harbour, down the long, broad river to the western seas. Lean and sleek, that first galley had been her passage to fame, and Shurq still regretted its fiery loss to that Mare escort in Laughter's End. But she was well pleased with the *Undying Gratitude*. Slightly too big for her crew, granted, but with their return to Letheras that problem could be solved easily enough. Her greatest sense of loss was with the departure of the Crimson Guard. Iron Bars had made it plain from the very start that they were working for passage. Even so, they'd been formidable additions on that wild crossing of the ocean, keeping the blood wake wide and unbroken as one merchant trader after another was taken, stripped of all valuables, then, more often than not, sent down into the dark. It hadn't been just their swords, deadly as those were, but the magery of Corlos – a magery far more refined, far more clever, than anything Shurq had witnessed before.

Such details opened her eyes, her mind as well. The world out there was huge. And in many fundamental ways, the empire of Lether, child of the First Empire, had been left in a kind of backwater, in its thinking, in its ways of working. A humbling revelation indeed.

The leavetaking with Iron Bars and his squad had not been quite as emotional or heartfelt for Shurq Elalle as it had probably seemed to everyone else, for the truth was, she had been growing ever more uneasy in their company. Iron Bars was not one to find subordination palatable for very long – oh, no doubt it was different when it came to his fellow Avowed among the Crimson Guard, or to their legendary commander, Prince K'azz. But she was not an Avowed, nor even one of that company's soldiers. So long as their goals ran in parallel, things were fine enough, and Shurq had made certain to never deviate, so as to avoid any confrontation.

They had deposited the mercenaries on a stony beach of the eastern shore of a land called Jacuruku, the sky squalling with sleeting rain. The landing had not been without witnesses, alas, and the last she'd seen of Iron Bars and his soldiers, they were turning inland to face a dozen massively armoured figures descending the broken slope, great-helmed with visors lowered. Brutal-looking bunch, and Shurq hoped all that belligerence was mostly for show. The grey sheets of rain had soon obscured all details from the strand as they pulled away on the oars back to the *Gratitude*.

Skorgen had sworn he'd caught the sound of blades clashing – a faint echo – with his one good ear, but Shurq herself had heard nothing.

In any case, they'd scurried from those waters, as pirates were wont to do when there was the risk of organized resistance lurking nearby, and Shurq consoled her agitated conscience by reminding herself that Iron Bars had spoken of Jacuruku with some familiarity – at least in so far as knowing its name. And as for Corlos's wide-eyed prayers to a few dozen divinities, well, he was prone to melodrama. A dozen knights wouldn't have been enough to halt Iron Bars and his Crimson Guard, determined as they were to do whatever it was they had to do, which, in this instance, was cross Jacuruku from one coast to the other, then find themselves another ship.

A huge world indeed.

The sweeps lifted clear of the water and were quietly shipped as the *Undying Gratitude* sidled up alongside the Edur wreck. Shurq Elalle moved to the rail and studied the visible deck of the Blackwood ship.

'Riding low,' Skorgen muttered.

No bodies amidst the clutter. But there *was* clutter. 'No orderly evacuation,' Shurq Elalle said, as grappling hooks sailed out, the tines biting as the lines were drawn taut. 'Six with us, weapons out,' she commanded, unsheathing her own rapier, then stepping up onto the rail.

She leapt across, landed lightly on the mid deck two strides from the splintered stump of the mainmast. Moments later Skorgen joined her, arriving with a grunt then a curse as he jarred his bad leg.

'This was a scrap,' he said, looking about. He limped back to the rail and tugged loose a splintered arrow shaft, then scowled as he studied it. 'Damned short and stubby – look at that head, that could punch through a bronze-sheeted shield. And this fletching – it's leather, like fins.'

So where were the bodies? Frowning, Shurq Elalle made her way to the cabin's hatchway. She paused at the hold, seeing that the hatch had been staved in. Nudging it aside with her boot, she crouched and looked down into the gloom of the hold.

The glimmer of water, and things floating. 'Skorgen, there's booty here. Come over and reach down for one of those amphorae.'

The second mate, Misery, called over from their ship, 'Captain! That hulk's lower in the water than it was when we arrived.'

She could now hear the soft groans of the hull.

Skorgen used his good arm to reach down and hook his hand through an ear of the amphora. Hissing with the weight, he lifted the hip-high object into view, rolling it onto the deck between himself and the captain.

The amphora itself was a gorgeous piece of work, Shurq observed. Foreign, the glaze cream in colour down to the inverted beehive base, where the coils were delineated in black geometric patterns on gleaming white. But it was the image painted on the shoulder and belly that captured her interest. Down low on one side there was a figure, nailed to an X-shaped cross. Whirling out from the figure's upturned head, there were crows. Hundreds, each one profoundly intricate, every detail etched – crows, flooding outward – or perhaps inward – to mass on the amphora's broad shoulders, encircling the entire object. Converging to feed on the hapless man? Fleeing him like his last, dying thoughts?

Skorgen had drawn a knife and was cutting away at the seal, stripping away the thick wax binding the stopper. After a moment he succeeded in working it loose. He tugged the stopper free, then leapt back as thick blood poured forth, spreading on the deck.

It looked fresh, and from it rose a scent of flowers, pungent and oversweet.

'Kagenza pollen,' Skorgen said. 'Keeps blood from thickening – the Edur use it when they paint temples in the forest – you know, on trees. The blood sanctifies. It's not a real temple, of course. No walls, or ceiling, just a grove—'

'I don't like first mates who babble,' Shurq Elalle said, straightening once more. 'Get the others out. The vessels alone will make us rich for a month or two.' She resumed her walk to the cabin.

The corridor was empty, the cabin door broken open and hanging from one leather hinge. As she made her way towards it, she glanced into the side alcoves and saw the layered bunks of the crew – but all were unoccupied, although dishevelled as if subject to searching.

In the cabin itself, more signs of looting, while on the floor was spreadeagled an Edur corpse. Hands and feet had been spiked into the floorboards, and someone had used a knife on him, methodically. The room stank of spilled wastes, and the expression frozen on the face was a twisted, agony-racked mask, the eyes staring out as if witness to a shattered faith, a terrible revelation at the moment of death.

She heard Skorgen come up behind her, heard his low curse upon seeing the body. 'Tortured 'im,' he said. 'Tortured the captain. This one was Merude, damn near an Elder. Errant save us, Captain, we're gonna get blamed if anyone else comes on this afore it all sinks. Torture. I don't get that—'

'It's simple,' she said. 'They wanted information.'

'About what?'

Shurq Elalle looked round. 'They took the log, the charts. Now, maybe pirates might do that, if they were strangers to Lether, but then they'd have no need to torture this poor bastard. Besides, they'd have taken the loot. No, whoever did this wanted more information – not what you could get from charts. And they didn't give a damn about booty.'

'Nasty bastards, whoever they were.'

She thought back to that amphora and its grisly contents. Then turned away. 'Maybe they had a good reason. Hole the hull, Skorgen. We'll wait around, though. Blackwood doesn't like sinking. We may have to fire it.'

'A pyre to bring 'em all in, Captain.'

'I am aware of the risks. Get on with it.'

Back on the deck, Shurq Elalle made her way to the forecastle, where she stood scanning the horizon while Skorgen and the crew began their demolition.

Strangers on the sea.

Who are no friends of the Tiste Edur. Even so, I think I'd rather not meet them. She turned to face the mid deck. 'Skorgen! When we're done here, we take to the sweeps. Back to the coast.'

His scarred brows rose. 'Letheras?'

'Why not? We can sell off and load up on crew.'

The battered man grinned.

Back to Letheras, aye. And fast.

CHAPTER FOUR

The mutiny came that fell dawn, when through
the heavy mists that had plagued us for ten days
we looked to the east, and there saw, rising vast
and innumerable on the cloud-bound horizon,
dragons. Too large to comprehend, their heads
above the sun, their folded wings reaching
down to cast a shadow that could swallow
all of Drene. This was too much, too frightening
even for the more seasoned soldiers in our
troop, for their dark eyes were upon us, an alien
regard that drained the blood from our hearts,
the very iron from our swords and spears.
    To walk into those shadows would quail
a champion of the First Empire. We not could face
such challenge, and though I voiced my fury,
my dismay, it was naught but the bolster
demanded of any expedition's leader, and indeed,
I had no intention of demanding of my party
the courage that I myself lacked. Bolster is
a dangerous thing, lest one succeeds where
one would not. And so I ceased my umbrage,
perhaps too easily yet none made account of
that, relieved as they all were as we broke camp,
packed our mules, and turned to the west.

Four Days Into the Wildlands
Thrydis Addanict

B ANISHMENT KILLED MOST VICTIMS, WHEN THE WORLD BEYOND WAS
harsh, when survival could not be purchased without the coin of
co-operation. No graver punishment was possible among the

tribal peoples, whether Awl or D'rhasilhani or Keryn. Yet it was the clan structure itself that imposed deadly intransigence, and with it a corresponding devastation when one was cast out, alone, bereft of all that gave meaning to life. Victims crumpled into themselves, abandoning all skills that could serve to sustain them; they withered, then died.

The Letherii, and their vast cities, the tumult of countless faces, were – beyond the chains of Indebtedness – almost indifferent to banishing. True, such people were not immune to the notion of spiritual punishment – they existed in families, after all, a universal characteristic of humans – yet such scars as were delivered from estrangement were survivable. Another village, another city – the struggle of beginning again could be managed and indeed, for some, beginning anew became an addiction in its own right. A way of absolving responsibility.

Redmask, his life that of the Awl, unsullied for generations, had come to believe that the nature of the Letherii – his most hated enemy – had nevertheless stained his spirit. Banishment had not proved a death sentence. Banishment had proved a gift, for with it he discovered freedom. The very lure that drew so many young warriors into the Lether Empire, where anonymity proved both bane and emancipation.

Driven away, he had wandered far, with no thought of ever returning. He was not as he had once been, no longer the son of his father, yet what he had become was, even to himself, a mystery.

The sky overhead was unmarred by clouds, the new season finding its heat, and jackrabbits raced from one thicket of momentary cover to another ahead of him as he rode the Letherii horse on the herd trail on its northeasterly route. A small herd, he had noted, with few fly-swarmed birth-stains along the path's outskirts, where rodara males would gather protectively until the newborn was able to find its legs. The clan guiding these beasts was probably small.

Redmask's guardian K'Chain Che'Malle were nowhere to be seen, but that was not unusual. The huge reptiles had prodigious appetites. At this time of year, the wild bhederin that had wintered in pocket forests – a solitary, larger breed than those of the plains to the south – ventured out from cover in search of mates. Massing more than two Letherii oxen, the bulls were ferocious and belligerent and would charge anything that approached too close, barring a female of its own kind. Sag'Churok, the male K'ell Hunter, delighted in meeting that thundering charge – Redmask had seen its pleasure, revealed in the slow sinuous lashing of the tail – as it stood in the bull's path, iron blades lifted high. As fast as the bhederin was, the K'Chain Che'Malle was faster. Each time after slaying the beast, Sag'Churok would yield the carcass to Gunth Mach, until she'd eaten her fill.

Redmask rode on through the day, his pace leisurely to ease the burden on the horse, and when the sun was descending towards the horizon, igniting distant storm clouds, he came within sight of the Awl encampment, situated on an ancient oxbow island between two dry eroded riverbeds. The herds were massed on the flanks of the valleys to either side and the sprawl of dome-shaped, sewn-hide huts huddled amidst the smoke of cookfires blanketing the valley.

No outriders. No pickets. And far too large a camp for the size of the herds.

Redmask reined in on the ridge line. He studied the scene below. Here and there, voices rose in ritual mourning. Few children were visible moving about between the huts.

After some time, as he sat motionless on the high Letherii saddle, someone saw him. Sudden cries, scurrying motion in the growing shadows, then a half-dozen warriors set out at a trot towards him.

Behind them, the camp had already begun a panicked breaking, sparks flying as hearths were kicked and stamped out. Hide walls rippled on the huts.

Herd and dray dogs appeared, racing to join the approaching warriors.

The Awl warriors were young, he saw as they drew closer. Only a year or two past their death nights. Not a single veteran among them. Where were the Elders? The shouldermen?

Halting fifteen paces downslope, the six warriors began conferring in hissed undertones, then one faced the encampment and loosed a piercing cry. All activity stopped below.

Faces stared up at Redmask. Not a single warrior among them seemed bold enough to venture closer.

The dogs were less cowed by the presence of a lone warrior. Growling, hackles raised, they crept in a half-circle towards him. Then, catching an unexpected scent, the beasts suddenly shrank back, tails dipping, thin whines coming from their throats.

Finally, one young warrior edged forward a step. 'You cannot be him,' he said.

Redmask sighed. 'Where is your war leader?' he demanded.

The youth filled his chest and straightened. 'I am this clan's war leader. Masarch, son of Nayrud.'

'When was your death night?'

'Those are the old ways,' Masarch said, baring his teeth in a snarl. 'We have abandoned such foolishness.'

Another spoke up behind the war leader. 'The old ways have failed us! We have cast them out!'

Masarch said, 'Remove that mask; it is not for you. You seek to deceive us. You ride a Letherii horse – you are one of the Factor's spies.'

Redmask made no immediate reply. His gaze slid past the war leader and his followers, fixing once more on the camp below. A crowd was

87

gathering at the near edge, watching. He was silent for another twenty heartbeats, then he said, 'You have set out no pickets. A Letherii troop could line this ridge and plunge down into your midst, and you would not be prepared. Your women cry out their distress, a sound that can be heard for leagues on a still night like this. Your people are starving, war leader, yet they light an excess of fires, enough to make above you a cloud of smoke that will not move, and reflects the light from below. You have been culling the newborn rodara and myrid, instead of butchering the ageing males and females past bearing. You must have no shouldermen, for if you did, they would bury you in the earth and force upon you the death night, so that you might emerge, born anew and, hopefully, gifted with new wisdom – wisdom you clearly lack.'

Masarch said nothing to that. He had finally seen Redmask's weapons. 'You are him,' he whispered. 'You have returned to the Awl'dan.'

'Which clan is this?'

'Redmask,' the war leader said, gesturing behind him. 'This clan . . . it is yours . . .'

Receiving naught but silence from the mounted warrior, Masarch added, 'We, we are all that remain. There are no shouldermen, Redmask. No witches.' He waved out towards the flanking herds. 'These beasts you see here, they are all that's left.' He hesitated, then straightened once more. 'Redmask, you have returned . . . for nothing. You do not speak, and this tells me that you see the truth of things. Great Warrior, *you are too late.*'

Even to this, Redmask was silent. He slowly dismounted. The dogs, which had continued their trepid circling, tails ducked, either picked up a fresh scent or heard something from the gloom beyond, for they suddenly broke and pelted back down the slope, disappearing into the camp. That panic seemed to ripple through the warriors facing him, but none fled, despite the fear and confusion gripping their expressions.

Licking his lips, Masarch said, 'Redmask, the Letherii are destroying us. Outrider camps have been ambushed, set upon and slaughtered, the herds stolen away. The Aendinar clan is no more. Sevond and Niritha remnants crawled to the Ganetok – only the Ganetok remains strong, for they are furthest east and, cowards that they are, they made pact with foreigners—'

'Foreigners.' Redmask's eyes narrowed in their slits. 'Mercenaries.'

Masarch nodded. 'There was a great battle, four seasons past, and those foreigners were destroyed.' He made a gesture. 'The Grey Sorcery.'

'Did not the victorious Letherii then march on the Ganetok camps?'

'No, Redmask, too few remained – the foreigners fought well.'

'Masarch,' he said, 'I do not understand. Did not the Ganetok fight alongside their mercenaries?'

The youth spat. 'Their war leader gathered from the clans fifteen thousand warriors. When the Letherii arrived, he fled, and the warriors followed. They abandoned the foreigners! Left them to slaughter!'

'Settle the camp below,' Redmask said. He pointed to the warriors standing behind Masarch. 'Stand first watch along this ridge line, here and to the west. I am now war leader to the Renfayar clan. Masarch, where hides the Ganetok?'

'Seven days to the east. They now hold the last great herd of the Awl.'

'Masarch, do you challenge my right to be war leader?'

The youth shook his head. 'You are Redmask. The Elders among the Renfayar who were your enemies are all dead. Their sons are dead.'

'How many warriors remain among the Renfayar?'

Masarch frowned, then gestured. 'You have met us, War Leader.'

'Six.'

A nod.

Redmask noted a lone dray dog sitting at the edge of the camp. It seemed to be watching him. He raised his left hand and the beast lunged into motion. The huge animal, a male, reached him moments later, dropping onto its chest and settling its wide, scarred head between Redmask's feet. He reached down and touched its snout – a gesture that, for most, would have risked fingers. The dog made no move.

Masarch was staring down at it with wide eyes. 'A lone survivor,' he said, 'from an outrider camp. It would not let us approach.'

'The foreigners,' Redmask said quietly, 'did they possess wardogs?'

'No. But they were sworn followers of the Wolves of War, and indeed, War Leader, it seemed those treacherous, foul beasts tracked them – always at a distance, yet in vast numbers. Until the Ganetok Elders invoked magic and drove them all away.' Masarch hesitated, then said, 'Redmask, the war leader among the Ganetok—'

Unseen behind the mask, a slow smile formed. 'Firstborn son of Capalah. Hadralt.'

'How did you know?'

'Tomorrow, Masarch, we drive the herds east – to the Ganetok. I would know more of those hapless foreigners who chose to fight for us. To die for the people of the Awl'dan.'

'We are to crawl to the Ganetok as did the Sevond and the Niritha?'

'You are starving. The herds are too weakened. I lead six youths none of whom has passed the death night. Shall the seven of us ride to war against the Letherii?'

Though young, it was clear that Masarch was no fool. 'You shall challenge Hadralt? Redmask, your warriors – we, we will all die. We are not enough to meet the hundreds of challenges that will be flung at us, and once we are dead, you will have to face those challenges, long before you are deemed worthy to cross weapons with Hadralt himself.'

'You will not die,' Redmask said. 'And none shall challenge any of you.'

'Then you mean to carve through a thousand warriors to face Hadralt?'

'What would be the point of that, Masarch? I need those warriors. Killing them would be a waste. No.' He paused, then said, 'I am not without guardians, Masarch. And I doubt that a single Ganetok warrior will dare challenge them. Hadralt shall have to face me, he and I, alone in the circle. Besides,' he added, 'we haven't the time for all the rest.'

'The Ganetok hold to the old ways, War Leader. There will be rituals. Days and days before the circle is made—'

'Masarch, we must go to war against the Letherii. Every warrior of the Awl—'

'War Leader! They will not follow you! Even Hadralt could only manage a third of them, and that with payment of rodara and myrid that halved his holdings!' Masarch waved at the depleted herds on the hillsides. 'We – we have nothing left! You could not purchase the spears of a hundred warriors!'

'Who holds the largest herds, Masarch?'

'The Ganetok themselves—'

'No. I ask again, who holds the largest herds?'

The youth's scowl deepened. 'The Letherii.'

'I will send three warriors to accompany the last of the Renfayar to the Ganetok. Choose two of your companions to accompany us.' The dray dog rose and moved to one side. Redmask collected the reins of his horse and set out down towards the camp. The dray fell in to heel on his left. 'We shall ride west, Masarch, and find us some herds.'

'We ride against the Letherii? War Leader, did you not moments ago mock the notion of seven warriors waging war against them? Yet now you say—'

'War is for later,' Redmask said. 'As you say, we need herds. To buy the services of the warriors.' He paused and looked back at the trailing youth. 'Where did the Letherii get their beasts?'

'From the Awl! From us!'

'Yes. They stole them. So we must steal them back.'

'Four of us, War Leader?'

'And one dray, and my guardians.'

'*What* guardians?'

Redmask resumed his journey. 'You lack respect, Masarch. Tonight, I think, you will have your death night.'

'The old ways are useless! I will not!'

Redmask's fist was a blur – it was questionable whether, in the gloom, Masarch even saw it – even as it connected solidly with the youth's jaw, dropping him in his tracks. Redmask reached down and grabbed a handful of hide jerkin, then began dragging the unconscious Masarch back down to the camp.

When the young man awoke, he would find himself in a coffin, beneath an arm's reach of earth and stones. None of the usual traditional, measured rituals prior to a death night, alas, the kind that served to prepare the chosen for internment. Of course, Masarch's loose reins displayed an appalling absence of respect, sufficient to obviate the gift of mercy, which in truth was what all those rituals were about.

Hard lessons, then. But becoming an adult depended on such lessons.

He expected he would have to pound the others into submission as well, which made for a long night ahead.

For us all.

The camp's old women would be pleased by the ruckus, he suspected. Preferable to wailing through the night, in any case.

The last tier of the buried city proved the most interesting, as far as Udinaas was concerned. He'd had his fill of the damned sniping that seemed to plague this fell party of fugitives, a testiness that seemed to be getting worse, especially from Fear Sengar. The ex-slave knew that the Tiste Edur wanted to murder him, and as for the details surrounding the abandonment of Rhulad – which made it clear that Udinaas himself had had no choice in the matter, that he had been as much a victim as Fear's own brother – well, Fear wasn't interested. Mitigating circumstances did not alter his intransigence, his harsh sense of right and wrong which did not, it appeared, extend to his own actions – after all, Fear had been the one to deliberately walk away from Rhulad.

Udinaas, upon regaining consciousness, should have returned to the Emperor.

To do what? Suffer a grisly death at Rhulad's hands? Yes, we were almost friends, he and I – as much as might be possible between slave and master, and of that the master ever feels more generous and virtuous than the slave – but I did not ask to be there, at the madman's side, struggling to guide him across that narrow bridge of sanity, when all Rhulad wanted to do was leap head-first over the side at every step. No, he had made do with what he had, and in showing that mere splinter of sympathy, he had done more for Rhulad than any of the Sengars – brothers, mother, father. More indeed than any Tiste Edur. *Is it any wonder none of you know happiness, Fear Sengar? You are all twisted branches from the same sick tree.*

There was no point in arguing this, of course. Seren Pedac alone might understand, might even agree with all that Udinaas had to say, but she wasn't interested in actually *being* one of this party. She clung to the role of Acquitor, a finder of trails, the reader of all those jealously guarded maps in her head. She liked not having to choose; better still, she liked not having to care.

A strange woman, the Acquitor. Habitually remote. Without friends *. . . yet she carries a Tiste Edur sword. Trull Sengar's sword. Kettle says he set it into her hands. Did she understand the significance of that gesture? She must have.* Trull Sengar had then returned to Rhulad. Perhaps the only brother who'd actually cared – where was he now? *Probably dead.*

Fresh, night-cooled air flowed down the broad ramp, moaned in the doorways situated every ten paces or so to either side. They were nearing the surface, somewhere in the saddleback pass – but on which side of the fort and its garrison? If the wrong side, then Silchas Ruin's swords would keen loud and long. The dead piled up in the wake of that walking white-skinned, red-eyed nightmare, didn't they just. The few times the hunters caught up with the hunted, they paid with their lives, yet they kept coming, and that made little sense.

Almost as ridiculous as this mosaic floor with its glowing armies. Images of lizard warriors locked in war, long-tails against short-tails, with the long-tails doing most of the dying, as far as he could tell. The bizarre slaughter beneath their feet spilled out into the adjoining rooms, each one, it seemed, devoted to the heroic death of some champion – *Fouled K'ell, Naw'rhuk A'dat and Matrons*, said Silchas Ruin as, enwreathed in sorcerous light, he explored each such side chamber, his interest desultory and cursive at best. In any case, Udinaas could read enough into the colourful scenes to recognize a campaign of mutual annihilation, with every scene of short-tail victory answered with a Matron's sorcerous conflagration. The winners never won because the losers refused to lose. *An insane war.*

Seren Pedac was in the lead, twenty paces ahead, and Udinaas saw her halt and suddenly crouch, one hand lifting. The air sweeping in was rich with the scent of loam and wood dust. The mouth of the tunnel was small, overgrown and half blocked by angled fragments of basalt from what had once been an arched gate, and beyond was darkness.

Seren Pedac waved the rest forward. 'I will scout out ahead,' she whispered as they gathered about just inside the cave mouth. 'Did anyone else notice that there were no bats in that last stretch? That floor was clean.'

'There are sounds beyond human hearing,' Silchas Ruin said. 'The flow of air is channelled through vents and into tubes behind the walls, producing a sound that perturbs bats, insects, rodents and the like. The Short-Tails were skilled at such things.'

'So, not magic, then?' Seren Pedac asked. 'No wards or curses here?'

'No.'

Udinaas rubbed at his face. His beard was filthy, and there were things crawling in the snarls of hair. 'Just find out if we're on the right side of that damned fort, Acquitor.'

'I was making sure I wouldn't trip some kind of ancient ward stepping outside, Indebted, something that all these broken boulders suggests has happened before. Unless of course you want to rush out there yourself.'

'Now why would I do that?' Udinaas asked. 'Ruin gave you your answer, Seren Pedac; what are you waiting for?'

'Perhaps,' Fear Sengar said, 'she waits for you to be quiet. We shall all, I suppose, end up waiting for ever in that regard.'

'Tormenting you, Fear, gives me my only pleasure.'

'A sad admission indeed,' Seren Pedac murmured, then edged forward, over the tumbled rocks, and into the night beyond.

Udinaas removed his pack and settled down on the littered floor, dried leaves crunching beneath him. He leaned against a tilted slab of stone and stretched out his legs.

Fear moved up to crouch at the very edge of the cave mouth.

Humming to herself, Kettle wandered off into a nearby side chamber.

Silchas Ruin stood regarding Udinaas. 'I am curious,' he said after a time. 'What gives your life meaning, Letherii?'

'That's odd. I was just thinking the same of you, Tiste Andii.'

'Indeed.'

'Why would I lie?'

'Why wouldn't you?'

'All right,' Udinaas said. 'You have a point.'

'So you will not answer my question.'

'You first.'

'I do not disguise what drives me.'

'Revenge? Well, fine enough, I suppose, as a motivation – at least for a while and maybe a while is all you're really interested in. But let's be honest here, Silchas Ruin: as the sole meaning for existing, it's a paltry, pathetic cause.'

'Whereas you claim to exist to torment Fear Sengar.'

'Oh, he manages that all on his own.' Udinaas shrugged. 'The problem with questions like that is, we rarely find meaning to what we do until well after we've done it. At that point we come up with not one but thousands – reasons, excuses, justifications, heartfelt defences. Meaning? Really, Silchas Ruin, ask me something interesting.'

'Very well. I am contemplating challenging our pursuers – no more of this unnecessary subterfuge. It offends my nature, truth be told.'

At the tunnel mouth, Fear turned to regard the Tiste Andii. 'You will kick awake a hornet's nest, Silchas Ruin. Worse, if this fallen god is

93

indeed behind Rhulad's power, you might find yourself suffering a fate far more dire than millennia buried in the ground.'

'Fear's turning into an Elder before our eyes,' Udinaas said. 'Jumping at shadows. You want to take on Rhulad and Hannan Mosag and his K'risnan, Silchas Ruin, you have my blessing. Grab the Errant by the throat and tear this empire to pieces. Turn it all into ash and dust. Level the whole damned continent, Tiste Andii – we'll just stay here in this cave. Come collect us when you're finished.'

Fear bared his teeth at Udinaas. 'Why would he bother sparing us?'

'I don't know,' the ex-slave replied, raising an eyebrow. 'Pity?'

Kettle spoke from the side chamber's arched doorway. 'Why don't any of you like each other? I like all of you. Even Wither.'

'It's all right,' Udinaas said, 'we're all just tortured by who we are, Kettle.'

No-one said much after that.

Seren Pedac reached the edge of the forest, keeping low to remain level with the stunted trees. The air was thin and cold at this altitude. The stars overhead were bright and sharp, the dust-shrouded crescent moon still low on the horizon to the north. Around her was whispered motion through the clumps of dead leaves and lichen – a kind of scaled mouse ruled the forest floor at night, a species she had never seen before. They seemed unusually fearless, so much so that more than one had scampered across her boots. No predators, presumably. Even so, their behaviour was odd.

Before her stretched a sloped clearing, sixty or more paces, ending at a rutted track. Beyond it was a level stretch of sharp, jagged stones, loose enough to be treacherous. The fort squatting in the midst of this moat of rubble was stone-walled, thick at the base and tapering sharply to twice the height of a man. The corner bastions were massive, squared and flat-topped. On those platforms were swivel-mounted ballestae. Seren could make out huddled figures positioned around the nearest one, while other soldiers were visible, shoulders and heads, walking the raised platform on the other side of the walls.

As she studied the fortification, she heard the soft clunk of armour and weapons to her left. She shrank back as a patrol appeared on the rutted track. Motionless, breath held, she watched them amble past.

After another twenty heartbeats, she turned about and made her way back through the stunted forest. She almost missed the entrance to the cave mouth, a mere slit of black behind high ferns beneath a craggy overhang of tilted, layered granite. Pushing through, she stumbled into Fear Sengar.

'Sorry,' he whispered. 'We were beginning to worry, or, at least,' he added, 'I was.'

She gestured him back into the cave.

'Good news,' she said once they were inside. 'We're behind the garrison – the pass ahead should be virtually unguarded—'

'There are K'risnan wards up the trail,' Silchas Ruin cut in. 'Tell me of this garrison, Acquitor.'

Seren closed her eyes. *Wards? Errant take us, what game is Hannan Mosag playing here?* 'I could smell horses from the fort. Once we trip those wards they'll be after us, and we can't outrun mounted soldiers.'

'The garrison,' Silchas said.

She shrugged. 'The fort looks impregnable. I'd guess there's anywhere between a hundred and two hundred soldiers there. And with that many there's bound to be mages, as well as a score or more Tiste Edur.'

'Silchas Ruin is tired of being chased,' Udinaas said from where he lounged, back resting on a stone slab.

Dread filled Seren Pedac at these words. 'Silchas, can we not go round these wards?'

'No.'

She glanced across at Fear Sengar, saw suspicion and unease in the warrior's expression, but he would not meet her eyes. *What conversation did I just miss here?* 'You are no stranger to sorcery, Silchas Ruin. Could you put everyone in that fort to sleep or something? Or cloud their minds, make them confused?'

He gave her an odd look. 'I know of no sorcery that can achieve that.'

'Mockra,' she replied. 'The warren of Mockra.'

'No such thing existed in my day,' he said. 'The K'risnan sorcery, rotted through with chaos as it is, seems recognizable enough to me. I have never heard of this Mockra.'

'Corlos, the mage with Iron Bars – the Crimson Guard mercenaries – he could reach into minds, fill them with false terrors.' She shrugged. 'He said the magic of Holds and Elder Warrens has, almost everywhere else, been supplanted.'

'I had wondered at the seeming weakness of Kurald Galain in this land. Acquitor, I cannot achieve what you ask. Although, I do intend to silence everyone in that fort. And collect for us some horses.'

'Silchas, there are hundreds of Letherii there, not just soldiers. A fort needs support staff. Cooks, scullions, smiths, carpenters, servants—'

'And the Tiste Edur,' Fear added, 'will have slaves.'

'None of this interests me,' the Tiste Andii said, moving past Seren and leaving the mouth of the cave.

Udinaas laughed softly. 'Red Ruin stalks the land. We must heed this tale of righteous retribution gone horribly wrong. So, Fear Sengar, your epic quest twists awry – what will you tell your grandchildren now?'

The Edur warrior said nothing.

Seren Pedac hesitated; she could hear Silchas Ruin walking away – a few strides crunching through leaves – then he was gone. She could hurry after him. Attempt one last time to dissuade him. Yet she did not move. In the wake of Ruin's passage the only sound filling the forest was the scurry and rustle of the scaled mice, in their thousands it seemed, all flowing in the same direction as the Tiste Andii. Sweat prickled like ice on her skin. *Look at us. Frozen like rabbits.*

Yet what can I do? Nothing. Besides, it's not my business, is it? I am but a glorified guide. Not one of these here holds to a cause that matters to me. They're welcome to their grand ambitions. I was asked to lead them out, that's all.

This is Silchas Ruin's war. And Fear Sengar's. She looked over at Udinaas and found him studying her from where he sat, eyes glittering, as if presciently aware of her thoughts, the sordid tracks each converging on a single, pathetic conclusion. *Not my business. Errant take you, Indebted.*

Mangled and misshapen, the K'risnan Ventrala reached up a scrawny, root-like forearm and wiped the sweat from his brow. Around him candles flickered, a forlorn invocation to Sister Shadow, but it seemed the ring of darkness in the small chamber was closing in on all sides, as inexorable as any tide.

He had woken half a bell earlier, heart pounding and breath coming in gasps. The forest north of the fort was seething with orthen, a rock-dwelling scaled creature unique to this mountain pass – since his arrival at the fort he had seen perhaps a half-dozen, brought in by the maned cats the Letherii locals kept. Those cats knew better than to attempt to eat the orthen, poison as they were, yet were not averse to playing with them until dead. Orthen avoided forest and soft ground. They dwelt among rocks. Yet now they swarmed the forest, and the K'risnan could feel something palpable from their presence, a stirring that tasted of bloodlust.

Should he crouch here in his room, terrified of creatures he could crush underfoot? He needed to master this unseemly panic – listen! He could hear nothing from the fort lookouts. No alarms shouted out.

But the damned orthen carpeted the forest floor up the pass, massing in unimaginable numbers, and that dread scaly flood was sweeping down, and Ventrala's panic rose yet higher, threatening to erupt from his throat in shrieks. He struggled to think.

Some kind of once in a decade migration, perhaps. Once in a century, even. A formless hunger. That and nothing more. The creatures would heave up against the walls, seethe for a time, then leave before the dawn. Or they'd flow around the fort, only to plunge from the numerous ledges and cliffs to either side of the approach. Some creatures were driven to suicide – yes, that was it . . .

The bloodlust suddenly burgeoned. The K'risnan's head rocked back, as if he'd just been slapped. Chills swept through him. He heard himself begin gibbering, even as he awakened the sorcery within him. His body flinched as chaotic power blossomed like poison in his muscles and bones. Sister Shadow had nothing to do with this magic racing through him, nothing at all, but he was past caring about such things.

Then, as shouts rose from the wall, K'risnan Ventrala sensed another presence in the forest beyond, a focus to all that bloodlust, a presence – and it was on its way.

Atri-Preda Hayenar awoke to distant shouts. An alarm was being raised, from the wall facing up-trail. And that, she realized as she quickly donned her uniform, made little sense. Then again, there wasn't much about this damned assignment that did. Pursue, she'd been told, but avoid contact. And now, one of those disgusting K'risnan had arrived, escorted by twenty-five Merude warriors. Well, if there was any real trouble brewing, she would let them handle it.

Their damned fugitives, after all. They could have them, with the Errant's blessing.

A moment later she was flung from her feet as a deafening concussion tore through the fort.

K'risnan Ventrala screamed, skidding across the floor to slam up against the wall, as a vast cold power swept over him, plucking at him as would a crow a rotted corpse. His own sorcery had recoiled, contracted into a trembling core deep in his chest – it had probed towards that approaching presence, probed until some kind of contact was achieved. And then Ventrala – and all that churning power within him – had been *rebuffed*.

Moments later, the fort's wall exploded.

Atri-Preda Hayenar stumbled from the main house and found the compound a scene of devastation. The wall between the up-trail bastions had been breached, the impact spilling huge pieces of stone and masonry onto the muster area. And the rock was burning – a black, sizzling coruscation that seemed to devour the stone even as it flared wild, racing across the rubble.

Broken bodies were visible amidst the wreckage, and from the stables – where the building's back wall leaned precariously inward – horses were screaming as if being devoured alive. Swarming over everything in sight were orthen, closing on fallen soldiers, and where they gathered, skin was chewed through and the tiny scaled creatures then burrowed in a frenzy into pulped meat.

Through the clouds of dust in the breach, came a tall figure with drawn swords.

White-skinned, crimson-eyed.

Errant take me – he's had enough of running – the White Crow—

She saw a dozen Tiste Edur appear near the barracks. Heavy throwing spears darted across the compound, converging on the ghastly warrior.

He parried them all aside, one after the other, and with each clash of shaft against blade the swords sang, until it seemed a chorus of deathly voices filled the air.

Hayenar, seeing a score of her Letherii soldiers arrive, staggered towards them. 'Withdraw!' she shouted, waving like a madwoman. 'Retreat, you damned fools!'

It seemed they had but awaited the command, as the unit broke into a rout, heading en masse for the down-trail gate.

One of the Tiste Edur closed on the Atri-Preda. '*What are you doing?*' he demanded. 'The K'risnan is coming – he'll slap this gnat down—'

'When he does,' she snarled, pulling back, 'we'll be happy to regroup!'

The Edur unsheathed his cutlass. 'Call them into battle, Atri-Preda – or I'll cut you down right here!'

She hesitated.

To their right, the other Tiste Edur had rushed forward and now engaged the White Crow.

The swords howled, a sound so filled with glee that Hayenar's blood turned to ice. She shook her head, watching, as did the warrior confronting her, as the White Crow carved his way through the Merude in a maelstrom of severed limbs, decapitations and disembowelling slashes that sent bodies reeling away.

'—your Letherii! Charge him, damn you!'

She stared across at the Edur warrior. 'Where's your K'risnan?' she demanded. '*Where is he?*'

Ventrala clawed his way into the corner of the room furthest from the conflagration outside. Endless, meaningless words were spilling from his drool-threaded mouth. His power had fled. Abandoning him here, in this cursed room. Not fair. He had done all that was asked of him. He had surrendered his flesh and blood, his heart and his very bones, all to Hannan Mosag.

There had been a promise, a promise of salvation, of vast rewards for his loyalty – once the hated youngest son of Tomad Sengar was torn down from the throne. They were to track Fear Sengar, the traitor, the betrayer, and when the net was finally closed around him it would not be Rhulad smiling in satisfaction. No, Rhulad, the fool, knew nothing about any of this. The gambit belonged to Hannan Mosag, the Warlock King, who had had his throne stolen from him. And it was Hannan who, with Fear Sengar in his hands – and the slave, Udinaas – would work out his vengeance.

The Emperor needed to be stripped, every familiar face twisted into a mask of betrayal, stripped, yes, until he was completely alone. Isolated in his own madness.

Only then—

Ventrala froze, curled tight into a foetal ball, at soft laughter spilling towards him . . . *from inside his room!*

'Poor K'risnan,' it then murmured. 'You had no idea this pale king of the orthen would turn on you, this strider of battlefields. His road is a river of blood, you pathetic fool, and . . . oh! look! his patience, his forbearance – *it's all gone!*'

A wraith, here with him, whispering madness. 'Begone,' he hissed, 'lest you share my fate! I did not summon you—'

'No, you didn't. My chains to the Tiste Edur have been severed. By the one out there. Yes, you see, I am his, not yours. The White Crow's – hah, the Letherii surprised me there – but it was the mice, K'risnan . . . seems a lifetime ago now. In the forest north of Hannan Mosag's village. And an apparition – alas, no-one understands, no-one *takes note*. But that is not my fault, is it?'

'Go away—'

'I cannot. Will not, rather. Can you hear? Outside? It's all quiet now. Most of the Letherii got away, unfortunately. Tumbling like drunk goats down the stairs, with their captain among them – she was no fool. As for your Merude, well, they're all dead. Now, listen! Boots in the hallway – he's on his way!'

The terror drained away from Ventrala. There was no point, was there? At least, finally, he would be delivered from this racked, twisted cage of a body. As if recalling the dignity it had once possessed, that body now lurched into motion, lifting itself into a sitting position, back pushed into the corner – it seemed to have acquired its own will, disconnected from Ventrala, from the mind and spirit that held to that name, that pathetic identity. Hannan Mosag had once said that the power of the Fallen One fed on all that was flawed and imperfect in one's soul, which in turn manifested in flesh and bone – what was then necessary was to teach oneself to exult in that power, even as it twisted and destroyed the soul's vessel.

Ventrala, with the sudden clarity that came with approaching death, now realized that it was all a lie. Pain was not to be embraced. Chaos was anathema to a mortal body. It ruined the flesh because it did not belong there. There was no exaltation in self-destruction.

A chorus of voices filled his skull, growing ever louder. *The swords* . . .

There was a soft scuffing sound in the hallway beyond, then the door squealed open.

Orthen poured in, flowing like grey foam in the grainy darkness. A moment later, the White Crow stepped into view. The song of the two swords filled the chamber.

Red, lambent eyes fixed on Ventrala.

The Tiste Andii then sheathed his weapons, muting the keening music. 'Tell me of this one who so presumes to offend me.'

Ventrala blinked, then shook his head. 'You think the Crippled God is interested in challenging you, Silchas Ruin? No, this . . . offence . . . it is Hannan Mosag's, and his alone. I understand that now, you see. It's why my power is gone. Fled. The Crippled God is not ready for the likes of you.'

The white-skinned apparition was motionless, silent, for a time. Then he said, 'If this Hannan Mosag knows my name, he knows too that I have reason to be affronted. By him. By all the Tiste Edur who have inherited the rewards of Scabandari's betrayal. Yet he provokes me.'

'Perhaps,' Ventrala said, 'Hannan Mosag presumed the Crippled God's delight in discord was without restraint.'

Silchas Ruin cocked his head. 'What is your name, K'risnan?'

Ventrala told him.

'I will let you live,' the Tiste Andii said, 'so that you may deliver to Hannan Mosag my words. The Azath cursed me with visions, its own memories, and so I was witness to many events on this world and on others. Tell Hannan Mosag this: a god in pain is not the same as a god obsessed with evil. Your Warlock King's obsessions are his own. It would seem, alas, that he is . . . confused. For that, I am merciful this night . . . and this night alone. Hereafter, should he resume his interference, he will know the extent of my displeasure.'

'I shall convey your words with precision, Silchas Ruin.'

'You should choose a better god to worship, Ventrala. Tortured spirits like company, even a god's.' He paused, then said, 'Then again, perhaps it is the likes of you who have in turn shaped the Crippled God. Perhaps, without his broken, malformed worshippers, he would have healed long ago.'

Soft rasping laughter from the wraith.

Silchas Ruin walked back through the doorway. 'I am conscripting some horses,' he said without turning round.

Moments later, the wraith slithered after him.

The orthen, which had been clambering about in seemingly aimless motion, now began to withdraw from the chamber.

Ventrala was alone once more. *To the stairs, find the Atri-Preda – an escort, for the journey back to Letheras. And I will speak to Hannan Mosag. And I will tell him about death in the pass. I will tell him of a Soletaken Tiste Andii with two knife wounds in his back, wounds that will not heal. Yet . . . he forbears.*

Silchas Ruin knows more of the Crippled God than any of us, barring perhaps Rhulad. But he does not hate. No, he feels pity.

Pity, even for me.

Seren Pedac heard the horses first, hoofs thumping at the walk up the forested trail. The night sky above the fort was strangely black, opaque, as if from smoke – yet there was no glow from flames. They had heard the concussion, the destruction of at least one stone wall, and Kettle had yelped with laughter, a chilling, grotesque sound. Then, distant screams and, all too quickly thereafter, naught but silence.

Silchas Ruin appeared, leading a dozen mounts, accompanied by sullen moaning from the scabbarded swords.

'And how many of my kin did you slay this time?' Fear Sengar asked.

'Only those foolish enough to oppose me. This pursuit,' he said, 'it does not belong to your brother. It is the Warlock King's. I believe we cannot doubt that he seeks what we seek. And now, Fear Sengar, the time has come to set our knives on the ground, the two of us. Perhaps Hannan Mosag's desires are a match to yours, but I assure you, such desires cannot be reconciled with mine.'

Seren Pedac felt a heaviness settle in the pit of her stomach. This had been a long time in coming, the one issue avoided again and again, ever excused to the demands of simple expediency. Fear Sengar could not win this battle – they all knew it. Did he intend to stand in Silchas Ruin's way? One more Tiste Edur to cut down? 'There is no compelling reason to broach this subject right now,' she said. 'Let's just get on these horses and ride.'

'No,' Fear Sengar said, eyes fixed on the Tiste Andii's. 'Let it be now. Silchas Ruin, in my heart I accept the truth of Scabandari's betrayal. You trusted him, and you suffered unimaginably in consequence. Yet how can we make reparation? We are not Soletaken. We are not ascendants. We are simply Tiste Edur, and so we fall like saplings before you and your swords. Tell me, how do we ease your thirst for vengeance?'

'You do not, nor is my killing your kin in any way an answer to my need. Fear Sengar, you spoke of reparation. Is this your desire?'

The Edur warrior was silent for a half-dozen heartbeats, then he said, 'Scabandari brought us to this world.'

'Yours was dying.'

'Yes.'

'You may not be aware of this,' Silchas Ruin continued, 'but Bloodeye was partly responsible for the sundering of Shadow. Nonetheless, of greater relevance, to me, are the betrayals that came before that particular crime. Betrayals against my own kin – my brother, Andarist – which set such grief upon his soul that he was driven mad.' He slowly cocked his head. 'Did you imagine me naive in fashioning an alliance with Scabandari Bloodeye?'

Udinaas barked a laugh. 'Naive enough to turn your back on him.'

Seren Pedac shut her eyes. *Please, Indebted, just keep your mouth shut. Just this once.*

'You speak truth, Udinaas,' Silchas Ruin replied after a moment. 'I was exhausted, careless. I did not imagine he would be so . . . public. Yet, in retrospect, the betrayal had to be absolute – and that included the slaughter of my followers.'

Fear Sengar said, 'You intended to betray Scabandari, only he acted first. A true alliance of equals, then.'

'I imagined you might see it that way,' the Tiste Andii replied. 'Understand me, Fear Sengar. I will not countenance freeing the soul of Scabandari Bloodeye. This world has enough reprehensible ascendants.'

'Without Father Shadow,' Fear said, 'I cannot free Rhulad from the chains of the Crippled God.'

'You could not, even with him.'

'I do not believe you, Silchas Ruin. Scabandari was your match, after all. And I do not think the Crippled God hunts you in earnest. If it is indeed Hannan Mosag behind this endless pursuit, then the ones he seeks are myself and Udinaas. Not you. It is, perhaps, even possible that the Warlock King knows nothing of you – of who you are, beyond the mysterious White Crow.'

'That does not appear to be the case, Fear Sengar.'

The statement seemed to rock the Tiste Edur.

Silchas Ruin continued, 'Scabandari Bloodeye's body was destroyed. Against me, now, he would be helpless. A soul without provenance is a vulnerable thing. Furthermore, it may be that his power is already being . . . used.'

'By whom?' Fear asked, almost whispering.

The Tiste Andii shrugged. 'It seems,' he said with something close to indifference, 'that your quest is without purpose. You cannot achieve what you seek. I will offer you this, Fear Sengar. The day I choose to move against the Crippled God, your brother shall find himself free, as will all the Tiste Edur. When that time comes, we can speak of reparation.'

Fear Sengar stared at Silchas Ruin, then glanced, momentarily, at

Seren Pedac. He drew a deep breath, then said, 'Your offer . . . humbles me. Yet I could not imagine what the Tiste Edur could gift you in answer to such deliverance.'

'Leave that to me,' the Tiste Andii said.

Seren Pedac sighed, then strode to the horses. 'It's almost dawn. We should ride until midday at least. Then we can sleep.' She paused, looked once more over at Silchas Ruin. 'You are confident we will not be pursued?'

'I am, Acquitor.'

'So, were there in truth wards awaiting us?'

The Tiste Andii made no reply.

As the Acquitor adjusted the saddle and stirrups on one of the horses to suit Kettle, Udinaas watched the young girl squatting on her haunches near the forest edge, playing with an orthen that did not seem in any way desperate to escape her attentions. The darkness had faded, the mists silver in the growing light.

Wither appeared beside him, like a smear of reluctant night. 'These scaled rats, Udinaas, came from the K'Chain Che'Malle world. There were larger ones, bred for food, but they were smart – smarter perhaps than they should have been. Started escaping their pens, vanishing into the mountains. It's said there are some still left—'

Udinaas grunted his derision. 'It's said? Been hanging round in bars, Wither?'

'The terrible price of familiarity – you no longer respect me, Indebted. A most tragic error, for the knowledge I possess—'

'Is like a curse of boredom,' Udinaas said, pushing himself to his feet. 'Look at her,' he said, nodding towards Kettle. 'Tell me, do you believe in innocence? Never mind; I'm not that interested in your opinion. By and large, I don't. Believe, that is. And yet, that child there . . . well, I am already grieving.'

'Grieving what?' Wither demanded.

'Innocence, wraith. When we kill her.'

Wither was, uncharacteristically, silent.

Udinaas glanced down at the crouching shade, then sneered. 'All your coveted knowledge . . .'

Seventeen legends described the war against the scaled demons the Awl called the Kechra; of those, sixteen were of battles, terrible clashes that left the corpses of warriors scattered across the plains and hills of the Awl'dan. Less a true war than headlong flight, at least in the first years. The Kechra had come from the west, from lands that would one day belong to the empire of Lether but were then, all those countless centuries ago, little more than blasted wastes – fly-swarmed marshlands

103

of peat and rotten ice. A ragged, battered horde, the Kechra had seen battle before, and it was held in some versions of those legends that the Kechra were themselves fleeing, fleeing a vast, devastating war that gave cause to their own desperation.

In the face of annihilation, the Awl had learned how to fight such creatures. The tide was met, held, then turned.

Or so the tales proclaimed, in ringing, stirring tones of triumph.

Redmask knew better, although at times he wished he didn't. The war ended because the Kechra's migration reached the easternmost side of the Awl'dan, and then continued onward. Granted, they had been badly mauled by the belligerent ancestors of the Awl, yet, in truth, they had been almost indifferent to them – an obstacle in their path – and the death of so many of their own kind was but one more ordeal in a history of fraught, tragic ordeals since coming to this world.

Kechra. K'Chain Che'Malle, the Firstborn of Dragons.

There was, to Redmask's mind, nothing palatable or sustaining about knowledge. As a young warrior, his world had been a single knot on the rope of the Awl people, his own deliberate binding to the long, worn history of bloodlines. He had never imagined that there were so many other ropes, so many intertwined threads; he had never before comprehended how vast the net of existence, nor how tangled it had become since the Night of Life – when all that was living came into being, born of deceit and betrayal and doomed to an eternity of struggle.

And Redmask had come to understand struggle – there in the startled eyes of the rodara, the timid fear of the myrid; in the disbelief of a young warrior dying on stone and wind-blown sand; in the staring comprehension of a woman surrendering her life to the child she pushed out from between her legs. He had seen elders, human and beast, curl up to die; he had seen others fight for their last breath with all the will they could muster. Yet in his heart, he could find no reason, no reward waiting beyond that eternal struggle.

Even the spirit gods of his people battled, flailed, warred with the weapons of faith, with intolerance and the sweet, deadly waters of hate. No less confused and sordid than any mortal.

The Letherii wanted, and want invariably transformed into a moral right to possess. Only fools believed such things to be bloodless, either in intent or execution.

Well, by the same argument – by its very fang and talon – there existed a moral right to defy them. And in such a battle, there would be no end until one side or the other was obliterated. More likely, both sides were doomed to suffer that fate. This final awareness is what came from too much knowledge.

Yet he would fight on.

These plains he and his three young followers moved through had once belonged to the Awl. Until the Letherii expanded their notion of self-interest to include stealing land and driving away its original inhabitants. Cairn markers and totem stones had all been removed, the boulders left in heaps; even the ring-stones that had once anchored huts were gone. The grasses were overgrazed, and here and there long rectangular sections had seen the earth broken in anticipation of planting crops, fence posts stacked nearby. But Redmask knew that this soil was poor, quickly exhausted except in the old river valleys. The Letherii might manage a generation or two before the topsoil blew away. He had seen the results east of the wastelands, in far Kolanse – an entire civilization tottering on the edge of starvation as desert spread like plague.

The blurred moon had lifted high in the star-spattered night sky as they drew closer to the mass of rodara. There was little point in going after the myrid – the beasts were not swift runners over any reasonable distance – but as they edged closer, Redmask could see the full extent of this rodara herd. Twenty thousand head, perhaps even more.

A large drover camp, lit by campfires, commanded a hilltop to the north. Two permanent buildings of cut-log walls and sod-capped roofs overlooked the shallow valley and the herds – these would, Redmask knew, belong to the Factor's foreman, forming the focus for the beginning of a true settlement.

Crouched in the grasses at the edge of a drainage gully cutting through the valley side, the three young warriors on his left, Redmask studied the Letherii for another twenty heartbeats; then he gestured Masarch and the others back into the gully itself.

'This is madness,' the warrior named Theven whispered. 'There must be a hundred Letherii in that camp – and what of the shepherds and their dogs? If the wind shifts . . .'

'Quiet,' said Redmask. 'Leave the dogs and the shepherds to me. As for the camp, well, they will soon be busy enough. Return to the horses, mount up, and be ready to flank and drive the herd when it arrives.'

In the moon's pale light, Masarch's expression was nerve-twisted, a wild look in his eyes – he had not done well on his death night, but thus far he appeared more or less sane. Both Theven and Kraysos had, Redmask suspected, made use of bledden herb smuggled with them into their coffins, which they chewed to make themselves insensate, beyond such things as panic and convulsions. Perhaps that was just as well. But Masarch had possessed no bledden herb. And, as was common to people of open lands, confinement was worse than death, worse than anything one could imagine.

Yet there was value in searing that transition into adulthood, rebirth that began with facing oneself, one's own demonic haunts that came clambering into view in grisly succession, immune to every denial. With the scars born of that transition, a warrior would come to understand the truth of imagination: that it was a weapon the mind drew at every turn, yet as deadly to its wielder as to its conjured foes. Wisdom arrived as one's skill with that weapon grew – *we fight every battle with our imaginations: the battles within, the battles in the world beyond. This is the truth of command, and a warrior must learn command, of oneself and of others.* It was possible that soldiers, such as the Letherii, experienced something similar in attaining rank, but Redmask was not sure of that.

Glancing back, he saw that his followers had vanished into the darkness. Probably, he judged, now at their horses. Waiting with fast, shallow breaths drawn into suddenly tight lungs. Starting at soft noises, gripping their reins and weapons in sweat-layered hands.

Redmask made a soft grunting sound and the dray, lying on its belly, edged closer. He settled a hand on its thick-furred neck, briefly, then drew it away. Together, the two set out, side by side, both low to the ground, towards the rodara herd.

Abasard walked slowly along the edge of the sleeping herd to keep himself alert. His two favoured dogs trotted in his wake. Born and raised as an Indebted in Drene, the sixteen-year-old had not imagined a world such as this – the vast sky, sprawling darkness and countless stars at night, enormous and depthless at day; the way the land itself reached out impossible distances, until at times he could swear he saw a curvature to the world, as if it existed like an island in the sea of the Abyss. And so much life, in the grasses, in the sky. In the spring tiny flowers erupted from every hillside, with berries ripening in the valleys. All his life, until his family had accompanied the Factor's foreman, he had lived with his father and mother, his brothers and sisters, with his grandmother and two aunts – all crowded into a house little more than a shack, facing onto a rubbish-filled alley that stank of urine. The menagerie of his youth was made up of rats, blue-eyed mice, meers, cockroaches, scorpions and silverworms.

But here, in this extraordinary place, he had discovered a new life. Winds that did not stink with rot and waste. And there was room, so much room. He had witnessed with his own eyes a return to health among the members of his family – his frail little sister now wiry and sun-darkened, ever grinning; his grandmother, whose cough had virtually vanished; his father, who stood taller now, no longer hunched beneath low-ceilinged shacks and worksheds. Only yesterday, Abasard had heard him laugh, for the very first time.

Perhaps, the youth dared believe, once the land was broken and crops were planted, there would be the chance to work their way free of debt. Suddenly, all things seemed possible.

106

His two dogs loped past him, vanished in the gloom ahead. A not unusual occurrence. They liked to chase jackrabbits, or low-flying rhinazan. He heard a brief commotion in the grasses just beyond a slight rise. Abasard adjusted his grip on the staff he carried, increased his pace – if the dogs had trapped and killed a jackrabbit, there would be extra meat in the stew tomorrow.

Reaching the rise, he paused, searched the darkness below for his dogs. They were nowhere to be seen. Abasard frowned, then let out a low whistle, expecting at any moment to hear them trot back to him. Yet only silence answered his summons. Confused, he slowly dropped into a crouch.

Ahead and to his right, a few hundred rodara shifted – awake and restless now.

Something was wrong. Wolves? The Bluerose cavalry the foreman kept under contract had hunted the local ones down long ago. Even the coyotes had been driven away, as had the bears.

Abasard crept forward, his mouth suddenly dry, his heart pounding hard in his chest.

His free hand, reaching out before him, came into contact with soft, warm fur. One of his dogs, lying motionless, still under his probing touch. Near its neck, the fur was wet. He reached down along it until his fingers sank into torn flesh where its throat should have been. The wound was ragged. *Wolf. Or one of those striped cats.* But of the latter he had only ever seen skins, and those came from the far south, near Bolkando Kingdom.

Truly frightened now, he continued on, and moments later found his other dog. This one had a broken neck. The two attacks, he realized, had to have been made simultaneously, else one or the other of the beasts would have barked.

A broken neck . . . but no other wounds, no slather of saliva on the fur.

The rodara heaved a half-dozen paces to one side again, and he could make out, at the very edge of his vision, their heads lifted on their long necks, their ears upright. Yet no fear-sounds came from them. So, no dangerous scent, no panic – *someone has their attention. Someone they're used to obeying.*

There was no mistaking this – the herd was being stolen. Abasard could not believe it. He turned about, retracing his route. Twenty paces of silent footfalls later, he set out into a run – back to the camp.

Redmask's whip snaked out to wrap round the shepherd's neck – the old Letherii had been standing, outlined well against the dark, staring mutely at the now-moving herd. A sharp tug from Redmask and the shepherd's head rolled from the shoulders, the body – arms jerking momentarily out to the sides – falling to one side.

The last of them, Redmask knew, as he moved up. Barring one, who had been smart enough to flee, although that would not save him in the end. Well, invaders had to accept the risks – they were thieves as well, weren't they? Luxuriating in their unearned wealth, squatting on land not their own, arrogant enough to demand that it change to suit their purposes. As good as pissing on the spirits in the earth – one paid for such temerity and blasphemy.

He pushed away that last thought as unworthy. The spirits could take care of themselves, and they would deliver their own vengeance, in time – for they were as patient as they were inexorable. It was not for Redmask to act on behalf of those spirits. No, that form of righteousness was both unnecessary and disingenuous. The truth was this: Redmask enjoyed being the hand of *Awl* vengeance. Personal and, accordingly, all the more delicious.

He had already begun his killing of the Letherii, back in Drene.

Drawing his knife as he crouched over the old man's severed head, he cut off the Letherii's face, rolled it up and stored it with the others in the salt-crusted bag at his hip.

Most of the herd dogs had submitted to the Awl dray's challenge – they now followed the larger, nastier beast as it worked to waken the entire herd, then drive it en masse eastward.

Straightening, Redmask turned as the first screams erupted from the drover camp.

Abasard was still forty paces from the camp when he saw one of the tents collapse to one side, poles and guides snapping, as an enormous two-legged creature thumped over it, talons punching through to the struggling forms beneath, and screams tore through the air. Head swivelling to one side, the fiend continued on in its loping, stiff-tailed gait. There were huge swords in its hands.

Another one crossed its path, fast, low, heading for the foreman's house. Abasard saw a figure dart from this second beast's path – but not quickly enough, as its head snapped forward, twisting so that its jaws closed to either side of the man's head. Whereupon the reptile threw the flailing form upward in a bone-breaking surge. The limp corpse sailed in the air, landing hard and rolling into the hearth fire in a spray of sparks.

Abasard stood, paralysed by the horror of the slaughter he saw before him. He had recognized that man. Another Indebted, a man who had been courting one of his aunts, a man who always seemed to be laughing.

Another figure caught his eye. His baby sister, ten years old, racing out from the camp – away from another tent whose inhabitants were dying beneath chopping swords – *our tent. Father*—

The reptile lifted its head, saw his sister's fleeting form, and surged after her.

All at once, Abasard found himself running, straight for the monstrous creature.

If it saw him converging, it was indifferent – until the very last moment, as Abasard raised his staff to swing overhand, hoping to strike the beast on its hind leg, imagining bones breaking—

The nearer sword lashed out, so fast, so—

Abasard found himself lying on sodden grasses, feeling heat pour from one side of his body, and as the heat poured out, he grew ever colder. He stared, seeing nothing yet, sensing how something was wrong – he was on his side, but his head was flattened down, his ear pressed to the ground. There should have been a shoulder below and beneath his head, and an arm, and it was where all the heat was pouring out.

And further down, the side of his chest, this too seemed to be gone.

He could feel his right leg, kicking at the ground. But no left leg. He did not understand.

Slowly, he settled onto his back, stared up at the night sky.

So much room up there, a ceiling beyond the reach of everyone, covering a place in which they could live. Uncrowded, room enough for all.

He was glad, he realized, that he had come here, to see, to witness, to understand. Glad, even as he died.

Redmask walked out of the dark to where Masarch waited with the Letherii horse. Behind him, the rodara herd was a mass of movement, the dominant males in the lead, their attention fixed on Redmask. Dogs barked and nipped from the far flanks. Distant shouts from the other two young warriors indicated they were where they should be.

Climbing into the saddle, Redmask nodded to Masarch then swung his mount round.

Pausing for a long moment, Masarch stared at the distant Letherii camp, where it seemed the unholy slaughter continued unabated. *His guardians, he'd said.*

He does not fear challenges to come. He will take the fur of the Ganetok war leader. He will lead us to war against the Letherii. He is Redmask, who forswore the Awl, only to now return.

I thought it was too late.

I now think I am wrong.

He thought again of his death night, and memories returned like winged demons. He had gone mad, in that hollowed-out log, gone so far mad that hardly any of him had survived to return, when the morning light blinded him. Now, the insanity was loose, tingling at the very ends of his limbs, loose and wild but as yet undecided, not yet ready to act, to show its face. There was nothing to hold it back. No-one.

No-one but Redmask. My war leader.
Who unleashed his own madness years ago.

CHAPTER FIVE

Denigration afflicted our vaunted ideals long
ago, but such inflictions are difficult to measure,
to rise up and point a finger to this place, this
moment, and say: here, my friends, this was
where our honour, our integrity died.

   The affliction was too insipid, too much a
product of our surrendering mindful regard
and diligence. The meanings of words lost their
precision – and no-one bothered taking to task
those who cynically abused those words to
serve their own ambitions, their own evasion
of personal responsibility. Lies went unchallenged,
lawful pursuit became a sham, vulnerable to graft,
and justice itself became a commodity, mutable
in imbalance. Truth was lost, a chimera reshaped
to match agenda, prejudices, thus consigning
the entire political process to a mummer's
charade of false indignation, hypocritical
posturing and a pervasive contempt for the
commonry.

   Once subsumed, ideals and the honour created
by their avowal can never be regained, except,
alas, by outright, unconstrained rejection,
invariably instigated by the commonry, at the
juncture of one particular moment, one single
event, of such brazen injustice that revolution
becomes the only reasonable response.

   Consider this then a warning. Liars will lie,
and continue to do so, even beyond being
caught out. They will lie, and in time, such
liars will convince themselves, will in all self-
righteousness divest the liars of culpability.

111

Until comes a time when one final lie is voiced,
the one that can only be answered by rage,
by cold murder, and on that day, blood shall
rain down every wall of this vaunted, weaning
society.

Impeached Guild Master's Speech
Semel Fural of the Guild of Sandal-Clasp Makers

O F THE TURTLES KNOWN AS VINIK THE FEMALES DWELT FOR THE most part in the uppermost reaches of the innumerable sources of the Lether River, in the pooled basins and high-ground bogs found in the coniferous forests crowding the base of the Bluerose Mountains. The mountain runoff, stemmed and backed by the dams built by flat-tailed river-rats, descended in modest steps towards the broader, conjoined tributaries feeding the vast river. Vinik turtles were long-shelled and dorsal-ridged, and their strong forelimbs ended in taloned hands bearing opposable thumbs. In the egg-laying season, the females – smaller by far than their male kin of the deep rivers and the seas – prowled the ponds seeking the nests of waterfowl. Finding one large enough and properly accessible, the female vinik would appropriate it. Prior to laying her own eggs, the turtle exuded a slime that coated the bird eggs, the slime possessing properties that suspended the development of those young birds. Once the vinik's clutch was in place, the turtle then dislodged the entire nest, leaving it free to float, drawn by the current. At each barrier juvenile male vinik were gathered, to drag the nests over dry ground so that they could continue their passive migration down to the Lether River.

Many sank, or encountered some fatal obstacle on their long, arduous journey to the sea. Others were raided by adult vinik dwelling in the depths of the main river. Of those nests that made it to sea, the eggs hatched, the hatchlings fed on the bird embryos, then slipped out into the salty water. Only upon reaching juvenile age – sixty or seventy years – would the new generation of vinik begin the years-long journey back up the river, to those distant, murky ponds of the Bluerose boreal forest.

Nests bobbed in the waters of the Lether River as it flowed past the Imperial City, Letheras, seat of the Emperor. Local fisher boats avoided them, since large vinik males sometimes tracked the nests just beneath the surface – and provided they weren't hungry enough to raid the nest, they would defend it. Few fisher folk willingly challenged a creature that could weigh as much as a river galley and was capable of tearing such a galley to pieces with its beak and its clawed forearms.

The arrival of the nests announced the beginning of summer, as did the clouds of midges swarming over the river, the settling of the water level and the reek of exposed silts along the banks.

On the faint rise behind the Old Palace, the dishevelled expanse where stood the foundations of ancient towers, and one in particular constructed of black stone with a low-walled yard, a hunched, hooded figure dragged himself towards the gateway step by aching, awkward step. His spine was twisted, pushed by past ravages of unconstrained power until the ridge of each vertebra was visible beneath the thread-bare cloak, the angle forcing his shoulders far forward so that the unkempt ground before him was within reach of his arms, which he used to pull his broken body along.

He came searching for a nest. A mound of ragged earth and dying grasses, a worm-chewed hole into a now dead realm. Questing with preternatural senses, he moved through the yard from one barrow to the next. Empty . . . empty . . . empty.

Strange insects edged away from his path. Midges spun in cavorting swirls over him, but would not alight to feed, for the searcher's blood was rotted with chaos. The day's dying light plucked at his misshapen shadow, as if seeking sense of a stain so malign on the yard's battered ground.

Empty . . .

But this one was not. He allowed himself a small moment of glee. Suspicions confirmed, at last. The place that was dead . . . was not entirely dead. Oh, the Azath was now nothing more than lifeless stone, all power and all will drained away. Yet some sorcery lingered, here, beneath this oversized mound ringed in shattered trees. Kurald for certain. Probably Galain – the stink of Tiste Andii was very nearly palpable. Binding rituals, a thick, interwoven skein to keep something . . . someone . . . *down*.

Crouched, the figure reached with his senses, then suddenly recoiled, breath hissing from between mangled lips.

It has begun unravelling! Someone has been here – before me! Not long. Sorcery, working the release of this imprisoned creature. *Father of Shadows, I must think!*

Hannan Mosag remained motionless, hunched at the very edge of this mound, his mind racing.

Beyond the ruined grounds, the river flowed on, down to the distant sea. Carried on its current, vinik nests spun lazily; milky green eggs, still warm with the day's heat, enclosed vague shapes that squirmed about, eager for the birth of light.

She lifted her head with a sharp motion, blood and fragments of human lung smearing her mouth and chin, sliding then dripping down into the

113

split-open ribcage of her victim – a fool who, consumed by delusions of domination and tyranny no doubt, had chosen to stalk her all the way from Up Markets. It had become a simple enough thing, a lone, seemingly lost woman of high birth, wandering through crowds unaware of the hooded looks and expressions of avarice tracking her. She was like the bait the fisher folk used to snare brainless fish in the river. True, while she remained hooded, her arms covered in shimmering silk the hue of raw ox-heart, wearing elegant calf-leather gloves, as well as close-wrapped leggings of black linen, there was no way anyone could see the cast of her skin, nor her unusual features. And, despite the Tiste Edur blood coursing diluted in her veins, she was not uncommonly tall, which well suited her apparent vulnerability, for it was clear that these Edur occupiers in this city were far too dangerous to be hunted by the common Letherii rapist.

She had led him into an alley, whereupon she drove one hand into his chest, tearing out his heart. But it was the lungs she enjoyed the most, the pulpy meat rich with oxygen and not yet soured by the rank juices of violent death.

The mortal realm was a delightful place. She had forgotten that.

But now, her feeding had been interrupted. Someone had come to the Azath grounds. Someone had probed her rituals, which had been dissolving the binding wards set by Silchas Ruin. There could be trouble there, and she was not inclined to suffer interference in her plans.

Probably the Errant, that meddling bastard. Or, even more alarming, that Elder God, Mael. A miserably crowded city, this Letheras – she had no intention of tarrying overlong here, lest her presence be discovered, her schemes knocked awry.

Wiping her mouth and chin with the back of one sleeved forearm, she straightened from her feast, then set off.

Rautos Hivanar, head of the Liberty Consign, squatted on the muddy bank of the river, the work crews finishing the day's excavation directly behind him, the pump crews already washing down, the sounds from the estate's back kitchen rising with the approaching demands of supper. He was making a point of feeding his diggers well, as much to ease their bemusement as to keep them working. They were now excavating way below the river level, after all, and if not for the constantly manned pumps, they would be working chest-deep in muddy water. As it was, the shoring on the walls needed continual attention, prone as they were to sag inward.

Eyes tracking a half-dozen vinik nests rafting down the river, Rautos Hivanar was lost in thought. There had been more mysterious objects, buried deep and disconnected, but he had begun to suspect that they all belonged together; that in an as yet inconceivable way they could be assembled into a kind of mechanism. Some central piece remained undiscovered, he believed. Perhaps tomorrow . . .

He heard slippered feet on the plank walkway leading down to the river, and a moment later came Venitt Sathad's voice. 'Master.'

'Venitt, you have allotted yourself two house guards for the journey. Take two more. And, accordingly, two more packhorses. You will travel without a supply wagon, as agreed, but that need not be a reason to reduce your level of comfort.'

'Very well, Master.'

'And remember, Venitt. Letur Anict is in every way the de facto ruler of Drene, regardless of the Edur governor's official status. I am informed that you will find Orbyn Truthfinder, the Invigilator's agent, a reliable ally. As to Letur Anict . . . the evidence points to the Factor's having lost . . . perspective. His ambition seems without restraint, no longer harnessed to reason or, for that matter, common sense.'

'I shall be diligent in my investigation, Master.'

Rautos Hivanar rose and faced his servant. 'If needs must, Venitt, err on the side of caution. I would not lose you.'

A flicker of something like surprise in the Indebted's lined face, then the man bowed. 'I will remain circumspect, Master.'

'One last thing,' Rautos said as he moved past Venitt on his way up to the estate. 'Do not embarrass me.'

The Indebted's eyes tracked his master for a moment, his expression once more closed.

Unseen behind them on the river, a huge shape lifted beneath one vinik nest, and breaking the water as the nest overturned was the prow ridge of an enormous shell, and below that a sinewy neck and a vast, gaping beak. Swallowing the nest entire.

The currents then carried the disturbance away, until no sign of it remained.

'You know, witnessing something is one thing. Understanding it another.'

Bugg turned away from his study of the distant river, where the setting sun's light turned the water into a rippled sheet of beaten gold, and frowned at Tehol Beddict. 'Very pondering of you, Master.'

'It was, wasn't it? I have decided that it is my normal eye that witnesses, while it is my blue eye that understands. Does that make sense to you?'

'No.'

'Good, I'm glad.'

'The night promises to be both heavy and hot, Master. And I suggest the mosquito netting.'

'Agreed. Can you get to it? I can't reach.'

'You could if you stretched an arm.'

'What's your point?'

'Nothing. I admit to some . . . distraction.'

'Just now?'

'Yes.'

'Are you over it yet?'

'Almost. Alas, certain individuals are stirring in the city this evening.'

'Well, are you going to do something about it or do I have to do everything around here?'

Bugg walked across the roof to stand beside the bed. He studied the reposed form of Tehol Beddict for a moment, then he collected the netting and draped it over his master.

Eyes, one brown, the other blue, blinked up at him. 'Shouldn't there be a frame or something? I feel I am being readied for my own funeral here.'

'We used the frame for this morning's fire.'

'Ah. Well, is this going to keep me from being bitten?'

'Probably not, but it looks rather fetching.'

Tehol closed his blue eye. 'I see . . .'

Bugg sighed. 'Gallows humour, Master.'

'My, you are in a state, aren't you?'

'I am undecided,' Bugg said, nodding. 'Yes I know, one of my eternal flaws.'

'What you require, old friend, is a mortal's perspective on things. So let's hear it. Lay out the dilemma for me, Bugg, so that I might provide you with a properly pithy solution.'

'The Errant follows the Warlock King, to see what he plans. The Warlock King meddles with nefarious rituals set in place by another ascendant, who in turn leaves off eating a freshly killed corpse and makes for an unexpected rendezvous with said Warlock King, where they will probably make each other's acquaintance then bargain to mutual benefit over the crumbling chains binding another ascendant – one soon to be freed, which will perturb someone far to the north, although that one is probably not yet ready to act. In the meantime, the long-departed Edur fleet skirts the Draconean Sea and shall soon enter the river mouth on its fated return to our fair city, and with it are two fell champions, neither of whom is likely to do what is expected of them. Now, to add spice to all of that, the secret that is the soul of one Scabandari Bloodeye will, in a depressingly short time, cease to be a secret, and consequently and in addition to and concomitant with, we are in for an interesting summer.'

'Is that all?'

'Not in the least, but one mouthful at a time, I always say.'

'No you don't. Shurq Elalle is the one always saying that.'

'Your penchant for disgusting images, Master, is as ever poorly timed and thoroughly inappropriate. Now, about that pithy solution of yours . . .'

'Well, I admit to disappointment. You didn't even mention my grand scheme to bankrupt the empire.'

'The Invigilator now hunts for you in earnest.'

'Karos Invictad? No wonder you put me under a shroud. I shall endeavour to be close to the roof's edge the day he clambers into view with his drooling henchmen, so that I can fling myself over the side, which, you'll agree, is far preferable to even one bell's worth of his infamous, ghastly inquisition. In the meantime, what's for supper?'

'Vinik eggs – I found a somewhat broken nest washed up under a dock.'

'But vinik eggs are poisonous, hence the clouds of complaining gulls constantly circling over every nasty little floating island.'

'It's a matter of proper cooking, Master, and the addition of a few essential herbs that serve to negate most of the ill effects.'

'Most?'

'Yes.'

'And do you have in your possession those life-sustaining herbs?'

'Well, no, but I thought I'd improvise.'

'There you have it.'

'There I have what, Master?'

'Why, my pithy reply, of course.'

Bugg squinted at Tehol Beddict, who winked, this time closing his brown eye. The Elder God scowled, then said, 'Thank you, Master. What would I ever do without you?'

'Scant little, I'd wager.'

Tanal Yathvanar set the package down on the Invigilator's desk. 'Delivered by a rat-faced urchin this morning. Sir, I expect it will prove no particular challenge. In any case,' he continued as he began unwrapping the package, 'I was instructed to treat it delicately, and to keep it upright. And you will, in moments, see why.'

Karos Invictad watched with heavy-lidded eyes as the grease-stained, poor quality ragweed wrapping was delicately pulled away, revealing a small, open-topped wooden box that seemed to possess layered sides. The Invigilator leaned forward to peer inside.

And saw a two-headed insect, such as were now appearing down by the river. Its legs were moving precisely, carrying it round . . . and round. The insides of the box were each of coloured, polished tiles, and it appeared that the tiles could be slid free, or rearranged, if one so chose.

'What were the instructions, Tanal?'

117

'The challenge is to halt the insect's motion. It will, apparently, continue walking in a circle, in the same place, until it dies of starvation – which, incidentally, is the fail point for the puzzle . . . approximately four months. While the creature rotates in place, it will not eat. As for water, a small clump of soaked moss will suffice. As you can see, the tiles on the inside can be rearranged, and presumably, once the proper order or sequence is discovered, the insect will stop. And you will have defeated the puzzle. The restrictions are these: no object may be placed inside the container; nor can you physically touch or make contact with the insect.'

Karos Invictad grunted. 'Seems direct enough. What is the record for the solution?'

'There is none. You are the first and only player, apparently.'

'Indeed. Curious. Tanal, three prisoners died in their cells last night – some contagion is loose down there. Have the corpses burned in the Receiving Ground west of the city. Thoroughly. And have the rest washed down with disinfectant.'

'At once, Invigilator.'

The ruins were far more extensive than is commonly imagined. In fact, most historians of the early period of the colony have paid little or no attention to the reports of the Royal Engineer, specifically those of Keden Qan, who served from the founding until the sixth decade. During the formulation of the settlement building plan, a most thorough survey was conducted. The three extant Jhag towers behind the Old Palace were in fact part of a far larger complex, which of course runs contrary to what is known of Jhag civilization. For this reason, it may be safe to assume that the Jhag complex on the bank of the Lether River represents a pre-dispersion site. That is, before the culture disintegrated in its sudden, violent diaspora. An alternative interpretation would be that the three main towers, four subterranean vaults, and what Qan called the Lined Moat all belonged to a single, unusually loyal family.

In either case, the point I am making here is this: beyond the Jhag – or more correctly, Jaghut – complex, there were other ruins. Of course, one need not point out the most obvious and still existing Azath structure – that lecture will have to wait another day. Rather, in an area covering almost the entire expanse of present-day Letheras could be found foundation walls, plazas or concourses, shaped wells, drainage ditches and, indeed, some form of cemetery or mortuary, and – listen carefully now – all of it not of human design. Nor Jaghut, nor even Tarthenal.

Now, what were the details of this unknown complex? Well, for one, it was self-contained, walled, entirely covered by multi-level roofing –

even the plazas, alleys and streets. As a fortress, it was virtually im-
pregnable. Beneath the intricately paved floors and streets, there was a
second even more defensible city, the corridors and tunnels of which
can now be found as an integral part of our sewer outflow.

In short, Letheras, the colony of the First Empire, was founded upon
the ruins of an earlier city, one whose layout seemed to disregard the
presence of the Jaghut towers and the Azath, suggesting that it pre-
dates both.

Even the first engineer, Keden Qan, was unable or unwilling to
attempt an identification of these early builders. Virtually no artifacts
were found – no potsherds, no sculptures, no remnants of metal-
working. One last interesting detail. It appeared that in the final stages
of occupation, the dwellers set about frantic alterations to their city.
Qan's analysis of these efforts led him to conclude that a catastrophic
climate change had occurred, for the efforts indicated a desperate
attempt to add insulation.

Presumably, that effort failed—

Her interior monologue ceased abruptly as she heard the faint scuff
of someone approaching. Lifting her head was a struggle, but Janath
Anar managed, just as the chamber's heavy door creaked open and light
flooded in from a lantern – dull and low yet blinding her nonetheless.

Tanal Yathvanar stepped into view – it would be none other but him,
she knew – and a moment later he spoke. 'I pray you've yet to drive
yourself mad.'

Through cracked, blistered lips, she smiled, then said in a croaking
voice, 'Lectures. I am halfway into the term. Early History. Mad? Oh
yes, without question.'

She heard him come closer. 'I have been gone from you too long –
you are suffering. That was careless of me.'

'Careless is keeping me alive, you miserable little wretch,' she said.

'Ah, perhaps I deserved that. Come, you must drink.'

'What if I refuse?'

'Then, with your inevitable death, you are defeated. By me. Are you
sure you want that, Scholar?'

'You urge me to stubborn resistance. I understand. The sadist needs
his victim alive, after all. For as long as humanly possible.'

'Dehydration is a most unpleasant way to die, Janath Anar.'

He lifted the spigot of a waterskin to her mouth. She drank.

'Not too quickly,' Tanal said, stepping back. 'You will just make
yourself sick. Which wouldn't, I see, be the first time for you.'

'When you see maggots crawl out of your own wastes, Yathvanar . . .
Next time,' she added, 'take your damned candle with you.'

'If I do that,' he replied, 'you will go blind—'

'And that matters?'

He stepped close once again and poured more water into her mouth. Then he set about washing her down. Sores had opened where stomach fluids had burned desiccated skin, and, he could see, she had been pulling on her bindings, seeking to squeeze her hands through the shackles. 'You are looking much worse for wear,' he said as he dabbed ointment on the wounds. 'You cannot get your hands through, Janath—'

'Panic cares nothing for what can and can't be done, Tanal Yathvanar. One day you will discover that. There was a priest once, in the second century, who created a cult founded on the premise that every victim tallied in one's mortal life awaits that one beyond death. From the slightest of wounds to the most grievous, every victim preceeding you into death . . . *waits*. For you.

'A mortal conducts spiritual economics in his or her life, amassing credit and debt. Tell me, Patriotist, how indebted are you by now? How vast the imbalance between good deeds and your endless acts of malice?'

'A bizarre, insane cult,' he muttered, moving away. 'No wonder it failed.'

'In this empire, yes, it's no wonder at all. The priest was set upon in the street and torn limb from limb. Still, it's said adherents remain, among the defeated peoples – the Tarthenal, the Fent and Nerek, the victims, as it were, of Letherii cruelty – and before those people virtually disappeared from the city, there were rumours that the cult was reviving.'

Tanal Yathvanar sneered. 'The ones who fail ever need a crutch, a justification – they fashion virtue out of misery. Karos Invictad has identified that weakness, in one of his treatises—'

Janath's laugh broke into ragged coughing. When she recovered, she spat and said, 'Karos Invictad. Do you know why he so despises academics? He is a failed one himself.' She bared her stained teeth. 'He calls them treatises, does he? Errant fend, how pathetic. Karos Invictad couldn't fashion a decent argument, much less a treatise.'

'You are wrong in that, woman,' Tanal said. 'He has even explained why he did so poorly as a young scholar – oh yes, he would not refute your assessment of his career as a student. Driven by emotions, back then. Incapable of a cogent position, leaving him rife with anger – but at himself, at his own failings. But, years later, he learned that all emotion had to be scoured from him; only then would his inner vision become clear.'

'Ah, he needed wounding, then. What was it? A betrayal of sorts, I expect. Some woman? A protégé, a patron? Does it even matter? Karos Invictad makes sense to me, now. Why he is what he has become.' She laughed again, this time without coughing, then said, 'Delicious irony. Karos Invictad became a *victim*.'

'Don't be—'

'A victim, Yathvanar! And he didn't like it, oh no, not at all. It hurt – the world hurt him, so now he's hurting it back. And yet, he has still to even the score. But you see, he never will, because in his mind, he's still that victim, still lashing out. And as you said earlier, the victim and his crutch, his virtue of misery – one feeds the other, without cessation. No wonder he bridles with self-righteousness for all his claims to emotionless intellect—'

He struck her, hard, her head snapping to one side, spittle and blood threading out.

Breathing fast, chest strangely tight, Tanal hissed, 'Rail at me all you will, Scholar. I expect that. But not at Karos Invictad. He is the empire's last true hope. Only Karos Invictad will guide us into glory, into a new age, an age without the Edur, without the mixed-bloods, without even the failed peoples. No, just the Letherii, an empire expanding outward with sword and fire, all the way back to the homeland of the First Empire. He has seen our future! Our destiny!'

She stared at him in the dull light. 'Of course. But first, he needs to kill every Letherii worthy of the name. Karos Invictad, the Great Scholar, and his empire of thugs—'

He struck her again, harder than before, then lurched back, raising his hand – it was trembling, skin torn and battered, a shard of one broken tooth jutting from one knuckle.

She was unconscious.

Well, she asked for it. She wouldn't stop. That means she wanted it, deep inside, she wanted me to beat her. I've heard about this – Karos has told me – they come to like it, eventually. They like the . . . attention.

So, I must not neglect her. Not again. Plenty of water, keep her clean and fed.

And beat her anyway.

But she was not unconscious, for she then spoke in a mumble. He could not make it out and edged closer.

'. . . on the other side . . . I will wait for you . . . on the other side . . .'

Tanal Yathvanar felt a slither deep in his gut. And fled from it. *No god waits to pass judgement. No-one marks the imbalance of deeds – no god is beyond its own imbalances – for its own deeds are as subject to judgement as any other. So who then fashions this afterlife? Some natural imposition? Ridiculous – there is no balance in nature. Besides, nature exists in this world and this world alone – its rules mean nothing once the bridge is crossed . . .*

Tanal Yathvanar found himself walking up the corridor, that horrid woman and her cell far behind him now – he had no recollection of actually leaving.

Karos has said again and again, justice is a conceit. It does not exist in nature. 'Retribution seen in natural catastrophes is manufactured by all too eager and all too pious people, each one convinced the world will end but spare them and them alone. But we all know, the world is inherited by the obnoxious, not the righteous.'

Unless, came the thought in Janath's voice, *the two are one and the same.*

He snarled as he hurried up the worn stone stairs. She was far below. Chained. A prisoner in her solitary cell. There was no escape for her.

I have left her down there, far below. Far behind. She can't escape.

Yet, in his mind, he heard her laughter.

And was no longer so sure.

Two entire wings of the Eternal Domicile were empty, long, vacated corridors and never-occupied chambers, storage rooms, administration vaults, servant quarters and kitchens. Guards patrolling these sections once a day carried their own lanterns, and left unrelieved darkness in their wake. In the growing damp of these unoccupied places, dust had become mould, mould had become rot, and the rot in turn leaked rank fluids that ran down plastered walls and pooled in dips in the floors.

Abandonment and neglect would soon defeat the ingenious innovations of Bugg's Construction, as they defeated most things raised by hands out of the earth, and Turudal Brizad, the Errant, considered himself almost unique in his fullest recognition of such sordid truths. Indeed, there were other elders persisting in their nominal existence, but they one and all fought still against the ravages of inevitable dissolution. Whereas the Errant could not be bothered.

Most of the time.

The Jaghut had come to comprehend the nature of futility, inspiring the Errant to a certain modicum of empathy for those most tragic of people. Where was Gothos now, he wondered. Probably long dead, all things considered. He had written a multiple-volumed suicide note – his *Folly* – that presumably concluded at some point, although the Errant had neither seen nor heard that such a conclusion existed. Perhaps, he considered with sudden suspicion, there was some hidden message in a suicidal testimonial without end, but if so, such meaning was too obscure for the mind of anyone but a Jaghut.

He had followed the Warlock King to the dead Azath, remained there long enough to discern Hannan Mosag's intentions, and had now returned to the Eternal Domicile, where he could walk these empty corridors in peace. Contemplating, among other things, stepping once again into the fray. To battle, one more time, the ravages of dissolution.

He thought he could hear Gothos laughing, somewhere. But no doubt that was only his imagination, ever eager to mock his carefully reasoned impulses.

Finding himself in a stretch of corridor awash with slime-laden water, the Errant paused. 'Well,' he said with a soft sigh, 'to bring a journey to a close, one must first begin it. Best I act whilst the will remains.'

His next step took him into a glade, thick verdant grasses underfoot, a ring of dazzling flowers at the very edges of the black-boled trees encircling the clearing. Butterflies danced from one bloom of colour to the next. The patch of sky visible overhead was faintly tinted vermilion and the air seemed strangely thin.

A voice spoke behind him. 'I do not welcome company here.'

The Errant turned. He slowly cocked his head. 'It's not often the sight of a woman inspires fear in my soul.'

She scowled. 'Am I that ugly, Elder?'

'To the contrary, Menandore. Rather . . . formidable.'

'You have trespassed into my place of refuge.' She paused, then asked, 'Does it so surprise you, that one such as myself needs refuge?'

'I do not know how to answer that,' he replied.

'You're a careful one, Errant.'

'I suspect you want a reason to kill me.'

She walked past him, long black sarong flowing from frayed ends and ragged tears. 'Abyss below,' she murmured, 'am I so transparent? Who but you could have guessed that I require justification for killing?'

'So your sense of sarcasm has survived your solitude, Menandore. It is what I am ever accused of, isn't it? My . . . random acts.'

'Oh, I know they're not random. They only seem that way. You delight in tragic failure, which leads me to wonder what you want with me? We are not well suited, you and I.'

'What have you been up to lately?' he asked.

'Why should I tell you?'

'Because I have information to impart, which you will find . . . *well suited* to your nature. And I seek recompense.'

'If I deny it you will have made this fraught journey for nothing.'

'It will only be fraught if you attempt something untoward, Menandore.'

'Precisely.'

Her unhuman eyes regarded him steadily.

He waited.

'Sky keeps,' she said.

'Ah, I see. Has it begun, then?'

'No, but soon.'

'Well, you are not one to act without long preparation, so I am not

123

that surprised. And which side will we, eventually, find you on, Menandore?'

'Why, mine of course.'

'You will be opposed.'

One thin brow arched.

The Errant glanced around. 'A pleasant place. What warren are we in?'

'You would not believe me if I told you.'

'Ah,' he nodded, '*that* one. Very well, your sisters conspire.'

'Not against me, Errant.'

'Not directly, or, rather, not immediately. Rest assured, however, that the severing of your head from your shoulders is the eventual goal.'

'Has she been freed, then?'

'Imminent.'

'And you will do nothing? What of the others in that fell city?'

Others? 'Mael is being . . . Mael. Who else hides in Letheras, barring your two sisters?'

'Sisters,' she said, then sneered as she turned away, walked to one edge of the glade, where she crouched and plucked a flower. Facing him once more, she lifted the flower to draw deep its scent.

From the snapped stem, thick red blood dripped steadily.

I've indeed heard it said that beauty is the thinnest skin.

She suddenly smiled. 'Why, no-one. I misspoke.'

'You invite me to a frantic and no doubt time-devouring search to prove your ingenuousness, Menandore. What possible reason could you have to set me on such a trail?'

She shrugged. 'Serves you right for infringing upon my place of refuge, Errant. Are we done here?'

'Your flower is bled out,' he said, as he stepped back, and found himself once more in the empty, flooded corridor of the Eternal Domicile's fifth wing.

Others. The bitch.

As soon as the Errant vanished from the glade, Menandore flung the wilted flower to one side, and two figures emerged from the forest, one from her left, the other from her right.

Menandore arched her back as she ran both hands through her thick red hair.

Both figures paused to watch.

She had known they would. 'You heard?' she asked, not caring which one answered.

Neither did. Menandore dropped her pose and scowled over to the scrawny, shadow-swarmed god to her left. 'That cane is an absurd affectation, you know.'

'Never mind my absurd affectations, woman. Blood dripping from a flower, for Hood's sake – oops—' The god known as Shadowthrone tilted a head towards the tall, cowled figure opposite. 'Humblest apologies, Reaper.'

Hood, Lord of Death, seemed to cock his head as if surprised. 'Yours?'

'Apologies? Naturally not. I but made a declarative statement. Was there a subject attached to it? No. We three fell creatures have met, have spoken, have agreed on scant little, and have concluded that our previous impressions of each other proved far too ... generous. Nonetheless, it seems we are agreed, more or less, on the one matter you, Hood, wanted to address. It's no wonder you're so ecstatic.'

Menandore frowned at the Lord of Death, seeking evidence of ecstasy. Finding none, she eyed Shadowthrone once more. 'Know that I have never accepted your claim.'

'I'm crushed. So your sisters are after you. What a dreadful family you have. Want help?'

'You too? Recall my dismissal of the Errant.'

Shadowthrone shrugged. 'Elders think too slowly. My offer is of another magnitude. Think carefully before you reject it.'

'And what do you ask in return?'

'Use of a gate.'

'Which gate?'

Shadowthrone giggled, then the eerie sound abruptly stopped, and in a serious tone he said, 'Starvald Demelain.'

'To what end?'

'Why, providing you with assistance, of course.'

'You want my sisters out of the way, too – perhaps more than I do. Squirming on that throne of yours, are you?'

'Convenient convergence of desires, Menandore. Ask Hood about such things, especially now.'

'If I give you access to Starvald Demelain, you will use it more than once.'

'Not I.'

'Do you so vow?'

'Why not?'

'Foolish,' Hood said in a rasp.

'I hold you to that vow, Shadowthrone,' Menandore said.

'Then you accept my help?'

'As you do mine in this matter. Convergence of desires, you said.'

'You're right,' Shadowthrone said. 'I retract all notions of "help". We are mutually assisting one another, as fits said convergence; and once finished with the task at hand, no other obligations exist between us.'

'That is agreeable.'

'You two,' Hood said, turning away, 'are worse than advocates. And you don't want to know what I do with the souls of advocates.' A heartbeat later and the Lord of Death was gone.

Menandore frowned. 'Shadowthrone, what are advocates?'

'A profession devoted to the subversion of laws for profit,' he replied, his cane inexplicably tapping as he shuffled back into the woods. 'When I was Emperor, I considered butchering them all.'

'So why didn't you?' she asked as he began to fade into a miasma of gloom beneath the trees.

Faintly came the reply, 'The Royal Advocate said it'd be a terrible mistake.'

Menandore was alone once again. She looked around, then grunted. 'Gods, I hate this place.' A moment later she too vanished.

Janall, once Empress of the Lether Empire, was now barely recognizable as a human. Brutally used as a conduit of the chaotic power of the Crippled God, her body had been twisted into a malign nightmare, bones bent, muscles stretched and bunched, and now, huge bulges of fat hung in folds from her malformed body. She could not walk, could not even lift her left arm, and the sorcery had broken her mind, the madness burning from eyes that glittered malevolently in the gloom as Nisall, carrying a lantern, paused in the doorway.

The chamber was rank with sweat, urine and other suppurations from the countless oozing sores on Janall's skin; the sweet reek of spoiled food, and another odour, pungent, that reminded the Emperor's Concubine of rotting teeth.

Janall dragged herself forward with a strange, asymmetrical shift of her hips, pivoting on her right arm. The motion made a sodden sound beneath her, and Nisall saw the streams of saliva easing out from the once-beautiful woman's misshapen mouth. The floor was pooled in the mucus and it was this, she realized, that was the source of the pungent smell.

Fighting back nausea, the Concubine stepped forward. 'Empress.'

'No longer!' The voice was ragged, squeezed out from a deformed throat, and drool spattered with every jerk of her misshapen jaw. 'I am Queen! Of his House, his honeyed House – oh, we are a contented family, oh yes, and one day, one day soon, you'll see, that pup on the throne will come here. For me, his Queen. You, whore, you're nothing – the House is not for you. You blind Rhulad to the truth, but his vision will clear, once,' her voice dropped to a whisper and she leaned forward, 'we are rid of you.'

'I came,' Nisall said, 'to see if you needed anything—'

'Liar. You came in search of allies. You think to steal him away. From me. From our true master. You will fail! Where's my son? Where is he?'

Nisall shook her head. 'I don't know. I don't even know if he's still alive – there are those in the court who claim he is, whilst others tell me he is long dead. But, Empress, I will seek to find out. And when I do, I will return. With the truth.'

'I don't believe you. You were never my ally. You were Ezgara's whore, not mine.'

'Has Turudal Brizad visited you, Empress?'

For a moment it seemed she would not answer. Then she managed something like a shrug. 'He does not dare. Master sees through my eyes – tell Rhulad that, and he will understand what must be. Through my eyes – look closer, if you would know a god. The god. The only god that matters now. The rest of them are blind, as blind as you've made Rhulad, but they're all in for a surprise, oh yes. The House is big – bigger than you imagine. The House is all of us, whore, and one day that truth will be proclaimed, so that all will hear. See me? I am on my knees, and that is no accident. Every human shall be on their knees, one day, and they will know me for their Queen. As for the King in Chains,' she laughed, a sound thick with phlegm, 'well, the crown is indifferent to whose skull it binds. The pup is failing, you know. Failing. There is . . . dissatisfaction. I should kill you, now, here. Come closer, whore.'

Instead, Nisall backed away a step, then two, until she was once more in the doorway. 'Empress, the Chancellor is the source of Rhulad's . . . failings. Your god should know that, lest it make a mistake. If you would kill anyone, it should be Triban Gnol, and, perhaps, Karos Invictad – they plot to usurp the Edur.'

'The Edur?' She spat. 'Master's almost done with them. Almost done.'

'I will send servants down,' Nisall said. 'To clean your chamber, Empress.'

'Spies.'

'No, from your own entourage.'

'Turned.'

'Empress, they will take care of you, for their loyalty remains.'

'But I don't want them!' Janall hunched lower. 'I don't want them . . . to see me like this.'

'A bed will be sent down. Canopied. You can draw the shroud when they arrive. Pass out the soiled bedding through a part in the curtain.'

'You would do this? I wanted you dead.'

'The past is nothing,' Nisall said. 'Not any more.'

'Get out,' Janall rasped, looking away. 'Master is disgusted with you. Suffering is our natural state. A truth to proclaim, and so I shall, when I win my new throne. Get out, whore, or come closer.'

'Expect your servants within the bell,' Nisall said, turning and walking from the grisly chamber.

127

As the echo of the whore's footsteps faded, Janall, Queen of the House of Chains, curled up into a ball on the slick, befouled floor. Madness flickered in her eyes, there, then gone, then there once more. Over and over again. She spoke, one voice thick, the other rasping.

'Vulnerable.'

'Until the final war. Watch the army, as it pivots round, entirely round. These sordid games here, the times are almost past, past us all. Oh, when the pain at last ends, then you shall see the truth of me. Dear Queen, my power was once the sweetest kiss. A love that broke nothing.'

'Give me my throne. You promised.'

'Is it worth it?'

'I beg you—'

'They all beg me, and call it prayer. What sour benediction must I swallow from this eternal fount of dread and spite and bald greed? Will you never see? Never understand? I must find the broken ones, just do not expect my reach, my touch. No-one understands, how the gods fear freedom. No-one.'

'You have lied to me.'

'You have lied to yourself. You all do, and call it faith. I am your god. I am what you made me. You all decry my indifference, but I assure you, you would greater decry my attention. No, make no procla- mations otherwise. I know what you claim to do in my name. I know your greatest fear is that I will one day call you on it – and that is the real game here, this knuckles of the soul. Watch me, mortal, watch me call you on it. Every one of you.'

'My god is mad.'

'As you would have me, so I am.'

'I want my throne.'

'You always want.'

'Why won't you give it to me?'

'I answer as a god: if I give you what you want, we all die. Hah, I know – *you don't care!* Oh, you humans, you are something else. You make my every breath agony. And my every convulsion is your ecstasy. Very well, mortal, I will answer your prayers. I promise. Just do not ever say I didn't warn you. Do not. *Ever.*'

Janall laughed, spraying spit. 'We are mad,' she whispered. 'Oh yes, quite mad. And we're climbing into the light . . .'

For all the scurrying servants and the motionless, helmed guards at various entrances, Nisall found the more populated areas of the Eternal Domicile in some ways more depressing than the abandoned corridors she'd left behind a third of a bell past. Suspicion soured the air, fear stalked like shadows underfoot between the stanchions of torchlight. The palace's name had acquired a taint of irony, rife as the Eternal Domicile was with paranoia, intrigue and incipient betrayal. As if humans could manage no better, and were doomed to such sordid existence for all time.

Clearly, there was nothing satisfying in peace, beyond the freedom it provided to get up to no good. She had been shaken by her visit to the supposedly insane once-empress, Janall. This Crippled God indeed lurked in the woman's eyes – Nisall had seen it, felt that chilling, un-human attention fixing on her, calculating, pondering her potential use. She did not want to be part of a god's plans, especially that god's. Even more frightening, Janall's ambitions remained, engorged with visions of supreme power, her tortured, brutalized body notwithstanding. The god was using her as well.

There were rumours of war hissing like wind in the palace, tales of a belligerent conspiracy of border kingdoms and tribes to the east. The Chancellor's reports to Rhulad had been anything but simple in their exhortations to raise the stakes. A formal declaration of war, the marching of massed troops over the borders in a pre-emptive campaign of conquest. Far better to spill blood on their lands than on Letherii soil, after all. *'If the Bolkando-led alliance wants war, we should give it to them.'* The Chancellor's glittering eyes belied the cool, almost tone-less enunciation of those words.

Rhulad had fidgeted on his throne, muttering his unease – the Edur were too spread out, the K'risnan were overworked. Why did the Bolkandans so dislike him? There had been no list of grievances. He had done nothing to spark this fire to life.

Triban Gnol had pointed out, quietly, that four agents of the conspiracy had been captured entering Letheras only the other day. Disguised as merchants seeking ivory. Karos Invictad had sent by courier their confessions and would the Emperor like to see them?

Shaking his head in denial, Rhulad had said nothing, his pain-racked eyes fixed on the tiles of the dais beyond his slippered feet.

So lost, this terrible Emperor.

As she turned onto the corridor leading to her private chambers, she saw a tall figure standing near her door. A Tiste Edur, one of the few who were resident in the palace. She vaguely recalled the warrior's having something to do with security.

He tilted his head in greeting as she approached. 'First Concubine Nisall.'

'Has the Emperor sent you?' she asked, stepping past and waving him behind her into the chambers. Few men could intimidate her – she knew too well their minds. She was less at ease in the company of women, and the virtually neutered men such as Triban Gnol.

'Alas,' the warrior said, 'I am not permitted to speak to my Emperor.'
She paused and glanced back at him. 'Are you out of favour?'

'I have no idea.'

Intrigued now, Nisall regarded the Edur for a moment, then asked, 'Would you like some wine?'

'No, thank you. Were you aware that a directive has been issued by Invigilator Karos Invictad to compile evidence leading to your arrest for sedition?'

She grew very still. Sudden heat flashed through her, then she felt cold, beads of sweat like ice against her skin. 'Are you here,' she whispered, 'to arrest me?'

His brows rose. 'No, nothing of the sort. The very opposite, in fact.'

'You wish, then, to join in my treason?'

'First Concubine, I do not believe you are engaged in any seditious acts. And if you are, I doubt they are directed against Emperor Rhulad.'

She frowned. 'If not the Emperor, then whom? And how could it be considered treasonous if they are not aimed at Rhulad? Do you think I resent the Tiste Edur hegemony? Precisely whom am I conspiring against?'

'If I was forced to hazard a guess . . . Chancellor Triban Gnol.'

She said nothing for a moment, then, 'What do you want?'

'Forgive me. My name is Bruthen Trana. I was appointed to oversee the operations of the Patriotists, although it is likely that the Emperor has since forgotten that detail.'

'I am not surprised. You've yet to report to him.'

He grimaced. 'True. The Chancellor has made certain of that.'

'He insists you report to *him* instead, yes? I'm beginning to understand, Bruthen Trana.'

'Presumably, Triban Gnol's assurances that he has conveyed said reports to Rhulad are false.'

'The only reports the Emperor receives regarding the Patriotists are those from the Invigilator, as vetted through the Chancellor.'

He sighed. 'As I suspected. First Concubine, it is said your relationship with the Emperor has gone somewhat beyond that of ruler and chosen whore – forgive me for the use of that term. Rhulad is being isolated – from his own people. Daily he receives petitions, but they are all from Letherii, and those are carefully selected by Triban Gnol and his staff. This situation had worsened since the fleets sailed, for with them went Tomad Sengar and Uruth, and many other Hiroth, including Rhulad's brother, Binadas. All who might have effectively opposed the Chancellor's machinations were removed from the scene. Even Hanradi Khalag . . .' His words fell away and he stared at her, then shrugged. 'I must speak to the Emperor, Nisall. Privately.'

'I may not be able to help you, if I am to be arrested,' she said.

'Only Rhulad himself can prevent that from occurring,' Bruthen Trana said. 'In the meantime, I can afford you some protection.'

She cocked her head. 'How?'

'I will assign you two Edur bodyguards.'

'Ah, so you are not entirely alone, Bruthen.'

'The only Edur truly alone here is the Emperor. And, perhaps, Hannan Mosag, although he still has his K'risnan – but it is anything but certain that the once-Warlock King is loyal to Rhulad.'

Nisall smiled without much humour. 'And so it turns out,' she said, 'that the Tiste Edur are no different from the Letherii after all. Do you know, Rhulad would have it . . . otherwise.'

'Perhaps, then, First Concubine, we can work together to help him realize his vision.'

'Your bodyguards had best be subtle, Bruthen. The Chancellor's spies watch me constantly.'

The Edur smiled. 'Nisall, we are children of Shadow . . .'

Once, long ago, she had walked for a time through Hood's Realm. In the language of the Eleint, the warren that was neither new nor Elder was known as Festal'rythan, the Layers of the Dead. She had found proof of that when traversing the winding cut of a gorge, the raw walls of which revealed innumerable strata evincing the truth of extinction. Every species that ever existed was trapped in the sediments of Festal'rythan, not in the same manner of similar formations of geology as could be found in any world; no, in Hood's Realm, the soul sparks persisted, and what she was witness to was their 'lives', abandoned here, crushed into immobility. The stone itself was, in the peculiar oxymoron that plagued the language of death, *alive*.

In the broken grounds surrounding the lifeless Azath of Letheras, many of those long-extinct creatures had crawled back through the gate, as insidious as any vermin. True, it was not a gate as such, just . . . rents, fissures, as if some terrible demon had slashed from both sides, talons the size of two-handed swords tearing through the fabric between the warrens. There had been battles here, the spilling of ascendant blood, the uttering of vows that could not be kept. She could still smell the death of the Tarthenal gods, could almost hear their outrage and disbelief, as one fell, then another, and another . . . until all were gone, delivered unto Festal'rythan. She did not pity them. It was too easy to be arrogant upon arriving in this world, to think that none could challenge the unleashing of ancient power.

She had long since discovered a host of truths in time's irresistible progression. Raw became refined, and with refinement, power grew ever deadlier. All that was simple would, in time and under sufficient pressure – and if random chance proved benign rather than malignant

131

– acquire greater complexity. And yet, at some point, a threshold was crossed, and complexity crumbled into dissolution. There was nothing fixed in this; some forms rose and fell with astonishing rapidity, while others could persist for extraordinarily long periods in seeming stasis.

Thus, she believed she comprehended more than most, yet found that she could do little with that knowledge. Standing in the overgrown, battered yard, her cold unhuman eyes fixed on the malformed shape squatting at the edge of the largest sundered barrow, she could see through to the chaos inside him, could see how it urged dissolution within that complex matrix of flesh, blood and bone. Pain radiated from his hunched, twisted back as she continued studying him.

He had grown aware of her presence, and fear whispered through him, the sorcery of the Crippled God building. Yet he was uncertain if she presented a threat. In the meantime, ambition rose and fell like crashing waves around the island of his soul.

She could, she decided, make use of this one.

'I am Hannan Mosag,' the figure said without turning. 'You . . . you are Soletaken. The cruellest of the Sisters, accursed among the Edur pantheon. Your heart is betrayal. I greet you, Sukul Ankhadu.'

She approached. 'Betrayal belongs to the one buried beneath, Hannan Mosag, to the Sister you once worshipped. How much, Edur, did that shape your destiny, I wonder? Any betrayals plaguing your people of late? Ah, I saw that flinch. Well, then, neither of us should be surprised.'

'You work to free her.'

'I always worked better with Sheltatha Lore than I did with Menandore . . . although that may not be the case now. The buried one has her . . . obsessions.'

The Tiste Edur grunted. 'Don't we all.'

'How long have you known your most cherished protectress was entombed here?'

'Suspicions. For years. I had thought – hoped – that I would discover what remained of Scabandari Bloodeye here as well.'

'Wrong ascendant,' Sukul Ankhadu said, her tone droll. 'Had you got it right as to who betrayed whom back then, you would have known that.'

'I hear the contempt in your voice.'

'Why are you here? So impatient as to add your power to the rituals I unleashed below?'

'It may be,' Hannan Mosag said, 'that we could work together . . . for a time.'

'What would be the value in that?'

The Tiste Edur shifted to look up at her. 'It seems obvious. Even now, Silchas Ruin hunts for the one I'd thought here. I doubt that either you or Sheltatha Lore would be pleased should he succeed. I can guide you onto his trail. I can also lend you . . . support, at the moment of confrontation.'

'And in return?'

'For one, we can see an end to your killing and eating citizens in the city. For another, we can destroy Silchas Ruin.'

She grunted. 'I have heard that determination voiced before, Hannan Mosag. Is the Crippled God truly prepared to challenge him?'

'With allies . . . yes.'

She considered his proposal. There would be treachery, but it would probably not occur until after Ruin was disposed of – the game would turn over the disposition of the Finnest. She well knew that Scabandari Bloodeye's power was not as it once was, and what remained would be profoundly vulnerable. 'Tell me, does Silchas Ruin travel alone?'

'No. He has a handful of followers, but of them, only one is cause for concern. A Tiste Edur, the eldest brother of the Sengar, once commander of the Edur Warriors.'

'A surprising alliance.'

'Shaky is a better way of describing it. He too seeks the Finnest, and will, I believe, do all he can to prevent its falling into Ruin's hands.'

'Ah, expedience plagues us all.' Sukul Ankhadu smiled. 'Very well, Hannan Mosag. We are agreed, but tell your Crippled God this: fleeing at the moment of attack, abandoning Sheltatha Lore and myself to Silchas Ruin and, say, making off with the Finnest during the fight, will prove a fatal error. With our dying breaths, we will tell Silchas Ruin all he needs to know, and he will come after the Crippled God, and he will not relent.'

'You will not be abandoned, Sukul Ankhadu. As for the Finnest itself, do you wish to claim it for yourselves?'

She laughed. 'To fight over between us? No, we'd rather see it destroyed.'

'I see. Would you object, then, to the Crippled God's making use of its power?'

'Will such use achieve eventual destruction?'

'Oh yes, Sukul Ankhadu.'

She shrugged. 'As you like.' *You must truly think me a fool, Hannan Mosag.* 'Your god marches to war – he will need all the help he can get.'

Hannan Mosag managed his own smile, a twisted, feral thing. 'He is incapable of marching. He does not even crawl. The war comes to him, Sister.'

If there was hidden significance to that distinction, Sukul Ankhadu was unable to discern it. Her gaze lifted, fixed on the river to the south. Wheeling gulls, strange islands of sticks and grasses spinning on the currents. And, she could sense, beneath the swirling surface, enormous, belligerent leviathans, using the islands as bait. Whatever came close enough . . .

She was drawn to a rumble of power from the broken barrow and looked down once more. 'She's coming, Hannan Mosag.'

'Shall I leave? Or will she be amenable to our arrangement?'

'On that, Edur, I cannot speak for her. Best you depart – she will, after all, be very hungry. Besides, she and I have much to discuss . . . old wounds to mend between us.'

She watched as the malformed warlock dragged himself away. *After all, you are much more her child than you are mine, and I'd rather she was, for the moment, without allies.*

It was all Menandore's doing, anyway.

CHAPTER SIX

The argument was this: a civilization shackled to the strictures of excessive control on its populace, from choice of religion through to the production of goods, will sap the will and the ingenuity of its people – for whom such qualities are no longer given sufficient incentive or reward. At face value, this is accurate enough. Trouble arrives when the opponents to such a system institute its extreme opposite, where individualism becomes godlike and sacrosanct, and no greater service to any other ideal (including community) is possible. In such a system rapacious greed thrives behind the guise of freedom, and the worst aspects of human nature come to the fore, a kind of intransigence as fierce and nonsensical as its maternalistic counterpart.

And so, in the clash of these two extreme systems, one is witness to brute stupidity and blood-splashed insensitivity; two belligerent faces glowering at each other across the unfathomed distance, and yet, in deed and in fanatic regard, they are but mirror reflections.

This would be amusing if it weren't so pathetically idiotic . . .

In Defence of Compassion
Denabaris of Letheras, 4th century

DEAD PIRATES WERE BETTER, SHURQ ELALLE MUSED. THERE WAS A twisted sort of justice in the dead preying upon the living, especially when it came to stealing all their treasured possessions. Her pleasure in prying those ultimately worthless objects from their hands was the sole reason for her criminal activities, more than sufficient incentive to maintain her new-found profession. Besides, she was good at it.

The hold of the *Undying Gratitude* was filled with the cargo from the abandoned Edur ship, the winds were fresh and steady, pushing them hard north out of the Draconean Sea, and it looked as if the huge fleet in her wake was not getting any closer.

Edur and Letherii ships, a hundred, maybe more. They'd come out of the southwest, driving at a converging angle towards the sea lane that led to the mouth of the Lether River. The same lane that Shurq Elalle's ship now tracked, as well as two merchant scows the *Undying Gratitude* was fast overhauling. And that last detail was too bad, since those Pilott scows were ripe targets, and without a mass of Imperial ships crawling up her behind, she'd have pounced.

Cursing, Skorgen Kaban limped up to where she stood at the aft rail. 'It's that infernal search, ain't it? The two main fleets, or what's left of 'em.' The first mate leaned over the rail and spat down into the churning foam skirling out from the keel. 'They're gonna be nipping our tails all the way into Letheras harbour.'

'That's right, Pretty, which means we have to stay nice.'

'Aye. Nothing more tragic than staying nice.'

'We'll get over it,' Shurq Elalle said. 'Once we're in the harbour, we can sell what we got, hopefully before the fleet arrives to do the same – because then the price will drop, mark my words. Then we head back out. There'll be more Pilott scows, Skorgen.'

'You don't think that fleet came up on the floating wreck, do you? They've got every stretch of canvas out, like maybe they was chasing us. We get to the mouth and we're trapped, Captain.'

'Well, you have a point there. If they were truly scattered by that storm, a few of them could have come up on the wreck before it went under.' She thought for a time, then said, 'Tell you what. We'll sail past the mouth. And if they ignore us and head upriver, we can come round and follow them in. But that means they'll offload before we will, which means we won't make as much—'

'Unless their haul ain't going to market,' the first mate cut in. 'Could be it's all to replenish the royal vaults, Captain, or maybe it goes to the Edur and nobody else. Blood and Kagenza, after all. We could always find a coastal port and do our selling there.'

'You get wiser with every body part you lose, Pretty.'

He grunted. 'Gotta be some kind of upside.'

'That's the attitude,' she replied. 'All right, that's what we'll do, but never mind the coastal port – they're all dirt poor this far north, surrounded by nothing but wilderness and bad roads where the bandits line up to charge tolls. And if a few Edur galleys take after us, we can always scoot straight up to that hold-out prison isle this side of Fent Reach – that's a tight harbour mouth, or so I've been told, and they got a chain to keep the baddies out.'

'Pirates ain't baddies?'

'Not as far as they're concerned. The prisoners are running things now.'

'I doubt it'll be that easy,' Skorgen muttered. 'We'd just be bringing trouble down on them – it's not like the Edur couldn't have conquered them long ago. They just can't be bothered.'

'Maybe, maybe not. The point is, we'll run out of food and water if we can't resupply somewhere. Edur galleys are fast, fast enough to stay with us. Anywhere we dock they'll be on us before the last line is drawn to the bollard. With the exception of the prison isle.' She scowled. 'It's a damned shame. I wanted to go home for a bit.'

'Then we'd best hope the whole damned fleet back there heads upriver,' Skorgen the Pretty said, scratching round an eye socket.

'Hope and pray – you pray to any gods, Skorgen?'

'Sea spirits, mostly. The Face Under the Waves, the Guardian of the Drowned, the Swallower of Ships, the Stealer of Winds, the Tower of Water, the Reef Hiders, the—'

'All right, Pretty, that'll do. You can keep your host of disasters to yourself . . . just make sure you do all the propitiations.'

'Thought you didn't believe in all that, Captain.'

'I don't. But it never hurts to make sure.'

'One day their names will rise from the water, Captain,' Skorgen Kaban said, making a complicated warding gesture with his one remaining hand. 'And with them the seas will lift high, to claim the sky itself. And the world will vanish beneath the waves.'

'You and your damned prophecies.'

'Not mine. Fent. Ever see their early maps? They show a coast leagues out from what it is now. All their founding villages are under hundreds of spans of water.'

'So they believe their prophecy is coming true. Only it's going to take ten thousand years.'

His shrug was lopsided. 'Could be, Captain. Even the Edur claim that the ice far to the north is breaking up. Ten thousand years, or a hundred. Either way, we'll be long dead by then.'

Speak for yourself, Pretty. Then again, what a thought. Me wandering round on the sea bottom for eternity. 'Skorgen, get young Burdenar down from the crow's nest and into my cabin.'

The first mate made a face. 'Captain, you're wearing him out.'

'I ain't heard him complain.'

'Of course not. We'd all like to be as lucky – your pardon, Captain, for me being too forward, but it's true. I was serious, though. You're wearing him out, and he's the youngest sailor we got.'

'Right, meaning I'd probably kill the rest of you. Call him down, Pretty.'

'Aye, Captain.'

She stared back at the distant ships. The long search was over, it seemed. What would they be bringing back to fair Letheras, apart from casks of blood? *Champions. Each one convinced they can do what no other has ever managed. Kill the Emperor. Kill him dead, deader than me, so dead he never gets back up.*

Too bad that would never happen.

On his way out of Letheras, Venitt Sathad, Indebted servant to Rautos Hivanar, halted the modest train outside the latest addition to the Hivanar holdings. The inn's refurbishment was well under way, he saw, as, accompanied by the owner of the construction company under hire, he made his way past the work crews crowding the main building, then out back to where the stables and other outbuildings stood.

Then stopped.

The structure that had been raised round the unknown ancient mechanism had been taken down. Venitt stared at the huge monolith of unknown metal, wondering why, now that it had been exposed, it looked so familiar. The edifice bent without a visible seam, three-quarters of the way up – at about one and a half times his own height – a seemingly perfect ninety degrees. The apex looked as if it awaited some kind of attachment, if the intricate loops of metal were anything more than decorative. The object stood on a platform of the same peculiar, dull metal, and again there was no obvious separation between it and the platform itself.

'Have you managed to identify its purpose?' Vennitt asked the old, mostly bald man at his side.

'Well,' Bugg conceded, 'I have some theories.'

'I would be interested in hearing them.'

'You will find others in the city,' Bugg said. 'No two alike, but the same nonetheless, if you know what I mean.'

'No, I don't, Bugg.'

'Same manufacture, same mystery as to function. I've never bothered actually mapping them, but it may be that there is some kind of pattern, and from that pattern, the purpose of their existence might be comprehended. Possibly.'

'But who built them?'

'No idea, Venitt. Long ago, I suspect – the few others I've seen myself are mostly underground, and further out towards the river bank. Buried in silts.'

'In silts . . .' Venitt continued staring, then his eyes slowly widened. He turned to the old man. 'Bugg, I have a most important favour to ask of you. I must continue on my way, out of Letheras. I need a message delivered, however, back to my master. To Rautos Hivanar.'

138

Bugg shrugged. 'I see no difficulty managing that, Venitt.'

'Good. Thank you. The message is this: he must come here, to see this for himself. And – and this is most important – he must bring his collection of artifacts.'

'Artifacts?'

'He will understand, Bugg.'

'All right,' the old man said. 'I can get over there in a couple days . . . or I can send a runner if you like.'

'Best in person, Bugg, if you would. If the runner garbles the message, my master might end up ignoring it.'

'As you like, Venitt. Where, may I ask, are you going?'

The Indebted scowled. 'Bluerose, and then on to Drene.'

'A long journey awaits you, Venitt. May it prove dull and uneventful.'

'Thank you, Bugg. How go things here?'

'We're waiting for another shipment of materials. When that arrives, we can finish up. Your master has pulled another of my crews over for that shoring-up project at his estate, but until the trusses arrive that's not as inconvenient as it might be.' He glanced at Venitt. 'Do you have any idea when Hivanar will be finshed with all of that?'

'Strictly speaking, it's not shoring-up – although that is involved.' He paused, rubbed at his face. 'More of a scholarly pursuit. Master is extending bulwarks out into the river, then draining and pumping the trenches clear so that the crews can dig down through the silts.'

Bugg frowned. 'Why? Is he planning to build a breakwater or a pier?'

'No. He is recovering . . . artifacts.'

Venitt watched the old man look back at the edifice, and saw the watery eyes narrow. 'I wouldn't mind seeing those.'

'Some of your foremen and engineers have done just that . . . but none were able to work out their function.' *And yes, they are linked to this thing here. In fact, one piece is a perfect replica of this, only on a much smaller scale.* 'When you deliver your message, you can ask to see what he's found, Bugg. I am sure he would welcome your observations.'

'Perhaps,' the old man said distractedly.

'Well,' Venitt said. 'I had best be going.'

'Errant ignore you, Venitt Sathad.'

'And you, Bugg.'

'If only . . .'

That last statement was little more than a whisper, and Venitt glanced back at Bugg as he crossed the courtyard on his way out. A peculiar thing to say.

But then, old men were prone to such eccentricities.

Dismounting, Atri-Preda Bivatt began walking among the wreckage. Vultures and crows clambered about from one bloated body to the next, as if confused by such a bounteous feast. Despite the efforts of the carrion eaters, it was clear to her that the nature of the slaughter was unusual. Huge blades, massive fangs and talons had done the damage to these hapless settlers, soldiers and drovers. And whatever had killed these people had struck before – the unit of cavalry that had pursued Redmask from Drene's North Gate had suffered an identical fate.

In her wake strode the Edur Overseer, Brohl Handar. 'There are demons,' he said, 'capable of this. Such as those the K'risnan conjured during the war . . . although they rarely use teeth and claws.'

Bivatt halted near a dead hearth. She pointed to a sweep of dirt beside it. 'Do your demons leave tracks such as these?'

The Edur warrior came to her side. 'No,' he said after a moment. 'This has the appearance of an oversized, flightless bird.'

'Oversized?' She glanced over at him, then resumed her walk.

Her soldiers were doing much the same, silent as they explored the devastated encampment. Outriders, still mounted, were circling the area, keeping to the ridge lines.

The rodara and myrid herds had been driven away, their tracks clearly visible heading east. The rodara herd had gone first, and the myrid had simply followed. It was possible, if the Letherii detachment rode hard, that they would catch up to the myrid. Bivatt suspected the raiders would not lag behind to tend to the slower-moving beasts.

'Well, Atri-Preda?' Brohl Handar asked from behind her. 'Do we pursue?'

She did not turn round. 'No.'

'The Factor will be severely displeased by your decision.'

'And that concerns you?'

'Not in the least.'

She said nothing. The Overseer was growing more confident in his appointment. More confident, or less cautious – there had been contempt in the Tiste Edur's tone. Of course, that he had chosen to accompany this expedition was evidence enough of his burgeoning independence. For all of that, she almost felt sorry for the warrior.

'If this Redmask is conjuring demons of some sort,' Brohl Handar continued, 'then we had best move in strength, accompanied by both Letherii and Edur mages. Accordingly, I concur with your decision.'

'It pleases me that you grasp the military implications of this, Overseer. Even so, in this instance even the desires of the Factor are of no importance to me. I am first and foremost an officer of the empire.'

'You are, and I am the Emperor's representative in this region. Thus.'

She nodded.

A few heartbeats later the Tiste Edur sighed. 'It grieves me to see so many slain children.'

'Overseer, we are no less thorough when slaying the Awl.'

'That, too, grieves me.'

'Such is war,' she said.

He grunted, then said, 'Atri-Preda, what is happening on these plains is not simply war. You Letherii have initiated a campaign of extermination. Had we Edur elected to cross that threshold, would you not have called us barbarians in truth? You do not hold the high ground in this conflict, no matter how you seek to justify your actions.'

'Overseer,' Bivatt said coldly, 'I care nothing about justifications, nor moral high ground. I have been a soldier too long to believe such things hold any sway over our actions. Whatever lies in our power to do, we do.' She gestured at the destroyed encampment around them. 'Citizens of Lether have been murdered. It is my responsibility to give answer to that, and so I shall.'

'And who will win?' Brohl Handar asked.

'We will, of course.'

'No, Atri-Preda. You will lose. As will the Awl. The victors are men such as Factor Letur Anict. Alas, such people as the Factor view you and your soldiers little differently from how they view their enemies. You are to be used, and this means that many of you will die. Letur Anict does not care. He needs you to win this victory, but beyond that his need for you ends . . . until a new enemy is found. Tell me, do empires exist solely to devour? Is there no value in peace? In order and prosperity and stability and security? Are the only worthwhile rewards the stacks of coin in Letur Anict's treasury? He would have it so – all the rest is incidental and only useful if it serves him. Atri-Preda, you are in truth less than an Indebted. You are a slave – I am not wrong in this, for I am a Tiste Edur who possesses slaves. A slave, Bivatt, is how Letur Anict and his kind see you.'

'Tell me, Overseer, how would you fare without your slaves?'

'Poorly, no doubt.'

She turned about and walked back to her horse. 'Mount up. We're returning to Drene.'

'And these dead citizens of the empire? Do you leave their bodies to the vultures?'

'In a month even the bones will be gone,' Bivatt said, swinging onto her horse and gathering the reins. 'The whittle beetles will gnaw them all to dust. Besides, there is not enough soil to dig proper graves.'

'There are stones,' Brohl Handar noted.

'Covered in Awl glyphs. To use them would be to curse the dead.'

'Ah, so the enmity persists, so that even the ghosts war with each other. It is a dark world you inhabit, Atri-Preda.'

She looked down at him for a moment, then said, 'Are the shadows any better, Overseer?' When he made no reply, she said, 'On your horse, sir, if you please.'

The Ganetok encampment, swollen with the survivors of the Sevond and Niritha clans, sprawled across the entire valley. Beyond to the east loomed vast dun-hued clouds from the main herds in the next few valleys. The air was gritty with dust and the acrid smell of hearth fires. Small bands of warriors moved back and forth like gangs of thugs, weapons bristling, their voices loud.

Outriders had made contact with Redmask and his paltry tribe earlier in the day, yet had kept their distance, seemingly more interested in the substantial herd of rodara trailing the small group. An unexpected wealth for so few Awl, leaving possession open to challenge, and it was clear to Redmask as he drew rein on a rise overlooking the encampment that word had preceded them, inciting countless warriors into bold challenge, one and all coveting rodara and eager to strip the beasts away from the mere handful of Renfayar warriors.

Alas, he would have to disappoint them. 'Masarch,' he now said, 'remain here with the others. Accept no challenges.'

'No-one has come close enough to see your mask,' the youth said. 'No-one suspects what you seek, War Leader. As soon as they do, we shall be under siege.'

'Do you fear, Masarch?'

'Dying? No, not any more.'

'Then you are a child no longer. Wait, do nothing.' Redmask nudged his horse onto the slope, gathering it into a collected canter as he approached the Ganetok encampment. Eyes fixed on him, then held, as shouts rose, the voices more angry than shocked. Until the nearer warriors made note of his weapons. All at once a hush fell over the encampment, rippling in a wave, and in its wake rose a murmuring, the anger he had first heard only now with a deeper timbre.

Dray dogs caught the burgeoning rage and drew closer, fangs bared and hackles stiff.

Redmask reined in. His Letherii horse tossed its head and stamped, snorting to warn off the huge dogs.

Someone was coming through the gathered crowd, like the prow of an unseen ship pushing through tall reeds. Settling back on the foreign saddle, Redmask waited.

Hadralt, firstborn son to Capalah, walked with his father's swagger but not his physical authority. He was short and lean, reputedly very fast with the hook-bladed shortswords cross-strapped beneath each arm. Surrounding him were a dozen of his favoured warriors, huge, hulking men whose faces had been painted in a simulacrum of scales, copper in tone yet clearly intended to echo Redmask's own. The expressions beneath that paint were now ones of chagrin.

His hands restless around the fetishes lining his belt, Hadralt glowered up at Redmask. 'If you are who you claim to be, then you do not belong here. Leave, or your blood will feed the dry earth.'

Redmask let his impassive gaze slide over the copper-faced warriors. 'You mouth the echoes, yet quail from the source.' He looked once more upon the war leader. 'I am before you now, Hadralt son of Capalah. Redmask, war leader of the Renfayar clan, and on this day I will kill you.'

The dark eyes widened, then Hadralt sneered. 'Your life was a curse, Redmask. You have not yet earned the right to challenge me. Tell me, will your pathetically few pups fight for you? Your ambition will see them all killed, and my warriors shall take the Renfayar herds. And the Renfayar women – but only of bearing age. The children and elders will die, for they are burdens we will not abide. The Renfayar shall cease to be.'

'For your warriors to gain the right to challenge my kin, Hadralt, they must first defeat my own champions.'

'And where are they hiding, Redmask? Unless you mean that scarred dray that followed you in.'

The laughter at that jest was overloud.

Redmask glanced back at the lone beast. Lying on the ground just to the right of the horse, it had faced down all the other dogs in the area without even rising. The dray lifted its head and met Redmask's eyes, as if the animal not only comprehended the words that had been spoken, but also welcomed the opportunity to face every challenger. He felt something stir in his chest. 'This beast understands courage,' he said, facing Hadralt once more. 'Would that I had ten thousand warriors to match it. Yet all I see before me is you, Hadralt, war leader of ten thousand cowards.'

The clamour that erupted then seemed to blister the air. Weapons flashed into sunlight, the massed crowd edging in. A sea of faces twisted with rage.

Hadralt had gone pale. Then he raised his arms and held them high until the outcry fell away. 'Every warrior here,' he said in a trembling voice, 'shall take a piece of your hide, Redmask. They deserve no less in answer to your words. You seek to take my place? You seek to lead? Lead . . . these *cowards*? You have learned nothing in your exile. Not a warrior here will follow you now, Redmask. Not one.'

'You hired an army,' Redmask said, unable to keep the contempt from his tone. 'You marched at their sides against the Letherii. And then, when the battle was offered and your new-found allies were engaged – fighting for *you* – you all fled. Cowards? That is too kind a word. In my eyes, Hadralt, you and your people are not Awl, not any more, for no true Awl warrior would do such a thing. I came upon their bodies. I was witness to your betrayal. The truth is this. When I am war leader here, before this day's sun touches the horizon, it will fall to every warrior present to prove his worth, to earn the right to follow me. And I shall not be easy to convince. Copper paint on the faces of cowards – no greater insult could you have delivered to me.'

'Climb down,' Hadralt said in a rasp. 'Down off that Letherii nag. Climb down, Redmask, to meet your end.'

Instead he drew out a hollowed rodara horn and lifted it to his lips. The piercing blast silenced all in the encampment except for the dogs, which began a mournful howling in answer. Redmask replaced the horn at his belt. 'It is the way of time,' he said, loud enough for his voice to carry, 'for old enemies to find peace in the passing of ages. We have fought many wars, yet it was the first that holds still in the memory of the Awl, here in this very earth.' He paused, for he could feel the reverberation beneath him – as did others now – as the two K'Chain Che'Malle approached in answer to his call. 'Hadralt, son of Capalah, you are about to stand alone, and you and I shall draw our weapons. Prepare yourself.'

From the ridge, where stood the modest line of Renfayar warriors, six in all, two other shapes loomed into view, huge, towering. Then, in liquid motion, the pair flowed down the slope.

Silence hung heavy, beyond the thump of taloned feet, and hands that had rested on the grips and pommels of weapons slowly fell away.

'My champions,' said Redmask. 'They are ready for your challengers, Hadralt. For your copper-faces.'

The war leader said nothing, and Redmask could see in the warrior's expression that he would not risk losing the force of his words, when his commands were disobeyed – as they would be, a truth to which all who were present were now aware. Destiny awaited, then, in this solitary clash of wills.

Hadralt licked his lips. 'Redmask, when I have killed you, what then of these Kechra?'

Making no reply, Redmask dismounted, walking to halt six paces in front of Hadralt. He unlimbered the rygtha crescent axe and centred his grip on the hafted weapon. 'Your father is gone. You must now let go of his hand and stand alone, Hadralt. The first and last time. You have failed as war leader. You led Awl warriors to battle, then led them in flight. You betrayed allies. And now, you hide here on the very edge of the wastelands, rather than meet the invading Letherii blade to blade, teeth to throat. You will now step aside, or die.'

'Step aside?' Hadralt tilted his head, then managed a rictus smile. 'That choice is not offered to an Awl warrior.'

'True,' Redmask said. 'Only to elders who can no longer defend themselves, or to those too broken by wounds.'

Hadralt bared his teeth. 'I am neither.'

'Nor are you an Awl warrior. Did your father step aside? No, I see that he did not. He looked into your soul, and knew you, Hadralt. And so, old as he was, he fought you. For his tribe. For his honour.'

Hadralt unsheathed his hook-blades. He was trembling once more.

One of the copper-faces then spoke. 'Capalah ate in the hut of his son. In a single night he sickened and died. In the morning, his face was the colour of blue lichen.'

'Trenys'galah?' Redmask's eyes narrowed in the mask's slits. 'You poisoned your father, Hadralt? Rather than meet his blades? How is it you stand here at all?'

'Poison has no name,' muttered the same copper-face.

Hadralt said, 'I am the reason the Awl still live! You will lead them to slaughter, Redmask! We are not yet ready to face the Letherii. I have been trading for weapons – yes, there are Letherii who believe our cause is just. We give up poor land, and receive fine iron weapons – and now you come, to undo all my plans!'

'I see those weapons,' Redmask said. 'In the hands of many of your warriors. Have they been tested in battle? You are a fool, Hadralt, to believe you won that bargain. The traders you meet are in the employ of the Factor – he profits on both sides of this war—'

'A lie!'

'I was in Drene,' Redmask said, 'less than two weeks ago. I saw the wagons and their crates of cast-off weapons, the iron blades that will shatter at the first blow against a shield. Weapons break, are lost, yet this is what you accepted, this is what you surrendered land for – land home to the dust of our ancestors. Home to Awl spirits, land that has drunk Awl blood.'

'Letherii weapons—'

'Must be taken from the corpses of soldiers – those are the weapons worthy of the term, Hadralt. If you must use their way of fighting, then you must use weapons of a quality to match. Lest you invite your warriors to slaughter. And this,' he added, 'is clearly what you were not prepared to do. Thus, Hadralt, I am led to conclude that you knew the truth. If so, then the traders paid you in more than weapons. Did you share out the coin, War Leader? Do your kin even know of the hoard you hide in your hut?'

Redmask watched as the copper-faces slowly moved away from Hadralt. Recognizing the betrayal their leader had committed upon them, upon the Awl.

'You intended surrender,' Redmask continued, 'didn't you? You were offered an estate in Drene, yes? And slaves and Indebted to do your bidding. You planned on selling off our people, our history—'

'*We cannot win!*'

Hadralt's last words. Three sword-blades erupted from his chest, thrust into his back by his own copper-faces. Eyes wide with shock, the firstborn son and slayer of Capalah, last worthy leader of the Ganetok, stared across at Redmask. Hook-blades fell from his hands, then he sagged forward, sliding from the swords with a ghastly sucking sound almost immediately replaced by the gush of blood.

Eyes blank now in death, the corpse of Hadralt then toppled face-first into the dust.

Redmask returned the rygtha to its harness. 'Seeds fall from the crown of the stalk. What is flawed there makes its every child weak. The curse of cowardice has ended this day. We are the Awl, and I am your war leader.' He paused, looked round, then said, 'And so I shall lead you to war.'

On the ridge overlooking the sprawling encampment, Masarch made a gesture to sun and sky, then earth and wind. 'Redmask now rules the Awl.'

Kraysos, standing on his right, grunted then said, 'Did you truly doubt he would succeed, Masarch? Kechra guard his flanks. He is the charging crest of a river of blood, and he shall flood these lands. And even as the Letherii drown in it, so shall we.'

'You cheated the death night, Kraysos, and so you still fear dying.'

On Masarch's other side, Theven snorted. 'The bledden herb had lost most of its potency. It took neither of us through the night. I screamed to the earth, Masarch. I screamed and screamed. So did Kraysos. We do not fear what is to come.'

'Hadralt was killed by his own warriors,' Masarch said. 'From behind. This does not bode well.'

'You are wrong,' Theven said. 'Redmask's words have turned them all. I did not think such a thing would be possible.'

'I suspect we will be saying that often,' noted Kraysos.

'We should walk down, now,' said Masarch. 'We are his first warriors, and behind us now there are tens of thousands.'

Theven sighed. 'The world has changed.'

'We will live a while longer, you mean.'

The young warrior glanced across at Masarch. 'That is for Redmask to decide.'

Brohl Handar rode at the Atri-Preda's side as the troop made its way down the trader track, still half a day from Drene's gates. The soldiers at their backs were silent, stoking anger and dreams of vengeance, no doubt. There had been elements of Bluerose cavalry stationed in Drene since shortly after the annexation of Bluerose itself. As far as Brohl Handar understood, the acquisition of Bluerose had not been as blood-less as Drene had been. A complicated religion had served to unite

146

disaffected elements of the population, led by a mysterious priesthood the Letherii had been unable to entirely exterminate. Reputedly some rebel groups still existed, active mostly in the mountains lining the western side of the territory.

In any case, the old Letherii policy of transferring Bluerose units to distant parts of the empire continued under Edur rule, certainly suggesting that risks remained. Brohl Handar wondered how the newly appointed Edur overseer in Bluerose was managing, and he reminded himself to initiate contact with his counterpart – stability in Bluerose was essential, for any disruption of Drene's principal supply route and trading partner could prove disastrous if the situation here in the Awl'dan ignited into full-out war.

'You seem thoughtful, Overseer,' Bivatt said after a time.

'Logistics,' he replied.

'If by that you mean military, such needs are my responsibility, sir.'

'Your army's needs cannot be met in isolation, Atri-Preda. If this conflict escalates, as I believe it will, then even the Factor cannot ensure that shortages will not occur, particularly among non-combatants in Drene and surrounding communities.'

'In all-out war, Overseer, the requirements of the military always take precedence. Besides, there is no reason to anticipate shortages. The Letherii are well versed in these matters. Our entire system of transport was honed by the exigencies of expansion. We possess the roads, the necessary sea lanes and merchant vessels.'

'There nonetheless remains a chokepoint,' Brohl Handar pointed out. 'The Bluerose Mountains.'

She shot him a startled glance. 'The primary eastward trade goods through that range are slaves and some luxury footstuffs from the far south. Bluerose of course is renowned for its mineral wealth, producing a quality of iron that rivals Letherii steel. Tin, copper, lead, lime and firerock, as well as cedar and spruce – all in abundance, while the Bluerose Sea abounds with cod. In return, Drene's vast farms annually produce a surplus harvest of grains. Overseer, you appear to have been misinformed with respect to the materiel demands in question. There will be no shortages—'

'Perhaps you are right.' He paused, then continued, 'Atri-Preda, it is my understanding that the Factor has instituted extensive trafficking of low-grade weapons and armour across the Bluerose Mountains. These weapons are in turn sold to the Awl, in exchange for land or at least the end of dispute over land. Over four hundred broad-bed wagonloads have been shipped thus far. Although the Factor holds the tithe seal, no formal acknowledgement nor taxation of these items has taken place. From this, I can only assume that a good many other supplies are moving to and fro across those mountains, none with official approval.'

147

'Overseer, regardless of the Factor's smuggling operations, the Bluerose Mountains are in no way a chokepoint when it comes to necessary supplies.'

'I hope you are right, especially given the recent failures of that route.'

'Excuse me? What failures?'

'The latest shipment of poor quality war materiel failed to arrive this side of the mountains, Atri-Preda. Furthermore, brigands struck a major fortress in the pass, routing the Letherii company stationed there.'

'What? I have heard nothing of this! An entire company – routed?'

'So it seems. Alas, that was the extent of the information provided me. Apart from the weapons, I was unsure what other items the Factor lost in that shipment. If, as you tell me, there was nothing more of consequence to fall into the hands of the brigands, then I am somewhat relieved.'

Neither spoke for a time. Brohl Handar was aware that the Atri-Preda's thoughts were racing, perhaps drawn into a tumult of confusion – uncertainty at how much Brohl knew, and by extension the Tiste Edur, regarding Letherii illegalities; and perhaps greater unease at the degree to which she herself had remained ignorant of recent events in Bluerose. That she'd been shaken told him she was not as much an agent of Letur Anict as he had feared.

He decided he had waited long enough. 'Atri-Preda, this imminent war with the Awl. Tell me, have you determined the complement of forces you feel will be necessary to effect victory?'

She blinked, visibly shifting the path of her thinking to address his question. 'More or less, Overseer. We believe that the Awl could, at best, field perhaps eight or nine thousand warriors. Certainly not more than that. As an army, they are undisciplined, divisive due to old feuds and rivalries, and their style of combat is unsuited to fighting as a unit. So, easily broken, unprepared as they are for any engagement taking longer than perhaps a bell. Generally, they prefer to raid and ambush, keeping to small troops and striving to remain elusive. At the same time, their almost absolute dependency on their herds, and the vulnerability of their main camps, will, inevitably, force them to stand and fight – whereupon we annihilate them.'

'A succinct preface,' Brohl Handar said.

'To answer you, we possess six companies of the Bluerose Battalion and near full complement of the reformed Artisan Battalion, along with detachments from the Drene Garrison and four companies from the Harridict Brigade. To ensure substantial numerical superiority, I will request the Crimson Rampant Brigade and at least half of the Merchants' Battalion.'

148

'Do you anticipate that this Redmask will in any way modify the tactics employed by the Awl?'

'No. He did not do so the first time. The threat he represents lies in his genius for superior ambushes and appallingly effective raids, especially on our supply lines. The sooner he is killed, the swifter the end of the war. If he succeeds in evading our grasp, then we can anticipate a long and bloody conflict.'

'Atri-Preda, I intend to request three K'risnan and four thousand Edur warriors.'

'Victory will be quick, then, Overseer, for Redmask will not be able to hide for long from your K'risnan.'

'Precisely. I want this war over as soon as possible, and with minimal loss of life – on both sides. Accordingly, we must kill Redmask at the first opportunity. And shatter the Awl army, such as it is.'

'You wish to force the Awl to capitulate and seek terms?'

'Yes.'

'Overseer, I will accept capitulation. As for terms, the only ones I will demand are complete surrender. The Awl will be enslaved, one and all. They will be scattered throughout the empire but nowhere near their traditional homelands. As slaves, they will be booty, and the right to pick first will be the reward I grant my soldiers.'

'The fate of the Nerek and the Fent and the Tarthenal.'

'Even so.'

'The notion does not sit well with me, Atri-Preda. Nor will it with any Tiste Edur, including the Emperor.'

'Let us argue this point once we have killed Redmask, Overseer.'

He grimaced, then nodded. 'Agreed.'

Brohl Handar silently cursed this Redmask, who had single-handedly torn through his hopes for a cessation of hostilities, for an equitable peace. Instead, Letur Anict now possessed all the justification he needed to exterminate the Awl, and no amount of tactical genius in ambushes and raids would, in the end, make any difference at all. *It is the curse of leaders to believe they can truly change the world.*

A curse that has even afflicted me, it seems. Am I too now a slave to Letur Anict and those like him?

The rage within him was the breath of ice, held deep and overlong, until its searing touch burned in his chest. Upon hearing the copper-face Natarkas's last words, he rose in silent fury and stalked from the hut, then stood, eyes narrowed, until his vision could adjust to the moonless, cloud-covered night. Nearby, motionless as carved sentinels of stone, stood his K'Chain Che'Malle guardians, their eyes faintly glowing smudges in the darkness. As Redmask pushed himself into motion, their heads turned in unison to watch as he set off through the encampment.

Neither creature followed, for which he was thankful. Every step taken by the huge beasts set the camp's dogs to howling and he was in no mood for their brainless cries.

Half the night was gone. He had called in the clan leaders and the most senior elders, one and all crowding into the hut that had once belonged to Hadralt. They had come expecting castigation, more condemnation from their new and much feared war leader, but Redmask had no interest in further belittling the warriors now under his command. The wounds of earlier that day were fresh enough. The courage they had lost could only be regained in battle.

For all of Hadralt's faults, he had been correct in one thing – the old way of fighting against the Letherii was doomed to fail. Yet the now-dead war leader's purported intent to retrain the Awl to a mode of combat identical to that of the Letherii was, Redmask told his followers, also doomed. The tradition did not exist, the Awl were skilled in the wrong weapons, and loyalties rarely crossed lines of clan and kin.

A new way had to be found.

Redmask had then asked about the mercenaries that had been hired, and the tale that unfolded had proved both complicated and sordid, details teased out from reluctant, shamefaced warriors. Oh, there had been plenty of Letherii coin delivered as part of the land purchase, and that wealth had been originally amassed with the intent of hiring a foreign army – one that had been found on the borderlands to the east. But Hadralt had then grown to covet all that gold and silver, so much so that he betrayed that army – led them to their deaths – rather than deliver the coin into their possession.

Such was the poison that was coin.

Where had these foreigners come from?

From the sea, it appeared, a landing on the north coast of the wastelands, in transports under the flag of Lamatath, a distant peninsular kingdom. Soldier priests and priestesses, sworn to wolf deities.

What had brought them to this continent?

Prophecy.

Redmask had started at that answer, which came from Natarkas, the spokesman among the copper-faces, the same warrior who had revealed Hadralt's murder of Capalah.

A prophecy, War Leader, Natarkas had continued. *A final war. They came seeking a place they called the Battlefield of the Gods. They called themselves the Grey Swords, the Reve of Togg and Fanderay. There were many women among them, including one of the commanders. The other is a man, one-eyed, who claims he has lost that eye three times—*

No, War Leader, this one still lives. A survivor of the battle. Hadralt imprisoned him. He lies in chains behind the women's blood-hut—

Natarkas had fallen silent then, recoiling at the sudden rage he clearly saw in Redmask's eyes.

And now the masked war leader strode through the Ganetok encampment, eastward to the far edge where trenches had been carved into the slope, taking away the wastes of the Awl; to the hut of blood that belonged to the women, then behind it, where, chained to a stake, slept a filthy creature, the lower half of his battered body in the drainage trench, where women's blood and urine trickled through mud, roots and stones on their way to the deep pits beyond.

Halting, then, to stand over the man, who awoke, turning his head to peer with one glittering eye up at Redmask.

'Do you understand me?' the war leader asked.

A nod.

'What is your name?'

The lone eye blinked, and the man reached up to scratch the blistered scar tissue around the empty socket where his other eye had been. He then grunted, as if surprised, and struggled into a sitting position. 'Anaster was my new name,' he said; a strange twist of his mouth that might have been a grin, then the man added, 'but I think my older name better suits me, with a slight alteration, that is. I am Toc.' The smile broadened. 'Toc the Unlucky.'

'I am Redmask—'

'I know who are you. I even know what you are.'

'How?'

'Can't help you there.'

Redmask tried again. 'What hidden knowledge of me do you think you possess?'

The smile faded, and the man looked down, seeming to study the turgid stream of thinned blood round his knees. 'It made little sense back then. Makes even less sense now. You're not what we expected, Redmask.' He coughed, then spat, careful to avoid the women's blood.

'Tell me what you expected?'

Another half-smile, yet Toc would not look up as he said, 'Why, when one seeks the First Sword of the K'Chain Che'Malle, well, one assumes it would be . . . K'Chain Che'Malle. Not human. An obvious assumption, don't you think?'

'First Sword? I do not know this title.'

Toc shrugged. 'K'ell Champion. Consort to the Matron. Hood take me, *King*. They're all the same in your case.' The man finally glanced up once more, and something glistened in his lone eye as he asked, 'So don't tell me the mask fooled them. Please . . .'

The gorge the lone figure emerged from was barely visible. Less than three man-heights across, the crevasse nestled between two steep mountainsides, half a league long and a thousand paces deep. Travellers thirty paces away, traversing the raw rock of the mountain to either side, would not even know the gorge existed. Of course, the likelihood of unwitting travellers anywhere within five leagues of the valley was virtually non-existent. No obvious trails wended through the Bluerose range this far north of the main passes; there were no high pastures or plateaux to invite settlement, and the weather was often fierce.

Clambering over the edge of the gorge into noon sunlight, the figure paused in a crouch and scanned the vicinity. Seeing nothing untoward, he straightened. Tall, thin, his midnight-black hair long, straight and unbound, his face unlined, the features somewhat hooded, eyes like firerock, the man reached into a fold in his faded black hide shirt and withdrew a length of thin chain, both ends holding a plain finger-ring – one gold, the other silver. A quick flip of his right index finger spun the rings round, then wrapped them close as the chain coiled tight. A moment later he reversed the motion. His right hand thus occupied, coiling and uncoiling the chain, he set off.

Southward he went, into and out of swaths of shadow and sunlight, his footfalls almost soundless, the snap of the chain the only noise accompanying him. Tied to his back was a horn and bloodwood bow, unstrung. At his right hip was a quiver of arrows, bloodwood shafts and hawk-feather fletching; at the quiver's moss-packed base, the arrowheads were iron, teardrop-shaped and slotted, the blades on each head forming an X pattern. In addition to this weapon he carried a baldric-slung plain rapier in a silver-banded turtleshell scabbard. The entire scabbard and its fastening rings were bound with sheepskin to deaden the noise as he padded along. These details to stealth were one and all undermined by the spinning and snapping chain.

The afternoon waned on, until he moved through unbroken shadow as he skirted the eastern flank of each successive valley he traversed, ever southward. Through it all the chain twirled, the rings clacking upon contacting each other, then whispering out and spinning yet again.

At dusk he came to a ledge overlooking a broader valley, this one running more or less east-west, whereupon, satisfied with his vantage point, he settled into a squat and waited. Chain whispering, rings clacking.

Two thousand spins later, the rings clattered, then went still, trapped inside the fist of his right hand. His eyes, which had held fixed on the western mouth of the pass, unmindful of the darkness, had caught movement. He tucked the chain and rings back into the pouch lining the inside of his shirt, then rose.

And began the long descent.

*

The Onyx Wizards, purest of the blood, had long since ceased to struggle against the strictures of the prison they had created for themselves. Antiquity and the countless traditions that were maintained to keep its memory alive were the chains and shackles they had come to accept. To accept, they said, was to grasp the importance of responsibility, and if such a thing as a secular god could exist, then to the dwellers of Andara, the last followers of the Black-Winged Lord, that god's name was Responsibility. And it had, over the decades since the Letherii Conquest, come to rival in power the Black-Winged Lord himself.

The young archer, nineteen years of age, was not alone in his rejection of the stolid, outdated ways of the Onyx Wizards. And like many of his compatriots of similar age – the first generation born to the Exile – he had taken a name for himself that bespoke the fullest measure of that rejection. Clan name cast away, all echoes of the old language – both the common tongue and the priest dialect – dispensed with. His clan was that of the Exiled, now.

For all these gestures of independence, a direct command delivered by Ordant Brid, Reve Master of the Rock among the Onyx Order, could not be ignored.

And so the young warrior named Clip of the Exiled had exited the eternally dark monastery of Andara, had climbed the interminable cliff wall and eventually emerged into hated sunlight to travel overland beneath the blinded stars of day, arriving at an overlook above the main pass.

The small party of travellers he now approached were not traders. No baggage train of goods accompanied them. No shackled slaves stumbled in their wake. They rode Letherii horses, yet even with the presence of at least three Letherii, Clip knew that this was no imperial delegation. No, these were refugees. And they were being hunted.

And among them walks the brother of my god.

As Clip drew nearer, as yet unseen by the travellers, he sensed a presence flowing alongside him. He snorted his disgust. 'A slave of the Tiste Edur, tell me, do you not know your own blood? We will tear you free, ghost – something you should have done for yourself long ago.'

'I am unbound,' came the hissing reply.

'Then I suppose you are safe enough from us.'

'Your blood is impure.'

Clip smiled in the darkness. 'Yes, I am a cauldron of failures. Nerek, Letherii – even D'rhasilhani.'

'And Tiste Andii.'

'Then greet me, brother.'

Rasping laughter. 'He has sensed you.'

'Was I sneaking up on them, ghost?'

'They have halted and now await.'

'Good, but can they guess what I will say to them? Can you?'

'You are impertinent. You lack respect. You are about to come face to face with Silchas Ruin, the White Crow—'

'Will he bring word of his lost brother? No? I thought not.'

Another hiss of laughter. 'Oddly enough, I believe you will fit right in with the ones you are about to meet.'

Seren Pedac squinted into the gloom. She was tired. They all were after long days traversing the pass, with no end in sight. Silchas Ruin's announcement that someone was approaching brought them all to a halt beside the sandy fringe of a stream, where insects rose in clouds to descend upon them. The horses snorted, tails flicking and hides rippling.

She dismounted a moment after Silchas Ruin, and followed him across the stream. Behind her the others remained where they were. Kettle slept in the arms of Udinaas, and he seemed disinclined to move lest he wake her. Fear Sengar slipped down from his horse but made no further move.

Standing beside the albino Tiste Andii, Seren could now hear a strange swishing and clacking sound, whispering down over the tumbled rocks beyond. A moment later a tall, lean form appeared, silhouetted against grey stone.

A smudge of deeper darkness flowed out from his side to hover before Silchas Ruin.

'Kin,' said the wraith.

'A descendant of my followers, Wither?'

'Oh no, Silchas Ruin.'

Breath slowly hissed from the Tiste Andii. 'My brother's. They were this close?'

The young warrior drew closer, his pace almost sauntering. The tone of his skin was dusky, not much different from that of a Tiste Edur. He was twirling a chain in his right hand, the rings on each end blurring in the gloom. 'Silchas Ruin,' he said, 'I greet you on behalf of the Onyx Order of Andara. It has been a long time since we last met a Tiste Andii not of our colony.' The broad mouth quirked slightly. 'You do not look at all as I had expected.'

'Your words verge on insult,' Silchas Ruin said. 'Is this how the Onyx Order would greet me?'

The young warrior shrugged, the chain snapping taut for a beat, then spinning out once more. 'There are K'risnan wards on the trail ahead of you – traps and snares. Nor will you find what you seek in Bluerose, not the city itself nor Jasp nor Outbound.'

'How is it you know what I seek?'

154

'He said you would come, sooner or later.'

'Who?'

Brows rose. 'Why, your brother. He didn't arrive in time to prevent your getting taken down, nor the slaughter of your followers—'

'Did he avenge me?'

'A moment,' Seren Pedac cut in. 'What is your name?'

A white smile. 'Clip. To answer you, Silchas Ruin, he was not inclined to murder all the Tiste Edur. Scabandari Bloodeye had been destroyed by Elder Gods. A curse was laid upon the lands west of here, denying even death's release. The Edur were scattered, assailed by ice, retreating seas and terrible storms. In the immediate aftermath of the Omtose Phellack curse, their survival was at risk, and Rake left them to it.'

'I do not recall my brother being so . . . merciful.'

'If our histories of that time are accurate,' Clip said, 'then he was rather preoccupied. The sundering of Kurald Emurlahn. Rumours of Osserc in the vicinity, a mercurial dalliance with Lady Envy, arguments and a shaky alliance with Kilmandaros, and then, finally, Silanah, the Eleint who emerged at his side from Emurlahn at the closing of the gate.'

'It seems much of that time is common knowledge among your Order,' Silchas Ruin observed, his tone flat. 'He stayed with you for a lengthy period, then.'

'He stays nowhere for very long,' Clip replied, clearly amused by something.

Seren Pedac wondered if the youth knew how close he was to pushing Ruin over the edge. A few more ill-chosen words and Clip's head would roll from his shoulders. 'Is it your mission,' she asked the Tiste Andii, 'to guide us to our destination?'

Another smile, another snap of the chain. 'It is. You will be, uh, welcomed as guests of the Andara. Although the presence of both Letherii and Tiste Edur in your party is somewhat problematic. The Onyx Order has been outlawed, as you know, subject to vicious repression. The Andara represents the last secret refuge of our people. Its location must not be compromised.'

'What do you suggest?' Seren asked.

'The remainder of this journey,' Clip replied, 'will be through warren. Through Kurald Galain.'

Silchas Ruin cocked his head at that, then grunted, 'I am beginning to understand. Tell me, Clip, how many wizards of the Order dwell in the Andara?'

'There are five, and they are the last.'

'And can they agree on anything?'

'Of course not. I am here by the command of Ordant Brid, Reve

155

Master of the Rock. My departure from the Andara was uneventful, else it is likely I would not be here—'

'Should another of the Order have intercepted you.'

A nod. 'Can you wait for the maelstrom your arrival will bring, Silchas Ruin? I can't.'

'Thus, your greeting earlier should have been qualified. The Order does not welcome us. Rather, this Ordant Brid does.'

'They all choose to speak for the Order,' Clip said, his eyes glittering, 'when it will most confound the others. Now, I can see how eager you all are.' From his right hand the chain whipped out, the silver ring round his index finger, and at the snap of the chain's full length, a gate into Darkness appeared to the warrior's right. 'Call the others here,' Clip said, 'at haste. Even now, bound wraiths serving the Tiste Edur are converging. Of course, they all dream of escape – alas, that we cannot give them. But their Edur masters watch through their eyes, and that won't do.'

Seren Pedac turned about and summoned the others.

Clip stepped to one side and bowed low. 'Silchas Ruin, I invite you to walk through first, and know once more the welcome embrace of true Darkness. Besides,' he added, straightening as Ruin strode towards the gate, 'you will make for us a bright beacon—'

One of Silchas Ruin's swords hissed out, a gleaming blur, the edge slashing across the space where Clip's neck had been, but the young warrior had leaned back . . . just enough, and the weapon sang through air.

A soft laugh from the youth, appallingly relaxed. 'He said you'd be angry.'

Silchas Ruin stared across at Clip for a long moment, then he turned and walked through the gate.

Drawing a deep breath to slow her heart, Seren Pedac glared at Clip. 'You have no idea—'

'Don't I?'

The others appeared, leading their horses. Udinaas, with Kettle tucked into one arm, barely glanced over at Clip before he tugged his horse into the rent.

'You wish to cross swords with a god, Clip?'

'He gave himself away – oh, he's fast all right, and with two weapons he'd be hard to handle, I'll grant you—'

'And will the Reve Master who sent you be pleased with your immature behaviour?'

Clip laughed. 'Ordant could have selected any of a hundred warriors at hand for this mission, Letherii.'

'Yet he chose you, meaning he is either profoundly stupid or he anticipated your irreverence.'

156

'You waste your time, Acquitor,' Fear Sengar said, coming up alongside her and eyeing Clip. 'He is Tiste Andii. His mind is naught but darkness, in which ignorance and foolishness thrive.'

To Fear the young warrior bowed again. 'Edur, please, proceed. Darkness awaits you.' And he waved at the gate.

As Fear Sengar led his horse into the gate, the chain on Clip's right index finger spun out once more, ending with a clash of rings.

'Why do you do that?' Seren demanded, irritated.

Brows lifted. 'Do what?'

Swearing under her breath, the Acquitor walked through the gate.

BOOK TWO

LAYERS OF THE DEAD

Who now strides on my trail
devouring the distance between
no matter how I flee, the wasted
breath of my haste cast into the wind
and these dogs will prevail
dragging me down with howling glee
for the beasts were born fated,
trained in bold vengeance
by my own switch and hand
and no god will stand in my stead,
nor provide me sanctuary, even
should I plead for absolution—
the hounds of my deeds belong
only to me, and they have long hunted
and now the hunt ends.

Songs of Guilt
Bet'netrask

CHAPTER SEVEN

Twice as far as you think
Half the distance you fear
Too thin to hold you
and well over your head
So much cleverer by far
yet witless beyond measure
will you hear my story now?

Tales of the Drunken Bard
Fisher

STANDING AT THE RAIL, ATRI-PREDA YAN TOVIS, KNOWN TO HER soldiers as Twilight, watched the sloping shoreline of the Lether River track past. Gulls rode the waves in the shallows. Fisher boats sculled among the reeds, the net-casters pausing to watch the battered fleet work its way towards the harbour. Along the bank birds crowded the leafless branches of trees that had succumbed to the last season's flood. Beyond the dead trees, riders were on the coast road, cantering towards the city to report to various officials, although Yan Tovis was certain that the palace had already been informed that the first of the fleets now approached, with another a bare half-day behind.

She would welcome solid ground beneath her boots again. And the presence of unfamiliar faces within range of her vision, rather than these tired features behind and to either side that she had come to know all too well, and at times, she had to admit, despise.

The last ocean they had crossed was far in their wake now, and for that she was profoundly relieved. The world had proved . . . immense. Even the ancient Letherii charts mapping the great migration route from the land of the First Empire had revealed but a fraction of the vast expanse that was this mortal realm. The scale had left them all belittled, as if their grand dramas were without consequence, as if true meaning was too thinly spread, too elusive for a single mind to grasp. And there had been a devastating toll paid for these fated journeys. Scores of ships lost, thousands of hands dead – there were belligerent and all too capable empires and peoples out there, few of whom were reluctant to test the prowess and determination of foreign invaders. If not for the formidable sorceries of the Edur and the new cadres of Letherii mages, there would have been more defeats than victories recorded in the ledgers, and yet fewer soldiers and sailors to rest eyes once more upon their homeland.

Hanradi Khalag, Uruth and Tomad Sengar would have dire news to deliver to the Emperor, sufficient to overwhelm their meagre successes, and Yan Tovis was thankful that she would not be present at that debriefing. She would have more than enough to deal with in her own capacity, besides. The Letherii Marines had been decimated – families would need to be informed, death-pensions distributed, lost equipment charged and debts transferred to heirs and kin. Depressing and tedious work and she already longed for the last scroll to be sealed and signed.

As the stands of trees and undergrowth dwindled, replaced by fisher shacks, jetties and then the walled estates of the elite, she stepped back from the rail and looked round the deck. Seeing Taralack Veed positioned near the stern, she walked over.

'We are very close now,' she said. 'Letheras, seat of the Emperor, the largest and richest city on this continent. And still your champion will not come on deck.'

'I see bridges ahead,' the barbarian observed, looking back up the length of the ship.

'Yes. The Tiers. There are canals in the city. Did I not tell you of the Drownings?'

The man grimaced, then swung about once more and spat over the stern rail. 'They die without honour and this entertains you. What is it you would wish Icarium to see, Twilight?'

'He shall need his anger,' she replied in a low voice.

Taralack Veed ran both hands over his scalp, flattening back his hair. 'When he is next awakened, matters of resolve will mean nothing. Your Emperor shall be annihilated, and likely most of this sparkling city with him. If you choose to witness, then you too will die. As will Tomad Sengar and Hanradi Khalag.'

'Alas,' she said after a moment, 'I will not be present to witness the clash. My duties will take me back north, back to Fent Reach.' She glanced across at him. 'A journey of over a month by horseback, Taralack Veed. Will that be distant enough?'

He shrugged. 'I make no promises.'

'But one,' she pointed out.

'Oh?'

'That he will fight.'

'You do not know Icarium as I do. He may remain below, but there is an excitement about him. Anticipation, now, unlike any I have ever seen before. Twilight, he has come to accept his curse; indeed, to embrace it. He sharpens his sword, again and again. Oils his bow. Examines his armour for flaws with every dawn. He has no more questions for me, and that is the most ominous detail of all.'

'He has failed us once,' she said.

'There was . . . intervention. That shall not occur again, unless your carelessness permits it.'

At a gentle bend in the river, Letheras revealed itself, sprawling up and back from the north shore, magnificent bridges arching over garishly painted buildings and the haze of innumerable cookfires. Domes and terraces, towers and platforms loomed, edges blurred in the gold-lit smoke. The imperial quays were directly ahead, just beyond a mole, and the first dromons of the fleet were shipping oars and swinging in towards berths. Scores of figures were gathering along the waterfront, including a bristling procession coming down from the Eternal Domicile, pennons and standards wavering overhead – the official delegation, although Yan Tovis noted that there were no Edur among it.

It seemed that Triban Gnol's quiet usurpation was all but complete. She was not surprised. The Chancellor had probably begun his plans long before King Ezgara Diskanar downed the fatal draught in the throne room. *Ensuring a smooth transition*, is how he would have defended himself. *The empire is greater than its ruler, and that is where lies the Chancellor's loyalty. Always and for ever more.* Laudable sentiments, no doubt, but the truth was never so clear. The lust for power was a strong current, roiling with clouds that obscured all to everyone, barring, perhaps, Triban Gnol himself, who was at the very centre of the maelstrom. His delusion of control had never been challenged, but Yan Tovis believed that it would not last.

After all, the Tiste Edur had returned. Tomad Sengar, Hanradi Khalag and three other former war chiefs of the tribes, as well as over four thousand seasoned warriors who'd long ago left their naivety behind, lost in Callows, in Sepik, Nemil, the Perish Coast, Shal-Morzinn and Drift Avalii, in a host of foreign waters, among the Meckros – the journey had been long. Fraught—

'The nest is about to be kicked awake,' Taralack Veed said, a rather ugly grin twisting his features.

Yan Tovis shrugged. 'To be expected. We have been absent a long time.'

'Maybe your Emperor is already dead. I see no Tiste Edur in that contingent.'

'I do not think that likely. Our K'risnan would have known.'

'Informed by their god? Yan Tovis, no gift from a god comes for free. More, if it sees fit, it will tell its followers nothing. Or, indeed, it will lie. The Edur do not understand any of this, but you surprise me. Is it not the very nature of your deity, this Errant, to deceive you at every turn?'

'The Emperor is not dead, Taralack Veed.'

'Then it is only a matter of time.'

'So you continually promise.'

But he shook his head. 'I do not speak of Icarium now. I speak of when a god's chosen one *fails*. And they always do, Twilight. We are never enough in their eyes. Never faithful enough, never fearful enough, never abject enough. Sooner or later we betray them, in weakness or in overwrought ambition. We see before us a city of bridges yet what I see and what you see are two different things. Do not let your eyes deceive you – the bridges awaiting us are all too narrow for mortals.'

Their ship slowly angled in towards the central imperial dock like a weary beast of burden, and a handful of Edur officers were now on deck, whilst sailors readied the lines along the port rail. The stench of effluent from the murky waters rose thick enough to sting the eyes.

Taralack Veed spat onto his hands and smoothed back his hair yet again. 'Almost time. I go to collect my champion.'

Noticed by no-one, Turudal Brizad, the Errant, stood with his back to a quayside warehouse thirty or so paces from the main pier. His gaze noted the disembarking of Tomad Sengar – the venerable warrior looking worn and aged – and his expression, as he observed the absence of Tiste Edur among the delegation from the palace, seemed to grow darker by the moment. But neither he nor any of the other Edur held the god's attention for long. His attention sharpened as the Atri-Preda in command of this fleet's Letherii Marines strode the length of the gangway, followed by a half-dozen aides and officers, for he sensed, all at once, that there was something fated about the woman. Yet the details eluded him.

The god frowned, frustrated by his diminishing percipience. He should have sensed immediately what awaited Yan Tovis. Five years ago he would have, thinking nothing of the gift, the sheer privilege of such ascendant power. Not since those final tumultuous days of the First Empire – the succession of ghastly events that led to the intercession of the T'lan Imass to quell the fatal throes of Dessimbelackis's empire – had the Errant felt so disconnected. Chaos was rolling towards Letheras with the force of a cataclysmic wave, an ocean surge that simply engulfed this river's currents – *yes, it comes from the sea. That*

164

much I know, that much I can feel. From the sea, just like this woman, this Twilight.

Another figure appeared on the plank. A foreigner, the skin of his forearms a swirl of arcane tattoos, the rest of his upper body wrapped in a roughly woven cape, the hood hiding his features. Barbaric, wary, the glitter of eyes taking it all in, pausing halfway down to hawk and spit over the side, a gesture that startled the Errant and, it seemed, most of those standing on the dock.

A moment later another foreigner rose into view, pausing at the top of the gangway. The Errant's breath caught, a sudden chill flowing through him, as if Hood himself had arrived, his cold breath whispering across the back of the god's neck.

Abyss take me, all that waits within him. The foment none other here can see, could even guess at. Dear son of Gothos and that overgrown hag, the stain of Azath blood is about you like a cloud. This was more than a curse – all that afflicted this fell warrior. Deliberate skeins were woven about him, the threads of some elaborate, ancient, and deadly ritual. And he knew their flavour. *The Nameless Ones.*

Two soldiers from Triban Gnol's Palace Guard moved to await the Jhag as he slowly walked down to the dock.

The Errant's heart was thudding hard in his chest. *They have delivered a champion, a challenger to the Emperor of a Thousand Deaths—*

The Jhag stepped onto solid ground.

From the buildings beyond the harbour front, birds rose suddenly, hundreds, then thousands, voicing a chorus of shrieks, and beneath the Errant's feet the stones shifted with a heavy, groaning sound. Something large collapsed far into the city, beyond Quillas Canal, and distant screams followed. The Errant stepped out from the wall and saw the bloom of a dust cloud rising behind the caterwauling, panicked pigeons, rooks, gulls and starlings.

The subterranean groaning then ceased and a heavy silence settled.

Icarium's tusked mouth revealed the faintest of smiles, as if pleased with the earth's welcome, and the Errant could not be sure – at this distance – if that smile was truly as childlike as it seemed, or if it was in fact ironic or, indeed, bitter. He repressed the urge to draw closer seeking an answer to that question, reminding himself that he did not want Icarium's attention. Not now, not ever.

Tomad Sengar, what your son will face . . .

It was no wonder, he suddenly realized, that all that was to come was obscured in a maelstrom of chaos. *They have brought Icarium . . . into the heart of my power.*

Among the delegation and other Letherii nearby, it was clear that no particular connection had been made between Icarium's first touch on solid ground and the minor earthquake rumbling through Letheras – yet such stirrings were virtually unknown for this region, and while the terror among the birds and the bawling of various beasts of burden continued unabated, already the consternation of those within the Errant's sight was diminishing. *Foolish mortals, so quick to disregard unease.*

In the river beyond, the water slowly lost its shivering agitation and the gulls further out began to settle once again amidst yet more ships angling towards shore. Yet somewhere in the city, a building had toppled, probably some venerable ancient edifice, its foundations weakened by groundwater, its mortar crumbled and supports rotted through.

There would have been casualties – *Icarium's first, but most assuredly not his last.*

And he smiles.

Still cursing, Taralack Veed turned to Yan Tovis. 'Unsettled lands – Burn does not rest easy here.'

The Atri-Preda shrugged to hide her queasy shock. 'To the north of here, along the Reach Mountains, the ground shakes often. The same can be said for the north side of the ranges to the far south, the other side of the Draconean Sea.'

She saw the glimmer of bared teeth in the hood's shadow. 'But not in Letheras, yes?'

'I've not heard of such before, but that means little,' she replied. 'This city is not my home. Not where I was born. Not where I grew up.'

Taralack Veed edged closer, facing away from Icarium, who stood listening to the two palace guards as they instructed him in what was to come. 'You fool,' he hissed at her. 'Burn's flesh flinched, Twilight. *Flinched* – because of *him*.'

She snorted.

The Gral cocked his head, and she could feel his contempt. 'What happens now?' he asked.

'Now? Very little. There are secure residences, for you and your champion. As for when the Emperor chooses to face his challengers, that is up to him. Sometimes, he is impatient and the clash occurs immediately. Other times, he waits, often for weeks. But I will tell you what will begin immediately.'

'What is that?'

'The burial urn for Icarium, and his place in the cemetery where resides every challenger Rhulad has faced.'

'Even that place will not survive,' Taralack Veed muttered.

The Gral, feeling sick to his stomach, walked over to Icarium. He did not want to think of the destruction to come. He had seen it once, after

166

all. *Burn, even in your eternal sleep, you felt the stabbing wound that is Icarium – and none of these people here countenanced it, none was ready for the truth. Their hands are not in the earth, the touch is lost – yet look at them: they would call me the savage.*

'Icarium, my friend—'

'Can you not feel it, Taralack Veed?' In his unhuman eyes, the gleam of anticipation. 'This place . . . I have been here before – no, not this city. From the time before this city was born. I have stood on this ground—'

'And it remembered,' growled Taralack Veed.

'Yes, but not in the way you believe. There are truths here, waiting for me. Truths. I have never been as close to them as I am now. Now I understand why I did not refuse you.'

Refuse me? You considered such a thing? Was it truly so near the edge? 'Your destiny will soon welcome you, Icarium, as I have said all along. You could no more refuse that than you could the Jaghut blood in your veins.'

A grimace. 'Jaghut . . . yes, they have been here. In my wake. Perhaps, even, on my trail. Long ago, and now again—'

'Again?'

'Omtose Phellack – the heart of this city is ice, Taralack Veed. A most violent imposition.'

'Are you certain? I do not understand—'

'Nor I. Yet. But I shall. No secret shall survive my sojourn here. It will change.'

'What will change?'

Icarium smiled, one hand resting on the pommel of his sword, and did not reply.

'You will face this Emperor then?'

'So it is expected of me, Taralack Veed.' A bright glance. 'How could I refuse them?'

Spirits below, my death draws close. It was what we wanted all along. So why do I now rail at it? Who has stolen my courage?

'It is as if,' Icarium whispered, 'my life awakens anew.'

The hand shot out in the gloom, snatching the rat from atop the wooden cage holding the forward pump. The scrawny creature had a moment to squeal in panic before its neck was snapped. There was a thud as the dead rat was flung to one side, where it slid down into the murky bilge water.

'Oh, how I hate you when you lose patience,' Samar Dev said in a weary tone. 'That's an invitation to disease, Karsa Orlong.'

'Life is an invitation to disease,' the huge warrior rumbled from the shadows. After a moment, he added, 'I'll feed it to the turtles.' Then he snorted. 'Turtles big enough to drag down this damned ship. These Letherii live in a mad god's nightmare.'

'More than you realize,' Samar Dev muttered. 'Listen. Shouts from shore. We're finally drawing in.'

'The rats are relieved.'

'Don't you have something you need to do to get ready?'

'Such as?'

'I don't know. Knock a few more chips off your sword, or something. Get it sharp.'

'The sword is unbreakable.'

'What about that armour? Most of the shells are broken – it's not worthy of the name and won't stop a blade—'

'No blade will reach it, witch. I shall face but one man, not twenty. And he is small – my people call you children. And that is all you truly are. Short-lived, stick-limbed, with faces I want to pinch. The Edur are little different, just stretched out a bit.'

'Pinch? Would that be before or after decapitation?'

He grunted a laugh.

Samar Dev leaned back against the bale in which something hard and lumpy had been packed – despite the mild discomfort she was not inclined to explore any further. Both the Edur and the Letherii had peculiar ideas about what constituted booty. In this very hold there were amphorae containing spiced human blood and a dozen wax-clad corpses of Edur 'refugees' from Sepik who had not survived the journey, stacked like bolts of cloth against a bloodstained conch-shell throne that had belonged to some remote island chieftain – whose pickled head probably resided in one of the jars Karsa Orlong leaned against. 'At least we're soon to get off this damned ship. My skin has all dried up. Look at my hands – I've seen mummified ones looking better than these. All this damned salt – it clings like a second skin, and it's moulting—'

'Spirits below, woman, you incite me to wring another rat's neck.'

'So I am responsible for that last rat's death, am I? Needless to say, I take exception to that. Was your hand that reached out, Toblakai. Your hand that—'

'And your mouth that never stops, making me need to kill something.'

'I am not to blame for your violent impulses. Besides, I was just passing time in harmless conversation. We've not spoken in a while, you and I. I find I prefer Taxilian's company, and were he not sick with homesickness and even more miserable than you . . .'

'Conversation. Is that what you call it? Then why are my ears numb?'

'You know, I too am impatient. I've not cast a curse on anyone in a long time.'

'Your squalling spirits do not frighten me,' Karsa Orlong replied. 'And they have been squalling, ever since we made the river. A thousand voices clamouring in my skull – can you not silence them?'

Sighing, she tilted her head back and closed her eyes. 'Toblakai . . . you will have quite an audience when you clash swords with this Edur Emperor.'

'What has that to do with your spirits, Samar Dev?'

'Yes, that was too obscure, wasn't it? Then I shall be more precise. There are gods in this city we approach. Resident gods.'

'Do they ever get a moment's rest?'

'They don't live in temples. Nor any signs above the doors of their residences, Karsa Orlong. They are in the city, yet few know of it. Understand, the spirits shriek because they are not welcome, and, even more worrying, should any one of those gods seek to wrest them away from me, well, there is little I could do against them.'

'Yet they are bound to me as well, aren't they?'

She clamped her mouth shut, squinted across at him in the gloom. The hull thumped as the ship edged up alongside the dock. She saw the glimmer of bared teeth, feral, and a chill rippled through her. 'What do you know of that?' she asked.

'It is my curse to gather souls,' he replied. 'What are spirits, witch, if not simply powerful souls? They haunt me . . . I haunt them. The candles I lit, in that apothecary of yours – they were in the wax, weren't they?'

'Released, then held close, yes. I gathered them . . . after I'd sent you away.'

'Bound them into that knife at your belt,' Karsa said. 'Tell me, do you sense the two Toblakai souls in my own weapon?'

'Yes, no. That is, I sense them, but I dare not approach.'

'Why?'

'Karsa, they are too strong for me. They are like fire in the crystal of that flint, trapped by your will.'

'Not trapped,' he replied. 'They dwell within because they choose to, because the weapon honours them. They are my companions, Samar Dev.' The Toblakai rose suddenly, hunching beneath the ceiling. 'Should a god be foolish enough to seek to steal our spirits, I will kill it.'

She regarded him from half-closed eyes. Declarative statements such as that one were not rare utterances from Karsa Orlong, and she had long since learned that they were not empty boasts, no matter how absurd the assertion might have sounded. 'That would not be wise,' she said after a moment.

'A god devoid of wisdom deserves what it gets.'

'That's not what I meant.'

Karsa stooped momentarily to retrieve the dead rat, then he headed for the hatch.

She followed.

When she reached the main deck, the Toblakai was walking towards the captain. She watched as he placed the sodden rat in the Letherii's hands, then turned away, saying, 'Get the hoists – I want my horse on deck and off this damned hulk.' Behind him, the captain stared down at the creature in his hands, then, with a snarl, he flung it over the rail.

Samar Dev contemplated a few quick words with the captain, to stave off the coming storm – a storm that Karsa had nonchalantly triggered innumerable times before on this voyage – then decided it was not worth the effort. It seemed that the captain concluded much the same, as a sailor hurried up with a bucket of seawater, into which the Letherii thrust his hands.

The main hatch to the cargo hold was being removed, while other hands set to assembling the winches.

Karsa strode to the gangway. He halted, then said in a loud voice, 'This city reeks. When I am done with its Emperor, I may well burn it to the ground.'

The planks sagged and bounced as the Toblakai descended to the landing.

Samar Dev hurried after him.

One of two fully armoured guards had already begun addressing Karsa in contemptuous tones. '—to be unarmed whenever you are permitted to leave the compound, said permission to be granted only by the ranking officer of the Watch. Our immediate task is to escort you to your quarters, where the filth will be scrubbed from your body and hair—'

He got no further, as Karsa reached out, closed his hand on the guard's leather weapons harness, and with a single heave flung the Letherii into the air. Six or more paces to the left he sailed, colliding with three stevedores who had been watching the proceedings. All four went down.

Voicing an oath, the second guard tugged at his shortsword.

Karsa's punch rocked his head back and the man collapsed.

Hoarse shouts of alarm, more Letherii soldiers converging.

Samar Dev rushed forward. 'Hood take you, Toblakai – do you intend to war with the whole empire?'

Glaring at the half-circle of guards closing round him, Karsa grunted then crossed his arms. 'If you are to be my escort,' he said to them, 'then be civil, or I will break you all into pieces.' Then he swung about, pushing past Samar. 'Where is my horse?' he bellowed to the crew still on deck. 'Where is Havok! I grow tired of waiting!'

Samar Dev considered returning to the ship, demanding that they sail

170

out, back down the river, back into the Draconean Sea, then beyond. Leaving this unpredictable Toblakai to Letheras and all its hapless denizens.

Alas, even gods don't deserve that.

Bugg stood thirty paces from the grand entrance to the Hivanar Estate, one hand out as he leaned against a wall to steady himself. In some alley garden a short distance away, chickens screeched in wild clamour and flung themselves into the grille hatches in frenzied panic. Overhead, starlings still raced back and forth en masse.

He wiped beads of sweat from his brow, struggled to draw a deep breath.

A worthy reminder, he told himself. Everything was only a matter of time. What stretched would then contract. Events tumbled, forces closed to collision, and for all that, the measured pace seemed to remain unchanged, a current beneath all else. Yet, he knew, even that slowed, incrementally, from one age to the next. *Death is written in birth – the words of a great sage. What was her name? When did she live? Ah, so much has whispered away from my mind, these memories, like sand between the fingers. Yet she could see what most cannot – not even the gods. Death and birth. Even in opposition the two forces are bound, and to define one is to define the other.*

And now *he* had come. With his first step, delivering the weight of history. This land's. His own. Two forces in opposition, yet inextricably bound. *Do you now feel as if you have come home, Icarium? I remember you, striding from the sea, a refugee from a realm you had laid to waste. Yet your father did not await you – he had gone, he had walked down the throat of an Azath. Icarium, he was Jaghut, and among the Jaghut no father reaches across to take his child's hand.*

'Are you sick, old man?'

Blinking, Bugg looked across to see a servant from one of the nearby estates, returning from market with a basket of foodstuffs balanced on his head. *Only with grief, dear mortal.* He shook his head.

'It was the floods,' the servant went on. 'Shifting the clay.'

'Aye.'

'Scale House fell down – did you hear? Right into the street. Good thing it was empty, hey? Though I heard there was a fatality – in the street.' The man suddenly grinned. 'A cat!' Laughing, he resumed his journey.

Bugg stared after him; then, with a grunt, he set off for the gate.

He waited on the terrace, frowning down at the surprisingly deep trench the crew had managed to excavate into the bank, then outward, through the bedded silts of the river itself. The shoring was robust, and

171

Bugg could see few leaks from between the sealed slats. Even so, two workers were on the pump, their bared backs slick with sweat.

Rautos Hivanar came to his side. 'Bugg, welcome. I imagine you wish to retrieve your crew.'

'No rush, sir,' Bugg replied. 'It is clear to me now that this project of yours is . . . ambitious. How much water is coming up from the floor of that pit?'

'Without constant pumping, the trench would overflow in a little under two bells.'

'I bring you a message from your servant, Venitt Sathad, who visited on his way out of the city. He came to observe our progress on the refurbishment of the inn you recently acquired, and was struck with something of a revelation upon seeing the mysterious mechanism we found inside an outbuilding. He further suggested it was imperative that you see it for yourself. Also, he mentioned a collection of artifacts . . . recovered from this trench, yes?'

The large man was silent for a moment, then he seemed to reach a decision, for he gestured Bugg to follow.

They entered the estate, passing through an elongated, shuttered room in which hung drying herbs, down a corridor and into a work-room dominated by a large table and prism lanterns attached to hinged arms so that, if desired, they could be drawn close or lifted clear when someone was working at the table. Resting on the polished wood surface were a dozen or so objects, both metal and fired clay, not one of which revealed any obvious function.

Rautos Hivanar still silent and standing now at his side, Bugg scanned the objects for a long moment, then reached out and picked up one in particular. Heavy, unmarked by pitting or rust, seamlessly bent almost to right angles.

'Your engineers,' Rautos Hivanar said, 'could determine no purpose to these mechanisms.'

Bugg's brows rose at the man's use of the word 'mechanism'. He hefted the object in his hands.

'I have attempted to assemble these,' the merchant continued, 'to no avail. There are no obvious attachment points, yet, somehow, they seem to me to be of a piece. Perhaps some essential item is still buried beneath the river, but we have found nothing for three days now, barring a wheelbarrow's worth of stone chips and shards – and these were recovered in a level of sediment far below these artifacts, leading me to believe that they pre-date them by centuries, if not millennia.'

'Yes,' Bugg muttered. 'Eres'al, a mated pair, preparing flint for tools, here on the bank of the vast marsh. He worked the cores, she did the more detailed knapping. They came here for three seasons, then she died in childbirth, and he wandered with a starving babe in his arms

172

until it too died. He found no others of his kind, for they had been scattered after the conflagration of the great forests, the wildfires sweeping out over the plains. The air was thick with ash. He wandered, until he died, and so was the last of his line.' He stared unseeing at the artifact, even as its weight seemed to burgeon, threatening to tug at his arms, to drag him down to his knees. 'But Icarium said there would be no end, that the cut thread was but an illusion – in his voice, then, I could hear his father.'

A hand closed on his shoulder and swung him round. Startled, he met Rautos Hivanar's sharp, glittering eyes. Bugg frowned. 'Sir?'

'You – you are inclined to invent stories. Or, perhaps, you are a sage, gifted with unnatural sight. Is this what I am hearing, old man? Tell me, who was this Icarium? Was that the name of the Eres'al? The one who died?'

'I am sorry, sir.' He raised the object higher. 'This artifact – you will find it is identical to the massive object at the inn, barring scale. I believe this is what your servant wanted you to realize – as he himself did when he first looked upon the edifice once we had brought down the walls enclosing it.'

'Are you certain of all this?'

'Yes.' Bugg gestured at the array of items on the table. 'A central piece is missing, as you suspected, sir. Alas, you will not find it, for it is not physical. The framework that will hold it together is one of energy, not matter. And,' he added, still in a distracted tone, 'it has yet to arrive.'

He set the artifact back down and walked from the chamber, back up the corridor, through the dry-rack room, out onto the terrace. Unmindful of the two workers pausing to stare across at him as Rautos Hivanar appeared as if in pursuit – the merchant's hands were spread, palms up, as if beseeching, although the huge man said not a word, his mouth working in silence, as though he had been struck mute. Bugg's glance at the large man was momentary. He continued on, along the passage between estate wall and compound wall, to the side postern near the front gate.

He found himself once more on the street, only remotely noticing the passers-by in the cooler shade of afternoon.

It has yet to arrive.

And yet, it comes.

'Watch where you're walking, old man!'

'Leave off him – see how he weeps? It's an old man's right to grieve, so leave him be.'

'Must be blind, the clumsy fool . . .'

And here, long before this city was born, there stood a temple, into which Icarium walked – as lost as any son, the child severed from the

173

thread. But the Elder God within could give him nothing. Nothing beyond what he himself was preparing to do.

Could you have imagined, K'rul, how Icarium would take what you did? Take it into himself as would any child seeking a guiding hand? Where are you, K'rul? Do you sense his return? Do you know what he seeks?

'Clumsy or not, it's a question of manners and proper respect.'

Bugg's threadbare tunic was grasped and he was dragged to one side, then flung up against a wall. He stared at a battered face beneath the rim of a helm. To one side, scowling, another guard.

'Do you know who we are?' the man holding him demanded, baring stained teeth.

'Karos Invictad's thugs, aye. His private police, the ones who kick in doors at the middle of night. The ones who take mothers from babes, fathers from sons. The ones who, in the righteous glory that comes with unchallenged power, then loot the homes of the arrested, not to mention raping the daughters—'

Bugg was thrown a second time against the wall, the back of his head crunching hard on the pitted brick.

'For that, bastard,' the man snarled, 'you'll Drown.'

Bugg blinked sweat from his eyes, then, as the thug's words penetrated, he laughed. 'Drown? Oh, that's priceless. Now, take your hands off me or I will lose my temper.'

Instead, the man tightened his hold on the front of Bugg's tunic, while the other said, 'You were right, Kanorsos, he needs beating.'

'The bully's greatest terror,' Bugg said, 'comes when he meets someone bigger and meaner—'

'And is that you?'

Both men laughed.

Bugg twisted his head, looked round. People were hurrying past – it was never wise to witness such events, not when the murderers of the Patriotists were involved. 'So be it,' he said under his breath. 'Gentlemen, allow me to introduce to you someone bigger and meaner, or, to be more accurate, some*thing*.'

A moment later Bugg was alone. He adjusted his tunic, glanced about, then set off once more for his master's abode.

It was inevitable, he knew, that someone had witnessed the sudden vanishing of two armed and amoured men. But no-one cried out in his wake, for which he was relieved, since he was not inclined to discuss much with anyone right at that moment.

Did I just lose my temper? It's possible, but then, you were distracted. Perturbed, even. These things happen.

*

174

Feather Witch wasted little time. Off the cursed ships and their countless, endlessly miserable crowds, the eyes always upon her, the expressions of suspicion or contempt and the stench of suffering that came of hundreds of prisoners – the fallen Edur of Sepik, mixed-blood one and all, worse in the eyes of the tribes than Letherii slaves; the scores of foreigners who possessed knowledge deemed useful – at least for now; the Nemil fisher folk; the four copper-skinned Shal-Morzinn warriors dragged from a floundering carrack; denizens of Seven Cities, hailing from Erhlitan, the Karang Isles, Pur Atrii and other places; Quon sailors who claimed to be citizens of an empire called Malaz; dwellers of Lamatath and Callows . . .

Among them there were warriors considered worthy enough to be treated as challengers. An axeman from the ruined Meckros City the fleet had descended upon, a Cabalhii monk and a silent woman wearing a porcelain mask the brow of which was marked with eleven arcane glyphs – she had been found near dead in a storm-battered scow south of Callows.

There were others, chained in the holds of other ships in other fleets, but where they came from and what they were was mostly irrelevant. The only detail that had come to fascinate Feather Witch – among all these pathetic creatures – was the bewildering array of gods, goddesses, spirits and ascendants they worshipped. Prayers in a dozen languages, voices reaching out into vast silences – all these forlorn fools and all the unanswered calls for salvation.

No end, in that huge, chaotic world, to the delusions of those who believed they were chosen. Unique among their kind, basking beneath the gaze of gods that gave a damn – as if they would, when the truth was, each immortal visage, for all its peculiar traits, was but a facet of one, and that one had long since turned away, only to fight an eternal battle against itself. From the heavens, only indifference rained down, like ash, stinging the eyes, scratching raw the throat. There was no sustenance in that blinding deluge.

Chosen – now *there* was a conceit of appalling proportions. *Either we all are, or none of us are. And if the former, then we will all face the same judge, the same hand of justice – the wealthy, the Indebted, the master, the slave, the murderer and the victim, the raper and the raped, all of us, so pray hard, everyone – if that helps – and look well to your own shadow.* More likely, in her mind, no-one was chosen, and there was no day of judgement awaiting every soul. Each and every mortal faced a singular end, and that was oblivion.

Oh, indeed, the gods existed, but not one cared a whit for the fate of a mortal's soul, unless they could bend that soul to their will, to serve as but one more soldier in their pointless, self-destructive wars.

For herself, she was past such thinking. She had found her own freedom, basking beneath that blessed rain of indifference. She would do as she willed, and not even the gods could stop her. It would be the gods themselves, she vowed, who would come to her. Beseeching, on their knees, snared in their own game.

She moved silently, now, deep in the crypts beneath the Old Palace. *I was a slave, once – many believe I still am, yet look at me – I rule this buried realm. I alone know where the hidden chambers reside, I know what awaits me within them. I walk this most fated path, and, when the time is right, I will take the throne.*

The Throne of Oblivion.

Uruth might well be looking for her right now, the old hag with all her airs, the smugness of a thousand imagined secrets, but Feather Witch knew all those secrets. There was nothing to fear from Uruth Sengar – she had been usurped by events. By her youngest son, by the other sons who then betrayed Rhulad. By the conquest itself. The society of Edur women was now scattered, torn apart; they went where their husbands were despatched; they had surrounded themselves in Letherii slaves, fawners and Indebted. They had ceased to care. In any case, Feather Witch had had enough of all that. She was in Letheras once more and like that fool, Udinaas, she was fleeing her bondage; and here, in the catacombs of the Old Palace, none would find her.

Old storage rooms were already well supplied, equipped a morsel at a time in the days before the long journey across the oceans. She had fresh water, wine and beer, dried fish and beef, fired clay jugs with preserved fruits. Bedding, spare clothes, and over a hundred scrolls stolen from the Imperial Library. Histories of the Nerek, the Tarthenal, the Fent and a host of even more obscure peoples the Letherii had devoured in the last seven or eight centuries – the Bratha, the Katter, the Dresh and the Shake.

And here, beneath the Old Palace, Feather Witch had discovered chambers lined with shelves on which sat thousands of mouldering scrolls, crumbling clay tablets and worm-gnawed bound books. Of those she had examined, the faded script in most of them was written in an arcane style of Letherii that proved difficult to decipher, but she was learning, albeit slowly. A handful of old tomes, however, were penned in a language she had never seen before.

The First Empire, whence this colony originally came all those centuries ago, seemed to be a complicated place, home to countless peoples each with their own languages and gods. For all the imperial claims to being the birth of human civilization, it was clear to Feather Witch that no such claim could be taken seriously. Perhaps the First Empire marked the initial nation consisting of more than a single city, probably born out of conquest, one city-state after another swallowed up by the rampaging founders. Yet even then, the fabled Seven Cities was an empire bordered by independent tribes and peoples, and there had been wars and then treaties. Some were broken, most were not. Imperial ambitions had been stymied, and it was this fact that triggered the age of colonization to distant lands.

The First Empire had met foes who would not bend a knee. This was, for Feather Witch, the most important truth of all, one that had been conveniently and deliberately forgotten. She had gained strength from that, but such details were themselves but confirmation of discoveries she had already made – out in the vast world beyond. There had been clashes, fierce seafarers who took exception to a foreign fleet's invading their waters. Letherii and Edur ships had gone down, figures amidst flotsam-filled waves, arms raised in hopeless supplication – the heave and swirl of sharks, dhenrabi and other mysterious predators of the deep – screams, piteous screams, they still echoed in her head, writhing at the pit of her stomach. Revulsion and glee both.

The storms that had battered the fleet, especially west of the Draconean Sea, had revealed the true immensity of natural power, its fickle thrashings that swallowed entire ships – there was delight in being so humbled, coming upon her with the weight of revelation. The Lether Empire was puny – like Uruth Sengar, it held to airs of greatness when it was but one more pathetic hovel of cowering mortals.

She would not regret destroying it.

Huddled now in her favoured chamber, the ceiling overhead a cracked dome, its plaster paintings obscured by stains and mould, Feather Witch sat herself down cross-legged and drew out a small leather pouch. Within, her most precious possession. She could feel its modest length through the thin hide, the protuberances, the slightly ragged end, and, opposite, the curl of a nail that had continued growing. She wanted to draw it out, to touch once again its burnished skin—

'Foolish little girl.'

Hissing, Feather Witch flinched back from the doorway. A twisted, malformed figure occupied the threshold – she had not seen it in a long time, had almost forgotten – 'Hannan Mosag. I do not answer to you. And if you think me weak—'

'Oh no,' wheezed the Warlock King, 'not that. I chose my word carefully when I said "foolish". I know you have delved deep into your Letherii magic. You have gone far beyond casting those old, chipped tiles of long ago, haven't you? Even Uruth has no inkling of your Cedance – you did well to disguise your learning. Yet, for all that, you are still a fool, dreaming of all that you might achieve – when in truth you are alone.'

'What do you want? If the Emperor were to learn that you're skulking around down here—'

'He will learn nothing. You and I, Letherii, we can work together. We can destroy that abomination—'

177

'With yet another in his place – you.'

'Do you truly think I would have let it come to this? Rhulad is mad, as is the god who controls him. They must be expunged.'

'I know your hunger, Hannan Mosag—'

'You do not!' the Edur snapped, a shudder taking him. He edged closer into the chamber, then held up a mangled hand. 'Look carefully upon me, woman. See what the Chained One's sorcery does to the flesh – oh, we are bound now to the power of chaos, to its taste, its seductive flavour. It should never have come to this—'

'So you keep saying,' she cut in with a sneer. 'And how would the great empire of Hannan Mosag have looked? A rain of flowers onto every street, every citizen freed of debt, with the benign Tiste Edur overseeing it all?' She leaned forward. 'You forget, I was born among your people, in your very tribe, Warlock King. I remember going hungry during the unification wars. I remember the cruelty you heaped upon us slaves – when we got too old, you used us as bait for beskra crabs – threw our old ones into a cage and dropped it over the side of your knarri. Oh, yes, drowning was a mercy, but the ones you didn't like you kept their heads above the tide line, you let the crabs devour them alive, and laughed at the screams. We were muscle and when that muscle was used up, we were meat.'

'And is Indebtedness any better—'

'No, for that is a plague that spreads to every family member, every generation.'

Hannan Mosag shook his misshapen head. 'I would not have succumbed to the Chained One. He believed he was using me, but I was using him. Feather Witch, there would have been no war. No conquest. The tribes were joined as one – I made certain of that. Prosperity and freedom from fear awaited us, and in that world the lives of the slaves would have changed. Perhaps, indeed, the lives of Letherii among the Tiste Edur would have proved a lure to the Indebted in the southlands, enough to shatter the spine of this empire, for we would have offered freedom.'

She turned away, deftly hiding the small leather bag. 'What is the point of this, Hannan Mosag?'

'You wish to bring down Rhulad—'

'I will bring you all down.'

'But it must begin with Rhulad – you can see that. Unless he is destroyed, and that sword with him, you can achieve nothing.'

'If you could have killed him, Warlock King, you would have done so long ago.'

'Oh, but I will kill him.'

She glared across at him. 'How?'

'Why, with his own family.'

Feather Witch was silent for a dozen heartbeats. 'His father cowers in fear. His mother cannot meet his eyes. Binadas and Trull are dead, and Fear has fled.'

'Binadas?' The breath hissed slowly from Hannan Mosag. 'I did not know that.'

'Tomad dreamed of his son's death, and Hanradi Khalag quested for his soul – and failed.'

The Warlock King regarded her with hooded eyes. 'And did my K'risnan attempt the same of Trull Sengar?'

'No, why would he? Rhulad himself murdered Trull. Chained him in the Nascent. If that was meant to be secret, it failed. We heard – we slaves hear everything—'

'Yes, you do, and that is why we can help each other. Feather Witch, you wish to see this cursed empire collapse – so do I. And when that occurs, know this: I intend to take my Edur home. Back to our northlands. If the south is in flames, that is of no concern to me – I leave the Letherii to the Letherii, for no surer recipe for obliteration do any of us require. I knew that from the very start. Lether cannot sustain itself. Its appetite is an addiction, and that appetite exceeds the resources it needs to survive. Your people had already crossed that threshold, although they knew it not. It was my dream, Feather Witch, to raise a wall of power and so ensure the immunity of the Tiste Edur. Tell me, what do you know of the impending war in the east?'

'What war?'

Hannan Mosag smiled. 'The unravelling begins. Let us each grasp a thread, you at one end, me at the other. Behind you, the slaves. Behind me, all the K'risnan.'

'Does Trull Sengar live?'

'It is Fear Sengar who seeks the means of destroying Rhulad. And I mean for him to find it. Decide now, Feather Witch. Are we in league?'

She permitted herself a small smile. 'Hannan Mosag, when the moment of obliteration comes . . . you had better crawl fast.'

'I don't want to see them.'

With these words the Emperor twisted on his throne, legs drawing up, and seemed to focus on the wall to his left. The sword in his right hand, point resting on the dais, was trembling.

Standing in an alcove to one side, Nisall wanted to hurry forward, reaching out for the beleaguered, frightened Edur.

But Triban Gnol stood facing the throne. This audience belonged to him and him alone; nor would the Chancellor countenance any interruption from her. He clearly detested her very presence, but on that detail Rhulad had insisted – Nisall's only victory thus far.

'Highness, I agree with you. Your father, alas, insisted I convey to you his wishes. He would greet his most cherished son. Further, he brings dire news—'

'His favourite kind,' Rhulad muttered, eyes flickering as if he was seeking an escape from the chamber. 'Cherished? His word? No, I thought not. What he cherishes is my power – he wants it for himself. Him and Binadas—'

'Forgive my interruption, Highness,' Triban Gnol said, bowing his head. 'There is news of Binadas.'

The Emperor flinched. Licked dry lips. 'What has happened?'

'It is now known,' the Chancellor replied, 'that Binadas was murdered. He was commanding a section of the fleet. There was a battle with an unknown enemy. Terrible sorcery was exchanged, and the remnants of both fleets were plunged into the Nascent, there to complete their battle in that flooded realm. Yet, this was all prelude. After the remaining enemy ships fled, a demon came upon Binadas's ship. Such was its ferocity that all the Edur were slaughtered. Binadas himself was pinned to his chair by a spear flung by that demon.'

'How,' Rhulad croaked, 'how is all this known?'

'Your father . . . dreamed. In that dream he found himself a silent, ghostly witness, drawn there as if by the caprice of a malevolent god.'

'What of that demon? Does it still haunt the Nascent? I shall hunt it down, I shall destroy it. Yes, there must be vengeance. He was my brother. I sent him, my brother, sent him. They all die by my word. All of them, and this is what my father will tell me – oh how he hungers for that moment, but he shall not have it! The demon, yes, the demon who stalks my kin . . .' His fevered ramble trickled away, and so ravaged was Rhulad's face that Nisall had to look away, lest she cry out.

'Highness,' the Chancellor said in a quiet voice.

Nisall stiffened – this is what Triban Gnol was working towards – all that had come before was for this precise moment.

'Highness, the demon has been delivered. It is here, Emperor.'

Rhulad seemed to shrink back into himself. He said nothing, though his mouth worked.

'A challenger,' Triban Gnol continued. 'Tarthenal blood, yet purer, Hanradi Khalag claims, than any Tarthenal of this continent. Tomad knew him for what he was the moment the giant warrior took his first step onto Edur bloodwood. Knew him, yet could not face him, for Binadas's soul is in the Tarthenal's shadow – along with a thousand other fell victims. They clamour, one and all, for both freedom and vengeance. Highness, the truth must now be clear to you. Your god has delivered him. To you, so that you may slay him, so that you may avenge your brother's death.'

'Yes,' Rhulad whispered. 'He laughs – oh, how he laughs. Binadas, are you close? Close to me now? Do you yearn for freedom? Well, if I cannot have it, why should you? No, there is no hurry now, is there? You wanted this throne, and now you learn how it feels – just a hint, yes, of all that haunts me.'

'Highness,' the Chancellor murmured, 'are you not eager to avenge Binadas? Tomad—'

'Tomad!' Rhulad jolted on the throne, glared at Triban Gnol – who visibly rocked back. 'He saw the demon slay Binadas, and now he thinks it will do the same to me! *That* is the desire for vengeance at work here, you fish-skinned fool! Tomad wants me to die because I killed Binadas! And Trull! I have killed his children! But whose blood burns in my veins? *Whose?* Where is Hanradi? Oh, I know why he will not be found in the outer room – he goes to Hannan Mosag! They plunge into Darkness and whisper of betrayal – I am past my patience with them!'

Triban Gnol spread his hands. 'Highness, I had intended to speak to you of this, but at another time—'

'Of what? Out with it!'

'A humble inquiry from Invigilator Karos Invictad, Highness. With all respect, I assure you, he asks your will in regard to matters of treason – not among the Letherii, of course, for he has that well in hand – but among the Tiste Edur themselves . . .'

Nisall's gasp echoed in the suddenly silent room. She looked across to where Edur guards were stationed, and saw them motionless as statues.

Rhulad looked ready to weep. 'Treason among the Edur? My Edur? No, this cannot be – has he proof?'

A faint shrug. 'Highness, I doubt he would have ventured this inquiry had he not inadvertently stumbled on some . . . sensitive information.'

'Go away. Get out. Get out!'

Triban Gnol bowed, then backed from the chamber. Perhaps he'd gone too far, yet the seed had been planted. In most fertile soil.

As soon as the outer doors closed, Nisall stepped from the alcove. Rhulad waved her closer.

'My love,' he whispered in a child's voice, 'what am I to do? The demon – they brought it here.'

'You cannot be defeated, Emperor.'

'And to destroy it, how many times must I die? No, I'm not ready. Binadas was a powerful sorceror, rival to the Warlock King himself. My brother . . .'

'It may be,' Nisall ventured, 'that the Chancellor erred in the details of that. It may indeed be that Tomad's dream was a deceitful sending – there are many gods and spirits out there who see the Crippled God as an enemy.'

'No more. I am cursed into confusion; I don't understand any of this. What is happening, Nisall?'

'Palace ambitions, beloved. The return of the fleets has stirred things up.'

'My own Edur . . . plotting treason . . .'

She reached out and set a hand on his left shoulder. The lightest of touches, momentary, then withdrawn once more. *Dare I?* 'Karos Invictad is perhaps the most ambitious of them all. He revels in his reign of terror among the Letherii, and would expand it to include the Tiste Edur. Highness, I am Letherii – I know men like the Invigilator, I know what drives them, what feeds their malign souls. He hungers for control, for his heart quails in fear at all that is outside his control – at chaos itself. In his world, he is assailed on all sides. Highness, Karos Invictad's ideal world is one surrounded by a sea of corpses, every unknown and unknowable obliterated. And even then, he will find no peace.'

'Perhaps he should face me in the arena,' Rhulad said, with a sudden vicious smile. 'Face to face with a child of chaos, yes? But no, I need him to hunt down his Letherii. The traitors.'

'And shall this Letherii be granted domination over Tiste Edur as well?'

'Treason is colourless,' Rhulad said, shifting uneasily on the throne once more. 'It flows unseen no matter the hue of blood. I have not decided on that. I need to think, to understand. Perhaps I should summon the Chancellor once again.'

'Highness, you once appointed an Edur to oversee the Patriotists. Do you recall?'

'Of course I do. Do you think me an idiot, woman?'

'Perhaps Bruthen Trana—'

'Yes, that's him. Not once has he reported to me. Has he done as I commanded? How do I even know?'

'Summon him, then, Highness.'

'Why does he hide from me? Unless he conspires with the other traitors.'

'Highness, I know for a truth that he seeks an audience with you almost daily.'

'You?' Rhulad glanced over at her, eyes narrowing. 'How?'

'Bruthen Trana sought me out, beseeching me to speak to you on his behalf. The Chancellor denies him an audience with you—'

'Triban Gnol cannot deny such things! He is a Letherii! Where are my Edur? Why do I never see them? And now Tomad has returned, and Hanradi Khalag! None of them will speak to me!'

'Highness, Tomad waits in the outer chamber—'

'He knew I would deny him. You are confusing me, whore. I don't need you – I don't need anyone! I just need time. To think. That is all. They're all frightened of me, and with good reason, oh yes. Traitors are always frightened, and when their schemes are discovered, oh how they plead for their lives! Perhaps I should kill everyone – a sea of corpses, then there would be peace. And that is all I want. Peace. Tell me, are the people happy, Nisall?'

She bowed her head. 'I do not know, Highness.'

'Are you? Are you happy with me?'

'I feel naught but love for you, Emperor. My heart is yours.'

'The same words you spoke to Diskanar, no doubt. And all the other men you've bedded. Have your slaves draw a bath – you stink of sweat, woman. Then await me beneath silks.' He raised his voice. 'Call the Chancellor! We wish to speak to him immediately! Go, Nisall, your Letherii stink makes me ill.'

As she backed away Rhulad raised his free hand. 'My dearest, the golden silks – you are like a pearl among those. The sweetest pearl . . .'

Bruthen Trana waited in the corridor until Tomad Sengar, denied audience with the Emperor, departed the Citizens' Chamber. Stepping into the elder's path he bowed and said, 'I greet you, Tomad Sengar.'

Distracted, the older Tiste Edur frowned at him. 'Den-Ratha. What do you wish from me?'

'A word or two, no more than that. I am Bruthen Trana—'

'One of Rhulad's sycophants.'

'Alas, no. I was appointed early in the regime to oversee the Letherii security organization known as the Patriotists. As part of my responsibilities, I was to report to the Emperor in person each week. As of yet, I have not once addressed him. The Chancellor has interposed himself and turns me away each and every time.'

'My youngest son suckles at Gnol's tit,' Tomad Sengar said in a low, bitter voice.

'It is my belief,' Bruthen Trana said, 'that the Emperor himself is not entirely away of the extent of the barriers the Chancellor and his agents have raised around him, Elder Sengar. Although I have sought to penetrate them, I have failed thus far.'

'Then why turn to me, Den-Ratha? I am even less able to reach through to my son.'

'It is the Tiste Edur who are being isolated from their Emperor,' Bruthen said. 'Not just you and I. All of us.'

'Hannan Mosag—'

'Is reviled, for it is well understood that the Warlock King is responsible for all of this. His ambition, his pact with an evil god. He sought the sword for himself, did he not?'

'Then Rhulad is truly alone?'

183

Bruthen Trana nodded, then added, 'There is a possibility . . . there is one person. The Letherii woman who is his First Concubine—'

'A Letherii?' Tomad snarled. 'You must be mad. She is an agent for Gnol, a spy. She has corrupted Rhulad – how else could she remain as First Concubine? My son would never have taken her, unless she had some nefarious hold over him.' The snarl twisted the elder's features. 'You are being used, warrior. You and I shall not speak again.'

Tomad Sengar pushed him to one side and marched down the corridor. Bruthen Trana turned to watch him go.

Drawing out a crimson silk cloth, Karos Invictad daubed at the sweat on his brow, his eyes fixed on the strange two-headed insect as it circled in place, round and round and round in its box cage. 'Not a single arrangement of tiles will halt this confounded, brainless creature. I begin to believe this is a hoax.'

'Were it me, sir,' Tanal Yathvanar said, 'I would have crushed the whole contraption under heel long ago. Indeed it must be a hoax – the proof is that you have not defeated it yet.'

The Invigilator's gaze lifted, regarded Tanal. 'I do not know which is the more disgusting, you acknowledging defeat by an insect, or your pathetic attempts at flattery.' He set the cloth down on the table and leaned back. 'The studied pursuit of solutions requires patience, and, more, a certain cast of intellect. This is why you will never achieve more than you have, Tanal Yathvanar. You totter at the very edge of your competence – ah, no need for the blood to so rush to your face, it is what you are that I find so useful to me. Furthermore, you display uncommon wisdom in restraining your ambition, so that you make no effort to attempt what is beyond your capacity. That is a rare talent. Now, what have you to report to me this fine afternoon?'

'Master, we have come very close to seeing our efforts extended to include the Tiste Edur.'

Karos Invictad's brows rose. 'Triban Gnol has spoken to the Emperor?'

'He has. Of course, the Emperor was shaken by the notion of traitors among the Edur. So much so that he ordered the Chancellor from the throne room. For a while.' Tanal Yathvanar smiled. 'A quarter-bell, apparently. The subject was not broached again that day, yet it is clear that Rhulad's suspicions of his fellow Edur have burgeoned.'

'Very well. It will not be long, then.' The Invigilator leaned forward again, frowning down at the puzzle box. 'It is important that all obstacles be removed. The only words the Emperor should be hearing should come from the Chancellor. Tanal, prepare a dossier on the First Concubine.' He looked up again. 'You understand, don't you, that your opportunity to free that scholar you have chained far below has passed? There is no choice now but that she must disappear.'

Unable to speak, Tanal Yathvanar simply nodded.

'I note this – and with some urgency – because you have no doubt grown weary of her in any case, and if not, you should have. I trust I am understood. Would you not enjoy replacing her with the First Concubine?' Karos smiled.

Tanal licked dry lips. 'Such a dossier will be difficult, Master—'

'Don't be a fool. Work with the Chancellor's agents. We're not interested in factual reportage here. Invent what we need to incriminate her. That should not be difficult. Errant knows, we have had enough practice.'

'Even so – forgive me, sir – but she is the Emperor's only lover.'

'You do not understand at all, do you? She is not Rhulad's first love. No, that woman, an Edur, killed herself – oh, never mind the official version, I have witness reports of that tragic event. She was carrying the Emperor's child. Thus, in every respect imaginable, she betrayed him. Tanal, for Rhulad the rains have just passed, and while the clay feels firm underfoot, it is in truth thin as papyrus. At the first intimation of suspicion, Rhulad will lose his mind to rage – we will be lucky to wrest the woman from his clutches. Accordingly, the arrest must take effect in the palace, in private, when the First Concubine is alone. She must then be brought here immediately.'

'Do you not believe the Emperor will demand her return?'

'The Chancellor will advise against it, of course. Please, Tanal Yathvanar, leave the subtle details of human – and Edur – natures to those of us who fully comprehend them. You shall have the woman, fear not. To do with as you please – once we have her confession, that is. Bloodied and bruised, is that not how you prefer them? Now, leave me. I believe I have arrived at a solution to this contraption.'

Tanal Yathvanar stood outside the closed door for a time, struggling to slow his heart, his mind racing. Murder Janath Anar? Make her disappear like all the others? *Fattening the crabs at the bottom of the river? Oh, Errant, I do not know ... if ... I do not know—*

From behind the office door came a snarl of frustration.

Oddly enough, the sound delighted him. *Yes, you towering intellect, it defeats you again. That two-headed nightmare in miniature. For all your lofty musings on your own genius, this puzzle confounds you. Perhaps, Invigilator, the world is not how you would have it, not so clear, not so perfectly designed to welcome your domination.*

He forced himself forward, down the hall. No, he would not kill Janath Anar. He loved her. Karos Invictad loved only himself – it had always been so, Tanal suspected, and that was not going to change. The Invigilator understood nothing of human nature, no matter how he might delude himself. Indeed, Karos had given himself away in that careless command to kill her. *Yes, Invigilator, this is my revelation. I am smarter than you. I am superior in all the ways that truly matter. You and your power, it is all compensation for what you do not understand about the world, for the void in your soul where compassion belongs. Compassion, and the love that one can feel for another person.*

He would tell her, now. He would confess the depth of his feelings, and then he would unchain her, and they would flee. Out of Letheras. Beyond the reach of the Patriotists. Together, they would make their lives anew.

He hurried down the damp, worn stairs, beyond the sight of everyone now, down into his own private world. Where his love awaited him.

The Invigilator could not reach everywhere – as Tanal was about to prove.

Down through darkness, all so familiar now he no longer needed a lantern. Where *he* ruled, not Karos Invictad, no, not here. This was why the Invigilator attacked him again and again, with ever the same weapon, the implicit threat of exposure, of defamation of Tanal Yathvanar's good name. But all these crimes, they belonged to Karos Invictad. Imagine the counter-charges Tanal could level against him, if he needed to – he had copies of records; he knew where every secret was buried. The accounts of the bloodstained wealth the Invigilator had amassed from the estates of his victims – Tanal knew where those records were kept. And as for the corpses of the ones who had disappeared . . .

Reaching the barred door to the torture chamber, he drew down the lantern he had left on a ledge and, after a few efforts, struck the wick alight. He lifted clear the heavy bar and pushed open the heavy door with one hand.

'Back so soon?' The voice was a raw croak.

Tanal stepped into the chamber. 'You have fouled yourself again. No matter – this is the last time, Janath Anar.'

'Come to kill me, then. So be it. You should have done that long ago. I look forward to leaving this broken flesh. You cannot chain a ghost. And so, with my death, you shall become the prisoner. You shall be the one who is tormented. For as long as you live, and I do hope it is long, I shall whisper in your ear—' She broke into a fit of coughing.

He walked closer, feeling emptied inside, his every determination stripped away by the vehemence in her words.

The manacles seemed to weep blood – she had been struggling against her fetters again. *Dreaming of haunting me, of destroying me. How is she any different? How could I have expected her to be any different?* 'Look at you,' he said in a low voice. 'Not even human any more – do you not care about your appearance, about how you want me to see you when I come here?'

'You're right,' she said in a grating voice, 'I should have waited until you arrived, until you came close. Then voided all over you. I'm sorry. I'm afraid my bowels are in bad shape right now – the muscles are weakening, inevitably.'

'You'll not haunt me, woman, your soul is too useless – the Abyss will sweep it away, I'm sure. Besides, I won't kill you for a long while yet—'

'I don't think it's up to you any more, Tanal Yathvanar.'

'It's *all* up to me!' he shrieked. 'All of it!'

He stalked over to her and began unshackling her arms, then her legs. She lost consciousness before he had freed her second wrist, and slid into a heap that almost snapped both her legs before he managed to work the manacles from her battered, torn ankles.

She weighed almost nothing, and he was able to move quickly, up twenty or so stairs, until he reached a side passage. The slimy cobble floor underfoot gradually sloped downward as he shambled along, the woman over one shoulder, the lantern swinging from his free hand. Rats scurried from his path, out to the sides where deep, narrow gutters had been cut by an almost constant flow of runoff.

Eventually, the drip of dark water from the curved ceiling overhead became a veritable rain. The droplets revived Janath momentarily, enough for her to moan, then cough for a half-dozen strides – he was thankful when she swooned once more, and the feeble clawing on his back ceased.

And now came the stench. *Disappeared? Oh no, they are here. All of them. All the ones Karos Invictad didn't like, didn't need, wanted out of the way.*

Into the first of the huge domed chambers with its stone walkway encircling a deep well, in which white-shelled crabs clambered amidst bones. This well was entirely filled, which is what had forced the opening of another, then another and another – there were so many of them, down here beneath the river.

Arriving at the last of the chambers, Tanal set her down, where he shackled one of her legs to the wall. On either side of her, she had company, although neither victim was alive. He stepped back as she stirred once more.

'This is temporary,' he said. 'You won't be joining your friends beside you. When I return – and it won't be long – I will move you again. To a new cell, known to no-one but me. Where I will teach you to love me. You'll see, Janath Anar. I am not the monster you believe me to be. Karos Invictad is the monster – he has twisted me, he has made me into what I am. But Karos Invictad is not a god. Not immortal. Not . . .

infallible. As we shall all discover. He thinks I want her, that whore of the Emperor's – that dirty, fallen bitch. He could not be more wrong. Oh, there's so much to do now, but I promise I won't be gone long. You'll see, my love . . .'

She awoke to the sound of his footfalls, dwindling, then lost to the trickle and drip of water. It was dark, and cold, colder than it had ever been before – she was somewhere else now, some other crypt, *but the same nightmare.*

She lifted a hand – as best she could – and wiped at her face. Her hand came away slick with slime. Yet . . . *the chains, they're gone.* She struggled to draw her limbs inward, then almost immediately heard the rattle of iron links snaking across stone. *Ah, not completely.*

And now pain arrived, in every joint, piercing fire. Ligaments and tendons, stretched for so long, now began contracting like burning ropes – *oh, Errant take me—*

Her eyes flickered open once more, and with returning consciousness she became aware of savage hunger, coiling in her shrunken stomach. Watery waste trickled loose.

There was no point in weeping. No point in wondering which of them was madder – him for his base appetites and senseless cruelty, or her for clinging so to this remnant of a life. A battle of wills, yet profoundly unequal – she knew that in her heart, had known it all along.

The succession of grand lectures she had devised in her mind all proved hollow conceits, their taste too bitter to bear. He had defeated her, because his were weapons without reason – *and so I answered with my own madness. I thought it would work. Instead, I ended up surrendering all that I had that was of any worth.*

And so now, the cold of death stealing over me, I can only dream of becoming a vengeful ghost, eager to torment the one who tormented me, eager to be to him as he was to me. Believing that such a balance was just, was righteous.

Madness. To give in kind is to be in kind.

So now, let me leave here, for ever gone—

And she felt that madness reach out to her, an embrace that would sweep away her sense of self, her knowledge of who she had been, once, that proud, smug academic with her pristine intellect ordering and reordering the world. Until even practicality was a quaint notion, not even worthy of discourse, because the world outside wasn't worth reaching out to, not really – besides, it was sullied, wasn't it? By men like Tanal Yathvanar and Karos Invictad – the ones who revelled in the filth they made, because only the stench of excess could reach through to their numbed senses—

—as it reaches through to mine. Listen! He returns, step by hesitant step—

A calloused hand settled on her brow.

Janath Anar opened her eyes.

Faint light, coming from every direction. Warm light, gentle as a breath. Looming above her was a face. Old, lined and weathered, with eyes deep as the seas, even as tears made them glisten.

She felt the chain being dragged close. Then the old man tugged with one hand and the links parted like rotted reeds. He reached down, then, and lifted her effortlessly.

Abyss, yours is such a gentle face . . .

Darkness, once more.

Beneath the bed of the river, below silts almost a storey thick, rested the remains of almost sixteen thousand citizens of Letheras. Their bones filled ancient wells that had been drilled before the river's arrival – before the drainage course from the far eastern mountains changed cataclysmically, making the serpent lash its tail, the torrent carving a new channel, one that inundated a nascent city countless millennia ago.

Letherii engineers centuries past had stumbled upon these submerged constructs, wondering at the humped corridors and the domed chambers, wondering at the huge, deep wells with their clear, cold water. And baffled to explain how such tunnels remained more or less dry, the cut channels seeming to absorb water like runners of sponge.

No records existed any more recounting these discoveries – the tunnels and chambers and wells were lost knowledge to all but a chosen few. And of the existence of parallel passages, the hidden doors in the walls of corridors, and the hundreds of lesser tombs, not even those few were aware. Certain secrets belonged exclusively to the gods.

The Elder God carried the starved, brutalized woman into one of those side passages, the cantilevered door swinging shut noiselessly behind him. In his mind there was recrimination, a seething torrent of anger at himself. He had not imagined the full extent of depravity and slaughter conducted by the Patriotists, and he was sorely tempted to awaken himself, unleashing his fullest wrath upon these unmitigated sadists.

Of course, that would lead to unwarranted attention, which would no doubt result in yet greater slaughter, and one that made no distinction between those who deserved death and those who did not. This was the curse of power, after all.

As, he well knew, Karos Invictad would soon discover.

You fool, Invigilator. Who has turned his deadly regard upon you? Deadly, oh my, yes indeed.

Though few might comprehend that, given the modestly handsome, thoroughly benign features surrounding that face.

Even so, Karos Invictad. Tehol Beddict has decided that you must go. And I almost pity you.

Tehol Beddict was on his knees on the dirt floor of the hovel, rummaging through a small heap of debris, when he heard a scuffling sound at the doorway. He glanced over a shoulder. 'Ublala Pung, good evening, my friend.'

The huge half-blood Tarthenal edged into the chamber, hunching beneath the low ceiling. 'What are you doing?'

'A wooden spoon – or at least the fragment thereof. Employed in a central role in the preparation of this morning's meal. I dread the possibility that Bugg tossed it into the hearth. Ah! Here, see that? A curdle of fat remains on it!'

'Looks like dirt to me, Tehol Beddict.'

'Well, even dirt has flavour,' he replied, crawling over to the pot simmering on the hearth. 'Finally, my soup acquires subtle sumptuousness. Can you believe this, Ublala Pung? Look at me, reduced to menial chores, even unto preparing my own meals! I tell you, my manservant's head has grown too large by far. He rises above his station, does Bugg. Perhaps you could box him about the ears for me. Now, I am not as indifferent as you think – there is the glow of heightened excitement in your rather blunt, dogged features. What has happened? Has Shurq Elalle returned, then?'

'Would I be here if she had?' Ublala asked. 'No, Tehol Beddict. She is gone. Out to the seas, with all her pirated young men. I was too big, you see. I had to sleep on the deck, no matter the weather, and that was no fun – and those pirates, they kept wanting to tie sails to me, laughing as if that was funny or something.'

'Ah well, sailors have simple minds, friend. And pirates are failed sailors, mostly, taking simpledom to profound extremes—'

'What? I have news, you know.'

'Do you now?'

'I do.'

'Can I hear it?'

'Do you want to?'

'Why yes, else I would not have asked.'

'Really want to?'

'Look, if you're not interested in telling me—'

'No, I'm interested. In telling you. That is why I'm here, although I will have some of that soup if you're offering.'

'Ublala Pung, you are most welcome to this soup, but first let me fish out this rag I fed into the broth, lest you choke or something.'

'Rag? What kind of rag?'

'Well, squarish, mostly. I believe it was used to wipe down a kitchen counter, thereby absorbing countless assorted foodstuffs.'

'Tehol Beddict, one of the pure blood has come to the city.'

'Is that your news?'

The huge man nodded solemnly.

'Pure blood?'

Another nod.

'So, a Tarthenal—'

'No,' Ublala Pung cut in. '*Pure* blood. Purer than any Tarthenal. And he carries a stone sword. On his face are the most terrifying tattoos, like a shattered tile. He is greatly scarred and countless ghosts swirl in his wake—'

'Ghosts? You could see ghosts following him around?'

'See them? Of course not. But I smelled them.'

'Really? So what do ghosts smell like? Never mind. A Tarthenal who's more Tarthenal than any Tarthenal has arrived in the city. What does he want?'

'You do not understand, Tehol Beddict. He is a champion. He is here to challenge the Emperor.'

'Oh, the poor man.'

'Yes. The poor man, but he's not a man, is he? He's a Tiste Edur.'

Tehol Beddict frowned across at Ublala Pung. 'Ah, we were speaking of two different poor men. Well, a short time earlier a runner from Rucket visited – it seems Scale House collapsed during that earthquake. But it was not your normal earthquake, such as never occur around here anyway. Ublala Pung, there is another champion, one far more frightening than any pure blood Tarthenal. There is great consternation among the Rat Catchers, all of whom seem to know more than they're letting on. The view seems to be that this time the Emperor's search has drawn in a most deadly haul.'

'Well, I don't know nothing about that,' Ublala Pung said, rubbing thoughtfully at the bristle on his chin. 'Only, this pure blood has a stone sword. Chipped, like those old spear-points people are selling in the Downs Market. It's almost as tall as he is, and he's taller than me. I saw him pick up a Letherii guard and throw him away.'

'Throw him away?'

'Like a small sack of . . . of mushrooms or something.'

'So his temper is even worse than yours, then.'

'Pure bloods know no fear.'

'Right. So how is it you know about pure bloods?'

'The Sereghal. Our gods, the ones I helped to kill, they were fallen pure bloods. Cast out.'

'So the one who has just arrived, he's the equivalent of one of your gods, Ublala Pung? Please, don't tell me you're planning on trying to kill him. I mean, he has a stone sword and all.'

'Kill him? No, you don't understand, Tehol Beddict. This one, this pure blood, he is worthy of true worship. Not the way we appeased the Sereghal – that was to keep them away. Wait and see, wait and see what is going to happen. My kin will gather, once the word spreads. They will gather.'

'What if the Emperor kills him?'

Ublala Pung simply shook his head.

They both looked over as Bugg appeared in the doorway, in his arms the body of a naked woman.

'Now really,' Tehol said, 'the pot's not nearly big enough. Besides, hungry as I am, there are limits and eating academics far exceeds them—'

The manservant frowned. 'You recognize this woman?'

'I do, from my former life, replete as it was with stern tutors and the occasional subjects of youthful crushes and the like. Alas, she looks much worse for wear. I had always heard that the world of scholars was cut-throat – what debate on nuances resulted in this, I wonder?'

Bugg carried her over and set her down on his own sleeping pallet.

As the manservant stepped back, Ublala Pung stepped close and struck Bugg in the side of the head, hard enough to send the old man reeling against a wall.

'Wait!' Tehol shouted to the giant. 'No more!'

Rubbing at his temple, Bugg blinked up at Ublala Pung. 'What was that all about?' he demanded.

'Tehol said—'

'Never mind what I said, Ublala. It was but a passing thought, a musing devoid of substance, a careless utterance disconnected in every way from physical action. Never intended—'

'You said he needed boxing about the head, Tehol Beddict. You asked me – because it'd got bigger or something, so I needed to puncture it so it'd get smaller again. It didn't look any bigger to me. But that's what you said. He was above his situation, you said—'

'Station, not situation. My point is – both of you – stop looking at me like that. My point was, I was but voicing a few minor complaints of a domestic nature here. Not once suspecting that Ublala Pung would take me so literally.'

'Master, he *is* Ublala Pung.'

'I know, I know. Clearly, all the once-finely honed edges of my intellect have worn off of late.' Then his expression brightened. 'But now I have a tutor!'

'A victim of the Patriotists,' Bugg said, eyeing Ublala askance as he made his way over to the pot on the hearth. 'Abyss below, Master, this barely passes as muddy water.'

'Aye, alas, in dire need of your culinary magic. The Patriotists? You broke her out of prison?'

'In a manner of speaking. I do not anticipate a city-wide manhunt, however. She was to have been one of the ones who simply vanished.'

Ublala Pung grunted a laugh. 'They'd never find her if it was a manhunt.'

The other two men looked across at him.

The half-blood Tarthenal gestured at the obvious. 'Look, she's got breasts and stuff.'

Bugg's tone was soft as he said to Tehol, 'She needs gentle healing, Master. And peace.'

'Well, no better refuge from the dreads of the world than Tehol Beddict's abode.'

'A manhunt.' Ublala laughed again, then shook his head. 'Them Patriotists are idiots.'

CHAPTER EIGHT

When stone is water, time is ice.
When all is frozen in place
fates rain down in fell torrent.

My face revealed, in this stone that is water.
The ripples locked hard to its shape
a countenance passing strange.

Ages will hide when stone is water.
Cycles bound in these depths
are flawed illusions breaking the stream.

When stone is water, time is ice.
When all is frozen in place
our lives are stones in the torrent.

And we rain down, rain down
like water on stone
with every strike of the hand.

Water and Stone
Elder Fent

THE REALM OF SHADOW WAS HOME TO BRUTAL PLACES, YET NOT ONE could match the brutality of shadows upon the soul. Such thoughts haunted Cotillion these days. He stood on a rise, before him a gentle, elongated slope reaching down to a lake's placid waters. A makeshift camp was visible on a level terrace forty paces to his left, a single longhouse flanked by half-buried outbuildings, including stable and coop. The entire arrangement – fortunately unoccupied at the time, excepting a dozen hens and a rooster, one irritated rook with a gimp leg and two milk cows – had been stolen from another realm, captured by some vagary of happenstance, or, more likely, the consequence of the breaking of mysterious laws, as seemed to occur sporadically during Shadow Realm's endless migration.

However it had arrived, Shadowthrone learned of it in time to despatch a flurry of wraiths to lay claim to the buildings and livestock, saving them from predation by roving demons or, indeed, one of the Hounds.

Following the disaster at the First Throne, the score of survivors had been delivered to this place, to wander and wonder at the strange artifacts left by the previous inhabitants: the curved wooden prows surmounting the peaks of the longhouse with their intricate, serpentine carvings; the mysterious totemic jewellery, mostly of silver although amber seemed common as well; the bolts of cloth, wool both coarse and fine; wooden bowls and cups of hammered bronze. Wandering through it all, dazed, a blankness in their eyes . . .

Recovering.

As if such a thing is possible.

Off to his right, a lone cape-shrouded figure stood at the water's edge, motionless, seeming to stare out on the unmarred expanse of the lake. There was nothing normal to this lake, Cotillion knew, although the scene it presented from this section of the shore was deceptively serene. Barring the lack of birds. And the absence of molluscs, crustaceans or even insects.

Every scrap of food to feed the livestock – and the miserable rook – was brought in by the wraiths Shadowthrone had assigned to the task. For all of that, the rooster had died mere days after arriving. *Died from grief, I expect. Not a single dawn to crow awake.*

He could hear voices from somewhere just beyond the longhouse. Panek, Aystar and the other surviving children – well, hardly children any more. They'd seen battle, they'd seen their friends die, they knew the world – every world – was an unpleasant place where a human's life was not worth much. They knew, too, what it meant to be used.

Further down the beach, well past the lone hooded figure, walked Trull Sengar and the T'lan Imass, Onrack the Broken. Like an artist with his deathless muse, or perhaps at his shoulder a critic of ghastly mien. An odd friendship, that one. But then, T'lan Imass were full of surprises.

Sighing, Cotillion set off down the slope.

The hooded head half turned at his approach. A face the hue of burnished leather, eyes dark beneath the felted wool rim of the hood. 'Have you come with the key, Cotillion?'

'Quick Ben, it is good to see that you have recovered.'

'More or less.'

'What key?'

The flash of a humourless smile. 'The one that sets me free.'

Cotillion stood beside the wizard and studied the murky expanse of water. 'I would imagine that you could leave here at any time. You are a High Mage, with more than one warren at your disposal. Force a gate, then walk through it.'

'Do you take me for a fool?' Quick Ben asked in a quiet voice. 'This damned realm is wandering. There's no telling where I would come out, although if I guess correctly, I would be in for a long swim.'

'Ah. Well, I'm afraid I pay little attention to such things these days. We are crossing an ocean, then?'

'So I suspect.'

'Then indeed, to journey anywhere you require our help.'

The wizard shot him a glance. 'As I thought. You have created pathways, gates with fixed exits. How did you manage that, Cotillion?'

'Oh, not our doing, I assure you. We simply stumbled onto them, in a manner of speaking.'

'The Azath.'

'Very good. You always were sharp, Ben Delat.'

A grunt. 'I've not used that version of my name in a long time.'

'Oh? When was the last time – do you recall?'

'These Azath,' Quick Ben said, clearly ignoring the question. 'The House of Shadow itself, here in this realm, correct? Somehow, it has usurped the gate, the original gate. Kurald Emurlahn. The House exists both as a cast shadow and as its true physical manifestation. No distinction can be made between the two. A nexus . . . but that is not unusual for Azath constructs, is it? What is, however, is that the gate to Kurald Emurlahn was vulnerable in the first place, to such a usurpation.'

'Necessity, I expect,' said Cotillion, frowning at seeing a slow sweep of broad ripples approach the shore, their source somewhere further out. *Not at all what it seems . . .*

'What do you mean?'

The god shrugged. 'The realm was shattered. Dying.'

'The Azath participated in healing the fragments? Intentional? By design, by intellect? Or in the manner that blood dries to create a scab? Is the Azath nothing more than some kind of natural immune system, such as our bodies unleash to fight illness?'

'The breadth of your scholarly knowledge is impressive, Quick Ben.'

'Never mind that. The warrens were K'rul's supreme sacrifice – his own flesh, his own blood. But not the *Elder* Warrens – or so we are to believe. Whose veins were opened to create those, Cotillion?'

'I wish I knew. No, rather, I don't. I doubt it is relevant, in any case. Does the Azath simply respond to damage, or is there a guiding intelligence behind its actions? I cannot answer you. I doubt anyone can. Does it even matter?'

'I don't know, to be honest. But not knowing makes me nervous.'

'I have a key for you,' Cotillion said after a moment. Trull Sengar and Onrack were now walking towards them. 'For the three of you, in fact. If you want it.'

'There's a choice?'

'Not for them,' Cotillion said, nodding in the direction of Trull and the T'lan Imass. 'And they could use your help.'

'The same was true of Kalam Mekhar,' Quick Ben said. 'Not to mention Adjunct Tavore.'

'They survived,' Cotillion replied.

'You cannot be sure, though – not with Kalam. You can't be entirely sure, can you?'

'He was alive when the Deadhouse took him.'

'So Shadowthrone claims.'

'He would not lie.'

The wizard barked a bitter laugh.

'Kalam still lives, Quick Ben. The Deadhouse has him, beyond the reach of time itself. Yet he will heal. The poison will degrade, become inert. Shadowthrone saved the assassin's life—'

'Why?'

'Now that is a harder question to answer,' Cotillion admitted. 'Perhaps simply to defy Laseen, and you should not be surprised if that is his only reason. Believe me, for Shadowthrone, it suffices.' *Be glad, Ben Adaephon Delat, that I do not tell you his real reason.*

Trull Sengar and Onrack drew close, then halted. The Tiste Edur's new stone-tipped spear was strapped to his back; he was wearing a long cape against the chill, the wool dyed deep burgundy – one of the more useful treasures found in the longhouse. It was held in place by an exquisite silver brooch depicting some sort of stylized hammer. At his side, Onrack the Broken's skeletal frame was so battered, dented and fractured it was a wonder that the warrior was still in one piece.

The T'lan Imass spoke, 'This lake, god. The shore opposite . . .'

'What of it?'

'It does not exist.'

Cotillion nodded.

Trull Sengar asked, 'How can that be? Onrack says it's not a gate, on the other side. It's not anything at all.'

Cotillion ran a hand through his hair, then scratched his chin – realizing he needed to shave – and squinted out on the water. 'The other side is . . . unresolved.'

'What does that mean?' Quick Ben demanded.

'To fully understand, you will have to go there, wizard. The three of you – that is the path of your journey. And you must leave soon.'

'Forgive us for being unimpressed,' the Tiste Edur said drily. 'The last nightmare you sent us into has made us rather reluctant adventurers. We need a better reason, Cotillion.'

'I imagine you do.'

'We're waiting,' Quick Ben said, crossing his arms.

'Alas, I cannot help you. Any explanation I attempt will affect your perception of what you will find, at your journey's end. And that must not be allowed to happen, because the manner in which you perceive will shape and indeed define the reality that awaits you.' He sighed again. 'I know, that's not very helpful.'

'Then summon Shadowthrone,' Trull Sengar said. 'Maybe he can do better.'

Cotillion shrugged, then nodded.

A dozen heartbeats later a mostly formless shadow rose in their midst, from which emerged a knobby cane at the end of a skinny, gnarled arm. The god glanced about, then down, to find itself ankle-deep in water. Hissing, Shadowthrone picked up the tattered ends of his cloak then pranced onto dry land. 'Oh, wasn't that amusing?' he sang. 'Wretches, all of you. What do you want? I'm busy. Do you understand? Busy.'

Onrack pointed one skeletal arm out towards the lake. 'Cotillion would send us across this water, on a mission he will not explain, to achieve goals he refuses to define, in a place he cannot describe. We therefore call upon you, formless one, to deliver what he will not.'

Shadowthrone giggled.

Cotillion glanced away, suspecting what was coming.

'Delighted to, bony one. I respond in this manner. It is as Cotillion believes. The rooster died of grief.'

A curse from Quick Ben as Shadowthrone then swirled into nothingness.

Cotillion turned away. 'Supplies await you outside the longhouse. When you return down here, a boat will have been readied. Make your goodbyes to Minala and the children as brief as possible. The way ahead is long and arduous, and we are running out of time.'

The *Undying Gratitude* heeled hard to starboard, the gale bitter with the cold reek of ice. Pulling and half climbing his way across the aft deck as the crew struggled against the sudden onslaught, First Mate Skorgen Kaban reached the pilot station where Shurq Elalle, held in place by a leather harness, stood with legs planted wide.

She seemed impervious to the plunging temperature, with not even a hint of colour slapped to her cheeks by the buffeting wind. An uncanny woman indeed. Uncanny, insatiable, unearthly, she was like a sea goddess of old, a glamoured succubus luring them all to their doom –

but no, that was not a good thought, not now, not ever. Or at least for as long as he sailed with her.

'Captain! It's going to be close – them mountains of ice are closin' on the cut, maybe faster than we are! Where in the Errant's name did they come from?'

'We'll make it,' Shurq Elalle asserted. 'Come round into the lee of the island – it's the northwest shore that's going to get hammered. I'd be amazed if the citadel's walls on that side survive what's coming. Look at the Reach, Pretty, it's nothing but fangs of ice – wherever all this has come from, it's devouring the entire coast.'

'Damned cold, is what it is,' Skorgen said in a growl. 'Maybe we should turn round, Captain. That fleet never came after us anyway – we could head for Lether Mouth—'

'And starve before we're halfway there. No, Pretty, Second Maiden Fort's an independent state now, and I'm finding that rather appealing. Besides, I'm curious. Aren't you?'

'Not enough to risk getting crushed by them white jaws, Captain.'

'We'll make it.'

The foment that was the crest of the heaving bergs was the colour of old leather, shredded by the churning fragments of ice, tree roots, shattered trunks and huge broken rocks that seemed to defy the pull to the deep – at least for long enough to appear atop the water, like the leading edge of a slide, rolling on across the surface of the tumult before reluctantly vanishing into the depths.

Tumbling out from this surge like rotted curtains was fog, plucked and torn by the ferocious winds, and Shurq Elalle, facing astern, watched as the maelstrom heaved in their wake. It was gaining, but not fast enough; they were moments from rounding the isle's rocky headland, which looked to be formidable enough to shunt the ice aside, down its length.

At least, she hoped so. If not, then Second Maiden's harbour was doomed. *And so is my ship and crew.* As for herself, well, if she managed to avoid being crushed or frozen in place, she could probably work her way clear, maybe even clamber aboard for the long ride to the mainland's coast.

It won't come to that. Islands don't get pushed around. Buried, possibly, but then Fent Reach is where it's all piling up – what's chasing us here is just an outer arm, and before long it'll be fighting the tide. Errant fend, imagine what happened to the Edur homeland – that entire coast must have been chewed to pieces – or swallowed up entire. So what broke up the dam, that's what I want to know.

Groaning, the *Undying Gratitude* rounded the point, the wind quickly dropping off as the ship settled and began its crawl into the high-walled harbour. A prison island indeed – all the evidence remained: the massive fortifications, the towers with lines of sight and fire arcs facing both to sea and inland. Huge ballistae, mangonels and scorpions mounted on every available space, and in the harbour itself rock-pile islands held miniature forts festooned with signal flags, fast ten-man pursuit galleys moored alongside.

A dozen ships rode at anchor in the choppy waters. Along the docks, she saw, tiny figures were racing in every direction, like ants on a kicked nest. 'Pretty, have us drop anchor other side of that odd-looking dromon. Seems like nobody's going to pay us much attention – hear that roar? That's the northwest shore getting hit.'

'The whole damned island could go under, Captain.'

'That's why we're staying aboard – to see what happens. If we have to run east, I want us ready to do so.'

'Look, there's a harbour scow comin' our way.'

Damn. 'Typical. World's falling in but that don't stop the fee-takers. All right, prepare to receive them.'

The anchor had rattled down by the time the scow fought its way alongside. Two officious-looking women climbed aboard, one tall, the other short. The latter spoke first. 'Who's the captain here and where d'you hail from?'

'I am Captain Shurq Elalle. We've come up from Letheras. Twenty months at sea with a hold full of goods.'

The tall woman, thin, pale, with stringy blond hair, smiled. 'Very accommodating of you, dear. Now, if you'll be so kind, Brevity here will head down into the hold to inspect the cargo.'

The short dark-haired woman, Brevity, then said, 'And Pithy here will collect the anchoring fee.'

'Fifteen docks a day.'

'That's a little steep!'

'Well,' Pithy said with a lopsided shrug, 'it's looking like the harbour's days are numbered. We'd best get what we can.'

Brevity was frowning at Shurq's first mate. 'You wouldn't be Skorgen Kaban the Pretty, would you?'

'Aye, that's me.'

'I happen to have your lost eye, Skorgen. In a jar.'

The man scowled across at Shurq Elalle, then said, 'You and about fifty other people.'

'What? But I paid good money for that! How many people lose an eye sneezing? By the Errant, you're famous!'

'Sneeze is it? That's what you heard? And you believed it? Spirits of the deep, lass, and you paid the crook how much?'

Shurq said to Pithy, 'You and your friend here are welcome to inspect the cargo – but if we're not offloading that's as far as it goes, and whether we offload or not depends on the kinds of prices your buyers are prepared to offer.'

'I'll prove it to you,' Brevity said, advancing on Skorgen Kaban. 'It's a match all right – I can tell from here.'

'Can't be a match,' the first mate replied. 'The eye I lost was a different colour from this one.'

'You had different-coloured eyes?'

'That's right.'

'That's a curse among sailors.'

'Maybe that's why it ain't there no more.' Skorgen nodded towards the nearby dromon. 'Where's that hailing from? I never seen lines like those before – looks like it's seen a scrap or two, asides.'

Brevity shrugged. 'Foreigners. We get a few—'

'No more of that,' Pithy cut in. 'Check the cargo, dearie. Time's a-wasting.'

Shurq Elalle turned and examined the foreign ship with more intensity after that peculiar exchange. The dromon looked damned weather-beaten, she decided, but her first mate's lone eye had been sharp – the ship had been in a battle, one involving sorcery. Black, charred streaks latticed the hull like a painted web. *A whole lot of sorcery. That ship should be kindling.*

'Listen,' Pithy said, facing inland. 'They beat it back, like they said they would.'

The cataclysm in the making seemed to be dying a rapid death, there on the other side of the island where clouds of ice crystals billowed skyward. Shurq Elalle twisted round to look out to the sea to the south, past the promontory. Ice, looking like a massive frozen lake, was piling up in the wake of the violent vanguard that had come so close to wrecking the *Undying Gratitude*. But its energy was fast dissipating. A gust of warm wind backed across the deck.

Skorgen Kaban grunted. 'And how many sacrifices did they fling off the cliff to earn this appeasement?' He laughed. 'Then again, you probably got no shortage of prisoners!'

'There are no prisoners on this island,' Pithy said, assuming a lofty expression as she crossed her arms. 'In any case, you ignorant oaf, blood sacrifices wouldn't have helped – it's just ice, after all. The vast sheets up north went and broke to pieces – why, just a week past and we was sweating uncommon here, and that's not something we ever get on Second Maiden. I should know, I was born here.'

'Born to prisoners?'

'You didn't hear me, Skorgen Kaban? No prisoners on this island—'

'Not since you ousted your jailers, you mean.'

'Enough of that,' Shurq Elalle said, seeing the woman's umbrage ratchet up a few more notches on the old hoist pole – and it was plenty high enough already. 'Second Maiden is now independent, and for that I have boundless admiration. Tell me, how many Edur ships assailed your island in the invasion?'

Pithy snorted. 'They took one look at the fortifications, and one sniff at the mages we'd let loose on the walls, and went right round us.'

The captain's brows rose a fraction. 'I had heard there was a fight.'

'There was, when our glorious liberation was declared. Following the terrible accidents befalling the warden and her cronies.'

'Accidents, hah! That's a good one.'

Shurq Elalle glared across at her first mate, but like most men he was impervious to such non-verbal warnings.

'I will take that fifteen docks now,' Pithy said, her tone cold. 'Plus the five docks disembarking fee, assuming you intend to come ashore to take on supplies or sell your cargo, or both.'

'You ain't never mentioned five—'

'Pretty,' Shurq Elalle interrupted, 'head below and check on Brevity – she may have questions regarding our goods.'

'Aye, Captain.' With a final glower at Pithy he stumped off for the hatch.

Pithy squinted at Shurq Elalle for a moment, then scanned the various sailors in sight. 'You're pirates.'

'Don't be absurd. We're independent traders. You have no prisoners on your island, I have no pirates on my ship.'

'What are you suggesting by that statement?'

'Clearly, if I had been suggesting anything, it was lost on you. I take it you are not the harbour master, just a toll-taker.' She turned as first Skorgen then Brevity emerged onto the deck. The short woman's eyes were bright.

'Pithy, they got stuff!'

'Now there's a succinct report,' Shurq Elalle said. 'Brevity, be sure to inform the harbour master that we wish a berth at one of the stone piers, to better effect unloading our cargo. A messenger out to potential buyers might also prove . . . rewarding.' She glanced at Pithy, then away, as she added, 'As for mooring and landing fees, I will settle up with the harbour master directly, once I have negotiated the master's commission.'

'You think you're smart,' Pithy snapped. 'I should have brought a squad with me – how would you have liked that, Captain? Poking in here and there, giving things a real look. How would you like that?'

'Brevity, who rules Second Maiden?' Shurq Elalle asked.

'Shake Brullyg, Captain. He's Grand Master of the Putative Assembly.'

'The Putative Assembly? Are you sure you have the right word there, lass? Putative?'

'That's what I said. That's right, isn't it, Pithy?'

'The captain thinks she's smart, but she's not so smart, is she? Wait until she meets Shake Brullyg, then won't she be surprised—'

'Not really,' Shurq said. 'I happen to know Shake Brullyg. I even know the crime for which he was sent away. The only surprise is that he's still alive.'

'Nobody kills Shake Brullyg easily,' Pithy said.

One of the crew burst into a laugh that he quickly converted into a cough.

'We'll await the harbour master's response,' Shurq Elalle said.

Pithy and Brevity returned to their scow, the former taking the oars.

'Strange women,' Skorgen Kaban muttered as they watched the wallowing craft pull away.

'An island full of inbred prisoners,' Shurq replied in a murmur. 'Are you at all surprised, Pretty? And if that's not enough, a full-blooded Shake – who just happens to be completely mad – is ruling the roost. I tell you this, our stay should be interesting.'

'I hate interesting.'

'And probably profitable.'

'Oh, good. I like profitable. I can swallow interesting so long as it's profitable.'

'Get the hands ready to ship the anchor. I doubt we'll have to wait overlong for the harbour master's signal flag.'

'Aye, Captain.'

Udinaas sat watching her clean and oil her sword. An Edur sword, set into her hands by a Tiste Edur warrior. All she needed now was a house so she could bury the damned thing. Oh yes, and the future husband's fateful return. Now, maybe nothing was meant by it; just a helpful gesture by one of Fear's brothers – the only Sengar brother Udinaas actually respected. Maybe, but maybe not.

The interminable chanting droned through the stone walls, a sound even grimmer than the blunt grunting of Edur women at mourning. The Onyx Wizards were in consultation. If such an assertion held any truth then the priestly version of their language was incomprehensible and devoid of the rhythm normally found in both song and speech. And if it was nothing but chanting, then the old fools could not even agree on the tempo.

And he had thought the Tiste Edur strange. They were nothing compared to these Tiste Andii, who had carried dour regard to unhuman extremes.

It was no wonder, though. The Andara was a crumbling blackstone edifice at the base of a refuse-cluttered gorge. As isolated as a prison. The cliff walls were honeycombed with caves, pocked with irregular chambers, like giant burst bubbles along the course of winding tunnels. There were bottomless pits, dead ends, passages so steep they could not be traversed without rope ladders. Hollowed-out towers rose like inverted spires through solid bedrock; while over subterranean chasms arched narrow bridges of white pumice, carved into amorphous shapes and set without mortar. In one place there was a lake of hardened lava, smoother than wind-polished ice, the obsidian streaked with red, and this was the Amass Chamber, where the entire population could gather – barefooted – to witness the endless wrangling of the Reve Masters, otherwise known as the Onyx Wizards.

Master of the Rock, of the Air, of the Root, of the Dark Water, of the Night. Five wizards in all, squabbling over orders of procession, hierarchies of propitiation, proper hem-length of the Onyx robes and Errant knew what else. With these half-mad neurotics any burr in the cloth became a mass of wrinkles and creases.

From what Udinaas had come to understand, no more than fourteen of the half-thousand or so denizens – beyond the wizards themselves – were pure Tiste Andii, and of those, only three had ever seen daylight – which they quaintly called the *blinded stars* – only three had ever climbed to the world above.

No wonder they'd all lost their minds.

'Why is it,' Udinaas said, 'when some people laugh it sounds more like crying?'

Seren Pedac glanced up from the sword bridging her knees, the oil-stained cloth in her long-fingered hands. 'I don't hear anyone laughing. Or crying.'

'I didn't necessarily mean out loud,' he replied.

A snort from Fear Sengar, where he sat on a stone bench near the portal way. 'Boredom is stealing the last fragments of sanity in your mind, slave. I for one will not miss them.'

'The wizards and Silchas are probably arguing the manner of your execution, Fear Sengar,' Udinaas said. 'You are their most hated enemy, after all. Child of the Betrayer, spawn of lies and all that. It suits your grand quest, for the moment at least, doesn't it? Into the viper's den – every hero needs to do that, right? And moments before your doom arrives, out hisses your enchanted sword and evil minions die by the score. Ever wondered what the aftermath of such slaughter must be? Dread depopulation, shattered families, wailing babes – and should that crucial threshold be crossed, then inevitable extinction is assured, hovering before them like a grisly spectre. Oh yes, I heard my share when I was a child, of epic tales and poems and all the rest. But I always started worrying . . . about those evil minions, the victims of those bright heroes and their intractable righteousness. I mean, someone invades your hide-out, your cherished home, and of course you try to kill and eat them. Who wouldn't? There they were, nominally ugly and shifty-looking, busy with their own little lives, plaiting nooses or some such thing. Then shock! The alarms are raised! The intruders have somehow slipped their chains and death is a whirlwind in every corridor!'

Seren Pedac sheathed the sword. 'I think I would like to hear your version of such stories, Udinaas. How you would like them to turn out. At the very least, it will pass the time.'

'I'd rather not singe Kettle's innocent ears—'

'She's asleep. Something she does a lot of these days.'

'Perhaps she's ill.'

'Perhaps she knows how to wait things out,' the Acquitor responded. 'Go on, Udinaas, how does the heroic epic of yours, your revised version, turn out?'

'Well, first, the hidden lair of the evil ones. There's a crisis brewing. Their priorities got all mixed up – some past evil ruler with no management skills or something. So, they've got dungeons and ingenious but ultimately ineffective torture devices. They have steaming chambers with huge cauldrons, awaiting human flesh to sweeten the pot – but alas, nobody's been by of late. After all, the lair is reputedly cursed, a place whence no adventurer ever returns – all dubious propaganda, of course. In fact, the lair's a good market for the local woodcutters and the pitch-sloppers – huge hearths and torches and murky oil lamps – that's the problem with underground lairs – they're dark. Worse than that, everyone's been sharing a cold for the past eight hundred years. Anyway, even an evil lair needs the necessities of reasonable existence. Vegetables, bushels of berries, spices and medicines, cloth and pottery, hides and well-gnawed leather, evil-looking hats. Of course I've not even mentioned all the weapons and intimidating uniforms.'

'You have stumbled from your narrative trail, Udinaas,' Seren Pedac observed.

'So I have, and that too is an essential point. Life is like that. We stumble astray. Just like those evil minions. A crisis – no new prisoners, no fresh meat. Children are starving. It's an unmitigated disaster.'

'What's the solution?'

'Why, they invent a story. A magical item in their possession, something to lure fools into the lair. It's reasonable, if you consider it. Every hook needs a wriggling worm. And then they choose one among them to play the role of the Insane Master, the one seeking to unlock the dire powers of that magical item and so bring about a utopia of animated corpses stumbling through a realm of ash and rejected tailings. Now, if this doesn't bring heroes in by the drove, nothing will.'

'Do they succeed?'

'For a time, but recall those ill-conceived torture implements. Invariably, some enterprising and lucky fool gets free, then crushes the skull of a dozing guard or three, and mayhem is let loose. Endless slaughter – hundreds, then thousands of untrained evil warriors who forgot to sharpen their swords and never mind the birch-bark shields that woodcutter with the hump sold them.'

Even Fear Sengar grunted a laugh at that. 'All right, Udinaas, you win. I think I prefer your version after all.'

Udinaas, surprised into silence, stared across at Seren Pedac, who smiled and said, 'You have revealed your true talent, Udinaas. So the hero wins free. Then what?'

'The hero does nothing of the sort. Instead, the hero catches a chill down in those dank tunnels. Makes it out alive, however, and retreats to a nearby city, where the plague he carries spreads and kills everyone. And for thousands of years thereafter, that hero's name is a curse to both people living above ground and those below.'

After a moment, Fear spoke. 'Ah, even your version has an implicit warning, slave. And this is what you would have me heed, but that leads me to wonder – what do you care for my fate? You call me your enemy, your lifelong foe, for all the injustices my people have delivered upon you. Do you truly wish me to take note of your message?'

'As you like, Edur,' Udinaas replied, 'but my faith runs deeper than you imagine, and on an entirely different course from what you clearly think. I said the hero wins clear, at least momentarily, but I mentioned nothing of his hapless followers, his brave companions.'

'All of whom died in the lair.'

'Not at all. In the aftermath there was dire need for new blood. They were one and all adopted by the evil ones, who were only evil in a relative sense, being sickly and miserable and hungry and not too bright. In any case, there was a great renaissance in the lair's culture, producing the finest art and treasures the world had ever seen.'

'And what happened then?' Seren asked.

'It lasted until a new hero arrived, but that's another tale for another time. I have talked myself hoarse.'

'Among the women of the Tiste Edur,' Fear Sengar said then, 'is told the tale that Father Shadow, Scabandari Bloodeye, chose of his own free will to die, freeing his soul to journey down the Grey Road, a journey in search of absolution, for such was the guilt of what he had done on the plains of the Kechra.'

'Now that is a convenient version.'

'Now it is you who lack subtlety, Udinaas. This alternative inter-pretation is itself allegorical, for what it truly represents is *our* guilt. For Scabandari's crime. We cannot take back the deeds of Father Shadow; nor were we in any position, ever, to gainsay him. He led, the Edur followed. Could we have defied him? Possibly. But not likely. As such, we are left with a guilt that cannot be appeased, except in an allegorical sense. And so we hold to legends of redemption.'

Seren Pedac rose and walked over to set her scabbarded sword down beside the food pack. 'Yet this was a tale held in private by the women of your tribes, Fear. Setting aside for the moment the curious fact that you know of it, how is it the promise of redemption belongs only to the women?'

'The warriors follow another path,' Fear replied. 'That I know of the story – and the truth of Scabandari – is due to my mother, who rejected the tradition of secrecy. Uruth does not flee knowledge, and she would her sons do not either—'

'Then how do you explain Rhulad?' Udinaas asked.

'Do not bait him,' Seren Pedac said to the slave. 'Rhulad is accursed. By the sword in his hand, by the god who made that sword.'

'Rhulad was young,' Fear said, unconsciously wringing his hands as he stared at the chamber's worn floor. 'There was so much still to teach him. He sought to become a great warrior, a heroic warrior. He was discomfited in the shadows of his three older brothers, and this made him precipitate.'

'I think the god chose him . . . over Hannan Mosag,' said Udinaas. 'Rhulad had no choice.'

Fear studied Udinaas for a long moment, then he nodded. 'If that is your belief, then you are far more generous towards Rhulad than any Tiste Edur. Again and again, Udinaas, you leave me unbalanced.'

Udinaas closed his eyes as he leaned back against the rough wall. 'He spoke to me, Fear, because I listened. Something the rest of you never bothered doing – which isn't that surprising, since your vaunted family order had just been shattered. Your precious hierarchy was in disarray. Shocking. Terrible. So, while he could not speak to you, you in turn were unwilling to hear him. He was silent and you were deaf to that silence. A typical mess – I don't regret having no family.'

'You lay all the blame at the foot of the chaotic god.'

Udinaas opened his eyes, blinked for a moment, then smiled. 'Too convenient by far. Now, if I was seeking redemption, I'd leap on the back of that one, and ride the beast all the way – to the cliff's edge, then right over, amen.'

'Then . . . what?'

'What to blame? Well, how should I know? I'm just a worn-out slave. But if I had to guess, I'd look first at that rigid hierarchy I mentioned earlier. It traps everyone, and everyone makes sure it traps everyone else. Until none of you can move, not side to side, not up either. You can move down, of course – just do something no-one else likes. Disapproval kicks out every rung of the ladder, and down you go.'

'So it is the way of living among the Tiste Edur.' Fear snorted, looked away.

'All right,' Udinaas said, sighing, 'let me ask you this. Why wasn't that sword offered to some Letherii – a brilliant officer of an army, a cold-blooded merchant prince? Why not Ezgara himself? Or better still, his son, Quillas? Now there was ambition and stupidity in perfect balance. And if not a Letherii, then why not a Nerek shaman? Or a Fent or a Tarthenal? Of course, all those others, well, those tribes were mostly obliterated – at least, all the taboos, traditions and rules of every sort that kept people in line – all gone, thanks to the Letherii.'

'Very well,' Seren Pedac said, 'why not a Letherii?'

Udinaas shrugged. 'The wrong fatal flaws, obviously. The Chained One recognized the absolute perfection of the Tiste Edur – their politics, their history, their culture and their political situation.'

'Now I understand,' Fear murmured, his arms crossed.

'Understand what?'

'Why Rhulad so valued you, Udinaas. You were wasted scraping fish scales all day when by the measure of your intelligence and your vision, you could sit tall on any kingdom's throne.'

The slave's grin was hard with malice. 'Damn you, Fear Sengar.'

'How did that offend you?'

'You just stated the central argument – both for and against the institution of slavery. I was wasted, was I? Or of necessity kept under firm heel. Too many people like me on the loose and no ruler, tyrant or otherwise, could sit assured on a throne. We would stir things up, again and again. We would challenge, we would protest, we would defy. By being enlightened, we would cause utter mayhem. So, Fear, kick another basket of fish over here, it's better for everyone.'

'Except you.'

'No, even me. This way, all my brilliance remains ineffectual, harmless to anyone and therefore especially to myself, lest my lofty ideas loose a torrent of blood.'

Seren Pedac grunted, 'You are frightened by your own ideas, Udinaas?'

'All the time, Acquitor. Aren't you?'

She said nothing.

'Listen,' Fear said. 'The chanting has stopped.'

As usual, the debate ended with everyone losing. The clash of intractable views produced no harmony, just exhaustion and an ache in the back of the skull. Clip, seated with his legs propped up on the back of the next lower bench, in the gloom of the uppermost tier overlooking the absurdly named Disc of Concordance on which stood five glowering Onyx Wizards, struggled to awaken his mind as the wizards turned as one to face Silchas Ruin.

Ordant Brid, Reve of the Rock, who had sent Clip to retrieve these fell wanderers, was the first to speak. 'Silchas Ruin, brother of blood to our Black-Winged Lord, we know what you seek.'

'Then you also know not to get in my way.'

At these cold words, Clip sat straighter.

'It is as I warned!' cried Rin Varalath, Reve of the Night, in his high-pitched, grating voice. 'He arrives like a leviathan of destruction! Which of the brothers was gifted the greater share of deliberation and wisdom? Well, the answer is clear!'

'Calm down,' said Penith Vinandas.

Clip smiled to himself, wondering yet again if the Reve aspects created the personalities of their masters – or, in the case of Penith, mistress – or was it the other way round? Of course the Mistress of the Root would advise calm, a settling of wild wills, for she was so assuredly . . . *rooted*.

'I am calm!' snarled Rin Varalath. He jabbed a finger at Silchas Ruin. 'We must not yield to this one, else all that we have achieved will be brought down upon our very heads. The balance is all that keeps us alive, and each of you knows that. And if you do not, then you are more lost than I ever imagined.'

Draxos Hulch, Reve of the Dark Water, spoke in his depthless baritone. 'The issue, my fellow wizards, is less open to debate than you would hope. Unless, of course, we can explain to this warrior the nature of our struggle and the uneasy balance we have but recently won.'

'Why should he be interested?' Rin Varalath asked. 'If this all collapses it is nothing to him. He will move on, uncaring – our deaths will be meaningless as far as he is concerned.'

Silchas Ruin sighed. 'I am not insensitive to the battle you have waged here, wizards. But your success is due entirely to the inevitable disintegration of the Jaghut's ritual.' He scanned the faces before him. 'You are no match to Omtose Phellack, when its wielder was none other than Gothos. In any case, the balance you believe you have achieved is illusory. The ritual fails. Ice, which had been held in check, held timeless, has begun to move once more. It falters in the warmth of this age, yet its volume is so vast that, even melted, it will effect vast change. As for the glaciers bound in the highest reaches of the moun-tains of Bluerose – those to the north – well, they have already begun their migration. Unmindful of the distant ocean's assault, they draw power from a wayward flow of cold air. These glaciers, Wizards, still hold the spear of the ritual, and soon it will drive for your heart. The Andara is doomed.'

'We care nothing for the Andara,' said Gestallin Aros, Reve of the Air. 'The balance you speak of is not the one that matters to us. Silchas

Ruin, the Jaghut's ritual was of ice only in the manner that fire is of wood – it was the means of achieving a specific goal, and that goal was the freezing in place of time. Of life, and of death.'

Clip's gaze narrowed on Silchas Ruin, as the albino Andii slowly cocked his head, then said, 'You speak of a different failing, yet the two are linked—'

'We are aware of that,' cut in Ordant Brid. Then, with a faint smile, 'Perhaps more so than you. You speak of a spear of ice, of Omtose Phellack's very core, still living, still powerful. That spear, Silchas Ruin, casts a shadow, and it is within that shadow that you will find what you seek. Although not, I think, in the way you desire.'

'Explain.'

'We will not,' snapped Rin Varalath. 'If you wish to understand, then look to your kin.'

'My kin? Are you then able to summon Anomander?'

'Not him,' replied Ordant Brid. He hesitated, then continued. 'We were visited, not so long ago, by an ascendant. Menandore. Sister Dawn—'

If anything, Ruin's voice grew even colder as he demanded, 'What has she to do with this?'

'Balance, you ignorant fool!' Rin Varalath's shriek echoed in the chamber.

'Where is she now?' Silchas Ruin asked.

'Alas,' replied Draxos Hulch, 'we do not know. But she is close, for reasons that are entirely her own. She will, I fear, oppose you, should you decide to force your way past us.'

'I seek the soul of Scabandari Bloodeye. I do not understand that you would object to such a goal.'

'We see the truth of that,' said Ordant Brid.

A long moment of silence. The five Onyx Wizards faced a nonplussed Silchas Ruin, who seemed at a loss for words.

'It is,' said Penith Vinandas, 'a question of . . . compassion.'

'We are not fools,' said Ordant Brid. 'We cannot oppose you. Perhaps, however, we can guide you. The journey to the place you seek is arduous – the path is not straight. Silchas Ruin, it is with some astonishment that I tell you that we have reached something of a consensus on this. You have no idea how rare such a thing is – granted, I speak of a compromise, one which sits uneasier with some of us than with others. Nonetheless, we have agreed to offer you a guide.'

'A guide? To lead me on this crooked path, or tug me ever astray from it?'

'Such deceit would not work for very long.'

'True; nor would I be merciful upon its discovery.'

'Of course.'

210

Silchas Ruin crossed his arms. 'You will provide us with a guide. Very well. Which of you has volunteered?'

'Why, none of us,' said Ordant Brid. 'The need for us here prevents such a thing. As you said, a spear of ice is directed at us, and while we cannot shatter it, perhaps we can . . . redirect it. Silchas Ruin, your guide shall be the Mortal Sword of the Black-Winged Lord.' At that, the wizard gestured.

Clip rose to his feet, then began his descent to the Disc of Concordance. The chain and its rings appeared in his hand, whirring, then snapping, then whirring out again.

'He is Anomander's Mortal Sword?' Silchas Ruin asked in obvious disbelief as he stared up at this meeting's audience of one.

Clip smiled. 'Do you think he would be displeased?'

After a moment, the brother of Rake grimaced, then shook his head. 'Probably not.'

'Come the morrow,' Ordant Brid said, 'we will begin preparing the way for the continuation of your journey.'

Reaching the edge of the lowest tier, Clip dropped lightly onto the polished stone of the Disc, then approached Silchas Ruin, the chain in his hand spinning and clacking.

'Must you always do that?' Silchas Ruin demanded.

'Do what?'

Silchas Ruin walked into the chamber, followed a moment later by the Tiste Andii, Clip.

Seren Pedac felt a sudden chill, although she could not determine its source. Clip was smiling, but it was a cynical smile, and it seemed his eyes held steady on Fear Sengar, as if awaiting some kind of challenge.

'Acquitor,' said Silchas Ruin, releasing the clasp of his cloak as he walked over to the stone table against a far wall, where waited wine and food, 'at least one mystery has been answered.'

'Oh?'

'The preponderance of wraiths here in the Andara, the countless ghosts of dead Tiste Andii – I know why they are here.'

'I am sorry, I did not know this place was crowded with wraiths. I've not even seen Wither lately.'

He glanced across at her, then poured himself a goblet of wine. 'It is extraordinary,' he murmured, 'how something as basic as the absence of a taste on the tongue can prove the most excruciating torture . . . when one is buried for thousands of years.'

She watched him take a mouthful of the watery wine, watched him savour it. Then he said, 'Time, Acquitor. The Omtose Phellack ritual, which froze all in place, defied Hood himself – apologies, Hood is the Lord of Death. The ghosts – they had nowhere to go. Easily captured and enslaved by the Tiste Edur, but many others managed to evade that fate, and they are here, among their mortal kin. The Onyx Wizards speak of compassion and balance, you see . . .'

No, I do not, but I think that is of no matter. 'Will the wizards help us?'

A wry grimace from Silchas Ruin, then he shrugged. 'Our fell party now has a new member, Acquitor, who is charged with guiding us to what we seek.'

Fear Sengar, suddenly tense, stepped close to Clip. 'Tiste Andii,' he said, 'know this, please. I possess no enmity towards you or your people. If indeed you will lead us to where the soul of Scabandari is bound, I will be in your debt – indeed, all of the Edur will be in your debt.'

Clip grinned. 'Oh, you don't want that, warrior.'

Fear seemed taken aback.

'You,' said Silchas Ruin to the Tiste Edur, 'pose the gravest threat to these Andii. Your kind has good reason to hunt down every last one of them; nor are the Letherii well disposed to them, given their resistance to the annexation – a resistance that continues to this day. Bluerose does not appreciate being occupied; nor do the humans who lived in peace alongside those possessing Andii blood in their veins hold any loyalty to the Letherii conquerors. When the Onyx Order ruled, it was a distant sort of rule, reluctant to interfere in daily activities and making few demands on the populace. And now, Fear Sengar, your kind rule the Letherii, compounding the resentment seething in Bluerose.'

'I cannot speak for the empire,' Fear said. 'Only for myself. Yet I believe that, should events transpire in the manner I desire, then true liberation may be the reward granted by the Edur for their assistance – to the entire province of Bluerose and all its inhabitants. Certainly, I would argue for that.'

Clip's laugh was sardonic.

The chain spun to wrap tight around his right hand, yet that served as his only comment to these grave pronouncements and bold promises.

Seren Pedac felt sick inside. Clip, this maddening pup with his chain and rings, his ever-mocking expression . . .

Oh, Fear Sengar, do not trust this one. Do not trust him at all.

'Are you certain you want to do this, Overseer?'

Brohl Handar glanced across at the Atri-Preda. 'This expedition is to be punitive, Bivatt. No formal proclamation of war has been made – the missive from Letheras is very clear on this. Apparently, it falls under my duties as Overseer to ensure that the engagement does not exceed its parameters. You march to hunt down and destroy those who slaughtered the settlers.'

Her eyes remained on the columns of Letherii and Edur troops marching along the road. Dust hung in the air, staining the sky's bright blue. The sound from the army reminded Brohl Handar of broken ice groaning and crunching its way down a river. Bivatt spoke. 'That is precisely my intention, Overseer. That and nothing more, as I have been commanded.'

He studied her for a moment longer, then shifted on the saddle to ease the strain on his lower back – he preferred admiring horses from afar to perching atop the damned things. It seemed they understood his distaste and reciprocated in kind, and this one was in the habit of tossing its head as it drew up from every canter, clearly seeking to crack Brohl's chin. The Atri-Preda told him he leaned too far forward, and the horse knew it and saw the error as an opportunity to inflict damage. The Tiste Edur was not looking forward to this journey. 'Nonetheless,' he finally said, 'I will accompany you.'

He knew she was unhappy with the prospect. Yet he had his own bodyguards, from his own tribe. His own carriage and driver and team of oxen. More than enough supplies to ensure they were not a burden on the military train.

'I remain concerned for your safety,' she said.

'No need. I have every confidence in my Arapay—'

'Forgive me, Overseer, but hunting seals is not the same as—'

'Atri-Preda,' Brohl Handar interrupted in turn, 'my warriors faced crack Letherii soldiers in the conquest, and it was your Letherii who broke. Seals? Indeed, some of them weighing as much as an ox, with tusks longer than a shortsword. And white-furred bears, and cave-dwelling bears. Short-legged wolves and pack wolves. And, one should not forget, Jheck shape-shifters. Did you imagine the white wastes of the north are empty lands? Against what an Arapay must face every day, the Letherii were no great threat. As for protecting me from the Awl, presumably such a need would only arise following the rout of your forces. We shall have a K'risnan of the Den-Ratha, as well as your mage cadre. In short,' he concluded, 'your concerns ring false. Tell me, Atri-Preda, what was the substance of your secret meeting with Factor Letur Anict?'

The question, voiced as an afterthought, seemed to strike her like a blow, and the eyes she fixed on him were wide, alarmed, until something darker swirled to life. 'Financial discussions, Overseer,' she said in a cold tone. 'An army needs to eat.'

'The financing of this punitive expedition is provided by the Imperial Treasury.'

'Said funds managed by the Factor. After all, that is the function of being a factor, sir.'

'Not in this instance,' Brohl Handar replied. 'Disbursement is being

213

managed by my office. In fact, it is Edur coin that is sponsoring this expedition. Atri-Preda, you should in the future be certain of the facts before you contrive to lie. Now, it would seem that you are to proceed under the burden of two sets of orders. I do hope for the sake of your peace of mind that the two do not prove conflicting.'

'I should imagine not,' she said tightly.

'Are you confident of that, Atri-Preda?'

'I am, sir.'

'Good.'

'Overseer, a number of the settlers killed originated from within the Factor's own household.'

Brohl's brows lifted. 'The desire for a most bloody vengeance must be overwhelming, then, for poor Letur Anict.'

'At that meeting, sir, I simply reiterated my intent to exact the necessary punishment against the murderers. The Factor sought reassurance, which I was pleased to give him under the circumstances.'

'In other words, Letur Anict was somewhat alarmed that his control over the management of the expedition had been taken away, for such a decision was unprecedented. One must assume he is intelligent enough to recognize – once he has calmed down somewhat – that the move indicates disapproval of his recent excesses.'

'I would not know, sir.'

'I shall be interested to gauge his humility upon our triumphant return, Atri-Preda.'

She said nothing.

Of course, he added to himself, there would probably be much more to Letur Anict's response at that time, given that there was, in fact, nothing truly official in any of this. The Factor's cronies in the palace – the Letherii servants of, it was likely, the Chancellor – would be outraged upon discovering this circumvention; but this time it was the Edur who had organized this minor usurpation, a working of the tribes, the linkage established via the K'risnan and the Edur staffs of various overseers. There was vast risk in all this – the Emperor himself knew nothing of it, after all.

Letur Anict needed to be reined in. No, more than that, the man needed hobbling. Permanently. If Brohl had his way, there would be a new Factor of Drene within a year, and as for Letur Anict's holdings, well, the crime for High Treason and corruption at the scale he had managed would without doubt result in their confiscation, with all familial rights stripped away, and restitution at such high level that the Anict line would be Indebted for generations to come.

He is corrupt. And he has spun a deadly web here, from Drene out into every bordering nation. He seeks war with all of our neighbours. Unnecessary war. Pointless beyond the covetous greed of one man.

Such corruption needed excision, for there were plenty of Letur Anicts in this empire, thriving under the protection of the Liberty Consign and, quite possibly, the Patriotists. This man here would be the example and the warning.

You Letherii think us fools. You laugh behind our backs. Mock us in our ignorance of your sophisticated deceptions. Well, there is more than one kind of sophistication, as you shall discover.

Finally, Brohl Handar no longer felt helpless.

Atri-Preda Bivatt fumed in silence. The damned fool at her side was going to get himself killed, and she would be made responsible for that failure to protect him. K'risnan and Arapay bodyguards would achieve nothing. The Factor's agents infected every Letherii legion on this march, and among those agents . . . *Errant-damned assassins. Masters of the Poison.*

She liked this warrior at her side, dour as he was – which seemed a trait of the Tiste Edur in any case. And though clearly intelligent, he was also . . . naive.

It was clear that Letur Anict had penetrated the pathetic unofficial efforts of Brohl Handar and a half-dozen other overseers, and the Factor intended to eliminate this nascent threat here and now. On this very expedition.

'*We have a problem with Brohl Handar,*' the factor had said, his pale round face looking like dusty stone in the habitual gloom of his inner sanctum.

'Sir?'

'Unsanctioned, he seeks to exceed his responsibilities, and in so doing undermine the traditional functions of a factor in a border province. His ambitions have drawn others into his web, which could, alas, have fatal repercussions.'

'Fatal? How?'

'Atri-Preda, I must tell you. No longer are the Patriotists focusing exclusively on the Letherii in the empire. There has come to light evidence of an emerging conspiracy among the Tiste Edur – against the state, possibly against the Emperor himself.'

Absurd. Do you truly take me for such a fool, Anict? Against the state and against the Emperor are two different things. The state is you and people like you. The state is the Liberty Consign and the Patriotists. The state is the Chancellor and his cronies. Against them, the notion of a conspiracy among the Tiste Edur to rid the empire of Letherii corruption seemed more than plausible. They had been occupiers long enough to come to understand the empire they had won; to begin to realize that a far more subtle conquest had taken place, of which they were the losers.

215

The Tiste Edur were, above all else, a proud people. Not likely to abide defeat, and the fact that the victors were, by their measure, cowards in the true sense of the term would sting all the more. So she was not surprised that Brohl Handar and his fellow Edur had at last begun a campaign of eradication against the Letherii running the state. *Not surprising, either, the extent to which the Edur have under-estimated their enemy.*

'Sir, I am an officer in the Imperial Army. My commander is the Emperor himself.'

'The Emperor rules us all, Atri-Preda,' Letur Anict had said with a faint smile. 'The conspiracy among his kind directly threatens his loyal support structure – those who endeavour, at great personal sacrifice, to maintain that apparatus.'

'People such as yourself.'

'Indeed.'

'What are you asking of me, sir?'

'Brohl Handar will insist on accompanying your punitive expedition. I believe it is his intent to claim territories reconquered for himself' – a wave of one hand – 'no doubt in the name of the empire or some such meaningless nonsense.'

You mean, as you have done?

'I will try to talk him out of it,' she said. 'It's not safe—'

'Indeed it isn't. Precisely my point.' After a moment, Letur Anict leaned back. 'You will, alas, not win your argument. The Overseer will march with you, accepting the risks.'

The risks, yes. Imagining they come from the Awl.

'I will do all I can to preserve his life,' Bivatt said.

A spread of hands. 'Of course. That is your duty, and we both know how treacherous the Awl can be, especially as they are now commanded by none other than Redmask. Who can say what dread ambushes he has contrived to spring upon you, with the principal aim of murdering commanders and other important personages. Indeed, Atri-Preda, you have your duty and I would expect no less from you. But I do remind you, Brohl Handar is engaged in treason.'

'Then have Orbyn Truthfinder arrest him.' *If he dares, for that will bring it all out into the open, and you're not ready for that.*

'We will,' the Factor then said, 'be prepared for his return.'

So soon? 'Has the Emperor been informed of these developments, sir?'

'He has. The Patriotists would not be engaged in this hunt were it not so – I am sure you understand that, Atri-Preda.'

She believed she did. Even Karos Invictad would not proceed without some sort of sanction. 'Is that all, sir?'

'It is. Errant smile on your hunt, Atri-Preda.'

216

'Thank you, sir.'

And now, everything had proceeded to match the Factor's predictions. Brohl Handar would accompany the expedition, refuting her every argument against the idea. Reading his expression, she saw a renewed confidence and will – the Overseer felt as if he had found, at last, firm footing. No error in his recognition of his true enemy. The unmitigated disaster lay in the Edur's belief that he had made the first move.

She said now to the Overseer, 'Sir, if you will excuse me. I must have words with my officers.'

'Of course,' Brohl Handar replied. 'When do you anticipate contacting the enemy?'

Oh, you fool, you already have. 'That depends, sir, on whether they're fleeing, or coming straight for us.'

The Overseer's brows lifted. 'Do you fear this Redmask?'

'Fear that yields respect is not a bad thing, sir. In that fashion, yes, I fear Redmask. As he will me, before too long.'

She rode away then, down to her troops, seeking out, not an officer, but one man in particular, a horseman among the Bluerose, taller and duskier than most.

After a time she found him, gestured him to ride out to her side, and they walked their horses along one edge of the road. She spoke of two things, one loud enough to be heard by others and concerning the health of the mounts and other such mundane details; the other in much quieter tones, which no-one but the man could hear.

'What can you see of the horizon's bruised smear, that cannot be blotted out by a raised hand?'

Redmask glanced over at the foreigner.

Anaster Toc smiled. 'Lying in a ditch amidst the wastes of humanity is something I would recommend to any nascent poet. The rhythms of ebb and flow, the legacy of what we discard. Wealth like liquid gold.'

Not entirely sane any more, Redmask judged, unsurprised. Skin and bones, scabbed and stained with fiery, peeling rashes. At least he could now stand without the aid of a stick, and his appetite had returned. Before long, Redmask believed, the foreigner would recover, at last physically. The poor man's mind was another matter.

'Your people,' Anaster Toc continued after a moment, 'do not believe in poetry, in the power of simple words. Oh, you sing with the coming of dawn and the fleeing sun. You sing to storm clouds and wolf tracks and shed antlers you find in the grass. You sing to decide the order of beads on a thread. But no words to any of them. Just tonal variations, as senseless as birdsong—'

'Birds sing,' cut in Natarkas who stood on the foreigner's other side, squinting westward to the dying sun, 'to tell others they exist. They sing to warn of hunters. They sing to woo mates. They sing in the days before they die.'

'Very well, the wrong example. You sing like whales—'

'Like what?' asked Natarkas and two other copper-faces behind them.

'Oh, never mind, then. My point was, you sing without words—'

'Music is its own language.'

'Natarkas,' said Anaster Toc, 'answer me this, if you will. The song the children use when they slip beads onto a thread, what does it mean?'

'There is more than one, depending on the pattern desired. The song sets the order of the type of bead, and its colour.'

'Why do such things have to be set?'

'Because the beads tell a story.'

'What story?'

'Different stories, depending on the pattern, which is assured by the song. The story is not lost, not corrupted, because the song never changes.'

'For Hood's sake,' the foreigner muttered. 'What's wrong with words?'

'With words,' said Redmask, turning away, 'meanings change.'

'Well,' Anaster Toc said, following as Redmask made his way back to his army's camp, 'that is precisely the point. That's their value – their ability to adapt—'

'Grow corrupt, you mean. The Letherii are masters at corrupting words, their meanings. They call war peace, they call tyranny liberty. On which side of the shadow you stand decides a word's meaning. Words are the weapons used by those who see others with contempt. A contempt which only deepens when they see how those others are deceived and made into fools because they chose to believe. Because in their naivety they thought the meaning of a word was fixed, immune to abuse.'

'Togg's teats, Redmask, that's a long speech coming from you.'

'I hold words in contempt, Anaster Toc. What do you mean when you say "Togg's teats"?'

'Togg's a god.'

'Not a goddess?'

'No.'

'Then its teats are—'

'Useless. Precisely.'

'What of the others? "Hood's Breath"?'

'Hood is the Lord of Death.'

'Thus . . . no breath.'

'Correct.'

'Beru's mercy?'

'She has no mercy.'

'Mowri fend?'

'The Lady of the Poor fends off nothing.'

Redmask regarded the foreigner. 'Your people have a strange relationship with your gods.'

'I suppose we do. Some decry it as cynical and they may have a point. It's all to do with power, Redmask, and what it does to those who possess it. Gods not excepted.'

'If they are so unhelpful, why do you worship them?'

'Imagine how much more unhelpful they'd be if we didn't.' At whatever Anaster Toc saw in Redmask's eyes, he then laughed.

Annoyed, Redmask said, 'You fought as an army devoted to the Lord and Lady of the Wolves.'

'And see where it got us.'

'The reason your force was slaughtered is because my people betrayed you. Such betrayal did not come from your wolf gods.'

'True, I suppose. We accepted the contract. We assumed we shared the meaning of the words we had exchanged with our employers—' At that he offered Redmask a wry smile. 'We marched to war believing in honour. So. Togg and Fanderay are not responsible – especially for the stupidity of their followers.'

'Are you now godless, Anaster Toc?'

'Oh, I heard their sorrowful howls every now and then, or at least I imagined I did.'

'Wolves came to the place of slaughter and took the hearts of the fallen.'

'What? What do you mean?'

'They broke open the chests of your comrades and ate their hearts, leaving everything else.'

'Well, I didn't know that.'

'Why did you not die with them?' Redmask asked. 'Did you flee?'

'I was the best rider among the Grey Swords. Accordingly, I was acting to maintain contact between our forces. I was, unfortunately, with the Awl when the decision was made to flee. They dragged me down from my horse and beat me senseless. I don't know why they didn't kill me there and then. Or just leave me for the Letherii.'

'There are levels to betrayal, Anaster Toc; limits to what even the Awl can stomach. They could run from the battle, but they could not draw a blade across your throat.'

'Well, that's a comforting relief. Apologies. I have always been prone to facetious commentary. I suppose I should be thankful, but I'm not.'

'Of course you're not,' Redmask said. They were approaching the broad hide awning protecting the rodara-skin maps the war leader had drawn – mostly from what he could recall of Letherii military maps he had seen. These new maps had been stretched out on the ground, pegged down, arrayed like pieces of a puzzle to create a single rendition of a vast area – one that included the south border kingdoms. 'But you are a soldier, Anaster Toc, and I have need of soldiers.'

'So, you seek an agreement between us.'

'I do.'

'A binding of words.'

'Yes.'

'And what if I choose to leave? To walk away?'

'You will be permitted and given a horse and supplies. You may ride east or southeast or indeed north, although there is nothing to be found to the north. But not west, not southwest.'

'Not to the Lether Empire, in other words.'

'Correct. I do not know what vengeance you hold close to your wounded soul. I do not know if you would betray the Awl – to answer their betrayal of you. For which I would not blame you in the least. I have no desire to have to kill you and this is why I forbid you to ride to Lether.'

'I see.'

Redmask studied the map in the crepuscular light. The black lines seemed to be fading into oblivion before him. 'It is my thought, however, to appeal to your desire for vengeance against the Letherii.'

'Rather than the Awl.'

'Yes.'

'You believe you can defeat them.'

'I shall, Anaster Toc.'

'By preparing fields of battle well in advance. Well, as a tactic I would not gainsay it. Assuming the Letherii are foolish enough to position themselves precisely where you want them.'

'They are arrogant,' Redmask said. 'Besides, they have no choice. They wish to avenge the slaughter of settlements and the theft of herds they call their property – even though they stole them from us. They wish to punish us, and so will be eager to cross blades.'

'Using cavalry, infantry, archers and mages.'

'Yes.'

'How do you intend to negate those mages, Redmask?'

'I will not tell you, yet.'

'In case I leave, circle round and somehow elude you and your hunters.'

'The chance of that is remote.'

At the foreigner's smile, Redmask continued, 'I understand you are a skilled rider, but I would not send Awl after you. I would send my K'Chain Che'Malle.'

Anaster Toc had turned and he seemed to be studying the encampment, the rows upon rows of tents, the wreathed dung smoke of the fires. 'You have fielded what, ten, twelve thousand warriors?'

'Closer to fifteen.'

'Yet you have broken up the clans.'

'I have.'

'In the manner needed to field something resembling a professional army. You must shift their loyalty from the old blood-ties. I've seen you badgering your troop commanders, ensuring that they will follow your commands in battle. I've seen them in turn badgering their squad leaders, and the squad leaders their squads.'

'You are a soldier, Anaster Toc.'

'And I hated every moment of it, Redmask.'

'That matters not. Tell me of your Grey Swords, the tactics they employed.'

'That won't be much help. I could, however, tell you of the army I originally belonged to, before the Grey Swords.' He glanced over with his one glittering eye, and Redmask saw amusement there, a kind of mad hilarity that left him uneasy. 'I could tell you of the Malazans.'

'I have not heard of that tribe.'

Anaster Toc laughed again. 'Not a tribe. An empire. An empire three, four times the size of Lether.'

'You will stay, then?'

Anaster Toc shrugged. 'For now.'

There was nothing simple to this man, Redmask realized. Mad indeed, but it could prove a useful madness. 'Then how,' he asked, 'do the Malazans win their wars?'

The foreigner's twisted smile gleamed in the dusk, like the flash of a knife. 'This could take a while, Redmask.'

'I will send for food.'

'And oil lamps – I can't make out a damned thing on your map.'

'Do you approve of my intent, Anaster Toc?'

'To create a professional army? Yes, it's essential, but it will change everything. Your people, your culture, everything.' He paused, then added in a dry, mocking tone, 'You'll need a new song.'

'Then you must create it,' Redmask replied. 'Choose one from among the Malazans. Something appropriate.'

'Aye,' the man muttered, 'a dirge.'

The white knife flashed again, and Redmask would rather it had remained sheathed.

CHAPTER NINE

Everywhere I looked I saw the signs of war upon the landscape. There
the trees had crested the rise, despatching skirmishers down the slope
to challenge the upstart low growth in the riverbed, which had been
dry as bone until the breaking of the ice dams high in the mountains,
where the savage sun had struck in unexpected ambush, a siege that
breached the ancient barricades and unleashed torrents of water upon
the lowlands.

And here, on this tuck and fold of bedrock, the old scars of glaciers
were vanishing beneath advancing mosses, creeping and devouring
colonies of lichen which were themselves locked in feuds with kin.

Ants flung bridges across cracks in the stone, the air above swirling
with winged termites, dying in silence in the serrated jaws of rhinazan
that swung and ducked as they evaded yet fiercer predators of the
sky.

All these wars proclaim the truth of life, of existence itself. Now we
must ask ourselves, are we to excuse all we do by citing such ancient
and ubiquitous laws? Or can we proclaim our freedom of will by
defying our natural urge to violence, domination and slaughter? Such
were my thoughts – puerile and cynical – as I stood triumphant over
the last man I had slain, his lifeblood a dwindling stream down the
length of my sword-blade, whilst in my soul there surged such
pleasure as to leave me trembling . . .

King Kilanbas in the Valley of Slate
Third Letheras Tide – the Wars of Conquest

THE RUINS OF A LOW WALL ENCIRCLED THE GLADE, THE BATTERED
rough-cut basalt dividing swaths of green grasses. Just beyond
rose a thin copse of young birch and aspen, spring leaves bright
and fluttering. Behind this stand the forest thickened, darkened,
grey-skinned boles of pine crowding out all else. Whatever the wall had

enclosed had vanished beneath the soft loam of the glade, although depressions were visible here and there to mark out cellar pits and the like.

The sunlit air seemed to spin and swirl, so thick were the clouds of flying insects, and there was a taint of something in the warm, sultry air that left Sukul Ankhadu with a vague sense of unease, as if ghosts watched from the black knots on the trees surrounding them. She had quested outward more than once, finding nothing but minute life-sparks – the natural denizens of any forest – and the low murmurings of earth spirits, too weak to do much more than stir restlessly in their eternal, dying sleep. Nothing to concern them, then, which was well.

Standing close to one of the shin-high walls, she glanced back at the makeshift shelter, repressing yet another surge of irritation and impatience.

Freeing her sister should have yielded nothing but gratitude from the bitch. Sheltatha Lore had not exactly fared well in that barrow – beaten senseless by Silchas Ruin and a damned Locqui Wyval, left near-drowned in a bottomless bog in some memory pocket realm of the Azath, where every moment stretched like centuries – so much so that Sheltatha had emerged indelibly stained by those dark waters, her hair a burnt red, her skin the hue of a betel nut, as waxy and seamed as that of a T'lan Imass. Wounds gaped bloodless. Taloned fingernails gleamed like elongated beetle carapaces – Sukul had found her eyes drawn to them again and again, as if waiting for them to split, revealing wings of exfoliated skin as they dragged the fingers loose to whirl skyward.

And her sister was fevered. Day after day, raving with madness. Dialogue – negotiation – had been hopeless thus far. It had been all Sukul had managed, just getting her from that infernal city out here to a place of relative quietude.

She now eyed the lean-to which, from this angle, hid the recumbent form of Sheltatha Lore, grimly amused by the sight. Hardly palatial, as far as residences were concerned, and especially given their royal blood – if the fiery draconean torrent in their veins could justify the appellation, and why wouldn't it? Worthy ascendants were few and far between in this realm, after all. Barring a handful of dour Elder Gods – and these nameless spirits of stone and tree, spring and stream. *No doubt Menandore has fashioned for herself a more stately abode – ripe for appropriation. Some mountain fastness, spired and impregnable, so high as to be for ever wreathed in clouds. I want to walk those airy halls and call them my own. Our own. Unless I have no choice but to lock Sheltatha in some crypt, where she can rave and shriek disturbing no-one—*

'I should tear your throat out.'

The croak, coming from beneath the boughed shelter, triggered a sigh from Sukul. She approached until she came round to the front and could look within. Her sister had sat up, although her head was bowed, that long, crimson hair obscuring her face. Her long nails at the end of her dangling hands glistened as if leaking oil. 'Your fever has broken – that is well.'

Sheltatha Lore did not look up. 'Is it? I called for you – when Ruin was clawing loose – when he turned upon me – that self-serving, heartless bastard! Turned on me! *I called on you!*'

'I heard, sister. Alas, too far away to do much about it – that fight of yours. But I came at last, didn't I? Came, and freed you.'

Silence for a long moment; then, her voice dark and brutal, 'Where is she, then?'

'Menandore?'

'It was her, wasn't it?' Lore looked up suddenly, revealing amber eyes, the whites stained like rust. A ghastly gaze, yet wide and searching. 'Striking me from behind – I suspected nothing – I thought you were there, I thought – you *were* there, weren't you!'

'As much a victim as you, Sheltatha. Menandore had prepared long for that betrayal, a score of rituals – to drive you down, to leave me helpless to intervene.'

'She struck first, you mean.' The statement was a half-snarl. 'Were we not planning the same, Sukul?'

'That detail is without much relevance now, isn't it?'

'And yet, dear sister, she didn't bury *you*, did she?'

'Not through any prowess on my part. Nor did I bargain for my freedom. No, it seemed Menandore was not interested in destroying me.' Sukul could feel her own sneer of hatred twisting her features. 'She never thought I was worth much. Sukul Ankhadu, Dapple, *the Fickle*. Well, she is about to learn otherwise, isn't she?'

'We must find an Azath,' Sheltatha Lore said, baring brown teeth. 'She must be made to suffer what I suffered.'

'I agree, sister. Alas, there are no surviving Azath in this place – on this continent, I mean. Sheltatha Lore – will you trust me? I have something in mind – a means of trapping Menandore, of exacting our long-awaited revenge. Will you join me? As true allies – together, there are none here powerful enough to stop us—'

'You fool, there is Silchas Ruin.'

'I have an answer for him as well, sister. But I need your help. We must work together, and in so doing we will achieve the demise of both Menandore and Silchas Ruin. Do you trust me?'

Sheltatha Lore's laugh was harsh. 'Cast that word away, sister. It is meaningless. I demand vengeance. You have something to prove – to us all. Very well, we shall work together, and see what comes of it. Tell me your grand plan, then. Tell me how we shall crush Silchas Ruin who is without equal in this realm—'

'You must conquer your fear of him,' Sukul said, glancing away, studying the glade, noting how the shafts of sunlight had lengthened, and the ruined wall surrounding them now hunched like crumbling darkness. 'He is not indomitable. Scabandari proved that well enough—'

'Are you truly so stupid as to believe that?' Sheltatha demanded, clambering free of the lean-to, straightening like some anthropomorphic tree. Her skin gleamed, polished and the colour of stained wood. 'I shared the bastard's barrow for a thousand eternities. I tasted his dreams, I sipped at the stream of his secretmost thoughts – he grew careless . . .'

Sukul scowled at her kin. 'What are you saying?'

The terrible eyes fixed mockingly on her. 'He stood on the field of battle. He stood, his back to Scabandari – whom he called Bloodeye and was that not hint enough? Stood, I tell you, and but waited for the knives.'

'I do not believe you – that must be a lie, it must be!'

'Why? Wounded, weaponless. Sensing the fast approach of this realm's powers – powers that would not hesitate in destroying him and Bloodeye both. Destroying in the absolute sense – Silchas was in no condition to defend against them. Nor, he well knew, was Scabandari, for all that idiot's pompous preening over the countless dead. So, join in Scabandari's fate, or . . . *escape*?'

'Millennia within a barrow of an Azath – you call that an escape, Sheltatha?'

'More than any of us – more even than Anomandaris,' she said, her eyes suddenly veiled, 'Silchas Ruin thinks . . . *draconean*. As cold, as calculating, as *timeless*. Abyss below, Sukul Ankhadu, you have no idea . . .' A shudder took Sheltatha then and she turned away. 'Be sure of your schemes, sister,' she added in a guttural tone, 'and, no matter how sure you make yourself, leave us a means of escape. For when we fail.'

Another faint groan, from the earth spirits on all sides, and Sukul Ankhadu shivered, assailed by uncertainty – and fear. 'You must tell me more of him,' she said. 'All you learned—'

'Oh, I shall. Freedom has left you . . . arrogant, sister. We must strip that from you, we must free your gaze of that veil of confidence. And refashion your plans accordingly.' A long pause, then Sheltatha Lore faced Sukul once again, an odd glint in her eyes. 'Tell me, did you choose in deliberation?'

'What?'

A gesture. 'This place . . . for my recovery.'

Sukul shrugged. 'Shunned by the local people. Private – I thought—'

'Shunned, aye. With reason.'

'And that would be?'

Sheltatha studied her for a long moment, then she simply turned away. 'Matters not. I am ready to leave here now.'

As am I, I think. 'Agreed. North—'

Another sharp glance, then a nod.

Oh, I see your contempt, sister. I know you felt as Menandore did – I know you think little of me. And you thought I would step forward once she struck? Why? I spoke of trust, yes, but you did not understand. I do indeed trust you, Sheltatha. I trust you to lust for vengeance. And that is all I need. For ten thousand lifetimes of slight and disregard . . . it will be all I need.

His tattooed arms bared in the humid heat, Taxilian walked to the low table where sat Samar Dev, ignoring the curious regard from other patrons in the courtyard restaurant. Without a word he sat, reached for the jug of watered, chilled wine and poured himself a goblet, then leaned closer. 'By the Seven Holies, witch, this damned city is a wonder – and a nightmare.'

Samar Dev shrugged. 'The word is out – a score of champions now await the Emperor's pleasure. You are bound to attract attention.'

He shook his head. 'You misunderstand. I was once an architect, yes? It is one thing' – he waved carelessly – 'to stand agape at the extraordinary causeways and spans, the bridges and that dubious conceit that is the Eternal Domicile – even the canals with their locks, inflows and outflows, the aqueduct courses and the huge blockhouses with their massive pumps and the like.' He paused for another mouthful of wine. 'No, I speak of something else entirely. Did you know, an ancient temple of sorts collapsed the day we arrived – a temple devoted, it seems, to *rats*—'

'Rats?'

'Rats, not that I could glean any hint of a cult centred on such foul creatures.'

'Karsa would find the notion amusing,' Samar Dev said with a half-smile, 'and acquire in such cultists yet another enemy, given his predilection for wringing the necks of rodents—'

Taxilian said in a low voice, 'Not just rodents, I gather . . .'

'Alas, but on that matter I would allow the Toblakai some steerage room – he warned them that no-one was to touch his sword. A dozen or more times, in fact. That guard should have known better.'

'Dear witch,' Taxilian sighed, 'you've been careless or, worse, lazy. It's to do with the Emperor, you see. The weapon destined to cross blades with Rhulad's own. The touch signifies a blessing – did you not know? The loyal citizens of this empire *want* the champions to succeed. They want their damned tyrant obliterated. They pray for it; they dream of it—'

'All right,' Samar Dev hissed, 'keep your voice down!'

Taxilian spread his hands, then he grimaced. 'Yes, of course. After all, every shadow hides a Patriotist—'

'Careful of whom you mock. That's a capricious, bloodthirsty bunch, Taxilian, and you being a foreigner only adds to your vulnerability.'

'You need to eavesdrop on more conversations, witch. The Emperor is unkillable. Karsa Orlong will join all the others in that cemetery of urns. Do not expect otherwise. And when that happens, why, all his . . . hangers-on, his companions – all who came with him will suffer the same fate. Such is the decree. Why would the Patriotists bother with us, given our inevitable demise?' He drained the last wine from his goblet, then refilled it. 'In any case, you distracted me. I was speaking of that collapsed temple, and what I saw of its underpinnings – the very proof for my growing suspicions.'

'I didn't know we're destined for execution. Well, that changes things – although I am not sure how.' She fell silent; then, considering Taxilian's other words, she said, 'Go on.'

Taxilian slowly leaned back, cradling the goblet in his hands. 'Consider Ehrlitan, a city built on the bones of countless others. In that, little different from the majority of settlements across all Seven Cities. But this Letheras, it is nothing like that, Samar Dev. No. Here, the older city never collapsed, never disintegrated into rubble. It still stands, following street patterns not quite obscured. Here and there, the ancient buildings remain, like crooked teeth. I have never seen the like, witch – it seems no regard whatsoever was accorded those old streets. At least two canals cut right through them – you can see the bulge of stonework on the canal walls, like the sawed ends of long-bones.'

'Peculiar indeed. Alas, a subject only an architect or a mason would find a source of excitement, Taxilian.'

'You still don't understand. That ancient pattern, that mostly hidden gridwork and the remaining structures adhering to it – witch, none of it is accidental.'

'What do you mean?'

'I should probably not tell you this, but among masons and architects there are secrets of a mystical nature. Certain truths regarding numbers and geometry reveal hidden energies, lattices of power. Samar Dev, there are such courses of energy, like twisted wires in mortar, woven through this city. The collapse of Scale House revealed it to my eyes: a gaping wound, dripping ancient blood – nearly dead blood, I'll grant you, but undeniable.'

'Are you certain of this?'

'I am, and furthermore, someone *knows*. Enough to ensure that the essential constructs, the buildings that form a network of fulcra – the fixing-points to the lattice of energy – they all remain standing—'

'Barring this Scale House.'

A nod. 'Not necessarily a bad thing – indeed, not necessarily *accidental*, that collapse.'

'Now you have lost me. That temple fell down on purpose?'

'I would not discount that. In fact, that accords precisely with my suspicions. We approach a momentous event, Samar Dev. For now, that is as far as I can take it. Something is going to happen. I only pray we are alive to witness it.'

'You've done little to enliven my day,' she said, eyeing her half-finished breakfast of bread, cheeses and unfamiliar fruit. 'At the very least you can order us another carafe of wine for your sins.'

'I think you should run,' Taxilian said under his breath, not meeting her eyes. 'I would, barring the event I believe is coming. But as you say, my interest is perhaps mostly professional. You, on the other hand, would do better to look to your own life – to maintaining it, that is.'

She frowned. 'It's not that I hold to an unreasoning faith in the martial prowess of Karsa Orlong. There have been enough hints that the Emperor has fought other great champions, other warriors of formidable skill, and none could defeat him. Nonetheless, I admit to a feeling of . . . well, loyalty.'

'Enough to join him at Hood's Gate?'

'I am not sure. In any case, don't you imagine that we're being watched? Don't you think that others have tried to flee their fate?'

'No doubt. But Samar Dev, to not even try . . .'

'I will think on it, Taxilian. Now, I've changed my mind – that second carafe of wine will have to wait. Let us walk this fair city. I am of a mind to see this ruined temple for myself. We can gawk like the foreigners we are, and the Patriotists will think nothing of it.' She rose from her seat.

Taxilian followed suit. 'I trust you've already paid the proprietor.'

'No need. Imperial largesse.'

'Generosity towards the condemned – that runs contrary to my sense of this fell empire.'

'Things are always more complex than they first seem.'

Tracked by the eyes of a dozen patrons, the two left the restaurant.

The sun devoured the last shadows in the sand-floored compound, heat rising in streaming waves along the length of the rectangular, high-walled enclosure. The sands had been raked and smoothed by servants, and that surface would remain unmarred until late afternoon, when the challengers in waiting would troop out to spar with each other and gather – those who shared a language – to chew and gnaw on these odd, macabre circumstances. Yet, leaning against a wall just within the inner entranceway, Taralack Veed watched Icarium move slowly alongside the compound's outer wall, one hand out to brush with fingertips the bleached, dusty stone and its faded frieze.

On that frieze, faded images of imperial heroes and glory-soaked kings, chipped and scarred now by the weapons of unmindful foreigners sparring with each other, each and every one of those foreigners intent upon the murder of the Emperor now commanding the throne.

Thus, a lone set of footprints now, tracking along that wall, a shadow diminished to almost nothing beneath the tall, olive-skinned warrior, who paused to look skyward as a flock of unfamiliar birds skittered across the blue gap, then continued on until he reached the far end, where a huge barred gate blocked the way into the street beyond. The figures of guards were just visible beyond the thick, rust-pitted bars. Icarium halted facing that gate, stood motionless, the sunlight bleaching him as if the Jhag had just stepped out from the frieze on his left, as faded and worn as any hero of antiquity.

But no, not a hero. Not in anyone's eyes. Not ever. A weapon and nothing more. Yet . . . *he lives, he breathes, and when something breathes, it is more than a weapon. Hot blood in the veins, the grace of motion, a cavort of thoughts and feelings in that skull, awareness like flames in the eyes.* The Nameless Ones had knelt on the threshold of stone for too long. Worshipping a house, its heaved grounds, its echoing rooms – why not the living, breathing ones who might dwell within that house? Why not the immortal builders? A temple was hallowed ground not to its own existence but to the god it would honour. But the Nameless Ones did not see it that way. *Worship taken to its absurd extreme . . . yet perhaps in truth as primitive as leaving an offering in a fold of rock, of blood-paint on that worn surface . . . oh, I am not the one for this, for thoughts that chill the marrow of my soul.*

A Gral, cut and scarred by the betrayals. The ones that wait in every man's shadow – for we are both house and dweller. Stone and earth. Blood and flesh. And so we will haunt the old rooms, walk the familiar corridors, until, turning a corner, we find ourselves facing a stranger, who can be none other than our most evil reflection.

And then the knives are drawn and a life's battle is waged, year after year, deed after deed. Courage and vile treachery, cowardice and bright malice.

The stranger has driven me back, step by step. Until I no longer know myself – what sane man would dare recognize his own infamy? Who would draw pleasure from the sensation of evil, satisfaction from its all too bitter rewards? No, instead we run with our own lies – do I not utter my vows of vengeance each dawn? Do I not whisper my curses against all those who wronged me?

And now I dare judge the Nameless Ones, who would wield one evil against another. And what of my place in this dread scheme?

He stared across at Icarium, who still faced the gate, who stood like a statue, blurred behind ripples of heat. *My stranger. Yet which one of us is the evil one?*

His predecessor, Mappo – the Trell – had long ago left such struggles behind, Taralack suspected. Choosing to betray the Nameless Ones rather than this warrior before the gate. An evil choice? The Gral was no longer so sure of his answer.

Hissing under his breath, he pushed himself from the wall and walked the length of the compound, through waves of heat, to stand at the Jhag's side. 'If you leave your weapons,' Taralack said, 'you are free to wander the city.'

'Free to change my mind?' Icarium asked with a faint smile.

'That would achieve little – except perhaps our immediate execution.'

'There might be mercy in that.'

'You do not believe your own words, Icarium. Instead, you speak to mock me.'

'That may be true, Taralack Veed. As for this city,' he shook his head, 'I am not yet ready.'

'The Emperor could decide at any moment—'

'He will not. There is time.'

The Gral scowled up at the Jhag. 'How are you certain?'

'Because, Taralack Veed,' Icarium said, quiet and measured as he turned to walk back, 'he is afraid.'

Staring after him, the Gral was silent. *Of you? What does he know? Seven Holies, who would know of this land's history? Its legends? Are they forewarned of Icarium and all that waits within him?*

Icarium vanished in the shadow beneath the building entranceway. After a dozen rapid heartbeats, Taralack followed, not to reclaim the Jhag's dour companionship, but to find one who might give him the answers to the host of questions now assailing him.

Varat Taun, once second in command to Atri-Preda Yan Tovis, huddled in a corner of the unfurnished room. His only reaction to Yan Tovis's arrival was a flinch. Curling yet tighter in that corner, he did not lift his head to look upon her. This man had, alone, led Taralack Veed and Icarium back through the warrens – a tunnel torn open by unknown magic, through every realm the expedition had traversed on their outward journey. The Atri-Preda herself had seen the blistering wound that had been the exit gate; she had heard its shrieking howl, a voice that seemed to reach into her chest and grip her heart; she had stared in disbelieving wonder at the three figures emerging from it, one dragged between two . . .

No other survivors. Not one. Neither Edur nor Letherii.

Varat Taun's mind had already snapped. Incapable of coherent explanations, he had babbled, shrieking at anyone who drew too close to his person, yet unable or unwilling to tear his wide eyes from the unconscious form of Icarium.

Taralack Veed's rasping words, then: *All dead. Everyone. The First Throne is destroyed, every defender slaughtered – Icarium alone was left standing, and even he was grievously wounded. He is . . . he is worthy of your Emperor.*

But so the Gral had been saying since the beginning. The truth was, no-one knew for certain. What had happened in the subterranean sepulchre where stood the First Throne?

The terrible claims did not end there. The Throne of Shadow had also been destroyed. Yan Tovis remembered the dismay and horror upon the features of the Tiste Edur when they comprehended Taralack Veed's badly accented words.

Another expedition was necessary. That much had been obvious. To see the truth of such claims.

The gate had closed shortly after spitting out the survivors, the healing almost as violent and fraught as the first wounding, with a cacophony of screams – like the lost souls of the damned – erupting from that portal at the last moment, leaving witnesses with the terrible conviction that others had been racing to get out.

Swift into the wake of that suspicion came the news of failures – on ship after ship of the fleet – by the warlocks of the Edur when they sought to carve new paths into the warrens. The trauma created by that chaotic rent had somehow sealed every possible path to the place of the Throne of Shadow, and that of the T'lan Imass First Throne. Was this permanent? No-one knew. Even to reach out, as the warlocks had done, was to then recoil in savage pain. *Hot*, they said; *the very flesh of existence rages like fire.*

Yet in truth Yan Tovis had little interest in such matters. She had lost soldiers, and none stung more than her second in command, Varat Taun.

She stared now upon his huddled form. *Is this what I will deliver to his wife and child in Bluerose?* Letherii healers had tended to him, unsuccessfully – the wounds on his mind were beyond their powers to mend.

The sounds of boots in the corridor behind her. She stepped to one side as the guard arrived with his barefooted charge. Another 'guest'. A monk from the archipelago theocracy of Cabal who had, oddly enough, volunteered to join the Edur fleet, following, it turned out, a tradition of delivering hostages to fend off potential enemies. The Edur fleet had been too damaged to pose much threat at that time, still licking its wounds after clashing with the denizens of Perish, but that had not seemed to matter much – the tradition announcing first contact with strangers was an official policy.

The Cabalhii monk standing now in the threshold of the doorway was no higher than Twilight's shoulder, slight of build, bald, his round face painted into a comical mask with thick, solid pigments, bright and garish, exaggerating an expression of hilarity perfectly reflected in the glitter of the man's eyes. Yan Tovis had not known what to expect, but certainly nothing like . . . this.

'Thank you for agreeing to see him,' she now said. 'I understand that you possess talent as a healer.'

The monk seemed moments from bursting into laughter at her every word, and Twilight felt a flash of irritation.

'Can you understand me?' she demanded.

Beneath the face paint the features were flat, unresponsive, as he said in fluid Letherii, 'I understand your every word. By the lilt of your accent, you come from the empire's north, on the coast. You have also learned the necessary intonation that is part of the military's own lexicon, which does not entirely amend the residue of your low birth, yet is of sufficient mediation to leave most of your comrades uncertain of your familial station.' The eyes, a soft brown, were brimming with silent mirth with each statement. 'This of course does not refer to the temporary taint that has come from long proximity among sailors, as well as the Tiste Edur. Which, you may be relieved to hear, is fast diminishing.'

Yan Tovis glanced at the guard standing behind the monk. A gesture sent her away.

'If that was your idea of a joke,' she said to the Cabalhii after the woman had left, 'then even the paint does not help.'

The eyes flashed. 'I assure you, no humour was intended. Now, I am told your own healers have had no success. Is this correct?'

'Yes.'

'And the Tiste Edur?'

'They are . . . uninterested in Varat Taun's fate.'

A nod, then the monk, drawing his loose silks closer, walked noiselessly towards the figure in the far corner.

Varat Taun squealed and began clawing at the walls.

The monk halted, cocking his head, then turned about and approached Yan Tovis. 'Do you wish to hear my assessment?'

'Go on.'

'He is mad.'

She stared down into those dancing eyes, and felt a sudden desire to throttle this Cabalhii. 'Is that all?' Her question came out in a rasping tone, rough with threat.

'All? It is considerable. Madness. Myriad causes, some the result of physical damage to the brain, others due to dysfunctioning organs which can be ascribed to traits of parentage – an inherited flaw, as it were. Other sources include an imbalance of the Ten Thousand Secretions of the flesh, a tainting of select fluids, the fever kiss of delusion. Such imbalances can be the result of aforementioned damage or dysfunction.'

'Can you heal him?'

The monk blinked. 'Is it necessary?'

'Well, that is why I sent for you – excuse me, but what is your name?'

'My name was discarded upon attaining my present rank within the Unified Sects of Cabal.'

'I see, and what rank is that?'

'Senior Assessor.'

'Assessing what?'

The expression did not change. 'All matters requiring assessment. Is more explanation required?'

Yan Tovis scowled. 'I'm not sure,' she muttered. 'I think we are wasting our time.'

Another wild cavort in the monk's eyes. 'The appearance of a foreign fleet among our islands required assessment. The empire that despatched it required assessment. The demands of this Emperor require assessment. And now, as we see, the condition of this young soldier requires assessment. So I have assessed it.'

'So where, precisely, does your talent for healing come in?'

'Healing must needs precede assessing success or failure of the treatment.'

'What treatment?'

'These things follow a progression of requirements, each of which must be fully met before one is able to proceed to the next. Thus. I have assessed this soldier's present condition. He is mad. I then, for your benefit, described the various conditions of madness and their possible causes. Thereafter we negotiated the issue of personal nomenclature – an aside with little relevance, as it turns out – and now I am ready to resume the task at hand.'

'Forgive my interruption, then.'

'There is no need. Now, to continue. This soldier has suffered a trauma sufficient to disrupt the normal balance of the Ten Thousand Secretions. Various organs within his brain are now trapped in a cycle of dysfunction beyond any measures of self-repair. The trauma has left a residue in the form of an infection of chaos – it is, I might add, never wise to sip the deadly waters between the warrens. Furthermore, this chaos is tainted with the presence of a false god.'

'A false god – what is false about it?'

'I am a monk of the Unified Sects of Cabal, and it now seems necessary that I explain the nature of my religion. Among the people of Cabal there are three thousand and twelve sects. These sects are devoted, one and all, to the One God. In the past, terrible civil wars plagued the islands of Cabal, as each sect fought for domination of both secular and spiritual matters. Not until the Grand Synod of New Year One was peace secured and formalized for every generation to come. Hence, the Unified Sects. The solution to the endless conflicts was, it turned out, brilliantly simple. "Belief in the One God occludes all other concerns." '

'How could there be so many sects and only one god?'

'Ah. Well, you must understand. The One God writes nothing down. The One God has gifted its children with language and thought in the expectation that the One God's desires be recorded by mortal hands and interpreted by mortal minds. That there were three thousand and twelve sects at New Year One is only surprising in that there were once tens of thousands, resulting from a previous misguided policy of extensive education provided to every citizen of Cabal – a policy since amended in the interests of unification. There is now one college per sect, wherein doctrine is formalized. Accordingly, Cabal has known twenty-three months of uninterrupted peace.'

Yan Tovis studied the small man, the dancing eyes, the absurd mask of paint. 'And which sect doctrine did you learn, Senior Assessor?'

'Why, that of the Mockers.'

'And their tenet?'

'Only this: the One God, having written nothing down, having left all matters of interpretation of faith and worship to the unguided minds of over-educated mortals, is unequivocally insane.'

'Which, I suppose, is why your mask shows wild laughter—'

'Not at all. We of the Mockers are forbidden laughter, for that is an invitation to the hysteria afflicting the One God. In the Holy Expression adorning my face you are granted a true image of the One Behind the Grand Design, in so far as our sect determines such.' The monk suddenly clasped his hands beneath his chin. 'Now, our poor soldier has suffered overlong as it is, whilst we digressed yet again. I have assessed the taint of a false god in the beleaguered mind of this wounded man. Accordingly, that false god must be driven out. Once this is done, I shall remove the blockages in the brain preventing self-repair, and so all imbalances will be redressed. The effects of said treatment will be virtually immediate and readily obvious.'

Yan Tovis blinked. 'You can truly heal him?'

'Have I not said so?'

'Senior Assessor.'

'Yes?'

'Are you aware of the purpose you are meant to serve here in Letheras?'

'I believe I will be expected to meet the Emperor on a pitch, where-upon we shall endeavour to kill each other. Furthermore, I am led to understand that this Emperor cannot be slain with any measure of finality, cursed as he is by a false god – the very same false god who has afflicted this soldier here, by the way. Thus, it is my assessment that I will be killed in that contest, to the dismay of no-one and everyone.'

'And your One God will not help you, a senior priest of its temple?'

The man's eyes glittered. 'The One God helps no-one. After all, should it help one then it must help all, and such potentially universal assistance would inevitably lead to irreconcilable conflict, which in turn would without question drive the One God mad. As indeed it did, long ago.'

'And that imbalance can never be redressed?'

'You lead me to reassess you, Atri-Preda Yan Tovis. You are rather clever, in an intuitive way. I judge that your Ten Thousand Secretions flow even and clear, probably the result of remorseless objectivity or some similar blasphemy of the spirit – for which, I assure you, I hold no particular resentment. So, we share this question, which enunciates the very core of the Mockers' Doctrine. It is our belief that, should every mortal in this realm achieve clarity of thought and a cogent regard of morality, and so acquire a profound humility and respect for all others and for the world in which they live, then the imbalance will be redressed, and sanity will return once more to the One God.'

'Ah . . . I see.'

'I am sure you do. Now, I believe a healing was imminent. A con-joining of the warrens of High Mockra and High Denul. Physiological amendment achieved by the latter. Expurgation of the taint and elimination of the blockages, via the former. Of course, said warrens are faint in their manifestation here in this city, for a variety of reasons. Nonetheless, I do indeed possess substantial talents, some of which are directly applicable to the matter at hand.'

Feeling slightly numbed, Yan Tovis rubbed at her face. She closed her eyes – then, at a ragged sigh from Varat Taun, opened them again, to see her second in command's limbs slowly unfold, the fierce clutch of muscles on his neck visibly ease as the man, blinking, slowly lifted his head.

And saw her.

'Varat Taun.'

A faint smile, worn with sorrow – but a natural sorrow. 'Atri-Preda. We made it back, then . . .'

She frowned, then nodded. 'You did. And since that time, Lieutenant, the fleet has come home.' She gestured at the room. 'You are in the Domicile's Annexe, in Letheras.'

'Letheras? What?' He struggled to rise, pausing a moment to look wonderingly at the Cabalhii monk; then, using the wall behind him, he straightened and met Twilight's eyes. 'But that is impossible. We'd two entire oceans to cross, at the very least—'

'Your escape proved a terrible ordeal, Lieutenant,' Yan Tovis said. 'You have lain in a coma for many, many months. I expect you are feeling weak—'

A grimace. 'Exhausted, sir.'

'What do you last recall, Lieutenant?'

Dread filled his wan features and his gaze fell away from hers. 'Slaughter, sir.'

'Yes. The barbarian known as Taralack Veed survived, as did the Jhag, Icarium—'

Varat Taun's head snapped up. 'Icarium! Yes – Atri-Preda, he – he is an *abomination*!'

'A moment!' cried the Senior Assessor, eyes now piercing as he stared at the lieutenant. 'Icarium, the Jhag Warrior? *Icarium, Lifestealer?*'

Suddenly frightened, Yan Tovis said, 'Yes, Cabalhii. He is here. Like you, he will challenge the Emperor—' She stopped then, in shock, as the monk, eyes bulging, flung both hands to his face, streaking across the thick paint, and, teeth appearing to clench down hard on his lower lip, bit. Until blood spurted. The monk reeled back until he struck the wall beside the doorway – then, all at once, he whirled about and fled the room.

'Errant take us,' Varat Taun hissed, 'what was all that about?'

Forbidden laughter? She shook her head. 'I don't know, Lieutenant.'

'Who . . . what . . . ?'

'A healer,' she replied in a shaky voice, forcing herself to draw a steadying breath. 'The one who awakened you, Varat. A guest of the Emperor's – from Uruth's fleet.'

Varat Taun licked chapped, broken lips. 'Sir.'

'Yes?'

'Icarium . . . Errant save us, he must not be awakened. Taralack knows, he was there, he saw. The Jhag . . . have him sent away, sir—'

She approached him, boots hard on the floor. 'The Gral's claim are not exaggerated, then? He will bring destruction?'

A whisper: '*Yes.*'

She could not help herself then, and reached out, gloved hands grasping the front of Varat's ragged shirt, dragging him close. 'Tell me, damn you! Can he kill him? *Can Icarium kill him?*'

Horror swirled in the soldier's eyes as he nodded.

Errant's blessing, maybe this time . . . 'Varat Taun. Listen to me. I am leading my company out in two days. Back to the north. You will ride with me, as far up the coast as necessary – then you ride east – to

Bluerose. I am assigning you to the Factor's staff there, understood? Two days.'

'Yes sir.'

She released him, suddenly embarrassed at her own outburst. Yet her legs were weak as reeds beneath her still. She wiped sweat from her eyes. 'Welcome back, Lieutenant,' she said in a rough voice, not meeting his gaze. 'Are you strong enough to accompany me?'

'Sir. Yes, I shall try.'

'Good.'

Emerging from the room, they came face to face with the Gral barbarian. Breath hissed from Varat Taun.

Taralack Veed had halted in the corridor and was staring at the lieutenant. 'You are ... recovered. I did not think—' He shook his head, then said, 'I am pleased, soldier—'

'You warned us again and again,' Varat Taun said.

The Gral grimaced and seemed ready to spit, then decided otherwise. Gravely, he said, 'I did. And yes, I was foolish enough to be an eager witness . . .'

'And next time?' The question from Varat Taun was a snarl.

'You do not need to ask me that.'

The lieutenant stared hard at the savage, then he seemed to sag, and Yan Tovis was astonished to see Taralack Veed move forward to take Varat's weight. *Ah, it is what they have shared. It is that. That.*

The Gral glared over at her. 'He is half dead with exhaustion!'

'Yes.'

'I will help him now – where would you lead us, Atri-Preda?'

'To more hospitable quarters. What are you doing here, Veed?'

'A sudden fear,' he said as he now struggled with Varat's unconscious form.

She moved to help him. 'What sort of fear?'

'That he would be stopped.'

'Who?'

'Icarium. That you would stop him – now, especially, now that this man is sane once more. He will tell you – tell you everything—'

'Taralack Veed,' she said in a harsh tone, 'the lieutenant and I leave this city in two days. We ride north. Between then and now, Varat Taun is under my care. No-one else's.'

'None but me, that is.'

'If you insist.'

The lieutenant between them, the Gral studied her. 'You know, don't you. He told you—'

'Yes.'

'And you mean to say nothing, to no-one. No warning—'

'That is correct.'

'Who else might suspect – your ancient histories of the First Empire. Your scholars—'

'I don't know about that. There is one, and if I am able he will be coming with us.' *That damned monk. It should be simple enough. The Cabal priests misunderstood. Sent us an ambassador, not a champion. No value in killing him – the poor fool cannot fight – imagine Rhulad's rage at wasting his time . . . yes, that should do it.*

'No scholars . . .'

She grimaced and said, 'Dead, or in prison.' She glared across at the Gral. 'What of you? Will you flee with us?'

'You know I cannot – I am to share Icarium's fate. More than any of them realize. No, Atri-Preda, I will not leave this city.'

'Was this your task, Taralack Veed? To deliver Icarium here?'

He would not meet her eyes.

'Who sent you?' she demanded.

'Does it matter? We are here. Listen to me, Twilight, your Emperor is being sorely used. There is war among the gods, and we are as nothing – not you, not me, not Rhulad Sengar. So ride, yes, as far away as you can. And take this brave warrior with you. Do this, and I will die empty of sorrow—'

'And what of regrets?'

He spat on the floor. His only answer, but she understood him well enough.

Sealed by a massive, thick wall of cut limestone at the end of a long-abandoned corridor in a forgotten passage of the Old Palace, the ancient Temple of the Errant no longer existed in the collective memory of the citizens of Letheras. Its beehive-domed central chamber would have remained unlit, its air still and motionless, for over four centuries, and the spoked branches leading off to lesser rooms would have last echoed to footfalls almost a hundred years earlier.

The Errant had walked out into the world, after all. The altar stood cold and dead and probably destroyed. The last priests and priestesses – titles held in secret against the plague of pogroms – had taken their gnostic traditions to their graves, with no followers left to replace them.

The Master of the Holds has walked out into the world. He is now among us. There can be no worship now – no priests, no temples. The only blood the Errant will taste from now on is his own. He has betrayed us.

Betrayed us all.

And yet the whispers never went away. They echoed like ghost-winds in the god's mind. With each utterance of his name, as prayer, as curse, he could feel that tremble of power – mocking all that he had once held in his hands, mocking the raging fires of blood sacrifice, of fervent, fearful faith. There were times, he admitted, that he knew regret. For all that he had so willingly surrendered.

Master of the Tiles, the Walker Among the Holds. *But the Holds have waned, their power forgotten, buried by the passing of age upon age. And I too have faded, trapped in this fragment of land, this pathetic empire in a corner of a continent. I walked into the world . . . but the world has grown old.*

He stood now facing the stone wall at the end of the corridor. Another half-dozen heartbeats of indecision, then he stepped through.

And found himself in darkness, the air stale and dry in his throat. Once, long ago, he had needed tiles to manage such a thing as walking through a solid stone wall. Once, his powers had seemed new, brimming with possibilities; once, it had seemed he could shape and reshape the world. Such arrogance. It had defied every assault of reality – for a time.

He still persisted in his conceit, he well knew – a curse among all gods. And he would amuse himself, a nudge here, a tug there, to then stand back and see how the skein of fates reconfigured itself, each strand humming with his intrusion. But it was getting harder. The world resisted him. *Because I am the last, I am myself the last thread reaching back to the Holds.* And if that thread was severed, the tension suddenly snapping, flinging him loose, stumbling forward into the day's light . . . what then?

The Errant gestured, and flames rose once more from the clamshell niches low on the dome's ring-wall, casting wavering shadows across the mosaic floor. A sledgehammer had been taken to the altar on its raised dais. The shattered stones seemed to bleed recrimination still in the Errant's eyes. *Who served whom, damn you? I went out, among you, to make a difference – so that I could deliver wisdom, whatever wisdom I possessed. I thought – I thought you would be grateful.*

But you preferred shedding blood in my name. My words just got in your way, my cries for mercy for your fellow citizens – oh, how that enraged you.

His thoughts fell silent. The hairs on the back of his neck rose. *What is this? I am not alone.*

A soft laugh from one of the passageways. He slowly turned.

The man crouched there was more ogre than human, broad shoulders covered in bristly black hair, a bullet head thrust forward on a short neck. The bottom half of the face was strangely pronounced beneath long, curling moustache and beard, and large yellowed tusks jutted from the lower jaw, pushing clear of lip and thick, ringleted hair. Stubby, battered hands hung down from long arms, the knuckles on the floor.

From the apparition came a bestial, rank stench.

The Errant squinted, seeking to pierce the gloom beneath the heavy brows, where small narrow-set eyes glittered dull as rough garnets. 'This is my temple,' he said. 'I do not recall an open invitation to . . . guests.'

Another low laugh, but there was no humour in it, the Errant realized. Bitterness, as thick and pungent as the smell stinging the god's nostrils.

'I remember you,' came the creature's voice, low and rumbling. 'And I knew this place. I knew what it had been. It was . . . safe. Who recalls the Holds, after all? Who knew enough to suspect? Oh, they can hunt me down all they want – yes, they will find me in the end – I know this. Soon, maybe. Sooner, now that you have found me, Master of the Tiles. He might have returned me, you know, along with other . . . gifts. But he has failed.' Another laugh, this time harsh. 'A common demise among mortals.'

Though he spoke, no words emerged from the ogre's mouth. That heavy, awkward voice was in the Errant's head, which was all for the best – those tusks would have brutalized every utterance into near incomprehensibility. 'You are a god.'

More laughter. 'I am.'

'You walked into the world.'

'Not by choice, Master of the Tiles. Not like you.'

'Ah.'

'And so my followers died – oh, how they have died. Across half the world, their blood soaked the earth. And I could do nothing. I *can* do nothing.'

'It is something,' the Errant observed, 'to hold yourself to such a modest form. But how much longer will that control last? How soon before you burst the confines of this temple of mine? How long before you heave yourself into the view of all, shouldering aside the clouds, shaking mountains to dust—'

'I will be long from here before then, Master of the Tiles.'

The Errant's smile was wry. 'That is a relief, god.'

'You have survived,' the god now said. 'For so long. How?'

'Alas,' said the Errant, 'my advice to you would be useless. My power quickly dissipated. It had already been terribly wounded – the Forkrul Assail's pogroms against my faithful saw to that. The thought of another failure like that one was too much . . . so I willingly relinquished most of what remained to me. It made me ineffectual, beyond, perhaps, this city and a modest stretch of river. And so not a threat to anyone.' *Not even you, tusked one.* 'You, however, cannot make a similar choice. They will want the raw power within you – in your blood – and they will need it spilled before they can drink, before they can bathe in what's left of you.'

240

'Yes. One last battle awaits me. That much, at least, I do not regret.'
Lucky you. 'A battle. And . . . a war?'

Amusement in his thoughts, then, 'Oh, indeed, Master of the Tiles. A war – enough to make my heart surge with life, with hunger. How could it not? I am the Boar of Summer, Lord of the Hosts on the Field of Battle. The chorus of the dying to come . . . ah, Master, be glad it will be nowhere close—'

'I am not so sure of that.'

A shrug.

The Errant frowned, then asked, 'How long do you intend to remain here, then?'

'Why, as long as I can, before my control crumbles – or I am summoned to my battle, my death, I mean. Unless, of course, you choose to banish me.'

'I would not risk the power revealed by that,' the Errant said.

A rumbling laugh. 'You think I would not go quietly?'

'I know it, Boar of Summer.'

'True enough.' Hesitation, then the war god said, 'Offer me sanctuary, Errant, and I will yield to you a gift.'

'Very well.'

'No bargaining?'

'No. I've not the energy. What is this gift, then?'

'This: the Hold of the Beasts is awakened. I was driven out, you see, and there was need, necessity, *insistence* that some inheritor arise to take my place – to assume the voices of war. Treach was too young, too weak. And so the Wolves awoke. They flank the throne now – no, they *are* the throne.'

The Errant could barely draw breath at this revelation. A Hold, *awakened*? From a mouth gone dry as dust, he said, 'Sanctuary is yours, Boar of Summer. And, for your trail here, my fullest efforts at . . . misdirection. None shall know, none shall even suspect.'

'Please, then, block those who call on me still. Their cries fill my skull – it is too much—'

'Yes, I know. I will do what I can. Your name – do they call upon the Boar of Summer?'

'Not often,' the god replied. 'Fener. They call upon Fener.'

The Errant nodded, then bowed low.

He passed through the stone wall and once more found himself in the disused corridor of the Old Palace. *Awakened? Abyss below . . . no wonder the Cedance whirls in chaos. Wolves? Could it be . . .*

This is chaos! It makes no sense! Feather Witch stared down at the chipped tiles scattered on the stone floor before her. *Axe, bound to both Saviour and Betrayer of the Empty Hold. Knuckles and the White*

Crow circle the Ice Throne like leaves in a whirlpool. Elder of Beast Hold stands at the Portal of the Azath Hold. Gate of the Dragon and Blood-Drinker converge on the Watcher of the Empty Hold – but no, this is all madness.

The Dragon Hold was virtually dead. Everyone knew this, every Caster of the Tiles, every Dreamer of the Ages. Yet here it vied for dominance with the Empty Hold – and what of Ice? Timeless, unchanging, that throne had been dead for millennia. *White Crow – yes, I have heard. Some bandit in the reaches of the Bluerose Mountains now claims that title. Hunted by Hannan Mosag – that tells me there is power to that bandit's bold claim. I must speak again to the Warlock King, the bent, broken bastard.*

She leaned back on her haunches, wiped chilled sweat from her brow. Udinaas had claimed to see a white crow, centuries ago it seemed now, there on the strand beside the village. A white crow in the dusk. And she had called upon the Wyval, her lust for power overwhelming all caution. Udinaas – he had stolen so much from her. She dreamed of the day he was finally captured, alive, helpless in chains.

The fool thought he loved me – I could have used that. I should have. My own set of chains to snap shut on his ankles and wrists, to drag him down. Together, we could have destroyed Rhulad long before he came to his power. She stared down at the tiles, at the ones that had fallen face up – none of the others were in play, as the fates had decreed. *Yet the Errant is nowhere to be seen – how can that be?* She reached down to one of the face-down tiles and picked it up, looked at its hidden side. *Shapefinder. See, even here, the Errant does not show his hand.* She squinted at the tile. *Fiery Dawn, these hints are new . . . Menandore. And I was thinking about Udinaas – yes, I see now. You waited for me to pick you up from this field. You are the secret link to all of this.*

She recalled the scene, the terrible vision of her dream, that horrendous witch taking Udinaas and . . . *Maybe the chains on him now belong to her. I did not think of that. True, he was raped, but men sometimes find pleasure in being such a victim. What if she is protecting him now? An immortal . . . rival. The Wyval chose him, didn't it? That must mean something – it's why she took him, after all. It must be.*

In a sudden gesture she swept up the tiles, replacing them in their wooden box, then wrapping the box in strips of hide before pushing the package beneath her cot. She then drew from a niche in one wall a leather-bound volume, easing back its stained, mouldy cover. Her trembling fingers worked through a dozen brittle vellum pages before she reached the place where she had previously left off memorizing the names listed within – names that filled the entire volume.

Compendium of the Gods.

242

The brush of cool air. Feather Witch looked up, glared about. Nothing. No-one at the entrance, no unwelcome shadows in the corners – lanterns burned on all sides. There had been a taint to that unseemly breath, something like wax . . .

She shut the book and slid it back onto its shelf, then, heartbeat rapid in her chest, she hurried over to a single pavestone in the room's centre, wherein she had earlier inscribed, with an iron stylus, an intricate pattern. *Capture.* 'The Holds are before me,' she whispered, closing her eyes. 'I see Tracker of the Beasts, footfalls padding on the trail of the one who hides, who thinks to flee. But no escape is possible. The quarry circles and circles, yet is drawn ever closer to the trap. It pulls, it drags – the creature screams, but no succour is possible – none but my mercy – *and that is never free!*' She opened her eyes, and saw a smudge of mist bound within the confines of the inscribed pattern. 'I have you! Ghost, spy – show yourself!'

Soft laughter.

The mist spun, wavered, then settled once more, tendrils reaching out tentatively – beyond the carved borders.

Feather Witch gasped. 'You mock me with your power – yet, coward that you are, you dare not show yourself.'

'Dear girl, this game will eat you alive.' The words, the faintest whisper – the touch of breath along both ears. She started, glared about, sensed a presence behind her and spun round – no-one.

'Who is here?' she demanded.

'Beware the gathering of names . . . it is . . . premature . . .'

'Name yourself, ghost! I command it.'

'Oh, compulsion is ever the weapon of the undeserving. Let us instead bargain in faith. That severed finger you keep round your neck, Caster, what do you intend with it?'

She clutched at the object. 'I will not tell you—'

'Then I in turn will reveal to you the same – nothing.'

She hesitated. 'Can you not guess?'

'Ah, and have I guessed correctly?'

'Yes.'

'Premature.'

'I am biding my time, ghost – I am no fool.'

'No indeed,' the ghost replied. 'Even so, let us extend the bargain—'

'Why? You have revealed nothing of yourself—'

'Patience. Caster of the Tiles, await my . . . encouragement. Before you do what you intend. Await me, and I will assist you.'

She snorted. 'You are a ghost. You have no power—'

'I am a ghost, and that is precisely why I have power. For what you seek, that is.'

'Why should I believe you? Why should I agree to anything you suggest?'

243

'Very well, my part of the bargain. You speak now with Kuru Qan, once Ceda to King Ezgara Diskanar.'

'Slain by Trull Sengar . . .'

Something like a chuckle. 'Well, *someone* needed to thrust the spear . . .'

'You knew it was coming?'

'Knowing and being able to do something about it are two different matters, Caster of the Tiles. In any case, lay the true blame at the Errant's feet. And I admit, I am of a mind to call him out on that, eventually. But like you, I understand the necessity of biding one's time. Have we a bargain?'

She licked her lips, then nodded. 'We have.'

'Then I shall leave you to your education. Be careful when casting your tiles – you risk much by so revealing your talents as a seer.'

'But I must know—'

'Knowing and being able to do something about it—'

'Yes,' she snapped, 'I heard you the first time.'

'You lack respect, girl.'

'And be glad of it.'

'You may have a point there. Worth some consideration, I think.'

'Do you now intend to spy on me my every moment down here?'

'No, that would be cruel, not to mention dull. When I come here, you shall be warned – the wind, the mist, yes? Now, witness its vanishing.'

She stared down at the swirling cloud, watched as it faded, then was gone.

Silence in the chamber, the air still beyond her own breath. *Kuru Qan, the Ceda! See how I gather allies. Oh, this shall be sweet vengeance indeed!*

The waning sun's shafts of dusty light cut across the space where the old temple had stood, although the wreckage filling the lower half of that gap was swallowed in gloom. Fragments of façade were scattered on the street – pieces of rats in dismaying profusion. Edging closer, Samar Dev kicked at the rubble, frowning down at the disarticulated stone rodents. 'This is most . . . alarming,' she said.

'Ah,' Taxilian said, smiling, 'now the witch speaks. Tell me, what do you sense in this fell place?'

'Too many spirits to count,' she murmured. 'And all of them . . . rats.'

'There was a D'ivers once, wasn't there? A terrible demonic thing that travelled the merchant roads across Seven Cities—'

'Gryllen.'

'Yes, that was its name! So, do we have here another such . . . Gryllen?'

She shook her head. 'No, this feels older, by far.'

'And what of that bleeding? Of power?'

'I'm not sure.' Glancing around, she saw a tall, cloaked man leaning against a wall on the other side of the street, watching them. 'Some things, long ago grinding to a halt, should never be reawakened. Alas . . .'

Taxilian sighed. 'You use that word a lot. "Alas."' You are too resigned, Samar Dev. You flee from your own curiosity – I do not think you were always like this.'

She squinted at him. 'Oh, my curiosity remains. It's my belief in my own efficacy that has taken a beating.'

'We spin and swirl on the currents of fate, do we?'

'If you like.' She sighed. 'Very well, I've seen enough. Besides, it will be curfew soon, and I gather guards kill law-breakers on sight.'

'You have seen – but you explain nothing!'

'Sorry, Taxilian. All of this requires . . . some thought. If I reach any spectacular conclusions any time soon, I will be sure to let you know.'

'Do I deserve such irony?'

'No, you don't. Alas.'

Bugg finally made his way round the corner, emerging from the alley's gloom then pausing in the sunlit street. He glanced over at Tehol, who stood leaning against a wall, arms crossed beneath his blanket, which he had wrapped about him like a robe. 'Master,' he said, 'why do you hesitate now?'

'Me? Why, this only appears to be hesitation. You know, you could have let me help you carry that.'

Bugg set the heavy sack down. 'You never offered.'

'Well, that would be unseemly. You should have insisted.'

'Are you sure you have that right, Master?'

'Not in the least, but some graciousness on your part would have helped us move past this awkward moment.'

From the bag came soft clucking sounds.

Tehol blinked down at it. 'Bugg, you said retired hens, correct?'

'I did. In exchange for some modest repairs to a water trough.'

'But . . . they're not dead.'

'No, Master.'

'But . . . that means one of us has to kill them. Wring their necks. See the light of life dim in their beady eyes. You are a hard man, Bugg.'

'Me?'

'Retired – their egg-laying days over. Isn't there some kind of pasture awaiting them? Some well-strewn pecking ground?'

'Only the one in the sky, Master. But I see your point. About killing them, I mean.'

'Blood on your hands, Bugg – I'm glad I'm not you.'

'This is ridiculous. We'll figure something out when we get back home.'

'We could build us a coop on the roof, as mad folk do for pigeons. That way the birds could fly in and out, back and forth, and see something of this fine city.'

'Chickens can't fly, Master.'

'Beats wringing their necks, though, don't you think?'

'Seeing the city?'

'Well, momentarily.'

Clearly satisfied with his solution, Tehol adjusted his blanket then walked out onto the street. Sighing, Bugg collected the sack with its dozen hens and followed at a somewhat slower pace.

'Well,' he said as he joined Tehol in front of the ruin, 'at least that foreign witch is gone.'

'She was a foreign witch? Rather pretty, in a stolid, earthy way. All right, handsome, then, although I assure you I would never say that to her face, knowing how women are so easily offended.'

'By a compliment?'

'Absolutely. If it is the *wrong* compliment. You have been . . . inactive far too long, dear Bugg.'

'Possibly. I am also reticent when it comes to compliments. They have a way of coming after you.'

Tehol glanced over at him, brows lifted. 'Sounds like you've been married once or twice.'

'Once or twice,' Bugg replied, grimacing. Glancing up at the ruined Scale House, he went very still. 'Ah, I see now what she no doubt saw.'

'If what you are seeing is the source for making the hairs of my neck stand on end every time I come here, then I would be pleased if you explained.'

'For someone to step inside,' Bugg said, 'of necessity there must be a door. And if one does not exist, one must be made.'

'How can a collapsed building be a door, Bugg?'

'I begin to comprehend what is coming.'

'Sufficient to suggest a course of action?'

'In this matter, Master, the best course is to do nothing.'

'Hold on, Bugg, that particular conclusion seems to crop up rather often with you.'

'We'd best get home before curfew, Master. Care to take a turn with this sack?'

'Errant's blessing, have you lost your mind?'

'I thought as much.'

There was little in Sirryn Kanar's thoughts that reached down to the depths of his soul – he had a sense of that, sufficient to make him recognize that he was blessed with a virtually untroubled life. He possessed a wife frightened enough to do whatever he told her to do. His three children held him in the proper mixture of respect and terror, and he had seen in his eldest son the development of similar traits of dominance and certainty. His position as a lieutenant in the Palace Cell of the Patriotists did not, as far as he was concerned, conflict with his official title of Sergeant of the Guard – protection of the powerful demanded both overt and covert diligence, after all.

The emotions commanding him were similarly simple and straight-forward. He feared what he could not understand, and he despised what he feared. But acknowledging fear did not make him a coward – for he had proclaimed for himself an eternal war against all that threatened him, be it a devious wife who had raised walls round her soul, or conspirators against the empire of Lether. His enemies, he well understood, were the true cowards. They thought within clouds that obscured all the harsh truths of the world. Their struggles to 'under-stand' led, inevitably, to seditious positions against authority. Even as they forgave the empire's enemies, they condemned the weaknesses of their own homeland – not recognizing that they themselves personified such weaknesses.

An empire such as Lether was ever under siege. This had been the first statement uttered by Karos Invictad during the recruitment and training process, and Sirryn Kanar had understood the truth of that with barely a moment's thought. A siege, inside and out, yes – the very privileges the empire granted were exploited by those who would see the empire destroyed. And there could be no room for 'understanding' such people – they were evil, and evil must be expurgated.

The vision of Karos Invictad had struck him with the force of revelation, yielding such perfect clarity and, indeed, peace in what had been, at times, a soul in turmoil – battered and assailed on occasion by a world blurry with confusion and uncertainty – that all that raged within him settled out as certainty arrived, blazing and blinding in its wondrous gift of release.

He now lived an untroubled life, and so set an example to his fellow agents in the palace. In their eyes he had seen, again and again, the glimmer of awe and fear, or, equally satisfying, a perfect reflection of his own – flat, remorseless, as impervious to every deceit the enemy might attempt as he himself was.

Untroubled, then, he gestured to two burly Patriotists who stepped forward and kicked in the door. It virtually flew off its flimsy hinges, crashing down into the opulent chamber beyond. A scream, then another, from the gloom to the left – where the handmaidens slept – but already the lead agents were crossing the room to the door opposite. More violence, wood splintering beneath heavy boots.

Sprawled in the hallway behind Sirryn was the corpse of a Tiste Edur – someone had set a guard. Curious, but of little consequence. Poisoned quarrels had proved both quick and virtually silent. Already two of his men were preparing to carry the corpse away – just one more Edur who mysteriously vanished.

Sirryn Kanar positioned himself in the centre of the first chamber, as another agent arrived with a hooded lantern to stand off to one side, shedding just enough light. Too much would not do – the shadows needed to be alive, writhing, confusion on all sides. Sirryn delighted in precision.

His men emerged from the inner room, a figure between them – half naked, hair tousled, a look of disbelief— No. Sirryn Kanar's eyes narrowed. Not disbelief. *Resignation. Good, the traitor knew her fate, knew she could never escape it.* Saying nothing, he gestured for his agents to take her out.

Three handmaidens, weeping now, huddled against the wall, near their sleeping pallets. 'Attend to them,' Sirryn commanded, and four from his squad moved towards them. 'The senior one will be questioned, the other two disposed of immediately.'

He looked around, pleased at the ease of this operation, barely noticing the death-cries of two women.

In a short while, he would deliver his two prisoners to the squad waiting at a side postern of the palace, who would move quickly through the night – alone on the streets this long after curfew – to the headquarters of the Patriotists. Deliver the two women into interrogation cells. And the work would begin, the only release from the ordeal full confession of their crimes against the empire.

A simple, straightforward procedure. Proven effective. Traitors were invariably weak of will.

And Sirryn Kanar did not think the First Concubine would be any different. If anything, even more flimsy of spirit than most.

Women delighted in their airs of mystery, but those airs vanished before the storm of a man's will. True, whores hid things better than most – behind an endless succession of lies that never fooled him. He knew they were contemptuous of him and men like him, believing him weak by simple virtue of his using them – as if that use came from actual, genuine need. But he had always known how to wipe the smirks from their painted faces.

He envied the interrogators. That bitch Nisall – she was no different from his wife, he suspected.

Our enemies are legion, Karos Invictad had said, *so you must understand, all of you – this war, it will last for ever. For ever.*

Sirryn Kanar was content with that notion. Kept things simple.

And it is our task, the Master of the Patriotists had continued, *to ensure that. So that we are never expendable.*

Somewhat more confusing, that part, but Sirryn felt no real compulsion to pursue the notion. Karos was very clever, after all. *Clever and on our side. The right side.*

His thoughts shifting to the bed that awaited him, and the whore he'd have delivered to him there, the lieutenant marched down the empty palace corridor, his men falling in behind him.

Bruthen Trana stepped into the chamber. His eyes settled on the corpses of the two handmaidens. 'How long ago?' he asked the Arapay warlock who was crouched over the bodies. Two other Edur entered the First Concubine's bedroom, emerged again a moment later.

The warlock muttered something inaudible under his breath, then said in a louder voice, 'A bell, perhaps. Shortswords. The kind used by the Palace Guard.'

'Gather ten more warriors,' Bruthen Trana said. 'We are marching to the headquarters of the Patriotists.'

The warlock slowly straightened. 'Shall I inform Hannan Mosag?'

'Not yet. We cannot delay here. Sixteen Edur warriors and a warlock should suffice.'

'You mean to demand the release of the woman?'

'There are two, yes?'

A nod.

'They will begin interrogations immediately,' Bruthen Trana said. 'And that is not a pleasant procedure.'

'And if they have wrung confessions from them?'

'I understand your concern, K'ar Penath. Do you fear violence this night?'

The other warriors in the chamber had paused, eyes fixed on the Arapay warlock.

'Fear? Not in the least. With confessions in hand, however, Karos Invictad and, by extension, Triban Gnol, will be able to assert righteous domain—'

'We are wasting time,' Bruthen Trana cut in. 'My patience with Karos Invictad is at an end.' *And where is the guard I set in the hallway outside? As if I cannot guess.*

A new voice spoke from the outer doorway: 'Personal enmity, Bruthen Trana, is a very dangerous guide to your actions.'

The Tiste Edur turned.

The Chancellor, with two bodyguards hovering in the corridor behind him, stood with hands folded. After a moment he took a step into the room and looked about. An expression of regret when he saw the two dead women. 'Clearly, there was some resistance. They were most loyal servants to the First Concubine, probably innocent of all wrongdoing – this is tragic indeed. Blood on Nisall's hands now.'

249

Bruthen Trana studied the tall, thin man for a long moment, then he walked past him and out into the hall.

Neither bodyguard was suspicious, and neither had time to draw their weapons before the Edur's knives – one in each hand – slid up under their jaws, points driven deep into their brains. Leaving the weapons embedded, Bruthen Trana spun round, both hands snapping out to grasp the Chancellor's heavy brocaded collar. The Letherii gasped as he was yanked from his feet, flung round to face Bruthen, then slammed hard against the corridor's opposite wall.

'My patience with you,' the Edur said in a low voice, 'is at an end as well. Tragic demise for your bodyguards. Blood on your hands, alas. And I am not of a mind, presently, to forgive you their deaths.'

Triban Gnol's feet dangled, the stiff-tipped slippers kicking lightly against Bruthen Trana's shins. The Letherii's face was darkening, eyes bulging as they stared into the Edur's hard, cold gaze.

I should kill him now. I should stand here and watch him suffocate in the drawn folds of his own robe. Better yet, retrieve a knife and slice open his guts – watch them tumble onto the floor.

Behind him, K'ar Penath said, 'Commander, as you said, we've no time for this.'

Baring his teeth, Bruthen Trana flung the pathetic man aside. An awkward fall: Triban Gnol threw a hand down to break his descent, and the snap of finger bones – like iron nails driven into wood – was followed immediately by a gasp and squeal of pain.

Gesturing for his warriors to follow, Bruthen Trana stepped over the Chancellor and marched quickly down the corridor.

As the footfalls echoed away, Triban Gnol, clutching one hand against his torso, slowly climbed to his feet. He glared down the now empty corridor. Licked dry lips, then hissed, 'You will die for that, Bruthen Trana. You and every other witness who stood back and did nothing. You will all die.'

Could he warn Karos Invictad in time? Not likely. Well, the Master of the Patriotists was a capable man. With more than just two incompetent, pathetic bodyguards. Perfunctory notes to their widows: *Your husbands failed in their responsibilities. No death-pensions will be forthcoming. Leave the family residences of the Palace Guard immediately – barring your eldest child who is now Indebted to the estate of the Chancellor.*

He despised incompetence – and to be made to suffer its consequences . . . well, someone paid. Always. *Two children, then, yes. Hopefully boys.* And now he would need two new bodyguards. From among the married guard, of course. *Someone to pay the debt should they fail me.*

His broken fingers were growing numb, although a heavy ache throbbed in his wrist and forearm now.

The Chancellor set off for the residence of his private healer.

Her nightgown half torn, Nisall was pushed into a windowless room that was lit by a single candle positioned on a small table in the centre. The chill, damp air stank of old fear and human waste. Shivering from the night's march through the streets, she stood unmoving for a moment, seeking to wrap the gauze-thin material closer about herself.

Two young innocent women were dead. Butchered like criminals. *And Tissin is next – as close to a mother as I have ever had. She has done nothing – no, stop that. None of us have. But that doesn't matter – I cannot think otherwise. I cannot pretend that anything I say will make a difference, will in any way change my fate. No, this is a death sentence. For me. For Tissin.*

The Emperor would not hear of this. She was certain of that. Triban Gnol would announce that she was missing from the palace. That she had fled – just one more betrayal. Rhulad would flinch back in his throne, seeming to shrink in upon himself, as the Chancellor carefully, remorselessly fed the Emperor's many insecurities, then stood back to observe how his poisoned words stole the life from Rhulad's tortured eyes.

We cannot win against this. They are too clever, too ruthless. Their only desire is to destroy Rhulad – his mind – to leave him gibbering, beset by unseen terrors, unable to do anything, unwilling to see anyone. Anyone who might help him.

Errant save him—

The door was thrown open, swinging to slam hard against the wall, where old cracks showed that this violent announcement was part of the pattern. But she had noted those, and so did not start at the cracking crunch, but merely turned to face her tormentor.

None other than Karos Invictad himself. A swirl of crimson silks, onyx rings on his fingers, the sceptre of his office held in one hand and resting between right shoulder and clavicle. A look of faint dismay in the mundane features. 'Dearest woman,' he said in his high voice, 'let us be quick about this, so that I can be merciful. I've no wish to damage you, lovely as you are. Thus, a signed statement outlining your treason against the empire, then a quick, private execution. Your handmaiden has already complied, and has been mercifully decapitated.'

Oh, well done, Tissin. Yet she herself struggled, seeking similar courage – to accept things as they were, to recognize that no other recourse was possible. 'Decapitation is not damage?'

An empty smile. 'The damage I was referring to, of course, concerned wresting from you your confession. Some advice: compose your features in the moment before the blade descends. It is an unfortunate fact that the head lives on a few moments after it has been severed from the neck. A few blinks, a roll or two of the eyes, and, if one is not . . . mindful, a rash of unpleasant expressions. Alas, your handmaiden was disinclined to heed such advice, too busy as she was with a pointless tirade of curses.'

'Pray the Errant heard her,' Nisall said. Her heart was thudding hard against her ribs.

'Oh, she did not curse me in the Errant's name, sweet whore. No, instead she revealed a faith long believed to be extinct. Did you know her ancestry was Shake? By the Holds, I cannot even recall the name of the god she uttered.' He shrugged and smiled his empty smile once more. 'No matter. Indeed, even had she called upon the Errant, I would have no cause to panic. Coddled as you are – or, rather, were – in the palace, you are probably unaware that the handful of temples in the city purportedly sanctified in the Errant's name are in truth private and wholly secular – businesses, in fact, profiting from the ignorance of citizens. Their priests and priestesses are actors one and all. I sometimes wonder if Ezgara Diskanar even knew – he seemed oddly devoted to the Errant.' He paused, then sighed. The sceptre began tapping in place. 'You seek to delay the inevitable. Understandable, but I have no wish to remain here all night. I am sleepy and desire to retire at the earliest opportunity. You look chilled, Nisall. And this is a dreadful room, after all. Let us return to my office. I have a spare robe that is proof against any draught. And writing materials at hand.' He gestured with the sceptre and turned about.

The door opened and Nisall saw two guards in the corridor.

Numbed, she followed Karos Invictad.

Up a flight of stairs, down a passageway, then into the man's office. As promised, Karos Invictad found a cloak and set it carefully on Nisall's shoulders.

She drew it tight.

He waved her to a chair in front of the huge desk, where waited a sheet of vellum, a horsehair brush and a pot of squid ink. Slightly off to one side of the ink pot was a small, strange box, opened at the top. Unable to help herself, Nisall leaned over for a look.

'That is none of your concern.' The words were a pitch higher than usual and she glanced over to see the man scowling.

'You have a pet insect,' Nisall said, wondering at the flush of colour in Karos Invictad's face.

'Hardly. As I said, not your concern.'

'Do you seek a confession from it as well? You will have to decapitate it twice. With a very small blade.'

'Are you amusing yourself, woman? Sit down.'

Shrugging, she did as he commanded. Stared down at the blank vellum, then reached over and collected the brush. Her hand trembled. 'What is it you wish me to confess?'

'You need not be specific. You, Nisall, admit to conspiring against the Emperor and the empire. You state this freely and with sound mind, and submit to the fate awaiting all traitors.'

She dipped the brush into the ink and began writing.

'I am relieved you are taking this so well,' Karos Invictad said.

'My concern is not for me,' she said as she completed the terse statement and signed it with a flourish that did not quite succeed in hiding the shakiness of her hand. 'It is for Rhulad.'

'He will spare you nothing but venom, Nisall.'

'Again,' she said, leaning back in the chair. 'I do not care for myself.'

'Your sympathy is admirable—'

'It extends to you, Karos Invictad.'

He reached out and collected the vellum, waved it in the air to dry the ink. 'Me? Woman, you insult me—'

'Not intended. But when the Emperor learns that you executed the woman who carried his heir, well, Master of the Patriotists or not . . .'

The vellum dropped from the man's fingers. The sceptre ceased its contented tapping. Then, a rasp: 'You lie. Easily proved—'

'Indeed. Call in a healer. Presumably you have at least one in attendance, lest the executioner be stung by a sliver – or, more likely, a burst blister, busy as he is.'

'When we discover your ruse, Nisall, well, the notion of mercy is dispensed with, regardless of this signed confession.' He leaned over and collected the vellum. Then scowled. 'You used too much ink – it has run and is now illegible.'

'Most missives I pen are with stylus and wax,' she said.

He slapped the sheet back down in front of her, the reverse side up. 'Again. I will be back in a moment – with the healer.'

She heard the door open and shut behind her. Writing out her confession once more, she set the brush down and rose. Leaned over the odd little box with its pivoting two-headed insect. *Round and round you go. Do you know dismay? Helplessness?*

A commotion somewhere below. Voices, something crashing to the floor.

The door behind her was flung open.

She turned.

Karos Invictad walked in, straight for her.

She saw him twist the lower half of the sceptre, saw a short knife-blade emerge from the sceptre's base.

Nisall looked up, met the man's eyes.

And saw, in them, nothing human.

253

He thrust the blade into her chest, into her heart. Then twice more as she sagged, falling to strike the chair.

She saw the floor come up to meet her face, heard the crack of her forehead, felt the vague sting, then darkness closed in. *Oh, Tissin—*

Bruthen Trana shouldered a wounded guard aside and entered Invictad's office.

The Master of the Patriotists was stepping back from the crumpled form of Nisall, the sceptre in his hand – the blade at its base – gleaming crimson. 'Her confession demanded—'

The Tiste Edur walked to the desk, kicking aside the toppled chair. He picked up the sheet of vellum, squinted to make out the Letherii words. A single line. A statement. A confession indeed. For a moment, he felt as if his heart stuttered.

In the corridor, Tiste Edur warriors. Bruthen Trana said without turning, 'K'ar Penath, collect the body of the First Concubine—'

'This is an outrage!' Karos Invictad hissed. *'Do not touch her!'*

Snarling, Bruthen Trana took one stride closer to the man, then lashed out with the back of his left hand.

Blood sprayed as Karos Invictad staggered, sceptre flying, his shoulder striking the wall – more blood, from mouth and nose, a look of horror in the man's eyes as he stared down at the spatter on his hands.

From the corridor, a warrior spoke in the Edur language. 'Commander. The other woman has been beheaded.'

Bruthen Trana carefully rolled the sheet of vellum and slipped it beneath his hauberk. Then he reached out and dragged Karos Invictad to his feet.

He struck the man again, then again. Gouts of blood, broken teeth, threads of crimson spit.

Again. Again.

The reek of urine.

Bruthen Trana took handfuls of the silk beneath the flaccid neck and shook the Letherii, hard, watching the head snap back and forth. He kept shaking him.

Until a hand closed on his wrist.

Through a red haze, Bruthen Trana looked over, met the calm eyes of K'ar Penath.

'Commander, if you continue so with this unconscious man, you will break his neck.'

'Your point, warlock?'

'The First Concubine is dead, by his hand. Is it for you to exact this punishment?'

'Sister take you,' Bruthen Trana growled, then he flung Karos Invictad to the floor. 'Both bodies come with us.'

'Commander, the Chancellor—'

'Never mind him, K'ar Penath. Wrap well the bodies. We return to the Eternal Domicile.'

'What of the dead Letherii below?'

'His guards? What of them? They chose to step into our path, warlock.'

'As you say. But with their healer dead, some of them will bleed out unless we call upon—'

'Not our concern,' Bruthen Trana said.

K'ar Penath bowed. 'As you say, Commander.'

Half blind with terror, Tanal Yathvanar approached the entrance to the headquarters. She was gone. Gone, from that place, that most hidden place – her shackle snapped, the iron bent and twisted, the links of the chain parted as if they were nothing but damp clay.

Karos Invictad, it was your work. Again. Yet another warning to me – do as you command. You know all, you see all. For you, nothing but games, ones where you make certain you always win. But she was not a game. Not for me, you bastard. I loved her – where is she? What have you done with her?

Slowly, it registered upon him that something was amiss. Guards running in the compound. Shouts, wavering torchlight. The front entrance to the building yawned wide – he saw a pair of boots, attached to motionless legs, prone across the threshold.

Errant take us, we have been attacked!

He hurried forward.

A guard emerged, stepping over the body.

'You!' shouted Tanal. 'What has happened here?'

A rough salute. The man's face was pale. 'We have called for healers, sir—'

'What has happened, damn you?'

'Edur – a vicious ambush – we did not expect—'

'The Master?'

'Alive. But beaten badly. *Beaten, sir, by a Tiste Edur!* The liasion – Trana – Bruthen Trana—'

Tanal Yathvanar pushed past the fool, into the hallway, to the stairs. More bodies, guards cut down without so much as their weapons drawn. *What initiated this from the Edur? Did they catch word of our investigations? Bruthen Trana – does his file remain? Damn him, why didn't he just kill the bastard? Choke the life from him – make his face as red as those damned silks? Oh, I would run this differently indeed. Given the chance—*

He reached the office, stumbled to a halt upon seeing the spattered blood on the walls, the pools of it on the floor. The reek of piss was heavy in the air. Looking small and broken, Karos Invictad sat hunched in his oversized chair, stained cloths held to his swollen, bruised face. In the man's eyes, a rage as sharp as diamonds. Fixing now upon Tanal Yathvanar.

'Master! Healers are on the way—'

From mashed lips, muffled words: '*Where were you?*'

'What? Why, at home. In bed.'

'We arrested Nisall tonight.'

Tanal looked about. 'I was not informed, sir—'

'No – *no-one could find you!* Not at your home – not anywhere!'

'Sir, has Bruthen Trana retrieved the whore, then?'

A hacking, muffled laugh. 'Oh yes. Her cold flesh – but not her spirit. But he carries her written confession – by the Holds, it hurts to speak! *He broke my face!*'

And how many times did your fist do the same to a prisoner? 'Will you risk some wine, sir?'

A glare above the cloths, then a sharp nod.

Tanal went quickly to the cabinet. Found a clay jug containing un-diluted wine. *A better smell than – the piss of your terror, little man.* He poured a goblet, then hesitated – and poured another for himself. *Damn you, why not?* 'The healers will be here soon – I informed the guards that any delay risks their lives.'

'Swift-thinking Tanal Yathvanar.'

He carried the goblet over to Karos Invictad, not sure if there was irony in that last statement, so distorted was the voice. 'The guards were struck unawares – vicious betrayal—'

'Those that aren't yet dead will wish they were,' the Master of the Patriotists said. 'Why weren't we warned? Chancellor or no, I will have his answer.'

'I did not think we'd take the whore yet,' Tanal said, retrieving his own wine. He watched over the rim of the goblet as Karos pulled the soaked cloth away, revealing the terrible assault done on his face as he gingerly sipped at the wine – wincing as the alcohol bit into gashes and cuts. 'Perhaps the Edur should have been first. Bruthen Trana – he did not seem such a viper. He said not a word, revealed nothing—'

'Of course not. Nor would I in his place. No. Wait, observe, then strike without warning. Yes, I underestimated him. Well, such a failing occurs but once. Tonight, Tanal Yathvanar, a war has begun. And this time the Letherii will not lose.' Another sip. 'I am relieved,' he then said, 'that you got rid of that academic – too bad you did not get Nisall to play with, but I needed to act quickly. Tell me how you disposed of her – the academic. I need some satisfying news for a change . . .'

Tanal stared at the man. *If not you . . .*

From the corridor, rushing feet. The healers had arrived.

'Commander,' K'ar Penath said as he hurried alongside Bruthen Trana, 'do we seek audience with the Emperor?'

'No. Not yet. We will watch all of this play out for a time.'

'And the bodies?'

'Hide them well, warlock. And inform Hannan Mosag that I wish to speak to him. As soon as possible.'

'Sir, he is not in the Emperor's favour at the moment—'

'You misunderstand me, warlock. This has nothing to do with Rhulad. Not yet. We conquered this empire. It seems the Letherii have forgotten that. The time has come to stir the Tiste Edur awake once more. To deliver terror, to make our displeasure clear. This night, K'ar, the weapons are drawn.'

'You speak of civil war, Commander.'

'In a manner of speaking, although I expect nothing overt from the Chancellor or Invictad. A war, yes, but one waged behind the Emperor's back. He will know nothing—'

'Commander—'

'Your shock at my words does not convince me. Hannan Mosag is no fool – nor are you or any of his other warlocks. Tell me now you anticipated nothing . . . ah, I thought as much.'

'I fear we are not ready—'

'We aren't. But neither were they. This taking Nisall – *this murder* – tells me something gave them reason to panic. We need to find out what. Something has happened, or is happening even now, that forced matters to a head. And that is the trail Hannan Mosag must pursue – no, I do not presume to command him—'

'I understand, Bruthen Trana. You speak as a Tiste Edur. I will support your advice to the Warlock King with all my zeal.'

'Thank you.'

'Tonight, Commander,' K'ar Penath said, 'in witnessing you . . . I was proud. We are . . . awakened, as you said. This civilization, it is a poison. A rot upon our souls. It must be excised.'

And now I hear Hannan Mosag speaking through you, warlock. Answering other . . . suspicions. So be it.

Nisall. First Concubine, I am sorry. But know this, I will avenge you in truth. As I will avenge my brave warrior – Sister take me, that was careless—

'The Chancellor will speak to the Emperor—'

'Only if he is stupid,' Bruthen Trana said, 'or inclined to panic. He is neither. No, he needs to be pushed, kept off balance – oh, we will deliver panic, yes, and sooner or later he will do as you say. Speak to Rhulad. And then we will have him. And Invictad. Two snakes in the same basket – a basket soaked in oil. And it will be Triban Gnol himself who strikes the spark.'

'How?'

'You will see.'

Tehol stared down through the roof hatch in unmitigated horror. 'That was a mistake,' he said.

Leaning beside him, also looking down, Bugg nodded. 'It was an act of mercy, Master. Twelve hens in a sack, half crushing each other, jostled about in fetid darkness. There was the risk of suffocation.'

'Precisely! Peaceful demise, remote, unseen. No wringing of necks required! But now look at them! They've taken over our room! My house. My abode, my very hearth—'

'About that – seems one of them has caught fire, Master.'

'It's smouldering, and too brainless to care. If we wait we can dine on roast chicken for breakfast. And which one laid that egg?'

'Hmm, a most gravid mystery indeed.'

'You may find this amusing right now, Bugg, but you are the one who will be sleeping down there. They'll peck your eyes out, you know. Evil has been bred into them, generation after generation, until their tiny black bean brains are condensed knots of malice—'

'You display unexpected familiarity with hens, Master.'

'I had a tutor who was a human version.'

Bugg leaned back and glanced over at the woman sleeping in Tehol's bed.

'Not her. Janath was only mildly vicious, as properly befits all instructors, plagued as they often are by mewling, lovestruck, pimply-faced students.'

'Oh, Master, I am sorry.'

'Be quiet. We're not talking about that. No, instead, Bugg, my house has been invaded by rabid hens, because of your habit of taking in strays and the like.'

'Strays? We're going to eat those things.'

'No wonder strays avoid you these days. Listen to them – how will we sleep with all that racket going on?'

'I suppose they're happy, Master. And in any case they are taking care of that cockroach infestation really fast.'

Creaking from the bed behind them drew their attention.

The scholar was sitting up, looking about in confusion.

Tehol hastily pushed Bugg towards her.

She frowned as the old man approached. 'Where am I? Who are you? Are we on a roof?'

'What do you last recall?' Bugg asked.

'Being alone. In the dark. He moved me . . . to a new place.'

'You have been freed,' he said.

Janath was examining her shapeless, rough tunic. 'Freed,' she said in a low voice.

'That shift was all we could find at short notice,' Bugg said. 'Of course, we will endeavour to, uh, improve your apparel as soon as we are able.'

'I have been healed.'

'Your physical wounds, yes.'

Grimacing, she nodded. 'The other kind is rather more elusive.'

'You seem remarkably . . . sound, Janath.'

She glanced up at him. 'You know me.'

'My master was once a student of yours.' He watched as she sought to look past him, first to one side, then the other. Bemused, Bugg turned, to see Tehol moving back and forth in an effort to keep the manservant between himself and the woman on the bed. 'Tehol? What are you doing?'

'Tehol? Tehol Beddict?'

Bugg spun round again, to see Janath gathering her tunic and stretching it out here and there in an effort to cover as much of her body as she could.

'That lecherous, pathetic worm? Is that you, Tehol? Hiding there behind this old man? Well, you certainly haven't changed, have you? Get out here, front and centre!'

Tehol stepped into view. Then bridled. 'Hold on, I am no longer your student, Janath! Besides, I'm well over you, I'll have you know. I haven't dreamt of you in . . . in . . . years! Months!'

Her brows rose. 'Weeks?'

Tehol drew himself straighter. 'It is well known that an adult man's adolescent misapprehensions often insinuate themselves when said man is sleeping, in his dreams, I mean. Or, indeed, nightmares—'

'I doubt I feature in your nightmares, Tehol,' Janath said. 'Although you do in mine.'

'Oh, really. I was no more pathetic than any other pathetic, lovestruck student. Was I?'

To that she said nothing.

Bugg said to her, 'You are indeed on a roof—'

'Above a chicken coop?'

'Well, as to that. Are you hungry?'

'The fine aroma of roasting chicken is making my mouth water,' she replied. 'Oh, please, have you no other clothes? I have no doubt at all what is going on in my former student's disgusting little brain right now.'

'Come the morning,' Bugg said, 'I will pay a visit to Selush – her wardrobe, while somewhat abysmal in taste, is nonetheless extensive.'

259

'Want my blanket?' Tehol asked her.

'Gods below, Master, you're almost leering.'

'Don't be insane, Bugg. I was making light. Ha ha, we're trapped in a dearth of attire. Ha ha. After all, what if that had been a child's tunic?'

In a deadpan voice, Janath said, 'What if it had.'

'Errant's blessing,' Tehol said with a loud sigh, 'these summer nights are hot, aren't they?'

'I know one hen that would agree with you,' Bugg noted, walking back to the hatch, from which a column of smoke was now rising.

'Tehol Beddict,' said Janath, 'I am glad you are here.'

'You are?' both Bugg and Tehol asked.

She nodded, not meeting their eyes. 'I was going mad – I thought I had already done so. Yathvanar – he beat me, he raped me . . . and told me of his undying love all the while. So, Tehol, you are as his opposite – harmless in your infatuation. You remind me of better days.' She was silent for a long moment. 'Better days.'

Bugg and Tehol exchanged a look, then the manservant made his way down the ladder. From above he heard Tehol say, 'Janath, are you not impressed with what I have done with my extensive education?'

'It is a very fine roof, Tehol Beddict.'

Nodding to himself, Bugg went in search of roasted chicken through clouds of acrid smoke. Surrounded on all sides by mindless clucking. *Abyss take me, I might as well be in a temple . . .*

The morning sun pushed through the slats on the shutters, stretching ribbons of light across the long, heavy table dominating the council room. Wiping his hands with a cloth, Rautos Hivanar entered and moved to stand behind his chair at one end of the table. He set the cloth down and studied the arrayed faces turned towards him – and saw in more than one expressions of taut fear and anxiety.

'My friends, welcome. Two matters on the agenda. We will first address the one that I suspect is foremost in your minds at the moment. We have reached a state of crisis – the dearth of hard coin, of silver, of gold, of cut gems and indeed of copper bars, is now acute. Someone is actively sabotaging our empire's economy—'

'We knew this was coming,' interrupted Uster Taran. 'Yet what measures were taken by the Consign? As far as I can see, none. Rautos Hivanar, as much on the minds of those assembled here is the question of your continued position as Master.'

'I see. Very well, present to me your list of concerns in that regard.'

Uster's craggy face reddened. 'List? Concerns? Errant take us, Rautos, have you not even set the Patriotists on the trail of this mad creature? Or creatures? Could this not be an effort from the outside –

from one of the border kingdoms – to destabilize us prior to invasion? News of this Bolkando Conspiracy should have—'

'A moment, please. One issue at a time, Uster. The Patriotists are indeed pursuing an investigation, without result to date. A general announcement to that effect, while potentially alleviating your anxieties, would have been, in my judgement, equally likely to trigger panic. Accordingly, I chose to keep the matter private. My own inquiries, in the meantime, have led me to eliminate external sources to this financial assault. The source, my friends, is here in Letheras—'

'Then why haven't we caught the bastard?' demanded Druz Thennict, his head seeming to bob atop its long, thin neck.

'The trails are most cleverly obscured, good Druz,' said Rautos. 'Quite simply, we are at war with a genius.'

From the far end of the table, Horul Rinnesict snorted, then said, 'Why not just mint more coins and take the pressure off?'

'We could,' Rautos replied, 'although it would not be easy. There is a fixed yield from the Imperial Mines and it is, of necessity, modest. And, unfortunately, rather inflexible. Beyond that concern, you might ask yourself: what would I do then, were I this saboteur? A sudden influx of new coin? If you sought to create chaos in the economy, what would you do?'

'Release my hoard,' Barrakta Ilk said in a growl, 'setting off runaway inflation. We'd be drowning in worthless coin.'

Rautos Hivanar nodded. 'It is my belief that our saboteur cannot hide much longer. He or she will need to become overt. The key will lie in observing which enterprise is the first to topple, for it is there that his or her trail will become readily discernible.'

'At which point,' said Barrakta, 'the Patriotists will pounce.'

'Ah, this leads me into the second subject. There has, I understand, been news from Drene – no, I have no specifics as yet, but it seems to have triggered something very much like panic among the Patriotists. Last night, here in Letheras, a number of unprecedented arrests occurred—'

Uster laughed. 'What could be unprecedented about the Patriotists arresting people?'

'Well, foremost among them was the First Concubine.'

Silence around the table.

Rautos Hivanar cleared his throat, working hard to keep the fury from his voice. 'It seems Karos Invictad acted in haste, which, as I am sure you all know, is quite unlike him. As a result, things went awry. There was a clash, both inside and outside the Eternal Domicile, between the Patriotists and the Tiste Edur.'

'That damned fool!' bellowed Barrakta, one fist pounding on the tabletop.

'The First Concubine is, I understand, dead. As are a number of guards – primarily those in the Patriotist compound, and at least two bodyguards to the Chancellor.'

'Has that damned snake turned suicidal as well?'

'It almost seems so, Barrakta,' Rautos conceded. 'All very troubling – especially Karos Invictad's reluctance to be forthcoming on what exactly happened. The only hint I possess of just how extreme events were last night is a rumour that Karos was beaten, nearly to death. I cannot confirm that rumour, since he was seeing no-one, and besides, no doubt healers visited in the aftermath.'

'Rautos,' murmured Druz, 'do we need to distance ourselves from the Patriotists?'

'It is worth considering,' Rautos replied. 'You might wish to begin preparations in that regard. In the meantime, however, we need the Patriotists, but I admit to worry that they may prove lacking come the day we most need their services.'

'Hire our own,' Barrakta said.

'I have done so.'

Sharp nods answered this quiet statement.

Uster Taran cleared his throat. 'My apologies, Rautos. You proceed on matters with your usual assurance. I regret my doubt.'

'As ever,' Rautos said, reaching once more for the cloth and wiping his hands, 'I welcome discourse. Indeed, even challenge. Lest I grow careless. Now, we need to assess the health of our own holdings, to give us all a better indication of our resilience . . .'

As the meeting continued, Rautos wiped at his hands again and again. A corpse had snagged on one of the mooring poles opposite the estate's landing this morning. Bloated and rotting, crawling with crayfish and seething with eels.

An occasional occurrence, but one that each time struck him with greater force, especially in the last few years. This morning it had been particularly bad, and though he had approached no closer than the uppermost tier in his yard, still it was as if some residue had reached him, making his hands oddly sticky – a residue that he seemed unable to remove, no matter how hard he tried.

CHAPTER TEN

The One God strode out – a puppet trailing
severed strings – from the conflagration. Another
city destroyed, another people cut down in their
tens of thousands. Who among us, witnessing
his emergence, could not but conclude that
madness had taken him? For all the power of
creation he possessed, he delivered naught but
death and destruction. Stealer of Life, Slayer and
Reaper, in his eyes where moments earlier there
had been the blaze of unreasoning rage, now
there was calm. He knew nothing. He could not
resolve the blood on his own hands. He begged
us for answers, but we could say nothing.
 We could weep. We could laugh.
 We chose laughter.

Creed of the Mockers
Cabal

LET'S PLAY A GAME, THE WIND WHISPERED. THEN IT LAUGHED IN THE
soft hiss of dust and sand.
 Hedge sat, listening, the crumbly stone block beneath him
eroded into a saddle shape, comforting enough, all things considered. It
might have been an altar once, fallen through some hole in the sky –
Hood knew, enough strange objects had tumbled down from the low,
impenetrable clouds during his long, meandering journey across this
dire world. Some of them far too close for comfort.

Yes, probably an altar. The depression wherein resided his behind felt
too even, too symmetrical to be natural. But he did not worry about
blasphemy – this was, after all, where the dead went. And the dead
included, on occasion, gods.

The wind told him as much. It had been his companion for so long, now, he had grown accustomed to its easy revelations, its quiet rasp of secrets and its caressing embrace. When he stumbled onto a scatter of enormous bones, hinting at some unhuman, monstrous god of long ago, the wind – as it slipped down among those bones, seeped between jutting ribs and slithered through orbitals and into the hollow caves of skulls – moaned that god's once-holy name. Names. It seemed they had so many, their utterances now and for ever more trapped in the wind's domain. Voiced in the swirl of dust, nothing but echoes now.

Let's play a game.

There is no gate – oh, you've seen it, I well know.

But it is a lie. It is what your mind builds, stone by stone.

For your kind love borders. Thresholds, divisions, delineations. To enter a place you believe you must leave another. But look around and you can see. There is no gate, my friend.

I show you this. Again and again. The day you comprehend, the day wisdom comes to you, you will join me. The flesh that encompasses you is your final conceit. Abandon it, my love. You once scattered yourself and you will do so again. When wisdom arrives. Has wisdom arrived yet?

The wind's efforts at seduction, its invitations to his accepting some kind of wilful dissolution, were getting irritating. Grunting, he pushed himself upright.

On the slope to his left, a hundred or more paces away, sprawled the skeleton of a dragon. Something had shattered its ribcage, puncturing blows driving shards and fragments inward – fatally so, he could see even from this distance. The bones looked strange, sheathed one and all in something like black, smoky glass. Glass that webbed down to the ground, then ran in frozen streams through furrows on the slope. As if the beast's melting flesh had somehow vitrified.

He had seen the same on the two other dragon remains he had come across.

He stood, luxuriating in his conceit – in the dull pain in his lower back, the vague earache from the insistent wind, and the dryness at the back of his throat that forced him to repeatedly clear it. Which he did, before saying, 'All the wonders and miseries of a body, wind, that is what you have forgotten. What you long for. You want me to join you? Ha, it's the other way round.'

You will never win this game, my love—

'Then why play it?'

He set off at an angle up the hillside. On the summit, he could see, more stone rubble, the remnants of a temple that had dropped through a hole in the earth, plucked from mortal eyes in a conflagration of dust and thunder. Like cutting the feet out from under a god. Like obliterat-ing a faith with a single slash of the knife. A hole in the earth, then, the

264

temple's pieces tumbling through the Abyss, the ethered layers of realm after realm, until they ran out of worlds to plunge through.

Knock knock, right on Hood's head.

Your irreverence will deliver unto you profoundest regret, beloved.

'My profoundest regret, wind, is that it never rains here. No crashing descent of water – to drown your every word.'

Your mood is foul today. This is not like you. We have played so many games together, you and I.

'Your breath is getting cold.'

Because you are walking the wrong way!

'Ah. Thank you, wind.'

A sudden bitter gust buffeted him, evincing its displeasure. Grit stung his eyes, and he laughed. 'Hood's secret revealed, at last. Scurry on back to him, wind, you have lost this game.'

You fool. Ponder this question: among the fallen, among the dead, will you find more soldiers – more fighters than non-fighters? Will you find more men than women? More gods than mortals? More fools than the wise? Among the Fallen, my friend, does the echo of marching armies drown all else? Or the moans of the diseased, the cries of the starving?

'I expect, in the end,' he said after a moment, 'it all evens out.'

You are wrong. I must answer you, even though it will break your heart. I must.

'There is no need,' he replied. 'I already know.'

Do you? whispered the wind.

'You want me to falter. In despair. I know your tricks, wind. And I know, too, that you are probably all that remains of some ancient, long-forgotten god. Hood knows, maybe you are all of them, their every voice a tangled mess, pushing dust and sand and little else. You want me to fall to my knees before you. In abject worship, because maybe then some trickle of power will come to you. Enough to make your escape.' He grunted a laugh. 'But this is for you to ponder, wind. Among all the fallen, why do you haunt *me*?'

Why not? You boldly assert bone and flesh. You would spit in Hood's face – you would spit in mine if you could think of a way to dodge my spitting it right back.

'Aye, I would at that. Which is my point. You chose wrongly, wind. Because I am a soldier.'

Let's play a game.

'Let's not.'

Among the Fallen, who—

'The answer is *children*, wind. More children than anyone else.'

Then where is your despair?

'You understand nothing,' he said, pausing to spit. 'For a man or a

265

woman to reach adulthood, they must first kill the child within them.'

You are a most vicious man, soldier.

'You still understand nothing. I have just confessed my despair, wind. You win the game. You win every game. But I will march on, into your icy breath, because that's what soldiers do.'

Odd, it does not feel as if I have won.

On a flat stretch of cold but not yet frozen mud, he came upon tracks. Broad, flattened and bony feet, one set, heading in the same direction. Someone . . . seeking perhaps what he sought. Water pooled in the deep prints, motionless and reflecting the pewter sky.

He crouched down, studying the deep impressions. 'Be useful, wind. Tell me who walks ahead of me.'

Silent. One who does not play.

'Is that the best you can do?'

Undead.

He squinted down at the tracks, noting the wide, slightly misaligned gait, the faint streaks left by dangling tufts of hide, skins, whatever. 'T'lan Imass?'

Broken.

'Two, maybe three leagues ahead of me.'

More. Water crawls slowly here.

'I smell snow and ice.'

My breath betrays all that I devour. Turn back to a sweeter kiss, beloved.

'You mean the reek of fly-swarmed swamp I've endured for the past two months?' He straightened, adjusted his heavy pack.

You are cruel. At least the one ahead says nothing. Thinks nothing. Feels nothing.

'T'lan Imass for certain, then.'

Broken.

'Yes, I understood you the first time.'

What will you do?

'If need be, I will give you a gift, wind.'

A gift? Oh, what is it?

'A new game – you have to guess.'

I will think and think and—

'Hood's breath – oh – oh! Forget I just said that!'

—and think and think . . .

They rode hard, westward at first, paralleling the great river for most of two days, before reaching the feeder track that angled northerly towards Almas, a modest town distinguished only by its garrison and stables, where Atri-Preda Yan Tovis, Varat Taun and their

Letherii company could rest, resupply and requisition fresh mounts.

Varat Taun knew flight when he saw it, when he found himself part of it. Away from Letheras, where, a day before their departure, the palace and barracks seemed caught in a rising storm of tension, the smell of blood heady in the air, a thousand rumours cavorting in all directions but none of them possessing much substance, beyond news relating the casting out of two families, the widows and children of two men who had been the Chancellor's bodyguards, and who were clearly no longer among the living.

Had someone tried to assassinate Triban Gnol? He'd wondered that out loud early in this journey and his commander had simply grunted, as if nothing in the notion surprised or even alarmed her. Of course she knew more than she was letting on, but Twilight had never been free with her words.

Nor am I, it turns out. The horrors of what I witnessed in that cavern – no, nothing I can say could possibly convey the . . . the sheer extremity of the truth. So best leave it. The ones who will witness will not live long past the experience. What then will remain of the empire?

And is this not why we are running away?

A foreigner rode with them. A Mocker, Yan Tovis had said, whatever that meant. A monk of some sort. *With the painted face of a cavorting mummer – what mad religion is that?* Varat Taun could not recall the strange little man saying a word – perhaps he was mute, perhaps his tongue had been cut out. Cultists did terrible things to themselves. The journey across the seas and oceans of the world had provided a seemingly endless pageantry of bizarre cultures and customs. No amount of self-mutilation in misguided service to some god would surprise Varat Taun. The Mocker had been among the challengers, but the absurdity of this was now obvious – after the first day of riding he had been exhausted, reeling in the saddle. He was, evidently, a healer.

Who healed me. Who guided me out from the terror and confusion. I have spoken my gratitude, but he just nodded. Did he witness the visions in my mind? Is he now struck mute, his very sanity under siege? In any case, he was no challenger to the Emperor, and that was why he now rode beside Yan Tovis, although what value she placed in this Mocker escaped the lieutenant.

Perhaps it's no different from how she views me. I ride in this company in an act of mercy. Soon to be sent to a posting in my home city. To be with my wife and my child. Twilight is not thinking as an Atri-Preda – not even her duty as a soldier was enough to compel her to report what she had learned to her superiors.

But this is not the first time, is it? Why should I be surprised? She surrendered Fent Reach to the Edur, didn't she? No battle, they just opened the gates.

267

'*Clearly, she loves the Edur so much she can go with them, to take command of the Letherii forces in the fleets.*' *So went the argument, dry and mocking.*

The truth may be that Yan Tovis is a coward.

Varat Taun did not like that thought, even as it now hounded him. He reminded himself of the battles, the skirmishes, both on water and ashore, where there had been nothing – not a single moment – when he had been given cause to doubt her courage.

Yet here, now, she was fleeing Letheras with her elite company.

Because I confirmed that Gral's claims. Besides, would I willingly stand beside Icarium again? No, not at his side, not in the same city, preferably not on the same damned continent. Does that make me a coward as well?

There had been a child, in that cavern, a strange thing, more imp than human. And it had managed what no-one else could – taking down Icarium, stealing away his rage and all the power that came with it. Varat Taun did not think there would be another such intervention. The defenders of the First Throne had possessed allies. The Emperor in Gold could not but refuse the same. There would be no-one there to stop Icarium. No-one but Rhulad himself, which was of course possible.

It is our lack of faith in our Emperor that has set us on this road.

But what if neither one will fall? What if Icarium finds himself killing Rhulad again and again? Ten times, fifty, a hundred – ten thousand? An endless succession of battles, obliterating all else. Could we not see the end of the world?

Icarium cannot yield. Rhulad will not. They will share that inevitability. And they will share the madness that comes of it.

Bluerose would not be far enough away. *No place will.*

He had left behind the one man who understood what was coming better than anyone else. The barbarian. Who wore a heavy hood to hide his features when among strangers. Who spat on his hands to smooth back his hair. Who greeted each and every dawn with a litany of curses against all who had wronged him. *Yet, now, I see him in my mind as if looking upon a brother.*

He and I alone survived. Together, we brought Icarium out.

His thoughts had brought him to this moment, this conflation of revelations, and he felt his heart grow cold in his chest. Varat Taun pushed his horse to a greater pace, until he came up alongside his commander. 'Atri-Preda.'

She looked across at him.

'I must go back,' he said.

'To warn them?'

'No, sir.'

268

'What of your family, Varat Taun?'

He glanced away. 'I have realized something. Nowhere is far enough.'

'I see. Then, would you not wish to be at her side?'

'Knowing I cannot save them . . .' Varat shook his head. 'The Gral and I – together – I don't know, perhaps we can do something – if we're there.'

'Can I talk you out of this?'

He shook his head.

'Very well. Errant's blessing on you, Varat Taun.'

'He is right,' said the Mocker behind them. 'I too must return.'

A heavy sigh gusted from Yan Tovis. 'So be it – I should have known better than to try to save anyone but myself – no, I'm not as bitter as that sounded. My apologies. You both have my blessing. Be sure to walk those horses on occasion, however.'

'Yes sir. Atri-Preda? Thank you.'

'What word do I send to your wife?'

'None, sir. Please.'

Yan Tovis nodded.

Varat Taun guided his mount off the road, reining in. The monk followed suited, somewhat more awkwardly. The lieutenant watched in some amusement. 'You have no horses in your lands?'

'Few. Cabal is an archipelago for the most part. The mainland holdings are on the sides of rather sheer cliffs, a stretch of coast that is severely mountainous. And what horses we do have are bred for labour and food.'

To that, Varat Taun said nothing.

They waited on the side of the track, watching the column of mounted soldiers ride past.

Errant take me, what have I done?

The lake stretched on with no end in sight. The three figures had rowed their well-provisioned boat for what passed for a day and most of a night in the Shadow Realm, before the craft ran aground in shallows. Unable to find a way past, they had shouldered the packs and disembarked, wading in silty, knee-deep water. Now, midway through the next day, they dragged exhausted, numbed legs through a calm lake that had been no deeper than their hips since dawn – until they reached a sudden drop-off.

Trull Sengar had been in the lead, using his spear to probe the waters ahead, and now he moved to one side, step by step, the butt of the weapon stirring the grey, milky silts along the edge. He continued on for a time, watched by his companions. 'Doesn't feel natural,' he finally said, making his way back to the others. 'The drop-away is smooth, even.' Moving past Onrack and Quick Ben, he resumed probing the ledge in the opposite direction. 'No change here.'

The wizard voiced a long, elaborate string of curses in his Malazan tongue, then said, 'I could take to the air, drawing on Serc – although how long I could manage that is anyone's guess.' He glared across at Onrack. 'You can just melt into silts, you damned T'lan Imass.'

'Leaving me,' said Trull, who then shrugged. 'I will swim, then – there may well be a resumption of the shallows ahead – you know, we've been walking on an unnaturally level bottom for some time. Imagine for the moment that we are on a submerged concourse of some sort – enormous, granted, but still. This drop-off could simply mark a canal. In which case I should soon find the opposite side.'

'A concourse?' Quick Ben grimaced. 'Trull, if this is a concourse beneath us it's the size of a city-state.'

Onrack said, 'You will find one such construct, Wizard, covering the southeast peninsula of Stratem. K'Chain Che'Malle. A place where ritual wars were fought – before all ritual was abandoned.'

'You mean when the Short-Tails rebelled.'

Trull swore under his breath. 'I hate it when everyone knows more than me.' Then he snorted. 'Mind you, my company consists of a mage and an undead, so I suppose it's no surprise I falter in comparison.'

'Falter?' Onrack's neck creaked loud as the warrior turned to regard the Tiste Edur. 'Trull Sengar, you are the Knight of Shadow.'

Quick Ben seemed to choke.

Above the wizard's sudden fit of coughing, Trull shouted: 'I am *what*? Was this Cotillion's idea? That damned upstart—'

'Cotillion did not choose you, friend,' Onrack said. 'I cannot tell you who made you what you now are. Perhaps the Eres'al, although I do not comprehend the nature of her claim within the realm of Shadow. One thing, however, is very clear – she has taken an interest in you, Trull Sengar. Even so, I do not believe the Eres'al was responsible. I believe you yourself were.'

'How? What did I do?'

The T'lan Imass slowly tilted its head to one side. 'Warrior, you stood before Icarium. You held the Lifestealer. You did what no warrior has ever done.'

'Absurd,' snapped Trull. 'I was finished. If not for Quick Ben here – and the Eres'al – I'd be dead, my chopped-up bones mouldering outside the throne room.'

'It is your way, my friend, to disarm your own achievements.'

'Onrack—'

Quick Ben laughed. 'He's calling you modest, Edur. And don't bother denying the truth of that – you still manage to startle me on that count. I've lived most of my life among mages or in the ranks of an army, and in neither company did I ever find much in the way of self-deprecation. We were all too busy pissing on each other's trees. One needs a certain level of, uh, bravado when it's your job to kill people.'

'Trull Sengar fought as a soldier,' Onrack said to the wizard. 'The difference between you two is that he is unable to hide his grief at the frailty of life.'

'Nothing frail about us,' Quick Ben muttered. 'Life stays stubborn until it has no choice but to give up, and even then it's likely to spit one last time in the eye of whatever's killed it. We're cruel in victory and cruel in defeat, my friends. Now, if you two will be quiet for a moment, I can go in search of a way out of here.'

'Not flying?' Trull asked, leaning on his spear.

'No, a damned gate. I'm beginning to suspect this lake doesn't end.'

'It must end,' the Edur said.

'The Abyss is not always twisted with wild storms. Sometimes it's like this – placid, colourless, a tide rising so slowly that it's impossible to notice, but rise it does, swallowing this tilted, dying realm.'

'The Shadow Realm is *dying*, Quick Ben?'

The wizard licked his lips – a nervous gesture Trull had seen before from the tall, thin man – then shrugged. 'I think so. With every border an open wound, it's not that surprising. Now, quiet everyone. I need to concentrate.'

Trull watched as Quick Ben closed his eyes.

A moment later his body grew indistinct, grainy at its edges, then began wavering, into and out of solidity.

The Tiste Edur, still leaning on his spear, grinned over at Onrack. 'Well, old friend, it seems we wander the unknown yet again.'

'I regret nothing, Trull Sengar.'

'It's virtually the opposite for me – with the exception of talking you into freeing me when I was about to drown in the Nascent – which, I've just realized, doesn't look much different from this place. Flooding worlds. Is this more pervasive than we realize?'

A clattering of bones as the T'lan Imass shrugged. 'I would know something, Trull Sengar. When peace comes to a warrior . . .'

The Edur's eyes narrowed on the battered undead. 'How do you just cast off all the rest? The surge of pleasure at the height of battle? The rush of emotions, each one threatening to overwhelm you, drown you? That sizzling sense of being alive? Onrack, I thought your kind felt . . . nothing.'

'With awakening memories,' Onrack replied, 'so too other . . . forces of the soul.' The T'lan Imass lifted one withered hand. 'This calm on all sides – it mocks me.'

'Better a wild storm?'

'I think, yes. A foe to fight. Trull Sengar, should I join this water as

271

dust, I do not think I would return. Oblivion would take me with the promise of a struggle ended. Not what I desire, friend, for that would mean abandoning you. And surrendering my memories. Yet what does a warrior do when peace is won?'

'Take up fishing,' Quick Ben muttered, eyes still closed, body still wavering. 'Now enough words from you two. This isn't easy.'

Wavering once more in and out of existence, then, suddenly – gone.

Ever since Shadowthrone had stolen him away – when Kalam needed him the most – Quick Ben had quietly seethed. Repaying a debt in one direction had meant betraying a friend in another. Unacceptable.

Diabolical.

And if Shadowthrone thinks he has my loyalty just because he pushed Kal into the Deadhouse, then he is truly as mad as we all think he is. Oh, I'm sure the Azath and whatever horrid guardian resides in there would welcome Kalam readily enough. Mount his head on the wall above the mantel, maybe – all right, that's not very likely. But the Azath collects. That's what it does, and now it has my oldest friend. So, how in Hood's name do I get him out?

Damn you, Shadowthrone.

But such anger left him feeling unbalanced, making concentration difficult. *And the skin rotting from my legs isn't helping either.* Still, they needed a way out. Cotillion hadn't explained much. *No, he'd just expected us to figure things out for ourselves. What that means is that there's only one real direction. Wouldn't do to have us get lost now, would it?*

Slightly emboldened – a momentary triumph over diffidence – Quick Ben concentrated, his senses reaching out to the surrounding ether. Solid, clammy, a smooth surface yielding like sponge under the push of imagined hands. The fabric of this realm, the pocked skin of a ravaged world. He began applying more pressure, seeking . . . *soft spots, weaknesses – I know you exist.*

Ah, you are now aware of me – I can feel that. Curious, you feel almost . . . feminine. Well, a first time for everything. What had been clammy beneath his touch was now simply cool. *Hood's breath, I'm not sure I like the images accompanying this thought of pushing through.*

Beyond his sense of touch, there was nothing. Nothing for his eyes to find; no scent in the tepid air; no sound beyond the faint swish of blood in the body – there one moment, gone the next as he struggled to separate his soul, free it to wander.

This isn't that bad—

A grisly tearing sound, then a vast, inexorable inhalation, tearing his spirit loose – yanking him forward and through, stumbling, into acrid swirling heat, thick clouds closing on all sides, soft sodden ground underfoot. He groped forward, his lungs filling with a pungent vapour that made his head reel. *Gods, what sickness is this? I can't breathe—*

The wind spun, drove him staggering forward – sudden chill, stones turning beneath his feet, blessed clean air that he sucked in with desperate gasps.

Down onto his hands and knees. On the rocky ground, lichen and mosses. On either side, a thinly spread forest in miniature – he saw oaks, spruce, alder, old and twisted and none higher than his hip. Dun-hued birds flitted among small green leaves. Midges closed in, sought to alight – but he was a ghost here, an apparition – *thus far. But this is where we must go.*

The wizard slowly lifted his head, then climbed to his feet.

He stood in a shallow, broad valley, the dwarf forest covering the basin behind him and climbing the slopes on all sides, strangely park-like in the generous spacing of the trees. And they swarmed with birds. From somewhere nearby came the sound of trickling water. Overhead, dragonflies with wingspans to match that of crows darted in their uncanny precision, feeding on midges. Beyond this feeding frenzy the sky was cerulean, almost purple near the horizons. Tatters of elongated clouds ran in high ribbons, like the froth of frozen waves on some celestial shore.

Primordial beauty – tundra's edge. Gods, I hate tundra. But so be it, as kings and queens say when it's all swirled down the piss-hole. Nothing to be done for it. Here we must come.

Trull Sengar started at the sudden coughing – Quick Ben had re-appeared, halfbent over, tears streaming from his eyes and something like smoke drifting from his entire body. He hacked, then spat and slowly straightened.

Grinning.

The proprietor of the Harridict Tavern was a man under siege. An affliction that had reached beyond months and into years. His establishment, once devoted to serving the island prison's guards, had since been usurped along with the rest of the port town following the prisoners' rebellion. Chaos now ruled, ageing honest folk beyond their years. But the money was good.

He had taken to joining Captain Shurq Elalle and Skorgen Kaban the Pretty at their preferred table in the corner during lulls in the mayhem, when the serving wenches and scull-boys rushed about with more purpose than panic, dull exhaustion replacing abject terror in their glazed eyes – and all seemed, for the moment, right and proper.

There was a certain calm with this here captain – *a pirate if the Errant pisses straight and he ain't missed yet* – and a marked elegance and civility to her manner that told the proprietor that she had stolen not just coins from the highborn but culture as well, which marked her as a smart, sharp woman.

He believed he was falling in love, hopeless as that was. Stress of the profession and too much sampling of inland ales had left him – in his honest, not unreasonably harsh judgement – a physical wreck to match his moral lassitude which on good days he called his *business acumen*. Protruding belly round as a stew pot and damned near as greasy. Bulbous nose – one up on Skorgen there – with burst veins, hair-sprouting blackheads and swirling bristles that reached down from the nostrils to entwine with his moustache – once a fashion among hirsute men but no more, alas. Watery close-set eyes, the whites so long yellow he was no longer sure they hadn't always been that colour. A few front teeth were left, four in all, one up top, three below. Better than his wife, then, who'd lost her last two stumbling into a wall while draining an ale casket – the brass spigot knocking the twin tombstones clean out of their sockets, and if she hadn't then choked on the damned things she'd still be with him, bless her. Times she was sober she'd work like a horse and bite just as hard and both talents did her well working the tables.

But life was lonely these days, wasn't it just, then in saunters this glorious, sultry pirate captain. A whole sight better than those foreigners, walking in and out of the Brullyg Shake's Palace as if it was their ancestral home, then spending their nights here, hunched down at the games table – the biggest table in the whole damned tavern, if you mind, with a single jug of ale to last the entire night no matter how many of them crowded round their strange, foreign, seemingly endless game.

Oh, he'd demanded a cut as was his right and they paid over peaceably enough – even though he could make no sense of the rules of play. And how those peculiar rectangular coins went back and forth! But the tavern's take wasn't worth it. A regular game of Bale's Scoop on any given night would yield twice as much for the house. And the ale quaffed – a player didn't need a sharp brain to play Bale's, Errant be praised. So these foreigners were worse than lumps of moss renting a rock, as his dear wife used to say whenever he sat down for a rest.

Contemplating life, my love. Contemplate this fist, dear husband. Wasn't she something, wasn't she just something. Been so quiet since that spigot punched her teeth down her throat.

'All right, Ballant,' Skorgen Kaban said in a sudden gust of beery breath, leaning over the table. 'You come and sit wi' us every damned night. And just sit. Saying nothing. You're the most tight-lipped tavernkeep I've ever known.'

'Leave the man alone,' the captain said. 'He's mourning. Grief don't need words for company. In fact, words is the last thing grief needs, so wipe your dripping nose, Pretty, and shut the toothy hole under it.'

The first mate ducked. 'Hey, I never knew nothing about grief, Captain.' He used the back of one cuff to blot at the weeping holes where his nose used to be, then said to Ballant, 'You just sit here, Keeper, and go on saying nothing to no-one for as long as you like.'

Ballant struggled to pull his adoring gaze from the captain, long enough to nod and smile at Skorgen Kaban, then looked back again to Shurq Elalle.

The diamond set in her forehead glittered in the yellowy lantern light like a knuckle sun, the jewel in her frown – oh, he'd have to remember that one – but she *was* frowning, and that was never good. Not for a woman.

'Pretty,' she now said in a low voice, 'you remember a couple of them Crimson Guard – in the squad? There was that dark-skinned one – sort of a more earthy colour than an Edur. And the other one, with that faint blue skin, some island mix, he said.'

'What about them, Captain?'

'Well.' She nodded towards the foreigners at the games table on the other side of the room. 'Them. Something reminds me of those two in Iron Bars's squad. Not just skin, but their gestures, the way they move – even some of the words I've overheard in that language they're speaking. Just . . . odd echoes.' She then fixed her dark but luminous gaze on Ballant. 'What do you know about them, Keeper?'

'Captain,' Skorgen objected, 'he's in mourning—'

'Be quiet, Pretty. Me and Ballant are having an inconsequential conversation.'

Yes, most inconsequential, even if that diamond blinded him, and that wonderful spicy aroma that was her breath made his head swim as if it was the finest liqueur. Blinking, he licked his lips – tasting sweat – then said, 'They have lots of private meetings with Brullyg Shake. Then they come down here and waste time.'

Even her answering grunt was lovely.

Skorgen snorted – wetly – then reached out with his one good hand and wiped clean the tabletop. 'Can you believe that, Captain? Brullyg an old friend of yours and you can't e'en get in to see him while a bunch of cheap foreigners can natter in his ear all day an' every day!' He half rose. 'I'm thinking a word with these here—'

'Sit down, Pretty. Something tells me you don't want to mess with that crowd. Unless you're of a mind to lose another part of your body.' Her frown deepened, almost swallowing that diamond. 'Ballant, you said they waste time, right? Now, that's the real curious part about all this. People like them don't waste time. No. They're waiting. For something or someone. And those meetings with the Shake – that sounds like negotiating, the kind of negotiating that Brullyg can't walk away from.'

'That don't sound good, Captain,' Skorgen muttered. 'In fact, it makes me nervous. Never mind avalanches of ice – Brullyg didn't run when that was coming down—'

Shurq Elalle thumped the table. 'That's it! Thank you, Pretty. It was something one of those women said. Brevity or Pithy – one of them. That ice was beaten back, all right, but not thanks to the handful of mages working for the Shake. No – those foreigners are the ones who saved this damned island. And that's why Brullyg can't bar his door against them. It isn't negotiation, because they're the ones doing all the talking.' She slowly leaned back. 'No wonder the Shake won't see me – Errant take us, I'd be surprised if he was still alive—'

'No, he's alive,' Ballant said. 'At least, people have seen him. Besides, he has a liking for Fent ale and orders a cask from me once every three days without fail, and that hasn't changed. Why, just yesterday—'

The captain leaned forward again. 'Ballant. Next time you're told to deliver one, let me and Pretty here do the delivering.'

'Why, I could deny you nothing, Captain,' Ballant said, then felt his face flush.

But she just smiled.

He liked these inconsequential conversations. Not much different from those he used to have with his wife. And . . . yes, here it was – that sudden sense of a yawning abyss awaiting his next step. Nostalgia rose within him, brimming his eyes.

Under siege, dear husband? One swing of this fist and those walls will come tumbling down – you do know that, husband, don't you?

Oh yes, my love.

Odd, sometimes he would swear she'd never left. Dead or not, she still had teeth.

Blue-grey mould filled pocks in the rotted ice like snow's own fur, shedding with the season as the sun's bright heat devoured the glacier. But winter, when it next came, would do little more than slow the inexorable disintegration. This river of ice was dying, an age in retreat.

Seren Pedac had scant sense of the age to come, since she felt she was drowning in its birth, swept along in the mud and refuse of long-frozen debris. Periodically, as their discordant, constantly bickering party climbed ever higher into the northern Bluerose Mountains, they would hear the thundering collapse of distant ice cliffs, calving beneath the besieging sun; and everywhere water streamed across bared rock, coughed its way along channels and fissures, swept past them in its descent into darkness – the journey to the sea just begun – swept past, to traverse subterranean caverns, shadowed gorges, sodden forests.

The mould was sporing, and that had triggered a recoil of Seren's senses – her nose was stuffed, her throat was dry and sore and she was racked with bouts of sneezing that had proved amusing enough to elicit even a sympathetic smile from Fear Sengar. That hint of sympathy alone earned her forgiveness – the pleasure the others took at her discomfort deserved nothing but reciprocation, when the opportunity arose, and she was certain it would.

Silchas Ruin, of course, was not afflicted with a sense of humour, in so far as she could tell. Or its dryness beggared a desert. Besides, he strode far enough ahead to spare himself her sneezing fits, with the Tiste Andii, Clip, only a few strides in his wake – like a sparrow harassing a hawk. Every now and then some fragment of Clip's monologue drifted back to where Seren and her companions struggled along, and while it was clear that he was baiting the brother of his god, it was equally evident that the Mortal Sword of the Black-Winged Lord was, as Udinaas had remarked, using the wrong bait.

Four days now, this quest into the ravaged north, climbing the spine of the mountains. Skirting huge masses of broken ice that slid – almost perceptibly – ever downslope, voicing terrible groans and gasps. *The leviathans are fatally wounded,* Udinaas once observed, *and will not go quietly.*

Melting ice exuded a stench beyond the acrid bite of the mould spores. Decaying detritus: vegetation and mud frozen for centuries; the withered corpses of animals, some of them beasts long extinct, leaving behind twisted hides of brittle fur every whisper of wind plucked into the air, fractured bones and bulging cavities filled with gases that eventually burst, hissing out fetid breath. It was no wonder Seren Pedac's body was rebelling.

The migrating mountains of ice were, it turned out, cause for the near-panic among the Tiste Andii inhabitants of the subterranean monastery. The deep gorge that marked its entrance branched like a tree to the north, and back down each branch now crawled packed snow and enormous blocks of ice, with streams of meltwater providing the grease, ever speeding their southward migration. And there was fetid magic in that ice, remnants of an ancient ritual still powerful enough to defeat the Onyx Wizards.

Seren Pedac suspected that there was more to this journey, and to Clip's presence, than she and her companions had been led to believe. *We walk towards the heart of that ritual, to the core that remains. Because a secret awaits us there.*

Does Clip mean to shatter the ritual? What will happen if he does?

And what if to do so ruins us? Our chances of finding the soul of Scabandari Bloodeye, of releasing it?

She was beginning to dread this journey's end.

There will be blood.

Swathed in the furs the Andii had provided, Udinaas moved up alongside her. 'Acquitor, I have been thinking.'

'Is that wise?' she asked.

'Of course not, but it's not as if I can help it. The same for you, I am sure.'

Grimacing, she said, 'I have lost my purpose here. Clip now leads. I . . . I don't know why I am still walking in your sordid company.'

'Contemplating leaving us, are you?'

She shrugged.

'Do not do that,' said Fear Sengar behind them.

Surprised, she half turned. 'Why?'

The warrior looked uncomfortable with his own statement. He hesitated.

What mystery is this?

Udinaas laughed. 'His brother offered you a sword, Acquitor. Fear understands – it wasn't just expedience. Nor was your taking it, I'd wager—'

'You do not know that,' Seren said, suddenly uneasy. 'Trull spoke – he assured me it was nothing more—'

'Do you expect everyone to speak plainly?' the ex-slave asked. 'Do you expect *anyone* to speak plainly? What sort of world do you inhabit, Acquitor?' He laughed. 'Not the same as mine, that's for certain. For every word we speak, are there not a thousand left unsaid? Do we not often say one thing and mean the very opposite? Woman, look at us – look at yourself. Our souls might as well be trapped inside a haunted keep. Sure, we built it – each of us – with our own hands, but we've forgotten half the rooms, we get lost in the corridors. We stumble into rooms of raging heat, then stagger back, away, lest our own emotions roast us alive. Other places are cold as ice – as cold as this frozen land around us. Still others remain for ever dark – no lantern will work, every candle dies as if starved of air, and we grope around, collide with unseen furniture, with walls. We look out through the high windows, but distrust all that we see. We armour ourselves against unreal phantasms, yet shadows and whispers make us bleed.'

'Good thing the thousand words for each of those were left unsaid,' Fear Sengar muttered, 'else we find ourselves in the twilight of all existence before you are through.'

Udinaas replied without turning. 'I tore away the veil of your reason, Fear, for asking the Acquitor to stay. Do you deny that? You see her as betrothed to your brother. And that he happens to be dead means nothing, because, unlike your *youngest* brother, you are an honourable man.'

A grunt of surprise from Udinaas, as Fear Sengar reached out to grasp the ex-slave, hands closing on the wrapped folds of fur. A surge of anger sent Udinaas sprawling onto the muddy scree.

As the Tiste Edur then whirled to advance on the winded Letherii, Seren Pedac stepped into his path. 'Stop. Please, Fear. Yes, I know he deserved it. But . . . stop.'

Udinaas had managed to sit up, Kettle crouching down at his side and trying to wipe the smears of mud from his face. He coughed, then said, 'That will be the last time I compliment you, Fear.'

Seren turned on the ex-slave. 'That was a rather vicious compliment, Udinaas. And I second your own advice – don't say anything like that again. Ever. Not if you value your life—'

Udinaas spat grit and blood, then said, 'Ah, but now we've stumbled into a dark room indeed. And, Seren Pedac, you are not welcome there.' He pushed himself upright. 'You have been warned.' Then he looked up, one hand settling on Kettle's shoulder. His eyes, suddenly bright, avid, scanned Seren, Fear, and then moved up the trail, to where Silchas Ruin and Clip now stood side by side, regarding those downslope. 'Here's a most telling question – the kind few dare utter, by the way. Which one among us, friends, is *not* haunted by a death wish? Perhaps we ought to discuss mutual suicide . . .'

No-one spoke for a half-dozen heartbeats. Until Kettle said, 'I don't want to die!'

Seren saw the ex-slave's bitter smile crumble, a sudden collapse into undeniable grief, before he turned away.

'Trull was blind to his own truth,' Fear said to her in a quiet voice. 'I was there, Acquitor. I know what I saw.'

She refused to meet his eyes. *Expedience. How could such a warrior proclaim his love for me? How could he even believe he knew me enough for that?*

And why can I see his face as clear in my mind as if he stood here before me? I am haunted indeed. Oh, Udinaas, you were right. Fear is an honourable man, so honourable as to break all our hearts.

But, Fear, there is no value in honouring one who is dead.

'Trull is dead,' she said, stunning herself with her own brutality as she saw Fear visibly flinch. 'He is dead.' *And so am I. There is no point in honouring the dead. I have seen too much to believe otherwise. Grieve for lost potential, the end of possibilities, the eternally silent demise of promise. Grieve for that, Fear Sengar, and you will under- stand, finally, how grief is but a mirror, held close to one's own face.*

And every tear springs from the choices we ourselves did not make.

When I grieve, Fear, I cannot even see the bloom of my own breath – what does that tell you?

They resumed walking. Silent.

A hundred paces above the group, Clip spun his chain and rings. 'What was all that about?' he asked.

'You have lived in your tidy cave for too long,' the white-skinned Tiste Andii said.

'Oh, I get out often enough. Carousing in Bluerose – the gods know how many bastards have been brewed by my seed. Why—'

'One day, Mortal Sword,' Silchas Ruin interrupted, 'you will discover what cuts deeper than any weapon of iron.'

'Wise words from the one who smells still of barrows and rotting cobwebs.'

'If the dead could speak, Clip, what would they tell you?'

'Little, I expect, beyond complaints about this and that.'

'Perhaps, then, that is all you deserve.'

'Oh, I lack honour, do I?'

'I am not sure what you lack,' Silchas Ruin replied, 'but I am certain I will comprehend before we are done.'

Rings and chain snapped taut. 'Here they come. Shall we continue onward and upward?'

There was so much that Toc the Younger – Anaster, Firstborn of the Dead Seed, the Thrice-blinded, Chosen by the Wolf Gods, the Unlucky – did not wish to remember. His other body for one; the body he had been born into, the first home to his soul. Detonations against Moon's Spawn above the doomed city of Pale, fire and searing, blazing heat – *oh, don't stand there*. Then that damned puppet, Hairlock, delivering oblivion, wherein his soul had found a rider, another force – a wolf, one-eyed and grieving.

How the Pannion Seer had lusted for its death. Toc recalled the cage, that spiritual prison, and the torment as his body was broken, healed, then broken yet again, a procession seemingly without end. But these were memories and pain and anguish persisted as little more than abstract notions. Yet, mangled and twisted as that body had beeen, *at least it was mine.*

Strip away years, course sudden in new blood, feel these strange limbs so vulnerable to cold. To awaken in another's flesh, to start against muscle memories, to struggle with those that were suddenly gone. Toc wondered if any other mortal soul had ever before staggered this tortured path. Stone and fire had marked him, as Tool once told him. To lose an eye delivers the gift of preternatural sight. And what of leaving a used-up body for a younger, healthier one? *Surely a gift – so the wolves desired, or was it Silverfox?*

But wait. A closer look at this Anaster – who lost an eye, was given a new one, then lost it yet again. Whose mind – before it was broken and flung away – was twisted with terror, haunted by a mother's terrible love; who had lived the life of a tyrant among cannibals – oh yes, look closely at these limbs, the muscles beneath, and remember –

this body has grown with the eating of human flesh. And this mouth, so eager with its words, it has tasted the succulent juices of its kin – remember that?

No, he could not.

But the body can. It knows hunger and desire on the battlefield – walking among the dead and dying, seeing the split flesh, the jutting bones, smelling the reek of spilled blood – ah, how the mouth waters.

Well, everyone had his secrets. And few are worth sharing. *Unless you enjoy losing friends.*

He rode apart from the train, ostensibly taking an outrider flank, as he had done as a soldier, long ago. The Awl army of Redmask, fourteen thousand or so warriors, half again as many in the trailing support train – weaponsmiths, healers, horsewives, elders, old women, the lame and the once-born children, and, of course, twenty or so thousand rodara. Along with wagons, travois, and almost three thousand herd dogs and the larger wolf-hunters the Awl called dray. If anything could trigger cold fear in Toc it was these beasts. Too many by far, and rarely fed, they ranged in packs, running down every creature on the plains for leagues around.

But let us not forget the K'Chain Che'Malle. Living, breathing ones. Tool – or perhaps it was Lady Envy – had told him that they had been extinct for thousands of years – tens, hundreds of thousands, even. Their civilization was dust. *And wounds in the sky that never heal; now there's a detail worth remembering, Toc.*

The huge creatures provided Redmask's bodyguard at the head of the vanguard – no risk of assassination, to be sure. The male – Sag'Churok – was a K'ell Hunter, bred to kill, the elite guard of a Matron. *So where is the Matron? Where is his Queen?*

Perhaps it was the young female in the K'ell's company. Gunth Mach. Toc had asked Redmask how he had come to know their names, but the war leader had refused him an answer. Reticent bastard. *A leader must have his secrets, perhaps more so than anyone else. But Redmask's secrets are driving me mad. K'Chain Che'Malle, for Hood's sake!*

Outcast, the young warrior had journeyed into the eastern wastelands. So went the tale, although after that initial statement it was a tale that in truth went nowhere, since virtually nothing else was known of Redmask's adventures during those decades – *yet at some point, this man donned a red-scaled mask. And found himself flesh and blood K'Chain Che'Malle. Who did not chop him to pieces. Who somehow communicated to him their names. Then swore allegiance. What is it, then, about this story that I really do not like?*

How about all of it.

The eastern wastelands. A typical description for a place the name-givers found inhospitable or unconquerable. *We can't claim it so it is*

281

worthless, a wasted land, a wasteland. Hah, and you thought us without imaginations!

Haunted by ghosts, or demons, the earth blasted, where every blade of grass clings to a neighbour in abject terror. The sun's light is darker, its warmth colder. Shadows are smudged. Water brackish and quite possibly poisonous. Two-headed babies are common. Every tribe needed such a place. For heroic war leaders to wander into on some fraught quest rife with obscure motivations that could easily be bludgeoned into morality tales. *And, alas, this particular tale is far from done. The hero needs to return, to deliver his people. Or annihilate them.*

Toc had his memories, a whole battlefield's worth, and as the last man left standing he held few illusions of grandeur, either as witness or as player. *So this lone eye cannot help but look askance. Is it any wonder I've taken to poetry?*

The Grey Swords had been cut to pieces. Slaughtered. Oh, they'd yielded their lives in blood enough to pay the Hound's Toll, as the Gadrobi were wont to say. But what had their deaths meant? *Nothing. A waste.* Yet here he rode, in the company of his betrayers.

Does Redmask offer redemption? He promises the defeat of the Letherii – but they were not our enemies, not until we agreed the contract. So, what is redeemed? The extinction of the Grey Swords? Oh, I need to twist and bend to bind those two together, and how am I doing thus far?

Badly. Not a whisper of righteousness – no crow croaks on my shoulder as we march to war.

Oh, Tool, I could use your friendship right now. A few terse words on futility to cheer me up.

Twenty myrid had been killed, gutted and skinned but not hung to drain their blood. The cavities where their organs had been were stuffed solid with a local tuber that had been sweated on hot stones. The carcasses were then wrapped in hides and loaded into a wagon that was kept apart from all the others in the train. *Redmask's plans for the battle to come. No more peculiar than all the others. The man has spent years thinking on this inevitable war. That makes me nervous.*

Hey, Tool, you'd think after all I've been through, I'd have no nerves left. But I'm no Whiskeyjack. Or Kalam. No, for me, it just gets worse.

Marching to war. Again. Seems the world wants me to be a soldier.

Well, the world can go fuck itself.

'A haunted man,' the elder said in his broken growl as he reached up and scratched the savage red scar marring his neck. 'He should not be with us. Fey in darkness, that one. He dreams of running with wolves.'

Redmask shrugged, wondering yet again what this old man wanted with him. An elder who did not fear the K'Chain Che'Malle, who was so bold as to guide his ancient horse between Redmask and Sag'Churok.

'You should have killed him.'

'I do not ask for your advice, Elder,' Redmask said. 'He is owed respite. We must redeem our people in his eyes.'

'Pointless,' the old man snapped. 'Kill him and we need redeem ourselves to no-one. Kill him and we are free.'

'One cannot flee the past.'

'Indeed? That belief must taste bitter for one such as you, Redmask. Best discard it.'

Redmask slowly faced the man. 'Of me, Elder, you know nothing.'

A twisted smile. 'Alas, I do. You do not recognize me, Redmask. You should.'

'You are Renfayar – my tribe. You share blood with Masarch.'

'Yes, but more than that. I am old. Do you understand? I am the oldest among our people, the last one left . . . who was there, who remembers. Everything.' The smile broadened, revealing rotted teeth, a pointed red – almost purple – tongue. 'I know your secret, Redmask. I know what she meant to you, and *I know why*.' The eyes glittered, black and red-rimmed. 'You had best fear me, Redmask. You had best heed my words – my advice. I shall ride your shoulder, yes? From this moment on, until the very day of battle. And I shall speak with the voice of the Awl, my voice the voice of their souls. And know this, Redmask: I shall not countenance their betrayal. Not by you, not by that one-eyed stranger and his bloodthirsty wolves.'

Redmask studied the old man a moment longer, then fixed his gaze ahead once more.

A soft, ragged laugh at his side, then, 'You dare say nothing. You dare do nothing. I am a dagger hovering over your heart. Do not fear me – there is no need, unless you intend evil. I wish you great glory in this war. I wish the end of the Letherii, for all time. Perhaps such glory shall come by your hand – together, you and I, let us strive for that, yes?'

A long moment of silence.

'Speak, Redmask,' the elder growled. 'Lest I suspect defiance.'

'An end to the Letherii, yes,' Redmask finally said, in a grating voice. 'Victory for the Awl.'

'Good,' grunted the old man. 'Good.'

The magic world had ended abruptly, an ending as sudden as the slamming of a trunk lid – a sound that had always shocked her, frozen her in place. Back in the city, that place of reeks and noise, there had

283

been a house steward, a tyrant, who would hunt down slave children who had, in his words, disappointed him. A night spent in the musty confines of the bronze box would teach them a thing or two, wouldn't it?

Stayandi had spent one such night, enclosed in cramped darkness, two months or so before the slaves joined the colonists out on the plain. The solid clunk of the lid had truly seemed, then, the end of the world. Her shrieks had filled the close air of the trunk until something broke in her throat, until every scream was naught but a hiss of air.

Since that time, she had been mute, yet this had proved a gift, for she had been selected to enter the Mistress's domain as a handmaiden in training. No secrets would pass her lips, after all. And she would have been there still, if not for the homesteading.

A magic world. So much space, so much air. The freedom of blue skies, unending wind and darkness lit by countless stars – she had not imagined such a world existed, all within reach.

And then one night, it ended. A fierce nightmare made real in screams of slaughter.

Abasard—

She had fled into the darkness, stunned with the knowledge of his death – her brother, who had flung himself into the demon's path, who had died in her place. Her bared feet, feather-light, carrying her away, the hiss of grasses soon the only sound to reach her ears. Stars glittering, the plain bathed silver, the wind cooling the sweat on her skin.

In her mind, her feet carried her across an entire continent. Away from the realm of people, of slaves and masters, of herds and soldiers and demons. She was alone now, witness to a succession of dawns, smeared sunsets, alone on a plain that stretched out unbroken on all sides. She saw wild creatures, always at a distance. Darting hares, antelope watching from ridgelines, hawks wheeling in the sky. At night she heard the howl of wolves and coyotes and, once, the guttural bellow of a bear.

She did not eat, and the pangs of hunger soon passed, so that she floated, and all that her eyes witnessed shone with a luminous clarity. Water she licked from dew-laden grasses, the cupped holes of deer and elk tracks in basins, and once she found a spring, almost hidden by thick brush in which flitted hundreds of tiny birds. It had been their chittering songs that had drawn her attention.

An eternity of running later, she had fallen. And found no strength to rise once more, to resume the wondrous journey through this glowing land.

Night then stole upon her, and not long after came the four-legged people. They wore furs smelling of wind and dust, and they gathered close, lying down, sharing the warmth of their thick, soft cloaks. There were children among them, tiny babes that crawled as did their parents, squirming and snuggling up against her.

And when they fed on milk, so did Stayandi.

The four-legged people were as mute as she was, until they began their mournful cries, when night was at its deepest; crying – she knew – to summon the sun.

They stayed with her, guardians with their gifts of warmth and food. After the milk, there was meat. Crushed, mangled carcasses – mice, shrews, a headless snake – she ate all they gave her, tiny bones crunching in her mouth, damp fur and chewy skin.

This too seemed timeless, a *foreverness*. The grown-ups came and went. The children grew burlier, and she now crawled with them when it was time to wander.

When the bear appeared and rushed towards them, she was not afraid. It wanted the children, that much was obvious, but the grown-ups attacked and drove it off. Her people were strong, fearless. They ruled this world.

Until one morning she awoke to find herself alone. Forcing herself to her hind legs, helpless whimpering coming from her throat in jolts of pain, she scanned the land in all directions—

And saw the giant. Bare above the waist, the deep hue of sun-darkened skin almost entirely obscured beneath white paint – paint that transformed his chest, shoulders and face into bone. His eyes, as he walked closer, were black pits in the caked mask skull. He carried weapons: a long spear, a sword with a broad, curved blade. The fur of the four-legged people was wrapped about his hips, and the small but deadly knives strung in a necklace about the warrior's neck, they too belonged to her people.

Frightened, angry, she bared her teeth at the stranger, even as she cowered in the fold of a small hummock – nowhere to run, knowing he could catch her effortlessly. Knowing that yet another of her worlds had shattered. Fear was her bronze box, and she was trapped, unable to move.

He studied her for a time, cocking his head as she snapped and snarled. Then slowly crouched down until his eyes were level with her own.

And she fell silent.

Remembering . . . things.

They were not kind eyes, but they were – she knew – like her own. As was his hairless face beneath that deathly paint.

She had run away, she now recalled, until it seemed her fleeing mind had outstripped her flesh and bone, had darted out into something unknown and unknowable.

And this savage face, across from her, was slowly bringing her mind back. And she understood, now, who the four-legged people were, what they were. She remembered what it was to stand upright, to run with two legs instead of four. She remembered an encampment, the digging of cellar pits, the first of the sod-walled houses. She remembered her family – her brother – and the night the demons came to steal it all away.

After a time of mutual silent regard, he straightened, settled the weapons and gear about himself once more, then set out.

She hesitated, then rose.

And, at a distance, she followed.

He walked towards the rising sun.

Scratching at the scarred, gaping hole where one eye had been, Toc watched the children running back and forth as the first cookfires were lit. Elders hobbled about with iron pots and wrapped foodstuffs – they were wiry, weathered folk, but days of marching had dulled the fire in their eyes, and more than a few snapped at the young ones who passed too close.

He saw Redmask, trailed by Masarch and Natarkas and another bearing the red face-paint, appear near the area laid out for the war leader's yurt. Seeing Toc, Redmask approached.

'Tell me, Toc Anaster, you flanked our march on the north this day – did you see tracks?'

'What sort do you mean?'

Redmask turned to Natarkas's companion. 'Torrent rode to the south. He made out a trail that followed an antelope track – a dozen men on foot—'

'Or more,' the one named Torrent said. 'They were skilled.'

'Not Letherii, then,' Toc guessed.

'Moccasined,' Redmask replied, his tone betraying slight irritation at Torrent's interruption. 'Tall, heavy.'

'I noted nothing like that,' said Toc. 'Although I admit I was mostly scanning horizon lines.'

'This place shall be our camp,' Redmask said after a moment. 'We will meet the Letherii three leagues from here, in the valley known as Bast Fulmar. Toc Anaster, will you stay with the elders and children or accompany us?'

'I have had my fill of fields of battle, Redmask. I said I'd found myself a soldier again, but even an army's train needs guards, and that is about all I am up to right now.' He shrugged. 'Maybe from now on.'

The eyes in that scaled mask held on Toc for a half-dozen heartbeats, then slowly turned away. 'Torrent, you too will stay here.'

The warrior stiffened in surprise. 'War Leader—'

'You will begin training those children who are close to their death nights. Bows, knives.'

Torrent bowed, stiffly. 'As you command.'

Redmask left them, trailed by Natarkas and Masarch.

Torrent glanced over at Toc. 'My courage is not broken,' he said.

'You're young still,' he replied.

'You will oversee the younger children, Toc Anaster. That and nothing more. You will keep them and yourself out of my way.'

Toc had had enough of this man. 'Torrent, you rode at your old war leader's side when you Awl abandoned us to the Letherii army. Be careful of your bold claims of courage. And when I came to you and pleaded for the lives of my soldiers, you turned away with the rest of them. I believe Redmask has just taken your measure, Torrent, and if I hear another threat from you I will give you reason to curse me – with what will be your last breath.'

The warrior bared his teeth in a humourless smile. 'All I see in that lone eye, Toc Anaster, tells me you are already cursed.' He pivoted and walked away.

Well, the bastard has a point. So maybe I'm not as good at this give and take as I imagined myself to be. For these Awl, it is a way of life, after all. Then again, the Malazan armies are pretty good at it, too – no wonder I never really fit.

A half-dozen children hurried past, trailed by a mud-smeared toddler struggling to keep up. Seeing the chattering mob vanish round a tent, the toddler halted, then let out a wail.

Toc grunted. *Aye, you and me both.*

He made a rude sound and the toddler looked over, eyes wide. Then laughed.

Eye socket fiercely itching once more, Toc scratched for a moment, then headed over, issuing yet another rude noise. *Oh, look at that – innocent delight. Well, Toc, take your rewards where and when you can.*

Redmask stood at the very edge of the sprawling encampment, studying the horizon to the south. 'Someone is out there,' he said in a low voice.

'So it seems,' Natarkas said. 'Strangers – who walk our land as if they owned it. War Leader, you have wounded Torrent—'

'Torrent must learn the value of respect. And so he will, as weapon master to a score of restless adolescents. When next he joins us, he will be a wiser man. Do you challenge my decisions, Natarkas?'

'Challenge? No, War Leader. But at times I will probe them, if I find the need to understand them better.'

Redmask nodded, then said to the warrior standing a short distance away. 'Heed those words, Masarch.'

'So I shall,' the young warrior replied.

'Tomorrow,' said Redmask, 'I lead my warriors to war. Bast Fulmar.'

Natarkas hissed, then said, 'A cursed valley.'

'We will honour the blood spilled there three hundred years ago, Natarkas. The past will die there, and from there on we shall look only to a new future. New in every way.'

'This new way of fighting, War Leader, I see little honour in it.'

'You speak true. There is none to be found. Such is necessity.'

'Must necessity be surrender?'

Redmask looked across at the warrior whose face was painted in the likeness of his own mask. 'When the ways surrendered hold naught but the promise of failure, then yes. It must be done. They must be cast away.'

'The elders will find that difficult to accept, War Leader.'

'I know. You and I have played this game before. This is not their war. It is mine. And I mean to win it.'

They were silent then, as the wind, a dirge through dead grasses, moaned ghostly across the land.

CHAPTER ELEVEN

Sea without water
spreads white bones
crumbled flat and bleached
like parchment
where I walked.

But this scrawl
scratching my wake
is without history
bereft of raiment
to clothe my fate.

Sky has lost its clouds
to some ragged wind
that never runs aground
these shoals revealed
on paths untrod.

Wind heaves waves
unseen in the shell
a cup of promise unfulfilled
the rank lie of salt
that bites my tongue.

I dwelt by a sea, once
etching histories
along the endless strand
in rolling scrolls
of flotsam and weed.

Rumours of the Sea
Fisher kel Tath

THERE HAD BEEN RAIN IN THE AFTERNOON, WHICH WAS JUST AS WELL since there wasn't much value in burning the entire forest down and besides, he wasn't popular at the best of times. They had mocked his antics, and they had said he stank, too, so much so that no-one ever came within reach of his huge, gnarled hands. Of course, had any of his neighbours done so, he might well have torn their limbs off to answer years of scorn and abuse.

Old Hunch Arbat no longer pulled his cart from farm to farm, from shack to shack, collecting the excrement with which he buried the idols of the Tarthenal gods that had commanded a mostly forgotten glade deep in the woods. The need had passed, after all. The damned hoary nightmares were dead.

His neighbours had not appreciated Arbat's sudden retirement, since now the stink of their wastes had begun to foul their own homes. Lazy wastrels that they were, they weren't of a mind to deepen their cesspits – didn't Old Hunch empty them out on a regular basis? Well, not any more.

That alone might have been reason enough to light out. And Arbat would have liked nothing better than to just vanish into the forest gloom, never to be seen again. Walk far, yes, until he came to a hamlet or village where none knew him, where none even knew of him. Rainwashed of all odour, just some kindly, harmless old mixed-blood Tarthenal who could, for a coin or two, mend broken things, including flesh and bone.

Walk, then. Leaving behind the old Tarthenal territories, away from the weed-snagged statues in the overgrown glades. And maybe, even, away from the ancient blood of his heritage. Not all healers were shamans, were they? They'd not ask any awkward questions, so long as he treated them right, and he could do that, easy.

Old bastards like him deserved their rest. A lifetime of service. Propitiations, the Masks of Dreaming, the leering faces of stone, the solitary rituals – all done, now. He could walk his last walk, into the unknown. A hamlet, a village, a sun-warmed boulder beside a trickling stream, where he could settle back and ease his tortured frame and not move, until the final mask was pulled away . . .

Instead, he had woken in darkness, in the moments before false dawn, shaking as if afflicted with ague, and before his eyes had hovered the slowly shredding fragments of a most unexpected Dream Mask. One he had never seen before, yet a visage of terrifying power. A mask crazed with cracks, a mask moments from shattering explosively—

Lying on his cot, the wood frame creaking beneath him as he trembled from head to foot, he waited for revelation.

The sun was high overhead when he finally emerged from his shack. Banks of clouds climbed the sky to the west – an almost-spent storm coming in from the sea – and he set about his preparations, ignoring the rain when it arrived.

Now, with dusk fast approaching, Arbat collected a bundled cane of rushes and set one end aflame from the hearth. He fired his shack, then the woodshed, and finally the old barn wherein resided his two-wheeled cart. Then, satisfied that each building was truly alight, he shouldered the sack containing those possessions and supplies he would need, and set out onto the trail leading down to the road.

A grunt of surprise a short time later, on the road, as he ran into a score of villagers hurrying in a mob towards him. In their lead, the Factor, who cried out in relief upon seeing Arbat.

'Thank the Errant you're alive, Hunch!'

Scowling, Arbat studied the man's horsey face for a moment, then scanned the pale smudges of the other faces, hovering behind the Factor. 'What is all this?' he demanded.

'A troop of Edur are staying at the inn tonight, Arbat. When word of the fires reached them they insisted we head up to help – in case the wood goes up, you see—'

'The wood, right. So where are the meddlers now, then?'

'They remained behind, of course. But I was ordered—' the Factor paused, then leaned closer to peer up at Arbat. 'Was it Vrager, then? The fool likes his fires, and is no friend of yours.'

'Vrager? Could be. He's been in the habit of sneaking in at night and pissing on my door. Doesn't accept me being retired and all. Says I got a duty to cart away his shit.'

'And so you do!' someone growled from the mob behind the Factor. 'Why else we let you live here anyway?'

'Well that's a problem solved now, ain't it?' Arbat said, grinning. 'Vrager burned me out, so I'm leaving.' He hesitated, then asked, 'What business was this of the Edur? It's just done rained – the chances of the blaze moving much ain't worth the worry. Didn't you tell them my place is cleared back eighty, a hundred paces on all sides? And there's the old settling pools – good as a moat.'

The Factor shrugged, then said, 'They asked about you, then decided maybe someone had torched you out of spite – and that's breaking the law and the Edur don't like it when that happens—'

'And they told you to do your job, did they?' Arbat laughed at the man. 'That'd be a first!'

'Vrager, you said – is that a formal accusation, Arbat? If it is, you gotta dictate and make your mark and stay round for the convening and if Vrager hires an advocate—'

'Vrager's got a cousin in Letheras who's just that,' someone said.

The Factor nodded. 'All this could take a damned while, Arbat, and ain't none of us obliged to give you a roof overhead, neither—'

'So best I don't cause trouble, right? You can tell the Edur I wasn't making no formal complaint, so that's that. And what with the shacks pretty much burnt down by now and the chill seeping into your bones and no sign the fire's jumped anywhere . . .' Arbat slapped the Factor on the shoulder – a gesture that nearly drove the man to his knees – then stepped past. 'Make way, the rest of you – could be I'm still contagious with all the sick you been dumping in my cart.'

That worked readily enough, and Arbat's way was suddenly clear. And on he walked.

They'd give Vrager some trouble – not good calling down the Edur's regard, after all – but it'd be nothing fatal. Pissing against a door don't forfeit the fool's life, now did it? Anyway, the Edur would ride on, to wherever it was they were going, and he'd leave them—

What now? Horses on the road, riders coming at the canter. Grumbling under his breath, Old Hunch Arbat worked his way to one verge, then waited.

Another damned troop. Letherii this time.

The lead rider, an officer, slowed her mount upon seeing Arbat, and the troop behind her did the same at her command. As she trotted her horse closer, she called out, 'You, sir – is there a village ahead?'

'There is,' Arbat replied, 'though you might have to fight for room at the inn.'

'And why's that?' she asked as she rode opposite.

'Some Edur staying the night there.'

At that the officer reined in, gesturing the rest to a halt. Twisting in her saddle, she eyed him from beneath the ridge of her iron helm. 'Tiste Edur?'

'That's them all right.'

'What are they doing there?'

Before he could answer, one of her soldiers said, 'Atri-Preda, something's blazing ahead – y'can see the glow and smell it.'

'That'd be my homestead,' Arbat replied. 'Accident. It won't spread, I'm sure of that as can be. Got nothing to do,' he added, 'with them Edur. They're just passing through.'

The Atri-Preda swore under her breath. 'Tarthenal, yes?'

'Mostly.'

'Can you think of anywhere we can camp for the night, then? Close by, but well off the trail.'

Arbat squinted at her. 'Off the trail, eh? Far enough off so's your privacy ain't disturbed, you mean?'

She nodded.

Arbat rubbed at the bristly hair covering his prognathous jaw. 'Forty or so paces up there's a trail, right side of the road. Leads through a thicket, then an old orchard, and beyond that there's an abandoned

292

homestead – barn's still got a roof, though I doubt it's weatherproof. There's a well too, which should be serviceable enough.'

'This close by, and no-one's occupied it or stripped it down?'

Arbat grinned. 'Oh, they'll get to that before long. It was downwind of my place, you see.'

'No, I don't.'

His grin broadened into a smile. 'Local colour kinda pales when told to outsiders. It's no matter, really. All you'll be smelling is woodsmoke this night, and that'll keep the bugs away.'

He watched as she thought about pressing the matter; then, as her horse tossed its head, she gathered the reins once more. 'Thank you, Tarthenal. Be safe in your journey.'

'And you, Atri-Preda.'

They rode on, and Arbat waited on the verge for the troop to pass.

Safe in my journey. Yes, safe enough, I suppose. Nothing on the road I can't handle.

No, it's the destination that's got my knees knocking together like two skulls in a sack.

Lying on his stomach, edging up to the trapdoor, peering down. A menagerie in the room below, yet comforting in its odd domesticity nonetheless. Why, he knew artists who would pay for such a scene. Ten hens wandering about, occasionally squawking from the path of a clumsily swung foot from Ublala Pung as the huge man paced back and forth. The scholar Janath sitting with her back to one wall, rolling chicken down or whatever it was called between the palms of her hands, prior to stuffing it into a burlap sack that was intended to serve as a pillow at some point – proving beyond all doubt that academics knew nothing about anything worth knowing about. Not to mention inserting a sliver of fear that Bugg's healing of her mind had not been quite up to scratch. And finally, Bugg himself, crouched by the hearth, using a clawed hen foot to stir the steaming pot of chicken soup, a detail which, Tehol admitted, had a certain macabre undercurrent. As did the toneless humming coming from his stalwart manservant.

True enough, the household was blessed with food aplenty, marking the continuation of their good run of luck. Huge capabara fish beside the canal a couple of weeks back, and now retired hens being retired one by one, as inexorable as the growl of a stomach. Or two or three. Or four, assuming Ublala Pung had but one stomach which was not in any way certain. Selush might know, having dressed enough bodies from the inside out. Tarthenal had more organs in those enormous bodies than regular folk, after all. Alas, this trait did not extend to brains.

Yet another formless, ineffable worry was afflicting Ublala Pung.

Could be lovestruck again, or struck to fear by love. The half-blood lived in a world of worry, which, all things considered, was rather surprising. Then again, that undeniable virtue between his legs garnered its share of worshippers, lighting feminine eyes with the gleam of possession, avarice, malicious competition – in short, all those traits most common to priesthoods. But it was worship for all the wrong reasons, as poor Ublala's fretful state of mind made plain. His paltry brain wanted to be loved for itself.

Making him, alas, a complete idiot.

'Ublala,' Bugg said from where he hovered over the soup pot, 'glance upward for me if you will to confirm that those beady eyes studying us belong to my master. If so, please be so kind as to invite him down for supper.'

Tall as he was, Ublala's face, lifting into view to squint upwards at Tehol, was within reach. Smiling and patting him on the head, Tehol said, 'My friend, if you could, step back from what serves as a ladder here – and given my manservant's lacklustre efforts at repair I am using the description advisedly – so that I may descend in a manner befitting my station.'

'What?'

'Get out of the way, you oaf!'

Ducking, edging away, Ublala grunted. 'Why is he so miserable?' he asked, jerking a thumb up at Tehol. 'The world is about to end but does he care about that? No. He doesn't. Care about that. The world ending. Does he?'

Tehol shifted round to lead with his feet on the uppermost rung of the ladder. 'Loquacious Ublala Pung, how ever will we follow the track of your thoughts? I despair.' He wiggled over the edge then groped with his feet.

Bugg spoke. 'Given the view you are presently providing us, master, despair is indeed the word. Best look away, Janath.'

'Too late,' she replied. 'To my horror.'

'I live in the company of voyeurs!' Tehol managed to find the rung with one foot and began making his way down.

'I thought they were chickens,' Ublala said.

A piercing avian cry, ending in a mangled crunch.

'Oh.'

Cursing from Bugg. 'Damn you, Pung! You're eating that one! All by yourself! And you can cook it yourself, too!'

'It just got in the way! If you built some more rooms, Bugg, it wouldn't have happened.'

'And if you did your damned pacing in the alley outside – better yet, if you just stopped worrying about things – or bringing those worries here – or always showing up around supper time – or—'

'Now now,' Tehol interjected, stepping free of the last rung and adjusting his blanket. 'Nerves are frayed and quarters are cramped and Ublala's cramped brain is fraying our nerves without quarter, so it would be best if we all—'

'Master, he just flattened a hen!'

'A voyeur,' Ublala insisted.

'—got along,' Tehol finished.

'Time, I think,' said Janath, 'for some mitigation, Tehol. I seem to recall you having some talent for that, especially working your way around the many attempts at expelling you.'

'Yeah,' said Ublala, 'where do we do that?'

'Do what?' Janath asked.

'I gotta go.'

'Over to the warehouse,' Tehol said, pushing Ublala towards the door – without much success. 'Ublala, do your expelling back of the warehouse, near the drain spout. Use the comfrey bush poking out of the rubbish heap then wash your hands in the tilted trough.'

Looking relieved, the huge man ducked his way out into the alley.

Turning, Tehol regarded Bugg. 'All right, a moment of silence, then, for the retired hen.'

Rubbing his brow, Bugg leaned back and sighed. 'Sorry. I'm not used to these . . . crowds.'

'What amazes me,' Tehol said, now studying the surviving hens, 'is their eerie indifference. They just walk around their crushed sister—'

'Wait a moment and they'll start ripping it apart,' Bugg said, shambling over to collect the carcass. 'Between the two, I prefer indifference.' He picked the limp form up, frowned at the dangling neck. 'Quiet in death, as with all things. Almost all things, I mean . . .' Abruptly he shook his head and tossed the dead creature onto the floor in front of Janath. 'More feathers for you, Scholar.'

'A most appropriate task,' Tehol murmured, 'plucking lovely plumage to reveal the pimpled nightmare beneath.'

'Sort of like inadvertently looking up your tunic, Tehol Beddict.'

'You are a cruel woman.'

She paused and looked up at him. 'Assuming those were just pimples.'

'Most cruel, leading me to suspect that you in fact fancy me.'

Janath shot Bugg a glance. 'What kind of healing did you do on me, Bugg? My world seems . . . smaller.' She tapped one temple. 'In here. My thoughts travel any distance – any distance at all – and they vanish in a . . . in a white nothing. Blissful oblivion. So, I do remember what happened, but not even a whisper of emotion reaches me.'

'Janath, most of those protections are of your own making. Things will . . . expand. But it will take time. In any case, it is not too surprising that you are developing an attachment to Tehol, seeing him as your protector—'

'Now hold on, old man! Attachment? To Tehol? To an ex-student? That is, in every way imaginable, disgusting.'

'I thought it was a common occurrence,' Tehol said. 'Why, some of the stories I've heard—'

'Common for those fools who confuse love with worship – all to feed their paltry egos, I might add. Usually men, too. Married men. It's pathetic—'

'Janath, did— No, never mind.' Rubbing his hands together, Tehol faced Bugg. 'My, that soup smells wonderful.'

Ublala Pung returned, shouldering his way through the doorway. 'That comfrey tasted awful,' he said.

The three stared at him for a long moment.

Then Bugg spoke. 'See those half-gourds, Ublala? Bring them over and get your voyeur soup.'

'I could eat a whole one all by myself, I'm so hungry.'

Tehol pointed. 'There's one right there, Ublala.'

The huge man paused, glanced over at the bedraggled carcass. Then pushed the gourds into Tehol's hands and said, 'Okay.'

'Leave me some feathers?' Janath asked.

'Okay.'

Tehol said, 'Do you mind, Ublala, if the rest of us eat . . . uh, up on the roof?'

'Go ahead.'

'After supper,' Tehol continued as the half-blood lowered himself into a cross-legged position, reached for the carcass and tore off a leg. 'After, I mean, Ublala, we can talk about what's worrying you, all right?'

'No point talking,' Ublala said around a mouthful of feathers, skin and meat. 'I got to take you to him.'

'Who?'

'A champion. The Toblakai.'

Tehol met Bugg's eyes, and saw in them unfeigned alarm.

'We got to break into the compound,' Ublala continued.

'Uh, right.'

'Then make sure he doesn't kill us.'

'I thought you said there was no point in talking!'

'I did. There isn't.'

Janath collected her gourd of soup. 'So we have to climb one-handed up that ladder? And I expect you want me to go first? Do you think me an idiot?'

Tehol scowled at her, then brightened. 'You have a choice, Janath. You follow me and Bugg, at the risk of your appetite, or we follow you, lifting you skyward with our sighs of admiration.'

'How about neither?' With that, she headed out into the alley.

Horrible crunching sounds came from where Ublala sat. After a moment, both Tehol and Bugg followed in Janath's wake.

Ormly, once Champion Rat Catcher, sat down opposite Rucket.

After a nod of greeting, she returned to her meal. 'I'd offer you some of these crisped hog ears, but as you can see, there's not many left and they are one of my favourites.'

'You do it on purpose, don't you?'

'Men always assume beautiful women think of nothing but sex, or, rather, are obsessed with the potential thereof, at any and every moment. But I assure you, food poses a sensuality rarely achieved in clumsy gropings on some flea-bitten mattress with errant draughts sending chills through you at every change of position.'

Ormly's withered face twisted into a scowl. 'Change of position? What does that mean?'

'Something tells there is no legion of beleaguered women bemoaning the loss of one Ormly.'

'I wouldn't know nothing about that. Listen, I'm nervous.'

'How do you think I feel? Care for some wine? Oh, I was hoping you'd decline. You know, hiding in this burial crypt has put a strain on select vintages. It's all very well for you, skulking in the shadows every night, but as the new commander of our insurgent organization, I have to hide down here, receiving and despatching all day, doing endless paperwork—'

'What paperwork?'

'Well, the paperwork I do to convince the minions how busy I am, so they don't come running to me every damned moment.'

'Yes, but what are you writing down, Rucket?'

'I record snatches of overheard conversations – the acoustics down here are impressive if a tad wayward. One can achieve sheer poetry on occasion, with judicial use of juxtaposition.'

'If it's random then it ain't poetry,' Ormly said, still scowling.

'Clearly you don't keep up with modern movements, then.'

'Just one, Rucket, and that's what I'm nervous about. It's Tehol Beddict, you see.'

'A most extraordinary juxtaposition there,' she replied, reaching for another hog's ear. 'Idiocy and genius. In particular, his genius for creating idiotic moments. Why, the last time we made love—'

'Rucket, please! Don't you see what's going on out there? Oh, sorry, I guess you don't. But listen to me, then. He's *too* successful! It's going too fast! The Patriotists are stirred up something awful, and you can be sure the Liberty Consign is backing them with every resource at its disposal. In the Low Markets they're starting to barter because there's no coin.'

297

'Well, that was the plan—'

'But we're not ready!'

'Ormly, Scale House collapsed, didn't it?'

He glared at her suspiciously, then grunted and looked away. 'All right, so we knew that was coming. We've been ready for that, yes. True enough. Even though we're no closer to knowing what'll happen when whatever it is happens, assuming we'll even know it's happening when it does. Anyway, you're just trying to confuse me, because you've lost all objectivity when it comes to Tehol.'

'Oh now really, do you take me for a fool?'

'Yes. Love, lust, whatever, it's affected your ability to think straight when it comes to that madman.'

'You're the one not thinking straight. Tehol's not the mystery here. Tehol's easy – no, not that kind of – oh, very well, that kind, too. Anyway, like I said. Easy. The true mystery before us, Ormly, is his damned manservant.'

'Bugg?'

'Bugg.'

'But he's just the front man—'

'You sure it's not the other way round? What does he do with all that coin they've leveraged into their hands? Bury it in the back yard? They don't even have a back yard. Ormly, we're talking tons of coinage here.' She waved a hand about. 'Could fill this crypt twenty times over. Now, sure, there're other crypts under the city, but we know them all. I've sent runners to every one of them, but they're empty, the dust underfoot not disturbed in years. We've sent rats into every fissure, every crevasse, every crack. Nothing.' She snapped her fingers. 'Gone. As if into thin air. And not just in this city, either.'

'So maybe Tehol's found a hiding place we ain't looked at yet. Something both clever and idiotic, like you said.'

'I thought of that, Ormly. Trust me when I tell you, it's all gone.'

His scowl suddenly cleared and reached for a refill of the wine. 'I figured it out. It's all dumped into the river. Simple. Easy.'

'Except that Tehol insists it can be recovered – to flood the market, if the Consign financiers panic and start minting more than the usual quota. And even that quota is proving inflationary, since there's no recycling of old coins taking place. There's no return for recasting. I hear even the Imperial Treasury is hurting. Tehol says he can dump it all back onto the streets, at a moment's notice.'

'Maybe he's lying.'

'Maybe he isn't.'

'Maybe I'll have that last hog ear.'

'Forget it.'

'Fine. We got another problem. Tensions are high between the Edur and the Patriotists – and the Chancellor and his army of thugs and spies. Blood was spilled.'

'Not surprising,' Rucket replied. 'It was bound to happen. And don't think the financial strain has nothing to do with it.'

'If it does it's only indirectly,' Ormly said. 'No, this clash was, I think, personal.'

'Can we make use of it?'

'Ah, finally we can discuss something and actually get somewhere.'

'You're just jealous of Tehol Beddict.'

'So what if I am. Forget it. Let's make plans.'

Sighing, Rucket gestured to one of her servants. 'Bring us another bottle, Unn.'

Ormly's brow lifted, and, as the huge man shambled off into a side chamber, he leaned closer. 'Unn? The one who . . . ?'

'Murdered Gerun Eberict? Indeed, the very man. With his own two hands, Ormly. His own two hands.' Then she smiled. 'And those hands, well, murdering isn't the only thing they're good at.'

'I knew it! It *is* all you ever think about!'

She settled back in her chair. *Make them feel clever. The only sure way to keep the peace.*

Beneath the city of Letheras was a massive core of ice. A fist of Omtose Phellack, clutching in its implacable grip an ancient spirit. Lured, then trapped by a startling alliance of Ceda Kuru Qan, a Jaghut sorceress and an Elder God. For the Errant, it was a struggle to appreciate that conjoining, no matter how advantageous the consequence. A spirit imprisoned, until such time as that hoary ritual weakened – or, more likely, was shattered in wilful malice. So, though temporary – and what truly wasn't? – it had prevented death and destruction on a colossal scale. All very well.

Kuru Qan treating with a Jaghut sorceress – surprising but not disturbing. No, it was Mael's involvement that gnawed ceaselessly in the Errant's thoughts.

An Elder God. But not K'rul, not Draconus, not Kilmandaros. No, this was the one Elder God who never got involved. Mael's curse was everyone else's blessing. So what changed? What forced the old bastard's hand, enough so that he forged alliances, that he unleashed his power in the streets of the city, that he emerged onto a remote island and battered a broken god senseless?

Friendship towards a pathetic mortal?

And what, dear Mael, do you now plan to do about all those worshippers? The ones so abusing your indifference? They are legion and their hands drip blood in your name. Does this please you? From them, after all, you acquire power. Enough to drown this entire realm.

War among the gods, but was the battle line so simply drawn as it seemed? The Errant was no longer sure.

He stood in solid rock, within reach of the enormous knot of ice. He could smell it, that gelid ancient sorcery that belonged to another era. The spirit imprisoned within it, frozen in the act of rising through a fetid lake, was a seething storm of helpless rage, blurred and indistinct at its centre. One of Mael's own kin, the Errant suspected, like a piece torn free only to suffer a geas of the Crippled God. Entirely unaware – so far – of the terrible fissures spread like crazed webs through that ice, fissures even now working their way inwards.

Shattered indeed. With intent? No, not this time, but in imagining a place of permanence they chose in error. And no, they could not have known. This . . . nudge . . . not mine. Just . . . dread circumstance.

Does Mael know? Abyss take me, I need to speak to him – ah, how I recoil at the notion! How much longer can I delay? What rotted commodity would my silence purchase? What meagre reward my warning?

Perhaps another word with that war god, Fener. But no, that poor creature probably knew even less than he did. Cowering, virtually usurped . . . *usurped, now there's an interesting notion. Gods at war . . . yes, possibly.*

The Errant withdrew, passing ghostly through rock. Sudden desire, impatience, pushed him onward. He would need a mortal's hand for what he planned. A mortal's blood.

He emerged onto a floor of mouldy, uneven pavestones. How far had he travelled? How much time had passed? Darkness and the muted sound of dripping water. He sniffed the air, caught the scent of life. Tainted acrid by delving into old magic. And knew where he was. Not far, then. Not long. *Never hide in the same place, child.* Mouth dry – something like anticipation – he hurried down the crooked corridor.

I can do nothing, weak as I am. Edging askew the course of fates – I was once far more. Master of the Tiles. All that power in those scribed images, the near-words from a time when no written words existed. They would have starved without my blessing. Withered. Does this mean nothing? Am I past bargaining?

He could feel now, within him, flaring to life, a once-dull ember of . . . of . . . *of what? Ah, yes, I see it clear. I see it.*

Ambition.

The Errant reached the secret chamber, could discern trickling heat at the entrance.

Crouched over a brazier, she spun round when he stepped into the room. The heady, damp air, thick with spices, made him feel half drunk. He saw her eyes widen.

'Turudal Brizad—'

The Errant staggered forward. 'It's this, you see. A bargain—'

He saw her hand edge out, hovering over the coals of the brazier. 'They all want to bargain. With me—'

'The Holds, witch. They clash, clumsy as crones. Against the young ones – the *Warrens*. Only a fool would call it a dance of equals. Power was robust, once. Now it is . . .' he smiled, taking another step closer, '*gracile*. Do you understand? What I offer you, witch?'

She was scowling to hide her fear. 'No. You stink like a refuse pit, Consort – you are not welcome here—'

'The tiles so want to play, don't they? Yet they clatter down in broken patterns, ever broken. There is no *flow*. They are outmoded, witch. *Outmoded*.'

A gesture with the hovering hand, and Feather Witch's eyes flicked past the Errant.

A faint voice behind him. '*Do not do this.*'

The Errant turned. 'Kuru Qan. She summoned *you*?' He laughed. 'I could banish you with the blink of an eye, ghost.'

'*She was not to know that. Heed my warning, Errant; you are driven to desperation. And the illusion of glory – do you not understand what has so afflicted you? You stood too close to the ice. Assailed by a storm of desire from the trapped demon. Its ambition. Its lust.*'

A sliver of doubt, stinging, then the Errant shook his head. 'I am the Master of the Tiles, Elder. No pathetic wellspring spirit could so infect me. My thoughts are clear. My purpose—' He turned again, dismissing the ghost behind him. And reeled slightly, needing a step to right himself.

The ghost of the Ceda spoke. '*Errant, you think to challenge the Warrens? Do you not realize that, as the Tiles once had a Master, so too the Warrens?*'

'Don't be a fool,' the Errant said. 'There are no tiles describing these warrens—'

'*Not Tiles. Cards. A Deck. And yes, there is a Master. Do you now choose to set yourself against him? To achieve what?*'

The Errant made no reply, although his answer whispered in his skull. *Usurpation. As a child before one such as myself. I might even pity him, as I wrest from him all power, every drop of blood, his very life.*

I shall retreat from this world no longer.

Kuru Qan continued, '*If you set the Holds to battle against the Warrens, Errant, you will shatter alliances—*'

The Errant snorted. 'They are already shattered, Ceda. What began as yet another march on the Crippled God to exact brutal punishment – as if the Fallen One commits a crime by virtue of his very existence – well, it is that no more. The Elders are awakened, awakened to

301

themselves – the memory of what they once were, what they could be again. Besides,' he added as he took another step towards the now trembling Letherii witch, 'the enemy is divided, confused—'

'*All strangers to you. To us. Are you so certain that what you sense is true? Not simply what your enemy wants you to believe?*'

'Now you play games, Kuru Qan. Ever your flaw.'

'*This is not our war, Errant.*'

'Oh, but it is. My war. Rhulad's war. The Crippled God's. After all, it is not the Elder Gods who so hunger to destroy the Fallen One.'

'*They would if they but understood, Errant. But they are blinded by the lure of resurrection – as blinded as you, here, now. All but one, and that is the maker of the Warrens. K'rul himself. Errant, listen to me! To set the Holds against the Warrens, you declare war upon K'rul—*'

'No. Just his children. Children who will kill him if they can. They don't want him. He was gone, but now he walks the realms again, and drags with him the Tiles, the Holds, the ancient places he knew so well – there is the real war, Ceda!'

'*True, and K'rul's idiotic nostalgia is proving a most virulent poison – although he is yet to realize that. I am dead, Errant – the paths I have wandered—*'

'Do not interest me.'

'*Do not do this. This is all the Crippled God's game!*'

Smiling, the Errant reached out, the motion a blur. Grasped the Letherii witch round the throat. Lifted her clear of the floor.

In his other hand, a knife appeared.

Blood. Mortal's gift to the Elder—

She held something in one hand. Thrashing, struggling against his life-stealing grip, her eyes bulging, face darkening, she lashed out with that hand.

And stabbed a severed finger into his left eye.

The Errant bellowed in shock, a spear of incandescence lancing into his brain.

His knife bit into the woman's body. He flung her away, then lurched, flailing at his own face – where blood streamed down, where something dangled at the end of a thread against his cheek. *Got her, never mind what she did to me – got her, that foul creature – her blood – my blood – Abyss take me, the* pain!

Then she was back. Clawed hands gouging against his face – grasping something, tearing it away – *pain!* And her vicious snarl, close – '*I'm collecting.*' Twisting away, even as he slashed again with the knife, cutting into flesh, the edge rippling along bones.

She had torn away an eye. Gone. Crushed in one bloody hand.

But her blood gleamed on his knife. Enough. More than enough.

The Errant, one hand outstretched, lone eye struggling to make

sense of a battered, broken perspective, staggered towards the doorway.
All I need.

Trailing blood, Feather Witch dragged herself to the far wall, where she curled up, in one stained hand the eye of a god, in the other the severed finger of Brys Beddict – it felt swollen now, as if it absorbed the Errant's blood. Warm, no, *hot.*

'*Collecting,*' she whispered.

The ghost of the Ceda drew close. '*You are dying, child. You need a healer.*'

She spat. 'Then find me one.'

The brazier's coals pulsed, but all she could feel was cold, deep in her body, spreading outward to steal all life from her limbs.

'Hurry,' she said in a mumble.

But no-one replied.

The Errant stumbled down the bridge. To either side, the tiles of the Cedance spun in confused mayhem. He barked out a laugh, holding the slick knife before him as if it was a torch – he could feel the heat searing his face, drying the blood and other fluids weeping down from his left socket.

Someone had been here. Not long past.

Hannan Mosag. Delving the mysteries of ancient power.

But he was Tiste Edur. A stranger to these forces.

No, they are mine. They were always mine. And now I come.

To reclaim them.

And I challenge you, Master of the Deck, whoever, whatever you are. Face me here, if you've the courage. I challenge you!

The Errant reached the centre dais, held the knife high, then flung it down onto the tiles.

The point sank deep into painted stone.

He stared down. One eye. Widening.

The knife had pierced the centre of a tile, nailing it in place. The others now began swirling round it, as if drawn into a vortex.

The centre of a tile.

His own. The blade buried in the chest of the image. *My chest. What does that mean? No matter. What other tile could it possibly choose?*

The world trembled – he could feel it, deep in its core, spreading in ripples, those ripples rising, devouring energy, lifting into waves. The waves heaving higher, gaining speed, lifting . . .

The Errant laughed as power burgeoned within him. 'Mortal blood!'

Was she dead now? He'd struck her twice. Driven the weapon deep. She would have spilled out by now. A corpse huddled in that cursed chamber. Until the rats found her. And this was well. She could not be allowed to survive – he wanted no High Priestess, no mortal bound to his resurrected godhood. *The other prayers I can swallow. Ignore. They all know I never answer. Never give a thing away. Expecting nothing, so they receive nothing, and I am not bound to them.*

But a High Priestess . . .

He would have to make sure. Go back. And make sure.

The Errant spun round, began walking.

'Bastard,' Feather Witch said, her mouth filled with the taste of blood. Running from her nostrils, bubbling at the back of her throat. Immense pressures crushing her chest on the right side.

She could wait no longer. The ghost was too late.

'I am dying.'

No. Errant, bastard god, forgotten god, hungry god.

Well, you are not the only hungry one around here.

She bared her teeth in a red smile, then pushed the mangled eyeball into her mouth.

And swallowed.

The Errant staggered, rebounded from a corridor wall, as something reached into his chest and tore free a welter of power. Stole it away. Leaving a cavern of agony.

'The bitch!'

The roar echoed against cold stone.

And he heard her voice, filling his skull: *'I am yours now. You are mine. Worshipper and worshipped, locked together in mutual hate. Oh, won't that twist things, yes?*

'You should have found someone else, Errant. I have read the histories. Destrai Anant, God Chosen, the Well of the Spirit. Feather Witch. You are mine. I am yours. And listen to my prayer – listen! Your Destrai demands it! In my hand, now, waits our Mortal Sword. He too has tasted your blood. Your power can heal him as it has done me. Do you not still feel his' – malicious delight – *'touch?'*

Her laughter rasped in his head, rebounding bitter with his stolen power.

'Summon him, Errant. We need him.'

'No.'

'We need him! And a Shield Anvil – a T'orrud Segul in the language of the First Empire. Which of us shall choose? Oh, of course, you would claim that right for yourself. But I have a candidate. Another wrapped tight in webs of spite – I utter his name and so find a face to my deepest hatred – is that not well suited?

'And yes, he still lives. Udinaas. Let us make of this priesthood a

company of betrayers. Let us claim the Empty Throne – it was ever rightfully ours, Errant – beloved.

'Udinaas. Claim him! Choose him! We can devour each other's souls across the span of a thousand years. Ten thousand!'

'Leave me, damn you!'

'Leave you? God of mine, I compel you!'

The Errant fell to his knees, tilted his head back, and screamed his rage. And the world trembled anew.

He had forgotten. The chains. The wills locked in an eternal tug of war. The flood waters of fierce emotion rising again and again. The deathless drowning. *I am in the world again. I surrendered my weakness, and am imprisoned by power.* 'Only the weak and useless are truly free,' he whispered.

She heard him. 'No need to be so maudlin, Errant. Go back to the Cedance and see for yourself. Blood now flows between the Tiles. Between them all. The Warrens. The Cedance, at last, maps the truth of things. The truth of things. To use your words, the Tiles now . . . flow.

'Can you not taste them? These new Warrens? Come, let us explore them, you and I, and choose our aspect. There are flavours . . . light, and dark, shadow and death, life and . . . oh, what is this? The Jesters of Chance, an Unaligned, Oponn? Oponn – dear Errant, you have upstarts standing in your stead. These Twins play your game, Errant.

'What will we do about that?'

'Abyss take me,' the god groaned, sinking down onto the cold, clammy pavestones.

'Summon him, Errant. He is needed. Now. Summon our Mortal Sword.'

'I cannot. You damned fool. He is lost to us.'

'I possess—'

'I know what you possess. Do you truly think it enough? To wrest him from Mael's grasp? You stupid, pathetic bitch. Now, cease this damned prayer, Destrai. Your every demand weakens me – and that is not smart. Not now. Too soon. I am . . . vulnerable. The Edur—'

'The Edur warlocks tremble and start at shadows now – they do not know what has happened. All they know is blind terror—'

'Silence!' the god bellowed. 'Who can reach through those warlocks, you blubbering capabara? *Leave me alone! Now!*'

He was answered with . . . nothing. Sudden absence, a presence recoiling.

'Better,' he snarled.

Yet he remained, slumped onto the cold floor, surrounded in darkness. Thinking. But even thoughts did not come free, without a price.

305

Abyss below, I think I have made a mistake. And now I must live with it.

And make plans.

Gadalanak stepped in behind and under his round-shield. A huge hand grasped his arm, wrapping round it just below his shoulder, and a moment later he was flying across the compound, landing hard, skidding then rolling until he crashed up against the wall.

The Meckros warrior groaned, shook his head, then released his short-handled double-bladed axe and reached up to tug clear his helm. 'Not fair,' he said, wincing as he sat up. He glared across at Karsa Orlong. 'The Emperor couldn't have done that.'

'Too bad for him,' the Toblakai rumbled in reply.

'I think you tore something in my arm.'

Samar Dev spoke from where she sat on a chair in the shade, 'Best find a healer, then, Gadalanak.'

'Who else will dare face me?' Karsa demanded, eyeing the half-dozen other warriors as he leaned on his sword. All eyes turned to the masked woman, who stood silent and motionless, worn and weathered like a forgotten statue in some ruin. She seemed indifferent to the attention. And she had yet to draw her two swords.

Karsa snorted. 'Cowards.'

'Hold on,' the one named Puddy said, his scarred face twisting. 'It ain't that, y'damned bhederin bull. It's your style of fighting. No point in learning to deal with it, since this Edur Emperor don't fight that way. He couldn't. I mean, he ain't got the strength. Nor the reach. Besides, he's civilized – you fight like an animal, Karsa, and you just might take the bastard down – only you won't have to, 'cause I'll do it before you.' He hefted the short javelin in one hand. 'I'll skewer him first – then let's see him fight with a shaft of wood impaling him. I skewer him from six paces, right? Then I close with my cutlass and chop him into pieces.'

Samar Dev stopped listening, since she had heard Puddy's boasts before, and held her gaze on the woman the Meckros warrior had called a Seguleh. First Empire word, that. *The Anvil.* Strange name for a people – probably some remnant clan from the colonial period of Dessimbelackis's empire. A fragment of an army, settled on some pleasant island as their reward for some great victory – those armies were each named, and 'the Anvil' was but a variation on a theme common among the First Empire military. The mask, however, was a unique affectation. Gadalanak said all Seguleh were so attired, and something in the glyphs and scratches on those enamel masks indicated rank. *But if those marks are writing, it's not First Empire. Not even close. Curious. Too bad she never says anything.*

Cradling his shield arm, Gadalanak used the wall to lever himself upright, then set off in search of a healer.

There had been events in the palace, sending tremors far enough to reach the challengers' compound. Perhaps the List had been formalized, the order of the battles decided. A rumour to please the idiotic warriors gathered here – although Karsa's only response to the possibility was a sour grunt. Samar Dev was inclined to agree with him – she was not convinced that the rumour was accurate. No, something else had happened, something messy. *Factions sniping like mongrels at a feast all could share had they any brains. But that's always the way, isn't it? Enough is never enough.*

She felt something then, a shivering along the strands – the bones – buried beneath the flesh of this realm. *This realm . . . and every other one. Gods below . . .* The witch found she was on her feet. Blinking. And in the compound's centre she saw Karsa now facing her, a fierce regard in his bestial eyes. The Toblakai bared his teeth.

Shaking her gaze free of the terrible warrior, she walked quickly into the colonnaded hallway, then through to the passage lined by the cells where the champions were quartered. Down the corridor.

Into her modest room.

She closed the door behind her, already muttering the ritual of sealing. Trouble out there, blood spilled and sizzling like acid. Dreadful events, something old beyond belief, exulting in new power—

Her heart stuttered in her chest. An apparition was rising from the floor in the centre of the room. Shouldering through her wards.

She drew her knife.

A damned ghost. The ghost of a damned mage, in fact.

Luminous but faint eyes fixed on her. 'Witch,' it whispered, '*do not resist, I beg you.*'

'You are not invited,' she said. 'Why would I not resist?'

'*I need your help.*'

'Seems a little late for that.'

'*I am Ceda Kuru Qan.*'

She frowned, then nodded. 'I have heard that name. You fell at the Edur conquest.'

'*Fell? A notion worth consideration. Alas, not now. You must heal someone. Please. I can lead you to her.*'

'Who?'

'*A Letherii. She is named Feather Witch—*'

Samar Dev hissed, then said, 'You chose the wrong person, Ceda Kuru Qan. Heal that blonde rhinazan? If she's dying, I am happy to help her along. That woman gives witches a bad name.'

Another tremor rumbled through the unseen web binding the world. She saw Kuru Qan's ghost flinch, saw the sudden terror in its eyes.

And Samar Dev spat on her knife blade, darted forward and slashed the weapon through the ghost.

The Ceda's shriek was short-lived, as the iron weapon snared the ghost, drew it inward, trapped it. In her hand the knife's hilt was suddenly cold as ice. Steam slithered from the blade.

She quickly added a few words under her breath, tightening the binding.

Then staggered back until her legs bumped against her cot. She sank down, shivering in the aftermath of the capture. Her eyes fell to the weapon in her hand. 'Gods below,' she mumbled. 'Got another one.'

Moments later the door swung open. Ducking, Karsa Orlong entered.

Samar Dev cursed at him, then said, 'Must you do that?'

'This room stinks, witch.'

'You walk through my wards as if they were cobwebs. Toblakai, it would take a damned god to do what you just did – yet you are no god. I would swear to that on the bones of every poor fool you've killed.'

'I care nothing for your damned wards,' the huge warrior replied, leaning his sword against a wall then taking a single step that placed him in the centre of the room. 'I know that smell. Ghosts, spirits, it's the stink of forgetting.'

'Forgetting?'

'When the dead forget they're dead, witch.'

'Like your friends in that stone sword of yours?'

The eyes that fixed on her were cold as ashes. 'They have cheated death, Samar Dev. Such was my gift. Such was theirs, to turn away from peace. From oblivion. They live because the sword lives.'

'Yes, a warren within a weapon. Don't imagine that as unique as you might want it to be.'

He bared his teeth. 'No. After all, you have that knife.'

She started. 'Hardly a warren in this blade, Karsa Orlong. It's just folded iron. Folded in a very specific way—'

'To fashion a prison. You civilized people are so eager to blunt the meaning of your words. Probably because you have so many of them, which you use too often and for no reason.' He looked round. 'So you have bound a ghost. That is not like you.'

'I could not argue that,' she admitted, 'since I am no longer sure who I am. What I'm supposed to be like.'

'You once told me you did not compel, you did not bind. You bargained.'

'Ah, that. Well, yes, given the choice. Seems that being in your company crushes under heel the privilege of choice, Toblakai.'

'You blame me for your greed?'

'Not greed. More like an overwhelming need for power.'

'To oppose me?'

'You? No, I don't think so. To stay alive, I think. You are dangerous, Karsa Orlong. Your will, your strength, your . . . disregard. You present the quaint and appalling argument that through wilful ignorance of the laws and rules of the universe you cannot suffer their influence. As you might imagine, your very success poses evidence of that tenet, and it is one I cannot reconcile, since it runs contrary to a lifetime of observation.'

'Too many words again, Samar Dev. State it plain.'

'Fine,' she snapped. 'Everything about you terrifies me.'

He nodded. 'And fascinates as well.'

'Arrogant bastard. Believe what you like!'

He turned back to the doorway. Collecting his sword, he said over one shoulder, 'The Seguleh has unsheathed her swords for me, witch.'

Then he was gone.

Samar Dev remained on her cot for another dozen heartbeats, then, 'Damn him!' And she rose, hurrying to arrive before the bout began. *Damn him!*

The sun had crawled far enough to one side of the sky to leave the compound in shadow. As she emerged from the covered colonnade Samar Dev saw the Seguleh standing in the middle of the exercise area, a thin-bladed longsword in each gloved hand. Her dark hair hung in greasy strands down her shoulders, and through the eye-holes of the mask her midnight gaze tracked Karsa Orlong as he strode to join her in the sand-floored clearing.

A full score of champions looked on, indicating that word had travelled, and Samar Dev saw – with shock – the Gral, Taralack Veed, and, behind him, Icarium. *Gods below, the name, the Jhag . . . all that I know, all that I have heard. Icarium is here. A champion.*

He will leave this city a heap of rubble. He will leave its citizens a mountain of shattered bones. Gods, look at him! Standing calm, so deep in shadow as to be almost invisible – Karsa does not see him, no. The Toblakai's focus rests on the Seguleh, as he circles her at a distance. And she moves like a cat to ever face him.

Oh, she is a fighter all right.

And Karsa will throw her over the damned wall.

If she dares close. As she must. Get inside that huge flint sword.

Over the wall. Or through it.

Her heart pounded, the beat rapid, disturbingly erratic.

She sensed someone at her side and saw, with a jolt of alarm, a Tiste Edur – and she then recognized him. *Preda . . . Tomad. Tomad Sengar.*

The Emperor's father.

Karsa, you don't want this audience—

*

An explosion of motion as the two contestants closed – afterwards, none could agree on who moved first, as if some instinctive agreement was reached between the Seguleh and Karsa, and acted upon faster than thought itself.

And, as iron rang on stone – or stone on iron – Karsa Orlong did something unexpected.

Pounded down with one foot. Hard onto the packed sand.

In the midst of the Seguleh's lithe dance.

Pounded down, hard enough to stagger onlookers as the entire compound floor thundered.

The Seguleh's perfect balance . . . vanished.

No doubt it was but a fraction, the dislodging so minor few would even register it, and no doubt her recovery was as instantaneous – but she was already reeling back to a savage blow with the flat of Karsa's blade, both wrists broken by the impact.

Yet, as she toppled, she twisted, one foot lashing upward towards the Toblakai's crotch.

He caught her kick with one hand, blocking the blow, then boldly lifted her into the air.

She swung the other foot.

And the Toblakai, laughing, released his sword and snagged that leg as well.

And held her there.

Dangling.

Behind Taralack Veed, there was a soft sigh, and the Gral, blinking, turned round.

Icarium smiled. Then said in a low voice, 'We have met, I think. He and I. Perhaps long ago. A duel that was interrupted.'

By Mappo. Has to be. Mappo, who saw a storm coming between these two. Oh, Trell . . .

Taralack licked dry lips. 'Would you resume that duel, Icarium?'

The Jhag's brows lifted fractionally. Then he shook his head, leaving that as his answer.

Thank the spirits.

From Preda Tomad Sengar, a grunt.

'These games,' Samar Dev ventured, drawing his attention, 'they are intended to entertain, yes? Each contest more challenging than the last.'

The Tiste Edur eyed her, expressionless, then he said, 'Among the audience, there are those who are entertained.'

'Yes.'

After a moment, he added, 'Yes, this Tarthenal will come last. The

310

decision was unanimous among our observers.' Then he shrugged and said, 'I came to see for myself. Although my judgement has no relevance.'

'That Seguleh was very good,' Samar Dev said.

'Perhaps. But she has sparred with no others.'

'They hold her in great respect.'

'Even now? When will he set her down?'

She shook her head.

Tomad Sengar turned away. 'The Tarthenal is superb.'

'And yet your son is better.'

This halted him once more and he stared back at her with narrowed eyes. 'Your Tarthenal is superb,' he repeated. 'But he will die anyway.'

The Tiste Edur walked away.

Finally responding to shouts and entreaties from the onlookers, Karsa Orlong set the woman down onto the ground.

Three Letherii healers rushed in to tend to her.

Collecting his sword, Karsa straightened, then looked round.

Oh, thought Samar Dev, *oh no*.

But Icarium was gone. As was his Gral keeper.

The Toblakai walked towards her.

'I didn't need to know,' she said.

'No, you knew already.'

Oh, gods!

Then he drew closer and stared down at her. 'The Jhag fled. The Trell who was with him is gone. Probably dead. Now there is a desert warrior I could break with one hand. There would have been none to stop us, this Icarium and me. He knew that. So he fled.'

'You damned fool, Karsa. Icarium is not the kind of warrior who *spars*. Do you understand me?'

'We would not have sparred, Samar Dev.'

'So why spend yourself against him? Is it not these Edur and their Letherii slaves you seek vengeance against?'

'When I am finished with their Emperor, I will seek out Icarium. We will finish what we began.'

'Beware gathering the men before the battering ram, Karsa Orlong.'

'A foolish saying,' he pronounced after a moment.

'Oh, and why is that?'

'Among the Teblor, men *are* the battering ram. Look upon me, Samar Dev. I have fought and won. See the sweat on my muscles? Come lie with me.'

'No, I feel sick.'

'I will make you feel better. I will split you in two.'

'That sounds fun. Go away.'

'Must I hunt down another whore?'

311

'They all run when they see you now, Karsa Orlong. In the opposite direction, I mean.'

He snorted, then looked round. 'Perhaps the Seguleh.'

'Oh, really! You just broke her arms!'

'She won't need them. Besides, the healers are mending her.'

'Gods below, I'm leaving.'

As she strode away, she heard his rumbling laugh. *Oh, I know you make sport of me. I know and yet I fall into your traps every time. You are too clever, barbarian. Where is that thick-skulled savage? The one to match your pose?*

Dragging mangled legs, every lurch stabbing pain along the length of his bent, twisted spine, Hannan Mosag squinted ahead, and could just make out the scree of river-polished stones rising like a road between the cliffs of the gorge. He did not know if what he was seeing was real.

Yet it felt right.

Like home.

Kurald Emurlahn, the Realm of Shadow. Not a fragment, not a torn smear riven through with impurities. Home, as it once was, before all the betrayals ripped it asunder. *Paradise awaits us. In our minds. Ghost images, all perfection assembled by will and will alone. Believe what you see, Hannan Mosag. This is home.*

And yet it resisted. Seeking to reject him, his broken body, his chaos-stained mind.

Mother Dark. Father Light. Look upon your crippled children. Upon me. Upon Emurlahn. Heal us. Do you not see the world fashioned in my mind? All as it once was. I hold still to this purity, to all that I sought to create in the mortal realm, among the tribes I brought to heel – the peace I demanded, and won.

None could have guessed my deepest desire. The Throne of Shadow – it was for me. And by my rule, Kurald Emurlahn would grow strong once again. Whole. Rightfully in its place.

Yes, there was chaos – the raw unbound power coursing like impassable rivers, isolating every island of Shadow. But I would have used that chaos – to heal.

Chains. Chains to draw the fragments together, to bind them together.

The Fallen God was a tool, nothing more.

But Rhulad Sengar had destroyed all that. In the reach of a child's hand. And now, everything was dying. Poisoned. Crumbling into dissolution.

He reached the base of the scree, smooth round pebbles clacking beneath his clawed fingers. Coarse sand under his nails, wet, biting. *My world.*

Rain falling in wisps of mist, the pungent smell of moss and rotting wood. And on the wind . . . the sea. Surmounting the steep slope of stones, the boles of Blackwood trees stood arrayed like sentinels.

There were no invasive demons here. This world was the world of the Tiste Edur.

The shadow of a gliding owl slipped over the glistening slide, crossing his intended path, and Hannan Mosag froze.

No. It cannot be. There is no-one alive to claim that title.

He is dead.

He was not even Tiste Edur!

And yet, who stood alone before Rhulad Sengar? *Yes, she has his severed finger. The owl – most ancient of omens – the owl, to mark the coming of the one.*

Yet anger surged within him.

It is for me to choose. Me! Mother Dark! Father Light! Guide me to the Throne of Shadow. Emurlahn reborn! It is this, I tell you both, this or the King in Chains, and behind him the Crippled God! Hear my offer!

'Andii, Liosan, Edur, the *Armies of the Tiste*. No betrayal. The betrayals are done – bind us to our words as you have bound each other. Light, Dark and Shadow, the first elements of existence. Energy and void and the ceaseless motion of the ebb and flow between them. These three forces – the first, the greatest, the purest. Hear me. I would so pledge the Edur to this alliance! Send to me those who would speak for the Andii. The Liosan. Send them – bring your children together!

'Mother Dark. Father Light. I await your word. I await . . .'

He could go no further.

Weeping, Hannan Mosag rested his head on the stones. 'As you say,' he muttered. 'I will not deny the omen. Very well, it is not for me to choose.

'He shall be our Mortal Sword of Emurlahn – no, not the old title. The new one, to suit this age. Mortal Sword.' *Madness – why would he even agree? Letherii . . .*

'So be it.'

Dusk had arrived. Yet he felt a sliver of warmth against one cheek, and he lifted his head. The clouds had broken, there, to the east – a welling band of darkness.

And, to the west, another slash parting the overcast.

The lurid glow of the sun.

'So be it,' he whispered.

Bruthen Trana stepped back as the prostrate Warlock King flinched, Hannan Mosag's legs drawing up like an insect in death.

A moment later, the warlock's bloodshot eyes prised open. And seemed to see nothing for a moment. Then they flicked upward. 'Warrior,' he said thickly, then grimaced and spat a throatful of phlegm onto the grimy pavestones. 'Bruthen Trana. K'ar Penath speaks boldly of your loyalty, your honour. You are Tiste Edur – as we all once were. Before – before Rhulad.' He coughed, then pushed himself into a sitting position, raising his head with obvious effort to glower up at Bruthen Trana. 'And so, I must send you away.'

'Warlock King, I serve this empire—'

'Errant take this damned empire! You serve the Tiste Edur!'

Bruthen Trana regarded the broken creature below, said nothing.

'I know,' Hannan Mosag said, 'you would lead our warriors – through the palace above us. Room by room, cutting down every one of the Chancellor's pernicious spies. Cutting Rhulad free of the snaring web spun about him – but that fool on his throne could not recognize freedom if it sprouted wings on his shoulders. He will see it as an attack, a rebellion. Listen to me! Leave the Chancellor to us!'

'And Karos Invictad?'

'All of them, Bruthen Trana. So I vow before you.'

'Where do you wish me to go, Warlock King? After Fear Sengar?'

Hannan Mosag started, then shook his head. 'No. But I dare not speak the name of the one you must find. Here, in this realm, the Crippled God courses in my veins – where I travelled a few moments ago, I was free then. To understand. To . . . pray.'

'How will I know where to look? How will I know when I find the one you seek?'

The Warlock King hesitated. He licked his lips, then said, 'He is dead. But not dead. Distant, yet is summoned. His tomb lies empty, yet was never occupied. He is never spoken of, though his touch haunts us all again and again.'

Bruthen Trana raised a hand – not surprised to see that it trembled. 'No more. Where shall I find the beginning of the path?'

'Where the sun dies. I think.'

The warrior scowled. 'West? But you are not sure?'

'I am not. I dare not.'

'Am I to travel alone?'

'For you to decide, Bruthen Trana. But before all else, you must get something – an item – from the Letherii slave. Feather Witch – she hides beneath the Old Palace—'

'I know those tunnels, Warlock King. What is this item?'

Hannan Mosag told him.

He studied the twisted warlock for a moment longer – the avid gleam in Hannan Mosag's eyes bright as fever – then spun round and strode from the chamber.

*

Bearing lanterns, the squad of guards formed a pool of lurid yellow light that glimmered along the waters of Quillas Canal as they trudged, amidst clanking weapons and desultory muttering, across the bridge. Once on the other side, the squad turned right to follow the main avenue towards the Creeper district.

As soon as the glow trundled away, Tehol nudged Ublala and they hurried onto the bridge. Glancing back at the half-blood, Tehol scowled, then hissed, 'Watch me, you fool! See? I'm skulking. No – hunch down, look about suspiciously, skitter this way and that. Duck down, Ublala!'

'But then I can't see.'

'*Quiet!*'

'Sorry. Can we get off this bridge?'

'First, let me see you skulk. Go on, you need to practise.'

Grumbling, Ublala Pung hunched low, his beetled brow rippling as he looked first one way, then the other.

'Nice,' Tehol said. 'Now, hurry up and skulk after me.'

'All right, Tehol. It's just that there's the curfew, and I don't want trouble.'

They reached the other side and Tehol led the way, thirty paces into the wake of the guards, then an abrupt cut to the left, coming within sight of the Tolls Repository. Into an alley, where he crouched, then gestured frantically for Ublala to do the same.

'All right,' he whispered, 'do you know which wing?'

Ublala blinked in the gloom. 'What?'

'Do you know where this Tarthenal is quartered?'

'Yes. With all the other champions.'

'Good. Where is that?'

'Well, it must be somewhere.'

'Good thinking, Ublala. Now, stay close to me. I am, after all, a master of this thieving skulduggery.'

'Really? But Bugg said—'

'What? What did my miserable manservant say? About me? Behind my back?'

Ublala shrugged. 'Lots of things. I mean, nothing. Oh, you misheard me, Tehol. I didn't say anything. You're not a clumsy oaf with a head full of grander delusions, or anything. Like that.' He brightened. 'You want me to box him about the ears again?'

'Later. Here's what I think. Near the Imperial Barracks, but a wing of the Eternal Domicile. Or between the Eternal Domicile and the Old Palace.'

Ublala was nodding.

'So,' Tehol continued, 'shall we get going?'

'Where?'

'Somehow I don't think this night is going to go well. Never mind, just stay with me.'

A quick peek into the street, up one way, down the other, then Tehol moved out, keeping low against the near wall. As they drew closer to the Eternal Domicile, the shadows diminished – lantern poles at intersections, broader streets, and there soldiers positioned at postern gates, outside corner blockhouses, soldiers, in fact, everywhere.

Tehol tugged Ublala into the last usable alley, where they crouched once more in gloom. 'This looks bad,' he whispered. 'There's people, Ublala. Well, listen, it was a good try. But we've been bested by superior security and that's that.'

'They're all standing in their own light,' Ublala said. 'They can't see nothing, Tehol. Besides, I got in mind a diversion.'

'A diversion like your usual diversions, Ublala? Forget it. Shurq Elalle's told me about that last time—'

'Yes, like that. It worked, didn't it?'

'But that was to get her inside the Gerrun Estate – her, not you. Aren't you the one who wants to talk to this champion?'

'That's why you're doing the diversion, Tehol.'

'Me? Are you mad?'

'It's the only way.'

They heard the scuff of boots from the street, then a loud voice: '*There! Who's skulking in that alley?*'

Ublala flinched down. 'How did he know?'

'We better run!'

They bolted, as a spear of lantern-light lanced across the alley mouth; then, pursued by shouting soldiers, the two fugitives reached the far end of the alley.

Where Tehol went left.

And Ublala went right.

Alarms resounded in the night.

The answering of his prayers was nothing like Bruthen Trana had imagined. Not through the grotesque creature that was Hannan Mosag, the Warlock King. The very man who had started the Edur down this path of dissolution. Ambition, greed and betrayal – it was all Bruthen could manage to stand still before Hannan Mosag, rather than strangle the life from the Warlock King.

Yet from that twisted mouth had come . . . hope. It seemed impossible. Macabre. Mocking Bruthen Trana's visions of heroic salvation. *Rhulad falls – the whole Sengar bloodline obliterated – and then . . . Hannan Mosag. For his crimes. Honour can be won – I will see to that.*

This is how it must be.

He was not unduly worried over the Letherii. The Chancellor would not live much longer. The palace would be purged. The Patriotists would be crushed, their agents slain, and those poor prisoners whose only crime, as far as he could tell, was to disagree with the practices of the Patriotists – those prisoners, Letherii one and all, could be freed. There was no real sedition at work here. No treason. Karos Invictad used such accusations as if they encompassed a guilt that needed no proof, as if they justified any treatment of the accused he desired. Ironically, in so doing he subverted humanity itself, making him the most profound traitor of all.

But not even that mattered much. Bruthen Trana did not like the man, a dislike that seemed reason enough to kill the bastard. Karos Invictad took pleasure in cruelty, making him both pathetic and dangerous. If he were permitted to continue, there was the very real risk that the Letherii people would rise up in true rebellion, and the gutters in every city of the empire would run crimson. *No matter. I do not like him. For years I was witness to his contempt for me, there in his eyes. I will brook the affront no longer.*

This, more than anything else, dismayed Bruthen Trana. Hannan Mosag's insisting he leave immediately – for some place where the sun dies. *West. But no, not west. The Warlock King misunderstood his own vision—*

A sudden thought, slowing his steps as he made his way down into the subterranean corridors and chambers beneath the Old Palace. *Who answered his prayers? Who showed him this path? He suggested it was not this Crippled God. Father Shadow? Has Scabandari Bloodeye returned to us?*

No, he has not. Then . . . who?

A moment later, Bruthen Trana scowled, then cursed under his breath and resumed his journey. *I am given hope and what do I do? Seek to kill it with my own hands. No, I understand the path – better than Hannan Mosag himself.*

Where the sun dies is not to the west.

It is beneath the waves. In the depths.

Did not a demon of the seas retrieve his body? No, Hannan Mosag, you dare not name him. He is not even Tiste Edur. Yet he must be our salvation.

He reached the sloping tunnel that would take him to the slave's supposedly secret abode. These Letherii were indeed pathetic.

We each carry a whisper of Emurlahn within us – each and every Tiste Edur. This is why no slave among the tribes could escape us.

Except for one, he corrected himself. Udinaas. But then, the K'risnan knew where he was – or so Bruthen Trana suspected. They knew, yet chose to do nothing.

317

It was no wonder Rhulad did not trust them.

Nor do I.

He could smell the stench of bitter magic as he drew nearer, and he heard her muttering in her chamber, and knew that something had changed. In the one named Feather Witch. In the power she possessed.

Well, he would give her no time to prepare.

Feather Witch looked up in fear and alarm as the Tiste Edur warrior strode in. Squealing, she backed away until brought short by a wall, then sank down and covered her face.

The stark intent in the warrior's face was fierce.

He grasped her by the hair and yanked her to her feet, then higher, the pain forcing a shriek from her.

With his other hand he grasped the small leather pouch between her breasts. When he tore it loose, the thong cut like wire across the back of her neck and behind one ear. She could feel blood. She thought that her ear had very nearly been cut loose, that it hung by a strand of—

He flung her back down. Her head cracked against the stone of the wall. She slumped onto the floor, ragged sobbing erupting from her heaving chest.

And listened – beyond the close roar of blood in her skull – to his dwindling footsteps.

He had taken the severed finger.

He goes to find the soul of Brys Beddict.

Tehol staggered into the single room, collapsed down near the hearth. Sheathed in sweat, gasping to gain his breath.

Bugg, seated with his back to a wall and sipping tea, slowly raised his brows. 'Afflicted with the delusion of competence, I see.'

'That – that what you said – to Ublala? You cruel, heartless—'

'The observation was made regarding all mortals, actually.'

'He didn't take it that way!'

Janath spoke from where she sat sipping from her own chipped clay cup. 'All those alarms ringing through the city are because of you, Tehol Beddict?'

'They will be on the lookout now,' Bugg observed, 'for a man wearing a blanket.'

'Well,' Tehol retorted, 'there must be plenty of those, right?'

There was no immediate reply.

'There must be,' Tehol insisted, a little wildly even to his own ears. He hastened on in a more reasonable tone. 'The ever growing divide between the rich and the poor and all that. Why, blankets are the new fashion among the destitute. I'm sure of it.'

Neither listener said anything, then both sipped from their cups.

Scowling, Tehol said, 'What's that you're drinking?'

'Hen tea,' Bugg said.

'Soup, you mean.'

'No,' said Janath. 'Tea.'

'Wait, where are all the chickens?'

'On the roof,' Bugg said.

'Won't they fall off?'

'One or two might. We do regular rounds. So far, they have displayed uncharacteristic cleverness. Rather unique for this household.'

'Oh right, kick the exhausted fugitive why don't you? They probably caught poor old Ublala.'

'Maybe. He did have a diversion in mind.'

Tehol's eyes narrowed on his manservant. 'Those wisps above your ears need trimming. Janath, find me a knife, will you?'

'No.'

'You *would* side with him, wouldn't you?'

'Bugg is actually a very capable man, Tehol. You don't deserve him, you know.'

'I assure you, Scholar, the undeservedness is mutual.'

'What does that mean?'

'You know, from the smell I think I could make a strong argument that hen tea is no different from watery chicken soup, or, at the very least, broth.'

'You never could grasp semantics, Tehol Beddict.'

'I couldn't grasp much of anything, I seem to recall. Yet I will defend my diligence, my single-minded lust for seductive knowledge, the purity of true academic . . . uh, pursuit – why, I could go on and on—'

'Ever your flaw, Tehol.'

'—but I won't, cursed as I am with an unappreciative audience. So tell me, Bugg, why was Ublala so eager to talk to this true blood Tarthenal?'

'He wishes to discover, I imagine, if the warrior is a god.'

'A what?'

'A new god, I mean. Or an ascendant, to be more precise. I doubt there are worshippers involved. Yet.'

'Well, Tarthenal only worship what terrifies them, right? This is just some warrior doomed to die by the Emperor's sword. Hardly the subject to inspire poor Ublala Pung.'

To that Bugg simply shrugged.

Tehol wiped sweat from his brow. 'Give me some of that hen tea, will you?'

'With or without?'

'With or without what?'

'Feathers.'

'That depends. Are they clean feathers?'

'They are now,' Bugg replied.

'All right, then, since I can't think of anything more absurd. With.'

Bugg reached for a clay cup, 'I knew I could count on you, Master.'

She woke to a metallic clang out in the corridor.

Sitting up, Samar Dev stared into the darkness of her room.

She thought she could hear breathing, just outside her door, then, distinctly, a muted whimper.

She rose, wrapping the blanket about her, and padded to the doorway. Lifted the latch and swung the flimsy barrier aside.

'Karsa?'

The huge figure spun to face her.

'No,' she then said. 'Not Karsa. Who are you?'

'Where is he?'

'Who?'

'The one like me. Which room?'

Samar Dev edged out into the corridor. She looked to the left and saw the motionless forms of the two palace guards normally stationed to either side of the corridor's entranceway. Their helmed heads were conspicuously close together, and those iron pots were both severely dented. 'You killed them?'

The huge man glanced over, then grunted. 'They were looking the wrong way.'

'You mean they didn't see you.'

'Maybe my hands.'

The nonsensical yet oddly satisfying exchange had been in whispers. Samar Dev gestured that he follow and set off up the corridor until she came to the door to Karsa Orlong's room. 'He's in here.'

'Knock,' the giant ordered. 'Then walk in ahead of me.'

'Or else?'

'Or else I knock your head . . . together.'

Sighing, she reached towards the door with one fist.

It opened and the point of a stone sword suddenly hovered in the hollow of her throat.

'Who is that behind you, witch?'

'You have a visitor,' she replied. 'From . . . outside.'

Karsa Orlong, naked above the waist, his escaped slave tattoos a crazed web reaching down to his shoulders and chest, withdrew the sword and stepped back.

The stranger pushed Samar Dev to one side and entered the small room.

Whereupon he sank down to his knees, head bowing. 'Pure one,' he said, the words like a prayer.

Samar Dev edged in and shut the door behind her, as Karsa Orlong tossed his sword on the cot, then reached down with one hand – and hammered the stranger in the side of the head.

Rocking the man. Blood started from his nostrils and he blinked stupidly up at Karsa.

Who said, 'There is Toblakai blood in you. Toblakai kneel to no one.'

Samar Dev crossed her arms and leaned back against the door. 'First lesson when dealing with Karsa Orlong,' she murmured. 'Expect the unexpected.'

The huge man struggled back to his feet, wiping at the blood on his face. He was not as tall as Karsa, but almost as wide. 'I am Ublala Pung, of the Tarthenal—'

'Tarthenal.'

Samar Dev said, 'A mixed-blood remnant of some local Toblakai population. Used to be more in the city – I certainly have not seen any others out in the markets and such. But they've virtually vanished, just like most of the other tribes the Letherii subjugated.'

Ublala half turned to glower at her. 'Not vanished. Defeated. And now those who are left live on islands in the Draconean Sea.'

At the word 'defeated', Samar Dev saw Karsa scowl.

Ublala faced the Toblakai once more, then said, with strange awkwardness, 'Lead us, War Leader.'

Sudden fire in Karsa's eyes and he met Samar Dev's gaze. 'I told you once, witch, that I would lead an army of my kind. It has begun.'

'They're not Toblakai—'

'If but one drop of Toblakai blood burns in their veins, witch, then they are Toblakai.'

'Decimated by Letherii sorcery—'

A sneer. 'Letherii sorcery? I care naught.'

Ublala Pung, however, was shaking his head. 'Even with our greatest shamans, Pure One, we could not defeat it. Why, Arbanat himself—'

This time it was Samar Dev who interrupted. 'Ublala, I have seen Karsa Orlong *push* his way through that sorcery.'

The mixed-blood stared at her, mouth agape. 'Push?' The word was mostly mouthed, the barest of whispers.

Despite herself, she nodded. 'I wish I could tell you otherwise, you poor bastard. I wish I could tell you to run away and hide with your kin on those islands, because this one here makes empty promises. Alas, I cannot. He does not make empty promises. Not so far, anyway. Of course,' she added with a shrug that belied the bitterness she felt, 'this Edur Emperor will kill him.'

To that, Ublala Pung shook his head.

Denial? Dismay?

Karsa Orlong addressed Ublala: 'You must leave when this is done,

321

warrior. You must travel to your islands and gather our people then bring them here. You are now my army. I am Karsa Orlong, Toblakai and Teblor. I am your war leader.'

'The marks on your face,' Ublala whispered.

'What of them?'

'As shattered as the Tarthenal. As the Toblakai – broken, driven apart. So the oldest legends say – scattered, by ice, by betrayal . . .'

An icy draught seemed to flow up around Samar Dev, like a cold wave engulfing a rock, and she shivered. *Oh, I dislike the sound of that, since it echoes the truth of things. Too clearly.*

'Yet see my face behind it,' Karsa said. 'Two truths. What was and what will be. Do you deny this, Ublala of the Tarthenal?'

A mute shake of the head. Then the warrior shot another glance at Samar Dev, before saying, 'War Leader, I have words. Of . . . of Rhulad Sengar, the Edur Emperor. Words . . . of his secret.'

'Leave us, witch,' Karsa said.

She started. 'What? Not a chance—'

'Leave us or I will instruct my warrior to knock your head together.'

'Oh, so now it's idiocy that inspires you?'

'Samar Dev,' Karsa said. 'This warrior has defeated every barrier surrounding this compound. I am not interested in his words. Did you not hear the alarms? He fights as would a Toblakai.'

'They tried Drowning me too, once,' Ublala said.

Samar Dev snorted. 'With him around, it truly is a struggle to remain solemn, never mind dignified. A cure for pomposity, Karsa Orlong – be sure to keep this one at your side.'

'Go.'

She gestured with sudden contempt. 'Oh, fine, on with you two, then. Later, Karsa, I will remind you of one thing.'

'What?'

She opened the door behind her. 'This oaf couldn't even find your room.'

Out in the corridor, Samar Dev heard a stirring from one of guards, then a groan and then, distinctly: 'What are all those lights?'

CHAPTER TWELVE

I looked to the west and saw a thousand suns setting.

Sidivar Trelus

T HE EARTHY SMELL OF THE DUNG-FIRES PRECEDED THE FIRST SIGHTING of the Awl army. Beneath the smudged light of a dull moon, the Atri-Preda and Brohl Handar rode with the scout troop to the base of a ridge, where they dismounted and, leaving one soldier with the horses, set out on foot up the slope.

The summit was almost devoid of grasses, knobs of angular bedrock pushing through where the ceaseless winds had eroded away the scant soil. Dropping down low, the half-dozen Letherii and one Tiste Edur edged up between the outcroppings, filling the spaces in the broken spine of basalt.

Beyond, perhaps a third of a league distant, burned the cookfires of the enemy. A sea of fallen, smouldering stars, spreading out to fill the basin of an entire valley, then up the far slope, defining its contours.

'How many do you judge?' Brohl Handar asked the Atri-Preda in a low voice.

Bivatt sighed. 'Combatants? Maybe ten, eleven thousand. These armies are more like migrations, Overseer. Everyone tags along.'

'Then where are the herds?'

'Probably the other side of the far valley.'

'So tomorrow, we ride to battle.'

'Yes. And again, I advise that you and your bodyguard remain with the train—'

'That will not be necessary,' Brohl Handar cut in, repeating words he had uttered a dozen times in the past three days and nights. 'There are Edur warriors with you, and they will be used, yes?'

'If needed, Overseer. But the fight awaiting us looks to be no different from all the others we Letherii have had against these people of the

323

plains. It looks as if Redmask was not able to sway the elders with any new schemes. It's the old tactics – the ones that fail them time and again.' She was silent for a moment, then she continued, 'The valley behind us is called Bast Fulmar. It has some arcane significance for the Awl. That is where we will meet.'

He turned his head and studied her in the gloom. 'You are content to let them choose the place of battle?'

She snorted. 'Overseer, if these lands were filled with defiles, canyons, arroyos or impassable rivers – or forests – then indeed I would think carefully about engaging the enemy where they want us to. But not here. Visibility is not an issue – with our mages the Awl cannot hide in any case. There are no difficult avenues of retreat, no blinds. The fight tomorrow will be brutal in its simplicity. Awl ferocity against Letherii discipline.'

'And with this Redmask leading them, they will be ferocious indeed.'

'Yes. But it will fail in the end.'

'You are confident, Atri-Preda.'

He caught her smile. 'Relieved, Overseer. This night, I see only what I have seen a dozen times before. Do not imagine, however, that I am dismissing the enemy. It will be bloody.' With that she gestured, and the group began withdrawing from the ridgeline.

As they made their way down to the waiting horses, Brohl Handar said, 'I saw no pickets, Atri-Preda. Nor mounted outriders. Does that not seem odd to you?'

'No. They know we are close. They wanted us to see that camp.'

'To achieve what? Some pointless effort to overawe us?'

'Something like that, yes.'

You invite me to feel contempt for these Awl. Why? So that you can justify not using the Tiste Edur? The K'risnan? You want this victory on the morrow to be Letherii. You do not want to find yourself beholden to the Edur – not for this grand theft of land and beast, this harvesting of slaves.

So, I suspect, the Factor instructed. Letur Anict is not one to share the spoils.

I, Atri-Preda, am not *relieved.*

'Stone-tipped arrows – you are truly a fool. They will break against Letherii armour. I can expect nothing from you. At least I discover that now, instead of in the midst of battle.'

Toc Anaster settled back on his haunches and watched Torrent march out of the firelight. Off . . . somewhere. *Somewhere important. Like the latrines.* He resumed examining the fletching on the Imass arrows. *Gift of an old friend. That clunking, creaking collection of droll bones.* He could barely recall the last time he was among friends. Gruntle, perhaps. Another continent. A drunken evening – was that Saltoan wine? Gredfallan ale? He couldn't recall.

Surrounding him, the murmur of thousands – their moving through the camp, their quiet conversations around the cookfires. Old men and old women, the lame, the young. A fire burning for each and every Awl.

And somewhere out on the plain, Redmask and his warriors – a night without fires, without conversations. Nothing, I imagine, but the soft honing of weapon edges. Iron and stone whispering in the night.

A simple deceit, its success dependent on Letherii expectations. Enemy scouts had spotted this camp, after all. As predicted. Countless fires in the darkness, appropriately close to Bast Fulmar, the site of the impending battle. All the way it was supposed to be.

But Redmask had other plans. And to aid in the deception, Toc suspected, some arcane sorcery from the K'Chain Che'Malle.

An elder appeared, walking into the fire's glow on bowed legs. Toc had seen this one speaking to Redmask, often riding at the war leader's side. He crouched down opposite Toc and studied him for a dozen heartbeats, then spat into the flames, nodded at the answering sizzle, and spoke: 'I do not trust you.'

'I'm crushed.'

'Those arrows, they are bound in ritual magic. Yet no spirit has blessed them. What sort of sorcery is that? Letherii? Are you a creature of the Tiles and Holds? A traitor in our midst. You plot betrayal, vengeance against our abandoning you.'

'Trying to inspire me, Elder? Sorry to disappoint you, but there are no embers in the ashes, nothing to stir to life.'

'You are young.'

'Not as young as you think. Besides, what has that to do with anything?'

'Redmask likes you.'

Toc scratched the scar where an eye had been. 'Are your wits addled by age?'

A grunt. 'I know secrets.'

'Me too.'

'None to compare with mine. I was there when Redmask's sister killed herself.'

'And I suckled at the tit of a K'Chain Che'Malle Matron. If tit is the right word.'

The old man's face twisted in disbelief. 'That is a good lie. But it is not the game I am playing. I saw with my own eyes the great sea canoes. Upon the north shore. Thousands upon thousands.'

Toc began returning the arrows to the hide quiver. 'These arrows were made by a dead man. Dead for a hundred thousand years, or more.'

The wrinkled scowl opposite him deepened. 'I have seen skeletons running in the night – on this very plain.'

'This body you see isn't mine. I stole it.'

'I alone know the truth of Bast Fulmar.'

'This body's father was a dead man – he gasped his last breath even as his seed was taken on a field of battle.'

'The victory of long ago was in truth a defeat.'

'This body grew strong on human meat.'

'Redmask will betray us.'

'This mouth waters as I look at you.'

The old man pushed himself to his feet. 'Evil speaks in lies.'

'And the good know only one truth. But it's a lie, because there's always more than one truth.'

Another throatful of phlegm into the campfire. Then a complicated series of gestures, the inscribing in the air above the flames of a skein of wards that seemed to swirl for a moment in the thin smoke. 'You are banished,' the elder then pronounced.

'You have no idea, old man.'

'I think you should have died long ago.'

'More times than I can count. Started with a piece of a moon. Then a damned puppet, then . . . oh, never mind.'

'Torrent says you will run. In the end. He says your courage is broken.'

Toc looked down into the flames. 'That may well be,' he said.

'He will kill you then.'

'Assuming he can catch me. If there's one thing I know how to do, it's ride a horse.'

With a snarl, the elder stormed off.

'Courage,' Toc muttered to himself. 'Yes, there is that. And maybe cowardice truly is bred in the very bones.' *Because let's face it, Anaster was no cold iron. Nor hot, for that matter.*

From somewhere in the night came the keening howl of a wolf.

Toc grunted. 'Yes, well, it's not as if I had the privilege of choice, is it? I wonder if any of us has. Ever.' He raised his voice slightly, 'You know, Torrent – yes, I see you hulking out there – it occurs to me, given the precedent, that the question of cowardice is one your Awl must face, tomorrow. I have no doubt Redmask – if he has any concerns – is thinking on that right now. Wondering. Can he bully all of you into honour?'

The vague shape that was Torrent moved off.

Toc fell silent, tossed yet another lump of rodara dung onto the fire, and thought about old friends long gone.

The lone line of scuffed footprints ended with a figure, trudging up the distant slope of clay and pebbles. That was the thing about following a trail, Hedge reminded himself. Easy to forget the damned prints

326

belonged to something real, especially after what seemed weeks of tracking the bastard.

T'lan Imass, as he had suspected. Those splayed, bony feet dragged too much, especially with an arch so high it left no imprint. True, some bowlegged Wickan might leave something similar, but not walking at a pace that stayed ahead of Hedge for this long. Not a chance of that. Still, it was odd that the ancient undead warrior was walking at all.

Easier traversing this wasteland as dust.

Maybe it's too damp. Maybe it's no fun being mud. I'll have to ask it that.

Assuming it doesn't kill me outright. Or try to, I mean. I keep forgetting that I'm already dead. If there's one thing the dead should remember, it's that crucial detail, don't you think, Fid? Bah, what would you know. You're still alive. And not here either.

Hood take me, I'm in need of company.

Not that damned whispering wind, though. Good thing it had fled, in tatters, unable to draw any closer to this T'lan Imass with – yes – but one arm. *Beat up thing, ain't it just?*

He was sure it knew he was here, a thousand paces behind it. *Probably knows I'm a ghost, too. Which is why it hasn't bothered attacking me.*

I think I'm getting used to this.

Another third of a league passed before Hedge was able to draw close enough to finally snare the undead warrior's regard. Halting, slowly turning about. The flint weapon in its lone hand was more a cutlass than a sword, its end strangely hooked. A hilt had been fashioned from the palmate portion of an antler, creating a shallow, tined bell-guard polished brown with age. Part of the warrior's face had been brutally smashed: but one side of its heavy jaw was intact, giving its ghastly mien a lopsided cant.

'Begone, ghost,' the T'lan Imass said in a ravaged voice.

'Well I would,' Hedge replied, 'only it seems we're heading in the same direction.'

'That cannot be.'

'Why?'

'Because you do not know where I am going.'

'Oh, perfect Imass logic. In other words, absurd idiocy. No, I don't know precisely where you are going, but it is undeniably to be found in the same direction as where I am headed. Is that too sharp an observation for you?'

'Why do you hold to your flesh?'

'The same reason, I suppose, why you hold on to what's left of yours. Listen, I am named Hedge. I was once a soldier, a Bridgeburner. Malazan marines. Are you some cast-off from Logros T'lan Imass?'

327

The warrior said nothing for a moment, then, 'I was once of Kron T'lan Imass. Born in the Season of Blood-from-the-Mountain to the clan of Eptr Phinana. My own blood arrived on the shores of Jagra Til. I am Emroth.'

'A woman?'

A clattering, uneven shrug.

'Well, Emroth, what are you doing walking across Hood's forgotten ice-pit?'

'There is no pit here.'

'As you say.' Hedge looked round. 'Is this where abandoned T'lan Imass go, then?'

'Not here,' Emroth replied. Then the cutlass lifted and slowly pointed.

Ahead. The direction Hedge had decided to call north. 'What, are we headed towards a huge pile of frozen bones, then?'

Emroth turned and began walking once more.

Hedge moved up alongside the undead creature. 'Were you beautiful once, Emroth?'

'I do not remember.'

'I was hopeless with women,' Hedge said. 'My ears are too big – yes, that's why I wear this leather cap. And I got knobby knees. It's why I became a soldier, you know. To meet women. And then I discovered that women soldiers are scary. I mean, a lot more scary than normal women, which is saying something. I guess with you Imass, well, everyone was a warrior, right?'

'I understand,' Emroth said.

'You do? Understand what?'

'Why you have no companions, Hedge of the Bridgeburners.'

'You're not going to turn into a cloud of dust on me, are you?'

'In this place, I cannot. Alas.'

Grinning, Hedge resumed, 'It's not like I died a virgin or anything, of course. Even ugly bastards like me – well, so long as there's enough coin in your hand. But I'll tell you something, Emroth, that's not what you'd call love now, is it? So anyway, the truth of it is, I never shared that with anybody. Love. I mean, from the time I stopped being a child, right up until I died.

'Now there was this soldier, once. She was big and mean. Named Detoran. She decided she loved me, and showed it by beating me senseless. So how do you figure that one? Well, I've got it worked out. You see, she was even less lovable than me. Poor old cow. Wish I'd understood that at the time. But I was too busy running away from her. Funny how that is, isn't it?

'She died, too. And so I had a chance to, you know, talk to her. Since we found ourselves in the same place. Her problem was, she couldn't put enough words together to make a real sentence. Not thick, much. Just inarticulate. People like that, how can you guess what's in their mind? They can't tell you, so the guessing stays guessing and most of the time you're so wrong it's pathetic. Well, we worked it out, more or less. I think. She said even less as a ghost.

'But that's the thing with it all, Emroth. There's the big explosion, the white, then black, then you're stirring awake all over again. A damned ghost with nowhere worthwhile to go, and all you're left with is realizations and regrets. And a list of wishes longer than Hood's—'

'No more, Hedge of the Bridgeburners,' Emroth interjected, the tremor of emotion in its voice. 'I am not a fool. I comprehend this game of yours. But my memories are not for you.'

Hedge shrugged. 'Not for you either, I gather. Gave them all away to wage war against the Jaghut. They were so evil, so dangerous, you made of yourselves your first victims. Kind of a backwards kind of vengeance, wouldn't you say? Like you went and done their work for them. And the real joke is, they weren't much evil or dangerous at all. Oh, maybe a handful, but those handful earned the wrath of their kin real fast – often long before you and your armies even showed up. They could police themselves just fine. They flung glaciers at you, so what did you do to defeat that? Why, you made your hearts even colder, even more lifeless than any glacier. Hood knows, that's irony for you.'

'I am unbound,' Emroth said in a rasp. 'My memories remain with me. It is these memories that have broken me.'

'Broken?'

Another shrug. 'Hedge of the Bridgeburners, unlike you, I remember love.'

Neither spoke for a time after that. The wind whipped bitter and dry. The crusted remnants of snow crackled underfoot in the beds of moss and lichen. On the horizon ahead there was a slate-grey ridge of some sort, angular like a massed line of toppled buildings. Above it the sky was milky white. Hedge gestured northward. 'So, Emroth, is that it?'

The half-shattered head lifted. 'Omtose Phellack.'

'Really? But—'

'We must cross it.'

'Oh, and what lies beyond?'

The T'lan Imass halted and stared at Hedge with its withered, shadow-shrunken eyes. 'I am not sure,' it replied. 'But, I now believe, it may be . . . home.'

Damn you, Emroth. You've just made things a lot harder.

The temple stood on a low hill, the land barren on all sides. Its huge cyclopean walls looked battered, shoved inward as if by ten thousand stone fists. Crooked fissures tracked the dark grey granite from ground level to the massive lintel stone leaning drunkenly above what had once been a grand, noble entranceway. The remnants of statues jutted from pedestals set to either side of the broad, now sagging steps.

Udinaas did not know where he was. Just another dream, or what started as a dream. Doomed, like all the others, to slide into something far worse.

And so he waited, trembling, his legs crippled, broken and lifeless beneath him – a new variation on the theme of incapacity. Bludgeoning symbol to his many flaws. The last time, he recalled, he had been squirming on the ground, limbless, a broken-backed snake. It seemed his subconscious lacked subtlety, a most bitter admission.

Unless, of course, someone or something else was sending these visitations.

And now, corpses had appeared on the stony slopes beneath the temple. Scores, then hundreds.

Tall, skin pale as the shell of turtle eggs, red-rimmed eyes set deep in elongated, chiselled faces, and too many joints on their long limbs, transforming their stiff expressions of death into something surreal, fevered – but that last detail was no surprise.

And now, a smudge of motion in the darkness beneath the lintel stone. A figure staggering into view. Unlike the dead. No, this one looked . . . *human.*

Splashed in blood from head to toe, the man reeled forward, halted at the top of the steps and looked round with wild, enraged eyes. Then, flinging his head back, he screamed at the colourless sky.

No words. Just fury.

Udinaas recoiled, sought to drag himself away.

And the figure saw him. One crimson, dripping hand, lifting, reaching out for him. Beckoning.

As if grasped by the throat, Udinaas lurched closer to the man, to the temple, to the cold scree of corpses. 'No,' he muttered, 'not me. Choose someone else. Not me.'

'Can you feel this grief, mortal?'

'Not for me!'

'But it is. You are the only one left. Are their deaths to be empty, forgotten, without meaning?'

Udinaas tried to hold on to the ground, but the stones pulled loose under his hands, the sandy soil broke free as his nails dragged furrows in his wake. 'Find someone else!' His shriek echoed, as if launched directly at the temple, in through the gaping entrance, and echoing within – trapped, stolen away, rebounding until it was no longer his own voice, but that of the temple itself – a mournful cry of dying, of desperate defiance. The temple, voicing its thirst.

And something shook the sky then. Lightning without fire, thunder without sound – an arrival, jarring loose the world.

The entire temple heaved sideways, clouds of dust gasping out from between mortarless joins. It was moments from collapse—

'*No!*' bellowed the figure at the top of the stairs, even as he staggered to regain his balance. '*This one is mine! My T'orrud Segul! Look at these dead – they must be saved, delivered, they must be—*'

And now another voice sounded, behind Udinaas, high, distant, a voice of the sky itself. 'No, Errant. These dead are Forkrul Assail. Dead by your own hand. You cannot kill them to save them—'

'*Dread witch, you know nothing! They're the only ones I can save!*'

'The curse of Elder Gods – look at the blood on your hands. It is all of your own making. All of it.'

A huge shadow swept over Udinaas then. Wheeled round.

Wind gusting, tossing tangled black hair upward from corpses, buffeting the torn fragments of their clothes; then, a sudden pressure, as of vast weight descending, and the dragon was there – between Udinaas and the Errant – long hind limbs stretching downward, claws plunging through cold bodies, crushing them in the snapping of bones as the enormous creature settled on the slope. Sinuous neck curling round, the huge head drawing closer to Udinaas, eyes of white fire.

Its voice filled his skull. 'Do you know me?'

Argent flames rippling along the golden scales, a presence exuding incandescent heat – Forkrul Assail bodies blackened beneath her, skin crinkling, peeling back. Fats melting, popping from sudden blisters, weeping from joints.

Udinaas nodded. 'Menandore. Sister Dawn. Rapist.'

Thick, liquid laughter. The head swung away, angled up towards the Errant. 'This one is mine,' she said. 'I claimed him long ago.'

'*Claim what you like, Menandore. Before we are done here, you will give him to me. Of your own will.*'

'Indeed?'

'*As . . . payment.*'

'For what?'

'*For news of your sisters.*'

She laughed again. 'Do you imagine I don't know?'

'*But I offer more.*' The god raised his red hands. '*I can ensure they are removed from your path, Menandore. A simple . . . nudge.*'

The dragon shifted round, regarded Udinaas once more. 'For this one?'

'*Yes.*'

'Very well, you can have him. But not our child.'

It was the Errant's turn to laugh. '*When last did you visit that . . . child, Menandore?*'

'What does that mean?'

'*Only this. He is grown now. His mind is his own. Not yours, Menandore. You are warned, and this time I demand nothing in return. Elder Gods, my dear, can on occasion know mercy.*'

She snorted – a gust of raw power. 'I have heard that. Fine propaganda, the morsel you feed to your starving, pathetic worshippers. This man, this father of my child, he will fail you. T'orrud Segul. He has no faith. The compassion within him is like a meer-rat in a pit of lions – dancing faster than you can see, ever but moments from annihilation. He has played with it for a long time, Errant. You will not catch it, cannot claim it, cannot bind it to your cause.' She voiced her cruel laughter once more. 'I took more from him than you realize.'

Including, bitch, my fear of you. 'You think you can give me away, Menandore?'

The eyes flared with amusement or contempt or both. 'Speak then, Udinaas, let us hear your bold claims.'

'You both think you summoned me here, don't you? For your stupid tug of war. But the truth is, I summoned the two of you.'

'You are mad—'

'Maybe so, Menandore. *But this is my dream.* Not yours. Not his. *Mine.*'

'You fool,' she spat. 'Just try banishing us—'

Udinaas opened his eyes, stared up at a cold, clear night sky, and allowed himself a smile. *My dream, your nightmare.* He pulled the furs tighter about himself, drawing up his legs – making sure they weren't broken. Stiffness in the knees – normal, what came of scrabbling over rock and ice – but warm with life. 'All is well,' he whispered.

'Good,' said Kettle.

Udinaas turned, looked up. She was crouched at his side. 'Why are you awake?' he demanded.

'I'm not. And neither are you. That temple, it fell over. After you left.'

'Hope it crushed the Errant flat, then.'

'No. You'd already sent him away. Her too.'

'But not you.'

'No. You didn't know I was there.'

'All right, so I am still dreaming. What do you want?'

'That temple. It couldn't have held all those souls. All that grief. It was broken and that's why it fell over. That was what you were supposed to see. So you'd understand when everything happens. And not be sad. And be able to do what he wants you to do, just not in the way he thought it would be. That's all.'

'Good. Now crawl back to your own dreams, Kettle.'

'Okay. Just remember, don't cry too soon. You have to wait.'

'Really. How long before I do this crying?'

But she was gone.

He'd caught some damn fever from the rotting ice. Shivering and hallucinating for three – maybe four – nights now. Bizarre dreams inside dreams and on and on. Delusions of warmth, the comfort of furs not sodden with sweat, the balm of mysterious conversations where meaning wasn't an issue. *I like this life. It's predictable. Mostly. And when it isn't, it feels no different. I take whatever comes at me. As if each night I receive lessons in . . . in taking control.*

Now it was time for the huge table heaped with all his favourite foods.

They said he was gaunt as a wraith.

But every night he ate his fill.

With the dawn light pushing the shadows into the clefts and valleys and transforming the snow-clad peaks into molten gold, Seren Pedac rose from her furs and stood, feeling grimy and dishevelled. The high altitude left her throat sore and her eyes dry, and her allergies only exasperated those conditions. Shivering in the cutting wind, she watched Fear Sengar struggling to relight the fire. Long-frozen wood was reluctant to burn. Kettle had been gathering grasses and she now squatted down beside the Tiste Edur with her offerings.

A ragged cough from where Udinaas lay still buried in furs. After a moment, he slowly sat up. Face flushed with fever, sweat on his brow, his eyes dull. He hacked out a noise Seren belatedly realized was laughter.

Fear's head snapped round as if wasp-stung. 'This amuses you? You'd rather another cold meal to start the day?'

Udinaas blinked over at the Tiste Edur, then shrugged and looked away.

Seren cleared her throat. 'Whatever amused him, Fear, had nothing to do with you.'

'Speaking for me now?' Udinaas asked her. He tottered weakly to his feet, still wrapped in the furs. 'This might be another dream,' he said. 'At any moment that white-skinned warrior perched over there might transform into a dragon. And the child Kettle will open her mouth like a door, into which Fear Sengar will plunge, devoured by his own hunger to betray.' The flat, murky eyes fixed on Seren Pedac. 'And you will conjure lost ages, Acquitor, as if the follies of history had any relevance, any at all.'

The whirl and snap of a chain punctuated the bizarre pronouncements.

Udinaas glanced over at Clip, and smiled. 'And you're dreaming of sinking your hands into a pool of blood, but not any old blood. The question is, can you manipulate events to achieve that red torrent?'

'Your fever has boiled your brain,' the Tiste Andii warrior said with an answering smile. He faced Silchas Ruin. 'Kill him or leave him behind.'

Seren Pedac sighed, then said, 'Clip, when will we begin our descent? Lower down, there will be herbs to defeat his fever.'

'Not for days,' he replied, spinning the chain in his right hand. 'And even then . . . well, I doubt you'll find what you're looking for. Besides,' he added, 'what ails him isn't entirely natural.'

Silchas Ruin, facing the trail they would climb this day, said, 'He speaks true. Old sorcery fills this fetid air.'

'What kind?' Seren asked.

'It is fragmented. Perhaps . . . K'Chain Che'Malle – they rarely used their magic in ways easily understood. Never in battle. I do recall something . . . necromantic.'

'And is that what this is?'

'I cannot say, Acquitor.'

'So why is Udinaas the one afflicted? What about the rest of us?'

No-one ventured a response, barring another broken laugh from Udinaas.

Rings clacked. 'I have made my suggestion,' Clip said.

Again, the conversation seemed to die. Kettle walked over to stand close to Udinaas, as if conferring protection.

The small campfire was finally alight, if feebly so. Seren collected a tin pot and set out to find some clean snow, which should have been a simple enough task. But the rotted patches were foul with detritus. Smears of decaying vegetation, speckled layers of charcoal and ash, the carcasses of some kind of ice-dwelling worm or beetle, wood and pieces of countless animals. Hardly palatable. She was surprised they weren't all sick.

She halted before a long, narrow stretch of ice-crusted snow that filled a crack or fold in the rock. She drew her knife, knelt down and began pecking at it. Chunks broke away. She examined each one, discarding those too discoloured with filth, setting the others into the pot. Not much like normal glaciers – those few she had seen up close. After all, they were made of successive snowfalls as much as creeping ice. Those snowfalls normally produced relatively pristine strata. But here, it was as if the air through which the snow fell had been thick with drifting refuse, clogging every descending flake. *Air thick with smoke, ash, pieces of once living things. What could have done that?* If just ash then she could interpret it as the result of some volcanic eruption. *But not damned fragments of skin and meat. What secret hides in these mountains?*

She managed to dig the knife-point deep into the ice, then settled her weight on it. The entire remaining slab of ice lifted suddenly, prised away from the crack. And there, lying beneath it, a spear.

The shaft, long as Seren was tall, was not wood. Polished, mottled amber and brown, it looked almost . . . scaled. The broad head was of one piece, blade and stem, ground jade, milky smooth and leaf-shaped. No obvious glue or binding held the socket onto the shaft.

She pulled the weapon loose. The scaled texture, she saw, was created by successive, intricate layering of horn, which explained the mottled appearance. Again, she could discern no indication of how the layers were fixed. The spear was surprisingly heavy, as if the shaft had mineralized.

A voice spoke behind her. 'Now that is an interesting find.'

She turned, studied Clip's mocking expression, and felt a flash of irritation. 'In the habit of following people around, Clip?'

'No, mostly I lead them. I know, that task serves to push you to one side. Leaves you feeling useless.'

'Any other bright observations you want to make?'

He shrugged, spinning the damned chain back and forth. 'That spear you found. It's T'lan Imass.'

'Is that supposed to mean something to me?'

'It will.'

'It's not a weapon *you* fight with, is it?'

'No. And I don't hide in trees and throw fruit either.'

She frowned.

He laughed, turning away. 'I was born in Darkness, Acquitor.'

'And?'

He paused, glanced back at her. 'Why do you think I am the Mortal Sword of the Black-Winged Lord? My good looks? My charming personality? My skill with these blades here?'

'Well,' she replied, 'you've just exhausted my list of reasons.'

'Ha ha. Hear me. Born in Darkness. Blessed by our Mother. The first in thousands of years – she turned away, you know. From her chosen sons. Thousands of years? More like tens of thousands. But not from me. I can *walk* the Darkness, Acquitor.' He waved his chain-spinning hand back towards the others. 'Not even Silchas Ruin can make that claim.'

'Does he know?'

'No. This is our secret for as long as you choose.'

'And why would I choose to not tell him this, Clip?'

'Because I am the only one here who can keep him from killing you. You and Udinaas – the two he considers most useless. Indeed, potential enemies.'

'Enemies? Why would he think that?' She shook her head in disbelief. 'We're just bugs he can crush underfoot any time he likes. An enemy is one who poses a threat. We don't.'

'Well, on that count, I see no need to enlighten you. Yet.'

Snorting, she turned and collected the pot with its chunks of glittering ice.

'Plan on keeping your find?' Clip asked.

She looked down at the weapon in her right hand. 'Udinaas can use it as a crutch.'

Clip's laugh was bitterly cruel. 'Oh, the injustice, Acquitor. For a storied weapon such as that one.'

She frowned at him. 'You speak as if you recognise it. Do you?'

'Let's just say it belongs with us.'

Frustrated, she moved past him, back towards the camp.

The spear drew attention, frighteningly fast from Silchas Ruin, who – before he spun round to face her – seemed to flinch. Udinaas, too – his head snapping up as she walked towards him. She felt her heart lurch in her chest and was suddenly afraid.

She sought to hide it by holding stubbornly to her original thought. 'Udinaas, I found this – you can use it to keep your balance.'

He grunted, then nodded. 'A ground-stone tip – can't have much of an edge, can it? At least I won't stumble and poke my eye out, unless I work hard at it, and why would I do that?'

'Do not mock it,' Silchas Ruin said. 'Use it in the manner the Acquitor has suggested, by all means. But know that it is not yours. You will have to surrender it – know that, Udinaas.'

'Surrender it – to you, perchance?'

Again the flinch. 'No.' And Silchas Ruin turned away once more.

Udinaas grinned weakly at Seren. 'Have you just given me a cursed weapon, Acquitor?'

'I don't know.'

He leaned on it. 'Well, never mind. I've a whole collection of curses – one more won't make much difference.'

Ice was melted, waterskins refilled. Another pot of frozen snow provided the water for a broth of herbs, rinds of myrid fat, berries and nuggets of sap taken from maple trees – the last of which they had seen ten days ago, at an elevation where the air was invigorating and sweetly pungent with life. Here, there were no trees. Not even shrubs. The vast forest surrounding them was barely ankle high – a tangled world of lichen and mosses.

Holding a bowl of the soup in trembling hands, Udinaas spoke to Seren. 'So, just to get things straight in this epic farce of ours, did you find this spear or did it find you?'

She shook her head. 'No matter. It's yours now.'

'No. Silchas is right. You've but loaned it to me, Acquitor. It slides like grease in my hands. I couldn't use it to fight – even if I knew how, which I don't.'

'Not hard,' Clip said. 'Just don't hold it at the sharp end and poke people with it until they fall over. I've yet to face a warrior with a spear I couldn't cut to pieces.'

Fear Sengar snorted.

And Seren knew why. It was enough to brighten this morning, enough to bring a wry smile to her lips.

Clip noted it and sneered, but said nothing.

'Pack up,' Silchas Ruin said after a moment. 'I weary of waiting.'

'I keep telling you,' Clip said, spinning the rings once more, 'it'll all come in its own time, Silchas Ruin.'

Seren turned to face the rearing peaks to the north. The gold had paled, as if drained of all life, all wonder. Another day of weary travel awaited them. Her mood plunged and she sighed.

Given the choice, this game should have been his own. Not Cotillion's, not Shadowthrone's. But enough details had drifted down to Ben Adaephon Delat, heavy and grim as the ash from a forest fire, to make him content, for the moment, to choke on someone else's problems. Since the Enfilade at Pale, his life had been rather headlong. He felt as if he was plunging down a steep hill, for ever but one step from bone-snapping, blood-spraying disaster.

Used to be he thrived on such feelings. Proof that he was alive.

Yet . . . too many friends had fallen to the wayside on the journey. Far too many, and he was reluctant to let others take their places – not even this humble Tiste Edur with his too-full heart, his raw wound of grief; nor that damned T'lan Imass who now waded through a turgid sea of memories, as if seeking one – *just one* – that did not sob with futility. The wrong company indeed for Quick Ben – they were such open invitations to friendship. Not pity – which would have been easier. No, their damned *nobility* demolished that possibility.

And look where all his friends had gone. Whiskeyjack, Hedge, Trotts, Dujek Onearm, Kalam . . . well, wasn't it always the way, that the pain of loss so easily overwhelmed the . . . *the not-yet-lost*? And that sad list was only the most recent version. All since Pale. What of all the others, from long ago? *Us damned survivors don't have it easy. Not even close.*

The thought made him sneer inside. What was this feeling sorry for himself? Pathetic indulgence and nothing else.

Skirting the edge of a submerged ravine, they sloshed through tepid, waist-deep water, their passage swirling up clouds of silts that had rested lightly on some unseen, interminably paved lake-bottom. Tracked now by some kind of fish, their humped backs appearing every now and then to one side or the other, the dorsal fin ribbed, the bulge of water hinting at sizes a little too large for restful contemplation.

Least pleasant of all, Trull Sengar's comment only moments past that these fish were probably the same kind that had once tried to eat him.

And Onrack the Broken had replied, 'Yes, they are the same as the ones we fought on the floodwall, although of course they were then in their land-dwelling stage of life.'

'So why are they here?' Trull then asked.

'Hungry,' Onrack answered.

Enough, right then and there, to stir Quick Ben from his morose taciturnity. 'Listen to you two! We're about to be attacked by giant wizard-eating fish and you're reminiscing! Look, are we in real danger or what?'

Onrack's robust, prognathous face swung to regard him for a moment, then the T'lan Imass said, 'We were assuming that you were warding us from them, Quick Ben.'

'Me?' He looked about, seeking any sign of dry land – but the milky water stretched on and on.

'Is it time, then, to make use of your gate?'

Quick Ben licked his lips. 'I think so. I mean, I've recovered from the last time, more or less. And I found somewhere to go. It's just . . .'

Trull Sengar leaned on his spear. 'You came out of that magical journey, Quick Ben, wearing the grin of the condemned. If indeed our destination is as fraught as it must be, I can understand your reluctance. Also, having observed you for some time now, it is clear to me that your battle against Icarium has weakened you at some fundamental level – perhaps you fear you will not be able to fashion a gate durable enough to permit the passage of all three of us? If so—'

'Wait,' the wizard interjected, silently cursing. 'All right, I am a little . . . fragile. Ever since Icarium. You see far too much, Trull Sengar. But I can take us all through. That's a promise. It's just . . .' He glanced over at Onrack. 'Well, there may be some . . . unanticipated, uh, developments.'

Onrack spoke, 'I am at risk?'

'I'm not sure. Maybe.'

'This should not unduly affect your decision,' the T'lan Imass replied. 'I am expendable. These fish cannot eat me, after all.'

'If we leave,' Quick Ben said, 'you will be trapped here for ever.'

'No. I will abandon this form. I will join oblivion in these waters.'

'Onrack—' Trull began in clear alarm.

But Quick Ben cut in, 'You're coming with us, Onrack. I'm just say-ing there's a little uncertainty with what will happen to you. I can't explain more. It just relates to where we will find ourselves. To the aspect of that realm, I mean.'

Trull Sengar snorted. 'Sometimes,' he said with a wry smile, 'you are truly hopeless, wizard. Best open the gate now, before we end up in the belly of a fish.' He then pointed behind Quick Ben. 'That one looks to be the biggest yet – see the others scatter – and it's coming straight for us.'

Turning, the wizard's eyes widened.

The waist-deep water did not even reach its eyes, and the monstrous fish was simply bulling its way through the shallows. A damned catfish of some sort, longer than a Napan galley—

Quick Ben raised his arms and shouted in a loud, oddly high-pitched voice: 'It's time to leave!'

Fragile. Oh yes, there is that. I poured too much through me trying to beat him back. There's only so much mortal flesh and bone can take. The oldest rule of all, for Hood's sake.

He forced open the gate, heard the explosive plunge of water into the realm beyond – the current wrapping round his legs – and he lunged forward, shouting, 'Follow me!'

Once again, that nauseating, dreadful moment of suffocation, then he was staggering through a stream, water splashing out on all sides, rushing away – and cold wintry air closed in amidst clouds of vapour.

Trull Sengar stumbled past him, using the spear to right himself a moment before falling.

Gasping, Quick Ben turned.

And saw a figure emerge from the white mists.

Trull Sengar's shout of surprise startled into the air birds from a nearby swath of knee-high trees, and as they raced skyward they spun in a half-circle over the head of Onrack the Broken. At their cries, at the swarm of tiny shadows darting around him, the warrior looked up, then halted.

Quick Ben saw Onrack's chest swell with an indrawn breath that seemed without end.

The head then tilted down once more.

And the wizard stared into a face of smooth, wind-burnished skin. Eyes of green glittered beneath the heavy ridge of the brow. Twin streams of cold air then plumed down from Onrack's broad, flattened, oft-broken nose.

From Trull Sengar, 'Onrack? By the Sisters, Onrack!'

The small eyes, buried in epicanthic folds, shifted. A low, reverberating voice rumbled from the flesh and blood warrior. 'Trull Sengar. Is this . . . is this mortality?'

The Tiste Edur drew a step closer. 'You don't remember? How it feels to be alive?'

'I – I . . . yes.' A sudden look of wonder in that heavy, broadly featured face. 'Yes.' Another deep breath, then a gust that was nearly savage in its exultation. The strange gaze fixed on Quick Ben once more. 'Wizard, is this illusion? Dream? A journey of my spirit?'

'I don't think so. I mean, I think it's real enough.'

'Then . . . this realm. It is Tellann.'

'Maybe. I'm not sure.'

Trull Sengar was suddenly on his knees, and Quick Ben saw tears streaming down the Tiste Edur's lean, dusky face.

The burly, muscled warrior before them, still wearing the rotted remnants of fur, slowly looked round at the withered landscape of open tundra. 'Tellann,' he whispered. '*Tellann.*'

'When the world was young,' Redmask began, 'these plains surrounding us were higher, closer to the sky. The earth was as a thin hide, covering thick flesh that was nothing but frozen wood and leaves. The rotted corpse of ancient forests. Beneath summer sun, unseen rivers flowed through that forest, between every twig, every crushed-down branch. And with each summer, the sun's heat was greater, the season longer, and the rivers flowed, draining the vast buried forest. And so the plains descended, settled as the dried-out forest crumbled to dust, and with the rains more water would sink down, sweeping away that dust, southward, northward, eastward, westward, following valleys, rising to join streams. All directions, ever flowing away.'

Masarch sat silent with the other warriors – a score or more now, gathering to hear the ancient tale. None, however – Masarch included – had heard it told in quite this way, the words emerging from the red-scaled mask – from a warrior who rarely spoke yet who spoke now with ease, matching the cadence of elders with perfect precision.

The K'Chain Che'Malle stood nearby, hulking and motionless like a pair of grotesque statues. Yet Masarch imagined that they were listening, even as he and his companions were.

'The land left the sky. The land settled onto stone, the very bone of the world. In this manner, the land changed to echo the cursed sorceries of the Shamans of the Antlers, the ones who kneel among boulders, the worshippers of stone, the weapon-makers.' He paused, then said, 'This was no accident. What I have just described is but one truth. There is another.' A longer hesitation, then a long, drawn-out sigh. 'Shamans of the Antlers, gnarled as tree roots, those few left, those few still haunting our dreams even as they haunt this ancient plain. They hide in cracks in the world's bone. Sometimes their bodies are all but gone, until only their withered faces stare out from those cracks, challenging eternity as befits their terrible curse.'

Masarch was not alone in shivering in the pre-dawn chill, at the images Redmask's words conjured. Every child knew of those twisted, malevolent spirits, the husks of shamans long, long dead, yet unable to truly die. Rolling stones into strange patterns beneath star-strewn night skies, chewing with their teeth the faces of boulders to make frightening

340

scenes that only appeared at dusk or dawn, when the sun's light was newborn or fading into death – and far more often the boulders were so angled that it was at the moments of dusk that the deep magic was awakened, the images rising into being from what had seemed random pecules in the stone. Magic to murder the wind in that place—

'In the time before the plains descended, the shamans and their dread followers made music at the sun's dying, on the night of its shortest passage, and at other holy times before the snows came. They did not use skin drums. There was no need. No, they used the hide of the earth, the buried forest beneath. They pounded the skin of the world until every beast of the plain trembled, until the bhederin burst into motion, tens of thousands as one, and ran wild through the night – and so they too echoed the music of the Shamans of the Antlers, feeding their dark power.

'But the land fell away in the end – in grasping eternity, the shamans slew the very earth itself. This curse is without rest. This curse would close about our necks – each and every one of us here – this very night, if it could.'

Redmask was silent for a time then, as if allowing the terror to run free through the hearts of his audience. Eventually he resumed. 'The Shamans of the Antlers gathered their deathless warriors then, and set out to wage war. Abandoning this plain – and from that time, only those who fell in battle were returned here. Broken pieces. Failed and withered as the plain itself, never again to reach or even look skyward. Such was their curse.

'We do not forgive. It is not in us to forgive. But nor will we forget.

'Bast Fulmar, the Valley of Drums. The Letherii believe we hold it in great awe. They believe this valley was the sight of an ancient war between the Awl and the K'Chain Che'Malle – although the Letherii know not the true name of our ancient enemy. Perhaps indeed there were skirmishes, such that memory survives, only to twist and bind anew in false shapes. Many of you hold to those new shapes, believing them true. An ancient battle. One we won. One we lost – there are elders who are bold with the latter secret, as if defeat was a knife hidden in their heart-hand.' Redmask shrugged at the notion, dismissing it. Pale light was creeping close. Birdsong rose from the low shrubs.

'Bast Fulmar,' Redmask said again. 'Valley of Drums. Here, then, is its secret truth. The Shamans of the Antlers drummed the hide of this valley before us. Until all life was stolen, all the waters fled. They drank deep, until nothing was left. For at this time, the shamans were not alone, not for that fell ritual. No, others of their kind had joined them – on distant continents, hundreds, thousands of leagues away, each and all on that one night. To sever their life from the earth, to sever this earth from its own life.'

341

Silence, then, not a single warrior even so much as drawing breath. Held – too long—

Redmask released them with another sigh. 'Bast Fulmar. We rise now to make war. In the Valley of Drums, my warriors, Letherii sorcery *will fail*. Edur sorcery *will fail*. In Bast Fulmar, there is no water of magic, no stream of power from which to steal. All used up, all taken to quench the fire that is life. Our enemy is not aware. They will find the truth this day. Too late. Today, my warriors, shall be iron against iron. That and nothing more.'

Redmask then rose. 'Release the truth – to every warrior. Then make ready. We march to battle. To victory.'

Courage surged through Masarch's chest, and he found he was on his feet, trembling, and now moving off into the fading gloom, whispering his words to all that he passed. Again and again.

'Bast Fulmar sings this day. It sings: there is no magic. There is no magic!'

Stablers gathering the horses and leading them across the courtyard behind her, Atri-Preda Yan Tovis left the reins of her mount in the hands of an aide, then strode towards the estate's squat, brooding entrance. Thirty leagues south of the port town of Rennis, Boaral Keep was the birthplace of the Grass Jackets Brigade, but that was a long century past and now some third or fourth son of a remotely related Boaral held this fortress, clinging to the antiquated noble title of Dresh-Preda, or Demesne Lord. And in his command, a garrison consisting of barely a dozen soldiers, at least two of whom – at the outer gate – were drunk.

Weary, saddlesore, and feeling decidedly short on patience, Yan Tovis ascended the four broad, shallow steps to the lintel-capped main doors. No guard in sight. She wrenched the latch clear, then kicked open the heavy door and marched into the gloomy foyer within, startling two old women with buckets and khalit vine mops.

They flinched back, eyes down, hastily genuflecting.

'Where is Dresh Boaral?' Twilight demanded as she tugged free her gauntlets.

The hags exchanged glances, then one attempted something like a curtsy before saying, 'Ma'am, he be well sleeping it off, aye. An' us, we be well cleaning up his supper.'

A muffled snort from the other servant.

Only now did Yan Tovis detect the acrid smell of bile beneath that of lye soap. 'Where then is the Master at Arms?'

'Ma'am,' another curtsy, then, 'he be ridin' off wi' four soljers, west as they say, t'reach the coast fast as a clam squirt, an' that's a cloud ain't e'en settled yet.'

'He left recently then? What was the reason? And how far is the coast from here?'

'Ma'am, would be unner a bell, fast-goin' as he was.'

'And the reason?'

Another mysterious exchange of glances, then, 'Ma'am, coast be well black an' whispery of late. Got fishers vanishin' an' demon eyes flashin' from the deeps. Got islands be well ice an' all, pale an' deathly as the innards of a murderer's skull.'

'The Master at Arms rode off after superstitious rumours?'

'Ma'am, I be well 'ave a cousin on the shore—'

'The ditsy one, aye,' interjected the other hag.

'Be well ditsy but that don't matter in this, in this being the voices of the sea, which she heard an' heard more'n once too. Voices, ma'am, like the ghosts of the drowned as she says, havin' heard them an' heard them more'n once too.'

Two of her sergeants were now behind the Atri-Preda, listening. Twilight loosened the strap on her helm. 'This Master stays sober?' she asked.

'One a them hast, be well an' all.'

'It be him,' the other agreed. 'An' that a curse what make us worse at bad times of the night like now—'

'Shush you! This ma'am be a soljer outrankin' Dresh himself!'

'You don't know that, Pully! Why—'

'But I do! Whose nephew dug latrines for the Grass Jackets, be well he did! It's ranks an' neck torcs an' the cut of the cape an' all—'

Yan Tovis turned to one of her sergeants. 'Are there fresh horses in the stables?'

A nod. 'Four, Atri-Preda.'

The first old woman pushed at the other at that and said, 'Tolya! Be well I did!'

Yan Tovis tilted her head back in an effort to loosen the muscles of her neck. She closed her eyes for a moment, then sighed. 'Saddle them up, Sergeant. Pick me three of the least exhausted riders. I am off to find our missing Master at Arms.'

'Sir.' The man saluted and departed.

Turning back to the old women, the Atri-Preda asked, 'Where is the nearest detachment of Tiste Edur?'

A half-dozen heartbeats of non-verbal communication between the two hags, then the first one nodded and said, 'Rennis, ma'am. An' they be well not once visited neither.'

'Be glad they haven't,' Twilight said. 'They would have separated Boaral's head from his shoulders.'

The second woman snorted. 'Not so's he'd notice—'

'Shush!' scolded the first one. Then, to Twilight, 'Ma'am, Dresh

Boaral, he lost mostly alla his kin when the Edur come down. Lost his wife, too, in Noose Bog, what, now be well three years—'

The other hag spat onto the floor they had just cleaned. 'Lost? Be well strangled and dumped, Pully, by his master himself! So now he drowns on his own drinkin'! But oh she was fire wasn't she – no time for mewlin' husbands only he likes his mewlin' and be well likes it enough to murder his own wife!'

Twilight said to the sergeant who had remained, 'We will stay for a few days. I want the Dresh here under house arrest. Send a rider to Rennis to request adjudication by the Tiste Edur. The investigation will involve some sorcery, specifically speaking with the dead.'

The sergeant saluted and left.

'Best be well not speak wi' the mistress, ma'am.'

Twilight frowned at the woman. 'Why not?'

'Liable she is t'start talkin' and ne'er stop. Master drunk an' she's fire, all fire – she's a might claw his eyes out, be well an' that.'

'Are you two witches?'

More silent communication between the two hags, then the first one edged one knobby, hairy foot forward and carefully wiped at the gobbet of spit on the pavestones. The toes, Twilight saw, were taloned.

'You are Shake? Shoulderwomen of the Old Ways?'

Wrinkled brows rose, then the one named Pully curtsied again. 'Local born you be well as we'd known, aye. It's there, ma'am, you're a child of the shore an' ain't you gone far, but not so far as to f'get. Mistress ne'er liked us much.'

'So who strangled her and dumped her corpse in Noose Bog, Pully?'

The other seemed to choke, then she said, 'Dresh give 'is orders plain as web on a trail, didn't he, Pully? Give 'is orders an' wi' us we be well here since the Keep's first black stone was laid. Loyal, aye. Boaral blood was Letherii blood, the first t'these lands, the first masters a'all. Dresh the First give us 'is blood in full knowing, t'blacken the Black Stone.'

'The first Dresh here found you and forced your blessing?'

A cackle from the second woman. 'What he be well think were blessing!'

Twilight looked away, then stepped to one side and leaned a shoulder against the grimy wall. She was too tired for this. Boaral line cursed by Shake witches – who remained, alive and watchful, through generation after generation. She closed her eyes. 'Pully, how many wives have you two murdered?'

'None wi'out Dresh's command, ma'am.'

'But your curse drives them mad, every one of them. Don't make me ask the question again.'

'Ma'am, be well twenty and one. Once their bearin' days are done. Mostly.'

'And you have been working hard at keeping the Tiste Edur away.'

'No business a theirs, ma'am.'

Nor mine. Yet . . . not entirely true, is it? 'End the curse, Pully. You've done enough.'

'Boaral killed more Shake than any other Dresh, ma'am. You know that.'

'End it,' Twilight said, opening her eyes and facing the two women, 'or your heads will be in sacks and buried deep in Noose Bog before this night is out.'

Pully and her companion grinned at each other.

'I am of the shore,' Yan Tovis said in a hard voice. 'My Shake name is Twilight.'

The hags suddenly backed away, then sank down onto their knees, heads bowed.

'End the curse,' Twilight said again. 'Will you defy a princess of the Last Blood?'

'Princess no longer,' Pully said to the floor.

Yan Tovis felt the blood drain from her face – if not for the wall she leaned against she would have staggered.

'Your mother died be well a year past,' Pully said in a soft, sad voice.

The other witch added, 'Crossin' from the Isle, the boat overturning. They say it was some demon o' the deep, pushed too close by dark magic out at sea – the same magic, my Queen, as could be well squirted Master at Arms west as they say. A demon, up unner the boat, an' all drowned. Whisperin' from the waters, my Queen, dark and well nigh black.'

Yan Tovis drew a deep breath. To be Shake was to know grief. Her mother was dead, now a face emptied of life. Well, she had not seen the woman in over a decade, had she? So, why this pain? *Because there is something else.* 'What is the name of the Master at Arms, Pully?'

'Yedan Derryg, Highness. The Watch.'

The half-brother I have never met. The one who ran – from his blood, from everything. Ran nearly as far as I did. And yet, was that old tale even true? The Watch was here, after all, a mere bell's ride from the shore. She understood now why he had ridden out on this night. *Something else, and this is it.*

Yan Tovis drew her cloak about herself, began pulling on her gauntlets. 'Feed well my soldiers. I will return with Derryg by dawn.' As she turned to the door she paused. 'The madness afflicting the Dresh, Pully.'

Behind her the witch replied, 'Be well too late for him, Highness. But we will scour the Black Stone this night. Before the Edur arrive.'

Oh, yes, I sent for them, didn't I? 'I imagine,' she said, her gaze fixed on the door, 'the summary execution of Dresh Boaral will be something of a mercy for the poor man.'

'You mean to do it before the Edur come here as they say, Highness?'

'Yes, Pully. He will die, I suppose, trying to flee arrest.' After a moment, she asked, 'Pully, how many shoulderwomen are left?'

'More than two hundred, Highness.'

'I see.'

'My Queen,' ventured the other, 'word will be sent out, cob to web as they say, before the sun's rise. You have been chosen a betrothed.'

'I have, have I? Who?'

'Shake Brullyg, of the Isle.'

'And does my betrothed remain on Second Maiden Fort?'

'We think so, Highness,' Pully replied.

At that she turned round. 'You don't know?'

'The web's been snapped, Highness. Almost a month now. Ice an' dark and whisperings, we cannot reach across the waves. The shore is blind to the sea, Highness.'

The shore is blind to the sea. 'Has such a thing ever occurred before?'

Both witches shook their heads.

Twilight swung about and hastened outside. Her riders awaited her, already mounted, silent with fatigue. She strode to the horse bearing her saddle – a chestnut gelding, the fittest of the lot, she could see in the torchlight – and pulled herself onto its broad back.

'Atri-Preda?'

'To the coast,' she said, gathering the reins. 'At the canter.'

'What's wrong with them?'

The Hound Master's face was ravaged with distress, tears streaming down his wind-burned cheeks and glistening like sweat in his beard. 'They've been poisoned, Atri-Preda! Poisoned meat, left on the ground – I'm going to lose them all!'

Bivatt cursed under her breath, then said, 'Then we shall have to do without.'

'But the Edur mages—'

'If our own cannot treat them, Bellict, then neither can the warlocks – the Edur tribes do not breed dogs for war, do they? I am sorry. Leave me now.'

Just one more unpleasant surprise to greet this dawn. Her army had marched through the last two bells of night to reach the valley – she wanted to be the first to array her troops for the battle to come, to force Redmask to react rather than initiate. Given the location of the Awl encampment, she had not felt rushed in conducting that march, anticipating it would be midday at the earliest before the savages appeared on the east side of Bast Fulmar, thus negating any advantage of a bright morning sun at their backs.

But that enemy encampment had been a deceit.

Less than a half-league from the valley, scouts had returned to the column to report enemy in strength at Bast Fulmar.

How had her mages not found them? They had no answer, barring a disquieting fear in their eyes. Even Brohl Handar's Den-Ratha K'risnan and his four warlocks had been at a loss to explain the success of Redmask's deception. The news had left the sour taste of self-recrimination in Bivatt – relying upon mages had been a mistake, laziness leaning heavy on past successes. Outriding scouts would have discovered the ruse days ago, had she bothered to send them beyond line of sight. Keeping them close ensured no raids or ambushes, both gambits for which the Awl were renowned. She had been following doctrine, to the letter.

Damn this Redmask. Clearly he knows that doctrine as well as I do. And used it against us.

Now, the battle awaiting them was imminent, and the bright dawn sun would indeed blaze into the eyes of her soldiers even as the first blood was spilled.

Rising in her stirrups, she squinted once more at the valley's far side. Mounted Awl in swirling motion, in seeming chaos, riding back and forth, lifting clouds of dust that burned gold in the morning light. Horse-archers for the most part. Tending to mass in front of one of the broader slopes to the south, on her right. A second gentle incline was situated slightly to her left, and there, shifting restlessly, were five distinct wedges of Awl warriors on foot, lining what passed for a ridge – and she could see their long spears waving like reeds on a shore. Spears, not those flimsy swords sold them by the Factor's agents. She judged around a thousand warriors per wedge formation – too disciplined even now, before the fighting began. *They should be drunk. Pounding on shields. Their shamans should be rushing about in front, down all the way to the riverbed. Showing us their backsides as they defecate. Screaming curses, dancing to summon dread spirits and all the rest. Instead, this . . .*

Well, how likely is it those wedges will survive contact with my soldiers? They are not trained to this kind of war – nor did Redmask have the time to manage anything but this thin shell of organization. I have over sixteen thousand with me. Eighteen if I include the Tiste Edur. This one army of mine outnumbers the entire Awl population of warriors – and while it looks indeed as if Redmask has gathered them all, still they are not enough.

But he wasn't making it easy to gauge numbers. The tumultuous back and forth of the horse-archers, the clouds of dust, the truncated line of sight beyond the valley's ridge – he was keeping her blind.

Brohl Handar reined in at her side, speaking loudly to be heard over the movement of her troops and the officers bellowing orders.

'Atri-Preda, you seem to intend to hold most of your medium infantry in reserve.' He gestured behind them to punctuate his words. Then, when it was clear she would not respond, he waved ahead. 'This valley's flanks, while not steeply inclined, are ribboned with drainage channels—'

'Narrow,' she cut in. 'Not deep.'

'True, but they serve to separate the field of battle into segments nonetheless.'

She glanced across at him. 'We have three such channels on our side, and all of them on my right. They have four, one to my right, two before me and one to my left – and in that direction, north, the valley narrows.' She pointed. 'See the bluff on our side there, where the Dresh ballistae are being emplaced? It cannot be assaulted from the valley floor. That shall be our rock in the stream. And before the day is through, not simply a rock, but an anvil.'

'Provided you can hold the debouch beneath it,' the Tiste Edur observed.

'I pray to the Errant that the Awl seek to flee down that defile. It may not look deadly but I assure you, push a few thousand panicking barbarians into that chokepoint and as many will die underfoot as we ourselves slaughter.'

'So you intend to sweep down and in with your right flank, pushing the enemy on the valley floor north to that narrowing. Cannot Redmask see the same?'

'He chose this site, Overseer.'

'Suggesting he sees what you see – that this place invites a half-encirclement to funnel his warriors north – to their deaths. You said, did you not, that this Redmask is no fool. How then will he counter what you seek?'

She faced the valley once again. 'Overseer, I am afraid I do not have time for this—'

'Would not a slow placing of your forces be to our advantage, given the sun's position?'

'I believe he is ready, even now,' she replied, biting back her irritation. 'He could advance at any time – and we are not ready.'

'Then why not withdraw?'

'Because the plain behind us is level for leagues – he will have more mounted warriors than I, lighter-armoured than my Bluerose lancers, and on rested horses – they can harry us at will, Overseer. Worse, we have lost our wardogs, while from the sounds of that barking, Redmask has hundreds if not thousands of his drays and herders. Your suggestion invites chaos, a messy succession of skirmishes, attacks, feints, raids—'

'Very well,' Brohl Handar interrupted. 'Atri-Preda, my K'risnan tells me this valley is dead.'

'What does he mean, *dead*?'

'Bereft of the energies one uses to create magic. It has been . . . murdered.'

'This is why none of the mages sensed the Awl army?'

Brohl Handar nodded.

Murdered? By Redmask? Never mind. 'Did you ask your K'risnan about the impending battle? Will he be able to use sorcery?'

'No. Nor can your mages. As he said, there will be no magic here. In this valley. That is why I again advise we withdraw. Even on the plain, exposed as you say we are, at least we will have sorcery.'

Bivatt was silent, considering. She had already known her mages would be ineffective in the valley below, although they could not explain why it was so. That the Edur warlocks had found the reason confirmed that spirit magic was involved. After a long moment, she swore and shook her head. 'We still outnumber them, with better-disciplined, better-armoured troops. Iron to iron, we will crush the Awl today. An end to this war, Overseer. Did you not counsel a quick, succinct campaign?'

'I did. But I am uneasy, Atri-Preda—'

'A battle awaits – we are all uneasy.'

'Not in that way.'

Bivatt grimaced. 'Retain your warriors, Overseer, midway between our baggage camp and my reserve units – those medium infantry, by the way, are arrayed into discrete platoons of five hundred at the minimum, and each one protects one of my mages. *They* are not in the valley.'

'Thus, if you are forced to retreat—'

'We will be positioned to blunt the pursuit with sorcery, yes.'

'Is this your plan? A feigned retreat, Atri-Preda?'

'One of them, but I do not believe it will be necessary.'

Brohl Handar studied her for a long moment, then he gathered his reins and swung his horse round. 'I will reposition my warriors, then.'

As he rode away, signal horns were sounding from various locations along the western side of the valley as units announced they were in place and at the ready. Bivatt rose once more on her stirrups and scanned her lines.

This section of the valley certainly invited a horned advance – the west edge curved, marking what had once been a broad bend in the course of the long-dead river. The enemy's side was more un-dulating, bulging in the centre. The widest approach for the Awl was to her right. To counter that she had set three legions of the Crimson Rampant Brigade in shield-wall formation at the top of the slope, fifteen hundred medium infantry, flanked on the nearer inside by five hundred heavies of the Harridict Brigade. To the furthest right and already edging down into the valley were a thousand skirmishing light

349

infantry of the Crimson Rampant. Inside of the heavies another fifteen hundred skirmishers, these of the Artisan Battalion, were likewise slowly, raggedly, working their way down. The foot soldiers on this side screened three wings of Bluerose cavalry: fifteen hundred lancers who would, when she gave the signal, sweep down between the south skirmishers and the Crimson Rampant shield-wall to begin the hard push of the enemy northward along the floor of the valley, even as that shield-wall advanced towards the riverbed.

On her immediate right, at a modest bulge in the ridge line, the Atri-Preda had positioned the Drene Garrison – fifteen hundred medium infantry – looking down on an approach narrowed by two drainage channels. Directly in front of her waited the conjoined wedges of a thousand heavy infantry of the Merchants' Battalion – a sawtooth formation that she would advance down then swing either right or left, depending on the state of battle. Rightward was problematic in that they would have to cross a drainage channel, but they would do that so early in the march down that she was not unduly concerned.

To her immediate left waited three half-legions of heavies from the Artisan Battalion, screened in front by a thousand Harridict skirmishers just beginning their move down towards the broad, flat riverbed. Just north of these units waited the Atri-Preda's mailed fist, a thousand heavies of the Crimson Rampant, again in sawtooth formation, against whom she expected Redmask to throw his main force of warriors – who were already directly opposite, still holding to their spearhead forms, five in all.

Behind this solid wall of heavy infantry waited the remaining three companies of Bluerose lancers, although this was a feint, since Bivatt intended to send them northward, round behind the ballistae knoll and down into the riverbed beyond the chokepoint.

North of the Crimson Rampant heavy infantry was another shield-wall of the brigade's medium infantry, positioned to guard the flank of the heavies to their right and the approach to the knoll to their left.

Settling back onto her saddle, Bivatt gestured and an aide hurried to her side. 'Signal the Crimson Rampant heavy to advance into the valley and halt midway between their present position and the riverbed. Confirm that the Dresh ballistae are properly sighted for enfilade.'

The runner rushed off to the block of flag signallers gathered on the raised platform behind her. Without mages they were resorting to the ancient practices of communication. Far from ideal, she admitted, and once the clouds of dust rose above the engagement . . . well, at that point such signalling often became irrelevant.

She waved another aide forward. 'Send the left flank lancers to north of the chokepoint.'

Right and left on the valley slope before her, Letherii skirmishers were reaching the flats of the riverbed, still unchallenged. The sound of masses of soldiers in motion rode in a whisper above the thunder of horse-hoofs from the other side of the valley.

On that side the clouds of sunlit dust obscured almost everything, but she noted that those clouds stretched both north and south, well beyond the battle site. *Well, one of those marks a feint, likely the north one. He knows which of my horns will strike deepest and turn.* She called out to a third message-bearer. 'Signal the right flank lancers to advance to the edge of the riverbed, widely arrayed in case the skirmishers need to withdraw in haste. Crimson Rampant mediums and the Harridict heavies to march down in their wake.'

Let's get this damned thing started, Redmask.

She couldn't see him. No knot of standards or banners marked his command position. No riders converging in one place then back out again.

But, finally, movement. Lightly armoured skirmishers were pelting down to meet her right advance. Slingers, shortbow archers, javelin-hurlers, round hide shields and scimitars. The mass of horse-archers that had been riding back and forth along that ridge line was suddenly gone.

'Have the south lancers hold!' Bivatt snapped. Those Awl skirmishers were an invitation to charge, at which point her cavalry's flank would be swept by those mounted archers – and whatever lurked hidden behind them.

Light engagement now between skirmishers, directly down from the Drene Garrison. The javelins were an unexpected inclusion, and were proving bloodily effective.

The southernmost Crimson Rampant skirmishers had crossed the riverbed and were angling northward – still a thousand or more paces from contacting their Awl counterparts. Then arrows began descending in their midst – horse-archers, crowding the ridge just above its steepest bank. Hardly clouds of missiles, but enough to make those lightly armoured skirmishers flinch, then contract slightly back towards the riverbed.

Where the hand-to-hand fighting was occurring, the Artisan skirmishers – weathering the javelin strike – were now driving the Awl back.

The early morning air remained infuriatingly still – no wind at all, and the dust swirled and rolled and spread in an ever-thickening haze.

At sighting the half-thousand heavy infantry of the Harridict appear at the west edge of the riverbed, the Awl skirmishers began a wholesale retreat, many flinging away their round-shields.

Redmask does not have their hearts. Oh, we can break them here. Hard and fast. 'Signal the Merchants' heavies to advance and swing south!'

351

To her left, the only movement was from her own forces, the skirmishers of the Harridict and, just north of them, the Crimson Rampant heavy infantry – almost to the riverbed now. She squinted at the valley's opposite side. Perhaps this chaos she was seeing was evidence of Redmask's loss of control. *No, wait on this. Wait until we take the valley's south end.*

The Artisan skirmishers were seeking to maintain contact with the retreating Awl, but Bivatt could see the sergeants holding them in check, keeping them just ahead of the advancing heavies on their right flank. *Still, throwing away their damned shields . . .*

Then, directly before her, horse-archers appeared, a narrow spear driving down the centre of the battlefield, with only skirmishers opposite them – who quickly backed up the slope at a southerly angle to draw in behind her advancing Merchants' Battalion of heavy infantry. *Is Redmask mad? That spear-point will be smashed against the heavies – this is not how cavalry charge – they're only horse-archers!*

Whereupon the mounted archers wheeled, the spear becoming a line – a thousand or more – suddenly sweeping southward.

Catching the Artisan skirmishers in the flank.

Arrows flashed.

The Letherii light infantry seemed to melt away, bodies tumbling down. Survivors ran for their lives.

That broad line of horse-archers then began a complicated, stunning manoeuvre, its tailing, easternmost end now slowing, swinging up, west, pulling to shift the line south-north, now launching sweeping arrow-fire across the front ranks of the Harridict heavy infantry, then the Crimson Rampant medium, before the head of the line swung back eastward, more missiles arcing across to the Bluerose lancers, who responded with a blare of horns, surging forward to close with the Awl.

Yet they were not interested in such an engagement. The line broke apart, as riders spurred hard back towards the east ridge.

'Halt that charge!' Bivatt shouted. *Stung, we lash out – who commands that wing?*

As the lancers spread out in their hard pursuit, three wings of heavier-armed and armoured Awl horse-warriors appeared on the ridge line, then plunged down the slope to take the Bluerose companies in the flank. Three wings, outnumbering the lancers by two to one.

Bivatt watched in fury as her cavalry sought to wheel to meet the attack, whilst others responded to her command – and so lost all momentum.

'Sound the withdrawal for those lancers!'

Too late.

The Awl horse-warriors swept through scattered skirmishers of the Crimson Rampant, then slammed into the Bluerose companies.

She heard animals scream, felt the impact tremble through the ground – enough to make her mount sidestep – and then dust obscured the scene. 'Advance the heavies at the double!'

'Which heavies, Atri-Preda?'

'Harridict and Merchants', you fool! And same command for the Crimson Rampant medium! Quickly!'

She saw riders and riderless horses plunge into view from the roiling dust clouds. Her lancers had been shattered – were the Awl pursuing? *Their blood must be high – oh, let them lose control, let them meet the fists of my heavies!*

But no, there they were, rising up the far slope, waving weapons in the air to announce their triumph.

She saw the Awl skirmishers reappearing on the ridge line, in blocks with avenues in between to let the riders pass through – but those light infantry were transformed. Equipped now with rectangular, copper-sheathed shields and bearing long spears, they closed ranks after the last horse-warriors were through, and steadied their line at the very edge of the ridge.

On the valley floor, dust climbed skyward, slowly revealing the devastating effects of that flank charge into the Bluerose companies. *Errant below, they've been wiped out.* Hundreds of dead and dying skirmishers covered the grounds to either side of that fateful impact.

Her right advance had been deeply wounded – *not yet mortal, even so* – 'Advance the medium and the two heavies across the valley – order to engage that line on the ridge. Wedge formations!' *Those skirmishers are too thinly arrayed to hold.*

'Atri-Preda!' called an aide. 'Movement to the north side!'

She cantered her horse to the very edge of the rise and scanned the scene below and to her left. 'Report!'

'Bluerose lancers in retreat, Atri-Preda – the valley floor beyond the chokepoint is theirs—'

'What? How many damned horse-archers does he have?'

The officer shook her head. 'Wardogs, sir. Close on two thousand of the damned things – moving through the high grasses in the basin – they were on the lancers before they knew it. The horses went wild, sir—'

'*Shit!*' Then, upon seeing the messenger's widening eyes, she steeled herself. 'Very well. Move the reserve medium to the north flank of the knoll.' *Seven hundred and fifty, Merchants' Battalion – I doubt they'd try sending dogs against that. I can still advance them to retake the chokepoint's debouch, when the time comes.*

As she thought this, she was scanning the array before her. Directly opposite, the thousand Harridict skirmishers had crossed the riverbed, even as the Crimson Rampant sawtooth advance moved onto level ground.

And Redmask's five wedges of warriors were marching to meet them. *Excellent. We'll lock that engagement – with ballistae enfilade to weaken their north flank – then down come the Crimson Rampant medium, to wheel into their flank.*

Surprisingly the Awl wedges more or less held to their formations, although they were each maintaining considerable distance from their flanking neighbours – once the space drew tighter, she suspected, the wedges would start mixing, edges pulled ragged. Marching in time was the most difficult battlefield manoeuvre, after all. Between each of them, then, could be found the weak points. Perhaps enough to push through with the saw's teeth and begin isolating each wedge.

'Wardogs on the knoll!'

She spun at the cry. 'Errant's kick!' Frenzied barking, shrieks from the weapon crews – 'Second reserve legion – the Artisan! Advance on the double – butcher those damned things!'

Obscurely, she suddenly recalled a scene months ago – wounded but alive, less than a handful of the beasts on a hill overlooking an Awl camp, watching the Letherii slaughtering the last of their masters. And she wondered, with a shiver of superstitious fear, if those beasts were now exacting ferocious vengeance. *Dammit, Bivatt – never mind all that.*

The Awl spear-heads were not drawing together, she saw – nor was there need to, now that she'd temporarily lost her ballistae. Indeed, the two northernmost of those wedges were now angling to challenge her Crimson Rampant medium. But this would be old-style fighting, she knew – and the Awl did not possess the discipline nor the training for this kind of steeled butchery.

Yet, Redmask is not waging this battle in the Awl fashion, is he? No, this is something else. He's treating this like a plains engagement in miniature – the way those horse-archers wheeled, reformed, then reformed again – a hit and run tactic, all on a compacted scale.

I see now – but it will not work for much longer.

Once his warriors locked with her mailed fist.

The Awl spear-heads were now nearing the flat of the riverbed – the two sides would engage on the hardpacked sand of the bed itself. No advantage of slope to either side – *until the tide shifts. One way or the other – no, do not think—*

A new reverberation trembled through the ground now. Deeper, rolling, ominous.

From the dust, between the Awl wedges, huge shapes loomed, rumbled forward.

Wagons. *Awl wagons, the six-wheeled bastards* – not drawn, but pushed. Their beds were crowded with half-naked warriors, spears bristling. The entire front end of each rocking, pitching wagon was a horizontal forest of oversized spears. Round-shields overlapped to form a half-turtleshell that encased the forward section.

They now thundered through the broad gaps between the wedges – twenty, fifty, a hundred – lumbering yet rolling so swiftly after the long descent into the valley that the masses of burly warriors who had been pushing them now trailed in their wake, sprinting to catch up.

The wagons plunged straight into the face of the Crimson Rampant heavy infantry.

Armoured bodies cartwheeled above the press as the entire saw-tooth formation was torn apart – and now the bare-chested fanatics riding those wagons launched themselves out to all sides, screaming like demons.

The three wedges facing the heavy infantry then thrust into the chaotic wake, delivering frenzied slaughter.

Bivatt stared, disbelieving, then snapped, 'Artisan heavy, advance down at the double, crescent, and prepare to cover the retreat.'

The aide beside her stared. 'Retreat, Atri-Preda?'

'You heard me! Signal general withdrawal and sound the Crimson Rampant to retreat! Quickly, before every damned one of them is butchered!'

Will Redmask follow? Oh, I'll lose heavily if he does – but I'll also hit back hard – on the plain. I'll see his bones burst into flames—

She heard more wagons, this time to her right. *My other advance –* 'Sound general withdrawal!'

Horns blared.

Shouts behind her. 'Attack on the baggage camp! Attack—'

'Quiet! Do you think the Edur cannot deal with that?' She prayed Brohl Handar could. Without supplies this campaign was over. *Without supplies, we'll never make it back to Drene. Errant fend, I have been outwitted at every turn—*

And now the sound behind her was rising to challenge that in the valley below. With sick dread, she tugged her horse round and rode back, past the signallers' platform.

Her remaining reserve units had all wheeled round, reversing their facing. Seeing an officer riding between two of the squares, Bivatt spurred to catch him.

'What in the Errant's name is happening over there?' she demanded. Distant screams, the reek of smoke, thunder—

The helmed head swung round, the face beneath it pale. 'Demons, Atri-Preda! The mages pursue them—'

'*They what?* Recall them, damn you! *Recall them now!*'

Brohl Handar sat astride his horse in the company of eight Arapay war leaders, four warlocks and the Den-Ratha K'risnan. The two thousand foot soldiers – Tiste Edur warriors, categorized in Letherii military terms as medium to light infantry – were arranged into eight distinct blocks, fully caparisoned in armour and awaiting the word to march.

The supply train's camp was sprawled on a broad, mostly level hill fifteen hundred paces to the west, the corralled beasts of burden milling beneath dust and slowly drifting dung-smoke. The Overseer could see hospital tents rising along the near side, the canvas sides bright in the morning light. Above another hill, north of the train's camp, wheeled two hawks or perhaps eagles. The sky was otherwise empty, a span of deep blue slowly paling as the sun climbed higher.

Butterflies flitted among small yellow flowers – their wings matched precisely the colour of the petals, Brohl realized, surprised that he had not noted such a detail before. *Nature understands disguise and deceit. Nature reminds us what it is to survive.* The Tiste Edur had well grasped those truths – grey as the shadows from which they had been born; grey as the boles of the trees in the murky forests of this world; grey as the shrouds of dusk.

'What have we forgotten?' he murmured.

An Arapay war leader – a Preda – turned his helmed head, the scarred face beneath its jutting rim hidden in shadow. 'Overseer? We are positioned as you commanded—'

'Never mind,' Brohl Handar cut in, inexplicably irritated by the veteran's attention. 'What is the guard at the camp?'

'Four hundred mixed infantry,' the warrior replied, then shrugged. 'These Letherii are ever confident.'

'Comes with overwhelming superiority,' another Arapay drawled.

The first Preda nodded. 'I do well recall, old friend, the surprise on their faces the day we shattered them outside Letheras. As if, all at once, the world revealed itself to be other than what they had always believed. That look – it was *disbelief.*' The warrior grunted a laugh. 'Too busy with their denial to adapt when it was needed most.'

'Enough of this,' Brohl Handar snapped. 'The Atri-Preda's forces have engaged the Awl – can you not hear?' He twisted on his saddle and squinted eastward. 'See the dust.' He was silent for a dozen heartbeats, then he turned to the first Arapay Preda. 'Take two cohorts to the camp. Four hundred Letherii are not enough.'

'Overseer, what if we are called on to reinforce the Atri-Preda?'

'If we are, then this day is lost. I have given you my order.'

A nod, and the Preda spurred his horse towards the arrayed Edur warriors.

Brohl Handar studied the K'risnan at his side for a moment. The bent creature sat hunched in his saddle like a bloated crow. He was hooded, no doubt to hide the twisted ravaging of his once-handsome features. A chief's son, transformed into a ghastly icon of the chaotic power before which the Tiste Edur now knelt. He saw the figure twitch. 'What assails you?' the Overseer demanded.

'Something, nothing.' The reply was guttural, the words misshaped by a malformed throat. It was the sound of pain, enduring and unyielding.

'Which?'

Another twitch, passing, Brohl realized, for a shrug. 'Footfalls on dead land.'

'An Awl war-party?'

'No.' The hooded head pivoted until the shadow-swallowed face was directed at the Overseer. 'Heavier.'

All at once Brohl Handar recalled the enormous taloned tracks found at the destroyed homestead. He straightened, one hand reaching for the Arapay scimitar at his side. 'Where? Which direction?'

A long pause, then the K'risnan pointed with a clawed hand.

Towards the supply camp.

Where sudden screams erupted.

'Cohorts at the double!' Brohl Handar bellowed. 'K'risnan, you and your warlocks – with me!' With that he spurred his horse, kicking the startled beast into a canter, then a gallop.

Ahead, he saw, the Arapay Preda who had been escorting the two cohorts had already commanded them into a half-jog. The warrior's helmed head turned and tracked the Overseer and his cadre of mages as they pounded past.

Ahead, the braying of terrified oxen and mules rose, mournful and helpless, above the sounds of slaughter. Tents had gone down, guide-ropes whipping into the air, and Brohl saw figures now, fleeing the camp, pelting northward—

—where a perfect Awl ambush awaited them. Rising from the high grasses. Arrows, javelins, sleeting through the air. Bodies sprawling, tumbling, then the savages, loosing war-cries, rushing to close with spears, axes and swords.

Nothing to be done for them – poor bastards. We need to save our supplies.

They reached the faint slope and rode hard towards the row of hospital tents.

The beast that burst into view directly before them was indeed a demon – an image that closed like talons in his mind – the shock of recognition. *Our ancient enemy – it must be – the Edur cannot forget –*

Head thrust forward on a sinuous neck, broad jaw open to reveal dagger fangs. Massive shoulders behind the neck, long heavily muscled arms with huge curved blades of iron strapped where hands should have been. Leaning far forward as it ran towards them on enormous hind legs, the huge tail thrust straight back for balance, the beast was suddenly in their midst.

Horses screamed. Brohl found himself to the demon's right, almost within reach of those scything sword blades, and he stared in horror as that viper's head snapped forward, jaws closing on the neck of a horse, closing, crunching, then tearing loose, blood spraying, its mouth still filled with meat and bone, the horse's spine half ripping loose from the horrid gap left in the wake of those savage jaws. A blade cut in half the warlock astride that mount. The other sword slashed down, chopping through another warlock's thigh, the saddle, then deep into the horse's shoulder, smashing scapula, then ribs. The beast collapsed beneath the blow, as the rider – the severed stump of his leg gushing blood – pitched over, balanced for a moment on the one stirrup, then sprawled to land on the ground, even as another horse's stamping hoof descended onto his upturned face.

The Overseer's horse seemed to collide with something, snapping both front legs. The animal's plunging fall threw Brohl over its head. He struck, rolled, the scimitar's blade biting into his left leg, and came to a stop facing his thrashing mount. The demon's tail had swept into and through their path.

He saw it wheel for a return attack.

A foaming wave of sorcery rose into its path, lifting, climbing with power.

The demon vanished from Brohl's view behind that churning wave.

Sun's light suddenly blotted—

—the demon in the air, arcing over the crest of the K'risnan's magic, then down, the talons of its hind feet outstretched. One closing on another warlock, pushing the head down at an impossible angle into the cup between the man's shoulders as the demon's weight descended – the horse crumpling beneath that overwhelming force, legs snapping like twigs. The other raking towards the K'risnan, a glancing blow that flung him from the back of his bolting horse, the claws catching the horse's rump before it could lunge out of reach, the talons sinking deep, then tearing free a mass of meat to reveal – in a gory flash – the bones of its hips and upper legs.

The horse crashed down in a twisting fall that cracked ribs, less than three strides away from where Brohl was lying. He saw the whites of the beast's eyes – shock and terror, death's own spectre—

The Overseer sought to rise, but something was wrong with his left leg – drained of all strength, strangely heavy, sodden in the tangled grass. He looked down. Red from the hip down – his own scimitar had opened a deep, welling gash at an angle over his thigh, the cut ending just above the knee.

A killing wound – blood pouring out – Brohl Handar fell back, staring up at the sky, disbelieving. *I have killed myself.*

He heard the thump of the demon's feet, swift, moving away – then a deeper sound, the rush of warriors, closing now around him, weapons drawn. Heads turned, faces stretched as words were shouted – he could not understand them, the sounds fading, retreating – a figure crawling to his side, hooded, blood dripping from its nose – the only part of the face that was visible – a gnarled hand reaching for him – and Brohl Handar closed his eyes.

Atri-Preda Bivatt sawed the reins of her horse as she came between two units of her reserve medium infantry, Artisan on her right, Harridict on her left, and beyond them, where another Artisan unit was positioned, there was the commotion of fighting.

She saw a reptilian monstrosity plunging into their ranks – soldiers seeming to melt from its path, others lifting into the air on both sides, in welters of blood, as the beast's taloned hands slashed right and left. Dark-hued, perfectly balanced on two massive hind legs, the demon tore a path straight to the heart of the packed square—

Reaching out, both hands closing on a single figure, a woman, a mage – plucking her flailing into the air, then dismembering her as would a child a straw doll.

Beyond, she could see, the southernmost unit, seven hundred and fifty medium infantry of the Merchants' Battalion, were a milling mass strewn with dead and dying soldiers.

'Sorcery!' she screamed, wheeling towards the Artisan unit on her right – seeking out the mage in its midst – motion, someone pushing through the ranks.

Dust clouds caught her eye – the camp – the Edur legion was nowhere in sight – they had rushed to its defence. *Against more of these demons?*

The creature barrelled free of the Artisan soldiers south of the now-retreating Harridict unit, where a second sorceror stumbled into view, running towards the other mage. She could see his mouth moving as he wove magic, adding his power to that of the first.

The demon had spun to its left instead of continuing its attack, launching itself into a run, wheeling round the unit it had just torn through, placing them between itself and the sorcery now bursting loose in a refulgent tumult from the ground in front of the mages.

Leaning far forward, the demon's speed was astonishing as it fled.

Bivatt heard the ritual sputter and die and she twisted on her saddle. 'Damn you! Hit it!'

'Your soldiers!'

'You took too long!' She spied a Preda from the Harridict unit. 'Draw all the reserves behind the mages! North, you fool – sound the order! Cadre, keep that damned magic at the ready!'

'We are, Atri-Preda!'

Chilled despite the burgeoning heat, Bivatt swung her horse round once more and rode hard back towards the valley. *I am outwitted. Flinching on every side, recoiling, reacting – Redmask, this one is yours.*

But I will have you in the end. I swear it.

Ahead, she could see her troops appearing on the rise, withdrawing in order, in what was clearly an uncontested retreat. Redmask, it seemed, was satisfied – he would not be drawn out from the valley, even with his demonic allies—

The camp. She needed to get her soldiers back to that damned camp – *pray the Edur beat off the attack. Pray Brohl Handar has not forgotten how to think like a soldier.*

Pray he fared better than I did this day.

The shore is blind to the sea. Might as well say the moon has for ever fled the night sky. Chilled, exhausted, Yan Tovis rode with her three soldiers down the level, narrow road. Thick stands of trees on either side, the leaves black where the moon's light did not reach, the banks high and steep evincing the antiquity of this trail to the shore, roots reaching down witch-braided, gnarled and dripping in the clammy darkness. Stones snapping beneath hooves, the gusts of breath from the horses, the muted crackle of shifting armour. Dawn was still two bells away.

Blind to the sea. The sea's thirst was ceaseless. The truth of that could be seen in its endless gnawing of the shore, could be heard in its hungry voice, could be found in the bitter poison of its taste. The Shake knew that in the beginning the world had been nothing but sea, and that in the end it would be the same. The water rising, devouring all, and this was an inexorable fate to which the Shake were helpless witness.

The shore's battle had ever been the battle of her people. The Isle, which had once been sacred, had been desecrated, made a fetid prison by the Letherii. *Yet now it is freed once again. Too late.* Generations past there had been land bridges linking the many islands south of the Reach. Now gone. The Isle itself rose from the sea with high cliffs, everywhere but the single harbour now. Such was the dying world.

Often among the Shake there had been born demon-kissed children. Some would be chosen by the coven and taught the Old Ways; the rest would be flung from those cliffs, down into the thirsty sea. Gift of mortal blood; momentary, pathetic easing of its need.

She had run, years ago, for a reason. The noble blood within her had burned like poison, the barbaric legacy of her people overwhelmed her with shame and guilt. With the raw vigour of youth she had refused to accept the barbaric brutality of her ancestors, refused to wallow in the cloying, suffocating nihilism of a self-inflicted crime.

All of the defiance within her was obliterated when she had seen for herself the birth of a demon-kissed monstrosity – the taloned hands and feet, the scaled, elongated face, the blunt tail twitching like a headless worm, the eyes of lurid green. If naught but the taloned hands and feet had marked the demon's seed, the coven would have chosen this new-born, for there was true power in demonic blood when no more than a single drop trickled in the child's veins. More than that, and the creation was an abomination.

Grotesque babes crawling in the muck of the sea's floor, claws gouging furrows in the dark, the sea's legion, the army awaiting us all.

The seeds thrived in the foaming waves where they met the land, generation upon generation. Flung high onto the shore, they sank into the ground. Dwelling within living creatures, prey and predator; bound inside plants; adhering to the very blades of grass, the leaves of the trees – these seeds could not be escaped: another bitter truth among the Shake. When they found a woman's womb where a child was already growing, the seed stole its fate. Seeking . . . something, yet yielding naught but a shape that warred with that of the human.

The demons had been pure, once. Birthing their own kind, a world of mothers and offspring. The seeds had dwelt in the sea found in demonic wombs. Until the war that saw the bellies of those mothers slit open, spilling what belonged inside out into this world – the seeds even the sea sought to reject. A war of slaughter – yet the demons had found a way to survive, to this very day. In the swirling spume of tidal pools, in the rush of tumbling, crashing waves. Lost, yet not defeated. Gone, yet poised to return.

Seeking the right mother.

So the witches remained. Yan Tovis had believed the coven obliterated, crushed into extinction – the Letherii well knew that resistance to tyranny was nurtured in schools of faith, espoused by old, bitter priests and priestesses, by elders who would work through the foolish young – use them like weapons, flung away when broken, melo-dramatically mourned when destroyed. Priests and priestesses whose version of faith justified the abuse of their own followers.

The birth of a priesthood, Yan Tovis now understood, forced a hierarchy upon piety, as if the rules of servitude were malleable, where such a scheme – shrouded in mysterious knowledge and learning – con-veyed upon the life of a priest or priestess greater value and virtue than those of the ignorant common folk.

In her years of Letherii education, Yan Tovis had seen how the arrival of shouldermen – of warlocks and witches – was in truth a devolution among the Shake, a devolution from truly knowing the god that was the shore. Artifice and secular ambition, witholding sacred knowledge from those never to be initiated – these were not the shore's will. *No, only what the warlocks and witches wanted.*

Taloned hands and feet have proved iconic indeed.

But power came with demonic blood. And so long as every child born with such power and allowed to survive was initiated into the coven, then that power remained exclusive.

The Letherii in their conquest of the Shake had conducted a pogrom against the coven.

And had failed.

With all her being, Yan Tovis wished they had succeeded.

The Shake were gone as a people. Even the soldiers of her company – each one carefully selected over the years on the basis of Shake remnants in their blood – were in truth more Letherii than Shake. She had done little, after all, to awaken their heritage.

Yet I chose them, did I not? I wanted their loyalty, beyond that of a Letherii soldier for his or her Atri-Preda.

Admit it, Twilight. You are a queen now, and these soldiers – these Shake – *know it. And it is what you sought in the depths of your own ambition.* And now, it seemed, she would have to face the truth of that ambition, the stirring of her noble blood – seeking its proper preeminence, its *right.*

What has brought my half-brother to the shore? Did he ride as a Shake, or a Letherii Master at Arms for a Dresh-Preda? But she found she could not believe her own question. She knew the answer, quivering like a knife in her soul. *The shore is blind . . .*

They rode on in the dark.

We were never as the Nerek, the Tarthenal and the others. We could raise no army against the invaders. Our belief in the shore held no vast power, for it is a belief in the mutable, in transformation. A god with no face but every face. Our temple is the strand where the eternal war between land and sea is waged, a temple that rises only to crumble yet again. Temple of sound, of smell, taste and tears upon every fingertip.

Our coven healed wounds, scoured away diseases, and murdered babies.

The Tarthenal viewed us with horror. The Nerek hunted our folk in the forests. For the Faered, we were child-snatchers in the night. They would leave us husks of bread on tree stumps, as if we were no better than malignant crows.

Of these people, these Shake, I am now Queen.

And a man who would be her husband awaited her. On the Isle.

Errant take me, I am too tired for this.

Horse-hoofs splashing through puddles where the old road dipped – they were nearing the shore. Ahead, the land rose again – some long-ago high tide mark, a broad ridge of smoothed stones and cobbles bedded in sandy clay – the kind of clay that became shale beneath the weight of time, pocked by the restless stones. In that shale one could find embedded shells, mollusc fragments, proof of the sea's many victories.

The trees were sparser here, bent down by the wind that she could not yet feel on her face – a calm that surprised her, given the season. The smell of the shore was heavy in the air, motionless and fetid.

They slowed their mounts. From the as yet unseen sea there was no sound, not even the whisper of gentle waves. As if the world on the other side of the ridge had vanished.

'Tracks here, sir,' one of her soldiers said as they drew to a halt close to the slope. 'Riders, skirting the bank, north and south both.'

'As if they were hunting someone,' another observed.

Yan Tovis held up a gauntleted hand.

Horses to the north, riding at the canter, approaching.

Struck by a sudden, almost superstitious fear, Yan Tovis made a gesture, and her soldiers drew their swords. She reached for her own.

The first of the riders appeared.

Letherii.

Relaxing, Yan Tovis released her breath. 'Hold, soldier!'

The sudden command clearly startled the figure and the three other riders behind it. Hoofs skidding on loose pebbles.

Armoured as if for battle – chain hauberks, the blackened rings glistening, visors drawn down on their helms. The lead rider held a long-handled single-bladed axe in his right hand; those behind him wielded lances, the heads wide and barbed as if the troop had been hunting boar.

Yan Tovis nudged her horse round and guided it a few steps closer. 'I am Atri-Preda Yan Tovis,' she said.

A tilt of the helmed head from the lead man. 'Yedan Derryg,' he said in a low voice, 'Master at Arms, Boaral Keep.'

She hesitated, then said, 'The Watch.'

'Twilight,' he replied. 'Even in this gloom, I can see it is you.'

'I find that difficult to believe – you fled—'

'Fled, my Queen?'

'The House of our mother, yes.'

'Your father and I did not get along, Twilight. You were but a toddler when last I saw you. But that does not matter. I see now in your face what I saw then. No mistaking it.'

Sighing, she dismounted.

After a moment, the others did the same. Yedan gestured with a tilt of his head and he and Yan Tovis walked off a short distance. Stood beneath the tallest tree this close to the ridge – a dead pine – as a light rain began to fall.

'I have just come from the Keep,' she said. 'Your Dresh attempted to escape arrest and is dead. Or will be soon. I have had a word with the witches. There will be Tiste Edur, from Rennis, but by the time they arrive the investigation will be over and I will have to apologize for wasting their time.'

Yedan said nothing. The grilled visor thoroughly hid his features, although the black snarl of his beard was visible – it seemed he was slowly chewing something.

'Watch,' she resumed, 'you called me "Queen" in front of your soldiers.'

'They are Shake.'

'I see. Then, you are here . . . at the shore—'

'Because I am the Watch, yes.'

'That title is without meaning,' she said, rather more harshly than she had intended. 'It's an honorific, some old remnant—'

'I believed the same,' he cut in – *like an older brother, damn him* – 'until three nights ago.'

'Why are you here, then? Who are you looking for?'

'I wish I could answer you better than I can. I am not sure why I am here, only that I am summoned.'

'By whom?'

He seemed to chew some more, then he said, 'By the shore.'

'I see.'

'As for who – or what – I am looking for, I cannot say at all. Strangers have arrived. We heard them this night, yet no matter where we rode, no matter how quickly we arrived, we found no-one. Nor any sign – no tracks, nothing. Yet . . . they are here.'

'Perhaps ghosts then.'

'Perhaps.'

Twilight slowly turned. 'From the sea?'

'Again, no tracks on the strand. Sister, since we have arrived, the air has not stirred. Not so much as a sigh. Day and night, the shore is still.' He tilted his head upward. 'Now, this rain – the first time.'

A murmur from the soldiers drew their attention. They were facing the ridge, six motionless spectres, metal and leather gleaming.

Beyond the ridge, the fitful rise and ebb of a glow.

'This,' Yedan said, and he set off.

Yan Tovis followed.

They scrambled through loose stones, stripped branches and naked roots, pulling themselves onto the rise. The six soldiers in their wake now on the slope, Yan Tovis moved to her half-brother's side, pushing through the soft brush until they both emerged onto the shoreline.

Where they halted, staring out to sea.

Ships.

A row of ships, all well offshore. Reaching to the north, to the south.

All burning.

'Errant's blessing,' Yan Tovis whispered.

Hundreds of ships. Burning.

Flames playing over still water, columns of smoke rising, lit from beneath like enormous ash-dusted coals in the bed of the black sky.

'Those,' Yedan said, 'are not Letherii ships. Nor Edur.'

'No,' Twilight whispered, 'they are not.'

Strangers have arrived.

'What means this?' There was raw fear in the question, and Yan Tovis turned to look at the soldier who had spoken. Faint on his features, the orange glow of the distant flames.

She looked back at the ships. 'Dromons,' she said. Her heart was pounding hard in her chest, a kind of febrile excitement – strangely dark with malice and . . . *savage delight.*

'What name is that?' Yedan asked.

'I know them – those prows, the rigging. Our search – a distant continent. An empire. We killed hundreds – thousands – of its subjects. We clashed with its fleets.' She was silent for a dozen breaths, then she turned to one of her soldiers. 'Ride back to the Keep. Make sure the Dresh is dead. The company is to leave immediately – we will meet you north of Rennis on the coast road. Oh, and bring those damned witches with you.'

Yedan said, 'What—'

She cut off her half-brother with cruel glee. 'You are the Watch. Your Queen needs you.' She glared at him. 'You will ride with us, Yedan. With your troop.'

The bearded jaw bunched, then, 'Where?'

'The Isle.'

'What of the Letherii and their masters? We should send warning.'

Eyes on the burning hulks in the sea, she almost snarled her reply. 'We killed their subjects. And clearly they will not let that pass. Errant take the Letherii and the Edur.' She spun round, making for her horse. The others scrambled after her. 'Strangers, Yedan? Not to me. They followed us.' She swung herself onto her horse and tugged it towards the north trail. 'We left a debt in blood,' she said, baring her teeth. 'Malazan blood. *And it seems they will not let that stand.*'

They are here. On this shore.

The Malazans are on our shore.

BOOK THREE

KNUCKLES OF THE SOUL

We are eager
to impugn the beast crouched
in our souls
but this creature is pure
with shy eyes
and it watches our frantic crimes
cowering
in the cage of our cruelty

I will take
for myself and your fate
in these hands
the grace of animal to amend
broken dreams –
freedom unchained and unbound
long running –
the beast will kill when I murder

In absolution
a list of unremarked distinctions
availed these hands
freedom without excuse
see how clean
this blood compared to yours
the death grin
of your bestial snarl mars the scape

Of your face
this is what sets us apart
in our souls
my beast and I chained together
as we must
who leads and who is the led is
never quite asked
of the charmed and the innocent

Dog in an Alley
Confessions
Tibal Feredict

CHAPTER THIRTEEN

Keel and half a hull remained of the wreck where us wreckers
gathered, and the storm of the night past remained like spit
in the air when we clambered down into that bent-rib bed.

I heard many a prayer muttered, hands flashing to ward
this and that as befits each soul's need, its conversation
with fear begun in childhood no doubt and, could I recall
mine, I too would have been of mind to mime flight from
terror.

As it was I could only look down at that crabshell harvest
of tiny skeletons, the tailed imps with the human-like faces,
their hawk talons and all sorts of strange embellishments to
give perfect detail to the bright sunny nightmare.

No wonder is it I forswore the sea that day. Storm and
broken ship had lifted a host most unholy and oh there
were plenty more no doubt, ringing this damned island.

As it was, it was me who then spoke a most unsavoury
tumble of words. 'I guess not all imps can fly.'

For all that, it was hardly cause to gouge out my eyes
now, was it?

Blind Tobor of the Reach

'NOW THERE, FRIENDS, IS ONE BEAUTIFUL WOMAN.'
'If that's how you like them.'
'Now why wouldn't I, y'damned barrow-digger? Thing is,
and it's always the way isn't it, look at that hopeless thug she's with. I
can't figure things like that. She could have anyone in here. She could
have me, even. But no, there she is, sittin' aside that limpin' one-armed,
one-eared, one-eyed and no-nosed cattle-dog. I mean, talk about ugly.'

The third man, who had yet to speak, gave him a surreptitious,
sidelong look, noting the birdnest hair, the jutting steering-oar ears, the

369

bulging eyes, and the piebald patches that were the scars of fire on features that reminded him of a squashed gourd – sidelong and brief, that glance, and Throatslitter quickly looked away. The last thing he wanted to do was break into another one of his trilling, uncanny laughs that seemed to freeze everyone within earshot.

Never used to have a laugh sounding like that. Damn thing scares even me. Well, he'd taken a throatful of oily flames and it'd done bad things to his voice-reed. The damage only revealed itself when he laughed, and, he recalled, in the months following . . . *all that stuff . . .* there had been few reasons for mirth.

'There goes that tavernkeeper,' Deadsmell observed.

It was easy talking about anything and everything, since no-one here but them understood Malazan.

'There's another one all moon-eyed over her,' Sergeant Balm said with a sneer. 'But who does she sit with? Hood take me, it don't make sense.'

Deadsmell slowly leaned forward on the table and carefully refilled his tankard. 'It's the delivery of that cask. Brullyg's. Looks like the pretty one and the dead lass have volunteered.'

Balm's bulging eyes bulged even more. 'She ain't dead! I'll tell you what's dead, Deadsmell, that puddle-drowned worm between your legs!'

Throatslitter eyed the corporal. '*If that's how you like them,*' he'd said. A half-strangled gulp escaped him, making both his companions flinch.

'What in Hood's name are you gonna laugh about?' Balm demanded. 'Just don't, and that's an order.'

Throatslitter bit down hard on his own tongue. Tears blurred his vision for a moment as pain shot round his skull like a pebble in a bucket. Mute, he shook his head. *Laugh? Not me.*

The sergeant was glaring at Deadsmell again. 'Dead? She don't look much dead to me.'

'Trust me,' the corporal replied after taking a deep draught. He belched. 'Sure, she's hiding it well, but that woman died some time ago.'

Balm was hunched over the table, scratching at the tangles of his hair. Flakes drifted down to land like specks of paint on the dark wood. 'Gods below,' he whispered. 'Maybe somebody should . . . I don't know . . . maybe . . . tell her?'

Deadsmell's mostly hairless brows lifted. 'Excuse me, ma'am, you have a complexion to die for and I guess that's what you did.'

Another squawk from Throatslitter.

The corporal continued, 'Is it true, ma'am, that perfect hair and expensive makeup can hide anything?'

A choked squeal from Throatslitter.

Heads turned.

Deadsmell drank down another mouthful, warming to the subject. 'Funny, you don't *look* dead.'

The high-pitched cackle erupted.

As it died, sudden silence in the main room of the tavern, barring that of a rolling tankard, which then plunged off a tabletop and bounced on the floor.

Balm glared at Deadsmell. 'You done that. You just kept pushing and pushing. Another word from you, corporal, and you'll be deader than she is.'

'What's that smell?' Deadsmell asked. 'Oh right. Essence of putrescence.'

Balm's cheeks bulged, his face turning a strange purple shade. His yellowy eyes looked moments from leaping out on their stalks.

Throatslitter tried squeezing his own eyes shut, but the image of his sergeant's face burst into his mind. He shrieked behind his hands. Looked round in helpless appeal.

All attention was fixed on them now, no-one speaking. Even the beautiful woman who'd shipped in with that maimed oaf and the oaf himself – whose one good eye glittered out from the folds of a severe frown – had paused, standing each to one side of the cask of ale the tavernkeeper had brought out. And the keeper himself, staring at Throatslitter with mouth hanging open.

'Well,' Deadsmell observed, 'there goes our credit as bad boys. Throaty here's making mating calls – hope there's no turkeys on this island. And you, sergeant, your head looks ready to explode like a cusser.'

Balm hissed, 'It was *your* fault, you bastard!'

'Hardly. As you see, I am calm. Although somewhat embarrassed by my company, alas.'

'Fine, we're shifting you off. Hood knows, Gilani's a damned sight prettier to look at—'

'Yes, but she happens to be alive, sergeant. Not your type at all.'

'I didn't know!'

'Now that is a most pathetic admission, wouldn't you say?'

'Hold on,' Throatslitter finally interjected. 'I couldn't tell about her either, Deadsmell.' He jabbed a finger at the corporal. 'Further proof you're a damned necromancer. No, forget that shocked look, we ain't buying no more. You knew she was dead because you can smell 'em, just like your name says you can. In fact, I'd wager that's why Braven Tooth gave you that name – doesn't miss a thing, ever, does he?'

The ambient noise was slowly resurrecting itself, accompanied by more than a few warding gestures, a couple of chairs scraping

371

back through filth as patrons made furtive escapes out of the front door.

Deadsmell drank more ale. And said nothing.

The dead woman and her companion headed out, the latter limping as he struggled to balance the cask on one shoulder.

Balm grunted. 'There they go. Typical, isn't it? Just when we're under strength, too.'

'Nothing to worry about, sergeant,' Deadsmell said. 'It's all in hand. Though if the keeper decides on following . . .'

Throatslitter grunted. 'If he does, he'll regret it.' He rose then, adjusting the marine-issue rain cape. 'Lucky you two, getting to sit here adding fat to your arses. It's damned cold out there, you know.'

'I'm making note of all this insubordination,' Balm grumbled. Then tapped his head. 'In here.'

'Well that's a relief,' Throatslitter said. He left the tavern.

Shake Brullyg, tyrant of Second Maiden Fort, would-be King of the Isle, slouched in the old prison prefect's high-backed chair and glared from under heavy brows at the two foreigners at the table beside the chamber's door. They were playing another of their damned games. Knuckle bones, elongated wooden bowl and split crow-feathers.

'Two bounces earns me a sweep,' one of them said, although Brullyg was not quite sure of that – picking up a language on the sly was no easy thing, but he'd always been good with languages. Shake, Letherii, Tiste Edur, Fent, trader's tongue and Meckros. And now, spatterings of this . . . this *Malazan*.

Timing. They'd taken it from him, as easily as they'd taken his knife, his war-axe. Foreigners easing into the harbour – not so many aboard as to cause much worry, or so it had seemed. Besides, there had been enough trouble to chew on right then. A sea filled with mountains of ice, bearing down on the Isle, more ominous than any fleet or army. They said they could take care of that – and he'd been a drowning man going down for the last time.

Would-be King of the Isle, crushed and smeared flat under insensate ice. Face to face with that kind of truth had been like dragon claws through his sail. After all he'd done . . .

Timing. He now wondered if these Malazans had brought the ice with them. Sent it spinning down on the season's wild current, just so they could arrive one step ahead and offer to turn it away. He'd not even believed them, Brullyg recalled, but desperation had spoken with its very own voice. *Do that and you'll be royal guests for as long as you like.* They'd smiled at that offer.

I am a fool. And worse.

And now, two miserable squads ruled over him and every damned resident of this island, and there was not a thing he could do about it.

Except keep the truth from everyone else. And that's getting a whole lot harder with every day that passes.

'Sweep's in the trough, pluck a knuckle and that about does it,' said the other soldier.

Possibly.

'It skidded when you breathed – I saw it, you cheat!'

'I ain't breathed.'

'Oh right, you're a Hood-damned corpse, are you?'

'No, I just ain't breathed when you said I did. Look, it's in the trough, you deny it?'

'Here, let me take a closer look. Ha, no it isn't!'

'You just sighed and moved it, damn you!'

'I didn't sigh.'

'Right, and you're not losing neither, are ya?'

'Just because I'm losing doesn't mean I sighed right then. And see, it's not in the trough.'

'Hold on while I breathe—'

'Then I'll sigh!'

'Breathing is what winners do. Sighing is what losers do. Therefore, I win.'

'Sure, for you cheating is as natural as breathing, isn't it?'

Brullyg slowly shifted his attention from the two at the door, regarded the last soldier in the chamber. By the coven she was a beauty. Such dark, magical skin, and those tilted eyes just glowed with sweet invitation – damn him, all the mysteries of the world were in those eyes. And that mouth! Those lips! If he could just get rid of the other two, and maybe steal away those wicked knives of hers, why then he'd discover those mysteries the way she wanted him to.

I'm King of the Isle. About to be. One more week, and if none of the dead Queen's bitch daughters show up before then, it all falls to me. King of the Isle. Almost. Close enough to use the title, sure. And what woman wouldn't set aside a miserable soldier's life for the soft, warm bed of a king's First Concubine? Sure, that is indeed a Letherii way, but as king I can make my own rules. And if the coven doesn't like it, well, there're the cliffs.

One of the Malazans at the table said, 'Careful, Masan, he's getting that look again.'

The woman named Masan Gilani straightened catlike in her chair, lifting her smooth, not-scrawny arms in an arching stretch that transformed her large breasts into round globes, tautening the worn fabric of her shirt. ''S long as he keeps thinking with the wrong brain, Lobe, we're good and easy.' She then settled back, straightening her perfect legs.

'We should bring him another whore,' the one named Lobe said as he gathered the knuckle bones into a small leather bag.

'No,' Masan Gilani said. 'Deadsmell barely revived the last one.'

But that's not the real reason, is it? Brullyg smiled. *No, you want me for yourself. Besides, I'm not usually like that. I was taking out some . . . frustrations. That's all.* His smile faded. *They sure do use their hands a lot when talking. Gestures of all sorts. Strange people, these Malazans.* He cleared his throat and spoke Letherii in the slow way they seemed to need. 'I could do with another walk. My legs want exercise.' A wink towards Masan Gilani, who responded with a knowing smile that lit him up low down, enough to make him shift in the chair. 'My people need to see me, you understand? If they start getting suspicious – well, if anybody knows what a house arrest looks like, it is the citizens of Second Maiden Fort.'

In terribly accented Letherii, Lobe said, 'You get your ale comes today, right? Best want to be waiting here for that. We walk you tonight.'

Like a Liberty mistress her pampered dog. Isn't that nice? And when I lift a leg and piss against you, Lobe, what then?

These soldiers here did not frighten him. It was the other squad, the one still up-island. The one with that scrawny little mute girl. And she had a way of showing up as if from nowhere. From a swirl of light – he wondered what the Shake witches would make of that cute trick. All Lobe needed to do – Lobe, or Masan Gilani, or Galt, any of them – all they needed to do was call her name.

Sinn.

A real terror that one, and not a talon showing. He suspected he'd need the whole coven to get rid of her. Preferably with great losses. The coven had a way of crowding the chosen rulers of the Shake. *And they're on their way, like ravens to a carcass, all spit and cackle. Of course, they can't fly. Can't even swim. No, they'll need boats, to take them across the strait – and that's assuming the Reach isn't now a jumbled mass of ice, which is how it looks from here.*

The soldier named Galt rose from his chair, wincing at some twinge in his lower back, then ambled over to what had been the prefect's prize possession, a tapestry that dominated an entire wall. Faded with age – and stained in the lower left corner with dried spatters of the poor prefect's blood – the hanging depicted the First Landing of the Letherii, although in truth that was not the colonizers' first landing. The fleet had come within sight of shore somewhere opposite the Reach. Fent canoes had ventured out to establish contact with the strangers. An exchange of gifts had gone awry, resulting in the slaughter of the Fent men and the subsequent enslavement of the women and children in the village. Three more settlements had suffered the same fate. The next four, southward down the coast, had been hastily abandoned.

The fleet had eventually rounded Sadon Peninsula on the north coast of the Ouster Sea, then sailed past the Lenth Arm and into Gedry Bay. The city of Gedry was founded on the place of the First Landing, at the mouth of the Lether River. This tapestry, easily a thousand years old, was proof enough of that. The general belief these days was that the landing occurred at the site of the capital itself, well up the river. Strange how the past was remade to suit the present. A lesson there Brullyg could use, once he was king. The Shake were a people of failure, fated to know naught but tragedy and pathos. Guardians of the shore, but incapable of guarding it against the sea's tireless hunger. All of that needed . . . revising.

The Letherii had known defeat. Many times. Their history on this land was bloody, rife with their betrayals, their lies, their heartless cruelties. All of which were now seen as triumphant and heroic.

This is how a people must see itself. As we Shake must. A blinding beacon on this dark shore. When I am king . . .

'Look at this damned thing,' Galt said. 'Here, that writing in the borders – that could be Erhlii.'

'But it isn't,' Lobe muttered. He had dismantled one of his daggers; on the table before him was the pommel, a few rivets and pins, a wooden handle wrapped in leather, a slitted hilt and the tanged blade. It seemed the soldier was now at a loss on how to put it all back together again.

'Some of the letters—'

'Ehrlii and Letherii come from the same language,' Lobe said.

Galt's glare was suspicious. 'How do you know that?'

'I don't, you idiot. It's just what I was told.'

'Who?'

'Ebron, I think. Or Shard. What difference does it make? Somebody who knows things, that's all. Hood, you're making my brain hurt. And look at this mess.'

'Is that my knife?'

'Was.'

Brullyg saw Lobe cock his head, then the soldier said, 'Footsteps bottom of the stairs.' And with these words, his hands moved in a blur, and even as Galt was walking towards the door, Lobe was twisting home the pommel and flipping the knife into Galt's path. Where it was caught one-handed – Galt had not even slowed in passing.

Brullyg settled back in his chair.

Rising, Masan Gilani loosened from their scabbards the vicious-looking long-bladed knives at her hips. 'Wish I was with my own squad,' she said, then drew a step closer to where Brullyg sat.

'Stay put,' she murmured.

Mouth dry, he nodded.

'It's likely the ale delivery,' Lobe said from one side of the door, while

Galt unlocked it and pushed it out wide enough to enable him to peer through the crack.

'Sure, but those boots sound wrong.'

'Not the usual drooling fart and his son?'

'Not even close.'

'All right.' Lobe reached under the table and lifted into view a crossbow. A truly foreign weapon, constructed entirely of iron – or something very much like Letherii steel. The cord was thick as a man's thumb, and the quarrel set into the groove was tipped with a x-shaped head that would punch through a Letherii shield as if it was birch bark. The soldier cranked the claw back and somehow locked it in place. Then he moved along the door's wall to the corner.

Galt edged back as the footsteps on the stairs drew nearer. He made a series of hand gestures to which Masan Gilani grunted in response and Brullyg heard ripping cloth behind him and a moment later the point of a knife pressed between his shoulder blades – thrust right through the damned chair. She leaned down. 'Be nice and be stupid, Brullyg. We know these two and we can guess why they're here.'

Glancing back at Masan Gilani, nodding once, Galt then moved into the doorway, opening wide the door. 'Well,' he drawled in his dreadful Letherii, 'if it isn't the captain and her first mate. Run out of money comes too soon? What you making to comes with ale?'

A heavy growl from beyond. 'What did he say, Captain?'

'Whatever it was, he said it badly.' A woman, and that voice – Brullyg frowned. That was a voice he had heard before. The knife tip dug deeper into his spine.

'We're bringing Shake Brullyg his ale,' the woman continued.

'That's nice,' Galt replied. 'We see he comes gets it.'

'Shake Brullyg's an old friend of mine. I want to see him.'

'He's busy.'

'Doing what?'

'Thinking.'

'Shake Brullyg? I really doubt that – and who in the Errant's name are you anyway? You're no Letherii, and you and those friends of yours hanging out at the tavern, well, none of you were prisoners here either. I asked around. You're from that strange ship anchored in the bay.'

'Why, Captain, it is simple. We comes to goes all the ice. So Brullyg he rewards us. Guests. Royal guests. Now we keep him company. He is smiles nice all the time. We nice too.'

'Nice idiots, I think,' the man outside – presumably the captain's first mate – said in a growl. 'Now, my arm's getting tired – move aside and let me deliver this damned thing.'

Galt glanced back over a shoulder at Masan Gilani, who said in

Malazan, 'Why you looking at me? I'm just here to keep this man's tongue hanging.'

Brullyg licked sweat from his lips. *So even knowing that, why does it still work? Am I that stupid?* 'Let them in,' he said in a low voice. 'So I can ease their minds and send them away.'

Galt looked at Masan Gilani again, and though she said nothing, some kind of communication must have passed between them, for he shrugged and stepped back. 'Comes the ale.'

Brullyg watched as the two figures entered the chamber. The one in the lead was Skorgen Kaban the Pretty. Which meant . . . yes. The would-be king smiled, 'Shurq Elalle. You've not aged a day since I last saw you. And Skorgen – put the cask down, before you dislocate your shoulder and add lopsided to your list of ailments. Broach the damned thing and we can all have a drink. Oh,' he added as he watched the two pirates take in the soldiers – Skorgen almost jumping when he saw Lobe in the corner, crossbow now cradled in his arms – 'these are some of my royal guests. At the door, Galt. In the corner, Lobe, and this lovely here with the one hand behind the back of my chair is Masan Gilani.'

Shurq Elalle collected one of the chairs near the door and dragged it opposite Brullyg. Sitting, she folded one leg over the other and laced her hands together on her lap. 'Brullyg, you half-mad cheating miser of a bastard. If you were alone I'd be throttling that flabby neck of yours right now.'

'Can't say I'm shocked by your animosity,' Shake Brullyg replied, suddenly comforted by his Malazan bodyguards. 'But you know, it was never as bad or ugly as you thought it was. You just never gave me the chance to explain—'

Shurq's smile was both beautiful and dark. 'Why, Brullyg, you were never one to explain yourself.'

'A man changes.'

'That'd be a first.'

Brullyg resisted shrugging, since that would have opened a nasty slit in the flesh of his back. Instead, he lifted his hands, palms up, as he said, 'Let's set aside all that history. The *Undying Gratitude* rests safe and sound in my harbour. Cargo offloaded and plenty of coin in your purse. I imagine you're itching to leave our blessed isle.'

'Something like that,' she replied. 'Alas, it seems we're having trouble getting, uh, permission. There's the biggest damned ship I've ever seen blocking the harbour mouth right now, and a sleek war galley of some kind is making for berth at the main pier. You know,' she added, with another quick smile, 'it's all starting to look like some kind of . . . well . . . *blockade*.'

The knife-point left Brullyg's back and Masan Gilani, sliding the weapon into its scabbard, stepped round. When she spoke this time, it was in a language Brullyg had never heard before.

Lobe levelled the crossbow again, aiming towards Brullyg, and answered Masan in the same tongue.

Skorgen, who had been kneeling beside the cask, thumping at the spigot with the heel of one hand, now rose. 'What in the Errant's name is going on here, Brullyg?'

A voice spoke from the doorway, 'Just this. Your captain's right. Our waiting's done.'

The soldier named Throatslitter was leaning against the door frame, arms crossed. He was smiling across at Masan Gilani. 'Good news ain't it? Now you can take your delicious curves and such and dance your way down to the pier – I'm sure Urb and the rest are missing 'em something awful.'

Shurq Elalle, who had not moved from her chair, sighed loudly then said, 'Pretty, I don't think we'll be leaving this room for a while. Find us some tankards and pour, why don't you?'

'We're hostages?'

'No no,' his captain replied. 'Guests.'

Masan Gilani, hips swaying considerably more than was necessary, sauntered out of the chamber.

Under his breath, Brullyg groaned.

'As I said earlier,' Shurq murmured, 'men don't change.' She glanced over at Galt, who had drawn up the other chair. 'I assume you won't let me strangle this odious worm.'

'Sorry, no.' A quick smile. 'Not yet anyway.'

'So, who are your friends in the harbour?'

Galt winked. 'We've a little work to do, Captain. And we've decided this island will do just fine as headquarters.'

'Your skill with Letherii has noticeably improved.'

'Must be your fine company, Captain.'

'Don't bother,' Throatslitter said from the doorway. 'Deadsmell says she's standing on the wrong side of Hood's gate, despite what you see or think you see.'

Galt slowly paled.

'Not sure what he means by all that,' Shurq Elalle said, her sultry eyes settling on Galt, 'but my appetites are as lively as ever.'

'That's . . . disgusting.'

'Explains the sweat on your brow, I suppose.'

Galt hastily wiped his forehead. 'This one's worse than Masan Gilani,' he complained.

Brullyg shifted nervously in his chair. Timing. These damned Malazans had it by the bucketful. *Freedom should've lasted longer than this.* 'Hurry up with that ale, Pretty.'

*

378

Finding yourself standing, alone, cut loose, with an unhappy army squirming in your hands, was a commander's greatest nightmare. *And when you got them running straight into the wilderness of an ocean at the time, it's about as bad as it can get.*

Fury had united them, for a while. Until the truth started to sink in, like botfly worms under the skin. Their homeland wanted them all dead. There'd be no seeing family – no wives, husbands, mothers, fathers. No children to bounce on one knee while working numbers in the head – wondering which neighbour's eyes you're looking down at. No chasms to cross, no breaches to mend. Every loved one as good as dead.

Armies get unruly when that happens. Almost as bad as no loot and no pay.

We were soldiers of the empire. Our families depended on the wages, the tax relief, the buy-outs and the pensions. And a lot of us were young enough to think about signing out, making a new life, one that didn't involve swinging a sword and looking in the eye of some snarling thug wanting to cut you in two. Some of us were damned tired.

So, what kept us together?

Well, no ship likes to sail alone, does it?

But Fist Blistig knew that there was more to it. Dried blood holding everyone in place like glue. The seared burn of betrayal, the sting of fury. And a commander who sacrificed her own love to see them all survive.

He had spent too many days and nights on the *Froth Wolf* standing no less than five paces from the Adjunct, studying her stiff back as she faced the surly seas. A woman who showed nothing, but some things no mortal could hide, and one of those things was grief. He had stared and he had wondered. Was she going to come through this?

Someone – might have been Keneb, who at times seemed to understand Tavore better than anyone else, maybe even Tavore herself – had then made a fateful decision. The Adjunct had lost her aide. In Malaz City. Aide, and lover. Now, maybe nothing could be done about the lover, but the role of aide was an official position, a necessary one for any commander. Not a man, of course – would have to be a woman for certain.

Blistig recalled that night, even as the eleventh bell was sounded on deck – the ragged fleet, flanked by the Perish Thrones of War, was three days east of Kartool, beginning a northward-wending arc to take them round the tumultuous, deadly straits between Malaz Island and the coast of Korel – and the Adjunct was standing alone just beyond the forecastle mast, the wind tugging fitfully at her rain cape, making Blistig think of a broken-winged crow. A second figure appeared, halting close to Tavore on her left. *Where T'amber would stand, where any aide to a commander would stand.*

379

Tavore's head had turned in startlement, and words were exchanged – too low for Blistig's ears – followed by a salute from the newcomer.

The Adjunct is alone. So too is another woman, seemingly as bound up in grief as Tavore herself, yet this one possesses an edge, an anger tempered like Aren steel. Short on patience, which might be precisely what's needed here.

Was it you, Keneb?

Of course, Lostara Yil, once a captain in the Red Blades, now just one more outlawed soldier, had revealed no inclinations to take a woman to her bed. Not anyone, in fact. Yet she was no torture to look at, if one had a taste for broken glass made pretty. That and Pardu tattoos. But it was just as likely that the Adjunct wasn't thinking in those terms. Too soon. Wrong woman.

Throughout the fleet, officers had been reporting talk of mutiny among the soldiers – excepting, oddly enough, the marines, who never seemed capable of thinking past the next meal or game of Troughs. A succession of reports, delivered in increasingly nervous tones, and it had seemed the Adjunct was unwilling or unable to even so much as care.

You can heal wounds of the flesh well enough, but it's the other ones that can bleed out a soul.

After that night, Lostara Yil clung to a resentful Tavore like a damned tick. Commander's aide. She understood the role. In the absence of actual direction from her commander, Lostara Yil assumed the task of managing nearly eight thousand miserable soldiers. The first necessity was clearing up the matter of pay. The fleet was making sail for Theft, a paltry kingdom torn to tatters by Malazan incursions and civil war. Supplies needed to be purchased, but more than that, the soldiers needed leave and for that there must be not only coin but the promise of more to come, lest the entire army disappear into the back streets of the first port of call.

The army's chests could not feed what was owed.

So Lostara hunted down Banaschar, the once-priest of D'rek. Hunted him down and cornered him. And all at once, those treasury chests were overflowing.

Now, why Banaschar? How did Lostara know?

Grub, of course. That scrawny runt climbing the rigging with those not-quite-right bhok'aral – I ain't once seen him come down, no matter how brutal the weather. Yet Grub somehow knew about Banaschar's hidden purse, and somehow got the word to Lostara Yil.

The Fourteenth Army was suddenly rich. Too much handed out all at once would have been disastrous, but Lostara knew that. Enough that it be seen, that the rumours were let loose to scamper like stoats through every ship in the fleet.

Soldiers being what they were, it wasn't long before they were griping about something else, and this time the Adjunct's aide could do nothing to give answer.

Where in Hood's name are we going?

Are we still an army and if we are, who are we fighting for? The notion of becoming mercenaries did not sit well, it turned out.

The story went that Lostara Yil had it out with Tavore one night in the Adjunct's cabin. A night of screams, curses and, maybe, tears. Or something else happened. Something as simple as Lostara wearing her commander down, like D'rek's own soldier worms gnawing the ankles of the earth, *snap snick right through*. Whatever the details, the Adjunct was . . . awakened. The entire Fourteenth was days from falling to pieces.

A call was issued for the Fists and officers ranking captain and higher to assemble on the *Froth Wolf*. And, to the astonishment of everyone, Tavore Paran appeared on deck and delivered a *speech*. Sinn and Banaschar were present, and through sorcery the Adjunct's words were heard by everyone, even crew high in the riggings and crow's nests.

A Hood-damned speech.

From Tavore. Tighter-lipped than a cat at Togg's teats, but she talked. Not long, not complicated. And there was no brilliance, no genius. It was plain, every word picked up from dusty ground, strung together on a chewed thong, not even spat on to bring out a gleam. Not a precious stone to be found. No pearls, no opals, no sapphires.

Raw garnet at best.

At best.

Tied to Tavore's sword belt, there had been a finger bone. Yellowed, charred at one end. She stood in silence for a time, her plain features looking drawn, aged, her eyes dull as smudged slate. When at last she spoke, her voice was low, strangely measured, devoid of all emotion.

Blistig could still remember every word.

'There have been armies. Burdened with names, the legacy of meetings, of battles, of betrayals. The history behind the name is each army's secret language – one that no-one else can understand, much less share. The First Sword of Dassem Ultor – the Plains of Unta, the Grissian Hills, Li Heng, Y'Ghatan. The Bridgeburners – Raraku, Black Dog, Mott Wood, Pale, Black Coral. Coltaine's Seventh – Gelor Ridge, Vathar Crossing and the Day of Pure Blood, Sanimon, the Fall.

'Some of you share a few of those – with comrades now fallen, now dust. They are, for you, the cracked vessels of your grief and your pride. And you cannot stand in one place for long, lest the ground turn to depthless mud around your feet.' Her eyes fell then, a heartbeat, another, before she looked up once more, scanning the array of sombre faces before her.

'Among us, among the Bonehunters, our secret language has begun.

381

Cruel in its birth at Aren, sordid in a river of old blood. Coltaine's blood. You know this. I need tell you none of this. We have our own Raraku. We have our own Y'Ghatan. We have Malaz City.

'In the civil war on Theft, a warlord who captured a rival's army then destroyed them – not by slaughter; no, he simply gave the order that each soldier's weapon hand lose its index finger. The maimed soldiers were then sent back to the warlord's rival. Twelve thousand useless men and women. To feed, to send home, to swallow the bitter taste of defeat. I was . . . I was reminded of that story, not long ago.'

Yes, Blistig thought then, *and I think I know by whom. Gods, we all do.*

'We too are maimed. In our hearts. Each of you knows this.

'And so we carry, tied to our belts, a piece of bone. Legacy of a severed finger. And yes, we cannot help but know bitterness.' She paused, held back for a long moment, and it seemed the silence itself grated in his skull.

Tavore resumed. 'The Bonehunters will speak in our secret language. We sail to add another name to our burden, and it may be it will prove our last. I do not believe so, but there are clouds before the face of the future – we cannot see. We cannot know.

'The island of Sepik, a protectorate of the Malazan Empire, is now empty of human life. Sentenced to senseless slaughter, every man, child and woman. We know the face of the slayer. We have seen the dark ships. We have seen the harsh magic unveiled.

'We are Malazan. We remain so, no matter the judgement of the Empress. Is this enough reason to give answer?

'No, it is not. Compassion is never enough. Nor is the hunger for vengeance. But, for now, for what awaits us, perhaps they will do. We are the Bonehunters, and sail to another name. Beyond Aren, beyond Raraku and beyond Y'Ghatan, we now cross the world to find the first name that will be truly our own. Shared by none other. We sail to give answer.

'There is more. But I will not speak of that beyond these words: *"What awaits you in the dusk of the old world's passing, shall go . . . unwitnessed."* T'amber's words.' Another long spell of pained silence.

'They are hard and well might they feed spite, if in weakness we permit such. But to those words I say this, as your commander: *we shall be our own witness, and that will be enough. It must be enough. It must ever be enough.'*

Even now, over a year later, Blistig wondered if she had said what was needed. In truth, he was not quite certain what she *had* said. The meaning of it. *Witnessed, unwitnessed, does it really make a difference?* But he knew the answer to that, even if he could not articulate precisely what it was he knew. Something stirred deep in the pit of his soul, as if his thoughts were black waters caressing unseen rocks, bending to shapes that even ignorance could not alter.

Well, how can any of this make sense? I do not have the words.

But damn me, she did. Back then. She *did.*

Unwitnessed. There was crime in that notion. A profound injustice against which he railed. *In silence. Like every other soldier in the Bonehunters. Maybe. No, I am not mistaken – I see something in their eyes. I can see it. We rail against injustice, yes. That what we do will be seen by no-one. Our fate unmeasured.*

Tavore, what have you awakened? And, Hood take us, what makes you think we are equal to any of this?

There had been no desertions. He did not understand. He didn't think he would ever understand. What had happened that night, what had happened in that strange speech.

She told us we would never see our loved ones again. That is what she told us. Isn't it?

Leaving us with what?

With each other, I suppose.

'We shall be our own witness.'

And was that enough?

Maybe. So far.

But now we are here. We have arrived. The fleet, the fleet burns – gods, that she would do that. Not a single transport left. Burned, sunk to the bottom off this damned shore. We are . . . cut away.

Welcome, Bonehunters, to the empire of Lether.

Alas, we are not here in festive spirit.

The treacherous ice was behind them now, the broken mountains that had filled the sea and clambered onto the Fent Reach, crushing everything on it to dust. No ruins to ponder over in some distant future, not a single sign of human existence left on that scraped rock. Ice was annihilation. It did not do what sand did, did not simply bury every trace. It was as the Jaghut had meant it: negation, a scouring down to bare rock.

Lostara Yil drew her fur-lined cloak tighter about herself as she followed the Adjunct to the forecastle deck of the *Froth Wolf*. The sheltered harbour was before them, a half-dozen ships anchored in the bay, including the *Silanda* – its heap of Tiste Andii heads hidden beneath thick tarpaulin. Getting the bone whistle from Gesler hadn't been easy, she recalled; and among the soldiers of the two squads left to command the haunted craft, the only one willing to use it had been that corporal, Deadsmell. Not even Sinn would touch it.

Before the splitting of the fleet there had been a flurry of shifting about among the squads and companies. The strategy for this war demanded certain adjustments, and, as was expected, few had been thrilled with the changes. *Soldiers are such conservative bastards.*

But at least we pulled Blistig away from real command – worse than a rheumy old dog, that one.

Lostara, still waiting for her commander to speak, turned for a glance back at the Throne of War blockading the mouth of the harbour. The last Perish ship in these waters, for now. She hoped it would be enough for what was to come.

'Where is Sergeant Cord's squad now?' the Adjunct asked.

'Northwest tip of the island,' Lostara replied. 'Sinn is keeping the ice away—'

'How?' Tavore demanded, not for the first time.

And Lostara could but give the same answer she had given countless times before. 'I don't know, Adjunct.' She hesitated, then added, 'Ebron believes that this ice is dying. A Jaghut ritual, crumbling. He notes the water lines on this island's cliffs – well past any earlier high water mark.'

To this the Adjunct said nothing. She seemed unaffected by the cold, damp wind, barring an absence of colour on her features, as if her blood had withdrawn from the surface of her flesh. Her hair was cut very short, as if to discard every hint of femininity.

'Grub says the world is drowning,' Lostara said.

Tavore turned slightly and looked up at the unlit shrouds high overhead. 'Grub. Another mystery,' she said.

'He seems able to communicate with the Nachts, which is, well, remarkable.'

'Communicate? It's become hard to tell them apart.'

The *Froth Wolf* was sidling past the anchored ships, angling towards the stone pier, on which stood two figures. Probably Sergeant Balm and Deadsmell.

Tavore said, 'Go below, Captain, and inform the others we are about to disembark.'

'Aye, sir.'

Remain a soldier, Lostara Yil told herself, a statement that whispered through her mind a hundred times a day. *Remain a soldier, and all the rest will go away.*

With dawn's first light paling the eastern sky, the mounted troop of Letherii thundered down the narrow coastal track, the berm of the old beach ridge on their left, the impenetrable, tangled forest on their right. The rain had dissolved into a clammy mist, strengthening the night's last grip of darkness, and the pounding of hoofs was oddly muted, quick to dwindle once the last rider was out of sight.

Puddles in the track settled once more, clouded with mud. The mists swirled, drifted into the trees.

An owl, perched high on a branch of a dead tree, had watched the troop pass. The echoes fading, it remained where it was, not moving, its large unblinking eyes fixed on a chaotic mass of shrubs and brambles amidst thin-boled poplars. Where something was not quite as it seemed. Unease sufficient to confuse its predatory mind.

The scrub blurred then, as if disintegrating in a fierce gale – although no wind stirred – and upon its vanishing, figures rose as if from nowhere.

The owl decided it would have to wait a little longer. While hungry, it nevertheless experienced a strange contentment, followed by a kind of tug on its mind, as of something . . . leaving.

Bottle rolled onto his back. 'Over thirty riders,' he said. 'Lancers, lightly armoured. Odd stirrups. Hood, but my skull aches. I hate Mockra—'

'Enough bitching,' Fiddler said as he watched his squad – barring a motionless Bottle – drawing in, with Gesler's doing the same beneath some trees a few paces away. 'You sure they didn't smell nothing?'

'Those first scouts nearly stepped right on us,' Bottle said. 'Something there . . . especially in one of them. As if he was somehow . . . I don't know, sensitized, I suppose. Him and this damned ugly coast where we don't belong—'

'Just answer the questions,' Fiddler cut in again.

'We should've ambushed the whole lot,' Koryk muttered, checking the knots on all the fetishes he was wearing, then dragging over his oversized supply pack to examine the straps.

Fiddler shook his head. 'No fighting until our feet dry. I hate that.'

'Then why are you a damned marine, Sergeant?'

'Accident. Besides, those were Letherii. We're to avoid contact with them, for now.'

'I'm hungry,' Bottle said. 'Well, no. It was the owl, dammit. Anyway, you would not believe what looking through an owl's eyes at night is like. Bright as noon in the desert.'

'Desert,' Tarr said. 'I miss the desert.'

'You'd miss a latrine pit if it was the last place you crawled out of,' Smiles observed. 'Koryk had his crossbow trained on those riders, Sergeant.'

'What are you, my little sister?' Koryk demanded. He then mimed Smiles's voice. 'He didn't shake his baby-maker when he'd done peeing, Sergeant! I *saw* it!'

'See it?' Smiles laughed. 'I'd never get that close to you, half-blood, trust me.'

'She's getting better,' Cuttle said to Koryk, whose only response was a grunt.

'Quiet everyone,' Fiddler said. 'No telling who else lives in these woods – or might be using the road.'

'We're alone,' Bottle pronounced, slowly sitting up, then gripping the sides of his head. 'Hiding fourteen grunting, farting soldiers ain't easy. And once we get to more populated areas it's going to be worse.'

'Getting one miserable mage to shut his mouth is even harder,' Fiddler said. 'Check your gear, everyone. I want us a ways deeper into these woods before we dig in for the day.' For the past month on the ships the Bonehunters had been shifting over into reversing their sleep cycles. A damned hard thing to do, as it turned out. But now at least pretty much everyone was done turning round. *Lost the tans, anyway.* Fiddler moved over to where Gesler crouched.

Except this gold-skinned bastard and his hairy corporal. 'Your people ready?'

Gesler nodded. 'Heavies are complaining their armour's gonna rust.'

'So long as they keep the squeaking to a minimum.' Fiddler glanced at the huddled soldiers of Gesler's squad, then back towards his own. 'Some army,' he said under his breath.

'Some invasion, aye,' Gesler agreed. 'Ever known anyone to do it this way?'

Fiddler shook his head. 'It makes a weird kind of sense, though, doesn't it? The Edur are spread thin, from all reports. The oppressed are legion – all these damned Letherii.'

'That troop just passed us didn't look much oppressed to me, Fid.'

'Well, I suppose we'll find out one way or the other, won't we? Now, let's get this invasion under way.'

'A moment,' Gesler said, settling a scarred hand on Fiddler's shoulder. 'She burned the fucking transports, Fid.'

The sergeant winced.

'Hard to miss the point of that, wouldn't you say?'

'Which meaning are you referring to, Gesler? The one about patrols on this coast seeing the flames or the one about for us there's no going back?'

'Hood take me, I can only chew on one piece of meat at a time, you know? Start with the first one. If I was this damned empire, I'd be flooding this coastline with soldiers before this day's sun is down. And no matter how much Mockra our squad mages now know, we're going to mess up. Sooner or later, Fid.'

'Would that be before or after we start drawing blood?'

'I ain't even thinking about once we start killing Hood-damned Tiste Edur. I'm thinking about today.'

'Someone stumbles onto us and we get nasty and dirty, then we bolt according to the plan.'

'And try to stay alive, aye. Great. And what if these Letherii ain't friendly?'

'We just keep going, and steal what we need.'

'We should've landed en masse, not just marines. With shields locked and see what they can throw at us.'

Fiddler rubbed at the back of his neck. Then sighed and said, 'You know what they can throw at us, Gesler. Only the next time, there won't be Quick Ben dancing in the air and matching them horror for horror. This is a night war we're looking at. Ambushes. Knives in the dark. Cut and bolt.'

'With no way out.'

'Aye. So I do wonder if she lit up our transports to tell 'em we're here, or to tell us there's no point in thinking about retreat. Or both.'

Gesler grunted. ' "Unwitnessed", she said. Is that where we are? Already?'

Shrugging, Fiddler half rose. 'Might be, Gesler. Let's get moving – the birds are twittering almost as loud as we are.'

But, as they tramped deeper into the wet, rotting forest, Gesler's last question haunted Fiddler. *Is he right, Adjunct? We there already? Invading a damned empire in two-squad units. Running alone, un-supported, living or dying on the shoulders of a single squad mage. What if Bottle gets killed in the first scrap? We're done for, that's what. Best keep Corabb nice and close to Bottle, and hope the old rebel's luck keeps pulling.*

At the very least, the waiting was over. Real ground underfoot – they'd all wobbled like drunks coming up from the strand, which might have been amusing in other circumstances. *But not when we could have staggered right into a patrol.* Things were feeling solid now, though. Thank Hood. Well, as solid as one could be stumping over moss, over-grown sinkholes and twisted roots. *Almost as bad as Black Dog. No, don't think like that. Look ahead, Fid. Keep looking ahead.*

Somewhere above them, through a mad witch's weave of branches, the sky was lightening.

'Any more complainin' from any of you and I'll cut off my left tit.'

A half-circle of faces ogled her. Good. She was pleased with the way that always worked.

'Good thing the swim put you out,' Bowl said.

Sergeant Hellian frowned at the huge soldier. Put out? 'Heavies are idiots, you know that? Now.' She looked down and tried counting the number of rum casks she'd managed to drag from the hold before the flames went wild. Six, maybe ten. Nine. She waved at the blurry array. 'Everybody make room in your packs. For one each.'

Touchy Brethless said, 'Sergeant, ain't we supposed to find Urb and his squad? They gotta be close.' Then her corporal spoke again, this time in a different voice, 'He's right. Bowl, where'd you come from again? Up the shore or down it?'

'I don't remember. It was dark.'

'Hold on,' Hellian said, taking a sidestep to maintain her balance on the pitching deck. No, the pitching ground. 'You're not in my squad, Bowl. Go away.'

'I'd like nothing better,' he replied, squinting at the wall of trees surrounding them. 'I ain't carrying no cask of damned ale. Look at you, Sergeant, you're scorched all over.'

Hellian straightened. 'Now hold on, we're talking 'ssential victuals. But I'll tell you what's a lot worse. I bet that fire was seen by somebody – and I hope the fool that started it is a heap of ash right now, that's what I hope. Somebody's seen it, that's for sure.'

'Sergeant, they lit up *all* the transports,' said another one of her soldiers. Beard, thick chest, solid as a tree trunk and probably not much smarter either. What was his name?

'Who are you?'

The man rubbed at his eyes. 'Balgrid.'

'Right, Baldy, now try explaining to me how some fool swam from ship to ship and set them afire? Well? That's what I thought.'

'Someone's coming,' hissed the squad sapper.

The one with the stupid name. A name she always had trouble remembering. Could be? No. Sometimes? Unsure? *Ah, Maybe. Our sapper's name is Maybe. And his friend there, that's Lutes. And there's Tavos Pond – he's too tall. Tall soldiers get arrows in their foreheads. Why isn't he dead?* 'Anybody got a bow?' she asked.

A rustling of undergrowth, then two figures emerged from the gloom.

Hellian stared at the first one, feeling an inexplicable surge of rage. She rubbed thoughtfully at her jaw, trying to remember something about this sad-looking soldier. The rage drained away, was replaced with heartfelt affection.

Bowl stepped past her. 'Sergeant Urb, thank Hood you found us.'

'Urb?' Hellian asked, weaving as she moved closer and peered up into the man's round face. 'That you?'

'Found the rum, did you?'

Lutes said from behind her, 'She's poisoning her liver.'

'My liver's fine, soldier. Just needs a squeezing out.'

'Squeezing out?'

She turned round and glared at the squad healer. 'I seen livers before, Cutter. Big sponges full of blood. Tumbles out when you cut someone open.'

'Sounds more like a lung, Sergeant. The liver's this flat thing, muddy brown or purple—'

'Doesn't matter,' she said, wheeling back to stare at Urb. 'If the first one dies the other one kicks in. I'm fine. Well,' she added with a loud sigh which seemed to make Urb reel back a step, 'I'm in the best of moods, my friends. The best of moods. And now we're all together, so let's march because I'm pretty sure we're supposed to march somewhere.' She smiled over at her corporal. 'What say you, Touchy Brethless?'

'Sounds good, Sergeant.

'Brilliant plan, Sergeant.'

'Why do you always do that, Corporal?'

'Do what?

'Do what?'

'Look, Baldy's the one who's half deaf—'

'I'm not half deaf any more, Sergeant.'

'You're not? So who here is half deaf?'

'Nobody, Sergeant.'

'No need to shout. Baldy can hear you and if he can't then we should've left him on the boat, along with that tall one there with the arrow in his skull, because neither one's no good to us. We're looking for grey-skinned murderers and they're hiding in these trees. Behind them, I mean. If they were in them, it'd hurt. So we need to start looking behind all these trees. But first, collect us a cask here, one each now, and then we can get going.

'What're you all staring at? I'm the one giving the orders and I got me a new sword which will make chopping off one of these here tits a whole lot easier. Get moving, everyone, we got us a war to fight. Behind those trees.'

Crouched before him, Gullstream had the furtive look of a weasel in a chicken coop. He wiped his runny nose with the back of one forearm, squinted, then said, 'Everyone accounted for, sir.'

Fist Keneb nodded, then turned as someone slid loudly down the beach ridge. 'Quiet over there. All right, Gullstream, find the captain and send her to me.'

'Aye, sir.'

The soldiers were feeling exposed, which was understandable. It was one thing for a squad or two to scout ahead of a column – at least retreat was possible in the traditional sense. Here, if they got into trouble, their only way out was to scatter. As the commander of what would be a prolonged, chaotic engagement, Keneb was worried. His attack unit of six squads would be the hardest one to hide – the mages with him were the weakest of the lot, for the simple reason that his platoon would be holding back on their inland march, with the primary objective being avoiding any contact. As for the rest of his legion, it was now scattered up and down thirty leagues of coastline. Moving in small units of a dozen or so soldiers and about to begin a covert campaign that might last months.

There had been profound changes to the Fourteenth Army since Malaz City. A kind of standardization had been imposed on the scores of wizards, shamans, conjurers and casters in the legions, with the intent of establishing sorcery as the principal means of communication. And, for the squad mages among the marines – a force that now had as many heavy infantry as sappers – certain rituals of Mockra were now universally known. Illusions to affect camouflage, to swallow sound, confuse scent.

And all of this told Keneb one thing. *She knew. From the very beginning. She knew where we were going, and she planned for it.* Once again there had been no consultation among the officers. The Adjunct's only meetings were with that Meckros blacksmith and the Tiste Andii from Drift Avalii. *What could they have told her about this land? None of them are even from here.*

He preferred to assume it was a simple stroke of fortune when the fleet had sighted two Edur ships that had been separated from the others following a storm. Too damaged to flee, they had been taken by the marines. Not easily – these Tiste Edur were fierce when cornered, even when half-starved and dying of thirst. Officers had been captured, but only after every other damned warrior had been cut down.

The interrogation of those Edur officers had been bloody. Yet, for all the information they provided, it had been the ship logs and charts that had proved the most useful for this strange campaign. *Ah, 'strange' is too mild a word for this. True, the Tiste Edur fleets clashed with our empire – or what used to be our empire – and they'd conducted wholesale slaughter of peoples under our nominal protection. But isn't all that Laseen's problem?*

The Adjunct would not relinquish her title, either. Adjunct to whom? The woman who had done all she could to try to murder her? What had happened that night up in Mock's Hold, anyway? The only other witnesses beyond Tavore and the Empress herself were dead. T'amber. Kalam Mekhar – *gods, that's a loss that will haunt us.* Keneb wondered then – and wondered still – if the entire debacle at Malaz City had not been planned out between Laseen and her cherished Adjunct. Each time this suspicion whispered through him, the same objections arose in his mind. *She would not have agreed to T'amber's murder. And Tavore damned near died at the harbour front. And what about Kalam?* Besides, even Tavore Paran was not cold enough to see the sacrifice of the Wickans, all to feed some damned lie. Was she?

But Laseen's done this before. With Dujek Onearm and the Host. And that time, the deal involved the annihilation of the Bridgeburners – at least that's how it looks. So . . . why not?

What would have happened if we'd just marched into the city?

Killing every damned fool who got in our way? If we'd gone in strength with Tavore up to Mock's Hold?

Civil war. He knew that to be the answer to those questions. Nor could he see a way out, even after months and months of second-guessing.

No wonder, then, that all of this was eating at Keneb's guts, and he knew he was not alone in that. Blistig believed in nothing any more, beginning with himself. His eyes seemed to reflect some spectre of the future that only he could see. He walked as a man already dead – the body refusing what the mind knew to be an irrevocable truth. And they'd lost Tene Baralta and his Red Blades, although perhaps that was not quite as tragic. *Well, come to think on it, Tavore's inner circle is pretty much gone. Carved out. Hood knows I never belonged there anyway – which is why I'm here, in this damned dripping swamp of a forest.*

'We're assembled and waiting, Fist.'

Blinking, Keneb saw that his captain had arrived. *Standing – waiting – how long?* He squinted up at the greying sky. *Shit.* 'Very well, we'll head inland until we find some dry ground.'

'Aye.'

'Oh, Captain, have you selected out the mage you want?'

Faradan Sort's eyes narrowed briefly, and in the colourless light the planes of her hard face looked more angular than ever. She sighed and said, 'I believe so, Fist. From Sergeant Gripe's squad. Beak.'

'Him? Are you sure?'

She shrugged. 'Nobody likes him, so you'll not rue the loss.'

Keneb felt a flicker of irritation. In a low tone he said, 'Your task is not meant to be a suicide mission, Captain. I am not entirely convinced this sorcerous communication system is going to work. And once the squads start losing mages, it will all fall apart. You will probably become the only link among all the units—'

'Once we find some horses,' she cut in.

'Correct.'

He watched as she studied him for a long moment, then she said, 'Beak has tracking skills, Fist. Of a sort. He says he can smell magic, which will help in finding our soldiers.'

'Very good. Now, it's time to move inland, Captain.'

'Aye, Fist.'

A short time later, the forty-odd soldiers of Keneb's command platoon were fighting their way through a bog of fetid, black water, as the day's heat grew. Insects swarmed in hungry clouds. Few words were exchanged.

None of us are sure of this, are we? Find the Tiste Edur – this land's oppressors – and cut them down. Free the Letherii to rebel. Aye, foment a civil war, the very thing we fled the Malazan Empire to avoid.

Odd, isn't it, how we now deliver upon another nation what we would not have done to ourselves.

About as much moral high ground as this damned swamp. No, we're not happy, Adjunct. Not happy at all.

Beak didn't know much about any of this. In fact, he would be the first to admit he didn't know much about anything at all, except maybe weaving sorcery. The one thing he knew for certain, however, was that no-one liked him.

Getting tied to the belt of this scary captain woman would probably turn out to be a bad idea. She reminded him of his mother, looks-wise, which should have killed quick any thoughts of the lustful kind. Should have, but didn't, which he found a little disturbing if he thought about it, which he didn't. Much. Unlike his mother, anyway, she wasn't the type to browbeat him at every turn, and that was refreshing.

'I was born a stupid boy to very rich noble-born parents.' Usually the first words he uttered to everyone he met. The next ones were: 'That's why I became a soldier, so's I could be with my own kind.' Conversations usually died away shortly after that, which made Beak sad.

He would have liked to talk with the other squad mages, but even there it seemed he couldn't quite get across his deep-in-the-bone love of magic. 'Mystery,' he'd say, nodding and nodding, 'mystery, right? And poetry. That's sorcery. *Mystery and poetry*, which is what my mother used to say to my brother when she crawled into his bed on the nights Father was somewhere else. "We're living in mystery and poetry, my dear one," she'd say – I'd pretend I was asleep, since once I sat up and she beat me real bad. Normally she never did that, with her fists I mean. Most of my tutors did that, so she wouldn't have to. But I sat up and that made her mad. The House healer said I almost died that night, and that's how I learned about poetry.'

The wonder that was sorcery was his greatest love, maybe his only one, so far, though he was sure he'd meet his perfect mate one day. A pretty woman as stupid as he was. In any case, the other mages usually just stared at him while he babbled on, which was what he did when getting nervous. On and on. Sometimes a mage would just up and hug him, then walk away. Once, a wizard he was talking to just started crying. That had frightened Beak.

The captain's interview of the mages in the platoon had ended with him, second in line.

'Where are you from, Beak, to have you so convinced you're stupid?'

He wasn't sure what that question meant, but he did try to answer. 'I was born in the great city of Quon on Quon Tali in the Malazan Empire, which is an empire ruled by a little Empress and is the most civilized place in the world. All my tutors called me stupid and they should know. Nobody didn't agree with them, either.'

'So who taught you about magic?'

'We had a Seti witch in charge of the stables. In the country estate. She said that for me sorcery was the lone candle in the darkness. The lone candle in the darkness. She said my brain had put out all the other candles, so this one would shine brighter and brighter. So she showed me magic, first the Seti way, which she knew best. But later, she always found other servants, other people who knew the other kinds. *Warrens.* That's what they're called. Different coloured candles for each and every one of them. Grey for Mockra, green for Ruse, white for Hood, yellow for Thyr, blue for—'

'You know how to use Mockra?'

'Yes. Want me to show you?'

'Not now. I need you to come with me – I am detaching you from your squad, Beak.'

'All right.'

'You and I, we are going to travel together, away from everyone else. We're going to ride from unit to unit, as best we can.'

'Ride, on horses?'

'Do you know how?'

'Quon horses are the finest horses in the world. We bred them. It was almost another candle in my head. But the witch said it was different, since I'd been born into it and riding was in my bones like writing in black ink.'

'Do you think you'll be able to find the other squads, even when they're using sorcery to hide themselves?'

'Find them? Of course. I smell magic. My candle flickers, then leans this way and whatever way the magic's coming from.'

'All right, Beak, you are now attached to Captain Faradan Sort. I've chosen you, over all the others.'

'All right.'

'Grab your gear and follow me.'

'How close?'

'Like you were tied to my sword-belt, Beak. Oh, and how old are you, by the way?'

'I've lost count. I was thirty but that was six years ago so I don't know any more.'

'The warrens, Beak – how many candles do you know about?'

'Oh, lots. All of them.'

'All of them.'

'We had a half-Fenn blacksmith for my last two years and he once asked me to list them, so I did, then he said that was all of them. He said: "That's all of them, Beak."'

'What else did he say?'

'Nothing much, only he made me this knife.' Beak tapped the large weapon at his hip. 'Then he told me to run away from home. Join the Malazan Army, so I wouldn't get beaten any more for being stupid. I was one year less than thirty when I did that, just like he told me to, and I haven't been beaten since. Nobody likes me but they don't hurt me. I didn't know the army would be so lonely.'

She was studying him the way most people did, then she asked, 'Beak, did you never use your sorcery to defend yourself, or fight back?'

'No.'

'Have you ever seen your parents or brother since?'

'My brother killed himself and my parents are dead – they died the night I left. So did the tutors.'

'What happened to them?'

'I'm not sure,' Beak admitted. 'Only, I showed them my candle.'

'Have you done that since, Beak? Showed your candle?'

'Not all of it, not all the light, no. The blacksmith told me not to, unless I had no choice.'

'Like that last night with your family and tutors.'

'Like that night, yes. They'd had the blacksmith whipped and driven off, you see, for giving me this knife. And then they tried to take it away from me. And all at once, I had no choice.'

So she said they were going away from the others, but here they were, trudging along with the rest, and the insects kept biting him, especially on the back of his neck, and getting stuck in his ears and up his nose, and he realized that he didn't understand anything.

But she was right there, right at his side.

The platoon reached a kind of island in the swamp, moated in black water. It was circular, and as they scrambled onto it Beak saw moss-covered rubble.

'Was a building here,' one of the soldiers said.

'Jaghut,' Beak called out, suddenly excited. 'Omtose Phellack. No flame, though, just the smell of tallow. The magic's all drained away and that's what made this swamp, but we can't stay here, because there's broken bodies under the rocks and those ghosts are hungry.'

They were all staring at him. He ducked his head. 'Sorry.'

But Captain Faradan Sort laid a hand on his shoulder. 'No need, Beak. These bodies – Jaghut?'

'No. Forkrul Assail and Tiste Liosan. They fought on the ruins. During what they called the Just Wars. Here, it was only a skirmish, but nobody survived. They killed each other, and the last warrior standing had a hole in her throat and she bled out right where the Fist is standing. She was Forkrul Assail, and her last thought was about how victory proved they were right and the enemy was wrong. Then she died.'

'It's the only dry land anywhere in sight,' Fist Keneb said. 'Can any mage here banish the ghosts? No? Hood's breath. Beak, what are they capable of doing to us anyway?'

'They'll eat into our brains and make us think terrible things, so that we all end up killing each other. That's the thing with the Just Wars – they never end and never will because Justice is a weak god with too many names. The Liosan called it Serkanos and the Assail called it Rynthan. Anyway, no matter what language it spoke, its followers could not understand it. A mystery language, which is why it has no power because all its followers believe the wrong things – things they just make up and nobody can agree and that's why the wars never end.' Beak paused, looking around at the blank faces, then he shrugged. 'I don't know, maybe if I talk to them. Summon one and we can talk to it.'

'I think not, Beak,' the Fist said. 'On your feet, soldiers, we're moving on.'

No-one complained.

Faradan Sort drew Beak to one side. 'We're leaving them now,' she said. 'Which direction do you think will get us out of this the quickest?'

Beak pointed north.

'How far?'

'A thousand paces. That's where the edge of the old Omtose Phellack is.'

She watched Keneb and his squads move down from the island, splashing their way further inland, due west. 'How long before they're out of this heading in that direction – heading west, I mean?'

'Maybe twelve hundred paces, if they stay out of the river.'

She grunted. 'Two hundred extra steps won't kill them. All right, Beak, north it is. Lead on.'

'Aye, Captain. We can use the old walkway.'

She laughed then. Beak had no idea why.

There was a sound in war that came during sieges, moments before an assault on the walls. The massed onagers, ballistae and catapults were let loose in a single salvo. The huge missiles striking the stone walls, the fortifications and the buildings raised a chaotic chorus of exploding stone and brick, shattered tiles and collapsing rooftops. The air itself seemed to shiver, as if recoiling from the violence.

Sergeant Cord stood on the promontory, leaning into the fierce, icy wind, and thought of that sound as he stared across at the churning bergs of ice warring across the strait. Like a city tumbling down, enormous sections looming over where Fent Reach used to be were splitting away, in momentary silence, until the waves of concussion rolled over the choppy waves of the sea, arriving in thunder. Roiling silver clouds, gouts of foamy water—

395

'A mountain range in its death-throes,' muttered Ebron at his side.

'War machines pounding a city wall,' Cord countered.

'A frozen storm,' said Limp behind them.

'You all have it wrong,' interjected Crump through chattering teeth. 'It's like big pieces of ice . . . falling down.'

'That's . . . simply stunning, Crump,' said Corporal Shard. 'You're a Hood-damned poet. I cannot believe the Mott Irregulars ever let you get away. No, truly, Crump. I cannot believe it.'

'Well, it's not like they had any choice,' the tall, knock-kneed sapper said, rubbing vigorously at both sides of his jaw before adding, 'I mean, I left when no-one was looking. I used a fish spine to pick the manacles – you can't arrest a High Marshal anyhow. I kept telling them. You can't. It's not allowed.'

Cord turned to his corporal. 'Any better luck at talking to your sister? Is she getting tired holding all this back? We can't tell. Widdershins doesn't even know how she's doing it in the first place, so he can't help.'

'Got no answers for you, Sergeant. She doesn't talk to me either. I don't know – she doesn't look tired, but she hardly sleeps any more anyway. There's not much I recognize in Sinn these days. Not since Y'Ghatan.'

Cord thought about this for a time, then he nodded. 'I'm sending Widdershins back. The Adjunct should be landing in the Fort by now.'

'She has,' said Ebron, pulling at his nose as if to confirm it hadn't frozen off. Like Widdershins, the squad mage had no idea how Sinn was managing to fend off mountains of ice. A bad jolt to his confidence, and it showed. 'The harbour's blocked, the thug in charge is contained. Everything is going as planned.'

A grunt from Limp. 'Glad you're not the superstitious type, Ebron. As for me, I'm getting down off this spine before I slip and blow a knee.'

Shard laughed. 'You're just about due, Limp.'

'Thanks, Corporal. I really do appreciate your concern.'

'Concern is right. I got five imperials on you living up to your name before the month's out.'

'Bastard.'

'Shard,' Cord said after they'd watched – with some amusement – Limp gingerly retreat from the promontory, 'where is Sinn now?'

'In that old lighthouse,' the corporal replied.

'All right. Let's get under some cover ourselves – there's more freezing rain on the way.'

'That's just it,' Ebron said in sudden anger. 'She's not just holding the ice back, Sergeant. She's *killing* it. And the water's rising and rising fast.'

'Thought it was all dying anyway.'

'Aye, Sergeant. But she's quickened that up – she just took apart that Omtose Phellack like reeds from a broken basket – but she didn't throw 'em away, no, she's weaving *something else*.'

Cord glared at his mage. 'Sinn ain't the only one not talking. What do you mean by "something else"?'

'I don't know! Hood's balls, I don't!'

'There's no baskets over there,' Crump said. 'Not that I can see. Marsh pigs, you got good eyes, Ebron. Even when I squint with one eye, I don't see—'

'That's enough, Sapper,' Cord cut in. He studied Ebron for a moment longer, then turned away. 'Come on, I got a block of ice between my legs and that's the warmest part of me.'

They headed down towards the fisher's shack they used as their base.

'You should get rid of it, Sergeant,' Crump said.

'What?'

'That block of ice. Or use your hands, at least.'

'Thanks, Crump, but I ain't that desperate yet.'

It had been a comfortable life, all things considered. True, Malaz City was hardly a jewel of the empire, but at least it wasn't likely to fall apart and sink in a storm. And he'd had no real complaints about the company he kept. Coop's had its assortment of fools, enough to make Withal feel as if he belonged.

Braven Tooth. Temper. Banaschar – and at least Banaschar was here, the one familiar face beyond a trio of Nachts and, of course, his wife. *Of course. Her.* And though an Elder God had told him to wait, the Meckros blacksmith would have been content to see that waiting last for ever. *Damn the gods, anyway, with their constant meddling, they way they just use us. As they like.*

Even after what had to be a year spent on the same ship as the Adjunct, Withal could not claim to know her. True, there had been that prolonged period of grief – Tavore's lover had been killed in Malaz City, he'd been told – and the Adjunct had seemed, for a time, like a woman more dead than alive.

If she was now back to herself, then, well, her self wasn't much.

The gods didn't care. They'd decided to use her as much as they had used him. He could see it, that bleak awareness in her unremarkable eyes. And if she had decided to stand against them, then she stood alone.

I would never have the courage for that. Not even close. But maybe, to do what she's doing, she has to make herself less than human. More than human? Choosing to be less to be more, perhaps. So many here might see her as surrounded by allies. Allies such as Withal himself,

Banaschar, Sandalath, Sinn and Keneb. But he knew better. *We all watch. Waiting. Wondering.*

Undecided.

Is this what you wanted, Mael? To deliver me to her? Yes, she was who I was waiting for.

Leading, inevitably, to that most perplexing question: *But why me?*

True, he could tell her of the sword. His sword. The tool he had hammered and pounded into life for the Crippled God. But there was no answering that weapon.

Yet the Adjunct was undeterred. Choosing a war not even her soldiers wanted. With the aim of bringing down an empire. And the Emperor who held that sword in his hands. An Emperor driven mad by his own power. Another tool of the gods.

It was hard to feel easy about all this. Hard to find any confidence in the Adjunct's bold decision. The marines had been flung onto the Letherii shore, not a single landing en masse, in strength, but one scattered, clandestine, at night. Then, as if to defy the tactic, the transports had been set aflame.

An announcement to be sure.

We are here. Find us, if you dare. But be assured, in time we will find you.

While most of another legion remained in ships well off the Letherii coast. And the Adjunct alone knew where the Khundryl had gone. And most of the Perish.

'You have taking to brooding, husband.'

Withal slowly lifted his head and regarded the onyx-skinned woman sitting opposite him in the cabin. 'I am a man of deep thoughts,' he said.

'You're a lazy toad trapped in a pit of self-obsession.'

'That, too.'

'We will soon be ashore. I would have thought you'd be eager at the gunnel, given all your groaning and moaning. Mother Dark knows, I would never have known you for a Meckros with your abiding hatred of the sea.'

'Abiding hatred, is it? No, more like . . . frustration.' He lifted his huge hands. 'Repairing ships is a speciality. But it's not mine. I need to be back doing what I do best, wife.'

'Horseshoes?'

'Precisely.'

'Shield-rims? Dagger-hilts? Swords?'

'If need be.'

'Armies always drag smiths with them.'

'Not my speciality.'

'Rubbish. You can fold iron into a blade as well as any weaponsmith.'

'Seen plenty of 'em, have you?'

'With a life as long as mine has been, I've seen too much of everything. Now, our young miserable charges are probably down in the hold again. Will you get them or will I?'

'Is it truly time to leave?'

'I think the Adjunct is already off.'

'You go. They still make my skin crawl.'

She rose. 'You lack sympathy, which is characteristic of self-obsession. These Tiste Andii are young, Withal. Abandoned first by Anomander Rake. Then by Andarist. Brothers and sisters fallen in pointless battle. Too many losses – they are caught in the fragility of the world, in the despair it delivers to their souls.'

'Privilege of the young, to wallow in world-weary cynicism.'

'Unlike your deep thoughts.'

'Completely unlike my deep thoughts, Sand.'

'You think they have not earned that privilege?'

He could sense her growing ire. She was, after all, no less Tiste Andii than they were. Some things needed steering around. *Volcanic island. Floating mountain of ice. Sea of fire. And Sandalath Drukorlat's list of sensitivities.* 'I suppose they have,' he replied carefully. 'But since when was cynicism a virtue? Besides, it gets damned tiring.'

'No argument there,' she said in a deadly tone, then turned and marched out.

'Brooding's different,' he muttered to the empty chair across from him. 'Could be any subject, for one thing. A subject not at all cynical. Like the meddling of the gods – no, all right, not like that one. Smithing, yes. Horseshoes. Nothing cynical about horseshoes . . . I don't think. Sure. Keeping horses comfortable. So they can gallop into battle and die horribly.' He fell silent. Scowling.

Phaed's flat, heart-shaped face was the colour of smudged slate, a hue unfortunate in its lifelessness. Her eyes were flat, except when filled with venom, which they were now as they rested on Sandalath Drukorlat's back as the older woman spoke to the others.

Nimander Golit could see the young woman he called his sister from the corner of his eye, and he wondered yet again at the source of Phaed's unquenchable malice, which had been there, as far as he could recall, from her very earliest days. Empathy did not exist within her, and in its absence something cold now thrived, promising a kind of brutal glee at every victory, real or imagined, obvious or subtle.

There was nothing easy in this young, beautiful woman. It began with the very first impression a stranger had upon seeing her, a kind of natural glamour that could take one's breath away. The perfection of art, the wordless language of the romantic.

This initial moment was short-lived. It usually died following the first polite query, which Phaed invariably met with cold silence. A silence that transformed that wordless language, dispelling all notions of romance, and filling the vast, prolonged absence of decorum with bald contempt.

Spite was reserved for those who saw her truly, and it was in these instances that Nimander felt a chill of premonition, for he knew that Phaed was capable of murder. Woe to the sharp observer who saw, unflinchingly, through to her soul – to that trembling knot of darkness veined with unimaginable fears – then chose to disguise nothing of that awareness.

Nimander had long since learned to affect a kind of innocence when with Phaed, quick with a relaxed smile which seemed to put her at ease. It was at these moments, alas, when she was wont to confide her cruel sentiments, whispering elaborate schemes of vengeance against a host of slights.

Sandalath Drukorlat was nothing if not perceptive, which was hardly surprising. She had lived centuries upon centuries. She had seen all manner of creatures, from the honourable to the demonic. It had not taken her long to decide towards which end of the spectrum Phaed belonged. She had answered cold regard with her own; the contempt flung her way was like pebbles thrown at a warrior's shield, raising not even a scratch. And, most cutting riposte of all, she had displayed amusement at Phaed's mute histrionics, even unto overt mockery. These, then, were the deep wounds suppurating in Phaed's soul, delivered by the woman who now stood as a surrogate mother to them all.

And now, Nimander knew, heart-faced Phaed was planning matricide.

He admitted to his own doldrums – long periods of flat indifference – as if none of this was in fact worth thinking about. He had his private host of demons, after all, none of which seemed inclined to simply fade away. Unperturbed by the occasional neglect, they played on in their dark games, and the modest hoard of wealth that made up Nimander's life went back and forth, until the scales spun without surcease. Clashing discord and chaos to mark the triumphant cries, the hissed curses, the careless scattering of coin. He often felt numbed, deafened.

It may have been that these were the traits of the Tiste Andii. *Introverts devoid of introspection. Darkness in the blood. Chimerae, even unto ourselves.* He'd wanted to care about the throne they had been defending, the one that Andarist died for, and he had led his charges into that savage battle without hesitation. Perhaps, even, with true eagerness.

Rush to death. The longer one lives, the less valued is that life. Why is that?

But that would be introspection, wouldn't it? Too trying a task, pursuing such questions. Easier to simply follow the commands of others. Another trait of his kind, this comfort in following? Yet who stood among the Tiste Andii as symbols of respect and awe? Not young warriors like Nimander Golit. Not wicked Phaed and her vile ambitions. *Anomander Rake, who walked away. Andarist, his brother, who did not. Silchas Ruin – ah, such a family!* Clearly unique among the brood of the Mother. They lived larger, then, in great drama. Lives tense and humming like bowstrings, the ferocity of truth in their every word, the hard, cruel exchanges that drove them apart when nothing else would. Not even Mother Dark's turning away. Their early lives were poems of epic grandeur. *And we? We are nothing. Softened, blunted, confused into obscurity. We have lost our simplicity, lost its purity. We are the Dark without mystery.*

Sandalath Drukorlat – who had lived in those ancient times and must grieve in her soul for the fallen Tiste Andii – now turned about and with a gesture beckoned the motley survivors of Drift Avalii to follow. Onto the deck – *'you have hair, Nimander, the colour of starlight'* – to look upon this squalid harbour town that would be their home for the *next little eternity*, to use Phaed's hissing words.

'It used to be a prison, this island. Full of rapists and murderers.' A sudden look into his eyes, as if seeking something, then she gave him a fleeting smile that was little more than a showing of teeth and said, 'A good place for murder.'

Words that, millennia past, could have triggered a civil war or worse, the fury of Mother Dark herself. Words, then, that barely stirred the calm repose of Nimander's indifference.

'You have hair, Nimander, the colour of—' But the past was dead. *Drift Avalii. Our very own prison isle, where we learned about dying.*

And the terrible price of following.

Where we learned that love does not belong in this world.

CHAPTER FOURTEEN

I took the stone bowl
in both hands
and poured out my time
onto the ground
drowning hapless insects
feeding the weeds
until the sun stood
looking down
and stole the stain.

Seeing in the vessel's cup
a thousand cracks
I looked back
the way I came
and saw a trail green
with memories lost
whoever made this bowl
was a fool but the greater
he who carried it.

Stone Bowl
Fisher kel Tath

THE PITCHED SWEEP OF ICE HAD GONE THROUGH SUCCESSIVE THAWS and freezes until its surface was pocked and sculpted like the colourless bark of some vast toppled tree. The wind, alternating between warm and cold, moaned a chorus of forlorn voices through this muricated surface, and it seemed to Hedge that with each crunching stamp of his boot, a lone cry was silenced for ever. The thought left him feeling morose, and this motley scatter of refuse dotting the plain of ice and granulated snow only made things worse.

Detritus of Jaghut lives, slowly rising like stones in a farmer's field. Mundane objects to bear witness to an entire people – if only he could make sense of them, could somehow assemble together all these disparate pieces. Ghosts, he now believed, existed in a perpetually confused state, the way before them an endless vista strewn with meaningless dross – the truths of living were secrets, the physicality of facts for ever withheld. A ghost could reach but could not touch, could move this and that, but never be moved by them. Some essence of empathy had vanished – but no, empathy wasn't the right word. He could *feel*, after all. The way he used to, when he had been alive. Emotions swam waters both shallow and deep. Tactile empathy perhaps was closer to the sense he sought. The comfort of mutual resistance.

He had willed himself this shape, this body in which he now dwelt, walking heavily alongside the withered, animate carcass that was Emroth. And it seemed he could conjure a kind of physical continuity with everything around him – like the crunching of his feet – but he now wondered if that continuity was a delusion, as if in picking up this curved shell of some ancient broken pot just ahead of him he was not in truth picking up *its* ghost. But for that revelation his eyes were blind, the senses of touch and sound were deceits, and he was as lost as an echo.

They continued trudging across this plateau, beneath deep blue skies where stars glittered high in the vault directly overhead, a world of ice seemingly without end. The scree of garbage accompanied them on all sides. Fragments of cloth or clothing or perhaps tapestry, potsherds, eating utensils, arcane tools of wood or ground stone, the piece of a musical instrument that involved strings and raised finger-drums, the splintered leg of a wooden chair or stool. No weapons, not in days, and the one they had discovered early on – a spear shaft – had been Imass.

Jaghut had died on this ice. Slaughtered. Emroth had said as much. But there were no bodies, and there had been no explanation forthcoming from the T'lan Imass. Collected then, Hedge surmised, perhaps by a survivor. Did the Jaghut practise ritual interment? He had no idea. In all his travels, he could not once recall talk of a Jaghut tomb or burial ground. If they did such things, they kept them to themselves.

But when they died here, they had been on the run. Some of those swaths of material were from tents. Flesh and blood Imass did not pursue them – not across this lifeless ice. No, they must have been T'lan. Of the Ritual. *Like Emroth here.*

'So,' Hedge said, his own voice startlingly loud in his ears, 'were you involved in this hunt, Emroth?'

'I cannot be certain,' she replied after a long moment. 'It is possible.'

'One scene of slaughter looks pretty much the same as the next, right?'

'Yes. That is true.'

Her agreement left him feeling even more depressed.

'There is something ahead,' the T'lan Imass said. 'We are, I believe, about to discover the answer to the mystery.'

'What mystery?'

'The absence of bodies.'

'Oh, that mystery.'

Night came abruptly to this place, like the snuffing out of a candle. The sun, which circled just above the horizon through the day, would suddenly tumble, like a rolling ball, beneath the gleaming, blood-hued skyline. And the black sky would fill with stars that only faded with the coming of strangely coloured brushstrokes of light, spanning the vault, that hissed like sprinkled fragments of fine glass.

Hedge sensed that night was close, as the wind's pockets of warmth grew more infrequent, the ember cast to what he assumed was west deepening into a shade both lurid and baleful.

He could now see what had caught Emroth's attention. A hump on the plateau, ringed in dark objects. The shape rising from the centre of that hillock at first looked like a spar of ice, but as they neared, Hedge saw that its core was dark, and that darkness reached down to the ground.

The objects surrounding the rise were cloth-swaddled bodies, many of them pitifully small.

As the day's light suddenly dropped away, night announced on a gust of chill wind, Hedge and Emroth halted just before the hump.

The upthrust spar was in fact a throne of ice, and on it sat the frozen corpse of a male Jaghut. Mummified by cold and desiccating winds, it nevertheless presented an imposing if ghastly figure, a figure of domination, the head tilted slightly downward, as if surveying a ring of permanently supine subjects.

'Death observing death,' Hedge muttered. 'How damned appropriate. He collected the bodies, then sat down and just died with them. Gave up. No thoughts of vengeance, no dreams of resurrection. Here's your dread enemy, Emroth.'

'More than you realize,' the T'lan Imass replied.

She moved on, edging round the edifice, her hide-wrapped feet plunging through the crust of brittle ice in small sparkling puffs of powdery snow.

Hedge stared up at the Jaghut on his half-melted throne. *All thrones should be made of ice, I think.*

Sit on that numb arse, sinking down and down, with the puddle of dissolution getting ever wider around you. Sit, dear ruler, and tell me all your grand designs.

Of course, the throne wasn't the only thing falling apart up there.

The Jaghut's green, leathery skin had sloughed away on the forehead, revealing sickly bone, almost luminescent in the gloom; and on the points of the shoulders the skin was frayed, with the polished knobs of the shoulder bones showing through. Similar gleams from the knuckles of both hands where they rested on the now-tilted arms of the chair.

Hedge's gaze returned to the face. Black, sunken pits for eyes, a nose broad and smashed flat, tusks of black silver. *I thought these things never quite died. Needed big rocks on them to keep them from getting back up. Or chopped to pieces and every piece planted under a boulder.*

I didn't think they died this way at all.

He shook himself and set off after Emroth.

They would walk through the night. Camps, meals and sleeping were for still-breathing folk, after all.

'Emroth!'

The head creaked round.

'That damned thing back there's not still alive, is it?'

'No. The spirit left.'

'Just . . . left?'

'Yes.'

'Isn't that, uh, unusual?'

'The Throne of Ice was dying. Is dying still. There was – is – nothing left to rule, ghost. Would you have him sit there for ever?' She did not seem inclined to await a reply, for she then said, 'I have not been here before, Hedge of the Bridgeburners. For I would have known.'

'Known what, Emroth?'

'I have never before seen the true Throne of Ice, in the heart of the Hold. The very heart of the Jaghut realm.'

Hedge glanced back. *The true Throne of Ice?* 'Who – who was he, Emroth?'

But she did not give answer.

After a time, however, he thought he knew. Had always known.

He kicked aside a broken pot, watched it skid, roll, then wobble to a halt. *King on your melting throne, you drew a breath, then let it go. And . . . never again. Simple. Easy. When you are the last of your kind, and you release that last breath, then it is the breath of extinction.*

And it rides the wind.

Every wind.

'Emroth, there was a scholar in Malaz City – a miserable old bastard named Obo – who claimed he was witness to the death of a star. And when the charts were compared again, against the night sky, well, one light was gone.'

'The stars have changed since my mortal life, ghost.'

'Some have gone out?'

'Yes.'

'As in . . . *died*?'

'The Bonecasters could not agree on this,' she said. 'Another obser-vation offered a different possibility. The stars are moving away from us, Hedge of the Bridgeburners. Perhaps those we no longer see have gone too far for our eyes.'

'Obo's star was pretty bright – wouldn't it have faded first, over a long time, before going out?'

'Perhaps both answers are true. Stars die. Stars move away.'

'So, did that Jaghut die, or did he move away?'

'Your question makes no sense.'

Really? Hedge barked a laugh. 'You're a damned bad liar, Emroth.'

'This,' she said, 'is not a perfect world.'

The swaths of colours sweeping overhead hissed softly, while around them the wind plucked at tufts of cloth and fur, moaning through miniature gullies and caverns of ice, and closer still, a sound shared by ghost and T'lan Imass, the crackling destruction of their footsteps across the plateau.

Onrack knelt beside the stream, plunging his hands into the icy water, then lifting them clear again to watch the runnels trickling down. The wonder had not left his dark brown eyes since his transformation, since the miracle of a life regained.

A man could have no heart if he felt nothing watching this rebirth, this innocent joy in a savage warrior who had been dead a hundred thousand years. He picked up polished stones as if they were treasure, ran blunt, calloused fingertips across swaths of lichen and moss, brought to his heavy lips a discarded antler to taste with his tongue, to draw in its burnt-hair scent. Walking through the thorny brush of some arctic rose, Onrack had then halted, with a cry of astonishment, upon seeing red scratches on his bowed shins.

The Imass was, Trull Sengar reminded himself yet again, nothing – *nothing* – like what he would have imagined him to be. Virtually hair-less everywhere barring the brown, almost black mane sweeping down past his broad shoulders. In the days since they had come to this strange realm, a beard had begun, thin along Onrack's jawline and above his mouth, the bristles wide-spaced and black as a boar's; but not growing at all on the cheeks, or the neck. The features of the face were broad and flat, dominated by a flaring nose with a pronounced bridge, like a knuckle bone between the wide-spaced, deeply inset eyes. The heavy ridge over those eyes was made all the more robust by the sparseness of the eyebrows.

Although not particularly tall, Onrack nevertheless seemed huge. Ropy muscles bound to thick bone, the arms elongated, the hands wide but the fingers stubby. The legs were disproportionately short, bowed so that the knees were almost as far out to the sides as his hips. Yet Onrack moved with lithe stealth, furtive as prey, eyes flicking in every direction, head tilting, nostrils flaring as he picked up scents on the wind. Prey, yet now he needed to satisfy a prodigious appetite, and when Onrack hunted, it was with discipline, a single-mindedness that was fierce to witness.

This world was his, in every way. A blend of tundra to the north and a treeline in the south that reached up every now and then to the very shadow of the huge glaciers stretching down the valleys. The forest was a confused mix of deciduous and coniferous trees, broken with ravines and tumbled rocks, springs of clean water and boggy sinkholes. The branches swarmed with birds, their incessant chatter at times overwhelming all else.

Along the edges there were trails. Caribou moved haphazardly between forest and tundra in their grazing. Closer to the ice, on higher ground where bedrock was exposed, there were goat-like creatures, scampering up ledges to look back down on the two-legged strangers passing through their domain.

Onrack had disappeared into the forest again and again in the first week of their wandering. Each time he reappeared his toolkit had expanded. A wooden shaft, the point of which he hardened in the fire of their camp; vines and reeds from which he fashioned snares, and nets that he then attached to the other end of the spear, displaying impressive skill at trapping birds on the wing.

From the small mammals caught in his nightly snares he assembled skins and gut. With the stomachs and intestines of hares he made floats for the weighted nets he strung across streams, and from the grayling and sturgeon harvested he gathered numerous spines which he then used to sew together the hides, fashioning a bag. He collected charcoal and tree sap, lichens, mosses, tubers, feathers and small pouches of animal fat, all of which went into the hide bag.

But all of these things were as nothing when compared with the burgeoning of the man himself. A face Trull had known only as dried skin taut over shattered bone was now animate with expression, and it was as if Trull had been blind to his friend in the time before, when even vocal inflection had been flat and lifeless.

Onrack now *smiled*. A sudden lighting of genuine pleasure that not only took Trull's breath away – and, he admitted, often filled his eyes with tears – but could silence Quick Ben as well, the wizard's dark face suddenly evincing ineffable wonder, an expression that a well-meaning adult might have upon seeing a child at play.

Everything about this Imass invited friendship, as if his smile alone cast some sorcery, a geas of charm, to which unquestioning loyalty was the only possible response. This glamour Trull Sengar had no interest in

407

resisting. *Onrack, after all, is the one brother I chose.* But the Tiste Edur could see, on occasion, the gleam of suspicion in the Malazan wizard, as if Quick Ben was catching himself at the edge of some inner precipice, some slide into a place Ben could not, by his very nature, wholly trust.

Trull felt no worry; he could see that Onrack was not interested in manipulating his companions. His was a spirit contained within itself, a spirit that had emerged from a haunted place and was haunted no longer. *Dead in a demonic nightmare. Reborn into a paradise. Onrack, my friend, you are redeemed, and you know it, with every sense – with your touch, your vision, with the scents of the land and the songs in the trees.*

The previous evening he had returned from a trip into the forest with a sheath of bark in his hands. On it were nuggets of crumbly yellow ochre. Later, beside the fire, while Quick Ben cooked the remaining meat from a small deer Onrack had killed in the forest two days previously, the Imass ground the nuggets into powder. Then, using spit and grease, he made a yellow paste. As he worked these preparations, he hummed a song, a droning, vibrating cadence that was as much nasal as vocal. The range, like his speaking voice, was unearthly. It seemed capable of carrying two distinct tones, one high and the other deep. The song ended when the task was done. There was a long pause; then, as Onrack began applying the paint to his face, neck and arms, a different song emerged, this one with a rapid beat, fast as the heart of a fleeing beast.

When the last daub of paint marked his amber skin, the song stopped.

'Gods below!' Quick Ben had gasped, one hand on his chest. 'My heart's about to pound right through my cage of bones, Onrack!'

The Imass, settling back in his cross-legged position, regarded the wizard with calm, dark eyes. 'You have been pursued often. In your life.'

A grimace from Quick Ben, then he nodded. 'Feels like years and years of that.'

'There are two names to the song. Agkor Raella and Allish Raella. The wolf song, and the caribou song.'

'Ah, so my cud-chewing ways are exposed at last.'

Onrack smiled. 'One day, you must become the wolf.'

'Might be I already am,' Quick Ben said after a long moment. 'I've seen wolves – plenty of them around here, after all. Those long-legged ones with the smallish heads—'

'Ay.'

'Aye, right. And they're damned shy. I'd wager they don't go for the kill until the odds are well in their favour. The worst kind of gamblers, in fact. But very good at survival.'

'Shy,' Onrack said, nodding. 'Yet curious. The same pack follows us now for three days.'

'They enjoy scavenging your kills – let you take all the risks. Makes for a sweet deal.'

'Thus far,' Onrack said, 'there have been few risks.'

Quick Ben glanced over at Trull, then shook his head and said, 'That mountain sheep or whatever you call it not only charged you, Onrack, but it sent you flying. We thought it'd broken every bone in your body, and you just two days into your new one at that.'

'The bigger the prey, the more you must pay,' Onrack said, smiling again. 'In the way of gambling, yes?'

'Absolutely,' the wizard said, prodding at the meat on the spit. 'My point was, the wolf is the caribou until necessity forces otherwise. If the odds are too bad, the wolf runs. It's a matter of timing, of choosing the right moment to turn round and hold your ground. As for those wolves tracking us, well, I'd guess they've never seen our kind before—'

'No, Quick Ben,' Onrack said. 'The very opposite is true.'

Trull studied his friend for a moment, then asked, 'We're not alone here?'

'The ay knew to follow us. Yes, they are curious, but they are also clever, and they remember. They have followed Imass before.' He lifted his head and sniffed loudly. 'They are close tonight, those ay. Drawn to my song, which they have heard before. The ay know, you see, that tomorrow I will hunt dangerous prey. And when the moment of the kill comes, well, we shall see.'

'Just how dangerous?' Trull asked, suddenly uneasy.

'There is a hunting cat, an emlava – we entered its territory today, for I found the scrapes of its claim, on stone and on wood. A male by the flavour of its piss. Today, the ay were more nervous than usual, for the cat will kill them at every opportunity, and it is a creature of ambush. But I have assured them with my song. I found Tog'tol – yellow ochre – after all.'

'So,' Quick Ben said, his eyes on the dripping meat above the flames, 'if your wolves know we are here, how about the cat?'

'He knows.'

'Well, that's just terrific, Onrack. I'm going to need some warrens close to hand all damned day, then. That happens to be exhausting, you know.'

'You need not worry with the sun overhead, wizard,' Onrack said. 'The cat hunts at night.'

'Hood's breath! Let's hope those wolves smell it before we do!'

'They won't,' the Imass replied with infuriating calm. 'In scenting its territory, the emlava saturates the air with its sign. Its own body scent is much weaker, freeing the beast to move wherever it will when inside its territory.'

'Why are dumb brutes so damned smart, anyway?'

'Why are us smart folk so often stupidly brutal, Quick Ben?' Trull asked.

'Stop trying to confuse me in my state of animal terror, Edur.'

An uneventful night passed and now, the following day, they walked yet further into the territory of the emlava. Halting at a stream in mid-morning, Onrack had knelt beside it to begin his ritual washing of hands. At least, Trull assumed it was a ritual, although it might well have been another of those moments of breathless wonder that seemed to afflict Onrack – and no surprise there; Trull suspected he'd be staggering about for months after such a rebirth. *Of course, he does not think like us. I am much closer in my ways of thought to this human, Quick Ben, than I am to any Imass, dead or otherwise. How can that be?*

Onrack then rose and faced them, his spear in one hand, sword in the other. 'We are near the emlava's lair. Although he sleeps, he senses us. Tonight, he means to kill one of us. I shall now challenge his claim to this territory. If I fail, he may well leave you be, for he will feed on my flesh.'

But Quick Ben was shaking his head. 'You're not doing this alone, Onrack. Granted, I'm not entirely sure of how my sorcery will work in this place, but dammit, it's just a dumb cat, after all. A blinding flash of light, a loud sound—'

'And I will join you as well,' Trull Sengar said. 'We begin with spears, yes? I have fought enough wolves in my time. We will meet its charge with spears. Then, when it is wounded and crippled, we close with bladed weapons.'

Onrack studied them for a moment, then he smiled. 'I see that I will not dissuade you. Yet, for the fight itself, you must not interfere. I do not think I will fail, and you will see why before long.'

Trull and the wizard followed the Imass up the slope of an outwash fan that filled most of a crevasse, up among the lichen-clad, tilted and folded bedrock. Beyond this black-stone ledge rose a sheer wall of grey shale pocked with caves where sediments had eroded away beneath an endless torrent of glacial melt. The stream in which Onrack had plunged his hands earlier poured out from this cliff, forming a pool in one cavern that extended out to fill a basin before continuing down-slope. To the right of this was another cave, triangular in shape, with one entire side formed by a collapse in the shale overburden. The flat ground before it was scattered with splintered bones.

As they skirted the pool Onrack suddenly halted, lifting a hand.

A massive shape now filled the cave mouth.

Three heartbeats later, the emlava emerged.

'Hood's breath,' Quick Ben whispered.

Trull had expected a hunting cat little different from a mountain lion – perhaps one of the black ones rumoured to live in the deeper forests of his homeland. The creature hulking into view, blinking sleep from its charcoal eyes, was the size of a plains brown bear. Its enormous upper canines projected down past its lower jaw, long as a huntsman's knife and polished the hue of amber. The head was broad and flat, the ears small and set far back. Behind the short neck, the emlava's shoulders were hunched, forming a kind of muscled hump. Its fur was striped, black barbs on deep grey, although its throat revealed a flash of white.

'Not quite built for speed, is it?'

Trull glanced over at Quick Ben, saw the wizard holding a dagger in one hand. 'We should get you a spear,' the Tiste Edur said.

'I'll take one of your spares – if you don't mind.'

Trull slipped the bound clutch from his shoulder and said, 'Take your pick.'

The emlava was studying them. Then it yawned and with that Onrack moved lightly forward in a half-crouch.

As he did so, pebbles scattered nearby and Trull turned. 'Well, it seems Onrack has allies in this after all.'

The wolves – *ay* in the Imass language – had appeared and were now closing on Onrack's position, heads lowered and eyes fixed on the huge cat.

The sudden arrival of seven wolves clearly displeased the emlava, for it then lowered itself until its chest brushed the ground, gathering its legs beneath it. The mouth opened again, and a deep hiss filled the air.

'We might as well get out of their way,' Quick Ben said, taking a step back with obvious relief.

'I wonder,' Trull said as he watched the momentary stand-off, 'if this is how domestication first began. Not banding together in a hunt for prey, but in an elimination of rival predators.'

Onrack had readied his spear, not to meet a charge, but to throw the weapon using a stone-weighted antler atlatl. The wolves to his either side had fanned out, edging closer with fangs bared.

'Not a growl to be heard,' Quick Ben said. 'Somehow that's more chilling.'

'Growls are to warn,' Trull replied. 'There is fear in growls, just as there is in that cat's hissing.'

The emlava's single lungful of breath finally whistled down into silence. It refilled its lungs and began again.

Onrack lunged forward, the spear darting from his hand.

Flinching back, the emlava screamed as the weapon drove deep into its chest, just to one side of the neck and beneath the clavicle. At that moment the wolves rushed in.

A mortal wound, however, was not enough to slow the cat as it lashed out with two staggered swings of its forepaws at one of the wolves. The first paw sank talons deep into the wolf's shoulder, snatching the entire animal closer, within the reach of the second paw, which dragged the yelping wolf closer still. The massive head then snapped down on its neck, fangs burying themselves in flesh and bone.

The emlava, lurching, then drove its full weight down on the dying wolf, probably breaking every bone in its body.

As it did so, four other wolves lunged for its soft belly, two to each side, their canines tearing deep, then pulling away as, screaming, the emlava spun round to fend them off.

Exposing its neck.

Onrack's sword flashed, point-first, into the cat's throat.

It recoiled, sending one wolf tumbling, then reared back on its hind legs – as if to wheel and flee back into its cave – but all strength left the emlava then. It toppled, thumped hard onto the ground, and was still.

The six remaining wolves – one limping – padded away, keeping a distance between themselves and the three men, and moments later were gone from sight.

Onrack walked up to the emlava and tugged free his gore-spattered spear. Then he knelt beside the cat's head.

'Asking forgiveness?' Quick Ben queried, his tone only slightly ironic.

The Imass looked over at them. 'No, that would be dishonest, wizard.'

'You're right, it would. I am glad you're not dumping any blessed spirit rubbish on us. It's pretty obvious, isn't it, that there were *wars* long before there were wars between people. You had your rival hunters to dispose of first.'

'Yes, that is true. And we found allies. If you wish to find irony, Quick Ben, know that we then hunted until most of our prey was extinct. And our allies then starved – those that did not surrender to our stewardship.'

'The Imass are hardly unique in that,' Trull Sengar said.

Quick Ben snorted. 'That's understating it, Trull. So tell us, Onrack, why are you kneeling beside that carcass?'

'I have made a mistake,' the Imass replied, climbing to his feet and staring into the cave.

'Seemed pretty flawless to me.'

'The killing, yes, Quick Ben. But this emlava, it is female.'

The wizard grunted, then seemed to flinch. 'You mean the male's still around?'

'I do not know. Sometimes they . . . wander.' Onrack looked down at the bloodied spear in his hands. 'My friends,' he said. 'I am now . . . hesitant, I admit. Perhaps, long ago, I would not have thought twice –

as you said, wizard, we warred against our competitors. But this realm – it is a gift. All that was lost, because of our thoughtless acts, now lives again. Here. I wonder, can things be different?'

In the silence following that question, they heard, coming from the cave, the first pitiful cry.

'Did you ever wish, Udinaas, that you could sink inside stone? Shake loose its vast memories—'

The ex-slave glanced at Wither – a deeper smear in the gloom – then sneered. 'And see what they have seen? You damned wraith, stones can't see.'

'True enough. Yet they swallow sound and bind it trapped inside. They hold conversations with heat and cold. Their skins wear away to the words of the wind and the lick of water. Darkness and light live in their flesh – and they carry within them the echoes of wounding, of breaking, of being cruelly shaped—'

'Oh, enough!' Udinaas snapped, pushing a stick further into the fire. 'Go melt away into these ruins, then.'

'You are the last one awake, my friend. And yes, I *have* been in these ruins.'

'Games like those are bound to drive you mad.'

A long pause. 'You know things you have no right to know.'

'How about this, then? Sinking into stone is easy. It's getting out again that's hard. You can get lost, trapped in the maze. And on all sides, all those memories pressing in, pressing down.'

'It is your dreams, isn't it? Where you learn such things. Who speaks to you? Tell me the name of this fell mentor!'

Udinaas laughed. 'You fool, Wither. My mentor? Why, none other than *imagination*.'

'I do not believe you.'

There seemed little point in responding to that declaration. Staring into the flames, Udinaas allowed its flickering dance to lull him. He was tired. He should be sleeping. The fever was gone, the nightmarish hallucinations, the strange nectars that fed the tumbling delusions all seeped away, *like piss in moss. The strength I felt in those other worlds was a lie. The clarity, a deceit. All those offered ways forward, through what will come, every one a dead end. I should have known better.*

'K'Chain Nah'ruk, these ruins.'

'You still here, Wither? Why?'

'This was once a plateau on which the Short-Tails built a city. But now, as you can see, it is shattered. Now there is nothing but these dread slabs all pitched and angled – yet we have been working our way downward. Did you sense this? We will soon reach the centre, the heart of this crater, and we will see what destroyed this place.'

413

'The ruins,' said Udinaas, 'remember cool shadow. Then concussion. Shadow, Wither, in a flood to announce the end of the world. The concussion, well, that belonged to the shadow, right?'

'You know things—'

'You damned fool, listen to me! We came to the edge of this place, this high plateau, expecting to see it stretch out nice and flat before us. Instead, it looks like a frozen puddle onto which someone dropped a heavy rock. *Splat.* All the sides caved inward. Wraith, I don't need any secret knowledge to work this out. Something big came down from the sky – a meteorite, a sky keep, whatever. We trudged through its ash for days. Covering the ancient snow. Ash and dust, eating into that snow like acid. And the ruins, they're all toppled, blasted outward, then tilted inward. Out first, in second. Heave out and down, then slide back. Wither, all it takes is for someone to just *look*. *Really look.* That's it. So enough with all this mystical sealshit, all right?'

His tirade had wakened the others. *Too bad. Nearly dawn anyway.* Udinaas listened to them moving around, heard a cough, then someone hawking spit. *Which? Seren? Kettle?* The ex-slave smiled to himself. 'Your problem, Wither, is your damned expectations. You hounded me for months and months, and now you feel the need to have made it – me – worth all that attention. So here you are, pushing some kind of sage wisdom on this broken slave, but I told you then what I'll tell you now. I'm nothing, no-one. Understand? Just a man with a brain that, every now and then, actually works. Yes, I work it, because I find no comfort in being stupid. Unlike, I think, most people. Us Letherii, anyway. *Stupid and proud of it.* Belongs on the Imperial Seal, that happy proclamation. No wonder I failed so miserably.'

Seren Pedac moved into the firelight, crouching down to warm her hands. 'Failed at what, Udinaas?'

'Why, everything, Acquitor. No need for specifics here.'

Fear Sengar spoke from behind him. 'You were skilled, I recall, at mending nets.'

Udinaas did not turn round, but he smiled. 'Yes, I probably deserved that. My well-meaning tormentor speaks. Well-meaning? Oh, perhaps not. Indifferent? Possibly. Until, at least, I did something wrong. A badly mended net – aaii! Flay the fool's skin from his back! I know, it was all for my own good. Someone's, anyway.'

'Another sleepless night, Udinaas?'

He looked across the fire at Seren, but she was intent on the flames licking beneath her outstretched hands, as if the question had been rhetorical.

'I can see my bones,' she then said.

'They're not real bones,' Kettle replied, settling down with her legs drawn up. 'They look more like twigs.'

414

'Thank you, dear.'

'Bones are hard, like rock.' She set her hands on her knees and rubbed them. 'Cold rock.'

'Udinaas,' Seren said, 'I see puddles of gold in the ashes.'

'I found pieces of a picture frame.' He shrugged. 'Odd to think of K'Chain Nah'ruk hanging pictures, isn't it?'

Seren looked up, met his eyes. 'K'Chain—'

Silchas Ruin spoke as he stepped round a heap of cut stone. 'Not pictures. The frame was used to stretch skin. K'Chain moult until they reach adulthod. The skins were employed as parchment, for writing. The Nah'ruk were obsessive recorders.'

'You know a lot about creatures you killed on sight,' Fear Sengar said.

Clip's soft laughter sounded from somewhere beyond the circle of light, followed by the snap of rings on a chain.

Fear's head lifted sharply. 'That amuses you, pup?'

The Tiste Andii's voice drifted in, eerily disembodied. 'Silchas Ruin's dread secret. He parleyed with the Nah'ruk. There was this civil war going on, you see . . .'

'It will be light soon,' Silchas said, turning away.

Before too long, the group separated as it usually did. Striding well ahead were Silchas Ruin and Clip. Next on the path was Seren Pedac herself, while twenty or more paces behind her straggled Udinaas – still using the Imass spear as a walking stick – and Kettle and Fear Sengar.

Seren was not sure if she was deliberately inviting solitude upon herself. More likely some remnant of her old profession was exerting on her a disgruntled pressure to take the lead, deftly dismissing the presence ahead of the two Tiste warriors. *As if they don't count. As if they're intrinsically unreliable as guides . . . to wherever it is we're going.*

She thought back, often, on their interminable flight from Letheras, the sheer chaos of that trek, its contradictions of direction and purpose; the times when they were motionless – setting down tentative roots in some backwater hamlet or abandoned homestead – but their exhaustion did not ease then, for it was not of blood and flesh. Scabandari Bloodeye's soul awaited them, like some enervating parasite, in a place long forgotten. Such was the stated purpose, but Seren had begun, at last, to wonder.

Silchas had endeavoured to lead them west, ever west, and was turned aside each time – as if whatever threat the servants of Rhulad and Hannan Mosag presented was too vast to challenge. And that made no sense. *The bastard can change into a damned dragon. And is Silchas a pacifist at heart? Hardly. He kills with all the compunction of a man*

415

swatting mosquitoes. Did he turn us away to spare our lives? Again, unlikely. A dragon doesn't leave behind anything alive, does it?

Driven north, again and again, away from the more populated areas.

To the very edge of Bluerose, a region once ruled by Tiste Andii – *hiding still under the noses of Letherii and Edur – no, I do not trust any of this. I cannot. Silchas Ruin sensed his kin. He must have.*

Suspecting Silchas Ruin of deceit was one thing, voicing the accusation quite another. She lacked the courage. As simple as that. *Easier, isn't it, to just go along, and to keep from thinking too hard. Because thinking too hard is what Udinaas has done, and look at the state he's in. Yet, even then, he's managing to keep his mouth shut. Most of the time. He may be an ex-slave, he may be 'no-one' – but he is not a fool.*

So she walked alone. Bound by friendship to none – none here, in any case – and disinclined to change that.

The ruined city, little more than heaps of tumbled stone, rolled past on all sides, the slope ahead becoming ever steeper, and she thought, after a time, that she could hear the whisper of sand, crumbled mortar, fragments of rubble, as if their passage was yet further pitching this landscape, and as they walked they gathered to them streams of sliding refuse. *As if our presence alone is enough shift the balance.*

The whispering could have been voices, uttered beneath the wind, and she felt – with a sudden realization that lifted beads of sweat to her skin – within moments of understanding the words. *Of stone and broken mortar. I am sliding into madness indeed—*

'When the stone breaks, every cry escapes. Can you hear me now, Seren Pedac?'

'Is that you, Wither? Leave me be.'

'Are any warrens alive? Most would say no. Impossible. They are forces. Aspects. Proclivities manifest as the predictable – oh, the Great Thinkers who are long since dust worried this in fevered need, as befits the obsessed. But they did not understand. One warren lies like a web over all the others, and its voice is the will necessary to shape magic. They did not see it. Not for what it was. They thought . . . chaos, a web where each strand was undifferentiated energy, not yet articulated, not yet given shape by an Elder God's intent.'

She listened, as yet uncomprehending, even as her heart thundered in her chest and her each breath came in a harsh rasp. This, she knew, was not Wither's voice. Not the wraith's language. Not its cadence.

'But K'rul understood. Spilled blood is lost blood, powerless blood in the end. It dies when abandoned. Witness violent death for proof of that. For the warrens to thrive, coursing in their appointed rivers and streams, there must be a living body, a grander form that exists in itself. Not chaos. Not Dark, nor Light. Not heat, not cold. No, a conscious* *aversion to disorder. Negation to and of all else, when all else is dead. For the true face of Death is dissolution, and in dissolution there is chaos until the last mote of energy ceases its wilful glow, its persistent abnegation. Do you understand?'*

'No. Who are you?'

'There is another way, then, of seeing this. K'rul realized he could not do this alone. The sacrifice, the opening of his veins and arteries, would mean nothing, would indeed fail. Without living flesh, without organized functionality.

'Ah, the warrens, Seren Pedac, they are a dialogue. Do you see now?'

'No!'

Her frustrated cry echoed through the ruins. She saw Silchas and Clip halt and turn about.

Behind her, Fear Sengar called out, 'Acquitor? What is it you deny?'

Knowing laughter from Udinaas.

'Disregard the vicious crowd now, the torrent of sound overwhelming the warrens, the users, the guardians, the parasites and the hunters, the complicit gods elder and young. Shut them away, as Corlos taught you. To remember rape is to fold details into sensation, and so relive each time its terrible truth. He told you this could become habit, an addiction, until even despair became a welcome taste on your tongue. Understand, then – as only you can here – that to take one's own life is the final expression of despair. You saw that. Buruk the Pale. You felt that, at the sea's edge. Seren Pedac, K'rul could not act alone in this sacrifice, lest he fill every warren with despair.

'Dialogue. Presupposition, yes, of the plural. One with another. Or succession of others, for this dialogue must be ongoing, indeed, eternal.

'Do I speak of the Master of the Holds? The Master of the Deck? Perhaps – the face of the other is ever turned away – to all but K'rul himself. This is how it must be. The dialogue, then, is the feeding of power. Power unimaginable, power virtually omnipotent, unassailable . . . so long as that other's face remains ... turned away.

'From you. From me. From all of us.'

She stared wildly about then, at these tilted ruins, this endless scree of destruction.

'The dialogue, however, can be sensed if not heard – such is its power. The construction of language, the agreement in principle of meaning and intent, the rules of grammar – Seren Pedac, what did you think Mockra was? If not a game of grammar? Twisting semantics, turning inference, inviting suggestion, reshaping a mind's internal language to deceive its own senses?

'Who am I?

'Why, Seren Pedac, I am Mockra.'

The others were gathered round her now. She found herself on her knees, driven there by revelation – there would be bruises, an appalling softness in the tissue where it pressed against hard pavestone. She registered this, as she stared up at the others. Reproachful communication, between damaged flesh and her mind, between her senses and her brain.

She shunted those words aside, then settled into a sweet, painless calm.

As easy as that.

'Beware, there is a deadly risk in deceiving oneself. You can blind youself to your own damage. You can die quickly in that particular game, Seren Pedac. No, if you must . . . experiment . . . then choose another.

'Corlos would have showed you that, had he the time with you.'

'So – so he knows you?'

'Not as intimately as you. There are few so . . . blessed.'

'But you are not a god, are you?'

'You need not ask that, Seren Pedac.'

'You are right. But still, you are *alive*.'

She heard amusement in the reply. *'Unless my greatest deceit is the announcement of my own existence! There are rules in language, and language is needed for the stating of the rules. As K'rul understood, the blood flows out, and then it returns. Weak, then enlivened. Round and round. Who then, ask yourself, who then is the enemy?'*

'I don't know.'

'Not yet, perhaps. You will need to find out, however, Seren Pedac. Before we are through.'

She smiled. 'You give me a purpose?'

'Dialogue, my love, must not end.'

'Ours? Or the other one?'

'Your companions think you fevered now. Tell me, before we part, which you would choose. For your experiments?'

She blinked up at the half-circle of faces. Expressions of concern, mockery, curiosity, indifference. 'I don't know,' she said. 'It seems . . . cruel.'

'Power ever is, Seren Pedac.'

'I won't decide, then. Not yet.'

'So be it.'

'Seren?' Kettle asked. 'What is wrong with you?'

She smiled, then pushed herself to her feet, Udinaas – to her astonishment – reaching out to help her regain her balance.

Seeing her wince, he half smiled. 'You landed hard, Acquitor. Can you walk?' His smile broadened. 'Perhaps no faster than the rest of us laggards, now?'

'You, Udinaas? No, I think not.'

He frowned. 'Just the two of us right now,' he said.

Her eyes flickered up to meet his, shied away, then returned again – hard. 'You heard?'

'Didn't need to,' he replied under his breath as he set the Imass walking stick into her hands. 'Had Wither sniffing at my heels long before I left the north.' He shrugged.

Silchas Ruin and Clip had already resumed the journey.

Leaning on the Imass spear, Seren Pedac walked alongside the ex-slave, struggling with a sudden flood of emotion for this broken man. *Perhaps, true comrades after all. He and I.*

'Seren Pedac.'

'Yes?'

'Stop shifting the pain in your knees into mine, will you?'

Stop – what? Oh.

'Either that or give me that damned stick back.'

'If I say "sorry" then, well . . .'

'You give it away. Well, say it if you mean it, and either way we'll leave it at that.'

'Sorry.'

His surprised glance delighted her.

The rising sea level had saturated the ground beneath the village. Anyone with half their wits would have moved to the stony, treed terrace bordering the flood plain, but the sordid remnants of the Shake dwelling here had simply levered their homes onto stilts and raised the slatted walkways, living above fetid, salty bog crawling with the white-backed crabs known as skullcaps.

Yan Tovis, Yedan Derryg and the troop of lancers reined in at Road's End, the ferry landing and its assorted buildings on their left, a mass of felled trees rotting into the ground on their right. The air was chill, colder than it should have been this late into spring, and tendrils of low-lying fog hid most of the salt marsh beneath the stilts and bridged walkways.

Among the outbuildings of the landing – all situated on higher ground – there was a stone-walled stable fronted by a courtyard of planed logs, and beyond that, facing the village, an inn without a name.

Dismounting, Yan Tovis stood beside her horse for a long moment, her eyes closing. *We have been invaded. I should be riding to every garrison on this coast – Errant fend, they must know by now. Truth delivered the hard way. The empire is at war.*

But she was now Queen of the Last Blood, Queen of the Shake. Opening her weary eyes she looked upon the decrepit fishing village. *My people, Errant help me.* Running away had made sense back then. It made even more sense now.

Beside her, Yedan Derryg, her half-brother, loosened the strap of his visored helm, then said, 'Twilight, what now?'

She glanced over at him, watched the rhythmic bunching of his bearded jaw. She understood the question in all its ramifications. *What now? Do the Shake proclaim their independence, rising eager in the chaos of a Malazan-Letherii war? Do we gather our arms, our young whom we would call soldiers? The Shake cry out their liberty, and the sound is devoured by the shore's rolling surf.*

She sighed. 'I was in command on the Reach, when the Edur came in their ships. We surrendered. I surrendered.'

To do otherwise would have been suicidal. Yedan should have said those words, then. For he knew the truth of them. Instead, he seemed to chew again for a moment, before turning to squint at the flat, broad ferry. 'That's not slipped its mooring in some time, I think. The coast north of Awl must be flooded.'

He gives me nothing. 'We shall make use of it, all the way out to Third Maiden Fort.'

A nod.

'Before that, however, we must summon the witches and warlocks.'

'You'll find most of them huddled in the village yonder, Queen. And Pully and Skwish will have announced your return. Taloned toes are tapping the floorboards, I would wager.'

'Go down there,' she commanded, facing the inn. 'Escort them back here – I will be in the tavern.'

'And if the tavern is not big enough?'

An odd concern. She began walking towards the entrance. 'Then they can perch on shoulders like the crows they are, Yedan.'

'Twilight.'

She half turned.

Yedan was tightening the straps of his helm once again. 'Do not do it.'

'Do not do what?'

'Send us to war, sister.'

She studied him.

But he said nothing more, and a moment later he had turned away and set off down towards the village.

She resumed her walk, while her soldiers led the mounts towards the stable, the beasts' hoofs slipping on the slick logs of the courtyard. They had ridden hard, these last horses drawn from a virtually empty garrison fort just north of Tulamesh – reports of bandits had sent the squads into the countryside and they'd yet to return. Yan Tovis believed they would never do so.

At the entranceway she paused, looking down at the slab of stone beneath her boots, on which were carved Shake runes.

'*This Raised Stone honours Teyan Atovis, Rise, who was claimed by the Shore 1113th Year of the Isle. Slain by the Letherii for Debts Unremitted.*'

Yan Tovis grunted. One of her kin, no less, dead a thousand years now. 'Well, Teyan,' she muttered, 'you died of drink, and now your stone straddles the threshold of a tavern.' True, some list of mysterious, crushing debts had invited his ignoble fall to alcohol and misery, but this grand commemoration had taken a slanted view on the hands guiding the man's fate. And now . . . *Brullyg would be Rise. Will you wear the crown as well as Teyan did?*

She pushed open the door and strode inside.

The low-ceilinged room was crowded, every face turned to her.

A familiar figure pushed into view, her face a mass of wrinkles twisted into a half-smile.

'Pully,' Twilight said, nodding. 'I have just sent the Watch down to the village to find you.'

'Be well he'll find Skwish and a score others. They be well weaving cob to web on th' close sea beyond the shore, Queen, an' all the truths writ there. Strangers—'

'I know,' Yan Tovis interjected, looking past the old hag and scanning the other witches and warlocks, the Shoulderfolk of the Old Ways. Their eyes glittered in the smoky gloom, and Twilight could now smell these Shake elders – half-unravelled damp wool and patchy sealskin, fish-oil and rank sweat, the breath coming from mouths dark with sickened gums or rotting teeth.

If there was a proprietor to this tavern he or she had fled. Casks had been broached and tankards filled with pungent ale. A huge pot of fish soup steamed on the centre hearth and there were countless gourd-shell bowls scattered on the tables. Large rats waddled about on the filthy floor.

Far more witches than warlocks, she noted. This had been a discernible trend among the demon-kissed – fewer and fewer males born bearing the accepted number of traits; most were far too demonic. *More than two hundred of the Shoulderfolk. Gathered here.*

'Queen,' Pully ventured, ducking her head. 'Cob to web, all of Shake blood know that you now rule. Barring them that's on the Isle, who only know that your mother's dead.'

'So Brullyg is there, anticipating . . .'

'Aye, Twilight, that be well he will be Rise, King of the Shake.'

Errant take me. 'We must sail to the Isle.'

A murmur of agreement amidst the eager quaffing of ale.

'You intend, this night,' Yan Tovis said, 'a ritual.'

'We are loosening the chains as they say, Queen. There are nets be strung across the path of the world, t'see what we catch.'

'No.'

Pully's black eyes narrowed. 'What's that?'

'No. There will be no ritual tonight. Nor tomorrow night, nor the next. Not until we are on the Isle, and perhaps not even then.'

Not a sound in the tavern now.

Pully opened her mouth, shut it, then opened it again. 'Queen, the shore be alive wi' voices as they say and the words they are for us. These – these they be the Old Ways, *our* ways—'

'And my mother was in the habit of looking away, yes. But I am not.' She lifted her head and scanned once more the array of faces, seeing the shock, the anger, the growing malice. 'The Old Ways failed us. Then and now. Your ways,' she told them in a hard voice, 'have failed us all. I am Queen. Twilight on the shore. At my side in my rule is the Watch. Brullyg would be Rise – that remains to be seen, for your proclamation is not cause enough, not even close. Rise is chosen by all the Shake. *All.*'

'*Do not mar us, Queen.*' Pully's smile was gone. Her face was a mask of venom.

Yan Tovis snorted. 'Will you send a curse my way, old woman? Do not even think it. I mean to see my people survive, through all that will happen. From all of you, I will need healing, I will need blessing. You rule no longer – no, do not speak to me of my mother. I know better than any of you the depths of her surrender. I am Queen. Obey me.'

They were not happy. They had been the true power for so long – if that pathetic curse-weaving in the shadows could be called power – and Yan Tovis knew that this struggle had but just begun, for all their apparent acquiescence. *They will begin planning my downfall. It is to be expected.*

Yedan Derryg, never mind watching the shore. You must now watch my back.

Fiddler opened his eyes. Dusk had just begun to settle. Groaning, he rolled onto his back. Too many years of sleeping on hard, cold ground; too many years of a tattered rain cape for a mattress, a single blanket of coarse wool for cover. At least now he was sleeping through the day, easing his old bones with the sun's warmth.

Sitting up, he looked round the glade. Huddled figures on all sides. Just beyond them was Koryk, the sleep's last watch, sitting on a tree stump. *Aye, woodcutters in this forest.*

Not that we've seen any.

Three nights since the landing. Ever moving eastward, inland. *A strange empire, this. Roads and tracks and the occasional farmstead, barely a handful of towns on the coast that we saw. And where in Hood's name are these Tiste Edur?*

Fiddler climbed to his feet, arching his back to work out the aches and twinges. He'd wanted to be a soldier named Strings, here among the Bonehunters, a different man, a new man. But that hadn't worked so well. The conceit had fooled no-one. Even worse, he could not convince himself that he had begun anew, that the legacy of past campaigns could be put aside. *A life don't work that way. Dammit.* He trudged over to Koryk.

The Seti half-blood glanced up. 'Some damned war we got ourselves here, Sergeant. I'd even take one of Smiles's knives in the leg just to get us the smell of blood. Let's forget these damned Edur and go ahead and start killing Letherii.'

'Farmers and swineherds, Koryk? We need them on our side, remember?'

'So far there ain't been enough of them to muster a damned squad. Least we should show ourselves—'

'Not yet. Besides, it's probably been just bad luck we haven't met the enemy yet. I'd wager other squads have already been in a scrap or two.'

Koryk grunted. 'I doubt it. All it takes is just one squad to kick the nest and these woods should be swarming. They ain't.'

Fiddler had nothing to say to that. He scratched himself, then turned away. 'Shut your eyes for a time now, soldier. We'll wake you when breakfast's ready.'

Do your complainin' now, Koryk, because when this lets loose we'll look back on sunsets like this one like it was idyllic paradise. Still, how many times could he make that promise? The legacy of the Bonehunters thus far was nothing to sing songs about. Even Y'Ghatan had been a mess, with them whistling a song while they walked right into a trap. It galled him still, that one. He should have smelled trouble. Same for Gesler – *aye, we let them down that day. Badly.*

Malaz City had been worse. True, weapons had been drawn. There'd even been a shield-line for a few squads of marines. *Against Malazans. An undisciplined mob of our own people.* Somehow, somewhere, this army needed to fight for real.

The Adjunct had thrown them onto this coast, like a handful of ticks onto a dog's back. Sooner or later the beast was going to scratch.

As the others wakened to the coming of night, Fiddler walked over to his pack. Stood studying it for a time. The Deck was in there, waiting. And he was sorely tempted. Just to get a taste of what was coming. *Don't be a fool, Fid. Remember Tattersail. Remember all the good it did her.*

'Bad idea, Sergeant.'

Fiddler glanced over, scowled. 'Stop reading my mind, Bottle. You're not as good at it as you think.'

'You're like a man who's sworn off drink but carries a flask in his pouch.'

'Enough of that, soldier.'

Bottle shrugged, looked round. 'Where's Gesler gone?'

'Probably off fertilizing the trees.'

'Maybe,' Bottle said, sounding unconvinced. 'It's just that I woke up earlier, and didn't see him then either.'

Gods below. Waving at midges, Fiddler walked over to the far end of the glade, where the other squad was positioned. He saw Stormy standing like a sleep-addled bear – his red hair and beard a wild mass of twig-filled tangles – repeatedly kicking the side of a loudly snoring Shortnose.

'Stormy,' Fiddler called out softly, 'where's your sergeant gone to?'

'No idea,' the huge man replied. 'He had last watch on this side, though. Hey, Fid, she wouldn't have burned the *Silanda*, would she?'

'Of course not. Listen, if Gesler ain't back soon you're going to have to go looking for him.'

Stormy's small porcine eyes blinked at him. 'Might be he's lost? I didn't think of that.'

'Never mind that dimwitted act, Corporal.'

'Yeah. That Koryk you got, he any good at tracking?'

'No. Damned near useless in fact, although don't say that to his face. Bottle—'

'Oh, him. That one gives me the creeps, Fid. Masturbates like I pick my nose. Now sure, soldiers will do that, but—'

'He says it's not him.'

'Well, if Smiles wants to reach in under the covers—'

'Smiles? What are you going on about, Stormy?'

'I mean—'

'Look, Bottle's haunted by a damned ghost of some kind – Quick Ben confirmed it, so stop giving me that look. Anyway, that ghost's, uh, female, and she likes him way too much—'

'Mages are sick, Fid.'

'Not a relevant point here, Stormy.'

'So you say,' the corporal said, shaking himself then turning away. ' "*Not a relevant point here,*" ' he mimicked under his breath.

'I can still hear you, Corporal.'

Stormy waved a wide, hairy hand but did not turn round, instead making his way towards the hearth. He paused in his first step to set his boot down on one of Shortnose's hands. There was an audible crack and the heavy infantryman made a small sound, then sat up. Stormy continued on, while Shortnose looked down at his hand, frowning at the oddly angled third finger, which he then reset with a tug, before rising and wandering off to find somewhere to empty his bladder.

Fiddler scratched at his beard, then swung about and walked back to his squad.

Aye, we're a lethal bunch.

Gesler wandered the strange ruins. The light was fast fading, making the place seem even more spectral. Round wells on all sides, at least a dozen scattered among the old trees. The stones were exquisitely cut, fitted without mortar – as he had discovered upon peeling back some moss. He had caught sight of the regular shapes from the edge of the glade, had first thought them to be the pedestals for some colonnaded structure long since toppled over. But the only other stone he found was paving, buckled by roots, making footing treacherous.

Seating himself on the edge of one of the wells, he peered down into the inky blackness, and could smell stagnant water. He felt oddly pleased with himself to find that his curiosity had not been as thoroughly dulled as he'd once believed. Not nearly as bad as, say, Cuttle. Now there was a grim bastard. Still, Gesler had seen a lot in his life, and some of it had permanently stained his skin – not to mention other, more subtle changes. But mostly that host of things witnessed, deeds done, not done, they just wore a man down.

He could not look at the tiny flames of the squad's hearth without remembering Truth and that fearless plunge into Y'Ghatan's palace. Or he'd glance down at the crossbow in his hands as they stumbled through this damned forest and recall Pella, skewered through the forehead, sagging against the corner of a building barely a hundred paces into Y'Ghatan itself. With every crow's cackle he heard the echoes of the screams when dread ghosts had assailed the camp of the Dogslayers at Raraku. A glance down at his bared hands and their battered knuckles, and the vision rose in his mind of that Wickan, Coltaine, down on the banks of the Vathar – *gods, to have led that mob that far, with more still to go, with nothing but cruel betrayal at the Fall.*

The slaughter of the inhabitants of Aren, when the Logros T'lan Imass rose from the dust of the streets and their weapons of stone began to rise and fall, rise and fall. If not for that ex-Red Blade driving open the gates and so opening a path of escape, there would have been no survivors at all. None. *Except us Malazans, who could only stand aside and watch the slaughter. Helpless as babes . . .*

A dragon through fire, a ship riding flames – his first sight of a Tiste Edur: dead, pinned to his chair by a giant's spear. Oar benches where sat decapitated rowers, hands resting on the sweeps, and their severed heads heaped in a pile round the mainmast, eyes blinking in the sudden light, faces twisting into appalling expressions—

So who built twelve wells in a forest? That's what I want to know. Maybe.

He recalled a knock at the door, and opening it to see, with absurd delight, a drenched T'lan Imass whom he recognized. *Stormy, it's for you. And aye, I dream of moments like this, you red-haired ox.* And what did that say about Gesler himself? *Wait, I'm not that curious.*

'There you are.'

Gesler looked up. 'Stormy. I was just thinking of you.'

'Thinking what?'

He waved at the well's black hole. 'If you'd fit, of course. Most of you would go, but not, alas, your head.'

'You keep forgetting, Gesler,' the corporal said as he drew nearer, 'I was one of the ones who punched back.'

'Got no recollection of that at all.'

'Want me to remind you?'

'What I want is to know why you're bothering me.'

'We're all gettin' ready to head out.'

'Stormy.'

'What?'

'What do you think about all this?'

'Someone liked building wells.'

'Not this. I mean, the war. This war, the one here.'

'I'll let you know once we start busting heads.'

'And if that never happens?'

Stormy shrugged, ran thick fingers through his knotted beard. 'Just another typical Bonehunter war, then.'

Gesler grunted. 'Go on, lead the way. Wait. How many battles have we fought, you and me?'

'You mean, with each other?'

'No, you damned idiot. I mean against other people. How many?'

'I lost count.'

'Liar.'

'All right. Thirty-seven, but not counting Y'Ghatan since I wasn't there. Thirty-eight for you, Gesler.'

'And how many did we manage to avoid?'

'Hundreds.'

'So maybe, old friend, we're just getting better at this.'

The huge Falari scowled. 'You trying to ruin my day, Sergeant?'

Koryk tightened the straps of his bulky pack. 'I just want to kill someone,' he growled.

Bottle rubbed at his face then eyed the half-blood Seti. 'There's always Smiles. Or Tarr, if you jump him when he's not looking.'

'You being funny?'

'No, just trying to deflect your attention from the weakest guy in this squad. Namely, me.'

'You're a mage. Sort of. You smell like one, anyway.'

'What does that mean?'

426

'If I kill you, you'd just curse me with your last breath, then I'd be miserable.'

'So what would change, Koryk?'

'Having a reason to be miserable is always worse than having no reason but being miserable anyway. If it's just a way of life, I mean.' He suddenly drew out the latest weapon in his arsenal, a long-knife. 'See this? Just like the kind Kalam used. It's a damned fast weapon, but I can't see it doing much against armour.'

'Where Kalam stuck them there wasn't no armour. Throat, armpit, crotch – you should give it to Smiles.'

'I grabbed it to *keep* it from her, idiot.'

Bottle looked over to where Smiles had, moments earlier, disappeared into the forest. She was on her way back, the placid expression on her face hiding all sorts of evil, no doubt. 'I hope we're not expected to stand against Edur the way heavies are,' he said to Koryk while watching Smiles. 'Apart from you and Tarr, and maybe Corabb, we're not a big mailed fist kind of squad, are we? So, in a way, this kind of war suits us – subterfuge, covert stuff.' He glanced over and saw the half-blood glaring at him. Still holding the long-knife. 'But maybe we're actually more versatile. We can be half mailed fist and half black glove, right?'

'Anyway,' Koryk said, resheathing the weapon, 'when I said I wanted to kill someone I meant the enemy.'

'Tiste Edur.'

'Letherii bandits will do – there must be bandits around here somewhere.'

'Why?'

'What do you mean, why? There's always bandits in the countryside, Bottle. Led by moustached rogues with fancy names. Zorala Snicker, or Pamby Doughty—'

A loud snort from Smiles, who had just arrived. 'I remember those stories. Pamby Doughty with the feather in his hat and his hunchback sidekick, Pomolo Paltry the Sly. Stealers of the Royal Treasure of Li Heng. Cutters of the Great Rope that held Drift Avalii in one place. And Zorala, who as a child climbed the tallest tree in the forest, then found he couldn't get back down, so that's where he lived for years, growing up. Until the woodsman came—'

'Gods below,' Cuttle growled from the blankets he remained under, 'someone cut her throat, please.'

'Well,' Smiles said with a tight, eponymous curve of her mouth, 'at least I started the night in a good mood.'

'She means she had a most satisfying—'

'Clack the teeth together, Koryk, or I'll cut those braids off when you're sleeping and trust me, you won't like what I'll use 'em for. And you, Bottle, don't let that give you any ideas, neither.

427

I took the blame for something you did once, but never again.'

'I wouldn't cut off Koryk's braids,' Bottle said. 'He needs them to sneeze into.'

'Get moving, Cuttle,' Fiddler said as he strode among them. 'Look at Corabb – he's the only one actually ready—'

'No I'm not,' the man replied. 'I just fell asleep in my armour, Sergeant, and now I need somewhere to pee. Only—'

'Never mind,' Fiddler cut in. 'Let's see if we can't stumble onto some Edur tonight.'

'We could start a forest fire,' Koryk said.

'But we happen to be in it,' Tarr pointed out.

'It was just an idea.'

Corabb Bhilan Thenu'alas admitted to himself that these Malazans were nothing like the soldiers of the Dogslayers, or the warriors of Leoman's army. He was not even sure if they were human. More like ... animals. Endlessly bickering ones at that, like a pack of starving dogs.

They pretty much ignored him, which was a good thing. Even Bottle, to whom the sergeant had instructed Corabb to stay close. Guarding someone else's back was something Corabb was familiar with, so he had no issue with that command. Even though Bottle was a mage and he wasn't too sure about mages. They made deals with gods – but one didn't have to be a mage to do that, he knew. No, one could be a most trusted leader, a commander whose warriors would follow him into the pit of the Abyss itself. Even someone like that could make deals with gods, and so doom his every follower in a fiery cataclysm even as that one ran away.

Yes, ran away.

He was pleased that he had got over all that. Old history, and old history was old so it didn't mean anything any more, because . . . well, because it was old. He had a new history, now. It had begun in the rubble beneath Y'Ghatan. Among these . . . animals. Still, there was Fiddler and Corabb knew he would follow his sergeant because the man was worth following. Not like some people.

An army of fourteen seemed a little small, but it would have to do for now. He hoped, however, that somewhere ahead – further inland – they'd come to a desert. Too many trees in this wet, bad-smelling forest. And he'd like to get on a horse again, too. All this walking was, he was certain, unhealthy.

As the squad left the glade, slipping into the deeper darkness beyond, he moved alongside Bottle, who glanced over and grimaced. 'Here to protect me from bats, Corabb?'

The warrior shrugged. 'If they try attacking you I will kill them.'

'Don't you dare. I happen to like bats. I talk to them, in fact.'

'The same as that rat and her pups you kept, right?'

'Exactly.'

'I was surprised, Bottle, that you left them to burn on the transports.'

'I'd never do that. I shipped them onto the *Froth Wolf*. Some time ago, in fact—'

'So you could spy on the Adjunct, yes.'

'It was an act of mercy – the one ship I knew would be safe, you see—'

'And so you could spy.'

'All right, fine. So I could spy. Let's move on to another subject. Did Leoman ever tell you about his bargain with the Queen of Dreams?'

Corabb scowled. 'I don't like that subject. It's *old history*, which means nobody talks about it any more.'

'Fine, so why didn't you go with him? I'm sure he offered.'

'I will kill the next bat I see.'

Someone hissed from up ahead: '*Stop that jabbering, idiots!*'

Corabb wished he was riding a fine horse, across a sun-blistered desert – no-one could truly understand the magic wonder of water, unless they had spent time in a desert. Here, there was so much of it a man's feet could rot off and that wasn't right. 'This land is mad,' he muttered.

Bottle grunted. 'More like deathless. Layer on layer, ghosts tangled in every root, squirming restlessly under every stone. Owls can see them, you know. Poor things.'

Another hiss from ahead of them.

It started to rain.

Even the sky holds water in contempt. Madness.

Trantalo Kendar, youngest son among four brothers in a coastal clan of the Beneda Tiste Edur, rode with surprising grace, unmatched by any of his Edur companions, alas. He was the only one in his troop who actually liked horses. Trantalo had been a raw fifteen years of age at the conquest, unblooded, and the closest he had come to fighting had been as an apprentice to a distantly related aunt who had served as a healer in Hannan Mosag's army.

Under her bitter command, he had seen the terrible damage war did to otherwise healthy warriors. The ghastly wounds, the suppurating burns and limbs withered from Letherii sorcery. And, walking the fields of battle in search of the wounded, he had seen the same horrid destruction among dead and dying Letherii soldiers.

Although young, something of the eagerness for battle had left him then, driving him apart from his friends. Too many spilled out intestines, too many crushed skulls, too many desperate pleas for help answered by naught but crows and gulls. He had bound countless wounds, had stared into the glazed eyes of warriors shocked by their own mortality, or, worse, despairing with the misery of lost limbs, scarred faces, lost futures.

He did not count himself clever, nor in any other way exceptional – barring, perhaps, his talent for riding horses – but he now rode with eleven veteran Edur warriors, four of them Beneda, including the troop commander, Estav Kendar, Trantalo's eldest brother. And he was proud to be at the column's head, first down this coastal track that led to Boaral Keep, where, as he understood it, some sort of Letherii impropriety demanded Edur attention.

This was as far south from Rennis as he had been since managing to flee his aunt's clutches just inland of the city of Awl. Trantalo had not seen the walls of Letheras, nor the battlefields surrounding it, and for that he was glad, for he had heard that the sorcery in those final clashes had been the most horrifying of them all.

Life in Rennis had been one of strange privilege. To be Tiste Edur alone seemed sufficient reason for both fear and respect among the subservient Letherii. He had exulted in the respect. The fear had dismayed him, but he was not so naive as not to understand that without that fear, there would be none of the respect that so pleased him. *'The threat of reprisal,'* Estav had told him the first week of his arrival. *'This is what keeps the pathetic creatures cowering. And there will be times, young brother, when we shall have to remind them – bloodily – of that threat.'*

Seeking to tug down his elation was the apprehension that this journey, down to this in-the-middle-of-nowhere keep, was just that – the delivery of reprisal. Blood-splashed adjudication. It was no wonder the Letherii strove to keep the Edur out of such disputes. *We are not interested in niceties. Details bore us. And so swords will be drawn, probably this very night.*

Estav would make no special demands of him, he knew. It was enough that he rode point on the journey. Once at the keep, Trantalo suspected he would be stationed to guard the gate or some such thing. He was more than satisfied with that.

The sun's light was fast fading on the narrow track leading to the keep. They had a short time earlier left the main coastal road, and here on this lesser path the banks were steep, almost chest-high were one standing rather than riding, and braided with dangling roots. The trees pressed in close from both sides, branches almost entwining overhead. Rounding a twist in the trail, Trantalo caught first sight of the stockade, the rough boles – still bearing most of their bark – irregularly tilted and sunken. A half-dozen decrepit outbuildings crouched against a stand of alders and birch to the left and a flatbed wagon with a broken axle squatted in high grasses just to the right of the gate.

Trantalo drew rein before the the entrance. The gate was open. The single door, made of saplings and a Z-shaped frame of planks, had been pushed well to one side and left there, its base snarled with grasses. The warrior could see through to the compound beyond, oddly lifeless. Hearing his fellow Edur draw closer at the canter, he edged his horse forward until he made out the smoke-stained façade of the keep itself. No lights from any of the vertical slit windows. And the front door yawned wide.

'Why do you hesitate, Trantalo?' Estav inquired as he rode up.

'Preda,' Trantalo said, delighting, as ever, in these new Letherii titles, 'the keep appears to be abandoned. Perhaps we have ridden to the wrong one—'

'Boaral,' affirmed a warrior behind Estav. 'I've been here before.'

'And is it always this quiet?' Estav asked, one brow lifting in the way Trantalo knew so well.

'Nearly,' the warrior said, rising gingerly on the swivelling Letherii stirrups to look round. 'There should be at least two torches, one planted above that wagon – then one in the courtyard itself.'

'No guards?'

'Should be at least one – could be he's staggered off to the latrine trench—'

'No,' said Estav, 'there's no-one here.' He worked his horse past Trantalo's and rode through the gate.

Trantalo followed.

The two brothers approached the stepped front entrance to the keep.

'Estav, something wet on those stairs.'

'You're right. Good eye, brother.' The Beneda warrior dismounted with obvious relief, passing the reins over to Trantalo, then strode towards the steps. 'Blood-trail.'

'Perhaps a mutiny?'

The other Edur had left their horses with one of their company and were now moving out across the courtyard to search the stables, smithy, coop and well-house.

Estav stood at the base of the steps, eyes on the ground. 'A body has been dragged outside,' he said, tracking the blood-trail.

Trantalo saw his brother's head lift to face the stable. As it did Estav grunted suddenly, then abruptly sat down.

'Estav?'

Trantalo looked out to the courtyard, in time to see four warriors crumple. Sudden shouts from the three near the stables, as something like a rock sailed down into their midst.

A flash of fire. A solid, *cracking* sound. The three were thrown onto their backs. As a small cloud bloomed, there was shrieking.

Trantalo kicked his boots free of the stirrups, swung one leg over then dropped down into a crouch. His mouth was dry as tinder. His heart pounded so hard in his chest he felt half deafened by its drumbeat. Drawing his sword, he hurried over to his brother.

'Estav?'

Sitting, legs out before him in the careless manner of a child, hands resting on the muddy ground. Something was jutting from his chest. A hand's length of a shaft, thicker than a normal arrow, the fletching curved fins of leather. Blood had poured down from Estav's mouth, covering his chin and soaking into the front of his woollen cloak. His staring eyes did not blink.

'*Estav?*'

In the courtyard, the sharp clash of blades.

Disbelieving, Trantalo dragged his eyes from his brother's corpse. Two Edur warriors were attempting a fighting withdrawal, backing towards the uneasy horses that still stood five or so paces in from the gate. The Edur who had been left with them was on his hands and knees, crawling for the opening. There was something jutting from the side of his head.

Difficult to make out who the attackers were in the darkness, but they were well armed and armoured, four in all, maintaining close contact with the last two Edur.

Smudged movement behind them – Trantalo leapt to his feet, about to cry out a warning, when sudden fire filled his throat. Gagging, he lurched away and felt something cold slide out from the side of his neck. Blood gushed down, inside and out. Coughing, drowning, he fell to one knee, almost within reach of his brother. Blindness closing in, he lunged towards Estav, arms outstretched.

Estav?

He never made it.

Managing a straight line, Hellian walked out from the stable. She was slightly shivering, now that the time of serious sweating had passed. Fighting always evened her out. She didn't know why that was the case, but it was and all in all probably a good thing, too. 'Someone light a damned lantern,' she growled. 'You, Maybe, put that sharper away – we got 'em all.' She let out a loud sigh. 'The big nasty enemy.'

Drawing nearer the two Edur down in front of the keep, she waved her sword. 'Tavos, check those two. It ain't enough to stab 'im then just stand there looking down. Might be one last bite in 'im, you know.'

'Both dead as my sex-life,' Tavos Pond said. 'Who sniped the first one, Sergeant? Damned fine shot.'

'Lutes,' she replied, now watching Urb lead the others on a walk-past of the Edur bodies in the courtyard. 'Leaned the weapon on my back.'

'Your back?'

'I was throwing up, if it's any of your business. Between heaves, he let go. Got him dead centre, didn't he?'

'Aye, Sergeant.'

'And you didn't want t'bring the rum. Well, that's why I'm in charge and you're not. Where's my corporal?'

'Here.

'Here.'

'Gather up them horses – I don't care what the Fist ordered, we're going to ride.'

At that Urb glanced over, then approached. 'Hellian—'

'Don't even try to sweet-talk me. I almost remember what you did.' She drew out her flask and drank down a mouthful. 'So be careful, Urb. Now, everybody who loosed quarrels go find them and that means all of them!' She looked back down at the two dead Edur by the entrance.

'Think we're the first to draw blood?' Tavos Pond asked, crouching to clean the blade of his sword on the cloak of the older Edur.

'Big fat war, Tavos Pond. That's what we got ourselves here.'

'They weren't so hard, Sergeant.'

'Wasn't expecting nothing either, were they? You think we can just ambush our way all the way to Letheras? Think again.' She drank a couple more mouthfuls, then sighed and glowered over at Urb. 'How soon before they're the ones doing the ambushin'? That's why I mean for us to ride – we're gonna stay ahead of the bad news 's long as we can. That way we can *be* the bad news, right? The way it's s'posed t'be.'

Corporal Reem walked up to Urb. 'Sergeant, we got us twelve horses.'

'So we get one each,' Hellian said. 'Perfect.'

'By my count,' said Reem with narrowed eyes, 'someone's going to have to ride double.'

'If you say so. Now, let's get these bodies dragged away – they got any coin? Anybody checked?'

'Some,' said Maybe. 'But mostly just polished stones.'

'Polished stones?'

'First I thought slingstones, but none of them's carrying slings. So, aye, Sergeant. Polished stones.'

Hellian turned away as the soldiers set off to dispose of the Edur corpses. Oponn's pull, finding this keep, and finding nobody in it but one freshly dead Letherii in the hallway. Place had been cleaned out, although there'd been some foodstocks in the cold-rooms. Not a drop of wine or ale, the final proof, as far as she was concerned, that this foreign empire was a mess and useless besides and pretty much worth destroying down to its very last brick.

Too bad they weren't going to get a chance to do so.

But then, it does a body good to misunderstand orders on occasion. So, let's go hunting Edur heads. Hellian faced the courtyard again. *Damn this darkness. Easy enough for the mages, maybe. And these grey-skins.* 'Urb,' she said in a low voice.

He edged closer, warily. 'Hellian?'

'We need us to arrange our ambushes for dusk and dawn.'

'Aye. You're right. You know, I'm glad our squads were paired up.'

'Of course you are. You unnerstand me, Urb. You're the only one who does, you know.' She wiped her nose with the back of one hand. 'It's a sad thing, Urb. A sad thing.'

'What? Killing these Tiste Edur?'

She blinked at him. 'No, you oaf. The fact that nobody else unnerstands me.'

'Aye, Hellian. Tragic.'

'That's what Banaschar always said to me, no matter what I was talking about. He'd just look at me, like you did there, and say *tragic*. So what's all that about?' She shook the flask – *still half full, but another mouthful means I'm running it down, so's I'll need to top it up. Gotta be measured about these things, in case something terrible happens and I can't get a fast refill.* 'Come on, it's time to ride.'

'And if we run into a troop of Letherii?'

Hellian frowned. 'Then we do as Keneb told us. We talk to 'em.'

'And if they don't like what we say?'

'Then we kill 'em, of course.'

'And we're riding for Letheras?'

She smiled at Urb. Then tapped the side of her slightly numb head with one finger. 'I memmored th'map – ized, memmized the map. There's towns, Urb. An' the closer we get t'Letheras, the more of them. Wha's in towns, Urb? Taverns. Bars. So, we're not takin' a straight, pre-dic-table route.'

'We're invading Lether from tavern to tavern?'

'Aye.'

'Hellian, I hate to say this, but that's kind of clever.'

'Aye. And that way we can eat real cooked food, too. It's the civilized way of conductin' war. Hellian's way.'

The bodies joined the lone Letherii in the latrine pit. Half naked, stripped of valuables, they were dumped down into the thick, turgid slop, which proved deeper than anyone had expected, as it swallowed up those corpses, leaving not a trace.

The Malazans threw the polished stones after them.

Then rode off down the dark road.

'That has the look of a way station,' the captain said under her breath.

Beak squinted, then said, 'I smell horses, sir. That long building over there.'

'Stables,' Faradan Sort said, nodding. 'Any Tiste Edur here?'

Beak shook his head. 'Deepest blue of Rashan – that's their candle, mostly. Not as deep as Kurald Galain. They call it Kurald Emurlahn, but these ones here, well, there's skuzzy foam on that blue, like what sits on waves outside a harbour. That's chaotic power. Sick power. Power like pain if pain was good, maybe even strong. I don't know. I don't like these Edur here.'

'They're here?'

'No. I meant this continent, sir. There's just Letherii in there. Four. In that small house beside the road.'

'No magic?'

'Just some charms.'

'I want to steal four horses, Beak. Can you cast a glamour on those Letherii?'

'The Grey Candle, yes. But they'll find out after we've gone.'

'True. Any suggestions?'

Beak was happy. He had never been so happy. This captain was asking him things. Asking for suggestions. Advice. And it wasn't just for show neither. *I'm in love with her.* To her question he nodded, then tilted up his skullcap helm to scratch in his hair, and said, 'Not the usual glamour, sir. Something lots more complicated. Finishing with the Orange Candle—'

'Which is?'

'Tellann.'

'Is this going to be messy?'

'Not if we take all the horses, Captain.'

He watched her studying him, wondered what she saw. She wasn't much for expressions on that hard but beautiful face. Not even her eyes showed much. He loved her, true, but he was also a little frightened of Faradan Sort.

'All right, Beak, where do you want me?'

'In the stables with all the horses ready to leave, and maybe two saddled. Oh, and feed for us to take along.'

'And I can do all that without an alarm's being raised?'

'They won't hear a thing, sir. In fact, you could go up right now and knock on their door and they won't hear it.'

Still she hesitated. 'So I can just walk over to the stables, right out in the open, right now?'

Beak nodded with a broad smile.

'Gods below,' she muttered, 'I don't know if I'll ever get used to this.'

'Mockra has their minds, sir. They've got no defences. They've never been glamoured before, I don't think.'

435

She set out in a half-crouch, moving quickly, although none of that was necessary, and moments later was inside the stables.

It would take some time, Beak knew, for her to do all that he'd asked – *I just told a captain what to do! And she's doing it! Does that mean she loves me right back?* He shook himself. Not a good idea, letting his mind wander just now. He edged out from the cover of the trees lining this side of the stony road. Crouched to pick up a small rock, which he then spat on and set back down – to hold the Mockra in place – as he closed his eyes and sought out the White Candle.

Hood. Death, a cold, cold place. Even the air was dead. In his mind he looked in on that realm as if peering through a window, the wooden sill thick with melted candle wax, the white candle itself flickering to one side. Beyond, ash-heaped ground strewn with bones of all sorts. He reached through, closed a hand on the shaft of a heavy longbone, and drew it back. Working quickly, Beak pulled as many bones as would fit through the wandering window, always choosing big ones. He had no idea what the beasts had been to which all these bones belonged, but they would do.

When he was satisfied with the white, dusty pile heaped on the road, Beak closed the window and opened his eyes. Glancing across he saw the captain standing at the stables, gesturing at him.

Beak waved back, then turned and showed the bones the Purple Candle. They lifted from the road like feathers on an updraught, and as the mage hurried over to join Faradan Sort the bones followed in his wake, floating waist-high above the ground.

The captain disappeared back inside the stables before Beak arrived, then emerged, leading the horses, just as he padded up to the broad doors.

Grinning, Beak went into the stables, the bones tracking him. Once inside, smelling that wonderful musty smell of horses, leather, dung and piss-damp straw, he scattered the bones, a few into each stall, snuffing out the purple candle when he was done. He walked over to the mound of straw at one end, closed his eyes to awaken the Orange Candle, then spat into the straw.

Rejoining the captain outside he said to her, 'We can go now.'

'That's it?'

'Yes sir. We'll be a thousand paces down the road before the Tellann lights up—'

'Fire?'

'Yes sir. A terrible fire – they won't even be able to get close – and it'll burn fast but go nowhere else and by the morning there'll be nothing but ashes.'

'And charred bones that might belong to horses.'

'Yes sir.'

'You've done well tonight, Beak,' Faradan Sort said, swinging up onto one of the saddled horses.

Feeling impossibly light on his feet, Beak leapt onto the other one then looked back, with pride, at the remaining seven beasts. Decent animals, just badly treated. Which made it good that they were stealing them. Malazans knew how to care for their horses, after all.

Then he frowned and looked down at his stirrups.

The captain was doing the same, he saw a moment later, with her own. 'What is this?' she demanded in a hiss.

'Broken?' Beak wondered.

'Not that I can see – and yours are identical to mine. What fool invented these?'

'Captain,' said Beak, 'I don't think we have to worry much about Letherii cavalry, do we?'

'You've that right, Beak. Well, let's ride. If we're lucky, we won't break our necks twenty paces up the road.'

The father of the man named Throatslitter used to tell stories of the Emperor's conquest of Li Heng, long before Kellanved was emperor of anywhere. True, he'd usurped Mock on Malaz Island and had proclaimed himself the island's ruler, but since when was Malaz Island anything but a squalid haven for pirates? Few on the mainland took much notice of such things. A new tyrannical criminal in place of the old tyrannical criminal.

The conquest of Li Heng changed all that. There'd been no fleet of ships crowding the river mouth to the south and east of the city; nothing, in fact, to announce the assault. Instead, on a fine spring morning no different from countless other such mornings, Throatslitter's father, along with thousands of other doughty citizens, had, upon a casual glance towards the Inner Focus where stood the palace of the Protectress, noted the sudden inexplicable presence of strange figures on the walls and battlements. Squat, wide, wearing furs and wielding misshapen swords and axes. Helmed in bone.

What had happened to the vaunted Guard? And why were tendrils of smoke rising from the barracks of the courtyard and parade ground? And was it – was it truly – the Protectress herself who had been seen plunging from the High Tower beside the City Temple at the heart of the cynosure?

Someone had cut off Li Heng's head in the Palace. Undead warriors stood sentinel on the walls and, a short time later, emerged in their thousands from the Inner Focus Gate to occupy the city. Li Heng's standing army – after a half-dozen suicidal skirmishes – capitulated that same day. Kellanved now ruled the city-state, and officers and nobles of the high court knelt in fealty, and the reverberations of this conquest

437

rattled the windows of palaces across the entire mainland of Quon Tali.

'*This, son, was the awakening of the Logros T'lan Imass. The Emperor's undead army. I was there, on the streets, and saw with my own eyes those terrible warriors with their pitted eyeholes, the stretched, torn skin, the wisps of hair bleached of all colour. They say, son, that the Logros were always there, below Reacher's Falls. Maybe in the Crevasse, maybe not. Maybe just the very dust that blew in from the west every damned day and night – who can say? But he woke them, he commanded them, and I tell you after that day every ruler on Quon Tali saw a skull's face in their silver mirror, aye.*

'*The fleet of ships came later, under the command of three madmen – Crust, Urko and Nok – but first to step ashore was none other than Surly and you know who she'd become, don't you?*'

Didn't he just. Command of the T'lan Imass didn't stop the knife in the back, did it? This detail was the defining revelation of Throatslitter's life. Command thousands, tens of thousands. Command sorcerors and imperial fleets. Hold in your hand the lives of a million citizens. The real power was none of this. The real power was the knife in the hand, the hand at a fool's back.

The egalitarian plunge. There, Father, you old crab, a word you've never heard among the fifty or so you knew about in your long, point-less life. Paint on pots, now there's a useless skill, since pots never survive, and so all those lovely images end up in pieces, on the pebbled beaches, in the fill between walls, on the fields of the farmers. And it's true enough, isn't it, Father, that your private firing of 'The Coming of the Logros' proved about as popular as a whore's dose of the face-eater?

Eldest son or not, mixing glazes and circling a kiln on firing day was not the future he dreamed about. *But you can paint me, Father, and call it 'The Coming of the Assassin'. My likeness to adorn funeral urns – those who fell to the knife, of course. Too bad you never understood the world well enough to honour me. My chosen profession. My war against inequity in this miserable, evil existence.*

And striking my name from the family line, well now, really, that was uncalled for.

Fourteen years of age, Throatslitter found himself in the company of secretive old men and old women. The why and the how were without relevance, even back then. His future was set out before him, in measured strides, and not even the gods could drive him from this cold path.

He wondered about his old masters from time to time. All dead, of course. Surly had seen to that. Not that death meant failure. Her agents had failed in tracking down Throatslitter, after all, and he doubted he was the only one to evade the Claws. He also wondered if indeed he was still on the path – torn away, as he had been, from the Malazan Empire. But he was a patient man; one in his profession had to be, after all.

Still, the Adjunct has asked for loyalty. For service to an unknown cause. We are to be unwitnessed, she said. That suits me fine. It's how assassins conduct their trade. So he would go along with her and this Oponn-pushed army of sorry fools. For now.

He stood, arms crossed, shoulders drawn forward as he leaned against the wall, and could feel the occasional touch, light as a mouse's paw, on his chest as he watched, with half-hearted interest, the proceedings in Brullyg's private chamber.

The poor Shake ruler was sweating and no amount of his favoured ale could still the trembling of his hands as he sat huddled in his high-backed chair, eyes on the tankard in his grip rather than on the two armoured women standing before him.

Lostara Yil, Throatslitter considered, was if anything better-looking than T'amber had been. Or at least more closely aligned with his own tastes. The Pardu tattoos were sensuality writ on skin, and the fullness of her figure – unsuccessfully disguised by her armour – moved with a dancer's grace (when she moved, which she wasn't doing now, although the promise of elegance was unmistakable). The Adjunct stood in grim contrast, the poor woman. Like those destined to dwell in the shadows of more attractive friends, she suffered the comparison with every sign of indifference, but Throatslitter – who was skilled at seeing unspoken truths – could read the pain that dull paucity delivered, and this was a human truth, no more or less sordid than all the other human truths. Those without beauty compensated in other ways, the formal but artificial ways of rank and power, and that was just how things were the world over.

Of course when you've finally got that power, it doesn't matter how ugly you are, you can breed with the best. Maybe this explained Lostara's presence at Tavore's side. But Throatslitter was not entirely sure of that. He didn't think they were lovers. He wasn't even convinced they were friends.

Aligned near the wall to the right of the door stood the rest of the Adjunct's retinue. Fist Blistig, his blunt, wide face shadowed with some kind of spiritual exhaustion. *Doesn't pay, Adjunct, to keep close a man like that – he drains life, hope, faith. No, Tavore, you need to get rid of him and promote some new Fists. Faradan Sort. Madan tul'Rada. Fiddler. Not Captain Kindly, though, don't even think that, woman. Not unless you want a real mutiny on your hands.*

Mutiny. Well, there, he'd said it. Thought it, actually, but that was close enough. To conjure the word was to awaken the possibility, like making the scratch to invite the fester. The Bonehunters were now

439

scattered to the winds and that was a terrible risk. He suspected that, at the end of this bizarre campaign, her soldiers would come trickling back in paltry few number, if at all.

Unwitnessed. Most soldiers don't like that idea. True, it made them hard – when she told them – but that fierceness can't last. The iron is too cold. Its taste too bitter. Gods, just look at Blistig for the truth of that.

Beside the Fist stood Withal, the Meckros blacksmith – *the man we went to Malaz City to get, and we still don't know why. Oh, there's blood in your shadow, isn't there? Malazan blood. T'amber's. Kalam's. Maybe Quick Ben's, too. Are you worth it?* Throatslitter had yet to see Withal speaking to a soldier. Not one, not a word of thanks, not an apology for the lives sacrificed. He was here because the Adjunct needed him. For what? *Hah, not like she's talking, is it? Not our cagey Tavore Paran.*

To Withal's right stood Banaschar, a deposed high priest of D'rek, if the rumours were true. Yet another passenger in this damned renegade army. But Throatslitter knew Banaschar's purpose. *Coin. Thousands, tens of thousands. He's our paymaster, and all this silver and gold in our pouches was stolen from somewhere. Has to be. Nobody's that rich. The obvious answer? Why, how about the Worm of Autumn's temple coffers?*

Pray to the Worm, pay an army of disgruntled malcontents. Somehow, all you believers, I doubt that was in your prayers.

Poor Brullyg had few allies in this chamber. Balm's source of lust, this Captain Shurq Elalle of the privateer *Undying Gratitude*, and her first mate, Skorgen Kaban the Pretty. And neither seemed eager to leap to Brullyg's side of the sandpit.

But that Shurq, she was damned watchful. Probably a lot more dangerous than the usurper of this cruddy island.

The Adjunct had been explaining, in decent traders' tongue, the new rules of governance on Second Maiden Fort, and with each statement Brullyg's expression had sagged yet further.

Entertaining, if one was inclined towards sardonic humour.

'Ships from our fleet,' she was now explaining, 'will be entering the harbour to resupply. One at a time, since it wouldn't do to panic your citizens—'

A snort from Shurq Elalle, who had drawn her chair to one side, almost in front of where Throatslitter leaned against the wall, to permit herself a clear view of host and guests. Beside her, Skorgen was filling his prodigious gut with Brullyg's favourite ale, the tankard in one hand, the finger of the other hand exploring the depths of one mangled, rose-red ear. The man had begun a succession of belches, each released in a heavy sigh, that had been ongoing for half a bell now, with no sign of ending. The entire room stank of his yeasty exhalations.

The captain's derisive expostulation drew the Adjunct's attention. 'I understand your impatience,' Tavore said in a cool voice, 'and no doubt you wish to leave. Unfortunately, I must speak to you and will do so shortly—'

'Once you've thoroughly detailed Brullyg's emasculation, you mean.' Shurq lifted one shapely leg and crossed it on the other, then laced together her hands on her lap, smiling sweetly up at the Adjunct.

Tavore's colourless eyes regarded the pirate captain for a long moment, then she glanced over to where stood her retinue. 'Banaschar.'

'Adjunct?'

'What is wrong with this woman?'

'She's dead,' the ex-priest replied. 'A necromantic curse.'

'Are you certain?'

Throatslitter cleared his throat and said, 'Adjunct, Corporal Deadsmell said the same thing when we saw her down in the tavern.'

Brullyg was staring at Shurq with wide, bulging eyes, his jaw hanging slack.

At Shurq's side, Skorgen Kaban was suddenly frowning, his eyes darting. Then he withdrew the finger that had been plugging one ear and looked down at the gunk smeared all over it. After a moment, Pretty slid that finger into his mouth.

'Well,' Shurq sighed up at Tavore, 'you've done it now, haven't you? Alas, the coin of this secret is the basest of all, namely *vanity*. Now, if you possess some unpleasant bigotry regarding the undead, then I must re-evaluate my assessment of you, Adjunct. And your motley companions.'

To Throatslitter's surprise, Tavore actually smiled. 'Captain, the Malazan Empire is well acquainted with undead, although few possessing your host of charms.'

Gods below, she's flirting with this sweet-scented corpse!

'Host indeed,' murmured Banaschar, then was so rude as to offer no elaboration. *Hood-damned priests. Good for nothing at all.*

'In any case,' Tavore resumed, 'we are without prejudice in this matter. I apologize for posing the question leading to this unveiling. I was simply curious.'

'So am I,' Shurq replied. 'This Malazan Empire of yours – do you have any particular reason for invading the Lether Empire?'

'I was led to understand that this island is independent—'

'So it is, since the Edur Conquest. But you're hardly invading one squalid little island. No. You're just using this to stage your assault on the mainland. So let me ask again, why?'

'Our enemy,' the Adjunct said, all amusement now gone, 'are the Tiste Edur, Captain. Not the Letherii. In fact, we would encourage a general uprising of Letherii—'

'You won't get it,' Shurq Elalle said.

'Why not?' Lostara Yil asked.

'Because we happen to like things the way they are. More or less.'

When no-one spoke, she smiled and continued, 'The Edur may well have usurped the rulers in their absurd half-finished palace in Letheras. And they may well have savaged a few Letherii armies on the way to the capital. But you will not find bands of starving rebels in the forests dreaming of independence.'

'Why not?' Lostara demanded again in an identical tone.

'They conquered, but we won. Oh, I wish Tehol Beddict was here, since he's much better at explaining things, but let me try. I shall imagine Tehol sitting here, to help me along. Conquest. There are different kinds of conquests. Now, we have Tiste Edur lording it here and there, the elite whose word is law and never questioned. After all, their sorcery is cruel, their judgement cold and terribly simplistic. They are, in fact, above all law – as the Letherii understand the notion—'

'And,' Lostara pressed, 'how do they understand the notion of law?'

'Well, a set of deliberately vague guidelines one hires an advocate to evade when necessary.'

'What were you, Shurq Elalle, before you were a pirate?'

'A thief. I've employed a few advocates in my day. In any case, my point is this. The Edur rule but either through ignorance or indifference – and let's face it, without ignorance you don't get to indifference – they care little about the everyday administration of the empire. So, that particular apparatus remains Letherii and is, these days, even less regulated than it has been in the past.' She smiled again, one leg rocking. 'As for us lower orders, well, virtually nothing has changed. We stay poor. Debt-ridden and comfortably miserable and, as Tehol might say, miserable in our comfort.'

'So,' Lostara said, 'not even the Letherii nobles would welcome a change in the present order.'

'Them least of all.'

'What of your Emperor?'

'Rhulad? From all accounts, he is insane, and effectively isolated besides. The empire is ruled by the Chancellor, and he's Letherii. He was also Chancellor in the days of King Diskanar, and he was there to ensure that the transition went smoothly.'

A grunt from Blistig, and he turned to Tavore. 'The marines, Adjunct,' he said in a half-moan.

And Throatslitter understood and felt a dread chill seeping through him. *We sent them in, expecting to find allies, expecting them to whip the countryside into a belligerent frenzy. But they won't get that.*

The whole damned empire is going to rise up all right. To tear out their throats.

Adjunct, you have done it again.

442

CHAPTER FIFTEEN

Crawl down sun this is not your time
Black waves slide under the sheathed moon
upon the shore a silent storm a will untamed
heaves up from the red-skirled foam
Scud to your mountain nests you iron clouds
to leave the sea its dancing refuse of stars
on this host of salty midnight tides
Gather drawn and swell tight your tempest
lift like scaled heads from the blind depths
all your effulgent might in restless roving eyes
Reel back you tottering forests this night
the black waves crash on the black shore
to steal the flesh from your bony roots
death comes, shouldering aside in cold legion
in a marching wind this dread this blood
this reaper's gale

The Coming Storm
Reffer

T HE FIST SLAMMED DOWN AT THE FAR END OF THE TABLE. FOOD-
crusted cutlery danced, plates thumped then skidded. The
reverberation – heavy as thunder – rattled the goblets and shook
all that sat down the length of the long table's crowded world.

Fist shivering, pain lancing through the numb shock, Tomad Sengar
slowly sat back.

Candle flames steadied, seeming eager to please with their regained
calm, the pellucid warmth of their yellow light an affront nonetheless
to the Edur's bitter anger.

Across from him, his wife lifted a silk napkin to her lips, daubed
once, then set it down and regarded her husband. 'Coward.'

Tomad flinched, his gaze shifting away to scan the plastered wall to his right. Lifting past the discordant object hanging there to some place less ... painful. Damp stains painted mottled maps near the ceiling. Plaster had lifted, buckled, undermined by that incessant leakage. Cracks zigzagged down like the after-image of lightning.

'You will not see him,' Uruth said.

'He will not see me,' Tomad replied, and this was not in agreement. It was, in fact, a retort.

'A disgusting, scrawny Letherii who sleeps with young boys has defeated you, husband. He stands in your path and your bowels grow weak. Do not refute my words – you will not even meet my eyes. You have surrendered our last son.'

Tomad's lips twisted in a snarl. 'To whom, Uruth? Tell me. Chancellor Triban Gnol, who wounds children and calls it love?' He looked at her then, unwilling to admit, even to himself, the effort that gesture demanded of him. 'Shall I break his neck for you, wife? Easier than snapping a dead branch. What do you think his bodyguards will do? Stand aside?'

'Find allies. Our kin—'

'Are fools. Grown soft with indolence, blind with uncertainty. They are more lost than is Rhulad.'

'I had a visitor today,' Uruth said, refilling her goblet with the carafe of wine that had nearly toppled from the table with Tomad's sudden violence.

'I am pleased for you.'

'Perhaps you are. A K'risnan. He came to tell me that Bruthen Trana has disappeared. He suspects that Karos Invictad – or the Chancellor – have exacted their revenge. They have murdered Bruthen Trana. A Tiste Edur's blood is on their hands.'

'Can your K'risnan prove this?'

'He has begun on that path, but admits to little optimism. But none of that is, truth be told, what I would tell you.'

'Ah, so you think me indifferent to the spilling of Edur blood by Letherii hands?'

'Indifferent? No, husband. Helpless. Will you interrupt me yet again?'

Tomad said nothing, not in acquiescence, but because he had run out of things to say. To her. To anyone.

'Good,' she said. 'I would tell you this. I believe the K'risnan was lying.'

'About what?'

'I believe he knows what has happened to Bruthen Trana, and that he came to me to reach the women's council, and to reach you, husband. First, to gauge my reaction to the news at the time of its telling, then to gauge our more measured reaction in the days to come. Second, by voicing his suspicion, false though it is, he sought to encourage our growing hatred for the Letherii. And our hunger for vengeance, thus continuing this feud behind curtains, which, presumably, will distract Karos and Gnol.'

'And, so distracted, they perchance will miss comprehension of some greater threat – which has to do with wherever Bruthen Trana has gone.'

'Very good, husband. Coward you may be, but you are not stupid.' She paused to sip, then said, 'That is something.'

'How far will you push me, wife?'

'As far as is necessary.'

'We were not here. We were sailing half this damned world. We return to find the conspiracy triumphant, dominant and well entrenched. We returned, to find that we have lost our last son.'

'Then we must win him back.'

'There is no-one left to win, Uruth. Rhulad is mad. Nisall's betrayal has broken him.'

'The bitch is better gone than still in our way. Rhulad repeats his errors. With her, so he had already done with that slave, Udinaas. He failed to learn.'

Tomad allowed himself a bitter smile. 'Failed to learn. So have we all, Uruth. We saw for ourselves the poison that was Lether. We perceived well the threat, and so marched down to conquer, thus annihilating that threat for ever more. Or so we'd thought.'

'It devoured us.'

He looked again to the wall on the right, where, hanging from an iron hook, there was a bundle of fetishes. Feathers, strips of sealskin, necklaces of strung shells, shark teeth. The bedraggled remnants of three children – all that remained to remind them of their lives.

Some did not belong, for the son who had owned certain of those items had been banished, his life swept away as if it had never been. Had Rhulad seen these, even the binding of filial blood would not spare the lives of Tomad and Uruth. Trull Sengar – the name itself was anathema, a crime, and the punishment of its utterance was death.

Neither cared.

'A most insipid poison indeed,' Uruth continued, eyeing her goblet. 'We grow fat. The warriors get drunk and sleep in the beds of Letherii whores. Or lie unconscious in the durhang dens. Others simply . . . disappear.'

'They return home,' Tomad said, repressing a pang at the thought. Home. Before all this.

'Are you certain?'

445

He met her eyes once more. 'What do you mean?'

'Karos Invictad and his Patriotists never cease their vigilant tyranny of the people. They make arrests every day. Who is to say they have not arrested Tiste Edur?'

'He could not hide that, wife.'

'Why not? Now that Bruthen Trana is gone, Karos Invictad does as he pleases. No-one stands at his shoulder now.'

'He did as he pleased before.'

'You cannot know that, husband. Can you? What constraints did Invictad perceive – real or imagined, it matters not – when he knew Bruthen Trana was watching him?'

'I know what you want,' Tomad said in a low growl. 'But who is to blame for all of this?'

'That no longer matters,' she replied, watching him carefully – fearing what, he wondered. Another uncontrolled burst of violence? Or the far more insipid display revealing his despair?

'I don't know how you can say that,' he said. 'He sent our sons to retrieve the sword. That decision doomed them all. Us all. And look, we now sit in the palace of the Lether Empire, rotting in the filth of Letherii excess. We have no defence against indolence and apathy, against greed and decadence. These enemies do not fall to the sword, do not skid away from a raised shield.'

'Hannan Mosag, husband, is our only hope. You must go to him.'

'To conspire against our son?'

'Who is, as you have said, insane. Blood is one thing,' Uruth said, slowly leaning forward, 'but we now speak of the survival of the Tiste Edur. Tomad, the women are ready – we have been ready for a long time.'

He stared at her, wondering who this woman was, this cold, cold creature. Perhaps he was a coward, after all. When Rhulad had sent Trull away, he had said nothing. But then, neither had Uruth. And what of his own conspiracy? With Binadas? Find Trull. Please. Find the bravest among us. Recall the Sengar bloodline, son. Our first strides onto this world. Leading a legion onto its stony ground, loyal officers of Scabandari. Who drew the first Andii blood on the day of betrayal? That is our blood. That – not this.

So, Tomad had sent Binadas away. Had sent a son to his death. *Because I had not the will to do it myself.*

Coward.

Watching him still, Uruth carefully refilled her goblet.

Binadas, my son, your slayer awaits Rhulad's pleasure. Is that enough?

Like any old fool who had once wagered mortal lives, the Errant wandered the corridors of enlivened power, muttering his litany of lost opportunities and bad choices. Exhalation of sorcery averted the eyes of those who strode past, the guards at various doorways and intersections, the scurrying servants who fought their losing battle with the crumbling residence known – now with irony – as the Eternal Domicile. They saw but did not see, and no after-image remained in their minds upon passing.

More than any ghost, the Elder God was forgettable. But not as forgettable as he would have liked. He had worshippers now, at the cost of an eye binding him and his power, warring with his will in the guise of faith. Of course, every god knew of that war – such subversion seemed the primary purpose of every priest. Reduction of the sacred into the mundane world of mortal rivalries, politics and the games of control and manipulation of as many people as there were adherents. Oh, and yes, the acquisition of wealth, be it land or coin, be it the adjudication of fate or the gathering of souls.

With such thoughts haunting him, the Errant stepped into the throne room, moving silently to one side to take his usual place against a wall between two vast tapestries, as unnoticed as the grandiose scenes woven into those frames – images in which could be found some figure in the background very closely resembling the Errant.

The Chancellor Triban Gnol – with whom the Errant had shared a bed when expedience demanded it – stood before Rhulad who slouched like some sated monstrosity, poignant with wealth and madness. One of the Chancellor's bodyguards hovered a few paces back from Gnol, looking bored as his master recited numbers. Detailing, once more, the growing dissolution of the treasury.

These sessions, the Errant understood, with some admiration, were deliberate travails intended to further exhaust the Emperor. Revenues and losses, expenses and the sudden peak in defaulted debts, piled up in droning cadence like the gathering of forces preparing to lay siege. An assault against which Rhulad had no defence.

He would surrender, as he always did. Relinquishing all management to the Chancellor. A ritual as enervating to witness as it was to withstand, yet the Errant felt no pity. The Edur were barbarians. Like children in the face of civilized sophistication.

Why do I come here, day after day? What am I waiting to witness here? Rhulad's final collapse? Will that please me? Entertain me? How sordid have my tastes become?

He held his gaze on the Emperor. Dulled coins luridly gleaming, a rhythm of smudged reflection rising and settling with Rhulad's breathing; the black sanguine promise of the sword's long, straight blade, tip dug into the marble dais, the grey bony hand gripping the wire-wrapped handle. Sprawled there on his throne, Rhulad was indeed a metaphor made real. Armoured in riches and armed with a weapon that promised both immortality and annihilation, he was impervious to everything but his own growing madness. When Rhulad fell, the Errant believed, it would be from the inside out.

The ravaged face revealed this truth in a cascade of details, from the seamed scars of past failures to which, by virtue of his having survived them, he was indifferent, to whatever lessons they might hold. Pocked flesh to mock the possession of wealth long lost. Sunken eyes wherein resided the despairing penury of his spirit, a spirit that at times pushed close to those glittering dark prisms and let loose its silent howl.

Twitches tracked this brutal mien. Random ripples beneath the mottled skin, a migration of expressions attempting to escape the remote imperial mask.

One could understand, upon looking at Rhulad on his throne, the lie of simplicity that power whispered in the beholder's ear. The seductive voice urging pleasurable and satisfying reduction, from life's confusion to death's clarity. This, murmured power, is how I am revealed. Stepping naked through all the disguises. I am threat and if threat does not suffice, then I act. Like a reaper's scythe.

The lie of simplicity. Rhulad still believed it. In that he was no different from every other ruler, through every age, in every place where people gathered to fashion a common, the weal of community with its necessity for organization and division. Power is violence, its promise, its deed. Power cares nothing for reason, nothing for justice, nothing for compassion. It is, in fact, the singular abnegation of these things – once the cloak of deceits is stripped away, this one truth is revealed.

And the Errant was tired of it. All of it.

Mael once said there was no answer. For any of this. He said it was the way of things and always would be, and the only redemption that could be found was that all power, no matter how vast, how centralized, no matter how dominant, will destroy itself in the end. What entertained then was witnessing all those expressions of surprise on the faces of the wielders.

This seemed a far too bitter reward, as far as the Errant was concerned. *I have naught of Mael's capacity for cold, depthless regard. Nor his legendary patience. Nor, for that matter, his temper.*

No Elder God was blind to the folly of those who would reign in the many worlds. Assuming it was able to think at all, of course, and for some that was in no way a certain thing. Anomander Rake saw it clearly enough, and so he turned away from its vastness, instead choosing to concentrate on specific, minor conflicts. And he denied his worshippers, a crime so profound to them that they simply rejected it out of hand. Osserc, on the other hand, voiced his own refusal – of the hopeless truth – and so tried again and again and failed every time. For Osserc, Anomander Rake's very existence became an unconscionable insult.

448

Draconus – ah, now he was no fool. He would have wearied of his tyranny – had he lived long enough. I still wonder if he did not in fact welcome his annihilation. To die beneath the sword made by his own hands, to see his most cherished daughter standing to one side, witness, wilfully blind to his need . . . Draconus, how could you not despair of all you once dreamed?

And then there was Kilmandaros. Now she liked the notion of . . . simplicity. The solid righteousness of her fist was good enough for her. But then, see where it took her!

And what of K'rul? Why, he was—

'Stop!' Rhulad shrieked, visibly jolting on the throne, the upper half of his body suddenly leaning forward, the eyes black with sudden threat. 'What did you just say?'

The Chancellor frowned, then licked his withered lips. 'Emperor, I was recounting the costs of disposing the corpses from the trench-pens—'

'Corpses, yes.' Rhulad's hand twitched where it folded over the throne's ornate arm. He stared fixedly at Triban Gnol, then, with a strange smile, he asked, 'What corpses?'

'From the fleets, sire. The slaves rescued from the island of Sepik, the northernmost protectorate of the Malazan Empire.'

'Slaves. Rescued. Slaves.'

The Errant could see Triban Gnol's confusion, a momentary flicker, then . . . comprehension.

Oh now, let us witness this!

'Your fallen kin, sire. Those of Tiste Edur blood who had suffered beneath the tyranny of the Malazans.'

'Rescued.' Rhulad paused as if to taste that word. 'Edur blood.'

'Diluted—'

'Edur blood!'

'Indeed, Emperor.'

'Then why are they in the trench-pens?'

'They were deemed fallen, sire.'

Rhulad twisted on the throne, as if assailed from within. His head snapped back. His limbs were seized with trembling. He spoke as one lost. 'Fallen? But they are our kin. In this entire damned world, our only kin!'

'That is true, Emperor. I admit, I was somewhat dismayed at the decision to consign them to those most terrible cells—'

'Whose decision, Gnol? Answer me!'

A bow, which the Errant knew hid a satisfied gleam in the Chancellor's eyes – quickly disguised as he looked up once more. 'The disposition of the fallen Sepik Edur was the responsibility of Tomad Sengar, Emperor.'

Rhulad slowly settled back. 'And they are dying.'

'In droves, sire. Alas.'

'We rescued them to deliver our own torment. Rescued them to kill them.'

'It is, I would suggest, a somewhat unjust fate—'

'Unjust? You scrawny snake – why did you not tell me of this before?'

'Emperor, you indicated no interest in the financial details—'

Oh, a mistake there, Gnol.

'The what?'

Beads of sweat on the back of the Chancellor's neck now. 'The varied expenses associated with their imprisonment, sire.'

'They are Tiste Edur!'

Another bow.

Rhulad suddenly clawed at his face and looked away. 'Edur blood,' he murmured. 'Rescued from slavery. Trench-pens is their reward.'

Triban Gnol cleared his throat. 'Many died in the holds of the ships, sire. As I understand it, their maltreatment began upon leaving Sepik Island. What is it would have me do, Emperor?'

And so deftly you regain ground, Triban Gnol.

'Bring me Tomad Sengar. And Uruth. Bring to me my father and mother.'

'Now?'

The sword scraped free, point lifting to centre on Triban Gnol. 'Yes, Chancellor. Now.'

Triban Gnol and his bodyguard quickly departed.

Rhulad was alone in his throne room, now holding his sword out on nothing.

'How? How could they do this? These poor people – they are of our own blood. I need to think.' The Emperor lowered the sword then shifted about on the throne, drawing his coin-clad legs up. 'How? Nisall? Explain this to me – no, you cannot, can you. You have fled me. Where are you, Nisall? Some claim you are dead. Yet where is your body? Are you just another bloated corpse in the canal – the ones I see from the tower – were you one of those, drifting past? They tell me you were a traitor. They tell me you were not a traitor. They all lie to me. I know that, I can see that. Hear that. They all lie to me—' He sobbed then, his free hand covering his mouth, his eyes darting about the empty room.

The Errant saw that gaze slide right over him. He thought to step forward then, to relinquish the sorcery hiding him, to say to the Emperor: *Yes, sire. They all lie to you. But I will not. Do you dare hear the truth, Emperor Rhulad? All of it?*

'Slaves. This – this is wrong. Tomad – Father – where did this cruelty come from?'

Oh, dear Rhulad . . .

'Father, we will talk. You and me. Alone. And Mother, yes, you too. The three of us. It has been so long since we did that. Yes, that is what we will do. And you must ... you must not lie to me. No, that I will not accept.

'Father, where is Nisall?

'Where is Trull?'

Could an Elder God's heart break? The Errant almost sagged then, as Rhulad's plaintive query echoed momentarily in the chamber, then quickly died, leaving only the sound of the Emperor's laboured breathing.

Then, a harder voice emerging from the Emperor: 'Hannan Mosag, this is all your fault. You did this. To us. To me. You twisted me, made me send them all away. To find champions. But no, that was my idea, wasn't it? I can't – can't remember – so many lies here, so many voices, all lying. Nisall, you left me. Udinaas – I will find you both. I will see the skin flayed from your writhing bodies, I will listen to your screams—'

The sound of boots in the hallway beyond.

Rhulad looked up guiltily, then settled into the throne. Righting the weapon. Licking his lips. Then, as the doors creaked open, he sat with a fixed grin, a baring of his teeth to greet his parents.

Dessert arrived at the point of a sword. A full dozen Letherii guards, led by Sirryn Kanar, burst into the private chambers of Tomad and Uruth Sengar. Weapons drawn, they entered the dining room to find the two Edur seated each at one end of the long table.

Neither had moved. Neither seemed surprised.

'On your feet,' Sirryn growled, unable to hide his satisfaction, his delicious pleasure at this moment. 'The Emperor demands your presence. Now.'

The tight smile on Tomad's face seemed to flicker a moment, before the old warrior rose to his feet.

Sneering, Uruth had not moved. 'The Emperor would see his mother? Very well, he may ask.'

Sirryn looked down at her. 'This is a command, woman.'

'And I am a High Priestess of Shadow, you pathetic thug.'

'Sent here by the Emperor's will. You will stand, or—'

'Or what? Will you dare lay hands on me, Letherii? Recall your place.'

The guard reached out.

'Stop!' Tomad shouted. 'Unless, Letherii, you wish your flesh torn from your bones. My wife has awakened Shadow, and she will not suffer your touch.'

Sirryn Kanar found he was trembling. With rage. 'Then advise her, Tomad Sengar, of her son's impatience.'

Uruth slowly drained her goblet of wine, set it carefully down, then rose. 'Sheathe your weapons, Letherii. My husband and I can walk to the throne room in your company, or alone. My preference is for the latter, but I permit you this single warning. Sheathe your swords, or I will kill you all.'

Sirryn gestured to his soldiers and weapons slid back into scabbards. After a moment, his did the same. *I will have an answer for this, Uruth Sengar. Recall my place? Of course, if the lie suits you, as it does me . . . for now.*

'Finally,' Uruth said to Tomad, 'we shall have an opportunity to tell our son all that needs to be told. An audience. Such privilege.'

'It may be you shall await his pleasure,' Sirryn said.

'Indeed? How long?'

The Letherii smiled at her. 'That is not for me to say.'

'This game is not Rhulad's. It is yours. You and your Chancellor.'

'Not this time,' Sirryn replied.

'I have killed Tiste Edur before.'

Samar Dev watched Karsa Orlong as the Toblakai examined the tattered clamshell armour shirt he had laid out on the cot. The pearlescent scales were tarnished and chipped, and large patches of the thick leather under-panels – hinged with rawhide – were visible. He had gathered a few hundred holed coins – made of tin and virtually worthless – and was clearly planning to use them to amend the armour.

Was this a gesture of mockery, she wondered. A visible sneer in Rhulad's face? Barbarian or not, she would not put it past Karsa Orlong.

'I cleared the deck of the fools,' he continued, then glanced over at her. 'And what of those in the forest of the Anibar? As for the Letherii, they're even more pathetic – see how they cower, even now? I will explore this city, with my sword strapped to my back, and none shall stop me.'

She rubbed at her face. 'There is a rumour that the first roll of champions will be called. Soon. Raise the ire of these people, Karsa, and you will not have to wait long to face the Emperor.'

'Good,' he grunted. 'Then I shall walk Letheras as its new emperor.'

'Is that what you seek?' she asked, her eyes narrowing on him in surprise.

'If that is what is needed for them to leave me be.'

She snorted. 'Then the last thing you want is to be emperor.'

He straightened, frowning down at the gaudy if bedraggled armour shirt. 'I am not interested in fleeing, witch. There is no reason for them to forbid me.'

'You can step outside this compound and wander where you will . . . just leave your sword behind.'

'That I will not do.'

'Then here you remain, slowly going mad at the Emperor's pleasure.'

'Perhaps I shall fight my way through.'

'Karsa, they just don't want you killing citizens. Given that you are so, uh, easily offended, it's not an unusual request.'

'What offends me is their lack of faith.'

'Right,' she snapped, 'which you have well earned by killing Edur and Letherii at every turn. Including a Preda—'

'I did not know he was that.'

'Would it have made a difference? No, I thought not. How about the fact that he was a brother to the Emperor?'

'I did not know that either.'

'And?'

'And what, Samar Dev?'

'Murdered him with a spear, wasn't it?'

'He assailed me with magic—'

'You have told me this tale, Karsa Orlong. You had just slaughtered his crew. Then kicked in the door to his cabin. Then crushed the skulls of his bodyguards. I tell you, in his place I too would have drawn upon my warren – assuming I had one, which I don't. And I would have thrown everything I had at you.'

'There is no point to this conversation,' the Toblakai said in a growl.

'Fine,' she said, rising from her chair. 'I am off to find Taxilian. At least his obdurate obsessions are less infuriating.'

'Is he your lover now?'

She halted at the doorway. 'And if he was?'

'Just as well,' Karsa said, now glowering down at his patchy armour. 'I would break you in two.'

Jealousy to join the host of other madnesses? Spirits below! She turned back to the door. 'I'd be more inclined towards Senior Assessor. Alas, he has taken vows of celibacy.'

'The fawning monk is still here?'

'He is.'

'You have sordid tastes, witch.'

'Well,' she said after a moment, 'I see no possible way of responding to that comment.'

'Of course not.'

Lips pressed tight together, Samar Dev left the room.

Karsa Orlong's mood was foul, but it did not occur to him that it in any way flavoured his conversation with Samar Dev. She was a woman and any exchange of words with a woman was fraught with her torturer's array of deadly implements, each one hovering at the very edge of a man's comprehension. Swords were simpler. Even the harried disaster of all-out war was simpler than the briefest, lightest touch of a woman's attention. What infuriated him was how much he missed that touch. True, there were whores aplenty for the champions awaiting the Emperor. But there was nothing subtle – nothing real – in that.

There must be a middle ground, Karsa told himself. Where the exchange exulted in all the sparks and feints that made things interesting, without putting his dignity at risk. Yet he was realistic enough to hold little hope of ever finding it.

The world was filled with weapons and combat was a way of life. Perhaps the only way of life. He'd bled to whips and words, to punches and glances. He'd been bludgeoned by invisible shields, blindsided by unseen clubs, and had laboured under the chains of his own vows. And as Samar Dev would say, one survives by withstanding this onslaught, this history of the then and the now. To fail was to fall, but falling was not always synonymous with a quick, merciful death. Rather, one could fall into the slow dissolution, losses heaped high, that dragged a mortal to his or her knees. That made them slow slayers of themselves.

He had come to understand his own traps, and, in that sense, he was probably not yet ready to encounter someone else's, to step awry and discover the shock of pain. Still, the hunger never went away. And this tumult in his soul was wearisome and so a most sordid invitation to a disgruntled mood.

Easily solved by mayhem.

Lacking love, the warrior seeks violence.

Karsa Orlong sneered as he slung the stone sword over his left shoulder and strode out into the corridor. 'I hear you, Bairoth Gild. You would be my conscience?' He grunted a laugh. 'You, who stole my woman.'

Perhaps you have found another, Karsa Orlong.

'I would break her in two.'

That has not stopped you before.

But no, this was a game. Bairoth Gild's soul was bound within a sword. These sly words filling Karsa's skull were his own. Lacking someone else's attention, he was now digging his own pitfalls. 'I think I need to kill someone.'

From the corridor to a broader hallway, then on to the colonnaded transept, into a side passage and on to the compound's north postern gate. Meeting no-one on the way, further befouling Karsa's mood. The gate was inset with a small guardhouse to its left where the heavy latch release could be found.

The Letherii seated within had time to glance up before the Toblakai's fist connected solidly with his face. Blood sprayed from a shattered nose and the hapless man sank down into his chair, then slid like a sack of onions to the floor. Stepping over him, Karsa lifted the latch and slid the bronze bar to his left, until its right-hand end cleared the gate itself. The bar dropped down into a wheeled recess with a clunk. Emerging outside once more, Karsa pushed the gate open and, ducking to clear the lintel, stepped out into the street beyond.

There was a flash as some sort of magical ward ignited the moment he crossed the threshold. Fires burgeoned, a whisper of vague pain, then the flames dwindled and vanished. Shaking his head to clear the spell's metallic reverberation from his mind, he continued on.

A few citizens here and there; only one noted his appearance and that one – eyes widening – quickened his pace and moments later turned a corner and was lost from sight.

Karsa drew a deep breath, then set off for the canal he had seen from the roof of the barracks.

Vast as a river barge, the enormous black-haired woman in mauve silks filled the entrance to the courtyard restaurant, fixed her eyes on Tehol Beddict, then surged forward with the singular intent of a hungry leviathan.

Beside him, Bugg seemed to cringe back in his chair. 'By the Abyss, Master—'

'Now now,' Tehol murmured as the woman drew closer. 'Pragmatism, dear Bugg, must now be uppermost among your, uh, considerations. Find Huldo and get his lads to drag over that oversized couch from the back of the kitchen. Quick now, Bugg!'

The manservant's departure was an uncharacteristic bolt.

The woman – sudden centre of attention with most conversations falling away – seemed for all her impressive girth to glide as she moved between the blessedly widely spaced tables, and in her dark violet eyes there gleamed a sultry confidence so at odds with her ungainly proportions that Tehol felt an alarming stir in his groin and sweat prickled in enough manly places to make him shift uneasily in his chair, all thoughts of the meal on the plate before him torn away like so many clothes.

He did not believe it possible that flesh could move in as many directions all at once, every swell beneath the silk seemingly possessed of corporeal independence, yet advancing in a singular chorus of overt sexuality. Her shadow engulfing him, Tehol loosed a small whimper, struggling to drag his eyes up, past the stacked folds of her belly, past the impossibly high, bulging, grainsack-sized breasts – lost for a moment in that depthless cleavage – then, with heroic will, yet higher to the smooth udder beneath her chin; higher still, neck straining, to that so round face with its broad, painted,

455

purple lips – higher – *Errant help me* – to those delicious, knowing eyes.

'You disgust me, Tehol.'

'I – what?'

'Where's Bugg with that damned couch?'

Tehol leaned forward, then recoiled again with instinctive self-preservation. 'Rucket? Is that you?'

'Quiet, you fool. Do you have any idea how long it took us to perfect this illusion?'

'B-but—'

'The best disguise is misdirection.'

'Misdirection? Oh, why . . . oh, well of course, when you put it that way. I mean, all the way. Sorry, that just tumbled out. Came out wrong, I mean—'

'Stop staring at my tits.'

'I'd be the only one in here not staring,' he retorted, 'which would be very suspicious. Besides, who decided on that particular . . . defiance of the earth's eternal pull? Probably Ormly – it's those piggy eyes of his, hinting at perverse fantasies.'

Bugg had arrived with two of Huldo's servers carrying the couch between them. They set it down then hastily retreated.

Bugg returned to his seat. 'Rucket,' he said under his breath, shaking his head, 'do you not imagine that a woman of your stature would not already be infamous in Letheras?'

'Not if I never went out, would I? As it turns out, there are plenty of recluses in this city—'

'Because most of them were the Guild's illusions – false personalities you could assume when necessity demanded it.'

'Precisely,' she said, as if settling the matter.

Which she then did with consummate grace, easing down fluidly into the huge couch, her massive alabaster arms spreading out along the back, which had the effect of hitching her breasts up still further then spreading them like the Gates of the Damned.

Tehol glanced at Bugg. 'There are certain laws regarding the properties of physical entities, yes? There must be. I'm sure of it.'

'She is a defiant woman, Master. And please, if you will, adjust your blanket. Yes, there, beneath this blessed table.'

'Stop that.'

'Whom or what are you addressing?' Rucket asked with a leer big enough for two women.

'Damn you, Rucket, we'd just ordered, you know. Bugg's purse, or his company's, that is. And now my appetite . . . well . . . it's—'

'Shifted?' she asked, thin perfect brows lifting above those knowing eyes. 'The problem with men elucidated right there: your inability to indulge in more than one pleasure at any one time.'

'Which you presently personify with terrible perfection. So, how precise is this illusion of yours? I mean, the couch creaked and everything.'

'No doubt you're most eager to explore that weighty question. But first, where's Huldo with my lunch?'

'He took one look at you and then went out to hire more cooks.'

She leaned forward and pulled Tehol's plate closer. 'This will do. Especially after that cruel attempt at humour, Tehol.' She began eating with absurd delicacy.

'There's no real way in there, is there?'

Morsel of food halted halfway to her open mouth.

Bugg seemed to choke on something.

Tehol wiped sweat from his brow. 'Errant take me, I'm losing my mind.'

'You force me,' Rucket said, 'to prove to you otherwise.' The dainty popped into her mouth.

'You expect me to succumb to an illusion?'

'Why not? Men do that a thousand times a day.'

'Without that, the world would grind to a halt.'

'Yours, maybe.'

'Speaking of which,' Bugg interjected hastily, 'your Guild, Rucket, is about to become bankrupt.'

'Nonsense. We have more wealth hidden away than the Liberty Consign.'

'That's good, because they're about to discover that most of their unadvertised holdings have been so thoroughly undermined that they're not only worthless, but fatal liabilities.'

'We transferred ours beyond the empire, Bugg. Months ago. Once we fully understood what you and Tehol were doing.'

'Where?' Bugg asked.

'Should I tell you?'

'We're not going after it,' Tehol said. 'Right, Bugg?'

'Of course not. I just want to be sure it's, uh, far enough removed.'

Rucket's eyes narrowed. 'Are you that close?'

Neither man replied.

She looked down at the plate for a moment, then settled back like a human canal lock, her belly re-emerging from the shadows in silky waves. 'Very well, gentlemen. South Pilott. Far enough away, Bugg?'

'Just.'

'That answer makes me nervous.'

'I am about to default on everything I owe,' Bugg said. 'This will cause a massive financial cascade that will not spare a single sector of industry, and not just here in Letheras, but across the entire empire and beyond. Once I do it, there will be chaos. Anarchy. People may actually die.'

'Bugg's Construction is that big?'

'Not at all. If it was, we'd have been rounded up long ago. No, there are about two thousand seemingly independent small- and middling-sized holdings, each one perfectly positioned according to Tehol's diabolical planning to ensure that dread cascade. Bugg's Construction is but the first gravestone to tip – and it's a very crowded cemetery.'

'Your analogy makes me even more nervous.'

'Your glamour fades a touch when you're nervous,' Tehol observed. 'Please, regain your confidence, Rucket.'

'Shut your mouth, Tehol.'

'In any case,' Bugg resumed, 'this meeting was to deliver to you and the Guild the final warning before the collapse. Needless to say, I will be hard to track down once it happens.'

Her eyes settled on Tehol. 'And you, Tehol? Planning on crawling into a hole as well?'

'I thought we weren't talking about that any more.'

'By the Abyss, Master,' Bugg muttered.

Tehol blinked, first at Bugg, then at Rucket. Then, 'Oh. Sorry. You meant, um, was I planning on going into hiding, right? Well, I'm undecided. Part of the satisfaction, you see, is in witnessing the mess. Because, regardless of how we've insinuated ourselves in the machinery of Lether's vast commerce, the most bitter truth is that the causes behind this impending chaos are in fact systemic. Granted, we're hastening things somewhat, but dissolution – in its truest sense – is an integral flaw in the system itself. It may well view itself as immortal, eminently adaptable and all that, but that's all both illusional and delusional. Resources are never infinite, though they might seem that way. And those resources include more than just the raw product of earth and sea. They also include labour, and the manifest conceit of a monetary system with its arbitrary notions of value – the two forces we set our sights on, by the way. Shipping out the lowest classes – the dispossessed – to pressure the infrastructure, and then stripping away hard currency to escalate a recession – why are you two staring at me like that?'

Rucket smiled. 'Defaulting to the comfort of your scholarly analysis to deflect us from your more pathetic fixations. That, Tehol Beddict, is perhaps the lowest you have gone yet.'

'But we've just begun.'

'You may wish to believe that to be the case. For myself, my own curiosity is fast diminishing.'

'But think of all the challenges in store for us, Rucket!'

She surged to her feet. 'I'm going out the back way.'

'You won't fit.'

'Alas, Tehol, the same will never be said of you. Good day, gentlemen.'

'Wait!'

'Yes, Tehol?'

'Well, uh, I trust this conversation will resume at a later date?'

'I'm not hanging around for that,' Bugg said, crossing his brawny arms in a show of . . . something. Disgust, maybe. Or, Tehol reconsidered, more likely abject envy.

'Nothing is certain,' Rucket told him. 'Barring the truth that men are wont to get lost in their illusions of grandeur.'

'Oh,' murmured Bugg, 'very nice, Rucket.'

'If that hadn't left me speechless,' Tehol said as she rolled away, 'I'd have said something.'

'I have no doubt of that, Master.'

'Your faith is a relief, Bugg.'

'Small comfort in comparison, I'd wager.'

'In comparison,' Tehol agreed, nodding. 'Now, shall we go for a walk, old friend?'

'Assuming your drape is now unmarred by unsightly bulges.'

'In a moment.'

'Master?'

Tehol smiled at the alarm on Bugg's face. 'I was just imaging her stuck there, wedged in Huldo's alleyway. Unable to turn. Helpless, in fact.'

'There it is,' he said with a sigh, 'you did indeed manage to sink lower.'

There was an old Gral legend that had begun to haunt Taralack Veed, although he could not quite grasp its relevance to this moment, here in Letheras, with the Lifestealer walking at his side as they pushed through the crowds mulling outside a row of market stalls opposite the Quillas Canal.

The Gral were an ancient people; their tribes had dwelt in the wild hills of the First Empire, and there had been Gral companies serving in Dessimbelackis's vaunted armies, as trackers, as skirmishers and as shock troops, although this manner of combat ill suited them. Even then, the Gral preferred their feuds, the spilling of blood in the name of personal honour. The pursuit of vengeance was a worthy cause. Slaughtering strangers made no sense and stained the soul, demanding tortured cleansing rituals. Further, there was no satisfaction in such murder.

Two months before the Great Fall, a commander named Vorlock Duven, leading the Karasch Legion deep into the untamed wastes of the southwest, had sent her seventy-four Gral warriors into the Tasse Hills to begin a campaign of subjugation against the tribe believed to rule that forbidding range. The Gral were to incite the Tasse to battle, then withdraw, with the savages hard on their heels, to a place of ambush at the very edge of the highlands.

Leading the Gral was a wise veteran of the Bhok'ar clan named Sidilack, called by many Snaketongue after a sword-thrust into his mouth had sliced down the length of his tongue. His warriors, well blooded after a three-year campaign of conquest among the desert and plains peoples south of Ugari, were skilled at finding the hidden trails leading into the rough heights, and before long they were coming upon rude dwellings and rock shelters in the midst of ancient ruins that hinted that some terrible descent from civilization had afflicted the Tasse long ago.

At dusk on the third day seven woad-painted savages ambushed the lead scouts, killing one before being driven off. Of the four Tasse who had fallen in the clash, only one was not already dead of his wounds. The language of his pain-stricken ravings was like nothing Sidilack and his warriors had ever heard before. Beneath the dusty blue paint the Tasse were physically unlike any other nearby tribes. Tall, lithe, with strangely small hands and feet, they had elongated faces, weak chins and oversized teeth. Their eyes were close-set, the irises tawny like dried grass, the whites blistered with so many blood vessels it seemed they might well weep red tears.

Among all four of the Tasse the signs of dehydration and malnutrition were obvious, and as fighters they had been singularly ineffective with their stone-tipped spears and knotted clubs.

The wounded savage soon died.

Resuming their hunt, the Gral pushed ever deeper, ever higher into the hills. They found ancient terraces that had once held crops, the soil now lifeless, barely able to sustain dry desert scrub. They found stone-lined channels to collect rainwater that no longer came. They found stone tombs with large capstones carved into phallic shapes. On the trail potsherds and white bleached bone fragments crunched underfoot.

At noon on the fourth day the Gral came upon the settlement of the Tasse. Twelve scraggy huts, from which rushed three warriors with spears, shrieking as they lined up in a pathetic defensive line in front of five starving females and a lone two- or three-year-old female child.

Sidilack, the wise veteran who had fought twenty battles, who had stained his soul with the slaughter of countless strangers, sent his Gral forward. The battle lasted a half-dozen heartbeats. When the Tasse men fell their women attacked with their hands and teeth. When they were all dead, the lone child crouched down and hissed at them like a cat.

A sword was raised to strike her down.

It never descended. The clearing was suddenly swallowed in shadows. Seven terrible hounds emerged to surround the child, and a man appeared. His shoulders so broad as to make him seem hunched, he was wearing an ankle-length coat of blued chain, his black hair long and unbound. Cold blue eyes fixed upon Sidilack and he spoke in the language of the First Empire: 'They were the last. I do not decry your slaughter. They lived in fear. This land – not their home – could not feed them. Abandoned by the Deragoth and their kind, they had failed in life's struggle.' He turned then to regard the child. 'But this one I will take.'

Sidilack, it was said, could feel then the deepest stain settling upon his soul. One that no cleansing ritual could eradicate. He saw, in that moment, the grim fate of his destiny, a descent into the madness of inconsolable grief. The god would take the last child, but it was most certainly the last. The blood of the others was on Sidilack's hands, a curse, a haunting that only death could relieve.

Yet he was Gral. Forbidden from taking his own life.

Another legend followed, that one recounting the long journey to Snaketongue's final end, his pursuit of questions that could not be answered, the pathos of his staggering walk into the Dead Man's Desert – realm of the fallen Gral – where even the noble spirits refused him, his soul, the hollow defence of his own crime.

Taralack Veed did not want to think of these things. Echoes of the child, that hissing, less-than-human creature who had been drawn into the shadows by a god – to what end? A mystery within the legend that would never be solved. But he did not believe there had been mercy in that god's heart. He did not want to think of young females with small hands and feet, with sloped chins and large canines, with luminous eyes the hue of savanna grasses.

He did not want to think of Sidilack and the endless night of his doom. The warrior with slaughter's blood staining his hands and his soul. That tragic fool was nothing like Taralack Veed, he told himself again and again. Truths did not hide in vague similarities, after all; only in the specific details, and he shared none of those with old Snaketongue.

'You speak rarely these days, Taralack Veed.'

The Gral glanced up at Icarium. 'I am frightened for you,' he said.

'Why?'

'I see nothing of the hardness in your eyes, friend, the hardness that perhaps none but a longtime companion would be able to detect. The hardness that bespeaks your rage. It seems to sleep, and I do not know if even Rhulad can awaken it. If he cannot, then you will die. Quickly.'

'If all you say of me is true,' the Jhag replied, 'then my death would be welcome. And justified in every sense of the word.'

'No other can defeat the Emperor—'

'Why are you so certain I can? I do not wield a magical sword. I do not return to life should I fall. These are the rumours regarding the Tiste Edur named Rhulad, yes?'

461

'When your anger is unleashed, Icarium, you cannot be stopped.'

'Ah, but it seems I can.'

Taralack Veed's eyes narrowed. 'Is this the change that has come to you, Icarium? Have your memories returned to you?'

'I believe if they had, I would not now be here,' the Jhag replied, pausing before one stall offering cord-wrapped pottery. 'Look upon these items here, Taralack Veed, and tell me what you see. Empty vessels? Or endless possibilities?'

'They are naught but pots.'

Icarium smiled.

It was, the Gral decided, a far too easy smile. 'Do you mock me, Icarium?'

'Something awaits me. I do not mean this mad Emperor. Something else. Answer me this. How does one measure time?'

'By the course of the sun, the phases of the moon, the wheel of the stars. And, of course, in cities such as this one, the sounding of a bell at fixed intervals – a wholly absurd conceit and, indeed, one that is spiritually debilitating.'

'The Gral speaks.'

'Now you truly mock me. This is unlike you, Icarium.'

'The sounding of bells, their increments established by the passing of sand or water through a narrowed vessel. As you say, a conceit. An arbitrary assertion of constancy. Can we truly say, however, that time is constant?'

'As any Gral would tell you, it is not. Else our senses lie.'

'Perhaps they do.'

'Then we are lost.'

'I appreciate your intellectual belligerence today, Taralack Veed.'

They moved on, wandering slowly alongside the canal.

'I understand your obsession with time,' the Gral said. 'You, who have passed through age after age, unchanging, unknowing.'

'Unknowing, yes. That is the problem, isn't it?'

'I do not agree. It is our salvation.'

They were silent for a few more strides. Many were the curious – at times pitying – glances cast their way. The champions were also the condemned, after all. Yet was there hope, buried deep behind those shying eyes? There must be. For an end to the nightmare that was Rhulad Sengar, the Edur Emperor of Lether.

'Without an understanding of time, history means nothing. Do you follow, Taralack Veed?'

'Yet you do not understand time, do you?'

'No, that is true. Yet I believe I have . . . pursued this . . . again and again. From age to age. In the faith that a revelation on the meaning of time will unlock my own hidden history. I would find its true measure,

Taralack Veed. And not just its measure, but its very nature. Consider this canal, and those linked to it. The water is pushed by current and tide from the river, then traverses the city, only to rejoin the river not far from where it first entered. We may seek to step out from the river and so choose our own path, but no matter how straight it seems, we will, in the end, return to that river.'

'As with the bells, then,' the Gral said, 'water tracks the passage of time.'

'You misunderstand,' Icarium replied, but did not elaborate.

Taralack Veed scowled, paused to spit thick phlegm onto his palms, then swept it back through his hair. Somewhere in the crowd a woman screamed, but the sound was not repeated. 'The canal's current cannot change the law that binds its direction. The canal is but a detour.'

'Yes, one that slows the passage of its water. And in turn that water changes, gathering the refuse of the city it passes through, and so, upon returning to the river, it is a different colour. Muddier, more befouled.'

'The slower your path, the muddier your boots?'

'Even so,' Icarium said, nodding.

'Time is nothing like that.'

'Are you so certain? When we must wait, our minds fill with sludge, random thoughts like so much refuse. When we are driven to action, our current is swift, the water seemingly clear, cold and sharp.'

'I'd rather, Icarium, we wait a long time. Here, in the face of what is to come.'

'The path to Rhulad? As you like. But I tell you, Taralack Veed, that is not the path I am walking.'

Another half-dozen strides.

Then the Gral spoke. 'They wrap the cord around them, Icarium, to keep them from breaking.'

Senior Assessor's eyes glittered as he stood amidst a crowd twenty paces from where Icarium and Taralack Veed had paused in front of a potter's stall. His hands were folded together, the fingers twitching. His breathing was rapid and shallow.

Beside him, Samar Dev rolled her eyes, then asked, 'Are you about to fall dead on me? If I'd known this walk involved skulking in that Jhag's shadow, I think I would have stayed in the compound.'

'The choices you make,' he replied, 'must needs be entirely of your own accord, Samar Dev. Reasonably distinct from mine or anyone else's. It is said that the history of human conflict resides exclusively in the clash of expectations.'

'Is it now?'

'Furthermore—'

'Never mind your "furthermore", Senior Assessor. Compromise is the negotiation of expectation. With your wayward notions we do not negotiate, and so all the compromising is mine.'

'As you choose.'

She thought about hitting him, decided she didn't want to make a scene. What was it with men and their obsessions? 'He is in all likelihood going to die, and soon.'

'I think not. No, most certainly I think not.'

Icarium and the Gral resumed their meander through the crowds, and after a moment Senior Assessor followed, maintaining his distance. Sighing, Samar Dev set off after him. She didn't like this mob. It felt wrong. Tense, overwrought. Strain was visible on faces, and the cries of the hawkers sounded strident and half desperate. Few passers-by, she noted, were buying.

'Something's wrong,' she said.

'There is nothing here that cannot be explained by impending financial panic, Samar Dev. Although you may believe I am unaware of anything but him, I assure you that I have assessed the condition of Letheras and, by extension, this entire empire. A crisis looms. Wealth, alas, is not an infinite commodity. Systems such as this are dependent upon the assumption of unlimited resources, however. These resources range from cheap labour and materials to an insatiable demand. Such demand, in turn, depends on rather more ethereal virtues, such as confidence, will, perceived need and the bliss of short-term thinking, any one of which is vulnerable to mysterious and often inexplicable influences. We are witness, here, to the effects of a complex collusion of factors which are serving to undermine said virtues. Furthermore, it is my belief that the situation has been orchestrated.'

Her mind had begun to drift with Senior Assessor's diatribe, but this last observation drew her round. 'Letheras is under economic assault?'

'Well put, Samar Dev. Someone is manipulating the situation to achieve a cascading collapse, yes. Such is my humble assessment.'

'Humble?'

'Of course not. I view my own brilliance with irony.'

'To what end?'

'Why, to make me humble.'

'Are we going to follow Icarium and his pet Gral all afternoon?'

'I am the only living native of Cabal, Samar Dev, to have seen with my own eyes our god. Is it any wonder I follow him?'

God? He's not a god. He's a damned Jhag from the Odhan west of Seven Cities. Suffering a tragic curse, but then, aren't they all? A figure well ahead of Icarium and Taralack Veed caught her attention. A figure tall, hulking, with a shattered face and a huge stone sword strapped to its back. 'Oh no,' she murmured.

'What is it?' Senior Assessor asked.

'He's seen him.'

'Samar Dev?'

But he was behind her now, and she was hurrying forward, roughly pushing past people. Expectations? Most certainly. Compromise? Not a chance.

One of the sconces had a faulty valve and had begun producing thick black tendrils of smoke that coiled like serpents in the air, and Uruth's coughing echoed like barks in the antechamber. His back to the door leading to the throne room, Sirryn Kanar stood with crossed arms, watching the two Tiste Edur. Tomad Sengar was pacing, walking a path that deftly avoided the other waiting guards even as he made a point of pretending they weren't there. His wife had drawn her dark grey robe about herself, so tight she reminded Sirryn of a vulture with its wings folded close. Age had made her shoulders slightly hunched, adding to the avian impression, sufficient to draw a half-smile to the guard's mouth.

'No doubt this waiting amuses you,' Tomad said in a growl.

'So you were watching me after all.'

'I was watching the door, which you happen to be standing against.'

Contemplating kicking through it, no doubt. Sirryn's smile broadened. *Alas, you'd have to go through me, and that you won't do, will you?* 'The Emperor is very busy.'

'With what?' Tomad demanded. 'Triban Gnol decides everything, after all. Rhulad just sits with a glazed look and nods every now and then.'

'You think little of your son.'

That struck a nerve, he saw, as husband and wife both fixed hard eyes on him.

'We think less of Triban Gnol,' Uruth said.

There was no need to comment on that observation, for Sirryn well knew their opinions of the Chancellor; indeed, their views on all Letherii. Blind bigotry, of course, all the more hypocritical for the zeal with which the Edur had embraced the Letherii way of living, even as they sneered and proclaimed their disgust and contempt. *If you are so disgusted, why do you still suckle at the tit, Edur? You had your chance at destroying all this. Us. And our own whole terrible civilization.* No, there was little that was worth saying to these two savages.

He felt more than heard the scratch at the door behind him, and slowly straightened. 'The Emperor will see you now.'

Tomad wheeled round to face the door, and Sirryn saw in the bastard's face a sudden strain beneath the haughty façade. Beyond him, Uruth swept her cloak back, freeing her arms. Was that fear in her eyes? He watched her move up to stand beside her husband, yet

465

it seemed all they drew from that proximity was yet another tension.

Stepping to one side, Sirryn Kanar swung open the door. 'Halt in the tiled circle,' he said. 'Step past it and a dozen arrows will find your body. No warning will be voiced. By the Emperor's own command. Now, proceed. Slowly.'

At this moment, a Tiste Edur and four Letherii soldiers approached the city's west gate on lathered horses. A shout from the Edur sent pedestrians scattering from the raised road. The five riders were covered in mud and two bore wounds. The swords of the two whose scabbards were not empty were blood-crusted. The Edur was one of those without weapons, and from his back jutted the stub of an arrow, its iron head buried in his right scapula. Blood soaked his cloak where the quarrel had pinned it to his back. This warrior was dying. He had been dying for four days.

Another hoarse shout from the Tiste Edur, as he led his ragged troop beneath the gate's arch, and into the city of Letheras.

The Errant studied Rhulad Sengar, who had sat motionless since the Chancellor had returned to announce the imminent arrival of Tomad and Uruth. Was it some faltering of courage that had kept the Emperor from demanding their immediate presence? There was no way to tell. Even the Chancellor's cautious queries had elicited nothing.

Lanterns burned on. The traditional torches breathed out smoke, their flickering light licking the walls. Triban Gnol stood, hands folded, waiting.

Within Rhulad's head battles were being waged. Armies of will and desire contested with the raving forces of fear and doubt. The field was sodden with blood and littered with fallen heroes. Or into his skull some blinding fog had rolled in, oppressive as oblivion itself, and Rhulad wandered lost.

He sat as if carved, clothed in stained wealth, the product of a mad artist's vision. Lacquered eyes and scarred flesh, twisted mouth and black strands of greasy hair. Sculpted solid to the throne to cajole symbols of permanence and imprisonment, but this madness had lost all subtlety – ever the curse of fascism, the tyranny of gleeful servility that could not abide subversion.

Look upon him, and see what comes when justice is vengeance. When challenge is criminal. When scepticism is treason. Call upon them, Emperor! Your father, your mother. Call them to stand before you in this inverted nightmare of fidelity, and unleash your wrath!

'Now,' Rhulad said in a croak.

The Chancellor gestured to a guard near the side door, who turned in a soft rustle of armour and brushed his gauntleted hand upon the ornate panel. A moment later it opened.

All of this was occurring to the Errant's left, along the same wall he leaned against, so he could not see what occurred then beyond, barring a few indistinct words.

Tomad and Uruth Sengar strode into the throne room, halting in the tiled circle. Both then bowed to their Emperor.

Rhulad licked his broken lips. 'They are kin,' he said.

A frown from Tomad.

'Enslaved by humans. They deserved our liberation, did they not?'

'From the Isle of Sepik, Emperor?' asked Uruth. 'Are these of whom you speak?'

'They were indeed liberated,' Tomad said, nodding.

Rhulad leaned forward. 'Enslaved kin. Liberated. Then why, dear Father, do they now rot in chains?'

Tomad seemed unable to answer, a look of confusion on his lined face.

'Awaiting your disposition,' Uruth said. 'Emperor, we have sought audience with you many times since our return. Alas,' she glanced over at Triban Gnol, 'the Chancellor sends us away. Without fail.'

'And so,' Rhulad said in a rasp, 'you proclaimed them guests of the empire as was their right, then settled them where? Why, not in our many fine residences surrounding the palace. No. You chose the trenches – the pits alongside debtors, traitors and murderers. Is this your notion of the Guest Gift in your household, Tomad? Uruth? Strange, for I do not recall in my youth this most profound betrayal of Tiste Edur custom. *Not in the House of my family!*'

'Rhulad. Emperor,' Tomad said, almost stepping back in the face of his son's rage, 'have you seen these kin of ours? They are . . . pathetic. To look upon them is to feel stained. Dirtied. Their spirits are crushed. They have been made a mockery of all that is Tiste Edur. This was the crime the humans of Sepik committed against our blood, and for that we answered, Emperor. That island is now dead.'

'Kin,' the Emperor whispered. 'Explain to me, Father, for I do not understand. You perceive the crime and deliver the judgement, yes, in the name of Edur blood. No matter how fouled, no matter how decrepit. Indeed, those details are without relevance – they in no way affect the punishment, except perhaps to make it all the more severe. All of this, Father, is a single thread of thought, and it runs true. Yet there is another, isn't there? A twisted, knotted thing. One where the victims of those humans are undeserving of our regard, where they must be hidden away, left to rot like filth.

'What, then, were you avenging?

'Where – oh where, Father – is the Guest Gift? Where is the honour

467

that binds all Tiste Edur? Where, Tomad Sengar, where, in all this, is my will? *I am Emperor and the face of the empire is mine and mine alone!*'

As the echoes of that shriek rebounded in the throne room, reluctant to fade, neither Uruth nor Tomad seemed able to speak. Their grey faces were the colour of ash.

Triban Gnol, standing a few paces behind and to the right of the two Edur, looked like a penitent priest, his eyes down on the floor. But the Errant, whose senses could reach out with a sensitivity that far surpassed that of any mortal, could hear the hammering of that old man's wretched heart; could almost smell the dark glee concealed behind his benign, vaguely rueful expression.

Uruth seemed to shake herself then, slowly straightening. 'Emperor,' she said, 'we cannot know your will when we are barred from seeing you. Is it the Chancellor's privilege to deny the Emperor's own parents? The Emperor's own blood? And what of all the other Tiste Edur? Emperor, a wall has been raised around you. A Letherii wall.'

The Errant heard Triban Gnol's heart stutter in its cage. 'Majesty!' the Chancellor cried in indignation. 'No such wall exists! You are protected, yes. Indeed. From all who would harm you—'

'Harm him?' Tomad shouted, wheeling on the Chancellor. 'He is our son!'

'Assuredly not you, Tomad Sengar. Nor you, Uruth. Perhaps the protection necessary around a ruler might seem to you a wall, but—'

'We would speak to him!'

'From you,' Rhulad said in a dreadful rasp, 'I would hear nothing. Your words are naught but lies. You both lie to me, as Hannan Mosag lies, as every one of my fellow Tiste Edur lies. Do you imagine I cannot smell the stench of your fear? Your hatred? No, I will hear neither of you. However, you shall hear me.'

The Emperor slowly leaned back in his throne, his eyes hard. 'Our kin will be set free. This I command. They will be set free. For you, my dear parents, it seems a lesson is required. You left them to rot in darkness. In the ships. In the trench-pits. From these egregious acts, I can only assume that you do not possess any comprehension of the horror of such ordeals. Therefore it is my judgement that you must taste something of what you inflicted upon our kin. You will both spend two months interred in the dungeon crypts of the Fifth Wing. You will live in darkness, fed once a day through chutes in the ceilings of your cells. You will have no-one but each other with whom to speak. You will be shackled. In darkness – do you understand, Uruth? True darkness. No shadows for you to manipulate, no power to whisper in your ear. In that time, I suggest you both think long of what Guest Gift means to a Tiste Edur, of honouring our kin no matter how far they have fallen. Of what it truly means to liberate.' Rhulad waved his free hand. 'Send them away, Chancellor. I am made ill by their betrayal of our own kin.'

The Errant, very nearly as stunned as were Tomad and Uruth, missed whatever gesture Triban Gnol used to summon forth the Letherii guards. They appeared quickly, as if conjured from thin air, and closed round Tomad and Uruth.

Letherii hands, iron-scaled and implacable, closed about Tiste Edur arms.

And the Errant knew that the end had begun.

Samar Dev's hope of ending things before they began did not last long. She was still four strides from Karsa Orlong when he reached Icarium and Taralack Veed. The Toblakai had approached from the side, almost behind the Jhag – who had turned to contemplate the canal's murky waters – and she watched as the huge warrior reached out one hand, grasped Icarium by an upper arm, and swung him round.

Taralack Veed lunged to break that grip and his head was snapped by a punch that seemed almost casual. The Gral collapsed onto the pavestones and did not move.

Icarium was staring down at the hand clutching his left arm, his expression vaguely perturbed.

'Karsa!' Samar Dev shouted, as heads turned and citizens – those who had witnessed Taralack Veed's fate – moved away. 'If you've killed the Gral—'

'He is nothing,' Karsa said in a growl, his eyes fixed on Icarium. 'Your last minder, Jhag, was far more formidable. Now you stand here with no-one to attack me from behind.'

'Karsa, he is unarmed.'

'But I am not.'

Icarium was still studying that battered hand gripping his arm – the red weals of scarring left by shackles encircling the thick wrist, the dots and dashes of old tattoos – as if the Jhag was unable to comprehend its function. Then he glanced over at Samar Dev, and his face brightened in a warm smile. 'Ah, witch. Both Taxilian and Varat Taun have spoken highly of you. Would that we had met earlier – although I have seen you from across the compound—'

'She is not your problem,' Karsa said. 'I am your problem.'

Icarium slowly turned and met the Toblakai's eyes. 'You are Karsa Orlong, who does not understand what it means to spar. How many comrades have you crippled?'

'They are not comrades. Nor are you.'

'What about me?' Samar Dev demanded. 'Am I not a comrade of yours, Karsa?'

He scowled. 'What of it?'

'Icarium is unarmed. If you kill him here you will not face the

Emperor. No, you will find yourself in chains. At least until your head gets lopped off.'

'I have told you before, witch. Chains do not hold me.'

'You want to face the Emperor, don't you?'

'And if this one kills him first?' Karsa demanded, giving the arm a shake that clearly startled Icarium.

'Is that the problem?' Samar Dev asked. *And is that why you're crippling other champions? Not that any will play with you any more, you brainless bully.*

'You wish to face Emperor Rhulad before I do?' Icarium inquired.

'I do not ask for your permission, Jhag.'

'Yet I give it nonetheless, Karsa Orlong. You are welcome to Rhulad.'

Karsa glared at Icarium who, though not as tall, somehow still seemed able to meet the Toblakai eye to eye without lifting his head.

Then something odd occurred. Samar Dev saw a slight widening of Karsa's eyes as he studied Icarium's face. 'Yes,' he said in a gruff voice. 'I see it now.'

'I am pleased,' replied Icarium.

'See what?' Samar Dev demanded.

On the ground behind her Taralack Veed groaned, coughed, then rolled onto his side and was sick.

Karsa released the Jhag's arm and stepped back. 'You are good to your word?'

Icarium bowed slightly then said, 'How could I not be?'

'That is true. Icarium, I witness.'

The Jhag bowed a second time.

'Keep your hands away from that sword!'

This shout brought them all round, to see a half-dozen Letherii guards edging closer, their weapons unsheathed.

Karsa sneered at them. 'I am returning to the compound, children. Get out of my way.'

They parted like reeds before a canoe's prow as the Toblakai marched forward, then moved into his wake, hurrying to keep up with Karsa's long strides.

Samar Dev stared after them, then loosed a sudden yelp, before clapping her hands to her mouth.

'You remind me of Senior Assessor, doing that,' Icarium observed with another smile. His gaze lifted past her. 'And yes, there he remains, my very own personal vulture. If I gesture him to us, do you think he will come, witch?'

She shook her head, still struggling with an overwhelming flood of relief and the aftermath of terror's cold clutch that even now made her hands tremble. 'No, he prefers to worship from a distance.'

'Worship? The man is deluded. Samar Dev, will you inform him of that?'

'As you like, but it won't matter, Icarium. His people, you see, they remember you.'

'Do they now.' Icarium's eyes narrowed slightly on the Senior Assessor, who had begun to cringe from the singular attention of his god.

Spirits below, why was I interested in this monk in the first place? There is no lure to the glow of fanatical worship. There is only smug intransigence and the hidden knives of sharp judgement.

'Perhaps,' said Icarium, 'I must speak to him after all.'

'He'll run away.'

'In the compound, then—'

'Where you can corner him?'

The Jhag smiled. 'Proof of my omnipotence.'

Sirryn Kanar's exultation was like a cauldron on the boil, the heavy lid moments from stuttering loose, yet he had held himself down on the long walk into the crypts of the Fifth Wing, where the air was wet enough to taste, where mould skidded beneath their boots and the dank chill reached tendrils to their very bones.

This, then, would be the home of Tomad and Uruth Sengar for the next two months, and Sirryn could not be more pleased. In the light of the lanterns the guards carried he saw, with immense satisfaction, that certain look on the Edur faces, the one that settled upon the expression of every prisoner: the numbed disbelief, the shock and fear stirring in the eyes every now and then, until they were once more overwhelmed by that stupid refusal to accept reality.

He would take sexual pleasure this night, he knew, as if this moment now was but one half of desire's dialogue. He would sleep satiated, content with the world. His world.

They walked the length of the lowest corridor until reaching the very end. Sirryn gestured that Tomad be taken to the cell on the left; Uruth into the one opposite. He watched as the Edur woman, with a last glance back at her husband, turned and accompanied her three Letherii guards. A moment later Sirryn followed.

'I know that you are the more dangerous,' he said to her as one of his guards bent to fix the shackle onto her right ankle. 'There are shadows here, so long as we remain.'

'I leave your fate to others,' she replied.

He studied her for a moment. 'You shall be forbidden visitors.'

'Yes.'

'The shock goes away.'

She looked at him, and he saw in her eyes raw contempt.

471

'In its place,' he continued, 'comes despair.'

'Begone, you wretched man.'

Sirryn smiled. 'Take her cloak. Why should Tomad be the only one to suffer the chill?'

She pushed the guard's hand away and unlocked the clasp herself.

'You were foolish enough to refuse the Edur Gift,' he said, 'so now you receive' – he waved at the tiny cell with its dripping ceiling, its streaming walls – 'the Letherii gift. Granted with pleasure.'

When she made no reply, Sirryn turned about. 'Come,' he said to his guards, 'let us leave them to their darkness.'

As the last echoes of their footfalls faded, Feather Witch moved out from the cell in which she had been hiding. Guests had arrived in her private world. Unwelcome. These were her corridors; the uneven stones beneath her feet, the slick, slimy walls within her reach, the sodden air, the reek of rot, the very darkness itself – these all belonged to her.

Tomad and Uruth Sengar. Uruth, who had once owned Feather Witch. Well, there was justice in that. Feather Witch was Letherii, after all, and who could now doubt that the grey tide had turned?

She crept out into the corridor, her moccasin-clad feet noiseless on the slumped floor, then hesitated. Did she wish to look upon them? To voice her mockery of their plight? The temptation was strong. But no, better to remain unseen, unknown to them.

And they were now speaking to each other. She drew closer to listen.

'. . . not long,' Tomad was saying. 'This, more than anything else, wife, forces our hand. Hannan Mosag will approach the women and an alliance will be forged—'

'Do not be so sure of that,' Uruth replied. 'We have not forgotten the truth of the Warlock King's ambition. This is of his making—'

'Move past that – there is no choice.'

'Perhaps. But concessions will be necessary and that will be difficult, for we do not trust him. Oh, he will give his word, no doubt. As you say, there is no choice. But what value Hannan Mosag's word? His soul is poisoned. He still lusts for that sword, for the power it holds. And that we will not give him. Never within his reach. Never!'

There was a rustle of chains, then Tomad spoke: 'He did not sound mad, Uruth.'

'No,' she replied in a low voice. 'He did not.'

'He was right in his outrage.'

'Yes.'

'As were we, on Sepik, when we saw how far our kin had fallen. Their misery, their surrender of all will, all pride, all identity. They were once Tiste Edur! Had we known that from the first—'

'We would have left them, husband?'

Silence, then: 'No. Vengeance against the Malazans was necessary. But for our sake, not that of our kin. Rhulad misunderstood that.'

'He did not. Tomad, those kin suffered the holds of the fleet. They suffered the pits. Rhulad did not misunderstand. We were punishing them for their failure. That, too, was vengeance. Against our very own blood.'

Bitterness now in Tomad's voice: 'You said nothing when judgement was cast, wife. Please yourself with this false wisdom if you like. If it is what I must hear from you, then I'd rather silence.'

'Then, husband, you shall have it.'

Feather Witch eased back. Yes, Hannan Mosag would be told. And what would he then do? Seek out the Edur women? She hoped not. If Feather Witch possessed a true enemy, it was they. Was the Warlock King their match? In deceit, most certainly. But in power? Not any more. Unless, of course, he had hidden allies.

She would need to speak with the Errant. With her god.

She would need to force some . . . concessions.

Smiling, Feather Witch slipped her way up the corridor.

The fate of Tomad and Uruth Sengar drifted through her mind, then passed on, leaving scarce a ripple.

One subterranean tunnel of the Old Palace stretched inland almost to the junction of the Main Canal and Creeper Canal. This passage had been bricked in at three separate locations, and these barriers Hannan Mosag had left in place, twisting reality with Kurald Emurlahn in order to pass through them, as he had done this time with Bruthen Trana in tow.

The Warlock King's followers had kept the warrior hidden for some time now, whilst Hannan Mosag worked his preparations, and this had not been an easy task. It was not as if the palace was astir with search parties and the like – the fever of confusion and fear was endemic these days, after all. People vanished with disturbing regularity, especially among the Tiste Edur. No, the difficulty resided with Bruthen Trana himself.

A strong-willed man. But this will do us well, provided I can pound into his skull the fact that impatience is a weakness. A warrior needed resolve, true enough, but there was a time and there was a place, and both had yet to arrive.

Hannan Mosag had led Bruthen to the chamber at the very end of the tunnel, an octagonal room of ill-fitted stones. The angular domed ceiling overhead, tiled in once bright but now black copper, was so low the room felt like a hut.

When the Warlock King had first found this chamber, it and at least forty paces of the tunnel had been under water, the depth following the

473

downward gradient until the black, murky sludge very nearly brushed the chamber's ceiling.

Hannan Mosag had drained the water through a modest rent that led into the realm of the Nascent, which he then closed, moving quickly in his crab-like scrabble to drag seven bundled arm-length shafts of Blackwood down the slimy corridor and into the chamber. It had begun refilling, of course, and the Warlock King sloshed his way to the centre, where he untied the bundle, then began constructing an octagonal fence, each stick a hand's width in from the walls, two to each side, held mostly upright in the thick sludge covering the floor. When he had completed this task, he called upon his fullest unveiling of Kurald Emurlahn.

At a dreadful cost. Seeking to purge the power of all chaos, of the poisonous breath of the Crippled God, he was almost unequal to the task. His malformed flesh, his twisted bones, the thin, blackened blood in his veins and arteries; these now served the malign world of the Fallen One, forming a symbiosis of life and power. It had been so long since he had last felt – truly felt – the purity of Kurald Emurlahn that, even in its fragmented, weakened state, he very nearly recoiled at its burning touch.

With the air reeking of scorched flesh and singed hair, Hannan Mosag sought to force sanctification upon the chamber. Trapping the power of Shadow in this, his new, private temple. An entire night of struggle, the cold water ever rising, his legs numb, he began to feel his concentration tearing apart. In desperation – feeling it all slipping away – he called upon Father Shadow.

Scabandari.

Despairing, knowing that he had failed—

And sudden power, pure and resolute, burgeoned in the chamber. Boiling away the water in roiling gusts of steam, until oven-dry heat crackled from the stone walls. The mud on the floor hardened, cementing the Blackwood shafts.

That heat reached into Hannan Mosag's flesh, down to grip his very bones. He had shrieked in agony, even as a new kind of life spread through him.

It had not healed him; had done nothing to straighten his bones or unclench scarred tissue.

No, it had been more like a promise, a whispering invitation to some blessed future. Fading in a dozen heartbeats, yet the memory of that promise remained with Hannan Mosag.

Scabandari, Father Shadow, still lived. Torn from bone and flesh, true, but the spirit remained. Answering his desperate prayer, gifting this place with sanctity.

I have found the path. I can see the end.

Now he crouched on the hard, desiccated ground and Bruthen Trana – forced to hunch slightly because of the low ceiling – stood at his side. The Warlock King gestured to the centre of the chamber. 'There, warrior. You must lie down. The ritual is readied, but I warn you, the journey will be long and difficult.'

'I do not understand this, Warlock King. This . . . this temple. It is true Kurald Emurlahn.'

'Yes, Bruthen Trana. Blessed by the power of Father Shadow himself. Warrior, your journey itself is so blessed. Does this not tell you that we are on the right path?'

Bruthen Trana stared down at him, was silent for a half-dozen heart-beats, then said, 'You, among all others, should have been turned away. By Father Shadow. Your betrayal—'

'My betrayal means nothing,' the Warlock King snapped. 'Warrior, we are blessed! This place, it is not simply a temple of Kurald Emurlahn! It is a temple of Scabandari! Of our god himself! The very first such temple in this realm – do you not grasp what that means? He is coming back. To us.'

'Then perhaps what we seek is pointless,' Bruthen replied.

'What?'

'Scabandari will return, and he will stand before Rhulad Sengar. Tell me, will your Crippled God risk that confrontation?'

'Do not be a fool, Bruthen Trana. You ask the wrong question. Will Scabandari risk that confrontation? Upon the very moment of his return? We cannot know Father Shadow's power, but I believe he will be weak, exhausted. No, warrior, it is for us to protect him upon his return. Protect, and nourish.'

'Has Fear Sengar found him then?'

Hannan Mosag's dark eyes narrowed. 'What do you know of that, Bruthen Trana?'

'Only what most Edur know. Fear left, to seek out Father Shadow. In answer to his brother. In answer to you, Warlock King.'

'Clearly,' Hannan Mosag said in a tight voice, 'there has been a reconciliation.'

'Perhaps there has. You did not answer my question.'

'I cannot. For I do not know.'

'Do you dissemble yet again?'

'Your accusation is unjust, Bruthen Trana.'

'Let us begin this ritual. Tell me, will I journey in the flesh?'

'No. You would die, and instantly, warrior. No, we must tug free your spirit.'

Hannan Mosag watched as Bruthen Trana moved to the centre of the chamber. The warrior divested himself of his sword and belt and lay down on his back.

'Close your eyes,' the Warlock King said, crawling closer. 'Lead your mind into the comfort of Shadow. You shall feel my touch, upon your chest. Shortly after, all sense of your physical body will vanish. Open your eyes then, and you will find yourself . . . elsewhere.'

'How will I know when I have found the path I seek?'

'By virtue of seeking, you will find, Bruthen Trana. Now, silence please. I must concentrate.'

A short time later the Warlock King reached out and settled his hand upon the warrior's chest.

As easy as that.

The body lying before him drew no breath. Left alone for too long it would begin to rot. But this was sanctified ground, alive now with the power of Kurald Emurlahn. There would be no decay. There would, for the body, be no passage of time at all.

Hannan Mosag pulled himself closer. He began searching Bruthen Trana's clothing. The warrior had something hidden on him – something with an aura of raw power that struck the Warlock King's senses like a stench. He worked through the pockets on the underside of the warrior's leather cloak and found naught but a tattered note of some kind. He emptied the coin pouch tied to the sword-belt. A lone polished stone, black as onyx but nothing more than wave-eroded obsidian. Three docks – the local Letherii currency. And nothing else. With growing irritation, Hannan Mosag began stripping the warrior.

Nothing. Yet he could smell it, permeating the clothing.

Snarling, Hannan Mosag settled back, his hands twitching.

He's taken it with him. That should have been impossible. Yet . . . what other possibility is there?

His fevered gaze found the crumpled note. Collecting it, he flattened the linen and read what had been written there.

At first he could make no sense of the statement – no, not a statement, he realized. A confession. A signature he had not seen before, so stylized in the Letherii fashion as to be indecipherable. Moments later, his mind racing, revelation arrived.

His eyes lifted, fixed upon Bruthen Trana's now naked form. 'What deceit were you planning with this, warrior? Perhaps you are cleverer than I had imagined.' He paused, then smiled. 'No matter now.'

The Warlock King drew his dagger. 'Some blood, yes, to seal the sacred life of my temple. Scabandari, you would understand this. Yes. The necessity.'

He crawled up beside Bruthen Trana. 'Deliver the one we seek, warrior. Yes. Beyond that, alas, my need for you ends.' He raised the knife, then drove it hard into the warrior's heart.

Glancing over at Bugg, Tehol Beddict saw his manservant complete an

476

entire turn, his eyes tracking the huge Tarthenal as if they had been nailed to the barbaric warrior with his absurd stone sword. The cordon of guards flanking the giant looked appropriately terrified. 'Well,' Tehol said, 'he's no Ublala Pung, now is he?'

Bugg did not even seem to hear him.

'Oh, be like that, then. I think I want to talk to that other one – what did you call him? Oh yes, the Jhag. Any person who would not flinch in the grip of that Tarthenal is either brainless or – oh, not a pleasant thought – even scarier. Perhaps it would do to hesitate at this moment, mindful as ever of loyal manservant's advice . . . no? No it is. So please, do stand there like a man whose heart has just dropped through to lodge somewhere underneath his spliver or some such organ I don't want to know about. Yes, then, do that.'

Tehol set off towards the Jhag. The other savage who had been punched unconscious by the Tarthenal – the Tarthenal whom Ublala Pung had broken into the compound to find – was now sitting up, looking dazedly about. Blood still streamed from his thoroughly broken nose. The woman, attractive in an earthy way, Tehol noted again, was speaking to the tattooed giant, while a dozen paces away a foreigner stood gazing with something like awe upon either the woman or the Jhag.

In all, Tehol decided, an interesting scenario. Interesting enough to interrupt in his usual charming manner. As he drew closer, he spread his arms and announced, 'Time, I think, for a more proper welcome to our fair city!' And his blanket slipped down to gather at his feet.

Bugg, alas, missed this delightful introduction, for even as his eyes had clung to the Toblakai, so he found himself walking, following, step after step, as the warrior and his escort marched towards the Champion's Compound – or whatever unintentionally ironic name the guileless officials of the palace had named it. They had come to within a street of the walled enclosure when all hopes of continuing came to a sudden but confused end. For the street was filled with people.

Emaciated, fouled with excrement, mostly naked flesh covered in welts and sores, they packed the street like abandoned children, lost and forlorn, blinking in the harsh afternoon sun. Hundreds of the wretched creatures.

The Toblakai's guards halted at this unexpected barrier, and Bugg saw the foremost one reel back as if assailed by a stench, then turn to argue with the others. Their 'prisoner', on the other hand, simply bellowed at the mob to clear way, then walked on, shouldering through the press.

He had gone perhaps twenty paces when he too drew to a halt. Shoulders and head above the crowd, he glared about, then shouted in a rude version of Malazan: 'I know you! Once slaves of Sepik Island! Hear me!'

Faces swung round. The crowd shifted on all sides, forming a rough circle.

They hear. They are desperate to hear.

'I, Karsa Orlong, will give answer! So I vow. Your kin refuse you. They cast you out. You live or you die and neither matters to them. Nor to any in this cursed land. To your fate I offer nothing! In vengeance for what has been done to you, I offer everything. Now, go your way – your chains are gone. Go, so that never again will they return to you!' With that, the Toblakai warrior moved on, towards the compound's main gate.

Not precisely what they needed to hear, I think. Not yet, anyway. In time, I suspect, it may well return to them.

No, this – here and now – this demands another kind of leadership.

The guards had retreated, seeking another route.

The few citizens within sight were doing the same. No-one wanted to see this legacy.

Bugg pushed himself forward. He drew upon his power, felt it struggle at this unseemly purpose. *Damn my worshippers – whoever, wherever you are. I will have my way here!* Power, devoid of sympathy, cold as the sea, dark as the depths. *I will have my way.*

'Close your eyes,' he said to the mob. The words were little more than a whisper, yet all heard them, solid and undeniable in their minds. *Close your eyes.*

They did. Children, women, men. Motionless now. Eyes closed tight, breaths held in sudden tension, perhaps even fear – but Bugg suspected that these people were beyond fear. They waited for what would come next. And did not move.

I will have my way. 'Hear me. There is a place of safety. Far from here. I will send you there. Now. Friends will find you. They will bring healing, and you will have food, clothing and shelter. When you feel the ground shift beneath you, open your eyes to your new home.'

The sea did not forgive. Its power was hunger and swelling rage. The sea warred with the shore, with the very sky. The sea wept for no-one.

Bugg did not care.

Like any tidal pool motionless under the hot sun, his blood had grown . . . heated. And the smallest pool was filled with the promise of an ocean, a score of oceans – all their power could be held in a single drop of water. Such was Denaeth Rusen, such was Ruse, the warren where life was first born. *And there, in that promise of life itself, will I find what I need.*

Of empathy.

Of warmth.

The power, when it came, was a true current. Angry, yes, yet true. Water had known life for so long it held no memory of purity. Power and gift had become one, and so it yielded to its god.

And he sent them away.

Bugg opened his eyes, and saw before him an empty street.

In his room once more, Karsa Orlong lifted free his shoulder scabbard, then, holding the weapon and its harness in his hands, he stared down at the long table, on which sat an oil lantern set on low burn. After a moment he laid the sword and rigging down. And grew still once more.

Many things to consider, a heaving of foam and froth from some struck well deep within him. The slaves. Cast out because their lives were meaningless. Both these Edur and the Letherii were heartless, yet cowards. Eager to turn away from witnessing the cost of their indifference. Content to strip fellowship from any whenever it suited them.

Yet they would call him the barbarian.

If so, then he was well pleased with the distinction.

And, true to his savagely clear vision of right and wrong, he would hold in his mind that scene – those starved faces, the liquid eyes that seemed to shine so bright he felt burned by their touch – hold to it when he faced Emperor Rhulad. When he then faced every Letherii and every Edur who chose to stand in his way.

So he had vowed, and so all would witness.

This cold thought held him motionless for another dozen heartbeats, then a second image returned to him. Icarium, the one they called Lifestealer.

He had been moments from breaking that Jhag's neck.

And then he had seen in the ash-skinned face . . . something. And with it, recognition.

He would yield to Karsa. He had given his word, and Karsa now knew that would not be broken.

There was Jhag blood in this Icarium, but of that Karsa knew little. Father or mother a Jaghut; it hardly mattered which.

Yet the other parent. Father or mother. Well, he had seen enough in Icarium's face to know that blood. To know it like the whisper of his very own.

Toblakai.

In his opulent office, Chancellor Triban Gnol slowly sat down with uncharacteristic caution. A dust-laden, sweat- and blood-stained Letherii soldier stood before him, flanked on his right by Sirryn Kanar, whose return from the crypts had coincided with the arrival of this messenger.

Triban Gnol looked away from the exhausted soldier. He would call in the scrub-slaves afterwards, to wash down the floor where the man now stood; to scent the air once again with pine oil. Eyes on a lacquered box on the desktop before him, he asked, 'How many did you come in with, Corporal?'

'Three others. And an Edur.'

Triban Gnol's head snapped up. 'Where is he now?'

'Died not three steps into the Domicile's grand entrance, sir.'

'Indeed? Died?'

'He was grievously wounded, sir. And I knew enough to prevent any healer reaching him in time. I moved close to help him as he staggered, and gave the arrow in his back a few twists, then a deeper push. He passed out with the pain of that, and as I caught him and lowered him to the floor, I closed my thumb upon the great artery in his neck. I was able to hold that grip for thirty or more heartbeats. That was more than the Edur could withstand.'

'And you a mere corporal in my employ? I think not. Sirryn, after we are done here, draft a promotion for this man.'

'Yes, Chancellor.'

'And so,' Triban Gnol resumed, 'being of rank among the remaining Letherii, the responsibility for reporting fell to you.'

'Yes sir.'

'I need the names of the others.'

The corporal seemed to flinch. 'Sir, without my soldiers, I would never have—'

'I understand your loyalty, and I commend you. Alas, we must face this situation with a clear eye. We must recognize necessity. Those soldiers are not mine. Not like you.'

'They are loyal, sir—'

'To whom? To what? No, the risk is too great. I will grant you this gift, however.' The Chancellor's gaze flicked to Sirryn. 'Quick and painless. No interrogation.'

Sirryn's brows rose. 'None?'

'None.'

'As you command, sir.'

The corporal licked his lips, and then, clearly forcing out the words, he said, 'I thank you, sir.'

The Chancellor's nod was distracted, his gaze once more on the gleaming box of Blackwood on his desk. 'I would ask again,' he said, 'there was no indication of who they were? No formal declaration of war?'

'Nothing like that at all, sir,' the corporal replied. 'Hundreds of burning ships – that was their declaration of war. And even then, they seemed . . . few. No army – no sign at all of the landing.'

'Yet there was one.'

'Errant fend, yes! Sir, I rode with twenty Letherii, veterans all, and six Tiste Edur of the Arapay. Edur magic or not, we were ambushed in a clearing behind an abandoned homestead. One moment – thinking to make our camp – we were reining in amidst the high grasses – alone – and the next there was thunder and fire, and bodies flying – flying, sir, through the air. Or just limbs. Pieces. And arrows hissing in the dusk.'

'Yet your troop recovered.'

But the corporal shook his head. 'The Edur commanding us – he knew that the news we were bringing to the capital – that of the burning ships and the dead Tiste bodies on the roads – that news demanded that we disengage. As many of us as could fight clear. Sir, with the Edur in the lead, we bolted. Seven of us at first – they had killed the other five Edur in the first breath of the attack – seven, then five.'

'Did this enemy pursue?' Triban Gnol asked in a quiet, thoughtful voice.

'No sir. They had no horses – none that we saw in any case.'

The Chancellor simply nodded at that. Then asked, 'Human?'

'Yes sir. But not Letherii, not tribal either, from what we could see. Sir, they used crossbows, but not the small, weak fisher bows such as we use in the shallows during the carp run. No, these were weapons of blackened iron, with thick cords and quarrels that punched through armour and shield. I saw one of my soldiers knocked flat onto his back by one such quarrel, dead in the instant. And—'

He halted when Triban Gnol raised a perfectly manicured finger.

'A moment, soldier. A moment. Something you said.' The Chancellor looked up. 'Five of the six Edur, killed at the very beginning of the ambush. And the discovery of Edur corpses on the roads leading in from the coast. No Letherii bodies on those roads?'

'None that we found, sir, no.'

'Yet the sixth Edur survived that initial strike in the glade – how?'

'It must have seemed that he didn't. The quarrel in his back, sir, the one that eventually killed him. He was sent tumbling from his saddle. I doubt any one expected him to rise again, to regain his mount—'

'You saw all this with your own eyes?'

'I did, sir.'

'That quarrel – before or after the thunder and fire?'

The corporal frowned, then said, 'Before. Just before – not even a blink from one to the next, I think. Yes, I am certain. He was the very first struck.'

'Because he was clearly in command?'

'I suppose so, sir.'

'This thunder and fire, where did the sorcery strike first? Let me answer that for myself. In the midst of the remaining Edur.'

'Yes sir.'

'You may go now, soldier. Sirryn, remain with me a moment.'

As soon as the door closed Triban Gnol was on his feet. 'Errant fend! A damned invasion! Against the Letherii Empire!'

'Sounds more like against the Edur,' Sirryn ventured.

The Chancellor glared across at him. 'You damned fool. That is incidental – an interesting detail at most. Without true relevance. Sirryn, the Edur rule us – perhaps only in name, yes, but they are our occupiers. In our midst. Able to command Letherii forces as befits their need.'

He slammed a fist down on the table. The lacquered box jumped, the lid clattering free. Triban Gnol stared at what lay within. 'We are at war,' he said. 'Not our war – not the one we planned for – no. War!'

'We will crush these invaders, sir—'

'Of course we will, once we meet their sorcery with our own. That too is not relevant.'

'I do not understand, sir.'

Triban Gnol glared at the man. *No, you don't. Which is why your rank will never rise higher, you pathetic thug.* 'When you are done with silencing the other soldiers, Sirryn – oh yes, and the promotion for our enterprising young corporal – I want you to deliver, by hand, a message to Karos Invictad.'

'Sir?'

'An invitation. He is to come to the palace.'

'When?'

'Immediately.'

Sirryn saluted. 'Yes, sir.'

'Go.'

As the door closed a second time, Triban Gnol stared down at his desk. Down into the box with its dislodged lid. Wherein sat a small, squat bottle. A third of its contents remaining.

Triban Gnol often drew satisfaction from the sight of it, the very knowledge of it when hidden within its box. He would recall pouring the contents into the vessel of wine from which he knew Ezgara Diskanar would drink, there on that last terrible day. In the throne room. Ezgara, and that pathetic First Eunuch. Nisall should have followed. Not Brys. No, anyone but Brys Beddict.

Regrettable, that.

CHAPTER SIXTEEN

Every field of battle
holds every cry uttered
Threaded like roots
between stones
and broken armour,
shattered weapons,
leather clasps rotting
into the earth.
Centuries are as nothing
to those voices,
those aggrieved souls.
They die in the now
And the now is for ever.

On the Deal Plains
Rael of Longspit

FIRE HAD TAKEN THE GRASSES. WIND AND WATER HAD TAKEN THE SOIL. The level stretch where the two drainage channels debouched was a scatter of button cacti, fist-sized cobbles and fire-cracked rock. The Letherii outrider's corpse had rolled down from the ridge leaving a path of spattered blood now black as ink on the rocks. Coyotes, wolves or perhaps Awl dogs had chewed away the softer tissues – face and gut, buttocks and inner thighs – leaving the rest to the flies and their maggot spawn.

Overseer Brohl Handar – who knew he should have died at Bast Fulmar, had indeed believed at that last moment that he would, absurdly killed by his own sword – gestured to two of his troop to remain on the ridge and waved the others to the highest rise thirty paces away, on the other side of one of the gullies, then walked his horse down onto the flat. Steeling himself against the stench of the dead soldier, he forced his reluctant mount closer.

The K'risnan had reached him in time. With the power to heal, a power pure – no stain of chaos – that was, Brohl Handar now understood, a blessing. Kurald Emurlahn. Darkness reborn. He would not question it, would not doubt it. *Blessing.*

The stub of an arrow jutted from the outrider's throat. His weapons had been taken, as had the vest of fine chain beneath the light tanned leather shirt. There was no sign of the Letherii's horse. The buzz of the flies seemed preternaturally loud.

Brohl Handar wheeled his mount round and guided it back up onto the ridge. He spoke to the Sollanta scout. 'Tracks?'

'Just his horse, Overseer,' the warrior replied. 'The ambusher was, I believe, on foot.'

Brohl nodded. This had been the pattern. The Awl were collecting horses, weapons and armour. The Atri-Preda had since commanded that no outrider scout alone. To this Redmask would no doubt add more ambushers.

'The Awl rode southeast, Overseer.'

Days ago, alas. There was no point in pursuing.

Eyes narrowed against the harsh sunlight, Brohl Handar scanned the plain on all sides. How could a warrior hide in this empty land? The drainage gullies had seemed an obvious answer, and as soon as one was spotted a troop would dismount, advance on foot, and plunge into it seeking to flush out the enemy. All they had found were bedded deer and coyote dens.

Areas of high grasses were virtually attacked, both mounted and on foot. Again, nothing but the occasional deer bolting almost from the feet of some startled, cursing soldier; or ptarmigan or thrushes exploding skyward in a flurry of feathers and drumming wings.

The mages insisted that sorcery was not at work here; indeed, much of the Awl'dan seemed strangely bereft of whatever was necessary to shape magic. The valley known as Bast Fulmar had been, it was becoming clear, in no way unique. Brohl Handar had begun with the belief that the plains were but southern versions of tundra. In some ways this was true; in others it was anything but. Horizons deceived, distances lied. Valleys hid from the eye until one was upon them. *Yet, so much like the tundra, a terrible place to fight a war.*

Redmask and his army had disappeared. Oh, there were trails aplenty; huge swaths of trodden ground wending this way and that. But some were from bhederin herds; others were old and still others seemed to indicate travel in opposite directions, overlapping back and forth until all sense was lost. And so, day after day, the Letherii forces set out, their supplies dwindling, losing outriders to ambushes, marching this way and that, as if doomed to pursue a mythic battle that would never come.

Brohl Handar had assembled thirty of his best riders, and each day he led them out from the column, pushing far onto the flanks – dangerously far – in hopes of sighting the Awl.

He now squinted at the Sollanta scout. 'Where have they gone?'

The warrior grimaced. 'I have given this some thought, Overseer. Indeed, it is all I have thought about this past week. The enemy, I believe, is all around us. After Bast Fulmar, Redmask split the tribes. Each segment employed wagons to make them indistinguishable – as we have seen from the countless trails, those wagons are drawn from side to side to side, eight or ten across, and they move last, thus obliterating signs of all that precedes them on the trail. Could be a hundred warriors ahead, could be five thousand.'

'If so,' Brohl objected, 'we should have caught up with at least one such train.'

'We do not move fast enough, Overseer. Recall, we remained encamped on the south side of Bast Fulmar for two entire days. That gave them a crucial head start. Their columns, wagons and all, move faster than ours. It is as simple as that.'

'And the Atri-Preda refuses to send out reconnaissance in force,' Brohl said, nodding.

'A wise decision,' the scout said.

'How so?'

'Redmask would turn on such a force. He would overwhelm it and slaughter every soldier in it. Either way, Overseer, we are playing his game.'

'That is . . . unacceptable.'

'I imagine the Atri-Preda agrees with you, sir.'

'What can be done?'

The warrior's brows lifted. 'I do not command this army, Overseer.'

Nor do I. 'If you did?'

Sudden unease in the scout's face and he glanced over at the other outrider with them on the ridge, but that man seemed intent on something else, far off on the horizon, as he tore loose bits of dried meat from the thin strip in his left hand, and slowly chewed.

'Never mind,' Brohl said, sighing. 'An unfair question.'

'Yet I would answer still, Overseer, if you like.'

'Go on.'

'Retreat, sir. Back to Drene. Resume claiming land, and protect it well. Redmask, then, will have to come to us, if he would contest the theft of Awl land.'

I agree. But she will not have it. 'Sound the recall,' he said. 'We're returning to the column.'

*

The sun had crawled past noon by the time the Tiste Edur troop came within sight of the Letherii column, and it was immediately evident that something had happened. Supply wagons were drawn into a hollow square formation, the oxen and mules already unhitched and led into two separate kraals within that defensive array. Elements of the various brigades and regiments were drawing into order both north and south of the square, with mounted troops well out east and west.

Brohl Handar led his troop into a quick canter. To his lead scout he said, 'Rejoin my Arapay – I see them to the west.'

'Yes sir.'

As the troop turned behind him, the Overseer kicked his horse into a gallop and rode for the small forest of standards marking the Atri-Preda's position, just outside the east barrier of wagons. The land here was relatively flat. Another ridge of slightly higher ground ran roughly east–west a thousand paces to the south, while the topography on this north side was more or less level with the trail, thick with the waist-high silver-bladed grass known as knifegrass, a direct translation of the Awl name, *masthebe*.

Redmask would be a fool to meet us here.

He eased his horse down to a fast trot as he drew nearer. He could see the Atri-Preda now, the flush of excitement on her face replacing the strain that had seemed to age her a year for every day since Bast Fulmar. She had gathered her officers, and they were now pulling away in answer to her orders. By the time the Overseer arrived only a few messengers remained, along with the standard bearer of Bivatt's own command.

He reined in. 'What has happened?'

'Seems he's grown weary of running,' Bivatt replied with a fiercely satisfied expression.

'You have found him?'

'He even now marches for us, Overseer.'

'But . . . why would he do that?'

There was a flicker of unease in her eyes, then she looked away, fixing her gaze to the southeast, where Brohl could now see a dust cloud on the horizon. 'He believes us tired, worn out. He knows we are short of food and decent forage, and that we have wagons crowded with wounded. He means to savage us yet again.'

The sweat on Brohl Handar's brow was plucked away by a gust of warm wind. Ceaseless breath of the plains, that wind, always from the west or northwest. It devoured every drop of moisture, turning the skin leathery and burnished. Licking chapped lips, the Overseer cleared his throat, then said, 'Can sorcery be unleashed here, Atri-Preda?'

Her eyes flashed. 'Yes. And with that, we will give answer.'

'And their shamans? What of the Awl shamans?'

486

'Useless, Overseer. Their rituals are too slow for combat. Nor can they make use of raw power. We will have at them this day, Brohl Handar.'

'You have positioned the Tiste Edur once again to the rear. Are we to guard the dung left by the oxen, Atri-Preda?'

'Not at all. I believe you will see plenty of fighting today. There are bound to be flanking strikes, seeking our supplies, and I will need you and your Edur to throw them back. Recall, as well, those two demons.'

'They are difficult to forget,' he replied. 'Very well, we shall position ourselves defensively.' He collected his reins. 'Enjoy your battle, Atri-Preda.'

Bivatt watched the Overseer ride off, irritated with his questions, his scepticism. Redmask was as mortal as any man. He was not immune to mistakes, and this day he had made one. The defender was ever at an advantage, and the general rule was that an attacker required substantial numerical superiority. Bivatt had lost to death or wounding over eight hundred of her soldiers in the debacle that was Bast Fulmar. Even with that, Redmask did not possess sufficient numbers, assuming he intended to advance beyond initial sighting.

Ideally, she would have liked to position her forces along the ridge to the south, but there had been no time for that; and by staying where she was, she would prevent that ridge from factoring in the battle to come. There was the chance that Redmask would simply take the ridge then await her, but she would not play into his hands again. If he sought battle this day, he would have to advance. And quickly. Standing and waiting on the ridge would not be tolerated, not when Bivatt had her mages. *Stand there if you dare, Redmask, in the face of wave upon wave of sorcery.*

But he was coming. Bivatt did not believe he would seek the ridge then simply wait, expecting her to yield her defensive formation in order to march upon him.

No, he has lost his patience. Revealed his weakness.

She scanned the positioning of her troops. Crimson Rampant heavy infantry to anchor the far left, the easternmost end of her line. Merchants' Battalion heavy infantry to the far right. Artisan Battalion heavy infantry at the centre. To their flanks, extending out and at double-depth – twenty rather than ten lines – were the assorted medium infantry of her force. Reserve elements of her remaining skirmishers, the Drene Garrison and medium infantry were arrayed closer to the square of wagons. The Bluerose cavalry, divided into two wings, she held back to await a quick response, as either counter-attack or riding to close a breach.

Brohl Handar's Tiste Edur guarded the north. They would be facing away from the main battle, yet Bivatt was certain there would be an attack on them, another strike for the supplies. And she suspected it would come from the high grasses on the north side of the track.

Rising on her stirrups, she studied the approaching dust cloud. Her scouts had confirmed that this was indeed Redmask, leading what had to be the majority of his warriors. That haze of dust seemed to be angling towards the ridge. The Atri-Preda sneered, then gestured a messenger over. 'Bring me my mages. On the double.'

The old man had been found dead in his tent that morning. The imprints of the hands that had strangled him left a mottled map of brutality below his bloated face and bulging eyes. His murderer had sat atop him, staring down to witness death's arrival. The last elder of the Renfayar, Redmask's own tribe, perhaps the most ancient man among the entire Awl. The Blind Stalker that was death should have reached out a most gentle touch upon such a man.

In the camp fear and dismay whistled and spun like a trapped wind in a gorge, punctuated by terrible wails from the crones and cries announcing ill omen. Redmask had arrived to look down upon the corpse when it had been carried into the open, and of course none could see what lay behind his scaled mask, but he did not fall to his knees beside the body of his kin, his wise adviser. He had stood, motionless, cadaran whip wrapped crossways about his torso, the rygtha crescent axe held loose in his left hand.

Dogs were howling, their voices awakened by the mourners, and on the flanks of the slopes to the south the rodara herds shifted this way and that, nervous and fretful.

Redmask had turned away, then. His copper-masked officers drew closer, along with Masarch and, trailing a few steps behind, Toc Anaster.

'We are done fleeing,' Redmask said. 'Today, we will spill yet more Letherii blood.'

This was what the Awl warriors had been waiting to hear. Their loyalty was not in question, not since Bast Fulmar, yet they were young and they had tasted blood. They wanted to taste it again. The elaborate hare-dance in which they had led the Letherii had gone on too long. Even the clever ambushes sprung on the enemy outriders and scouts had not been enough. The wending, chaotic march had seemed too much like flight.

The warriors were assembled north of the encampment with dawn still fresh in the air, the dog-masters and their helpers leashing the snapping, restless beasts and positioning their charges slightly to the east. Horses stamped on the dew-smeared ground, clan pennons wavering like tall reeds. Scouts were sent off with horse-archers to make contact with the Letherii outriders and drive them back to their nest.

This would ensure that the specific presentation of Redmask's forces would remain unknown for as long as possible.

Moments before the army set out, Torrent arrived to position himself at Toc's side. The warrior was scowling, as he did most mornings – and afternoons and evenings – when he had forgotten to don his mask of paint. Since it had begun to give him a blotchy rash on cheeks, chin and forehead, he 'forgot' more often these days – and Toc answered that belligerent expression with a bright smile.

'Swords unsheathed this day, Torrent.'

'Has Redmask given you leave to ride to battle?'

Toc shrugged. 'He's said nothing either way, which I suppose is leave enough.'

'It is not.' Torrent backed his horse away, then swung it round to ride to where Redmask sat astride his Letherii mount beyond the rough line of readied riders.

Settling back in the strange boxy Awl saddle, Toc examined once again his bow, then the arrows in the quiver strapped to his right thigh. He wasn't much interested in actually fighting, but at the very least he would be ready to defend himself if necessary. *Ill omens.* Clearly Redmask was indifferent to such notions. Toc scratched at the lurid tissue surrounding his eyeless socket. *I miss that eye, gift of High Denul in what seems ages past. Gods knew, made me a real archer again – these days I'm damned near useless. Fast and inaccurate, that's Toc the Unlucky.*

Would Redmask forbid him his ride this day? Toc did not think so. He could see Torrent exchanging words with the war leader, the unmasked warrior's horse sidestepping and tossing its head. *True enough, how the beast comes to resemble its master. Imagine all the one-eyed dogs I might have owned.* Torrent then wheeled his mount and made his way back towards Toc at a quick canter.

The scowl had darkened. Toc smiled once more. 'Swords unsheathed this day, Torrent.'

'You've said that before.'

'I thought we might start over.'

'He wants you out of danger.'

'But I can still ride with the army.'

'I do not trust you, so do not think that anything you do will not be unwitnessed.'

'Too many nots there, I think, Torrent. But I'm feeling generous this morning so I'll leave the reins loose.'

'One must never knot his reins,' Torrent said. 'Any fool knows that.'

'As you say.'

The army set out, all mounted for the moment – including the dog-masters – but that would not last. Nor, Toc suspected, would the force remain united. Redmask saw no battle as a singular event. Rather, he

489

saw a collection of clashes, an engagement of wills; where one was blunted he would shift his attention to resume the sparring elsewhere, and it was in the orchestration of these numerous meetings that a battle was won or lost. Flanking elements would spin off from the main column. More than one attack, more than one objective.

Toc understood this well enough. It was, he suspected, the essence of tactics among successful commanders the world over. Certainly the Malazans had fought that way, with great success. Eschewing the notion of feints, every engagement was deliberate and deliberately intended to lock an enemy down, into fierce, desperate combat.

'*Leave feints to the nobility,*' Kellanved had once said. '*And they can take their clever elegance to the barrow.*' That had been while he and Dassem Ultor had observed the Untan knights on the field of battle east of Jurda. Riding back and forth, back and forth. Tiring their burdened warhorses, sowing confusion in the dust-clouds engulfing their own ranks. Feint and blind. Dassem had ignored the pure blood fools, and before the day's battle was done he had shattered the entire Untan army, including those vaunted, once-feared knights.

The Letherii did not possess heavy cavalry. But if they did, Toc believed, they would play feint and blind all day long.

Or perhaps not. Their sorcery in battle was neither subtle nor elegant. Ugly as a Fenn's fist, in fact. This suggested a certain pragmatism, an interest in efficiency over pomp, and, indeed, a kind of impatience regarding the mannerisms of war.

Sorcery. Had Redmask forgotten the Letherii mages?

The vast level plain where the enemy waited – the Awl called it Pradegar, Old Salt – was not magically dead. Redmask's shamans had made use of the residual magic there to track the movements of the enemy army, after all.

Redmask, have you lost your mind?

The Awl rode on.

More than swords unsheathed this day, I fear. He scratched again at his gaping socket, then kicked his horse into motion.

Orbyn Truthfinder disliked the feel of soft ground beneath him. Earth, loam, sand, anything that seemed uneasy beneath his weight. He would suffer a ride in a carriage, since the wheels were solid enough, the side to side lurching above the rocky trail serving to reassure him whenever he thought of that uncertainty below. He stood now on firm stone, a bulge of scraped bedrock just up from the trail that wound the length of the valley floor.

The air's breath was sun-warmed, smelling of cold water and pine. Midges wandered in swarms along the streams of ice-melt threading down the mountainsides, slanting this way and that whenever a dragonfly darted into their midst. The sky was cloudless, the blue so sharp and clean compared to the dusty atmosphere of Drene – or any other city for that matter – that Orbyn found himself glancing upward again and again, struggling with something like disbelief.

When not looking skyward, the Patriotist's eyes were fixed on the three riders descending from the pass ahead. They had moved well in advance of his company, climbing the heights, then traversing the spine of the mountains to the far pass, where a garrison had been slaughtered. Where, more importantly, a certain shipment of weapons had not arrived. In the grander scheme, such a loss meant little, but Factor Letur Anict was not a man of grand schemes. His motivations were truncated, parsed into a language of precision, intolerant of deviation, almost neurotic when faced with anything messy. And this, indeed, was messy. In short, Letur Anict, for all his wealth and power, was a bureaucrat in the truest sense of the word.

The advance riders were returning, at long last, but Orbyn was not particularly pleased by that. They would have nothing good to say, he knew. Tales of rotting corpses, charred wood, squalling ravens and mice among mouldering bones. At the very least, he could force himself once again into the Factor's carriage to sit opposite that obnoxious number-chewer, and counsel – with greater veracity this time – that they turn their column round and head back to Drene.

Not that he would succeed, he knew. For Letur Anict, every insult was grievous, and every failure was an insult. Someone would pay. Someone always did.

Some instinct made Orbyn glance back at the camp and he saw the Factor emerging from his carriage. Well, that was a relief, since Orbyn was in the habit of sweating profusely in Letur's cramped contrivance. He watched as the washed-out man picked a delicate path up to where stood Orbyn. Overdressed for the mild air, his lank, white hair covered by a broad-rimmed hat to keep the sun from pallid skin, his strangely round face already flushed with exertion.

'Truthfinder,' he said as soon as he reached the bulge of bedrock, 'we both know what our scouts will tell us.'

'Indeed, Factor.'

'So . . . where are they?'

Orbyn's thin brows rose, and he blinked to clear the sudden sweat stinging his eyes. 'As you know, they never descended farther than this – where we are camped right now. Leaving three possibilities. One, they turned round, back up and through the pass—'

'They were not seen to do that.'

'No. Two, they left the trail here and went south, perhaps seeking the Pearls Pass into south Bluerose.'

'Travelling the spine of the mountains? That seems unlikely, Truthfinder.'

'Three, they went north from here.'

The Factor licked his lips, as if considering something. Inflectionless, he asked, 'Why would they do that?'

Orbyn shrugged. 'One could, if one so desired, skirt the range until one reached the coast, then hire a craft to take one to virtually any coastal village or port of the Bluerose Sea.'

'Months.'

'Fear Sengar and his companions are well used to that, Factor. No fugitive party has ever fled for as long within the confines of the empire as have they.'

'Not through skill alone, Truthfinder. We both know that the Edur could have taken them a hundred times, in a hundred different places. And further, we both know why they have not done so. The question you and I have danced round for a long, long time is what, if anything, are we going to do regarding all of that.'

'That question, alas,' said Orbyn, 'is one that can only be addressed by our masters, back in Letheras.'

'Masters?' Letur Anict snorted. 'They have other, more pressing concerns. We must act independently, in keeping with the responsibilities granted us; indeed, in keeping with the very expectation that we will meet those responsibilities. Do we stand aside while Fear Sengar searches for the Edur god? Do we stand aside while Hannan Mosag and his so-called hunters work their deft incompetence in this so-called pursuit? Is there any doubt in your mind, Orbyn Truthfinder, that Hannan Mosag is committing treason? Against the Emperor? Against the empire?'

'Karos Invictad, and, I'm sure, the Chancellor, are dealing with the matter of the Warlock King's treason.'

'No doubt. Yet what might occur to their plans if Fear Sengar should succeed? What will happen to all of our plans, should the Edur God of Shadows rise again?'

'That, Factor, is highly unlikely.' *No, it is in fact impossible.*

'I am well acquainted,' Letur Anict said testily, 'with probabilities and risk assessment, Truthfinder.'

'What is it you desire?' Orbyn asked.

Letur Anict's smile was tight. He faced north. 'They are hiding. And we both know where.'

Orbyn was not happy. 'The extent of your knowledge surprises me, Factor.'

'You have underestimated me.'

'It seems I have at that.'

'Truthfinder. I have with me twenty of my finest guard. You have forty soldiers and two mages. We have enough lanterns to cast out

492

darkness and so steal the power of those decrepit warlocks. How many remain in that hidden fastness? If we strike quickly, we can rid ourselves of this damnable cult and that alone is worth the effort. Capturing Fear Sengar in the bargain would sweeten the repast. Consider the delight, the accolades, should we deliver to Karos and the Chancellor the terrible traitor, Fear Sengar, and that fool, Udinaas. Consider, if you will, the *rewards*.'

Orbyn Truthfinder sighed, then he said, 'Very well.'

'Then you know the secret path. I suspected as much.'

And you do not, and I knew as much. He withdrew a handkerchief and mopped the sweat from his face, then along the wattle beneath his chin. 'The climb is strenuous. We shall have to leave the carriages and horses here.'

'Your three scouts can serve to guard the camp. They have earned a rest. When do we leave, Truthfinder?'

Orbyn grimaced. 'Immediately.'

Two of the three scouts were sitting beside a fire on which sat a soot-stained pot of simmering tea, while the third one rose, arched to ease his back, then sauntered towards the modest train that had spent most of the day descending into the valley.

The usual greetings were exchanged, along with invitations to share this night and this camp. The leader of the train walked wearily over to join the scout.

'Is that not the Drene Factor's seal on that carriage?' he asked.

The scout nodded. 'So it is.' His gaze strayed past the rather un-impressive man standing opposite him. 'You are not traders, I see. Yet, plenty of guards.'

'A wise investment, I should judge,' the man replied, nodding. 'The garrison fort gave proof enough of that. It stands abandoned still, half burnt down and strewn with the bones of slaughtered soldiers.'

The scout shrugged. 'The west side of the range is notorious for bandits. I heard they was hunted down and killed.'

'Is that so?'

'So I heard. And there's a new detachment on its way, along with carpenters, tree-fellers and a blacksmith. The fort should be rebuilt before season's end.' He shrugged. 'It's the risk of the road.'

Venitt Sathad nodded again. 'We passed no-one on the trail. Is the Factor coming to join you here, then?'

'He is.'

'Is it not unusual, this journey? Drene, after all, is on the far side of the sea.'

'Factor's business is his own,' the scout replied, a little tersely. 'You never answered me, sir.'

493

'I did not? What was your question again?'

'I asked what you were carrying, that needs so few packs and so many guards.'

'I am not at liberty to tell you, alas,' Venitt Sathad said, as he began scanning the camp. 'You had more soldiers here, not long ago.'

'Went down the valley yesterday.'

'To meet the Factor?'

'Just so. And I've had a thought – if they come up this night, the campsite here won't be big enough. Not for them and your group.'

'I expect you are correct.'

'Perhaps it'd be best, then, if you moved on. There's another site two thousand paces down the valley. You've enough light, I should think.'

Venitt Sathad smiled. 'We shall do as you have asked, then. Mayhap we will meet your Factor on the way.'

'Mayhap you will, sir.'

In the man's eyes, Venitt Sathad saw the lie. Still smiling, he walked back to his horse. 'Mount up,' he told his guards. 'We ride on.'

A most displeasing command, but Venitt Sethad had chosen his escort well. Within a very short time, the troop was once more on its way.

He had no idea why the man he was sent to meet was on this trail, so far from Drene. Nor did Venitt know where Anict had gone, since on all sides but ahead there was naught but rugged, wild mountains populated by little more than rock-climbing horned sheep and a few cliff-nesting condors. Perhaps he would find out eventually. As it was, sooner or later Letur Anict would return to Drene, and he, Venitt Sathad, agent of Rautos Hivanar and the Letheras Liberty Consign, would be waiting for him.

With some questions from his master.

And some answers.

A shriek echoed in the distance, then faded. Closer to hand, amidst flickering lantern-light and wavering shadows, the last cries of the slaughtered had long since fallen away, as soldiers of Orbyn's guard walked among the piled bodies – mostly the young, women and the aged in this chamber – ensuring that none still breathed.

None did. Orbyn Truthfinder had made certain of that himself. In a distracted way, torn as he was by distaste and the necessity that no carelessness be permitted. They had been four bells in this subterranean maze, at the most, to mark the first breach of wards at the entranceway in the crevasse and all that followed, from room to room, corridor to corridor, the assault of light and refulgent sorcery.

Whatever elaborate organization of power had held fast in this buried demesne had been obliterated with scarce the loss of a single Letherii life, and all that then remained was simple butchery. Hunting down the ones who hid, who fled to the farthest reaches, the smallest storage rooms, the children huddling in alcoves and, for one, in an amphora half filled with wine.

Less than four bells, then, to annihilate the Cult of the Black-Winged Lord. These degenerate versions of Tiste Edur. Hardly worth the effort, as far as Orbyn Truthfinder was concerned. Even more bitter to the tongue, there had been no sign of Fear Sengar or any of his companions. No sign, indeed, that they had ever been here.

His gaze resting upon the heaped corpses, he felt sullied. Letur Anict had used him in his obsessive pursuit of efficiency, of cruel simplification of his world. One less nagging irritant for the Factor of Drene. And now they would return, and Orbyn wondered if this journey to track down a few wagonloads of cheap weapons had, in fact, been nothing more than a ruse. One that fooled him as easily as it would a wide-eyed child.

He drew out a cloth to wipe the blood from his dagger, then slipped the long-bladed weapon back into its sheath below his right arm.

One of his mages approached. 'Truthfinder.'

'Are we done here?'

'We are. We found the chamber of the altar. A half-dozen tottering priests and priestesses on their knees beseeching their god for deliverance.' The mage made a sour face. 'Alas, the Black-Winged Lord wasn't home.'

'What a surprise.'

'Yes, but there was one, sir. A surprise, that is.'

'Go on.'

'That altar, sir, it was truly sanctified.'

Orbyn glanced at the mage with narrowed eyes. 'Meaning?'

'Touched by Darkness, by the Hold itself.'

'I did not know such a Hold even existed. Darkness?'

'The Tiles possess an aspect of Darkness, sir, although only the oldest texts make note of that. Of the Fulcra, sir. The White Crow.'

Orbyn's breath suddenly caught. He stared hard at the mage standing before him, watched the shadows flit over the man's lined face. 'The White Crow. The strange Edur who accompanies Fear Sengar is so named.'

'If that stranger is so named, then he is not Tiste Edur, sir.'

'Then what?'

The mage gestured at the bodies lying on all sides. 'Tiste Andii, they call themselves. Children of Darkness. Sir, I know little of this . . . White Crow, who travels with Fear Sengar. If indeed they walk together, then something has changed.'

'What do you mean?'

'The Edur and the Andii, sir, were most vicious enemies. If what we have gleaned from Edur legends and the like holds any truth, then they

495

warred, and that war ended with betrayal. With the slaying of the White Crow.' The mage shook his head. 'That is why I do not believe in this White Crow who is with Fear Sengar – it is but a name, a name given in error, or perhaps mockery. But if I am wrong, sir, then an old feud has been buried in a deep grave, and this could prove . . . worrisome.'

Orbyn looked away. 'We have slaughtered the last of these Andii, have we not?'

'In this place, yes. Should we be confident that they are the last Andii left? Even in Bluerose? Did not the Edur find kin across the ocean? Perhaps other contacts were made, ones our spies in the fleets did not detect. I am made uneasy, sir, by all of this.'

You do not stand alone in that, mage. 'Think more on it,' he said.

'I shall.'

As the mage turned to leave Orbyn reached out a huge, plump hand to stay him. 'Have you spoken with the Factor?'

A frown, as if the mage had taken offence at the question. 'Of course not, sir.'

'Good. Of the altar, and the sanctification, say nothing.' He thought for a moment, then added, 'Of your other thoughts, say nothing as well.'

'I would not have done otherwise, sir.'

'Excellent. Now, gather our soldiers. I would we leave here as soon as we can.'

'Yes sir, with pleasure.'

Leave Letur Anict to his world made simpler. What he would have it to be and what it is, are not the same. And that, dear Factor, is the path to ruin. You will walk it without me.

Clip stood facing south. His right hand was raised, the chain and its rings looped tight. He'd not spun it for more than dozen heartbeats. His hair, left unbound, stirred in the wind. A few paces away, Silchas Ruin sat on a boulder, running a whetstone along the edge of one of his singing swords.

Snow drifted down from a pale blue sky, some high-altitude version of a sun-shower, perhaps, or winds had lifted the flakes from the young peaks that reared on all sides but directly ahead. The air was bitter, so dry that wool sparked and crackled. They had crossed the last of the broken plateau the day before, leaving behind the mass of shattered black stone that marked its cratered centre. The climb this morning had been treacherous, as so many slabs of stone under foot were sheathed in ice. Reaching the crest of the caldera in late afternoon light, they found themselves looking upon a vast descending slope, stretching north for half a league or more to a tundra plain. Beyond that the horizon reached in a flat, hazy white line. Ice fields, Fear Sengar had said, to which Udinaas had laughed.

Seren Pedac paced restlessly along the ridge. She had been walking with the others, well behind Clip and Silchas Ruin. There was light left to continue, yet the young Tiste Andii had perched himself on the crest to stare back the way they had come. Silent, expressionless.

She walked over to stand before Udinaas, who had taken to carrying the Imass spear again and was now seated on a rock poking the spear's point into the mossy turf. 'What is happening here?' she asked him in a low voice. 'Do you know?'

'Familiar with the jarack bird, Acquitor? The grey-crested thief and murderer of the forest?'

She nodded.

'And what happens when a jarack female finds a nest containing some other's bird's hatchlings? An unguarded nest?'

'It kills and eats the chicks.'

He smiled. 'True. Commonly known. But jaracks do something else on occasion, earlier in the season. They push out an egg and leave one of their own. The other birds seem blind to the exchange. And when the jarack hatches, of course it kills and eats its rivals.'

'Then sounds its call,' she said. 'But it's a call that seems no different from those of the other bird's chicks. And those birds come with food in their beaks.'

'Only to be ambushed by the two adult jaracks waiting nearby and killed in the nest. Another meal for their hatchling.'

'Jaracks are in every way unpleasant birds. Why are we talking about jaracks, Udinaas?'

'No reason, really. But sometimes it's worth reminding ourselves that we humans are hardly unique in our cruelty.'

'The Fent believed that jaracks are the souls of abandoned children who died alone in the forest. And so they yearn for a home and a family, yet are so driven to rage when they find them they destroy all that they desire.'

'The Fent were in the habit of abandoning children?'

Seren Pedac grimaced. 'Only in the last hundred or so years.'

'Impediments to their self-destructive appetites, I should think.'

She said nothing to that comment, yet in her mind's eye she saw Hull Beddict suddenly standing beside her, drawing to his full height, reaching down to take Udinaas by the throat and dragging the man upright.

Udinaas suddenly bolted forward, choking, one hand clawing up towards her.

Seren Pedac stepped back. *No, dammit!* She struggled to cast the vision away.

It would not leave.

Eyes bulging, face blackening, Udinaas closed his own hands about his neck, but there was nothing to pull away—

'Seren!' Kettle shrieked.

Errant fend! What, how . . . oh, I'm killing him! Hull Beddict stood, crushing the life from Udinaas. She wanted to reach out to him, drag his grip loose, but she knew she would not be strong enough. No, she realized, she needed someone else—

And conjured into the scene within her mind another figure, stepping close, lithe and half seen. A hand flashing up, striking Hull Beddict in his own throat. The Letherii staggered back, then fell to one knee, even as he released Udinaas. Hull then reached for his sword.

A spear shaft scythed into view, caught Hull flat on the forehead, snapping his head back. He toppled.

The Edur warrior now stood between Hull Beddict and Udinaas, spear held in a guard position.

Seeing him, seeing his face, sent Seren reeling back. *Trull Sengar? Trull—*

The vision faded, was gone.

Coughing, gasping, Udinaas rolled onto his side.

Kettle rushed to crouch beside the ex-slave.

A hand closed on Seren's shoulder and swung her round. She found herself staring up into Fear's face, and wondered at the warrior's strange expression. *He – he could not have seen. That would be—*

'Shorn,' Fear whispered. 'Older. A sadness—' He broke off then, unable to go on, and twisted away.

She stared after him. *A sadness upon his eyes.*

Upon his eyes.

'Deadly games, Acquitor.'

She started, looked over to see that Silchas Ruin was now studying her from where he sat. Beyond him, Clip had not turned round, had not even moved. 'I did not. I mean. I didn't—'

'Imagination,' Udinaas grated from the ground to her right, 'is ever quick to judge.' He coughed again, then laughter broke from his ravaged throat. 'Ask any jealous man. Or woman. Next time I say something that annoys you, Seren Pedac, just swear at me, all right?'

'I'm sorry, Udinaas. I didn't think—'

'You thought all right, woman.'

Oh, Udinaas. 'I'm sorry,' she whispered.

'What sorcery have you found?' Fear Sengar demanded, his eyes slightly wild as he glared at her. 'I saw—'

'What did you see?' Silchas Ruin asked lightly, slipping one sword into its scabbard, then drawing the other.

Fear said nothing, and after a moment he pulled his gaze from Seren Pedac. 'What is Clip doing?' he demanded.

'Mourning, I expect.'

This answer brought Udinaas upright into a sitting position. Glancing at Seren, he nodded, mouthed *Jarack*.

'Mourning what?' Fear asked.

'All who dwelt within the Andara,' Silchas Ruin replied, 'are dead. Slaughtered by Letherii soldiers and mages. Clip is the Mortal Sword of Darkness. Had he been there, they would now still be alive – his kin. And the bodies lying motionless in the darkness would be Letherii. He wonders if he has not made a terrible mistake.'

'That thought,' the young Tiste Andii said, 'was fleeting. They were hunting for you, Fear Sengar. And you, Udinaas.' He turned, his face appalling in its calm repose. The chains spun out, snapped in the cold air, then whirled back inward again. 'My kin would have made certain there would remain no evidence that you were there. Nor were the Letherii mages powerful enough – nor clever enough – to desecrate the altar, although they tried.' He smiled. 'They brought their lanterns with them, you see.'

'The gate didn't stay there long enough anyway,' Udinaas said in a cracking voice.

Clip's hard eyes fixed on the ex-slave. 'You know nothing.'

'I know what's spinning from your finger, Clip. You showed us once before, after all.'

Silchas Ruin, finished with the second sword, now sheathed it and rose. 'Udinaas,' he said to Clip, 'is as much a mystery as the Acquitor here. Knowledge and power, the hand and the gauntlet. We should move on. Unless,' he paused, facing Clip, 'it is time.'

Time? Time for what?

'It is,' Udinaas said, using the Imass spear to get to his feet. 'They knew they were going to die. Hiding in that deep pit took them nowhere. Fewer young, ever weaker blood. But that blood, well, spill enough of it . . .'

Clip advanced on the ex-slave.

'No,' Silchas Ruin said.

The Mortal Sword stopped, seemed to hesitate, then shrugged and turned away. Chain spinning.

'Mother Dark,' Udinaas resumed with a tight smile. 'Open your damned gate, Clip, it's been paid for.'

And the spinning chain snapped taut. Horizontally. At each end a ring, balanced as if on end. Within the band closest to them there was . . . darkness.

Seren Pedac stared, as that sphere of black began growing, spilling out from the ring.

'She has this thing,' Udinaas muttered, 'about birth canals.'

Silchas Ruin walked into the Dark and vanished. A moment later there was a ghostly flit as Wither raced into the gate. Kettle took Udinaas's hand and led him through.

Seren glanced over at Fear. *We leave your world behind, Tiste Edur. And yet, I can see the realization awaken in your eyes. Beyond. Through that gate, Fear Sengar, waits the soul of Scabandari.*

He settled a hand on his sword, then strode forward.

As Seren Pedac followed, she looked at Clip, met his eyes as he stood there, waiting, the one hand raised, the gate forming a spiralling tunnel out from the nearest ring. In some other world, she imagined, the gate emerged from the other ring. *He's carried it with him. Our way through to where we needed to go. All this time.*

Clip winked.

Chilled by that gesture, the Acquitor stepped forward and plunged into darkness.

Third Maiden Isle was dead astern, rising into view on the swells then falling away again in the troughs. The ferry groaned like a floundering beast, twisting beneath its forest of masts and their makeshift sails, and the mass of Shake huddled sick and terrified on the deck. Witches and warlocks, on their knees, wailed their prayers to be heard above the gale's swollen fury, but the shore was far away now and they were lost.

Yedan Derryg, drenched by the spume that periodically thrashed over the low gunnels with what seemed demonic glee, was making his way towards Yan Tovis, who stood beside the four men on the steering oar. She was holding on to a pair of thick ratlines, legs set wide to take the pitch and yawl, and as she studied her half-brother's face as he drew nearer, she saw what she already knew to be truth.

We're not going to make it.

Cleaving the lines once past the salt marsh, then up, rounding the peninsula and out along the north edge of the reefs, a journey of three days and two nights before they could tie up in one of the small coves on the lee side of Third Maiden Isle. The weather had held, and at dawn this day all had seemed possible.

'The seams, Twilight,' Yedan Derryg said upon reaching her. 'These waves are hammering 'em wide open. We're going down—' He barked a savage laugh. 'Beyond the shore, be well as they say! More bones to the deep!'

He was pale – as pale as she no doubt was – yet in his eyes there was a dark fury. 'Tour's Spit lies two pegs off the line, and there're shoals, but, sister, it's the only dry land we might reach.'

'Oh, and how many on the deck there know how to swim? Any?' She shook her head, blinking salty spray from her eyes. 'What would you have us do, crash this damned thing onto the strand? Pray to the shore

500

that we can slip through the shoals untouched? Dear Watch, would you curl up in the lap of the gods?'

Bearded jaw bunched, cabled muscles growing so tight she waited to hear bone or teeth crack, then he looked away. 'What would *you* have us do, then?'

'Get the damned fools to bail, Yedan. We get any lower and the next wave'll roll us right over.'

Yet she knew it was too late. Whatever grand schemes of survival for her people she had nurtured, deep in her heart, had come untethered. By this one storm. It had been madness, flinging this coast-creeping ferry out beyond the shore, even though the only truly dangerous stretch had been . . . *this one, here, north from Third Maiden Isle to the lee of Spyrock Island. The only stretch truly open to the western ocean.*

The gale lifted loose suddenly, slammed a fist into the port side of the craft. A mast splintered, the sail billowing round, sheets snapping, and like a huge wing the sail tore itself loose, carrying the mast with it. Rigging snatched up hapless figures from the deck and flung them skyward. A second mast toppled, this one heavy enough to tug its sail downward. Yet more tinny screams reaching through the howl.

The ferry seemed to slump, as if moments from plunging into the deep. Yan Tovis found herself gripping the lines as if they could pull her loose, into the sky – as if they could take her from all of this. *The Queen commands. Her people die.*

At least I will join—

A shout from Yedan Derryg, who had gone forward into the chaos of the deck, a shout that reached her.

And now she saw. Two enormous ships had come upon them from astern, one to each side, heaving like hunting behemoths, their sails alone dwarfing the ferry pitching in their midst. The one to port stole the gale's fierce breath and all at once the ferry righted itself amidst choppy waves.

Yan Tovis stared across, saw figures scrambling about side-mounted ballistae, saw others moving to the rail beneath huge coils of rope.

Pirates? Now?

The crew of the ship to starboard, she saw with growing alarm, was doing much the same.

Yet it was the ships that most frightened her. For she recognized them.

Perish. What were they called? Yes, Thrones of War. She well remembered that battle, the lash of sorceries ripping the crests of waves, the detonations as Edur galleys disintegrated before her very eyes. The cries of drowning warriors—

Ballistae loosed their robust quarrels, yet the missiles arced high, clearing the deck by two or more man-heights. And from them snaked

501

out ropes. The launching had been virtually simultaneous from both ships. She saw those quarrels rip through the flimsy sails, slice past rigging, then the heavy-headed missiles dipped down to the seas in between.

She saw as the ropes were hauled taut. She felt the crunching bite of the quarrels as they lifted back clear of the water and anchored barbs deep into the gunnels of the ferry.

And, as the wind pushed them all onward now, the Thrones of War drew closer.

Massive fends of bundled seaweed swung down to cushion the contact of the hulls.

Sailors from the Perish ships scrambled along the lines, many of them standing upright as they did so – impossibly balanced despite the pitching seas – and dropped down onto the ferry deck with ropes and an assortment of tools.

The ropes were cleated to stanchions and pills on the ferry.

An armoured Perish emerged from the mass of humanity on the main deck and climbed her way to where stood Yan Tovis.

In the language of the trader's tongue, the woman said, 'Your craft is sinking, Captain. We must evacuate your passengers.'

Numbed, Yan Tovis nodded.

'We are sailing,' said the Perish, 'for Second Maiden Isle.'

'As were we,' Yan Tovis responded.

A sudden smile, as welcome to Yan Tovis's eyes as dawn after a long night. 'Then we are most well met.'

Well met, yes. And well answered. Second Maiden Fort. The silent Isle has been conquered. Not just the Malazans then. The Perish. Oh, look what we have awakened.

He'd had months to think things over, and in the end very little of what had happened back in the Malazan Empire surprised Banaschar, once Demidrek of the Worm of Autumn. Perhaps, if seen from the outside, from some borderland where real power was as ephemeral, as elusive, as a cloud on the face of the moon, there would be a sense of astonishment and, indeed, disbelief. That the mortal woman commanding the most powerful empire in the world could find herself so . . . helpless. So bound to the ambitions and lusts of the faceless players behind the tapestries. Folk blissfully unaware of the machinations of politics might well believe that someone like Empress Laseen was omnipotent, that she could do entirely as she pleased. And that a High Mage, such as Tayschrenn, was likewise free, unconstrained in his ambitions.

For people with such simplistic world views, Banaschar knew, catastrophes were disconnected things, isolated in and of themselves. There was no sense of cause and effect beyond the immediate, beyond the directly observable. A cliff collapses onto a village, killing hundreds. The effect: death. The cause: the cliff's collapse. Of course, if one were to then speak of cutting down every tree within sight, including those above that cliff, as the true cause of the disaster – a cause that, in its essence, lay at the feet of the very victims, then fierce denial was the response; or, even more pathetic, blank confusion. And if one were to then elaborate on the economic pressures that demanded such rapacious deforestation, ranging from the need for firewood among the locals and the desire to clear land for pasture to increase herds all the way to the hunger for wood to meet the shipbuilding needs of a port city leagues distant, in order to go to war with a neighbouring kingdom over contested fishing areas – contested because the shoals were vanishing, leading to the threat of starvation in both kingdoms, which in turn might destabilize the ruling families, thus raising the spectre of civil war . . . well, then, the entire notion of cause and effect, suddenly revealing its true level of complexity, simply overwhelmed.

Rebellion in Seven Cities, followed by terrible plague, and suddenly the heart of the Malazan Empire – Quon Tali – was faced with a shortage of grain. But no, Banaschar knew, one could go yet further back. Why did the rebellion occur at all? Never mind the convenient prophecies of apocalypse. The crisis was born in the aftermath of Laseen's coup, when virtually all of Kellanved's commanders vanished – drowned, as the grisly joke went. She sat herself down on the throne, only to find her most able governors and military leaders gone. And into the vacuum of their departure came far less capable and far less reliable people. She should not have been surprised at their avarice and corruption – for the chapter she had begun in the history of the empire had been announced with betrayal and blood. *Cast bitter seeds yield bitter fruit*, as the saying went.

Corruption and incompetence. These were rebellion's sparks. Born in the imperial palace in Unta, only to return with a vengeance.

Laseen had used the Claw to achieve her coup. In her arrogance she clearly imagined no-one could do the same; could infiltrate her deadly cadre of assassins. Yet, Banaschar now believed, that is what had happened. And so the most powerful mortal woman in the world had suddenly found herself emasculated, indeed trapped by a host of exigencies, unbearable pressures, inescapable demands. And her most deadly weapon of internal control had been irrevocably compromised.

There had been no civil war – the *Adjunct* had seen to that – yet the enfilade at Malaz City might well have driven the final spike into the labouring heart of Laseen's rule. The Claw had been decimated, perhaps so much so that *no-one* could use it for years to come.

The Claw had declared war on the wrong people. And so, at long last, Cotillion – who had once been Dancer – had his revenge on the organization that had destroyed his own Talon and then lifted Laseen onto the throne. For, that night in Malaz City, there had been a Shadow Dance.

Causes and effects, they were like the gossamer strands spanning the towers of Kartool City, a deadly web, a skein tethered to a thousand places. And to imagine that things were simple was to be naive, often fatally so.

A crime that he himself had been guilty of, Banaschar now understood. D'rek's rage against her worshippers had not been an isolated, internal event. It belonged to a vast war, and in war people died. Perhaps, unlike Banaschar, Tayschrenn had not been greatly affected by the tragedy. Perhaps, indeed, the Imperial High Mage had known all along.

Such unpleasant thoughts were in the habit of wandering into his mind when the sun had long fled the sky, when he should have been asleep – plummeted into the drunken stupor of oblivion here in the decrepit room he had rented opposite the Harridict Tavern on this damned island. Instead he stood by the window, wide awake, listening to the cold wind creak its way through the shutters. And even if it had been a warm night, he doubted he would have opened those shutters. Better to see nothing but those weathered slats; better to be reminded that there was no way out.

The Worm of Autumn stirred in his gut; an immortal parasite and he its mortal host. The goddess was within him once more, after all these years. Again, no surprise. *After all, I'm the only one left.* Yet D'rek remained as no more than a presence, a faint taste on his tongue. There had been no battle of wills; but he knew it would come. The goddess needed him and sooner or later she would reach out and close a cold fist about his soul.

This was no way to be called by one's god.

He heard skittering noises behind him and slowly closed his eyes.

'Smells. Smells, smells, smells.'

The words were a whining whisper in Banaschar's head.

'That's the problem, Telorast. With this island. With this entire continent! Oh, why did we come here? We should have stolen the bodies of two gulls, never mind these rotting stick-things with empty bellies we can't never fill! How many rats have we killed, Telorast? Answer me!'

'So we couldn't eat them,' muttered Telorast. 'Killing them was fun, wasn't it? Cleanest ships in the world. Enough of your complaining, Curdle. Can't you feel how close we are?'

'She's walked here!' Now there was terror in Curdle's voice. '*What are we doing in this place?*'

Banaschar turned. The two knee-high skeletal reptiles were pacing back and forth the length of the cot, clambering awkwardly amidst the dishevelled folds of bedding. 'A good question,' he said. 'What *are* you doing here? In my room? And who is "she"?'

Curdle's head bobbed, jaws clacking. 'Not-Not-Apsalar drove us away. But we need to tell someone!'

'Anyone!' chimed Telorast. 'Even you!'

'Her name is Lostara Yil,' Banaschar said. 'Not Not-Not-Apsalar – gods, did I just say that?'

' "She",' Curdle said, tail whipping, 'is the one who walked here. Long ago. More long ago than you could even think of, that long ago. Telorast is mad. She's excited, but how can anyone be excited when we're so close to *her*? Madness!'

'Just because she walked here,' Telorast said, 'doesn't mean she's still hanging around. Got no big skulls to push her fist through, not for a long time, right? And look at us, Curdle. We could dance in the palm of her hand. Either one. Or both, one for me and one for you – and she wouldn't be able to tell anything about us, not anything.' The creature swung to face Banaschar again. 'So there's no reason to panic, and that's what you need to tell Curdle, Wormfood. So, go on, tell her.'

Banaschar slowly blinked, then said, 'There's nothing to worry about, Curdle. Now, will you two leave? I have more brooding to do and half the night's gone.'

Telorast's razor-beaked head swung to Curdle. 'See? Everything's fine. We're close because we have to be. Because it's where Edgewalker wants—'

'Quiet!' Curdle hissed.

Telorast ducked. 'Oh. We have to kill him now, don't we?'

'No, that would be messy. We just have to hope for a terrible accident. Quick, Telorast, think of a terrible accident!'

'I've never heard of Edgewalker,' Banaschar said. 'Relax and go away and forget thinking about killing me. Unless you want to awaken D'rek, that is. The goddess might well know who this Edgewalker is, and from that might be able to glean something of your deadly secret mission, and from that she might decide it would be better if you two were crushed into dust.'

Curdle leapt down from the cot, crept closer to Banaschar, then began to grovel. 'We didn't mean anything by any of that. We never mean anything, do we, Telorast? We're most useless and tiny besides.'

'We can smell the Worm all right,' Telorast said, head bobbing. 'On you. In you. Just one more dread smell hereabouts. We don't like it at all. Let's go, Curdle. He's not the one we should be talking to. Not as dangerous as Not-Apsalar, but just as scary. Open those shutters, Wormfood; we'll go out that way.'

'Easy for you,' Banaschar muttered, turning back to pull the slatted barriers aside. The wind gusted in like Hood's own breath, and the reborn priest shivered.

In a flash the two reptiles were perched on the sill.

'Look, Telorast, pigeon poo.'

Then the two creatures leapt from sight. After a moment, Banaschar closed the shutters once more. Making right his vision of the world. His world, at least.

*

'Shillydan the dark-eyed man
Pokes his head up for a look round
Hillyman the black-clawed man
Came up the well for a look round

"Well and and!" says the twelve-toed man
And round down the hill he bound
Still-me-hand the dead-smile man
Went bounding bound down he did bound

Shillydan the red-water man
Croaks and kisses the lass's brow
Hillyman the blue-cocked man—'

'For Hood's sake, Crump, stop that damned singing!'

The gangly sapper straightened, stared with mouth agape, then ducked down once more and resumed digging the pit. Under his breath he began humming his mad, endless swamp song.

Corporal Shard watched the dirt flying out, caught by the whipping wind in wild swirls, for a moment longer. Twenty paces beyond the deep hole and Crump's flashing shovel squatted the low-walled stone enclosure where the squad had stashed their gear, and where now crouched Sergeant Cord, Masan Gilani, Limp and Ebron, taking shelter from the blustery wind. In a short while, Cord would call everyone to their feet, and the patrol of this part of the coast would begin.

In the meantime, Crump was digging a pit. A deep pit, just like the sergeant ordered. Just like the sergeant had been ordering every day for nearly a week now.

Shard rubbed at his numbed face, sick with worry over his sister. The Sinn he knew was gone and no sign of her remained. She'd found her power, creating something avid, almost lurid, in her dark eyes. He was frightened of her and he was not alone in that. Limp's bad knees knocked together whenever she came too close, and Ebron made what he thought were subtle, unseen gestures of warding behind her back. Masan Gilani seemed unaffected – that at least was something, maybe

506

a woman thing at that, since Faradan Sort had been pretty much the same.

That simple? Terrifying to men but not women? But why would that be the case?

He had no answer for that.

Crump's humming was getting louder, drawing Shard's attention once again. Loud enough to very nearly overwhelm the distant groans of dying ice from the other side of the strait. Worth yelling at the fool again? Maybe not.

Dirt flying out, skirling skyward then racing out on the wave of the gelid wind.

There were holes dotted along half a league of this island's north coast. Crump was proud of his achievement, and would go on being proud, probably for ever. Finest holes ever dug. Ten, fifty, a hundred, however many the sergeant wanted, yes sir.

Shard believed that Cord's fervent hope that one such pit would collapse, burying the damned idiot once and for all, was little more than wishful thinking.

After all, Crump digs great holes.

He heard a piping shriek from some way behind him and turned. And there she was. Sinn, the girl he used to throw onto a shoulder like a sack of tubers – a giggling sack – and rush with through room after room as her laughter turned to squeals and her legs started kicking. Straggly black hair whipping about, a bone flute in her hands, its music flung out into the bitter tumult like inky strands, as she cavorted in the face of the weather as if spider-bitten.

Sinn, the child witch. The High Mage with a thirst for blood.

Child of the rebellion. Stolen from the life she should have lived, fashioned by horror into something new. Child of Seven Cities, of the Apocalyptic, oh yes. Dryjhna's blessed spawn.

He wondered how many such creatures were out there, stumbling through the ruins like starved dogs. Uprising, grand failure, then plague: how many scars could a young soul carry? Before it twisted into something unrecognizable, something barely human?

Did Sinn find salvation in sorcery? Shard held no faith that such salvation was in truth benign. A weapon for her will, and how far could a mortal go with such a weapon in their hands? How vast the weight of their will, unbound and unleashed?

They were right to fear. So very right.

A gruff command from Sergeant Cord and it was time to begin the patrol. A league's worth of blasted, wind-torn coastline. Crump climbed out of the pit and dusted his palms, his face shining as he looked down on his handiwork.

'Isn't she fine, Corporal? A hole dug by a High Marshal of Mott

Wood, and we know how to dig 'em, don't we just. Why, I think it might be the best one yet! Especially with all the baby skulls on the bottom, like cobbles they are, though they break too easy – need to step light! Step light!'

Suddenly chilled in a place far deeper than any wind could reach, Shard walked to the edge of the pit and looked down. Moments later the rest of the squad joined him.

In the gloom almost a man's height down, the glimmer of rounded shapes. *Like cobbles they are.*

And they were *stirring.*

A hiss from Ebron and he glared across at Sinn, whose music and dancing had reached a frenzied pitch. 'Gods below! Sergeant—'

'Grab that shovel again,' Cord growled to Crump. 'Fill it in, you fool! Fill it in! Fill them all in!'

Crump blinked, then collected up his shovel and began pushing the dry soil back into the hole. 'Best hole-fillers t'be found anywhere! You'll see, Sergeant! Why, you won't never see holes filled so good as them's done by a High Marshal of Mott Wood!'

'Hurry up, you damned fool!'

'Yes sir, hurry up. Crump can do that!'

After a moment, the sapper began singing.

> *'Shillydan the red-water man*
> *Croaks and kisses the lass's brow*
> *Hillyman the blue-cocked man*
> *Strokes and blessings t'thank 'er now!'*

*

Nimander Golit, wrapped in a heavy dark blue woollen cloak, stood at one end of the winding street. Decrepit harbour buildings leaned and sagged, a brick grimace curling down to the waterfront that glittered a hundred paces distant. Shreds of cloud scudded beneath a night sky of bleary stars, rushing southward like advance runners of snow and ice.

Tiste Andii, sentinel to the dark; he would have liked such grand notions wrapped about him as tightly as this cloak. A mythic stance, heavy with . . . with something. And the sword at his side, a weapon of heroic will, which he could draw forth when dread fate arrived with its banshee wail, and use with a skill that could astound – like the great ones of old, a consummate icon of power unveiled in Mother Dark's name.

But it was all a dream. His skill with the sword was middling, a symbol of mediocrity as muddied as his own bloodline. He was no soldier of darkness, just a young man standing lost in a strange street, a man with nowhere to go – yet driven, driven on at this very moment – to go *somewhere.*

No, even that was untrue. He stood in the night because of a need to escape. Phaed's malice had become rabid, and Nimander was the one in whom she had chosen to confide. Would she murder Sandalath Drukorlat here in this port city, as she had vowed? More to the point, was he, Nimander, going to permit it? Did he even have the courage to betray Phaed – knowing how swiftly she would turn, and how deadly her venom?

Anomander Rake would not hesitate. No, he would kick down the door to Phaed's room and drag the squealing little stoat out by her neck. And he'd then shake the life from her. He'd have no choice, would he? One look into Phaed's eyes and the secret would be revealed. The secret of the vast empty space within her, where her conscience should be. He would see it plain, and then into her eyes would come the horror of exposure – moments before her neck snapped.

Mother Dark would wait for Phaed's soul, then, for its shrieking delivery, the malign birth of just execution, of choices that were not choices at all. Why? *Because nothing else can be done. Not for one such as her.*

And Rake would accept the blood on his hands. He would accept that terrible burden as but one more amidst countless others he carried across a hundred thousand years. Childslayer. A child of one's own blood.

The courage of one with power. And that was Nimander's very own yawning emptiness in the heart of his soul. *We may be his children, his grandchildren, we may be of his blood, but we are each incomplete. Phaed and her wicked moral void. Nenanda and his unreasoning rage. Aranatha with her foolish hopes. Kedeviss who screams herself awake every morning. Skintick for whom all of existence is a joke. Desra who would spread her legs for any man if it could boost her up one more rung on the ladder towards whatever great glory she imagines she deserves. And Nimander, who imagines himself the leader of this fell family of would-be heroes, who will seek out the ends of the earth in his hunt for . . . for courage, for conviction, for a reason to do, to feel* anything.

Oh, for Nimander, then, an empty street in the dead of night. With the denizens lost in their fitful, pathetic sleep – as if oblivion offered any escape, any escape at all. For Nimander, these interminable moments in which he could contemplate actually making a decision, actually stepping between an innocent elder Tiste Andii and Nimander's own murderous little sister. To say *No, Phaed. You will not have this. No more. You shall be a secret no longer. You shall be known.*

If he could do that. If he could but do that.

He heard a sound. Spinning, the whisper of fine chain cutting a path through the air – close, so close that Nimander spun round – but there was no-one. He was alone. *Spinning, twirling, a hiss* – then a sudden snap, two distinct, soft clicks as of two tiny objects held out at each end of that fine chain – *yes, this sound, the prophecy – Mother fend, is this the prophecy?*

Silence now, yet the air felt febrile on all sides, and his breath was coming in harsh gasps. *'He carries the gates, Nimander, so it is said. Is this not a worthy cause? For us? To search the realms, to find, not our grandsire, but the one who carries the gates?*

'Our way home. To Mother Dark, to her deepest embrace – oh, Nimander, my love, let us—'

'Stop it,' he croaked. 'Please. Stop.'

She was dead. On the Floating Isle. Cut down by a Tiste Edur who'd thought nothing of it. Nothing. She was dead.

And she had been his courage. And now there was nothing left.

The prophecy? Not for one such as Nimander.

Dream naught of glory. She too is dead.

She was everything. And she is dead.

A cool wind sighed, plucking away that tension – a tension he now knew he but imagined. A moment of weakness. Something skittering on a nearby roof.

These things did not come to those who were incomplete. He should have known better.

Three soft chimes sounded in the night, announcing yet another shift of personnel out in the advance pickets. Mostly silent, soldiers rose, dark shapes edging out from their positions, quickly replaced by those who had come to guard in their stead. Weapons rustled, clasps and buckles clicked, leather armour making small animal sounds. Figures moved back and forth on the plain. Somewhere in the darkness beyond, on the other side of that rise, out in the sweeps of high grasses and in the distant ravines, the enemy hid.

The soldiers knew that Bivatt had believed the battle was imminent. Redmask and his Awl were fast approaching. Blood would be spilled in the late afternoon on the day now gone. Oh, as the Letherii soldiers along the advance pickets well knew, the savages had indeed arrived. And the Atri-Preda had arrayed her mages to greet them. Foul sorceries had crackled and spat, blackening whole swaths of grassland until ash thickened the air.

Yet the enemy would not close, the damned Awl would not even show their faces. Even as they moved, just beyond line of sight, to encircle the Letherii army. This sounded deadlier than it was – no Awl line of barbarians would be able to hold against a concerted break-out, and the hundreds of low-ranking tactical geniuses common to all armies had predicted again and again that Bivatt would do just that: drive a solid wedge into contact with the Awl, scattering them to the winds.

510

Those predictions began falling away as the afternoon waned, as dusk gathered, as night closed in round them with its impenetrable cloak.

Well, they then said, *of course she ain't bitten. It's an obvious trap, so clumsy it almost beggars belief. Redmask wants us out of our positions, moving this way and that. Wants the confusion, d'you see? Bivatt's too smart for that.*

So now they sat the night, tired, nervous, and heard in every sound the stealthy approach of killers in the dark. Yes, friends, there was movement out there, no doubt of that. So what were the bastards doing?

They're waiting. To draw swords with the dawn, like they did the last time. We're sitting out here, wide awake, for nothing. And come the morrow we'll be sand-eyed and stiff as corpses, at least until the fighting starts for real, then we'll tear their hides off. Blade and magic, friends. To announce the day to come.

The Atri-Preda paced. Brohl Handar could see her well enough, although even if he couldn't he would be able to track her by the mutter of her armour. And, despite the diminishment of details, the Tiste Edur knew she was overwrought; knew she held none of the necessary calm expected of a commander; and so it was well, he concluded, that the two of them were twenty or more paces away from the nearest bivouac of troops.

More than a little exposed, in fact. If the enemy had infiltrated the pickets, they might be hiding not ten paces distant, adjusting grips on their knives moments before the sudden rush straight for them. Slaying the two leaders of this invading army. Of course, to have managed that, the savages would have had to deceive the magical wards woven by the mages, and that seemed unlikely. Bivatt was not unique when it came to fraught nerves, and he needed to be mindful of such flaws.

Redmask excelled in surprises. He had already proved that, and it had been foolish to expect a sudden change, a dramatic failure in his deviousness. Yet was this simply a matter of seeking battle with the sun's rise? That seemed too easy.

The Atri-Preda walked over. 'Overseer,' she said in a low voice, 'I would you send your Edur out. I need to know what he's doing.'

Startled, Brohl said nothing for a moment.

She interpreted that, rightly, as disapproval. 'Your kind are better able to see in the dark. Is that not correct? Certainly better than us Letherii; but more important, better than the Awl.'

'And their dogs, Atri-Preda? They will smell us, hear us – they will raise their heads and awaken the night. Like your soldiers,' he

511

continued, 'mine are in position, facing the high grasses and expecting to sight the enemy at any moment.'

She sighed. 'Yes, of course.'

'He plays with us,' Brohl Handar said. 'He wants us second-guessing him. He wants our minds numbed with exhaustion come the dawn, and so slowed in our capacity to react, to respond with alacrity. Redmask wants us confused, and he has succeeded.'

'Do you imagine that I don't know all that?' she demanded in a hiss.

'Atri-Preda, you do not even trust your mages just now – the wards they have set to guard us this night. Our soldiers should be sleeping.'

'If I have reason to lack confidence in my mages,' Bivatt said dryly, 'I have good cause. Nor has your K'risnan impressed me thus far, Overseer. Although,' she added, 'his healing talents have proved more than adequate.'

'You sound very nearly resentful of that,' Brohl said.

She waved a dismissive hand and turned away to resume her pacing.

A troubled commander indeed.

Redmask would be delighted.

Toc leaned along the length of the horse's neck. He was riding bareback, and he could feel the animal's heat and its acrid yet gentle smell filled his nostrils as he let the beast take another step forward. From the height of the horse's shoulder he could see just above the line of the ridge off to his left.

The modest defensive berms were like humped graves along the flat this side of the Letherii camp. There had been a change of guard – the chimes had been readily audible – meaning yet another ideal time for the attack had slipped past.

He was no military genius, but Toc believed that this night could not have been more perfect as far as the Awl were concerned. They had their enemy confused, weary and frayed. Instead, Redmask exhausted his own warriors by sending them one way and then the next, with the seemingly sole purpose of raising dust no-one could even see. No command to initiate contact had been issued. No concerted gathering to launch a sudden strike into the Letherii camp. Not even any harassing flights of arrows to speed down in the dark.

He thought he understood the reason for Redmask's inconstancy. The Letherii mages. His scouts had witnessed that impatient, deadly sorcery, held ready to greet the Awl attack. They had brought back stories of blistered land, rocks snapping in the incandescent heat, and these tales had spread quickly, driving deep into the army a spike of fear. The problem was simple. Here, in this place, Redmask had no answer to that magic. And Toc now believed that Redmask would soon sound the retreat, no matter how galling – no spilling of blood, and the great advantage of advancing well beyond reach of the Letherii column and so avoiding detection had been surrendered, uselessly thrown away. No battle, yet a defeat nonetheless.

His horse, unguided by the human on its back, took another step, head dipping so that the animal could crop grass. Too much of that and the beast would find its bowels in knots.

Oh, we take you into slaughter without a moment's thought. And yes, some of you come to enjoy it, to lust for that cacophony, that violence, the reek of blood. And so we share with you, dear horse, our peculiar madness. But who judges us for this crime against you and your kind? No-one.

Unless you horses have a god.

He wondered if there might a poem somewhere in that. *But poems that remind us of our ghastlier traits are never popular, are they? Best the bald lies of heroes and great deeds. The slick comfort of someone else's courage and conviction. So we can bask in the righteous glow and so feel uplifted in kind.*

Aye, I'll stay with the lies. Why not? Everyone else does.

And those who don't are told they think too much. Hah, now there's a fearsome attack enough to quail any venturesome soul. See me tremble.

His horse heard a whinny from off to the right and in whatever language the beasts shared that sound was surely a summons, for it lifted its head, then walked slowly towards it. Toc waited a few moments longer, then, when he judged they were well clear of the ridge line behind them, he straightened and gathered the reins.

And saw before him a solid line of mounted warriors, lances upright.

In front of the row was the young Renfayar, Masarch.

Toc angled his horse on an approach.

'What is this, Masarch? A cavalry charge in the dark?'

The young warrior shrugged. 'We've readied three times this night, Mezla.'

Toc smiled to himself. He'd thrown that pejorative out in a fit of self-mockery a few days past, and now it had become an honorific. Which, he admitted, appealed to his sense of irony. He edged his horse closer and in a low tone asked: 'Do you have any idea what Redmask is doing, Masarch?'

A hooded glance, then another shrug.

'Well,' Toc persisted, 'is this the main concentration of forces? No? Then where?'

'To the northwest, I think.'

'Is yours to be a feint attack?'

'Should the horn sound, Mezla, we ride to blood.'

Toc twisted on the horse and looked back at the ridge. The Letherii would feel the drumming of hoofs, and then see the silhouettes as the Awl crested the line. And those soldiers had dug pits – he could already hear the snapping of leg bones and the animal screaming. 'Masarch,' he said, 'you can't charge those pickets.'

'We can see them well enough to ride around them—'

'Until the animal beside you jostles yours into one.'

At first Toc thought he was hearing wolves howling, but the sudden cry levelled out – Redmask's rodara horn.

Masarch raised his lance. 'Do you ride with us, Mezla?'

Bareback? 'No.'

'Then ride fast to one side!'

Toc kicked his horse into motion, and as he rode down the line he saw the Awl warriors ready their weapons above suddenly restless mounts. Breaths gusted like smoke into the air. From somewhere on the far side of the Letherii encampment there was the sudden reverberation of clashing arms.

He judged that Masarch led six or seven hundred Awl riders. Urging his horse into a gallop, Toc drew clear just as the mass of warriors surged forward. 'This is madness!' He spun the mount round, tugging his bow loose from his shoulder even as he looped the reins over his left wrist. Jamming one end of the bow onto his moccasined foot – between the big toe and the rest – he leaned down his weight to string it. Weapon readied and in his right hand, he deftly adjusted his hold on the reins and knotted them to ensure that they did not fall and foul the horse's front legs.

As the beast cantered into the dusty wake of the cavalry charge, Toc Anaster drew out from the quiver at his hip the first stone-tipped arrow. *What in Hood's name am I doing?*

Getting ready to cover the retreat I know is coming? Aye, a one-eyed archer . . .

With the pressure of his thighs and a slight shifting of weight, he guided his horse in the direction of the rise – where the Awl warriors had arrived in a dark mass, only now voicing their war-cries. Somewhere in the distance rose the sound of dogs, joining that ever-growing cacophony of iron on iron and screaming voices.

Redmask had finally struck, and now there was chaos in the night.

The cavalry, reaching the rise, swept down the other side and moments later were lost from sight.

Toc urged his horse forward, nocking the arrow. He had no stirrups to stand in while shooting, making this whole exercise seem ridiculous, yet he quickly approached the crest. Moments before arriving, he heard the clash ahead – the shouts, the piercing shrieks of injured horses, and beneath it all the thunder of hoofs.

Although difficult to discern amidst the darkness and dust, Toc could see that most of the lancers had swept round the outlying pickets, continuing on to crash into the camp itself. He saw soldiers emerging from those entrenchments, many wounded, some simply dazed. Younger Awl warriors rode among them, slashing down with scimitars in a grotesque slaughter.

Coruscating light burgeoned off to the right – the foaming rise of sorcery – and Toc saw the Awl cavalry begin to withdraw, pulling away like fangs from flesh.

'No!' he shouted, riding hard now towards them. 'Stay among the enemy! Go back! Attack, you damned fools! Attack!'

But, even could they hear him, they had seen the magic, the tumult building into a writhing wave of blistering power. And fear took their hearts. Fear took them and then fled—

Still Toc rode forward, now among the berms. Bodies sprawled, horses lying on their sides, kicking, ears flat and teeth bared; others broken heaps filling pits.

The first of the retreating Awl raced past, unseeing, their faces masks of terror.

A second wave of sorcery had appeared, this one from the left, and he watched it roll into the first of the horse-warriors on that side. Flesh burst, fluids sprayed. The magic climbed, slowed as it seemed to struggle against all the flesh it contacted. Screams, the sound reaching Toc on its own wave, chilling his very bones. Hundreds died before the magic spent itself, and into the dust now swirled white ash – all that was left of human and horse along the entire west flank.

Riders swarming past Toc, along with riderless horses surging ahead in the grip of panic. Dust biting his lone eye, dust seeking to claw down his throat, and all around him shadows writhing in their own war of light and dark as sorceries lifted, rolled then fell in gusting clouds of ash.

And then Toc Anaster was alone, arrow still nocked, in the wasteland just inside the berms. Watching another wave of sorcery sweep past his position, pursuing the fleeing Awl.

Before he could think either way, Toc found himself riding hard, in behind that dread wave, into the scalding, brittle air of the magic's wake – and there, sixty paces away, within a mass of advancing soldiers, he saw the mage. The latter clenched his hands and power tumbled from him, forming yet another excoriating conjuration of raw destruction that rose up to greet Toc, then heaved for him.

One eye or not, he could see that damned wizard.

An impossible shot, jostled as he was on the horse's back as the beast weaved between pits and suspect tufts of grass, as its head lifted in sudden recognition of terrible danger.

Silver-veined power surging towards him.

Galloping now, mad as any other fool this night, and he saw, off to his left, a deep, elongated trench – drainage for the camp's latrines – and he forced his mount towards it, even as the sorcery raced for him on a convergent path from his right.

The horse saw the trench, gauged its width, then stretched out a moment before gathering to make the leap.

He felt the beast lift beneath him, sail through the air – and for that one moment all was still, all was smooth, and in that one moment Toc twisted at the hips, knees hard against the animal's shoulders, drew the bow back, aimed – damning this flat, one-eyed world that was all he had left – then loosed the stone-tipped arrow.

The horse landed, throwing Toc forward onto its neck. Bow in his right hand, legs stretching out now along the length of the beast's back, and his left arm wrapping, desperately tight, about the animal's muscle-sheathed neck – behind them and to the right, the heat of that wave, reaching out, closer, closer—

The horse screamed, bolting forward. He held on.

And felt a gust of cool air behind him. Risked a glance.

The magic had died. Beyond it, at the front line of the advancing – now halted and milling – Letherii troops, a body settling onto its knees. A body without a head; a neck from which rose, not blood, but something like smoke—

A detonation? Had there been a detonation – a thumping crack, bludgeoning the air – yes, maybe he had heard—

He regained control of his horse, took the knotted reins in his left hand and guided the frightened creature round, back towards the crest.

The air reeked of cooked meat. Other flashes lit the night. Dogs snarled. Soldiers and warriors died. And among Masarch's cavalry, Toc would later learn, half were not there to see the dawn.

High overhead, night and its audience of unblinking stars had seen enough, and the sky paled, as if washed of all blood, as if drained of the last life.

The sun was unkind in lighting the morning sky, revealing the thick, biting ash of incinerated humans, horses and dogs. Revealing, as well, the strewn carnage of the battle just done. Brohl Handar walked, half numbed, along the east edge of the now-dishevelled encampment, and approached the Atri-Preda and her retinue.

She had dismounted, and was now crouched beside a corpse just inside the berms – where, it seemed, the suicidal Awl had elected to charge. He wondered how many had died to Letherii sorcery here. Probably every damned one of them. Hundreds for certain, perhaps thousands – there was no way to tell in this kind of aftermath, was there? A handful of fine ash to mark an entire human. Two for a horse. Half for a dog. Just so. The wind took it all away, less than an orator's echo, less than a mourner's gut-deep grunt of despair.

He staggered to a halt opposite Bivatt, the corpse – headless, it turned out – between them.

She looked up, and perhaps it was the harsh sunlight, or the dust in a thin sheath – but her face was paler than he had ever seen before.

Brohl studied the headless body. One of the mages.

'Do you know, Overseer,' Bivatt asked in a rough voice, 'what could have done this?'

He shook his head. 'Perhaps his sorcery returned to him, uncontrolled—'

'No,' she cut in. 'It was an arrow. From a lone archer with the audacity to outrun . . . to slip between – Overseer, an archer riding bareback, loosing his arrow whilst his horse leapt a trench . . .'

She stared up at him, disbelieving, as if challenging him to do other than shake his head. He was too tired for this. He had lost warriors last night. Dogs rushing from the high grasses. Dogs . . . and two Kechra – two, there were only two, weren't there? The same two he had seen before. Only one with those strapped-on swords.

Swords that had chopped his K'risnan in half, one swinging in from one side, the other from the opposite side. Not that the blades actually met. The left one had been higher, from the top of the shoulder down to just below the ribcage. The right blade had cut into ribs, down through the gut, tearing free below the hip and taking a lot of that hip out with it. So, to be accurate, not in half. In three.

The other Kechra had just used its talons and jaws, proving no less deadly – in fact, Brohl thought this one more savage than its larger companion, more clearly delighting in its violent mayhem. The other fought with perfunctory grace. The smaller, swordless Kechra revelled in the guts and limbs it flung in every direction.

But those beasts were not immortal. They could bleed. Take wounds. And enough spears and swords had managed to cut through their tough hides to drive both of them off.

Brohl Handar blinked down at the Atri-Preda. 'A fine shot, then.'

Rage twisted her features. 'He was bound with another of my mages, both drawing their powers together. They were exhausted . . . all the wards.' She spat. 'The other one, Overseer, his head burst apart too. Same as this one here. I've lost two mages, to one damned arrow.' She clambered stiffly to her feet. 'Who was that archer? *Who?*'

Brohl said nothing.

'Get your K'risnan to—'

'I cannot. He is dead.'

That silenced her. For a moment. 'Overseer, we mauled them. Do you understand? Thousands died, to only a few hundred of our own.'

'I lost eighty-two Tiste Edur warriors.'

He was pleased at her flinch, at the faltering of her hard gaze. 'An arrow. A lone rider. Not an Awl – the eye-witnesses swear to that. A mage-killer.'

The only thorn from this wild ride through the night. I see, yes. But I cannot help you. Brohl Handar turned away. Ten, fifteen strides across cracked, crackling, ash-laden ground.

Sorcery had taken the grasses. Sorcery had taken the soil and its very life. The sun, its glory stolen before it could rise this day, looked down, one-eyed. Affronted by this rival.

Yes. Affronted.

CHAPTER SEVENTEEN

When I go in search
The world cries out
And spins away
To walk is to reach
But the world turns
Shied into sublime fend
Flinching to my sting
So innocent a touch
This is what it is to search
The world's answer
Is a cornered retort
It does not want seeing
Does not suffer knowing
To want is to fail
And die mute
Ever solitary these steps
Yielding what it is
To be alone
Crying out to the world
Spinning away
As in its search
It finds you out.

Search
Gaullag of the Spring

HE MIGHT WELL SPEAK OF MYSTERY AND SHOW A MASK OF delighted wonder, but the truth of it was, mystery frightened Beak. He could smell sorcery, yes, and sense its poetic music, so orderly and eloquent, but its heat could so easily burn, right down to a mortal man's core. He was not much for bravery; oh, he could see it well enough among other soldiers – he could see it in every detail of Captain Faradan Sort, who now sat her horse at his side – but he knew he possessed none of it himself.

Coward and stupid were two words that went together, Beak believed, and both belonged to him. Smelling magic had been a way of avoiding it, of running from it, and as for all those candles within him, well, he was happiest when nothing arrived that might send their flames flickering, brightening, bursting into a conflagration. He supposed it was just another stupid decision, this being a soldier, but there was nothing he could do about it now.

Marching across that desert in that place called Seven Cities (although he'd only seen two cities, he was sure there were five more somewhere), Beak had listened to all the other soldiers complaining. About . . . well, everything. The fighting. Not fighting. The heat of the day, the cold at night, the damned coyotes yipping in the dark sounding so close you thought they were standing right beside you, mouth at your ear. The biting insects, the scorpions and spiders and snakes all wanting to kill you. Yes, they'd found lots to complain about. That terrible city, Y'Ghatan, and the goddess who'd opened one eye that night and so stolen away that evil rebel, Leoman. And then, when all had seemed lost, that girl – Sinn – showing her own candle. Blindingly bright, so pure that Beak had cowered before it. They'd complained about all of that, too. Sinn should have snuffed that firestorm out. The Adjunct should have waited a few days longer, because there was no way those marines would have died so easily.

And what about Beak? Hadn't he sensed them? Well, maybe. That mage, Bottle, the one with all the pets. Maybe Beak had smelled him, still alive under all those ashes. But then he was a coward, wasn't he? To go up to, say, the Adjunct, or Captain Kindly, and tell them – no, that was too much. Kindly was like his own father, who didn't like to listen whenever it was something he wasn't interested in hearing. And the Adjunct, well, even her own soldiers weren't sure of her.

He'd listened with all the rest to her speech after they'd left Malaz City (a most terrifying night, that, and he was so glad he'd been far away from it, out on a transport), and he remembered how she talked about going it alone from now on. And doing things nobody else would ever know about. *Unwitnessed*, she said. As if that was important. Such talk usually confused Beak, but not this time. His entire life was, he knew, *unwitnessed*. So, she had made all the other soldiers just like him, just like Beak, and that had been an unexpected gift from that cold, cold woman. Coward or no and stupid as he was, she'd won him that night. Something she wouldn't think much of, obviously, but it meant a lot to him.

Anyway, his heart had slowed its wild run, and he lifted his head and glanced over at the captain. She sat her horse in the deep shadow, unmoving just as he had been, and yet, in an instant, he thought he caught from her a sound – the hammering of waves against stone, the screams of soldiers in battle, swords and slaughter, lances like ice piercing hot flesh, and the waves – and then all of that was gone.

She must have sensed his attention, for she asked in a low voice: 'Are they well past, Beak?'

'Aye.'

'Caught no scent of us?'

'None, Captain. I hid us with grey and blue. It was easy. That mage she kneels in front of the Holds. She knows nothing about the grey and blue warrens.'

'The Letherii were supposed to join us,' Faradan Sort muttered. 'Instead, we find them riding with Tiste Edur, doing their work for them.'

'All stirred up, aye. Especially round here.'

'And that's the problem,' she replied, gathering her reins and nudging her mount out from beneath the heavy branches where they had hidden – fifteen paces off the trail – while the war-party rode past. 'We're well ahead of the other squads. Either Hellian or Urb has lost their mind, or maybe both of them.'

Beak followed on his own horse, a gentle bay he'd named Lily. 'Like a hot poker, Captain, pushing right to the back of the forge. Do that and you burn your hand, right?'

'The hand, yes. Keneb. You and me. All the other squads.'

'Um, your hand, I meant.'

'I am learning to tell those moments,' she said, now eyeing him.

'What moments?' Beak asked.

'When you've convinced yourself how stupid you are.'

'Oh.' *Those moments.* 'I ain't never been so loyal, Captain. Never.'

She gave him a strange look then, but said nothing.

They rode up onto the trail and faced their mounts east. 'They're up there somewhere ahead,' the captain said. 'Causing all sorts of trouble.'

Beak nodded. They'd been tracking those two squads for two nights now. And it was truly a trail of corpses. Sprung ambushes, dead Letherii and Tiste Edur, the bodies dragged off into cover, stripped down and so naked Beak had to avert his eyes, lest evil thoughts sneak into his mind. All the places his mother liked him to touch that one night – no, all that was evil thinking, evil memories, the kind of evil that could make him hang himself as his brother had done.

'We have to find them, Beak.'

He nodded again.

'We have to rein them in. Tonight, do you think?'

'It's the one named Balgrid, Captain. And the other named Bowl – who's learned magic real fast. Balgrid's got the white candle, you see,

521

and this land ain't had no white candle for a long time. So he's dragging the smell off all the bodies they're leaving and that's muddying things up – those ears they're cutting off, and the fingers and stuff that they're tying to their belts. That's why we're going from ambush to ambush, right? Instead of straight to them.'

'Well,' she said after a moment and another long, curious look, 'we're on damned horses, aren't we?'

'So are *they* now, Captain.'

'Are you sure?'

'I think so. Just tonight. It's the Holds. There's one for beasts. And if the Letherii mages figure things out, they could turn with that and find them real fast.'

'Hood's breath, Beak. And what about us?'

'Us too. Of course, there's plenty of people riding horses round here, bad stirrups or no. But if they get close, then maybe even grey and blue candles won't work.'

'You might end up having to show a few more, then.'

Oh, he didn't like that idea. 'I hope not. I really hope not.'

'Let's get going then, Beak.'

Don't burn me down to the core, Captain. Please. It won't be nice, not for anyone. I can still hear their screams and there's always screams and I start first. My screams scare me the most, Captain. Scare me stupid, aye.

'Wish Masan Gilani was with us,' Scant said, pulling up clumps of moss to wash the blood from his hands.

Hellian blinked at the fool. Masan who?

'Listen, Sergeant,' Balgrid said again.

He was always saying that and so she'd stopped listening to him. It was like pissing in the fire, the way men could do when women couldn't. Just a hiss into sudden darkness and then that awful smell. *Listen, Sergeant* and hiss, she stopped listening.

'You've got to,' Balgrid insisted, reaching out to prod her with a finger. 'Sergeant?'

She glared down at that finger. 'Want me t'cut off my left cheek, soldier? Touch me again and you'll be sorry 's what I'm sayin'.'

'Someone's tracking us.'

She scowled. 'For how long?'

'Two, maybe three nights going,' Balgrid replied.

'So you decide to tell me *now*? All my soljers are idiots. How they trackin' us? You and Bowl said you had it covered, had something covered, anyway. What was it you had covered? Right, you been pissing all over our trail or something.' She glared at him. 'Hiss.'

'What? No. Listen, Sergeant—'

And there it went again. She rose to her feet, wobbling on the soft, loamy ground. Where one could fall at every damned step if one wasn't careful. 'Someone – you, Corporal, drag them bodies away.'

'Aye Sergeant.

'Right away, Sergeant.'

'And you two. Maybe. Louts—'

'Lutes.'

'Help the corporal. You all made a mess killing these ones.' And that was right enough, wasn't it? This one had been nasty. Sixteen Letherii and four Edur. Quarrels to the heads did for them Edur what it does for normal people. Like sacks of stones on a big drop, whoo, toppling right off them horses. Then a pair of sharpers, one front of the Letherii column, the other at the tail end. Boom boom and the dusk was nothing but screaming and thrashing limbs human and horse and some couldn't tell which.

Damned Letherii had recovered a little too fast for her liking. Dead sure too fast for Hanno's liking, since Hanno went down with only half a skull left after one of the meanest sword swings she'd ever seen. Threw the soldier right off balance, though, with those stupid stirrups, and so it'd been easy for Urb to reach up one of those giant hands of his, grasp a belt or something and drag the fool right off. Throwing him down with such force that all wind rushed out of him both ends. At which point Urb pushed a mailed fist so hard into the face under the helmet that Urb hurt his knuckles on the back of the man's skull – low, just above the vertables or whatever they were called. Teeth and bone splinters and meat spurting out everywhere.

The first loss in the squads, that'd been. All because Hanno jumped in close thinking the Letherii were still confused and useless. But no, these soldiers, they'd been veterans. They'd come round damned quick.

Saltlick was bad cut up, though Balgrid had worked on him and he wasn't bleeding out and unconscious any more. And Corporal Reem went and got two fingers of his left hand cut off – a bad fend with his shield. Poor Urb wasn't doing too well as sergeant.

Hellian worked round carefully until she faced another direction, and could see Urb sitting on a rotting log, looking miserable. She drank down a mouthful of rum then ambled over. 'We're both sergeants now, right? Let's go find some bushes t'crawl under. I'm in the mood for sweat and grunts with somebody, and since we're the same rank an' all it's only obvious and ain't nobody here gonna c'mplain.'

He blinked up at her, wide-eyed as an owl.

'Wha's your probbem, Urb? I ain't as ugly as you, am I?'

'Urb ain't ugly,' Reem said with an incredulous laugh. 'Masan couldn't think straight around him! Probably why she let herself get shifted over to Balm's squad.'

Hellian grunted, then said, 'Be quiet, Reem. You're a corporal. This is sergeant business.'

'You want a roll with Urb, Sergeant,' Reem said. 'Got nothing to do with you two being sergeants and everything t'do with Urb looking like some goddamned god and you drunk enough to get hungry for the sweats and grunts.'

'Still ain't your business.'

'Maybe not, but we gotta listen to those grunts. Like Scant said, if Masan was around we could all of us dream those dreams and maybe even try, hoping she'd be so frustrated trying to get anywhere with Urb she just might—'

'Since when you find that runaway mouth of yours, Reem?' Balgrid demanded. 'You was better being silent and mysterious. So now you lose a couple fingers and what happens?'

'Quiet allaya,' Hellian said. 'You want another patrol coming down on us and us not ready for 'em this time? Now, the rest of you, not countin' Urb here, check your gear and get your trophies and all that and if you wanna listen then just don't make too many groanin' noises. Of envy and the like.'

'We won't be groaning outa envy, Hellian. More like—'

'Silent and mysterious, damn you, Reem!'

'I feel like talking, Balgrid, and you can't stop me—'

'But I can, and you won't like it at all.'

'Damned necromancer.'

'Just the other side of Denul, Reem, like I keep telling you. Denul's giving, Hood's taking away.'

Hellian closed in on Urb, who suddenly looked terrified. 'Relax,' she said. 'I ain't gonna cut anything off. Not anything of yours, anyway. But if I get clobbered with terrible rejection here . . .'

'Nice bed of moss over here,' Scant said, straightening and moving away with a gesture in his wake.

Hellian reached down and tugged Urb to his feet.

Balgrid was suddenly beside him. 'Listen, Sergeant—'

She dragged Urb past the mage.

'No, Sergeant! Those ones tracking us – I think they've found us!'

All at once weapons were drawn, figures scattering to defensive positions – a rough circle facing outward with Hellian and Urb in the centre.

'Balgrid,' she hissed. 'You coulda said—'

Horse hoofs, the heavy breath of an animal, then a voice called out, low, in Malazan: 'Captain Faradan Sort and Beak. We're coming in so put your damned sharpers away.'

'Oh, that's just great,' Hellian sighed. 'Ease down, everyone, it's that scary captain.'

Marines all right. Beak didn't like the look of them. Mean, hungry, scowling now that the captain had found them. And there was a dead one, too.

Faradan Sort guided her horse into their midst, then dismounted. Beak remained where he was for the moment, not far from where two soldiers stood, only now sheathing their swords. He could see the necromancer, the man's aura white and ghostly. Death was everywhere here, the still air heavy with last breaths, and he could feel this assault of loss like a tight fist in his chest.

It was always this way where people died. He should never have become a soldier.

'Hellian, Urb, we need to talk. In private.' Cool and hard, the captain's voice. 'Beak?'

'Captain?'

'Join us.'

Oh no. But he rode forward and then slipped down from the saddle. Too much attention on him all at once, and he ducked as he made his way to the captain's side.

Faradan Sort in the lead, the group set off into the wood.

'We ain't done nothin' wrong,' Sergeant Hellian said as soon as they halted twenty or so paces from the others. She seemed to be weaving back and forth like a flat-headed snake moments from spitting venom.

'You were supposed to pace yourselves, not get too far ahead of the other squads. At any moment now, Sergeant, we won't be running onto patrols of twenty, but two hundred. Then two thousand.'

'Tha's not the probbem,' Hellian said – an accent Beak had never heard before. 'The probbem is, Cap'in, the Letherii are fightin' alongside them Edur—'

'Have you attempted to make contact with those Letherii?'

'We have,' Urb said. 'It got messy.' He shook his head. 'There's no sign, Captain, that these people want to be liberated.'

'Like Urb said,' Hellian added, nodding vigorously.

The captain looked away. 'The other squads have said much the same.'

'Maybe we can convince them or something,' Urb said.

Hellian leaned against a tree. 'Seems t'me, Cap'in, we got two things we can do and ony two. We can retreat back t'the coast. Build ten thousand rafts and paddle away 's fast as we can. Or we go on. Fast, vicious mean. And iffin they come at us two thousand at once, then we run an' hide like we was trained t'do. Fast and vicious mean, Cap'in, or a long paddle.'

'There is only one thing worse than arguing with a drunk,' Faradan Sort said, 'and that's arguing with a drunk who's right.'

Hellian beamed a big smile.

She was drunk? She was drunk. A drunk sergeant, only, as the captain had just said, no fool either.

Faradan Sort continued, 'Do you have enough horses for your squads?'

'Aye, sir,' Urb replied. 'More than enough.'

'I still want you to slow down, for a few days at least. I intend to contact the other squads and get them to start doing what you're doing, but that will take some time—'

'Captain,' Urb said. 'I got a feeling they're learning already. There's lots more patrols now and they're getting bigger and a lot more wary. We've been expecting to walk into an ambush at any time, and that's what's got us worried. Next time you ride to find us you might find a pile of corpses. Malazan corpses. We ain't got the munitions to carry us all the way – no-one has – so it's going to start getting a lot harder, sir.'

'I know, Sergeant. You lost one in that fight, didn't you?'

'Hanno.'

'Got careless,' Hellian said.

Urb frowned, then nodded. 'Aye, that's true.'

'Then let us hope that one hard lesson is enough,' the captain said.

'Expect it is,' Urb confirmed.

Faradan Sort faced Beak. 'Tell them about the Holds, Beak.'

He flinched, then sighed and said, 'Letherii mages – they might be able to find us by the horses, by smelling them out, I mean.'

'Balgrid's covering our trail,' Urb said. 'Are you saying it won't work?'

'Might be,' Beak said. 'Necromancy's one thing they can't figure. Not Letherii. Not Tiste Edur. But there's a Beast Hold, you see.'

Hellian withdrew a flask and drank down a mouthful, then said, 'We need to know for certain. Next time, Urb, we get us one of them Letherii mages alive. We ask some questions, and in between the screams we get answers.'

Beak shivered. Not just drunk but bloodthirsty, too.

'Be careful,' the captain said. 'That could go sour very quickly.'

'We know allabout careful, sir,' Hellian said with a bleary smile.

Faradan Sort studied the sergeant the way she sometimes studied Beak himself, then she said, 'We're done. Slow down some, and watch out for small patrols – they might be bait.' She hesitated, then added, 'We're in this, now. Understand?'

'No rafts?'

'No rafts, Hellian.'

'Good. If'n I never see another sea I'm going to die happy.'

She would, too, Beak knew. Die happy. She had that going for her.

'Back to your squads,' the captain said. 'Set your nervous soldiers at ease.'

'It's not the smell,' Beak said.

The others turned inquiringly.

'That's not what's making them nervous, I mean,' Beak explained. 'The death smell – they're carrying all that with them, right? So they're used to it now. They're only nervous because they've been sitting around too long. In one place. That's all.'

'Then let us not waste any more time,' Faradan Sort said.

Good idea. That was why she was a captain, of course. Smart enough to make her ways of thinking a mystery to him – but that was one mystery he was happy enough with. Maybe the only one.

They flung themselves down at the forest's edge. Edge, aye – too many damned edges. Beyond was a patchwork of farmland and hedgerows. Two small farms were visible, although no lantern- or candle-light showed through the tiny, shuttered windows. Heart pounding painfully in his chest, Fiddler rolled onto his side to see how many had made it. A chorus of harsh breaths from the scatter of bodies in the gloom to either side of the sergeant. All there. Thanks to Corabb and the desert warrior's impossible luck.

The ambush had been a clever one, he admitted. Should have taken them all down. Instead, half a league back, in a small grassy glade, there was the carcass of a deer – a deer that Corabb had inadvertently flushed out – with about twenty arrows in it. Cleverly planned, poorly executed.

The Malazans had quickly turned it. Sharpers cracking in the night, crossbows thudding, the flit of quarrels and the punch of impact. Shrieks of agony. A rush from Gesler's heavies had broken one side of the ambush—

And then the sorcery had churned awake, something raw and terrible, devouring trees like acid. Grey tongues of chaotic fire, heaving into a kind of standing wave. Charging forward, engulfing Sands – his scream had been mercifully short. Fiddler, not ten paces away from where Sands had vanished, saw the Letherii mage, who seemed to be screaming with his own pain, even as the wave hurled forward. Bellowing, he'd swung his crossbow round, felt the kick in his hands as he loosed the heavy quarrel.

The cusser had struck a bole just above and behind the mage's head. The explosion flattened nearby trees, shredded a score of Letherii soldiers. Snuffed the sorcery out in an instant. As more trees toppled, branches thrashing down, the Malazans had pulled back, fast, and then they ran.

Movement from Fiddler's left and a moment later Gesler dragged himself up alongside. 'Hood's damned us all, Fid. We're running out of forest – how's Cuttle?'

'Arrow's deep,' Fiddler replied, 'but not a bleeder. We can dig it out when we get a chance.'

'Think they're tracking us?'

Fiddler shook his head. He had no idea. If there were enough of them left. He twisted round. 'Bottle,' he hissed, 'over here.'

The young mage crawled close.

'Can you reach back?' Fiddler asked. 'Find out if they're after us?'

'Already did, Sergeant. Used every damned creature in our wake.'

'And?' Gesler wanted to know.

'That cusser did most of them, Sergeant. But the noise brought others. At least a dozen Tiste Edur and maybe a few hundred Letherii. Are they tracking us now? Aye, but still a way behind – they've learned to be cautious, I guess.'

'We losing the dark,' Gesler said. 'We need a place to hide, Fid – only that's probably not going to work this time, is it? They're not going to rest.'

'Can we lose them?' Fiddler asked Bottle.

'I'm pretty tired, Sergeant—'

'Never mind. You've done enough. What do you think, Gesler? Time to get messy?'

'And use up our few cussers?'

'Don't see much choice, to be honest. Of course, I always hold one back. Same for Cuttle.'

Gesler nodded. 'We had ours distributed – good thing, too, the way Sands went up. Still, he had munitions on him, yet they didn't ignite—'

'Oh, but they did,' Fiddler said. 'Just not in this realm. Am I right, Bottle? That sorcery, it's like a broken gate, the kind that chews up whoever goes through it.'

'Spirits below, Fid, you smelled it out about dead right. That magic, it started as one thing, then became another – and the mage was losing control, even before you minced him.'

Fiddler nodded. He'd seen as much. Or thought he had. 'So, Bottle, what does that mean?'

The young mage shook his head. 'Things are getting out of hand . . . somewhere. There was old stuff, primitive magic, at first. Not as ancient as spirit-bound stuff. Still, primitive. And then something chaotic grabbed it by the throat . . .'

A short distance away, Koryk rolled onto his back. He was bone tired. Let Bottle and the sergeants mutter away, he knew they were neck-deep in Hood's dusty shit.

'Hey, Koryk.'

'What is it, Smiles?'

'You damned near lost it back there, you know.'

'I did, did I?'

'When them four came at you all at once, oh, you danced quite a jig, half-blood.' She laughed, low and brimming with what sounded like malice. 'And if I hadn't come along to stick a knife in that one's eye – the one who'd slipped under your guard and was ready to give you a wide belly smile – well, you'd be cooling fast back there right now.'

'And the other three?' Koryk asked, grinning in the gloom. 'Bet you never knew I was that quick, did you?'

'Something tells me you didn't either.'

He said nothing, because she was right. He'd been in something like a frenzy, yet his eye and his hand had been cold, precise. Through it all it had been as if he had simply watched, every move, every block, every shift in stance and twist, every slash of his heavy blade. Watched, yes, yet profoundly in love with that moment, with each moment. He'd felt some of this at the shield wall on the dock that night in Malaz City. But what had begun as vague euphoria was now transformed into pure revelation. *I like killing. Gods below, I do like it, and the more I like it, the better at it I get.* He never felt more alive, never more perfectly *alive.*

'Can't wait to see you dance again,' Smiles murmured.

Koryk blinked in the gloom, then shifted to face her. Was she stirred? Had he somehow kissed her awake between those muscled legs of hers? Because he'd killed well? *Did I dance* that *jig, Smiles?* 'You get scarier, woman, the more I know you.'

She snorted. 'As it should be, half-blood.'

Tarr spoke from Koryk's other side: 'I think I'm going to be sick.'

A slightly more distant laugh from Cuttle, 'Aye, Tarr, it's what happens when your entire world view collapses. Of course,' he added, 'if you could manage to dance like poetry when killing people, who knows—'

'Enough of that. Please.'

'No worries,' Cuttle persisted. 'You ain't the dancing kind. You're as rooted as a tree, and just about as slow, Tarr.'

'I may be slow, Cuttle, but the fools go down eventually, don't they?'

'Oh aye, that they do. Not suggesting otherwise. You're a one-man shield-wall, you are.'

Corporal Stormy was spitting blood. A damned elbow had cracked his mouth, and now two teeth were loose and he'd bitten his tongue. The elbow might have been his own – someone had collided hard with him in the scrap and he'd had his weapon arm lifted high with the sword's point angled downward. Nearly wrenched his shoulder out of its damned socket.

A savage back-swing with the pommel had crunched the attacker's

529

temple and he'd reeled away, one eye half popped out. Shortnose had then cut the Letherii down.

That had been some charge, him and his heavies, Shortnose and the trio of dread ladies each one of whom could both stare down a rutting bhederin bull and beat it into a pulp if it came to that. Making Stormy a very happy sergeant. Bad luck about Sands, though. *But we ain't gonna lose any more. Not one. I got my heavies and we can take down whatever they throw at us.*

And not just us neither. That Tarr and Koryk . . . Fid's got a good mean pair in those. And that Smiles, she's got the blackrock heart of a Claw. Good squads here, for this kinda work. And now we're gonna turn round and kick 'em dead in the jaw, I can feel it. Fid and Gesler, cooking in Kellanved's old cauldron.

He was delighted the Adjunct had finally cut them loose. In just this way, too. To Hood with damned marching in column. No, cut in fast and low and keep going, aye, and keep their heads spinnin' every which way. So the fools on their trail were coming for them, were they? And why not? Just two puny squads. And them probably in the hundreds by now.

'Kellanved's curse,' he muttered with a grin.

Flashwit's round face loomed into view, 'Say something, Corporal?'

'Malazan marines, my dear, that's us.'

'Not heavies? I thought—'

'You're both, Flash. Relax. It's this, you see – the Malazan marines haven't done what they was trained to do in years, not since before Kellanved died. Trained, y'see. To do exactly what we're doing right now, praise Fener. Them poor bastards Letherii and Edur, gods below, them poor ignorant fools.'

'Smart enough to ambush us,' Uru Hela said from beyond Flashwit.

'Didn't work though, did it?'

'Only because—'

'Enough from you, Uru Hela. I was talking here, right? Your corporal. So just listen.'

'I was just askin'—'

'Another word and you're on report, soldier.'

If she snorted she fast turned it into a cough.

From Gesler up with Fiddler: '*Quiet down there!*'

Point proved. Stormy nodded.

Malazan marines. Hah.

Fiddler nodded at the narrow, wending track snaking towards the nearest farmhouse and its meagre outbuildings. 'We jog good and heavy, dragging our wounded, down there. Straight for the farmhouse along that cart path.'

'Like we was still running scared, panicked,' Gesler said. 'Aye. Of course, we got to clear that farmhouse, which means killing civilians, and I have to say, Fid, I don't like that.'

'Maybe we can figure a way round that,' Fiddler replied. 'Bottle?'

'Aye, Sergeant. I'm tired, but I could probably glamour them. Maybe even throw some false ideas in their heads. Like, we went north when we really went south. Like that.'

'Don't ever die on us, Bottle,' Gesler said. To Fiddler, he added, 'I'll go collect munitions from my squad, then.'

'Me and Cuttle,' Fiddler said, nodding again.

'Trip wires?'

'No, it'll be daylight by then. No, we'll do the drum.'

'Hood take me,' Gesler breathed. 'You sure? I mean, I've heard about it—'

'You heard because me and Hedge invented it. And perfected it, more or less.'

'More or less?'

Fiddler shrugged. 'It either works or it doesn't. We've got Bottle's deception, in case it doesn't—'

'But there'll be no coming back to retrieve those cussers, though, will there?'

'Not unless you want to see the bright white light, Gesler.'

'Well,' the amber-hued man said with grin, 'since there's a chance at seeing the legend come real, with the genius who invented it right here . . . I ain't gonna talk you out of it, Fid.'

'Half the genius, Gesler. Hedge was the other.'

'Second thoughts?'

'Second, ninth and tenth, friend. But we're doing it anyway. When everyone's ready, you lead them ahead, excepting me and Cuttle. To that farmhouse – the near one. I think the far one's abandoned. Could be the owner rebuilt. The fields look damned well kept, don't they?'

'Yeah, especially given how small the homestead is.'

'Let Bottle sniff it out before you go charging in.'

'Aye. You hear that, mage?'

'What? Sorry, I think I fell asleep.'

Gesler glared across at Fiddler. 'Our lives are in this man's hands? Hood help us.'

Orders were given, passed down the ragged row of supine soldiers. Dawn was just tingeing the air when Gesler, Bottle at his side and trailed by Corabb Bhilan Thenu'alas, led his now oversized squad onto the cart path. Scuffing the ground, dragging furrows here and there – not too obvious, just enough – as they made their way towards the modest farmhouse.

Fiddler and Cuttle watched them for a time, until they were well enough away from the place they'd decided was best for the trap. Shrubs running close to the cart path, narrowing lines of sight for that span. Beyond the bushes, two middle-aged trees on the left and one old ancient on the right.

Four cussers for this. Two close together, then one, and then the last.

Cuttle, his face sheathed in sweat from the arrow-head lodged in his shoulder, was strangely lacking in commentary as Fiddler directed the sapper to pace the track from this side of the narrowing to twenty strides beyond it, and set sticks in the ground when Fiddler so commanded. Once this was done, Cuttle's task was to dig holes in the packed earth where the sticks had been. Shallow holes.

A sapper who trusted to Oponn's pull might have left it at that, praying to the fickle Twins that a horse hoof would descend on at least one of the planted cussers. But that was not how the drum worked. All that was needed was vibration. If the cussers were thinned on one side just right; if the sharp stone against that spot was sharp enough and angled just right so that the reverberation would drive its tip into the clay shell. The real challenge, Fiddler and Hedge had discovered, was down to shaving the cusser – right down to eggshell thin – without breaking it and so painting leaves in the highest trees with one's own blood and guts.

As soon as Cuttle finished the first scooped-out hole, Fiddler headed towards it with a cusser cradled in his hands. Setting it down carefully on the ground, he drew a knife and made some minute adjustments to the hole. Then he turned his attention to the cusser. This one, furthest down along the track, would be the one to go first. Which would trigger the others, in the midst of the troop, with two at the back end in case the column was especially long.

He set the cusser into the hole, then settled down onto his stomach and brought his knife close to one side of the mine. And began scraping clay.

The sun had risen, and although the air was still cool sweat streamed down Fiddler's face as he shaved away minute slivers of the fine-grained clay. He wished for direct sunlight on the cusser, the side he was working on, so he could work until he saw that faint glow reaching through to the bright yellow incendiary powder with its shards of iron. But no such luck. All remained in shadow.

Finally, one last scrape, then he carefully edged the blade away. Found the sharp stone and set it down beside the thinned shell. Point against the clay, he made a half-twist – breath held, eyes squeezed shut – then slowly withdrew his hand. Opened his eyes. Studied his handiwork.

A few more deep breaths to settle his nerves, then he began filling the hole with small handfuls of earth. Then scattered detritus over the spot.

Fiddler belly-crawled away, until he reached the edge of the track where he'd left the other cussers. Glancing up the path, he saw Cuttle waiting at the far end, arms wrapped about his torso, looking like he'd just pissed himself. *Aye, he knows why we're a dying breed.*

Taking the second cusser, Fiddler made his way – lightly – to the second hole. Not as thin this time, but thin enough. Each one in turn slightly easier, which made shaving each of them increasingly dangerous – the risk of getting careless, sloppy, just in that wash of relief at having managed the first one . . . well, he knew all the dangers in all this, didn't he?

Teeth gritted, he arrived at the second hole in the path, slowly sank to his knees. Set the cusser down, and reached for his knife.

Cuttle was as close to pissing himself as he had ever been. Not at the prospect of dying – he was fine enough with that and had been ever since finding himself in the Fourteenth – but at what he was witnessing here.

The last great Malazan sapper. No-one else came close. Imagine, shaving cusser shells. With a knife. Eggshell thin. Cuttle had watched, unable to make out much from this distance, as Fiddler had set to work on the first one, the deadliest one of all. And he had prayed, to every god he could think of, to gods he didn't even know the names of, to spirits and ghosts and every sapper living or dead, each name a benediction to one man's brilliance. Praying that the one man he truly worshipped wouldn't . . . wouldn't what?

Let me down.

How pathetic. He knew that. He kept telling himself that, in between the breathed-out beseechings. As if he'd have time to rue the failing of his faith.

So there was Fiddler, closer now, at the second hole, doing it all over again. Imagine, Fid and Hedge, the way they must have been together. Gods, those Bridgeburners must have been holy terrors. But now . . . just Fiddler, and Cuttle here poorer than a shadow of the famous Hedge. It was all coming to an end. But so long as Fiddler stayed alive, well then, damn them all, it was worth holding on. And this arrow lodged in his left shoulder, well, true he'd seen it coming, but he hadn't exactly leaned into it, had he? Might have looked that way. Might have at that. As if he'd had time to even think, with everything going on around him. He wasn't superhuman, was he?

Edging back from the second set mine, Fiddler glanced over at Cuttle. The man's face was white as death. Well, thinking on it, he didn't need the man that close any more, did he?

He hand-signalled *Leave, rejoin the squads.*

Cuttle shook his head.

Shrugging – this was no time to argue and if Cuttle had a death-wish it wasn't news to Fiddler – he rose and set off to collect the third cusser. Even footfalls were now risky, forcing him to move slowly along the verge of the track. There was plenty of superstition about where to stash munitions when working. Hedge would have insisted the cussers be ahead of the work at all times, but the less Fiddler handled them the better he felt. No matter what, there was back and forth with the damned things, wasn't there?

He reached the spot and looked down at the two remaining cussers. More superstition. Which one? Heart side or head side? Facing the hole or with the hole behind him as it was now? Hood's breath, Hedge was clambering around in his skull like a fiend. Enough of the superstition! Fiddler crouched and collected a cusser.

Heart side.

And was random chance really any more than just that? The Moranth were fanatics when it came to precision. Every class of munitions perfect beyond belief. No variation at all. With variation, being a sapper would be nothing more than being a rock-thrower – with explosive rocks, mind, but even so. No real talent involved, no hard-earned skill.

Fiddler remembered, with the appalling clarity of a god-touched revelation, his first encounter with Moranth munitions. Northern Genabackis, a week before the march on the city of Mott followed by the twin nightmares of Mott Wood and Blackdog Swamp. There had been rumours of contact and extensive negotiations with a strange people ruling a place called Cloud Forest, far to the south. An isolated people, said to be terrifying and inhuman in appearance, who rode enormous domesticated four-winged insects – giant dragonflies – and could rain death upon enemies from great heights.

The Malazan negotiators had included Tayschrenn, some nobleborn dignitary named Aragan, and a lone T'lan Imass named Onos T'oolan. The Second and Third Armies had been encamped on Nathii farmland two days from the landing south of Malyntaeas. A crate had been carried – gingerly, by sweating soldiers from the quartermaster's unit – and set down ten paces from the squad's hearth fire. Whiskeyjack had gestured Hedge and Fiddler over.

'You two do most of the sapping in this miserable squad,' the sergeant had said, grimacing as if he'd swallowed something unpleasant – which he had, by virtue of legitimizing Fid and Hedge's destructive anarchy. 'In yon box there are grenados and nastier stuff, come from the Moranth now that we're allied with 'em. Seems to make sense – in an insane way – to hand 'em over to you two. Now, obviously, you need to do some experimenting with what's in that box. Just make sure you do it half a league or more from this here camp.' He hesitated, scratched at his bearded jaw, then added, 'The big ones are too big to throw far enough, far enough to survive them exploding, I mean. So you'll need to crack your heads together to work out trying them. As a final order, soldiers, don't kill yourselves. This squad's under strength as it is and I'd need to pick out two others to hump these damned things around. And the only two I could use are Kalam and Trotts.'

Aye, Trotts.

Fiddler and Hedge had pried the lid loose, then had stared down, bemused, at the well-packed grenados, nestled in frames and matted straw. Small round ones, long tapered ones, spike-shaped ones of exquisite glass – not a bubble to be seen – and, at the bottom, much larger ones, big enough to ride a catapult cup if one was so inclined (and, it turned out, suicidal, since they tended to detonate as soon as the catapult arm struck the brace. Great for destroying catapults and their hapless crews, though).

Experimentation indeed. Hedge and Fid had set out, the crate between them, on a long, exhausting walk into some out-of-the-way place, where they threw the small ones they decided to call sharpers because when detonated too close they had a tendency to pepper the thrower with slivers of iron and made the ears bleed; where they discovered the incendiary properties of the burners, to the wailing protestations of a farmer who'd witnessed the fiery destruction of a hay wagon (at least until they'd handed over four gold imperial sceptres – Kellanved's newly minted currency – which was enough money to buy a new farm). Crackers, driven into elongated wedge-shaped holes in hard-packed earth, did sweet mayhem on foundation stones, mortared or otherwise. And, finally, the cussers, the ugliest, nastiest munitions ever created. They were intended to be dropped from high overhead by the Moranth on their Quorls, and Hedge and Fid had used up most of their allotted supply trying to work out an alternative means of practical, non-fatal use. And, in the end, had needed twenty more – two crates' worth – to finally conclude that a fool would have to be Oponn-kissed by the Lady to try anything but secondary usage; add-ons to crackers and burners and, if the chance presented itself, a well-thrown sharper.

The oversized crossbows came much later, as did maniacal variations like the drum and the slow burn. And through all of that, the Lady's Pull always remained as the last resort. Had Fiddler been a religious man, he would have been obliged, he well knew, to drop every single coin of pay and loot he earned into the coffers of the Lady's temples, given how many times he had loosed a cusser at targets well within blast range of himself and countless other Malazans. Hedge had been even less . . . restrained. And, alas, his demise had therefore been of a nature succinctly unsurprising.

Reminiscing had a way of arriving at the worst of moments, a glamour of nostalgia no doubt infused with subtle but alluring suicidal inclinations, and Fiddler was forced to push all such remembrances aside as he approached Cuttle and the last hole in the path.

'You should have hightailed it out of here,' Fiddler said as he settled down beside the modest excavation.

'No chance of that,' Cuttle replied in a low voice.

'As you like, then, but don't be standing there at Hood's Gate if I mess this one up.'

'I hear you, Fid.'

And, trying not to think of Hedge, of Whiskeyjack, Trotts and all the rest; trying not to think of the old days, when the world still seemed new and wondrous, when taking mad risks was all part of the game, Fiddler, the last great saboteur, went to work.

Bottle squinted at the farmhouse. Someone or ones inside there, he was sure enough of that. Living, breathing folk, oh yes. But . . . something, a faint odour, charnel recollections, or . . . whatever. He wasn't sure, couldn't be sure, and that made him seriously uneasy.

Gesler had moved up beside him, had lain there patient as a tick on a blade of grass, at least to start. But now, a hundred or more heart-beats on, Bottle could sense the man growing restless. Fine enough for him, with that gold skin that didn't burn once in Y'Ghatan – of course, Truth had shown that the strange skin wasn't truly impervious, especially when it came to Moranth munitions. Even so, Gesler was a man who had walked through fire, in every permutation of the phrase Bottle could think of, so all of this skulking and trickery and brutal slaughter was fine for him.

But I'm the one they're all counting on, and I couldn't use this stupid sword at my belt to hack my way clear of a gaggle of puritanical do-gooders with their pointing fingers and sharp nails and all – gods below, where did that image come from? Damned Mockra, someone's leaking thoughts. Bottle glanced over at Gesler. 'Sergeant?' he whispered.

'What?'

'Got strange notions in your skull, by any chance?'

A suspicious glance, then Gesler shook his head. 'Was thinking of an old mage I knew. Kulp. Not that you remind me of him or anything, Bottle. You're more like Quick Ben, I think, than any of us are comfortable with. Last I saw of Kulp, though, was the poor bastard flung head over heels off the stern rail of a ship – in a firestorm. Always wondered what happened to him. I like to think he made it just fine, dropping out of that furnace of a warren and finding himself in some young widow's back garden, waist-deep in the cool waters of her fountain. Just as she was on her knees praying for salvation or something.' All at once he looked embarrassed and his gaze flicked away. 'Aye, I paint pretty pictures of what could be, since what is always turns out so damned bad.'

Bottle's grunt was soft, then he nodded. 'I like that, Sergeant. Kind of . . . relieves me.'

'Meaning?'

'Only, shows that you're not as far from the rest of us as it sometimes seems.'

Gesler grimaced. 'Then you'd be wrong, soldier. I'm a sergeant, which makes me as far from you and these other idiots as a cave bear from a damned three-legged stoat. Understood?'

'Aye, Sergeant.'

'Now why are we still hiding here? There's smoke trickling up from that chimney, meaning we got folks inside. So, give us the damned go-ahead on this, Bottle, then your task's done, for now.'

'All right. I think there's two in there. Quiet, contemplative thoughts, no conversation yet.'

'Contemplative? As in what a cow thinks with a bellyful of feed in her and a calf tugging wet and hard at a teat? Or like some kind of giant two-headed snake that's just come down the chimney and swallowed up old Crud-nails and his missus?'

'Somewhere in between, I'd say.'

Gesler's expression turned into a glare; then, with a snort, he twisted round and hand-signalled. A moment later Uru Hela crawled past Corabb Bhilan Thenu'alas – who was directly behind the sergeant – and came up on Gesler's left.

'Sergeant?'

'Bottle says there's two in there. I want you to walk up peaceful-like and call 'em out – you're thirsty and want to ask for a ladle or two from that well there.'

'I ain't thirsty, Sergeant.'

'Lie, soldier.'

Bottle could see the notion upset her. *Spirits fend, the things you find out . . .*

'How about I just ask to refill my waterskin?'

'Aye, that will do.'

'Of course,' she said, frowning, 'I'll need to empty it out first.'

'Why don't you do that?'

'Aye, Sergeant.'

Gesler twisted to look at Bottle, and the young mage could plainly see the man's battle with pathos and despair. 'Get yourself ready,' he said, 'to hit 'em with a glamour or something, in case things go all wrong.'

Bottle nodded, then, seeing an entirely new expression on Gesler's face, he asked, 'What's wrong, Sergeant?'

'Well, either I just wet myself or Uru Hela's draining her waterskin. On some level,' he added, 'I think the distinction's moot.'

That's it, Sergeant. You've just won me. Right there. Won me, so I'll give you what I got. From now on. Yet, even with that quasi-serious notion, he had to turn his head away and bite hard on the sleeve of his tanned leather shirt. *Better yet, Sergeant, wait till we all see that fine wet patch on your crotch. You won't live this one down, no sir, not a chance of that. Oh, precious memory!*

Strapping her now empty waterskin onto her belt, Uru Hela then squirmed forward a little further, and climbed to her feet. Adjusting her heavy armour and plucking twigs and grass from metal joins and hinges, she tightened the helm strap and set out for the farmhouse.

'Oh,' Bottle muttered.

'What?' Gesler demanded.

'They're suddenly alert – I don't know, maybe one of them saw her through a crack in the window shutters – no, that's not right.'

'*What?*'

'Still not talking, but moving around now. A lot. Fast, too. Sergeant, I don't think they saw her. I think they *smelled* her. And us.'

'Smelled? Bottle—'

'Sergeant, I don't think they're human—'

Uru Hela was just passing the well, fifteen paces from the farm-house's door, when that door flew open – pushed hard enough to tear it from its leather hinges – and the creature that surged into view seemed too huge to even fit through the frame, coming up as if from stairs sunk steep below ground level – coming up, looming massive, dragging free an enormous single-bladed two-handed wood-axe—

Uru Hela halted, stood motionless as if frozen in place.

'Forward!' Gesler bellowed, scrambling upright as he swung up his crossbow—

Corabb Bhilan Thenu'alas charged past the sergeant, blade out—

Bottle realized his mouth was moving, yet no sounds came forth. He stared, struggling to comprehend. A demon. A Hood-damned Kenryll'ah demon!

It had lunged clear of the doorframe and now charged straight for Uru Hela.

She threw her waterskin at it, then spun to flee, even as she tugged at her sword.

Not nearly fast enough to escape – the demon's huge axe slashed in a gleaming, blurred arc, caught the soldier solid in her left shoulder. Arm leapt away. Blood spurted from joins in the scales right across her entire back, as the blade's broad wedge drove yet deeper. Deeper, severing her spine, then further, tearing loose with her right scapula – cut halfway through – jammed on the gory blade as it whipped clear of Uru Hela's body.

More blood, so much more, yet the sudden overwhelming gouts of red quickly subsided – the soldier's heart already stopped, the life that was her mind already fleeing this corporeal carnage – and she was collapsing, forward, the sword in her right hand half drawn and never to go further, head dipping, chin to chest, then down, face-first onto the ground. A heavy sound. A thump. Whereupon all motion from her ceased.

Gesler's crossbow thudded, releasing a quarrel that sliced past Corabb, not a hand's breadth from his right shoulder.

A bellow of pain from the demon – the finned bolt sunk deep into its chest, well above its two hearts.

Corabb Bhilan Thenu'alas closed fast, yelling something in the tribal tongue, something like '*Leoman's balls!*'

Gesler reloading on one knee. Stormy, Saltlick and Shortnose thundering past him, followed by Koryk and Tarr. Smiles swinging wide, crossbow in her hands – one of Fid's weapons, this one headed with a sharper – which she then trained on the farmhouse entrance, where a second demon had appeared. Oh, she was fast indeed, that quarrel flitting across the intervening space, making a strange warbling sound as it went, and the second demon, seeing it, somehow swinging his weapon – a tulwar – into its path – not much use, that gesture, as the sharper exploded.

Another scream of pain, the huge demon knocked back, off its feet, crashing into the side of the farmhouse. Wood, sod and chinking bowed inward, and as the demon fell, the entire wall on that side of the door-frame went with it.

And what am I doing? Damn me, what am I doing? Bottle leapt upright, desperately drawing on whatever warren first answered his summons.

The axe-wielding demon surged towards Corabb. The wedge-blade slashed its deadly arc. Struck Corabb's shield at an oblique angle, caromed upward and would have caught the side of Corabb's head if not for the man's stumbling, left knee buckling as he inadvertently stepped into a groundhog hole, losing his balance and pitching to one side. His answering sword-swing, which should have been batted aside by the demon's swing-through, dipped well under it, the edge *thunking* hard into the demon's right knee.

It howled.

In the next instant Stormy, flanked by his heavies, arrived. Swords chopping, shields clattering up against the wounded Kenryll'ah. Blood and pieces of meat spattered the air.

Another bellow from the demon as it launched itself backward, clear of the deadly infighting, gaining room to swing the wood-axe in a horizontal slash that crumpled all three shields lifting to intercept it. Banded metal and wood exploded in all directions. Saltlick grunted from a broken arm.

'Clear!' someone shouted, and Stormy and his heavies flung themselves backward. Corabb, still lying on the ground, rolled after them.

The demon stood, momentarily confused, readying its axe.

Smiles's hand-thrown sharper struck it on its left temple.

Bright light, deafening crack, smoke, and the demon was reeling away, one side of its bestial face obliterated into red pulp.

Yet Bottle sensed the creature's mind already righting itself.

Gesler was yelling. 'Withdraw! Everyone!'

Summoning all he had, Bottle assailed the demon's brain with Mockra. Felt it recoil, stunned.

From the ruined farmhouse, the second Kenryll'ah was beginning to clamber free.

Smiles tossed another sharper into the wreckage. A second snapping explosion, more smoke, more of the building falling down.

'We're pulling out!'

Bottle saw Koryk and Tarr hesitate, desperate to close in on the stunned demon. At that moment Fiddler and Cuttle arrived.

'Hood's balls!' Fiddler swore. 'Get moving, Koryk! Tarr! Move!'

Gesler was making some strange gesture. 'We go south! South!'

Saltlick and Shortnose swung in that direction, but Stormy pulled them back. 'That's called misdirection, y'damned idiots!'

The squads reforming as they moved, eastward, now in a run. The shock of Uru Hela's death and the battle that followed keeping them quiet now, just their gasping breaths, the sounds of armour like broken crockery underfoot. Behind them, smoke billowing from the farmhouse. An axe-wielding demon staggering about in a daze, blood streaming from its head.

Damned sharper should have cracked that skull wide open, Bottle well knew. *Thick bones, I guess.* Kenryll'ah, aye, not their underlings. No, Highborn of Aral Gamelon, he was sure of that.

Stormy started up. 'Hood-damned demon farmers! They got Hood-damned demon farmers! Sowing seeds, yanking teats, spinnin' wool – and chopping strangers to pieces! Gesler, old friend, I hate this place, you hear me? *Hate it!*'

'Keep quiet!' Fiddler snarled. 'We was lucky enough all those sharpers didn't mince us on the road – now your bleating's telling those demons exactly where we're going!'

'I wasn't going to lose any more,' Stormy retorted in a bitter growl. 'I'd swore it—'

'Should've known better,' Gesler cut in. 'Damn you, Stormy, don't make promises you can't keep – we're in a fight here and people are going to die. No more promises, got me?'

A surly nod was his only answer.

They ran on, the end of a long, long night now tumbled over into day. For the others, Bottle knew, there'd be rest ahead. Somewhere. But not him. No, he'd need to work illusions to hide them. He'd need to flit from creature to creature out in the forest, checking on their backtrail. He needed to keep these fools alive.

Crawling from the wreckage of the farmhouse, the demon prince spat out some blood, then settled back onto his haunches and looked blearily around. His brother stood nearby, cut and lashed about the body and half his face torn away. Well, it had never been much of a face anyway, and most of it would grow back. Except maybe for that eye.

His brother saw him and staggered over. 'I'm never going to believe you again,' he said.

'Whatever do you mean?' The words were harsh, painful to utter. He'd inhaled some flames with that second grenade.

'You said farming was peaceful. You said we could just retire.'

'It was peaceful,' he retorted. 'All our neighbours ran away, didn't they?'

'These ones didn't.'

'Weren't farmers, though. I believe I can say that with some assurance.'

'My head hurts.'

'Mine too.'

'Where did they run to?'

'Not south.'

'Should we go after them, brother? As it stands, I'd have to venture the opinion that they had the better of us in this little skirmish, and that displeases me.'

'It's worth considering. My ire is awakened, after all. Although I suggest you find your matlock, brother, instead of that silly wood-axe.'

'Nearest thing within reach. And now I'll have to dig into our crumpled, smouldering abode – all that digging we did, all for nothing!'

At that moment they heard, distinctly, the sound of horses. Coming fast up the track.

'Listen, there's more of them. No time to find your matlock, brother. Let us set forth and commence our sweet vengeance, shall we?'

'Superior notion indeed. One of my eyes still works, which should suffice.'

The two Kenryll'ah demon princes set out for the cart path.

It was really not their day.

A quarter of a league now from the farmhouse, and Fiddler swung round, confirming for Bottle yet again that the old sergeant had hidden talents. 'Horses,' he said.

Bottle had sensed the same.

The squads halted, under bright sunlight, alongside a cobbled road left in bad repair. Another cluster of farm buildings awaited them a thousand paces to the east. No smoke rising from the chimney. *No surprise with demons for neighbours, I suppose.*

The detonations were a drumbeat of thunderous concussions that shook the earth beneath them.

'Four!' Fiddler said with a savage grin.

Bottle saw Cuttle staring at the sergeant with undisguised awe and more than a little worship.

Smoke now, billowing in the distance, an earthen blot rising above the treeline.

'Let's make for that farm ahead,' Fiddler said. 'We'll rest up there for the day – I don't think our pursuers are in any condition to do much.'

'The drum,' Cuttle whispered. 'I seen it. The drum. Now I can die happy.'

Damned sappers. Bottle shook his head. There was pain there, now, in that mangled stretch of track a quarter-league away. Human, beast, and . . . oh, and *demon. You'd have done better chasing us. Even so, what a mess we've made.*

Yes, plenty of pain, but more death. Flat, dwindling death, spreading dark as that dust in the air. Fiddler's drum. No better announcement imaginable, that the Malazans were here.

Thom Tissy's descent from the tree was a little loud, a little fast. In a skein of snapped branches, twigs, leaves and one abandoned wasp nest, the sergeant landed heavy and hard on his backside. 'Ow, gods below, gods below!'

'Ain't no god at that end, just a tailbone,' a soldier called out from the nearby squads.

Keneb waited for a few more heartbeats, then asked, 'Sergeant, tell me what you saw.'

Thom Tissy slowly, carefully, regained his feet. He walked about on his short bandy legs, squat as an ogre, replete with pocked face and warty hands. 'Smoke, Fist, and plenty of it. Counted ten spots in all, one of 'em big – probably the thunder we heard a little while back – more than one cusser for sure. Maybe three, maybe more.'

Meaning someone was in desperate trouble. Keneb glanced away, scanned the motley soldiers hunkered down in the forest glade. 'Ten?'

'Aye, Fist. I guess we stirred 'em up some, enough so that the fighting's getting fierce. When the captain gets back, we'll find out some details, I suppose.'

Yes. Faradan Sort. But she and Beak had been away for days, almost a week now.

'Ten.'

'Expecting more, Fist?' Thom Tissy asked. 'My line of sight wasn't bad, but not perfect. I saw six on the north side, four on the south, putting us near dead centre and a half a night's travel behind. Anyway, the outermost smokes were right on the horizons, so we're still spread well out, the way we should be. And the smoke just tells us where bigger fights happened, not all the other little ambushes and the like. Something wrong, Fist?'

'Settle the squads in,' Keneb replied, turning away. Oh, aye, there was fighting going on. But nothing evenly matched. His marines were outnumbered; no chance of acquiring the allies they'd thought they'd get. True, they were loaded down with munitions, but the more mages arriving with the Edur and Letherii troops the more the sheer overwhelming imbalance would start to tell. His squads, even paired up, couldn't afford losses. Four or five dead and that threshold of effectiveness would have been crossed. There would have to be convergence, merging of survivors – and this leagues-long line of advance would start thinning out. Instead of gaining in strength and momentum as the advance began to close in on this empire's capital, the Malazan marines would in fact be weaker.

Of course, this invasion was not simply Keneb's covert marine advance. There were other elements – the Adjunct and Blistig's regular infantry, who would be led in the field, when that time came, by the terrifying but competent Captain Kindly. There were the Khundryl Burned Tears and the Perish – although they were, for the moment, far away. A complicated invasion indeed.

For us, here, all we need to do is sow confusion, cut supplies to the capital whenever we can, and just keep the enemy off balance, guessing, reacting rather than initiating. The fatal blows will come from elsewhere, and I need to remind myself of that. So that I don't try to do too much. What counts is keeping as many of my marines alive as possible – not that the Adjunct's tactics with us give me much chance of that. I think I'm starting to understand how the Bridgeburners felt, when they were being thrown into every nightmare, again and again.

Especially at the end. Pale, Darujhistan, that city called Black Coral.

But no, this is different. The Adjunct doesn't want us wiped out. That would be insanity, and she may be a cold, cold bitch, but she's not mad. At least not so it's showed, anyway.

Keneb cursed himself. The strategy had been audacious, yes, yet founded on sound principles. On traditional principles, in fact.

543

Kellanved's own, in the purpose behind the creation of the marines; in the way the sappers rose to pre-eminence, once the Moranth munitions arrived to revolutionize Malazan-style warfare. This was, in fact, the old, original way of employing the marines – although the absence of supply lines, no matter how tenuous or stretched, enforced a level of commitment that allowed no deviation, no possibility of retreat – *she burned the transports and not a Quorl in sight* – creating a situation that would have made the Emperor squirm.

Or not. Kellanved had known the value of gambles, had known how an entire war could shift, could turn on that single unexpected, outrageous act, the breaking of protocol that left the enemy reeling, then, all at once, entirely routed.

Such acts were what made military geniuses. Kellanved, Dassem Ultor, Sher'arah of Korel, Prince K'azz D'avore of the Crimson Guard. Caladan Brood. Coltaine. Dujek.

Did Adjunct Tavore belong in this esteemed company? *She's not shown it yet, has she? Gods above, Keneb, you've got to stop thinking like this. You'll become another Blistig and one Blistig is more than enough.*

He needed to focus on the matters at hand. He and the marines were committed to this campaign, this bold gamble. Leave the others to do their part, believing at all times that they would succeed, that they would appear in their allotted positions when the moment arrived. They would appear, yes, with the expectation that he, Keneb, would do the same. With the bulk of his marines.

Game pieces, aye. Leave the deciding hand to someone else. To fate, to the gods, to Tavore of House Paran, Adjunct to No-one. So bringing me round, damn this, to faith. Again. Faith. That she's not insane. That she's a military genius to rival a mere handful of others across the span of Malazan history.

Faith. Not in a god, not in fate, but in a fellow mortal. Whose face he knew well, remembering with grim clarity its limited range of expression, through grief to anger, to her ferocious will to achieve . . . *whatever it is she seeks to achieve. Now, if only I knew what that was.*

Perhaps this kind of fighting was suited to the marines. But it was not suited to Keneb himself. Not as commander, not as Fist. It was hard not to feel helpless. He wasn't even in contact with his army, beyond sporadic murmurings among the squad mages. *I'll feel better when Faradan Sort returns.*

If she returns.

'Fist.'

Keneb turned. 'You following me round, Sergeant?'

'No sir,' Thom Tissy replied. 'Just thought I'd say, before I sack out, that, well, we understand.'

544

'Understand what? Who is "we"?'

'All of us, sir. It's impossible. I mean, for you. We know that.'

'Do you now?'

'Aye. You can't lead. You're stuck with following, and not knowing what in Hood's name is happening to your soldiers, because they're all over the place—'

'Go get some sleep, Sergeant. And tell the rest, I am not aware that any of this is impossible. We maintain the advance, and that is that.'

'Well, uh—'

'You presume too much, Sergeant. Now return to your squad, tell your soldiers to stow all the theorizing, and go get some sleep.'

'Aye, sir.'

Keneb watched the squat man walk away. Decent of him, all that rubbish. Decent, but pointless and dangerous. *We're not friends, Thom Tissy. Neither of us can afford that.*

After a moment, he allowed himself a wry smile. All of his complaints regarding Tavore, and here he was, doing the same damned thing that she did – pushing them all away.

Because it was necessary. Because there was no choice.

So, if she's mad, then so am I.

Hood take me, maybe we all are.

The long descent of the ice field stretched out before them, studded with the rubble and detritus that was all that remained of the Age of the Jaghut. They stood side by side, a body without a soul and a soul without a body, and Hedge wished he could be more mindful of that delicious irony, but as long as he could not decide which of them was more lost, the cool pleasure of that recognition evaded his grasp.

Beyond the ice field's ragged demise two thousand paces distant, copses of deciduous trees rose in defiant exuberance, broken here and there by glades green with chest-high grasses. This patchwork landscape extended onward, climbing modest hills until those hills lifted higher, steeper, and the forest canopy, unbroken now, was the darker green of conifers.

'I admit,' Hedge said, finally breaking the silence between them, 'I didn't expect anything like this. Broken tundra, maybe. Heaps of gravel, those dry dusty dunes stirred round by the winds. Mostly lifeless. Struggling, in other words.'

'Yes,' Emroth said in her rasping voice. 'Unexpected, this close to the Throne of Ice.'

They set out down the slope.

'I think,' Hedge ventured after a time, 'we should probably get around to discussing our respective, uh, destinations.'

The T'lan Imass regarded him with her empty, carved-out eyes. 'We have travelled together, Ghost. Beyond that, nothing exists to bind you to me. I am a Broken, an Unbound, and I have knelt before a god. My path is so ordained, and all that would oppose me will be destroyed by my hand.'

'And how, precisely, do you plan on destroying me, Emroth?' Hedge asked. 'I'm a Hood-forsaken ghost, after all.'

'My inability to solve that dilemma, Ghost, is the only reason you are still with me. That, and my curiosity. I now believe you intend something inimical to my master – perhaps, indeed, your task is to thwart me. And yet, as a ghost, you can do nothing—'

'Are you so sure?'

She did not reply. They reached to within thirty or so paces from the edge of the ice, where they halted again and the T'lan Imass shifted round to study him.

'Manifestation of the will,' Hedge said, smiling as he crossed his arms. 'Took me a long time to come up with that phrase, and the idea behind it. Aye, I am a ghost, but obviously not your usual kind of ghost. I persist, even unto fashioning this seemingly solid flesh and bone – where does such power come from? That's the question. I've chewed on this for a long time. In fact, ever since I opened my non-existent eyes and realized I wasn't in Coral any longer. I was someplace else. And then, when I found myself in, uh, familiar company, well, things got even more mysterious.' He paused, then winked. 'Don't mind me talking now, Emroth?'

'Go on,' she said.

Hedge's smile broadened, then he nodded and said, 'The Bridgeburners, Emroth. That's what we were called. An elite division in the Malazan Army. Pretty much annihilated at Coral – our last official engagement, I suppose. And that should have been that.

'But it wasn't. No. Some Tanno Spiritwalker gave us a song, and it was a very powerful song. The Bridgeburners, Emroth – the dead ones, that is; couldn't say either way for the few still alive – us dead ones, we *ascended*.

'Manifestation of the will, T'lan Imass. I'd hazard you understand that notion, probably better than I do. But such power didn't end with your cursed Ritual. No, maybe you just set the precedent.'

'You are not flesh without soul.'

'No, I'm more like your reflection. Sort of *inverted*, aye?'

'I sense no power from you,' Emroth said, head tilting a fraction. 'Nothing. You are not even here.'

Hedge smiled again, and slowly withdrew a cusser from beneath his raincape. He held it up between them. 'Is this, Emroth?'

'I do not know what that is.'

'Aye, but is it even here?'

'No. Like you it is an illusion.'

'An illusion, or a manifestation of the will? My will?'

'There is no value in the distinction,' the T'lan Imass asserted.

'You cannot see the truth within me, for the vision you'd need to see it is not within you. You threw it away, at the Ritual. You wilfully blinded yourselves to the one thing that can destroy you. That is, perhaps, destroying your kind even now – some trouble on the continent of Assail, yes? I have vague recollections of somebody hearing something . . . well, never mind that. The point here, Emroth, is this: you cannot understand me because you cannot *see* me. Beyond, that is, what I have willed into existence – this body, this cusser, this face—'

'In which,' Emroth said, 'I now see my destruction.'

'Not necessarily. A lot depends on our little conversation here. You say you have knelt before a god – no, it's all right, I've already worked out who, Emroth. And you're now doing its bidding.' Hedge eyed the cusser in his hand. Its weight felt just right. *It's here, just like back at the Deragoth statues. No different at all.* 'I've walked a long way,' he resumed, 'starting out in the Jaghut underworld. I don't recall crossing any obvious borders, or stepping through any gates. And the ice fields we've been crossing for what must have been weeks, well, that made sense, too. In fact, I'm not even much surprised we found the Ice Throne – after all, where else would it be?' With his free hand he gestured at the forest-clad expanse before them. 'But this . . .'

'Yes,' said the T'lan Imass. 'You held to the notion of distinction, as do all your kind. The warrens. As if each was separate—'

'But they are,' Hedge insisted. 'I'm not a mage, but I knew one. A very good one, with more than a few warrens at his disposal. Each one is an aspect of power. There are barriers between them. And chaos at their roots, and threading in between.'

'Then what do you see here, Ghost?'

'I don't know, but it isn't Jaghut. Yet now, well, I'm thinking it's Elder, just like Jaghut. An Elder Warren. Which doesn't leave many options, does it? Especially since this is your destination.'

'In that you would be wrong,' Emroth replied.

'But you recognize it.'

'Of course. It is Tellann. Home.'

'Yet it's here, trapped in the Jaghut underworld, Emroth. How can that be?'

'I do not know.'

'If it's not your destination, then, I think I need to know if our finding it changes anything. For you, I mean.'

The head cocked yet further. 'And upon my answer hangs my fate, Ghost?'

Hedge shrugged. The cusser was too real all right: his arm had begun to ache.

'I have no answer for you,' Emroth said, and Hedge might have heard something like regret in the creature's voice, although more likely that was just his imagination. 'Perhaps, Ghost,' she continued after a moment, 'what we see here is an example of this *manifestation of the will.*'

The sapper's eyes widened. 'Whose?'

'In the Jaghut Wars, many T'lan Imass fell. Those who could not flee what remained of their bodies were left where they fell, for they had failed. On rare occasions, a Fallen would be gifted, so that its eternal vision looked out upon a vista rather than a stretch of ground or the darkness of earth. The T'lan Imass who were more thoroughly destroyed were believed to have found oblivion. True non-existence, which we came to hold as the greatest gift of all.'

Hedge glanced away. These damned T'lan Imass were heartbreakers, in every sense of the term.

'Perhaps,' Emroth continued, 'for some, oblivion was not what they found. Dragged down into the Jaghut underworld, the Jaghut realm of death. A place without the war, without, perhaps, the Ritual itself.'

'Without the war? This is the Jaghut underworld – shouldn't it be filled with Jaghut? Their souls? Their spirits?'

'The Jaghut do not believe in souls, Ghost.'

Hedge stared, dumbfounded. 'But . . . that's ridiculous. If no souls, then how in Hood's name am I here?'

'It occurs to me,' Emroth said with rasping dryness, 'that manifestation of the will can go both ways.'

'Their disbelief annihilated their own souls? *Then why create an underworld?*'

'Verdith'anath is an ancient creation. It may be that the first Jaghut souls found it not to their liking. To create a realm of death is the truest manifestation of will, after all. And yet, what is created is not always solely what was willed. Every realm finds . . . resident beings. Every realm, once formed, is rife with bridges, gates, portals. If the Jaghut did not find it to their liking, other creatures did.'

'Like your T'lan Imass.'

'In the ages of ice that beset our kind,' Emroth said, 'there existed pockets of rich land, often surrounded in ice, yet resisting its fierce power. In these pockets, Ghost, the old ways of the Imass persisted. Places of forests, sometimes tundra, and, always, the beasts we knew so well. Our name for such a place was Farl ved ten ara. A refugium.'

Hedge studied the forested hills. 'There are Imass in there.'

'I believe that is so.'

'Do you intend to seek them out, Emroth?'

'Yes. I must.'

'And what of your new god?'

'If you would destroy me, do it now, Ghost.' With that she turned and began walking towards the Refugium.

Hedge stood, shifted the cusser to his right hand, and gauged distance. *The Crippled God would welcome more allies, wouldn't he just? You go, Emroth, to meet this timeless kin. With your words marshalled to sway them, to offer them a new faith. Your kin. Could be thousands of them. Tens of thousands.*

But they're not what you came for.

Like me, Emroth, you're heading for the gate. Starvald Demelain. Where anything is possible.

Including the destruction of the warrens.

It's the blood, you see. The blood of dragons. Outside and inside. Dead and living. Aye, amazing the things you figure out once you're dead. But not dead. Aye, it's all about the will.

The cusser returned to his left hand.

Arm angled back. Then swung forward. He watched the cusser's arc for the briefest of moments, then, as habit demanded, he pitched sideways, onto the ground—

Even as it lurched up to meet him, a stone cracking hard against his chin. The concussion had of course deafened him, and he stared about, spitting blood from his tooth-sliced tongue. His left arm was gone, as was most of his left hip and thigh. Snow and dust drifting down, sparkling in the sunlight. Pebbles and clods of frozen earth now landing all around him, bouncing, skittering. The snow in the air, sparkling like magic.

He spat more blood, felt his chin with his one remaining hand and found a deep gash there, studded with gravel. He scowled, dismissed these absurd details. No more blood, a tongue whole and ever eager to wag. Smooth chin, unmarred by any gash – well, more or less smooth, under all that stubble. New left leg, hip, arm. *Aye, that's better.*

The sapper climbed to his feet.

The crater was appropriately large, suitably deep, reaching down past the skin of ice and snow to the ground underneath, that now steamed sodden and glistening. Pieces of Emroth here and there. Not many. Cussers were like that, after all.

'Aye,' Hedge muttered, 'Fid's the sentimental one.'

Thirty, then thirty-five paces on, reaching the first sward of riotous grass, the sapper came upon one more fragment of Emroth's body. And he halted. Stared down for some time. Then slowly turned and studied the way he had come, the borderline between ice and earth.

Farl ved ten ara. Refugium indeed. 'Shit,' he muttered. Worse yet, she'd told him. *A place without the Ritual itself.*

After a long moment, Hedge turned back to the forest ahead. He stepped over the torn, severed left leg lying bleeding in the grass. Flesh and blood, aye. A woman's leg. Damned shapely at that.

'Shit,' he said again, hurrying on. 'Fid's the soft-hearted one, that he is. Fiddler. Not me. Not me.' Wiping at his cheeks, cursing the ghost tears on his ghost face, and alone once more in this insipid, uninspiring realm of the dead, the Bridgeburner went on. Undead for a few hundred thousand years. Broken, Fallen, then resurrected, enough to walk once more. And, finally, thirty or so paces from a return to life . . .

A grim lesson about keeping the wrong company.

Seeking the forest. Beneath the thick branches at last, the heavy fluttering of a new season's painfully green leaves. Spin and whirl of insects, the chitter of birds. Into the forest, aye, beyond the sight of that severed limb, the borderland, the steaming crater.

Shit!

'Damned soft of you, Fid. But we're at war, like I keep telling you. We're at war. And I don't care of it's a damned Jaghut Bridge of Death, it's still a bridge, and you know what we do to bridges, don't you?'

Refugium.

But no refuge for me.

The emlava kittens were heavy as cattle dogs but shorter of leg and nowhere near as energetic. All they wanted to do was sleep. And feed. For the first few days, carrying them invited deadly fits of lashing talons and terrifying lunges with jaws opened wide. Unmindful of macabre irony, Onrack used their mother's skinned hide to fashion a sack. Ends affixed to a cut sapling, the Imass and either Quick Ben or Trull would then carry between them the two hissing, thrashing creatures in their ghastly bag.

The ay never came close again.

A male and a female, their grey fur not yet banded and the pale hue of ashes rather than the dark iron of their mother. In the cave there had been a third one, dead a week or more. From the condition of its body, its siblings had decided on eliminating it. So fared the weak in this and every other world.

Trull's sense of wonder was reawakened every time he glanced across at Onrack. A friend in the flesh was truly a revelation. He had imagined himself long past such profound, prolonged astonishment. The day he had been Shorn by his brother, it had seemed to him that his heart had died. Chained to stone, awaiting the cold water and the rot that it promised, the muscle that forged the tides of his blood seemed to beat on in some kind of waning inertia.

The desiccated corpse that was Onrack, walking up to where he had been bound, had even then seemed an unlikely salvation.

Trull recalled he'd had to argue with the T'lan Imass to win his own release. The thought amused him still. Creaking sinew and cabled muscle and torque-twisted bone, Onrack had been the personification of indifference. As unmindful of life and its struggle to persist as only a lifeless thing could be.

And so Trull had simply tagged along, unwilling to admit to himself the burgeoning truth of his salvation – his reluctant return to life in the company of an undead warrior who had begun to discover his own life, the memories once thought surrendered, to time and cruel ritual, to wilful denial spanning tens of thousands of years.

What had bound them together? What improbable menagerie of terse conversations, unanticipated emotions and the shared extremity of combat had so thoroughly entwined them together, now as brothers yet more a brother than any of those with whom Trull Sengar shared blood? *We stood side by side, together facing certain defeat. Only to find blessing in the timid hand of a creature not even half human. Oh, I know her well, that one.*

Yet she is a secret I find I cannot share with Onrack, with my friend. Now, if only he was as coy, as guarded. Not this . . . this open regard, this casting away of every natural, reasonable defence. This childness – by the Sisters, Trull, at least find yourself a word that exists. But he seems so young! Not of age, but of cast. A species of unmitigated innocence – is such a thing even possible?

Well, he might know the answer to that soon enough. They had found signs as they trekked this youthful world. Camps, hearthstones lining firepits. Places where stone tools had been made, a flat boulder where an Imass had sat, striking flakes from flint, leaving behind a half-circle scatter of splinters. Refuse pits, filled with bones charred white or boiled to extract the fat, leaving them crumbly and light as pumice; scorched shell fragments from the gourds used to heat the bones in water; and the shattered rocks that had been plunged hot into that water to bring it to a boil. Signs of passing this way, some only a few weeks old, by Onrack's estimations.

Did those Imass know that strangers had come among them? To this even Onrack had no answer. His kind were shy, he explained, and cunning. They might watch from hiding places for days, nights, and only when they so chose would they reveal enough to touch Onrack's senses, his animal awareness with its instinctive whispering. *Eyes are upon us, friends. It is time.*

Trull waited for those words.

The emlava kits yowled, announcing their hunger.

Trull, who had taken point whilst Onrack and the wizard carried the beasts in their sack, halted and turned about.

Time for feeding. Else not a single moment of peace.

Groaning, Quick Ben set down his end of the sling-pole, watched bemusedly as the two kits spat and clawed their way free of the skin, hissing at each other then at Onrack, who began withdrawing leaf-wrapped hunks of raw antelope. The meat was foul, but clearly this was no deterrent for the emlava cubs as they lunged towards him.

The Imass flung the meat onto the ground to spare his own hands, and then stepped away with an odd smile on his face.

Too many odd smiles these days, the wizard thought. As if the blinding wonder and joy had begun to dim – not much, only a fraction, yet Quick Ben believed it was there, a hint of dismay. He was not surprised. No-one could sustain such pure pleasure indefinitely. And, for all this seeming paradise – at least a paradise by Imass standards – there remained something vaguely unreal about it. As if it was no more than an illusion, already begun to fray at the edges.

No real evidence of that, however. The wizard could *feel* the health of this place. It was strong, and, he now suspected, it was growing. As Omtose Phellack waned on all sides. The end of an age, then. An age that had ended everywhere else long, long ago. *But isn't Tellann itself dead everywhere else? Maybe it isn't. Maybe it's just changed, grown into itself. Maybe, everywhere else, what we're seeing – what we're living in – is Tellann ascendant, victor in the war of millennia past, dominant and secure in its maturity. Is that possible?*

Yet that did not mesh with Onrack, with how he had been and how he was now. Unless . . . *gods below, unlike everywhere else, this is one fragment of Tellann that lies, somehow, beyond the Ritual. That is why he is flesh and blood here. In this place, there was no Ritual of Tellann, no severing of Imass souls. Suggesting that the Imass living here know nothing about it.*

So what would happen if Logros led his thousands here? If Kron— But no, Silverfox wouldn't permit that. She needed them for something else. For another war.

It'd be nice to know how this fragment related to the one created for the Wolves at the end of the Pannion War. From what Quick Ben had understood, that Beast Hold, or whatever it had been called, had been seeded with the souls of T'lan Imass. Or at least the memories of those souls – *could be that's all a soul really is: the bound, snarled mass of memories from one life. Huh. Might explain why mine is such a mess. Too many lives, too many disparate strands all now tangled together . . .*

Trull Sengar had set off in search of water – springs bubbled up from bedrock almost everywhere, as if even the stone itself was saturated with glacial melt.

Onrack eyed the cats for another moment then turned to Quick Ben. 'There is a sweep of ice beyond these hills,' he said. 'I can smell its rot – an ancient road, once travelled by Jaghut. Fleeing slaughter. This intrusion, wizard, troubles me.'

'Why? Presumably that battle occurred thousands of years ago and the Jaghut are all dead.'

'Yes. Still, that road reminds me of . . . things. Awakens memories . . .'

Quick Ben slowly nodded. 'Like shadows, aye.'

'Just so.'

'You had to know it couldn't last.'

The Imass frowned, the expression accentuating his strangely un-human, robust features. 'Yes, perhaps I did, deep within me. I had . . . forgotten.'

'You're too damned hard on yourself, Onrack. You don't need to keep yourself shining so bright all the time.'

Onrack's smile held sadness. 'I gift my friend,' he said quietly, 'for all the gifts he has given me.'

Quick Ben studied the warrior's face. 'The gift loses its value, Onrack, if it goes on too long. It begins to exhaust us, all of us.'

'Yes, I see that now.'

'Besides,' the wizard added, watching the two emlava, their bellies full, now mock-fighting on the blood-smeared grass, 'showing your fallible side is another kind of gift. The kind that invites empathy instead of just awe. If that makes any sense.'

'It does.'

'You've been making lots of paints, haven't you?'

A sudden smile. 'You are clever. When I find a wall of stone that speaks . . . yes, a different kind of gift. My forbidden talents.'

'Forbidden? Why?'

'It is taboo among my people to render our own forms in likeness to truth. Too much is captured, too much is trapped in time. Hearts can break, and betrayals breed like vermin.'

Quick Ben glanced up at Onrack, then away. *Hearts can break. Aye, the soul can haunt, can't it just.*

Trull Sengar returned, waterskins sloshing. 'By the Sisters,' he said to Onrack, 'is that a frown you're wearing?'

'It is, friend. Do you wish to know why?'

'Not at all. It's just, uh, well, a damned relief, to be honest.'

Onrack reached down and snagged one of the cubs, lifting it by the scruff of its neck. The beast hissed in outrage, writhing as he held it up. 'Trull Sengar, you may explain to our friend why Imass are forbidden to paint likenesses of themselves. You may also tell him my story, so that he understands, and need not ask again why I am awakened to pain within me, recalling now, as I do, that mortal flesh is only made real when fed by the breath of love.'

Quick Ben studied Onrack with narrowed eyes. *I don't recall asking anything like that. Well, not out loud, anyway.*

Trull Sengar's relieved expression fell away and he sighed, but it was a loose sigh, the kind that marked the unbinding of long-held tensions. 'I shall. Thank you, Onrack. Some secrets prove a heavy burden. And when I am done revealing to Quick Ben one of the details of your life that has served to forge our friendship, I will then tell you both of my own secret. I will tell you of the Eres'al and what she did to me, long before she appeared to us all in the cavern.'

A moment of long silence.

Then Quick Ben snorted. 'Fine. And I'll tell a tale of twelve souls. And a promise I made to a man named Whiskeyjack – a promise that has brought me all this way, with farther still to go. And then, I suppose, we shall all truly know each other.'

'It is,' Onrack said, collecting the second cub so he could hold both beasts up side by side, 'a day for gifts.'

From beyond the hills there came the sound of thunder. That faded, and did not repeat.

The emlava were suddenly quiet.

'What was that?' Trull Sengar asked.

Quick Ben could feel his heart pound in his chest. 'That, friends, was a cusser.'

Fiddler made his way across the dirt floor of the barn to where Bottle slept. He stared down at the young soldier curled up beneath a dark grey blanket. *Poor bastard.* He nudged with his foot and Bottle groaned. 'Sun's set,' Fiddler said.

'I know, Sergeant. I watched it going down.'

'We've rigged a stretcher. Just get up and eat something and then you've got a mobile bed for the rest of the night.'

'Unless you need me.'

'Unless we need you, aye.'

Bottle sat up, rubbed at his face. 'Thanks, Sergeant. I don't need the whole night – half will do.'

'You take what I give you, soldier. Cut it short and we could all end up regretting it.'

'All right, fine, make me feel guilty, then. See if I care.'

Smiling, Fiddler turned away. The rest of the squad was readying the gear, a few muted words drifting between the soldiers. Gesler and his crew were in the abandoned farmhouse – no point in crowding up all in one place. Poor tactics anyway.

There had been no pursuit. The drum had done its work. But that was four cussers lost, to add to the others they'd already used. Down to two left and that was bad news. If another enemy column found them . . . *we're dead or worse.* Well, marines weren't supposed to have it easy. Good enough that they were still alive.

554

Cuttle approached. 'Tarr says we're ready, Fid.' He glanced over at Bottle. 'I got the sorry end of the stretcher to start, soldier. You better not have gas.'

Bottle, a mouthful of nuts and lard bulging his cheeks, simply stared up at the sapper.

'Gods below,' Cuttle said, 'you're eating one of those Khundryl cakes, ain't ya? Well, Fid, if we need us a torch to light the way—'

'Permission denied, Cuttle.'

'Aye, probably right. It'd light up half the night sky. Hood's breath, why do I always get the short twig?'

'So long as you face off against Corabb on that kind of thing,' Fiddler said, 'short's your middle name.'

Cuttle edged closer to Fiddler and said in a low voice, 'That big bang yesterday's gonna draw down a damned army—'

'Assuming they've fielded one. So far, we're running into companies, battalion elements – as if an army's dispersed, which is more or less what we expected them to do. No point in maintaining a single force when your enemy's scattered right across Hood's pimply backside. If they were smart they'd draw up reserves and saturate the region, leave us not a single deer trail to slink along.'

'So far,' Cuttle said, squinting through the gloom at the rest of the squad and massaging his roughly healed shoulder, 'they ain't been very smart.'

'Moranth munitions are new to them,' Fiddler pointed out. 'So's our brand of magic. Whoever's in command here is probably still reeling, still trying to guess our plans.'

'My guess is whoever was in command, Fid, is now Rannalled in tree branches.'

Fiddler shrugged, then lifted his pack onto his shoulders and collected his crossbow.

Corporal Tarr checked his gear one last time, then straightened. He drew his left arm through the shield straps, adjusted his sword belt, then tightened the strap of his helm.

'Most people just carry their shields on their backs,' Koryk said from where he stood by the barn's entrance.

'Not me,' said Tarr. 'Get ambushed and there's no time to ready, is there? So I stay readied.' He then rolled his shoulders to settle his scaled hauberk, a most familiar, satisfying rustle and clack of iron. He felt unsteady on his feet without that solid, anchoring weight. He had quick-release clasps for his pack of equipment, could drop all that behind him one-handed even as he stepped forward and drew his sword. At least one of them in this squad had to be first to the front, after all, to give them time to bring whatever they had to bear.

This was what he had been trained to do, from the very beginning. Braven Tooth had seen it true enough, seen into Tarr's stolid, stubborn soul, and he'd said as much, hadn't he? *'Your name's Tarr, soldier. It's under your feet and you're stuck fast. When needs be. It's your job, from now on. You hold back the enemy at that first blink of contact, you make your squad survive that moment, aye? Now, you ain't solid enough yet. Strap on these extra weights, soldier, then get sparring . . .'*

He liked the idea of being immovable. He liked the idea of being corporal, too, especially the way he hardly ever had to say anything. He had a good squad for that. Fast learners. Even Smiles. Corabb he wasn't too sure about. Aye, the man had Oponn's wink true enough. And no shortage of courage. But it seemed he always had to get there first, before Tarr himself. Trying to prove something, of course. No mystery there. As far as the squad was concerned, Corabb was a recruit. More or less. Well, maybe he was a bit past that – nobody called him Recruit, did they? Even if Tarr still thought of him that way.

But Corabb had dragged Fiddler out. All by himself. A damned prisoner, and he'd done that. Saved the sergeant's life. Almost enough to excuse him being at Leoman's side as the two of them lured the Bonehunters into Y'Ghatan's fiery nightmare.

Almost.

Aye, Tarr knew he wasn't the forgiving kind. Not the forgetting kind, either. And he knew, deep down inside, that he'd stand for every soldier in his squad, stand till he fell. Except, maybe, for Corabb Bhilan Thenu'alas.

Koryk taking far point, they headed out into the night.

Along the edge of the nearest stand of trees, on the path between those boles and the edge of the fallow field, they silently merged with Gesler and his squad. Setting out in darkness beneath burgeoning stars.

Stormy's heavies were good to have around, Tarr decided. Almost as tough and stubborn as he was. Too bad, though, about Uru Hela. But she'd been careless, hadn't she? Even if you're carrying a waterskin, the least you should have at the ready was a shield. Even more appalling, she'd turned and run, exposing her back.

Should've sent me to do all that. Demon or no, I'd have stood to meet the bastard. Stood, and held.

'Remember your name, Tarr. And just to help you remember it, come over here and listen to your Master Sergeant, while I tell you a tale. About another soldier with tar under his feet. His name was Temper, and on the day Dassem Ultor fell, outside Y'Ghatan, well, here then is that tale . . .'

Tarr had listened, all right. Enough to know that a man like that couldn't have existed, except in the mind of Master Sergeant Braven Tooth. But it had been inspiring anyway. Temper, a good name, a damned good name. Almost as good as Tarr.

Three paces behind her corporal, Smiles scanned to either side as they moved along the trail, eyes restless with unease, senses awakened to such acuity her skull ached. Bottle was sleeping. Which meant no tiny spying eyes checking out the area, no forest animals tricked into succumbing to Bottle's puny will, that empathy of similar brain size and intelligence that had so well served them all thus far.

And their damned corporal, all clicking scales and creaking leather, who probably couldn't put fifteen words together in any reasonable, understandable order. Fine enough jamming a breach, with his ridiculous oversized shield – the only one left after that demon took care of the ones used by the heavies – and his short thick-bladed sword. The kind of soldier who'd hold his ground even when dead. Useful, aye, but as a corporal? She couldn't figure that.

No, Fid would have been better served with a quick-witted, fast, nasty and hard-to-hit kind of corporal. Well, there was one consolation, and that was anyone could see she was next in line. And it'd been close back there, hadn't it? Could've been Tarr sent out to say hello to that demon, and that would have been that. She'd now be Corporal Smiles, and look sharp there, y'damned fish-sniffers.

But never mind Tarr. It was Koryk who was riding her, uh, mind. A killer, oh yes, a real killer. Sort of like her but without the subtlety, and that made the two of them a good match. Dangerous, scary, the core of the nastiest squad in the Bonehunters. Oh, Balm's crew might argue that, especially that yelping Throatslitter, but they were lounging round on a damned island right now, weren't they? Not out here doing what marines were supposed to do, infiltrating, kicking the white squirmy balls outa Edur and Letherii and blowing up the occasional company just to remind Hood who did all the delivering.

She liked this life, yes she did. Better than that squalid existence she'd climbed out of back home. Poor village girl cowering in the ghostly shadow of a dead sister. Wondering when the next vanishing of the shoals would spell her watery demise. Oh, but the boys had wanted her once she'd been the only one left, wanted to fill that shadow with their own, as if that was even possible.

But Koryk here, well, that was different. Felt different, anyway. Because she was older now, she supposed. More experienced, so much so that she now knew what stirred her little winged flutter-bird. Watching Koryk kill people, ah, that had been so sweet, and lucky everyone else was too busy to have heard her moan and nearly squeal and guess what it'd meant.

Revelations were the world's sharpest spice, and she'd just had a noseful. Making the night somehow clearer, cleaner. Every detail blade-edged, eager to be seen, noted by her glittering eyes. She heard the small creatures moving through the scrub of the fallow field, heard the frogs race up the boles of nearby trees. Mosquito hum and—

A sudden blinding flash to the south, a bloom of fiery light lifting skyward above a distant treeline. A moment later the rumble of twin detonations reached them. Everyone motionless now, crouched down. The small creatures frozen, quivering, terrified.

'Bad time for an ambush,' Koryk muttered as he worked his way back, slipping past Tarr.

'So not one sprung by Malazan marines,' Fiddler said, moving up to meet Koryk and Tarr. 'That was a league away, maybe less. Anyone recall which squads were to our right first night?'

Silence.

'Should we head over, Sergeant?' Tarr asked. He had drawn his shortsword. 'Could be they need our help.'

Gesler arrived. 'Stormy says he heard sharpers after the cussers,' the sergeant said. 'Four or five.'

'Could be the ambush got turned,' Smiles said, struggling to control her breathing. *Oh, take us there, you damned sergeant. Let me see Koryk fight again. It's this itch, you see . . .*

'Not in our orders,' Fiddler said. 'If they've been mauled, the survivors will swing north or south and come looking for friends. We keep going.'

'They come up to find us and they might have a thousand enemy on their heels,' Gesler said.

'Always a possibility,' Fiddler conceded. 'All right, Koryk, back on point. We go on, but with extra stealth. We're not the only ones to see and hear that, so we might run into a troop riding hard across our path. Set us a cautious pace, soldier.'

Nodding, Koryk set out along the trail.

Smiles licked her lips, glowered at Tarr. 'Put the damned pig-sticker away, Tarr.'

'That's "Corporal" to you, Smiles.'

She rolled her eyes. 'Hood's breath, it's gone to his head.'

'And those aren't knives in your hands?'

Smiles sheathed them, said nothing.

'Go on,' Fiddler ordered them. 'Koryk's waiting.'

Corabb picked up his end of the stretcher again and set out after the others. Bottle had slept through that distant succession of explosions. Sign of just how exhausted the poor man was. Still, it was unnerving not having him awake and keeping an eye on things, the way he could leap from animal to animal. Birds, too. And even insects. Although Corabb wondered just how far an insect could see.

He reached up and crushed a mosquito against one eyelid. The stretcher pitched behind him and he heard Cuttle swear under his breath. Corabb quickly regained his hold on the sapling. Damned insects, he needed to stop thinking about them. Because thinking about them led to hearing and feeling them, crawling and biting everywhere and him with both hands used up. This wasn't like the desert. You could see chigger fleas coming on the wind, could hear a bloodfly from five paces, could pretty much guess that under every rock or stone there was a scorpion or a big hairy spider or a snake all of which wanted to kill you. Simple and straightforward, in other words. None of this devious whispering in the night, this whining at the ear, this winged flit up a man's nostril. Or crawling into the hair to take nips of flesh that left a swollen, oozing, damnably itching hole.

And then there were the slithery things that sucked blood. Hid under leaves waiting for some poor bastard handless soldier to go past. And ticks. And plants that, when one brushed innocently against them, started up an awful itching rash that then leaked some kind of oil – this was a true underworld, peopled by demon farmers and every life form of the night a raving, rapacious devourer of desert-born men. And never mind the Tiste Edur and the spineless Letherii. Imagine, fighting at the behest of tyrannical masters. Had they no pride? Might be smart to take a prisoner or two, just to get some answers. A Letherii. He might mention the idea to the sergeant. Fiddler was all right with suggestions. In fact, the entire Malazan Army seemed all right with that kind of thing. Sort of a constant warrior gathering, when anyone could speak up, anyone could argue, and thus decisions were forged. Of course, among the tribes, when that gathering was done, argument ended.

No, the Malazans did almost everything differently, their own way. Corabb wasn't bothered by that any more. It was probably a good thing he had held to so many ignorant, outrageous beliefs about them back when he was among the rebels. Otherwise, he might have found it hard to hate the enemy the way he was supposed to, the way it needed to be.

But now I know what it means to be a marine in the Malazan Army, even if the empire's decided we're outlaws or something. Still marines. Still the elite and that's worth fighting for – the soldier at your side, the one in the stretcher, the one on point. Not sure about Smiles, though. Not sure about her at all. Reminds me of Dunsparrow, with that knowing look in her eyes and the way she licks her lips whenever someone talks about killing. And those knives – no, not sure about her at all.

At least they had a good corporal, though. A tough bastard not interested in words. Shield and sword did all Tarr's talking, and Corabb always found himself rushing forward to stand at the man's side in every scrap. Sword-arm side, but a step forward since Tarr used that short-bladed sticker so his parrying was foreshortened and that risked too much close-in stuff, the quick dirty underhanded kind – the style the desert tribes would use against a shield-wall soldier like Tarr – when there was no shield-wall, when it was just the one man, flank exposed and guard too tight. Batter and wail at the shield until his knees bent a fraction more and he ducked in behind and below that shield, left leg forward – then just sidestep and slip round the shield, over or under that stabbing shortsword, to take arm tendons or the unprotected underarm.

Corabb knew he needed to protect Tarr on that side, even if it meant disobeying Fiddler's orders about staying close to Bottle. So long as Bottle looked to be out of trouble, Corabb would move forward, because he understood Tarr and Tarr's way of fighting. Not like Koryk, who was more the desert warrior than any other in these two squads, and what he needed fending his flanks was someone like Smiles, with her flicking knives, crossbow quarrels and the like. Staying back and to one side, out of range of Koryk's frenzied swings of his longsword, and take down the enemy that worked in from the flanks. A good pairing, that.

Cuttle, the miserable old veteran, he had his cussers, and if Bottle got in danger the sapper would take care of things. Was also pretty sharp and quick with the crossbow, an old hand at the release and load-while-you-run.

It was no wonder Seven Cities was conquered the first time round, with Malazan marines in the field. Never mind the T'lan Imass. They'd only been let loose at the Aren uprising, after all. *And if Fiddler's telling the truth, that wasn't the Emperor at all. No, it was Laseen who'd given the order.*

Gesler ain't convinced, so the truth is, no-one knows the truth. About Aren. Just like, I suppose, pretty soon no-one will know the truth about Coltaine and the Chain of Dogs, or – spirits below – the Adjunct and the Bonehunters at Y'Ghatan, and at Malaz City.

He felt a chill whisper through him then, as if he'd stumbled onto something profound. About history. As it was remembered, as it was told and retold. As it was lost to lies when the truth proved too unpleasant. *Something, aye . . . Something . . . Damn! Lost it!*

From the stretcher behind him, Bottle muttered in his sleep, then said, distinctly: 'He never sees the owl. That's the problem.'

Poor bastard. Raving in delirium. Exhausted. Sleep easy, soldier, we need you.

I need you. Like Leoman never needed me, that's how I need you. Because I'm a marine now. I suppose.

'Ask the mice,' Bottle said. 'They'll tell you.' He then mumbled something under his breath, before sighing and saying: 'If you want to live, pay attention to the shadow. The shadow. The owl's shadow.'

At the other end of the stretcher, Cuttle grunted then shook the handles until Bottle groaned again and edged onto his side. Whereupon the young mage fell silent.

They continued on through the night. And once more, sometime later, they heard detonations in the distance again. These ones to the north.

Oh, they'd stirred 'em awake all right.

Shurq Elalle's herbs were getting stale. It had been all right out on the *Undying Gratitude*, on a wind-whipped deck and in the privacy of her cabin. And with a man with no nose for company. But now she found herself in a cramped map room with a half-dozen foreigners and Shake Brullyg, the eponymous king of this miserable little island, and – especially among the women – she could see their nostrils wrinkle as they caught unpleasant aromas in the turgid, over-warm air.

Oh well. If they wanted to deal with her, they'd have to live with it. And be grateful for that 'living' part. She eyed the Adjunct, who never seemed to want to actually sit down; and although she stood behind the chair she had claimed at one end of the long, scarred table, hands resting on its back, she revealed none of the restlessness one might expect from someone for whom sitting felt like a sentence in a stock in the village square.

When it came to looks, there was not much to this Tavore Paran. Studious drab, sexless indifference, the wardrobe of the uncaring. A woman for whom womanly charms had less value than the lint in the creases of a coin purse. She could have made herself more attractive – almost feminine, in fact – if she so chose. But clearly such charms did not count as valuable assets to the Adjunct's notions of command. And this was interesting, in a vague, academic sort of way. A leader who sought to lead without physical presence, without heroic or lustful or any other sort of imaginable grandeur. And so, with nary a hint of personality, what was Tavore left with?

Well, Shurq considered, there was her mind. Some kind of tactical genius? She wasn't sure of that. From what Shurq had gathered from the fragmented mutterings of Balm's squad, some vast error in judgement had already occurred. Seemed there had been an advance landing of some sort. Elite troops, creeping onto the wild shore and its tangled swamps and forests in the dead of night. Soldiers with a mission to sow confusion and destabilize the Edur rule, and so stir the downtrodden Letherii into uprising.

Tactical genius? More like bad intelligence. The Letherii liked things just fine. This Tavore may well have condemned to slaughter a vital element of her army. They'd burned the transports – *and what was that about? Leaving her own troops with no choice but to go on? That stinks of distrust, of no confidence – aye, that stinks worse than I do. Unless I'm reading it all wrong. Which is a distinct possibility. There's nothing simple about these Malazans.*

· The Malazan Empire, aye. But nothing like the Letherii Empire, with its petty games of bloodlines and racial hierarchy. No, these Malazans came in all styles indeed. Look at Tavore's aide – a stunning tattooed barbarian whose every movement was sensuality personified. Anyone looking that savage and primitive would be cleaning stalls here in the Letherii Empire. And there was Masan Gilani, another invitation to manly blubbering – oh, how Shurq wished she had skin that luscious, burnished hue, and the graceful, leonine lines of those long legs and full thighs, the swell of unsagging breasts with nipples that made her think of overripe figs – *not that I needed to peek, she's got less modesty than me and that's saying a lot indeed. So, Tavore keeps the pretty ones close. Now that might be a telling hint.*

'What are we waiting for?' Shake Brullyg demanded, close to being drunk enough to start slurring his words. He slouched in the chair at the other end of the long table, directly opposite the Adjunct but with his heavy-lidded eyes fixed on Masan Gilani. The man truly believed that lascivious leers could make a woman swoon with desire. Yet Masan Gilani hid her disgust well, playing it along to keep the pathetic king dangling. The barbaric soldier was following very specific orders, Shurq suspected. To keep Brullyg from getting belligerent. Until they didn't need him any more.

Well, that wouldn't work with her, now, would it? Unless these Malazans had an Ublala Pung hidden nearby. Oh, that would be unfortunate indeed, to see her dissolving into an insatiable rutting animal in front of everyone. That was one secret she had better keep to herself. 'Relax, Brullyg,' she said. 'All of this has to do with those huge trimarans that sailed into harbour last night.' She'd love to have one of those, too, although she'd need two crews which meant less coin for everyone – *damned logistics, always getting in the way of my dreams.*

The Adjunct was eyeing her now, one of those gauging regards she settled on Shurq Elalle whenever the undead pirate said anything. Her own fault, actually – Shurq had sent Skorgen back to the *Undying Gratitude.* Her first mate's unfortunate assortment of afflictions had proved far too distracting for everyone else, until she realized he was becoming a liability, undermining her . . . professionalism. *Yes, that's the word I was looking for. Got to be taken seriously here. I suspect my very existence depends on it.* But she now found herself missing his weeping hole in the face, his mangled ear, blinded eye, stumped arm and bad leg – anything to swing away Tavore's attention every time she was unwise enough to voice an opinion or observation.

Throatslitter, who sat opposite Shurq, now cleared his throat – producing an odd squeak – and smiled across at her.

562

She looked away, pointedly. That man was not a nice man. The way Gerun Eberict hadn't been a nice man. Took too much pleasure in his job, she suspected. And even for a soldier, that wasn't sensible. People like that tended to linger when lingering wasn't good. Tended to put other soldiers at risk. Tended to get carried away. No, she didn't like Throatslitter.

Yet her glance away had inadvertently shifted her attention to Corporal Deadsmell. *Oh, funny name, that.* In some ways, that man was even worse. No secrets from him, she suspected, no matter how coy she was – yes, he could smell her, and not stale herbs either. *Had* smelled her, from the very start. *Had it been some bastard like him who wove the curse now afflicting me?* No, that wasn't right. Deadsmell had talents unknown here on Lether. Talents that made her think of that dying tower in Letheras, and Kettle, and the barrows in the yard.

Fortunately, he was dozing at the moment, bearded chin on his broad chest, thus sparing her his knowing look.

Ah, if only Tehol Beddict was here with me – he'd have them all reeling. In confusion or laughter? Laughter would be bad, very bad. For me. For anyone sitting too close to me. Very well, forget Tehol Beddict. I must be losing my mind.

The Adjunct addressed her. 'Captain, I have spoken at length with Shake Brullyg, seeking to complete my understanding of this Letherii Empire. Yet I find his replies increasingly unsatisfactory—'

'Poor Brullyg's despondent,' Shurq said. 'And lovelorn. Well, perhaps unrequited lust is more accurate a description for his sordid, uncommunicative state of mind.' *Hah, she could out-Tehol Tehol Beddict! With no risk of laughing either!*

Brullyg blinked at her.

Sergeant Balm leaned towards Throatslitter. 'What did she just say?'

'The Emperor,' said Tavore.

Shurq frowned, but waited.

'Of a Thousand Deaths.'

'The title's an exaggeration, I'm sure. Maybe a few hundred. Champions. They all die, eventually.'

'Presumably he is well protected by his Edur in the palace.'

Shurq Elalle shrugged. 'Not many details creep out of the Eternal Domicile, Adjunct. The Chancellor and his entire staff – Letherii – were retained after the conquest. There is also, now, a very powerful secret police, also Letherii. As for the economic apparatus, well, that too is Letherii.'

The tattooed woman named Lostara Yil snorted. 'Then what in Hood's name are the Edur doing? Where do they fit?'

'On top,' Shurq replied. 'Wobbling.'

There was a long moment of silence.

'Yet,' Tavore finally said, 'the Edur Emperor cannot be killed.'

'That is true.' Shurq watched as these details worked their way through the Malazans, with the exception of Deadsmell, of course, whose snores were waves rolling ashore in the little dank cavern of a room.

'Is that,' Tavore asked, 'irrelevant?'

'Sometimes seems that way,' Shurq conceded. Oh, she wished she could drink wine without its draining out everywhere. She could do with a tankard or two.

'An Emperor whose very rule is dictated by the sword,' Tavore said. 'What remain unhoned, however, are the necessities of administering an empire.'

'Very dull necessities, aye,' Shurq said, smiling.

'The Tiste Edur, leaning hard against the undying solidity of their ruler, exist under the delusion of mastery,' Tavore continued. 'But reality is not so generous.'

Nodding, Shurq Elalle said, 'The Tiste Edur were fisher folk, seal-hunters. Builders in wood. A half-dozen or so tribes. There was someone called the Warlock King, Hannan Mosag, who waged a war of subjugation – why he didn't end up with that dreadful sword only the Edur know and it is not something they talk about.'

'Does this Hannan Mosag still live?' Tavore asked.

'The Emperor's new Ceda.'

Deadsmell's snores ceased. 'Imperial High Mage,' he said. 'Ceda, a degradation of "Cedance", I'd wager. "Cedance" was some sort of ritual back in the days of the First Empire.' His eyes opened halfway. 'Ebron won't be at all surprised. These Letherii are some lost colony of the First Empire.' The heavy lids slid down once more, and a moment later his snores groaned back to life.

Shurq Elalle thought to clear her throat, changed her mind. Things were rank enough as it was. 'The point I was making, Adjunct, is that the Tiste Edur couldn't administer their way through a mooring tithe. They're warriors and hunters – the males, that is. The females are, as far as I can tell, completely useless mystics of some sort, and since the conquest they've virtually disappeared from sight.'

Boots echoed from the corridor and moments later the door opened. Accompanied by Galt and the odd little man named Widdershins, two Letherii soldiers strode into the chamber. One of them was an Atri-Preda.

Shake Brullyg lurched back in his chair, almost toppling it. Face twisting, he rose. 'Damn every damned witch to the deep!'

'It gets worse,' the Atri-Preda replied with a faint smile on her lips. 'I choose my own Rise, and you are not him. Yedan, throw this fool out on his arse – any window will do.'

Sudden alarm in Brullyg's eyes as he stared at the soldier at the captain's side, who made to move forward.

Galt's sword was out of its scabbard in a blur, settled flat against the soldier's stomach, halting the man in his tracks. 'Maybe we should all back this up a few steps,' he said in a drawl. 'Adjunct, allow me to present Atri-Preda Yan Tovis and Shore Watch Yedan Derryg – which I take it is some kind of sergeant in charge of some kind of coastal patrol. What's "Atri-Preda"? Captain? Commander? Whatever, they was in charge of that half-drowned bunch the Perish plucked from the storm.'

The Adjunct was frowning at Yan Tovis. 'Atri-Preda, welcome. I am Adjunct Tavore Paran of the Malazan Empire—'

Yan Tovis glanced across at her. 'You're commanding this invasion? How many soldiers did you land on the coast, Adjunct? Ten thousand? Twenty? I saw the ships, the burning ships – you followed our fleets all the way from your empire? That's a long way for a little vengeful blood-letting, isn't it?'

Shurq dreamed of downing another tankard of wine. At least the Malazans weren't looking her way any more.

The Adjunct's frown deepened, accentuating her drab plainness. 'If you wish,' she said coolly, 'we can formalize your status as prisoners of war. Yet I find it difficult to characterize your sinking ferry as a punitive invasion expedition. According to the reports I have received, your status is better likened as refugees, yes? A modest company of soldiers overseeing a sizeable collection of old men and women, children and other non-combatants. Were you sailing here assuming the island remained independent?' She flicked her gaze across to Brullyg, who stood leaning against the far wall. 'That you and Shake Brullyg are acquainted suggests you are here to resolve some private matter between you.'

Yan Tovis's eyes were flat as she shrugged and said, 'Hardly private. "Shake" is a tribe's name and could, if desired, precede the names of myself and Yedan here, as well as our "collection" of "refugees". The Shake were the original inhabitants of the central west coast and some of the islands off shore. We were long ago subjugated by the Letherii.' She shrugged again. 'My issue with Brullyg refers to a matter of succession.'

Tavore's brows rose. 'Succession? You retain such things even when subjugated?'

'More or less. The line is maintained through the women. The Queen – my mother – has recently died. It was Brullyg's hope that I not return to claim the title. Brullyg wanted to rule the Shake for himself. He also wanted, I suspect, to make some bold claim to independence, riding the wave of your invasion – assuming it proves successful. Casting off the Letherii yoke and creating a new centre for our people, on this

565

once-holy island. Although a murderer and a betrayer, Brullyg is an ambitious creature. Alas, his rule on this island has come to an end.'

Throatslitter hissed laughter. 'Hear that, Masan Gilani? You can stop showing all that sweet flesh now.'

'I am not sure,' the Adjunct said, 'the decision is yours to make, Atri-Preda.'

'That rank is now gone. You may address me as Queen or, if you like, as Twilight.'

Shurq Elalle saw Deadsmell's eyes flick open then, saw them fix hard and unblinking on Yan Tovis.

The Adjunct missed nothing, for she glanced at Deadsmell for a moment, then away again.

'Twilight, Watch and Rise,' Deadsmell muttered. 'Covered the whole night, haven't ya? But damn me, the blood's awful thin. Your skin's the colour of clay – couldn't have been more than a handful at the start, probably refugees hiding among the local savages. A pathetic handful, but the old titles remained. Guarding the Shores of Night.'

Yan Tovis licked her lips. 'Just the Shore,' she said.

Deadsmell smiled. 'Lost the rest, did you?'

'Corporal,' Tavore said.

'Our squad spent time on the right ship,' Deadsmell explained. 'Enough for me to do plenty of talking with our black-skinned guests. Twilight,' he said to Yan Tovis, 'that's a Letherii word you use. Would you be surprised if I told you the word for "twilight", in your original language, was "yenander"? And that "antovis" meant "night" or even "dark"? Your own name is your title, and I can see by your expression that you didn't even know it. Yedan Derryg? Not sure what "derryg" is – we'll need to ask Sandalath – but "yedanas" is "watch", both act and title. Gods below, what wave was that? The very first? And why the Shore? Because that's where newborn K'Chain Che'Malle came from, isn't it? The ones not claimed by a Matron, that is.' His hard eyes held on Yan Tovis a moment longer, then he settled back once more and closed his eyes.

Errant fend, is he going to do that all evening?

'I do not know what he is talking about,' Yan Tovis said, but it was clear that she had been rattled. 'You are all foreigners – what can you know of the Shake? We are barely worth mentioning even in Letherii history.'

'Twilight,' said Tavore, 'you are here to assert your title as Queen – will you also proclaim this island sovereign?'

'Yes.'

'And, in that capacity, do you seek to treat with us?'

'The sooner I can negotiate you Malazans off this island, the happier I will be. And you, as well.'

'Why is that?'

The mage named Widdershins spoke up, 'Those refugees of hers,

Adjunct. One big squall of witches and warlocks. Oh, squiggily stuff for the most part – fouling water and cursin' us with the runs and boils and the like. Mind, they could get together and work nastier rituals . . .'

Shurq Elalle stared at the strange man. *Squiggily?*

'Yes,' said Yan Tovis. 'They could become troublesome.'

Galt grunted. 'So saving all their lives don't count for nothing?'

'It does, of course. But, like all things, even gratitude wanes in time, soldier. Especially when the deed hangs over us like an executioner's axe.'

Galt's scowl deepened, then he prodded Yedan Derryg with his sword. 'I need to keep this here?' he asked.

The bearded, helmed soldier seemed to chew on his reply before answering, 'That is for my Queen to decide.'

'Belay my last order,' Yan Tovis said. 'We can deal with Brullyg later.'

'Like demon-spawn you will!' Brullyg drew himself up. 'Adjunct Tavore Paran, I hereby seek your protection. Since I have co-operated with you from the very start, the least you can do is keep me alive. Sail me to the mainland if that suits. I don't care where I end up – just not in that woman's clutches.'

Shurq Elalle smiled at the fool. *Only everything you don't deserve, Brullyg. Mercy? In the Errant's fart, that's where you'll find that.*

Tavore's voice was suddenly cold. 'Shake Brullyg, your assistance is duly noted, and you have our gratitude, although I do seem to recall something about this island's imminent destruction beneath a sea of ice – which we prevented and continue to prevent. It may please the Queen that we do not intend to remain here much longer.'

Brullyg paled. 'But what about that ice?' he demanded. 'If you leave—'

'As the season warms,' Tavore said, 'the threat diminishes. Literally.'

'So what holds you here?' Yan Tovis demanded.

'We seek a pilot to the Lether River. And Letheras.'

Silence again. Shurq Elalle, who had been gleefully observing Brullyg's emotional dissolution, slowly frowned. Then looked round. All eyes were fixed on her. What had the Adjunct just said? Oh. The Lether River and Letheras.

And a pilot to guide their invasion fleet.

'What's that smell?' Widdershins suddenly asked.

Shurq scowled. 'The Errant's fart, is my guess.'

CHAPTER EIGHTEEN

The view thus accorded was a vista to answer
my last day in the mortal world. The march
down of hewn stones, menhirs and rygoliths
showed in these unrelieved shadows the
array of stolid faces, the underworld grimaces
and hisses, bared teeth to threaten, the infinite
rows of rooted gods and spirits stretching
down the slope, across hill after hill, all the
way, yes, to the limitless beyond sight,
beyond the mirror of these misshapen,
squinting eyes. And in these stalwart
belligerents, who each in their day of eminence
reached out clawed, grasping hands, the
crimson touch of faith in all its demands
on our time, our lives, our loves and our
fears, were naught but mystery now, all
recognition forgotten, abandoned to the
crawl of remorseless change. Did their lost
voices ride this forlorn wind? Did I tremble
to the echo of blood beseechings, the tearing
of young virgin flesh and the wonder of an
exposed heart, the bemused last beats of
insistent outrage? Did I fall to my knees
before this ghastly succession of holy
tyranny, as might any ignorant cowerer
in crowded shadows?
   The armies of the faithful were gone.
They marched away in lifted waves of dust
and ash. Priests and priestesses, the succumbers
to hope who conveyed their convictions with
the desperate thirst of demons hoarding
fearful souls in their private meanings of

wealth, they remained couched in the cracks of their idols, bits of crumbling bone lodged in the stone's weaknesses, that and nothing more.

The view thus accorded, is the historian's curse. Lessons endless on the pointlessness of games of intellect, emotion and faith.

The only worthwhile historians, I say, are those who conclude their lives in succinct acts of suicide.

Sixth Note, Volume II
Collected Suicide Notes
Historian Brevos (the Indecisive)

HIS MOTHER HAD LOVED HIS HANDS. A MUSICIAN'S HANDS. A sculptor's hands. An artist's hands. Alas, they had belonged on someone else, for Chancellor Triban Gnol was without such talents. Yet his fondness for his hands, tainted as it might be by the mockery of a physical gift without suitable expression, had grown over the years. They had, in a sense, become his own works of art. When lost in thought, he would watch them, their sinuous movements filled with grace and elegance. No artist could capture the true beauty of these pointless instruments, and although there was darkness to such appreciation, he had long since made peace with that.

Yet now, the perfection was gone. The healers had done what they could, but Triban Gnol could see the misshapen marring of once-flawless lines. He could still hear the snap of his finger bones, the betrayal of all that his mother had loved, had worshipped in their secret ways.

His father, of course, would have laughed. A sour grunt of a laugh. Well, not his true father, anyway. Simply the man who had ruled the household with thick-skulled murky cruelty. He had known that his wife's cherished son was not his own. His hands were thick and clumsy – all the more viciously ironic in that artistic talent resided within those bludgeon tools. No, Triban Gnol's once-perfect hands had come from his mother's lover, the young (so young, then) consort, Turudal Brizad, a man who was anything but what he seemed to be. Anything, yes, and nothing as well.

She would have approved, he knew, of her son's finding in the consort – his father – a perfect lover.

Such were the sordid vagaries of palace life in King Ezagara Diskanar's cherished kingdom, all of which seemed aged now, exhausted, bitter as ashes in Triban Gnol's mouth. The consort was gone, yet not gone. Touch withdrawn, probably for ever now, a consort whose existence had become as ephemeral as his timeless beauty.

Ephemeral, yes. As with all things that these hands had once held; as with all things that had passed through these long, slim fingers. He knew he was feeling sorry for himself. An old man, beyond all hopes of attraction for anyone. Ghosts crowded him, the array of stained hues that had once painted his cherished works of art, layer upon layer – oh, the only time they had been truly soaked in blood had been the night he had murdered his father. All the others had died somewhat removed from such direct effort. A host of lovers who had betrayed him in some way or other, often in the simple but terrible crime of not loving him enough. And now, like a crooked ancient, he took children to his bed, gagging them to silence their cries. Using them up. Watching his hands do their work, the failed and ever-failing artist in pursuit of some kind of perfection, yet destroying all that he touched.

The crowding ghosts were accusation enough. They did not need to whisper in his skull.

Triban Gnol watched his hands as he sat behind his desk, watched their hunt for beauty and perfection, lost now and for ever more. *He broke my fingers. I can still hear—*

'Chancellor?'

He looked up, studied Sirryn, his newly favoured agent in the palace. Yes, the man was ideal. Stupid and unimaginative, he had probably tormented weaker children outside the tutor's classroom, to compensate for the fog in his head that made every attempt at learning a pointless waste of time. A creature eager for faith, suckling at someone's tit as if begging to be convinced that anything – absolutely anything – could taste like nectar.

'It draws close to the eighth bell, sir.'

'Yes.'

'The Emperor—'

'Tell me nothing of the Emperor, Sirryn. I do not need your observations on the Emperor.'

'Of course. My apologies, Chancellor.'

He would see these hands before him painted crimson again, he now knew. In a most literal fashion. 'Have you found Bruthen Trana?'

Sirryn's gaze flickered, then fell to the floor. 'No. He has truly vanished, sir.'

'Hannan Mosag sent him away,' Triban Gnol said, musing. 'Back up to the Edur homeland, I suspect. To dig in the middens.'

'The middens, sir?'

'Heaps of garbage, Sirryn.'

'But – why—'

'Hannan Mosag did not approve of Bruthen's precipitous stupidity. The fool very nearly launched a palace bloodbath. At the very least, sent away or not, Bruthen Trana has made it plain to all that such a bloodbath is imminent.'

'But the Emperor cannot be killed. There can be no—'

'That means nothing. It never has. I rule this empire. Besides, there is now a champion . . .' Triban Gnol fell silent, then shook his head and slowly rose. 'Come, Sirryn, it is time to tell the Emperor of the war we are now in.'

Outside in the corridor waited seven Letherii mages, called in from the four armies massing just west of Letheras. The Chancellor experienced a moment of regret that Kuru Qan was gone. And Enedictal and Nekal Bara, mages of impressive prowess. These new ones were but pale shadows, mostly supplanted by Hannan Mosag's Cedance of Tiste Edur. Yet they would be needed, because there weren't enough K'risnan left. And soon, the Chancellor suspected as he set out for the throne room, the others falling in behind him, soon there would be still fewer K'risnan.

The foreign enemy was deadly. They killed mages as a matter of course. Using explosive incendiaries, grenados. Able to somehow hide from the sorcery seeking them, they sprang deadly ambushes that rarely left behind a corpse of their own.

But the most important detail was one that Triban Gnol would keep from the Emperor. These foreigners were making a point of killing Tiste Edur. So, although Letherii soldiers were assembling to march west against the invaders, the Chancellor had prepared secret instructions to the commanders. He could see a way through all of this. *For the Letherii, that is.*

'Have you readied your gear, Sirryn?' he asked as they approached the throne room doors.

'Yes,' the soldier said bemusedly.

'I need someone I can rely on with the armies, Sirryn, and that someone is you.'

'Yes, Chancellor!'

Just convey my words to the letter, idiot. 'Fail me, Sirryn, and do not bother coming back.'

'Understood, sir.'

'Get the doors.'

Sirryn rushed ahead.

Inside the throne room was an unexpected, unwelcome surprise. Crouched in a desultory heap of twisted bone and mangled flesh was Hannan Mosag and four of his K'risnan. As emblems of the foul sorcery feeding these Edur, there could be no better image to burn its bitter way into the Chancellor's brain. His father would have appreciated the scene, would indeed have gathered huge chunks of marble from which he would hack out life-sized likenesses, as if in mimicking reality he could somehow discover what lay beneath it, the turgid currents of soul. A waste of time, as far as Triban Gnol was concerned. Besides, some things should never be revealed.

Hannan Mosag's deformed face seemed to leer at the Chancellor as he strode past the Ceda and his four Tiste Edur warlocks, but there was fear in the Ceda's eyes.

Sword-tip skittering on the cracked, scarred and gouged tiles, the Emperor of a Thousand Deaths shifted uneasily on his throne. 'Chancellor,' Rhulad rasped, 'how good of you to come. And Letherii mages, a most impressive if useless gathering.'

Triban Gnol bowed, then said, 'Allied with Hannan Mosag's formidable Cedance, sire, our sorcerous prowess should be more than sufficient to rid ourselves of these foreign interlopers.'

Coins clicked on Rhulad's face as he grimaced. 'And the mages of the Borthen Brigade, were they sufficient? What of the Brigade itself, Chancellor? They have been mauled! Letherii mages, Letherii soldiers! Tiste Edur! Your foreign interlopers are carving through a damned army!'

'Unanticipated,' Triban Gnol murmured, eyes downcast, 'that the imperial fleets in their search for champions should have so riled a distant empire. As to that empire's belligerence, well, it seems almost unmatched; indeed, virtually insane, given the distances spanned to prosecute vengeance. Odd, as well, that no formal declaration of war was received – although, of course, it is doubtful our fleets ventured the same preceding the slaughter of that empire's citizens. Perhaps,' he added, glancing up, 'negotiation remains possible. Some form of financial compensation, should we prove able to arrange a truce—'

Hacking laughter from Hannan Mosag. 'You provincial fool, Gnol. Would that you were even capable of expanding that puny, melo-dramatic theatre of your mind, then mayhap humility would still that flapping tongue of yours.'

Brows raised, the Chancellor half turned to regard the Ceda. 'And what secret knowledge of this enemy do you possess? And would you care to enlighten myself and your Emperor?'

'This is not punitive,' Hannan Mosag said. 'Although it might seem that way. Empires get their noses bloodied all the time, and there were enough clashes at sea to deliver the message that this Malazan Empire was not to be trifled with. Our fleets were sent scurrying from their waters – Hanradi Khalag was brutally honest in his assessment. Malazan mages are more than a match for us, and for the Letherii.'

'If not punitive,' Triban Gnol asked, 'then what?'

Hannan Mosag faced the Emperor. 'Sire, my answer is best reserved for you alone.'

Rhulad bared his teeth. 'I am not deceived by your games, Ceda. Speak.'

'Sire—'

'Answer him!'

'I must not!'

Silence, in which Triban Gnol could hear naught but his own heart, thudding hard against his ribs. Hannan Mosag had made a terrible mistake here, victim of his own self-importance. Seeking to use this information of his as a means to crawl back to the Emperor's side. But the effort . . . *so clumsy!*

'Tell me,' Rhulad said in a whisper, 'why this must be our secret.'

'Sire, this matter belongs among the Tiste Edur.'

'Why?'

Ah. Because, dear Emperor, these Malazans, they are coming for you. Triban Gnol cleared his throat and clasped his hands together above his robe's belt. 'This is unnecessary,' he said in his smoothest voice. 'I am not so provincial as Hannan Mosag would like to believe. Emperor, your fleets set out across the world in search of champions, and so indeed they have gathered the best, most capable fighters from a host of peoples. What they could not have anticipated is that an entire *empire* would proclaim itself a champion. And set itself against you, sire. Our reports have made it clear,' he added, 'that the enemy is converging on Letheras, on this very city.' He regarded Hannan Mosag as he added, 'They are – and yes, Ceda, I see the truth plain on your face – they are coming for the Emperor of a Thousand Deaths. Alas, I do not expect they will elect to challenge him one soldier at a time.'

Rhulad seemed to have shrunk back into the throne. His red-shot eyes were wide with terror. 'They must be stopped,' he said in a trembling hiss. 'You will stop them. You, Hannan Mosag! And you, Chancellor! Our armies must stop them!'

'And so we shall,' Triban Gnol said, bowing again, before straightening and glancing across at the Ceda. 'Hannan Mosag, for all of our . . . disputes, do not for a moment fear that we Letherii will abandon our Emperor to these foreign dogs. We must unite, you and I, and bring all that we have together, and so annihilate these Malazans. Such audacity must be punished, thoroughly. Truly united, the Tiste Edur and the Letherii cannot be defeated.'

'Yes,' said Rhulad. 'That is true. Array the armies in an unbroken line outside the city – it is clear, isn't it, that they do not have the numbers to challenge such a thing?'

'Sire,' Triban Gnol ventured, 'perhaps it would be best to advance a little distance nonetheless. Westward. In that way we can, if need be, assemble our reserves in case there is a breach. Two lines of defence, sire, to make certain.'

'Yes,' Rhulad said, 'those tactics are sound. How far away are these Malazans? How long do we have?'

'Weeks,' Triban Gnol said.

'Good. That is well. Yes, we must do that. All of that, as you say. Ceda! You will second yourself and your K'risnan to the Chancellor—'

'Sire, he is no military commander—'

'Quiet! You have heard my will, Hannan Mosag. Defy me again and I will have you flailed.'

Hannan Mosag did not quail at the threat. Why would he in that destroyed body? Clearly, the Ceda, once Warlock King, was familiar with agony; indeed, at times it seemed the deadly magic that poured through him transformed pain into ecstasy, lighting Hannan Mosag's eyes with fervent fire.

Triban Gnol said to the Emperor, 'Sire, we shall protect you.' He hesitated, just long enough, then half raised a hand as if struck by a sudden thought. 'Emperor, I wonder, perhaps it would be best to begin the Challenges? Soon? Their presence is a distraction, an irritant for my guards. There have been incidents of violence, a growing impatience.' He paused again, two heartbeats, then said in a lower tone: 'Speculation, sire, that you fear to face them . . .'

Hannan Mosag's sneer produced a bestial growl. 'You pathetic creature, Gnol—'

'Not another word, Ceda!' Rhulad hissed. Spasms rippled across the Emperor's mottled face. The sword skittered again.

Yes, Rhulad, you understand what it is to fear death more than any of us. Perhaps more than any mortal creature this world has seen. But you flinch not from some vague notion of oblivion, do you? No, for you, dear Emperor, death is something different. Never an end, only that which precedes yet another pain-filled rebirth. Even in death you cannot lose yourself, cannot escape – does anyone else here, apart from me, truly grasp the sheer horror of that?

'The Challenges,' said the Emperor, 'will begin in four days. Chancellor, have your assessors agreed on an order?'

'Yes, sire. Three of the least skilled to begin. It is likely you will kill all three in a single day. They will tax you, of that we can be sure, but not unduly so. The second day is reserved for one champion. A masked woman. Exceptional speed but perhaps lacking imagination. Yet she will be difficult.'

'Good.'

'Sire . . .'

'Yes? What is it?'

'There are the two we have spoken of before. The Tarthenal with the flint sword. Undefeated by any other champion – in fact, no-one dares spar with him any more. He has the habit of breaking bones.'

'Yes. The arrogant one.' Rhulad smiled. 'But I have faced Tarthenal before.'

'But not one with Karsa Orlong's prowess, sire.'

'No matter, that.'

'He may succeed in killing you, sire. Perhaps more than once. Not seven. Such days are long past. But, perhaps, three or four. We have allotted three days.'

'Following the masked woman?'

'No, there are six others to span two days.'

Hannan Mosag was staring at the Chancellor now. 'Three days for this Tarthenal? No champion has yet been accorded *three* days.'

'Nonetheless, my assessors were unanimous, Ceda. This one is . . . unique.'

Rhulad was trembling once more. Slain by Karsa Orlong three, four times. *Yes, sire, the sheer horror of that . . .*

'There remains one more,' the Emperor said.

'Yes. The one named Icarium. He will be the last. If not the eighth day, then the ninth.'

'And the number of days with him, Chancellor?'

'Unknown, sire. He does not spar.'

'Then how do we know he can fight?'

Triban Gnol bowed again. 'Sire, we have discussed this before. The report of Varat Taun, corroborated by Icarium's companion, Taralack Veed. And now, I learned today, something new. Something most extraordinary.'

'What? Tell me!'

'Among the rejected champions, Sire, a monk from a distant archipelago. It would appear, sire, that this monk – and indeed all of his people – worship a single god. And this god is none other than Icarium.'

Rhulad flinched as if struck across the face. The sword's point leapt up from the floor, then cracked down again. Marble chips clattered down the dais step. 'I am to cross blades with a *god*?'

The Chancellor shrugged. 'Do such claims hold veracity, sire? A primitive, ignorant people, these Cabalhii. No doubt seeing in dhenrabi the soul of sea-storms and in crab carapaces the faces of the drowned. I should add, Emperor, that this monk believes his god to be insane, to which the only answer is a painted mask denoting laughter. Savages possess the strangest notions.'

'A god . . .'

Triban Gnol risked a glance at Hannan Mosag. The Warlock King's expression was closed as he studied Rhulad. Something about that awakened a worm of unease in the Chancellor's gut.

'I shall slay a god . . .'

'There is no reason to believe otherwise,' Triban Gnol said in a calm, confident voice. 'It will serve timely, sire, in pronouncing your own godhood.'

Rhulad's eyes widened.

'Immortality,' the Chancellor murmured, 'already well established. Worshipped? Oh yes, by every citizen of this empire. Too modest, oh yes, to make the pronouncement of what is obvious to us all. But, when you stand over Icarium's destroyed corpse, well, that will be pronouncement enough, I should imagine.'

'Godhood. A god.'

'Yes, sire. Most assuredly. I have instructed the guild of sculptors, and their finest artists have already begun work. We shall announce the end of the Challenge in a most appropriate, a most glorious, manner.'

'You are wise indeed,' Rhulad said, slowly leaning back. 'Yes, wise.'

Triban Gnol bowed, ignoring the sour grunt from Hannan Mosag. *Oh, Ceda, you are mine now, and I shall use you. You and your foul Edur. Oh yes.* His eyes focused on his hands, folded so serenely where they rested on the clasp of his belt. 'Sire, orders must be delivered to our armies. The Ceda and I must discuss the disposition of mages and K'risnan.'

'Yes, of course. Leave me, all of you. Attend to your tasks.'

Gesturing behind him, Triban Gnol backed away, head still lowered, eyes now on the floor with its chips of marble and streaks of dust.

He could hear Hannan Mosag and his collection of freaks dragging their way towards the doors, like gigantic migrating toads. The simile brought a faint smile to his lips.

Out in the corridor, the doors shutting behind them, Triban Gnol turned to study Hannan Mosag. But the Ceda was continuing on, toads crowding his wake.

'Hannan Mosag,' the Chancellor called out. 'You and I have—'

'Save your crap for Rhulad,' the Ceda snapped.

'He will be displeased to hear of your lack of co-operation.'

'Flap away with that tongue of yours, Gnol. The displeasures yet to come will overwhelm your pathetic bleatings, I am sure.'

'What do you mean?'

But Hannan Mosag did not answer.

Triban Gnol watched as they plunged into a side passage and were gone from sight. *Yes, I will deal with you, Ceda, with great satisfaction.* 'Sirryn, assemble your entourage in the compound and be on your way within the bell. And take these mages with you.'

'Yes sir.'

The Chancellor remained where he was until they too were gone, then he set off for his office, well pleased. That worm of unease was, however, reluctant to cease its gnawing deep inside him. He would have

576

to think on that – too dangerous to just ignore such instincts, after all. But not right now. It was important to reward oneself, promptly, and so he released that flow of satisfaction. Everything was proceeding nicely – that detail about the Emperor himself being the final target of these foreigners simply sweetened the scenario. The Tiste Edur would of course stand to defend their Emperor – *they would, certainly.*

Yet, Rhulad's own brothers, the day of the accession. The worm writhed, forcing a twitch to his face, and he quickened his pace, eager for the sanctuary of his office.

Only to discover it occupied.

Triban Gnol stood in the doorway, surprised and discomfited by the sight of the man standing to one side of the huge desk. The crimson silks, the onyx rings, that damned sceptre of office tapping rhythmically on one rounded shoulder. 'What in the Errant's name are you doing here, Invigilator?'

Karos Invictad sighed. 'I share your displeasure, Chancellor.'

Triban Gnol entered the room, walked round his desk and sat. 'I am in the habit of assuming that your control of the city is well in hand—'

'Where is Bruthen Trana?'

The Chancellor pursed his lips. 'I haven't the time for this. Put your panic to rest – Bruthen Trana is no longer in Letheras.'

'Then where has he gone? What road? How long ago? What is the size of his escort?'

Sighing, Triban Gnol leaned back, eyes settling on his hands where they rested palms down on the desktop. 'Your need for vengeance, Invigilator, is compromising your responsibilities in maintaining order. You must step back, draw a few deep breaths—'

The sceptre cracked down on the desktop, directly between the Chancellor's hands. Triban Gnol lurched back in alarm.

Karos Invictad leaned far forward, seeking an imposing, threatening posture that, alas, failed. The man was, simply put, too small. Sweat glistened on his brow, beads glinting from his nose and to either side of that too-full mouth. 'You patronizing piece of shit,' the Invigilator whispered. 'I was given leave to hunt down Tiste Edur. I was given leave to make arrests. I wanted that K'risnan who accompanied Bruthen Trana, only to find him beyond my reach because of Hannan Mosag and this damned invasion from the west. Fine. He can wait until the trouble passes. But Bruthen Trana . . . no, I will not put that aside. I want him. *I want him!*'

'He has been whisked away, Invigilator, and no, we have no information on when, or which road or ship he set out on. He is gone. Will he return? I imagine he will, and when that time comes, of course he is yours. In the meantime, Karos, we are faced with far more important concerns. I have four armies massing west of the city for which wages are now two weeks overdue. Why? Because the treasury is experiencing a shortage of coin. Even as you and your favourite agents line the walls of your new estates with stolen loot, even as you assume control of one confiscated enterprise after another. Tell me, Invigilator, how fares the treasury of the Patriotists these days? Minus the loot?' The Chancellor then rose from his chair, making full use of his superior height and seeing with grim pleasure the small man step back. It was now Triban Gnol's turn to lean across the desk. 'We have a crisis! The threat of financial ruin looms over us all – and you stand here fretting over one Tiste Edur barbarian!' He made a show of struggling to master his fury, then added, 'I have received increasingly desperate missives from the Liberty Consign, from Rautos Hivanar himself – the wealthiest man in the empire. Missives, Invigilator, imploring me to summon you – so be it, here you are, and you *will* answer my questions! And if those answers do not satisfy me, I assure you they will not satisfy Rautos Hivanar!'

Karos Invictad sneered. 'Hivanar. The old fool has gone senile. Obsessing over a handful of artifacts dug up from the river bank. Have you seen him of late? He has lost so much weight his skin hangs like drapery on his bones.'

'Perhaps you are the source of his stress, Invigilator—'

'Hardly.'

'Rautos has indicated you have been . . . excessive, in your use of his resources. He begins to suspect you are using his coin for the payroll of the entire Patriotist organization.'

'I am and will continue to do so. In pursuit of the conspirators.' Karos smiled. 'Chancellor, your opinion that Rautos Hivanar is the wealthiest man in the empire is, alas, in error. At least, if it was once so, it is no longer.'

Triban Gnol stared at the man. At his flushed, triumphant expression. 'Explain yourself, Karos Invictad.'

'At the beginning of this investigation, Chancellor, I perceived the essential weakness in our position. Rautos Hivanar himself. As leader of the Liberty Consign. And, by extension, the Consign itself was, as an organization, inherently flawed. We were faced with a looming collision, one that I could not will myself blind to, and accordingly it was incumbent on me to rectify the situation as quickly as possible. You see, the power lay with me, but the wealth resided in the clutches of Hivanar and his Consign. This was unacceptable. In order to meet the threat of the conspirators – or, as I now see, conspirator – yes, there is but one – in order to meet his threat, I needed to attack from a con-solidated position.'

Triban Gnol stared, disbelieving even as he began to comprehend the direction of the Invigilator's pompous, megalomaniacal monologue.

'The sweetest irony is,' Karos Invictad continued, sceptre once more tapping a beat on his shoulder, 'that lone criminal and his pathetically simplistic efforts at financial sabotage provided me with the greatest inspiration. It was not difficult, for one of my intelligence, to advance and indeed to elaborate on that theme of seeming destabilization. Of course, the only people being destabilized were Rautos Hivanar and his fellow bloated blue-bloods, and was I supposed to be sympathetic? I, Karos Invictad, born to a family crushed by murderous debt? I, who struggled, using every talent I possessed to finally rid myself of that inherited misery – no,' he laughed softly, 'there was no sympathy in my heart. Only bright revelation, brilliant inspiration – do you know who was my greatest idol when I fought my war against Indebtedness? Tehol Beddict. Recall him? Who could not lose, whose wealth shot skyward with such stunning speed, achieving such extraordinary height, before flashing out like a spent star in the night sky. Oh, he liked his games, didn't he? Yet, a lesson there, and one I heeded well. Such genius, sparking too hot, too soon, left him a gutted shell. And that, Chancellor, I would not emulate.'

'You,' Triban Gnol said, 'are the true source of this empire-wide sabotage.'

'Who better positioned? Oh, I will grant you, my fellow conspirator has displayed increasingly impressive deviousness of late. And there is no doubt that I could not have achieved quite the level of success as I have without him or her. Triban Gnol, standing before you at this moment is the wealthiest man ever to have lived in Lether. Yes, appalling stacks of coin have indeed vanished. Yes, the strain has sent fatal fissures through every merchant house in the empire. And yes, many great families are about to fall and nothing can save them, even were I so inclined. Which I am not. Thus.' The sceptre settled motionless onto that shoulder. 'I am both the power and the wealth, and I am poised to save this empire from financial ruin – should I so choose.'

The Chancellor's hands, there on the desktop, had gone white, the veins and arteries prominent in their sickly blue and green hues. The hands – his hands – felt cold as death. 'What do you want, Karos Invictad?'

'Oh, I mostly have it already, Chancellor. Including, I am pleased to see, your fullest understanding of the situation. As it stands now. As it will stand in the future.'

'You seem to forget there is a war on.'

'There always is. Opportunities for yet more profit and power. In the next week or two, Chancellor, I will become more famous, more beloved, more *powerful* than even you could imagine, or, should I say, *fear*.' His smile broadened. 'I assume it's fear, but relax, Chancellor, I

579

do not have you next on my list. Your position is secure, and, once these damned Tiste Edur are taken care of, including the Emperor, it shall be you and I in control of this empire. No, you will see plain enough, as will everyone else. The saboteur arrested. The coins recovered. The invaders bought off. The Liberty Consign obliterated and the Patriotists dominant. You see, my agents will control the internal matters, while you will possess the armies – well-paid armies, I assure you – and absolute mastery of the palace.'

'What?' Triban Gnol asked dryly. 'You do not seek the throne for yourself?'

The sceptre waved dismissively. 'Not in the least. Throw a fop on it if you feel the need. Or better still, salute the legend and leave it empty.'

Triban Gnol folded his hands together. 'You are about to arrest your conspirator?'

'I am.'

'And my armies?'

'They will be paid. At once.'

The Chancellor nodded. 'Invigilator,' he then said, with a slight frown as he studied his hands, 'I have heard disturbing reports . . .'

'Oh?'

'Yes. It seems that, in a manner distressingly similar to Rautos Hivanar, you too have succumbed to a peculiar obsession.' He glanced up searchingly, innocently. 'Something about a puzzle?'

'Who has told you that?'

The Chancellor shrugged.

After a moment the flush in Invictad's round face faded to blotches on the cheeks, and the man shrugged. 'An idle pursuit. Amusing. A quaint challenge which I will solve in a few days. Unlike Rautos Hivanar, you see, I have found that this puzzle has in fact sharpened my mind. The world has never been clearer to my eyes. Never as clean, as precise, as perfect. That puzzle, Chancellor, has become my inspiration.'

'Indeed. Yet it haunts you – you cry out in your sleep—'

'Lies! Someone mocks you with such untruths, Triban Gnol! I have come here, have I not, to inform you of the impending triumph of my plans. Every detail coming to fullest fruition. This effort of yours now, pathetically transparent as it is, is entirely unnecessary. As I told you, your position is secure. You are, and will remain, entirely essential.'

'As you say, Invigilator.'

Karos Invictad turned to leave. 'As soon as you learn of Bruthen Trana's return . . .'

'You shall be informed at once.'

'Excellent. I am pleased.' He paused at the door but did not turn round. 'Regarding that K'risnan under the Ceda's protection . . .'

'I am sure something can be arranged.'

'I am doubly pleased, Chancellor. Now, fare you well.'

The door closed. The odious, insane creature was gone.

Odious and insane, yes, but . . . *now the wealthiest man in the empire.* He would have to play this carefully, very carefully indeed. *Yet Karos Invictad has revealed his own flaw. Too eager to gloat and too ready to give in to that eagerness. All too soon.*

The Emperor of a Thousand Deaths remains on the throne.

A foreign army uninterested in negotiation approaches.

A champion who is a god will soon draw his sword.

Karos Invictad has the hands of a child. A vicious child, crooning as he watches them pull out the entrails of his still-alive pet cat. Or dog. Or abject prisoner in one of his cells. A child, yes, but one unleashed, free to do and be as he pleases.

By the Errant, children are such monsters.

Tonight, the Chancellor realized, he would summon a child for himself. For his own pleasure. And he would destroy that child, as only an adult with beautiful hands could. Destroy it utterly.

It was the only thing one could do with monsters.

The one-eyed god standing unseen in the throne room was furious. Ignorance was ever the enemy, and the Errant understood that he was under assault. By Chancellor Triban Gnol. By Hannan Mosag. The clash of these two forces of the empire was something that the Emperor on his throne barely sensed – the Errant was sure of that. Rhulad was trapped in his own cage of emotions, terror wielding all its instruments of torture, poking, jabbing, twisting deep. Yet the Errant had witnessed with clear eyes – *no, a clear eye* – in the fraught audience now past, just how vicious this battle was becoming.

But I cannot fathom their secrets. Neither Triban Gnol's nor Hannan Mosag's. This is my realm. Mine!

He might renew one old path. The one leading into the Chancellor's bedroom. But even then, when that relationship had been in fullest bloom, Triban Gnol held to his secrets. Sinking into his various personas of innocent victim and wide-eyed child, he had become little more than a simpleton when with the Errant – with Turudal Brizad, the Consort to the Queen, who never grew old – and would not be moved from the games he so needed. *No, that would not work, because it never had.*

Was there any other way to the Chancellor?

Even now, Triban Gnol was a godless creature. Not one to bend knee to the Errant. So that path, too, was closed. *I could simply follow him. Everywhere. Piece together his scheme by listening to the orders he delivers, by reading the missives he despatches. By hoping he talks in his sleep. Abyss below!*

Furious, indeed. At his own growing panic as the convergence drew ever closer. His knowledge was no better when it came to Hannan Mosag, although some details were beyond dissembling. The power of the Crippled God, for one. Yet even there, the Warlock King was no simple servant, no mindless slave to that chaotic promise. He had sought the sword now in Rhulad's hands, after all. As with any other god, the Fallen One played no favourites. First to arrive at the altar . . . No, Hannan Mosag would hold to no delusions there.

The Errant glanced once more at Rhulad, this Emperor of a Thousand Deaths. The fool, for all his bulk, now sat on that throne in painful insignificance – so obvious it hurt to just look at him. Alone in this vast domed chamber, the thousand deaths refracted into ten thousand flinches in those glittering eyes.

The Chancellor and his retinue were gone. The Ceda away with his broken handful as well. Not a guard in sight, yet Rhulad remained. Sitting, burnished coins gleaming. And on his face all that had been private, unrevealed, was now loosed in expressive array. All the pathos, the abject hauntings – the Errant had seen, had always seen, in face after face spanning too many years to count, the divide of the soul, the difference between the face that knew it was being watched, and the face that believed in its solitude. Bifurcation. And he had witnessed when inside crawled outside to a seemingly unseeing world.

Divided soul. Yours, Rhulad, has been cut in two. By that sword, by the spilled blood between you and each of your brothers, between you and your parents. Between you and your kind. What would you give me, Rhulad Sengar of the Hiroth Tiste Edur, to be healed?

Assuming I could manage such a thing, of course. Which I cannot.

But it was clear to the Errant now that Rhulad had begun to understand one thing at least. The fast approach of convergence, the dread gathering and inevitable clash of powers. Perhaps the Crippled God had been whispering in his sword-bearer's ear. Or perhaps Rhulad was not quite the fool most believed him to be. *Even me, on occasion – and who am I to sneer in contempt? A damned Letherii witch swallowed one of my eyes!*

The growing fear was undisguised in the Emperor's face. Coins bedded in burnt skin. Mottled pocking where the coins were gone. Brutal wealth and wounded penury, two sides of yet another curse to plague this modern age. *Yes, divide humanity's soul. Into the haves, the have-nots. Rhulad, you are in truth a living symbol. But that is a weight no-one can bear for very long. You see the end coming. Or, many endings, and yes, one of them is yours.*

Shall it be this foreign army that has, in Triban Gnol's clever words, proclaimed itself a champion?

Shall it be Icarium, Stealer of Life? The Wanderer through Time?

Or something far more sordid – some perfect ambush by Hannan Mosag; or one final betrayal to annihilate you utterly, as would one committed by your Chancellor?

And why do I believe the answer will be none of those? Not one. Not a single thing so . . . so direct. So obvious.

And when will this blood stop seeping from this socket? When will these crimson tears end?

The Errant melted into the wall behind him. He'd had enough of Rhulad's private face. Too much, he suspected, like his own. *Imagined unwatched – but am I too being watched? Whose cold gaze is fixed on me, calculating meanings, measuring weaknesses?*

Yes, see where I weep, see what I weep.

And yes, this was all by a mortal's hand.

He moved quickly, unmindful of barriers of mortar and stone, of tapestry and wardrobe, of tiled floors and ceiling beams. Through darkness and light and shadows in all their flavours, into the sunken tunnels, where he walked through ankle-deep water without parting its murky surface.

Into her cherished room.

She had brought stones to build platforms and walkways, creating a series of bridges and islands over the shallow lake that now flooded the chamber. Oil lamps painted ripples and the Errant stood, taking form once more opposite the misshapen altar she had erected, its battered top crowded with bizarre votive offerings, items of binding and investiture, reliquaries assembled to give new shape to the god's worship. *To the worship of me.* The gnostic chthonic nightmare might have amused the Errant once, long ago. But now he could feel his face twisting in disdain.

She spoke from the gloomy corner to his left. 'Everything is perfect, Immortal One.'

Solitude and insanity, most natural bedmates. 'Nothing is perfect, Feather Witch. Look, all around you in this place – is it not obvious? We are in the throes of dissolution—'

'The river is high,' she said dismissively. 'A third of the tunnels I used to wander are now under water. But I saved all the old books and scrolls and tablets. I saved them all.'

Under water. Something about that disturbed him – not the obvious thing, the dissolution he had spoken of, but . . . something else.

'The names,' she said. 'To release. To bind. Oh, we shall have many servants, Immortal One. Many.'

'I have seen,' the god said, 'the fissures in the ice. The meltwater. The failing prison of that vast demon of the sea. We cannot hope to enslave such a creature. When it breaks free, there will be devastation. Unless, of course, the Jaghut returns – to effect repairs on her ritual. In any case

583

– and fortunately for everyone – I do not believe that Mael will permit it to get even that far – to escape.'

'You must stop him!' Feather Witch said in a hiss.

'Why?'

'Because I want that demon!'

'I told you, we cannot hope to—'

'*I can!* I know the names! All of the names!'

He stared across at her. 'You seek an entire pantheon, Feather Witch? Is one god under your heel not enough?'

She laughed, and he heard something splash in the water near her. 'The sea remembers. In every wave, every current. The sea, Immortal One, remembers the shore.'

'What – what does that mean?'

Feather Witch laughed again. 'Everything is perfect. Tonight, I will visit Udinaas. In his dreams. By morning he will be mine. Ours.'

'This web you cast,' the Errant said, 'it is too thin, too weak. You have stretched it beyond all resilience, and it *will* snap, Feather Witch.'

'I know how to use your power,' she replied. 'Better than you do. Because us mortals understand certain things far better than you and your kind.'

'Such as?' the Errant asked, amused.

'The fact that worship is a weapon, for one.'

At those dry words, chill seeped through the god.

Ah, poor Udinaas.

'Now go,' she said. 'You know what must be done.'

Did he? *Well . . . yes. A nudge. What I do best.*

The sceptre cracked hard against the side of Tanal Yathvanar's head, exploding stars behind his eyes, and he staggered, then sank down onto one knee, as the blood began flowing. Above him, Karos Invictad said in a conversational tone: 'I advise you, next time you are tempted to inform on my activities to one of the Chancellor's agents, to reconsider. Because the next time, Tanal, I will see you killed. In a most unpleasant fashion.'

Tanal watched the blood fall in elongated droplets, spattering on the dusty floor. His temple throbbed, and his probing fingers found a flap of mangled skin hanging down almost to his cheek. His eye on that side ebbed in and out of focus in time with the throbbing. He felt exposed, vulnerable. He felt like a child among cold-faced adults. 'Invigilator,' he said in a shaky voice, 'I have told no-one anything.'

'Lie again and I will dispense with mercy. Lie again and the breath you use to utter it will be your last.'

Tanal licked his lips. What could he do? 'I'm sorry, Invigilator. Never again. I swear it.'

'Get out, and send for a servant to clean up the mess you've left in my office.'

Nauseated, his throat tightening against an eager upswell of vomit, Tanal Yathvanar hurried out in a half-crouch.

I've done nothing. Nothing to deserve this. Invictad's paranoia has driven him into the abyss of madness. Even as his power grows. Imagine, threatening to sweep away the Chancellor's own life, in Triban Gnol's own office! Of course, that had been but the Invigilator's version of what had transpired. But Tanal had seen the bright gleam in Invictad's eyes, fresh from the glory of his visit to the Eternal Domicile.

It had all gone too far. All of it.

Head spinning, Tanal set out to find a healer. There was much still to do this day. An arrest to be made, and, split-open skull or no, Karos Invictad's precise schedule had to be kept. This was to be a triumphant day. For the Patriotists. For the great Letherii Empire.

It would ease the pressure, the ever-tightening straits that gripped the people – and not just here in Letheras, but across the entire empire. Too many fraught rumours, of battles and defeats suffered. The strictures of not enough hard coin, the strange disappearance of unskilled labour, the tales of once-secure families falling into Indebtedness. The whisper of huge financial holdings tottering like trees with rotted roots. Heroic victories were needed, and this day would mark one. Karos Invictad had found the greatest traitor ever, and he, Tanal Yathvanar, would make the arrest. *And they will hear that detail. My name, central to all that will happen this day. I intend to make certain of it.*

Karos Invictad was not the only man skilled at reaping glory.

Ancient cities possessed many secrets. The average citizen was born, lived, and died in the fugue of vast ignorance. The Errant knew he had well learned his contempt for humanity, for the dross of mortal existence that called blindness vision, ignorance comprehension, and delusion faith. He had seen often enough the wilful truncation people undertook upon leaving childhood (and the wonder of its endless possibilities), as if to exist demanded the sacrifice of both unfettered dreams and the fearless ambition needed to achieve them. As if those self-imposed limitations used to justify failure were virtues, to add to those of pious self-righteousness and the condescension of the flagellant.

Oh, but look at himself, here and now, look at what he was about to do. The city's ancient secrets made into things to be used, and used to achieve cruel ends. Yet was he not a god? Was this not his realm? If all that existed was not open to use and, indeed, *abuse*, then what was its purpose?

He walked through the ghostly walls, the submerged levels,

acknowledging a vague awareness of hidden, mostly obscured patterns, structures, the array of *things* that held significance, although such comprehension was not for him, not for his cast of mind, but something alien, something long lost to the dead ages of the distant past.

No end to manifestations, however, few of which captured the awareness of the mortals he now walked among – walked unseen, less than a chill draught against the neck – and the Errant continued on, observing such details as snared his attention.

Finding the place he sought, he halted. Before him stood the walls of an estate. None other than the one that had belonged to the late Gerun Eberict. It stood abandoned, ownership mired in a legal tangle of claims that had stretched on and on. Gerun Eberict had, it seemed, taken all his wealth with him, a detail that amused the Errant no end.

The huge main building's footprint cut across the unremarked lines of an older structure that had once stood bordered on three sides by open water: two cut channels and a stream born of deep artesian wells filled with cold black water beneath a vast shelf of limestone that itself lay below a thick layer of silts, sand lenses and beds of clay. There had been significance to these channels, and to the fact that the fourth side had possessed, beneath what passed for a street seven thousand years ago, a buried tunnel of fire-hardened clay. In this tunnel, kept distinct from all other local sources, there had flowed water from the depths of the river. Thus, all four sides, the precious lifeblood of the Elder God who had been worshipped in the temple that had once squatted in this place.

Eberict should have been mindful of that detail, in which a hired seer might well have discerned Gerun's eventual demise at the blunt hands of a half-breed giant. It was no accident, after all, that those of Tarthenal blood were so drawn to Mael, even now – some whispering of instinct of that first alliance, forged on the water, between Imass and Tarthenal – or Toblakai, to use their true name. Before the Great Landings that brought the last of the giants who had chosen to remain pure of blood to this and other shores, where the first founders would become the vicious, spiteful gods of the Tarthenal.

But it was not just Gerun Eberict and the countless other citizens of Letheras who dwelt here who were unmindful – or, perhaps, forgetful – of the ancient significance of all that had been swept clean from the surface in this city.

The Errant moved forward. Through the estate's outer wall. Then down, through the cobbles of the compound, sliding ghostly past the rubble and sand of fill, down into the foul, motionless air of the clay-lined tunnel. Knee-deep in thick, soupy water.

He faced the inner sloping wall of the tunnel, gauging his position relative to whatever remnants of the old temple remained beyond. And strode forward.

Shattered stone, jammed and packed tight, stained black by the thick, airless clays now filling every space. Evidence of fire in the burst cracks of foundation blocks. Remnants of ore-laden paints still clinging to fragments of plaster. Ubiquitous pieces of pottery, shapeless clumps of green copper, the mangled black knuckles of silver, the defiant gleam of red-tinged gold – all that remained of past complexities of mortal life, reminders of hands that had once touched, shaped, pressed tips to indent and nails to incise, brushed glaze and paint and dust from chipped rims; hands that left nothing behind but these objects poignant with failure.

Disgusted, nauseated, the god pushed his way through the detritus, and clawed his way clear: a steeply angled space, created by the partially collapsed inner wall. Blue tesserae to paint an image of unbroken sea, but various pieces had fallen away, revealing grey plaster still bearing the grooved patterns left by the undersides of the minute cut tiles. In this cramped space the Errant crouched, gasping. Time told no bright tales. No, time delivered its mute message of dissolution with unrelieved monotony.

By the Abyss, such crushing weight!

The Errant drew a deep breath of the stale, dead air. Then another.

And sensed, not far away, the faint whisper of power. Residual, so meagre as to be meaningless, yet it started the god's heart pounding hard in his chest. The sanctification remained. No desecration, making what he sought that much simpler. Relieved at the thought of being quickly done with this ghastly place, the Errant set out towards that power.

The altar was beneath a mass of rubble, the limestone wreckage so packed down that it must have come from a collapsing ceiling, the huge weight slamming down hard enough to shatter the stones of the floor beneath that runnelled block of sacred stone. *Even better. And . . . yes, bone dry.* He could murmur a thousand nudges into that surrounding matrix. Ten thousand.

Edging closer, the Errant reached down and settled one hand on the altar. He could not feel those runnels, could not feel the water-worn basalt, could not feel the deep-cut channels that had once vented living blood into the salty streams filling the runnels. *Ah, we were thirsty in those days, weren't we?*

He awakened his own power – as much as she would give him, and for this task it was more than enough.

The Errant began weaving a ritual.

Advocate Sleem was a tall, thin man. Covering most of his forehead and spreading down onto his left cheek, reaching the line of the jaw, was a skin ailment that created a cracked scale pattern reminiscent of the bellies of newly hatched alligators. There were ointments that could heal this condition, but it was clear that the legendary advocate of Letherii law in fact cultivated this reptilian dermatosis, which so cleverly complemented both his reputation and his cold, lifeless eyes.

He stood now in Bugg's office, hunched at the shoulders as if to make himself even narrower, and the high collar of his dark green cloak flared out like a snake's hood behind his elongated, small-eared and hairless head. His regard was languid in that lifeless way of his as he studied Bugg. 'Did I hear you correctly?' the advocate asked in a voice that he tried hard to make sibilant, but which instead came out awkward and wavering. The effect, Bugg realized with a faint start, precisely matched what he would imagine a snake would sound like with words emerging from a lipless mouth. Although, he added to himself, the specific question hardly seemed one he would expect a snake to utter. *Snakes don't ask for clarification.*

Do they?

'You wear a most odd expression,' Sleem said after a moment. 'Did my inability to understand you leave you confused, Master Bugg?'

'Did you truly misunderstand?'

'That is why I sought reiteration.'

'Ah. Well, what did you think you heard?'

The eyes blinked. 'Have we truly uttered all these words to return to my original query?'

'I invite you to use some more, Sleem.'

'Rather than simply repeating yourself.'

'I hate repeating myself.'

Advocate Sleem, Bugg knew, despised discombobulation, although that was in all probability not even a word.

'Master Bugg, as you know, I despise discombobulation.'

'Oh, I'm sorry to hear that.'

'You should be, since I charge by the word.'

'Both our words, or just yours?'

'It is a little late to ask that now, isn't it?' Sleem's folded hands did something sinuous and vaguely disreputable. 'You have instructed me, if I understand you correctly – and correct me if I am in error – you have instructed me, then, to approach your financier to request yet another loan with the stated intention to use it to pay a portion of the interest on the previous loan, which if I recall accurately, and I do, was intended to address in part the interest on yet another loan. This leads me to wonder, since I am not your only advocate, just how many loans you have arranged to pay interest on yet other loans?'

'Well, that was expensive.'

'I become loquacious when I get nervous, Master Bugg.'

'Dealing with you gets more costly when you're nervous? That, Sleem, is really quite clever.'

'Yes, I am. Will you now answer my question?'

'Since you insist. There are perhaps forty loans outstanding with respect to addressing interest payments on still other loans.'

The advocate licked suitably dry lips. 'It was reasons of courtesy and respect, Master Bugg – and, I now see, certain misapprehensions as to your solvency – that encouraged me to refrain from asking for payment up front – for my services, that is, which have been substantial. Although not as substantial, proportionately, as I was led to believe.'

'I don't recall leading you into any such assumptions, Sleem.'

'Of course you don't. They were assumptions.'

'As an advocate, you might have been expected to make very few assumptions indeed. About anything.'

'Permit me to be blunt, Master Bugg. Where in this financial scheme of yours is the money you owe me?'

'Nowhere as of yet, Sleem. Perhaps we should arrange another loan.'

'This is most distressing.'

'I am sure it is, but how do you think I feel?'

'I am resisting asking myself that question, because I fear the answer will be something like: "He feels fine." Now, were I to cling with great faith to those particular assumptions we spoke of earlier, I would now insist that this next loan be devoted exclusively to addressing my fees. No matter what lies I deliver to your financier. Which returns us, alas, to my original utterance, which was voiced in a tone of abject disbelief. You see, your financiers' present state of panic is what has brought me here, for they have reached a level of harassment of my office with respect to you, Master Bugg, that has reached absurd proportions. I have had to hire bodyguards, in fact – at your expense. Dare I ask you then, how much money is in your possession?'

'Right now?'

'Yes.'

Bugg drew out his tattered leather purse, prised it open and peered inside. Then he looked up. 'Two docks.'

'I see. Surely you exaggerate.'

'Well, I cut a sliver off one of them, to pay for a haircut.'

'You have no hair.'

'That's why it was just a sliver. Nose hairs. Ear hairs, a trim of the eyebrows. It's important to be presentable.'

'At your Drowning?'

Bugg laughed. 'That would be fun.' Then he grew sober and leaned forward across his desk. 'You don't think it will come to that, surely. As your client, I expect a most diligence defence at my trial.'

'As your advocate, Master Bugg, I will be first in line demanding your blood.'

'Oh, that's not very loyal of you.'

'You have not paid for my loyalty.'

'But loyalty is not something one pays for, Advocate Sleem.'

'Had I known that delusions accompanied your now-apparent incompetence, Master Bugg, I would never have agreed to represent you in any matter whatsoever.'

Bugg leaned back. 'That makes no sense,' he said. 'As Tehol Beddict has observed on countless occasions, delusions lie at the very heart of our economic system. Indenture as ethical virtue. Pieces of otherwise useless metal – beyond decoration – as wealth. Servitude as freedom. Debt as ownership. And so on.'

'Ah, but those stated delusions are essential to my well-being, Master Bugg. Without them my profession would not exist. All of civilization is, in essence, a collection of contracts. Why, the very nature of society is founded upon mutually agreed measures of value.' He stopped then, and slowly shook his head – a motion alarmingly sinuous. 'Why am I even discussing this with you? You are clearly insane, and your insanity is about to trigger an avalanche of financial devastation.'

'I don't see why, Master Sleem. Unless, of course, your faith in the notion of social contract is nothing more than cynical self-interest.'

'Of course it is, you fool!'

So much for awkward sibilance.

Sleem's fingers wriggled like snared, blind and groping worms. 'Without cynicism,' he said in a strangled voice, 'one becomes the system's victim rather than its master, and I am too clever to be a victim!'

'Which you must prove to yourself repeatedly in the measuring by your wealth, your ease of life, of the necessary contrast with the victims – a contrast that you must surround yourself with at every moment, as represented by your material excesses.'

'Wordy, Master Bugg. Smug ostentation will suffice.'

'Brevity from you, Advocate Sleem?'

'You get what you pay for.'

'By that token,' Bugg observed, 'I am surprised you're saying anything at all.'

'What follows is my gift. I will set forth immediately to inform your financiers that you are in fact broke, and I will in turn offer my services in the feeding frenzy over your material assets.'

'Generous of you.'

Sleem's lips disappeared into a bony grimace. One eye twitched. The worms at the ends of his hands had gone white and deathly. 'In the meantime, I will take those two docks.'

'Not quite two.'

'Nonetheless.'

'I can owe you that missing sliver.'

'Be certain that I will have it, eventually.'

'All right.' Bugg reached into the purse and fished out the two coins. 'This is a loan, yes?'

'Against my fees?'

'Naturally.'

'I sense you are no longer playing the game, Master Bugg.'

'Which game would that be?'

'The one where winners win and losers lose.'

'Oh, that game. No, I suppose not. Assuming, of course, I ever did.'

'I have a sudden suspicion – this very real truth behind all the rumours of impending market collapse – it is all your doing, isn't it?'

'Hardly. Countless winners jumped in, I assure you. Believing, naturally, that they would win in the end. That's how these things work. Until they stop working.' Bugg snapped his fingers. 'Poof!'

'Without those contracts, Master Bugg, there will be chaos.'

'You mean the winners will panic and the losers will launch themselves into their own feeding frenzy. Yes. Chaos.'

'You are truly insane.'

'No, just tired. I've looked into the eyes of too many losers, Sleem. Far too many.'

'And your answer is to make losers of us all. To level the playing field? But it won't do that, you know. You must know that, Bugg. It won't. Instead, the thugs will find the top of every heap, and instead of debt you will have true slavery; instead of contracts you will have tyranny.'

'All the masks torn off, yes.'

'Where is the virtue in that?'

The Elder God shrugged. 'The perils of unfettered expansion, Advocate Sleem, are revealed in the dust and ashes left behind. Assume the species' immortality since it suits the game. Every game. But that assumption will not save you in the end. No, in fact, it will probably kill you. That one self-serving, pious, pretentious, arrogant assumption.'

'The bitter old man speaks.'

'You have no idea.'

'Would that I carried a knife. For I would kill you with it, here and now.'

'Yes. The game always ends at some point, doesn't it?'

'And you dare call me the cynical one.'

'Your cynicism lies in your willing abuse of others to consolidate your superiority over them. My cynicism is in regard to humanity's wilful blindness with respect to its own extinction.'

'Without that wilful blindness there is naught but despair.'

'Oh, I am not that cynical. In fact, I do not agree at all. Maybe when the wilful blindness runs its inevitable course, there will be born wilful wisdom, the revelation of seeing things as they are.'

'Things? To which things are you referring, old man?'

'Why, that everything of true value is, in fact, free.'

Sleem placed the coins in his own bulging purse and walked to the door. 'A very quaint notion. Alas, I will not wish you a good day.'

'Don't bother.'

Sleem turned at the hard edge in Bugg's voice. His brows lifted in curiosity.

Bugg smiled. 'The sentiment wouldn't be free now, would it?'

'No, it would not.'

As soon as the hapless advocate was gone, Bugg rose. *Well, it's begun. Almost to the day when Tehol said it would. The man's uncanny. And maybe in that, there lies some hope for humanity. All those things that cannot be measured, cannot be quantified in any way at all.*

Maybe.

Bugg would have to disappear now. Lest he get torn limb from limb by a murder of advocates, never mind the financiers. And that would be a most unpleasant experience. But first, he needed to warn Tehol.

The Elder God glanced around his office with something like affectionate regret, almost nostalgia. It had been fun, after all. This game. Like most games. He wondered why Tehol had stopped short the first time. But no, perhaps that wasn't at all baffling. Come face to face with a brutal truth – with any brutal truth – and it was understandable to back away.

As Sleem said, there is no value in despair.

But plenty of despair in value, once the illusion is revealed. Ah, I am indeed tired.

He set out from his office, to which he would never return.

'How can there be only four hens left? Yes, Ublala Pung, I am looking directly at you.'

'For the Errant's sake,' Janath sighed, 'leave the poor man alone. What did you expect to happen, Tehol? They're hens that no longer lay eggs, making them as scrawny and dry and useless as the gaggle of matronly scholars at my old school. What Ublala did was an act of profound bravery.'

'Eat my hens? Raw?'

'At least he plucked their feathers.'

'Were they dead by that point?'

'Let's not discuss those particular details, Tehol. Everyone is permitted one mistake.'

'My poor pets,' Tehol moaned, eyeing Ublala Pung's overstuffed pillow at one end of the reed mat that served as the half-blood Tarthenal's bed.

'They were not pets.'

He fixed a narrow gaze on his ex-tutor. 'I seem to recall you going on and on about the terrors of pragmatism, all through history. Yet what do I now hear from you, Janath? "They were not pets." A declarative statement uttered in most pragmatic tones. Why, as if by words alone you could cleanse what must have been an incident of brutal avian murder.'

'Ublala Pung has more stomachs than both you and me combined. They need filling, Tehol.'

'Oh?' He placed his hands on his hips – actually to make certain that the pin was holding the blanket in place, recalling with another pang his most public display a week past. 'Oh?' he asked again, and then added, 'And what, precisely and pragmatically, was wrong with my famous Grit Soup?'

'It was gritty.'

'Hinting of most subtle flavours as can only be cultivated from diligent collection of floor scrapings, especially a floor pranced upon by hungry hens.'

She stared up at him. 'You are not serious, are you? That really *was* grit from the floor? *This floor?*'

'Hardly reason for such a shocked expression, Janath. Of course,' he threw in offhandedly as he walked over to stand next to the blood-splotched pillow, 'creative cuisine demands a certain delicacy of the palate, a culture of appreciation—' He kicked at the pillow and it squawked.

Tehol spun round and glared at Ublala Pung, who sat, back to a wall, and now hung his head.

'I was saving one for later,' the giant mumbled.

'Plucked or unplucked?'

'Well, it's in there to stay warm.'

Tehol looked over at Janath and nodded, 'See? Do you see, Janath? Finally see?'

'See what?'

'The deadly slope of pragmatism, Mistress. The very proof of your arguments all those years ago. Ublala Pung's history of insensitive rationalizations – if you could call anything going on in that skull rational – leading him – and, dare I add, innumerable unsuspecting hens – into the inevitable, egregious extreme of . . . of abject nakedness inside a pillow!'

Her brows lifted. 'Well, that scene last week really scarred you, didn't it?'

'Don't be absurd, Janath.'

Ublala had stuck out his tongue – a huge, pebbled slab of meat – and was trying to study it, his eyes crossing with the effort.

'What are you doing now?' Tehol demanded.

The tongue retreated and Ublala blinked a few times to right his eyes. 'Got cut by a beak,' he said.

'You ate their beaks?'

'Easier to start with the head. They ain't so restless with no heads.'

'Really?'

Ublala Pung nodded.

'And I suppose you consider that merciful?'

'What?'

'Of course not,' Tehol snapped. 'It's just *pragmatic*. "Oh, I'm being eaten. But that's all right. I have no head!"'

Ublala frowned at him. 'Nobody's eating you, Tehol. And your head's still there – I can see it.'

'I was speaking for the hens.'

'But they don't speak Letherii.'

'You are not eating my last four hens.'

'What about the one in the pillow, Tehol? Do you want it back? Its feathers might grow back, though it might catch a cold or something. I can give it back if you like.'

'Generous of you, Ublala, but no. Put it out of its misery, but mind the beak. In the meantime, however, I think you need to get yourself organized – you were supposed to leave days ago, after all, weren't you?'

'I don't want to go to the islands,' Ublala said, dragging a chipped nail through the grit on the floor. 'I sent word. That's good enough, isn't it? I sent word.'

Tehol shrugged. 'If it's good enough, it's good enough. Right, Janath? By all means, stay with us, but you have to set out now to find food. For all of us. A hunting expedition and it won't be easy, Ublala. Not at all easy. There's not been a supply ship on the river for days now, and people have started hoarding things, as if some terrible disaster were imminent. So, as I said, Ublala, it won't be easy. And I hate to admit it, but there are people out there who don't think you can succeed.'

Ublala Pung's head snapped up, fire in his eyes. 'Who? Who?'

The four hens paused in their scratchings and cocked heads in unison.

'I better not say,' Tehol said. 'Anyway, we need food.'

The Tarthenal was on his feet, head crunching on the ceiling before he assumed his normal hunched posture when indoors. Plaster dust sprinkled his hair, drifted down to settle on the floor. The hens pounced, crowding his feet.

'If you fail,' Tehol said, 'we'll have to start eating, uh, plaster.'

'Lime is poisonous,' Janath said.

'And hen guano isn't? Did I hear you complain when you were slurping down my soup?'

'You had your hands over your ears, Tehol, and I wasn't slurping anything down, I was spewing it back up.'

'I can do it,' Ublala said, hands bunching into fists. 'I can get us food. I'll show you.' And with that he pushed through the doorway, out into the narrow alley, and was gone.

'How did you do that, Tehol?'

'I won't take credit. It's how Shurq Elalle manages him. Ublala Pung has an eagerness to show what he can do.'

'You prey on his low self-esteem, you mean.'

'Now that's rather hypocritical coming from a tutor, isn't it?'

'Ooh, all the old wounds still smarting, are they?'

'Never mind old wounds, Janath. You need to leave.'

'What? Are there rumours I'm incapable of something?'

'No, I'm serious. Any day now, there is going to be trouble. Here.'

'Where am I supposed to go?'

'You need to contact who's left of your scholarly friends – find one you can trust—'

'Tehol Beddict, really now. I have no friends among my fellow scholars, and certainly not one I can trust. You clearly know nothing of my profession. We crush beaks between our teeth as a matter of course. In any case, what kind of trouble are you talking about? This economic sabotage of yours?'

'Bugg should really learn to keep quiet.'

She was studying him in a most discomforting way. 'You know, Tehol Beddict, I never imagined you for an agent of evil.'

Tehol smoothed back his hair and swelled his chest.

'Very impressive, but I'm not convinced. Why are you doing all this? Is there some wound from the past that overwhelms all the others? Some terrible need for vengeance to answer some horrendous trauma of your youth? No, I am truly curious.'

'It was all Bugg's idea, of course.'

She shook her head. 'Try again.'

'There are all kinds of evil, Janath.'

'Yes, but yours will see blood spilled. Plenty of it.'

'Is there a difference between spilled blood and blood squeezed out slowly, excruciatingly, over the course of a foreshortened lifetime of stress, misery, anguish and despair – all in the name of some amorphous god that no-one dares call holy? Even as they bend knee and repeat the litany of sacred duty?'

'Oh my,' she said. 'Well, that is an interesting question. Is there a difference? Perhaps not, perhaps only as a matter of degree. But that hardly puts you on a moral high ground, does it?'

'I have never claimed a moral high ground,' Tehol said, 'which in itself sets me apart from my enemy.'

'Yes, I see that. And of course you are poised to destroy that enemy with its own tools, using its own holy scripture; using it, in short, to kill itself. You are at the very end of the slope on which perches your enemy. Or should I say "clings". Now, that you are diabolical comes as no surprise, Tehol. I saw that trait in you long ago. Even so, this blood-thirstiness? I still cannot see it.'

'Probably something to do with your lessons on pragmatism.'

'Oh now, don't you dare point a finger at me! True pragmatism, in this instance, would guide you to vast wealth and the reward of indolence, to the fullest exploitation of the system. The perfect parasite, and be damned to all those lesser folk, the destitute and the witless, the discarded failures squatting in every alley. You certainly possess the necessary talent and genius and indeed, were you now the wealthiest citizen of this empire, living in some enormous estate surrounded by an army of bodyguards and fifty concubines in your stable, I would not in the least be surprised.'

'Not surprised,' Tehol said, 'but, perhaps, disappointed nonetheless?'

She pursed her lips and glanced away. 'Well, that is another issue, Tehol Beddict. One we are not discussing here.'

'If you say so, Janath. In any case, the truth is, I *am* the wealthiest citizen in this empire. Thanks to Bugg, of course, my front man.'

'Yet you live in a hovel.'

'Disparaging my abode? You, an un-paying guest! I am deeply hurt, Janath.'

'No you're not.'

'Well, the hens are and since they do not speak Letherii . . .'

'Wealthiest citizen or not, Tehol Beddict, your goal is not the ostentatious expression of that wealth, not the fullest exploitation of the power it grants you. No, you intend the collapse of this empire's fundamental economic structure. And I still cannot fathom why.'

Tehol shrugged. 'Power always destroys itself in the end, Janath. Would you contest that assertion?'

'No. So, are you telling me that all of this is an exercise in power? An exercise culminating in a lesson no-one could not recognize for what it is? A metaphor made real?'

'But Janath, when I spoke of power destroying itself I was not speaking in terms of metaphor. I meant it literally. So, how many generations of Indebted need to suffer – even as the civilized trappings multiply and abound on all sides, with an ever-increasing proportion of those material follies out of their financial reach? How many, before we all collectively stop and say, "Aaii! That's enough! No more suffering, please! No more hunger, no more war, no more inequity!" Well, as far as I can see, there are never enough generations. We just scrabble on, and on, devouring all within reach, including our own kind, as if it was nothing more than the undeniable expression of some natural law, and as such subject to no moral context, no ethical constraint – despite the ubiquitous and disingenuous blathering over-invocation of those two grand notions.'

'Too much emotion in your speechifying, Tehol Beddict. Marks deducted.'

'Retreating to dry humour, Janath?'

'Ouch. All right, I begin to comprehend your motivations. You will trigger chaos and death, for the good of everyone.'

'If I were the self-pitying kind, I might now moan that no-one will thank me for it, either.'

'So you accept responsibility for the consequences.'

'Somebody has to.'

She was silent for a dozen heartbeats, and Tehol watched her eyes – lovely eyes indeed – slowly widen. '*You* are the metaphor made real.'

Tehol smiled. 'Don't like me? But that makes no sense! How can I not be likeable? Admirable, even? I am become the epitome of triumphant acquisitiveness, the very icon of this great unnamed god! And if I do nothing with all my vast wealth, why, I have earned the right. By every rule voiced in the sacred litany, *I have earned it!*'

'But where is the virtue in then destroying all that wealth? In destroying the very system you used to create it in the first place?'

'Janath, *where is the virtue in any of it?* Is possession a virtue? Is a lifetime of working for some rich toad a virtue? Is loyal employment in some merchant house a virtue? Loyal to what? To whom? Oh, have they paid for that loyalty with a hundred docks a week? Like any other commodity? But then, which version is truer – the virtue of self-serving acquisitiveness or the virtue of loyalty to one's employer? Are not the merchants at the top of their treasure heaps not ruthless and cut-throat as befits those privileges they have purportedly earned? And if it's good enough for them, why not the same for the lowest worker in their house? Where is the virtue in two sets of rules at odds with each other, and why are those fancy words like "moral" and "ethical" the first ones to bleat out from the mouths of those who lost sight of both in their climb to the top? Since when did ethics and morality become weapons of submission?'

She was staring up at him, her expression unreadable.

Tehol thought to toss up his hands to punctuate his harangue, but he shrugged instead. 'Yet my heart breaks for a naked hen.'

'I'm sure it does,' she whispered.

'You should have left,' Tehol said.

'What?'

Boots clumping in the alley, rushing up to the doorway. The flimsy broken shutter – newly installed by Bugg in the name of Janath's modesty – torn aside. Armoured figures pushing in.

A soft cry from Janath.

Tanal Yathvanar stared, disbelieving. His guards pushed in around him until he was forced to hold his arms out to the sides to block still more crowding into this absurd room with its clucking, frightened chickens and two wide-eyed citizens.

Well, *she* at least was wide-eyed. The man, who had to be the infamous Tehol Beddict, simply watched, ridiculous in his pinned blanket, as Tanal fixed his gaze on Janath and smiled. 'Unexpected, this.'

'I – I know you, don't I?'

Tehol asked in a calm voice, 'Can I help you?'

Confused by Janath's question, it was a moment before Tanal registered Tehol's words. Then he sneered at the man. 'I am here to arrest your manservant. The one named Bugg.'

'Oh, now really, his cooking isn't that bad.'

'As it turns out, it seems I have stumbled upon another crime in progress.'

Tehol sighed, then bent to retrieve a pillow. Into which he reached, dragging out a live chicken. Mostly plucked, only a few tufts remaining here and there. The creature tried flapping flabby pink wings, its head bobbing this way and that atop a scrawny neck. Tehol held the chicken out. 'Here, then. We never really expected the ransom in any case.'

Behind Tanal a guard grunted a quickly choked-off laugh.

Tanal scowled, reminding himself to find out who had made that noise. On report and a week of disciplinary duty should serve notice that such unprofessionalism was costly in Tanal Yathvanar's presence. 'You are both under arrest. Janath, for having escaped the custody of the Patriotists. And Tehol Beddict, for harbouring said fugitive.'

'Ah, well,' Tehol said, 'if you were to check the Advocacy Accounts for the past month, sir, you will find the official pardon granted Janath Anar, in absentia. The kind of pardon your people always issue when someone has thoroughly and, usually, *permanently* disappeared. So, the scholar here is under full pardon, which in turn means I am not harbouring a fugitive. As for Bugg, why, when you track him down, tell him he's fired. I will brook no criminals in my household. Speaking of which, you may leave now, sir.'

Oh no, she will not escape me a second time. 'If said pardon exists,' Tanal said to Tehol Beddict, 'then of course you will both be released,

with apologies. For the moment, however, you are now in my custody.'
He gestured to one of his guards. 'Shackle them.'

'Yes sir.'

Bugg turned the corner leading into the narrow lane only to find it blocked by a freshly killed steer, legs akimbo, white tongue lolling as Ublala Pung – an arm wrapped about the beast's broken neck – grunted and pulled, his face red and the veins on his temples purple and bulging. The odd multiple pulsing of his hearts visibly throbbed on both sides of the Tarthenal's thick neck as he endeavoured to drag the steer to Tehol's door.

His small eyes lit upon seeing Bugg. 'Oh good. Help.'

'Where did you get this? Never mind. It will never fit in through the door, Ublala. You'll have to dismember it out here.'

'Oh.' The giant waved one hand. 'I'm always forgetting things.'

'Ublala, is Tehol home?'

'No. Nobody is.'

'Not even Janath?'

The Tarthenal shook his head, eyeing the steer, which was now thoroughly jammed in the lane. 'I'll have to rip its legs off,' he said. 'Oh, the hens are home, Bugg.'

Bugg had been growing ever more nervous with each step that had brought him closer to their house, and now he understood why. But he should have been more than just nervous. He should have *known*. *My mind – I have been distracted. Distant worshippers, something closer to hand . . .*

Bugg clambered over the carcass, pushing past Ublala Pung, which, given the sweat lathering the huge man, proved virtually effortless, then hurried to the doorway.

The shutter was broken, torn from its flimsy hinges. Inside, four hens marched about on the floor like aimless soldiers. Ublala Pung's pillow was trying to do the same.

Shit. They've got them.

There would be a scene at the headquarters of the Patriotists. Couldn't be helped. Wholesale destruction, an Elder God's rage unleashed – oh, this was too soon. Too many heads would look up, eyes narrowing, hunger bursting like juices under the tongue. *Just stay where you are. Stay where you are, Icarium. Lifestealer. Do not reach for your sword, do not let your brow knit. No furrows of anger to mar your unhuman face. Stay, Icarium!*

He entered the room, found a large sack.

Ublala Pung filled the doorway. 'What is happening?'

Bugg began throwing their few possessions into the sack.

'Bugg?'

He snatched up a hen and stuffed it in, then another.

'Bugg?'

The mobile pillow went last. Knotting the sack, Bugg turned about and gave it to Ublala Pung. 'Find somewhere else to hide out,' Bugg said. 'Here, it's all yours—'

'But what about the cow?'

'It's a steer.'

'I tried but it's jammed.'

'Ublala – all right, stay here, then, but you're on your own. Understand?'

'Where are you going? Where is everyone?'

Had Bugg told him then, in clear terms that Ublala Pung would comprehend, all might well have turned out differently. The Elder God would look back on this one moment, over all others, during his extended time of retrospection that followed. *Had he spoken true* – 'They're just gone, friend, and none of us will be back. Not for a long time. Maybe never. Take care of yourself, Ublala Pung, and 'ware your new god – he is much more than he seems.'

With that, Bugg was outside, climbing over the carcass once more and to the mouth of the alley. Where he halted.

They would be looking for him. On the streets. Did he want a running battle? No, just one single strike, one scene of unveiled power to send Patriotist body parts flying. Fast, then done. *Before I awaken the whole damned menagerie.*

No, I need to move unseen now.

And quickly.

The Elder God stirred power to life, power enough to pluck at his material being, disassembling it. No longer corporeal, he slipped down through the grimy cobbles of the street, into the veins of seepwater threading the entire city.

Yes, much swifter here, movement as fast as thought—

He tripped the snare before he was even aware that he had been pulled off course, drawn like an iron filing to a lodestone. Pulled, hard and then as if in a whirlpool, down to a block of stone buried in darkness. A stone of power – of Mael's very own power – *a damned altar!*

Eagerly claiming him, chaining him as all altars sought to do to their chosen gods. Nothing of sentience or malice, of course, but a certain proclivity of structure. The flavour of ancient blood fused particle by particle into the stone's crystalline latticework.

Mael resisted, loosing a roar that shivered through the foundations of Letheras, even as he sought to reassert his physical form, to focus his strength—

And the trap was so sprung – by that very act of regaining his body. The altar, buried beneath rubble, the rubble grinding and shifting, a thousand minute adjustments ensnaring Mael – he could not move, could no longer even so much as cry out.

Errant! You bastard!

Why?

Why have you done this to me?

But the Errant had never shown much interest in lingering over his triumphs. He was nowhere close, and even if he had been, he would not have answered.

A player had been removed from the game.

But the game played on.

In the throne room of the Eternal Domicile, Rhulad Sengar, Emperor of a Thousand Deaths, sat alone, sword in one hand. In wavering torch-light he stared at nothing.

Inside his mind was another throne room, and in that place he was not alone. His brothers stood before him; and behind them, his father, Tomad, and his mother, Uruth. In the shadows along the walls stood Udinaas, Nisall, and the woman Rhulad would not name who had once been Fear's wife. And, close to the locked doors, one more figure, too lost in the dimness to make out. Too lost by far.

Binadas bowed his head. 'I have failed, Emperor,' he said. 'I have failed, my brother.' He gestured downward and Rhulad saw the spear transfixing Binadas's chest. 'A Toblakai, ghost of our ancient wars after the fall of the Kechra. Our wars on the seas. He returned to slay me. He is Karsa Orlong, a Teblor, a Tartheno Toblakai, Tarthenal, Fenn – oh, they have many names now, yes. I am slain, brother, yet I did not die for you.' Binadas looked up then and smiled a dead man's smile. 'Karsa waits for you. He waits.'

Fear took a single step forward and bowed. Straightening, he fixed his heavy gaze on Rhulad – who whimpered and shrank back into his throne. 'Emperor. Brother. You are not the child I nurtured. You are no child I have nurtured. You betrayed us at the Spar of Ice. You betrayed me when you stole my betrothed, my love, when you made her with child, when you delivered unto her such despair that she took her own life.' As he spoke his dead wife walked forward to join him, their hands clasping. Fear said, 'I stand with Father Shadow now, brother, and I wait for you.'

Rhulad cried out, a piteous sound that echoed in the empty chamber.

Trull, his pate pale where his hair had once been, his eyes the eyes of the Shorn – empty, unseen by any, eyes that could not be met by those of any other Tiste Edur. Eyes of *alone*. He raised the spear in his hands, and Rhulad saw the crimson gleam on that shaft, on the broad iron blade. 'I led warriors in your name, brother, and they are now all dead. All dead.

'I returned to you, brother, when Fear and Binadas could not. To beg for your soul, your soul of old, Rhulad, for the child, the brother you had once been.' He lowered the spear, leaned on it. 'You drowned me, chained to stone, while the Rhulad I sought hid in the darkness of your mind. But he will hide no longer.'

From the gloom of the doors, the vague figure moved forward, and Rhulad on his throne saw himself. A youth, weaponless, unblooded, his skin free of coins, his skin smooth and clear.

'We stand in the river of Sengar blood,' Trull said. 'And we wait for you.'

'*Stop!*' Rhulad shrieked. '*Stop!*'

'Truth,' said Udinaas, striding closer, 'is remorseless, Master. Friend?' The slave laughed. 'You were never my friend, Rhulad. You held my life in your hand – either hand, the empty one or the one with the sword, makes no difference. My life was yours, and you thought I had opened my heart to you. Errant take me, why would I do that? Look at my face, Rhulad. This is a slave's face. No more memorable than a clay mask. This flesh on my bones? It works limbs that are naught but tools. I held my hands in the sea, Rhulad, until all feeling went away. All life, gone. From my once-defiant grasp.' Udinaas smiled. 'And now, Rhulad Sengar, who is the slave?

'I stand at the end of the chains. The end but one. One set of shackles. Here, do you see? I stand, and I wait for you.'

Nisall spoke, gliding forward naked, motion like a serpent's in candle-light. 'I spied on you, Rhulad. Found out your every secret and I have them with me now, like seeds in my womb, and soon my belly will swell, and the monsters will emerge, one after another. Spawn of your seed, Rhulad Sengar. Abominations one and all. And you imagined this to be love? I was your whore. The coin you dropped in my hand paid for my life, but it wasn't enough.

'I stand where you will never find me. I, Rhulad, do not wait for you.'

Remaining silent, then, at the last, his father, his mother.

He could remember when last he saw them, the day he had sent them to dwell chained in the belly of this city. Oh, that had been so clever, hadn't it?

But moments earlier one of the Chancellor's guards had begged audience. A terrible event to relate. The Letherii's voice had quavered like a badly strung lyre. Tragedy. An error in rotation among the jailers, a week passing without anyone descending to their cells. No food, but, alas, plenty of water.

A rising flood, in fact.

'*My Emperor. They were drowned. The cells, chest-deep, sire. Their chains . . . not long enough. Not long enough. The palace weeps. The palace cries out. The entire empire, sire, hangs its head.*

'Chancellor Triban Gnol is stricken, sire. Taken to bed, unable to give voice to his grief.'

Rhulad could stare down at the trembling man, stare down, yes, with the blank regard of a man who has known death again and again, known past all feeling. And listen to these empty words, these proper expressions of horror and sorrow.

And in the Emperor's mind there could be these words: *I sent them down to be drowned. With not a single wager laid down.*

The rising waters, this melting, this sinking palace. This Eternal Domicile. I have drowned my father. My mother. He could see those cells, the black flood, the gouges in the walls where they had clawed at the very ends of those chains. He could see it all.

And so they stood. Silent. Flesh rotted and bloated with gases, puddles of slime spreading round their white, wrinkled feet. A father on whose shoulders Rhulad had ridden, shrieking with laughter, a child atop his god as it ran down the strand with limitless power and strength, with the promise of surety like a gentle kiss on the child's brow.

A mother – no, enough. *I die and die. More deaths, yes, than anyone can imagine. I die and I die, and I die.*

But where is my peace?

See what awaits me? See them!

Rhulad Sengar, Emperor of a Thousand Deaths, sat alone on his throne, dreaming peace. But even death could not offer that.

At that moment his brother, Trull Sengar, stood near Onrack, the emlava cubs squalling in the dirt behind them, and watched with wonder as Ben Adaephon Delat, a High Mage of the Malazan Empire, walked out across the shallow river. Unmindful of the glacial cold of that stream that threatened to leave numb his flesh, his bones, the very sentiments of his mind – nothing could deter him from this.

Upon seeing the lone figure appear from the brush on the other side, Quick Ben had halted. And, after a long moment, he had smiled, and under his breath he had said something like: 'Where else but here? Who else but him?' Then, with a laugh, the High Mage had set out.

To meet an old friend who himself strode without pause into that broad river.

Another Malazan.

Beside Trull, Onrack settled a hand on his shoulder and said, 'You, my friend, weep too easily.'

'I know,' Trull sighed. 'It's because, well, it's because I dream of such things. For myself. My brothers, my family. My people. The gifts of peace, Onrack – this is what breaks me, again and again.'

'I think,' said Onrack, 'you evade a deeper truth.'

603

'I do?'

'Yes. There is one other, is there not? Not a brother, not kin, not even Tiste Edur. One who offers another kind of peace, for you, a new kind. And this is what you yearn for, and see the echo of, even in the meeting of two friends such as we witness here.

'You weep when I speak of my ancient love.

'You weep for this, Trull Sengar, because your love has not been answered, and there is no greater anguish than that.'

'Please, friend. Enough. Look. I wonder what they are saying to each other?'

'The river's flow takes their words away, as it does us all.' Onrack's hand tightened on Trull's shoulder. 'Now, my friend, tell me of her.'

Trull Sengar wiped at his eyes, then he smiled. 'There was, yes, a most beautiful woman . . .'

BOOK FOUR

REAPER'S GALE

I went in search of death
In the cast down wreckage
Of someone's temple nave
I went in search among flowers
Nodding to the wind's words
Of woeful tales of war
I went among the blood troughs
Behind the women's tents
All the children that never were

And in the storm of ice and waves
I went in search of the drowned
Among bony shells and blunt worms
Where the grains swirled
Each and every one crying out
its name its life its loss
I went on the current roads
That led me nowhere known

And in the still mists afield
Where light itself crept uncertain
I went in search of wise spirits
Moaning their truths in dark loam
But the moss was silent, too damp
to remember my search
Finding at last where the reapers sow
Cutting stalks to take the season
I failed in my proud quest

To a scything flint blade
And lying asward lost to summer
Bared as its warm carapace
of youthful promise was sent away
into autumn's reliquary sky
Until the bones of night
Were nails glittering in the cold
oblivion, and down the darkness
death came to find me

Before Q'uson Tapi
Toc Anaster

CHAPTER NINETEEN

The great conspiracy among the kingdoms of Saphinand, Bolkando, Ak'ryn, and D'rhasilhani that culminated in the terrible Eastlands War was in numerous respects profoundly ironic. To begin with, there had been no conspiracy. This fraught political threat was in fact a falsehood, created and fomented by powerful economic interests in Lether; and more, it must be said, than just economic. Threat of a dread enemy permitted the imposition of strictures on the population of the empire that well served the brokers among the elite; and would no doubt have made them rich indeed if not for the coincidental financial collapse occurring at this most inopportune of moments in Letherii history. In any case, the border kingdoms and nations of the east could not but perceive the imminent threat, especially with the ongoing campaign against the Awl on the north plains. Thus a grand alliance was indeed created, and with the aforementioned foreign incentives, the war exploded across the entire eastern frontier.

Combined, not entirely accidentally, with the punitive invasion begun on the northwest coast, it is without doubt that Emperor Rhulad Sengar felt beleaguered indeed . . .

The Ashes of Ascension,
History of Lether, Vol. IV
Calasp Hivanar

S HE HAD BEEN NO DIFFERENT FROM ANY OTHER CHILD WITH HER childish dreams of love. Proud and tall, a hero to stride into her life, taking her in his arms and sweeping away all her fears like silts rushing down a stream to vanish in some distant ocean. The benediction of clarity and simplicity, oh my, yes, that had been a most cherished dream.

Although Seren Pedac could remember that child, could remember the twisting anguish in her stomach as she yearned for salvation, an anguish delicious in all its possible obliterations, she would not indulge in nostalgia. False visions of the world were a child's right, not something to be resented, but neither were they worthy of any adult sense of longing.

In Hull Beddict, after all, the young Seren Pedac had believed, for a time – a long time, in fact, before her foolish dream finally withered away – that she had found her wondrous hero, her majestic conjuration whose every glance was a blessing on her heart. So she had learned how purity was poison, the purity of her faith, that is, that such heroes existed. For her. For anyone.

Hull Beddict had died in Letheras. Or, rather, his body had died there. The rest had died in her arms years before then. In a way, she had used him and perhaps not just used him, but raped him. Devouring his belief, stealing away his vision – of himself, of his place in the world, of all the meaning that he, like any other man, sought for his own life. She had found her hero and had then, in ways subtle and cruel, destroyed him under the siege of reality. Reality as she had seen it, as she still saw it. That had been the poison within her, the battle between the child's dream and the venal cynicism that had seeped into adulthood. And Hull had been both her weapon and her victim.

She had in turn been raped. Drunk in a port city tearing itself apart as the armies of the Tiste Edur swept in amidst smoke, flames and ashes. Her flesh made weapon, her soul made victim. There could be no surprise, no blank astonishment, to answer her subsequent attempt to kill herself. Except among those who could not understand, who would never understand.

Seren killed what she loved. She had done it to Hull, and if the day ever arrived when that deadly flower opened in her heart once more, she would kill again. Fears could not be swept away. Fears returned in drowning tides, dragging her down into darkness. *I am poison.*

Stay away. All of you, stay away.

She sat, the shaft of the Imass spear athwart her knees, but it was the weight of the sword belted to her left hip that threatened to pull her down, as if that blade was not a hammered length of iron, but links in a chain. *He meant nothing by it. You meant nothing, Trull. I know that. Besides, like Hull, you are dead. You had the mercy of not dying in my arms. Be thankful for that.*

608

Nostalgia or no, the child still within her was creeping forward, in timid increments. It was safe, wasn't it, safe to cup her small unscarred hands and to show, in private oh-so-secret display, that old dream shining anew. Safe, because Trull was dead. No harm, none at all.

Loose the twist deep in her stomach – no, further down. She was now, after all, a grown woman. Loose it, yes, why not? For one who is poison, there is great pleasure in anguish. In wild longing. In the meaningless explorations of delighted surrender, subjugation – well, subjugation that was in truth domination – *no point in being coy here. I surrender in order to demand. Relinquish in order to rule. I invite the rape because the rapist is me and this body here is my weapon and you, my love, are my victim.*

Because heroes die. As Udinaas says, it is their fate.

The voice that was Mockra, that was the Warren of the Mind, had not spoken to her since that first time, as if, somehow, nothing more needed to be said. The discipline of control was hers to achieve, the lures of domination hers to resist. And she was managing both. Just.

In this the echoes of the past served to distract her, lull her into moments of sensual longing for a man now dead, a love that could never be. In this, even the past could become a weapon, which she wielded to fend off the present and indeed the future. But there were dangers here, too. Revisiting that moment when Trull Sengar had drawn his sword, had then set it into her hands. *He wished me safe. That is all. Dare I create in that something more? Even to drip honey onto desire?*

Seren Pedac glanced up. The fell gathering – her companions – were neither gathered nor companionable. Udinaas was down by the stream, upending rocks in search of crayfish – anything to add variety to their meals – and the icy water had turned his hands first red, then blue, and it seemed he did not care. Kettle sat near a boulder, hunched down to fend off the bitter wind racing up the valley. She had succumbed to an uncharacteristic silence these past few days, and would not meet anyone's eyes. Silchas Ruin stood thirty paces away, at the edge of an overhang of layered rock, and he seemed to be studying the white sky – a sky the same hue as his skin. *'The world is his mirror,'* Udinaas had said earlier, with a hard laugh, before walking down to the stream. Clip sat on a flat rock about halfway between Silchas Ruin and everyone else. He had laid out his assortment of weapons for yet another intense examination, as if obsession was a virtue. Seren Pedac's glance found them all in passing, before her gaze settled on Fear Sengar.

Brother of the man she loved. Ah, was that an easy thing to say? Easy, perhaps, in its falsehood. Or in its simple truth. Fear believed that Trull's gift was more than it seemed; that even Trull hadn't been entirely aware of his own motivations. That the sad-faced Edur warrior had

609

found in her, in Seren Pedac, Acquitor, a Letherii, something he had not found before in anyone. Not one of the countless beautiful Tiste Edur women he must have known. Young women, their faces unlined by years of harsh weather and harsher grief. Women who were not strangers. Women with still-pure visions of love.

This realm they now found themselves in, was it truly that of Darkness? Kurald Galain? Then why was the sky white? Why could she see with almost painful clarity every detail for such distances as left her mind reeling? The Gate itself had been inky, impenetrable – she had stumbled blindly, cursing the uneven, stony ground underfoot – twenty, thirty strides, and then there had been light. A rock-strewn vista, here and there a dead tree rising crooked into the pearlescent sky.

At what passed for dusk in this place that sky assumed a strange, pink tinge, before deepening to layers of purple and blue and finally black. So thus, a normal passage of day and night. Somewhere behind this cloak of white, then, a sun.

A sun in the Realm of Dark? She did not understand.

Fear Sengar had been studying the distant figure of Silchas Ruin. Now he turned and approached the Acquitor. 'Not long, now,' he said.

She frowned up at him. 'Until what?'

He shrugged, his eyes fixing on the Imass spear. 'Trull would have appreciated that weapon, I think. More than you appreciated his sword.'

Anger flared within her. 'He told me, Fear. He gave me his sword, not his heart.'

'He was distracted. His mind was filled with returning to Rhulad – to what would be his final audience with his brother. He could not afford to think of . . . other things. Yet those other things claimed his hands and the gesture was made. In that ritual, my brother's soul spoke.'

She looked away. 'It no longer matters, Fear.'

'It does to me.' His tone was hard, bitter. 'I do not care what you make of it, what you tell yourself now to avoid feeling anything. Once, a brother of mine demanded the woman I loved. I did not refuse him, and now she is dead. Everywhere I look, Acquitor, I see her blood, flowing down in streams. It will drown me in the end, but that is no matter. While I live, while I hold madness at bay, Seren Pedac, I will protect and defend you, for a brother of mine set his sword into your hands.'

He walked away then, and still she could not look at him. *Fear Sengar, you fool. A fool, like any other man, like every other man. What is it with your gestures? Your eagerness to sacrifice? Why do you all give yourselves to us? We are not pure vessels. We are not innocent. We will not handle your soul like a precious, fragile jewel. No, you fool, we'll abuse it as if it was our own, or, indeed, of lesser value than that – if that is possible.*

The crunch of stones, and suddenly Udinaas was crouching before her. In his cupped hands, a minnow. Writhing trapped in a tiny, diminishing pool of water.

'Plan on splitting it six ways, Udinaas?'

'It's not that, Acquitor. Look at it. Closely now. Do you see? It has no eyes. It is *blind*.'

'And is that significant?' But it was, she realized. She frowned up at him, saw the sharp glitter in his gaze. 'We are not seeing what is truly here, are we?'

'Darkness,' he said. 'The cave. The womb.'

'But . . . how?' She looked round. The landscape of broken rock, the pallid lichen and mosses and the very dead trees. The sky.

'Gift, or curse,' Udinaas said, straightening. 'She took a husband, didn't she?'

She watched him walking back to the stream, watched him tenderly returning the blind minnow to the rushing water. A gesture Seren would not have expected from him. *She? Who took a husband?*

'Gift or curse,' said Udinaas as he approached her once again. 'The debate rages on.'

'Mother Dark . . . and Father Light.'

He grinned his usual cold grin. 'At last, Seren Pedac stirs from her pit. I've been wondering about those three brothers.'

Three brothers?

He went on as if she knew of whom he was speaking. 'Spawn of Mother Dark, yes, but then, there were plenty of those, weren't there? Was there something that set those three apart? Andarist, Anomander, Silchas. What did Clip tell us? Oh, right, nothing. But we saw the tapestries, didn't we? Andarist, like midnight itself. Anomander, with hair of blazing white. And here, Silchas, our walking bloodless abomination, whiter than any corpse but just as friendly. So what caused the great rift between sons and mother? Maybe it wasn't her spreading her legs to Light like a stepfather none of them wanted. Maybe that's all a lie, one of those sweetly convenient ones. Maybe, Seren Pedac, it was finding out who their father was.'

She could not help but follow his gaze to where stood Silchas Ruin. Then she snorted and turned away. 'Does it matter?'

'Does it matter? Not right now,' Udinaas said. 'But it will.'

'Why? Every family has its secrets.'

He laughed. 'I have my own question. If Silchas Ruin is all Light on the outside, what must he be on the inside?'

'The world is his mirror.'

But the world we now look upon is a lie.

'Udinaas, I thought the *Tiste Edur* were the children of Mother Dark and Father Light.'

'Successive generations, probably. Not in any obvious way connected to those three brothers.'

'Scabandari.'

'Yes, I imagine so. Father Shadow, right? Ah, what a family that was! Let's not forget the sisters! Menandore with her raging fire of dawn, Sheltatha Lore the loving dusk, and Sukul Ankhadu, treacherous bitch of night. Were there others? There must have been, but they've since fallen by the wayside. Myths prefer manageable numbers, after all, and three always works best. Three of this, three of that.'

'But Scabandari would be the fourth—'

'Andarist is dead.'

Oh. 'Andarist is dead.' And how does he know such things? Who speaks to you, Udinaas, in your nightly fevers?

She could find out, she suddenly realized. She could slide in, like a ghost. She could, with the sorcery of Mockra, steal knowledge. *I could rape someone else's mind, is what I mean. Without his ever knowing.*

There was necessity, wasn't there? Something terrible was coming. Udinaas knew what it would be. What it might be, anyway. And Fear Sengar – he had just vowed to protect her, as if he too suspected some awful confrontation was close at hand. *I remain the only one to know nothing.*

She could change that. She could use the power she had found within her. It was nothing more than self-protection. To remain ignorant was to justly suffer whatever fate awaited her; yes, in lacking ruthlessness she would surely deserve whatever befell her. For ignoring what Mockra offered, for ignoring this gift.

No wonder it had said nothing since that first conversation. She had been in her pit, stirring old sand to see what seeds might spring to life, but there was no light reaching that pit, and no life among the chill grains. An indulgent game and nothing more.

I have a right to protect myself. Defend myself.

Clip and Silchas Ruin were walking back. Udinaas was studying them with the avidness he had displayed when examining the blind minnow.

I will have your secrets, slave. I will have those, and perhaps much, much more.

Udinaas could not help but see Silchas Ruin differently. *In a new light, ha ha.* The aggrieved son. One of them, anyway. *Aggrieved sons, daughters, grandchildren, their children, on and on until the race of Shadow wars against that of Darkness. All on a careless word, an insult, the wrong look a hundred thousand years ago.*

But, then, where are the children of Light?

Well, a good thing, maybe, that they weren't around. Enough trouble brewing as it was, with Silchas Ruin and Clip on one side and Fear Sengar and – possibly – Scabandari on the other. *But of course Fear Sengar is no Mortal Sword of Shadow. Although he probably wants to be, even believes himself to be. Oh, this will play badly indeed, won't it?*

Silent, they walked on. Across this blasted, lifeless landscape. *But not quite! There are . . . minnows.*

The quest was drawing to a close. Just as well. Nothing worse, as far as he was concerned, than those legends of old when the stalwart, noble adventurers simply went on and on, through one absurd episode after another, with each one serving some arcane function for at least one of the wide-eyed fools, as befitted the shining serrated back of morality that ran the length of the story, from head to tip of that long, sinuous tail. *Legends that bite. Yes, they all do. That's the point of them.*

But not this one, not this glorious quest of ours. No thunderous message driving home like a spike of lightning between the eyes. No tumbling cascade of fraught scenes ascending like some damned stairs to the magical tower perched on the mountain's summit, where all truths were forged into the simple contest of hero against villain.

Look at us! What heroes? We're all villains, and that tower doesn't even exist.

Yet.

I see blood dripping between the stones. Blood in its making. So much blood. You want that tower, Silchas Ruin? Fear Sengar? Clip? You want it that much? You will have to make it, and so you shall.

Fevers every night. Whatever sickness whispered in his veins preferred the darkness of the mind that was sleep. Revelations arrived in torn fragments, pieces hinting of some greater truth, something vast. But he did not trust any of that – those revelations, they were all lies. *Someone's* lies. The Errant's? Menandore's? The fingers poking into his brain were legion. *Too many contradictions, each vision warring with the next.*

What do you all want of me?

Whatever it was, he wasn't going to give it. He'd been a slave but he was a slave no longer.

This realm had not been lived in for a long, long time. At least nowhere in this particular region. The trees were so long dead they had turned to brittle stone, right down to the thinnest twigs with their eternally frozen buds awaiting a season of life that never came. And that sun up there, somewhere behind the white veil, well, it too was a lie. Somehow. *After all, Darkness should be* dark, *shouldn't it?*

He thought to find ruins or something. Proof that the Tiste Andii had once thrived here, but he had not seen a single thing that had been shaped by an intelligent hand, guided by a sentient mind. No roads, no trails of any kind.

When the hidden sun began its fade of light, Clip called a halt. Since arriving in this place, he had not once drawn out the chain and its two rings, the sole blessing to mark this part of their grand journey. There was nothing to feed a fire, so the dried remnants of smoked deer meat found no succulence in a stew and lent no warmth to their desultory repast.

What passed for conversation was no better.

Seren Pedac spoke. 'Clip, why is there light here?'

'We walk a road,' the young Tiste Andii replied. 'Kurald Liosan, Father Light's gift of long, long ago. As you can see, his proud garden didn't last very long.' He shrugged. 'Silchas Ruin and myself, well, naturally we don't need this, but leading you all by hand . . .' His smile was cold.

'Thought you were doing that anyway,' Udinaas said. The gloom was deepening, but he found that there was little effect on his vision, a detail he kept to himself.

'I was being kind in not stating the obvious, Letherii. Alas, you lack such tact.'

'Tact? Fuck tact, Clip.'

The smile grew harder. 'You are not needed, Udinaas. I trust you know that.'

A wince tightened Seren Pedac's face. 'There's no point in—'

'It's all right, Acquitor,' Udinaas said. 'I was getting rather tired of the dissembling bullshit anyway. Clip, where does this road lead? When we step off it, where will we find ourselves?'

'I'm surprised you haven't guessed.'

'Well, I have.'

Seren Pedac frowned across at Udinaas and asked, 'Will you tell me, then?'

'I can't. It's a secret – and yes, I know what I said about dissembling, but this way maybe you stay alive. Right now, and with what's to come, you have a chance of walking away, when all's said and done.'

'Generous of you,' she said wearily, glancing away.

'He is a slave,' Fear Sengar said. 'He knows nothing, Acquitor. How could he? He mended nets. He swept damp sheaves from the floor and scattered new ones. He shelled oysters.'

'And on the shore, one night,' Udinaas said, 'I saw a white crow.'

Sudden silence.

Finally, Silchas Ruin snorted. 'Means nothing. Except perhaps a presentiment of my rebirth. Thus, Udinaas, it may be you are a seer of sorts. Or a liar.'

'More likely both,' Udinaas said. 'Yet there was a white crow. Was it flying through darkness, or dusk? I'm not sure, but I think the distinction is, well, important. Might be worth some effort, remembering

614

exactly, I mean. But my days of working hard at anything are done.' He glanced over at Silchas Ruin. 'We'll find out soon enough.'

'This is pointless,' Clip announced, settling back until he was supine on the hard ground, hands laced behind his head, staring up at the black, blank sky.

'So this is a road, is it?' Udinaas asked – seemingly of no-one in particular. 'Gift of Father Light. That's the interesting part. So, the question I'd like to ask is this: are we travelling it alone?'

Clip sat back up.

Udinaas smiled at him. 'Ah, you've sensed it, haven't you? The downy hair on the back of your neck trying to stand on end. Sensed. Smelled. A whisper of air as from some high wind. Sending odd little chills through you. All that.'

Silchas Ruin rose, anger in his every line. 'Menandore,' he said.

'I would say she has more right to this road than we do,' Udinaas said. 'But Clip brought us here out of the goodness of his heart. Such noble intentions.'

'She tracks us,' Silchas Ruin muttered, hands finding the grips of his singing swords. Then he glared skyward. 'From the sky.'

'For your miserable family feuds are the only things worth living for, right?'

There was alarm in Fear Sengar's expression. 'I do not understand. Why is Sister Dawn following us? What cares she for the soul of Scabandari?'

'The Finnest,' Clip said under his breath. Then, louder, 'Bloodeye's soul, Edur. She seeks to claim it for herself. Its power.'

Udinaas sighed. 'So, Silchas Ruin, what terrible deed did you commit on your sun-locked sister? Or daughter, or whatever relation she is? Why is she out for your blood? Just what did you all do to each other all those millennia ago? Can't you kiss and make up? No, I imagine not.'

'There was no crime,' Silchas Ruin said. 'We are enemies in the name of ambition, even when I would not have it so. Alas, to live as long as we have, it seems there is naught else to sustain us. Naught but rage and hunger.'

'I suggest a huge mutual suicide,' Udinaas said. 'You and all your wretched kin, and you, Clip, you could just jump in to appease your ego or something. Vanish from the mortal realms, all of you, and leave the rest of us alone.'

'Udinaas,' Clip said with amusement, 'this is not a mortal realm.'

'Rubbish.'

'Not as you think of one, then. This is a place of elemental forces. Unfettered, and beneath every surface, the potential for chaos. This is a realm of the Tiste.'

Seren Pedac seemed startled. 'Just "Tiste"? Not Andii, Edur—'

'Acquitor,' Silchas Ruin said, 'The Tiste are the first children. The very first. Ours were the first cities, the first civilizations. Rising here, in realms such as this one. As Clip has said, *elemental*.'

'Then what of the Elder Gods?' Seren Pedac demanded.

Neither Clip nor Silchas Ruin replied, and the silence stretched, until Udinaas snorted a laugh. 'Unwelcome relatives. Pushed into closets. Bar the door, ignore the knocking and let's hope they move on. It's ever the problem with all these creation stories. "We're the first, isn't it obvious? Those others? Ignore them. Imposters, interlopers, and worse! Look at us, after all! Dark, Light, and the gloom in between! Could anyone be purer, more elemental, than that?" The answer, of course, is yes. Let's take an example, shall we?'

'Nothing preceded Darkness,' said Clip, irritation sharpening his pronouncement.

Udinaas shrugged. 'That seems a reasonable enough assertion. But then, is it? After all, Darkness is not just absence of light, is it? Can you have a negative definition like that? But maybe Clip wasn't being nearly so offhand as he sounded just there. "*Nothing preceded Darkness.*" *Nothing* indeed. True absence, then, of anything. Even Darkness. But wait, where does chaos fit in? Was that *Nothing* truly empty, or was it filled with chaos? Was Darkness the imposition of order on chaos? Was it the *only* imposition of order on chaos? That sounds presumptuous. Would that Feather Witch was here – there's too much of the Tiles that I've forgotten. All that birth of this and birth of that stuff. But chaos also produced Fire. It must have, for without Fire there is no Light. One might also say that without Light there is no Dark, and without both there is no Shadow. But Fire needs fuel to burn, so we would need matter of some kind – solids – born of Earth. And Fire needs air, and so—'

'I am done listening to all of this nonsense,' Silchas Ruin said.

The Tiste Andii walked off into the night, which wasn't night at all – at least not in the eyes of Udinaas, and he found he could watch Silchas Ruin as the warrior went on for another forty or so paces, then spun round to face the camp once more. *Ah, White Crow, you would listen on, would you? Yet with none to see your face, none to challenge you directly.*

My guess is, Silchas Ruin, you are as ignorant as the rest of us when it comes to the birth of all existence. That your notions are as quaint as ours, and just as pathetic, too.

Fear Sengar spoke. 'Udinaas, the Edur women hold that the Kechra bound all that exists to time itself, thus assuring the annihilation of everything. Their great crime. Yet that death – I have thought hard on this – that death, it does not have the face of chaos. The very opposite, in fact.'

'Chaos pursues,' Clip muttered with none of his characteristic arrogance. 'It is the Devourer. Mother Dark scattered its power, its armies, and it seeks ever to rejoin, to become one again, for when that happens no other power – not even Mother Dark – can defeat it.'

'Mother Dark must have had allies,' Udinaas said. 'Either that, or she ambushed chaos, caught her enemy unawares. Was all existence born of betrayal, Clip? Is that the core of your belief? No wonder you are all at each other's throats.' *Listen well, Silchas Ruin; I am closer on your trail than you ever imagined.* Which, he thought then, might not be wise; might, in fact, prove fatal. 'In any case, Mother Dark herself had to have been born of something. A conspiracy within chaos. Some unprecedented alliance where all alliances were forbidden. So, yet another betrayal.'

Fear Sengar leaned forward slightly. 'Udinaas, how did you know we were being followed? By Menandore.'

'Slaves need to hone their every sense, Fear Sengar. Because our masters are fickle. You might wake up one morning with a toothache, leaving you miserable and short-tempered, and in consequence an entire family of slaves might suffer devastation before the sun's at mid-day. A dead husband or wife, a dead parent, or both. Beaten, maimed for life, blinded, dead – every possibility waits in our shadows.'

He did not think Fear was convinced, and, granted, the argument was thin. True, those heightened senses might be sufficient to raise the hackles, to light the instincts that *something* was on their trail. But that was not the same as knowing that it was Menandore. *I was careless in revealing what I knew. I wanted to knock the fools off balance, but that has just made them more dangerous. To me.*

Because now they know – or will know, soon enough – that this useless slave does not walk alone.

For the moment, however, no-one was inclined to challenge him.

Drawing out bedrolls, settling in for a passage of restless sleep. Dark that was not dark. Light that was not light. Slaves who might be masters, and somewhere ahead of them all, a bruised stormcloud over-head, filled with thunder, lightning, and crimson rain.

She waited until the slave's breathing deepened, lengthened, found the rhythm of slumber. The wars of conscience were past. Udinaas had revealed enough secret knowledge to justify this. He had never left his slavery behind, and now his Mistress was Menandore, a creature by all accounts as treacherous, vicious and cold-blooded as any other in that ancient family of what-might-be-gods.

Mockra whispered into life in her mind, as free as wandering thought, unconstrained by a shell of hard bone, by the well-worn path-ways of the mind. A tendril lifting free, hovering in the air above her, she gave it the shape of a serpent, head questing, tongue flicking to find the scent of Udinaas, of the man's very soul – there, sliding forward to close, a touch—

Hot!

Seren Pedac felt that serpent recoil, felt the ripples sweep back into her in waves of scalding heat.

Fever dreams, the fire of Udinaas's soul. The man stirred in his blankets.

She would need to be more subtle, would need the essence of the serpent she had chosen. Edging forward once more, finding that raging forge, then burrowing down, through hot sand, beneath it. Oh, there was pain, yes, but it was not, she now realized, some integral furnace of his soul. It was the realm his dream had taken him into, a realm of blistering light—

Her eyes opened onto a torn landscape. Boulders baked red and brittle. Thick, turgid air, the breath of a potter's kiln. Blasted white sky overhead.

Udinaas wandered, staggering, ten paces away.

She sent her serpent slithering after him.

An enormous shadow slid over them – Udinaas spun and twisted to glare upward as that shadow flowed past, then on, and the silver and gold scaled dragon, gliding on stretched wings, flew over the ridge directly ahead, then, a moment later, vanished from sight.

Seren saw Udinaas waiting for it to reappear. And then he saw it again, now tiny as a speck, a glittering mote in the sky, fast dwindling. The Letherii slave cried out, but Seren could not tell if the sound had been one of rage or abandonment.

No-one likes being ignored.

Stones skittered near the serpent and in sudden terror she turned its gaze, head lifting, to see a woman. Not Menandore. No, a Letherii. Small, lithe, hair so blonde as to be almost white. Approaching Udinaas, tremulous, every motion revealing taut, frayed nerves.

Another intruder.

Udinaas had yet to turn from that distant sky, and Seren watched as the Letherii woman drew still closer. Then, five paces away, she straightened, ran her hands through her wild, burnished hair. In a sultry voice, the strange woman spoke. 'I have been looking for you, my love.'

He did not whirl round. He did not even move, but Seren saw something new in the lines of his back and shoulders, the way he now held his head. In his voice, when he replied, there was amusement. ' "My love"?' And then he faced her, with ravaged eyes, a bleakness like defiant ice in this world of fire. 'No longer the startled hare, Feather Witch – yes, I see the provocative way you now look at me, the brazen confidence, the *invitation*. And in all that, the truth that is your contempt still burns through. Besides,' he added, 'I heard you scrabbling closer, could smell, even, your fear. What do you want, Feather Witch?'

'I am not frightened, Udinaas,' the woman replied.

That name, yes. Feather Witch. The fellow slave, the Caster of the Tiles. Oh, there is history between them beyond what any of us might have imagined.

'But you are,' Udinaas insisted. 'Because you expected to find me alone.'

She stiffened, then attempted a shrug. 'Menandore feels nothing for you, my love. You must realize that. You are naught but a weapon in her hands.'

'Hardly. Too blunted, too pitted, too fragile by far.'

Feather Witch's laugh was high and sharp. 'Fragile? Errant take me, Udinaas, you have never been *that*.'

Seren Pedac certainly agreed with her assessment. What reason this false modesty?

'I asked what you wanted. Why are you here?'

'I have changed since you last saw me,' Feather Witch replied. 'I am now Destra Irant to the Errant, to the last Elder God of the Letherii. Who stands behind the Empty Throne—'

'It's not empty.'

'It will be.'

'Now there's your new-found faith getting in the way again. All that hopeful insistence that you are once more at the centre of things. Where is your flesh hiding right now, Feather Witch? In Letheras, no doubt. Some airless, stinking hovel that you have proclaimed a temple – yes, that stings you, telling me I am not in error. About you. Changed, Feather Witch? Well, fool yourself if you like. But don't think I'm deceived. Don't think I will now fall into your arms gasping with lust and devotion.'

'You once loved me.'

'I once pressed red-hot coins into Rhulad's dead eyes, too. But they weren't dead, alas. The past is a sea of regrets, but I have crawled a way up the shore now, Feather Witch. Quite a way, in fact.'

'We belong together, Udinaas. Destra Irant and T'orrud Segul, and we will have, at our disposal, a Mortal Sword. Letherii, all of us. As it should be, and through us the Errant rises once more. Into power, into domination – it is what our people need, what we have needed for a long time.'

'The Tiste Edur—'

'Are on their way out. Rhulad's Grey Empire – it was doomed from the start. Even you saw that. It's tottering, crumbling, falling to pieces. But we Letherii will survive. We always do, and now, with the rebirth

619

of the faith in the Errant, our empire will make the world tremble. Destra Irant, T'orrud Segul and Mortal Sword, we shall be the three behind the Empty Throne. Rich, free to do as we please. We shall have Edur for slaves. Broken, pathetic Edur. Chained, beaten, we shall use them up, as they once did to us. Love me or not, Udinaas. Taste my kiss or turn away, it does not matter. You are T'orrud Segul. The Errant has chosen you—'

'He tried, you mean. I sent the fool away.'

She was clearly stunned into silence.

Udinaas half turned with a dismissive wave of one hand. 'I sent Menandore away, too. They tried using me like a coin, something to be passed back and forth. But I know all about coins. I've smelled the burning stench of their touch.' He glanced back at her again. 'And if I am a coin, then I belong to no-one. Borrowed, occasionally. Wagered, often. Possessed? Never for long.'

'T'orrud Segul—'

'Find someone else.'

'You have been chosen, you damned fool!' She started forward suddenly, tearing at her own threadbare slave's tunic. Cloth ripped, fluttered on the hot wind like the tattered fragments of some imperial flag. She was naked, reaching out to drag Udinaas round, arms encircling his neck—

His push sent her sprawling onto the hard, stony ground. 'I'm done with rapes,' he said in a low, grating voice. 'Besides, I told you we have company. You clearly didn't completely understand me—' And he walked past her, walked straight towards the serpent that was Seren Pedac.

She woke with a calloused hand closed about her throat. Stared up into glittering eyes in the gloom.

She could feel him trembling above her, his weight pinning her down, and he lowered his face to hers, then, wiry beard bristling along her cheek, brought his mouth to her right ear, and began whispering.

'I have been expecting something like that, Seren Pedac, for some time. Thus, you had my admiration . . . of your restraint. Too bad, then, it didn't last.'

She was having trouble breathing; the hand wrapping her throat was an iron band.

'I meant what I said about rapes, Acquitor. If you ever do that again, I will kill you. Do you understand me?'

She managed a nod, and she could see now, in his face, the full measure of the betrayal he was feeling, the appalling *hurt*. That she would so abuse him.

'Think nothing of me,' Udinaas continued, 'if that suits the miserable little hole you live in, Seren Pedac. It's what wiped away your restraint in the first place, after all. But I have had goddesses use me. And gods try to. And now a scrawny witch I once lusted after, who dreams her version of tyranny is preferable to everyone else's. I was a slave – I am used to being used, remember? But – and listen carefully, woman – *I am a slave no longer*—'

Fear Sengar's voice came down from above them. 'Release her throat, Udinaas. That which you feel at the back of your own neck is the tip of my sword – and yes, that trickle of blood belongs to you. The Acquitor is Betrothed to Trull Sengar. She is under my protection. Release her now, or die.'

The hand gripping her throat loosened, lifted clear—

And Fear Sengar had one hand in the slave's hair, was tearing him back, flinging him onto the ground, the sword hissing in a lurid blur—

'NO!' Seren Pedac shrieked, clawing across to throw herself down onto Udinaas. 'No, Fear! Do not touch him!'

'Acquitor—'

Others awake now, rising on all sides—

'Do not hurt him!' *I have done enough of that this night.* 'Fear Sengar – Udinaas, he had that right—' *Oh, Errant save me* – 'He had that right,' she repeated, her throat feeling torn on the inside from that first shriek. 'I – listen, don't, Fear, you don't understand. I . . . I did something. Something terrible. Please . . .' she was sitting up now, speaking to everyone, 'please, this is my fault.'

Udinaas pushed her weight to one side, and she scraped an elbow raw as he clambered free. 'Make it day again, Silchas Ruin,' he said.

'The night—'

'*Make it day again, damn you! Enough sleep – let's move on. Now!*'

To Seren Pedac's astonishment, the sky began to lighten once more. *What? How?*

Udinaas was at his bedroll, fighting to draw it together, stuff it into his pack. She saw tears glittering on his weathered cheeks.

Oh, what have I done. Udinaas—

'You understand too much,' Clip said in that lilting, offhand tone of his. 'Did you hear me, Udinaas?'

'Go fuck yourself,' the slave muttered.

Silchas Ruin said, 'Leave him, Clip. He is but a child among us. And he will play his childish games.'

Ashes drifting down to bury her soul, Seren Pedac turned away from all of them. *No, the child is me. Still. Always.*

Udinaas . . .

Twelve paces away, Kettle sat, legs drawn under her, and held hands with Wither, ghost of an Andii, and there was neither warmth nor chill in that grip. She stared at the others as the light slowly burgeoned to begin a new day.

'What they do to each other,' she whispered.

Wither's hand tightened around hers. 'It is what it is to live, child.'

She thought about that, then. The ghost's words, the weariness in the tone, and, after a long time, she finally nodded.

Yes, this is what it is to live.

It made all that she knew was coming a little easier to bear.

In the litter-scattered streets of Drene, the smell of old smoke was bitter in the air. Black smears adorned building walls. Crockery, smashing down from toppled carts, had flung pieces everywhere, as if the sky the night before had rained glazed sherds. Bloodstained cloth, shredded and torn remnants of tunics and shirts, were blackening under the hot sun. Just beyond the lone table where sat Venitt Sathad, the chaos of the riot that had ignited the previous day's dusk was visible on all sides.

The proprietor of the kiosk bar limped back out from the shadowed alcove that served as kitchen and storehouse, bearing a splintered tray with another dusty bottle of Bluerose wine. The stunned look in the old man's eyes had yet to retreat, giving his motions an oddly disarticulated look as he set the bottle down on Venitt Sathad's table, bowed, then backed away.

The few figures that had passed by on the concourse this morning had each paused in their furtive passage to stare at Venitt – not because, he knew, he was in any way memorable or imposing, but because in sitting here, eating a light breakfast and now drinking expensive wine, the servant of Rautos Hivanar presented a scene of civil repose. Such a scene now jarred, now struck those who had weathered the chaos of the night before, as if lit with its very own madness.

A hundred versions clouded the riot's beginning. A money-lender's arrest. A meal overcharged and an argument that got out of hand. A sudden shortage of this or that. Two Patriotist spies beating someone, and then being set upon by twenty bystanders. Perhaps none of these things had occurred; perhaps they all had.

The riot had destroyed half the market on this side of the city. It had then spilled into the slums northwest of the docks, where, judging from the smoke, it raged on unchecked.

The garrison had set out into the streets to conduct a brutal campaign of pacification that was indiscriminate at first, but eventually found focus in a savage assault on the poorest people of Drene. At times in the past, the poor – being true victims – had been easily cowed by a few dozen cracked skulls. But not this time. They had had enough, and they had fought back.

In this morning's air, Venitt Sathad could still smell the shock – sharper by far than the smoke, colder than any bundle of bloody cloth that might still contain pieces of human meat – the shock of guards

622

screaming with fatal wounds, of armoured bullies being cornered then torn apart by frenzied mobs. The shock, finally, of the city garrison's ignoble retreat to the barracks.

They had been under strength, of course. Too many out with Bivatt in the campaign against the Awl. And they had been arrogant, emboldened by centuries of precedent. And that arrogance had blinded them to what had been happening out there, to what was about to happen.

The one detail that remained with Venitt Sathad, lodged like a sliver of wood in infected flesh that no amount of wine could wash away, was what had happened to the resident Tiste Edur.

Nothing.

The mobs had left them alone. Extraordinary, inexplicable. *Frightening.*

No, instead, half a thousand shrieking citizens had stormed Letur Anict's estate. Of course, the Factor's personal guards were, one and all, elite troops – recruited from every Letherii company that had ever been stationed in Drene – and the mob had been repulsed. It was said that corpses lay in heaps outside the estate's walls.

Letur Anict had returned to Drene two days before, and Venitt Sathad suspected that the Factor had been as unprepared for the sudden maelstrom as had the garrison. In Overseer Brohl Handar's absence, Letur governed the city and its outlying region. Whatever reports his agents might have delivered upon his return would have been rife with fears but scant on specifics – the kind of information that Letur Anict despised and would summarily dismiss. Besides, the Patriotists were supposed to take care of such things in their perpetual campaign of terror. A few more arrests, some notable disappearances, the confiscation of properties.

Of course, Rautos Hivanar, his master, had noted the telltale signs of impending chaos. Tyrannical control was dependent on a multitude of often disparate forces, running the gamut from perception to overt viciousness. The sense of power needed to be pervasive in order to create and maintain the illusion of omniscience. Invigilator Karos Invictad understood that much, at least, but where the thug in red silks failed was in understanding that thresholds existed, and to cross them – with ever greater acts of brutality, with paranoia and fear an ever-rising fever – was to see the illusion shattered.

At some point, no matter how repressive the regime, the citizenry will come to comprehend the vast power in their hands. The destitute, the Indebted, the beleaguered middle classes; in short, the myriad victims. Control was sleight of hand trickery, and against a hundred thousand defiant citizens, it stood no real chance. All at once, the game was up.

The threshold, this time, was precisely as Rautos Hivanar had feared.

The pressure of a crumbling, overburdened economy. Shortage of coin, the crushing weight of huge and ever-growing debts, the sudden inability to pay for anything. The Patriotists could draw knives, swords, could wield their knotted clubs, but against desperate hunger and a sense of impending calamity, they might as well have been swinging reeds at the wind.

In the face of all this, the Tiste Edur were helpless. Bemused, uncomprehending, and wholly unprepared. *Unless, that is, their answer will be to begin killing. Everyone.*

Another of Karos Invictad's blind spots. The Invigilator's contempt for the Tiste Edur could well prove suicidal. Their Emperor could not be killed. Their K'risnan could unleash sorcery that could devour every Letherii in the empire. And the fool thought to target them in a campaign of arrests?

No, the Patriotists had been useful; indeed, for a time, quite necessary. But—

'Venitt Sathad, welcome to Drene.'

Without looking up, Venitt gestured with one hand as he reached for the wine bottle. 'Find yourself a chair, Orbyn Truthfinder.' A glance upward. 'I was just thinking about you.'

The huge, odious man smiled. 'I am honoured. If, that is, your thoughts were of me specifically. If, however, they were of the Patriotists, well, I suspect that "honour" would be the wrong word indeed.'

The proprietor was struggling to drag another chair out to the table, but it was clear that whatever had caused the limp was proving most painful. Venitt Sathad set the bottle back down, rose, and walked over to help him.

'Humble apologies, kind sir,' the old man gasped, his face white and beads of sweat spotting his upper lip. 'Had a fall yestereve, sir—'

'Must have been a bad one. Here, leave the chair to me, and find us another unbroken bottle of wine – if you can.'

'Most obliged, sir . . .'

Wondering where the old man had found this solid oak dining chair – one large enough to take Orbyn's mass – Venitt Sathad pulled it across the cobbles and positioned it opposite his own chair with the table in between, then he sat down once more.

'If not honour,' he said, retrieving the bottle again and refilling the lone clay cup, 'then what word comes to mind, Orbyn?'

Truthfinder eased down into the chair, gusting out a loud, wheezing sigh. 'We can return to that anon. I have been expecting your arrival for some time now.'

'Yet I found neither you nor the Factor in the city, Orbyn, upon my much-anticipated arrival.'

A dismissive gesture, as the proprietor limped up with a cup and a second bottle of Bluerose wine, then retreated with head bowed. 'The Factor insisted I escort him on a venture across the sea. He has been wont to waste my time of late. I assure you, Venitt, that such luxuries are now part of the past. For Letur Anict.'

'I imagine he is in a most discomfited state at the moment.'

'Rattled.'

'He lacks confidence that he can restore order?'

'Lack of confidence has never been Letur Anict's weakness. Reconciling it with reality is, alas.'

'It is unfortunate that the Overseer elected to accompany Atri-Preda Bivatt's campaign to the east.'

'Possibly fatally so, yes.'

Venitt Sathad's brows lifted. 'Have some wine, Orbyn. And please elaborate on that comment.'

'There are assassins in that company,' Truthfinder replied, frowning to indicate his distaste. 'Not mine, I assure you. Letur plays his own game with the Overseer. Political. In truth, I do not expect Brohl Handar to return to Drene, except perhaps as a wrapped, salted corpse.'

'I see. Of course, this sparring of his has now put him at a great disadvantage.'

Orbyn nodded as he poured his cup full. 'Yes, with Brohl nowhere in sight, the blame for last night's riot rests exclusively with the Factor. There will be repercussions, no doubt?'

'Truthfinder, that riot is not yet over. It will continue into this night, where it will boil out from the slums with still greater force and ferocity. There will be more assaults on Letur's estate, and before long on all of his properties and holdings throughout Drene, and those he will not be able to protect. The barracks will be under siege. There will be looting. There will be slaughter.'

Orbyn was leaning forward, rubbing at his oily brow. 'So it is true, then. Financial collapse.'

'The empire reels. The Liberty Consign is mortally wounded. When the people learn that there have been other riots, in city after city—'

'The Tiste Edur will be stirred awake.'

'Yes.'

Orbyn's eyes fixed on Venitt Sathad's. 'There are rumours of war in the west.'

'West? What do you mean?'

'An invasion from the sea, that seems to be focused on the Tiste Edur themselves. Punitive, in the wake of the fleets. A distant empire that did not take kindly to the murder of its citizens. And now, reports of the Bolkando and their allies, massing along the border.'

A tight smile from Venitt Sathad. 'The alliance we forged.'

'Indeed. Another of Letur Anict's brilliant schemes gone awry.'

'Hardly his exclusively, Orbyn. Your Patriotists were essential participants in that propaganda.'

'I wish I could deny that. And so we come to that single word, the one that filled my mind in the place of "honour". I find you here, in Drene. Venitt Sathad, understand me. I know what you do for your master, and I know just how well you do it. I know what even Karos Invictad does not – nor have I any interest in enlightening him. Regarding you, sir.'

'You wish to speak for yourself, now? Rather than the Patriotists?'

'To stay alive, yes.'

'Then the word is indeed not honour.'

Orbyn Truthfinder, the most feared man in Drene, drained his cup of wine. He leaned back. 'You sit here, amidst carnage. People hurry past and they see you, and though you are, in features and in stature, barely worth noting, notice you they do. And a chill grips their hearts, and they do not know why. But I do.'

'You comprehend, then, that I must pay Letur Anict a visit.'

'Yes, and I wish you well in that.'

'Unfortunately, Orbyn, we find ourselves in a moment of crisis. In the absence of Overseer Brohl Handar, it falls to Letur Anict to restore order. Yes, he may well fail, but he must be given the opportunity to succeed. For the sake of the empire, Orbyn, I expect you and your agents to assist the Factor in every way possible.'

'Of course. But I have lost thirty-one agents since yesterday. And those among them who had families . . . well, no-one was spared retribution.'

'It is a sad truth, Orbyn, that all who have been rewarded by tyranny must eventually share an identical fate.'

'You sound almost satisfied, Venitt.'

The Indebted servant of Rautos Hivanar permitted a faint smile to reach his lips as he reached for his cup of wine.

Orbyn's expression flattened. 'Surely,' he said, 'you do not believe a mob is capable of justice?'

'They have been rather restrained, thus far.'

'You cannot be serious.'

'Orbyn, not one Tiste Edur has been touched.'

'Because the rioters are not fools. Who dares face Edur sorcery? It was the very inactivity of the local Edur that incited the mobs to ever more vicious extremes – and I assure you, Letur Anict is well aware of that fact.'

'Ah, so he would blame the Tiste Edur for this mess. How convenient.'

'I am not here to defend the Factor, Venitt Sathad.'

'No, you are here to bargain for your life.'

'I will of course assist Letur Anict in restoring order. But I am not confident that he will succeed, and I will not throw away my people.'

'Actually, you will do just that.'

Orbyn's eyes widened. Sweat was now trickling down his face. His clothes were sticking patchily to the folds of fat beneath.

'Truthfinder,' Venitt Sathad continued, 'the Patriotists have outlived their usefulness, barring one last, most noble sacrifice. As the focus of the people's rage. I understand there is a Drene custom, something to do with the season of storms, and the making of seaweed fisher folk – life-sized dolls with shells for eyes, dressed in old clothes and the like. Sent out to mark the season's birth, I believe, in small boats. An offering to the sealords of old – for the storms to drown. Quaint and unsurprisingly bloodthirsty, as most old customs are. The Patriotists, Orbyn, must become Drene's seaweed fisher folk. We are in a season of storms, and sacrifices are necessary.'

Truthfinder licked his lips. 'And what of me?' he asked in a whisper.

'Ah, that particular session of bargaining is not yet complete.'

'I see.'

'I hope so.'

'Venitt Sathad, my agents – there are wives, husbands, children—'

'Yes, I am sure there are. Just as there were wives, husbands and children of all those you happily arrested, tortured and murdered all in the name of personal financial gain. The people, Orbyn, do understand redressing an imbalance.'

'This is as Rautos Hivanar demands—'

'My master leaves the specifics to me. He respects my record of . . . efficiency. While the authority he represents no doubt bolsters compliance, I rarely make overt use of it. By that I mean I rarely find the need. You said you know me, Truthfinder, did you not?'

'I know you, Venitt Sathad, for the man who found Gerun Eberict's murderer and sent that half-blood away with a chest full of coins. I know you for the killer of a hundred men and women at virtually every level of society, and, no matter how well protected, they die, and you emerge unscathed, your identity unknown—'

'Except, it seems, to you.'

'I stumbled onto your secret life, Venitt Sathad, many years ago. And I have followed your career, not just within the empire, but in the many consulates and embassies where your . . . skills . . . were needed. To advance Letherii interests. I am a great admirer, Venitt Sathad.'

'Yet now you seek to cast in the coin of your knowledge in order to purchase your life. Do you not comprehend the risk?'

'What choice do I have? By telling you all I know, I am also telling

627

you I have no illusions – I know why you are here, and what you need to do; indeed, my only surprise is that it has taken Rautos Hivanar so long to finally send you. In fact, it might be you have arrived too late, Venitt Sathad.'

To that, Venitt slowly nodded. Orbyn Truthfinder was a dangerous man. Yet, for the moment, still useful. As, alas, was Letur Anict. But such things were measured day by day, at times moment by moment. *Too late. You fool, Orbyn, even you have no real idea just how true that statement is – too late.*

Tehol Beddict played a small game, once, to see how it would work out. But this time – with that damned manservant of his – he has played a game on a scale almost beyond comprehension.

And I am Venitt Sathad. Indebted, born of Indebted, most skilled slave and assassin of Rautos Hivanar, and you, Tehol Beddict – and you, Bugg – need never fear me.

Take the bastards down. Every damned one of them. Take them all down.

It seemed Orbyn Truthfinder saw something in his expression then that drained all colour from the man's round, sweat-streamed face.

Venitt Sathad was amused. *Orbyn, have you found a truth?*

Scattered to either side of the dark storm front, grey clouds skidded across the sky, dragging slanting sheets of rain. The plains were greening along hillsides and in the troughs of valleys, a mottled patchwork of lichen, mosses and matted grasses. On the summit of a nearby hill was the carcass of a wild bhederin, hastily butchered after dying to a lightning strike. The beast's legs were sticking up into the air and on one hoof was perched a storm-bedraggled crow. Eviscerated entrails stretched out and down the slope facing Brohl Handar and his troop as they rode past.

The Awl were on the run. Warriors who had died of their wounds were left under heaps of stones, and they were as road-markers for the fleeing tribe, although in truth unnecessary since with the rains the trail was a broad swath of churned ground. In many ways, this uncharacteristic carelessness worried the Overseer, but perhaps it was as Bivatt had said: the unseasonal bank of storms that had rolled across the plains in the past three days had caught Redmask unprepared – there could be no hiding the passage of thousands of warriors, their families, and the herds that moved with them. That, and the bloody, disastrous battle at Praedegar had shown Redmask to be fallible; indeed, it was quite possible that the masked war leader was now struggling with incipient mutiny among his people.

They needed an end to this, and soon. The supply train out of Drene had been disrupted, the cause unknown. Bivatt had this day despatched a hundred Bluerose lancers onto their back-trail, seeking out those burdened wagons and their escort. Food shortage was imminent and no army, no matter how loyal and well trained, would fight on an empty stomach. Of course, bounteous feasts were just ahead – the herds of rodara and myrid. Battle needed to be joined. Redmask and his Awl needed to be destroyed.

A cloud scudded into their path with sleeting rain. Surprisingly cold for this late in the season. Brohl Handar and his Tiste Edur rode on, silent – this was not the rain of their homeland, nothing soft, gentle with mists. Here, the water lanced down, hard, and left one drenched in a score of heartbeats. *We are truly strangers here.*

But in that we are not alone.

They were finding odd cairns, bearing ghastly faces painted in white, and in the cracks and fissures of those tumuli there were peculiar offerings – tufts of wolf fur, teeth, the tusks from some unknown beast and antlers bearing rows of pecules and grooves. None of this was Awl – even the Awl scouts among Bivatt's army had never before seen the like.

Some wandering people from the eastern wastelands, perhaps, yet when Brohl had suggested that, the Atri-Preda had simply shaken her head. *She knows something. Another damned secret.*

They rode out of the rain, into steaming hot sunlight, the rich smell of soaked lichen and moss.

The broad swath of churned ground was on their right. To draw any closer was to catch the stench of manure and human faeces, a smell he had come to associate with desperation. *We fight our wars and leave in our wake the redolent reek of suffering and misery. These plains are vast, are they not? What terrible cost would we face if we just left each other alone? An end to this squabble over land – Father Shadow knows, no-one really owns it. The game of possession belongs to us, not to the rocks and earth, the grasses and the creatures walking the surface in their fraught struggle to survive.*

A bolt of lightning descends. A wild bhederin is struck and nearly explodes, as if life itself is too much to bear.

The world is harsh enough. It does not need our deliberate cruelties. Our celebration of viciousness.

His scout was returning at the gallop. Brohl Handar raised a hand to halt his troop.

The young warrior reined in with impressive grace. 'Overseer, they are on Q'uson Tapi. They did not go round it, sir – we have them!'

Q'uson Tapi, a name that was found only on the oldest Letherii maps; the words themselves were so archaic that even their meaning was unknown. The bed of a dead inland sea or vast salt lake. Flat, not a single rise or feature spanning leagues – or so the maps indicated. 'How far ahead is this Q'uson Tapi?'

The scout studied the sky, eyes narrowing on the sun to the west. 'We can reach it before dusk,' he said.

'And the Awl?'

'They were less than a league out from the old shoreline, Overseer. Where they go, there is no forage – the herds are doomed, as are the Awl themselves.'

'Has the rain reached Q'uson Tapi?'

'Not yet, but it will, and those clays will turn into slime – the great wagons will be useless against us.'

As will cavalry on both sides, I would wager.

'Ride back to the column,' Brohl Handar told the scout, 'and report to the Atri-Preda. We will await her at the old shoreline.'

A Letherii salute – yes, the younger Edur had taken quickly to such things – and the scout nudged his horse into motion.

Redmask, what have you done now?

Atri-Preda Bivatt had tried, for most of the day, to convince herself that what she had seen had been conjured from an exhausted, overwrought mind, the proclivity of the eye to find shapes in nothing, all in gleeful service to a trembling imagination. With dawn's light barely a hint in the air she had walked out, alone, to stand before a cairn – these strange constructions they now came across as they pushed ever further east. Demonic faces in white on the flatter sides of the huge boulders. Votive offerings on niches and between the roughly stacked stones.

They had pried apart one such cairn two days earlier, finding at its core . . . very little. A single flat stone on which rested a splintered fragment of weathered wood – seemingly accidental, but Bivatt knew differently. She could recall, long ago on the north shores, on a day of fierce seas crashing that coast, a row of war canoes, their prows dismantled – and the wood, the wood was as this, here in the centre of a cairn on the Awl'dan.

Standing before this new cairn, with dawn attempting to crawl skyward as grey sheets of rain hammered down, she had happened to glance up. And saw – a darker grey, man-shaped yet huge, twenty, thirty paces away. Solitary, motionless, watching her. The blood in her veins lost all heat and all at once the rain was as cold as those thrashing seas on the north coast years past.

A gust of wind, momentarily making the wall of water opaque, and when it had passed, the figure was gone.

Alas, the chill would not leave her, the sense of gauging, almost unhuman regard.

A ghost. A shape cast by her mind, a trick of the rain and wind and dawn's uncertain birth. *But no, he was there. Watching. The maker of the cairns.*

Redmask. Myself. The Awl and the Letherii and Tiste Edur, here we duel on this plain. Assuming we are alone in this deadly game. Witnessed by naught but carrion birds, coyotes and the antelope grazing on the valley floors that watch us pass by day after day.

But we are not alone.

The thought frightened her, in a deep, childlike way – the fear born in a mind too young to cast anything away, be it dreams, nightmares, terrors or dread of all that was for ever unknowable. She felt no different now.

There were thousands. There must have been. How, then, could they hide? How could they have hidden for so long, all this time, invisible to us, invisible to the Awl?

Unless Redmask knows. And now, working in league with the strangers from the sea, they prepare an ambush. Our annihilation.

She was right to be frightened.

There would be one more battle. Neither side had anything left for more than that. And, barring more appalling displays of murderous skill from the mage-killer, Letherii sorcery would achieve victory. Brohl Handar's scout had returned with the stunning news that Redmask had led his people out onto Q'uson Tapi, and there would be no negation of magic on the flat floor of a dead sea. *Redmask forces the issue. Once we clash on Q'uson Tapi, our fates will be decided. No more fleeing, no more ambushes – even those Kechra will have nowhere to hide.*

Errant, heed me please. If you are indeed the god of the Letherii, deliver no surprises on that day. Please. Give us victory.

The column marched on, towards the ancient shore of a dead sea. Clouds were gathering on the horizon ahead. Rain was thrashing down on that salt-crusted bed of clay and silt. They would fight in a quagmire, where cavalry was useless, where no horse would be quick enough to outrun a wave of deadly magic. Where warriors and soldiers would lock weapons and die where they stood, until one side stood alone, triumphant.

Soon now, they would have done with it. Done with it all.

Since noon Redmask had driven his people hard, out onto the seabed, racing ahead of the rain-clouds. A league, then two, beneath searing sun and air growing febrile with the coming storm. He had then called a halt, but the activity did not cease, and Toc Anaster had watched, bemused at first and then in growing wonder and, finally, admiration, as the Awl warriors set down weapons, divested themselves of their armour, and joined with the elders and every other non-combatant in pulling free from the wagons the tents and every stretch of hide they could find.

And the wagons themselves were taken apart, broken down until virtually nothing remained but the huge wheels and their axles, which were then used to transport the planks of wood. Hide and canvas were stretched out, pegged down, the stakes driven flush with the ground itself. Wooden walkways were constructed, each leading back to a single, centrally positioned wagon-bed that had been left intact and raised on legs of bundled spear-shafts to create a platform.

The canvas and hides stretched in rows, with squares behind each row, linked by flattened wicker walls that had been used for hut-frames. But no-one would sleep under cover this night. No, all that took shape here served but one purpose – the coming battle. *The final battle.*

Redmask intended a defence. He invited Bivatt and her army to close with him, and to do so the Letherii and the Tiste Edur would need to march across open ground – Toc sat astride his horse, watching the frenzied preparations and occasionally glancing northwestward, to those closing stormclouds – open ground, then, that would be a sea of mud.

She might decide to wait. *I would, if I were her.* Wait until the rains had passed, until the ground hardened once again. But Toc suspected that she would not exercise such restraint. Redmask was trapped, true, but the Awl had their herds – thousands of beasts most of whom were now being slaughtered – so, Redmask could wait, his warriors well fed, whilst Bivatt and her army faced the threat of real starvation. She would need all that butchered meat, but to get to it she had to go through the Awl; she had to destroy her hated enemy.

Besides, she might be less dismayed than Redmask would think, come the day of battle. She has her mages, after all. Not as many as before, true, but still posing a significant threat – sufficient to win the day, in fact.

Redmask would have his warriors standing on those islands of dry ground. But such positions – with reserves on the squares behind them – offered no avenue of retreat. A final battle, then, the fates decided one way or the other. Was this what Redmask had planned? *Hardly. Praedegar was a disaster.*

Torrent rode up. No mask of paint again, a swath of red hives spanning his forehead. 'The sea will live once more,' he said.

'Hardly,' Toc replied.

'The Letherii will drown nonetheless.'

'Those tarps, Torrent, will not stay dry for long. And then there are the mages.'

'Redmask has his Guardians for those cowards.'

'Cowards?' Toc asked, amused. 'Because they wield sorcery instead of swords?'

'And hide behind rows of soldiers, yes. They care nothing for glory. For honour.'

'True: the only thing they care about is winning. Leaving them free to talk about honour and glory afterwards. The chief spoil of the victors, that privilege.'

'You speak like one of them, Mezla. That is why I do not trust you, and so I will remain at your side during the battle.'

'My heart goes out to you – I am tasked with guarding the children, after all. We'll be nowhere close to the fighting.' *Until the fighting comes to us, which it will.*

'I shall find my glory in slitting your miserable throat, Mezla, the moment you turn to run. I see the weakness in your soul; I have seen it all along. You are broken. You should have died with your soldiers.'

'Probably. At least then I'd be spared the judgements of someone with barely a whisker on his spotty chin. Have you even lain with a woman yet, Torrent?'

The young warrior glowered for a moment, then slowly nodded. 'It is said you are quick with your barbed arrows, Mezla.'

'A metaphor, Torrent? I'm surprised at this turn to the poetic.'

'You have not listened to our songs, have you? You have made yourself deaf to the beauty of the Awl, and in your deafness you have blinded that last eye left to you. We are an ancient people, Mezla.'

'Deaf, blind, too bad I'm not yet mute.'

'You will be when I slit your throat.'

Well, Toc conceded, he had a point there.

Redmask had waited for this a long time. And no old man of the Renfayar with his damned secrets would stand poised to shatter everything. No, with his own hands Redmask had taken care of that, and he could still see in his mind that elder's face, the bulging eyes, vessels bursting, the jutting tongue as the lined face turned blue, then a deathly shade of grey above his squeezing hands. That throat had been as nothing, thin as a reed, the cartilage crumpling like a papyrus scroll in his grip. And he had found himself unable to let go, long after the fool was dead.

Too many memories of his childhood had slithered into his hands, transforming his fingers into coiling serpents that seemed not satisfied with lifeless flesh in their grip, but sought that touch of cold that came long after the soul's flight. Of course, there had been more to it than that. The elder had imagined himself Redmask's master, his overseer to use the Letherii word, standing at the war leader's shoulder, ever ready to draw breath and loose words that held terrible truths, truths that would destroy Redmask, would destroy any chance he had of leading the Awl to victory.

Yet now the time drew near. He would see Bivatt's head on a spear. He would see mud and Letherii and Tiste Edur corpses in their thousands. Crows wheeling overhead, voicing delighted cries. And he would stand on the wooden platform, witness to it all. To his scaled Guardians, who had found him, had chosen him, rending mages limb from limb, scything through enemy lines—

And the face of the elder rose once more in his mind. He had revelled in that vision, at first, but now it had begun to haunt him. A face to greet his dreams; a face hinted at in every smear of stormcloud, the bruised grey and blue hues cold as iron filling the sky. He had thought himself rid of that fool and his cruel secrets, in that weighing look – like a father's regard on a wayward son, as if nothing the child did could be good enough, could be *Awl* in the ways of the people as they had been and would always be.

As the work continued on all sides, Redmask mounted the platform. Cadaran whip at his belt. Rygtha axe slung from its leather straps. *The weapons we were once born to, long ago. Is that not Awl enough? Am I not more Awl than any other among the Renfayar? Among the warriors gathered here? Do not look so at me, old man. You have not the right. You were never the man I have become – look at my Guardians!*

Shall I tell you the tale, Father?

But no. You are dead. And I feel still your feeble neck in my hands – ah, an error. That detail belongs to the old man. Who died mysteriously in his tent. Last of the Renfayar elders, who knew, yes, knew well my father and all his kin, and the children they called their own.

Fool, why did you not let the years blur your memories? Why did you not become like any other doddering, hopeless ancient? What kept your eyes honed so sharp? But no longer, yes. Now you stare at stone and darkness. Now that sharp mind rots in its skull, and that is that.

Leave me be.

The first spatters of rain struck him and he looked up at the sky. Hard drops, bursting against his mask, this scaled armour hiding dread truth. *I am immune. I cannot be touched. Tomorrow, we shall destroy the enemy.*

The Guardians will see to that. They chose me, did they not? Theirs is the gift of glory, and none but me has earned such a thing.

By the lizard eyes of the K'Chain Che'Malle, I will have my victory.

The deaf drummer began his arrhythmic thunder deep within the stormclouds, and the spirits of the Awl, glaring downward to the earth, began drawing their jagged swords.

CHAPTER TWENTY

We live in waiting
For this most precious thing:
Our god with clear eyes
Who walks into the waste
Of our lives
With the bound straw
Of a broom
And with a bright smile
This god brushes into a corner
Our mess of crimes
the ragged expostulations
We spit out on the morn
With each sun's rise

We live in waiting, yes
In precious abeyance
Cold-eyed our virtues
Sowing the seeds of waste
In life's hot earth
In hand the gelid iron
Of weapons
And with bright recompense
We soak this ground
Under the clear sky
With the blood of our god
Spat out and heaved
In rigour'd disgust

Our Waiting God
Cormor Fural

TOWERS AND BRIDGES, SKELETALLY THIN AND NOWHERE THE SIGN OF guiding hands, of intelligence or focused will. These constructs, reaching high towards the so-faint bloom of light, were entirely natural, rough of line and raw in their bony elegance. To wander their spindly feet was to overwhelm every sense of proportion, of the ways the world was supposed to look. There was no air, only water. No light, only the glow of some unnatural gift of spiritual vision. Revealing these towers and arching bridges, so tall, so thin, that they seemed but moments from toppling into the fierce, swirling currents.

Bruthen Trana, tugged loose from the flesh and bone that had been home to his entire existence, now wandered lost at the bottom of an ocean. He had not expected this. Visions and prophecies had failed them; failed Hannan Mosag especially. Bruthen had suspected that his journey would find him in a strange, unanticipated place, a realm, perhaps, of myth. A realm peopled by gods and demons, by sentinels defending long-dead demesnes with immortal stolidity.

'Where the sun's light will not reach.' Perhaps his memory was not perfect, but that had been the gist of that fell prophecy. And he was but a warrior of the Tiste Edur – now a warrior bereft of flesh beyond what his spirit insisted out of some wilful stubbornness, as obstinate in its conceits as any sentinel.

And so now he walked, and he could look down upon his limbs, his body; he could reach up and touch his face, feel his hair – now unbound – sweeping out on the current like strands of seaweed. He could feel the cold of the water, could feel even the immense pressure besieging him in this dark world. But there were no paths, no road, no obvious trail wending around these stone edifices.

The rotted wood of ship timbers burst into clouds beneath his feet. Clotted rivets turned underfoot. Fragments that might be bone skittered and danced along the muddy bottom, carried every which way by the currents. Dissolution seemed to be the curse of the world, of all the worlds. All that broke, all that failed, wandered down to some final resting place, lost to darkness, and this went beyond ships on the sea and the lives on those ships. Whales, dhenrabi, the tiniest crustacean. Plans, schemes and grandiose visions. Love, faith and honour. Ambition, lust and malice. He could reach down and scoop it all into his hands, watching the water tug it away, fling it out into a swirling, momentary path of glittering glory, then gone once more.

Perhaps this was the truth he had been meant to see, assuming the presumption of his worthiness, of course – which was proving a struggle to maintain indeed. Instead, waves of despair swept over him, swept through him, spun wild out of his own soul.

He was lost.

What am I looking for? Who am I looking for? I have forgotten. Is this a curse? Am I dead and now wandering doomed? Will these towers topple and crush me, leave me yet one more broken, mangled thing in the muck and silt?

I am Tiste Edur. This much I know. My true body is gone, perhaps for ever.

And something, some force of instinct, was driving him on, step by step. There was a goal, a thing to be achieved. He would find it. He had to find it. It had to do with Hannan Mosag, who had sent him here – he did recall that, along with the faint echoes of prophecy.

Yet he felt like a child, trapped in a dream that was an endless search for a familiar face, for his mother, who was out there, unmindful of his plight, and indifferent to it had she known – for that was the heart of such fearful dreams – a heart where love is revealed to be necrotic, a lie, the deepest betrayal possible. Bruthen Trana understood these fears for what they were, for the weakness they revealed, even as he felt helpless against them.

Wandering onward, leaving, at last, those dread monuments in his wake. He might have wept for a time, although of course he could not feel his own tears – they were one with the sea around him – but he voiced muted cries, enough to make his throat raw. And at times he staggered, fell, hands plunging deep into the muck, and struggled to regain his feet, buffeted by the currents.

All of this seemed to go on for a long time.

Until something loomed out of the darkness ahead. Blockish, heaped on one side with what seemed to be detritus – drifts of wreckage, tree branches and the like. Bruthen Trana stumbled closer, trying to make sense of what he was seeing.

A house. Enclosed by a low wall of the same black stone. Dead trees in the yard, their trunks thick, stubby, each rising from a root-heaved mound. A snaking path leading to three sagging, saddled steps and a recessed, narrow door. To either side of this entrance there were square windows, shuttered in strips of slate. To the right, forming a rounded corner, rose a squat, flat-topped tower. A small corniced window at the upper level was lit from within with a dull yellow glow, fitful, wavering.

A house. On the floor of the ocean.

And someone is home.

Bruthen Trana found himself standing before the gate, his eyes on the snaking path of pavestones leading to the steps. He could see blooms of silts rising from the mounds to either side, as if the mud was seething with worms. Closer now to the house, he noted the thick green slime bearding the walls, and the prevailing current – which had heaped up rubbish against one side – had done its work on the ground there as well, uprooting one of the dead trees and sculpting out the mound until it was no more than a scatter of barnacled boulders. The tree leaned against the house with unyielding branches from which algae streamed and swirled against the backwash of the current.

This is not what I seek. He knew that with sudden certainty. And yet ... he glanced up once more at the tower, in time to see the light dim, as if withdrawing, then vanish.

Bruthen Trana walked onto the path.

The current seemed fiercer here, as if eager to push him off the trail, and some instinct told the Tiste Edur that losing his footing in this yard would be a bad thing. Hunching down, he pushed on.

Upon reaching the steps, Bruthen Trana was buffeted by a sudden roil of the current and he looked up to see that the door had opened. And in the threshold stood a most extraordinary figure. As tall as the Tiste Edur, yet so thin as to seem emaciated. Bone-white flesh, thin and loose, a long, narrow face, seamed with a mass of wrinkles. The eyes were pale grey, surrounding vertical pupils.

The man wore rotted, colourless silks that hid little, including the extra joints on his arms and legs, and what seemed to be a sternum horizontally hinged in the middle. The ripple of too many ribs, a set of lesser collarbones beneath the others. His hair – little more than wisps on a mottled pate – stirred like cobwebs. In one lifted hand the man held a lantern in which sat a stone that burned with golden fire.

The voice that spoke in Bruthen Trana's mind was strangely childlike. 'Is this the night for spirits?'

'Is it night then?' Bruthen Trana asked.

'Isn't it?'

'I don't know.'

'Well,' the figure replied with a smile, 'neither do I. Will you join us? The house has not had a guest for a long time.'

'I am not for this place,' Bruthen Trana said, uncertain. 'I think . . .'

'You are correct, but the repast is timely. Besides, some current must have brought you here. It is not as if just any old spirit can find the house. You have been led here, friend.'

'Why? By whom?'

'The house, of course. As to why,' the man shrugged, then stepped back and gestured. 'Join us, please. There is wine, suitably . . . dry.'

Bruthen Trana ascended the steps, and crossed the threshold.

The door closed of its own accord behind him. They were in a narrow hallway, directly ahead a T-intersection.

'I am Bruthen Trana, a Tiste Edur of—'

'Yes, yes, indeed. The Empire of the Crippled God. Well, one of them, anyway. An Emperor in chains, a people in thrall' – a quick glance over the shoulder as the man led him into the corridor to the right – 'that would be you, Edur, not the Letherii, who are in thrall to a far crueller master.'

'Coin.'

'Well done. Yes.'

They halted before a door set in a curved wall.

'This leads to the tower,' Bruthen Trana said. 'Where I first saw your light.'

'Indeed. It is, alas, the only room large enough to accommodate my guest. Oh,' he stepped closer, 'before we go in, I must warn you of some things. My guest possesses a weakness – but then, don't we all? In any case, it has fallen to me to, uh, celebrate that weakness – now, yes, soon it will end, as all things do – but not quite yet. Thus, you must not distract my dear guest from the distraction I already provide. Do you understand me?'

'Perhaps I should not enter at all, then.'

'Nonsense. It is this, Bruthen Trana. You must not speak of *dragons*. No dragons, do you understand?'

The Tiste Edur shrugged. 'That topic had not even occurred to me—'

'Oh, but in a way it has, and continues to do so. The spirit of Emurlahnis. Scabandari. Father Shadow. This haunts you, as it does all the Tiste Edur. The matter is delicate, you see. Very delicate, for both you and my guest. I must needs rely upon your restraint, or there will be trouble. Calamity, in fact.'

'I shall do my best, sir. A moment – what is your name?'

The man reached for the latch. 'My name is for no-one, Bruthen Trana. Best know me by one of my many titles. The Letherii one will do. You may call me Knuckles.'

He lifted the latch and pushed open the door.

Within was a vast circular chamber – far too large for the modest tower's wall that Bruthen Trana had seen from outside. Whatever ceiling existed was lost in the gloom. The stone-tiled floor was fifty or more paces across. As Knuckles stepped inside, the glow from his lantern burgeoned, driving back the shadows. Opposite them, abutting the curved wall, was a raised dais on which heaps of silks, pillows and furs were scattered; and seated at the edge of that dais, leaning forward with forearms resting on thighs, was a giant. An ogre or some such demon, bearing the same hue of skin as Knuckles yet stretched over huge muscles and a robust frame of squat bones. The hands dangling down over the knees were disproportionately oversized even for that enormous body. Long, unkempt hair hung down to frame a heavy-featured face with deep-set eyes – so deep that even the lantern's light could spark but a glimmer in those ridge-shelved pits.

'My guest,' Knuckles murmured. 'Kilmandaros. Most gentle, I assure you, Bruthen Trana. When . . . distracted. Come, she is eager to meet you.'

639

They approached, footfalls echoing in this waterless chamber. Knuckles shifted his route slightly towards a low marble table on which sat a dusty bottle of wine. 'Beloved,' he called to Kilmandaros, 'see who the house has brought to us!'

'Stuff it with food and drink and send it on its way,' the huge woman said in a growl. 'I am on the trail of a solution, scrawny whelp of mine.'

Bruthen Trana could now see, scattered on the tiles before Kilmandaros, a profusion of small bones, each incised in patterns on every available surface. They seemed arrayed without order, nothing more than rubbish spilled out from some bag, yet Kilmandaros was frowning down at them with savage concentration.

'The solution,' she repeated.

'How exciting,' Knuckles said, procuring from somewhere a third goblet into which he poured amber wine. 'Double or nothing, then?'

'Oh yes, why not? But you owe me the treasuries of a hundred thousand empires already, dear Setch—'

'Knuckles, my love.'

'Dear Knuckles.'

'I am certain it is you who owes me, Mother.'

'For but a moment longer,' she replied, now rubbing those huge hands together. 'I am so close. You were a fool to offer double or nothing.'

'Ah, my weakness,' Knuckles sighed as he walked over to Bruthen Trana with the goblet. Meeting the Tiste Edur's eyes, Knuckles winked. 'The grains run the river, Mother,' he said. 'Best hurry with your solution.'

A fist thundered on the dais. 'Do not make me nervous!'

The echoes of that impact were long in fading.

Kilmandaros leaned still further, glowering down at the array of bones. 'The pattern,' she whispered, 'yes, almost there. Almost . . .'

'I feel magnanimous,' Knuckles said, 'and offer to still those grains . . . for a time. So that we may be true hosts to our new guest.'

The giant woman looked up, a sudden cunning in her expression. 'Excellent idea, Knuckles. Make it so!'

A gesture, and the wavering light of the lantern ceased its waver. All was still in a way Bruthen Trana could not define – after all, nothing had changed. And yet his soul knew, somehow, that the grains Knuckles had spoken of were *time*, its passage, its unending journey. He had just, with a single gesture of one hand, stopped time.

At least in this chamber. Surely not everywhere else. And yet . . .

Kilmandaros leaned back with a satisfied smirk and fixed her small eyes on Bruthen Trana. 'I see,' she said. 'The house anticipates.'

'We are as flitting dreams to the Azath,' Knuckles said. 'Yet, even though we are but momentary conceits, as our sorry existence might well be defined, we have our uses.'

'Some of us,' Kilmandaros said, suddenly dismissive, 'prove more useful than others. This Tiste Edur' – a wave of one huge, scarred hand – 'is of modest value by any measure.'

'The Azath see what we do not, in each of us. Perhaps, Mother, in *all* of us.'

A sour grunt. 'You think this house let me go of its own will – proof of your gullibility, Knuckles. Not even the Azath could hold me for ever.'

'Extraordinary,' Knuckles said, 'that it held you at all.'

This exchange, Bruthen Trana realized, was an old one, following well-worn ruts between the two.

'Would never have happened,' Kilmandaros said under her breath, 'if he'd not betrayed me—'

'Ah, Mother. I have no particular love for Anomander Purake, but let us be fair here. He did not betray you. In fact, it was *you* who jumped *him* from behind—'

'Anticipating his betrayal!'

'Anomander does not break his word, Mother. Never has, never will.'

'Tell that to Osserc—'

'Also in the habit of "anticipating" Anomander's imminent betrayal.'

'What of Draconus?'

'What of him, Mother?'

Kilmandaros rumbled something then, too low for Bruthen Trana to catch.

Knuckles said, 'Our Tiste Edur guest seeks the place of Names.'

Bruthen Trana started. *Yes!* It was true – a truth he had not even known before just this moment, before Knuckle's quiet words. *The place of Names. The Names of the Gods.*

'There will be trouble, then,' Kilmandaros said, shifting in agitation, her gaze drawn again and again to the scatter of bones. 'He must remember this house, then. The path – every step – he must remember, or he will wander lost for all time. And with him, just as lost as they have ever been, the names of every forgotten god.'

'His spirit is strong,' Knuckles said, then faced Bruthen Trana and smiled. 'Your spirit is strong. Forgive me – we often forget entirely the outside world, even when, on rare occasions such as this one, that world *intrudes*.'

The Tiste Edur shrugged. His head was spinning. *The place of Names.* 'What will I find there?' he asked.

'He forgets already,' Kilmandaros muttered.

'The path,' Knuckles answered. 'More than that, actually. But when all is done – for you, in that place – you must recall the path, Bruthen Trana, and you must walk it without a sliver of doubt.'

'But, Knuckles, all my life, I have walked no path without a sliver of doubt – more than a sliver, in fact—'

'Surprising,' Kilmandaros cut in, 'for a child of Scabandari—'

'I must begin the grains again,' Knuckles suddenly announced. 'Into the river – the pattern, Mother, it calls to you once more.'

She swore in some unknown language, bent to scowl down at the bones. 'I was there,' she muttered. 'Almost there – so close , so—'

A faint chime echoed in the chamber.

Her fist thundered again on the dais, and this time the echoes seemed unending.

At a modest signal from Knuckles, Bruthen Trana drained the fine wine and set the goblet down on the marble tabletop.

It was time to leave.

Knuckles led Bruthen Trana back into the corridor. A final glance back into that airy chamber and the Tiste Edur saw Kilmandaros, hands on knees, staring directly at him with those faintly glittering eyes, like two lone, dying stars in the firmament. Chilled to the depths of his heart, Bruthen Trana pulled his gaze away and followed the son of Kilmandaros back to the front door.

At the threshold, he paused for a moment to search Knuckles's face. 'The game you play with her – tell me, does such a pattern exist?'

Brows arched. 'In the casting of bones? Damned if I know.' A sudden smile, then. 'Our kind, ah, but we *love* patterns.'

'Even if they don't exist?'

'Don't they?' The smile grew mischievous. 'Go, Bruthen Trana, and mind the path. Always mind the path.'

The Tiste Edur walked down onto the pavestones. 'I would,' he muttered, 'could I find it.'

Forty paces from the house, he turned to look upon it, and saw nothing but swirling currents, spinning silts in funnels.

Gone. As if I had imagined the entire thing.

But I was warned, wasn't I? Something about a path.

'Remember . . .'

Lost. Again. Memories tugged free, snatched away by the ferocious winds of water.

He swung round again and set off, staggering, step by step, towards something he could not dredge up from his mind, could not even imagine. Was this where life ended? In some hopeless quest, some eternal search for a lost dream?

Remember the path. Oh, Father Shadow, remember . . . something. Anything.

*

642

Where the huge chunks of ice had been, there were now stands of young trees. Alder, aspen, dogwood, forming a tangled fringe surrounding the dead Meckros City. Beyond the trees were the grasses of the plains, among them deep-rooted bluestems and red-lipped poppies that cloaked the burial mounds where resided the bones of thousands of people.

The wreckage of buildings still stood here and there on their massive pylons of wood, while others had tilted, then toppled, spilling out their contents onto canted streets. Weeds and shrubs now grew everywhere, dotting the enormous, sprawling ruin, and among the broken bones of buildings lay a scatter of flowers, a profusion of colours on all sides.

He stood, balanced on a fallen pillar of dusty marble allowing him a view of the vista, the city stretching to his left, the ragged edge and green-leafed trees with the mounds beyond on his right. His eyes, a fiery amber, were fixed on something on the far horizon directly ahead. His broad mouth held its habitual downturn at the corners, an expression that seemed ever at war with the blazing joy within his eyes. *His mother's eyes*, it was said. But somehow less fierce and this, perhaps, was born of his father's uneasy gift – a mouth that did not expect to smile, ever.

His second father, his true father. The thread of blood. The one who had visited in his seventh week of life. Yes, while it had been a man named Araq Elalle who had raised him, whilst he lived in the Meckros City, it had been the other – the stranger in the company of a yellow-haired bonecaster – who had given his seed to Menandore, Rud Elalle's mother. His Imass minders had not been blind to such truths, and oh how Menandore had railed at them afterwards.

'*I took all that I needed from Udinaas! And left him a husk and nothing more. He can never sire another child – a husk! A useless mortal – forget him, my son. He is nothing.*' And from the terrible demand in her blazing eyes, her son had recoiled.

Rud Elalle was tall now, half a hand taller than even his mother. His hair, long and wild in the fashion of the Bentract Imass warriors, was a sun-bleached brown. He wore a cloak of ranag hide, deep brown and amber-tipped the fur. Beneath that was a supple leather shirt of deer-skin. His leggings were of thicker, tougher allish hide. On his feet were ranag leather moccasins that reached to just below his knees.

A scar ran down the right side of his neck, gift of a boar's dying lunge. The bones of his left wrist had been broken and were now mis-aligned, the places of the breaks knotted protrusions bound in thick sinews, but the arm had not been weakened by this; indeed, it was now stronger than its opposite. Menandore's gift, that strange response to any injury, as if his body sought to armour itself against any chance of the same injury's recurring. There had been other breaks, other wounds

– life among the Imass was hard, and though they would have protected him from its rigour, he would not permit that. He was among the Bentract, he was of the Bentract. Here, with these wondrous people, he had found love and fellowship. He would live as they lived, for as long as he could.

Yet, alas, he felt now . . . that time was coming to an end. His eyes remained fixed on that distant horizon, even as he sensed her arrival, now at his side. 'Mother,' he said.

'Imass,' she said. 'Speak our own language, my son. Speak the language of dragons.'

Faint distaste soured Rud Elalle. 'We are not Eleint, Mother. That blood is stolen. Impure—'

'We are no less children of Starvald Demelain. I do not know who has filled your mind with these doubts. But they are weaknesses, and now is not the time.'

'Now is not the time,' he repeated.

She snorted. 'My sisters.'

'Yes.'

'They want me. They want him. Yet, in both schemes, they have not counted you a threat, my son. Oh, they know you are grown now. They know the power within you. But they know nothing of your will.'

'Nor, Mother, do you.'

He heard her catch her breath, was inwardly amused at the suddenly crowded silence that followed.

He nodded to the far horizon, 'Do you see them, Mother?'

'Unimportant. Mayhap they will survive, but I would not wager upon it. Understand me, Rud, with what is to come, not one of us is safe. Not one. You, me, your precious Bentract—'

He turned at that, and his eyes were all at once a mirror of his mother's – bright with rage and menace.

She very nearly flinched, and he saw that and was pleased. 'I will permit no harm to come to them, Mother. You wish to understand my will. Now you do.'

'Foolish. No, insanity. They are not even alive—'

'In their minds, they are. In my mind, Mother, they are.'

She sneered. 'Do the new ones now among the Bentract hold to such noble faith, Rud? Have you not seen their disdain? Their contempt for their own deluded kin? It is only a matter of time before one of them speaks true – shattering the illusion for all time—'

'They will not,' Rud said, once more eyeing the distant party of wanderers who were now, without question, approaching the ruined city. 'You do not visit often enough,' he said. 'Disdain and contempt, yes, but now, too, you will see fear.'

'Of you? Oh, my son, you fool! And do your adopted kin know to guard your back against them? Of course not, for that would reveal too much, would invite awkward questions – and the Imass are not ones to be easily turned away when seeking truth.'

'My back will be guarded,' Rud said.

'By whom?'

'Not you, Mother?'

She hissed in a most reptilian manner. 'When? While my sisters are busy trying to kill me? When he has the Finnest in his hand and casts eyes upon all of us?'

'If not you,' he said easily, 'then someone else.'

'Wiser to kill the newcomers now, Rud.'

'And my kin would have no questions then?'

'None but you alive to answer, and you of course may tell them anything you care to. Kill those new Imass, those strangers with their sly regard, and be quick about it.'

'I think not.'

'Kill them, or I will.'

'No, Mother. The Imass are mine. Shed blood among my people – any of them – and you will stand alone the day Sukul and Sheltatha arrive, the day of Silchas Ruin who comes to claim the Finnest.' He glanced across at her. Could white skin grow still paler? 'Yes, all in a single day. I have been to the Twelve Gates – maintaining my vigil as you have asked.'

'And?' The query was almost breathless.

'Kurald Galain is most perturbed.'

'They draw close?'

'You know that as well as I do – my father is with them, is he not? You steal his eyes when it suits you—'

'Not as easy as you think.' Her tone was genuine in its bitterness. 'He . . . baffles me.'

Frightens you, you mean. 'Silchas Ruin will demand the Finnest.'

'Yes, he will! And we both know what he will do with it – *and that must not be permitted!*'

Are you sure of that, Mother? Because, you see, I am not. Not any more. 'Silchas Ruin may well demand. He may well make dire threats, Mother. You have said so often enough.'

'And if we stand side by side, my son, he cannot hope to get past us.'

'Yes.'

'*But who will be guarding your back?*'

'Enough, Mother. I warned them to silence and I do not think they will attempt anything. Call it faith – not in the measure of their fear. Instead, my faith rests in the measure of . . . wonder.'

She stared at him, clearly confused.

He felt no inclination to elaborate. She would see, in time. 'I would go to welcome these new ones,' he said, eyes returning to the approaching strangers. 'Will you join me, Menandore?'

'You must be mad.' Words filled with affection – yes, she could never rail at him for very long. Something of his father's ethereal ease, perhaps – an ease even Rud himself could remember from that single, short visit. An ease that would slip over the Letherii's regular, unimpressive features, whenever the wave of pain, dismay – or indeed any harsh emotion – was past and gone, leaving not a ripple in its wake.

That ease, Rud now understood, was the true face of Udinaas. The face of his soul.

Father, I do so look forward to seeing you again.

His mother was gone – at least from his side. At a sudden gust of wind Rud Elalle glanced up and saw the white and gold mass of her dragon form, lurching skyward with every heave of the huge wings.

The strangers had all halted, still three hundred paces away, and were staring up, now, as Menandore lunged yet higher, slid across currents of air for a moment, until she faced them, and then swept down, straight for the small party. Oh, how she loved to intimidate lesser beings.

What happened then without doubt surprised Menandore more than even Rud – who gave an involuntary shout of surprise as two feline shapes launched into the air from the midst of the party. Dog-sized, forelegs lashing upward as Rud's mother sailed overhead – and she snapped her hind legs up tight against her belly in instinctive alarm, even as a thundering beat of her wings lifted her out of harm's way. At sight of her neck twisting round, eyes flashing in an outraged glare – indignant indeed – Rud Elalle laughed, and was satisfied to see that the sound reached his mother, enough to draw her glare and hold it, until the dragon's momentum carried her well past the strangers and their defiant pets, out of the moment when she might have banked hard, jaws hingeing open to unleash deadly magic down on the obstreperous emlava and their masters.

The threat's balance tilted away – as Rud had sought with that barking laugh – and on she flew, dismissing all in her wake, including her son.

And, were it in his nature, he would then have smiled. For he knew his mother was smiling, now. Delighted to have so amused her only son, her child who, like any Imass, saved his laughter for the wounds his body received in the ferocious games of living. And even her doubts, etched in by this conversation just past, would smooth themselves over for a time.

A little time. When they returned, Rud also knew, they would sting like fire. But by then, it would be too late. *More or less.*

He climbed down from the toppled column. It was time to meet the strangers.

'That,' Hedge announced, 'is no Imass. Unless they breed 'em big round here.'

'Not kin,' Onrack observed with narrowed eyes.

Hedge's ghostly heart was still pounding hard in his ghostly chest in the wake of that damned dragon. If it hadn't been for the emlava cubs and their brainless lack of fear, things might well have got messy. A cusser in Hedge's left hand. Quick Ben with a dozen snarly warrens he might well have let loose all at once. Trull Sengar and his damned spears – *aye, dragon steaks raining down from the sky.*

Unless she got us first.

No matter, the moment had passed, and he was thankful for that. 'Maybe he's no kin, Onrack, but he dresses like an Imass, and those are stone chips at the business end of that bone club he's carrying.' Hedge glanced across at Quick Ben – feeling once again the surge of delight upon seeing a familiar face, the face of a friend – and said, 'I wish Fid was here, because just looking at that man has the hairs standing on the back of my neck.'

'If you've already got a bad feeling about this,' the wizard replied, 'why do you need Fid?'

'Confirmation, is why. The bastard was talking to a woman, who then veered into a dragon and thought to give us a scare. Anybody keeping scaly company makes me nervous.'

'Onrack,' said Trull Sengar as the man drew closer, walking with a casual, almost loose stride, 'I think we approach the place where Cotillion wanted us to be.'

At that, Hedge scowled. 'Speaking of scaly – dealing with Shadowthrone's lackey makes all this stink even worse—'

'Leaving once more unspoken the explanation for what you're doing here, Hedge,' the Tiste Edur replied with a faint smile at the sapper – that damned smile, so bloody disarming that Hedge almost spilled out every secret in his head, just to see that smile grow into something more welcoming. Trull Sengar was like that, inviting friendship and camaraderie like the sweet scent of a flower – probably a poisonous one – *but that might be just me. My usual paranoia. Well earned, mind. Still, there doesn't seem to be anything poisonous about Trull Sengar.*

It's just that I don't trust nice people. There, it's said – at least here in my head. And no, I don't need any Hood-kissed reason either. He stepped too close to one of the emlava cubs and had to dance away to avoid lashing talons. He glared at the hissing creature. 'Your hide's mine, you know that? Mine, kitty. Take good care of it in the meantime.'

The eyes burned up at him, and the emlava cub opened wide its jaws to loose yet another whispering hiss.

Damn, those fangs are getting long.

Onrack had moved out ahead, and now the Imass stopped. Moments later they had all drawn up to stand a few paces behind him.

The tall, wild-haired warrior walked closer. Five paces from Onrack he halted, smiled and said something in some guttural language.

Onrack cocked his head. 'He speaks Imass.'

'Not Malazan?' Hedge asked with mock incredulity. 'What's wrong with the damned fool?'

The man's smile broadened, those amber nugget eyes fixing on Hedge, and in Malazan he said, 'All the children of the Imass tongue are as poetry to this damned fool. As are the languages of the Tiste,' he added, gaze shifting to Trull Sengar. Then he spread his hands out to the sides, palms exposed. 'I am Rud Elalle, raised among the Bentract Imass as a child of their own.'

Onrack said, 'They have yet to show themselves, Rud Elalle. This is not the welcome I expected from kin.'

'You have been watched, yes, for some time. Many clans. Ulshun Pral sent out word that none were to block your path.' Rud Elalle looked down at the tethered cubs to either side of Trull Sengar. 'The ay flee your scent, and now I see why.' He then lowered his hands and stepped back. 'I have given you my name.'

'I am Onrack, of Logros T'lan Imass. The one who restrains the emlava is Trull Sengar, Tiste Edur of the Hiroth tribe. The dark-skinned man is Ben Adaephon Delat, born in a land called Seven Cities; and his companion is Hedge, once a soldier of the Malazan Empire.'

Rud's eyes found Hedge again. 'Tell me, soldier, do you bleed?'

'What?'

'You were dead, yes? A spirit willing itself the body it once possessed. But now you are here. Do you bleed?'

Bemused, Hedge looked to Quick Ben. 'What's he mean? Like a woman bleeds? I'm too ugly to be a woman, Quick.'

'Forgive me,' Rud Elalle said. 'Onrack proclaims himself a T'lan Imass – yet here he stands, clothed in flesh and bearing the scars of your journey in this realm. And there have been other such guests. T'lan Imass – lone wanderers who have found this place – and they too are clothed in flesh.'

'Other guests?' Hedge asked. 'You almost had one more of those, and she would have been a viper in your midst, Rud Elalle. For what it's worth, I wouldn't be trusting those other T'lan Imass, were I you.'

'Ulshun Pral is a wise leader,' Rud answered with another smile.

'I'm still a ghost,' Hedge said.

'Are you?'

The sapper frowned. 'Well, I ain't gonna cut myself to find out one way or the other.'

'Because you intend to leave this place, eventually. Of course, I understand.'

'Sounds like you do at that,' Hedge snapped. 'So, maybe you live with these Bentract Imass, Rud Elalle, but that's about as far as this kinship thing goes. So, who are you?'

'A friend,' the man replied with yet another smile.

Aye, and if you knew how I felt about friendly people.

'You have given me your names, and so now I welcome you among the Bentract Imass. Come, Ulshun Pral is eager to meet you.'

He set off.

They followed. With hand signals, Hedge drew Quick Ben closer to his side and they dropped back a bit from the others. The sapper spoke in very low tones. 'That furry tree's standing on the ruins of a dead city, Quick, like he was its Hood-damned prince.'

'A Meckros City,' the wizard murmured.

'Aye, I guessed as much. So where's the ocean? Glad I never saw the wave that carried it here.'

Quick Ben snorted. 'Gods and Elder Gods, Hedge. Been here kicking pieces around, I'd wager. And, just maybe, a Jaghut or two. There's a real mess of residual magic in this place – not just Imass. More Jaghut than Imass, in fact. And . . . other stuff.'

'Quick Ben Delat, lucid as a piss-hole.'

'You really want to know why Cotillion sent us here?'

'No. Just knowing snares me in his web and I ain't gonna dance for any god.'

'And I do, Hedge?'

The sapper grinned. 'Aye, but you dance, and then you *dance.*'

'Rud has a point, by the way.'

'No, he has a club.'

'About you bleeding.'

'Hood above, Quick—'

'Oh, now that's a giveaway, Hedge. What's Hood doing "above"? Just how deep was that hole you crawled out of? And more important, why?'

'My company soured already? I liked you least, you know. Even Trotts—'

'Now who's dancing?'

'Better we know nothing about why we're here, is what I'm trying to say.'

'Relax. I have already figured you out, Hedge, and here's something that might surprise you. Not only do I have no problem with you being here – neither does Cotillion.'

'Bastard! What – you and Cotillion sending pigeons back and forth on all this?'

'I'm not saying Cotillion knows anything about you, Hedge. I'm just saying that if he did, he'd be fine. So would Shadowthrone—'

'Gods below!'

'Calm down!'

'Around you, Quick, that's impossible. Always was, always will be! Hood, I'm a ghost and I'm *still* nervous!'

'You never were good at being calm, were you? One would think dying might have changed you, some, but I guess not.'

'Funny. Ha ha.'

They were now skirting the ruined city, and came within sight of the burial mounds. Quick Ben grunted. 'Looks like the Meckros didn't survive the kick.'

'Dead or no,' Hedge said, 'you'd be nervous too if you was carrying a sack of cussers on your back.'

'Damn you, Hedge – that *was* a cusser in your hand back there! When the dragon—'

'Aye, Quick, so you just keep them kitties away from me, lest I jump back and turn an ankle or something. And stop talking about Shadowthrone and Cotillion, too.'

'A sack full of cussers. Now I *am* nervous – you may be dead, but I'm not!'

'Just so.'

'I wish Fid was here, too. Instead of you.'

'That's not a very nice thing to say! You're hurting my feelings. Anyway. What I was wanting to tell you was about that T'lan Imass I was travelling with, for a time.'

'What happened to it? Let me guess, you tossed it a cusser.'

'Damned right I did, Quick. She was trailing chains, big ones.'

'Crippled God?'

'Aye. Everyone wants in on this game here.'

'That'd be a mistake,' the wizard asserted as they walked towards a series of rock outcroppings behind which rose thin tendrils of hearth smoke. 'The Crippled God would find himself seriously outclassed.'

'Think highly of yourself, don't you? Some things never change.'

'Not me, idiot. I meant the dragon. Menandore. Rud Elalle's mother.'

Hedge dragged the leather cap from his head and pulled at what was left of his hair. 'This is what drives me mad! You! Things like that, just dropped out like a big stinking lump of – ow!' He let go of his hair. 'Hey, that actually hurt!'

'Tug hard enough to bleed, Hedge?'

Hedge glared across at the wizard, who was now smirking. 'Look, Quick, this would all be fine if I was planning on building a homestead here, planting a few tubers and raising emlava for their cuddly fur or something. But damn it, I'm just passing through, right? And when I come out the other side, well, I'm back being a ghost, and that's something I need to get used to, and *stay* used to.'

Quick Ben shrugged. 'Just stop pulling your hair and you'll be fine, then.'

The emlava cubs had grown and were now strong enough to pull Trull Sengar off balance as they strained on their leather leashes, their attention fixed yet again on the Malazan soldier named Hedge, for whom they had acquired a mindless hate. Trull leaned forward to drag the beasts along – it always worked better when the sapper walked ahead, rather than lagging back as he was doing now.

Onrack, noting his struggles, turned and quickly clouted both cubs on their flat foreheads. Suitably cowed, the two emlava ceased their efforts and padded along, heads lowered.

'Their mother would do the same,' Onrack said.

'The paw of discipline,' Trull said, smiling. 'I wonder if we might believe the same for our guide here.'

Rud Elalle was ten paces ahead of them – perhaps he could hear, perhaps not.

'Yes, they share blood,' Onrack said, nodding. 'That much was clear when they were standing side by side. And if there is Eleint blood in the mother, then so too in the son.'

'Soletaken?'

'Yes.'

'I wonder if he anticipated this complication?' Trull meant Cotillion when saying *he*.

'Unknown,' Onrack replied, understanding well enough. 'The task awaiting us grows ever less certain. Friend Trull, I fear for these Imass. For this entire realm.'

'Leave the wizard and his sapper to address our benefactor's needs, then, and we will concern ourselves with protecting this place, and your kin who call it home.'

The Imass glanced across with narrowed eyes. 'You say this, with such ease?'

'The wizard, Onrack, is the one who needs to be here. His power – he will be our benefactor's hand in what is to come. You and me, we were but his escort, his bodyguards, if you will.'

'You misunderstand me, Trull Sengar. My wonder is in your willingness to risk your life, again. This time for a people who are nothing to you. For a realm not your own.'

'They are your kin, Onrack.'

'Distant. Bentract.'

'If it had been, say, the Den-Ratha tribe of the Edur to gain supremacy among our tribes, Onrack, instead of my own Hiroth,

651

would I not give my life to defend them? They are still my people. For you it is the same, yes? Logros, Bentract – just tribes – but the same people.'

'There is too much within you, Trull Sengar. You humble me.'

'Perhaps there lies your own misunderstanding, friend. Perhaps all you see here is my search for a cause, for something to fight for, to die for.'

'You will not die here.'

'Oh, Onrack—'

'I may well fight to protect the Bentract and this realm, but they are not why I am here. You are.'

Trull could not meet his friend's eyes, and in his heart there was pain. Deep, old, awakened.

'The son,' Onrack said after a moment, 'seems . . . very young.'

'Well, so am I.'

'Not when I look into your eyes. It is not the same with this Soletaken,' he continued, seemingly unmindful of the wound he had just delivered. 'No, those yellow eyes are *young*.'

'Innocent?'

A nod. 'Trusting, as a child is trusting.'

'A gentle mother, then.'

'She did not raise him,' Onrack said.

Ah, the Imass, then. And now I begin to see, to understand. 'We will be vigilant, Onrack.'

'Yes.'

Rud Elalle led them into a split between two upthrust knobs of layered rock, a trail that then wound between huge boulders before opening out into the Imass village.

Rock shelters along a cliff. Tusk-framed huts, the spindly frames of drying racks on which were stretched hides. Children running like squat imps in the midst of a gathering of perhaps thirty Imass. Men, women, elders. One warrior stood before all the others, while off to one side stood three more Imass, their garb rotted and subtly different in cut and style from that of the Bentract – the strangers, Trull realized – guests yet remaining apart.

Upon seeing them, Onrack's benign expression hardened. 'Friend,' he murmured to Trull, ' 'ware those three.'

'I decided the same myself,' Trull replied under his breath.

Rud Elalle moved to stand at the Bentract leader's side. 'This is Ulshun Pral,' he said, setting a hand on the man's thick shoulder – a gesture of open affection that seemed blissfully unmindful of the growing tension at the edge of this village.

Onrack moved forward. 'I am Onrack the Broken, once of the Logros T'lan Imass, child of the Ritual. I ask that we be made guests among your tribe, Ulshun Pral.'

The honey-skinned warrior frowned over at Rud Elalle, then said something in his own language.

Rud nodded and faced Onrack. 'Ulshun Pral asks that you speak in the First Language.'

'He asked,' Onrack said, 'why I chose not to.'

'Yes.'

'My friends do not share the knowing of that language. I cannot ask for guesting on their behalf without their understanding, for to be guest is to be bound to the rules of the tribe, and this they must know, before I would venture a promise of peace on their behalf.'

'Can you not simply translate?' Rud Elalle asked.

'Of course, yet I choose to leave that to you, Rud Elalle, for Ulshun Pral knows and trusts you, while he does not know me.'

'Very well, I shall do so.'

'Enough with all this,' Hedge called out, gingerly setting down his pack. 'We'll all be good boys, so long as no-one tries to kill us or worse, like making us eat some horrible vegetable rightly extinct on every other realm in the universe.'

Rud Elalle was displaying impressive skill and translating Hedge's words almost as fast as the sapper spoke them.

Ulshun Pral's brows lifted in seeming astonishment, then he turned and with a savage gesture yelled at a small crowd of elderly women at one side of the crowd.

Hedge scowled at Onrack, 'Now what did I say?' he demanded.

But Trull saw his friend smiling. 'Ulshun Pral has just directed the cooks to fish the baektar from the stew they have prepared for us.'

'The baek-what?'

'A vegetable, Hedge, that will be found nowhere but here.'

All at once the tension was gone. There were smiles, shouts of apparent welcome from other Imass, and many came forward to close, first on Onrack, and then – with expressions of delight and wonder, on Trull Sengar – no, he realized, not on him – *on the emlava cubs*. Who began purring deep in their throats, as thick, short-fingered hands reached out to stroke fur and scratch behind the small, tufted ears.

'Look at that, Quick!' Hedge was staring in disbelief. 'Now is that fair?'

The wizard slapped the sapper on the back. 'It's true, Hedge, the dead stink.'

'You're hurting my feelings again!'

Sighing, Trull released the leather leashes and stepped back. He smiled across at Hedge. 'I smell nothing untoward,' he said.

But the soldier's scowl only deepened. 'Maybe I like you now, Trull Sengar, but you keep being nice and that'll change, I swear it.'

'Have I offended you—'

'Ignore Hedge,' Quick Ben cut in, 'at least when he's talking. Trust me, it was the only way the rest of us in the squad stayed sane. Ignore him . . . until he reaches into that damned sack of his.'

'And then?' Trull asked in complete bewilderment.

'Then run like Hood himself was on your heels.'

Onrack had separated himself from his welcomers and was now walking towards the strangers.

'Yes,' Quick Ben said in a low voice. 'They're trouble indeed.'

'Because they were like Onrack? T'lan Imass?'

'Of the Ritual, aye. The question is, why are they here?'

'I would imagine that whatever mission brought them to this place, Quick Ben, the transformation they experienced has shaken them – perhaps, as with Onrack, their spirits have reawakened.'

'Well, they look unbalanced enough.'

Their conversation with Onrack was short, and Trull watched as his old friend approached.

'Well?' the wizard demanded.

Onrack was frowning. 'They are Bentract, after all. But from those who joined the Ritual. Ulshun Pral's clan were among the very few who did not, who were swayed by the arguments set forth by Kilava Onass – this is why,' Onrack added, 'they greet the emlava as if they were Kilava's very own children. Thus, there are ancient wounds between the two groups. Ulshun Pral was not a clan chief back then – indeed, the T'lan Bentract do not even know him.'

'And that is a problem?'

'It is, because one of the strangers is a chosen chief – chosen by Bentract himself. Hostille Rator.'

'And the other two?' Quick Ben asked.

'Yes, even more difficult. Ulshun Pral's Bonecaster is gone. Til'aras Benok and Gr'istanas Ish'ilm, who stand to either side of Hostille Rator, are Bonecasters.'

Trull Sengar drew a deep breath. 'They contemplate usurpation, then.'

Onrack the Broken nodded.

'Then what had stopped them?' Quick Ben asked.

'Rud Elalle, wizard. The son of Menandore terrifies them.'

The rain thundered down, every moment another hundred thousand iron-tipped lances crashing down out of the dark onto slate rooftops, exploding on the cobbled streets where streams now rushed down, racing for the harbour.

The ice north of the island had not died quietly. Sundered by the magic of a wilful child, the white and blue mountains had lifted skyward in pillars of steam that roiled into massive stormclouds, which had then marched south freed from the strictures of refusal, and those clouds now erupted over the beleaguered city with rage and vengeance. Late afternoon had become midnight and now, as the half-drowned chimes of midnight's bells sounded, it seemed as if this night would never end.

On the morrow – if it ever came – the Adjunct would set sail with her motley fleet. Thrones of War, a score of well-armed fast escorts, the last of the transports holding the rest of the Fourteenth Army, and one sleek black dromon propelled by the tireless oars manned by headless Tiste Andii. Oh, and of course, in the lead would be a local pirate's ship, captained by a dead woman – but never mind her. Return, yes, to that black-hulled nightmare.

Their hosts had worked hard to keep the dread truth of that Quon dromon from Nimander Golit and his kin. The severed heads on the deck, mounded around the mainmast, well, they had kept them covered. No point in encouraging hysteria, should their living Tiste Andii guests see the faces of their kin, their true kin, for were they not of Drift Avalii? Oh yes, they were indeed. Uncles, fathers, mothers, oh, a play on words now would well serve the notion – they were, yes, heads of families, cut away before their time, before their children had grown old enough, wise enough, hard enough to survive in this world. Cut away, ha ha. Now, death would have been one thing. Dying was one thing. Just one and there were other things, always, and you didn't need any special wisdom to know that. But those heads had not died, not stiffened then softened with rot. The faces had not fallen away to leave just bone, just the recognition that came with a sharing of what-is, what-was and what-would-be. No, the eyes stared on, the eyes blinked because some memory told them that blinking was necessary. The mouths moved, resuming interrupted conversations, the sharing of jests, the gossip of parents, yet not a single word could claw free.

But hysteria was a complicated place in which a young mind might find itself. It could be deafening with screams, shrieks, the endless bursts of horror again and again and again – a tide surging without end. Or it could be quiet – silent in that awful way of some silences – like that of gaping mouths, desperate but unable to draw breath, the eyes above bulging, the veins standing prominent in their need, but no breath would come, nothing to slide life into the lungs. This was the hysteria of drowning. Drowning inside oneself, inside horror. The hysteria of a child, blank-eyed, drool smearing the chin.

Some secrets were impossible to keep. The truth of that ship, for one. The *Silanda*'s lines were known, were profoundly familiar. The ship that had taken their parents on a pathetic journey in search of the one whom every Tiste Andii of Drift Avalii called Father. Anomander Rake. Anomander of the silver hair, the dragon's eyes. Didn't find him, alas.

Never the chance to plead for help, to ask all the questions that needed asking, to stab fingers in accusation, condemnation, damnation. All that, yes yes.

Take to your oars, brave parents, there is more sea to cross. Can you see the shore? Of course not. You see the sunlight when there is sunlight through canvas weave, and in your heads you feel the ache of your bodies, the strain in your shoulders, the bunch and loose, bunch and loose of every draw on the sweeps. You feel the blood welling up to pool in the neck as if it was a gilded cup, only to sink back down again. *Row, damn you! Row for the shore!*

Aye, the shore. Other side of this ocean, and this ocean, dear parents, is endless.

So row! Row!

He might have giggled, but that would be a dangerous thing, to break the silence of his hysteria, which he had held on to for so long now it had become warm as a mother's embrace.

Best to carry on, working to push away, shut away, all thought of the *Silanda*. Easier on land, in this inn, in this room.

But, on the morrow, they would sail. Again. Onto the ships, oh the spray and wind enlivens so!

And this was why, on this horrid night of vengeful rain, Nimander was awake. For he knew Phaed. He knew Phaed's own stain of hysteria, and what it might lead her to do. Tonight, in the sodden ashes of midnight's bell.

She could make her footfalls very quiet, as she crept out of her bed and padded barefoot to the door. *Blessed sister blessed daughter blessed mother blessed aunt, niece, grandmother – blessed kin, blood of my blood, spit of my spit, gall of my gall. I hear you.*

For I know your mind, Phaed. The ever-surging bursts in your soul – yes, I see your bared teeth, the smear of intent. You imagine yourself unseen, yes, unwitnessed, and so you reveal your raw self. There in that blessed slash of grey-white, so poetically echoed by the gleam of the knife in your hand.

To the door, darling Phaed. Lift the latch, and out you go, to slide down the corridor all slithering limbs as the rain lashes the roof above and water trickles down the walls in dirty tears. Cold enough to see your breath, Phaed, reminding you not just that you are alive, but that you are sexually awakened; that this journey is the sweetest indulgence of under-the-cover secrets, fingers ever playful on the knife, and on the rocking ship in the harbour eyes stare at blackness beneath drenched canvas, water trickling down . . .

She worries, yes, about Withal. Who might awaken. Before or after. Who might smell the blood, the iron stench, the death riding out on Sandalath Drukorlat's last breath. Who might witness when all that

Phaed was, truly was, could never be witnessed – because such things were not allowed, never allowed, and so she might have to kill him, too.

Vipers strike more than once.

Now at the door, the last barrier – *row you fools – the shore lies just beyond!* – and of course there is no lock binding the latch. No reason for it. Save one murderous child whose mother's head stares at canvas on a pitching deck. The one child who went to see that for herself. And we are drawn to pilgrimage. Because to live is to hunt for echoes. Echoes of what? No-one knows. But the pilgrimage is taken, yes, ever taken, and every now and then those echoes are caught – just a whisper – creaking oars, the slap and chop of waves like fists against the hull, clamouring to get in, and the burbling blood, the spitting suck as it sinks back down. And we hear, in those echoes, some master's voice: *Row! Row for the shore! Row for your lives!*

He remembered a story, the story he always remembered, would ever remember. An old man alone in a small fisher boat. Rowing into the face of a mountain of ice. Oh, he did love that story. The pointless glory of it, the mindless magic – he would grow chilled at the thought, at the vision he conjured of that wondrous, profound and profoundly useless scene. *Old man, what do you think you are doing? Old man – the ice!*

Inside, a shadow among shadows, gloom in the gloom, teeth hidden now, but the knife is a lurid gleam, catching reflections of rain from the window's pitted rainbow glass. And a shudder takes her then, pulling her down into a crouch as sensations flood up through her belly, lancing upward into her brain and her breath catches – oh, Phaed, don't scream now. Don't even moan.

They have drawn their cots together – on this night, then, the man and the bitch have shared the spit of their loins, isn't that sweet. She edges closer, eyes searching. Finding Sandalath's form on the left, closest to her. Convenient.

Phaed raises the knife.

In her mind, flashes, scene after scene, the sordid list of this old woman's constant slights, each one belittling Phaed, each one revealing to all nearby too many of Phaed's secret terrors – no-one has the right to do that, no-one has the right to then laugh – laugh in the eyes if not out loud. All those insults, well, the time has come to pay them back. Here, with one hard thrust of the knife.

She lifts the knife still higher, draws in her breath and holds it.

And stabs down.

Nimander's hand snaps out, catches her wrist, hard, tightening as she twists round, lips peeled back, eyes blazing with rage and fear. Her wrist is a tiny thing, like a bony snake, caught, frenzied, seeking to turn the knife, to set the edge against Nimander's hand. He twists again and bones break, an awful crunching, grinding sound.

657

The knife clunks on the wooden floor.

Nimander bears down on her, using his weight to crumple Phaed onto the floor beside the bed. She tries to scratch at his eyes and he releases the broken limb to grasp the other one. He breaks that one too.

She has not screamed. Amazing, that. Not a sound but her panting breath.

Nimander pins her down and takes her neck in his hands. He begins to squeeze.

No more, Phaed. I now do as would Anomander Rake. As would Silchas Ruin. As would Sandalath herself were she awake. I do this, because I know you – yes, even now, there, in your bulging eyes where all your awareness now gathers in a flood, I can see the truth of you.

The emptiness inside.

Your mother stares in horror. At what she has spawned. She stares, disbelieving, clinging desperately to the possibility that she has got it wrong, that we all have, that you are not as you are. But that is no help. Not to her. Not to you.

Yes, stare up into my eyes, Phaed, and know that I see you.

I see you—

He was being dragged away. Off Phaed. His hands were being pried loose, twisted painfully to break his grip – and he falls back, muscled arms wrapped about him now, and is dragged from Phaed, from her bloated face and the dreadful gasping – poor Phaed's throat hurts, maybe is torn, even. To breathe is to know agony.

But she lives. He has lost his chance, and now they will kill him.

Sandalath screams at him – she has been screaming at him for some time, he realizes. She first screamed when he broke Phaed's second wrist – awakened by Phaed's own screams – oh, of course she had not stayed quiet. Snapping bones would never permit that, not even from a soulless creature as was Phaed. She had screamed, and he'd heard nothing, not even echoes – *hands on the oar and squeeze!*

Now what would happen? Now what would they do?

'*Nimander!*'

He started, stared across at Sandalath, studied her face as if it were a stranger's.

Withal held him, arms trapped against his sides, but Nimander was not interested in struggling. It was too late for that.

Phaed had thrown up and the stink of her vomit was thick in the air.

Someone was pounding on the door – which in his wisdom Nimander had locked behind him after following Phaed into the room.

Sandalath yelled that it was all right, everything was fine – an accident, but everything is fine now.

But poor Phaed's wrists are broken. That will need seeing to.

Not now, Withal.

He stands limp in my arms, wife. Can I release him now?

Yes, but be wary—

I shall, no doubt of that.

And now Sandalath, positioned between Nimander and the still-coughing, gagging Phaed, took Nimander's face in her hands and leaned closer to study his eyes.

What do you see, Sandalath Drukorlat? Gems bright with truths and wonders? Pits whispering at you that no bottom will ever be found, that the plunge into a soul never ends? *Row, you fools! We're sinking!* Oh, don't giggle, Nimander, don't do that. Remain as you are, outwardly numb. Blank. What do you see? Why, nothing, of course.

'Nimander.'

'It's all right,' he said. 'You can kill me now.'

A strange look on her face. Something like horror. 'Nimander, no. Listen to me. I need to know. What has happened here? Why were you in our room?'

'Phaed.'

'Why were you both in our room, Nimander?'

Why, I followed her. I stayed awake – I've been doing that a lot. I've been watching her for days and days, nights and nights. Watching her sleep, waiting for her to wake up, to take out her knife and smile a greeting to the dark. The dark that is our heritage, the dark of betrayal.

I don't remember when last I slept, Sandalath Drukorlat. I needed to stay awake, always awake. Because of Phaed.

Did he answer her then? Out loud, all those tumbling statements, those reasonable explanations. He wasn't sure. 'Kill me now, so I can sleep, I so want to sleep.'

'No-one is going to kill you,' Sandalath said. Her hands, pressed to the sides of his face, were slick with sweat. Or rain, perhaps. Not tears – *leave that to the sky, to the night.*

'I am sorry,' Nimander said.

'I think that apology should be saved for Phaed, don't you?'

'I am sorry,' he repeated to her, then added, 'that she's not dead.'

Her hands pulled away, leaving his cheeks suddenly cold.

'Hold a moment,' Withal said, stepping to the foot of the bed and bending down to pick up something. Gleaming, edged. Her knife. 'Now,' he said in a murmur, 'which one does this toy belong to, I wonder?'

'Nimander's still wearing his,' Sandalath said, and then she turned to stare down at Phaed.

A moment later, Withal grunted. 'She's been a hateful little snake around you, Sand. But this?' He faced Nimander. 'You just saved my wife's life? I think you did.' And then he moved closer, but there was nothing of the horror of Sandalath's face in his own. No, this was a hard expression, that slowly softened. 'Gods below, Nimander, you knew this was coming, didn't you? How long? When did you last sleep?' He stared a moment longer, then spun. 'Move aside, Sand, I think I need to finish what Nimander started—'

'No!' his wife snapped.

'She'll try again.'

'I understand that, you stupid oaf! Do you think I've not seen into that fanged maw that is Phaed's soul? Listen, there is a solution—'

'Aye, wringing her scrawny neck—'

'We leave them here. On the island – we sail tomorrow without them. Withal – husband—'

'And when she recovers – creatures like this one always do – she'll take this damned knife and do to Nimander what she's tried to do to you. He saved your life, and I will not abandon him—'

'She won't kill him,' Sandalath said. 'You don't understand. She cannot – without him, she would be truly alone, and that she cannot abide – it would drive her mad—'

'Mad, aye, mad enough to take a knife to Nimander, the one who betrayed her!'

'No.'

'Wife, are you so certain? Is your faith in understanding the mind of a sociopath so strong? That you would leave Nimander with her?'

'Husband, her arms are broken.'

'And broken bones can be healed. A knife in the eye cannot.'

'She will not touch him.'

'Sand—'

Nimander spoke. 'She will not touch me.'

Withal's eyes searched his. 'You as well?'

'You must leave us here,' Nimander said, then winced at the sound of his own voice. So weak, so useless. He was no Anomander Rake. No Silchas Ruin. Andarist's faith in choosing him to lead the others had been a mistake. 'We cannot go with you. With *Silanda*. We cannot bear to see that ship any longer. Take it away, please, take *them* away!'

Oh, too many screams this night, in this room. More demands from outside, in growing alarm.

Sandalath turned and, drawing a robe about her – she had been, Nimander suddenly realized, naked – *a woman of matronly gifts, the body of a woman who had birthed children, a body such as young men dream of. And might there be wives who might be mothers who might be lovers . . . for one such as me? Stop, she is dead* – robe drawn, Sandalath walked to the door, quickly unlocked it and slipped outside, closing the door behind her. More voices in the corridor.

Withal was staring down at Phaed, who had ceased her coughing, her

660

whimpers of pain, her fitful weeping. 'This is not your crime, Nimander.'

What?

Withal reached down and grabbed Phaed by her upper arms. She shrieked.

'Don't,' Nimander said.

'Not your crime.'

'She will leave you, Withal. If you do that. She will leave you.'

He stared across at Nimander, then pushed Phaed back down onto the floor. 'You don't know me, Nimander. Maybe she doesn't, either – not when it comes to what I will do for her sake – and, I suppose,' he added with a snarl, 'for yours.'

Nimander had thought his words had drawn Withal back, had kept him from doing what he had intended to do, and so he was unprepared, and so he stood, watching, as Withal snatched Phaed up, surged across the room – carrying her as if she was no more than a sack of tubers – and threw her through the window.

A punching shatter of the thick, bubbled glass, and body, flopping arms and bared lower limbs – with dainty feet at the end – were gone, out into the night that howled, spraying the room with icy rain.

Withal stumbled back in the face of that wind, then he spun to face Nimander. 'I am going to lie,' he said in a growl. 'The mad creature ran, flung herself through – do you hear me?'

The door opened and Sandalath charged into the room, behind her the Adjunct's aide, Lostara Yil, and the priest, Banaschar – and, pushing close behind them, the other Tiste Andii – eyes wide with fear, confusion – and Nimander lurched towards them, one step, then another—

And was pulled round to face Sandalath.

Withal was speaking. A voice filled with disbelief. Expostulations.

But she was staring into his eyes. 'Did she? Nimander! *Did she?*'

Did she what? Oh, yes, go through the window.

Shouts from the street below, muted by the wailing winds and lashing rain. Lostara Yil moved to stand at the sill, leaned out. A moment later she stepped back and turned, her expression grave. 'Broken neck. I'm sorry, Sandalath. But I have questions . . .'

Mother, wife, Withal's lover, was still staring into Nimander's eyes – a look that said loss was rearing from the dark, frightened places in her mind, rearing, yes, to devour the love she held for her husband – for the man with the innocent face; that told him, with the answer he might give to her question, two more lives might be destroyed. *Did she? Through the window? Did she . . . die?*

Nimander nodded. 'Yes,' he said.

Another dead woman screamed in his skull and he almost reeled. Dead eyes, devouring all love. *'You have lied, Nimander!'*

Yes. To save Withal. To save Sandalath Drukorlat—
'To save yourself!'
Yes.
'My love, what has happened to you?'
I heard a spinning sound. A whispering promise – we must stay here,
you see. We must. Andarist chose me. He knew he was going to die. He
knew that there would be no Anomander Rake, no Silchas Ruin, no
great kin of our age of glory – no-one to come to save us, take care of
us. There was only me.

My love, to lead is to carry burdens. As did the heroes of old, with
clear eyes.

So look at my eyes, my love. See my burden? Just like a hero of old—
Sandalath reached up again, those two long-fingered hands. Not to
take his face, but to wipe away the rain streaming down his cheeks.
My clear eyes.

We will stay here, on this island – we will look to the Shake, and see
in them the faint threads of Tiste Andii blood, and we will turn them
away from the barbarity that has taken them and so twisted their
memories.

We will show them the shore. The true shore.

Burdens, my love. This is what it is to live, while your loved ones die.
Sandalath, still ignoring Lostara Yil's questioning, now stepped back
and turned to settle into her husband's arms.

And Withal looked across at Nimander.

Outside, the wind screamed.

Yes, my love, see it in his eyes. Look what I have done to Withal. All
because I failed.

Last night's storm had washed the town clean, giving it a scoured
appearance that made it very nearly palatable. Yan Tovis, Twilight,
stood on the pier watching the foreign ships pull out of the harbour. At
her side was her half-brother, Yedan Derryg, the Watch.

'Glad to see them go,' he said.

'You are not alone in that,' she replied.

'Brullyg's still dead to the world – but was that celebration or self-
pity?'

Yan Tovis shrugged.

'At dawn,' Yedan Derryg said after a long moment of silence between
them, 'our black-skinned cousins set out to build the tomb.' His
bearded jaw bunched, molars grinding, then he said, 'Only met the girl
once. Sour-faced, shy eyes.'

'Those broken arms did not come from the fall,' Yan Tovis said. 'Too
bruised – the tracks of fingers. Besides, she landed on her head, bit
through her tongue clean as a knife cut.'

662

'Something happened in that room. Something sordid.'

'I am pleased we did not inherit such traits.'

He grunted, said nothing.

Yan Tovis sighed. 'Pully and Skwish seem to have decided their sole purpose in living these days is to harry me at every turn.'

'The rest of the witches have elected them as their representatives. You begin your rule as Queen in a storm of ill-feeling.'

'It's worse than that,' she said. 'This town is crowded with ex-prisoners. Debt-runners and murderers. Brullyg managed to control them because he could back his claim to being the nastiest adder in the pit. They look at me and see an Atri-Preda of the Imperial Army – just another warden – and you, Derryg, well, you're my strong-arm Finadd. They don't care a whit about the Shake and their damned queen.'

'Which is precisely why you need the witches, Twilight.'

'I know. And if that's not misery enough, *they* know it, too.'

'You need clout,' he said.

'Clever man.'

'Even as a child, you were prone to sarcasm.'

'Sorry.'

'The answer, I think, will be found with these Tiste Andii.'

She looked across at him. 'What do you mean?'

'Who knows more of our past than even the witches? Who knows it as a clean thing? A thing not all twisted by generations of corruption, of half-remembrances and convenient lies?'

'Your tongue runs away with you, Yedan.'

'More sarcasm.'

'No, I find myself somewhat impressed.'

The jaw bunched as he studied her.

She laughed. Could not help it. 'Oh, brother, come – the foreigners are gone and probably won't be back – ever.'

'They sail to their annihilation?'

'What do you think?'

'I'm not sure, Twilight. That child mage, Sinn . . .'

'You may be right. News of her imminent departure had Pully and Skwish dancing.'

'She destroyed a solid wall of ice half as long as Fent Reach. I would not discount these Malazans.'

'The Adjunct did not impress me,' Yan Tovis said.

'Maybe because she didn't need to.'

Twilight thought about that, then thought about it some more.

Neither spoke as they turned away from the glittering bay and the now-distant foreign ships.

The morning sun was actually beginning to feel warm – the final, most poignant proof that the ice was dead, the threat past. The Isle would live on.

On the street ahead the first bucket of night-soil slopped down onto the clean cobbles from a second-storey window, forcing passers-by to dance aside.

'The people greet you, Queen.'

'Oh, be quiet, Yedan.'

Captain Kindly stood by the port rail, staring across the choppy waves to the *Silanda*. Soldiers from both of the squads on that haunted ship were visible on the deck, a handful gathered about a game of bones or some such nefarious activity, whilst the sweeps churned the water in steady rhythm. Masan Gilani was up near the steering oar, keeping Sergeant Cord company.

Lucky bastard, that Cord. Lieutenant Pores, positioned on Kindly's right, leaned his forearms on the rail, eyes fixed on Masan Gilani – as were, in all likelihood, the eyes of most of the sailors on this escort, those not busy readying the sails at any rate.

'Lieutenant.'

'Sir?'

'What do you think you are doing?'

'Uh, nothing, sir.'

'You're leaning on the gunnel. At ease. Did I at any time say "at ease", Lieutenant?'

Pores straightened. 'Sorry, sir.'

'That woman should be put up on report.'

'Aye, she's not wearing much, is she?'

'Out of uniform.'

'Damned distracting, isn't it, sir?'

'Disappointing, you mean, surely, Lieutenant.'

'Ah, that's the word I was looking for, all right. Thank you, sir.'

'The Shake make the most extraordinary combs,' Kindly said. 'Turtleshell.'

'Impressive, sir.'

'Expensive purchases, but well worth it, I should judge.'

'Yes sir. Tried them yet?'

'Lieutenant, do you imagine that to be amusing?'

'Sir? No, of course not!'

'Because, as is readily apparent, Lieutenant, your commanding officer has very little hair.'

'If by that you mean on your head, then yes sir, that is, uh, apparent indeed.'

'Am I infested with lice, then, that I might need to use a comb elsewhere on my body, Lieutenant?'

'I wouldn't know, sir. I mean, of course not.'

'Lieutenant, I want you to go to my cabin and prepare the disciplinary report on that soldier over there.'

'But sir, she's a marine.'

'Said report to be forwarded to Fist Keneb when such communication is practicable. Well, why are you still standing here? Get out of my sight, and no limping!'

'Limp's long gone, sir!'

Pores saluted then hurried away, trying not to limp. The problem was, it had become something of a habit when he was around Captain Kindly. Granted, a most pathetic attempt at eliciting some sympathy. Kindly had no sympathy. He had no friends, either. Except for his combs. 'And they're all teeth and no bite,' he murmured as he descended to Kindly's cabin. 'Turtleshell, ooh!'

Behind him, Kindly spoke, 'I have decided to accompany you, Lieutenant. To oversee your penmanship.'

Pores cringed, hitched a sudden limp then rubbed at his hip before opening the cabin hatch. 'Yes sir,' he said weakly.

'And when you are done, Lieutenant, my new turtleshell combs will need a thorough cleansing. Shake are not the most fastidious of peoples.'

'Nor are turtles.'

'Excuse me?'

'I will be most diligent, sir.'

'And careful.'

'Absolutely, sir.'

'In fact, I think I had better oversee that activity as well.'

'Yes sir.'

'That wasn't a limp I saw, was it?'

'No sir, I'm much better now.'

'Otherwise we would have to find a good reason for your limping, Lieutenant. For example, my finding a billy club and shattering your legs into pieces. Would that do, do you think? No need to answer, I see. Now, best find the ink box, yes?'

'I'm telling you, Masan, that was Kindly himself over there. Drooling over you.'

'You damned fool,' she said, then added, 'Sergeant.'

Cord just grinned. 'Even at that distance, your charms are, uh, unmistakable.'

'Sergeant, Kindly has probably not lain with a woman since the night of his coming of age, and that time was probably with a whore his father or uncle bought for the occasion. Women can tell these things. The man's repressed, in all the worst ways.'

'Oh, and what are the good ways of being repressed?'

'For a man? Well, decorum for one, as in not taking advantage of your rank. Listen closely now, if you dare. All real acts of chivalry are forms of repressed behaviour.'

'Where in Hood's name did you get that? Hardly back on the savannas of Dal Hon!'

'You'd be surprised what the women in the huts talk about, Sergeant.'

'Well, soldier, I happen to be steering this damned ship, so it was you who walked up here to stand with me, not the other way round!'

'I was just getting away from Balm's squad – not to mention that sapper of yours, Crump, who's decided I'm worthy of worship. Says I've got the tail of some salamander god.'

'You've what?'

'Aye. And if he grabs it it's liable to come off. I think he means he thinks I'm too perfect for the likes of him. Which is something of a relief. Doesn't stop him ogling me, though.'

'You get the ogles because you want the ogles, Masan Gilani. Keep your armour on and we'll all forget about you quick enough.'

'Armour on a ship? No thanks. That's a guarantee of a fast plunge to the mucky bottom, Sergeant.'

'We won't be seeing any battle on the waves,' Cord pronounced.

'Why not? The Letherii got a fleet or three, don't they?'

'Mostly chewed up by years at sea, Masan Gilani. Besides, they're not very good at the ship-to-ship kind of fighting – without their magic, that is.'

'Well, without our marines, neither are we.'

'They don't know that, do they?'

'We haven't got Quick Ben any more either.'

Cord leaned on the steering oar and looked across at her. 'You spent most of your time in the town, didn't you? Just a few trips back and forth to us up the north side of the island. Masan Gilani, Quick Ben had all the moves, aye, and even the look of an Imperial High Mage. Shifty, mysterious and scary as Hood's arse-crack. But I'll tell you this – Sinn, well, she's the real thing.'

'If you say so.' All Masan Gilani could think of, when it came to Sinn, was the little mute child curling up in the arms of every woman in sight, suckling on tits like a newborn. Of course, that was outside Y'Ghatan. Long ago, now.

'I do say so,' Cord insisted. 'Now, if you ain't interested in getting unofficial with this sergeant here, best take your swaying hips elsewhere.'

'You men really are all the same.'

'And so are you women. Might interest you,' he added as she

turned to leave, 'Crump's no whiskered shrew under those breeches.'

'That's disgusting.' But she paused at the steps leading down to the main deck and glanced back at the sergeant. 'Really?'

'Think I'd lie about something like that?'

He watched Masan Gilani sashay her way up the main deck to where Balm and the rest were gambling, Crump with all the winnings, thus far. They'd reel him in later, of course. Although idiots had a way of being damnably lucky.

In any case, the thought of Masan Gilani ending up with Crump, of all people, was simply too hilarious to let pass. If she wasn't interested in decent men like Sergeant Cord, well, she could have the sapper and so deserve everything that came with him. *Aye, he'll worship you all right. Even what you cough up every morning and that sweet way you clear your nose before going into battle. Oh, wait till I tell Shard about this. And Ebron. And Limp. We'll set up a book, aye. How long before she runs screaming. With Crump loping desperate after her, knees at his ears.*

Ebron climbed onto the aft deck. 'What's got you looking so cheerful, Sergeant?'

'I'll tell you later. Dropped out of the game?'

'Crump's still winning.'

'Ain't turned it yet?'

'We tried, half a bell ago, Sergeant. But the damned fool's luck's gone all uncanny.'

'Really? He's not a mage or something, is he?'

'Gods no, the very opposite. All my magics go awry – the ones I tried on him and on the bones and scull. Those Mott Irregulars, they were mage-hunters, you know. High Marshal this and High Marshal that – if Crump really is a Bole, one of the brothers, well, they were legendary.'

'You saying we're underestimating the bastard, Ebron?'

The squad mage looked morose. 'By about three hundred imperial jakatas and counting, Sergeant.'

Hood's balls, maybe Masan Gilani will like being Queen of the Universe.

'What was that you were going to tell me about, Sergeant?'

'Never mind.'

Shurq Elalle stood on the foredeck of the *Froth Wolf* and held a steady, gauging eye on the *Undying Gratitude* five reaches ahead. All sails out, riding high. Skorgen Kaban was captaining her ship and would continue to do so until they reached the mouth of the Lether River. Thus far, he'd not embarrassed himself – or, more important, her.

She wasn't very happy about all of this, but these Malazans were paying her well indeed. Good-quality gold, and a chestful of that would come in handy in the days, months and probably years to come.

Yet another invasion of the Letherii Empire, and in its own way possibly just as nasty as the last one. Were these omens, then, signalling the decline of a once great civilization? Conquered by barbaric Tiste Edur, and now in the midst of a protracted war that might well bleed them out, right down to a lifeless corpse.

Unless, of course, those hapless abandoned marines – whatever 'marines' were; soldiers, anyway – were already jellied and dissolving into the humus. A very real possibility, and Shurq was not privy to any details of the campaign so she had no way of knowing either way.

So, here she was, returning at last to Letheras . . . maybe just in time to witness its conquest. *Witness – now really, darling Shurq, you've a bigger role than that. Like leading the damned enemy right up to the docks. And how famous will that make you then? How many more curses on your name?*

'There is a ritual,' said a voice behind her.

She turned. That odd man, the one in the ratty robes, whose face was so easily forgotten. The priest. 'Banaschar, is it?'

He nodded. 'May I join you, Captain?'

'As you please, but at the moment I am not a captain. I'm a passenger, a guest.'

'As am I,' he replied. 'As I mentioned a moment ago, there is a ritual.'

'Meaning what?'

'To find and bind your soul to your body once more – to remove your curse and make you alive again.'

'A little late for that, even if I desired such a thing, Banaschar.'

His brows rose. 'You do not dream of living again?'

'Should I?'

'I am probably the last living High Priest of D'rek, the Worm of Autumn. The face of the aged, the dying and the diseased. And of the all-devouring earth that takes flesh and bone, and the fires that transform into ashes—'

'Yes, fine, I grasp the allusions.'

'I, more perhaps than most, do understand the tension between the living and the dead, the bitterness of the season that finds each and every one of us—'

'Do you always go on like this?'

He looked away. 'No. I am trying to resurrect my faith—'

'By the Tiles, Banaschar, don't make me laugh. Please.'

'Laugh? Ah, yes, the play on words. Accidental—'

'Rubbish.'

That elicited a mocking smile – which was better than the grave misery that had been there a moment earlier. 'Very well, Shurq Elalle, why do you not wish to live once again?'

'I don't get old, do I? I stay as I am, suitably attractive—'

'Outwardly, yes.'

'And have you taken the time to look *inward*, Banaschar?'

'I would not do such a thing without your permission.'

'I give it. Delve deep, High Priest.'

His gaze fixed on her, but slowly surrendered its focus. A moment passed, then he paled, blinked and stepped back. 'Gods below, what is *that*?'

'I don't know what you mean, good sir.'

'There are . . . roots . . . filling your entire being. Every vein and artery, the thinnest capillaries . . . alive . . .'

'My ootooloo – they said it would take over, eventually. Its appetites are' – she smiled – 'boundless. But I have learned to control them, more or less. It possesses its own rigour, yes?'

'You are dead and yet not dead, not any more – but what lives within you, what has claimed your entire body, Shurq Elalle, it is *alien*. A parasite!'

'Beats fleas.'

He gaped.

She grew impatient with his burgeoning alarm. 'Errant take your rituals. I am content enough as I am, or will be once I get scoured out and some new spices stuffed—'

'Stop, please.'

'As you like. Is there something else you wanted to discuss? Truth is, I have little time for high priests. As if piety comes from gaudy robes and self-righteous arrogance. Show me a priest who knows how to dance and I might bask in his measure, for a time. Otherwise . . .'

He bowed. 'Forgive me, then.'

'Forget trying to resurrect your faith, Banaschar, and try finding for yourself a more worthy ritual of living.'

He backed away, and very nearly collided with the Adjunct and Tavore's ever-present bodyguard, Lostara Yil. Another hasty bow, then flight down the steps.

The Adjunct frowned at Shurq Elalle. 'It seems you are upsetting my other passengers, Captain.'

'Not my concern, Adjunct. I would be of better service if I was on my own ship.'

'You lack confidence in your first mate?'

'My incomplete specimen of a human? Why would you imagine that?'

Lostara Yil snorted, then pointedly ignored the Adjunct's quick warning glance.

'I will have many questions to ask you, Captain,' Tavore said. 'Especially the closer we get to Letheras. And I will of course value your answers.'

'You are being too bold,' Shurq Elalle said, 'heading straight for the capital.'

'Answers, not advice.'

Shurq Elalle shrugged. 'I had an uncle who chose to leave Letheras and live with the Meckros. He wasn't much for listening to advice either. So off he went, and then, not so long ago, there was a ship, a Meckros ship from one of their floating cities south of Pilott – and they told tales of a sister city being destroyed by ice, then vanishing – almost no wreckage left behind at all – and no survivors. Probably straight down to the deep. That hapless city was the one my uncle lived on.'

'Then you should have learned a most wise lesson,' Lostara Yil said in a rather dry tone that hinted of self-mockery.

'Oh?'

'Yes. People who make up their minds about something never listen to advice – especially when it's to the contrary.'

'Well said.' Shurq Elalle smiled at the tattooed woman. 'Frustrating, isn't it?'

'If you two are done with your not very subtle complaints,' the Adjunct said, 'I wish to ask the captain here about the Letherii secret police, the Patriotists.'

'Ah well,' Shurq Elalle said, 'that is not a fun subject. Not fun at all.'

'I am not interested in fun,' Tavore said.

And one look at her, Shurq Elalle reflected, was proof enough of that.

With twelve of his most loyal guards from the Eternal Domicile, Sirryn marched up Kravos Hill, the west wall of Letheras two thousand paces behind him. The tents of the Imperial Brigade dominated in the midst of ancillary companies and lesser brigades, although the Tiste Edur encampment, situated slightly apart from the rest, to the north, looked substantial – at least two or three thousand of the damned savages, Sirryn judged.

Atop Kravos Hill stood half a dozen Letherii officers and a contingent of Tiste Edur, among them Hanradi Khalag. Sirryn withdrew a scroll and said to the once-king, 'I am here to deliver the Chancellor's orders.'

Expressionless, Hanradi reached out for the scroll, then passed it on to one of his aides without looking at it.

Sirryn scowled. 'Such orders—'

'I do not read Letherii,' Hanradi said.

'If you'd like, I can translate—'

'I have my own people for that, Finadd.' Hanradi Khalag looked across at the officers of the Imperial Brigade. 'In the future,' he said, 'we Edur will patrol the boundaries of our own camp. The parade of Letherii whores is now at an end, so your pimp soldiers will have to make their extra coin elsewhere.'

The Edur commander led his troop away, down off the summit of the hill. Sirryn stared after them for a moment, until he was certain they would not return. He then withdrew a second scroll and approached the Preda of the Imperial Brigade. 'These, too,' he said, 'are the Chancellor's orders.'

The Preda was a veteran, not just of battle, but of the ways of the palace. He simply nodded as he accepted the scroll. 'Finadd,' he asked, 'will the Chancellor be commanding us in person when the time comes?'

'I imagine not, sir.'

'That could make things awkward.'

'In some matters, I will speak for him, sir. As for the rest, you will find, once you have examined that scroll, that you are given considerable freedom for the battle itself.'

'And if I find myself at odds with Hanradi?'

'I doubt that will be a problem,' Sirryn said.

He watched the Preda mull that over, and thought he saw a slight widening of the man's eyes.

'Finadd,' the Preda said.

'Sir?'

'How fares the Chancellor, at the moment?'

'Well indeed, sir.'

'And . . . in the future?'

'He is most optimistic, sir.'

'Very good. Thank you, Finadd.'

Sirryn saluted. 'Begging your leave, sir, I wish to oversee the establishment of my camp.'

'Make it close to this hill, Finadd – this is where we will command the battle – and I will want you close.'

'Sir, there is scant room left—'

'You have my leave to move people out at your discretion, Finadd.'

'Thank you, sir.'

Oh, he would enjoy that. Grubby soldiers with dust on their boots – they always imagined themselves superior to their counterparts in the palace. Well, a few cracked skulls would change that quick enough. *By leave of their very own Preda.* He saluted again and led his troops back down the hill.

The man looked familiar. Had he been a student of hers? Son of a neighbour, son of another scholar? These were the questions in Janath's mind as the troop dragged them from Tehol's home. Of the journey to the compound of the Patriotists, she now recalled very little. But that man, with the familiar face – a face that stirred oddly intimate feelings within her – would not leave her.

Chained in her cell, chained in the darkness that crawled with vermin, she had been left alone for some time now. Days, perhaps even a week. A single plate of watery stew slid through the trap at the foot of the door at what seemed irregular intervals – it would not be pushed into her cell if she did not leave the empty plate from the last meal within easy reach of the guard. The ritual had not been explained to her, but she had come to admire its precision, its eloquence. Disobedience meant hunger; or, rather, starvation – hunger was always there, something that she had not experienced in the household of Bugg and Tehol. There had been a time, back then, when she had come to loathe the taste of chicken. Now she dreamed of those damned hens.

The man, Tanal Yathvanar, had visited but once, apparently to gloat. She'd no idea she had been wanted for sedition, although in truth that did not surprise her much. When thugs were in power, educated people were the first to feel their fists. It was so pathetic, really, how so much violence came from someone feeling *small*. Small of mind, and it did not matter how big the sword in hand, that essential *smallness* remained, gnawing with very sharp teeth.

Both Bugg and Tehol had hinted, occasionally, that things would not go well if the Patriotists found her. Well, *them*, as it turned out. Tehol Beddict, her most frustrating student, who had only attended her lectures out of adolescent lust, now revealed as the empire's greatest traitor – so Tanal Yathvanar had said to her, the glee in his voice matched by the lurid reflections in his eyes as he stood with his lantern in one hand and the other touching his private parts whenever he thought she wasn't looking. She had been sitting with her back to the stone wall, head tilted down chin to chest, with her filthy hair hanging ragged over her face.

Tehol Beddict, masterminding the empire's economic ruin – well, that was still a little hard to believe. Oh, he had the talent, yes. And maybe even the inclination. But for such universal collapse as was now occurring, there was a legion of co-conspirators. Unwitting for the most part, of course, barring that niggling in their guts that what they were doing was, ultimately, destructive beyond measure. But greed won out, as it always did. So, Tehol Beddict had paved the road, but hundreds – thousands? – had freely chosen to walk it. And now they cried out, indignant and appalled, even as they scurried for cover lest blame spread its crimson pool.

As things stood at the moment, the entire crime now rested at Tehol's feet – and Bugg's, the still elusive manservant.

'But we will find him, Janath,' Tanal Yathvanar had said. 'We find everyone, eventually.'

Everyone but yourselves, she had thought to reply, for that search leads you onto a far too frightening path. Instead, she had said nothing, given him nothing at all. And watched as the sword got ever smaller in his hand – yes, that sword, too.

'Just as we found you. Just as I found you. Oh, it's well known now. I was the one to arrest Tehol Beddict and Scholar Janath. Me. Not Karos Invictad, who sits day and night drooling over his box and that blessed two-headed insect. It has driven him mad, you know. He does nothing else.' He then laughed. 'Did you know he is now the richest man in the empire? At least, he thinks he is. But I did the work for him. I made the transactions. I have copies of everything. But the real glory is this – I am his beneficiary, and he doesn't even know it!'

Yes, the two-headed insect. One drooling, the other nattering.

Tanal Yathvanar. She knew him – that was now a certainty. She knew him, because he had done all this to her before. There had been no dissembling when he had talked about that – it was the source for his gloating over her, after all, so it could not be a lie.

And now her memories – of the time between the end of the semester at the academy, and her awakening in the care of Tehol and Bugg – memories that had been so fragmented, images blurred beyond all understanding, began to coalesce, began to draw into focus.

She was wanted, because she had escaped. Which meant that she had been arrested – her first arrest – and her tormentor had been none other than Tanal Yathvanar.

Logical. Reasonable intuitions from the available facts and her list of observations. Cogent argument and standing before her – some time ago now – the one man who offered the most poignant proof as he babbled on, driven by her lack of reaction. 'Dear Janath, we must resume where we left off. I don't know how you got away. I don't even know how you ended up with Tehol Beddict. But once more you are mine, to do with as I please. And what I will do with you will not, alas, please you, but your pleasure is not what interests me. This time, you will beg me, you will promise anything, you will come to worship me. And that is what I will leave you with, today. To give you things to think about, until my return.'

Her silence, it had turned out, had been a weak defence.

She was beginning to remember – past those ordered details arranged with clinical detachment – and with those memories there was . . . pain.

Pain beyond comprehension.

I was driven mad. That is why I could not remember anything. Entirely mad – I don't know how Bugg and Tehol healed me, but they must have. And Tehol's consideration, his very uncharacteristic *gentleness with me – not once did he seek to take advantage of me, although he must have known that he could have, that I would have welcomed it. That should have awakened suspicion in me, it should have, but I was too happy, too strangely content, even as I waited and waited for Tehol to find himself in my arms.*

Ah, now isn't that an odd way of putting it?

She wondered where he was. In another cell? There were plenty of moaners and criers for neighbours, most beyond all hope of communication. Was one of them Tehol Beddict? Broken into a bleeding, gibbering thing?

She did not believe it. Would not. No, for the Great Traitor of the Empire, there would have to be spectacle. A Drowning of such extravagance as to burn like a brand into the collective memory of the Letherii people. He would need to be broken publicly. Made the singular focus for this overwhelming tide of rage and fear. Karos Invictad's crucial act to regain control, to quell the anarchy, the panic, to restore order.

What irony, that even as Emperor Rhulad prepared to slaughter champions – among them some reputed to be the most dangerous Rhulad would ever face – Karos Invictad could so easily usurp the attention of everyone – well, among the Letherii, that is – with this one arrest, this one trial, this one act of bloodletting.

Doesn't he realize? That to kill Tehol Beddict this way will be to make of him a martyr? One such as has never been seen before? Tehol Beddict sought to destroy the Letherii system of Indebtedness. Sought to destroy the unholy union of coin and power. He will be the new Errant, but a new kind of Errant. One bound to justice, to freedom, to the commonality of humans. Regardless of whether he was right, regardless even if these were his aims – none of that will matter. He will be written of, a thousand accounts, and in time but a handful will survive, drawn together to forge the heart of a new cult.

And you, Karos Invictad, oh, how your name will ride the breath of curses, for ever more.

Make someone a martyr and surrender all control, of what that someone was in life, of what that someone becomes in death. Do this, Karos Invictad, and you will have lost, even as you lick the man's blood from your hands.

Yet, perhaps the Invigilator understood all of that. Enough to have already murdered Tehol Beddict, murdered him and dumped the body into the river, weighted down with stones. Unannounced, all in the darkness of night.

But no – the people wanted, needed, demanded that public, ritualized execution of Tehol Beddict.

And so she went round and round, in the swirling drain of her mind, the bottomless well that was her spirit's defensive collapse sucking her down, ever down.

Away from the memories.

From Tanal Yathvanar.

And what he had done to her before.

And what he would do to her now.

The proud, boisterous warrior who had been Gadalanak returned to the compound barely recognizable as human. The kind of failure, Samar Dev was led to understand, that infuriated this terrible, terrifying Emperor. Accordingly, Gadalanak had been cut to pieces. Long after he was dead, Rhulad's dread sword had swung down, chopping, slashing, stabbing and twisting. Most of the man's blood had probably drained into the sand of the arena floor, since the corpse carried by the burial retinue of Indebted did not even drip.

Puddy and other warriors, still waiting their turn – the masked woman included – stood nearby, watching the bearers and their reed stretcher with its grisly heap of raw meat and jutting bone cross the compound on their way to what was known as the Urn Room, where Gadalanak's remains would be interred. Another Indebted trailed the bearers, carrying the warrior's weapon and shield, virtually clean of any blood, spattered or otherwise. Word had already come of the contest's details. The Emperor had cut off Gadalanak's weapon-arm with the first blow, midway between hand and elbow, sending the weapon flying off to one side. Shield-arm followed, severed at the shoulder. It was said the attending Tiste Edur – and the few Letherii dignitaries whose blood-lust overwhelmed panic at sudden financial straits – had then voiced an ecstatic roar, as if answering Gadalanak's own screams.

Silent, sober of expression and pale as bleached sand, Puddy and the others watched this grim train, as did Samar Dev herself. Then she turned away. Into the side corridor, down its dusty, gloomy length.

Karsa Orlong was lying on the oversized cot that had been built for some previous champion – a full-blood Tarthenal, although still not as tall as the Teblor now sprawled down its length, bared feet jutting over the end with the toes pressed against the wall – a wall stamped with the grime of those toes and feet, since Karsa Orlong had taken to doing very little, ever since the announcement of the contests.

'He's dead,' she said.

'Who?'

'Gadalanak. Within two or three heartbeats – I think it was a mistake, all of you deciding not to attend – you need to see the one you will fight. You need to know his style. There might be weaknesses—'

Karsa snorted. 'Revealed in two heartbeats?'

'The others, I suspect, will now change their minds. They will go, see for themselves—'

'Fools.'

'Because they won't follow your lead in this?'

'I wasn't even aware they had, witch. What do you want? Can't you see I'm busy?'

She stepped into the room. 'Doing what?'

'You are dragging your ghosts with you.'

'More like they're clinging to my heels, gibbering – something is building within you, Karsa Orlong—'

'Climb onto me and we can relieve that, Samar Dev.'

'Amazing,' she breathed.

'Yes.'

'No, you idiot. I was just commenting on how you can still manage to shock me on occasion.'

'You only pretend to innocence, woman. Take your clothes off.'

'If I did, it would only be because you have worn me down. But I won't, because I am tougher than you think. One look at the odious stains your feet have left on that wall is enough to quench any ardour I might – in sudden madness – experience.'

'I did not ask you to make love to my feet.'

'Shouldn't you be exercising – no, not that kind. I mean, staying limber, stretching and the like.'

'What do you want?'

'Reassurance, I think.'

He turned to look at her, then slowly sat up, the cot groaning beneath him. 'Samar Dev, what is it you fear the most?'

'Well, you dying, I think. Infuriating as you are, you are a friend. To me, at least. That, and the fact that, uh, after you, they will call upon Icarium. As you can see, the two fears are closely bound together.'

'Is this what the spirits crowding you fear as well?'

'An interesting question. I'm not sure, Karsa.' And, a moment later, she added, 'Yes, I see now how that might be important – worth knowing, I mean.'

'I have my own ghosts,' he said.

'I know. And what are they feeling? Can you tell?'

'Eager.'

She frowned. 'Truly, Karsa Orlong? *Truly?*'

He laughed. 'Not for what you think. No, they delight in the end that is coming to them, to the sacrifice they will make.'

'What kind of sacrifice?'

'When the time comes, witch, you must draw your iron knife. Give it your blood. Free the spirits you have bound.'

'What time, damn you?'

'You will know. Now, take off your clothes. I will see you naked.'

'No. Gadalanak is dead. Never again will we hear his laughter—'

'Yes, so it is for us to laugh, now, Samar Dev. We must remind ourselves what it is to live. For him. For Gadalanak.'

She stared at him, then hissed in anger. 'You almost had me, Karsa Orlong. It's when you get too convincing, you know, that you become the most dangerous.'

'Perhaps you'd rather I just took you, then. Tore your clothes away with my own hands. Flung you down on the bed.'

'I'm leaving now.'

Taralack Veed had once dreamt of the time now imminent, when Icarium Lifestealer would step onto the sand of the arena, amidst the eager roar of unwitting onlookers – and those derisive cries would change very quickly, oh yes, to ones of astonishment, then terror. As the rage was awakened, unleashed.

As the world began its gory end. An emperor, a palace, a city, the heart of an empire.

But this Rhulad would not die. Not with finality. No, each time he would rise again, and two forces would lock together in battle that might never end. Unless . . . could Icarium be killed? Could he die? He was not immortal, after all – although it could be argued that his rage was, the rage of the victim, generation after generation, a rage against injustice and inequity, and such a thing was without end.

No, if Taralack Veed pushed his thoughts far enough, he ever came to the same place. Rhulad would kill Icarium. A hundred clashes, a thousand – at some point, on a continent of ashes, the burgeoning chaos would strike through, into the heart of Icarium's rage. And Lifestealer would fall.

There was logic to this. The victim might awaken to fury, but the victim was doomed to be just that: a victim. This was the true cycle, the one to which every culture, every civilization, was witness, century upon century. *A natural force, the core of the struggle to exist is the desire to not just survive, but thrive. And to thrive is to feed on victims, ever more victims.*

'It is the language itself,' Senior Assessor said, kneeling over a basin of still water to study his reflection as he applied gaudy paint. 'Life pushes forward, when it succeeds. Life halts or falls to the wayside, when it fails. Progression, Taralack Veed, implies a journey, but not necessarily one through a fixed interval of time. That is, the growth and ageing of an individual person, although that too is quickly sewn into the cloth. No, the true journey is one of procreation, one's seed moving from host to host in a succession of generations, each of which must be successful to some degree, lest the seed . . . halt, fall to the wayside. Of course, it is not in a single man's mind to think in terms of generation upon generation, although the need to sow his seed is ever paramount. Other concerns, all of which support that which is paramount, generally occupy the mind on a moment to moment basis. The acquisition of food, the security of one's shelter, the support of one's family, relatives and allies, the striving to fashion a predictable world, peopled with predictable people – the quest, if you will, for comfort.'

Taralack Veed looked away, back to the window, where stood Finadd Varat Taun, watching something in the compound below. 'Monk,' Taralack said in a growl, 'among my tribe, each of the things you describe was but part of a war, a feud that could never end. Each was desperate and vicious. No love, no loyalty could be wholly trusted, because the ground churned beneath our feet. Nothing is certain. Nothing.'

'One thing is,' Varat Taun said, facing them. 'The warrior named Gadalanak is dead. And now so too is the one named Puddy, the quick one who loved to boast.'

Taralack Veed nodded. 'You come to believe as I now do, Finadd. Yes, you and I, we have seen Icarium in his anger. But this Emperor, this Rhulad . . .'

The monk made a strange grunting noise, then pivoted on the stool – away from them both – and hugged himself.

Varat Taun frowned and took a step forward. 'Senior Assessor? Priest? Is something wrong?'

A vigorous shake of the head, then: 'No, please. Let us change the subject. Blessed God, I almost failed – the mirth, you see, it very nearly burst from me. Ah, it is all I can do to restrain myself.'

'Your faith in your god is unshaken.'

'Yes, Taralack Veed. Oh yes. Is it not said Rhulad is mad? Driven insane by countless deaths and rebirths? Well, my friends, I tell you, Lifestealer, my most beloved god – the one god – well, he too is mad. And remember this, please, it is Icarium who has come here. Not Rhulad – my god has made this journey. To delight in his own madness.'

'Rhulad is—'

'No, Varat Taun, Rhulad is *not*. A god. *The* god. He is a cursed creature, as mortal as you or me. The power lies in the sword he wields. The distinction, my friends, is essential. Now, enough, lest my vow is sundered. You are both too grave, too poisoned by fear and dread. My heart is near to bursting.'

Taralack Veed stared at the monk's back, saw the trembling that would not still. *No, Senior Assessor, it is you who is mad. To worship Icarium? Does a Gral worship the viper? The scorpion?*

Spirits of the rock and sand, I cannot wait much longer. Let us be done with this.

'The end,' Senior Assessor said, 'is never what you imagine. Be comforted by that, my friends.'

Varat Taun asked the monk, 'When do you intend to witness your first contest?'

'If any – and I am not yet decided – if any, then the Toblakai, of course,' Senior Assessor murmured, finally in control of his amusement – so much so that he twisted round to look up at the Finadd with calm, knowing eyes. 'The Toblakai.'

Rhulad Sengar, Emperor of a Thousand Deaths, stood above the corpse of his third victim. Splashed in blood not his own, sword trembling in his hand, he stared down at the still face with its lifeless eyes as the crowd dutifully roared its pleasure, gave voice to his bitter triumph.

That onrushing wall of noise parted around him, left him untouched. It was, he well knew, a lie. Everything was a lie. The challenge, which had proved anything but. The triumph, which was in truth a failure. The words uttered by his Chancellor, by his bent and twisted Ceda – and every face turned his way was as this one below. A mask, a thing of death, an expression of hidden laughter, hidden mockery. For if it was not death that mocked him, then what?

When last did he see something genuine in a subject's face? *When you did not think of them as subjects. When they were not. When they were friends, brothers, fathers and mothers. I have my throne, I have my sword, I have an empire. But I have . . . no-one.*

He so wanted to die. A true death. To fall and not find his spirit flesh cast up on the strand of that dread god's island.

But it will be different this time. I can feel it. Something . . . will be different.

Ignoring the crowd and its roar now creeping towards hysteria, Rhulad walked from the arena, through the shimmering ripples rising from the sun-baked sand. His own sweat had thinned the blood splashed upon him, sweat seeping out from between tarnished coins, glistening from the ringed ridges of pocked scars. Sweat and blood merged into these streams of sour victory that could but temporarily stain the surfaces of the coins.

Chancellor Triban Gnol could not understand that, Rhulad knew. How gold and silver outlived the conceits of mortal lives. Nor could Invigilator Karos Invictad.

In many ways Rhulad found himself admiring this Great Traitor, Tehol Beddict. *Beddict, yes, the brother of the one honourable Letherii warrior I was privileged to meet. One, only one. Brys Beddict, who defeated me truly – and in that too he was like no other.* Karos Invictad had wanted to drag Tehol Beddict out here into the arena, to stand before the Emperor, to be shamed and made to hear the frenzied hunger of the crowd. Karos Invictad had thought that such a thing would humiliate Tehol Beddict. *But if Tehol is like Brys, he would but stand, he would but smile, and that smile would be his challenge. To me. His invitation to execute him, cut him down as I never did to Brys. And yes, I would see that knowing, there in his eyes.* Rhulad had forbidden that. Leave Tehol to the Drownings. To that circus of savagery transformed into a game of wagers.

In the meantime, the empire's foundations wobbled, spat dust in grinding protest; the once-firm cornerstones shook as if revealed to be nothing more than clay, still wet from the river. Men who had been wealthy had taken their own lives. Warehouses had been besieged by an ever-growing mob – this thousand-headed beast of need rising in every city and town of the empire. Blood had spilled over a handful of docks, a crust of stale bread, and in the poorest slums mothers smothered their babies rather than see them bloat then wither with starvation.

Rhulad left the harsh sunlight and stood in the tunnel entrance, swallowed by shadows.

My grand empire.

The Chancellor stood before him each day, and lied. All was well, all would be well with the execution of Tehol Beddict. The mines were working overtime, forging more currency, but this needed careful control, because Karos Invictad believed that all that Tehol had stolen would be retrieved. Even so, better a period of inflation than the chaos now plaguing Lether.

But Hannan Mosag told him otherwise, had indeed fashioned rituals permitting Rhulad to see for himself – the riots, the madness, scenes blurred, at times maddeningly faded, yet still they stank of the truth. Where the Ceda lied was in what he would not reveal.

'What of the invasion, Ceda? Show me these Malazans.'

'I cannot, alas, Emperor. They protect themselves with strange magics. See, the water in the bowl grows cloudy when I quest their way. As if they could cast in handfuls of flour. Blinding all the water might reveal.'

Lies. Triban Gnol had been more blunt in his assessment – a directness that unveiled the Chancellor's growing concern, perhaps even his fear. The Malazans who had landed on the west coast, who had begun their march inland – towards Letheras itself – were proving themselves both cunning and deadly. To clash with them was to reel back bloodied and battered, a retreat strewn with dead soldiers and dead Tiste Edur. Yes, they were coming for Rhulad. Could the Chancellor stop them?

'Yes, Emperor. We can. We shall. Hanradi has divided his Edur forces. One waits with our main army just west of the city. The other has travelled fast and light northward and is even now swinging westward, like a sweeping arm, to appear behind these Malazans – but not as has been attempted before. No, your Edur do not ride in column, do not travel the roads now. They fight as they once did, during the unification wars. War-parties, moving silent in the shadows, matching the Malazans and perhaps going one better in their stealth—'

'Yes! We adapt, not into something new, but into something old – the very heart of our prowess. Whose idea was this? Tell me!'

A bow from Triban Gnol. 'Sire, did you not place me in charge of this defence?'

'Then, you.'

Another bow. 'As I said, Emperor, the guiding hand was yours.'

To be so unctuous was to reveal contempt. Rhulad understood that much. The Ceda lacked such civilized nuances in his reply: 'The idea was mine and Hanradi's, Emperor. After all, I was the Warlock King and he was my deadliest rival. This can be remade into a war we Edur understand and know well. It is clear enough that attempting to fight these Malazans in the manner of the Letherii has failed—'

'But there will be a clash, a great battle.'

'It seems so.'

'Good.'

'Perhaps not. Hanradi believes . . .'

And there the dissembling had begun, the half-truths, the poorly veiled attacks upon the Chancellor and his new role as military commander.

To fashion knowledge to match the reality was difficult, to sift through the lies, to shake free the truths – Rhulad was exhausted by it, yet what else could he do? He was learning, damn them all. He was learning.

'Tell me, Ceda, of the Bolkando invasion.'

'Our border forts have been overrun. There have been two battles and in both the Letherii divisions were forced to withdraw, badly wounded. That alliance among the eastern kingdoms is now real, and it appears that they have hired mercenary armies . . .'

The Bolkando Conspiracy . . . now real. Meaning it had begun as a lie. He recalled Triban Gnol's shocked expression when Rhulad had repeated Hannan Mosag's words – as if they were his own. 'That alliance among the eastern kingdoms is now real, Chancellor . . .'

Triban Gnol's mask had cracked then – no illusion there, no game brought to a yet deeper level. The man had looked . . . guilty.

We must win these wars. To the west and to the east. We must, as well, refashion this empire. The days of the Indebted will be gone. The days of the coins ruling this body are over. I, Rhulad, Emperor, shall set my hands upon this clay, and make of it something new.

So, let the plague of suicides among the once-rich continue. Let the great merchant houses crash down into ruin. Let the poor rend

681

the nobles limb from limb. Let estates burn. When the ashes have set-tled, have cooled, then shall Rhulad find fertile ground for his new empire.

Yes, that is what is different, this time. I sense a rebirth. Close. Imminent. I sense it, and maybe it will be enough, maybe it will give me reason again to cherish this life. My life.

Oh, Father Shadow, guide me now.

Mael had been careless. It had been that carelessness that the Errant had relied upon. The Elder God so fixed on saving his foolish mortal companion, blundering forward into such a simple trap. A relief to have the meddling bastard out of the way, serving as a kind of counter-balance to the lurid acquisitiveness of Feather Witch, whose disgusting company the Errant had just left.

And now he stood in the dark corridor. Alone.

'*We will have our Mortal Sword,*' she had announced from her perch on the altar that squatted like an island amidst black floodwater. '*The idiot remains blind and stupid.*'

Which idiot would that be, Feather Witch? Our imminent Mortal Sword?

'*I do not understand your sarcasm, Errant. Nothing has gone astray. Our cult grows day by day, among the Letherii slaves, and now the Indebted—*'

The disaffected, you mean. And what is it you are promising them, Feather Witch? In my name?

'*The golden age of the past. When you stood ascendant among all other gods. When yours was the worship of all the Letherii. Our glory was long ago, and to that we must return.*'

There was never a golden age. Worship of me to the exclusion of all other gods has never existed among the Letherii. The time you speak of was an age of plurality, of tolerance, a culture flowering—

'*Never mind the truth. The past is what I say it is. That is the free-dom of teaching the ignorant.*'

He had laughed then. *The High Priestess stumbles upon a vast wisdom. Yes, gather your disaffected, ignorant fools, then. Fill their heads with the noble glory of a non-existent past, then send them out with their eyes blazing in stupid – but comforting – fervour. And this will begin our new golden age, an exultation in the pleasures of repression and tyrannical control over the lives of everyone. Hail the mighty Errant, the god who brooks no dissent.*

'*What you do with your power is up to you. I know what I plan to do with mine.*'

Udinaas has rejected you, Feather Witch. You have lost the one you wanted the most.

She had smiled. '*He will change his mind. You will see. Together, we shall forge a dynasty. He was an Indebted. I need only awaken the greed within him.*'

*Feather Witch, listen well to your god. To this modest sliver of wisdom. The lives of others are not yours to use. Offer them bliss, yes, but do not be disappointed when they choose misery – because the misery is theirs, and in deciding to choose someone else's path or their own, they will choose their own. The Shake have a saying: '*Open to them your hand to the shore, watch them walk into the sea.*'*

'*No wonder they were wiped out.*'

Feather Witch—

'*Listen to my wisdom now, Errant. Wisdom the Shake should have heeded. When it comes to using the lives of others, the first thing to take from them is the privilege of choice. Once you have done that, the rest is easy.*'

He had found his High Priestess. Indeed. *Bless us all.*

CHAPTER TWENTY-ONE

Open to them your hand to the shore, watch them walk into the sea.
Press upon them all they need, see them yearn for all they want
Gift to them the calm pool of words, watch them draw the sword.
Bless upon them the satiation of peace, see them starve for war.
Grant them darkness and they will lust for light.
Deliver to them death and hear them beg for life.
Beget life and they will murder your kin.
Be as they are and they see you different.
Show wisdom and you are a fool.
The shore gives way to the sea.
And the sea, my friends,
Does not dream of you.

Shake Prayer

ANOTHER HOOD-DAMNED VILLAGE, WORSE THAN MUSHROOMS AFTER
a rain. Proof, if they'd needed it – and they didn't – that they
were drawing ever closer to the capital. Hamlets, villages, towns,
traffic on the roads and cart trails, the thundering passage of horses,
horns sounding in the distance like the howl of wolves closing in for the
kill.

'Best life there is,' Fiddler muttered.

'Sergeant?'

He rolled onto his back and studied his exhausted, cut-up, bloodstained, wild-eyed excuses for soldiers. What were they now? And
what, as they stared back at him, were they seeing? *Their last hope, and
if that isn't bad news . . .*

He wondered if Gesler and his squad were still alive. They'd been
neatly divided the night before by a clever thrust in strength of Edur,
bristling with weapons and sniffing the air like the hounds they had
become. Edur on their trail, delivering constant pressure, pushing them

ever forward, into what Fiddler damn well knew was a wall of soldiers somewhere ahead – no slipping past when that time came. No squeezing north or south either – the Edur bands filled the north a dozen to a copse and not too far away on the south was the wide Lether River grinning like the sun's own smile. Finally, aye, someone on the other side had got clever, had made the necessary adjustments, had turned this entire invasion into a vast funnel about to drive the Malazans into a meat-grinder.

Well, no fun lasts for ever. After Gesler and his Fifth had been pushed away, there had been sounds of fighting somewhere in that direction. And Fiddler had faced the hard choice between leading his handful of soldiers into a flanking charge to break through and relieve the poor bastards, or staying quiet and hurrying on, east on a southerly tack, right into that waiting maw.

The splitting *cracks* of sharpers had decided him – suicide running into that, since those sharpers tended to fly every which way, and they meant that Gesler and his squad were running, carving a path through the enemy, and Fiddler and his squad might simply end up stumbling into their wake, in the sudden midst of scores of enraged Edur.

So I left 'em to it. And the detonations died away, but the screams continued, Hood take me.

Sprawled in the high grasses at the edge of the treeline, his squad. They stank. The glory of the Bonehunters, this taking to the grisliest meaning of that name. *Koryk's curse, aye. Who else?* Severed fingers, ears, pierced through and dangling from belts, harness clasps, rawhide ties. His soldiers: one and all degraded into some ghastly blood-licking barely human savages. No real surprise there. It was one thing to go covert – as marines this was, after all, precisely what they had been trained to do. But it had gone on too long, without relief, with the only end in sight nothing other than Hood's own gate. Fingers and ears, except for Smiles, who'd added to the mix with that which only males could provide. '*My blecker worms,*' she'd said, referring to some off-shore mud-dwelling worm native to the Kanese coast. '*And just like the worms, they start out purple and blue and then after a day or two in the sun they turn grey. Bleckers, Sergeant.*'

Didn't need to lose the path to lose their minds, that much was obvious. *Gods below, look at these fools – how in Hood's name have we lasted this long?*

They'd not seen the captain and her runt of a mage in some time, which didn't bode well. Still, threads of brown telltale smoke drifting around here and there in the mornings, and the faint sounds of munitions at night. So, at least some of them were still alive. But even those signs were growing scarce, when they should have been, if anything, increasing as things got nastier.

685

We've run out. We're used up. Bah, listen to me! Starting to sound like Cuttle there. 'I'm ready to die now, Fid. Happy to, aye. Now that I seen—'

'Enough of that,' he snapped.

'Sergeant?'

'Stop asking me anything, Bottle. And stop looking at me like I've gone mad or something.'

'You'd better not, Sergeant. Go mad, that is. You're the only sane one left.'

'Does that assessment include you?'

Bottle grimaced, then spat out another wad of the grass he'd taken to chewing. Reached for a fresh handful.

Aye, answer enough.

'Almost dark,' Fiddler said, eyeing once more the quaint village ahead. Crossroads, tavern and stable, a smithy down the main street, in front of a huge pile of tailings, and what seemed too many residences, rows of narrow-laned mews, each abode looking barely enough for a small family. Could be there was some other industry, a quarry or potter's manufactury, somewhere on the other side of the village – he thought he could see a gravel road wending up a hill past the eastern edge.

Strangely quiet for dusk. *Workers still chained to their workbenches? Maybe. But still, not even a damned dog in that street.* 'I don't like the looks of this,' he said. 'You sure you smell nothing awry, Bottle?'

'Nothing magical. Doesn't mean there isn't a hundred Edur crouched inside those houses, just waiting for us.'

'So send in a squirrel or something, damn you.'

'I'm looking, Sergeant, but if you keep interrupting me . . .'

'Lord Hood, please sew up the mouths of mages, I implore you.'

'Sergeant, I'm begging you. We've got six squads of Edur less than a league behind us, and I'm damned tired of dodging javelins. Let me concentrate.'

Aye, concentrate on this fist down your throat, y'damned rat-kisser. Oh, I'm way too tired, way too old. Maybe, if we get through this – hah! – I'll just creep away, vanish into the streets of this Letheras. Retire. Take up fishing. Or maybe knitting. Funeral shawls. Bound to be a thriving enterprise for a while, I'd wager. Once the Adjunct arrives with the rest of us snarly losers and exacts a pleasant revenge for all us dead marines. No, stop thinking that way. We're still alive.

'Found a cat, Sergeant. Sleeping in the kitchen of that tavern. It's having bad dreams.'

'So become its worse nightmare, Bottle, and quick.'

Birds chirping in the trees behind them. Insects busy living and dying in the grasses around them. The extent of his world now, a tiresome travail punctuated by moments of profound terror. He itched with filth and could smell the stale stench of old fear, like redolent stains in the skin.

Who in Hood's name are these damned Letherii anyway? So this damned empire with its Edur overlords scrapped with the Malazan Empire. Laseen's problem, not ours. Damn you, Tavore, we get to this point and vengeance ain't enough—

'Got her,' Bottle said. 'Awake . . . stretching – yes, got to stretch, Sergeant, don't ask me why. All right, three people in the kitchen, all sweating, all rolling their eyes – they look terrified, huddling that way. I hear sounds in the tavern. Someone's singing . . .'

Fiddler waited for more.

And waited.

'Bottle—'

'Slipping into the tavern – ooh, a cockroach! Wait, no, stop playing with it – just eat the damned thing!'

'Keep your voice down, Bottle!'

'Done. Woah, crowded in here. That song . . . up onto the rail, and there—' Bottle halted abruptly, then, swearing under his breath, he rose. Stood for a moment, then snorted and said, 'Come on, Sergeant. We can just walk right on in.'

'Marines holding the village? Spit Hood on a stake, yes!'

The others heard that and as one they were on their feet, crowding round in relief.

Fiddler stared at all the stupid grins and was suddenly sober again. 'Look at you! A damned embarrassment!'

'Sergeant.' Bottle plucked at his arm. 'Fid, trust me, no worries on that front.'

Hellian had forgotten which song she was singing. Whatever it was, it wasn't what everyone else was singing, not that they were still singing, much. Though her corporal was somehow managing a double warble, stretching out some bizarre word in Old Cawn – foreigners shouldn't sing, since how could people understand them so it could be a mean song, a nasty, insulting song about sergeants, all of which meant her corporal earned that punch in the head and at least the warbling half stopped.

A moment later she realized that the other half had died away, too. And that she herself was the only one still singing, although even to her it sounded like some foreign language was blubbering from her numbed lips – something about sergeants, maybe – well, she could just take out this knife and—

More soldiers suddenly, the tavern even more crowded. Unfamiliar faces that looked familiar and how could that be well it was it just was, so there. Damn, another sergeant – how many sergeants did she have to deal with here in this tavern? First there was Urb, who seemed to have been following her around for weeks now, and then Gesler, staggering in at noon with more wounded than walking. And now here was another one, with the reddish beard and that battered fiddle on his back and there he was, laughing and hugging Gesler like they was long lost brothers or lovers or something – everyone was too damned happy as far as she was concerned. Happier than her, which was of course the same thing.

Things had been better in the morning. Was it this day? Yesterday? No matter. They'd been magicked hard to find – was that Balgrid's doing? Tavos Pond's? And so the three squads of Edur had pretty much walked right on top of them. Which made the killing easier. That wonderful sound of crossbows letting loose. *Thwok! Thwok! Thwokthwokthwok!* And then the swordwork, the in-close stabbing and chopping and slashing then poking and prodding but nope ain't nobody moving any more and that's a relief and being relieved was the happiest feeling.

Until it made you depressed. Standing around surrounded by dead people did that on occasion. The blood on the sword in your hand. The grunt twist and pull of removing quarrels from stubborn muscle, bone and organs. All the flies showing up like they was gathered on a nearby branch just waiting. And the stink of all that stuff poured out of bodies.

Stinking almost as bad as what was on all these marines. Who'd started all that? The fingers and cocks and ears and stuff?

A sudden flood of guilt in Hellian. *It was me!* She stood, reeled, then looked over at the long table that served large parties of travellers, the table that went along the side wall opposite the bar. Edur heads were piled high on it, amidst plenty of buzzing, crawling flies and maggots. *Too heavy on the belt – pulled Maybe's breeches down, hah! No wait, I'm supposed to be feeling bad. There's going to be trouble, because that's what comes when you get nasty with the corpses of your enemies. It just . . . what's the word?* 'Escalates!'

Faces turned, soldiers stared. Fiddler and Gesler who had been slapping each other on the back pulled apart and then walked over.

'Hood's pecker, Hellian,' Fiddler said under his breath, 'what happened to all the townfolk? As if I can't guess,' he added, glancing over at the heaped heads. 'They've all run away.'

Urb had joined them and he said, 'They were all those Indebted we heard about. Fifth, sixth generations. Working on blanks.'

'Blanks?' Gesler asked.

'For weapons,' Fiddler explained. 'So, they were slaves, Urb?'

'In everything but name,' the big man replied, scratching at his beard from which dangled one severed finger, grey and black. 'Under all those

Edur heads is the local Factor's head, some rich bastard in silks. We killed him in front of the Indebted and listened to them cheer. And then they cut off the poor fool's head as a gift, since we come in with all these Edur ones. And then they looted what they could and headed out.'

Gesler's brows had risen at all that. 'So you've managed what the rest of us haven't – arriving as damned liberators in this town.'

Hellian snorted. 'We worked that out weeks back. Never mind the Lurrii soljers, since they're all perfessionals and so's they like things jus' fine so's they's the one y'gotta kill no diff 'rent from the Edur. No, y'go into the hamlets and villages and kill all the 'ficials—'

'The what?' Gesler asked.

Urb said, 'Officials. We kill the officials, Gesler. And anybody with money, and the advocates, too.'

'The what?'

'Legal types. Oh, and the money-lenders and debt-holders, and the record-keepers and toll-counters. We kill them all—'

'Along with the soljers,' Hellian added, nodding – and nodding, for some reason finding herself unable to stop. She kept nodding as she said, 'An' what happens then is simple. Looting, lotsa sex, then everybody skittles out, and we sleep in soft beds and drink an' eat in the tavern an' if the keepers hang round we pays for it all nice an' honest—'

'Keepers like the ones hiding in the kitchen?'

Hellian blinked. 'Hiding? Oh, maybe we've gotten a little wild –'

'It's the heads,' Urb said, then he shrugged sheepishly. 'We're getting outa hand, Gesler, I think. Living like animals in the woods and the like—'

'Like animals,' Hellian agreed, still nodding. 'In soft beds and lotsa food and drink an' it's not like we carry them heads on our belts or anything. We just leave 'em in the taverns. Every village, right? Jus' to let 'em know we been through.' Unaccountably dizzy, Hellian sat back down, then reached for the flagon of ale on the table – needing to twist Balgrid's fingers from the handle and him fighting as if it was his flagon or something, the idiot. She swallowed a mouthful and leaned back – only it was a stool she was sitting on so there was no back to it, and now she was staring up at the ceiling and puddled whatever was soaking through her ragged shirt all along her back and faces were peering down at her. She glowered at the flagon still in her hand. 'Did I spill? Did I? Did I spill, dammit?'

'Not a drop,' Fiddler said, shaking his head in wonder. This damned Sergeant Hellian, who by Urb's account had crossed all the way from the coast in an inebriated haze – this soft-featured woman, soft just on the edge of dissolute, with the bright always wet lips – this Hellian had managed to succeed where every other squad – as far as Fiddler knew – had failed miserably. And since Urb was adamant on who was leading whom, it really *had* been her. This drunken, ferocious marine.

Leaving severed heads in every tavern, for Hood's sake!

But she had cut loose the common people, all these serfs and slaves and Indebted, and had watched them dance off in joy and freedom. *Our drunk liberator, our bloodthirsty goddess – what in Hood's name do all those people think when they first see her? Endless rumours of a terrible invading army. Soldiers and Edur dying in ambushes, chaos on the roads and trails. Then she shows up, dragging heads in sacks, and her marines break down every door in town and drag out all the ones nobody else has any reason to like. And then? Why, the not-so-subtle cutting away of all burdens for all these poor folk. 'Give us the bar for a couple nights and then we'll just be on our way.*

'Oh, and if you run into any Edur in the woods, send somebody back to warn us, right?'

Was it any wonder that Hellian and Urb and their squads had marched so far ahead of the others – or so Captain Sort had complained – with hardly any losses among her marines? The drunk, bright-eyed woman with all the rounded excesses of a well-fed, never sober but still young harlot had somehow managed to co-opt all the local help they'd needed to stay alive.

In a strange kind of floating wonder, the near-euphoria of relief, exhaustion and plenty of admiration that certainly wasn't innocent of sudden sexual desire – *for a damned drunk* – Fiddler found a table and moments later was joined by Gesler and Stormy, the latter arriving with a loaf of rye bread, a broached cask of ale and three dented pewter flagons with inscriptions on them.

'Can almost read this,' he said, squinting at the side of his cup. 'Like old Ehrlii.'

'Maker's stamp?' Gesler asked as he tore off a hunk of bread.

'No. Maybe something like "Advocate of the Year". Then a name. Could be Rizzin Purble. Or Wurble. Or Fizzin.'

'Could be that's the name of this village,' Gesler suggested. 'Fizzin Wurble.'

Stormy grunted, then nudged Fiddler. 'Stop dreaming of her, Fid. She's trouble and a lost cause too. Besides, it's Urb who's all dreamy 'bout her and he looks too dangerous to mess with.'

Fiddler sighed. 'Aye to all of that. It's just been a long time, that's all.'

'We'll get our rewards soon enough.'

He eyed Stormy for a moment, then glanced over to Gesler.

Who was scowling at his corporal. 'You lost your mind, Stormy? The only rewards we're going to reap are the crow feathers Hood hands out as we march through his gate. Sure, we're drawing up here, gaining in strength as we do it, but those Edur on our trail will be doing the same, outnumbering us five, ten to one by the time we run out of open ground.'

Stormy waved a dismissive hand. 'You do a count, Gesler? Look at Urb's squad. At Hellian's. Look at Fid's and ours. We're all damned near unscathed, given what we've been through. More living than dead in every squad here. So who's to say the other squads aren't in the same shape? We're damn near at strength, and you couldn't say that about the Letherii and the Edur, could you?'

'There's a whole lot more of them than us,' Gesler pointed out as he collected the cask and began pouring the ale into the flagons.

'Ain't made that much difference, though. We bulled through that last ambush—'

'And left the scene so cut up and bleeding a vole could've tracked us—'

'Sharper scatter, is all—'

'Mayfly's back was a shredded mess—'

'Armour took most of it—'

'Armour she doesn't have any more—'

'You two are worse than married,' Fiddler said, reaching for his ale.

'All right,' Koryk pronounced, 'there's no disagreement possible. Those bleckers of yours, Smiles, reek the worst of all. Worse than fingers, worse than ears, worse even than tongues. We've all voted. All us in the squad, and you've got to get rid of them.'

Smiles sneered. 'You think I don't know why you want me to toss 'em, Koryk? It's not the smell, oh no. It's the sight of them, and the way that makes you squirm inside, makes your balls pull up and hide. That's what this is all about. Pretty soon, none of us will be smelling much at all – everything's drying out, wrinkling up—'

'Enough,' groaned Tarr.

Koryk glanced across at Bottle. The fool looked to be asleep, his face hanging slack. Well, fair enough. Without Bottle they'd never have come this far. Virtually unscathed at that. He tapped the finger bone strung round his neck – the bone from the pit outside what was left of Y'Ghatan. Always worth a touch or two with thoughts like those.

And he knew they were headed for trouble. They all knew, which was why they'd talk about anything else but that huge grisly beast crouched right there in the forefront of their thoughts. The one with dripping fangs and jagged talons and that smeared grin of knowing. Aye. He touched the bone again.

'Come through not bad,' Cuttle said, eyeing the other marines in the crowded main room. 'Anybody here been thinking about how we're going to besiege a city the size of Unta? We're pretty much out of munitions – Fid's got a cusser left and maybe I do, too, but that's it. We can hardly try anything covert, since they know we're coming—'

'Magic, of course,' Smiles said. 'We'll just walk right in.'

691

Koryk winced at this turn in the conversation. Besieging Letheras? And nobody standing ranks-deep in their way? Not likely. Besides, the Edur were pushing them right along, and where the marines ended up was not going to be a pleasure palace, now was it? Had Cuttle lost his mind? Or was this just his way of dealing with the death looming in all their minds?

Probably. The sapper had little or no imagination, and he was making his biggest leap possible all the way to a siege that was never going to happen and wouldn't work anyway if it did, which it wouldn't. But it gave Cuttle something to think about.

'The sergeant will figure something out,' Cuttle concluded suddenly, with a loud sigh, as he settled back in his chair.

Hah, yes, Fiddler, Lord of the Sappers. Hie and fall on your knees!

Bottle sat looking through the ever-sharp eyes of a cat. Perched on the ridge of the tavern roof, gaze fixing and tracking on birds whenever the mage's concentration slipped – which was getting too often, but exhaustion did that, didn't it?

But now, there was movement there, along the edge of the forest there – where the squad had been hiding not so long ago. And more, to the north of that. And there, an Edur scout, edging out from the south end, other side of the road. Sniffing the air as was their wont – no surprise, the Malazans carried a carrion reek with them everywhere they went these days.

Oh, they were cautious, weren't they? *They don't want a real engagement. They just want us to bolt. Again. Once their strength's up, they'll show themselves more openly. Show their numbers, lances at the ready.*

A little time yet, then. For the other marines to relax. But not too much, lest they all got so drunk they couldn't stand, much less fight. Although, come to think on it, that Hellian seemed capable of fighting no matter how sodden she got – one of her corporals had talked about how she sobered up and turned into ice whenever the fighting started. Whenever orders needed delivering. That was a singular talent indeed. Her soldiers worshipped her. As did Urb and his squad. Worship all bound up with terror and probably more than a little lust, so a mixed-up kind of worship, which probably made it thick as armour and that was why so many were still alive.

Hellian, like a more modest version of, say, Coltaine. Or even Dujek during the Genabackan campaigns. Greymane in Korel. Prince K'azz for the Crimson Guard – from what I've heard.

But not, alas, the Adjunct. And that's too bad. That's worse than too bad—

Twenty Tiste Edur visible now, all eyeing the village – ooh, look at

692

that bird! No, that wasn't them. That was the damned cat. He needed to focus.

More of the barbaric warriors appearing. Another twenty. And there, another group as big as the first two combined.

A third one, coming down from due north and maybe even a little easterly—

Bottle shook himself, sat up, blinked across at his fellow marines. 'They're coming,' he said. 'We got to run.'

'How many?' Koryk demanded.

Three hundred and climbing. 'Too many—'

'Bottle!'

'Hundreds, damn you!'

He glared around the room, in the sudden silence following his scream. *Well now, that sobered 'em up.*

Beak's eyes felt full of sand. His tongue was thick in his mouth and he felt slightly nauseous. He wasn't used to keeping a candle lit for so long, but there had been little choice. The Tiste Edur were everywhere now. He had been muffling the sounds of horse hoofs from their mounts, he had been blurring their passage to make them little more than deeper shadows amidst the dappled cascade beneath branches. And he had been reaching out, his every sense awakened to almost painful precision, to find these stealthy hunters as they closed in on their trail. On everyone's trail. And to make matters worse, they were fighting in the same way as the Malazans – fast, vicious clashes, not even worrying about actually killing because wounding was better. Wounding slowed the marines down. Left blood trails. They cut then withdrew. Then did it all over again, later. Nights and into the days now, so there was no time to rest. Time only to . . . run.

And now he and the captain were riding in daylight, trying to find a way back to Fist Keneb and all the squads that had linked up with his company. Four hundred marines as of two days ago. Beak and the captain had pushed east in an effort to contact those squads that had moved faster and farther than all the others, but they had been driven back – too many Tiste Edur bands in between. He now knew that Faradan Sort feared those squads lost, if not dead already then as good as.

He was also pretty sure that this invasion was not quite going as planned. Something in the look in the captain's dark eyes told him that it wasn't just the two of them who kept stumbling into trouble. They'd found three squads, after all, that had been butchered – oh, they'd charged a high toll for the privilege, as Faradan Sort had said after wandering the glade with its heaps of corpses and studying the blood trails leading off into the woods. Beak could tell just by the silent howl of death roiling in the air, that cold fire that was the breath of every field of battle. A howl frozen like shock into the trees, the trunks, the branches and the leaves. And in the ground underfoot, oozing like sap, and Lily, his sweet bay, didn't want to take a single step into that clearing and Beak knew why.

A high toll, yes, just like she'd said, although of course no real coins were paid. Just lives.

They worked their weary mounts up an embankment all overgrown with bushes, and Beak was forced to concentrate even harder to mute the sounds of scrabbling hoofs and snapping brush, and the candle in his head flared suddenly and he very nearly reeled from his saddle.

The captain's hand reached across and steadied him. 'Beak?'

'It's hot,' he muttered. And now, all at once, he could suddenly see where all this was going, and what he would need to do.

The horses broke the contact between them as they struggled up the last of the ridge.

'Hold,' Faradan Sort murmured.

Yes. Beak sighed. 'Just ahead, Captain. We found them.'

A score of trees had been felled and left to rot directly ahead, and on this side of that barrier was a scum-laden pool on which danced glittering insects. Two marines smeared in mud rose from the near side of the bank, crossbows at the ready.

The captain raised her right hand and made a sequence of gestures, and the crossbows swung away and they were waved forward.

There was a mage crouched in a hollow beneath one of the felled trees, and she gave Beak a nod that seemed a little nervous. He waved back as they reined in ten paces from the pool.

The mage called out from her cover: 'Been expecting you two. Beak, you got a glow so bright it's damned near blinding.' Then she laughed. 'Don't worry, it's not the kind the Edur can see, not even their warlocks. But I'd dampen it down some, Beak, lest you burn right up.'

The captain turned to him and nodded. 'Rest now, Beak.'

Rest? No, there could be no rest. Not ever again. 'Sir, there are hundreds of Edur coming. From the northwest—'

'We know,' the other mage said, clambering out like a toad at dusk. 'We was just getting ready to pack our travelling trunks and the uniforms are pressed and the standards restitched in gold.'

'Really?'

She sobered and there was a sudden soft look in her eyes, reminding Beak of that one nurse his mother had hired, the one who was then raped by his father and had to go away. 'No, Beak, just havin' fun.'

Too bad, he considered. He would like to have seen that gold thread.

They dismounted and walked their horses round one end of the felled trees, and there, before them, was the Fist's encampment. 'Hood's mercy,' Faradan Sort said, 'there's more.'

'Six hundred and seventy-one, sir,' Beak said. And like the mage had said, there were getting ready to leave, swarming like ants on a kicked mound. There had been wounded – lots of them – but the healers had done their work and all the blood smelled old and the smell of death stayed where it belonged, close to the dozen graves on the far side of the clearing.

'Come along,' said the captain as two soldiers arrived to take charge of the horses, and Beak followed her as she made her way to where stood Fist Keneb and Sergeant Thom Tissy.

It felt strange to be walking after so long seated in those strange Letherii saddles, as if the ground was crumbling underfoot, and everything looked oddly fragile. *Yes. My friends. All of them.*

'How bad?' Keneb asked Faradan Sort.

'We couldn't reach them,' she replied, 'but there is still hope. Fist, Beak says we have to hurry.'

The Fist glanced at Beak and the young mage nearly wilted. Attention from important people always did that to him.

Keneb nodded, then sighed. 'I want to keep waiting, in case . . .' He shook his head. 'Fair enough. It's time to change tactics.'

'Yes sir,' said the captain.

'We push hard. For the capital, and if we run into anything we can't handle . . . we handle it.'

'Yes sir.'

'Captain, gather ten squads with full complement of heavies. Take command of our rearguard.'

'Yes sir.' She turned and took Beak by the arm. 'I want you on a stretcher, Beak,' she said as she led him along. 'Sleeping.'

'I can't, sir—'

'You will.'

'No, I really can't. The candles, they won't go out. Not any more. They won't go out.' *Not ever, Captain, and it isn't that I don't love you because I do and I'd do anything you asked. But I just can't and I can't even explain. Only, it's too late.*

He wasn't sure what she saw in his eyes, wasn't sure how much of all that he didn't say got heard anyway, but the grip of her hand on his arm loosened, became almost a caress, and she nodded and turned her head away. 'All right, Beak. Help us guard Keneb's back, then.'

'Yes sir, I will. You just watch me, I will.' He waited a moment, as they walked side by side through the camp, and then asked, 'Sir, if there's something we can't handle how do we handle it anyway?'

She either grunted or laughed from the same place that grunts came from. 'Sawtooth wedges and keep going, Beak. Throw back whatever is thrown at us. Keep going, until . . .'

'Until what?'

'It's all right, Beak, to die alongside your comrades. It's all right. Do you understand me?'

'Yes sir, I do. It is all right, because they're my friends.'

'That's right, Beak.'

And that's why no-one needs to worry, Captain.

Keneb watched as his marines fell into formation. Fast march, now, as if these poor souls weren't beat enough. But they couldn't dart and hide any more. The enemy had turned the game round and they had the advantage in numbers and maybe, finally, they were also a match for the ferocity of his Malazans.

It had been inevitable. No empire just rolls over, legs splaying. After enough pokes and jabs, it turns and snarls and then the fangs sink deep. And now it was his marines who were doing the bleeding. *But not nearly as bad as I'd feared. Look at them, Keneb. Looking meaner than ever.*

'Fist,' Thom Tissy said beside him, 'they're ready for you.'

'I see that, Sergeant.'

'No sir. I meant, *they're ready.*'

Keneb met the squat man's dark, beady eyes, and wasn't sure what he saw in them. Whatever it was, it burned bright.

'Sir,' Thom Tissy said, 'it's what we're meant for. All' – he waved one grimy hand – 'this. Trained to play more than one game, right? We stuck 'em enough to get 'em riled up and so here they are, all those damned Edur drawn right to us like we was a lodestone. Now we're about to knock 'em off balance all over again, and Hood take me, it's got my blood up! Same for us all! So, please, sir, sound us the order to march.'

Keneb stared at the man a moment longer, then he nodded.

To the sound of laughter, Koryk barrelled into the three Edur warriors, his heavy longsword hammering aside two of the out-thrust spears jabbing for his midsection. With his left hand he caught the shaft of the third one and used it to pull himself forward. Edge of his blade into the face of the warrior on his right – not deep enough to cause serious damage, but enough to spray blinding blood. Against the one in the middle, Koryk dropped one shoulder and hit him hard in the centre of his chest – hard enough to lift the Edur from his feet and send him sprawling back. Still gripping the third spear, Koryk twisted the warrior round and drove the point of his sword into the Edur's throat.

Koryk spun to slash at the first warrior, only to see her tumble back with a throwing knife skewering one eye socket. So he lunged after the middle Edur, sword chopping down in a frenzy until the Edur's smashed-up arms – raised to fend off the attack – fell away, freeing the half-blood Seti to deliver a skull-crushing blow.

Then he whirled. '*Will you in Hood's name stop that laughing!*'

But Smiles was on one knee, convulsing with hilarity even as she pulled out her throwing knife. 'Gods! I can't breathe! Wait – just wait—'

Snarling, Koryk turned to face the cloister again – these narrow-laned mews created perfect cul-de-sacs – lead them in at a run, flank out then turn and cut the bastards down. Even so, nobody had planned on making this ugly village the site of their last stand. Except maybe the Edur, who now entirely surrounded it and were working their way in, house by house, lane by lane.

Felt good kicking back, though, whenever they got too spread out in their eagerness to spill Malazan blood.

'They stink at fighting in groups,' Smiles said, coming up alongside him. She glanced up into his face and then burst out laughing again.

'What's so funny?'

'You! Them! The look in their eyes – the surprise, I mean, oh, gods of the deep! I can't stop!'

'You'd better,' Koryk warned, shaking the blood from his sword. 'I'm hearing movement – that lane mouth there – come on.'

Three quarrels flitted out, two of them taking down onrushing Edur. Two lances arced in retaliation, both darting straight for Fiddler. And then Tarr's huge shield shifted into their path, and the sergeant was pushed hard to one side – grunts from the corporal as both lances slammed solidly against the bronze-scaled face, one of them punching through a finger's length to pierce Tarr's upper arm. The corporal swore.

Fiddler ducked down behind the smithy's quenching barrel as a third lance cracked into it. Water gushed out onto the ground.

The crossfire ambush then caught the half-dozen charging Edur unawares – quarrels sleeting out from the narrow alley mouths on both sides. Moments later all were down, dead or dying.

'Pull back!' Fiddler shouted, turning to exchange his unloaded cross-bow for the loaded one Bottle now set into his hands.

Tarr covering the three of them, they retreated back through the smithy, across the dusty compound with its piled tailings and slag, through the kicked-down fence, and back towards the tavern.

Where, from the sounds, Stormy and his heavies were in a fight.

Motion on their flanks – the rest of the ambush converging. Cuttle, Corabb, Maybe, Gesler, Balgrid and Brethless. Reloading on the run.

'Gesler! Stormy's—'

'I can hear it, Fid! Corabb – hand that damned crossbow over to Brethless – you're useless with it. Join up with Tarr there and you two in first!'

'I got my target!' Corabb protested even as he gave one of Hellian's corporals the heavy weapon.

'By bouncing your quarrel off the cobbles and don't tell me that was a planned shot!'

Corabb was already readying the Edur spear he had picked up.

Fiddler waved Tarr forward as soon as Corabb arrived. 'Go, you two! Fast in and hard!'

Only by leaving his feet and throwing his entire weight on the shaft was the Edur able to drive the spear entirely through Stormy's left shoulder. An act of extraordinary courage that was rewarded with a thumb in his left eye – that dug yet deeper, then deeper still. Shrieking, the warrior tried to jerk his head away, but the huge red-bearded corporal now clutched a handful of hair and was holding him tight.

With a still louder shriek and even greater courage, the Edur tore his head back, leaving Stormy with a handful of scalp and a thumb smeared in gel and blood.

'Not so fast,' the corporal said in a strangely matter-of-fact tone, as he lunged forward to grapple the Edur. Both went down onto the smeared floorboards of the tavern – and the impact pushed the spear in Stormy's shoulder almost entirely through. Drawing his gutting knife, Stormy drove the blade into the warrior's side, just beneath the ribcage, under the heart, then cut outward.

Blood gushed in a flood.

Staggering, slipping, Stormy managed to regain his feet – the spear falling from his back – and tottered until he came up against the table with its pile of severed Edur heads. He reached for one and threw it across the room, into the crowd of Edur pushing in through the doorway where Flashwit and Bowl had been holding position until a spear skewered Bowl through the man's neck and someone knocked off Flashwit's helm and laid open her head. She was lying on her back, not moving as the moccasin-clad feet of the Edur stamped all over her in the inward rush.

The head struck the lead warrior in the face, and he howled in shock and pain, reeling to one side.

Mayfly stumbled up to take position beside Stormy. Stabbed four times already, it was a wonder the heavy was still standing.

'Don't you die, woman,' Stormy rumbled.

She set his sword into his hands. 'Found this, Sergeant, and thought you might want it.'

698

There was no time to answer as the first three Edur reached them.

Emerging from the kitchen entrance – a kitchen now emptied of serving staff – Corabb saw that charge, and he leapt forward to take it from the flank.

And tripped headlong over the body of the Edur that Stormy had just stabbed. His hands went forward, still holding the spear. The point drove through the right thigh of the nearest warrior, missing the bone, and plunged out the other side to stab into the next Edur's left knee, the triangular head sliding under the patella and neatly separating the joint on its way through. Angling downward, the point sticking fast between two floorboards, until the far one sprang loose, in time to foul the steps of the third Edur, and that warrior seemed to simply throw himself onto Stormy's out-thrust sword.

As Corabb landed amidst falling enemy, Tarr arrived, his shortsword hacking down here and there as he worked forward to plant himself in the path of the rest of the Edur.

Flashwit then stood up in their midst and she had a kethra knife in each hand.

Fiddler led the charge through the kitchen doorway, crossbow ready, to find Tarr cutting down the last standing Edur. The room was piled with bodies, only a few still moving, and crawling out from beneath two Edur corpses was Corabb Bhilan Thenu'alas, coughing in all the blood that had spilled over him.

Brethless moved past to the window. 'Sergeant! Another mob of 'em!'

'Crossbows up front!' Fiddler snapped.

Hellian squinted across the street at the fancy house. The Factor's house, she recalled. Had that look. Expensive, tasteless. She pointed with a dripping sword. 'Over in there, that's where we'll make our stand.'

Urb grunted, then spat out a red stream – taken to chewing betel nut, maybe. The things some people would do to their bodies beggared belief. She drank down another mouthful of the local whatever that tasted like bamboo shoots some dog had pissed on, but what a kick. Then waved him forward.

And then the others, except for Lutes and Tavos Pond who'd both been cut to pieces trying to hold a flank at that alley mouth back there. 'I'll take up rearguard,' she said by way of explanation as the six remaining marines staggered past. 'In a smart line, now!'

Another mouthful. Just got worse, this stuff. Who would come up with a drink like that?

She set out. Was halfway there or maybe just halfway along when a hundred or so Tiste Edur appeared thirty or so paces down the main street. So she threw the clay bottle away and planted her feet to meet the charge. Was what rearguard did, right? Hold 'em back.

The first row, about ten of them, halted and raised their lances.

'Not fair!' Hellian shouted, pulling her shield up and getting ready to duck behind it – oh, this wasn't a shield at all. It was the lid of an ale cask, the kind with a handle. She stared at it. 'Hey, I wasn't issued this.'

Three straight days and nights on the run from the river bank and now the sounds of fighting somewhere ahead. Since he'd lost his corporal two nights past – the fool fell down an abandoned well, one moment there at his side, the next gone. Went through a net of roots at least most of the way, until he jammed his head and pop went the neck and wasn't it funny how Hood never forgot since it'd been join the marines or dance the gibbet for the corporal and now the fool had done both. Since Badan Gruk lost his corporal, then, he now dragged Ruffle with him – not quite a promotion, Ruffle was not the promoting type, but she kept a cool eye when she wasn't busy eating everything in sight.

And now it was with a wheeze that Ruffle settled down beside Badan Gruk, 5th Squad sergeant, 3rd Company, 8th Legion, and lifted her pale rounded face up to his with that cold grey regard. 'We're kind of tired, Sergeant.'

Badan Gruk was Dal Honese, but not from the north savanna tribes. He had been born in the south jungle, half a day from the coast. His skin was as black as a Tiste Andii's, and the epicanthic folds of his eyes were so pronounced that little more than slits of white were visible; and he was not a man to smile much. He felt most comfortable on moonless nights, although Skim always complained about how their sergeant just damn disappeared, usually when he was needed the most.

But now here they were, in bright daylight, and oh how Badan Gruk wished for the gloom of the tropical rainforest of his homeland. 'Stay here, Ruffle,' he now said, then turned and scrabbled back to where Sergeant Primly crouched with the rest of the marines. Primly's squad, the 10th, was also but one short, while the 4th was down two, including Sergeant Sinter and that sent yet another pang through Badan Gruk. She'd been from his own tribe, after all. Damn, she'd been the reason he'd joined up in the first place. Following Sinter had always been way too easy.

Drawing close, Badan Gruk waved Primly over and the Quon noble's corporal, Hunt, tagged along. The three settled a short distance from the others. 'So,' Badan breathed, 'do we go round this?'

Primly's long ascetic face soured, which is what it always did whenever anyone spoke to him. Badan wasn't too sure of the man's history, beyond the obvious, which was that Primly had done something bad, once – bad enough to get him disowned and maybe even on the run. At least he'd left the highborn airs behind. To Badan's whispered question, Corporal Hunt snorted, then looked away.

'You're here,' Badan said to the Kartoolii, 'so talk.'

Hunt shrugged. 'We been running since the river, Sergeant. Ducking and dodging till all three of our mages are used up and worse than walking dead.' He nodded northwards. 'Those are marines up there, and they're in a fight. We're only down one heavy and one sapper—'

'And a sergeant and a corporal,' Badan added.

'Seventeen of us, Sergeant. Now, I seen what your heavies can do, and both me and Sergeant Primly can tell you that Lookback, Drawfirst and Shoaly are easy matches to Reliko and Vastly Blank. And Honey's still got three cussers and half again all the sharpers since Kisswhere left 'em behind when she and Sinter went and—'

'All right,' Badan cut in, not wanting to hear again what had happened to Sinter and Kisswhere, since it had been Kisswhere who had been the reason for Sinter's joining. Nothing good following a woman who was following another woman with worship in her eyes – even a sister – but that had been that and they were both gone now, weren't they? 'Primly?'

The Quon rubbed at what passed for a beard on his face – gods, showed just how young the poor bastard was – and cast a searching gaze back on the waiting soldiers. Then he smiled suddenly. 'Look at Skulldeath, Badan. Here we got a soldier that Toothy himself named first day on Malaz Island, and I still don't know – was it a joke? Skulldeath's yet to draw a drop of blood, barring mosquitoes and that blood was his own. Besides, Badan Gruk, you've got what looks like some kind of Dal Honese grand council here and you moonless night-shades seem to put holy terror in the Edur, like you were ghosts or something and sometimes I start wondering myself, the way you all manage to vanish in the dark. In any case, there's you, Nep Furrow, Reliko and Neller and Strap Mull and Mulvan Dreader's halfway there besides, and, well, we've come to fight, haven't we? So let's fight.'

Maybe you came to fight, Primly. I'm just trying to stay alive. Badan Gruk studied the two men beside him for a moment longer, then he rose to his full height, coming to very nearly Primly's shoulder, and drew out the two-handed sickle sword from its deer-hide harness on his broad back. Adjusting his grip on the ivory handle, he eyed the two thin otataral blades inset on both sides of the curved and carved tusk. *Vethbela*, the weapon was called in his own language, *Bonekisser*, the blades not deep enough to do more than touch the long bones of a normal warrior's legs, since those femurs were prized trophies, to be polished and carved with scenes of the owner's glorious death – and any

701

warrior seeking the heart of a woman needed to place more than a few at the threshold of her family's hut, as proof of his prowess and courage.

Never did manage to use this thing properly, did I? Not a single thigh bone to show Sinter. He nodded. 'Time to collect some trophies, then.'

Fifteen paces away, Honey nudged Skim. 'Hey, beloved, looks like we get to toss sharpers today.'

'Stop calling me that,' the other sapper replied in a bored tone, but she watched as Badan Gruk headed back up to where Ruffle hid, and she watched as Corporal Hunt went back down-trail to collect the 4th Squad's corporal, Pravalak Rim, who had been guarding their butts with Shoaly and Drawfirst. And pretty soon something less than whispered was dancing through every soldier and she saw weapons being drawn, armour straps tightened, helms adjusted, and finally she grunted. 'All right, Honey – Hood take me, how I hate saying that – looks like you've sniffed it just right—'

'Just let me prove it—'

'You're never prying my legs apart, Honey. Why don't you get that?'

'What a miserable attitude,' the 10th's sapper complained as he loaded his crossbow. 'Now Kisswhere, she was—'

'So tired of your advances, Honey, that she went and blew herself up – and took her sister with her, too. And now here I am wishing I'd been with them in that scull.' With that she rose and scrabbled over to Nep Furrow.

The old Dal Honese mage lifted one yellowy eye to squint at her, then both eyes opened wide when he saw the sharper she held in each hand. 'Eggit'way fra meen, tit-woman!'

'Relax,' she said, 'we're heading into a fight. You got anything left in that bent reed of yours?'

'Wha'?'

'Magicks, Nep, magicks – comes from the bleckers in men. Every woman knows that,' and she winked.

'You teasin' tit-woman you! Eggit'way fra meen!'

'I'm not eggitin' away from you, Nep, until you bless these two sharpers here.'

'Bliss 'em clay balls? Ya mad, tit-woman? Less time I done that—'

'They blew up, aye. Sinter and Kisswhere. Into pieces but nice and quick, right? Listen, it's my only way to escape Honey's advances. No, seriously, I want one of your blissin' curses or cursed blissin's. Please, Nep—'

'Eggit'way fra meen!'

*

Reliko, who was half a hand shorter even than his sergeant and therefore, by Toothy's own assertion, the smallest heavy infantry soldier in the history of the Malazan Empire, grunted upright and drew out his shortsword as he swung his shield into position. He glanced over at Vastly Blank. 'Time again.'

The oversized Seti warrior, still sitting on the bed of wet moss, looked up. 'Huh?'

'Fighting again.'

'Where?'

'Us, Vastly. Remember Y'Ghatan?'

'No.'

'Well, won't be like Y'Ghatan. More like yesterday only harder. Remember yesterday?'

Vastly Blank stared a moment longer, then he laughed his slow *ha ha ha* laugh and said, 'Yesterday! I remember yesterday!'

'Then pick up your sword and wipe the mud off it, Vastly. And take your shield – no, not mine, yours, the one on your back. Yes, bring it round. That's it – no, sword in the other hand. There, perfect. You ready?'

'Who do I kill?'

'I'll show you soon enough.'

'Good.'

'Seti should never breed with bhederin, I think.'

'What?'

'A joke, Vastly.'

'Oh. Ha ha ha! Ha.'

'Let's go join up with Lookback – we'll be on point.'

'Lookback's on point?'

'He's always on point for this kind of thing, Vastly.'

'Oh. Good.'

'Drawfirst and Shoaly at our backs, right? Like yesterday.'

'Right. Reliko, what happened yesterday?'

Strap Mull stepped close to Neller and they both eyed their corporal, Pravalak Rim, who was just sending Drawfirst and Shoaly up to the other heavies.

The two soldiers spoke in their native Dal Honese. 'Broke-hearted,' Strap said.

'Broker than broke,' Neller agreed.

'Kisswhere, she was lovely.'

'Lovelier than lovely.'

'Like Badan says, though.'

'Like he says, yes.'

'And that's that, is what he says.'

'I know that, Strap, you don't need to tell me anything. You think Letheras will be like Y'Ghatan? We didn't do nothing in Y'Ghatan. And,' Neller suddenly added, as if struck by something, 'we haven't done nothing here either, have we? Nothing not yet, anyway. If it's going to be like Y'Ghatan, though—'

'We're not even there yet,' Strap Mull said. 'Which sword you going to use?'

'This one.'

'The one with the broken handle?'

Neller looked down, frowned, then threw the weapon into the bushes and drew out another one. 'This one. It's Letherii, was on the cabin wall—'

'I know. I gave it to you.'

'You gave it to me because it howls like a wild woman every time I hit something with it.'

'That's right, Neller, and that's why I asked what sword you were going to use.'

'Now you know.'

'Now I know so I'm stuffing my ears with moss.'

'Thought they already were.'

'I'm adding more. See?'

Corporal Pravalak Rim was a haunted man. Born in a northern province of Gris to poor farmers, he had seen nothing of the world for most of his life, until the day a marine recruiter had come through the nearby village on the very day Pravalak was there with his older brothers, all of whom sneered at the marine on their way to the tavern. But Pravalak himself, well, he had stared in disbelief. His first sight of someone from Dal Hon. She had been big and round and though she was decades older than him and her hair had gone grey he could see how she had been beautiful and indeed, to his eyes, she still was.

Such dark skin. Such dark eyes, and oh, she spied him out and gave him that gleaming smile, before leading him by the hand into a back room of the local gaol and delivering her recruiting pitch sitting on him and rocking with exalted glee until he exploded right into the Malazan military.

His brothers had expressed their disbelief and were in a panic about how to explain to their ma and da how their youngest son had gone and got himself signed up and lost his virginity to a fifty-year-old demoness in the process – and was, in fact, not coming home at all. But that was their problem, and Pravalak had trundled off in the recruiter's wagon, one hand firmly snuggled between her ample legs, without a backward look.

That first great love affair had lasted the distance to the next town, where he'd found himself transferred onto a train of about fifty other Grisian farm boys and girls and marching an imperial road down to Unta, and from there out to Malaz Island for training as a marine. But he had not been as heartbroken as he would have thought, for the Malazan forces were crowded for a time with Dal Honese recruits – some mysterious population explosion or political upheaval had triggered an exodus from the savanna and jungles of Dal Hon. And he had soon realized that his worship of midnight skin and midnight eyes did not doom him to abject longing and eternal solitude.

Until he first met Kisswhere, who had but laughed at his attempts, as smooth and honed as they had become by then. And it was this rejection that stole his heart for all time.

Yet what haunted him now was, perhaps surprisingly, not all of that unrequited adoration. It was what he had seen, or maybe but imagined, in that dark night on the river, after the blinding flash of the munitions and the roar that shook the water, that one black-skinned hand, reaching up out of the choppy waves, the spinning swirl of the current awakening once more in the wake of the tumult, parting round the elegant wrist – and then that hand slipped away, or was simply lost to his straining sight, his desperate, anguished search in the grainy darkness – the hand, the skin, the dark, dark skin that so defeated him that night . . .

Oh, he wanted to die, now. To end his misery. She was gone. Her sister was gone, too – a sister who had drawn him to one side just two nights earlier and had whispered in his ear, *'Don't give up on her, Prav. I know my sister, you see, and there's a look growing in her eyes when she glances your way . . . so, don't give up . . .'*

Both gone, and that, as Badan repeated again and again when he thought no-one else was close enough to hear him, *is that. And that is that.*

Sergeant Primly came up then and slapped Pravalak on one shoulder. 'Ready, Corporal? Good. Lead your squad, just like Sinter would've done. Lead 'em, Prav, and let's go gut some Edur.'

Skulldeath, whose name had once been Tribole Futan, last surviving male of the Futani royal line of the Gilani tribe of southeast Seven Cities, slowly straightened as he watched the heavies work their way up the slope towards the sounds of fighting.

He readied his two Gilani tulwars, which had once belonged to a Falah'dan champion – his great-uncle – who had fallen to an assassin's poison three years before the Malazan invasion, when Tribole had been a child not yet cast out onto the mortal sands. Weapons he had inherited as last of the line in a family shattered by a feud, such as were common throughout all of Seven Cities before the conquest. The tulwars seemed large in his hands, almost oversized for his wrists – but he was Gilani and his tribe were a people characterized by bodies virtually devoid of fat. Muscles like ropes, long, gracile and far stronger than they appeared.

The softness of his feminine eyes did not change as he studied the tulwars, remembering when he had been a very young child and these weapons, if balanced on their curved tips, could be made to stand if he set the silver pommels into his armpits, and, gripping the handles just above the hilts, he would pitch himself round the camp like an imp with but one leg. Not long after that, he was using weighted sticks carved to match these tulwars of his great-uncle's. Working the patterns in the Gilani style, both afoot and atop a desert horse where he learned to perch on the balls of his feet and practise the lishgar efhanah, the leaping attack, the Edged Net. Many a night with bruised shoulders, then, until he learned how to roll clean after the mid-air attack was done, the three stuffed-grass dummies each sliced into pieces, the wind plucking at those golden grasses as they drifted in the dusty air. And he, rolling, upright once more, weapons at the ready.

He was not tall. He was not outspoken and his smile – rare as it was – was as shy as a young maiden's. Men wanted him in their beds. So did women. But he was of the royal line, and his seed was the last seed, and one day he would give it to a queen, perhaps even an empress, as befitted his true station. In the meantime, he would let men use him as they would, and even find pleasure in that, harmless as it was. But he refused to spill his seed.

He stood now, and when the signal was given, he moved forward, light on his feet.

Skulldeath was twenty-three years old. Such was his discipline that he had not spilled seed once, not even in his sleep.

As the squad mage Mulvan Dreader would say later, Skulldeath was truly a man about to explode.

And a certain Master Sergeant on Malaz Island had got it right. Again.

Urb ran back from the Factor's house as fast as he could, angling his shield to cover his right shoulder. The damned woman! Standing there with a damned cask lid with a flight of lances about to wing her way. Oh, her soldiers worshipped her all right, and so blind was that worship that not one of them could see all that Urb did just to keep the fool woman alive. He was exhausted and a nervous wreck besides and now – this time – it looked as if he would be too late.

Five paces from Hellian and out went a half-dozen lances, two winging to intercept Urb. Skidding as he pivoted round behind his shield, he lost sight of her.

One lance darted past a hand's width from his face. The other struck true against the shield, the iron head punching through to impale his upper arm, pinning it to his side. The impact spun Urb round and he staggered as the lance pulled at him, and, grunting, he slid down on his knees, the hard cobbles driving shocks up his legs. He slammed his sword-hand down – still clutching the weapon – to keep from pitching forward, and heard a knuckle crack.

At that instant, the world exploded white.

Four lances speeding Hellian's way came close to sobering her up. Crouching, she lifted her flimsy, undersized shield, only to have it hammered from her hand in a splintering concussion that sent it spinning, the snapped foreshafts of two lances buried deep in the soaked, heavy, wonderful-smelling wood. Then her helm was torn from her head with a deafening clang, even as she was struck a glancing blow on her right shoulder that ripped away the leather shingles of her armour. That impact turned her right round so that she faced up the street, and, upon seeing the clay bottle she had thrown away moments earlier, she dived towards it.

Better to die with one last mouthful—

The air above her whistled as she sailed through the air and she saw maybe a dozen lances flit overhead.

She slammed chest-first on the dusty cobbles, all breath punched from her lungs and stared, bug-eyed, as the bottle leapt of its own accord into the air. Then she was lifted by her feet and flipped straight over to thump hard on her back, and above her the blue sky was suddenly grey with dust and gravel, stone chips, red bits, all raining down.

She could not hear a thing, and that first desperate breath was so thick with dust that she convulsed in a fit of coughing. Twisting onto her side, she saw Urb maybe six paces away. The idiot had got himself skewered and looked even more stunned than usual. His face was white with dust except the blood on his lips from a tooth gash, and he was staring dumbly down the street to where all the Edur were – might be they were charging them now so she'd better find her sword—

She'd just sat up when a hand slapped her shoulder and she glared up at an unfamiliar face – a Kanese woman frowning intently at her. With a voice that seemed far away she said, 'Still with us, Sergeant? You shouldn't ever be that close to a cusser, you know.'

And then she was gone.

Hellian blinked. She squinted down the street and saw an enormous crater where the Edur had been. And body parts, and drifting dust and smoke.

And four more marines, two of them Dal Honese, loosing quarrels

707

into a side street then scattering as one of them threw a sharper in the same direction.

Hellian crawled over to Urb.

He'd managed to pull the lance out of his arm which had probably hurt, and there was plenty of blood now, pooling beneath him. His eyes had the look of a butchered cow though maybe not as dead as that but getting there.

Another marine arrived, another stranger. Black-haired, pale skin. He knelt down beside Urb.

'You,' Hellian said.

The man glanced over. 'None of your wounds look to kill you, Sergeant. But your friend here is going fast, so let me do my work.'

'What squad, damn you?'

'Tenth. Third Company.'

A healer. Well, good. Fix Urb right up so she could kill him. 'You're Nathii, aren't you?'

'Sharp woman,' he muttered as he began weaving magic over the huge torn hole in Urb's upper arm. 'Probably even sharper when you're sober.'

'Never count on that, Cutter.'

'I'm not really a cutter, Sergeant. I'm a combat mage, but we can't really be picky about those things any more, can we? I'm Mulvan Dreader.'

'Hellian. Eighth Squad, the Fourth.'

He shot her a sudden look. 'Really. You one of the ones crawled out under Y'Ghatan?'

'Yeah. Urb's gonna live?'

The Nathii nodded. 'Be on a stretcher for a while, though. All the lost blood.' He straightened and looked round. 'Where are the rest of your soldiers?'

Hellian looked over at the Factor's house. The cusser explosion seemed to have knocked it flat. She grunted. 'Damned if I know, Mulvan. You don't happen to have a flask of something on you, do you?'

But the mage was frowning at the wreckage of the collapsed house. 'I hear calls for help,' he said.

Hellian sighed. 'Guess you found 'em after all, Mulvan Dreader. Meaning we're gonna have to dig 'em out.' Then she brightened. 'But that'll work us up a thirst now, won't it?'

The multiple *crack* of sharpers outside the tavern and the biting snap of shrapnel striking the building's front sent the Malazans inside flinching back. Screams erupted outside, wailing up into the street's dust-filled air. Fiddler watched Gesler grab Stormy to keep him from charging out there – the huge Falari was reeling on his feet – then he turned to Mayfly, Corabb and Tarr. 'Let's meet our allies, then, but stay sharp. Rest of you, stay here, bind wounds – Bottle, where's Koryk and Smiles?'

But the mage shook his head. 'They went east side of the village, Sergeant.'

'All right, you three with me, then. Bottle – can you do something for Stormy?'

'Aye.'

Fiddler readied his crossbow, then led the way to the tavern entrance. At the threshold he crouched down, peering through the dust.

Allies all right. Blessed marines, a half-dozen, walking through the sprawled Edur bodies and silencing the screamers with quick thrusts of their swords. Fiddler saw a sergeant, South Dal Honese, short and wide and black as onyx. The woman at his side was half a head taller, pale-skinned and grey-eyed, and nearly round but in a way that had yet to sag. Behind these two stood another Dal Honese, this one wrinkled with pierced everything – ears, nose, wattle, cheeks – the gold ornaments a startling contrast to his dark scowling face. *A damned shaman.*

Fiddler approached, his eyes on the sergeant. There was fighting still going on, but nowhere close. 'How many of you?'

'Seventeen to start,' the man replied. He paused to look down at the barbaric tusk-sword in his hands. 'Just took off an Edur's head with this,' he said, then looked up. 'My first kill.'

Fiddler gaped. 'How in Hood's name did you get this far from the damned coast, then? What are you all, Soletaken bats?'

The Dal Honese grimaced. 'We stole a fisher boat and sailed up.'

The woman at his side spoke. 'We were the southmost squads, moving east till we hit the river, then it was either wading waist-deep in swamp muck or taking to the water. Worked fine until a few nights ago, when we ran straight into a Letherii galley. We lost a few that night,' she added.

Fiddler stared at her a moment longer. All round and soft-looking, except for those eyes. *Hood take me, this one could pluck the skin off a man one tiny strip at a time with one hand while doing herself with the other.* He looked away, back to the sergeant. 'What company?'

'Third. I'm Badan Gruk, and you're Fiddler, aren't you?'

'Yeggetan,' muttered the shaman with a warding gesture.

Badan Gruk turned to the pale woman. 'Ruffle, take Vastly and Reliko and work west until you meet up with Primly. Then back here.' He faced Fiddler again. 'We caught 'em good, I think.'

'Thought I heard a cusser a while back.'

A nod. 'Primly had the sappers. Anyway, the Edur pulled back, so I suppose we scared 'em.'

'Moranth munitions will do that.'

Badan Gruk glanced away again. He seemed strangely skittish. 'We never expected to run into any squads this far east,' he said. 'Not unless they took to the water like we did.' He met Fiddler's eyes. 'You're barely a day from Letheras, you know.'

Seven Edur had turned the game on Koryk and Smiles, pushing them into a less than promising lane between decrepit, leaning tenements, that then led to a most quaint killing ground blocked by stacks of timber on all sides but the one with the alley mouth.

Pushing Smiles behind him as he backed away from the Edur – who crowded the alley, slowly edging forward – Koryk readied his sword. Hand-and-a-half fighting now that he'd lost his shield. If the bastards threw lances, he'd be in trouble.

The thought made him snort. Him against seven Tiste Edur and all he had behind him was a young woman who'd used up all her throwing knives and was left with a top-heavy gutter that belonged in the hands of a butcher. Trouble? Only if they threw lances.

But these Edur weren't interested in skewering them from a distance. They wanted to close, and Koryk was not surprised by that. *Like Seti, these grey gaunts. Face to face, aye. That is where true glory is found.* As they reached the mouth of the alley, Koryk lifted the tip of his sword and waved them forward.

'Stay right back,' he said to Smiles who crouched behind him. 'Give me plenty of room—'

'To do what, you oaf? Die in style? Just cut a few and I'll slide in low and finish 'em.'

'And get a pommel through the top of your head? No, stay back.'

'I ain't staying back t'get raped by all the ones you were too incompetent to kill before dying yourself, Koryk.'

'Fine! *I'll* punch my pommel through your thick skull, then!'

'Only time you're ever gettin' inside of me, so go ahead and enjoy it.'

'Oh, believe me, I will—'

They might have gone on, and on, but the Edur had fanned out, four in front and three behind, and now they rushed forward.

Koryk and Smiles argued often, later, about whether their saviour descended on wings or just had a talent for leaping extraordinary distances, for he arrived in a blur, sailing right across the path of the first four Tiste Edur, and in that silent flight he seemed to writhe, amidst flashing heavy iron blades. A flurry of odd *snicking* sounds and then the man was past – and should have collided badly with a stack of rough-barked wood. Instead, one of those tulwars touched down tip first on a log, and pivoting on that single point of contact the man twisted round to land in a cat-like crouch against the slope of timbers – at an impossible to maintain angle, but that didn't matter since he was already springing back the way he had come, this time sailing over the collapsing, blood-drenched forms of four Tiste Edur. *Snick snick snick-snick* – and the back three Edur toppled.

He landed again, just short of the opposite timber wall this time, head ducking and shoulder seeming to barely brush the ground before he tumbled right over, touched one foot on a horizontal log and used it to twist round before landing balanced on the other foot now drawn tight beneath him. Facing the seven corpses he had just felled.

And facing two Malazan marines who, for once and just this once, had precisely nothing to say.

The marines of the 3rd and 4th Companies gathered in front of the tavern, stood or sat on the bloodstained cobbles of the main street. Wounds were tended to here and there, while others repaired armour or filed the nicks from sword edges.

Fiddler sat on the edge of a water trough near the hitching post to one side of the tavern entrance, taking stock. Since the coast, the three other squads of 4th Company had taken losses. Gone from Gesler's squad were Sands and Uru Hela. From Hellian's, Lutes and Tavos Pond, both of whom had died in this cursed village, while from Urb's both Hanno and now Bowl were dead, and Saltlick had lost his left hand. Fiddler's own squad had, thus far, come through unscathed, and that made him feel guilty. *Like one of Hood's minions, one in the row just the other side of the gate. Crow feathers in hand, or wilted roses, or sweetcakes, or any of the countless other gifts the dead were eager to hand their newly arrived kin – gods below, Smiles is turning me into another Kanese with all these absurd beliefs. Ain't nobody waiting other side of Hood's Gate, unless it's to jeer.*

The two sergeants from the 3rd came over. Badan Gruk, whom Fiddler had met earlier, and the Quon, Primly. They made an odd pair, but that was always the way, wasn't it?

Primly gave Fiddler a strangely deferential nod. 'We're fine with this,' he said.

'With what?'

'Your seniority, Fiddler. So, what do we do now?'

Grimacing, Fiddler looked away. 'Any losses?'

'From this scrap? No. Those Edur pulled out fast as hares in a kennel. A lot shakier than we'd expected.'

'They don't like the shield to shield fighting,' Fiddler said, scratching at his filthy beard. 'They'll do it, aye, especially when they've got Letherii troops with them. But of late they dropped that tactic, since with our munitions we made it a costly one. No, they've been hunting us, ambushing us, driving us hard. Their traditional way of fighting, I'd guess.'

711

Primly grunted. 'Driving you, you said. So, likely there's a damned army waiting for us this side of Letheras. The anvil.'

'Aye, which is why I think we should wait here a bit. It's risky, I know, since the Edur might return and next time there might be a thousand of them.'

Badan Gruk's thinned eyes grew yet thinner. 'Hoping your Fist is going to catch up with a lot more marines.'

'Your Fist now, too, Badan Gruk.'

A sharp nod, then a scowl. 'We only got thrown into the mix because of the 4th's losses at Y'Ghatan.'

'The Adjunct keeps making changes,' Primly said. 'We don't have Fists in charge of nothing but marines – not since Crust's day—'

'Well, we do now. We're not in the Malazan Army any more, Primly.'

'Yes, Fiddler, I'm aware of that.'

'That's my suggestion,' Fiddler repeated. 'Wait here for a while. Let our mages get some rest. And hope Keneb shows and hope he's got more than a few dozen marines with him. Now, I'm not much for this seniority thing. I'd rather we sergeants just agreed on matters, so I'm not holding you to anything.'

'Gesler agrees with you, Fiddler?'

'Aye.'

'What of Hellian and Urb?'

Fiddler laughed. 'Tavern's still wet, Primly.'

The sun had gone down, but no-one seemed eager to go anywhere. Traffic in and out of the tavern occurred whenever another cask needed bringing out. The tavern's main room was a slaughterhouse no-one was inclined to stay in for very long.

Smiles walked over to where Koryk sat. 'His name's Skulldeath, if you can believe that.'

'Who?'

'Nice try. You know who. The one who could kill you with his big toe.'

'Been thinking about that attack,' Koryk said. 'Only works if they're not expecting it.'

Smiles snorted.

'No, really. I see someone flying at me I cut him in half. It's not like he can retreat or change his mind, is it?'

'You're an idiot,' she said, then nudged him. 'Hey, met your twin brother, too. His name is Vastly Blank and between you two I'd say he got all the brains.'

Koryk glowered at her. 'What is it you want with me, Smiles?'

She shrugged. 'Skulldeath. I'm going to make him mine.'

'Yours?'

'Yes. Did you know he's saving himself for a woman of royal blood?'

'That's not what the men inclined that way are saying.'

'Where'd you hear that?'

'Besides, you're hardly royal blood, Smiles. Queen of shell-shuckers won't cut it.'

'That's why I need you to lie for me. I was a Kanese princess – sent into the Malazan Army to keep the Claw from finding me—'

'Oh, for Hood's sake!'

'Shh! Listen, the rest in the squad said they'd be happy to lie for me. What's wrong with you?'

'Happy . . . ha, that's good. Very good.' He then turned to study her. 'You're eager for Skulldeath to take one of those flying leaps straight between your legs? You want to get pregnant with some prince from some Seven Cities flying squirrel tribe?'

'Pregnant? Aye, when dolphins walk and fish nest in trees. I won't get pregnant,' she pronounced. 'Bottle's giving me some herbs to take care of that. My beloved Skulldeath can empty gallons of his seed into me for Hood-damned ever and there won't be any little jackrabbits jumping round.'

'He's got the face of a girl,' Koryk said. 'And the men say he kisses like one, too.'

'Who's telling you all this?'

'Saving his seed, that's a laugh.'

'Listen, those men, they don't mean nothing. Now, am I a Kanese princess or not?'

'Oh, aye. Rival to the empire's throne, in fact. Be the flying fish to the flying squirrel and make your nest in some tree, Smiles. When all's done what's needed doing.'

She surprised him with a bright smile. 'Thanks, Koryk. You're a true friend.'

He stared after her as she hurried off. Poor lass. *The squirrel's saving his seed because he doesn't know what to do with it, is my guess.*

A figure walked past in the gloom and Koryk squinted until he recognized the man's gait. 'Hey, Bottle.'

The young mage halted, looked over, then, feet dragging, approached.

Koryk said, 'You're supposed to be asleep.'

'Thanks.'

'So you're giving Smiles special herbs, are you. Why do you—'

'I'm what?'

'Herbs. So she won't get pregnant.'

'Look, if she doesn't want to get pregnant, she should just stop straddling every—'

'Hold on, Bottle! Wait. I thought she'd talked to you. About herbs which you promised to give her—'

'Oh, those herbs. No, you got it all wrong, Koryk. Those aren't to keep her from getting pregnant. In fact, it's some concoction of my grandmother's and I've no idea if it even works, but anyway, it's got nothing to do with not getting pregnant. Why, if she'd asked me about that kind of stuff, sure, there's some very reliable—'

'Stop! What – what does this concoction you're giving her do to her, then?'

'She'd better not be taking it! It's for a man—'

'For Skulldeath?'

'Skulldeath? What . . .' Bottle stared down for a long moment. 'Do you know what skulldeath is, Koryk? It's a plant that grows on Malaz Island and maybe Geni, too. You see, normally there's male plants and there's female plants and that's how you get fruit and the like, right? Anyway, not so with the sweet little skulldeath. There's only males – no females at all. Skulldeaths loose their – well, they spill it all out into the air, and it ends up somehow getting into the seeds of other plants and just riding along, hiding, until that seed sprouts, then it takes over and suddenly, another nice skulldeath with that grey flower that's not really a flower at all, just a thin sack filled with—'

'So, that concoction Smiles asked for – what does it do?'

'Supposed to change a man who prefers other men into one who prefers women. Does it work? I have no idea.'

'Skulldeath may be a plant,' Koryk said, 'but it's also the name for a soldier in Primly's squad. A pretty one.'

'Oh, and that name . . .'

'Is obviously very appropriate, Bottle.'

'Oh. Poor Smiles.'

The Factor's house might have looked nice, but it might as well have been made of straw, the way it fell down. Astonishing that no-one had died beneath all that wreckage. Urb at the least was certainly relieved by that, though his mood wilted somewhat after Hellian was through yelling at him.

In any case, thereafter satisfied and pleasantly feeling . . . pleasant, Hellian was anything but pleased when Balgrid's appallingly unattractive face loomed into view directly in front of her. She blinked at him. 'You're shorter than I'd thought.'

'Sergeant, I'm kneeling. What are you doing under the bar?'

'I'm not the one who keeps movin' it, Baldy.'

'The other sergeants have agreed that we're staying here for a while. You with them on that, Sergeant?'

'Why not?'

'Good. Oh, did you know, in the new squads, there's another Kartoolii.'

'Probbly a spy – they're still after me, y'know.'

'Why would they be after you?'

''Cause I did something, that's why. Can't 'member 'xactly what, but it was bad 'nough to get me sent here, wasn't it? A damned spy!'

'I doubt he's anything—'

'Yeah? Fine, make him come 'ere and kiss my feet, then! Tell 'im I'm the Queen of Kartool! An' I want my kissed feet! My feeted kiss, I mean. Go on, damn you!'

Less than six paces away, tucked beneath the bar at the other end, sat Skulldeath. Hiding from that pretty but way too lustful woman in Fiddler's squad. And at Hellian's words his head snapped round and his dark, almond-shaped eyes, which had already broken so many hearts, slowly widened on the dishevelled sergeant crouched in a pool of spilled wine.

Queen of Kartool.

On such modest things, worlds changed.

The women were singing an ancient song in a language that was anything but Imass. Filled with strange clicks and phlegmatic stops, along with rhythmic gestures of the hands, and the extraordinary twin voices emerging from each throat, the song made the hair on the back of Hedge's neck stand on end. *'Eres'al,'* Quick Ben had whispered, looking a little ashen himself. *'The First Language.'*

No wonder it made the skin crawl, awakening faint echoes in the back of his skull – as if stirring to life the soft murmurings of his mother a handful of days after he'd been born, even as he clung by the mouth to her tit and stared stupidly up at the blur of her face. A song to make a grown man feel horribly vulnerable, weak in the limbs and desperate for comfort.

Muttering under his breath, Hedge plucked at Quick Ben's sleeve.

The wizard understood well enough and they both rose, then backed away from the hearth and all the gathered Imass. Out into the darkness beneath a spray of glittering stars, up into the sprawl of tumbled boulders away from the rock shelters of the cliff face.

Hedge found a flat stone the size of a skiff, lying at the base of a scree. He sat down on it. Quick Ben stood nearby, bending down to collect a handful of gravel, then pacing as he began examining his collection – more by feel than sight – flinging rejections off into the gloom to bounce and skitter. 'So, Hedge.'

'What?'

'How's Fiddler these days?'

'It's not like I'm squatting on his shoulder or anything.'

'Hedge.'

'All right, I catch things occasionally. Whiffs. Echoes. He's still alive, I can say that much.'

Quick Ben paused. 'Any idea what the Adjunct's up to?'

'Who? No, why should I – never met her. You're the one should be doing the guessing, wizard. She shackled you into being her High Mage, after all. Me, I've been wandering for what seems for ever, in nothing but the ashes of the dead. At least until we found this place, and it ain't nearly as far away from the underworld as you might think.'

'Don't tell me what I think, sapper. I already know what I think and it's not what you think.'

'Well now, you're sounding all nervous again, Quick. Little heart going pitterpat?'

'She was taking them to Lether – to the Tiste Edur empire – once she managed to extricate them from Malaz harbour. Now, Cotillion says she managed that, despite my disappearing at the worst possible moment. True, some nasty losses. Like Kalam. And T'amber. Me. So, Lether. Pitching her measly army against an empire spanning half a continent or damn near, and why? Well, maybe to deliver some vengeance on behalf of the Malazan Empire and every other kingdom or people who got cut up by those roving fleets. But maybe that's not it at all, because, let's face it, as a motive it sounds, well, insane. And I don't think the Adjunct is insane. So, what's left?'

'Sorry, was that actually a question? For me?'

'Of course not, Hedge. It was rhetorical.'

'That's a relief. Go on, then.'

'Seems more likely she's set herself against the Crippled God.'

'Oh yeah? What's this Lether Empire got to do with the Crippled God?'

'A whole lot, that's what.'

'Meaning me and Fiddler are back fighting the same damned war.'

'As if you didn't already know that, Hedge – and no, wipe that innocent look off your face. It's not dark enough and you know that so that look is for me and it's a damned lie so get rid of it.'

'Ouch, the wizard's nerves are singing!'

'This is why I liked you least of all, Hedge.'

'I remember once you being scared witless of a recruit named Sorry, because she was possessed by a god. And now here you are, working for that god. Amazing, how things can turn right round in ways you'd never expect nor even predict.'

The wizard stared long and hard at the sapper. Then he said, 'Now hold on, Hedge.'

'You really think Sorry was there to get at the Empress, Quick? Some

sordid plan for vengeance against Laseen? Why, that would be . . .
insane.'

'What are you getting at?'

'Just wondering if you should be as sure of the ones you're working
for as you think you are. Because, and it only seems this way to me, all
this confusion you're feeling about the Adjunct might just be coming
from some wrong-footed, uh, misapprehensions about the two gods
crouching in your shadow.'

'Is all this just another one of your feelings?'

'I ain't Fiddler.'

'No, but you've been so close to him – in his damned shadow –
you're picking up all his uncanny, whispered suspicions, and don't even
try to deny it, Hedge. So now I better hear it straight from you. You and
me, are we fighting on the same side, or not?'

Hedge grinned up at him. 'Maybe not. But, just maybe, more than
you know, wizard.'

Quick Ben had selected out a half-dozen water-worn pebbles. Now
he flung the rest away. 'That answer was supposed to make me feel
better?'

'How do you think I feel?' Hedge demanded. 'Been at your damned
side, Quick, since Raraku! And I still don't know who or even *what* you
are!'

'What's your point?'

'It's this. I'm beginning to suspect that even Cotillion – and
Shadowthrone – don't know you half as well as they might think.
Which is why they're now keeping you close. And which is why, too,
they maybe made sure you ended up without Kalam right there guarding your back.'

'If you're right – about Kalam – there's going to be trouble.'

Hedge shrugged. 'All I'm saying is, maybe the plan was for Sorry to
be right there, right now, beside Fiddler.'

'The Adjunct didn't even have an army then, Hedge. What you're
suggesting is impossible.'

'Depends on how much Kellanved and Dancer saw – and came to
understand – when they left their empire and went in search of
ascendancy.' The sapper paused, then said, 'They walked the paths
of the Azath, didn't they?'

'Almost no-one knows that, Hedge. You sure didn't . . . before you
died. Which brings us back to the path you ended up walking, after
you'd gone and blown yourself up in Black Coral.'

'You mean, after I did my own ascending?'

'Yes.'

'I already told you most of it. The Bridgeburners ascended. Blame
some Spiritwalker.'

'And now there's more of you damned fools wandering around. Hood take you all, Hedge, there were some real nasty people in the Bridgeburners. Brutal and vicious and outright evil—'

'Rubbish. And I'll tell you a secret and maybe one day it'll do you good, too. Dying humbles ya.'

'I don't need any humbling, Hedge, which is fine since I don't plan on dying any time soon.'

'Best stay light on your toes, then.'

'You guarding my back, Hedge?'

'I ain't no Kalam, but aye, I am.'

'For now.'

'For now.'

'That will have to do, I suppose—'

'Mind you, only if you're guarding mine, Quick.'

'Of course. Loyalty to the old squad and all that.'

'So what are damned pebbles for? As if I couldn't guess.'

'We're heading into an ugly scrap, Hedge.' He rounded on the sapper. 'And listen, about those damned cussers – if you blow me into tiny pieces I *will* come back for you, Hedge. That's a vow, sworn by every damned soul in me.'

'Now that raises a question, don't it? Just how long do all of those souls plan on hiding in there, Ben Adaephon Delat?'

The wizard eyed him, and, predictably, said nothing.

Trull Sengar stood at the very edge of the fire's light, beyond the gathered Imass. The women's song had sunk into a series of sounds that a mother might make to her babe, soft sounds of comfort, and Onrack had explained how this Eres'al song was in fact a kind of traverse, back into the roots of language, beginning with the bizarre yet clearly complex adult Eres language with its odd clicks and stops and all the gestures that provided punctuation, then working backward and growing ever more simplified even as it became more musical. The effect was eerie and strangely disturbing to the Tiste Edur.

Music and song among his people was a static thing, fixated within ritual. If the ancient tales were true, there had once been a plethora of instruments in use among the Tiste Edur, but most of these were now unknown, beyond the names given them. Voice now stood in their stead and Trull began to sense that, perhaps, something had been lost.

The gestures among the women had transformed into dance, sinuous and swaying and now, suddenly, sexual.

A low voice beside him said, 'Before the child, there is passion.'

Trull glanced over and was surprised to see one of the T'lan, the clan chief, Hostille Rator.

An array of calcified bones were knotted in the filthy long hair dangling from the warrior's mottled, scarred pate. His brow ridge dominated the entire face, burying the eyes in darkness. Even clothed in the flesh of life, Hostille Rator seemed deathly.

'Passion begets the child, Tiste Edur. Do you see?'

Trull nodded. 'Yes. I think so.'

'So it was, long ago, at the Ritual.'

Ah.

'The child, alas,' the clan chief continued, 'grows up. And what was once passion is now . . .'

Nothing.

Hostille Rator resumed. 'There was a Bonecaster here, among these clans. She saw, clearly, the illusion of this realm. And saw, too, that it was dying. She sought to halt the bleeding away, by sacrificing herself. But she is failing – her spirit and her will, they are failing.'

Trull frowned at Hostille Rator. 'How did you come to know of this place?'

'She gave voice to her pain, her anguish.' The T'lan was silent a moment, then he added, 'It was our intention to answer the call of the Gathering – but the need in her voice was undeniable. We could not turn aside, even when what we surrendered was – possibly – our final rest.'

'So now you are here, Hostille Rator. Onrack believes you would usurp Ulshun Pral, but for Rud Elalle's presence – the threat he poses you.'

A glitter from the darkness beneath those brow ridges. 'You do not even whisper these things, Edur. Would you see weapons drawn this night, even after the gift of the First Song?'

'No. Yet, perhaps, better now than later.'

Trull now saw that the two T'lan Bonecasters had moved up behind Hostille Rator. The singing from the women had ceased – had it been an abrupt end? Trull could not recall. In any case, it was clear that all those present were now listening to this conversation. He saw Onrack emerge from the crowd, saw his friend's stone sword gripped in both hands.

Trull addressed Hostille Rator once more, his tone even and calm. 'You three have stood witness to all that you once were—'

'It will not survive,' the clan chief cut in. 'How can we embrace this illusion when, upon its fading, we must return to what we truly are?'

From the crowd Rud Elalle spoke, 'No harm shall befall my people – not by your hand, Hostille Rator, nor that of your Bonecasters. Nor,' he added, 'that of those who are coming here. I intend to lead the clans away – to safety.'

'There is no safety,' Hostille Rator said. 'This realm dies, and so too will all that is within it. And there can be no escape. Rud Elalle, without this realm, your clans do not even exist.'

Onrack said, 'I am T'lan, like you. Feel the flesh that now clothes you. The muscle, the heat of blood. Feel the breath in your lungs, Hostille Rator. I have looked into your eyes – each of you three – and I see what no doubt resides in mine. The wonder. The *remembering.*'

'We cannot permit it,' said the Bonecaster named Til'Aras Benok. 'For when we leave this place, Onrack . . .'

'Yes,' Trull's friend whispered. 'It will be . . . too much. To bear.'

'There was passion once,' Hostille Rator said. 'For us. It can never return. We are children no longer.'

'None of you understand!'

Rud Elalle's sudden shriek startled everyone, and Trull saw Ulshun Pral – on his face an expression of distress – reach out a hand to his adopted son, who angrily brushed it away as he stepped forward, the fire in his eyes as fierce as that in the hearth beyond. 'Stone, earth, trees and grasses. Beasts. The sky and the stars! None of this is an illusion!'

'A trapped memory—'

'No, Bonecaster, you are wrong.' He struggled to hold back his anger, and spun to face Onrack. 'I see your heart, Onrack the Broken. I know, you will stand with me – in the time that comes. You will!'

'Yes, Rud Elalle.'

'Then you believe!'

Onrack was silent.

Hostille Rator's laugh was a soft, bitter rasp. 'It is this, Rud Elalle. Onrack of the Logros T'lan Imass chooses to fight at your side, chooses to fight for these Bentract, because he cannot abide the thought of returning to what he once was, and so he would rather die here. And death is what Onrack the Broken anticipates – indeed, what he now yearns for.'

Trull studied his friend, and saw on Onrack's firelit face the veracity of Hostille Rator's words.

The Tiste Edur did not hesitate. 'Onrack will not stand alone,' he said.

Til'Aras Benok faced Trull. 'You surrender your life, Edur, to defend an illusion?'

'That, Bonecaster, is what we mortals delight in doing. You bind yourself to a clan, to a tribe, to a nation or an empire, but to give force to the illusion of a common bond, you must feed its opposite – that all those not of your clan, or tribe, or empire, do not share that bond. I have seen Onrack the Broken, a T'lan Imass. And now I have seen him, mortal once again. To the joy and the life in the eyes of my friend, I will fight all those who deem him their enemy. For the bond between us is one of friendship, and that, Til'Aras Benok, is *not* an illusion.'

Hostille Rator asked Onrack, 'In your mercy, as you have now found it alive once more in your soul, will you now reject Trull Sengar of the Tiste Edur?'

And the warrior bowed his head and said, 'I cannot.'

'Then, Onrack the Broken, your soul shall never find peace.'

'I know.'

Trull felt as if he had been punched in the chest. It was all very well to make his bold claims, in ferocious sincerity that could only come of true friendship. It was yet another thing to discover the price it demanded in the soul of the one he called friend. 'Onrack,' he whispered in sudden anguish.

But this moment would not await all that might have been said, all that needed to be said, for Hostille Rator had turned to face his Bonecasters, and whatever silent communication passed among these three was quick, decisive, for the clan chief swung round and walked towards Ulshun Pral. Whereupon he fell to one knee and bowed his head. 'We are humbled, Ulshun Pral. We are shamed by these two strangers. You are the Bentract. As were we, once, long ago. We now choose to remember. We now choose to fight in your name. In our deaths there will be naught but honour, this we vow.' He then rose and faced Rud Elalle. 'Soletaken, will you accept us as your soldiers?'

'As soldiers? No. As friends, as Bentract, yes.'

The three T'lan bowed to him.

All of this passed in a blur before Trull Sengar's eyes. Since Onrack the Broken's admission, it seemed as if Trull's entire world had, with grinding, stone-crushing irresistibility, turned on some vast, unimagined axis – yet he was drawn round again by a hand on his shoulder, and Onrack, now standing before him.

'There is no need,' the Imass warrior said. 'I know something even Rud Elalle does not, and I tell you this, Trull Sengar, there is no need. Not for grief. Nor regret. My friend, listen to me. *This world will not die.*'

And Trull found no will within him to challenge that assertion, to drive doubt into his friend's earnest gaze. After a moment, then, he simply sighed and nodded. 'So be it, Onrack.'

'And, if we are careful,' Onrack continued, 'neither shall we.'

'As you say, friend.'

Thirty paces away in the darkness, Hedge turned to Quick Ben and hissed, 'What do you make of all that, wizard?'

Quick Ben shrugged. 'Seems the confrontation has been averted, if Hostille Rator's kneeling before Ulshun Pral didn't involve picking up a dropped fang or something.'

'A dropped – what?'

'Never mind. That's not the point at all, anyway. But I now know I am right in one thing and don't ask me how I know. I just do. Suspicion into certainty.'

'Well, go on, damn you.'

'Just this, Hedge. The Finnest. Of Scabandari Bloodeye. It's here.'

'Here? What do you mean, here?'

'*Here*, sapper. *Right here.*'

The gate was a shattered mess on one side. The huge cyclopean stones that had once formed an enormous arch easily five storeys high had the appearance of having been blasted apart by multiple impacts, flinging some of the shaped blocks a hundred paces or more from the entrance-way. The platform the arch had once spanned was heaved and buckled as if some earthquake had rippled through the solid bedrock beneath the pavestones. The other side was dominated by a tower of still standing blocks, corkscrew-twisted and seemingly precariously balanced.

The illusion of bright daylight had held during this last part of the journey, as much by the belligerent insistence of Udinaas as by the amused indulgence of Clip. Or, perhaps, Silchas Ruin's impatience. The foremost consequence of this was that Seren Pedac was exhausted – and Udinaas looked no better. Like the two Tiste Andii, however, Kettle seemed impervious – with all the boundless energy of a child, Seren supposed, raising the possibility that at some moment not too far off she would simply collapse.

Seren could see that Fear Sengar was weary as well, but probably that had more to do with the unpleasant burden settling ever more heavily upon his shoulders. She had been harsh and unforgiving of herself in relating to the Tiste Edur the terrible crime she had committed upon Udinaas, and she had done so in the hope that Fear Sengar would – with a look of unfeigned and most deserving disgust in his eyes – choose to reject her, and his own vow to guard her life.

But the fool had instead held to that vow, although she could see the brutal awakening of regret. He would not – could not – break his word.

It was getting easier to disdain these bold gestures, the severity so readily embraced by males of any species. Some primitive holdover, she reasoned, of the time when possessing a woman meant survival, not of anything so prosaic as one's own bloodline, but *possession* in the manner of ownership, and survival in the sense of power. There had been backward tribes all along the fringe territories of the Letherii kingdom where such archaic notions were practised, and not always situations where men were the owners and wielders of power – for sometimes it was the women. In either case, history had shown that such systems could only survive in isolation, and only among peoples for whom magic had stagnated into a chaotic web of proscriptions, taboos and the artifice of nonsensical rules – where the power offered by sorcery had been usurped by profane ambitions and the imperatives of social control.

Contrary to Hull Beddict's romantic notions of such people, Seren Pedac had come to feel little remorse when she thought about their inevitable and often bloody extinction. Control was ever an illusion, and its maintenance could only persist when in isolation. Not to say, of course, that the Letherii system was one of unfettered freedom and the liberty of individual will. Hardly. One imposition had been replaced by another. *But at the very least it's not one divided by gender.*

The Tiste Edur were different. Their notions . . . primitive. Offer a sword, bury it at the threshold of one's home, the symbolic exchange of vows so archaic no words were even necessary. In such a ritual, no negotiation was possible, and if marriage did not involve negotiation then it was not marriage. *No, just mutual ownership. Or not-so-mutual ownership.* Such a thing deserved little respect.

And now, here, it was not even a prospective husband laying claim to her life, but that prospective husband's damned brother. And, to make the entire situation yet more absurd, the prospective husband was dead. *Fear will defend to the death my right to marry a corpse. Or, rather, the corpse's right to claim me. Well, that is madness and I will not – I do not – accept it. Not for a moment.*

Yes, I have moved past self-pity. Now I'm just angry.

Because he refused to let his disgust dissuade him.

For all her notions of defiance, that last thought stung her.

Udinaas had moved past her to study the ruined gate, and now he turned to Clip. 'Well, does it yet live?'

The Tiste Andii's chain and rings were spinning from one finger again, and he offered the Letherii slave a cool smile. 'The last road to walk,' he said, 'lies on the other side of the gate.'

'So who got mad and kicked it to pieces, Clip?'

'Of no consequence any more,' Clip replied, his smile broadening.

'You have no idea, in other words,' Udinaas said. 'Well, if we're to go through it, let's stop wasting time. I've almost given up hoping that you'll end up garrotting yourself with that chain. Almost.'

His last comment seemed to startle Clip for some reason.

And all at once Seren Pedac saw that chain with its rings differently. *By the Errant! Why did I not see it before? It* is *a garrotte. Clip is a damned assassin!* She snorted. 'And you claim to be a Mortal Sword! You're nothing but a murderer, Clip. Yes, Udinaas saw that long ago – which is why you hate him so. He was never fooled by all those weapons you carry. And now, neither am I.'

'We're wasting time indeed,' Clip said, once more seemingly un-perturbed, and he turned and approached the huge gate. Silchas Ruin set out after him, and Seren saw that the White Crow had his hands on the grips of his swords.

'Danger ahead,' Fear Sengar announced and yes, damn him, he then moved from his position just behind Seren's right shoulder to directly in front of her. And drew his sword.

Udinaas witnessed all this and grunted dismissively, then half turned and said, 'Silchas Ruin's earned his paranoia, Fear. But even that doesn't mean we're about to jump into a pit of dragons.' He then smiled without any humour. 'Not that dragons live in pits.'

When he walked after the two Tiste Andii, Kettle ran up to take his hand. At first Udinaas reacted as if her touch had burned him, but then his resistance vanished.

Clip reached the threshold, stepped forward and disappeared. A moment later Silchas Ruin did the same.

Neither Udinaas nor Kettle hesitated.

Reaching the same point, Fear Sengar paused and eyed her. 'What is in your mind, Acquitor?' he asked.

'Do you think I might abandon you all, Fear? Watch you step through and, assuming you can't get back, I just turn round and walk this pointless road – one I probably would never leave? Is that choice left to me?'

'All choices are left to you, Acquitor.'

'You too, I would say. Except, of course, for the ones you willingly surrendered.'

'Yes.'

'You admit that so easily.'

'Perhaps it seems that way.'

'Fear, if anyone should turn round right now, it is you.'

'We are close, Acquitor. We are perhaps a few strides from Scabandari's Finnest. How can you imagine I would even consider such a thing?'

'Some stubborn thread of self-preservation, perhaps. Some last surviving faith of mine that you actually possess a brain, one that can reason, that is. Fear Sengar, you will probably die. If you pass through this gate.'

He shrugged. 'Perhaps I shall, if only to confound Udinaas's expectations.'

'Udinaas?'

A faint smile. 'The hero fails the quest.'

'Ah. And that would prove satisfying enough?'

'Remains to be seen, I suppose. Now, you will follow?'

'Of course.'

'You then willingly surrender this choice?'

In answer she set a hand against his chest and pushed him, step by step, into the gate. All pressure vanished when he went through, and Seren stumbled forward, only to collide with the Tiste Edur's broad, muscled chest.

He righted her before she could fall.

And she saw, before them all, a most unexpected vista. Black volcanic ash, beneath a vast sky nearly as black, despite at least three suns blazing in the sky overhead. And, on this rough plain, stretching on all sides in horrific proliferation, there were dragons.

Humped, motionless. Scores – hundreds.

She heard Kettle's anguished whisper. '*Udinaas! They're all dead!*'

Clip, standing twenty paces ahead, was now facing them. The chain spun tight, and then he bowed. 'Welcome, my dear companions, to Starvald Demelain.'

CHAPTER TWENTY-TWO

The shadows lie on the field like the dead
From night's battle as the sun lifts high its standard
Into the dew-softened air

The children rise like flowers on stalks
To sing unworded songs we long ago surrendered
And the bees dance with great care

You might touch this scene with blessing
Even as you settle the weight of weapon in hand
And gaze across this expanse

And vow to the sun another day of blood

Untitled
Toc Anaster

GASKARAL TRAUM WAS THE FIRST SOLDIER IN ATRI-PREDA BIVATT'S army to take a life that morning. A large man with faint threads of Tarthenal blood in his veins, he had pitched his tent the night before forty paces from the Tiste Edur encampment. Within it he had lit a small oil lamp and arranged his bedroll over bundles of clothing, spare boots and spare helm. Then he had lain down beside it, on the side nearest the Edur tents, and let the lamp devour the last slick of oil until the darkness within the tent matched that of outside.

With dawn's false glow ebbing, Gaskaral Traum drew a knife and slit the side of the tent beside him, then silently edged out into the wet grasses, where he laid motionless for a time.

Then, seeing at last what he had been waiting for, he rose and, staying low, made his way across the sodden ground. The rain was still thrumming down on the old seabed of Q'uson Tapi – where waited the hated Awl – and the air smelled of sour mud. Although a large man, Gaskaral could move like a ghost. He reached the first row of Edur tents, paused with held breath for a moment, then edged into the camp.

The tent of Overseer Brohl Handar was centrally positioned, but otherwise unguarded. As Gaskaral came closer, he saw that the flap was untied, hanging loose. Water from the rain just past streamed down the oiled canvas like tears, pooling round the front pole and in the deep footprints crowding the entrance.

Gaskaral slipped his knife beneath his outer shirt and used the grimy undergarment to dry the handle and his left hand – palm and fingers – before withdrawing the weapon once more. Then he crept for that slitted opening.

Within was grainy darkness. The sound of breathing. And there, at the far end, the Overseer's cot. Brohl Handar was sleeping on his back. The furs covering him had slipped down to the floor. Of his face and chest, Gaskaral could see naught but heavy shadow.

Blackened iron gleamed, betrayed by the honed edge.

Gaskaral Traum took one more step, then he surged forward in a blur.

The figure standing directly over Brohl Handar spun, but not in time, as Gaskaral's knife sank deep, sliding between ribs, piercing the assassin's heart.

The black dagger fell and stuck point-first into the floor, and Gaskaral took the body's weight as, with a faint sigh, the killer slumped.

Atri-Preda Bivatt's favoured bodyguard – chosen by her outside Drene to safeguard the Overseer against just this eventuality – froze for a moment, eyes fixed on Brohl Handar's face, on the Edur's breathing. No stirring awake. And that was good. Very good.

Angling beneath the dead assassin's weight, Gaskaral slowly sheathed his knife, then reached down and retrieved the black dagger. This was the last of the bastards, he was sure. Seven in all, although only two before this one had got close enough to attempt Brohl's murder – and both of those had been in the midst of battle. Letur Anict was ever a thorough man, one prone to redundancy in assuring that his desires were satisfied. Alas, not this time.

Gaskaral lowered himself yet further until he could fold the body over one shoulder, then, rising into a bent-knee stance, he padded silently back to the tent-flap. Stepping to avoid the puddle and the upright pole, he carefully angled his burden through the opening.

Beneath overcast clouds with yet another fall of rain beginning, Gaskaral Traum quickly made his way back to the Letherii side of the camp. The body could remain in his tent – the day now approaching was going to be a day of battle, which meant plenty of chaos, plenty of opportunities to dispose of the corpse.

He was somewhat concerned, however. It was never a good thing to not sleep the night before a battle. But he was ever sensitive to his instincts, as if he could smell the approach of an assassin, as if he could slip into their minds. Certainly his uncanny timing proved the talent – another handful of heartbeats back there and he would have been too late—

Occasionally, of course, instincts failed.

The two figures that suddenly rushed him from the darkness caught Gaskaral Traum entirely by surprise. A shock blessedly short-lived, as it turned out. Gaskaral threw the body he had been carrying at the assassin on his right. With no time to draw out his knife, he simply charged to meet the other killer. Knocked aside the dagger stabbing for his throat, took the man's head in both hands and twisted hard.

Hard enough to spin the assassin's feet out from under him as the neck snapped.

The other killer had been thrown down by the corpse and was just rolling back into a crouch when, upon looking up, he met Gaskaral's boot – under his chin. The impact lifted the man into the air, arms flung out to the sides, his head separated from his spine, and dead before he thumped back onto the ground.

Gaskaral Traum looked round, saw no more coming, then permitted himself a moment of self-directed anger. Of course they would have realized that someone was intercepting them. So in went one while the other two remained back to see who their unknown hunter was, and then they would deal with that hunter in the usual way.

'Yeah? Like fuck they did.'

He studied the three bodies for a moment longer. Damn, it was going to be a crowded tent.

The sun would brook no obstacle in its singular observation of the Battle of Q'uson Tapi, and as it rose it burned away the clouds and drove spears of heat into the ground until the air steamed. Brohl Handar, awakening surprisingly refreshed, stood outside his tent and watched as his Arapay Tiste Edur readied their armour and weapons. The sudden, unrelieved humidity made iron slick and the shafts of spears oily, and already the ground underfoot was treacherous – the seabed would be a nightmare, he feared.

In the evening before, he and his troop had watched the Awl preparations, and Brohl Handar well understood the advantages Redmask was seeking in secure footing, but the Overseer suspected that such efforts would fail in the end. Canvas and hide tarps would before long grow as muddy and slippery as the ground beyond. At the initial shock of contact, however, there would likely be a telling difference . . . but not enough.

I hope.

A Letherii soldier approached – an oversized man he'd seen before – with a pleasant smile on his innocuous, oddly gentle face. 'The sun is most welcome, Overseer, is it not? I convey the Atri-Preda's invitation to join her – be assured that you will have time to return to your warriors and lead them into battle.'

'Very well. Proceed, then.'

The various companies were moving into positions all along the edge of the seabed opposite the Awl. Brohl saw that the Bluerose lancers were now dismounted, looking a little lost with their newly issued shields and spears. There were less than a thousand left and the Overseer saw that they had been placed as auxiliaries and would only be thrown into battle if things were going poorly. 'Now there's a miserable bunch,' he said to his escort, nodding towards the Bluerose Battalion.

'So they are, Overseer. Yet see how their horses are saddled and not too far away. This is because our scouts cannot see the Kechra in the Awl camp. The Atri-Preda expects another flanking attack from those two creatures, and this time she will see it met with mounted lancers. Who will then pursue.'

'I wish them well – those Kechra ever remain the gravest threat and the sooner they are dead the better.'

Atri-Preda Bivatt stood in a position at the edge of the old shoreline that permitted her a view of what would be the field of battle. As was her habit, she had sent away all her messengers and aides – they hovered watchfully forty paces back – and was now alone with her thoughts, her observations, and would remain so – barring Brohl's visit – until just before the engagement commenced.

His escort halted a short distance away from the Atri-Preda and waved Brohl Handar forward with an easy smile.

How can he be so calm? Unless he's one of those who will be standing guarding horses. Big as he is, he hasn't the look of a soldier – well, even horse-handlers are needed, after all.

'Overseer, you look . . . well rested.'

'I appear to be just that, Atri-Preda. As if the spirits of my ancestors held close vigil on me last night.'

'Indeed. Are your Arapay ready?'

'They are. Will you begin this battle with your mages?'

'I must be honest in this matter. I cannot rely upon their staying alive throughout the engagement. Accordingly, yes, I will use them immediately. And if they are still with me later, then all the better.'

'No sign of the Kechra, then.'

'No. Observe, the enemy arrays itself.'

'On dry purchase—'

'To begin, yes, but we will win that purchase, Overseer. And that is the flaw in Redmask's tactic. We will strike hard enough to knock them back, and then it will be the Awl who find themselves mired in the mud.'

Brohl Handar turned to study the Letherii forces. The various brigades, companies and battalion elements had been merged on the basis of function. On the front facing the Awl, three wedges of heavy infantry. Flanks of skirmishers mixed with medium infantry and archers. Blocks of archers between the wedges, who if they moved down onto the seabed would not go very far. Their flights of arrows would be intended to perforate the Awl line so that when the heavies struck they would drive back the enemy, one step, two, five, ten and into the mud.

'I do not understand this Redmask,' Brohl said, frowning back at the Awl lines.

'He had no choice,' Bivatt replied. 'Not after Praedegar. And that was, for him, a failure of patience. Perhaps this is, as well, but as I said: no choice left. We have him, Overseer. Yet he will make this victory a painful one, given the chance.'

'Your mages may well end it before it's begun, Atri-Preda.'

'We will see.'

Overhead, the sun continued its inexorable climb, heating the day with baleful intent. On the seabed lighter patches had begun appearing as the topmost surface dried. But immediately beneath, of course, the mud would remain soft and deep enough to cause trouble.

Bivatt had two mages left – the third had died two days past, fatally weakened by the disaster at Praedegar – one lone mounted archer had succeeded in killing three mages with one damned arrow. Brohl Handar now saw those two figures hobbling like ancients out to the old shore-line's edge. One at each end of the outermost heavy infantry wedge. They would launch their terrible wave of magic at angles intended to converge a dozen or so ranks deep in the centre formation of Awl, so as to maximize the path of destruction.

The Atri-Preda evidently made some gesture that Brohl did not see, for all at once her messengers had arrived. She turned to him. 'It is time. Best return to your warriors, Overseer.'

Brohl Handar grimaced. 'Rearguard again.'

'You will see a fight this day, Overseer. I am sure of that.'

He was not convinced, but he turned away then. Two strides along and he paused and said, 'May this day announce the end of this war.'

The Atri-Preda did not reply. It was not even certain she had heard him, as she was speaking quietly to the soldier who had been his escort. He saw surprise flit across her features beneath the helm, then she nodded.

Brohl Handar glared up at the sun, and longed for the shadowed forests of home. Then he set out for his Arapay.

Sitting on a boulder, Toc Anaster watched the children play for a moment longer, then he rolled the thinned flat of hide into a scroll and slipped it into his satchel, and added the brush of softened wood and the now-resealed bowl of charcoal, marrow and gaenth-berry ink. He rose, squinted skyward for a moment, then walked over to his horse. Seven paces, and by the time he arrived his moccasins were oversized clumps of mud. He tied the satchel to the saddle, drew a knife and bent down to scrape away as much of the mud as he could.

The Awl were gathered in their ranks off to his left, standing, waiting as the Letherii forces five hundred paces away jostled into the formations they would seek to maintain in the advance. Redmask's warriors seemed strangely silent – of course, this was not their kind of battle. 'No,' Toc muttered. 'This is the Letherii kind.' He looked across at the enemy.

Classic wedges in sawtooth, Toc observed. Three arrowheads of heavy infantry. Those formations would be rather messy by the time they reached the Awl. Moving slow, with soldiers falling, stumbling and slipping with every stride they attempted. All to the good. There would be no heaving push at the moment of contact, not without entire front ranks of heavily armoured soldiers falling flat on their faces.

'You will ride away,' Torrent said behind him. 'Or so you think. But I will be watching you, Mezla—'

'Oh, put it to rest,' Toc said. 'It's hardly my fault Redmask doesn't think you're worth much, Torrent. Besides,' he added, 'it's not as if a horse could do much more than walk in this. And finally, Redmask has said he might want me close to hand – with my arrows – in case the K'Chain Che'Malle fail.'

'They will not fail.'

'Oh, and what do you know of K'Chain Che'Malle, Torrent?'

'I know what Redmask tells us.'

'And what does he know? More to the point, *how* does he know? Have you not wondered that? Not even once? The K'Chain Che'Malle are this world's demons. Creatures of the far past. Virtually everywhere else they are extinct. So what in Hood's name are they doing here? And why are they at Redmask's side, seemingly eager to do as he bids?'

'Because he is Redmask, Mezla. He is not as we are and yes, I see how the envy burns in your eye. You will ever despise those who are better than you.'

Toc leaned his forearms across the back of his horse. 'Come closer, Torrent. Look into the eyes of this mare here. Tell me, do you see envy?'

'A mindless beast.'

'That will probably die today.'

'I do not understand you, Mezla.'

'I know. Anyway, I see that same look in your eyes, Torrent. That same blind willingness. To believe everything you need to believe. Redmask is to you as I am to this poor horse.'

'I will listen to you no longer.'

The young warrior headed off, the stiffness of his strides soon deteriorating in the conglomeration of mud on his feet.

Nearby the children were flinging clumps of the stuff at each other and laughing. *The younger ones, that is.* Those carrying a few more years were silent, staring over at the enemy forces, where horns had begun sounding, and now, two well-guarded groups edging out to the very edge of the ancient shore. The mages.

We begin, then.

Far to the west the sun had yet to rise. In a nondescript village a day's fast march from Letheras, where too many had died in the past two days, three Falari heavy infantry from 3rd Company sat on one edge of a horse trough outside the only tavern. Lookback, Drawfirst and Shoaly were cousins, or so the others thought of them, given their shared Falar traits of fiery red hair and blue eyes, and the olive-hued skin of the main island's indigenous people, who called themselves the Walk. The idea seemed convenient enough, although none had known the others before enlisting in the Malazan Army.

The Walk civilization had thrived long ago, before the coming of iron, in fact, and as miners of tin, copper and lead it had once dominated all the isles of the archipelago in the trade of bronze weapons and ornamentation. Had they been of pure Walk blood, the soldiers would have been squatter, black-haired and reputedly laconic to the point of somnolent; as it was, they all possessed the harder, fiercer blood of the Falari invaders who had conquered most of the islands generations past. The combination, oddly enough, made for superb marines.

At the moment, amidst darkness and a pleasantly cool breeze coming in from the river to the south, the three were having a conversation, the subjects of which were Sergeant Gesler and Corporal Stormy. Those two names – if not their pathetic ranks – were well known to all natives of Falar.

'But they've changed,' Lookback said. 'That gold skin, it's not natural at all. I think we should kill them.'

Drawfirst, who possessed the unfortunate combination of large breasts and a tendency to perspire profusely, had taken advantage of the darkness to divest herself of her upper armour and was now mopping beneath her breasts with a cloth. Now she said, 'But what's the point of that, Look? The cult is dead. It's been dead for years.'

'Ain't dead for us, though, is it?'

'Mostly,' answered Shoaly.

'That's you all right, Shoaly,' Lookback said. 'Always seeing the dying and dead side of things.'

'So go ask 'em, Look. And they'll tell you the same. Fener cult's finished.'

'That's why I think we should kill them. For betraying the cult. For betraying us. And what's with that gold skin anyway? It's creepy.'

'Listen,' Shoaly said, 'we just partnered with these squads. In case you forgot, Lookback, this is the company that crawled out from under Y'Ghatan. And then there's Fiddler. A Hood-damned Bridgeburner and maybe the only one left. Gesler was once high-ranked and so was Stormy, but just like Whiskeyjack they got busted down and down, and down, and now here you are wanting to stick 'em. The cult got out-lawed and now Fener ain't nowhere a god's supposed to be but that ain't Gesler's fault. Not Stormy's neither.'

'So what are you saying?' Lookback retorted. 'We should just leave 'em and that's that?'

'Leave 'em? Drawfirst, explain it to this fool.'

She had pushed her breasts back into their harness and was making some final adjustments. 'It's simple, Look. Not only are we stuck here, with Fid and the rest. We're all gonna die with 'em, too. Now, as for me – and probably Shoaly here – we're gonna stand and fight, right at their sides. Gesler, Stormy, those cute heavies they got. And when we finally fall, nobody's gonna be able to say we wasn't worth that standing there beside 'em. Now, maybe it's because you're the last heavy in Primly's squad. Maybe if Masker was still with you, you'd not be talking the way you're talking. So now you gotta choose, Lookback. Fight with us, fight with Reliko and Vastly Blank in Badan Gruk's squad, or fight on your own as the sole fist in Primly's. But every one of those choices is still fighting. Creep up behind Ges or Stormy and I'll lop your head off myself.'

'All right all right, I was just making conversation—'

Sounds from their left drew the heavies upright, reaching for weapons. Three figures padding down the main street towards them. Strap Mull, Skim and Neller.

Skim called out in a low voice, 'Soldiers on the way. Look sharp.'

'Letherii?' Shoaly asked.

'No,' she replied, halting opposite them while the other two marines continued on into the tavern. 'Picture in your heads the ugliest faces you ever seen, and you then kissin' them big and wet.'

'Finally,' Drawfirst sighed, 'some good news for a change.'

733

Beak and the captain made their way back to where Fist Keneb waited at the head of the column. There had been Tiste Edur ahead of them for some time, unwilling to engage, but now they were gone, at least between here and yon village.

The captain drew close to the Fist. 'Beak says they're marines, Fist. Seems we found some of them.'

'All of them,' Beak said. 'The ones who got far ahead of the rest. They're in the village and they've been killing Tiste Edur. Lots of Tiste Edur.'

'The munitions we heard yesterday.'

'Just so, Fist,' Beak said, nodding.

'All right, finally some good news. How many?'

'Seven, eight squads,' Beak replied. He delighted in being able to talk, in person, with a real Fist. Oh, he'd imagined scenes like this, of course, with Beak there providing all kinds of information to make the Fist do all the heroic things that needed doing, and then at last Beak himself being the biggest hero of all. He was sure everyone had dreams like that, the sudden revealing of some hidden, shy side that no-one else knew anything about and couldn't ever have guessed was even there. Shy, until it was needed, and then out it came, amazing everyone!

'Beak?'

'Fist?'

'I was asking, do they know we're here?'

'Yes sir, I think so. They've got some interesting mages, including an old style warlock from the Jakata people who were the first people on Malaz Island after the Stormriders retreated. He can see through the eyes of all sorts of creatures and that must have been helpful since the coast. There's also a Dal Honese bush shaman and a Dal Honese Grass Dancer. And a Nathii swamp necromancer.'

'Beak,' said Keneb, 'do these squads include Fiddler? Gesler and Stormy?'

'Fiddler's the one with the fiddle who played so sadly in Malaz City? The one with the Deck games in his head? Yes sir, he's there. Gesler and Stormy, they're the Falari ones, but with skins of gold and muscles and all that, the ones who were reforged in the fires of Tellann. Telas, Kurald Liosan, the fires, the ones dragons fly through to gain immunities and other proofs against magic and worse. Yes, they're there, too.'

See how they stared at him in wonder! Oh, just like the dream!

And he knew, all too well, how all this was going to turn out and even that couldn't make him anything but proud. He squinted up at the darkness overhead. 'It'll be dawn in a bell or so.'

Keneb turned to Faradan Sort. 'Captain, take Beak with you and head into the village. I'd like to see these squads presented – barring whatever pickets they've set out.'

'Yes, Fist. Plan on dressing 'em down, sir?'

Keneb's brows lifted. 'Not at all, Faradan. No. I might end up kissing every damned one of them, though.'

So once more Beak walked alongside Captain Faradan Sort, and that felt good and proper now, as if he'd always belonged with her, always being useful when that was what she needed. False dawn was just beginning and the air smelled wonderfully fresh – at least until they came to the pits where the Edur bodies had been dumped. That didn't smell good at all.

'Gods below,' the captain muttered as they skirted one of the shallow pits.

Beak nodded. 'Moranth munitions do that. Just . . . parts of people, and everything chewed up.'

'Not in this pit,' she said, pointing as they passed another mass grave. 'These ones were cut down. Swords, quarrels . . .'

'Aye, Captain, we're good at that, too, aren't we? But that's not why the Edur left – there was almost a thousand of them gathered here, planning on one more push. But then orders came to withdraw and so they did. They're now a league behind us, joining up with still more Edur.'

'The hammer,' Faradan Sort said, 'and somewhere ahead, the anvil.'

He nodded again.

She paused to search his face in the gloom. 'And the Adjunct and the fleet? Beak?'

'Don't know, sir. If you're wondering if they'll get to us in time to relieve us, then no. Not a chance. We're going to have to hold out, Captain, for so long it's impossible.'

She scowled at that. 'And if we just squat here? Right in this village?'

'They'll start pushing. There'll be four or five thousand Edur by then. That many can push us, sir, whether we want them to or not. Besides, didn't the Fist say he wanted to engage and hold down as many of the enemy as possible? To keep them from going anywhere else, like back behind the city walls which would mean the Adjunct's got to deal with another siege and nobody wants that.'

She glared at him for a moment longer, then set out again. Beak fell in step behind her.

From just behind a black heap of tailings at the edge of the village a voice called out, 'Nice seeing you again, Captain.'

Faradan Sort went on.

Beak saw Corporal Tarr rise from behind the tailings, slinging his crossbow back over a shoulder then dusting himself off before approaching on an intercept course.

'Fist wants to knock before coming in, does he?'

The captain halted in front of the stolid corporal. 'We've been fast-marching for a while now,' she said. 'We're damned tired, but if we're going to march into this village, we're not going to drag our boots. So the Fist called a short halt. That's all.'

Tarr scratched at his beard, making the various depending bones and such rustle and click. 'Fair enough,' he said.

'I am so relieved that you approve, Corporal. Now, the Fist wants the squads here all out in the main street.'

'We can do that,' Tarr replied, grinning. 'Been fighting for a while now and we're damned tired, Captain. So the sergeants got most of us resting up in the, uh, the tavern. But when the Fist sees us, well, we'll be looking smart as can be, I'm sure.'

'Get your arse into that tavern, Corporal, and wake the bastards up. We'll wait right here – but not for long, understood?'

A quick, unobtrusive salute and Tarr headed off.

'See what happens when an officer's not around enough? They get damned full of themselves, that's what happens, Beak.'

'Yes sir.'

'Well, when they hear all the bad news they won't be anywhere near as arrogant.'

'Oh, they know, sir. Better than we do.' *But that's not completely true. They don't know what I know, and neither, Captain my love, do you.*

They both turned at the sound of the column, coming up fast. Faster than it should be, in fact.

The captain's comment was succinct. 'Shit.' Then she added, 'Go on ahead, Beak – get 'em ready to move!'

'Yes sir!'

The problem with owls was that, even as far as birds went, they were profoundly stupid. Getting them to even so much as turn their damned heads was a struggle, no matter how tightly Bottle gripped their tiny squirming souls.

He was locked in such a battle at the moment, so far past the notion of sleep that it seemed it belonged exclusively to other people and would for ever remain beyond his reach.

But all at once it did not matter where the owl was looking, nor even where it *wanted* to look. Because there were figures moving across the land, through the copses, the tilled grounds, swarming the slopes of the old quarry pits and on the road and all its converging tracks. Hundreds, thousands. Moving quiet, weapons readied. And less than half a league behind Keneb's column.

Bottle shook himself, eyes blinking rapidly as he refocused – the pitted wall of the tavern, plaster chipped where daggers had been thrown against it, the yellow runnels of leakage from the thatched roof above the common room. Around him, marines pulling on their gear. Someone, probably Hellian, spitting and gagging somewhere behind the bar.

One of the newly arrived marines appeared in front of him, pulling up a chair and sitting down. The Dal Honese mage, the one with the jungle still in his eyes.

'Nep Furrow,' he now growled. 'Mimber me?

'Mimber what?'

'Me!'

'Yes. Nep Furrow. Like you just said. Listen, I've got no time to talk—'

A fluttering wave of one gnarled hand. 'We'en know! Bit the Edur! We'en know all'at.' A bent finger stabbed at Bottle. 'Issn this. You. Used dup! An'thas be-ad! Be-ad! We all die! Cuzzin you!'

'Oh, thanks for that, you chewed-up root! We weren't taking the scenic leg like you bastards, you know. In fact, we only got this far because of me!'

'Vlah! Iss th'feedle! The feedle orn your sergeant! Issn the song, yeseen – it ain't done-done yeet. Ain't yeet done-done! Hah!'

Bottle stared at the mage. 'So this is what happens when you pick your nose but never put anything back, right?'

'Pick'n back! Hee hee! Een so, Bauble, yeen the cause alla us dyin, s'long as yeen know.'

'And what about the unfinished song?'

An elaborate shrug. 'Oonoes when, eh? Oonoes?'

Then Fiddler was at the table. 'Bottle, now's not the time for a Hood-damned conversation. Out into the street and look awake, damn you – we're all about to charge out of this village like a herd of bhederin.'

Yeah, and right over a cliff we go. 'Wasn't me started this conversation, Sergeant—'

'Grab your gear, soldier.'

Koryk stood with the others of the squad, barring Bottle who clearly thought he was unique or something, and watched as the leading elements of the column appeared at the end of the main street, a darker mass amidst night's last, stubborn grip. No-one on horses, he saw, which wasn't too surprising. Food for Keneb and his tail-end company must have been hard to find, so horses went into the stew – there, a few left, but loaded down with gear. Soon there'd be stringy, lean meat to add flavour to the local grain that tasted the way goat shit smelled.

He could feel his heart thumping strong in his chest. Oh, there would be fighting today. The Edur to the west were rolling them up all right. And ahead, on this side of the great capital city, there'd be an army or two. *Waiting just for us and isn't that nice of 'em.*

Fiddler loomed directly in front of Koryk and slapped the half-blood on the side of his helm. 'Wake up, damn you!'

'I *was* awake, Sergeant!'

But that was all right. Understandable, even, as Fiddler went down the line snapping at everyone. Aye, there'd been way too much drinking in this village and wits were anything but sharp. Of course, Koryk felt fine enough. He'd mostly slept when the others were draining the last casks of ale. Slept, aye, knowing what was coming.

The new marines from 3rd Company had provided some novelty but not for long. They'd taken the easy route and they knew it and now so did everyone else, and it gave them all a look in the eyes, one that said they still had something to prove and this little help-out here in this village hadn't been nearly enough. *Gonna have to dive across a few hundred more Edur, sweetie, before any of us but Smiles gives you a nod or two.*

At the head of the column, which had now arrived, there was Fist Keneb and the sergeant, Thom Tissy, along with Captain Sort and her brainless mage, Beak.

Keneb eyed the squads then said, 'Sergeants, to me, please.'

Koryk watched Fiddler, Hellian, Gesler, Badan Gruk and Primly all head over to gather in a half-circle in front of the Fist.

'Typical,' muttered Smiles beside him. 'Now we all go up on report. Especially you, Koryk. You don't think anybody's forgotten you murdering that official in Malaz City – so they know you're the one to watch for.'

'Oh, be quiet,' Koryk muttered. 'They're just deciding now which squad dies first.'

That shut her up quick enough.

'You've all done damned well,' Keneb said in a low voice, 'but now the serious work begins.'

Gesler snorted. 'Think we didn't know that, Fist?'

'Still in the habit of irritating your superiors, I see.'

Gesler flashed his typical grin. 'How many you bring with you, sir, if I might ask? Because, you see, I'm starting to smell something and it's a bad smell. We can handle two to one odds. Three to one, even. But I've got a feeling we're about to find ourselves outnumbered what, ten to one? Twenty? Now, maybe you've brought us some more munitions, but unless you've got four or five wagons full hidden back of the column, it won't be enough—'

'That's not our problem,' Fiddler said, pulling a nit from his beard and cracking it between his teeth. 'There'll be mages and I know for a fact, Fist, that ours are used up. Even Bottle, and that's saying a lot.' Fiddler then scowled at Beak. 'What in Hood's name are you smiling about?'

Beak wilted, moved to hide behind Faradan Sort.

The captain seemed to bridle. 'Listen, Fiddler, maybe you know nothing about this mage here, but I assure you he has combat magicks. Beak, can you hold your own in what's to come?'

A low murmuring reply: 'Yes sir. You'll see. Everyone will because you're all my friends and friends are important. The most important thing in the world. And I'll show you.'

Fiddler winced and looked away, then squinted. 'Shit, we're losing the night.'

'Form up for the march,' Keneb ordered and damn, Fiddler observed, the Fist was looking old right now. 'We'll alternate to double-time every hundred paces – from what I understand, we don't have very far to go.'

'Until the way ahead is full of enemy,' Gesler said. 'Hope at least it's within sight of Letheras. I'd like to see the damned walls before I feed the weeds.'

'Enough of that, Sergeant. Dismissed.'

Fiddler didn't respond to Gesler's grin when they headed back to their squads.

'Come on, Fid, all those talents of yours got to be all screaming the same thing right now, aren't they?'

'Aye, they're all screaming at you to shut your damned mouth, Ges.'

Corabb Bhilan Thenu'alas had collected almost more weapons than he could carry. Four of the better spears, two javelins. A single-edged sword something like a scimitar; a nice long, straight Letherii longsword with a sharply tapered point, filed down from what had been a blunted end; two sticker knives and a brace of gutters as well. Strapped to his back was a Letherii shield, wood, leather and bronze. He also carried a crossbow and twenty-seven quarrels. And one sharper.

They were headed, he well knew, to their last stand, and it would be heroic. Glorious. It would be as it should have been with Leoman of the Flails. They would stand side by side, shoulder to shoulder, until not one was left alive. And years from now, songs would be sung of this dawning day. And there would be, among the details, a tale of one soldier, wielding spears and javelins and swords and knives and heaps of bodies at his feet. A warrior who had come from Seven Cities, yes, from thousands of leagues away, to finally give the proper ending to the Great Uprising of his homeland. A rebel once more, in the outlawed, homeless Fourteenth Army who were now called the Bonehunters, and whose own bones would be hunted, yes, for their magical properties, and sold for stacks of gold in markets. Especially Corabb's own skull, larger than all the others, once home to a vast brain filled with genius and other brilliant thoughts. A skull not even a king could afford, yes, especially with the sword blade or spear clove right through it as lasting memento to Corabb's spectacular death, the last marine standing—

'For Hood's sake, Corabb,' snapped Cuttle behind him, 'I'm dodging more spear butts now than I will in a bell's time! Get rid of some of them, will you?'

'I cannot,' Corabb replied. 'I shall need them all.'

'Now that doesn't surprise me, the way you treat your weapons.'

'There will be many enemy that need killing, yes.'

'That Letherii shield is next to useless,' Cuttle said. 'You should know that by now, Corabb.'

'When it breaks I shall find another.'

He so looked forward to the imminent battle. The screams, the shrieks of the dying, the shock of the enemy as it reeled back, repulsed again and again. The marines had earned it, oh yes. The fight they had all been waiting for, outside the very walls of Letheras – and the citizens would line them to watch, with wonder, with astonishment, with awe, as Corabb Bhilan Thenu'alas unleashed such ferocity as to sear the souls of every witness . . .

Hellian was never drinking *that* stuff again. Imagine, sick, still drunk, thirsty and hallucinating all at once. Almost as bad as that night of the Paralt Festival in Kartool, with all those people wearing giant spider costumes and Hellian, in a screaming frenzy, trying to stamp on all of them.

Now, she was trudging at the head of her paltry squad in the grainy half-light of dawn, and from the snatches of conversation that penetrated her present state of disrepair she gathered that the Edur were right behind them, like ten thousand giant spiders with fangs that could shoot out and skewer innocent seagulls and terrified women. And even worse, this damned column was marching straight for a giant web eager to ensnare them all.

Meanwhile, there were the hallucinations. Her corporal splitting in two, for example. One here, one there, both talking at once but not the same thing and not even in the same voice. And what about that doe-eyed fool with the stupid name who was now always hovering close? Scab Breath? Skulldent? Whatever, she had ten years on him easy, maybe more, or that's how it seemed since he had that smooth baby-skin – Babyskin? – face that made him look, gods, fourteen or so. All breathless with some bizarre story about being a prince and the last of a royal line and saving seeds to plant in perfect soil where cacti don't grow and now he wanted . . . wanted what? She couldn't be sure, but he was triggering all sorts of nasty thoughts in her head, above all an overwhelming desire to corrupt the boy so bad he'd never see straight ever again, just to prove that she wasn't someone anybody messed with without getting all messed up themselves. So maybe it all came down to power. The power to crush innocence and that was something even a terrified woman could do, couldn't she?

Passing through another village and oh, this wasn't a good sign. It'd been systematically flattened. Every building nothing but rubble. Armies did things like that to remove cover, to eliminate the chance of establishing redoubts and all that sort of thing. No trees beyond, either, just a level stretch of ploughed fields with the hedgerows cut down to stumps and the crops all burnt to blackened stubble and already the morning sun was lancing deadly darts into her skull, forcing her to down a few mouthfuls of her dwindling supply of Falari rum from the transports.

Steadying her some, thank Hood.

Her corporal merged back into one, which was a good sign, and he was pointing ahead and talking about something—

'What? Wait, Touchy Breath, wha's that you're saying?'

'The rise opposite, Sergeant! See the army waiting for us? See it? Gods above, we're finished! Thousands! No, worse than thousands—'

'Be quiet! I can see 'em well enough—'

'But you're looking the wrong way!'

'That's no matter either way, Corporal. I still see 'em, don't I? Now stop crowding me and go find Urb – got to keep 'im close to keep 'im alive, the clumsy fool.'

'He won't come, Sergeant.'

'Wha' you talkin' 'bout?'

'It's Skulldeath, you see. He's announced that he's given his heart to you—'

'His what? Listen, you go an' tell Hearty Death that he can have his skull back cause I don't wannit, but I'll take his cock once we're done killing all these bassards or maybe even before then if there's a chance, but in the meantime, drag Urb here because I'm 'sponsible for 'im, you see, for letting' 'im kick in that temple door.'

'Sergeant, he won't—'

'How come your voice keeps changin'?'

'So,' said the commander of the Letherii forces arrayed along the ridge, 'there they are. What do you judge, Sirryn Kanar? Under a thousand? I would believe so. All the way from the coast. Extraordinary.'

'They have survived thus far,' Sirryn said, scowling, 'because they are unwilling to stand and fight.'

741

'Rubbish,' the veteran officer replied. 'They fought the way they needed to, and they did it exceptionally well, as Hanradi and his Edur would attest. Under a thousand, by the Errant. What I could do with ten thousand such soldiers, Finadd. Pilott, Korshenn, Descent, T'roos, Isthmus – we could conquer them all. Two campaign seasons, no more than that.'

'Be that as it may,' Sirryn said, 'we're about to kill them all, sir.'

'Yes, Finadd,' the commander sighed. 'So we are.' He hesitated, then cast Sirryn an oddly sly glance. 'I doubt there will be much opportunity to excessively bleed the Tiste Edur, Finadd. They have done their task, after all, and now need only dig in behind these Malazans – and when the poor fools break, as they will, they will be routing right into Hanradi's Edur spears, and that will be the end of that.'

Sirryn Kanar shrugged. 'I still do not understand how these Malazans could have believed a thousand of their soldiers would be enough to conquer our empire. Even with their explosives and such.'

'You forget their formidable sorcery, Finadd.'

'Formidable at stealth, at hiding them from our forces. Naught else. And now, such talents have no use at all. We see our enemy, sir, and they are exposed, and so they will die.'

'Best we get on with it, then,' the commander said, somewhat shortly, as he turned to gesture his mages forward.

Below, on the vast plain that would be the killing field for this invading army – if it could even be called that – the Malazan column began, with alacrity, reforming into a defensive circle. The commander grunted. 'They hold to no illusions, Finadd, do they? They are finished and they know it. And so, there will be no rout, no retreat of any sort. Look at them! There they will stand, until none stand.'

Gathered now into their defensive circle, in very nearly the centre of the killing field, the force suddenly seemed pathetically small. The commander glanced at his seven mages, now arrayed at the very crest of the ridge and beginning the end of their ritual – which had been a week in the making. Then back to the distant huddle of Malazans. 'Errant bless peace upon their souls,' he whispered.

It was clear that Atri-Preda Bivatt, impatient as she no doubt was, had at the last moment decided to draw out the beginning of battle, to let the sun continue its assault on the mud of the seabed. Alas, such delay was not in Redmask's interest, and so he acted first.

The Letherii mages each stood within a protective ring of soldiers carrying oversized shields. They were positioned beyond arrow range, but Bivatt well knew their vulnerability nonetheless, particularly once they began their ritual summoning of power.

Toc Anaster, seated on his horse to permit him a clearer view, felt the scarring of his missing eye blaze into savage itching, and he could feel how the air grew charged, febrile, as the two mages bound their wills together. They could not, he suspected, maintain control for very long. The sorcery would need to erupt, would need to be released. To roll in foaming waves down into the seabed, blistering their way across the ground to crash into the Awl lines. Where warriors would die by the hundreds, perhaps by the thousands.

Against such a thing, Redmask's few shamans could do nothing. All that had once given power to the plains tribe was torn, very nearly shredded by displacement, by the desecration of holy grounds, by the deaths of countless warriors and elders and children. The Awl culture, Toc now understood, was crumbling, and to save it, to resurrect his people, Redmask needed victory this day, and he would do anything to achieve it.

Including, if need be, the sacrifice of his K'Chain Che'Malle.

Beneath their strange armour, beneath the fused swords at the end of the K'ell Hunter's arms, beneath their silent language and inexplicable alliance with Redmask of the Awl, the K'Chain Che'Malle were reptiles, and their blood was cold, and deep in their brains, perhaps, could be found ancient memories, recollections of a pre-civilized existence, a wildness bound in the skein of instincts. And so the patience of a supreme predator coursed in that chill blood.

Reptiles. *Damned lizards.*

Thirty or so paces from where stood the mages and their guardian soldiers, the slope reached down to the edge of the ancient sea, where the mud stretched out amidst tufts of smeared, flattened grasses, and where run-off had pooled before slowly ebbing away into the silts beneath.

The K'Chain Che'Malle had wallowed down into that mud, quite possibly even as the rains continued to thrash down in darkness. Huge as they were, they had proved skilled at burying themselves so that no sign was visible of their presence – no sign at least to a casual viewer. And after all, who could have imagined such enormous beasts were capable of simply disappearing from sight?

And Redmask had guessed more or less correctly where the mages would position themselves; indeed, he had invited such placements, where waves of magic would converge to maximum effect against his waiting warriors. Neither Sag'Churok nor Gunth Mach rose to find themselves too far away for that sudden, devastating rush upslope.

Screams of terror as the flat clay seemed to erupt at the old shoreline, and then, mud cascading from their backs, the demonic creatures were racing upslope, each closing in on one of the mages.

Panicked retreat – flight from the guards, flinging shields and swords away – exposing the hapless mages, both of whom sought to unleash their sorcery—

743

—no time, as Sag'Churok's twin blades slashed out and the first mage seemed to vanish in a bloom of blood and meat—

—no time, as Gunth Mach leapt high in the air then landed with splayed talons directly atop the second, cowering mage, crushing him in a snap of bones—

And then the beasts wheeled, racing back in zigzag patterns as flights of arrows descended. Those that struck bounced or, rarely, penetrated the thick scaled hide enough to hold fixed in place, until the creature's motion worked them loose.

In the wake of this sudden horror, the Letherii horns sounded like cries of rage, and all at once the wedges were moving down the slope, and some battle song lifted skyward to set cadence – but it was a shrill sound, erupting from the throats of shaken soldiers—

As easily as that, Toc Anaster reflected, *this battle begins.*

Behind him, Torrent was dancing in gleeful frenzy.

Shouting: '*Redmask! Redmask! Redmask!*'

The wedges edged out onto the seabed and visibly sagged as momentum slowed. Between them milled the archers, skirmishers and some medium infantry, and Toc saw soldiers slipping, falling, boots skidding out as they sought purchase to draw bowstrings – *chaos.* The heavy infantry in front were now sinking to their knees, while those at the back stumbled into those before them, as the rhythm broke, then utterly collapsed.

A second set of horns sounded as soon as each entire wedge was on the flat, and all forward motion ceased. A moment of relative silence as the wedges reformed, then a new song emerged from the soldiers, this one deeper, more assured, and carrying a slower cadence, a drawn-out beat that proved the perfect match to an advance of one step at a time, with a settling pause between it and the next.

Toc grunted in admiration. That was impressive control indeed, and it looked to be working.

They will reach the Awl lines intact. Still, no solid footing to fix shields or swing weapons with strength. Gods, this is going to be bloody.

For all of Redmask's creativity, he was not, in Toc's judgement, a tactical genius. Here, he had done all he could to gain advantage, displaying due competence. Without the K'Chain Che'Malle, this battle might already be over. In any case, Redmask's second surprise could not – for anyone – have been much of a surprise at all.

Natarkas, face slick with sweat behind his red mask, eased his horse into a canter. Surrounding him was the sound of thunder. Two thousand chosen warriors rode with him across the plain. As the canter was loosed into a gallop, lances were set, shields settled to cover groin, hip and chest.

Natarkas had led his cavalry through the night's rain, east of the seabed, then north and finally, as false dawn licked the darkness, westward.

At dawn, they were positioned a third of a league behind the Letherii forces. Arrayed into a wedge with Natarkas himself positioned in the centre of the sixth row. Awaiting the first sounds of battle.

Redmask had been adamant with his instructions. If enemy scouts found them, they were to wait, and wait yet longer, listening to the sounds of battle for at least two turns of the wheel. If they believed themselves undiscovered – if the opportunity for surprise remained – when the sounds of fighting commenced, Natarkas was to immediately lead his cavalry into an attack on the rear formations of the enemy forces – on, no doubt, the Tiste Edur. There was to be no deviation from these instructions.

At dawn, his own scouts had ridden to Natarkas to announce that a mounted troop of Edur had discovered them. And he thought back to Redmask the night before. *'Natarkas, do you understand why, if you are seen, I want you to hold? To not immediately charge? No? Then I will explain. If you are seen, I must be able to exploit that in the battle on the seabed. At least two wheels you must wait, doing nothing. This will lock the Tiste Edur in place. It may even draw out the Bluerose cavalry – and should they approach you, invite them to the chase – lead them away, yes, and keep leading them away. Do not engage them, Natarkas! You will be savaged! Run their horses into the dust – you see, they will cease to matter by then, and Bivatt will not have them at her disposal. This is important! Do you understand my commands?'*

Yes, he did understand them. If surprise was lost, he was to lead his Awl . . . away. Like cowards. But they had played the cowards before, and that was a truth that burned in his heart. Flaring into agony whenever he saw the Mezla, Toc Anaster, yes, the one-eyed foreigner who stood as living proof to a time of such darkness among the Awl that Natarkas could barely breathe whenever he thought about it.

And he knew his fellow warriors felt the same. The hollowness inside, the terrible need to give answer, to reject the past in the only way now left to them.

They had been seen, yes.

But they would not run. Nor would they wait. They would ride to the sounds of battle. They would sight the hated enemy, and they would charge.

Redemption. Do you understand that word, Redmask? No? Then, we shall show you its meaning.

*

'Sister Shadow, they're coming.' Brohl Handar tightened the strap of his helm. 'Ready your spears!' he bellowed to his warriors, and along the entire front line, two ranks deep, the iron points of the spears flashed downward. The foremost rank knelt, angling their points to the chest height of the approaching horses, while the row behind them remained standing, ready to thrust. 'Shields to guard!' The third rank edged forward half a step to bring their shields into a guard position beneath the weapon arms of the warriors in the second row.

Brohl turned to one of his runners. 'Inform the Atri-Preda that we face a cavalry charge, and I strongly advise she order the Bluerose to mount up for a flank attack – the sooner we are done with this the sooner we can join the fight on the seabed.'

He watched as the youth rushed off.

The wedges were on the flat now, he understood, employing the step and settle advance Bivatt had devised in order to adjust to the mud. They were probably nearing the Awl lines, although yet to clash. The Atri-Preda had another tactic for that moment, and Brohl Handar wished her well.

The slaying of the mages had been a grim opening to this day's battle, but the Overseer's confidence had, if anything, begun to grow.

These fools charge us! They charge a forest of spears! It is suicide!

Finally, he realized, they could end this. Finally, this absurd war could end. By day's close, not a single Awl would remain alive. Not one.

The thunder of hoofs. Lances lowered, the horses with necks stretched out, the warriors hunching down – closer, closer, then, all at once, *chaos.*

No horse could be made to run into a wall of wall of bristling spears. In the midst of the Awl lancers were mounted archers, and as the mass of riders drew to within a hundred paces of Edur, these archers rose on their stirrups and released a swarm of arrows.

The first row of Edur, kneeling with spears planted, had leaned their rectangular Letherii shields against their shoulders – the best they could manage with both hands on the spear shaft. Those immediately behind them were better protected, but the spear-hedge, as the Letherii called it, was vulnerable.

Warriors screamed, spun round by the impact of arrows. The row rippled, wavered, was suddenly ragged.

Horses could not be made to run into a wall of bristling spears. But, if sufficiently trained, they could be made to hammer into a mass of human flesh. And, among those still facing spears positioned at chest height, they could jump.

A second flight of arrows slanted out at forty or so paces. Then a third at ten paces.

The facing side of the Edur square was a ragged mess by the time the charge struck home. Beasts launched themselves into the air, straining to clear the first spears, only to intercept other iron-headed points – but none of these were butted into the ground, and while serrated edges slashed through leather plates and the flesh beneath, many were driven aside or punched back. In the gaps in the front line, the horses plunged into the ranks of Edur, flinging warriors away, trampling others. Lances thudded into reeling bodies, skidded from desperate shield blocks, kissed faces and throats in a welter of blood.

Brohl Handar, positioned behind his Edur square, stared in horror as the entire block of Arapay warriors seemed to recoil, flinch back, then inexorably fold inward from the facing side.

The Awl wedge had driven deep and was now exploding from within the disordered square. The impact had driven warriors back, fouling those behind them, in a rippling effect that spread through the entire formation.

Among the Awl, in the midst of jostling, stumbling Edur, heavy cutting swords appeared as lances were shattered, splintered or left in bodies. In screaming frenzy, the savages were hacking down on all sides.

Horses went down, kicking, lashing out in their death-throes. Spears stabbed upwards to lift Awl warriors from their saddles.

The square was seething madness.

And horses continued to go down, whilst others backed, despite the shrieking commands of their riders. More spears raked riders from their saddles, crowds closing about individuals.

All at once, the Awl were seeking to withdraw, and the Edur warriors began pushing, the square's flanks advancing in an effort to enclose the attackers.

Someone was screaming at Brohl Handar. Someone at his side, and he turned to see one of his runners.

Who was pointing westward with frantic gestures.

Bluerose cavalry, forming up.

Brohl Handar stared at the distant ranks, the sun-lashed lance-heads held high, the horses' heads lifting and tossing, then he shook himself. 'Sound close ranks! The square does not pursue! Close ranks and let the enemy withdraw!'

Moments later, horns blared.

The Awl did not understand. Panic was already among them, and the sudden recoiling of those now advancing Edur struck them as an opportunity. Eager to disengage, the horse-warriors sprang away from all contact – twenty paces – archers twisting in their saddles to loose arrows – forty, fifty paces, and a copper-faced officer among them yelling at his troops to draw up, to reform for another charge – and there was

747

thunder in the west, and that warrior turned in his saddle, and saw, descending upon his milling ranks, his own death.

His death, and that of his warriors.

Brohl Handar watched as the commander frantically tried to wheel his troops, to set them, to push the weary, bloodied beasts and their equally weary riders into a meeting charge – but it was too late. Voices cried out in fear as warriors saw what was descending upon them. The confusion redoubled, and then riders were breaking, fleeing—

All at once, the Bluerose lancers swept into them.

Brohl Handar looked down upon his Arapay – *Sister Shadow, but we have been wounded.* 'Sound the slow advance!' he commanded, stepping forward and drawing his sword. 'We will finish what the Bluerose have begun.' *I want those bastards. Every damned one of them. Screaming in pain, dying by our blades!*

Something dark and savage swirled awake within him. Oh, there would be pleasure in killing. Here. Now. *Such pleasure.*

As the Bluerose charge rolled through the Awl cavalry, a broad-bladed lance caught Natarkas – still shrieking his commands to wheel – in the side of the head. The point punched through low on his left temple, beneath the rim of the bronze-banded helm. It shattered that plate of the skull, along with his cheekbone and the orbit of the eye. Then drove still deeper, through brain and nasal cavity.

Blackness bloomed in his mind.

Beneath him – as he toppled, twisted round when the lance dragged free – his horse staggered before the impact of the attacker's own mount; then, as the weight of Natarkas's body rolled away, the beast bolted, seeking a place away from this carnage, this terror.

All at once, open plain ahead and two other riderless horses racing away, heads high in sudden freedom.

Natarkas's horse set off after them.

The chaos in its heart dwindled, faded, fluttered away with every exultant breath the beast drew into its aching lungs.

Free!

Never! Free!

Never again!

On the seabed, the heavy infantry wedges advanced beneath the now constant hail of descending arrows. Skittering on raised shields, glancing from visored helms, stabbing down through gaps in armour and chance ricochets. Soldiers cried out, stumbled, recovered or sought to fall – but these latter were suddenly grasped by hands on either side and bodies closed in, keeping them upright, feet now dragging as life poured its crimson gift to the churned mud below. Those hands then began pushing the dead and the dying forward, through the ranks. Hands reaching back, grasping, tugging and pulling, then pushing into yet more waiting hands.

Through all of this, the chant continued, the wait beat marked each settling step.

Twelve paces from the Awl on their islands of dry, able now to see into faces, to see the blazing eyes filled with fear or rage.

This slow advance could not but unnerve the waiting Awl. Human spear-heads, edging ever closer. Massive iron fangs, inexorably looming, step, wait, step, wait, step.

And now, eight paces away, arrow-riddled corpses were being flung forward from the front ranks, the bodies sprawling into the mud. Shields followed here and there. Boots settled atop these things, pushing them into the mud.

Bodies and shields, appearing in a seemingly unending stream.

Building, there in the last six strides, a floor of flesh, leather, wood and armour.

Javelins sleeted into those wedges, driving soldiers back and down, only to have their bodies thrust forward with chilling disregard. The wounded bled out. The wounded drowned screaming in the mud. And each wedge seemed to lift itself up and out of the mud, although the cadence did not change.

Four steps. Three.

And, at a bellowing shout, the points of those enormous wedges suddenly drove forward.

Into human flesh, into set shields, spears. Into the Awl.

Each and every mind dreamed of victory. Of immortality. And, among them all, not one would yield.

The sun stared down, blazing with eager heat, on Q'uson Tapi, where two civilizations locked throat to throat.

One last time.

A fateful decision, maybe, but he'd made it now. Dragging with him all the squads that had been in the village, Fiddler took over from some of Keneb's more beat-up units the west-facing side of their turtleback defence. No longer standing eye to eye with that huge Letherii army and its Hood-cursed sorcerers. No, here they waited, and opposite them, drawing up in thick ranks, the Tiste Edur.

Was it cowardice? He wasn't sure, and from the looks he caught in the eyes of his fellow sergeants – barring Hellian who'd made a temporarily unsuccessful grab at Skulldeath, or more precisely at his crotch, before Primly intervened – they weren't sure, either.

Fine, then, I just don't want to see my death come rolling down on me. Is that cowardly? Aye, by all counts it couldn't be anything but. Still, there's this. I don't feel frightened.

No, all he wanted right now, beyond what Hellian so obviously wanted, of course, all he wanted, then, was to die fighting. To see the face of the bastard who killed him, to pass on, in that final meeting of eyes, all that dying meant, must have meant and would always mean ... *whatever that was, and let's hope I do a better job of letting my killer know whatever it is – better, that is, than all those whose eyes I've looked into as they died at my hand. Aye, seems a worthy enough prayer.*

But I ain't praying to you, Hood.

In fact, damned if I know who I'm praying to, but even that doesn't seem to matter.

His soldiers were digging holes but not saying much. They'd received a satchelful of munitions, including two more cussers, and while that wasn't nearly enough it made it advisable to dig the holes where they could crouch for cover when those sharpers, cussers and all the rest started going off.

All of this, dammit, assumed there would be fighting.

Far more likely, magic would sweep over the Malazans, one and all, grabbing at their throats even as it burned away skin, muscle and organs, burned away even their last desperate, furious screams.

Fiddler vowed to make his last scream a curse. A good one, too.

He stared across at the rows of Tiste Edur.

Beside him, Cuttle said, 'They don't like it neither, you know.'

Fiddler replied with a wordless grunt.

'That's their leader, that old one with the hunched shoulders. Too many paying him too much attention. I plan to take him out, Fid – with a cusser. Listen – are you listening? As soon as that wave of magic starts its roll, we should damn well up and charge these bastards.'

Not a bad idea, actually. Blinking, Fiddler faced the sapper, and then nodded. 'Pass the word, then.'

At that moment one of Thom Tissy's soldiers jogged into their midst. 'Fist's orders,' he said, looking round. 'Where's your captain?'

'Holding Beak's hand, somewhere else,' Fiddler replied. 'You can give those orders to me, soldier.'

'All right. Maintain the turtleback – do not advance on the enemy—'

'That's fucking—'

'Enough, Cuttle!' Fiddler snapped. To the runner he nodded and said, 'How long?'

A blank expression answered that question.

Fiddler waved the idiot on, then turned once more to stare across at the Tiste Edur.

'Damn him, Fid!'

'Relax, Cuttle. We'll set out when we have to, all right?'

'Sergeant?' Bottle was suddenly crawling out of the hole he'd dug, and there was a strained look on his face. 'Something . . . something's happening—'

At that moment, from the ridge to the east, a blood-chilling sound – like ten thousand anchor chains ripping up from the ground, and there rose a virulent wall of swirling magic. Dark purple and shot through with crimson veins, black etchings like lightning darting along the crest as it rose, higher, yet higher—

'Hood's balls!' Cuttle breathed, eyes wide.

Fiddler simply stared. This was the sorcery they'd seen off the north coast of Seven Cities. Only, then they'd had Quick Ben with them. And Bottle had his – he reached out and pulled Bottle close. 'Listen! Is she—'

'No, Fid! Nowhere! She's not been with me since we landed. I'm sorry—'

Fiddler flung the man back down.

The wall heaved itself still higher.

The Tiste Edur along the western edge of the killing field were suddenly pulling back.

Cuttle yelled, '*We need to go now! Fiddler! Now!*'

Yet he could not move. Could not answer, no matter how the sapper railed at him. Could only stare, craning, ever upward. Too much magic. 'Gods above,' he muttered, '*talk about overkill.*'

Run away from this? Not a chance.

Cuttle dragged him round.

Fiddler scowled and pushed the man back, hard enough to make the sapper stumble. 'Fuck running, Cuttle! You think we can out-run *that*?'

'But the Edur—'

'It's going to take them too – can't you see that?' *It has to – no-one can control it once it's released – no-one.* 'Those Hood-damned Edur have been set up, Cuttle!' *Oh yes, the Letherii wanted to get rid of their masters – they just didn't want to do it with us as allies. No, they'll do it their way and take out both enemies at the same damned time . . .*

Three hundred paces to the west, Hanradi stared up at that Letherii magic. And understood, all at once. He *understood.*

'We have been betrayed,' he said, as much to himself as to the warriors standing close by. 'That ritual – it has been days in the making. Maybe weeks. Once unleashed . . .' *the devastation will stretch for leagues westward.*

What to do?

751

Father Shadow, what to do? 'Where are my K'risnan?' he suddenly demanded, turning to his aides.

Two Edur hobbled forward, their faces ashen.

'Can you protect us?'

Neither replied, and neither would meet Hanradi's eyes.

'Can you not call upon Hannan Mosag? Reach through to the Ceda, damn you!'

'You do not understand!' one of the once-young K'risnan shouted. 'We are – all – we are all abandoned!'

'But Kurald Emurlahn—'

'Yes! Awake once more! But we cannot reach it! Nor can the Ceda!'

'And what of that *other* power? The chaos?'

'Gone! Fled!'

Hanradi stared at the two warlocks. He drew his sword and lashed the blade across the nearest one's face, the edge biting through bridge of nose and splitting both eyeballs. Shrieking, the figure reeled back, hands at his face. Hanradi stepped forward and drove his sword into the creature's twisted chest, and the blood that gushed forth was almost black.

Tugging the weapon free, Hanradi turned to the other one, who cowered back. 'You warlocks,' the once-king said in a grating voice, 'are the cause of this. All of this.' He took another step closer. 'Would that you were Hannan Mosag crouched before me now—'

'Wait!' the K'risnan shrieked, suddenly pointing eastward. 'Wait! One gives answer! One gives answer!'

Hanradi turned, eyes focusing with some difficulty on the Malazans – so overwhelming was the wave of Letherii magic that a shadow had descended upon the entire killing field.

Rising from that huddled mass of soldiers, a faint, luminous glow. Silver, vaguely pulsing.

Hanradi's laugh was harsh. 'That pathetic thing is an answer?' He half raised his sword.

'No!' the K'risnan cried. 'Wait! Look, you stupid fool! *Look!*'

And so he did, once again.

And saw that dome of silver light burgeoning, spreading out to engulf the entire force – and it thickened, became opaque—

The last K'risnan clutched at Hanradi's arm. 'Listen to me! Its power – Father Shadow! *Its power!*'

'Can it hold?' Hanradi demanded. '*Can it hold against the Letherii?*'

He saw no answer in the K'risnan's red-rimmed eyes.

It cannot – look, still, it is tiny – against that ever-growing wave—

But . . . it need be no larger than that, need it? It engulfs them all.

'Sound the advance!' he shouted. 'At the double!'

Wide eyes fixed on Hanradi, who pointed at that scintillating dome of ethereal power. 'At the very least we can crouch in its shadow! Now, move forward! Everyone!'

Beak, who had once possessed another name, a more boring name, had been playing in the dirt that afternoon, on the floor of the old barn where no-one went any more and that was far away from the rest of the buildings of the estate, far enough away to enable him to imagine he was alone in an abandoned world. A world without trouble.

He was playing with the discarded lumps of wax he collected from the trash heap below the back wall of the main house. The heat of his hands could change their shape, like magic. He could mould faces from the pieces and build entire families like those families down in the village, where boys and girls his age worked alongside their parents and when not working played in the woods and were always laughing.

This was where his brother found him. His brother with the sad face so unlike the wax ones he liked to make. He arrived carrying a coil of rope, and stood just inside the gaping entrance with its jammed-wide doors all overgrown.

Beak, who had a more boring name back then, saw in his brother's face a sudden distress, which then drained away and a faint smile took its place which was a relief since Beak always hated it when his brother went off somewhere to cry. Older brothers should never do that and if he was older, why, he'd never do that.

His brother then walked towards him, and still half smiling he said, 'I need you to leave, little one. Take your toys and leave here.'

Beak stared with wide eyes. His brother never asked such things of him. His brother had always shared this barn. 'Don't you want to play with me?'

'Not now,' his brother replied, and Beak saw that his hands were trembling which meant there'd been trouble back at the estate. Trouble with Mother.

'Playing will make you feel better,' Beak said.

'I know. But not now.'

'Later?' Beak began collecting his wax villagers.

'We'll see.'

There were decisions that did not seem like decisions. And choices could just fall into place when nobody was really looking and that was how things were in childhood just as they were for adults. Wax villagers cradled in his arms, Beak set off, out the front and into the sunlight. Summer days were always wonderful – the sun was hot enough to make the villagers weep with joy, once he lined them up on the old border stone that meant nothing any more.

The stone was about eighteen of Beak's small paces away, toppled down at one corner of the track before it turned and sank down towards the bridge and the stream where minnows lived until it dried up and then they died because minnows could only breathe in water. He had just set his toys down in a row when he decided he needed to ask his brother something.

Decisions and choices, falling.

What was it he had wanted to ask? There was no memory of that. The memory of that was gone, melted down into nothing. It had been a very hot day.

Reaching the entrance he saw his brother – who had been sitting with legs dangling from the loft's edge – slide over to drop down onto the floor. But he didn't drop all the way. The rope round his neck caught him instead.

And then, his face turning dark as his eyes bulged and his tongue pushed out, his brother danced in the air, kicking through the shafts of dusty sunlight.

Beak ran up to him – the game his brother had been playing with the rope had gone all wrong, and now his brother was choking. He threw his arms about his brother's kicking legs and tried with all his might to hold him up.

And there he stood, and perhaps he was screaming, but perhaps he wasn't, because this was an abandoned place, too far away from any-one who might help.

His brother tried to kick him away. His brother's fists punched down on the top of Beak's head, hard enough to hurt but not so much since those hands couldn't but barely reach him, short as he was being still younger than his brother. So he just held on.

Fire awoke in the muscles of his arms. In his shoulders. His neck. His legs shook beneath him, because he needed to stand on his toes – if he tried to move his arms further down to well below his brother's knees, then his brother simply bent those knees and started choking again.

Fire everywhere, fire right through Beak's body.

His legs were failing. His arms were failing. And as they failed his brother choked. Pee ran down to burn against Beak's wrists and his face. The air was suddenly thick with worse smells and his brother never did things like this – all this mess, the terrible mistake with the rope.

Beak could not hold on, and this was the problem with being a younger brother, with being as he was. And the kicking finally stilled, the muscles of his brother's legs becoming soft, loose. Two fingertips from one of his brother's hands lightly brushed Beak's hair, but they only moved when Beak himself moved, so those fingers were as still as the legs.

It was good that his brother wasn't fighting any more. He must have loosened the rope from round his neck and was now just resting. And that was good because Beak was now on his knees, arms wrapped tight about his brother's feet.

And there he stayed.

Until, three bells after dusk, one of the stable hands from the search party came into the barn with a lantern.

By then, the sun's heat earlier that afternoon had ruined all his villagers, had drawn down their faces into expressions of grief, and Beak did not come back to collect them up, did not reshape them into nicer faces. Those lumps remained on the border stone that meant nothing any more, sinking down in the day after day sun.

After that last day with his brother, there was trouble aplenty in the household. But it did not last long, not long at all.

He did not know why he was thinking about his brother now, as he set ablaze every candle within him to make the world bright and to save all his friends. And before long he no longer sensed anyone else, barring the faint smudges they had become. The captain, the Fist, all the soldiers who were his friends, he let his light unfold to embrace them all, to keep them safe from that frightening, dark magic so eager to rush down upon them.

It had grown too powerful for those seven mages to contain. They had created something that would now destroy them, but Beak would not let it hurt his friends. And so he made his light burn yet brighter. He made of it a solid thing. Would it be enough? He did not know, but it had to be, for without friends there was nothing, no-one.

Brighter, hotter, so hot the wax of the candles burst into clouds of droplets, flaring bright as the sun, one after another. And, when every coloured candle was lit, why, there was white.

And yet more, for as each joined the torrent emanating from him, he felt in himself a cleansing, a scouring away, what priests called *purification* only they really knew nothing about purification because it had nothing to do with offerings of blood or coin and nothing to do with starving yourself and whipping your own back or endlessly chanting until the brain goes numb. Nothing like any of that. Purification, Beak now understood, was final.

Everything glowed, as if lit from fires within. The once-black stubble of crops blazed back into fierce life. Stones shone like precious gems. Incandescence raged on all sides. Fiddler saw his soldiers and he could see through, in pulsing flashes, to their very bones, the organs huddled within their cages. He saw, along one entire side of Koryk, old fractures on the ribs, the left arm, the shoulder blade, the hip. He saw three knuckle-sized dents on Cuttle's skull beneath the now translucent helm – a rap he had taken when still a babe, soft-boned and vulnerable. He saw the damage between Smiles's legs from all the times she savaged herself. He saw in Corabb Bhilan Thenu'alas the coursing blood that held in it the power to destroy every cancer that struck him, and he was a man under siege from that disease, but it would never kill. Would not even sicken him.

He saw in Bottle coruscating waves of raw power, a refulgence devoid of all control – but that would come. *It will come.*

Corporal Tarr crouched down in the hole he'd dug, and the light emanating from him looked solid as iron.

Among the others he saw more than any mortal would want to see, yet he could not close his eyes, could not look away.

Gesler and Stormy were lit in gold fire. Even Stormy's beard and hair – all spun gold now – a brutal beauty cascading round his face, and the damned fool was laughing.

The world beyond had vanished behind an opaque, curved wall of silver fire. Vague shapes on the other side – yes, he'd seen the Tiste Edur approaching, seeking some kind of shelter.

Fiddler found he was standing, facing that wall, and now he was walking forward. *Because some things matter more than others.* Stepping into that silver fire, feeling it lance through his entire body, neither hot nor cold, neither pain nor joy.

He staggered suddenly, blinking, and not fifteen paces from him crouched hundreds of Tiste Edur. Waiting to die.

Hanradi knelt with his gaze fixed on the sky, half of which had vanished behind a blackened wall of writhing madness. The crest had begun its toppling advance.

Sudden motion drew his eyes down.

To see a Malazan – now transformed into an apparition of white – beard, hair – the dangling finger bones were now polished, luminous, as was his armour, his weapons. Scoured, polished, even the leather of his harness looked new, supple.

The Malazan met his gaze with silver eyes, then he lifted one perfect hand, and waved them all forward.

Hanradi rose, flinging his sword aside.

His warriors saw. His warriors did the same, and as they all moved forward, the dome of silver fire all at once rushed towards them.

A piercing shriek and Hanradi turned to see his last K'risnan burst into flames – a single blinding instant, then the hapless warlock was simply ash, settling onto the ground—

Beak was happy to save them. He had understood that old sergeant. The twisted mage, alas, could not embrace such purification. Too much of his soul had been surrendered. The others – oh, they were wounded, filled with bitterness that he needed to sweep away, and so he did.

Nothing was difficult any more. Nothing—

At that moment, the wave of Letherii magic descended.

The Letherii commander could not see the killing field, could indeed see nothing but that swirling, burgeoning wall of eager sorcery. Its cruel hunger poured down in hissing clouds.

When it heaved forward, all illusion of control vanished.

The commander, with Sirryin Kanar cowering beside him, saw all seven of his mages plucked from the ground, dragged up into the air, into the wake of that charging wall. Screaming, flailing, then streaks of whipping blood as they were torn apart moments before vanishing into the dark storm.

The sorcery lurched, then plunged down upon the killing field.

Detonation.

Soldiers were thrown from their feet. Horses were flung onto their sides, riders tumbling or pinned as the terrified beasts rolled onto their backs. The entire ridge seemed to ripple, then buckle, and sudden slumping pulled soldiers from the edge, burying them in slides racing for the field below. Mouths were open, screams unleashed in seeming silence, the horror in so many eyes—

The collapsing wave blew apart—

Beak was driven down by the immense weight, the horrible hunger. Yet he would not retreat. Instead, he let the fire within him lash out, devouring every candle, igniting *everything*.

His friends, yes, the only ones he had ever known.

Survival, he realized, could only be found through purity. Of his love for them all – how so many of them had smiled at him, laughed with him. How hands clapped him on the shoulder and even, now and then, tousled his hair.

He would have liked to see the captain one last time, and maybe even kiss her. On the cheek, although of course he would have liked something far more . . . brave. But he was Beak, after all, and he could hold on to but one thing at a time.

Arms wrapped tight, even as the fire began to burn the muscles of his arms. His shoulders and neck. His legs.

He could hold on, now, until they found him.

Those fires were so hot, now, burning – but there was no pain. Pain had been scoured away, cleansed away. Oh, the weight was vast, getting heavier still, but he would not let go. Not of his brothers and his sisters, the ones he so loved.

My friends.

*

The Letherii sorcery broke, bursting into clouds of white fire that corkscrewed skyward before vanishing. Fragments crashed down to either side of the incandescent dome, ripped deep into the earth in black spewing clouds. And, everywhere, it died.

The commander struggled back onto his feet, stared uncomprehending at the scene on the killing field.

To either side his soldiers were stumbling upright once again. Runners appeared, one nearly colliding with him as he careened off a still-kneeling Sirryn Kanar, the woman trying to tell him something. Pointing southward.

'—landing! Another Malazan army, sir! Thousands more! From the river!'

The veteran commander frowned at the woman, whose face was smeared with dirt and whose eyes were brittle with panic.

He looked back down at the killing field. The dome was flickering, dying. But it had held. Long enough, it had held. 'Inform my officers,' he said to the runner. 'Prepare to wheel and fast march to the river – how far? Have they managed a beach-head?'

'If we march straight to the river, sir, we will meet them. And yes, as I was saying, they have landed. There are great warships in the river – scores of them! And—'

'Go, damn you! To my officers!'

Sirryn was now on his feet. He rounded on the commander. 'But sir – these ones below!'

'Leave them to the damned Edur, Sirryn! You wanted them mauled, then you shall have your wish! We must meet the larger force, and we must do so immediately!'

Sword and shield, at last, a battle in which a soldier could die with honour.

Captain Faradan Sort had, like so many other soldiers relatively close to where Beak had sat, been driven to the ground by the ferocity of his magic. She was slow to recover, and even as the silver glow pulsed in fitful death, she saw . . . *white*.

Gleaming armour and weapons. Hair white as snow, faces devoid of all scars. Figures, picking themselves up in a half-daze, rising like perfect conjurations from the brilliant green shoots of some kind of grass that now snarled everything and seemed to be growing before her eyes.

And, turning, she looked upon Beak.

To burn, fire needed fuel.

To save them all, Beak had used all the fuel within him.

In horror, Faradan Sort found herself staring at a collapsed jumble of ashes and scorched bone. But no, there was pattern within that, a configuration, if she could but focus through her tears. *Oh.* The bones of the arms seemed to be hugging the knees, the crumpled skull settled on them.

Like a child hiding in a closet, a child seeking to make himself small, so small . . .

Beak. Gods below . . . Beak.

'Plan on returning to your weapons?' Fiddler asked the Edur war leader. 'If you're wanting to start again, that is, we're willing.'

But the elderly warrior shook his head. 'We are done with empire.' Then he added, 'If you would permit us to leave.'

'I can think of quite of few of us who'd be more inclined to kill you all, right now.'

A nod.

'But,' Fiddler then said, as his soldiers gathered behind him, all staring at the Tiste Edur – who were staring back – 'we're not here to conduct genocide. You would leave your Emperor defenceless?'

The war leader pointed northward. 'Our villages lie far away. Few remain there, and they suffer for our absence. I would lead my warriors home, Malazan. To rebuild. To await the return of our families.'

'Go on, then.'

The Tiste Edur elder bowed. Then said, 'Would that we could . . . take back . . . all that we have done.'

'Tell me this. Your Emperor – can he be killed?'

'No.'

Nothing more was said. Fiddler watched as the Edur set off.

Behind him a grunt from Koryk, who then said, 'I was damned sure we'd get a fight today.'

'Fiddler. The Letherii army's marched off,' Gesler said.

'The Adjunct,' Fiddler said, nodding. 'She'll hammer them into the ground.'

'My point is,' Gesler continued, 'our way to Letheras . . . it's an open road. Are we going to let the Adjunct and all those salty soldiers of hers beat us there?'

'Good question,' Fiddler said, turning at last. 'Let's go ask the Fist, shall we?'

'Aye, and maybe we can find out why we're all still alive, too.'

'Aye, and white, too.'

Gesler tugged off his helm and grinned at Fiddler. 'Speak for yourself, Fid.'

Hair of spun gold. 'Hood take me,' Fiddler muttered, 'that's about as obnoxious a thing as I've ever seen.'

Another helping hand, lifting Beak to his feet. He looked round.

Nothing much to see. White sand, a gate of white marble ahead, within which swirled silver light.

The hand gripping his arm was skeletal, the skin a strange hue of green. The figure, very tall, was hooded and wearing black rags. It seemed to be studying the gate.

'Is that where I'm supposed to go, now?' Beak asked.

'Yes.'

'All right. Are you coming with me?'

'No.'

'All right. Well, will you let go of my arm, then?'

The hand fell away. 'It is not common,' the figure then said.

'What?'

'That I attend to . . . arrivals. In person.'

'My name is Beak.'

'Yes.'

'What's through there?'

'Your brother waits for you, Beak. He has been waiting a long time.'

Beak smiled and stepped forward, all at once in a great hurry – the silver light within that gate was beautiful, reminding him of something.

The stranger's voice brought him round: 'Beak.'

'Yes?'

'Your brother. He will not know you. Yet. Do you understand?'

Beak nodded. 'Why aren't you coming with me?'

'I choose to wait . . . for another.'

'My brother,' Beak said, his smile broadening. 'I'm taller now. Stronger. I can save him, can't I?'

A long pause, and then the figure said, 'Yes, Beak, you can save him.'

Yes, that made sense. He set out again. With sure strides. To the gate, into that silver glow, to emerge on the other side in a glade beside a trickling stream. And kneeling near the bank, his brother. The same as he remembered. On the ground on all sides there were hundreds of small wax figures. Smiling faces, an entire village, maybe even a whole town.

Beak walked up to his brother.

Who said, too shy to look up, 'I made all of these, for him.'

'They're beautiful,' Beak said, and he found tears running down his face, which embarrassed him so he wiped them away. Then asked, 'Can I play with you?'

His brother hesitated, scanning all the figures, then he nodded. 'All right.'

And so Beak knelt, down beside his brother.

While, upon the other side of the gate, the god Hood stood, motionless.

Waiting.

*

760

A third army rose from the seabed to conquer the others. An army of mud, against whom no shield could defend, through whom no sword could cut to the quick. The precious islands of canvas were now twisted jumbles, fouling the foot, wrapping tight about legs, or pushed down entirely beneath thick silts. Grey-smeared soldier struggled against grey-smeared warrior, locked together in desperation, rage and terror.

The seething mass had become an entity, a chaotic beast writhing and foundering in the mud, and from it rose the deafening clangour of clashing metal and voices erupting in pain and dying.

Soldiers and warriors fell, were then pushed down amidst grey and red, where they soon merged with the ground. Shield walls could not hold, advances were devoured; the battle had become that of individuals sunk to their knees, thrashing in the press.

The beast heaved back and forth, consuming itself in its madness, and upon either side those who commanded sent yet more into the maelstrom.

The wedge of Letherii heavy infantry should have swept the Awl aside, but the weight of their armour became a curse – the soldiers could not move fast enough to exploit breaches, were sluggish in shoring up their own. Fighters became mired, finding themselves suddenly separated from their comrades, and the Awl would then close in, surrounding the soldier, cutting and stabbing until the Letherii went down. Wherever the Letherii could concentrate in greater numbers – from three to thirty – they delivered mayhem, killing scores of their less disciplined enemy. But always, before long, the mud reached up, pulled the units apart.

Along the western edge, for a time, the K'Chain Che'Malle appeared, racing along the flank, unleashing dreadful slaughter.

Bivatt sent archers and spear-wielding skirmishers and, with heavy losses, they drove the two demons away – studded with arrows, the female limping from a deeply driven spear in her left thigh. The Atri-Preda would have then despatched her Bluerose cavalry to pursue the creatures, but she had lost them somewhere to the northeast – where they still pursued the few surviving Awl cavalry – and in any case, the Kechra remained on the seabed, spraying mud with every elongated stride, circling round towards the eastern side of the locked armies.

And, should they attack there, the Atri-Preda had few soldiers left to give answer: only two hundred skirmishers who, without the protection of archers, could do little more than provide a modest wall of spears guarding barely a quarter of the Letherii flank.

Seated atop her restless horse on the rise of the old shoreline, Bivatt cursed in the name of every god she could think of – those damned Kechra! Were they truly unkillable? *No, see the wounded one! Heavy spears can hurt them – Errant take me, do I have a choice?*

761

She beckoned to one of her few remaining runners. 'Finadd Treval is to lead his skirmishers down to the east flank,' she said. 'Defensive line in case the demons return.'

The messenger raced off.

Bivatt settled her gaze once more upon the battle before her. *At least there's no dust to obscure things.* And the evidence was plain to see. The Letherii were driving the Awl back, slowly advancing wings, at last, to form encircling horns. The fighting had lost none of its ferocity – indeed, the Awl on the outside edges seemed to be redoubling their desperate efforts, recognizing what was happening. Recognizing . . . *the beginning of the end.*

She could not see Redmask. He and his bodyguards had left the central platform half a bell past, rushing into the battle to fill a breach.

The fool had surrendered his overview of the battle, had surrendered his command. His aides carried no standard upon which his warriors could rally. If Redmask was not already dead, he would be covered in mud like all the rest, unrecognizable, useless.

She wanted so to feel exultant, triumphant. But she could see that she'd lost a third – perhaps more – of her entire army.

Because the Awl would not accept the truth. Of course, there could be no surrender – this day was for annihilation – but the fools would not even flee, when clearly they could, remaining on the seabed to prevent any pursuit from cavalry and easily outdistancing their heavier foes on foot. They could flee, damn them, in the hopes to fight another day.

Instead, the bastards stood, fought, killed and then died.

Even the women and elders had joined, adding their torn flesh and spilled blood to the churned morass.

Gods how she hated them!

Brohl Handar, Overseer of the Drene province, tasted the woman's blood in his mouth and, in a rush of pleasure, he swallowed it down. She had poured herself onto him as he'd leaned forward to drive his sword right through her midsection. Into his face, a hot, thick torrent. Tugging his weapon free as she fell back onto the ground, he spun, seeking yet another victim.

His warriors stood on all sides, few moving now beyond struggling to regain their breaths. The slaughtering of the unhorsed and the wounded had seemed fevered, as if every Arapay Tiste Edur had charged into the same nightmare, and yet there had been such glee in this slaying of Awl that its sudden absence filled the air with heavy, turgid shock.

This, Brohl Handar realized, was nothing like killing seals on the shores of his homeland. Necessity yielded a multitude of flavours, some bitter, others excruciatingly sweet. He could still taste that woman's blood, like honey coating his throat.

Father Shadow, have I gone mad?

He stared about. Dead Awl, dead horses. Edur warriors with weapons slick and dripping. And already crows were descending to feed.

'Are you injured, Overseer?'

Brohl wiped blood from his face and shook his head. 'Form ranks. We now march to the battle, to kill some more. To kill them all.'

'Yes sir!'

Masarch stumbled his way clear, half blinded by the mud. Where was Redmask? Had he fallen? There was no way to tell. Clutching his side, where a sword-point had punched through the leather armour, and hot blood squeezed between his fingers, the young Renfayar warrior fought through the mud towards the platform – but the enemy were nearly upon it on the east flank, and atop that platform no-one remained.

No matter.

All he desired, at this moment, was to pull away from this mud, to clamber onto those wooden boards. Too many of his comrades had vanished into the cloying sodden silts, raising in his mind horrifying memories of being buried alive – his death night – when madness reached into his brain. No, he would not fall, would not sink down, would not drown with blackness filling his eyes and mouth.

Disbelief raged through him. Redmask, their great leader, who had returned, who had promised them triumph – the end of the Letherii invaders – he had failed the Awl. *And now, we die. Our people. These plains, this land, will surrender even the echoes of our lives. Gone, for ever more.*

He could not accept that.

Yet it is the truth.

Redmask, you have slain us.

He reached the edge of the platform, stretched out his free hand – the one that should have held a weapon – where had it gone?

A bestial scream behind him and Masarch half turned, in time to see the twisted, grey, cracked face beneath the helm, the white of eyes staring out from thick scales of mud.

Fire burst in Masarch's chest and he felt himself lifted up, balanced on a sword's hilt and its sliding stream of molten iron, thrown onto his back – onto the boards of the platform – and the Letherii was pulling himself up after him, kicking mud from his boots, still pushing with his shortsword – although it could go no further, no deeper, and the weapon was now jammed, having thrust through Masarch's back and gouging deep into the wood. On his knees straddling the Renfayar, the Letherii, smeared teeth bared, stared down into Masarch's eyes, and began tugging at his sword.

He was speaking, the Awl realized, words repeated over and over again in that foul Letherii tongue. Masarch frowned – he needed to understand what the man was saying as the man killed him.

But the world was fading, too fast—

No, I hear you, soldier, yes. I hear, and yes, I know—

The Letherii watched the life leave the Awl bastard's young eyes. And though the Letherii's teeth were bared as if in a smile, though his eyes were wide and bright, the words coming from him repeated their litany: 'Keep me alive, please, keep me alive, please, *keep me alive . . .*'

Seventy paces away, Redmask pulled himself onto the back of his horse – one of the few left – and sawed at the reins to swing the beast round. He'd lost his whip, but the crescent axe remained in his hands, gore-spattered, the edges notched.

Gods, he had killed so many, so many, and there were more to come. He knew it, felt it, hungered for it. Heels pounded into the horse's flanks and it surged forward, hoofs kicking up mud. Madness to ride on this, but there was no choice, none at all.

Thousands of Letherii slain, more yet to butcher. Bivatt herself, yes – he rode towards the eastern side of the seething mass, well outside the encircling horn – oh, that would not last, his warriors would break through. Shattering the bastards and their flimsy lines.

Redmask would – once he was done with Bivatt – return to that slaughter – and yes, here were his K'Chain Che'Malle, thundering to join him. The three of them, together, thrusting like an enormous sword into the Letherii ranks. Again and again, killing all within reach.

Sag'Churok closing in from his right – see those huge arm-swords lift, readying themselves. And Gunth Mach, swinging round to his inside flank, placing herself between Redmask and the jostling line of skirmishers with their pathetic spears – Gunth Mach was limping, but the spear had worked itself loose – or she had dragged it free. These beasts felt no pain.

And they were almost with him, here, yet again, for they had chosen him.

Victory this day! Victory!

Sag'Churok drew yet closer, matching the pace of Redmask's horse, and he saw it swing its head to regard him. Those eyes, so cold, so appallingly empty—

The sword lashed out in a blur, taking the horse from the front, at the neck, just above its collarbones. A blow of such savagery and strength that it tore entirely through, cracking hard against the wooden rim of the high saddle. Knocking Redmask back, over the beast's rump, even as the headless horse ran on another half-dozen strides before wavering to one side then collapsing.

He struck the muddy ground on one shoulder, skidded, then rolled to a halt – and onto his feet, straightening, even as Sag'Churok slashed its second blade, taking him above the knees. Blood fountained as he toppled onto his back, and found himself staring at his severed legs, still standing upright in the mud.

Gunth Mach loomed over him, the talons of a hind foot plunging down to close round his chest. The talons punched deep, ribs crushing in that embrace, and Redmask was lifted then thrown through the air – where he intersected the path of one of Sag'Churok's swords. It chopped through his right shoulder, sending the arm spinning away – still gripping the crescent axe.

Redmask thumped onto the ground once more, already dead.

Three hundred paces to the east, Toc Anaster rose on his stirrups, ignoring Torrent's shrieks of horror, and watched as the two K'Chain Che'Malle padded once more towards what was left of Redmask. The female one kicked at the body, lightly nudging it, then stepped back.

A moment later and the two creatures were thumping away, northeast, heads stretched out, tails horizontal and stiff as spears behind them.

'He failed them,' Toc whispered. What other reason could there be for such a thing? Perhaps, many reasons. Only Redmask could have answered all the mysteries surrounding the K'Chain Che'Malle. Their presence here, their alliance – an alliance now at an end. *Because he failed.*

The suddenness of the execution remained within him, reverberating, a shock.

Beyond, the last of the Awl – no more than a few hundred now – were surrounded, and were dying in their cemetery of mud.

A score of skirmishers had moved out and were drawing nearer – they had seen this last remnant. Toc Anaster on his horse. Torrent. Twenty-odd children deemed too young to die with a weapon in hand – so now they would die anyway.

Still ignoring Torrent's screams of anguish, Toc turned in his saddle, in his mind the thought of killing these children with his own hands – quick thrusts, with his hand over the eyes – and instead he saw, to the southeast, an odd, seething line – bhederin?

No. That is an army.

Lone eye squinting, he watched that line drawing closer – yes, they were coming here. *Not Letherii – I see no standards, nothing at all. No, not Letherii.*

Toc glanced back at the skirmishers now jogging towards them. Still a hundred paces away.

One final look, down at the huddled, crying or mute children, and then he untied from his saddle the leather satchel containing his poems. 'Torrent!' he snapped, flinging the bag to the warrior – who caught it, his rash-mottled face streaked with mud and tears, his eyes wide and uncomprehending.

Toc pointed to the distant line. 'See? An army – not Letherii. Was there not word of the Bolkando and allies? Torrent, listen to me, damn you! You're the last – you and these children. Take them, Torrent – take them and if there's a single guardian spirit left to your people, then this need not be the last day of the Awl. Do you understand?'

'But—'

'Torrent – just go, damn you!' Toc Anaster, last of the Grey Swords of Elingarth, a Mezla, drew out his bow and nocked the first stone-tipped arrow on the gut string. 'I can buy you some time – but you have to go *now*!'

And he looped the reins round the saddle horn, delivering pressure with his knees as he leaned forward, and he rode – for the Letherii skirmishers.

Mud flew out as the horse stretched out into a gallop. *Hood's breath, this won't be easy.*

Fifty paces away from the foot soldiers, he rose on his stirrups, and began loosing arrows.

The seabed that Torrent guided the children along was a gentle, drawn-out slope, rising to where that army was, the mass of dark figures edging ever closer. No standards, nothing to reveal who they were, but he saw that they did not march in ordered ranks. Simply a mass, as the Awl might march, or the Ak'ryn or D'rhasilhani plains tribes of the south.

If this army belonged to either of those two rival tribes, then Torrent was probably leading these children to their deaths. *So be it, we are dead anyway.*

Another ten slogging paces, then he slowed, the children drawing in round him. One hand settling on the head of one child, Torrent halted, and turned about.

Toc Anaster deserved that much. A witness. Torrent had not believed there was courage left in the strange man. He had been wrong.

The horse was unhappy. Toc was unhappy. He had been a soldier, once, but he was no longer. He had been young – had felt young – and that had fed the fires of his soul. Even a shard of burning stone stealing his handsome face, not to mention an eye, had not proved enough to tear away his sense of invulnerability.

Prisoner to the Domin had changed all of that. The repeated destruction delivered upon his bones and flesh, the twisted healing that followed each time, the caging of his soul until even his own screams sounded like music – this had taken his youthful beliefs, taken them so far away that even nostalgia triggered remembrances of nothing but agony.

Arising in the body of another man should have given him all that a new life promised. But inside, he had remained Toc the Younger. Who had once been a soldier, but was one no longer.

Life with the Grey Swords had not altered that. They had travelled to this land, drawn by the Wolves with gifts of faint visions, murky prophecies born in confused dreams: some vast conflagration awaited them – a battle where they would be needed, desperately needed.

Not, it had turned out, alongside the Awl.

A most fatal error in judgement. The wrong allies. The wrong war.

Toc had never trusted the gods anyway. Any god. In truth, his list of those whom he did trust was, after all he had been through, pathetically short.

Tattersail. Ganoes Paran. Gruntle.

Tool.

A sorceress, a mediocre captain, a caravan guard and a damned T'lan Imass.

Would that they were with him now, riding at his side.

His horse's charge was slow, turgid, slewing. Perched over the press of his knees against the beast's shoulders, Toc sent arrow after arrow towards the skirmishers – though he knew it was hopeless. He could barely see, so jostled was he atop the saddle, with mud flying up on all sides as the horse careered in a wild struggle to stay upright.

As he drew closer, he heard screams. With but two arrows left, he rose higher still on his stirrups, drawing on his bowstring—

His arrows, he saw with astonishment, had not missed. Not one. Eight skirmishers were down.

He sent another hissing outward, saw it take a man in the forehead, the stone point punching through bronze and then bone.

Last arrow.

Gods—

He was suddenly among the Letherii. Driving his last arrow at near point-blank range into a woman's chest.

A spear tore into his left leg, cut through and then gouged along his horse's flank. The beast screamed, launched itself forward—

Tossing the bow away, Toc unsheathed his scimitar – *damn, should've brought a shield* – and hacked from side to side, beating away the thrusting spears.

His horse pulled through into the clear. And would have rushed on, straight into the Letherii ranks two hundred paces ahead, but Toc grasped the reins and swerved the animal round.

Only to find a dozen or so skirmishers right behind him – pursuing on foot.

Two spears drove into his mount, one skidding off a shoulder blade, the other stabbing deep into the animal's belly.

Squealing piteously, the horse foundered, then fell onto its side, hind legs already fouled with spilled out intestines, each frantic kick tearing more loose from the body cavity. Toc, with legs still drawn high, was able to throw himself from the beast, landing clear.

Skidding in the mud, struggling to regain his feet.

A spear drove into his right hip, lifting him from the muck before throwing him onto his back.

He hacked at the shaft. It splintered and the pressure pinning him down vanished.

Slashing blindly, Toc fought his way back onto his feet. There was blood pouring down both legs.

Another lunging attack. He parried the spear thrust, lurched close and chopped his scimitar into the side of the soldier's neck.

A point slammed into his back, punched him forward.

And onto a shortsword that slid up under his ribs, cutting his heart in half.

Toc Anaster sank down onto his knees, and, releasing his last breath, would have fallen forward into the mud, but for a hand grasping him, yanking him back. The flash of a knife before his lone eye. Sudden heat along the line of his jaw—

Torrent watched as the Letherii skirmisher cut away Toc Anaster's face. One more trophy. The task was quick, well-practised, and then the soldier pushed his victim away, and the red wound that had once been Toc's face plunged down into the mud.

The children were crying, and yes, he realized – in watching, in waiting, he had perhaps condemned them all to the Letherii knives. Still, they could—

Torrent turned round—

And found strangers before him.

Not Ak'rynnai.

Not D'rhasilhanii.

No, he had never before seen such people.

The clans of the White Face Barghast approached the scene of the battle – a battle nearing its grisly end. Who won, who lost, was without meaning to them. They intended to kill everyone.

Two hundred paces ahead of the ragged lines was their vanguard, walking within a stream of the Tellann Warren, which was strong in this place, where beneath the silts of the ancient shoreline could be found stone tools, harpoons made of antler, bone and ivory, and the hulks of dugout canoes. And out here, on the old seabed, there were offerings buried deep now in the silts. Polished stones, pairs of antlers locked together, animal skulls daubed in red ochre – countless gifts to a dwindling sea.

There were other reasons for such a powerful emanation of Tellann, but these were known to but one of the three in the vanguard, and she had ever been close with her secrets.

Emerging from the warren, the three had stood not far from the Awl warrior and the Awl children. They had watched, in silence, the extraordinary bravery of that lone warrior and his horse. To charge more than a score of skirmishers – the horse's skill at staying upright had been exceptional. The warrior's ability to guide the beast with but his legs, whilst loosing arrow after arrow – none of which did not find a target – was simply breathtaking.

That warrior – and his horse – had given their lives to save these last Awl, and it was that fact alone which stayed – for the moment – the hand of Tool, chosen now among all the White Face Barghast – with Humbrall Taur's tragic death at the landing – as war leader, even though he was not Barghast at all. But Imass. That he had taken as his mate Taur's daughter, Hetan, had without doubt eased the ascension to rule; but more than that, it had been owing to Tool himself.

His wisdom. His will.

The joy of life that could burn in his eyes. The fire of vengeance that could blaze in its stead – that blazed even now – when at last he had judged the time aright, the time to answer for all that had been done.

To the Grey Swords.

An answer delivered unto the betrayers.

An answer delivered unto the slayers.

If not for that brave warrior and his brave horse, then Tool would have killed these Awl immediately. The youth with the mottled face. The muddy children huddled around him. He probably still planned to.

Hetan knew all of this, in her heart; she knew her husband. And, had he drawn his flint sword, she would not have tried to stop him.

The White Faces had been hiding for too long. Their scouting expeditions to the east had long since told them all they needed to know, of the path that awaited them, the journey they must soon undertake. It had been vengeance keeping them in place. That, and the vast, uncanny patience of Tool.

Within the Tellann Warrens, the Barghast had watched this latest war, the protracted engagement that had begun with the massing of the two armies far to the west.

They had not come in time to save the Grey Swords, but Hetan well recalled her and her husband coming upon the killing ground where the company had fallen. Indeed, they had witnessed the plains wolves engaged in their ghastly excision of human hearts – an act of honour? There was no way of knowing – each animal had fled with its prize as soon as it was able. The slaughter of those betrayed soldiers had been particularly brutal – faces had been cut away. It had been impossible to identify anyone among the fallen – and this had delivered upon Tool the deepest wound of all. He had lost a friend there.

The betrayal.

The slaying.

There would be, in Tool, no room for mercy. Not for the Awl. Not for the Letherii army so far from home.

And now they stood, well able to see the last of the Awl warriors fall, to see their wardogs dying in the mud, to hear the triumphant roars of the Letherii, even as the nearby skirmishers – having seen the Barghast forces, were hastily retreating back to their lines.

Hetan studied that vast, churned killing field, and said, 'I cannot tell them apart.'

Torrent stared, not knowing what to think. Both women, flanking the lone man, were to his eyes terrifying. The one who had just spoken – in some infernal foreign tongue – was like an apparition from an adolescent boy's nightmare. Danger and sensuality, a bloodthirstiness that simply took Torrent's breath away – and with the loss of that breath, so too the loss of courage. Of manhood itself.

The other woman, dark, short yet lithe, wrapped in the furs of a panther. And the blue-black glint of that beast's skin seemed to be reflected in the heart of her eyes beneath that robust brow. A shaman, a witch, oh yes. A most dreadful witch.

The man was her kin – the resemblances were unmistakable in their features, as well as their modest heights and the bowing of their legs. And for all that the women terrified Torrent, the stolidity of the warrior's expression chilled the Awl's soul.

The taller woman, with her face streaked in white paint, now settled her gaze upon Torrent and said, in halting trader's tongue, 'You still live. Because of the horse warrior's sacrifice. But,' she nodded towards the savage with the flint sword, 'he remains undecided. Do you understand?'

Torrent nodded.

The man then said something, and the white-faced woman glanced away, eyes thinning. Then her gaze settled on the satchel Torrent still held, dangling from a strap, in his left hand. She pointed down at it. 'What do you carry?'

The Awl blinked, then looked down at the leather bag. Shrugging, he tossed it aside. 'Scribblings,' he said. 'He painted many words, like a woman. But he was not the coward I thought. He was not.'

'Scribblings?'

Torrent found that there were tears on his cheeks. He wiped them away. 'The horse-warrior,' he said. 'The Mezla.'

Hetan saw her husband's head slowly turn at that word, saw his eyes fix on the Awl warrior, then watched as a cascade of realizations took hold of Tool's expression, ending with a terrible scream as he brought his hands to his face, then fell to his knees.

And she was suddenly at his side, cradling his head against her belly as he loosed another piercing cry, clawing at his own face.

The Awl stared as if in shock.

Barghast warriors were rushing out from the line behind them, the young ones with their ancient single-edged hook-swords drawn, Tool's most beloved whom he saw as his own children. Faces filled with consternation, with fear, they converged towards Tool.

Hetan held out a hand, halted them all in their tracks.

Beside the two of them now, drawing her panther skin about her shoulders, Kilava Onass. Her husband's sister, whose heart held more sorrow and loss than Hetan could comprehend, who would weep every night as if it was ritually demanded of her with the sun's setting. Who would walk out beyond the camp and sing wordless songs to the night sky – songs that would send the ay howling with voices of mourning and grief.

She stood, now, on her brother's right. But did not reach down a hand, did not even cast upon Tool a glance of sympathy. Instead, her dark eyes were scanning the Letherii army. 'They prepare for us,' she said. 'The Tiste Edur join the ranks. The cavalry wait along the old shoreline. Onos Toolan, we are wasting time. You know I must leave soon. Very soon.'

Tool drew himself from Hetan's embrace. Saying nothing, he straightened, then began walking.

To where his friend had fallen.

The Awl warrior took a half-step towards him. 'No!' he shouted, turning pleading eyes upon Hetan. 'He must not! The Mezla – he was a friend, yes? Please, he must not!'

Tool walked on.

'*Please! They cut off his face!*'

Hetan flinched. 'He knows,' she said.

And then Tool did halt, looking back, meeting Hetan's eyes. 'My love,' he said in a ragged voice. 'I do not understand.'

She could but shake her head.

'They betrayed him,' Tool continued. 'Yet, see. This day. He rode to the enemy.'

'To save the lives of these children,' Hetan said. 'Yes.'

'I do not understand.'

'You have told me many tales, husband, of your friend. Of Toc the Younger. Of the honour within him. I ask you this: how could he not?'

Her heart came near to bursting as she gazed upon her beloved. These Imass – they were unable to hide anything they felt. They possessed none of the masks, the disguises, that were the bitter gifts of others, including her own Barghast. And they were without control, without mastery, which left grieving to wound the soul deeper than anything Hetan could imagine. *As with grieving, so too love. So too friendship. So too, alas, loyalty.*

'They live,' Tool then said.

She nodded.

Her husband turned and resumed his dreadful journey.

A snort of impatience from Kilava.

Hetan walked over to the leather satchel the Awl warrior had discarded. She picked it up, slung it over one shoulder. 'Kilava,' she said. 'Bonecaster. Lead our Barghast into this battle. I go down to my husband.'

'They will not—'

'Don't be absurd. Terror alone will ensure their obedience. Besides, the sooner they are done slaughtering, the sooner you will part our company.'

Her sudden smile revealed a panther's canines.

Sending a chill through Hetan. *Thank the spirits you smile so rarely, Kilava.*

Atri-Preda Bivatt had commanded her forces to withdraw from the seabed. Back onto more solid ground. Their triumph this day had grown sour with the taste of fear. Another damned army, and it was clear that they intended to do battle against her exhausted, bruised and battered forces. She had allowed herself but a few moments' silent raging at the injustice, before forcing upon herself the responsibilities of her command.

They would fight with courage and honour, although as the barbaric enemy continued massing she could see that it would be hopeless. Seventy thousand, perhaps more. The ones who landed on the north coast, but also, perhaps, the rumoured allies of the Bolkando. Returned here to the north – but why? To join with the Awl? But for that, their main army had come too late. Bivatt had done what she had set out to do; had done what had been commanded of her. She had exterminated the Awl.

Seventy thousand or two hundred thousand. The destruction of Bivatt and her army. Neither mattered in the greater scheme of things. The Letherii Empire would throw back these new invaders. Failing that, they would bribe them away from the Bolkando; indeed, turn them round to fashion an alliance that would sweep into the border kingdoms in waves of brutal slaughter.

Perhaps, she suddenly realized, there was a way through this . . . She glanced about until she saw one of her Finadds. Walked over. 'Prepare a delegation, Finadd. We will seek parley with this new enemy.'

'Yes sir.' The man rushed off.

'Atri-Preda!'

Bivatt turned to see Brohl Handar approach. The Overseer did not, at this moment, look like an imperial governor. He was covered in gore, gripping his sword in one hand thick with dried blood.

'It seems we are not too late after all,' he said.

'These are not Awl, Overseer.'

'I see that clearly enough. I see also, Atri-Preda, that you and I will die here today.' He paused, then grunted a laugh. 'Do you recall, Bivatt, warning me that Letur Anict sought to kill me? Yet here I have marched with you and your army, all this way—'

'Overseer,' she cut in. 'The Factor infiltrated my forces with ten assassins. All of whom are dead.'

His eyes slowly widened.

Bivatt continued, 'Have you seen the tall soldier often at your side? I set him the task of keeping you alive, and he has done all that I commanded. Unfortunately, Overseer, I believe that he shall soon fail at it.' *Unless I can negotiate our way out of this.*

She faced the advancing enemy once more. They were now raising standards. Only a few, and identical to each other. Bivatt squinted in the afternoon light.

And recognized those standards.

She went cold inside. 'Too bad,' she said.

'Atri-Preda?'

'I recognize those standards, Overseer. There will be no parley. Nor any chance of surrender.'

'Those warriors,' Brohl Handar said after a moment, 'are the ones who have been raising the cairns.'

'Yes.'

'They have been with us, then, for some time.'

'Their scouts at the least, Overseer. Longer than you think.'

'Atri-Preda.'

She faced him, studied his grave expression. 'Overseer?'

'Die well, Bivatt.'

'I intend to. And you. Die well, Brohl Handar.'

Brohl walked away from her then, threading through a line of soldiers, his eyes fixed on one in particular. Tall, with a gentle face streaked now in mud.

The Tiste Edur caught the man's gaze, and answered the easy smile with one of his own.

'Overseer, I see you have had an exciting day.'

'I see the same on you,' Brohl replied, 'and it seems there is more to come.'

'Yes, but I tell you this, I am pleased enough. For once, there is solid ground beneath me.'

The Overseer thought to simply thank the soldier, for keeping him alive this long. Instead, he said nothing for a long moment.

The soldier rubbed at his face, then said, 'Sir, your Arapay await you, no doubt. See, the enemy readies itself.'

And yes, this is what Brohl Handar wanted. 'My Arapay will fight well enough without me, Letherii. I would ask one final boon of you.'

'Then ask, sir.'

'I would ask for the privilege of fighting at your side. Until we fall.'

The man's soft eyes widened slightly, then all at once the smile returned. 'Choose, then, Overseer. Upon my right or upon my left.'

Brohl Handar chose the man's left. As for guarding his own un-protected flank, he was indifferent.

Somehow, the truth of that pleased him.

In the city of Drene at this time, riots raged over the entire north half of the city, and with the coming night the mayhem would spread into the more opulent south districts.

Venitt Sathad, granted immediate audience with Factor Letur Anict – who awaited him standing before his desk, his round, pale face glisten-ing with sweat, and in whose eyes the steward saw, as he walked towards the man, a kind of bemusement at war with deeper stresses – walked forward, in neither haste nor swagger. Rather, a walk of singular purpose.

He saw Letur Anict blink suddenly, a rapid reassessment, even as he continued right up to the man.

And drove a knife into the Factor's left eye, deep into the brain.

The weight of Letur Anict, as he collapsed, pulled the weapon free.

Venitt Sathad bent to clean the blade off on the Factor's silk robe; then he straightened, turned for the door, and departed.

Letur Anict had a wife. He had children. He'd had guards, but Orbyn Truthfinder had taken care of them.

Venitt Sathad set out to eliminate all heirs.

He no longer acted as an agent of the Liberty Consign. Now, at this moment, he was an Indebted.

Who had had enough.

Hetan left her husband kneeling beside the body of Toc the Younger. She could do no more for him, and this was not a failing on her part. The raw grief of an Imass was like a bottomless well, one that could snatch the unsuspecting and send them plummeting down into unending darkness.

Once, long ago now, Tool had stood before his friend, and his friend had not known him, and for the Imass – mortal once more, after thousands upon thousands of years – this had been the source of wry amusement, in the manner of a trickster's game where the final pleasure but awaited revelation of the truth.

Tool, in his unhuman patience, had waited a long time to unveil that revelation. Too long, now. His friend had died, unknowing. The trickster's game had delivered a wound from which, she suspected, her husband might never recover.

And so, she now knew in her heart, there might be other losses on this tragic day. A wife losing her husband. Two daughters losing their adopted father, and one son his true father.

She walked to where Kilava Onass had stationed herself to watch the battle, and it was no small mercy that she had elected not to veer into her Soletaken form, that, indeed, she had left the clans of the White Face Barghast the freedom to do what they did best: kill in a frenzy of explosive savagery.

Hetan saw that Kilava stood near where a lone rider had fallen – killed by the weapons of the K'Chain Che'Malle, she noted. A typically vicious slaying, stirring in her memories of the time when she herself had stood before such terrible creatures, a memory punctuated with the sharp pang of grief for a brother who had fallen that day.

Kilava was ignoring the legless, one-armed body lying ten paces to her left. Hetan's gaze settled upon it in sudden curiosity.

'Sister,' she said to Kilava – deliberate in her usage of the one title that Kilava most disliked – 'see how this one wears a mask. Was not the war leader of the Awl so masked?'

'I imagine so,' Kilava said, 'since he was named Redmask.'

'Well,' Hetan said, walking to the corpse, 'this one is wearing the garb of an Awl.'

'But he was slain by the K'Chain Che'Malle.'

'Yes, I see that. Even so . . .' She crouched down, studied that peculiar mask, the strange, minute scales beneath the spatters of mud. 'This mask, Kilava, it is the hide of a K'Chain, I would swear it, although the scales are rather tiny—'

'Matron's throat,' Kilava replied.

Hetan glanced over. 'Truly?' Then she reached down and tugged the mask away from the man's face. A long look down into those pale features.

Hetan rose, tossing the mask to one side. 'You were right, it's not Redmask.'

Kilava asked, 'How do you know that?'

'Well, Awl garb or not, this man was Letherii.'

Hood, High King of Death, Collector of the Fallen, the undemanding master of more souls than he could count – even had he been so inclined, which he was not – stood over the body, waiting.

Such particular attention was, thankfully, a rare occurrence. But some deaths arrived, every now and then, bearing certain . . . eccentricities. And the one lying below was one such arrival.

Not least because the Wolves wanted his soul, yet would not get it, but also because this mortal had evaded Hood's grasp again and again, even though any would see and understand well the sweet gift the Lord of Death had been offering.

Singular lives, yes, could be most . . . singular.

Witness that of the one who had arrived a short time earlier. There were no gifts in possessing a simple mind. There was no haze of calming incomprehension to salve the terrible wounds of a life that had been ordained to remain, until the very end, profoundly innocent.

Hood had not begrudged the blood on Beak's hands. He had, however, most succinctly begrudged the heartless actions of Beak's mother and father.

Few mortal priests understood the necessity for redress, although they often spouted the notion in their sermons of guilt, with their implicit extortions that did little more than swell the temple coffers.

Redress, then, was a demand that even a god could not deny. And so it had been with the one named Beak.

And so it was, now, with the one named Toc the Younger.

'Awaken,' Hood said. 'Arise.'

And Toc the Younger, with a long sigh, did as Hood commanded.

Standing, tottering, squinting now at the gate awaiting them both. 'Damn,' Toc muttered, 'but that's a poor excuse for a gate.'

'The dead see as they see, Toc the Younger. Not long ago, it shone white with purity.'

'My heart goes out to that poor, misguided soul.'

'Of course it does. Come. Walk with me.'

They set out towards that gate.

'You do this for every soul?'

'I do not.'

'Oh.' And then Toc halted – or tried to, but his feet dragged onward – 'Hold on, my soul was sworn to the Wolves—'

'Too late. Your soul, Toc the Younger, was sworn to me. Long ago.'

'Really? Who was the fool who did that?'

'Your father,' Hood replied. 'Who, unlike Dassem Ultor, remained loyal.'

'Which you rewarded by killing him? You bastard piece of pigsh—'

'You will await him, Toc the Younger.'

'He lives still?'

'Death never lies.'

Toc the Younger tried to halt again. 'Hood, a question – please.'

The god stopped, looked down at the mortal.

'Hood, why do I still have only one eye?'

The God of Death, Reaper of Souls, made no reply. He had been wondering that himself.

Damned wolves.

CHAPTER TWENTY-THREE

I have seen the face of sorrow
She looks away in the distance
Across all these bridges
From whence I came
And those spans, trussed and arched
Hold up our lives as we go back again
To how we thought then
To how we thought we thought then
I have seen sorrow's face,
But she is ever turned away
And her words leave me blind
Her eyes make me mute
I do not understand what she says to me
I do not know if to obey
Or attempt a flood of tears
I have seen her face
She does not speak
She does not weep
She does not know me
For I am but a stone fitted in place
On the bridge where she walks

Lay of the Bridgeburners
Toc the Younger

ONCE, LONG AGO, ONRACK THE BROKEN COMMITTED A CRIME. HE had professed his love for a woman in fashioning her likeness on the wall of a cave. There had been such talent in his hands, in his eyes, he had bound two souls into that stone. His own . . . that was his right, his choice. But the other soul, oh, the selfishness of that act, the cruelty of that theft . . .

He stood, now, before another wall of stone, within another cave, looking upon the array of paintings, the beasts with every line of muscle, every hint of motion, celebrating their veracity, the accuracy of genius. And in the midst of these great creatures of the world beyond, awkward stick figures, representing the Imass, cavorted in a poor mime of dance. Lifeless as the law demanded. He stood, then, still Broken, still the stealer of a woman's life.

In the darkness of his captivity, long ago, someone had come to him, with gentle hands and yielding flesh. He so wanted to believe that it had been she, the one whose soul he had stolen. But such knowledge was now lost to him; so confused had the memory become, so infused with all that his heart wished to believe.

And, even if it had indeed been she, well, perhaps she had no choice. Imprisoned by his crime, helpless to defy his desire. In his own breaking, he had destroyed her as well.

He reached out, settled fingertips lightly upon one of the images. Ranag, pursued by an ay. In the torch's wavering light both beasts seemed in motion, muscles rippling. In celebrating the world, which held no regrets, the Imass would gather shoulder to shoulder in this cavern, and with their voices they would beat out the rhythm of breaths, the *huffing* of the beasts; while others, positioned in selected concavities, pounded their hands on drums of hollowed-out wood and skin, until the echoes of hoofbeats thundered from all sides.

We are the witnesses. We are the eyes trapped for ever on the outside. We have been severed from the world. And this is at the heart of the law, the prohibition. We create ourselves as lifeless, awkward, apart. Once, we were as the beasts, and there was no inside, no outside. There was only the one, the one world, of which we were its flesh, its bone, flesh little different from grasses, lichens and trees. Bones little different from wood and stone. We were its blood, in which coursed rivers down to the lakes and seas.

We give voice to our sorrow, to our loss.

In discovering what it is to die, we have been cast out from the world.

In discovering beauty, we were made ugly.

We do not suffer in the manner that beasts suffer – for they surely do. We suffer with the memory of how it was before suffering came, and this deepens the wound, this tears open the pain. There is no beast that can match our anguish.

So sing, brothers. Sing, sisters. And in the torch's light, floating free from the walls of our minds – of the caves within us – see all the faces of sorrow. See those who have died and left us. And sing your grief until the very beasts flee.

Onrack the Broken felt the tears on his cheeks, and cursed himself for a sentimental fool.

Behind him, Trull Sengar stood in silence. In humouring a foolish Imass, he was without impatience. Onrack knew he would simply wait, and wait. Until such time as Onrack might stir from his grim memories, recalling once more the gifts of the present. He would—

'There was great skill in the painting of these beasts.'

The Imass, still facing the stone wall, still with his back to the Tiste Edur, found himself smiling. *So, even here and now, I indulge silly fantasies that are, even if comforting, without much meaning.* 'Yes, Trull Sengar. True talent. Such skill is passed down in the blood, and with each generation there is the potential for . . . burgeoning. Into such as we see here.'

'Is the artist among the clans here? Or were these painted long ago, by someone else?'

'The artist,' Onrack said, 'is Ulshun Pral.'

'And is it this talent that has earned him the right to rule?'

No. Never that. 'This talent,' the Imass replied, 'is his weakness.'

'Better than you, Onrack?'

He turned about, his smile now wry. 'I see some flaws. I see hints of impatience. Of emotion free and savage as the beasts he paints. I see also, perhaps, signs of a talent he had lost and has not yet rediscovered.'

'How does one lose talent like that?'

'By dying, only to return.'

'Onrack,' and there was a new tone to Trull's voice, a gravity that unnerved Onrack, 'I have spoken with these Imass here. Many of them. With Ulshun himself. And I do not think they ever died. I do not think they were once T'lan, only to have forgotten in the countless generations of existence here.'

'Yes, they say they are among those who did not join the Ritual. But this cannot be true, Trull Sengar. They must be ghosts, willed into flesh, held here by the timelessness of the Gate at the end of this cave. My friend, they do not know themselves.' And then he paused. *Can this be true?*

'Ulshun Pral says he remembers his mother. He says she is still alive. Although not here right now.'

'Ulshun Pral is a hundred thousand years old, Trull Sengar. Or more. What he remembers is false, a delusion.'

'I do not believe that, not any more. I think the mystery here is deeper than any of us realize.'

'Let us go on,' Onrack said. 'I would see this Gate.'

They left the chamber of the beasts.

Trull was filled with unease. Something had been awakened in his friend – by the paintings – and its taste was bitter. He had seen, in the lines of Onrack's back, his shoulders, a kind of slow collapse.

The return of some ancient burden. And, seeing this, Trull had forced himself to speak, to break the silence before Onrack could destroy himself.

Yes. The paintings. The crime. Will you not smile again, Onrack? Not the smile you gave me when you turned to face me just now – too broken, too filled with sorrow – but the smile I have grown to treasure since coming to this realm.

'Onrack.'

'Yes?'

'Do we still know what we are waiting for? Yes, threats approach. Will they come through the Gate? Or from across the hills beyond the camp? Do we know in truth if these Imass are indeed threatened?'

'Prepare yourself, Trull Sengar. Danger draws close . . . on all sides.'

'Perhaps then we should return to Ulshun Pral.'

'Rud Elalle is with them. There is time yet . . . to see this Gate.'

Moments later, they came to the edge of the vast, seemingly limitless cavern, and both halted.

Not one Gate. *Many gates.*

And all were seething with silent, wild fire.

'Onrack,' Trull said, unslinging his spear. 'Best return to Rud Elalle and let him know – this is not what he described.'

Onrack pointed towards a central heap of stones. 'She has failed. This realm, Trull Sengar, is dying. And when it dies . . .'

Neither spoke for a moment.

Then Onrack said, 'I will return quickly, my friend, so that you do not stand alone – against what may come through.'

'I look forward to your company,' Trull replied. 'So . . . hurry.'

Forty-odd paces beyond the camp rose a modest hill, stretched out as if it had once been an atoll, assuming the plains had once been under water and that, Hedge told himself as he kicked his way through a ribbon of sand studded with broken shells, was a fair assumption. Reaching the elongated summit, he set down his oversized crossbow near an outcrop of sun-bleached limestone, then walked over to where Quick Ben sat cross-legged, facing the hills two thousand paces to the south.

'You're not meditating or something, are you?'

'If I had been,' the wizard snapped, 'you'd have just ruined it and possibly killed us all.'

'It's all the posturing, Quick,' Hedge said, flopping down onto the gravel beside him. 'You turn picking your nose into a Hood-damned ritual, so it gets I just give up on knowing when to talk to you or not.'

'If that's the case, then don't ever talk to me and we'll both be happy.'

'Miserable snake.'

781

'Hairless rodent.'

The two sat in companionable silence for a time, then Hedge reached out and picked up a shard of dark brown flint. He peered at one serrated edge.

'What are you doing?' Quick Ben demanded.

'Contemplating.'

'Contemplating,' Quick Ben mimed, head wagging from side to side in time with each syllable.

'I could cut your throat with this. One swipe.'

'We never did get along, did we? Gods, I can't believe how we hugged and slapped each other on the back, down at that river—'

'Stream.'

'Watering hole.'

'Spring.'

'Will you please cut my throat now, Hedge?'

The sapper tossed the flint away and dusted his hands with brisk slaps. 'What makes you so sure the baddies are coming up from the south?'

'Who says I'm sure of anything?'

'So we could be sitting in the wrong place. Facing the wrong direction. Maybe everybody's getting butchered right now even as I speak.'

'Well, Hedge, if you hadn't of interrupted my meditating, maybe I'd have figured out where we should be right now!'

'Oh, nice one, wizard.'

'They're coming from the south because it's the best approach.'

'As what, rabbits?'

'No, as dragons, Hedge.'

The sapper squinted at the wizard. 'There always was a smell of Soletaken about you, Quick. We finally gonna see what scrawny beastie you got hiding in there?'

'That's a rather appalling way of putting it, Hedge. And the answer is: no.'

'You still feeling shaky?'

The wizard glanced over, his eyes bright and half mad – his normal look, in other words. 'No. In fact, the very opposite.'

'How so?'

'I stretched myself, way more than I'd ever done before. It's made me . . . nastier.'

'Really.'

'Don't sound so impressed, Hedge.'

'All I know is,' the sapper said, grunting to his feet, 'when they roll over you, there's just me and an endless supply of cussers. And that suits me just fine.'

'Don't blast my body to pieces, Hedge.'

'Even if you're already dead?'

'Especially then, because I won't be, will I? You'll just think it, because thinking it is convenient, because then you can go wild with your damned cussers until you're standing in a Hood-damned crater *a Hood-damned league across*!'

This last bit had been more or less a shriek.

Hedge continued his squinting. 'No reason to get all testy,' he said in a hurt tone, then turned and walked back to his crossbow, his beloved lobber. And said under his breath, 'Oh, this is going to be so much fun, I can't wait!'

'Hedge!'

'What?'

'Someone's coming.'

'From where?' the sapper demanded, readying a cusser in the cradle of the crossbow.

'Ha ha. From the south, you bloated bladder of piss.'

'I knew it,' Hedge said, coming to the wizard's side.

She had chosen to remain as she was, rather than veer into her Soletaken form. That would come later. And so she walked across the plain, through the high grasses of the basin. On a ridge directly ahead stood two figures. One was a ghost, but maybe something more than just a ghost. The other was a mage, and without question more than just a mage.

A sliver of disquiet stirred Menandore's thoughts. Quickly swept away. If Rud Elalle had selected these two as allies, then she would accept that. Just as he had recruited the Tiste Edur and the one known as Onrack the Broken. All . . . complications, but she would not be alone in dealing with them, would she?

The two men watched as she ascended the gentle slope. One was cradling a bizarre crossbow of some kind. The other was playing with a handful of small polished stones, as if trying to choose one as his favourite.

They're fools. Idiots.

And soon, they will both be dust.

She fixed on them her hardest glare as she drew up to the edge of the crest. 'You two are pathetic. Why stand here – do you know who approaches? Do you know they will come from the south? Meaning that you two will be the first they see. And so, the first they kill.'

The taller, darker-skinned one turned slightly, then said, 'Here comes your son, Menandore. With Ulshun Pral.' He then frowned. 'That's a familiar walk . . . Wonder why I never noticed that before.'

Walk? Familiar walk? He is truly mad.

'I have summoned them,' she said, crossing her arms. 'We must prepare for the battle.'

The shorter one grunted, then said, 'We don't want any company. So pick somewhere else to do your fighting.'

'I am tempted to crush your skull between my hands,' Menandore said.

'Doesn't work,' the wizard muttered. 'Everything just pops back out.'

The one with the crossbow gave her a wide smile.

Menandore said, 'I assure you, I have no intention of being anywhere near you, although it is my hope I will be within range to see your grisly deaths.'

'What makes you so sure they'll be grisly?' the wizard asked, now studying one pebble in particular, holding it up to the light as if it was a gem of some sort, but Menandore could see that it was not a gem. Simply a stone, and an opaque one at that.

'What are you doing?' she demanded.

He glanced across at her, then closed his hand round the stone and brought it down behind his back. 'Nothing. Why? Anyway, I asked you a question.'

'And I am obliged to answer it?' She snorted.

Rud Elalle and Ulshun Pral arrived, halting a few paces behind the wizard and his companion.

Menandore saw the hard expression in her son's face. *Could I have seen anything else? No. Not for this.* 'Beloved son—'

'I care nothing for the Finnest,' Rud Elalle said. 'I will not join you in your fight, Mother.'

She stared, eyes widening even as they filled with burning rage. 'You must! I cannot face them both!'

'You have new allies,' Rud Elalle said. 'These two, who even now guard the approach—'

'These brainless dolts? My son, you send me to my death!'

Rud Elalle straightened. 'I am taking my Imass away from here, Mother. They are all that matters to me—'

'More than the life of your mother?'

'More than the fight she chooses for herself!' he snapped. 'This clash – this feud – it is not mine. It is yours. It was *ever* yours! I want nothing to do with it!'

Menandore flinched back at her son's fury. Sought to hold his eyes, then failed and looked away. 'So be it,' she whispered. 'Go then, my son, and take your chosen kin. Go!'

As Rud Elalle nodded and turned away, however, she spoke again, in a tone harder than anything that had come before. '*But not him.*'

Her son swung round, saw his mother pointing towards the Imass at his side.

Ulshun Pral.

Rud Elalle frowned. 'What? I do not—'

'No, my son, *you do not*. Ulshun Pral must remain. Here.'

'I will not permit—'

And then the Bentract leader reached out a hand to stay Rud Elalle – who was moments from veering into his dragon form, to lock in battle with his own mother.

Menandore waited, outwardly calm, reposed, even as her heart thudded fierce in her chest.

'She speaks true,' Ulshun Pral said. 'I must stay.'

'But why?'

'For the secret I possess, Rud Elalle. The secret they all seek. If I go with you, all will pursue. Do you understand? Now, I beg you, lead my people away from here, to a safe place. Lead them away, Rud Elalle, and quickly!'

'Will you now fight at my side, my son?' Menandore demanded. 'To ensure the life of Ulshun Pral?'

But Ulshun Pral was already pushing Rud Elalle away. 'Do as I ask,' he said to Menandore's son. 'I cannot die fearing for my people – please, *lead them away*.'

The wizard then spoke up, 'We'll do our best to safeguard him, Rud Elalle.'

Menandore snorted her contempt. 'You risk such a thing?' she demanded of her son.

Rud Elalle stared across at the wizard, then at the smiling one with the crossbow, and she saw a strange calm slip over her son's expression – and that sliver of disquiet returned to her, stinging.

'I shall,' Rud Elalle then said, and he reached out to Ulshun Pral. A gentle gesture, a hand resting lightly against one side of the Imass's face. Rud Elalle then stepped back, swung round, and set off back for the camp.

Menandore spun on the two remaining men. 'You damned fools!'

'Just for that,' the wizard said, 'I'm not giving you my favourite stone.'

Hedge and Quick Ben watched her march back down the slope.

'That was odd,' the sapper muttered.

'Wasn't it.'

They were silent for another hundred heartbeats, then Hedge turned to Quick Ben. 'So what do you think?'

'You know exactly what I'm thinking, Hedge.'

'Same as me, then.'

'The same.'

'Tell me something, Quick.'

'What?'

'Was that really your favourite stone?'

'Do you mean the one I had in my hand? Or the one I slipped into her fancy white cloak?'

With skin wrinkled and stained by millennia buried in peat, Sheltatha Lore did indeed present an iconic figure of dusk. In keeping now with her reddish hair and the murky hue of her eyes, she wore a cloak of deep burgundy, black leather leggings and boots. Bronze-studded vest drawn tight across her chest.

At her side – like Sheltatha facing the hills – stood Sukul Ankhadu, Dapple, the mottling of her skin visible on her bared hands and forearms. On her slim shoulders a Letherii night-cloak, as was worn now by the noble born and the women of the Tiste Edur in the empire, although this one was somewhat worse for wear.

'Soon,' said Sheltatha Lore, 'this realm shall be dust.'

'This pleases you, sister?'

'Perhaps not as much as it pleases you, Sukul. Why is this place an abomination in your eyes?'

'I have no love for Imass. Imagine, a people grubbing in the dirt of caves for hundreds of thousands of years. Building nothing. All history trapped as memory, twisted as tales sung in rhyme every night. They are flawed. In their souls, there must be a flaw, a failing. And these ones here, they have deluded themselves into believing that they actually exist.'

'Not all of them, Sukul.'

Dapple waved dismissively. 'The greatest failing here, Sheltatha, lies with the Lord of Death. If not for Hood's indifference, this realm could never have lasted as long as it has. It irritates me, such carelessness.'

'So,' Sheltatha Lore said with a smile, 'you will hasten the demise of these Imass, even though, with the realm dying anyway, they are already doomed.'

'You do not understand. The situation has . . . changed.'

'What do you mean?'

'Their conceit,' said Sukul, 'has made them real. Mortal, now. Blood, flesh and bone. Capable of bleeding, of dying. Yet they remain ignorant of their world's imminent extinction. My slaughtering them, sister, will be an act of mercy.'

Sheltatha Lore grunted. 'I cannot wait to hear them thank you.'

At that moment a gold and white dragon rose into view before them, sailing low over the crests of the hills.

Sukul Ankhadu sighed. 'It begins.'

The Soletaken glided down the slope directly towards them. Looming huge, yet still fifty paces away, the dragon tilted its wings

786

back, crooked them as its hind limbs reached downwards, then settled onto the ground.

A blurring swirl enveloped the beast, and a moment later Menandore walked out from that spice-laden disturbance.

Sheltatha Lore and Sukul Ankhadu waited, saying nothing, their faces expressionless, while Menandore approached, finally halting five paces from them, her blazing eyes moving from one sister to the other, then back again. She said, 'Are we still agreed, then?'

'Such glorious precedent, this moment,' Sheltatha Lore observed.

Menandore frowned. 'Necessity. At least we should be understood on that matter. I cannot stand alone, cannot guard the soul of Scabandari. The Finnest must not fall in his hands.'

A slight catch of breath from Sukul. 'Is he near, then?'

'Oh yes. I have stolen the eyes of one travelling with him. Again and again. They even now draw to the last gate, and look upon its wound, and stand before the torn corpse of that foolish Imass Bonecaster who thought she could seal it with her own soul.' Menandore sneered. 'Imagine such effrontery. Starvald Demelain! The very chambers of K'rul's heart! Did she not know how that weakened him? Weakened *everything*?'

'So we three kill Silchas Ruin,' Sheltatha Lore said. 'And then the Imass.'

'My son chooses to oppose us in that last detail,' Menandore said. 'But the Imass have outlived their usefulness. We shall wound Rud if we must, but we do not kill him. Understood? I will have your word on this. Again. Here and now, sisters.'

'Agreed,' Sheltatha Lore said.

'Yes,' said Sukul Ankhadu, 'although it will make matters more difficult.'

'We must live with that.,' Menandore said, and then turned. 'It is time.'

'Already?'

'A few pathetic mortals seek to stand in our way – we must crush them first. And Silchas Ruin has allies. Our day's work begins now, sisters.'

With that she walked towards the hills, and began veering into her dragon form.

Behind her, Sheltatha Lore and Sukul Ankhadu exchanged a look, and then they moved apart, giving themselves the room they needed.

Veering into dragons.

Dawn, Dusk and the one known as Dapple. A dragon of gold and white. One stained brown and looking half-rotted. The last mottled, neither light nor dark, but the uneasy interplay between the two. Soletaken with the blood of Tiam, the Mother. Sail-winged and serpent-necked, taloned and scaled, the blood of *Eleint*.

787

Lifting into the air on gusts of raw sorcery. Menandore leading the wedge formation. Sheltatha Lore on her left. Sukul Ankhadu on her right.

The hills before them, now dropping away as they heaved their massive bulks yet higher.

Clearing the crests, the ancient ridge of an ancient shore, and the sun caught gleaming scales, bloomed through the membranes of wings, while beneath three shadows raced over grass and rock, shadows that sent small mammals scurrying for cover, that launched birds into screeching flight, that made hares freeze in their tracks.

Beasts in the sky were hunting, and nothing on the ground was safe.

A flat landscape studded with humped mounds – dead dragons, ghastly as broken barrows, from which bones jutted, webbed by desiccated skin and sinew. Wings snapped like the wreckage of foundered ships. Necks twisted on the ground, heads from which the skin had contracted, pulled back to reveal gaunt hollows in the eye sockets and beneath the cheekbones. Fangs coated in grey dust were bared as if in eternal defiance.

Seren Pedac had not believed there had once been so many dragons. Had not, in truth, believed that the creatures even existed, barring those who could create such a form from their own bodies, like Silchas Ruin. Were these, she had first wondered, all Soletaken? For some reason, she knew the answer to be *no*.

True dragons, of which Silchas Ruin, in his dread winged shape, was but a mockery. Devoid of majesty, of purity.

The shattering of bones and wings had come from age, not violence. None of these beasts were sprawled out in death. None revealed gaping wounds. They had each settled into their final postures.

'Like blue flies on the sill of a window,' Udinaas had said. *'Wrong side, trying to get out. But the window stayed closed. To them, maybe to everyone, every* thing. *Or . . . maybe not every thing.'* And then he had smiled, as if the thought had amused him.

They had seen the gate that was clearly their destination from a great distance away, and indeed it seemed the dragon mounds were more numerous the closer they came, crowding in on all sides. The flanks of that arch were high as towers, thin to the point of skeletal, while the arch itself seemed twisted, like a vast cobweb wrapped around a dead branch. Enclosed by this structure was a wall smooth and grey, yet vaguely swirling widdershins – the way through, to another world. Where, it was now understood by all, would be found the remnant soul of Scabandari, Father Shadow, the Betrayer. *Bloodeye.*

The lifeless air tasted foul to Seren Pedac, as if immeasurable grief tainted every breath drawn in this realm, a bleak redolence that would not fade even after countless millennia. It sickened her, sapped the strength from her limbs, from her very spirit. Daunting as that portal was, she longed to claw through the grey, formless barrier. Longed for an end to this. All of it.

There was a way, she was convinced – there *had* to be a way – of negotiating through the confrontation fast approaching. Was this not her sole talent, the singular skill she would permit herself to acknowledge?

Three strides ahead of her, Udinaas and Kettle walked, her tiny hand nestled in his much larger, much more battered one. The sight – which had preceded her virtually since their arrival in this grim place – was yet another source of anguish and unease. Was he alone capable of setting aside all his nightmares, to comfort this lone, lost child?

Long ago, at the very beginning of this journey, Kettle had held herself close to Silchas Ruin. For he had been the one who had spoken to her through the dying Azath. And he had made vows to protect her and the burgeoning life that had come to her. And so she had looked upon her benefactor with all the adoration one might expect of a foundling in such a circumstance.

This was no longer true. Oh, Seren Pedac saw enough small gestures to underscore that old allegiance, the threads linking these two so-different beings – their shared place of birth, the precious mutual recognition that was solitude, estrangement from all others. But Silchas Ruin had . . . revealed more of himself. Had revealed, in his cold disregard, a brutality that could take one's breath away. *Oh, and how different is that from Kettle's tales of murdering people in Letheras? Of draining their blood, feeding their corpses into the hungry, needy grounds of the Azath?*

Still, Kettle expressed none of those desires any more. In returning to life, she had abandoned her old ways, had become, with each passing day, more and more simply a young girl. An orphan.

Witness, again and again, to her adopted family's endless quarrelling and bickering. To the undeniable threats, the promises of murder. *Yes, this is what we have offered her.*

And Silchas Ruin is hardly above all of that, is he?

But what of Udinaas? Revealing no great talent, no terrible power. Revealing, in truth, naught but a profound vulnerability.

Ah, and this is what draws her to him. What he gifts back to her in that clasping of hands, the soft smile that reaches even his sad eyes.

Udinaas, Seren Pedac realized with a shock, was the only truly likeable member of their party.

She could in no way include herself as one with even the potential for genuine feelings of warmth from any of the others, not since her rape of Udinaas's mind. But even before then, she had revealed her paucity of skills in the area of camaraderie. Ever brooding, prone to despondency – these were the legacies of all she had done – and not done – in her life.

Kicking through dust, with Clip and Silchas Ruin well ahead of the others, with the massive humps of dead dragons on all sides, they drew yet closer to that towering gate. Fear Sengar, who had been walking two strides behind her on her left, now came alongside. His hand was on the grip of his sword.

'Do not be a fool,' she hissed at him.

His face was set in stern lines, lips tight.

Ahead, Clip and Silchas reached the gate and there they halted. Both seemed to be looking down at a vague, smallish form on the ground.

Udinaas slowed as the child whose hand he was holding began pulling back. Seren Pedac saw him look down and say something in a very low tone.

If Kettle replied it was in a whisper.

The ex-slave nodded then, and a moment later they carried on, Kettle keeping pace without any seeming reluctance.

What had made her shrink away?

What had he said to so easily draw her onward once more?

They came closer, and Seren Pedac heard a low sigh from Fear Sengar. 'They look upon a body,' he said.

Oh, Errant protect us.

'Acquitor,' continued the Tiste Edur, so low that only she could hear. 'Yes?'

'I must know . . . how you will choose.'

'I don't intend to,' she snapped in sudden irritation. 'Do we come all this way together only to kill each other now?'

He grunted in wry amusement. 'Are we that evenly matched?'

'Then, if it is truly hopeless, why attempt anything at all?'

'Have I come this far only to step away, then? Acquitor, I must do what I must. Will you stand with me?'

They had halted, well back from the others, all of whom were now gathered around that corpse. Seren Pedac unstrapped her helm and pulled it off, then clawed at her greasy hair.

'Acquitor,' Fear persisted, 'you have shown power – you are no longer the weakest among us. What you choose may prove the difference between our living and dying.'

'Fear, what is it you seek with the soul of Scabandari?'

'Redemption,' he answered immediately. 'For the Tiste Edur.'

'And how do you imagine Scabandari's broken, tattered soul will grant you such redemption?'

'I will awaken it, Acquitor – and together we will purge Kurald

790

Emurlahn. We will drive out the poison that afflicts us. And we will, perhaps, shatter my brother's cursed sword.'

Too vague, you damned fool. Even if you awaken Scabandari, might he not in turn be enslaved by that poison, and its promise of power? And what of his own desires, hungers – what of the vengeance he himself will seek? 'Fear,' she said in sudden, near-crippling weariness, 'your dream is hopeless.'

And saw him flinch back, saw the terrible retreat in his eyes.

She offered him a faint smile. 'Yes, let this break your vow, Fear Sengar. I am not worth protecting, especially in the name of a dead brother. I trust you see that now.'

'*Yes,*' he whispered.

And in that word was such anguish that Seren Pedac almost cried out. Then railed at herself. *It is what I wanted! Damn it! What I wanted. Needed. It is what must be!*

Oh, blessed Errant, how you have hurt him, Seren Pedac. Even this one. No different from all the others.

And she knew, then, that there would be no negotiation. No way through what was to come.

So be it. Do not count on me, Fear Sengar. I do not even know my power, nor my control of it. So, do not count on me.

But I shall do, for you, what I can.

A promise, yet one she would not voice out loud, for it was too late for that. She could see as much in his now cold eyes, his now hardened face.

Better that he expect nothing, yes. So that, should I fail . . . But she could not finish that thought, not with every word to follow so brightly painted in her mind – with cowardice.

Fear Sengar set out, leaving her behind. She saw, as she followed, that he no longer held on to his sword. Indeed, he suddenly seemed, looser, more relaxed, than she had ever seen him before.

She did not, at that moment, understand the significance of such a transformation. In a warrior. In a warrior who knew how to kill.

Perhaps he had always known where this journey would end. Perhaps that seemingly accidental visit the first time had been anything but, and Udinaas had been shown where his every decision in the interval would take him, as inevitable as the tide. And now, at last, here he had washed up, detritus in the silt-laden water.

Will I soon be dining on ranag calf? I think not.

The body of the female Imass was a piteous thing. Desiccated, limbs drawn up as tendons contracted. The wild masses of her hair had grown like roots from a dead tree, the nails of her stubby fingers like flattened talons the hue of tortoiseshell. The smudged garnets that were her eyes had sunk deep within their sockets, yet still seemed to stare balefully at the sky.

Yes, the Bonecaster. The witch who gave her soul to staunch the wound. So noble, this failed, useless sacrifice. No, woman, for you I will not weep. You should have found another way. You should have stayed alive, among your tribe, guiding them out from their dark cave of blissful ignorance.

'The world beyond dies,' said Clip, sounding very nearly pleased by the prospect. Rings sang out on the ends of the chain. One silver, one gold, spinning in blurs.

Silchas Ruin eyed his fellow Tiste Andii. 'Clip, you remain blind to . . . necessity.'

A faint, derisive smile. 'Hardly, O White Crow. Hardly.'

The albino warrior then turned to fix his uncanny red-rimmed eyes upon Udinaas. 'Is she still with us?'

Kettle's hand tightened in the ex-slave's, and it was all he could do to squeeze back in reassurance. 'She gauged our location moments ago,' Udinaas replied, earning a hiss from Clip. 'But now, no.'

Silchas Ruin faced the gate. 'She prepares for us, then. On the other side.'

Udinaas shrugged. 'I imagine so.'

Seren Pedac stirred and asked, 'Does that mean she holds the Finnest? Silchas? Udinaas?'

But Silchas Ruin shook his head. 'No. That would not have been tolerated. Not by her sisters. Not by the powerful ascendants who saw it fashioned in the first place—'

'Then why aren't they here?' Seren demanded. 'What makes you think they'll accept your possessing it, Silchas Ruin, when they will not stand for Menandore's owning it – we are speaking of Menandore, aren't we?'

Udinaas snorted. 'Left no stone unturned in my brain, did you, Acquitor?'

Silchas did not reply to her questions.

The ex-slave glanced over at Fear Sengar, and saw a warrior about to go into battle. *Yes, we are that close, aren't we? Oh, Fear Sengar, I do not hate you. In fact, I probably even like you. I may mock the honour you possess. I may scorn this path you've chosen.*

As I scorned this Bonecaster's, and yes, Edur, for entirely the same reasons.

Because I cannot follow.

Udinaas gently disengaged his hand from Kettle's, then lifted free the Imass spear strapped to his back. He walked over to Seren Pedac. Set the weapon into her hands, ignoring her raised brows, the confusion sliding into her gaze.

Yes, Acquitor, if you will seek to aid Fear Sengar – and I believe you will – then your need is greater than mine.

After all, I intend to run.

Silchas Ruin drew his two swords, thrust them both point-first into the ground. And then began tightening the various buckles and straps on his armour.

Yes, no point in rushing in unprepared, is there? You will need to move quickly, Silchas Ruin, won't you? Very quickly indeed.

He found his mouth was dry.

Dry as this pathetic corpse at his feet.

Seren Pedac gripped his arm. 'Udinaas,' she whispered.

He shook his arm free. 'Do what you must, Acquitor.' *Our great quest, our years of one foot in front of the other, it all draws now to a close.*

So hail the blood. Salute the inevitability.

And who, when all is done, will wade out of this crimson tide?

Rud Elalle, my son, how I fear for you.

Three specks in the sky above the hills to the south. The one named Hedge now half turned and squinted at Ulshun Pral, then said, 'Best withdraw to the cave. Stay close to Onrack the Broken. And Trull Sengar.'

Ulshun Pral smiled.

The man scowled. 'Quick, this oaf doesn't understand Malazan.' He then pointed back towards the rocks. 'Go there! Onrack and Trull. Go!'

The taller man snorted. 'Enough, Hedge. That oaf understands you just fine.'

'Oh, so why ain't he listening to me?'

'How should I know?'

Ulshun waited a moment longer, fixing into his memory the faces of these two men, so that death would not take all of them. He hoped they were doing the same with him, although of course they might well not understand the gift, nor even that they had given it.

Imass knew many truths that were lost to those who were, in every sense, their children. This, alas, did not make Imass superior, for most of those truths were unpleasant ones, and these children could not defend themselves against them, and so would be fatally weakened by their recognition.

For example, Ulshun Pral reminded himself, he had been waiting for this time, understanding all that was coming to this moment, all the truths bound within what would happen. Unlike his people, he had not been a ghost memory. He had not lived countless millennia in a haze of self-delusion. Oh, his life had spanned that time, but it had been just that: a life. Drawn out to near immortality, not through any soul-destroying ritual, but because of this realm. This deathless realm.

That was deathless no longer.

He set out, then, leaving these two brave children, and made his way towards the cave.

It might begin here, beneath this empty sky. But it would end, Ulshun Pral knew, before the Gates of Starvald Demelain.

Where a Bentract Bonecaster had failed. Not because the wound proved too virulent, or too vast. But because the Bonecaster had been nothing more than a ghost to begin with. A faded, pallid soul, a thing with barely enough power to hold on to itself.

Ulshun Pral was twenty paces from the entrance to the cave when Onrack the Broken emerged, and in Ulshun's heart there burgeoned such a welling of pride that tears filled his eyes.

'So I take it,' Hedge said, locking the foot of his crossbow, 'that what we were both thinking means neither of us is much surprised.'

'She gave in too easily.'

Hedge nodded. 'That she did. But I'm still wondering, Quick, why didn't she grab that damned Finnest a long time ago? Squirrel it away some place where Silchas Ruin would never find it? Answer me that!'

The wizard grunted as he moved out to the crest of the slope. 'She probably thought she'd done just as you said, Hedge.'

Hedge blinked, then frowned. 'Huh. Hadn't thought of that.'

'That's because you're thick, sapper. Now, if this goes the way I want it to, you won't be needed at all. Keep that in mind, Hedge. I'm begging you.'

'Oh, just get on with it.'

'Fine then. I will.'

And Ben Adaephon Delat straightened, then slowly raised his arms. *His scrawny arms.* Hedge laughed.

The wizard glared back at him over a shoulder. '*Will you stop that?*'

'Sorry! Had no idea you were so touchy.'

Quick Ben cursed, then turned and walked back to Hedge.

And punched him in the nose.

Stunned, eyes filling with tears, the sapper staggered back. Brought a hand to his face to stem the sudden gushing of blood. 'You broke my damned nose!'

'So I did,' the wizard answered, shaking one hand. 'And look, Hedge, you're bleeding.'

'Is it any surprise? Ow—'

'Hedge. You are *bleeding.*'

I'm – oh, gods.

'Get it now?'

And Quick turned and walked back, resumed his stance at the crest.

Hedge stared down at his bloody hand. 'Shit!'

Their conversation stopped then.

Since the three dragons were now no longer tiny specks.

Menandore's hatred of her sisters in no way diminished her respect for their power, and against Silchas Ruin that power would be needed. She knew that the three of them, together, could destroy that bastard. Utterly. True, one or two of them might fall. But not Menandore. She had plans to ensure that she would survive.

Before her now, minuscule on the edge of that rise, a lone mortal – the other one was crouching as if in terror, well behind his braver but equally stupid companion – a lone mortal, raising his hands.

Oh, mage, to think that will be enough.

Against us!

Power burgeoned within her and to either side she felt the same – sudden pressure, sudden promise.

Angling downward now, three man-heights from the basin's tawny grasses, huge shadows drawing closer, yet closer. Sleeting towards that slope.

She unhinged her jaws.

Hedge wiped blood from his face, blinked to clear his vision as he swore at his own throbbing head, and then lifted the crossbow. Just in case. Sweet candy for the middle one, aye.

The trio of dragons, wings wide, glided low above the ground, at a height that would bring them more or less level with the crest of this ancient atoll. They were, Hedge realized, awfully big.

In perfect unison, all three dragons opened their mouths.

And Quick Ben, standing there like a frail willow before a tsunami, unleashed his magic.

The very earth of the slope lifted up, *heaved* up to hammer the dragons like enormous fists into their chests. Necks whipped. Heads snapped back. Sorcery exploded from those jaws, waves lashing skyward – flung uselessly into the air, where the three sorceries clashed, writhing in a frenzy of mutual destruction.

Where the slope had been there were now clouds of dark, dusty earth, pieces of sod still spinning upward, long roots trailing like hair, and the hill lurched as the three dragons, engulfed by tons of earth, crashed into the ground forty paces from where stood Quick Ben.

And down, into that chaotic storm of soil and dragon, the wizard marched.

Waves erupted from him, rolling amidst the crackle of lightning, sweeping down in charging crests. Striking the floundering beasts with a succession of impacts that shook the entire hill. Black fire gouted, rocks sizzled as they were launched into the air, where they simply shattered into dust.

Wave after wave unleashed from the wizard's hands.

Hedge, staggering drunkenly to the edge, saw a dragon, hammered full on, flung onto its back, then pushed, skidding, kicking, like a flesh and blood avalanche, down onto the basin, gouging deep grooves across the flat as it was driven back, and back.

Another, with skin seeming afire, sought to lift itself into the air.

Another wave rose above it, slapped the beast back down with a bone-snapping crunch.

The third creature, half buried beneath steaming soil, suddenly turned then and launched itself straight for the dragon beside it. Jaws opening, magic ripping forth to lance into the side of its once-ally. Flesh exploded, blood spraying in a black cloud.

An ear-piercing shriek, the struck one's head whipping – even as enormous jaws closed on its throat.

Hedge saw that neck collapse in a welter of blood.

More blood poured from the stricken dragon's gaping mouth, a damned fountain of the stuff—

Quick Ben was walking back up the slope, seemingly indifferent to the carnage behind him.

The third dragon, the one driven far out on the basin, at the end of a torn-up track that stretched across the grass like a wound, now lifted itself into the air, streaming blood, and, climbing still higher, banked south and then eastward.

The warring dragons at the base of the slope slashed and tore at each other, yet the attacker would not release its death-grip on the other's neck, and those huge fangs were sawing right through. Then the spine crunched, snapped, and suddenly the severed head and its arm-length's worth of throat fell to the churned ground with a heavy thud. The body kicked, gouging into its slayer's underbelly for a moment longer, then sagged down as a spraying exhalation burst from the severed neck.

Quick Ben staggered onto the summit.

Hedge dragged his eyes from the scene below and stared at the wizard. 'You look like Hood's own arse-wipe, Quick.'

'Feel like it too, Hedge.' He pivoted round, the motion like an old man's. 'Sheltatha – what a nasty creature – turned on Menandore just like that!'

'When she realized they weren't getting past you, aye,' Hedge said. 'The other one's going for the Imass, I'd wager.'

'Won't get past Rud Ellalle.'

'No surprise, since you turned her into one giant bruise.'

Below, Sheltatha Lore, her belly ripped open, was dragging herself away.

Hedge eyed the treacherous beast.

'Aye, sapper,' Quick Ben said in a hollow voice. 'Now you get to play.'

Hedge grunted. 'Damn short playtime, Quick.'

'And then you nap.'

'Funny.'

Hedge raised the crossbow, paused to gauge the angle. Then he settled his right index finger against the release. And grinned. 'Here, suck on this, you fat winged cow.'

A solid *thunk* as the cusser shot out, then down.

Landing within the gaping cavity of Sheltatha Lore's belly.

The explosion sent chunks of dragon flesh in all directions. The thick, red, foul rain showered down on Hedge and Quick Ben. And what might have been a vertebra hammered Hedge right between the eyes, knocking him out cold.

Flung onto his hands and knees by the concussion, Quick Ben stared across at his unconscious friend, then began laughing. Higher-pitched than usual.

As they strode into the cave of paintings, Onrack reached out a hand to stay Ulshun Pral. 'Remain here,' he said.

'That is never easy,' Ulshun Pral replied, yet he halted nonetheless.

Nodding, Onrack looked at the images on the walls. 'You see again and again the flaws.'

'The failing of my hand, yes. The language of the eyes is ever perfect. Rendering it upon stone is where weakness is found.'

'These, Ulshun Pral, show few weaknesses.'

'Even so . . .'

'Remain, please,' Onrack said, slowly drawing his sword. 'The Gate . . . there will be intruders.'

'Yes.'

'Is it you they seek?'

'Yes, Onrack the Broken. It is me.'

'Why?'

'Because a Jaghut gave me something, once, long ago.'

'A Jaghut?'

Ulshun Pral smiled at the astonishment on Onrack's face. 'Here, in this world,' he said, 'we long ago ended our war. Here, we chose peace.'

'Yet that which the Jaghut gave you now endangers you, Ulshun Pral. And your clans.'

Deep thundering concussions suddenly shook the walls around them. Onrack bared his teeth. 'I must go.'

A moment later Ulshun Pral was alone, in the cave with all the paintings he had fashioned, and there was no light now that Onrack and the torch he had been carrying were gone. As the drums of grim magic reverberated through the rock surrounding him, he remained where he was, motionless, for a dozen heartbeats. Then he set out, after Onrack. On the path to the Gate.

There was, in truth, no choice.

Rud Elalle had led the Imass deeper into the rugged hills, then down the length of a narrow, crooked defile where some past earthquake had broken in half an entire mass of limestone, forming high, angled walls flanking a crack through its heart. At the mouth of this channel, as Rud Elalle urged the last few Imass into the narrow passage, Hostille Rator, Til'Aras Benok and Gr'istanas Ish'ilm halted.

'Quickly!' cried Rud Elalle.

But the clan chief was drawing out his cutlass-length obsidian sword with his right hand and a bone-hafted, groundstone maul with his left. 'An enemy approaches,' Hostille Rator said. 'Go on, Rud Elalle. We three will guard the mouth of this passage.'

They could hear terrible thunder from just south of the old camp.

Rud Elalle seemed at a loss.

Hostille Rator said, 'We did not come to this realm . . . expecting what we have found. We are now flesh, and so too are those Imass you call your own. Death, Rud Elalle, has arrived.' He pointed southward with his sword. 'A lone dragon has escaped the High Mage. To hunt down you and the Bentract. Rud Ellale, even as a dragon, she must land here. She must then semble into her other form. So that she can walk this passageway. We will meet her here, the three of us . . . strangers.'

'I can—'

'No, Rud Elalle. This dragon may not prove the only danger to you and the clans. You must go, you must prepare to stand as their final protector.'

'Why – why do you do this?'

'Because it pleases us.' *Because you please us, Rud Elalle. So too Ulshun Pral. And the Imass . . .*

And we came here with chaos in our hearts.

'Go, Rud Elalle.'

Sukul Ankhadu knew her sisters were dead, and for all the shock this realization engendered – the shattering of their plan to destroy Silchas Ruin, to enslave the Finnest of Scabandari and subject that torn, vulnerable soul to endless cruelty – a part of her was filled with glee. Menandore – whom she and Sheltatha Lore had intended to betray in any case – would never again befoul Sukul's desires and ambitions. Sheltatha – well, she had done what was needed, turning upon

Menandore at the moment of her greatest weakness. And had she survived that, Sukul would have had to kill the bitch herself.

Extraordinary, that a lone mortal human could unleash such venomous power. No, not a mere mortal human. There were other things hiding inside that scrawny body, she was certain of that. If she never encountered him again, she would know a life of peace, a life without fear.

Her wounds were, all things considered, relatively minor. One wing was shattered, forcing her to rely almost entirely on sorcery to keep her in the air. An assortment of scrapes and gouges, but already the bleeding had ebbed, the wounds were closing.

She could smell the stench of the Imass, could follow their trail with ease as it wound through the broken hills below.

Rud Elalle was a true child of Menandore. A Soletaken. But so very young, so very naive. If brute force could not defeat him, then treachery would. Her final act of vengeance – and betrayal – against Menandore.

The trail led into a high-walled, narrow channel, one that seemed to lead downward, perhaps to caves. Before its mouth was a small, level clearing, bounded on both sides by boulders.

She dropped down, slowed her flight.

And saw, standing before the defile's entrance, an Imass warrior.

Good. I can kill. I can feed.

Settling down into the clearing – a tight fit, her one working wing needing to draw in close – and then sembling, drawing her power inward. Until she stood, not twenty paces from the Imass.

Mortal. Nothing more than what he appeared.

Sukul Ankhadu laughed. She would walk up to him, wrest his stone weapons away, then sink her teeth into his throat.

Still laughing, she approached.

He readied himself, dropping into a crouch.

At ten paces, he surprised her. The maul, swung in a loop underhand, shot out from his extended arm.

Sukul threw herself to one side – had that weapon struck, it would have shattered her skull – then, as the Imass leapt forward with his sword, she reached out and caught his wrist. Twisted, snapping the bones. With her other hand she grasped his throat and lifted him from his feet.

And saw, in his face, a smile – even as she crushed that throat.

Behind her, two Bonecasters, veered into identical beasts – long-legged bears with vestigial tails, covered in thick brown and black hair, with flattened snouts, at their shoulders the height of a Tiste – emerged from the cover of the boulders and, as Hostille Rator died, the Soletaken arrived at a full charge.

Slamming into Sukul Ankhadu, one on her left, the other on her right. Huge talons slashing, massive forelimbs closing about her as jaws, opened wide, tore into her.

Lower canines sank under her left jawline, the upper canines punching down through flesh and bone, and as the beast whipped its head to one side, Sukul's lower jaw, left cheekbones and temporal plate all went with it.

The second beast bit through her right upper arm as it closed its jaws about her ribcage, clamping round a mouthful of crushed ribs and pulped lung.

As the terrible pain and pressure suddenly ripped away from her head, Sukul twisted round. Her left arm – the only one still attached to her – had been holding up the warrior, and now, releasing the dying Imass, she swung that arm backhand, striking the side of the giant bear's head. And with that impact, she released a surge of power.

The beast's head exploded in a mass of bone shards, brains and teeth.

As it fell away, Sukul Ankhadu tried twisting further, to reach across for the second beast's snout.

It lurched back, tearing away ribs and lung.

She spun, driving her hand between the creature's clavicles. Through thick hide, into a welter of spurting blood and soft meat, fingers closing on the ridged windpipe—

A taloned paw struck the side of her head – the same side as had been mauled by the first beast – and where the temporal plate had been, cerebral matter now sprayed out with the impact. The claws caught more bone and hard cartilage, raked through forebrain on its way back out.

The upper front of Sukul's head and the rest of her face was ripped away, spilling brains out from the gaping space.

At that moment, the other paw hammered what remained from the other side. When it had completed its passage, all that was left was a section of occipital plate attached to a flopping patch of scalp, dangling from the back of the neck.

Sukul Ankhadu's knees buckled. Her left hand exited the wound in the second beast's throat with a sobbing sound.

She might have remained on her knees, balanced by the sudden absence of any weight above her shoulders, but then the creature that had finally killed her lurched forward, its enormous weight crushing her down as the Soletaken, who had once been Til'Aras Benok, collapsed, slowly suffocating from a crushed windpipe.

Moments later, the only sound from this modest clearing was the dripping of blood.

Trull Sengar could hear the faint echoes of sorcery and he feared for his friends. Something was seeking to reach this place, and if it – or they –

got past Hedge and Quick Ben, then once more Trull would find himself standing before unlikely odds. Even with Onrack at his side . . .

Yet he held his gaze on the gates. The silent flames rose and ebbed within the portals, each to its own rhythm, each tinted in a different hue. The air felt charged. Static sparks crackled in the dust that had begun swirling up from the stone floor.

He heard a sound behind him and turned. Relief flooded through him. 'Onrack—'

'They seek Ulshun Pral,' his friend replied, emerging from the tunnel mouth, two paces, three, then he halted. 'You are too close to those gates, my friend. Come—'

He got no further.

The fires within one of the gates winked out, and from within the suddenly dark portal figures emerged.

Two strides behind Silchas Ruin, Seren Pedac was the next in their group to cross the threshold. She did not know what prompted her to push past Fear Sengar – and attributed no special significance to Clip's hanging back. A strange tug took hold of her soul, a sudden, excruciating yearning that overwhelmed her growing dread. All at once, the stone spear she held in her hands felt light as a reed.

Darkness, a momentary flicker, as of distant light, then she was stepping onto gritty stone.

A cavern. To either side, the raging maws of more gates, flooding all with light.

Before her, Silchas Ruin halted and his swords hissed from their scabbards. Someone was standing before him, but in that moment Seren Pedac's view was blocked by the White Crow.

She saw a barbaric warrior standing further back, and behind him, a lone silhouette standing in the mouth of a tunnel.

To her left Fear Sengar appeared.

She took another step, to bring her round Silchas Ruin, to see the one who had made the albino Tiste Andii pause.

And all at once, the terror began.

On Fear Sengar's face, an expression of profound horror – even as he surged past Seren Pedac. A knife in his raised hand. The blade flashing down towards Silchas Ruin's back.

Then all of Fear's forward motion ceased. The out-thrust arm with its knife flailed, slashed the air even as Silchas Ruin – as if entirely unaware of the attack – took a single step forward.

A terrible gurgling sound from Fear Sengar.

Spinning round, Seren Pedac saw Clip standing immediately behind Fear. Saw the chain between Clip's hands slide almost effortlessly through Fear Sengar's throat. Blood lashed out.

Beyond Clip, Udinaas, with Kettle now held tight in his arms, sought to lunge away, even as a shadow erupted beneath him, writhed about his lower limbs, and dragged the Letherii down to the stone floor, where Wither then swarmed over Udinaas.

Clip released one end of his chain and whipped the length free of Fear Sengar's throat. Eyes staring, the expression of fierce intent fixed upon his face, the Tiste Edur's head sagged back, revealing a slash reaching all the way back to his spine. As Fear Sengar fell, Clip slid in a deadly blur towards Udinaas.

Frozen in shock, Seren Pedac stood rooted. Disbelieving, as a scream of raw denial tore from her throat.

Silchas Ruin's swords were singing as he closed in deadly battle with whomever stood before him. Staccato impacts as those blades were parried with impossible speed.

Wither had wrapped shadow hands around Udinaas's neck. Was choking the life from the ex-slave.

Kettle pulled herself free, then twisted round to pound tiny hands against the wraith.

All at once, a ferocious will burgeoned within Seren Pedac. *The will to kill.* Launched like a javelin towards Wither.

The wraith exploded in shreds—

—as Clip arrived, standing over Udinaas and reaching down one hand to grasp Kettle's tunic between the girl's shoulder blades.

Clip threw the child across the floor. She struck, skidded then rolled like a bundle of rags.

With focused punches of Mockra, Seren Pedac hammered at Clip, sending him staggering. Blood sprayed from his nose, mouth and ears. Then he whipped round, a hand lashing out.

Something pounded Seren Pedac high on her left shoulder. Sudden agony radiated out from the point of impact and all her concentration vanished beneath those overwhelming waves. She looked down and saw a dagger buried to the hilt – stared down at it in disbelief.

There had been no time to think. Trull Sengar was left with naught but recognition. One, then another, arriving in shocks that left him stunned.

From the gate emerged an apparition – and Trull Sengar had stood before this one before, long ago, during a night's vigil over fallen kin. Ghost of darkness. The Betrayer. No longer weaponless, as he had been the first time. No longer half rotted, yet the coals of those terrifying eyes remained, fixed now upon him in bright familiarity.

And, in a low voice, almost a whisper, the Betrayer said, 'Of course it is you. But this battle, it is not—'

At that moment, Trull Sengar saw his brother. Fear, the god of his childhood, the stranger of his last days among the Tiste Edur. Fear, meeting Trull's wide eyes. Seeing the battle about to begin. Comprehending – and then there was a knife in his hand, and, as he surged forward to stab the Betrayer in the back, Trull saw in his brother's face – in an instant – the full measure of Fear's sudden self-awareness, the bitter irony, the truth of generations past returned once more, one last time. *Silchas Ruin, an Edur knife seeking his back.*

When Fear was tugged backward, when his throat opened wide, Trull Sengar felt his mind, his soul, obliterated, inundated by incandescent fury, and he was moving forward, the tip of his spear seeking the slayer of his brother—

And the Betrayer was in his way.

A slash opened up the Betrayer's skin at the base of his throat, the tip skittering away across one clavicle; then a thrust, punching into the apparition's left shoulder muscle.

And all at once the Betrayer's swords wove a skein of singing iron, parrying the spear's every lightning thrust and sweep. And suddenly Trull Sengar's advance stalled, and then he was being driven back, as those swords, hammering the shaft of his spear, tore away bronze sheathing, began splintering the wood.

And Trull Sengar recognized, before him, his own death.

Onrack the Broken saw his friend's attack fail, saw the fight turn, and saw that Trull Sengar was doomed to fall.

Yet he did not move. Could not.

He felt his own heart tearing itself to pieces, for the man behind him – the Imass, Ulshun Pral – was, Onrack knew at once, of his own blood. A revelation, the summation of a thousand mysterious sensations, instincts, the echoing of gestures – Ulshun Pral's very stance, his manner of walking, and the talent of eyes and hand – he was, oh he was . . .

Trull Sengar's spear exploded in the warrior's hands. A sword lashed out—

The blow to her shoulder had driven Seren Pedac down to her knees, then pitched her sideways – and she saw, there before Silchas Ruin, Trull Sengar.

Clip, blood streaming down his face, had turned back to pursue Udinaas, who was crawling, scrabbling towards Kettle.

And before her rose a choice.

Trull

Or Udinaas.

But, alas, Seren Pedac was never good with choices.

With her hands she sent the stone spear skittering towards Trull Sengar – even as his own weapon shattered into pieces. And, tearing the dagger from her shoulder, she renewed her Mockra assault on Clip – staggering the bastard once more.

As the sword swung to take Trull in the side of his head, he dropped down, then rolled to evade the second weapon that chopped down. He wasn't fast enough. The edge slammed deep into his right hip, stuck fast in solid bone.

Trull took hold of the Betrayer's forearm and pulled as he twisted – the pain as he sought to trap that embedded sword momentarily blinded him, filling his skull with white fire – and against the other sword he could do nothing—

But the Betrayer, pulled slightly off balance, took a step to the side to right himself – onto the shaft of the stone spear which promptly rolled beneath his weight.

And down he went.

Trull saw the spear, reached for it. Closed both hands about the shaft, then, still lying on his side, one of the singing swords pinned beneath him – the Betrayer's arm stretched out as he sought to maintain his grip – Trull drove the butt end of the spear into his opponent's midsection.

Punching all the air from his lungs.

He plunged backward, rolled, and the sword under Trull slapped down as the Betrayer's hand involuntarily released it. And Trull pounded a hand down on the weapon, dislodging it from the bone of his hip.

The white fire remained in his mind, even as he forced himself onto his knees, then upward. The leg beneath the wound refused to obey him and he snarled in sudden rage, willing himself into a standing position – then, leg dragging, he closed in on the Betrayer—

Seren Pedac – all her efforts at incinerating Clip's brain failing – shrank back as the now grinning Tiste Andii, abandoning his hunt for Udinaas, turned about and advanced on her, drawing out knife and rapier. Crimson teeth, crimson streaks from his eyes like tears—

At that moment, impossibly, Trull Sengar hurt Silchas Ruin – drove the White Crow onto his back where his head snapped back to crunch against the floor, stunning him.

And Clip turned, saw, and raced in a low blur towards Trull.

Meeting a spear that lashed out. Clip parried it at the last moment, surprise on his features, and he skidded to a halt, and was suddenly fighting for his life.

Against a crippled Tiste Edur.

Who drove him back a step.

Then another.

Wounds blossomed on Clip. Left arm. Across the ribs on the right side. Laying open his right cheek.

In a sudden, appallingly fast-shifting attack, Trull Sengar reversed the spear and the stone shaft cracked hard into Clip's right forearm, breaking it. Another *crack*, dislocating the right shoulder – and the knife spun away. Third time, this one on the upper left thigh, hard enough to splinter the femur. A final one, against Clip's left temple – a spray of blood, the head rocking to one side, the body collapsing utterly beneath it. Rapier clunking from a senseless hand.

And Trull then whirled back to Silchas Ruin—

But his wounded leg failed him and he fell – Seren heard his curse like a sharp retort—

The white-skinned Tiste Andii advanced to where Onrack stood. The lone sword in his right hand howled as he readied it.

'Step aside, Imass,' he said. 'The one behind you is mine.'

Onrack shook his head. *He is mine. Mine!*

It was clear that the Tiste Andii saw Onrack's refusal in the face of the Imass warrior, for he suddenly snarled—a sound of raw impatience – and lashed out with his left hand.

Sorcery hammered into Onrack. Lifting him from his feet, high into the air, then slamming him into a wall of stone.

As he dropped down hard onto the floor, a single thought drifted through his mind before unconsciousness took him: *Not again.*

Trull Sengar, lying helpless on the floor, cried out upon seeing Onrack engulfed in magic and then flung away. He struggled to regain his feet, but the leg was a dead weight now, and he was leaving a thick trail of blood as he dragged himself closer to Silchas Ruin.

Then someone was kneeling at his side. Hands soft on one shoulder—

'Stop,' a woman's voice murmured. 'Stop, Trull Sengar. It is too late.'

Udinaas struggled to breathe. Wither's shadowy hands had crushed something in his throat. He felt himself weakening, darkness closing in on all sides.

He had failed.

Even knowing, he had failed.

This is the truth of ex-slaves, because even that word is a lie. Slavery settles into the soul. My master now is naught but failure itself.

Forcing himself to remain conscious, he lifted his head. *Drag the breath in, dammit. Lift the head – fail if need be, but do not die. Not yet. Lift the head!*

And watch.

*

Silchas Ruin sheathed his remaining sword, walked up to Ulshun Pral.

And took him by the throat.

A low woman's voice spoke from his left. 'Harm my son, Tiste Andii, and you will not leave here.'

He turned to see a woman, an Imass, clothed in the skin of a panther. She was standing over the prone form of the warrior he had just flung aside.

'That this one lives,' she said, with a gesture down to the Imass at her bared feet, 'is the only reason I have not already torn you to pieces.'

A Bonecaster, and the look in her feline eyes was a dark promise.

Silchas Ruin loosened his hold on the Imass before him, then reached down and deftly plucked free a flint dagger. 'This,' he said, 'is all I need.' And as soon as he held the primitive weapon in his hand, he knew the truth of his claim.

Stepping away, eyes holding the woman's.

She made no move.

Satisfied, Silchas Ruin turned about.

Seren, kneeling beside Trull Sengar, watched the White Crow walk over to where Kettle sat on the stone floor. With his free hand he reached down to her.

A fistful of tunic, a sudden lift, pulling the child into the air, then back down, hard, onto the flat of her back, her head cracking hard on the stone, even as he drove the flint knife into the centre of her chest.

Her small legs kicked, then went still.

Silchas Ruin slowly straightened. Stepped back.

Udinaas turned his head away, his vision filling with tears. Of course, the child had known, just as *he* had known. Kettle was, after all, the last desperate creation of an Azath.

And here, in this brutal place, she had been joined to a Finnest.

He heard Seren Pedac cry out. Looked once more, blinking to clear his eyes.

Silchas Ruin had backed away, towards one of the gates.

Where Kettle lay, the leather-wrapped handle of the flint knife jutting up from her chest, the air had begun to swirl, darkness condensing. And the small body was moving in fitful jerks, then a slow writhing of limbs as roots snaked out, sank tendrils into the very stone. Rock hissed, steamed.

Silchas Ruin looked on for a moment longer, then he swung about, collected his second sword, sheathed it, and walked into a gate, vanishing from sight.

His breathing less ragged, Udinaas twisted round, looked for Clip's body – but the bastard was gone. A blood trail leading to one of the

806

gates. *It figures. But oh, I saw Trull Sengar – I saw him take you on, Clip. You, sneering at that paltry weapon, the lowly spear. I saw, Clip.*

The dark cloud surrounding Kettle's body had burgeoned, grown. Stone foundations, black roots, the trickle of water spreading in a stain.

An Azath, to hold for ever the soul of Scabandari. Silchas Ruin, you have your vengeance. Your perfect exchange.

And, because he could not help himself, Udinaas lowered his head and began to weep.

Somehow, Trull Sengar forced himself back onto his feet. Although without Seren Pedac at his side, taking much of his weight – and without the spear on which he leaned – she knew that that would have been impossible.

'Please,' he said to her, 'my brother.'

She nodded, wincing as the wound in her shoulder pulsed fresh blood, and began helping him hobble across to where Fear Sengar's body was sprawled, almost at the foot of the now darkened gate.

'What am I to do?' Trull asked, suddenly hesitating and looking to where stood the squat woman wearing the skin of a panther. She and the Imass who had carried the Finnest were both now crouched at the form of a third Imass, a warrior. The woman was cradling the dead or unconscious warrior's head. 'Onrack . . . my friend . . .'

'Kin first,' Seren Pedac said. Then she raised her voice and called out to the Imass. 'Does the fallen one live?'

'Yes,' the warrior replied. 'My father lives.'

A sob broke from Trull Sengar and he sagged against her. Seren staggered beneath his weight for a moment, then straightened. 'Come, my love.'

This caught Trull's attention as, perhaps, nothing else would. He searched her face, her eyes.

'We must return to my house,' she said, even as dread clawed at her heart – *another, after all I have done to those who came before him. Errant forgive me. Another.* 'I carry a sword,' she added. 'And would bury it before the threshold.' *And shall I then kneel there, dirt on my hands, and cover my eyes? Shall I cry out in grief for what is to come? For all that I will bring to you, Trull Sengar? My burdens—*

'I have dreamed you would say that, Seren Pedac.'

She closed her eyes for a long moment, and then nodded.

They resumed their journey, and when they reached Fear Sengar, she let Trull settle down onto the ground, and he set the spear down, then reached out to touch his brother's ashen, lifeless face.

From nearby, Udinaas – his face streaked in tears – spoke in a harsh, grating voice. 'I greet you, Trull Sengar. And I must tell you . . . your brother, Fear . . . he died as a hero would.'

Trull lifted his head, stared across at the Letherii. 'Udinaas. You are wrong. My brother sought . . . betrayal.'

'No. He saw you, Trull, and he knew the mind of Silchas Ruin. Knew you could never stand against the White Crow. Do you understand me? He saw you.'

'Is that helpful?' Seren Pedac snapped.

Udinaas bared bloodstained teeth. 'With the only alternative *betrayal*, Acquitor, then yes. Trull, I am . . . sorry. And yet . . . Fear – I am proud of him. Proud to have known him.'

And she saw her beloved nod, then manage a sorrow-filled smile at the ex-slave. 'Thank you, Udinaas. Your journey – all of you – your journey, it must have been long. Difficult.' He glanced to her, then back to Udinaas. 'For remaining at my brother's side, I thank you both.'

Oh, Trull, may you never know the truth.

Onrack the Broken opened his eyes to an ancient dream, and its conjuration twisted like a knife in his soul. *Not oblivion, then. Such peace is denied me. Instead, my crimes return. To haunt.*

And yet . . . Ulshun Pral—

An ancient dream, yes, and hovering just beyond, a far younger dream – one he had not even known to exist. The Ritual of Tellann had stolen from so many men of the Imass this reaching into the future, this creation of sons, daughters, this rooting of life into the soil that lived on.

Yes, that had indeed been a dream—

Kilava Onass suddenly frowned. 'You stare, Onrack, with all the intelligence of a bhederin. Have you lost your wits?'

Dreams did not berate, did they?

'Ah,' she then said, nodding, 'now I see you of old – I see the panic that ever fills a man's eyes, when all he longed for is suddenly within reach. But know this, I too have longed, and I too now feel . . . panic. To love in absence is to float on ever still waters. No sudden currents. No treacherous tides. No possibility of drowning. You and I, Onrack, have floated so for a very long time.'

He stared up at her – yes, he was lying on hard stone. In the cavern of the gates.

Then Kilava smiled, revealing those deadly canines. 'But I fared better, I think. For you gave me a gift, from that one night. You gave me Ulshun Pral. And when I found this . . . this illusion, I found for our son a home, a haven.'

'This realm . . . dies,' Onrack said. 'Are we all illusions now?'

Kilava shook her head, the luxuriant black hair shimmering. 'Gothos gave to our son the Finnest. As for the rest, well, your son has explained it to me. The white-skinned Tiste Andii, Silchas Ruin, delivered the seed of an Azath, a seed in the guise of a child. To accept the Finnest, to use its power to grow. Onrack, soon these gates will be sealed, each and all drawn into the House, into a squat, clumsy tower. And this realm – with an Azath House here, this realm no longer wanders, no longer fades. It is rooted, and so it will remain.'

Behind her, Ulshun Pral said, 'Gothos said Silchas Ruin would one day come for the Finnest. Gothos thought that was . . . funny. Jaghut,' he then said, 'are strange.'

Kilava Onass added, 'To win his freedom, Silchas Ruin bargained with an Azath, an Azath that was dying. And now he has done what was asked of him. And the Azath is reborn.'

'Then . . . we need not have fought.'

Kilava scowled. 'Never trust a Tiste Andii.' Her luminous eyes flickered away briefly. 'It seems there were other . . . issues.'

But Onrack was not ready to think of those. He continued staring up at Kilava Onass. 'You, then, that night in darkness.'

Her scowl deepened. 'Were you always this thick? I cannot remember – by the spirits, my panic worsens. Of course it was me. You bound me to stone, with your eyes and hand. With, Onrack, your love. Yours was a forbidden desire and it wounded so many. But not me. I knew only that I must give answer. I must let my heart speak.' She laid a hand on his chest. 'As yours now does. You are flesh and blood, Onrack. The Ritual has relinquished your soul. Tell me, what do you seek?'

He held his eyes on hers. 'I have found it,' he said.

Every bone in his body ached as he forced himself to his feet. At once his gaze was drawn to where he had last seen Trull Sengar; and a growing dread was swept from his mind upon seeing his friend.

Trull Sengar, you are as hard to kill as I am.

A moment later, he saw the tears on his friend's face, and it seemed there would be grief this day, after all.

At the mouth of a fissure not far away, in a small clearing, Rud Elalle stood in the midst of carnage. Where one of his mother's sisters had died. Where three Imass had died.

And somewhere beyond, he knew in his heart, he would find the body of his mother.

He stood on blood-soaked ground, and wondered what it was that had just died within his own soul.

Some time later, much later, he would find the word to describe it.

Innocence.

Quick Ben still hobbled like an old man, amusing Hedge no end. 'There you are,' he said as they made their way towards the cave and its tunnel leading to the Gates of Starvald Demalain, 'exactly how you'll look twenty years from now. Creepy and gamey. Pushing wobbly teeth with a purple tongue and muttering rhymes under your breath—'

'Keep talking, sapper, and you'll know all about loose teeth. In fact, I'm surprised a few weren't knocked right out when that bone hit you. Gods below, that is probably the funniest thing I have ever seen.'

Hedge reached and gingerly touched the huge lump on his forehead. 'So, we did our task today. How do you think the others fared?'

'We'll soon find out,' the wizard replied. 'One thing, though.'

'What?'

'There is now an Azath House growing in this damned realm.'

'Meaning?'

'Oh, lots of things. First, this place is now real. And it will live on. These Imass will live on.'

Hedge grunted. 'Rud Elalle will be pleased. Onrack, too, I imagine.'

'Aye. And here's another thing, only I don't think it'll please anyone. In that Azath House there will be a tower, and in that tower, all the gates.'

'So?'

Quick Ben sighed. 'You damned idiot. The Gates of Starvald Demelain.'

'And?'

'Just this. Shadowthrone, and Cotillion. Who like using the Azath whenever it suits them. Now they've got a way in. Not just to this realm, either.'

'Into Starvald Demelain? Gods below, Quick! *Is that why we just did all that? Is that what brought you here?*'

'No need to scream, sapper. When it came to planting that House, we weren't even witnesses. Were we? But you know, it what's those two sneaky bastards know, or seem to know, that really worries me. See my point?'

'Oh, Hood piss in your boots, Ben Adaephon Delat.'

'Got all your gear there, Hedge? Good. Because once we get to the Gates, we're going through one of them.'

'We are?'

'We are.' And the wizard grinned across at the sapper. 'Fid's never been the same without you.'

Silchas Ruin stood among ancient foundations – some Forkrul Assail remnant slumping its slow way down the mountainside – and lifted his face to the blue sky beyond the towering trees.

He had fulfilled his vow to the Azath.

And delivered unto the soul of Scabandari a reprieve Bloodeye did not deserve.

Vengeance, he well knew, was a poisoned triumph.

One task remained. A minor one, intended to serve little more than his own sense of redressing an egregious imbalance. He knew little of this Crippled God. But what little he knew, Silchas Ruin did not like.

Accordingly, he now spread his arms. And veered into his dragon form.

Surged skyward, branches torn away from the trees he shouldered aside. Into the crisp mountain air – far to the west, a pair of condors banked away in sudden terror. But the direction Silchas Ruin chose was not to the west.

South.

To a city called Letheras.

And this time, in truth, there was blood on his mind.

CHAPTER TWENTY-FOUR

If these were our last days
If all whose eyes can look inward
Now passed from ken
Who would remain to grieve?

As we hang our heads
Beset by the failure of ambition
Eyes see and are indifferent
Eyes witness and they are uncaring.

The stone regard of the statues
Guarding the perfected square
Is carved as warm
As history's soft surrender,

And the dancing creatures
In and out of our gaping mouths
Alone hear the wind moaning
Its hollow, hallowed voice.

So in these our last days
The end of what we see is inside
Where it all began and begins never again
A moment's reprieve, then darkness falls.

The Unwitnessed Dance
Fisher kel Tath

BEAK'S BARROW BEGAN WITH A FEW BONES TOSSED INTO THE ASH AND charred, splintered skeleton that was all that remained of the young mage. Before long, other objects joined the heap. Buckles, clasps, fetishes, coins, broken weapons. By the time Fist Keneb was ready to give the command to march, the mound was nearly the height of a man. When Captain Faradan Sort asked Bottle for a blessing, the squad mage had shaken his head, explaining that the entire killing field that had been enclosed by Bottle's sorcery was now magically dead. Probably permanently. At this news the captain had turned away, although Keneb thought he heard her say: '*Not a candle left to light, then.*'

As the marines set out for the city of Letheras, they could hear the rumble of detonations from the south, where the Adjunct had landed with the rest of the Bonehunters and was now engaging the Letherii armies. That thunder, Keneb knew, did not belong to sorcery.

He should be leading his troops to that battle, to hammer the Letherii rearguard, and then link up with Tavore and the main force. But Keneb agreed with the captain and with Fiddler and Gesler. He and his damned marines had earned this, had earned the right to be the first to assail this empire's capital city.

'Might be another army waiting on the walls,' Sergeant Thom Tissy had said, making his face twist in his singular expression of disapproval, like a man who'd just swallowed a nacht turd.

'It's possible there are,' the Fist had conceded. And that particular conversation went no further.

Up onto the imperial road with its well-set cobbles and breadth sufficient to accommodate a column ten soldiers wide. Marching amidst discarded accoutrements and the rubbish left by the Letherii legions as the day drew to a close and the shadows lengthened.

Dusk was not far off and the last sleep had been some time past, yet his soldiers, Keneb saw, carried themselves – and their gear – as if fresh from a week's rest.

A few hundred paces along, the column ran into the first refugees.

Smudged, frightened faces. Sacks and baskets of meagre provisions, wide-eyed babies peering from bundles. Burdened mules and two-wheeled carts creaking and groaning beneath possessions. No command was given, yet the Letherii shuffled to the roadsides, pulling whatever gear they had with them, as the column continued on. Eyes downcast, children held tight. Saying nothing at all.

Faradan Sort moved alongside Keneb. 'This is odd,' she said.

The Fist nodded. 'They have the look of people fleeing something that's already happened. Find one, Captain, and get some answers.'

'Aye, sir.'

Studying the refugees he passed, Keneb wondered what was behind the glances a few of them furtively cast on these marching soldiers, these white-haired foreigners in their gleaming armour. *Do they see saviours? Not a chance. Yet, where is the hostility? They are more frightened of what they've just left behind in Letheras than they are of us. What in Hood's name is happening there?*

And where are the Tiste Edur?

The crowds got thicker, more reluctant to move aside. Fiddler adjusted the pack on his shoulder and settled a hand on the grip of his short-sword. The column's pace had slowed, and the sergeant could feel the growing impatience among his troops.

They could see the end – Hood's breath – it was behind that white wall to the northeast, now a league or less distant. The imperial road stretching down towards them from a main gate was, in the red glare of sunset, a seething serpent. *Pouring out by the thousands.*

And why?

Riots, apparently. An economy in ruins, people facing starvation.

'Never knew we could cause such trouble, eh Fid?'

'Can't be us, Cuttle. Not just us, I mean. Haven't you noticed? There are no Tiste Edur in this crowd. Now, either they've retreated behind their estate walls, or to the palace keep or whatever it is where the Emperor lives, or they were the first to run.'

'Like those behind us, then. Heading back to their homelands in the north.'

'Maybe.'

'So, if this damned empire is already finished, why are we bothering with the capital?'

Fiddler shrugged. 'Bottle might have hidden one of his rats in the Adjunct's hair – why not ask him?'

'Adjunct ain't got enough hair for that,' Cuttle muttered, though he did glance back at the squad mage. Bottle did not deign to reply. 'See anybody on those walls, Fid? My eyes are bad in bad light.'

'If there are, they're not holding torches,' Fiddler replied.

There had been so little time to think. About anything, beyond just staying alive. Ever since the damned coast. But now, as he walked on this road, Fiddler found his thoughts wandering dusty paths. They had set out on this invasion in the name of vengeance. And, maybe, to eradicate a tyrannical Emperor who viewed anyone not his subject as meat for the butcher's cleaver. *All very well, as far as it goes. Besides, that hardly makes this Emperor unique.*

So why is this our *battle? And where in Hood's name do we go from here?* He so wanted to believe the Adjunct knew what she was doing. And that, whatever came and however it ended, there would be some meaning to what they did.

'We must be our own witness.' To what, dammit?

'Soldiers on the wall,' Koryk called out. 'Not many, but they see us clear enough.'

Fiddler sighed. *First to arrive, and maybe that's as far as we'll get. An army of eight hundred camped outside one gate. They must be pissing in their boots.* He drew another deep breath, then shook himself. 'Fair enough. We finally got an appreciative audience.'

Smiles didn't much like the look of these refugees. The pathetic faces, the shuffling gaits, they reminded her too much of . . . *home.* Oh, there'd been nothing in the way of hopeless flight back then, so it wasn't that, exactly. Just the dumb animal look in these eyes. The uncomprehending children dragged along by one hand, or clinging to mother's ratty tunic.

The Bonehunters marched to Letheras – why weren't these fools screaming and wailing in terror? *They're like slaves, pushed into free-dom like sheep into the wilds, and all they expect ahead is more slavery. That, or dying in the tangles of empty forests. They've been beaten down. All their lives.*

That's what's so familiar. Isn't it?

She turned her head and spat onto the road. *Hood take all empires. Hood take all the prod and pull. If I get to you, dear Emperor of Lether – if I get to you first, I'm going to slice you into slivers. Slow, with lots of pain. For every one of these wretched citizens on this stinking road.*

Now, the sooner all these fools get out of our way, the sooner I can torture their Emperor.

'We head for the palace,' Koryk said to Tarr. 'And let nothing get in our way.'

'You're smoke-dreaming, Koryk,' the corporal replied. 'We'd have to cut through a few thousand stubborn Letherii to do that. And maybe even more Edur. And if that's not enough, what about that wall there? Plan on jumping it? We haven't got enough munitions to—'

'Rubbish—'

'I mean, there's no way Keneb's going to allow the sappers to use up all their stuff, not when all we have to do is wait for the Adjunct, then do a siege all proper.'

Koryk snorted. 'Proper like Y'Ghatan? Oh, I can't wait.'

'There's no Leoman of the Flails in Letheras,' Tarr said, tugging at his chin strap. 'Just some Edur on the throne. Probably drunk. Insane. Drooling and singing lullabies. So, why bother with the palace? Won't be anything of interest there. I say we loot some estates, Koryk.'

'Malazan soldiers don't loot.'

'But we're not any more, are we? I mean, soldiers of the Malazan Empire.'

Koryk sneered at his corporal. 'So that means you just sink back down to some frothing barbarian, Tarr? Why am I not surprised?

815

I never believed all those civilized airs you're always putting on.'

'What airs?'

'Well, all right, maybe it's just how everybody sees you. But now I'm seeing you different. A damned thug, Tarr, just waiting to get nasty on us.'

'I was just thinking out loud,' Tarr said. 'It's not like Fid's gonna let us do whatever we want, is it?'

'*I'm* not gonna let you do whatever you want, Tarr.'

'Just making conversation, Koryk. That's all it was.'

Koryk grunted.

'You being insolent with your corporal, Koryk?'

'I'm thinking of pushing all your armour – and your shield – right up your bung hole, Corporal. Is that insolent?'

'Once I'm used to telling the difference, I'll let you know.'

'Listen, Corabb,' Bottle said, 'you can stop looking out for me now, all right?'

The round-shouldered warrior at his side shook his head. 'Sergeant Fiddler says—'

'Never mind that. We're in column. Hundreds of marines on all sides, right? And I'm almost rested up, ready to make trouble in case we get ambushed or whatever. I'm safe here, Corabb. Besides, you keep hitting me with that scabbard – my leg's all bruised.'

'Better a bruise than a chopped-off head,' Corabb said.

'Well, that's a fact.'

Corabb nodded, as if the issue was now closed.

Bottle rubbed at his face. The memory of Beak's sacrifice haunted him. He'd not known the mage very well. Just a face with a gawking expression or a wide smile, a pleasant enough man not much older than Bottle himself. For some – for the rarest few – the paths to power were smooth, uncluttered, and yet the danger was always there. *Too easy to draw too much, to let it just pour through you.*

Until you're nothing but ashes.

Yet Beak had won their lives. The problem was, Bottle wondered if it had been worth it. That maybe the lives of eight hundred marines weren't worth the life of a natural High Mage. Whatever was coming, at the very end of this journey, was going to be trouble. The Adjunct had Sinn and that was it. Another natural talent – *but I think she's mad.*

Adjunct, your High Mage is insane. Will that be a problem?

He snorted.

Corabb took that sound as an invitation to talk. 'See the fear in these people, Bottle? The Bonehunters turn their hearts to ice. When we reach the gate, it will swing wide open for us. The Letherii soldiers will throw down their arms. The people shall deliver to us the Emperor's head on a copper plate, and roses will be flung into our path—'

'For Hood's sake, Corabb, enough. You keep looking for glory in war. But there is no glory. And heroes, like Beak back there, they end up dead. Earning what? A barrow of rubbish, that's what.'

But Corabb was shaking his head. 'When I die—'

'It won't be in battle,' Bottle finished.

'You wound me with your words.'

'You've got the Lady in your shadow, Corabb. You'll keep scraping through. You'll break weapons or they'll fly from your hand. Your horse will flip end over end and land right side up, with you still in the saddle. In fact, I'd wager all my back pay that you'll be the last one of us standing at the very end.'

'You believe there will be a fight in this city?'

'Of course there will, you idiot. In fact, I'd be surprised if we even get inside the walls, until the Adjunct arrives. But then, aye, we're in for a messy street-by-street battle, and the only thing certain about that is a lot of us are going to get killed.'

Corabb spat on his hands, rubbed them together.

Bottle stared. The fool was actually smiling.

'You need fear nothing,' Corabb assured him, 'for I will guard you.'

'Wonderful.'

Hellian scowled. Damned crowded road, was it always like this? Must be a busy city, and everybody going on about things like there wasn't a column of foreign invaders pushing through them. She was still feeling the heat of shame – she'd fallen asleep back on that killing field. Supposed to be ready to fight and if not fight, then die horribly in a conflagration of piss-reeking magic, and what does she do?

Fall asleep. And dream of white light, and fires that don't burn, and because everybody had known she was dreaming they'd all decided to pull out their hidden supplies of aeb root paste and bleach their hair, and then polish all their gear. Well. Ha ha. Damned near the most elaborate joke ever pulled on her. But she wasn't going to let on about any of it. Pretend, aye, that nothing looked any different, and when her soldiers went over to where that one marine had died – the only casualty in the entire battle and there must have been some kind of battle since the evil Letherii army had run away – well, she'd done the same. Left on the mound an empty flask and if that wasn't honouring the idiot then what was?

But it was getting dark, and all these moon faces peering at them from the roadsides was getting eerie. She'd seen one baby, in an old woman's scrawny arms, stick out its tongue at her, and it had taken all her self-control to keep from pulling her sword and lopping off the tyke's little round head or maybe just twisting its ears or even tickling it to death, and so it was a good thing that nobody else could listen in on her thoughts because then they'd know she'd been rattled bad by that joke and her falling asleep when she should have been sergeant.

My polished sword at that. Which I can use to cut off all my white hair if I want to. Oh yes, they did it all to me and mine, too.

Someone stumbled on the back of her heel and she half turned. 'Get back, Corpor—' But it wasn't Touchbreath. It was that sultry dark-eyed lad, the one she'd already had fantasies about and maybe they weren't fantasies at all, the way he licked his lips when their eyes met. *Scupperskull. No, Skulldeath.* 'You in my squad now?' she asked.

A broad delicious smile answered her.

'The fool's besotted,' her corporal said from behind Skulldeath. 'Might as well adopt him, Sergeant,' he added in a different voice. 'Or marry him. Or both.'

'You ain't gonna confuse me, Corporal, talking back and forth like that. Just so you know.'

All at once the crowds thinned on the road, and there, directly ahead, the road was clear, rising to the huge double gates of the city. The gates were barred. 'Oh,' Hellian said, 'that's just terrific. We gotta pay a toll now.'

The commander of the Letherii forces died with a quarrel in his heart, one of the last to fall at the final rally point four hundred paces in from the river. Shattered, the remaining soldiers flung away their weapons and fled the battle. The enemy had few mounted troops, so the pursuit was a dragged-out affair, chaotic and mad as the day's light ebbed, and the slaughter pulled foreign soldiers well inland as they hunted down their exhausted, panic-stricken foes.

Twice, Sirryn Kanar had barely eluded the ruthless squads of the enemy, and when he heard the unfamiliar horns moan through the dusk, he knew the recall had been sounded. Stumbling, all his armour discarded, he scrabbled through brush and found himself among the levelled ruins of one of the shanty-towns outside the city wall. All these preparations for a siege, and now it was coming. He needed to get back inside, he needed to get to the palace.

Disbelief and shock raced on the currents of his pounding heart. He was smeared in sweat and the blood of fallen comrades, and un-controllable shivers rattled through him as if he was plagued with a fever. He had never before felt such terror. The thought of his life end-ing, of some cowardly bastard driving a blade into his precious body. The thought of all his dreams and ambitions gushing away in a red torrent to soak the ground. These had pushed him from the front lines, had sent him running as fast as his legs could carry him. There was no honour in dying alongside one's comrades – he'd not known any of them anyway. Strangers, and strangers could die in droves for all he cared. No, only one life mattered: his own.

And, Errant be praised, Sirryn had lived. Escaping that dark slaughter.

The Chancellor would have an answer to all of this. The Emperor – his Tiste Edur – Hannan Mosag – they would all give answer to these foreign curs. And in a year, maybe less, the world would be right once more, Sirryn ranking high in the Chancellor's staff, and higher still in the Patriotists. Richer than he'd ever been before. A score of soft-eyed whores within his reach. He could grow fat if he liked.

Reaching the wall, he made his way along its length. There were sunken posterns, tunnels that invited breaching yet were designed to flood with the pull of a single lever. He knew the thick wooden doors would be manned on the inside. Working his way along the foot of the massive wall, Sirryn continued his search.

He finally found one, the recessed door angled like a coal trap, thick grasses snarled on all sides. Muttering his thanks to the Errant, Sirryn slipped down into the depression, and leaned against the wood for a long moment, his eyes shut, his breathing slowing.

Then he drew out his one remaining weapon, a dagger, and began tapping the pommel against the wood.

And thought he heard a sound on the other side.

Sirryn pressed his cheek against the door. *'Tap if you can hear me!'* His own rasp sounded frighteningly loud in his ears.

After a half-dozen heartbeats, he heard a faint tap.

'I'm Finadd Sirryn Kanar, an agent of the Chancellor's. There's no-one else about. Let me through in the name of the Empire!'

Again, another long wait. Then he heard the sound of the bar scraping clear, and then a weight pushed against him and he scrabbled back to let the door open.

The young face of a soldier peered up at him. 'Finadd?'

Very young. Sirryn edged down into the entranceway, forcing the soldier back. *So young I could kiss him, take him right here, by the Errant!* 'Close this door, quickly!'

'What has happened?' the soldier asked, hastening to shut the portal, then, in the sudden darkness, struggling with the heavy bar. 'Where is the army, sir?'

As the bar clunked back in place, Sirryn allowed himself, at last, to feel safe. Back to his old form. He reached out, grasped a fistful of tunic, and dragged the soldier close. 'You damned fool! Anybody calling himself a Finadd and you open the damned door? I should have you flailed alive, soldier! In fact, I think I will!'

'P-please, sir, I just—'

'Be quiet! You're going to need to convince me another way, I think.'

'Sir?'

There was still time. That foreign army was a day away, maybe more. And he was feeling so very alive at this moment. He reached up and stroked the lad's cheek. And heard a sudden intake of breath. Ah, a quick-witted lad, then. It would be easy to—

A knife-tip pricked just under his right eye, and all at once the soldier's young voice hardened. 'Finadd, you want to live to climb out the other end of this tunnel, then you'll leave off right here. Sir.'

'I'll have your name—'

'You're welcome to it, Finadd, and may the Errant bless your eternal search – because I wasn't behind this door as a guard, sir. I was readying to make my escape.'

'Your what?'

'The mob rules the streets, Finadd. All we hold right now are the walls and gate houses. Oh, and the Eternal Domicile, where our insane Emperor keeps killing champions like it was a civic holiday. Nobody's much interested in besieging that place. Besides, the Edur left yesterday. All of them. Gone. So, Finadd, you want to get to your lover Chancellor, well, you're welcome to try.'

The knife pressed down, punctured skin and drew out a tear of blood. 'Now, sir. You can make for the dagger at your belt, and die. Or you can let go of my shirt.'

Insolence and cowardice were hardly attractive qualities. 'Happy to oblige, soldier,' Sirryn said, releasing his hold on the man. 'Now, if you're going out, then I had better remain here and lock the door behind you, yes?'

'Finadd, you can do whatever you please once I'm gone. So back away, sir. No, farther. That's good.'

Sirryn waited for the soldier to escape. He could still feel that knife-tip and the wound stung as sweat seeped into it. It was not cowardice, he told himself, that had forced him back, away from this hot-headed bastard busy disgracing his uniform. Simple expedience. He needed to get to the Chancellor, didn't he? That was paramount.

And now, absurdly, he would have to face making his way, unescorted, through the very city where he had been born, in fear for his life. The world had turned on its end. *I could just wait here, yes, in this tunnel, in the dark – no, the foreigners are coming. The Eternal Domicile – where, if surrender is demanded, Triban Gnol can do the negotiating, can oversee the handing over of the Emperor. And the Chancellor will want his loyal guards at his side. He'll want Finadd Sirryn Kanar, the last survivor of the battle at the river – Sirryn Kanar, who broke through the enemy lines to rush back to his Chancellor, bearer, yes, of grim news. Yet he won through, did he not?*

The soldier lowered the door back down from the other side. Sirryn moved up to it, found the bar and lifted it into place. He could reach the Eternal Domicile, even if it meant swimming the damned canals.

I still live. I can win through all of this.

There's not enough of these foreigners to rule the empire.

They'll need help, yes.

He set out along the tunnel.

The young soldier was twenty paces from the hidden door when dark figures rose on all sides and he saw those terrifying crossbows aimed at him. He froze, slowly raised his hands.

One figure spoke, then, in a language the soldier did not understand, and he flinched as someone stepped round him from behind – a woman, grinning, daggers in her gloved hands. She met his eyes and winked, then mimed a kiss.

'We not yet decide let you live,' the first one then said in rough Letherii. 'You spy?'

'No,' the soldier replied. 'Deserter.'

'Honest man, good. You answer all our questions? These doors, tunnels, why do sappers' work for us? Explain.'

'Yes, I will explain everything. I don't want to die.'

Corporal Tarr sighed, then turned from the prisoner to face Koryk. 'Better get Fid and the captain, Koryk. Looks like maybe we won't have to knock down any walls after all.'

Smiles snorted, sheathing her knives. 'No elegant back stab. And no torture. This isn't any fun at all.' She paused, then added, 'Good thing we didn't take down the first one, though, isn't it? Led us right to this.'

Their horses had not been exercised nearly enough, and were now huffing, heads lifting and falling as Sergeant Balm led his small troop inland. Too dark now to hunt Letherii and besides, the fun had grown sour awfully fast. Sure, slaughter made sense when on the enemy's own soil, since every soldier who got away was likely to fight again, and so they'd chased down the miserable wretches. But it was tiring work.

When magic wasn't around in a battle, Moranth munitions took its place, and the fit was very nice indeed. *As far as we're concerned, anyway. Gods, just seeing those bodies – and pieces of bodies – flying up into the air – and I was getting all confused, at the beginning there. Bits of Letherii everywhere and all that ringing in my ears.*

He'd come around sharp enough when he saw Cord's idiot sapper, Crump, running up the slope straight at the enemy line, with a Hood-damned cusser in each hand. If it hadn't been for all those blown-up Letherii absorbing so much of the twin blasts then Crump would still be standing there. His feet, anyway. The rest of him would be red haze drifting into the sunset. As it was, Crump was flattened beneath an avalanche of body parts, eventually clambering free like one of Hood's own revenants. Although Balm was pretty sure revenants didn't smile.

Not witless smiles, anyway.

Where the cussers had not obliterated entire companies of the enemy, the main attack – wedges of advancing heavies and medium infantry with a thin scattering of skirmishers and sappers out front – had closed with a hail of sharpers, virtually disintegrating the Letherii front ranks. And then it was just the killing thrust with those human wedges, ripping apart the enemy's formations, driving the Letherii soldiers back until they were packed tight and unable to do anything but die.

The Adjunct's Fourteenth Army, the Bonehunters, had shown, at long last, that they knew how to fight. She'd gotten her straight-in shield to shield dragged-out battle, and hadn't it been just grand?

Riding ahead as point was Masan Gilani. Made sense, using her. First off, she was the best rider by far, and secondly, there wasn't a soldier, man or woman, who could drag their eyes off her delicious round behind in that saddle, which made following her easy. Even in the gathering dark, aye. *Not that it actually glows. I don't think. But . . . amazing how we can all see it just fine. Why, could be a night without any other moon and no stars and nothing but the Abyss on all sides, and we'd follow that glorious, jiggling—*

Balm sawed his reins, pulling off to one side, just missing Masan Gilani's horse – which was standing still, and Masan suddenly nowhere in sight.

Cursing, he dragged his weary horse to a halt, raising a hand to command those behind him to draw up.

'Masan?'

'Over here,' came the luscious, heavenly voice, and a moment later she emerged out of the gloom ahead. 'We're on the killing field.'

'Not a chance,' Throatslitter said from behind Balm. 'No bodies, Masan, no nothing.'

Deadsmell rode a few paces ahead, then stopped and dismounted. He looked round in the gloom. 'No, she's right,' he said. 'This was where Keneb's marines closed ranks.'

They'd all seen the strange glow to the north – seen it from the ships, in fact, when the transports did their neat turn and surged for the shore-line. And before that, well, they'd seen the Letherii sorcery, that terrifying wave climbing into the sky and it was then that everyone knew the marines were finished. No Quick Ben to beat it all back, even if he could have, and Balm agreed with most everyone else that, good as he was, he wasn't that good. No Quick Ben, and no Sinn – aye, there she was, perched on the bow of the *Froth Wolf* with Grub at her side, staring at that dreadful conjuration.

When the thing rolled forward and then crashed down, well, curses rang in the air, curses or prayers and sometimes both, and this, soldiers said, was worse even than Y'Ghatan, and those poor damned marines, always getting their teeth kicked in, only this time nobody was coming out. The only thing that'd be pushing up from the ground in a few days' time would be slivers of burnt bone.

So the Bonehunters on the transports had been a mean-spirited bunch by the time they emptied the water out of their boots and picked up their weapons. Mean, aye, as that Letherii army could attest to, oh yes.

After the Letherii magic had faded, crashed away as if to nothing in the distance, there had been a cry from Sinn, and Balm had seen with his own eyes Grub dancing about on the foredeck. And then everyone else had seen that blue-white dome of swirling light, rising up from where the Letherii magic had come down.

What did it mean?

Cord and Shard had gone up to Sinn, but she wasn't talking which was a shock to them all. And all Grub said was something that nobody afterwards could even agree on, and since Balm hadn't heard it himself he concluded that Grub probably hadn't said anything at all, except maybe '*I got to pee*' which explained all that dancing.

'Could it be that Letherii magic turned them all into dust?' Throatslitter wondered now as he walked on the dew-laden field.

'And left the grasses growing wild?' Masan Gilani countered.

'Something over here,' Deadsmell said from ten or so paces on.

Balm and Throatslitter dismounted and joined Masan Gilani – slightly behind her to either side. And the three of them set off after Deadsmell, who was now fast disappearing in the gloom.

'Slow up there, Corporal!' *It's not like the Universal Lodestone is bouncing up there with you, is it?*

They saw that Deadsmell had finally halted, standing before a grey heap of something.

'What did you find?' Balm asked.

'Looks like a shell midden,' Throatslitter muttered.

'Hah, always figured you for a fisher's spawn.'

'Spawn, ha ha, that's so funny, Sergeant.'

'Yeah? Then why ain't you laughing? On second thought, don't – they'll hear it in the city and get scared. Well, scareder than they already are.'

They joined Deadsmell.

'It's a damned barrow,' said Throatslitter. 'And look, all kinds of Malazan stuff on it. Gods, Sergeant, you don't think all that's left of all those marines is under this mound?'

Balm shrugged. 'We don't even know how many made it this far. Could be six of 'em. In fact, it's a damned miracle any of 'em did in the first place.'

'No no,' Deadsmell said. 'There's only one in there, but that's about all I can say, Sergeant. There's not a whisper of magic left here and probably never will be. It's all been sucked dry.'

'By the Letherii?'

The corporal shrugged. 'Could be. That ritual was a bristling pig of a spell. Old magic, rougher than what comes from warrens.'

Masan Gilani crouched down and touched a badly notched Malazan shortsword. 'Looks like someone did a lot of hacking with this thing, and if they made it this far doing just that, well, beat-up or not, a soldier doesn't just toss it away like this.'

'Unless the dead one inside earned the honour,' Deadsmell said, nodding.

'So,' Masan concluded, 'a Malazan. But just one.'

'Aye, just the one.'

She straightened. 'So where are the rest of them?'

'Start looking for a trail or something,' Balm said to Masan Gilani.

They all watched her head off into the gloom.

Then smiled at each other.

Lostara Yil walked up to where stood the Adjunct. 'Most of the squads are back,' she reported. 'Pickets are being set now.'

'Has Sergeant Balm returned?'

'Not yet, Adjunct.' She hesitated, then added, 'Fist Keneb would have sent a runner.'

Tavore turned slightly to regard her. 'Would he?'

Lostara Yil blinked. 'Of course. Even at full strength – which we know would be impossible – he doesn't have the soldiers to take Letheras. Adjunct, having heard nothing, we have to anticipate the worst.'

During the battle, Lostara Yil had remained close to her commander, although at no point was the Adjunct in any danger from the Letherii. The landing had been quick, professional. As for the battle, classic Malazan, even without the usual contingent of marines to augment the advance from the shoreline. *Perfect, and brutal.*

The Letherii were already in poor shape, she saw. Not from any fight, but from a fast march from well inland – probably where the wave of sorcery had erupted. Disordered in their exhaustion, and in some other, unaccountable way, profoundly rattled.

Or so had been the Adjunct's assessment, after watching the enemy troops form ranks.

And she had been proved right. The Letherii had shattered like thin ice on a puddle. And what had happened to their mages? Nowhere in sight, leading Lostara to believe that those mages had used themselves up with that terrible conflagration they'd unleashed earlier.

Moranth munitions broke the Letherii apart – the Letherii commander had sent archers down the slope and the Bonehunters had had to wither a hail of sleeting arrows on their advance. There had been three hundred or so killed or wounded but there should have been more. Malazan armour, it turned out, was superior to the local armour; and once the skirmishers drew within range of their crossbows and sharpers, the enemy archers took heavy losses before fleeing back up the slope.

The Malazans simply followed them.

Sharpers, a few cussers sailing over the heads of the front Letherii ranks. Burners along the slope of the far left flank to ward off a modest cavalry charge. Smokers into the press to sow confusion. And then the wedges struck home.

Even then, had the Letherii stiffened their defence along the ridge, they could have bloodied the Malazans. Instead, they melted back, the lines collapsing, writhing like a wounded snake, and all at once the rout began. And with it, unmitigated slaughter.

The Adjunct had let her soldiers go, and Lostara Yil understood that decision. So much held down, for so long – *and the growing belief that Fist Keneb and all his marines were dead. Murdered by sorcery. Such things can only be answered one sword-swing at a time, until the arm grows leaden, until the breaths are gulped down ragged and desperate.*

And now, into the camp, the last of the soldiers were returning from their slaughter of Letherii. Faces drawn, expressions numbed – as if each soldier had but just awakened from a nightmare, one in which he or she – surprise – was the monster.

She hardens them, for that is what she needs.

The Adjunct spoke, 'Grub does not behave like a child who has lost his father.'

Lostara Yil snorted. 'The lad is addled, Adjunct. You saw him dance. You heard him singing about candles.'

'Addled. Yes, perhaps.'

'In any case,' Lostara persisted, 'unlike Sinn, Grub has no talents, no way of knowing the fate of Fist Keneb. As for Sinn, well, as you know, I have little faith in her. Not because I believe her without power. She has that, Dryjhna knows.' Then she shrugged. 'Adjunct, they were on their own – entirely on their own – for so long. Under strength to conduct a full-scale invasion.' She stopped then, realizing how critical all of this sounded. *And isn't it just that? A criticism of this, and of you, Adjunct. Didn't we abandon them?*

'I am aware of the views among the soldiers,' Tavore said, inflectionless.

'Adjunct,' Lostara said, 'we cannot conduct much of a siege, unless we use what sappers we have and most of our heavier munitions – I sense you're in something of a hurry and have no interest in settling in. When will the rest of the Perish and the Khundryl be joining us?'

'They shall not be joining us,' Tavore replied. 'We shall be joining them. To the east.'

The other half of this campaign. Another invasion, then. Damn you, Adjunct, I wish you shared your strategies. With me. Hood, with anyone! 'I have wondered,' she said, 'at the disordered response from the Tiste Edur and the Letherii.'

The Adjunct sighed, so low, so drawn out that Lostara Yil barely caught it. Then Tavore said, 'This empire is unwell. Our original assessment that the Tiste Edur were unpopular overseers was accurate. Where we erred, with respect to Fist Keneb's landing, was in not sufficiently comprehending the complexities of that relationship. The split has occurred, Captain. It just took longer.'

At the expense of over a thousand marines.

'Fist Keneb would not send a runner,' Tavore said. 'He would, in fact, lead his marines straight for Letheras. "First in, last out," as Sergeant Fiddler might say.'

'Last in, looking around,' Lostara said without thinking, then winced. 'Sorry, Adjunct—'

'The Bonehunters' motto, Captain?'

She would not meet her commander's eyes. 'Not a serious one, Adjunct. Coined by some heavy infantry soldier, I am told—'

'Who?'

She thought desperately. 'Nefarrias Bredd, I think.'

And caught, from the corner of her eye, a faint smile twitch Tavore's thin lips. Then it was gone and, in truth, might never have been.

'It may prove,' the Adjunct said, 'that Fist Keneb will earn us that ironic motto – those of us here, that is, in this camp.'

A handful of marines to conquer an imperial capital? 'Adjunct—'

'Enough. You will command for this night, Captain, as my representative. We march at dawn.' She turned. 'I must return to the *Froth Wolf*.'

'Adjunct?'

Tavore grimaced. 'Another argument with a certain weaponsmith and his belligerent wife.' Then she paused, 'Oh, when or if Sergeant Balm returns, I would hear his report.'

'Of course,' Lostara Yil replied. *If?*

She watched the Adjunct walk away, down towards the shore.

Aboard the *Froth Wolf*, Shurq Elalle leaned against the mainmast, her arms crossed, watching the three black, hairless, winged ape-like demons fighting over a shortsword. The scrap, a tumbling flurry of biting, scratching and countless inadvertent cuts and slices from the weapon itself, had migrated from the stern end of the mid deck and was now climbing up onto the foredeck.

Sailors stood here and there, keeping well clear, and trading wagers on which demon would win out – an issue of some dispute since it was hard to tell the three beasts apart.

'—with the cut across the nose – wait, Mael's salty slick! Now another one's got the same cut! Okay, the one without—'

'—which one just lost that ear? Cut nose and missing ear, then!'

Close beside Shurq Elalle, a voice said, 'None of it's real, you know.'

She turned. 'Thought she had you chained below.'

'Who, the Adjunct? Why—'

'No. Your wife, Withal.'

The man frowned. 'That's how it looks, is it?'

'Only of late,' Shurq replied. 'She's frightened for you, I think.'

To that he made no response.

'A launch is returning,' Shurq observed, then straightened. 'I hope it's the Adjunct – I'm ready to leave your blessed company. No offence, Withal, but I'm nervous about my first mate and what he might be doing with the *Undying Gratitude*.'

The Meckros weaponsmith turned to squint out into the darkness of the main channel. 'Last I saw, he'd yet to drop anchor and was just sailing back and forth.'

'Yes,' Shurq said. 'Sane people pace in their cabin. Skorgen paces with the whole damned ship.'

'Why so impatient?'

'I expect he wants to tie up in Letheras well before this army arrives. And take on panicky nobles with all their worldly goods. Then we head back out before the Malazan storm, dump the nobles over the side and share out the spoils.'

'As any proper pirate would do.'

'Precisely.'

'Do you enjoy your profession, Captain? Does it not get stale after a time?'

'No, that's me who gets stale after a time. As for the profession, why yes, I do enjoy it, Withal.'

'Even throwing nobles overboard?'

'With all that money they should have paid for swimming lessons.'

'Belated financial advice.'

'Don't make me laugh.'

A sudden outcry from the sailors. On the foredeck, the demons had somehow managed to skewer themselves on the sword. The weapon pinned all three of them to the deck. The creatures writhed. Blood poured from their mouths, even as the bottom-most one began strangling from behind the one in the middle, who followed suit with the one on top. The demon in the middle began cracking the back of its head into the bottom demon's face, smashing its already cut nose.

Shurq Elalle turned away. 'Errant take me,' she muttered. 'I nearly lost it there.'

'Lost what?'

'You do not want to know.'

The launch arrived, thumping up against the hull, and moments later the Adjunct climbed into view. She cast a single glance over at the pinned demons, then nodded greeting to Shurq Elalle as she walked up to Withal.

'Is it time?' he asked.

'Almost,' she replied. 'Come with me.'

Shurq watched the two head below.

Withal, you poor man. Now I'm frightened for you as well.

Damn, forgot to ask permission to leave. She thought to follow them, then decided not to. *Sorry, Skorgen, but don't worry. We can always outsail a marching army. Those nobles aren't going anywhere, after all, are they?*

A short time later, while the sailors argued over who'd won what, the three nachts – who had been lying motionless as if dead – stirred and deftly extricated themselves from the shortsword. One of them kicked the weapon into the river, held its hands over its ears at the soft splash.

The three then exchanged hugs and caresses.

Amused and curious from where he sat with his back to a rail on the foredeck, Banaschar, the last Demidrek of the Worm of Autumn, continued watching. And was nevertheless caught entirely by surprise when the nachts swarmed over the side and a moment later there followed three distinct splashes.

He rose and went to the rail, looking down. Three vague heads bobbed on their way to the shore.

'Almost time,' he whispered.

Rautos Hivanar stared down at the crowded array of objects on the tabletop, trying once more to make sense of them. He had rearranged them dozens of times, sensing that there was indeed a pattern, somewhere, and could he but place the objects in their proper position, he would finally understand.

The artifacts had been cleaned, the bronze polished and gleaming. He had assembled lists of characteristics, seeking a typology, groupings based on certain details – angles of curvature, weight, proximity of where they had been found, even the various depths at which they had been buried.

For they had indeed been buried. Not tossed away, not thrown into a pit. No, each one had been set down in a hole sculpted into the clays – he had managed to create moulds of those depressions, which had helped him establish each object's cant and orientation.

The array before him now was positioned on the basis of spatial location, each set precisely in proper relation to the others – at least he believed so, based on his map. The only exception was with the second and third artifacts. The dig at that time – when the first three had been recovered – had not been methodical, and so the removal of the objects had destroyed any chance of precisely specifying their placement. And so it was two of these three that he now moved, again and again. Regarding the third one – the very first object found – he well knew where it belonged.

Meanwhile, outside the estate's high, well-guarded walls, the city of Letheras descended into anarchy.

Muttering under his breath, Rautos Hivanar picked up that first artifact. Studied its now familiar right angle bend, feeling its sure weight in his hands, and wondering anew at the warmth of the metal. Had it grown hotter in the last few days? He wasn't sure and had no real way of measuring such a thing.

Faint on the air in the room was the smell of smoke. Not woodsmoke, as might come from a hundred thousand cookfires, but the more acrid reek of burnt cloth and varnished furniture, along with – so very subtle – the sweet tang of scorched human flesh.

He had sent his servants to their beds, irritated with their endless reports, the fear in their meek eyes. Was neither hungry nor thirsty, and it seemed a new clarity was taking hold of his vision, his mind. The most intriguing detail of all was that he had now found twelve full-scale counterparts throughout the city; and each of these corresponded perfectly with the layout before him – excepting the two, of course. So, what he had on this table was a miniature map, and this, he knew, was important.

Perhaps the most important detail of all.

If he only knew why.

Yes, the object was growing warmer. Was it the same with its much larger companion, there in the back yard of his new inn?

He rose. No matter how late it was, he needed to find out. Carefully replacing the artifact onto the tabletop map, matching the position of the inn, he then made his way to his wardrobe.

The sounds of rioting in the city beyond had moved away, back into the poorer districts to the north. Donning a heavy cloak and collecting his walking stick – one that saw little use under normal circumstances, but there was now the possible need for self-protection – Rautos Hivanar left the room. Made his way through the silent house. Then outside, turning left, to the outer wall.

829

The guards standing at the side postern gate saluted.

'Any nearby trouble?' Rautos asked.

'Not of late, sir.'

'I wish to go out.'

The guard hesitated, then said. 'I will assemble an escort—'

'No no. I intend to be circumspect.'

'Sir—'

'Open the door.'

The guard complied.

Passing through, he paused in the narrow avenue, listening to the guard lock the door behind him. The smell of smoke was stronger here, a haze forming haloes round those few lamps still lit atop their iron poles. Rubbish lined the gutters, a most unpleasant detail evincing just how far all order and civil conduct had descended. Failure to keep the streets clean was symbolic of a moribund culture, a culture that had, despite loud and public exhortations to the contrary, lost its sense of pride, and its belief in itself.

When had this happened? The Tiste Edur conquest? No, that defeat had been but a symptom. The promise of anarchy, of collapse, had been whispered long before then. But so soft was that whisper that none heard it. *Ah, that is a lie. We were just unwilling to listen.*

He continued looking round, feeling a heavy lassitude settle on his shoulders.

As with Letheras, so with empire.

Rautos Hivanar set out, to walk a dying city.

Five men meaning no good were camped out in the old Tarthenal cemetery. Frowning, Ublala Pung strode out of the darkness and into their midst. His fists flew. A few moments later he was standing amidst five motionless bodies. He picked up the first one and carried it to the pit left behind by a huge fallen tree, threw it in the sodden hole. Then went back for the others.

A short time later he stamped out the small fire and began clearing a space, pulling grass, tossing stones. He went down on his knees to tug loose the smaller weeds, and slowly crawled in an expanding spiral.

Overhead, the hazy moon was still on the rise, and somewhere to the north buildings burned. He needed to be done by dawn. The ground cleared, a wide, circular space of nothing but bared earth. It could be lumpy. That was all right, and it was good that it was all right since cemeteries were lumpy places.

Hearing a moan from the hole where the tree had been, Ublala rose, brushed the dirt from his knees and then his hands, and walked over. Edging down into the pit, he stared at the grey forms until he figured out which one was coming round. Then he crouched and punched the man in the head a few more times, until the moaning stopped. Satisfied, he returned to his clearing.

By dawn, yes.

Because at dawn, Ublala Pung knew, the Emperor would lift his cursed sword, and standing across from him, on that arena floor, would be Karsa Orlong.

In a secret chamber – what had once been a tomb of some kind – Ormly, the Champion Ratcatcher, sat down opposite an enormously fat woman. He scowled. 'You don't need that down here, Rucket.'

'True,' she replied, 'but I've grown used to it. You would not believe the power being huge engenders. The intimidation. You know, when things finally get better and there's plenty of food to be had again, I'm thinking of doing this for real.'

'But that's just my point,' Ormly replied, leaning forward. 'It's all padding and padding don't weigh anything like the real thing. You'll get tired walking across a room. Your knees will hurt. Your breaths will get shorter because the lungs can't expand enough. You'll get stretch marks even though you've never had a baby—'

'So if I get pregnant too then it'll be all right?'

'Except for all that other stuff, why yes, I suppose it would. Not that anybody could tell.'

'Ormly, you are a complete idiot.'

'But good at my job.'

To that, Rucket nodded. 'And so? How did it go?'

Ormly squinted across at her, then scratched his stubbly jaw. 'It's a problem.'

'Serious?'

'Serious.'

'How serious?'

'About as serious as it can get.'

'Hmmm. No word from Selush?'

'Not yet. And you're right, we'll have to wait for that.'

'But our people are in the right place, yes? No trouble with all the riots and such?'

'We're good on that count, Rucket. Hardly popular sites, are they?'

'So has there been any change in the time of execution?'

Ormly shrugged. 'We'll see come dawn, assuming any criers are still working. I sure hope not, Rucket. Even as it is, we may fail. You do know that, don't you?'

She sighed. 'That would be tragic. No, heartbreaking.'

'You actually love him?'

'Oh, I don't know. Hard not to, really. I'd have competition, though.'

'That scholar? Well, unless they're in the same cell, I don't think you need worry.'

'Like I said, you're an idiot. Of course I'm worrying, but not about competition. I'm worried for him. I'm worried for her. I'm worried that all this will go wrong and Karos Invictad will have his triumph. We're running out of time.'

Ormly nodded.

'So, do you have any good news?' she asked.

'Not sure if it's good but it's interesting.'

'What?'

'Ublala Pung's gone insane.'

Rucket shook her head. 'Not possible. He hasn't enough brains to go insane.'

'Well, he beat up five scribers hiding out from the riots in the Tarthenal cemetery, and now he's crawling around on his hands and knees and pinching weeds.'

'So what's all that about?'

'No idea, Rucket.'

'He's gone insane.'

'Impossible.'

'I know,' she replied.

They sat in silence for a time, then Rucket said, 'Maybe I'll just keep the padding. That way I can have it without all the costs.'

'Is it real padding?'

'Illusions and some real stuff, kind of a patchwork thing.'

'And you think he'll fall in love with you looking like that? I mean, compared to Janath who's probably getting skinnier by the moment which, as you know, some men like since it makes their women look like children or some other ghastly secret truth nobody ever admits out loud—'

'He's not one of those.'

'Are you sure?'

'I am.'

'Well, I suppose you would know.'

'I would,' she replied. 'Anyway, what you're talking about is making me feel kind of ill.'

'Manly truths will do that,' Ormly said.

They sat. They waited.

Ursto Hoobutt and his wife and sometime lover Pinosel clambered onto the muddy bank. In Ursto's gnarled hands was a huge clay jug. They paused to study the frozen pond that had once been Settle Lake, the ice gleaming in the diffuse moonlight.

'It's melting, Cherrytart,' he said.

'Well you're just getting smarter day by day, dearie. We knowed it was melting. We knowed that a long time coming. We knowed it sober and we knowed it drunk.' She lifted her hamper. 'Now, we looking at a late supper or are we looking at an early breakfast?'

'Let's stretch it out and make it both.'

'Can't make it both. One or the other and if we stretch it out it'll be neither so make up your mind.'

'What's got you so touchy, love?'

'It's melting, dammit, and that means ants at the picnic.'

'We knew it was coming—'

'So what? Ants is ants.'

They settled down onto the bank, waving at mosquitoes. Ursto unstoppered the jug as Pinosel unwrapped the hamper. He reached for a tidbit and she slapped his hand away. He offered her the jug and she scowled, then accepted it. With her hands full, he snatched the tidbit then leaned back, content as he popped the morsel into his mouth.

Then gagged. 'Errant's ear, what is this?'

'That was a clay ball, love. For the scribing. And now, we're going to have to dig us up some more. Or, you are, since it was you who ate the one we had.'

'Well, it wasn't all bad, really. Here, give me that jug so's I can wash it down.'

A pleasant evening, Ursto reflected somewhat blearily, to just sit and watch a pond melt.

At least until the giant demon trapped in the ice broke loose. At that disquieting thought, he shot his wife and sometime lover a glance, remembering the day long ago when they'd been sitting here, all peaceful and the like, and she'd been on at him to get married and he'd said – oh well, he'd said it and now here they were and that might've been the Errant's nudge but he didn't think so.

No matter what the Errant thought.

'I seen that nostalgic look in your eyes, hubby-bubby. What say we have a baby?'

Ursto choked a second time, but on nothing so prosaic as a ball of clay.

The central compound of the Patriotists, the Lether Empire's knotted core of fear and intimidation, was under siege. Periodically, mobs heaved against the walls, rocks and jugs of oil with burning rag wicks sailing over to crash down in the compound. Flames had taken the stables and four other outbuildings three nights past, and the terrible sound of screaming horses had filled the smoky air. It had been all the trapped Patriotists could do to keep the main block from catching fire.

Twice the main gate had been breached, and a dozen agents had died pushing the frenzied citizens back. Now an enormous barricade of rubble, charred beams and furniture blocked the passage. Through the stench and sooty puddles of the compound, figures walked, armoured as soldiers might be and awkward in the heavy gear. Few spoke, few met the eyes of others, in dread of seeing revealed the haunted, stunned disbelief that resided in their own souls.

The world did not work like this. The people could always be cowed, the ringleaders isolated and betrayed with a purse of coin or, failing that, quietly removed. But the agents could not set out into the streets to twist the dark deals. There were watchers, and gangs of thugs nearby who delighted in beating hapless agents to death, then flinging their heads back over the wall. And whatever operatives remained at large in the city had ceased all efforts at communicating – either had gone into hiding or were dead.

The vast network had been torn apart.

If it had been simple, Tanal Yathvanar knew, if it had been as easy as negotiating the release of prisoners according to the demands of the mob, then order could be restored. But those people beyond the compound wall were not friends and relatives of the scores of scholars, intellectuals and artists still locked up in the cells below. They didn't care a whit about the prisoners and would be just as happy to see them all burn along with the main block. So there was no noble cause to all of this. It was, he now understood, nothing but bloodlust.

Is it any wonder we were needed? To control them. To control their baser instincts. Now look what has happened.

He stood near the front door, watching the pike-wielding agents patrolling the filthy compound. A number of times, in fact, they'd heard shouted demands for Tehol Beddict. The mob wanted him for themselves. They wanted to tear him to pieces. The Grand Drowning at dusk on the morrow was not enough to appease their savage need.

But there would be no releasing Tehol Beddict. Not as long as Karos Invictad remained in charge.

Yet, if we gave him up, they might all calm down and go away. And we could begin again. Yes. Were I in charge, they could have Tehol Beddict, with my blessing.

But not Janath. Oh no, she is mine. For ever now. He had been shocked to discover that she had few memories of her previous incarceration, but he had taken great pleasure in re-educating her. *Ha, re-educating the teacher. I like that one.* At least Karos Invictad had been generous there, giving her to him. And now she resided in a private cell, chained to a bed, and he made use of her day and night. Even when the crowds raged against the walls and agents were dying keeping them out, he would lie atop her and have his way. And she'd fast learned to say all the right things, how to beg for more, whispering

834

her undying desire (no, he would not force her to speak of love, because that word was dead now between them. For ever dead) until those words of desire became real for her.

The attention. The end to loneliness. She had even cried out the last time, cried out his name as her back arched and her limbs thrashed against the manacles.

Cried out for him: Tanal Yathvanar, who even as a child had known he was destined for greatness – for was that not what they all told him, over and over again? Yes, he had found his perfect world, at last. And what had happened? The whole damned city had collapsed, threatening all he now possessed.

All because of Karos Invictad. Because he refused to hand over Tehol Beddict and spent all his waking time staring into a small wooden box at a two-headed insect that had – hah – outwitted him in its dim, obstinate stupidity. *There is a truth hidden in that, isn't there? I'm certain of it. Karos and his two-headed insect, going round and round and round and so it will go until it dies. And when it does, the great Invigilator will go mad.*

But he now suspected he would not be able to wait for that. The mob was too hungry.

Beyond the walls there was quiet, for the moment, but something vast and thousand-headed was seething on the other side of Creeper Canal, and would soon cross over from Far Reaches and make its way down to North Tiers. He could hear its heavy susurration, a tide in the darkness pouring down streets, gushing into and out of alleys, spreading bloody and black into avenues and lanes. He could smell its hunger in the bitter smoke.

And it comes for us, and it will not wait. Not even for Karos Invictad, the Invigilator of the Patriotists, the wealthiest man in all the empire.

He allowed himself a soft laugh, then he turned about and entered the main block. Down the dusty corridor, walking unmindful over crusted streaks left behind when the wounded and dying had been dragged inside. The smell of stale sweat, spilled urine and faeces – as bad as the cells below – *and yes, are we not prisoners now, too? With bare scraps for food and well water fouled with ashes and blood. Trapped here with a death sentence hanging round our necks with the weight of ten thousand docks, and nothing but deep water on all sides.*

Another thought to amuse him; another thought to record in his private books.

Up the stairs now, his boots echoing on the cut limestone, and into the corridor leading to the Invigilator's office, Karos Invictad's sanctum. *His own private cell.* No guards in the passage – Karos no longer trusted them. In fact, he no longer trusted anyone. *Except me. And that will prove his greatest error.*

Reaching the door he pushed it open without knocking and stepped inside, then halted.

The room stank, and its source was sprawled in the chair opposite the Invigilator and his desk.

Tehol Beddict. Smeared in filth, cut and scabbed and bruised – Karos Invictad's prohibition against such treatment was over, it seemed.

'I have a guest,' the Invigilator snapped. 'You were not invited, Tanal Yathvanar. Furthermore, I did not hear you knock, yet another sign of your growing insolence.'

'The mob will attack again,' Tanal said, eyes flicking to Tehol. 'Before dawn. I thought it best to inform you of our weakened defences. We have but fourteen agents remaining still able to defend us. This time, I fear, they will break through.'

'Fame is murderous,' Tehol Beddict said through split lips. 'I hesitate in recommending it.'

Karos Invictad continued glaring at Tanal for a moment longer, then he said, 'In the hidden room – yes, you know of it, I'm aware, so I need not provide any more details – in the hidden room, then, Tanal, you will find a large chest filled with coins. Stacked beside it are a few hundred small cloth bags. Gather the wounded and have them fill sacks with coins. Then deliver them to the agents at the walls. They will be their weapons tonight.'

'That could turn on you,' Tehol observed, beating Tanal Yathvanar to the thought, 'if they conclude there's more still inside.'

'They'll be too busy fighting each other to conclude anything,' Karos said dismissively. 'Now, Tanal, if there is nothing else, go back to your sweet victim, who will no doubt plead desperately for your sordid attention.'

Tanal licked his lips. Was it time? Was he ready?

And then he saw, in the Invigilator's eyes, an absolute awareness, chilling Tanal's bones. *He read my mind. He knows my thoughts.*

Tanal quickly saluted, then hurried from the room. *How can I defeat such a man? He is ever ten steps ahead of me. Perhaps I should wait, until the troubles have passed, then make my move when he relaxes, when he feels most secure.*

He had gone to Invictad's office to confirm that the man remained alone with his puzzle. Whereupon he had planned to head down to the cells and collect Tehol Beddict. Bound, gagged and hooded, up and out into the compound. To appease the mob, to see them away and so save his own life. Instead, the Invigilator had Tehol in his very office.

For what? A conversation? An extended gloat? Oh, each time I think I know that man . . .

He found an agent and quickly conveyed Invictad's instruction, as well as directions to the once-hidden room. Then he continued on, only faintly aware of the irony in following the Invigilator's orders to the letter.

Onto a lower level, down another corridor, this one thicker with dust than most of the others, barring where his own boots had scraped an eager path. To the door, where he drew a key and unlocked the latch. Stepping inside.

'I knew you'd be lonely,' he said.

The lantern's wick had almost burned down and he went over to the table where it sat. 'Thirsty? I'm sure you are.' He glanced over his shoulder and saw her watching him, saw the desire in her eyes. 'There's more trouble in the city, Janath. But I will protect you. I will always protect you. You are safe. You do understand that, yes? For ever safe.'

She nodded, and he saw her spread her legs wider on the bed, then invite him with a thrust of her pelvis.

And Tanal Yathvanar smiled. He had his perfect woman.

Karos Invictad regarded Tehol Beddict from above steepled fingers. 'Very close,' he said after a time.

Tehol, who had been staring dazedly at the puzzle box on the desk, stirred slightly then looked up with his mismatched eyes.

'Very close,' Karos repeated. 'The measure of your intelligence, compared with mine. You are, I believe, the closest to my equal of any man I have met.'

'Really? Thank you.'

'I normally do not express my admiration for intelligence in others. Primarily because I am surrounded by idiots and fools—'

'Even idiots and fools need supreme leaders,' Tehol cut in, then smiled, then winced as cuts opened on his lips, then smiled more broadly than before.

'Attempts at humour, alas,' Karos said with a sigh, 'poorly disguise the deficiencies of one's intelligence. Perhaps that alone is what distinguishes the two of us.'

Tehol's smile faded and suddenly he looked dismayed. 'You never attempt humour, Invigilator?'

'The mind is capable of playing countless games, Tehol Beddict. Some are useful. Others are worthless, a waste of time. Humour is a prime example of the latter.'

'Funny.'

'Excuse me?'

'Oh, sorry, I was just thinking. Funny.'

'What is?'

'You wouldn't get it, alas.'

'You actually imagine yourself brighter than me?'

'I have no idea regarding that. But, since you abjure all aspects of humour, anything I might consider and then observe with the word "funny" is obviously something you would not understand.' Tehol then leaned slightly forward. 'But wait, that's just it!'

'What nonsense are you—'

'It's why I am, after all, much smarter than you.'

Karos Invictad smiled. 'Indeed. Please, do explain yourself.'

'Why, without a sense of humour, you are blind to so much in this world. To human nature. To the absurdity of so much that we say and do. Consider this, a most poignant example: a mob approaches, seeking my head because I stole all their money, and what do you do to appease them? Why, throw them all the money *you've* stolen from them! And yet, it's clear that you were completely unaware of just how hilarious that really is – you made your decision unmindful of what, eighty per cent of its delicious nuances. Ninety per cent! Ninety-three per cent! And a half or just shy of a half, but more than a third but less than . . . oh, somewhere close to a half, then.'

Karos Invictad waggled a finger. 'Incorrect, I'm afraid. It is not that I was unmindful. It was that I was indifferent to such nuances, as you call them. They are, in fact, entirely meaningless.'

'Well, you may have a point there, since you seem capable of being appreciative of your own brilliance despite your ignorance. But let's see, perhaps I can come up with another example.'

'You are wasting your time, Tehol Beddict. And mine.'

'I am? It didn't seem you were very busy. What is so occupying you, Invigilator? Apart from anarchy in the streets, economic collapse, invading armies, dead agents and burning horses, I mean.'

The answer was involuntary, as Karos Invictad's eyes flicked down to the puzzle box. He corrected himself – but too late, for he saw a dawning realization in Tehol's bruised face, and the man leaned yet farther forward in his chair.

'What's this, then? Some magic receptacle? In which will be found all the solutions to this troubled world? Must be, to so demand all of your formidable genius. Wait, is something moving in there?'

'The puzzle is nothing,' Karos Invictad said, waving one bejewelled hand. 'We were speaking of your failings.'

Tehol Beddict leaned back, grimacing. 'Oh, *my* failings. Was that the topic of this sizzling discourse? I'm afraid I got confused.'

'Some puzzles have no solution,' Karos said, and he could hear how his own voice had grown higher-pitched. He forced himself to draw a deep breath, then said in a lower tone, 'Someone sought to confound me. Suggesting that a solution was possible. But I see now that no solution was ever possible. The fool did not play fair, and I so dislike such creatures and could I find him or her I would make an immediate arrest, and this entire building would echo with the fool's screams and shrieks.'

Karos paused when he saw Tehol frowning at him. 'What is it?'

'Nothing. Funny, though.'

The Invigilator reached for his sceptre and lifted it from the desktop, pleased as ever with the solid weight of the symbol, how it felt in his hand.

'Okay, not funny. Sorry I said anything. Don't hit me with that thing again. Please. Although,' Tehol added, 'considering it's the symbol of your office, hitting me with it, while somewhat heavy-handed, is nevertheless somewhat . . . funny.'

'I am thinking of giving you over to the citizens of Letheras,' Karos said, glancing up to gauge how the man would react to that statement. And was surprised to see the fool smiling again. 'You think I jest?'

'Never. Obviously.'

'Then you would enjoy being torn apart by the mob?'

'I doubt it. But then, I wouldn't be, would I? Torn apart, I mean.'

'Oh, and why not?'

'Because, not only do I have more money than you, Invigilator, I am – unlike you – entirely indifferent regarding who ends up owning it. Hand me over, by all means, sir. And watch me buy my life.'

Karos Invictad stared at the man.

Tehol wagged a broken finger. 'People with no sense or appreciation of humour, Invigilator, always take money too seriously. Its possession, anyway. Which is why they spend all their time stacking coins, counting this and that, gazing lovingly over their hoards and so on. They're compensating for the abject penury everywhere else in their lives. Nice rings, by the way.'

Karos forced himself to remain calm in the face of such overt insults. 'I said I was thinking of handing you over. Alas, you have just given me reason not to. So, you assure your own Drowning come the morrow. Satisfied?'

'Well, if my satisfaction is essential, then might I suggest—'

'Enough, Tehol Beddict. You no longer interest me.'

'Good, can I go now?'

'Yes.' Karos rose, tapping the sceptre onto one shoulder. 'And I, alas, must needs escort you.'

'Good help is hard to keep alive these days.'

'Stand up, Tehol Beddict.'

The man had some difficulty following that instruction, but the Invigilator waited, having learned to be patient with such things.

As soon as Tehol fully straightened, however, a look of astonishment lit his features. 'Why, it's a two-headed insect! Going round and round!'

839

'To the door now,' Karos said.

'What's the challenge?'

'It is pointless—'

'Oh now, really, Invigilator. You claim to be smarter than me, and I'm about to die – I like puzzles. I design them, in fact. Very difficult puzzles.'

'You are lying. I know all the designers and you do not number among them.'

'Well, all right. I designed just one.'

'Too bad, then, you will be unable to offer it to me, for my momentary pleasure, since you are now returning to your cell.'

'That's all right,' Tehol replied. 'It was more of a joke than a puzzle, anyway.'

Karos Invictad grimaced, then waved Tehol towards the door with the sceptre.

As he slowly shuffled over, Tehol said, 'I figured out the challenge, anyway. It's to make the bug stop going round and round.'

The Invigilator blocked him with the sceptre. 'I told you, there is no solution.'

'I think there is. I think I know it, in fact. Tell you what, sir. I solve that puzzle there on your desk and you postpone my Drowning. Say, by forty years or so.'

'Agreed. Because you cannot.' He watched Tehol Beddict walk like an old man over to the desk. Then lean over. 'You cannot touch the insect!'

'Of course,' Tehol replied. And leaned yet farther over, lowering his face towards the box.

Karos Invictad hurried forward to stand beside him. 'Do not touch!'

'I won't.'

'The tiles can be rearranged, but I assure you—'

'No need to rearrange the tiles.'

Karos Invictad found his heart pounding hard in his chest. 'You are wasting more of my time.'

'No, I'm putting an end to your wasting your time, sir.' He paused, cocked his head. 'Probably a mistake. Oh well.'

And lowered his face down directly over the box, then gusted a sharp breath against one of the tiles. Momentarily clouding it. And the insect, with one of its heads facing that suddenly opaque, suddenly non-reflective surface, simply stopped. Reached up a leg and scratched its abdomen. As the mist cleared on the tile, it scratched once more, then resumed its circling.

Tehol straightened. 'I'm free! Free!'

Karos Invictad could not speak for ten, fifteen heartbeats. His chest was suddenly tight, sweat beading on his skin, then he said in a rasp, 'Don't be a fool.'

'You lied? Oh, I can't believe how you lied to me! Well then, piss on you and your pissy stupid puzzle, too!'

The Invigilator's sceptre swept in an arc, intersecting with that box on the desk, shattering it, sending its wreckage flying across the room. The insect struck a wall and stayed there, then it began climbing towards the ceiling.

'*Run!*' whispered Tehol Beddict. '*Run!*'

The sceptre swung next into Tehol's chest, snapping ribs.

'Pull the chain tighter on my ankles,' Janath said. 'Force my legs wider.'

'You enjoy being helpless, don't you?'

'Yes. Yes!'

Smiling, Tanal Yathvanar knelt at the side of the bed. The chain beneath ran through holes in the bed frame at each corner. Pins held the lengths in place. To tighten the ones snaring her ankles all he needed to do was pull a pin on each side at the foot of the bed, drawing the chain down as far as he could, and, as he listened to her moans, replace the pins.

Then he rose and sat down on the edge of the bed. Stared down at her. Naked, most of the bruises fading since he no longer liked hurting her. A beautiful body indeed, getting thinner which he preferred in his women. He reached out, then drew his hand away again. He didn't like any touching until he was ready. She moaned a second time, arching her back.

Tanal Yathvanar undressed. Then he crawled up onto the bed, loomed over her with his knees between her legs, his hands pressing down on the mattress to either side of her chest.

He saw how the manacles had torn at her wrists. He would need to treat that – those wounds were looking much worse.

Slowly, Tanal settled onto her body, felt her shiver beneath him as he slid smoothly inside. So easy, so welcoming. She groaned, and, studying her face, he said, 'Do you want me to kiss you now?'

'*Yes!*'

And he brought his head down as he made his first deep thrust.

Janath, once eminent scholar, had found in herself a beast, prodded awake as if from a slumber of centuries, perhaps millennia. A beast that understood captivity, that understood that, sometimes, what needed doing entailed excruciating pain.

Beneath the manacles on her wrists, mostly hidden by scabs, blood and torn shreds of skin, the very bones had been worn down, chipped, cracked. By constant, savage tugging. Animal rhythm, blind to all else, deaf to every scream of her nerves. Tugging, and tugging.

Until the pins beneath the frame began to bend. Ever so slowly, bending, the wood holes chewed into, the pins bending, gouging through the holes.

And now, with the extra length of chain that came when Tanal Yathvanar had reset the pins at the foot of the bed frame, she had enough slack.

To reach with her left hand and grasp a clutch of his hair. To push his head to the right, where she had, in a clattering blur, brought most of the length of the chain through the hole, enough to wrap round his neck and then twist her hand down under and then over; and in sudden, excruciating determination, she pulled her left arm up, higher and higher with that arm – the manacle and her right wrist pinned to the frame, tugged down as far as it could go.

He thrashed, sought to dig his fingers under the chain, and she reached ever harder, her face brushing his own, her eyes seeing the sudden blue hue of his skin, his bulging eyes and jutting tongue.

He could have beaten against her. He could have driven his thumbs into her eyes. He could probably have killed her in time to survive all of this. But she had waited for his breath to release, which ever came at the moment he pushed in his first thrust. That breath, that she had heard a hundred times now, close to her ear, as he made use of her body, that breath is what killed him.

He needed air. He had none. Nothing else mattered. He tore at his own throat to get his fingers under the chain. She pushed her left arm straight, elbow locking, and loosed her own scream as the manacle round her right wrist shifted as a bolt slipped down into the hole.

That blue, bulging face, that flooding burst from his penis, followed by the hot gush of urine.

Staring eyes, veins blossoming red, then purple until the whites were completely filled.

She looked right into them. Looked into, seeking his soul, seeking to lock her gaze with that pathetic, vile, dying soul.

I kill you. I kill you. I kill you!

The beast's silent words.

The beast's gleeful, savage assertion. Her eyes shouted it at him, shouted it into his soul.

Tanal Yathvanar. I kill you!

Taralack Veed spat into his hands, rubbed them together to spread out the phlegm, then raised them and swept his hair back. 'I smell more smoke,' he said.

Senior Assessor, who sat opposite him at the small table, raised his thin brows. 'It surprises me that you can smell anything, Taralack Veed.'

'I have lived in the wild, Cabalhii. I can follow an antelope's spore that's a day old. This city is crumbling. The Tiste Edur have left. And suddenly the Emperor changes his mind and slaughters all the challengers until but two remain. And does anyone even care?' He rose suddenly and walked to the bed, on which he had laid out his weapons. He unsheathed his scimitar and peered down at the edge once again.

'You could trim your eyelashes with that sword by now.'

'Why would I do that?' Taralack asked distractedly.

'Just a suggestion, Gral.'

'I was a servant of the Nameless Ones.'

'I know,' Senior Assessor replied.

Taralack turned, studied with narrowed eyes the soft little man with his painted face. 'You do?'

'The Nameless Ones are known in my homeland. Do you know why they are called that? I will tell you as I see that you do not. The Initiated must surrender their names, in the belief that to know oneself by one's own name is to give it too much power. The name becomes the identity, becomes the face, becomes the self. Remove the name and power returns.'

'They made no such demands of me.'

'Because you are little more than a tool, no different from that sword in your hands. Needless to say, the Nameless Ones do not give names to their tools. And in a very short time you will have outlived your usefulness—'

'And I will be free once more. To return home.'

'Home,' mused Senior Assessor. 'Your tribe, there to right all your wrongs, to mend all the wounds you delivered in your zealous youth. You will come to them with wizened eyes, with slowed heart and a gentling hand. And one night, as you lie sleeping in your furs in the hut where you were born, someone will slip in and slide a blade across your throat. Because the world within your mind is not the world beyond. You are named Taralack Veed and they have taken of its power. From the name, the face. From the name, the self, and with it all the history, and so by your own power – so freely given away long, long ago – you are slain.'

Taralack Veed stared, the scimitar trembling in his hands. 'And this, then, is why you are known only as Senior Assessor.'

The Cabalhii shrugged. 'The Nameless Ones are fools for the most part. Said proof to be found in your presence here, with your Jhag companion. Even so, we share certain understandings, which is not too surprising, since we both came from the same civilization. From the First Empire of Dessimbelackis.'

'It was a common joke in Seven Cities,' the Gral said, sneering. 'One day the sun will die and one day there will be no civil war in the Cabal Isles.'

843

'Peace has at long last been won,' Senior Assessor replied, folding his hands together on his lap.

'Then why does every conversation I have with you of late make me want to throttle you?'

The Cabalhii sighed. 'Perhaps I have been away from home too long.'

Grimacing, Taralack Veed slammed the scimitar back in its scabbard.

From the corridor beyond a door thumped open and the two men in the room stiffened, their gazes meeting.

Soft footsteps, passing the door.

With a curse Taralack began strapping on his weapons. Senior Assessor rose, adjusting his robe before heading to the door and opening it just enough to peer outside. Then he ducked back in. 'He is on his way,' he said in a whisper.

Nodding, Taralack joined the monk who opened the door a second time. They went out into the corridor, even as they heard the sound of a momentary scuffle, then a grunt, after which something crunched on the stone floor.

Taralack Veed in the lead, they padded quickly down the corridor.

At the threshold of the practice yard's door was a crumpled heap – the guard. From the compound beyond there was a startled shout, a scuffle, then the sound of the outer gate opening.

Taralack Veed hurried out into the darkness. His mouth was dry. His heart pounded heavy in his chest. Senior Assessor had said that Icarium would not wait. That Icarium was a god and no-one could hold back a god, when it had set out to do what it would do. *They will find him gone. Will they search the city? No, they do not even dare unbar the palace gate.*

Icarium? Lifestealer, what do you seek?

Will you return to stand before the Emperor and his cursed sword?

The monk had told Taralack to be ready, to not sleep this night. *And this is why.*

They reached the gate, stepped over the bodies of two guards, then edged outside.

And saw him, standing motionless forty paces down the street, in its very centre. A group of four figures, wielding clubs, were converging on him. At ten paces away they halted, then began backing away. Then they whirled about and ran, one of the clubs clattering on the cobbles.

Icarium stared up at the night sky.

Somewhere to the north, three buildings were burning, reflecting lurid crimson on the bellies of the clouds of smoke seething overhead. Distant screams lifted into the air. Taralack Veed, his breath coming in gasps, drew out his sword. Thugs and murderers might run from Icarium, but that was no assurance that they would do the same for himself and the monk.

Icarium lowered his gaze, then looked about, as if only now discovering where he was. Another moment's pause, then he set out.

Silent, the Gral and the Cabalhii followed.

Samar Dev licked dry lips. He was lying on his bed, apparently asleep. And come the dawn, he would take his flint sword, strap on his armour, and walk in the midst of Letherii soldiers to the Imperial Arena. And he would walk, alone, out onto the sand, the few hundred onlookers on the marble benches raising desultory hooting and catcalls. There would be no bet-takers, no frenzied shouting of odds. Because this game always ended the same. And now, did anyone even care?

In her mind she watched him stride to the centre of the arena. Would he be looking at the Emperor? Studying Rhulad Sengar as he emerged from the far gate? The lightness of his step, the unconscious patterns the sword made at the end of his hands, patterns that whispered of all that muscles and bones had learned and were wont to do?

No, he will be as he always is. He will be Karsa Orlong. He'll not even look at the Emperor, until Rhulad draws closer, until the two of them begin.

Not overconfident. Not indifferent. Not even contemptuous. No easy explanations for this Toblakai warrior. He would be within himself, entirely within himself, until it was time . . . *to witness.*

But nothing would turn out right, Samar Dev knew. Not all of Karsa Orlong's prowess, nor that ever-flooding, ever-cascading torrent that was the Toblakai's will; nor even this host of spirits trapped in the knife she now held, and those others who trailed the Toblakai's shadow – souls of the slain, desert godlings and ancient demons of the sands and rock – spirits that might well burst forth, enwreathing their champion god (and was he truly that? A god? She did not know) with all their power. No, none of it would matter in the end.

Kill Rhulad Sengar. Kill him thrice. Kill him a dozen times. *In the end he will stand, sword bloodied, and then will come Icarium, the very last.*

To begin it all again.

Karsa Orlong, reduced to a mere name among the list of the slain. Nothing more than that. *For this extraordinary warrior. And this is what you whisper, Fallen One, as your holy credo. Grandness and potential and promise, they all break in the end.*

Even your great champion, this terrible, tortured Tiste Edur – you see him broken again and again. You fling him back each time less than what he was, yet with ever more power in his hands. He is there, yes, for us all. The power and its broken wielder broken by his power.

Karsa Orlong sat up. 'Someone has left,' he said.

Samar Dev blinked. 'What?'

845

He bared his teeth. 'Icarium. He is gone.'

'What do you mean, gone? *He's left?* To go where?'

'It does not matter,' the Toblakai replied, swinging round to settle his feet on the floor. He stared across at her. 'He knows.'

'Knows what, Karsa Orlong?'

The warrior stood, his smile broadening, twisting the crazed tattoos on his face. 'That he will not be needed.'

'Karsa—'

'You will know when, woman. You will know.'

Know what, damn you? 'They wouldn't have just let him go,' she said. 'So he must have taken down all the guards. Karsa, this is our last chance. To head out into the city. Leave all this—'

'You do not understand. The Emperor is nothing. The Emperor, Samar Dev, *is not the one he wants.*'

Who? Icarium? No – 'Karsa Orlong, what secret do you hold? What do you know about the Crippled God?'

The Toblakai rose. 'It is nearly dawn,' he said. 'Nearly time.'

'Karsa, please—'

'Will you witness?'

'Do I have to?'

He studied her for a moment, and then his next words shocked her to the core of her soul: 'I need you, woman.'

'*Why?*' she demanded, suddenly close to tears.

'To witness. To do what needs doing when the time comes.' He drew a deep, satisfied breath, looking away, his chest swelling until she thought his ribs would creak. 'I live for days like these,' he said.

And now she did weep.

Grandness, promise, potential. Fallen One, must you so share out your pain?

'Women always get weak once a month, don't they?'

'Go to Hood, bastard.'

'And quick to anger, too.'

She was on her feet. Pounding a fist into his solid chest.

Five times, six – he caught her wrist, not hard enough to hurt, but stopping those swings as if a manacle had snapped tight.

She glared up at him.

And he was, for *his* sake, not smiling.

Her fist opened and she found herself almost physically pulled up and into his eyes – seeing them, it seemed, for the first time. Their immeasurable depth, their bright ferocity and joy.

Karsa Orlong nodded. 'Better, Samar Dev.'

'You patronizing shit.'

He released her arm. 'I learn more each day about women. Because of you.'

'You still have a lot to learn, Karsa Orlong,' she said, turning away and wiping at her cheeks.

'Yes, and that is a journey I will enjoy.'

'I really should hate you,' she said. 'I'm sure most people who meet you hate you, eventually.'

The Toblakai snorted. 'The Emperor will.'

'So now I must walk with you. Now I must watch you die.'

From outside there came shouts.

'They have discovered the escape,' Karsa Orlong said, collecting his sword. 'Soon they will come for us. Are you ready, Samar Dev?'

'No.'

The water had rotted her feet, he saw. White as the skin of a corpse, shreds hanging loose to reveal gaping red wounds, and as she drew them onto the altar top and tucked them under her, the Errant suddenly understood something. About humanity, about the seething horde in its cruel avalanche through history.

The taste of ashes filling his mouth, he looked away, studied the runnels of water streaming down the stone walls of the chamber. 'It rises,' he said, looking back at her.

'He was never as lost as he thought he was,' Feather Witch said, reaching up distractedly to twirl the filthy strands of her once-golden hair. 'Are you not eager, dear god of mine? This empire is about to kneel at your feet. And,' she suddenly smiled, revealing brown teeth, 'at mine.'

Yes, at yours, Feather Witch. Those rotting, half-dead appendages that you could have used to run. Long ago. The empire kneels, and lips quiver forth. A blossom kiss. So cold, so like paste, and the smell, oh, the smell . . .

'Is it not time?' she asked, with an oddly coy glance.

'For what?'

'You were a consort. You know the ways of love. Teach me now.'

'Teach you?'

'I am unbroken. I have never lain with man or woman.'

'A lie,' the Errant replied. 'Gribna, the lame slave in the Hiroth village. You were very young. He used you. Often and badly. It is what has made you what you now are, Feather Witch.'

And he saw her eyes shy away, saw the frown upon her brow, and realized the awful truth that she had not remembered. *Too young, too wide-eyed. And then, every moment buried in a deep hole at the pit of her soul. She, by the Abyss, did not remember.* 'Feather Witch—'

'Go away,' she said. 'I don't need anything from you right now. I have Udinaas.'

'You have lost Udinaas. You never had him. Listen, please—'

'He's alive! Yes he is! And all the ones who wanted him are dead – the sisters, all dead! Could you have imagined that?'

'You fool. Silchas Ruin is coming here. To lay this city to waste. To destroy it utterly—'

'He cannot defeat Rhulad Sengar,' she retorted. 'Not even Silchas Ruin can do that!'

The Errant said nothing to that bold claim. Then he turned away. 'I saw gangrene at your feet, Feather Witch. My temple, as you like to call it, reeks of rotting flesh.'

'Then heal me.'

'The water rises,' he said, and this time the statement seemed to burgeon within him, filling his entire being. *The water rises. Why?* 'Hannan Mosag seeks the demon god, the one trapped in the ice. That ice, Feather Witch, is melting. Water . . . everywhere. *Water . . .*'

By the Holds, was it possible? Even this? *But no, I trapped the bastard. I trapped him!*

'He took the finger,' Feather Witch said behind him. 'He took it and thought that was enough, to just take it. But how could I go where he has gone? I couldn't. So I needed him, yes. I needed him, and he was never as lost as he thought he was.'

'And what of the other one?' the Errant asked, still with his back to her.

'Never found—'

The Elder God whirled round. '*Where is the other finger?*'

He saw her eyes widen.

Is it possible? Is it—

He found himself in the corridor, the water at his hips, though he passed through it effortlessly. *We have come to the moment – Icarium walks – where? A foreign army and a horrifying mage approaches. Silchas Ruin wings down from the north with eyes of fire. Hannan Mosag – the fool – crawls his way to Settle Lake even as the demon god stirs – and she says he was never as lost as he thought he was.*

Almost dawn, somewhere beyond these sagging, weeping walls.

An empire on its knees.

The blossom kiss, but moments away.

The word came to Varat Taun, newly appointed Finadd in the Palace Guard, that Icarium, along with Taralack Veed and Senior Assessor, had escaped. At that statement his knees had weakened, a flood rushing through him, but it was a murky, confused flood. Relief, yes, at what had been averted – at least for the moment, for might Icarium not return? – relief that was quickly engulfed by his growing dread for this invading army encamped barely two leagues away.

There would be a siege, and with virtually no-one left to hold the walls it would be a short one. And then the Eternal Domicile itself would be assailed, and by the time all was done, Emperor Rhulad Sengar would likely be standing alone, surrounded by the enemy.

An Emperor without an empire.

Five Letherii armies on the Bolkando borderlands far to the east had seemingly vanished. Not a word from a single mage among those forces. They had set out, under a competent if not brilliant commander, to crush the Bolkando and their allies. That should have been well within the woman's capabilities. The last report had come half a day before the armies clashed.

What else could anyone conclude? *Those five armies were shattered. The enemy marches on, into the empire's very heart. And what has happened east of Drene? More silence, and Atri-Preda Bivatt was considered by most as the next Preda of the Imperial Armies.*

Rebellion in Bluerose, riots in every city. Wholesale desertion of entire units and garrisons. The Tiste Edur vanishing like ghosts, fleeing back to their homeland, no doubt. *By the Errant, why did I not ride with Yan Tovis? Return to my wife – I am a fool, who will die here, in this damned palace. Die for nothing.*

He stood, positioned beside the throne room's entranceway, and watched from under the rim of his helm the Emperor of a Thousand Deaths pace in front of the throne. Filthy with blood and spilled fluids from a dozen dead challengers, a dozen cut through in a whirlwind frenzy, Rhulad shrieking as his sword whirled and chopped and severed and seemed to drink in the pain and blood of its victims.

And now, dawn was beginning on this day, and the sleepless Emperor paced. Blackened coins shifting on his ravaged face as emotions worked his features in endless cycles of disbelief, distress and fear.

Before Rhulad Sengar, standing motionless, was the Chancellor.

Thrice, the Emperor paused to glare at Triban Gnol. Thrice he made as if to speak, only to resume his pacing, the sword-tip dragging across the tiles.

His own people had abandoned him. He had inadvertently drowned his own mother and father. Killed all of his brothers. Driven the wife he had stolen to suicide. Been betrayed by the First and only Concubine he had possessed, Nisall.

An economy in ruins, all order crumbling, and armies invading.

And his only answer was to force hapless foreigners onto the sands of the arena and butcher them.

Pathos or grand comedy?

It will not do, Emperor. All that blood and guts covering you will not do. When you are but the hands holding the sword, the sword rules, and the sword knows nothing but what it was made for. It can achieve no resolutions, can manage no subtle diplomacy, can solve none of the problems afflicting people in their tens of thousands, hundreds of thousands.

Leave a sword to rule an empire and the empire falls. Amidst war, amidst anarchy, amidst a torrent of blood and a sea of misery.

Coin-clad, the wielder of the sword paced out the true extent of his domain, here in this throne room.

Halting, facing the chancellor once more. 'What has happened?'

A child's question. A child's voice. Varat Taun felt his heart give slightly, felt its hardness suddenly soften. *A child.*

The Chancellor's reply was measured, so reassuring that Varat Taun very nearly laughed at the absurdity of that tone. 'We are never truly conquered, Emperor. You will stand, because none can remove you. The invaders will see that, understand that. They will have done with their retribution. Will they occupy? Unknown. If not them, then the coalition coming from the eastern kingdoms will – and such coalitions inevitably break apart, devour themselves. They too will be able to do nothing to you, Emperor.'

Rhulad Sengar stared at Triban Gnol, his mouth working but no sounds coming forth.

'I have begun,' the Chancellor resumed, 'preparing our conditional surrender. To the Malazans. At the very least, they will enforce peace in the city, an end to the riots. Likely working in consort with the Patriotists. Once order is restored, we can begin the task of resurrecting the economy, minting—'

'Where are my people?' Rhulad Sengar asked.

'They will return, Emperor. I am sure of it.'

Rhulad turned to face the throne. And suddenly went perfectly still. '*It is empty,*' he whispered. 'Look!' He spun round, pointing his sword back at the throne. 'Do you see? It is *empty*!'

'Sire—'

'Like my father's chair in our house! Our house in the village! Empty!'

'The village is no longer there, Emperor—'

'But the chair remains! I see it! With my own eyes – my father's chair! The paint fades in the sun. The wood joins split in the rain. Crows perch on the weathered arms! *I see it!*'

The shout echoed in silence then. Not a guard stirring. The Chancellor with bowed head, and who knew what thoughts flickered behind the serpent's eyes?

Surrender. Conditional. Rhulad Sengar remains. Rhulad Sengar and, oh yes, Chancellor Triban Gnol. And the Patriotists. 'We cannot be conquered. We are for ever. Step into our world and it devours you.'

Rhulad's broad shoulders slowly sagged. Then he walked up to the throne, turned about and sat down. Looked out with bleak eyes. In a croaking voice he asked, 'Who remains?'

The Chancellor bowed. 'But one, Emperor.'

'One? There should be two.'

'The challenger known as Icarium has fled, Emperor. Into the city. We are hunting him down.'

Liar.

But Rhulad Sengar seemed indifferent, his head turning to one side, eyes lowering until they fixed on the gore-spattered sword. 'The Toblakai.'

'Yes, Emperor.'

'Who murdered Binadas. My brother.'

'Indeed, sire.'

The head slowly lifted. 'Is it dawn?'

'It is.'

Rhulad's command was soft as a breath. *'Bring him.'*

They let the poor fool go once he had shown them the recessed door leading under the city wall. It was, of course, locked, and while the rest of the squads waited in the slowly fading darkness – seeking whatever cover they could find and it wasn't much – Fiddler and Cuttle went down into the depression to examine the door.

'Made to be broken down,' Cuttle muttered, 'so it's like the lad said – we go in and then the floodgates open and we drown. Fid, I don't see a way to do this, not quietly enough so as no-one hears and figures out we've taken the trap.'

Fiddler scratched at his white beard. 'Maybe we could dismantle the entire door, frame and all.'

'We ain't got the time.'

'No. We pull back and hide out for the day, then do it tomorrow night.'

'The Adjunct should be showing up by then. Keneb wants us first in and he's right, we've earned it.'

At that moment they heard a thump from behind the door, then the low scrape of the bar being lifted.

The two Malazans moved to either side, quickly cocking their crossbows.

A grinding sound, then the door was pushed open.

The figure that climbed into view was no Letherii soldier. It was wearing plain leather armour that revealed, without question, that it was a woman, and on her face an enamel mask with a modest array of painted sigils. Two swords strapped across her back. One stride, then two. A glance to Fiddler on her right, then to Cuttle on her left. Pausing, brushing dirt from her armour, then setting out. Onto the killing field, and away.

Bathed in sweat, Fiddler settled back into a sitting position, the crossbow trembling in his hands.

Cuttle made a warding gesture, then sat down as well. 'Hood's breath was on my neck, Fid. Right there, right then. I know, she didn't even reach for those weapons, didn't even twitch . . .'

'Aye,' Fid answered, the word whispered like a blessing. *A Hood-damned Seguleh. High ranked, too. We'd never have got our shots off – no way. Our heads would have rolled like a pair of oversized snowballs.*

'I looked away, Fid. I looked right down at the ground when she turned my way.'

'Me too.'

'And that's why we're still alive.'

'Aye.'

Cuttle turned and peered down into the dark tunnel. 'We don't have to wait till tomorrow night after all.'

'Go back to the others, Cuttle. Get Keneb to draw 'em up. I'm heading in to check the other end. If it's unguarded and quiet, well and good. If not . . .'

'Aye, Fid.'

The sergeant dropped down into the tunnel.

He moved through the dark as fast as he could without making too much noise. The wall overhead was damned thick and he'd gone thirty paces before he saw the grey blur of the exit at the end of a sharp slope. Crossbow in hands, Fiddler edged forward.

He need not have worried.

The tunnel opened into a cramped blockhouse with no ceiling. One bench lined the wall to his right. Three bodies were sprawled on the dusty stone floor, bleeding out from vicious wounds. *Should've averted your eyes, soldiers.* Assuming she even gave them the time to decide either way – she'd wanted out, after all.

The door opposite him was ajar and Fiddler crept to it, looked out through the crack. A wide street, littered with rubbish.

They'd been listening to the riots half the night, and it was clear that mobs had swept through here, if not this night then other nights. The garrison blocks opposite were gutted, the windows soot-stained. *Better and better.*

He turned round and hastened back down the tunnel.

At the other end he found Cuttle, Faradan Sort and Fist Keneb, all standing a few paces in from the door.

Fiddler explained to them what he had found. Then said, 'We got to go through right away, I think. Eight hundred marines to come through and that'll take a while.'

Keneb nodded. 'Captain Faradan Sort.'

'Sir.'

'Take four squads through and establish flanking positions. Send one squad straight across to the nearest barracks to see if they are indeed abandoned. If so, that will be our staging area. From there, I will lead the main body to the gate, seize and secure it. Captain, you and four squads will strike into the city, as far as you can go, causing trouble all the way – take extra munitions for that.'

'Our destination?'

'The palace.'

'Aye, sir. Fiddler, collect Gesler and Hellian and Urb – you're the first four – and take your squads through. At a damned run if you please.'

In the grey light of early dawn, four figures emerged from a smear of blurred light twenty paces from the dead Azath Tower behind the Old Palace. As the portal swirled shut behind them, they stood, looking round.

Hedge gave Quick Ben a light push to one side, somewhere between comradely affection and irritation. 'Told you, it's reunion time, wizard.'

'Where in Hood's name are we?' Quick Ben demanded.

'We're in Letheras,' Seren Pedac said. 'Behind the Old Palace – but something's wrong.'

Trull Sengar wrapped his arms about himself, his face drawn with the pain of freshly healed wounds, his eyes filled with a deeper distress.

Hedge felt some of his anticipation dim like a dying oil lamp as he studied the Tiste Edur. *The poor bastard. A brother murdered in front of his eyes. Then, the awkward goodbye with Onrack – joy and sadness there in plenty, seeing his old friend and the woman at his side – a woman Onrack had loved for so long. So long? Damned near incomprehensible, that's how long.*

But now – 'Trull Sengar.'

The Tiste Edur slowly looked over.

Hedge shot Quick Ben a glance, then he said, 'We've a mind to escort you and Seren. To her house.'

'This city is assailed,' Trull Sengar said. 'My youngest brother – the Emperor—'

'That can all wait,' Hedge cut in. He paused, trying to figure out how to say what he meant, then said, 'Your friend Onrack stole a woman's heart, and it was all there. In her eyes, I mean. The answer, that is. And if you'd look, just look, Trull Sengar, into the eyes of Seren Pedac, well—'

'For Hood's sake,' Quick Ben sighed. 'He means you and Seren need to get alone before anything else, and we're going to make sure that happens. All right?'

The surprise on Seren Pedac's face was almost comical.

But Trull Sengar then nodded.

Hedge regarded Quick Ben once again. 'You recovered enough in case we walk into trouble?'

'Something your sharpers can't handle? Yes, probably. Maybe. Get a sharper in each hand, Hedge.'

'Good enough . . . since you're a damned idiot,' Hedge replied. 'Seren Pedac – you should know, I'm well envious of this Tiste Edur here, but anyway. Is your house far?'

'No, it is not, Hedge of the Bridgeburners.'

'Then let's get out of this spooky place.'

Silts swirled up round his feet, spun higher, engulfing his shins, then whirled away like smoke on the current. Strange pockets of luminosity drifted past, morphing as if subjected to unseen pressures in this dark, unforgiving world.

Bruthen Trana, who had been sent to find a saviour, walked an endless plain, the silts thick and gritty. He stumbled against buried detritus, tripped on submerged roots. He crossed current-swept rises of hardened clay from which jutted polished bones of long-dead leviathans. He skirted the wreckage of sunken ships, the ribs of the hulls splayed out and cargo scattered about. And as he walked, he thought about his life and the vast array of choices he had made, others he had refused to make.

No wife, no single face to lift into his mind's eye. He had been a warrior for what seemed all his life. Fighting alongside blood kin and comrades closer than any blood kin. He had seen them die or drift away. He had, he realized now, watched his entire people pulled apart. With the conquest, with the cold-blooded, anonymous nightmare that was Lether. As for the Letherii themselves, no, he did not hate them. More like pity and yes, compassion, for they were as trapped in the nightmare as anyone else. The rapacious desperation, the gnawing threat of falling, of drowning beneath the ever-rising, ever-onrushing torrent that was a culture that could never look back, could not even slow its headlong plunge into some gleaming future that – if it came at all – would ever only exist for but a privileged few.

This eternal seabed offered its own commentary, and it was one that threatened to drag him down into the silts, enervated beyond all hope of continuing, of even moving. Cold, crushing, this place was like history's own weight – history not of a people or a civilization, but of the entire world.

Why was he still walking? What saviour could liberate him from all of this? He should have remained in Letheras. Free to launch an assault on Karos Invictad and his Patriotists, free to annihilate the man and his thugs. And then he could have turned to the Chancellor. Imagining his hands on Triban Gnol's throat was most satisfying – for as long as the image lasted, which was never long enough. A bloom of silts up into his eyes, another hidden object snagging his foot.

And here, now, looming before him, pillars of stone. The surfaces, he saw, cavorted with carvings, unrecognizable sigils so intricate they spun and shifted before his eyes.

As he drew closer, silts gusted ahead, and Bruthen Trana saw a figure climbing into view. Armour green with verdigris and furred with slime. A closed helm covering its face. In one gauntleted hand was a Letherii sword.

And a voice spoke in the Tiste Edur's head: '*You have walked enough, Ghost.*'

Bruthen Trana halted. 'I am not a ghost in truth—'

'*You are, stranger. Your soul has been severed from now cold, now rotting flesh. You are no more than what stands here, before me. A ghost.*'

Somehow, the realization did not surprise him. Hannan Mosag's legacy of treachery made all alliances suspect. And he had, he realized, felt . . . severed. For a long time, yes. The Warlock King likely did not waste any time in cutting the throat of Bruthen Trana's helpless body.

'Then,' he said, 'what is left for me?'

'*One thing, Ghost. You are here to summon him. To send him back.*'

'But was not his soul severed as well?'

'*His flesh and bones are here, Ghost. And in this place, there is power. For here you will find the forgotten gods, the last holding of their names. Know this, Ghost, were we to seek to defy you, to refuse your summoning, we could. Even with what you carry.*'

'Will you then refuse me?' Bruthen Trana asked, and if the answer was *yes*, then he would laugh. To have come all this way. To have sacrificed his life . . .

'*No. We understand the need. Better, perhaps, than you.*' The armoured warrior lifted his free hand. All but the foremost of the metal-clad fingers folded. '*Go there,*' it said, pointing towards a pillar. '*The side with but one name. Draw forth that which you possess of his flesh and bone. Speak the name so written on the stone.*'

Bruthen Trana walked slowly to the standing stone, went round to the side with the lone carving. And read thereon the name inscribed: ' "Brys Beddict, Saviour of the Empty Hold." I summon you.'

The face of the stone, cleaned here, seeming almost fresh, all at once began to ripple, then bulge in places, the random shapes and movement coalescing to create a humanoid shape, pushing out from the stone. An arm came free, then shoulder, then head, face – eyes closed, features twisted as if in pain – upper torso. A leg. The second arm – Bruthen saw that two fingers were missing on that hand.

He frowned. *Two?*

As the currents streamed, Brys Beddict was driven out from the pillar. He fell forward onto his hands and knees, was almost swallowed in billowing silts.

The armoured warrior arrived, carrying a scabbarded sword, which he pushed point-first into the seabed beside the Letherii.

'Take it, Saviour. Feel the currents – they are eager. Go, you have little time.'

Still on his hands and knees, head hanging, Brys Beddict reached out for the weapon. As soon as his hand closed about the scabbard a sudden rush of the current lifted the man from the seabed. He spun in a flurry of silts and then was gone.

Bruthen Trana stood, motionless. That current had rushed right through him, unimpeded. *As it would through a ghost.*

All at once he felt bereft. He'd not had a chance to say a word to Brys Beddict, to tell him what needed to be done. An Emperor, to cut down once more. An empire, to resurrect.

'You are done here, Ghost.'

Bruthen Trana nodded.

'Where will you go?'

'There is a house. I lost it. I would find it again.'

'Then you shall.'

'Oh, Padderunt, look! It's twitching!'

The old man squinted over at Selush through a fog of smoke. She was doing that a lot of late. Bushels of rustleaf ever since Tehol Beddict's arrest. 'You've dressed enough dead to know what the lungs of people who do too much of that look like, Mistress.'

'Yes. No different from anyone else's.'

'Unless they got the rot, the cancer.'

'Lungs with the rot all look the same and that is most certainly true. Now, did you hear what I said?'

'It twitched,' Padderunt replied, twisting in his chair to peer up at the bubbly glass jar on the shelf that contained a stubby little severed finger suspended in pink goo.

'It's about time, too. Go to Rucket,' Selush said between ferocious pulls on the mouthpiece, her substantial chest swelling as if it was about to burst. 'And tell her.'

'That it twitched.'

'Yes!'

'All right.' He set down his cup. 'Rustleaf tea, Mistress.'

'I'd drown.'

'Not inhaled. Drunk, in civil fashion.'

'You're still here, dear servant, and I don't like that at all.'

He rose. 'On my way, O enwreathed one.'

She had managed to push the corpse of Tanal Yathvanar to one side, and it now lay beside her as if cuddled in sleep, the bloated, blotched face next to her own.

There would be no-one coming for her. This room was forbidden to all but Tanal Yathvanar, and unless some distaster struck this compound in the next day or two, leading Karos Invictad to demand Tanal's presence and so seek him out, Janath knew it would be too late for her.

Chained to the bed, legs spread wide, fluids leaking from her. She stared up at the ceiling, strangely comforted by the body lying at her side. Its stillness, the coolness of the skin, the flaccid lack of resistance from the flesh. She could feel the shrivelled thing that was his penis pressing against her right thigh. And the beast within her was pleased.

She needed water. She needed that above all else. A mouthful would be enough, would give her the strength to once again begin tugging at the chains, dragging the links against the wood, dreaming of the entire frame splintering beneath her – but it would take a strong man to do that, she knew, strong and healthy. Her dream was nothing more than that, but she held on to it as her sole amusement that would, she hoped, follow her into death. Yes, right up until the last moment.

It would be enough.

Tanal Yathvanar, her tormentor, was dead. But that would be no escape from her. She meant to resume her pursuit, her soul – sprung free of this flesh – demonic in its hunger, in the cruelty it wanted to inflict on whatever whimpering, cowering thing was left of Tanal Yathvanar.

A mouthful of water. That would be so sweet.

She could spit it into the staring face beside her.

Coins to the belligerent multitude brought a larger, more belligerent multitude. And, at last, trepidation awoke in Karos Invictad, the Invigilator of the Patriotists. He sent servants down into the hidden-most crypts below, to drag up chest after chest. In the compound his agents were exhausted, now simply flinging handfuls of coins over the walls since the small sacks were long gone. And a pressure was building against those walls that, it now seemed, no amount of silver and gold could relieve.

He sat in his office, trying to comprehend that glaring truth. Of course, he told himself, there were simply too many in the mob. Not enough coins was the problem. They'd fought like jackals over the sacks, had they not?

He had done and was doing what the Emperor should have done. Emptied the treasury and buried the people in riches. That would have purchased peace, yes. An end to the riots. Everyone returning to their homes, businesses opening once more, food on the stalls and whores

857

beckoning from windows and plenty of ale and wine to flow down throats – all the pleasures that purchased apathy and obedience. Yes, festivals and games and Drownings and that would have solved all of this. Along with a few quiet arrests and assassinations.

But he was running out of money. His money. Hard-won, a hoard amassed solely by his own genius. And they were taking it all.

Well, he would start all over again. Stealing it back from the pathetic bastards. Easy enough for one such as Karos Invictad.

Tanal Yathvanar had disappeared, likely hiding with his prisoner, and he could rot in her arms for all that the Invigilator cared. Oh, the man schemed to overthrow him, Karos knew. Pathetic, simplistic schemes. But they would come to naught, because the next time Karos saw the man, he would kill him. A knife through the eye. Quick, precise, most satisfying.

He could hear the shouts for Tehol Beddict, somewhat less fierce now – and that was, oddly enough, vaguely disturbing. Did they no longer want to tear him to pieces? Was he indeed hearing cries for the man's release?

Desperate knocking on his office door.

'Enter.'

An agent appeared, his face white. 'Sir, the main block—'

'Are we breached?'

'No—'

'Then go away – wait, check on Tehol Beddict. Make sure he's regained consciousness. I want him able to walk when we march to the Drownings.'

The man stared at him for a long moment, then he said, 'Yes sir.'

'Is that all?'

'No, the main block—' He gestured out into the corridor.

'What is it, you damned fool?'

'It's filling with rats, sir!'

Rats?

'They're coming from over the walls – we throw coins and rats come back. Thousands!'

'*That guild no longer exists!*'

The shriek echoed like a woman's scream.

The agent blinked, and all at once his tone changed, steadied. 'The mob, sir, they're calling for Tehol Beddict's release – can you not hear it? They're calling him a hero, a revolutionary—'

Karos Invictad slammed his sceptre down on his desk and rose. '*Is this what my gold paid for?*'

Feather Witch sensed the rebirth of Brys Beddict. She stopped plucking at the strips of skin hanging from her toes, drawing a deep breath as she felt him rushing closer, ever closer. So fast!

Crooning under her breath, she closed her eyes and conjured in her mind that severed finger. That fool the Errant had a lot to learn, still. About his formidable High Priestess. The finger still belonged to her, still held drops of her blood from when she had pushed it up inside her. Month after month, like a waterlogged stick in a stream, soaking her up.

Brys Beddict belonged to her, and she would use him well.

The death that was a non-death, for Rhulad Sengar, the insane Emperor. The murder of Hannan Mosag. And the Chancellor. And everyone else she didn't like.

And then . . . the handsome young man kneeling before her as she sat on her raised temple throne – in the new temple that would be built, sanctified to the Errant – kneeling, yes, while she spread her legs and invited him in. To kiss the place where his finger had been. To drive his tongue deep.

The future was so very bright, so very—

Feather Witch's eyes snapped open. Disbelieving.

As she felt Brys Beddict being pulled away, pulled out of her grasp. By some other force.

Pulled away!

She screamed, lurching forward on the dais, hands plunging into the floodwater – as if to reach down into the current and grasp hold of him once more – but it was deeper than she'd remembered. Unbalanced, she plunged face-first into the water. Involuntarily drew in a lungful of the cold, biting fluid.

Eyes staring into the darkness, as she thrashed about, her lungs contracting again and again, new lungfuls of water, one after another.

Deep – where was up?

A knee scraped the stone floor and she sought to bring her legs under her, but they were numb, heavy as logs – they would not work. One hand then, onto the floor, pushing upward – but not high enough to break the surface. The other hand, then, trying to guide her knees together – but one would drift out as soon as she left it seeking the other.

The darkness outside her eyes flooded in. Into her mind.

And, with blessed relief, she ceased struggling.

She would dream now. She could feel the sweet lure of that dream – almost within reach – and all the pain in her chest was gone – she could breathe this, she could. In and out, in and out, and then she no longer had to do even that. She could grow still, sinking down onto the slimy floor.

Darkness in and out, the dream drifting closer, almost within reach. Almost . . .

*

859

The Errant stood in the waist-deep water, his hand on her back. He waited, even though her struggles had ceased.

Sometimes, it was true, a nudge was not enough.

The malformed, twisted thing that was Hannan Mosag crawled up the last street before the narrow, crooked alley that led to Settle Lake. Roving bands had come upon the wretched Tiste Edur in the darkness before dawn and had given him wide berth, chased away by his laughter.

Soon, everything would return to him. All of his power, purest Kurald Emurlahn, and he would heal this mangled body, heal the scars of his mind. With the demon-god freed of the ice and bound to his will once more, who could challenge him?

Rhulad Sengar could remain Emperor – that hardly mattered, did it? The Warlock King would not be frightened of him, not any more. And, to crush him yet further, he possessed a certain note, a confession – oh, the madness unleashed then!

Then, these damned invaders – well, they were about to find themselves without a fleet.

And the river shall rise, flooding, a torrent to cleanse this accursed city. Of foreigners. Of the Letherii themselves. I will see them all drowned.

Reaching the mouth of the alley, he dragged himself into its gloom, pleased to be out of the dawn's grey light, and the stench of the pond wafted down to him. Rot, dissolution, the dying of the ice. At long last, all his ambitions were about to come true.

Crawling over the slick, mould-slimed cobblestones. He could hear thousands in the streets, somewhere near. Some name being cried out like a chant. Disgust filled Hannan Mosag. He never wanted anything to do with these Letherii. No, he would have raised an impenetrable wall between them and his people. He would have ruled over the tribes, remaining in the north, where the rain fell like mist and the forests of sacred trees embraced every village.

There would have been peace, for all the Tiste Edur.

Well, he had sent them all back north, had he not? He had begun his preparations. And soon he would join them, as Warlock King. And he would make his dream a reality.

And Rhulad Sengar? Well, I leave him a drowned empire, a wasteland of mud and dead trees and rotting corpses. Rule well, Emperor.

He found himself scrabbling against a growing stream of icy water that was working its way down the alley, the touch numbing his hands, knees and feet. He began slipping. Cursing under his breath, Hannan Mosag paused, staring down at the water flowing round him.

860

From up ahead there came a loud *crack!* and the Warlock King smiled. *My child stirs.*

Drawing upon the power of the shadows in this alley, he resumed his journey.

'Ah, the fell guardians,' Ormly said as he strode to the muddy bank of Settle Lake. The Champion Ratcatcher had come in from the north side, where he'd been busy in Creeper District, hiring random folk to cry out the name of the empire's great revolutionary, the hero of heroes, the this and that and all the rest. *Tehol Beddict! He's taken all the money back – from all the rich slobs in their estates! He's going to give it all to every one of you – he's going to clear all your debts! And are you listening? I've more rubbish to feed you – wait, come back!* True, he'd just added on that last bit.

What a busy night! And then a runner from Selush had brought him the damned sausage that a man had once used to pick his nose or something.

All right, there was some disrespect in that and it wasn't worthy, not of Brys Beddict – the Hero's very own brother! – nor of himself, Ormly of the Rats. So, enough of that, then.

'Oh, look, sweetcakes, it's him.'

'Who, dove-cookie?'

'Why, I forget his name. Tha's who.'

Ormly scowled at the pair lolling on the bank like a couple of gaping fish. 'I called you guardians? You're both drunk!'

'You'd be too,' Ursto Hoobutt said, 'if 'n you had to listen to this simperin' witch 'ere.' He wagged his head to mime his wife as he said: 'Ooh, I wanna baby! A big baby, with only one upper lip but a bottom one too to clamp onto you know where an' get even bigger! Ooh, syrup-smoochies, oh, *please? Can I? Can I? Can I!*'

'You poor man,' Ormly commiserated, walking up to them. He paused upon seeing the heaved and cracked slabs of ice crowding the centre of the lake. 'It's pushing, is it?'

'Took your time, too,' Pinosel muttered, casting her husband her third glowering look since Ormly had arrived. She swished whatever was in the jug in her left hand, then tilted it back to drink deep. Then wiped at her mouth, leaned forward and glared up at Ormly from lowered brows. 'Ain't gonna have no jus' one upper lip, neither. Gonna be healthy—'

'Really, Pinosel,' Ormly said, 'the likelihood of that—'

'You don't know nothing!'

'All right, maybe I don't. Not about the likes of two, anyway. But here's what I do know. In the Old Palace there's a panel in the baths that was painted about six hundred years ago. Of Settle Lake or something

861

a lot like it, with buildings in the background. And who's sitting there in the grasses on the bank, sharing a jug? Why, an ugly woman and an even uglier man – both looking a lot like you two!'

'Watchoo yer callin' ugly,' Pinosel said, lifting her head with an effort, taking a deep breath to compose her features, then patting at her crow's nest hair. 'Sure,' she said, 'I've had better days.'

'Ain't that the truth,' mumbled Ursto.

'An' I 'eard that! An' oose fault is that, porker-nose?'

'Only the people that ain't no more 'ere t'worship us an' all that.'

''Zactly!'

Ormly frowned at the pond and its ice. At that moment a huge slab buckled with a loud *crack!* And he found himself involuntarily stepping back, one step, two. 'Is it coming up?' he demanded.

'No,' Ursto said, squinting one-eyed at the groaning heap of ice. 'That'd be the one needing his finger back.'

The meltwater fringing the lake was bubbling and swirling now, bringing up clouds of silt as some current swept round the solid mass in the middle. Round and round, like a whirlpool only in reverse.

And all at once there was a thrashing, a spray of water, and a figure in its midst – struggling onto the bank, coughing, streaming muddy water, and holding in one incomplete hand a scabbarded sword.

Pinosel, her eyes bright as diamonds, lifted the jug in a wavering toast. 'Hail the Saviour! Hail the half-drowned dog spitting mud!' And then she crowed, the cry shifting into a cackle, before drinking deep once more.

Ormly plucked the severed finger from his purse and walked down to where knelt Brys Beddict. 'Looking for this?' he asked.

There had been a time of sleep, and then a time of pain. Neither had seemed to last very long, and now Brys Beddict, who had died of poison in the throne room of the Eternal Domicile, was on his hands and knees beside a lake of icy water. Racked with shivers, still coughing out water and slime.

And some man was crouched beside him, trying to give him a severed finger swollen and dyed pink.

He felt his left hand gripping a scabbard, and knew it for his own. Blinking to clear his eyes, he flitted a glance to confirm that the sword still resided within it. It did. Then, pushing the man's gift away, he slowly settled onto his haunches, and looked round.

Familiar, yes.

The man beside him now laid a warm hand on his shoulder, as if to still his shivering. 'Brys Beddict,' he said in a low voice. 'Tehol is about to die. Brys, *your brother needs you now.*'

And, as Brys let the man help him to his feet, he drew out his sword, half expecting to see it rusted, useless – but no, the weapon gleamed with fresh oil.

'Hold on!' shouted another voice.

The man steadying Brys turned slightly. 'What is it, Ursto?'

'The demon god's about to get free! Ask 'im!'

'Ask him what?'

'The name! Ask 'im what's its name, damn you! We can't send it away without its name!'

Brys spat grit from his mouth. Tried to think. The demon god in the ice, the ice that was failing. Moments from release, moments from . . . 'Ay'edenan of the Spring,' he said. 'Ay'edenan tek' velut !enan.'

The man beside him snorted. 'Try saying that five times fast! Errant, try saying it once!'

But someone was cackling.

'Brys—'

He nodded. *Yes. Tehol. My brother* – 'Take me,' he said. 'Take me to him.'

'I will,' the man promised. 'And on the way, I'll do some explaining. All right?'

Brys Beddict, Saviour of the Empty Throne, nodded.

'Imagine,' Pinosel said with a gusty sigh, 'a name in the old tongue. Oh now, ain't this one come a long way!'

'You stopped being drunk now, munch-sweets?'

She stirred, clambered onto her feet, then reached down and tugged at her husband. 'Come on.'

'But we got to wait – to use the name and send it away!'

'We got time. Let's perch ourselves down top of Wormface Alley, have another jug, an' we can watch the Edur crawl up t'us like the Turtle of the Abyss.'

Ursto snorted. 'Funny how that myth didn't last.'

A deeper, colder shadow slid over Hannan Mosag and he halted his efforts. Almost there, yes – where the alley opened out, he saw two figures seated in careless sprawls and leaning against one another. Passing a jug between them.

Squalid drunks, but perhaps most appropriate as witnesses – to the death of this gross empire. The first to die, too. Also fitting enough.

He made to heave himself closer, but a large hand closed about his cloak, just below his collar, and he was lifted from the ground.

Hissing, seeking his power—

Hannan Mosag was slowly turned about, and he found himself staring into an unhuman face. Grey-green skin like leather. Polished

863

tusks jutting from the corners of the mouth. Eyes with vertical pupils, regarding him now without expression.

Behind him the two drunks were laughing.

The Warlock King, dangling in the air before this giant demoness, reached for the sorcery of Kurald Emurlahn to blast this creature into oblivion. And he felt it surge within him—

But now her other hand took him by the throat.

And squeezed.

Cartilage crumpled like eggshells. Vertebrae crunched, buckled, broke against each other. Pain exploded upward, filling Hannan Mosag's skull with white fire.

As the sun's bright, unforgiving light suddenly bathed his face.

Sister Dawn – you greet me—

But he stared into the eyes of the demoness, and saw still nothing. A lizard's eyes, a snake's eyes.

Would she give him nothing at all?

The fire in his skull flared outward, blinding him, then, with a soft, fading roar, it contracted once more, darkness rushing into its wake.

But Hannan Mosag's eyes saw none of this.

The sun shone full on his dead face, highlighting every twist, every marred flare of bone, and the unseeing eyes that stared out into that light were empty.

As empty as the Jaghut's own.

Ursto and Pinosel watched the Jaghut fling the pathetic, mangled body away.

Then she faced them. 'My ritual is sundered.'

Pinosel laughed through her nose, which proved a messy outburst the cleaning of which occupied her for the next few moments.

Ursto cast her a disgusted glance, then nodded to the Jaghut sorceress. 'Oh, they all worked at doing that. Mosag, Menandore, Sukul Ankhadu, blah blah.' He waved one hand. 'But we're here, sweetness. We got its name, y'see.'

The Jaghut cocked her head. 'Then, I am not needed.'

'Well, that's true enough. Unless you care for a drink?' He tugged the jug free of Pinosel's grip, raised it.

The Jaghut stared a moment longer, then she said, 'A pleasing offer, thank you.'

The damned sun was up, but on this side the city's wall was all shadow. Except, Sergeant Balm saw, for the wide open gate.

Ahead, Masan Gilani did that unthinkable thing again and rose in her stirrups, leaning forward as she urged her horse into a gallop.

From just behind Balm, Throatslitter moaned like a puppy under a brick. Balm shook his head. Another sick thought just popping into his head like a squeezed tick. Where was he getting them from anyway? And why was that gate open and why were they all riding hard straight for it?

And was that corpses he saw just inside? Figures moving about amidst smoke? Weapons?

What was that sound from the other side of that gate?

'Sharpers!' Deadsmell called out behind him. 'Keneb's in! He's holding the gate!'

Keneb? Who in Hood's name was Keneb?

'Ride!' Balm shouted. 'They're after us! Ride for Aren!'

Masan Gilani's rising and lowering butt swept into the shadow of the gate.

Throatslitter cried out and that was the sound all right, when the cat dives under the cartwheel and things go squirt and it wasn't his fault he'd hardly kicked at all. 'It dived out there, Ma! Oh, I hate cities! Let's go home – ride! Through that hole! What's it called? The big false-arched cantilevered hole!'

Plunging into gloom, horse hoofs suddenly skidding, the entire beast slewing round beneath him. *Impact.* Hip to rump, and Balm was thrown, arms reaching out, wrapping tight round a soft yielding assembly of perfected flesh – and she yelped, pulled with him as he plunged past dragging Masan Gilani from her saddle.

Hard onto cobbles, Balm's head slamming down, denting and dislodging his helm. Her weight deliciously flattening him for a single exquisite moment before she rolled off.

Horses stumbling, hoofs cracking down way too close. Soldiers rushing in, pulling them clear.

Balm stared up into a familiar face. 'Thom Tissy, you ain't dead?'

The ugly face spread into a toad's grin – *toad under a brick oh they smile wide then don't they* – and then a calloused hand slapped him hard. 'You with us, Balm? Glad you arrived – we're getting pressed here – seems the whole damned city garrison is here, tryin' to retake the gate.'

'Garrison? What's Blistig thinking? We're on his side! Show me the famous dancing girls of Aren, Tissy, that's what I'm here to see and maybe more than see, hey?'

Thom Tissy dragged Balm onto his feet, set the dented helm back onto Balm's head, then he took him by the shoulders and turned him round.

And there was Keneb, and there, just beyond, barricades of wreckage and soldiers crouching down reloading crossbows while others hacked at Letherii soldiers trying to force a breach. Somewhere to the right a sharper detonated in an alley mouth where the enemy had been gathering for another rush. People screamed.

865

Fist Keneb stepped up to Balm. 'Where are the rest, Sergeant?'

'Sir?'

'The Adjunct and the army!'

'In the transports, sir, where else? Worst storm I've ever seen and now all the ships are upside down—'

Behind Balm Deadsmell said, 'Fist, they should be on the march.'

'Get Masan Gilani back on her horse,' Keneb said and Balm wanted to kiss the man, 'and I don't care if she kills the beast but I want her to reach the Adjunct – they need to step it up. Send their cavalry ahead riding hard.'

'Yes sir.'

'We're running low on munitions and quarrels and there's more of the Letherii gathering with every damned breath and if they find a decent commander we won't be able to hold.'

Was the Fist talking to Balm? He wasn't sure, but he wanted to turn round to watch Masan Gilani jump with her legs spread onto that horse's back, oh yes he did, but these hands on his shoulders wouldn't let him and someone was whimpering in his ear—

'Stop making that sound, Sergeant,' Keneb said.

Someone rode back out through the gate and where did they think they were going? There was a fight here! '*Boyfriends of the dancing girls*,' he whispered, reaching for his sword.

'Corporal,' Keneb said. 'Guide your sergeant here to the barricade to the left. You too, Throatslitter.'

Deadsmell said, 'He'll be fine in a moment, sir—'

'Yes, just go.'

'Aye, Fist.'

Boyfriends. Balm wanted to kill every one of them.

'This city looks like a hurricane went through it,' Cuttle said in a low mutter.

He had that right. The looting and all the rest was days old, however, and now it seemed that word of the Malazan breach was sweeping through in yet another storm – this one met with exhaustion – as the squad crouched in shadows near one end of an alley, watching the occasional furtive figure rush across the street.

They'd ambushed one unit forming up to march for the western gate. Quarrels and sharpers and a burner under the weapons wagon – still burning back there by the column of black smoke lifting into the ever-brightening sky. Took them all out, twenty-five dead or wounded, and before he and Gesler had pulled away locals were scurrying out to loot the bodies.

The captain had commandeered Urb and his squad off to find Hellian and her soldiers – the damned drunk had taken a wrong turn somewhere – which left Fiddler and Gesler to keep pushing for the palace.

Forty paces down the street to their right was a high wall with a fortified postern. City Garrison block and compound, and now that gate had opened and troops were filing out to form up ranks in the street.

'That's where we find the commander,' Cuttle said. 'The one organizing the whole thing.'

Fiddler looked directly across from where he and his marines were hiding and saw Gesler and his soldiers in a matching position in another alley mouth. *It'd be nice if we were on the roofs.* But no-one was keen to break into these official-looking buildings and maybe end up fighting frenzied clerks and night watch guards. Noise like that and there'd be real troops pushing in from behind them.

Maybe closer to the palace – tenement blocks there, and crowded together. It'd save us a lot of this ducking and crawling crap.

And what could be messy ambushes.

'Hood's breath, Fid, there's a hundred out there and still more coming.' Cuttle pointed. 'There, that's the man in charge.'

'Who's our best shot with the crossbow?' Fiddler asked.

'You.'

Shit.

'But Koryk's all right. Though, if I'd pick anyone, it'd be Corabb.'

Fiddler slowly smiled. 'Cuttle, sometimes you're a genius. Not that it'll ever earn you rank of corporal or anything like that.'

'I'll sleep easy tonight, then.' Cuttle paused, then mused, 'Forty paces and a clear shot, but we'd blow any chance of ambush.'

Fiddler shook his head. 'No, this is even better. He looses his quarrel, the man goes down. We rush out, throw five or six sharpers, then wheel and back into the alley – away as fast as we can. The survivors rush up, crowd the alley mouth, and Gesler hits 'em from behind with another five or six sharpers.'

'Beautiful, Fid. But How's Gesler gonna know—'

'He'll work it out.' Fiddler turned and gestured Corabb forward.

A freshly appointed Finadd of the Main Garrison, standing five paces from Atri-Preda Beshur, turned from reviewing his squads to see an aide's head twitch, sparks flying from his helm, and then Finadd Gart, who was beside the Atri-Preda, shrieked. He was holding up one hand, seemingly right in Beshur's face, and there was a quarrel stub jutting from that hand, and blood was gushing down Beshur's face – as the Atri-Preda staggered back, the motion pulling Gart's hand with him. For the quarrel was buried in Beshur's forehead.

The new Finadd, nineteen years of age and now the ranking officer of this full-strength unit, stared in disbelief.

Shouts, and he saw figures appearing at the mouth of an alley a ways down the street. Five, six in all, rushing forward with rocks in their hands—

Pointing, the Finadd screamed the order to counter-charge, and then he was running at the very head of his soldiers, waving his sword in the air.

Thirty paces.

Twenty.

The rocks flew out, arced towards them. He ducked one that sailed close past his right shoulder and then, suddenly deaf, eyes filled with grit, he was lying on the cobbles and there was blood everywhere. Someone stumbled into his line of sight, one of his soldiers. The woman's right arm dangled from a single thin strip of meat, and the appendage swung wildly about as the woman did a strange pirouette before promptly sitting down.

She looked across at him, and screamed.

The Finadd sought to climb to his feet, but something was wrong. His limbs weren't working, and now there was a fire in his back – someone had lit a damned fire there – why would they do that? Searing heat reaching down, through a strange numbness, and the back of his head was wet.

Struggling with all his will, he brought one hand up behind, to settle the palm on the back of his head.

And found his skull entirely gone.

Probing, trembling fingers pushed into some kind of pulped matter and all at once the burning pain in his back vanished.

He could make things work again, he realized, and pushed some more, deeper.

Whatever he then touched killed him.

As Fiddler led his squad into a seeming rout, with fifty or sixty Letherii soldiers charging after them, Gesler raised his hand, which held a burner. Aye, messy, but there were a lot of them, weren't there?

Fiddler and his marines made it into the alley, tore off down it.

A crowd of Letherii reached the mouth, others pushing up behind them.

And munitions flew, and suddenly the street was a conflagration.

Without waiting, and as a gust of fierce heat swept over them, Gesler turned and pushed Stormy to lead the retreat.

Running, running hard.

They'd find the next street and swing right, come up round the other side of the walled compound. Expecting to see Fiddler and his own soldiers waiting opposite them again. More alley mouths, and just that much closer to the palace.

'We got gold, damn you!'

'Everybody's got that,' replied the barkeep, laconic as ever.

Hellian glared at him. 'What kinda accent is that?'

'The proper kind for the trader's tongue, which makes one of us sound educated and I suppose that's something.'

'Oh, I'll show you something!' She drew out her corporal's sword, giving him a hard push on the chest to clear the weapon, then hammered the pommel down on the bartop. The weapon bounced up from her hand, the edge scoring deep across Hellian's right ear. She swore, reached up and saw her hand come away red with blood. 'Now look what you made me do!'

'And I suppose I also made you invade our empire, and this city, and—'

'Don't be an idiot, you ain't that important. It was the winged monkeys did that.'

The barkeep's thin, overlong face twisted slightly as he arched a single brow.

Hellian turned to her corporal. 'What kinda sword you using, fool? One that don't work right, that's what kind, I'd say.'

'Aye, Sergeant.

'Sorry, Sergeant.'

'Aye and sorry don't cut it with me, Corporal. Now get that sword outa my sight.'

'Did you hear it coming?' another one of her soldiers asked.

'What? What's that supposed to mean, Boatsnort?'

'Uh, my name's—'

'I just told you your name!'

'Nothing, Sergeant. I didn't mean nothing.'

The barkeep cleared his throat. 'Now, if you are done with jabbering amongst yourselves, you can kindly leave. As I said before, this tavern is dry—'

'They don't make taverns dry,' Hellian said.

'I'm sure you didn't say that quite right—'

'Corporal, you hearing all this?'

'Yes.

'Aye.'

'Good. String this fool up. By his nostrils. From that beam right there.'

'By his nostrils, Sergeant?'

'That you again, Snortface?'

Hellian smiled as the corporal used four arms to grab the barkeep and drag him across the counter. The man was suddenly nowhere near as laconic as he was a moment ago. Sputtering, clawing at the hands gripping him, he shouted, 'Wait! *Wait!*'

Everyone halted.

'In the cellar,' the man gasped.

'Give my corporal directions and proper ones,' Hellian said, so very satisfied now, except for her dribbling ear, but oh, if any of her soldiers got out of line she could pick the scab and bleed all over them and wouldn't they feel just awful about it and then do exactly what she wanted them to do, 'which is guard the door.'

'Sergeant?'

'You heard me, guard the door, so we're not disturbed.'

'Who are we on the lookout for?' Snivelnose asked. 'Ain't nobody—'

'The captain, who else? She's probably still after us, damn her.'

Memories, Icarium now understood, were not isolated things. They did not exist within high-walled compartments in a mind. Instead, they were like the branches of a tree, or perhaps a continuous mosaic on a floor that one could play light over, illuminating patches here and there. Yet, and he knew this as well, for others that patch of light was vast and bright, encompassing most of a life, and although details might be blurred, scenes made hazy and uncertain with time, it was, nevertheless, a virtual entirety. And from this was born a sense of a self.

Which he did not possess and perhaps had never possessed. And in the grip of such ignorance, he was as malleable as a child. To be used; to be, indeed, abused. And many had done so, for there was power in Icarium, far too much power.

Such exploitation was now at an end. All of Taralack Veed's exhortations were as wind in the distance, and he was not swayed. The Gral would be Icarium's last companion.

He stood in the street, all of his senses awakened to the realization that he knew this place, this modest patch of the mosaic grey with promise. And true illumination was finally at hand. The measuring of time, from this moment and for ever onward. A life begun again, with no risk of losing his sense of self.

My hands have worked here. In this city, beneath this city.

And now awaits me, to be awakened.

And when I have done that, I will begin anew. A life, a host of tesserae to lay down one by one.

He set out, then, for the door.

The door into his machine.

He walked, unmindful of those scurrying in his wake, of the figures and soldiers moving out of his path. He heard but held no curiosity for the sounds of fighting, the violence erupting in the streets to either side, the detonations as of lightning although this dawn was breaking clear and still. He passed beneath diffused shadows cast down by billowing smoke from burning buildings, wagons and barricades. He heard screams and shouts but did not seek out where they came from, even to lend succour as he would normally have done. He stepped over bodies in the street.

He walked alongside an ash-laden greasy canal for a time, then reached a bridge and crossed over into what was clearly an older part of the city. Down another street to an intersection, whereupon he swung left and continued on.

There were more people here in this quarter – with the day growing bolder and all sounds of fighting a distant roar to the west – yet even here the people seemed dazed. None of the usual conversations, the hawkers crying their wares, beasts pulling loaded carts. The drifting smoke wafted down like an omen, and the citizens wandered through it as if lost.

He drew nearer the door. Of course, it was nothing like a door in truth. More like a wound, a breach. He could feel its power stir to life, for as he sensed it so too did it sense him.

Icarium then slowed. A wound, yes. His machine was wounded. Its pieces had been twisted, shifted out of position. Ages had passed since he had built it, so he should not be surprised. Would it still work? He was no longer so sure.

This is mine. I must make it right, no matter the cost.

I will have this gift. I will have it.

He started forward once more.

The house that had once disguised this nexus of the machine had collapsed into ruin and no efforts had been made to clear the wreckage. There was a man standing before it.

After a long moment, Icarium realized that he recognized this man. He had been aboard the ships, and the name by which he had been known was Taxilian.

As Icarium walked up to him, Taxilian, his eyes strangely bright, bowed and stepped back. 'This, Icarium,' he said, 'is your day.'

My day? Yes, my first day.

Lifestealer faced the ruin.

A glow was now rising from somewhere inside, shafts slanting up between snapped timbers and beams, lancing out in spears from beneath stone and brick. The glow burgeoned, and the world beneath him seemed to tremble. But no, that was no illusion – buildings groaned, shuddered. Splintering sounds, shutters rattling as from a gust of wind.

Icarium drew a step closer, drawing a dagger.

Thunder sounded beneath him, making the cobbles bounce in puffs of dust. Somewhere, in the city, structures began to break apart, as sections and components within them stirred into life, into inexorable motion. Seeking to return to a most ancient pattern.

More thunder, as buildings burst apart.

Columns of dust corkscrewed skyward.

And still the white glow lifted, spread out in a fashion somewhere between liquid and fire, pouring, leaping, the shafts and spears twisting in the air. Engulfing the ruin, spilling out onto the street, lapping around Icarium, who drew the sharp-edged blade diagonally, deep, up one forearm; then did the same with the others – holding the weapon tight in a blood-soaked hand.

Who then raised his hands.

To measure time, one must begin. To grow futureward, one must root. *Deep into the ground with blood.*

I built this machine. This place that will forge my beginning. No longer outside the world. No longer outside time itself. Give me this, wounded or not, give me this. If K'rul can, why not me?

All that poured from his wrists flared incandescent. And Icarium walked into the white.

Taxilian was thrown back as the liquid fire exploded outward. A moment of surprise, before he was incinerated. The eruption tore into the neighbouring buildings, obliterating them. The street in front of what had once been Scale House became a maelstrom of shattered cobbles, the shards of stone racing outward to stipple walls and punch through shutters. The building opposite tilted back, every brace snapping, then collapsed inward.

Fleeing the sudden storm, Taralack Veed and Senior Assessor ran – a half-dozen strides before both were thrown from their feet.

The Cabalhii monk, lying on his back, had a momentary vision of a mass of masonry rushing down, and in that moment he burst out laughing – a sound cut short as the tons of rubble crushed him.

Taralack Veed had rolled with his tumble, narrowly avoiding that descending wall. Deafened, half blind, he used his hands to drag himself onward, tearing his nails away and lacerating his palms and fingers on the broken cobbles.

And there, through the dust, the billowing white fire, he saw his village, the huts, the horses in their roped kraal, and there, on the hill beyond, the goats huddled beneath the tree, sheltering from the terrible sun. Dogs lying in the shade, children on their knees playing with the tiny clay figurines that some travelling Malazan scholar had thought to be of great and sacred significance, but were in truth no more than toys for all children loved toys.

Why, he had had his very own collection and this was long before he killed his woman and her lover, before killing the man's brother who had proclaimed the feud and had drawn the knife.

But now, all at once, the goats were crying out, crying out in dread pain and terror – dying! The huge tree in flames, branches crashing down.

The huts were burning and bodies sprawled in the dust with faces red with ruin. And this was death, then, death in the breaking of what had always been, solid and predictable, pure and reliable. The breaking – devastation, to take it all away.

Taralack Veed screamed, bloodied hands reaching for those toys – those beautiful, so very sacred toys—

The enormous chunk of stone that slanted down took the top of Taralack Veed's head at an angle, crushing bone and brain, and, as it skidded away, it left a greasy smear of red- and grey-streaked hair.

Throughout the city, buildings erupted into clouds of dust. Stone, tile, bricks and wood sailed outward, and white fire poured forth, shafts of argent light arcing out through walls, as if nothing could exist that could impede them. A shimmering, crazed web of light, linking each piece of the machine. And the power flowed, racing in blinding pulses, and they all drew inward, to one place, to one heart.

Icarium.

The north and west outer walls detonated as sections of their foundations shifted, moved four, five paces, twisting as if vast pieces of a giant puzzle were being moved into place. Rent, sundered, parts of those walls toppled and the sound of that impact rumbled beneath every street.

In the courtyard of an inn that had, through nefarious schemes, become the property of Rautos Hivanar, a huge piece of metal, bent at right angles, now lifted straight upward to twice the height of the man standing before it. Revealing, at its base, a hinge of white fire.

And the structure then tilted, dropped forward like a smith's hammer.

Rautos Hivanar dived to escape, but not quickly enough, as the massive object slammed down onto the backs of his legs.

Pinned, as white fire licked out towards him, Rautos could feel his blood draining down from his crushed legs, turning the compound's dust into mud.

Yes, he thought, *as it began with mud, so it now ends—*

The white fire enveloped him.

And sucked out from his mind every memory he possessed.

The thing that died there a short time later was not Rautos Hivanar.

The vast web's pulsing lasted but a half-dozen heartbeats. The shifting of the pieces of the machine, with all the destruction that entailed, was even more short-lived. Yet, in that time, all who were devoured by the white fire emptied their lives into it. Every memory, from the pain of birth to the last moment of death.

The machine, alas, was indeed broken.

As the echoes of groaning stone and metal slowly faded, the web flickered, then vanished. And now, dust warred with the smoke in the air above Letheras.

A few remaining sections of stone and brick toppled, but these were but modest adjustments in the aftermath of what had gone before.

And in this time of settling, the first voices of pain, the first cries for help, lifted weakly from heaps of rubble.

The ruins of Scale House were naught but white dust, and from it nothing stirred.

The bed of a canal had cracked during the earthquake, opening a wide fissure into which water plunged, racing down veins between compacted bricks and fill. And in the shaking repercussions of falling structures, buried foundations shifted, cracked, slumped.

Barely noticed amidst all the others, then, the explosion that tore up through that canal in a spray of sludge and water was relatively minor, yet it proved singular in one detail, for as the muddy rain of the canal's water sluiced down onto the still-buckling streets, a figure clawed up from the canal, hands reaching for mooring rungs, pulling itself from the churning foam.

An old man.

Who stood, ragged tunic streaming brown water, and did not move while chaos and spears of blinding light tore through Letheras. Who remained motionless, indeed, after those terrifying events vanished and faded.

An old man.

Torn between incandescent rage and dreadful fear.

Because of who he was, the fear won out. Not for himself, of course, but for a mortal man who was, the old man knew, about to die.

And he would not reach him in time.

Well, so it would be rage after all. Vengeance against the Errant would have to wait its turn. First, vengeance against a man named Karos Invictad.

Mael, Elder God of the Seas, had work to do.

Lostara Yil and the Adjunct rode side by side at the head of the column of cavalry. Directly ahead they could see the west wall of the city. Enormous cracks were visible through the dust, and the gate before them remained open.

The horses were winded, their breaths gusting from foam-flecked nostrils.

Almost there.

'Adjunct, was that munitions?'

Tavore glanced across, then shook her head.

'Not a chance,' Masan Gilani said behind them. 'Only a handful of crackers in the whole lot. Something else did all that.'

Lostara twisted in her saddle.

Riding beside Masan Gilani was Sinn. Not riding well, either. Gilani was staying close, ready to reach out a steadying hand. The child seemed dazed, almost drunk. Lostara swung back. 'What's wrong with her?' she asked the Adjunct.

'I don't know.'

As the road's slope climbed towards the gate, they could see the river on their left. Thick with sails. The Malazan fleet and the two Thrones of War had arrived. The main army was only two or three bells behind the Adjunct's column, and Fist Blistig was pushing them hard.

They drew closer.

'That gate's not going to close ever again,' Lostara observed. 'In fact, I'm amazed it's still up.' Various carved blocks in the arch had slipped down, jamming atop the massive wooden doors, which served to bind them in place.

As they rode up, two marines emerged from the shadows. Had the look of heavies, and both were wounded. The Dal Honese one waved.

Reining in before them, the Adjunct was first to dismount, one gloved hand reaching for her sword as she approached.

'We're holding still,' the Dal Honese marine said. Then he raised a bloodied arm. 'Bastard cut my tendon – it's all rolled up under the skin – see? Hurts worse than a burr in the arse . . . sir.'

The Adjunct walked past both marines, into the shadow of the gate. Lostara gestured for the column to dismount, then set out after Tavore. As she came opposite the marines, she asked, 'What company are you?'

'Third, Captain. Fifth Squad. Sergeant Badan Gruk's squad. I'm Reliko and this oaf is Vastly Blank. We had us a fight.'

Onward, through the dusty gloom, then out into dusty, smoke-filled sunlight. Where she halted, seeing all the bodies, all the blood.

The Adjunct stood ten paces in, and Keneb was limping towards her and on his face was desperate relief.

Aye, they had them a fight all right.

Old Hunch Arbat walked into the cleared space and halted beside the slumbering figure in its centre. He kicked.

A faint groan.

He kicked again.

Ublala Pung's eyes flickered open, stared up uncomprehendingly for a long moment, then the Tarthenal sat up. 'Is it time?'

'Half the damned city's fallen down which is worse than Old Hunch predicted, isn't it? Oh yes it is, worse and more than worse. Damned gods. But that's no mind to us, Old Hunch says.' He cast a critical eye on the lad's efforts, then grudgingly nodded. 'It'll have to do. Just my luck, the last Tarthenal left in Letheras and he's carrying a sack of sun-baked hens.'

Frowning, Ublala stretched a foot over and nudged the sack. There was an answering cluck and he smiled. 'They helped me clean,' he said.

Old Hunch Arbat stared for a moment, then he lifted his gaze and studied the burial grounds. 'Smell them? Old Hunch does. Get out of this circle, Ublala Pung, unless you want to join in.'

Ublala scratched his jaw. 'I was told not to join in on things I know nothing about.'

'Oh? And who told you that?'

'A fat woman named Rucket, when she got me to swear fealty to the Rat Catchers' Guild.'

'The Rat Catchers' Guild?'

Ublala Pung shrugged. 'I guess they catch rats, but I'm not sure really.'

'Out of the circle, lad.'

Three strides by the challenger onto the sands of the arena and the earthquake had struck. Marble benches cracked, people cried out, many falling, tumbling, and the sand itself shimmered then seemed to transform, as conglomerated, gritty lumps of dried blood rose into view like garnets in a prospector's tin pan.

Samar Dev, shivering despite the sun's slanting light, held tight to one edge of a bouncing bench, eyes fixed on Karsa Orlong who stood, legs wide to keep his balance but otherwise looking unperturbed – and there, at the other end of the arena, a swaying, hulking figure emerged from a tunnel mouth. Sword sweeping a furrow in the sand.

White fire suddenly illuminated the sky, arcing across the blue-grey sky of sunrise. Flashing, pulsing, then vanishing, as trembles rippled in from the city, then faded away. Plumes of dust spiralled skyward from close by – in the direction of the Old Palace.

On the imperial stand the Chancellor – his face pale and eyes wide with alarm – was sending runners scurrying.

Samar Dev saw Finadd Varat Taun standing near Triban Gnol. Their gazes locked – and she understood. *Icarium.*

Oh, Taxilian, did you guess aright? Did you see what you longed to see?

'What is happening?'

The roar brought her round, to where stood the Emperor. Rhulad Sengar was staring up at the Chancellor. 'Tell me! What has happened?'

Triban Gnol shook his head, then raised his hands. 'An earthquake, Emperor. Pray to the Errant that it has passed.'

'Have we driven the invaders from our streets?'

'We do so even now,' the Chancellor replied.

'I will kill their commander. With my own hands I will kill their commander.'

Karsa Orlong drew his flint sword.

The act captured the Emperor's attention, and Samar Dev saw Rhulad Sengar bare his teeth in an ugly smile. 'Another giant,' he said. 'How many times shall you kill me? You, with the blood of my kin already on your hands. Twice? Three times? It will not matter. *It will not matter!*'

Karsa Orlong, bold with his claims, brazen in his arrogance, uttered but five words in reply: 'I will kill you . . . once.' And then he turned to look at Samar Dev – a moment's glance, and it was all that Rhulad Sengar gave him.

With a shriek, the Emperor of a Thousand Deaths rushed forward, his sword a whirling blur over his head.

Ten strides between them.

Five.

Three.

The gleaming arc of that cursed weapon slashed out, a decapitating swing – that rang deafeningly from Karsa's stone sword. Sprang back, chopped down, was blocked yet again.

Rhulad Sengar staggered back, still smiling his terrible smile. 'Kill me, then,' he said in a ragged rasp.

Karsa Orlong made no move.

With a scream the Emperor attacked again, seeking to drive the Toblakai back.

The ringing concussions seemed to leap from those weapons, as each savage attack was blocked, shunted aside. Rhulad pivoted, angled to one side, slashed down at Karsa's right thigh. Parried. A back-bladed swing up towards the Toblakai's shoulder. Batted away. Stumbling off balance from that block, the Emperor was suddenly vulnerable. A hack downward would take him, a thrust would pierce him – a damned fool could have cut Rhulad down at that moment.

Yet Karsa did nothing. Nor had he moved, beyond turning in place to keep the Emperor in front of him.

Rhulad stumbled clear, then spun round, righting his sword. Chest heaving beneath the patchwork of embedded coins, eyes wild as a boar's. '*Kill me then!*'

Karsa remained where he was. Not taunting, not even smiling.

Samar Dev stared down on the scene, transfixed. *I do not know him. I have never known him.*

Gods, we should have had sex – then I'd know!

Another whirling attack, again the shrieking reverberation of iron and flint, a flurry of sparks cascading down. And Rhulad staggered back once more.

The Emperor was now streaming with sweat.

Karsa Orlong did not even seem out of breath.

Inviting a fatal response, Rhulad Sengar dropped down onto one knee to regain his wind.

Invitation not accepted.

After a time, in which the score or fewer onlookers stared on, silent and confused; in which Chancellor Triban Gnol stood, hands clasped, like a crow nailed to a branch, the Emperor straightened, lifted his sword once more, and resumed his fruitless flailing – oh, there was skill, yes, extraordinary skill, yet Karsa Orlong stood his ground, and not once did that blade touch him.

Overhead, the sun climbed higher.

Karos Invitad, his shimmering red silks stained and smudged with grit and dust, dragged Tehol Beddict's body across the threshold. Back into his office. From down the corridor, someone was screaming about an army in the city, ships crowding the harbour, but none of that mattered now.

Nothing mattered but this unconscious man at his feet. Beaten until he barely clung to life. By the Invigilator's sceptre, his symbol of power, and was that not right? Oh, but it was.

Was the mob still there? Were they coming in now? An entire wall of the compound had collapsed, after all, nothing and no-one left to stop them. Motion caught his eye and his head snapped round – just another rat in the corridor, slithering past. *The Guild.* What kind of game were those fools playing? He'd killed dozens of the damned things, so easily crushed under heel or with a savage downward swing of his sceptre.

Rats. They were nothing. No different from the mob outside, all those precious citizens who understood nothing about anything, who needed leaders like Karos Invictad to guide them through the world. He adjusted his grip on the sceptre, flakes of blood falling away, his palm seemingly glued to the ornate shaft, but that glue had not set and wouldn't for a while, would it? Not until he was truly done.

Where was that damned mob? He wanted them to see – this final skull-shattering blow – their great hero, their revolutionary.

Martyrs could be dealt with. A campaign of misinformation, rumours of vulgarity, corruption, oh, all that was simple enough.

I stood alone, yes, did I not? Against the madness of this day. They will remember that. More than anything else. They will remember that, and everything else I choose to give them.

Slaying the Empire's greatest traitor – with my own hand, yes.

He stared down at Tehol Beddict. The battered, split-open face, the shallow breaths that trembled from beneath snapped ribs. He could put a foot down on the man's chest, settle some weight, until those broken ribs punctured the lungs, left them lacerated, and the red foam would spill out from Tehol's mashed nose, his torn lips. And, surprise. He would drown after all.

Another rat in the corridor? He turned.

The sword-point slashed across his stomach. Fluids gushed, organs following. Squealing, Karos Invictad fell to his knees, stared up at the man standing before him, stared up at the crimson-bladed sword in the man's hand.

'No,' he said in a mumble, 'but you are dead.'

Brys Beddict's calm brown eyes shifted from the Invigilator's face, noted the sceptre still held in Karos's right hand. His sword seemed to writhe.

Burning pain in the Invigilator's wrist and he looked down. Sceptre was gone. Hand was gone. Blood streamed from the stump.

A kick to the chest sent Karos Invictad toppling, trailing entrails that flopped down like an obscene, malformed penis between his legs.

He reached down with his one hand to pull it all back in, but there was no strength left.

Did I kill Tehol? Yes, I must have. The Invigilator is a true servant of the empire, and always will be, and there will be statues in courtyards and city squares. Karos Invictad, the hero who destroyed the rebellion.

Karos Invictad died then, with a smile on his face.

Brys Beddict sheathed his sword, knelt beside his brother, lifted his head into his lap.

Behind him, Ormly said, 'A healer's on the way.'

'No need,' Brys said. And looked up. 'An Elder God comes.'

Ormly licked his lips. 'Saviour—'

A cough from Tehol.

Brys looked down to see his brother's eyes flick open. One brown, one blue. Those odd eyes stared up at him for a long moment, then Tehol whispered something.

Brys bent lower. 'What?'

'I said, does this mean I'm dead?'

'No, Tehol. Nor am I, not any longer, it seems.'

'Ah. Then . . .'

'Then what?'

'Death – what's it like, Brys?'

And Brys Beddict smiled. 'Wet.'

'I always said cities were dangerous places,' Quick Ben said, brushing plaster dust from his clothes. The collapsing building had nearly flattened them both, and the wizard was still trembling – not from the close call, but from the horrendous sorcery that had lit the morning sky – a devouring, profoundly hungry sorcery. Had that energy reached for him, he was not sure he could have withstood it.

'What in Hood's name was that?' Hedge demanded.

'All I know, it was *old*. And vicious.'

'We gonna get any more, you think?'

Quick Ben shrugged. 'I hope not.'

They went on, through streets filled with rubble, and on all sides the cries of the wounded, figures staggering in shock, dust and smoke lifting into the sunlight.

Then Hedge held up a hand. 'Listen.'

Quick Ben did as he was bid.

And, from somewhere ahead – closer to the Eternal Domicile – the echo of 'Sharpers!'

'Aye, Quick, aye. Come on, let's go find 'em!'

'Wait – hold it, sapper – what are—'

'It's the Fourteenth, you thick-skulled halfwit!'

They began hurrying.

'Next time I see Cotillion,' Quick Ben hissed, 'I'm going to strangle him with his own rope.'

Six leagues to the north, a bone-white dragon with eyes of lurid red sailed through the morning sky. Wings creaking, muscles bunching, the wind hissing against scales and along bared fangs that were the length of shortswords.

Returning, after all this time, to the city of Letheras.

Hannan Mosag had been warned. The Crippled God had been warned. And yet neither had heeded Silchas Ruin. No, instead, they had conspired with Sukul Ankhadu and Sheltatha Lore, and possibly with Menandore herself. To get in his way, to oppose him and what he had needed to do.

More than this, the Letherii Empire had been hunting them for an inordinate amount of time, and out of forbearance Silchas Ruin had ignored the affront. For the sake of the Acquitor and the others.

Now, he was no longer ignoring anything.

An empire, a city, a people, a Tiste Edur Ceda and a mad Emperor.

The brother of Anomander and Andarist, for ever deemed the coldest of the three, the cruellest, Silchas Ruin flew, a white leviathan with murder in its heart.

White as bone, with eyes red as death.

Rhulad Sengar stumbled away, dragging his sword. Sweat streamed from him, his hair hanging ragged and dripping. He had struck again and again, not once piercing the defensive net of his challenger's stone sword. Six paces between them now, chewed-up sand soaked and clumped with nothing but spatters from the glistening oil that made the coins gleam.

Silent as all the other witnesses, Samar Dev watched on, wondering how all this would end, wondering how it *could* end. As long as Karsa refused to counter-attack . . .

And then the Toblakai raised his sword and walked forward.

Straight for the Emperor.

As easy as that, then.

Who rose with a sudden smile and lifted his weapon into a guard position.

The flint sword lashed out, an awkward cut, yet swung with such strength that Rhulad's block with his own weapon knocked one of his hands loose from the grip, and the iron blade flailed outward, and then, all at once, that cursed sword seemed to acquire a will of its own, the point thrusting into a lunge that dragged the Emperor forward with a scream.

And the blade sank into Karsa's left thigh, through skin, muscle, narrowly missing the bone, then punching out the back side. The Toblakai pivoted round, even as with appalling fluidity he brought his sword in a downward cut that sliced entirely through Rhulad's shoulder above the sword-arm.

As the arm, its hand still gripping the weapon now bound – trapped in Karsa's leg – parted from Rhulad's body, the Toblakai back-swung the flat of his blade into Rhulad's face, sending him sprawling onto the sand.

And Samar Dev found that she held the knife, the blade bared, and as Karsa turned to face her, she was already slicing deep across her palm, hissing the ancient words of release—letting loose the imprisoned spirits, the desert godlings and all those who were bound to the old knife—

Spirits and ghosts of the slain poured forth, freed by the power in her blood, streaming down over the rows of benches, down onto the floor of the arena.

To the terrible sounds of Rhulad Sengar's shrieking, those spirits rushed straight for Karsa, swept round, engulfed him – swirling chaos – a blinding moment as of fires unleashed—

—and Karsa Orlong, the Emperor's sword and the arm still holding it, vanished.

Lying alone on the sands of the arena, Rhulad Sengar spilled crimson from the stump of his shoulder.

And no-one moved.

881

To dwell within an iron blade had proved, for the ghost of Ceda Kuru Qan, a most interesting experience. After an immeasurable time of exploration, sensing all the other entities trapped within, he had worked out a means of escaping whenever he wished. But curiosity had held him, a growing suspicion that all dwelt in this dark place for some hidden purpose. *And they were waiting.*

Anticipation, even eagerness. And, indeed, far more bloodlust than Kuru Qan could abide.

He had considered a campaign of domination, of defeating all the other spirits, and binding them to his will. But a leader, he well understood, could not be ignorant, and to compel the revelation of the secret was ever a chancy proposition.

Instead, he had waited, patient as was his nature whether living or dead.

Sudden shock, then, upon the gushing taste of blood in his mouth, and the frenzied ecstasy that taste unleashed within him. Sour recognition – most humbling – in discovering such bestial weakness within him – and when the summoning arrived in the language of the First Empire, Kuru Qan found himself rising like a demon to roar his domination over all others, then lunging forth from the iron blade, into the world once again, leading a dread host—

To the one standing. Thelomen Tartheno Toblakai.

And the sword impaling his leg.

Kuru Qan understood, then, what needed to be done. Understood the path that must be forged, and understood, alas, the sacrifice that must be made.

They closed round the Toblakai warrior. They reached for that cursed sword and grasped hold of its blade. They drew with ferocious necessity on the blood streaming down the Toblakai's leg, causing him to stagger, and, with Kuru Qan in the forefront, the spirits tore open a gate.

A portal.

Chaos roared in on all sides, seeking to annihilate them, and the spirits began surrendering their ghostly lives, sacrificing themselves to the rapacious hunger assailing them. Yet, even as they did so, they pushed the Toblakai forward, forging the path, demanding the journey.

Other spirits awakened, from all around the warrior – the Toblakai's own slain, and they were legion.

Death roared. The pressure of the chaos stabbed, ripped spirits to pieces – even with all their numbers, the power of their will, they were slowing, they could not get through – Kuru Qan screamed – to draw more of the Toblakai's power would kill him. They had failed.

Failed—

*

882

In a cleared circle in an old Tarthenal burial ground, a decrepit shaman seated cross-legged in its centre stirred awake, eyes blinking open. He glanced up to see Ublala Pung standing just beyond the edge.

'Now, lad,' he said.

Weeping, the young Tarthenal rushed forward, a knife in his hands – one of Arbat's own, the iron black with age, the glyphs on the blade so worn down as to be almost invisible.

Arbat nodded as Ublala Pung reached him and drove the weapon deep into the shaman's chest. Not on the heart side – Old Hunch needed to take a while to die, to bleed out his power, to feed the multitude of ghosts now rising from the burial grounds.

'Get away from here!' Arbat shouted, even as he fell onto his side, blood frothing at his mouth. '*Get out!*'

Loosing a childlike bawl, Ublala Pung ran.

The ghosts gathered, pure-blooded and mixed-bloods, spanning centuries upon centuries and awake after so long.

And Old Hunch Arbat showed them their new god. And then showed them, with the power of his blood, the way through.

Kuru Qan felt himself lifted on a tide, shoved forward as if by an enormous wave, and all at once there were spirits, an army of them.

Thelomen Tartheno Toblakai.

Tarthenal—

Surging forward, the chaos thrust back, recoiling, then attacking once more.

Hundreds vanishing.

Thousands voicing wailing cries of agony.

Kuru Qan found himself close to the Toblakai warrior, directly in front of the flailing figure, and he reached back, as if to grab the Toblakai's throat. Closed his hand, and *pulled*.

Water, a crashing surf, coral sand shifting wild underfoot. Blinding heat from a raging sun.

Staggering, onto the shore – and yes, this was as far as Kuru Qan could go.

Upon the shore.

He released the warrior, saw him stumble onto the island's beach, dragging that sword-impaled leg—

Behind the old Ceda, the sea reached out, snatched Kuru Qan back with a rolling, tumbling inhalation.

Water everywhere, swirling, pulling him ever deeper, ever darker.

They were done.

We are done.

And the sea, my friends, does not dream of you.

*

On the arena floor, Emperor Rhulad Sengar lay dead. Bled out, his flesh where visible pale as river clay, and as cold. Sand dusted the sweaty coins and all the blood that had poured from him was turning black.

And the onlookers waited.

For the Emperor of a Thousand Deaths to rise again.

The sun rose higher, the sounds of fighting in the city drew closer.

And, had anyone been looking, they would have seen a speck above the horizon to the north. Growing ever larger.

One street away from the Eternal Domicile, Fiddler led his squad onto the rooftop of some gutted public building. Flecks of ash swirled in the hot morning air and all the city that they could see was veiled behind dust and smoke.

They'd lost Gesler and his squad, ever since the garrison ambush, but Fiddler was not overly concerned. All opposition was a shambles. He ran in a crouch to the edge facing the Eternal Domicile, looked across, and then down to the street below.

There was a gate, closed, but no guards in sight. *Damned strange. Where is everyone?*

He returned to where his soldiers waited, catching their breaths in the centre of the flat rooftop. 'All right,' he said, setting down his crossbow and opening his satchel, 'there's a gate that I can take out with a cusser from here. Then down we go and straight across and straight in, fast and mean. Kill everyone in sight, understood?' He drew out his cusser quarrel and carefully loaded the crossbow. Then resumed his instructions. 'Tarr takes up the rear crossing the street. Bottle, keep everything you got right at hand—'

'Sergeant—'

'Not now, Corabb. Listen! We're heading for the throne room. I want Cuttle out front—'

'Sergeant—'

'—with sharpers in hand. Koryk, you're next—'

'Sergeant—'

'*What in Hood's name is it, Corabb?*'

The man was pointing. Northward.

Fiddler and the others all turned.

To see an enormous white dragon bearing down on them.

An infrequent scattering of cut-down Letherii soldiers and small fires left behind by munitions had provided enough of a trail for Quick Ben and Hedge, and they were now crouched at the foot of a door to a burnt-out building.

'Listen,' Hedge was insisting, 'the roof here's right opposite the gate. I know Fid and I'm telling you, he's on that Hood-damned roof!'

'Fine, fine, lead on, sapper.' Quick Ben shook his head. *Something . . . I don't know . . .*

They plunged inside. The stench of smoke was acrid, biting. Charred wreckage lay all about, the detritus of a ruined empire.

'There,' Hedge said, then headed on into a corridor, down to a set of stairs leading upward.

Something . . . oh, gods!

'*Move it!*' Quick Ben snarled, shoving the sapper forward.

'What—'

'Hurry!'

The huge dragon angled down, straight for them.

Fiddler stared for a moment longer, seeing the beast opening its mouth, knowing what was coming, then he raised his crossbow and fired.

The bolt shot upward.

A hind limb of the dragon snapped out to bat the quarrel aside.

And the cusser detonated.

The explosion flattened the marines on the rooftop, sent Fiddler tumbling backward.

The roof itself sagged beneath them with grinding, crunching sounds.

Fiddler caught a glimpse of the dragon, streaming blood, its chest torn open, sliding off to one side, heading towards the street below, shredded wings flailing like sails in a storm.

A second bolt flew out to intercept it.

Another explosion, sending the dragon lurching back, down, into a building, which suddenly folded inward on that side, then collapsed with a deafening roar.

Fiddler twisted round—

—and saw Hedge.

—and Quick Ben, who was running towards the roof's edge, his hands raised and sorcery building round him as if he was the prow of a ship cutting through water.

Fiddler leapt to his feet and followed the wizard.

From the wreckage of the building beside the Eternal Domicile, the dragon was pulling itself free. Lacerated, bones jutting and blood leaking from terrible wounds. And then, impossibly, it rose skyward once more, rent wings flapping – but Fiddler knew that it was sorcery that was lifting the creature back into the air.

As it cleared the collapsed building, Quick Ben unleashed his magic. A wave of crackling fire crashed into the dragon, sent it reeling back.

Another.

And then another – the dragon was now two streets away, writhing under the burgeoning assault.

885

Then, with a piercing cry, it wheeled, climbed higher, and flew away, in full retreat.

Quick Ben lowered his arms, then fell to his knees.

Staring after the fast-diminishing dragon, Fiddler leaned his crossbow onto his shoulder.

'This ain't your fight,' he said to the distant creature. '*Fucking dragon.*'

Then he turned and stared at Hedge.

Who, grinning, stared back.

'No ghost?'

'No ghost. Aye, Fid, *I'm back.*'

Fiddler scowled, then shook his head. 'Hood help us all.' Then he turned to Quick Ben. 'And where in the Abyss have *you* been?'

Picking himself up from the buckled rooftop, Bottle stared across at those three soldiers. Didn't know one of them except that he was a sapper. And a damned Bridgeburner.

Beside him, Koryk groaned, then spat. 'Look at 'em,' he said.

Bottle nodded.

And, oddly enough, for all the soldiers in the squad, nothing more about it needed saying.

Bottle squinted at the fast-dwindling dragon. *Allow us to introduce ourselves . . .*

Trull Sengar gently lifted Seren's arms and stepped back from her embrace. She almost sagged forward, not wanting the moment to end, and something cold formed a fist in her stomach. Wincing, she turned away.

'Seren—'

She waved a hand, then met his eyes once more.

'My brother. My parents.'

'Yes,' she said.

'I cannot pretend that they are not there. That they mean nothing to me.'

She nodded, not trusting herself to speak.

He crossed the dusty room, kicking through rubbish – the place had been stripped of virtually everything, no matter how worthless. They had lain together on their cloaks, watched by spiders in the corners near the ceiling and bats slung in a row beneath a window sill. He picked up the Imass spear from where it leaned against a wall and faced her, offering a faint smile. 'I can protect myself. And alone, I can move quickly—'

'Go, then,' she said, and felt anguish at the sudden hardness in her voice.

His half-smile held a moment longer, then he nodded and walked into the corridor that led to the front door.

After a moment Seren Pedac followed. 'Trull—'

He paused at the doorway. 'I understand, Seren. It's all right.'

No it's not all right! 'Please,' she said, 'come back.'

'I will. I can do nothing else. You have all there is of me, all that's left.'

'Then I have all I need,' she replied.

He reached out, one hand brushing her cheek.

And then was gone.

Emerging from the pathway crossing the yard, Trull Sengar, the butt of the spear ringing like the heel of a staff on the cobbles, walked out into the street.

And set off in the direction of the Eternal Domicile.

From the shadows of an alley opposite, the Errant watched him.

'I feel much better.'

Brys Beddict smiled across at his brother. 'You look it. So, Tehol, your manservant is an Elder God.'

'I'll take anybody I can find.'

'Why are your eyes two different colours now?'

'I'm not sure, but I think Bugg may be colour blind. Blue and green, green and blue, and as for brown, forget it.'

Said manservant who happened to be an Elder God walked into the room. 'I found her.'

Tehol was on his feet. 'Where? Is she alive?'

'Yes, but we've work to do . . . again.'

'We need to find that man, that Tanal—'

'No need for that,' Bugg replied, eyes settling on the corpse of Karos Invictad.

Brys did the same. A two-headed insect was slowly making its way towards the spilled entrails. 'What in the Errant's name is that?'

And Bugg hissed through his teeth. 'Yes,' he said, 'he's next.'

Outside, in the compound, in the street beyond, a mass of citizens were gathering. Their sound was like an advancing tide. There had been some thunderous explosions, and the unmistakable roar of sorcery, from the direction of the Eternal Domicile, but that had all been short-lived.

Tehol faced Bugg, 'Listen to that mob. We going to be able to leave here alive? I'm really not in the mood for a Drowning. Especially my own.'

Brys grunted. 'You've not been paying attention, brother. You're a hero. They want to see you.'

'I am? Why, I never imagined that they had it in them.'

'They didn't,' Bugg replied, with a sour expression. 'Ormly and Rucket have spent a fortune on criers.'

Brys smiled. 'Humbled, Tehol?'

'Never. Bugg, take me to Janath. Please.'

At that, Brys Beddict's brows rose. *Ah, it is that way, then.*

Well.

Good.

A surviving officer of the city garrison formally surrendered to the Adjunct just inside the west gate, and now Tavore led her occupying army into Letheras.

Leaving Fist Blistig in charge of the main force, she assembled the five hundred or so surviving marines, along with Fist Keneb, and her own troop of mounted cavalry, and set out for the imperial palace. This ill-named 'Eternal Domicile'.

Sinn, riding behind Lostara Yil, had cried out when the dragon had appeared over the city; then had laughed and clapped her hands when at least two cussers and then wave after wave of ferocious sorcery routed the creature.

Captain Faradan Sort's advance squads were still active – that much had been made abundantly clear. And they were at the palace, or at least very close. *And they were in a mood.*

Most commanders would have raged at this – uncontrolled soldiers raising mayhem somewhere ahead, a handful of grubby marines who'd lived in the wilds for too long now battering at the palace door, frenzied with bloodlust and eager to deliver vengeance. Was this how she wanted to announce her conquest? Would the damned fools leave anything still breathing in that palace?

And what of this un-killable Emperor? Lostara Yil did not believe such a thing was even possible. *A cusser in the bastard's crotch there on that throne and he'll be giving to the people for days and days.* She wouldn't put it past Fiddler, either. One step into the throne room, the *thwock* of that oversized crossbow, and then the sergeant diving back, trying to get clear as the entire room erupted. He'd probably happily kill himself for that pleasure.

Yet, while without doubt the Adjunct shared such visions, Tavore said nothing. Nor did she urge her troops to any haste – not that any of them were in shape for that, especially the marines. Instead, they advanced at a measured pace, and citizens began appearing from the side lanes, alleys and avenues, to watch them march past. Some even cried out a welcome, with voices breaking with relief.

The city was a mess. Riots and earthquakes and Moranth munitions. Lostara Yil began to realize that, if the arrival of the Bonehunters signified anything, it was the promise of a return to order, a new settling of civilization, of laws and, ironically, of peace.

But Adjunct, if we tarry here too long, that will turn. It always does. Nobody likes being under an occupier's heel. Simple human nature, to take one's own despair and give it a foreigner's face, then let loose the hounds of blood.

See these citizens? These bright, gladdened faces? Any one of them, before long, could turn. The reapers of violence can hide behind the calmest eyes, the gentlest of smiles.

The column's pace was slowing, with ever more crowds before them. Chants were rising and falling here and there. Letherii words, the tone somewhere between hope and insistence.

'Adjunct, what is it they're all saying?'

'A name,' she replied. 'Well, two names, I think. One they call the Saviour. The other . . .'

'The other . . . what, sir?'

She cast Lostara a quick glance, then her mouth set, before she said, '*Emperor.*'

Emperor? 'But I thought—'

'A *new* Emperor, Captain. By proclamation, it would seem.'

Oh, and have we nothing to say on this?

Directly ahead was a wall of citizens, blocking all hopes of passage, through which a small group was moving, pushing its way to the forefront.

The Adjunct raised a gloved hand to signal a halt.

The group emerged, an enormously fat woman in the lead, followed by a gnarled little man who seemed to be carrying rats in the pockets of his cloak, and then two men who looked like brothers. Both lean, one in the uniform of an officer, the other wearing a tattered, blood-stained blanket.

Tavore dismounted, gesturing for Lostara to do the same.

The two women approached the group. As they drew closer, the fat woman stepped to one side and with a surprisingly elegant wave of one plump hand she said, 'Commander, I present to you Brys Beddict, once Champion to King Ezgara Diskanar – before the Edur conquest – now proclaimed the Saviour. And his brother, Tehol Beddict, financial genius, liberator of the oppressed and not half bad in bed, even now being proclaimed the new Emperor of Lether by his loving subjects.'

The Adjunct seemed at a loss for a reply.

Lostara stared at this Tehol Beddict – although, truth be told, she'd rather let her eyes linger on Brys – and frowned at the disgusting blanket wrapped about him. *Financial genius?*

Brys Beddict now stepped forward and, as had the huge woman, spoke in the trader's tongue. 'We would escort you to the Eternal

Domicile, Commander, where we will, I believe, find an emperor without an empire, who will need to be ousted.' He hesitated, then added, 'I assume you come as liberators, Commander. And, accordingly, have no wish to over-stay your welcome.'

'By that,' the Adjunct said, 'you mean to imply that I have insufficient forces to impose a viable occupation. Were you aware, Brys Beddict, that your eastern borderlands have been overrun? And that an army of allies now marches into your empire?'

'Do you come as conquerors, then?' Brys Beddict asked.

The Adjunct sighed, then unstrapped and pulled off her helm. She drew her hand from its glove and ran it through her short, sweat-damp hair. 'Hood forbid,' she muttered. 'Find us a way through these people, then, Brys Beddict.' She paused, cast her gaze to Tehol Beddict, and slowly frowned. 'You are rather shy for an emperor,' she observed.

Tehol refuted that with the brightest smile, and it transformed him, and suddenly Lostara forgot all about the man's martial-looking brother.

Spirits of the sand, those eyes . . .

'I do apologize, Commander. I admit I have been somewhat taken aback.'

The Adjunct slowly nodded. 'By this popular acclaim, yes, I imagine—'

'No, not that. She said I was not half bad in bed. I am crushed by the other half, the "half good" bit—'

'Oh, Tehol,' the fat woman said, 'I was being modest for your sake.'

'Modesty from you, Rucket? You don't know the meaning of the word! I mean, I just look at you and it's hard not to, if you know what I mean.'

'No.'

'Anyway!' Tehol clapped his hands together. 'We've had the fireworks, now let's get this parade started!'

Sirryn Kanar ran down the corridor, away from the fighting. The damned foreigners were in the Eternal Domicile, delivering slaughter – no calls for surrender, no demands to throw down weapons. Just those deadly quarrels, those chopping shortswords and those devastating grenados. His fellow guards were dying by the score, their blood splashing the once pristine walls.

And Sirryn vowed he was not going to suffer the same fate.

They wouldn't kill the Chancellor. They needed him, and besides, he was an old man. Obviously unarmed, a peaceful man. Civilized. And the guard they'd find standing at his side, well, even he carried naught but a knife at his belt. No sword, no shield, no helm or even armour.

I can stay alive there, right at the Chancellor's side.

But where is he?

The throne room had been empty.

The Emperor is in the arena. The mad fool is still fighting his pointless, pathetic fights. And the Chancellor would be there, attending, ironic witness to the last Tiste Edur's drooling stupidity. *The last Tiste Edur in the city. Yes.*

He hurried on, leaving the sounds of fighting well behind him.

A day of madness – would it never end?

Chancellor Triban Gnol stepped back. The realization had come suddenly to him, with the force of a hammer blow. *Rhulad Sengar will not return. The Emperor of a Thousand Deaths . . . has died his last death.*

Toblakai. Karsa Orlong, I do not know what you have done, I do not know how – but you have cleared the path.

You have cleared it and for that I bless you.

He looked about, and saw that the meagre audience had fled – yes, the Eternal Domicile was breached, the enemy was within. He turned to the Finadd standing nearby. 'Varat Taun.'

'Sir?'

'We are done here. Gather your soldiers and escort me to the throne room, where we will await the conquerors.'

'Yes sir.'

'And we bring that witch with us – I would know what has happened here. I would know why she laid open her hand with that knife. I would know *everything*.'

'Yes, Chancellor.'

The captain was surprisingly gentle taking the pale woman into his custody, and indeed, he seemed to whisper something to her that elicited a weary nod. Triban Gnol's eyes narrowed. No, he did not trust this new Finadd. Would that he had Sirryn with him.

As they made their way from the arena, the Chancellor paused for one look back, one last look at the pathetic figure lying on the bloody sand. *Dead. He is truly dead.*

I believe I always knew Karsa Orlong would be the one. Yes, I believe I did.

He was almost tempted to head back, down onto the arena floor, to walk across the pitch and stand over the body of Rhulad Sengar. And spit into the Emperor's face.

No time. Such pleasure will have to wait.

But I vow I will do it yet.

Cuttle waved them to the intersection. Fiddler led the rest of his squad to join the sapper.

'This is the main approach,' Cuttle said. 'It's got to be.'

Fiddler nodded. The corridor was ornately decorated, impressively wide, with an arched ceiling gleaming with gold leaf. There was no-one about. 'So where are the guards, and in which direction is the throne room?'

'No idea,' Cuttle replied. 'But I'd guess we go left.'

'Why?'

'No reason, except everyone who tried to get away from us was more or less heading that way.'

'Good point, unless they were all headed out the back door.' Fiddler wiped sweat from his eyes. Oh, this had been a nasty bloodletting, but he'd let his soldiers go, despite the disapproving looks from Quick Ben. Damned High Mage and his nose in the air – and where in Hood's name did all that magic come from? Quick had never showed anything like that before. Not even close.

He looked across at Hedge.

Same old Hedge. No older than the last time Fiddler had seen him. *Gods, it doesn't feel real. He's back. Living, breathing, farting . . .* He reached out and cuffed the man in the side of the head.

'Hey, what's that for?'

'No reason, but I'm sure I was owed doing that at least once.'

'Who saved your skin in the desert? And under the city?'

'Some ghost up to no good,' Fiddler replied.

'Hood, that white beard makes you look ancient, Fid, you know that?'

Oh, be quiet.

'Crossbows loaded, everyone? Good. Lead on, Cuttle, but slow and careful, right?'

They were five paces into the corridor when a side entrance ahead and to their right was suddenly filled with figures. And mayhem was let loose once more.

Tarr saw the old man first, the one in the lead, or even if he didn't see him first, he got off his shot before anyone else. And the quarrel sank into the side of the man's head, dead in the centre of his left temple. And everything sprayed out the other side.

Other quarrels caught him, at least two, spinning his scrawny but nice-robed body round before it toppled.

A handful of guards who had been accompanying the old man reeled back, at least two stuck good, and Tarr was already rushing forward, drawing his shortsword and bringing his shield round. He bumped hard against Corabb who was doing the same and swore as the man got in front of him.

Tarr raised his sword, a sudden, overwhelming urge to hammer the blade down on the bastard's head – but no, save that for the enemy—

Who were throwing down their weapons as they backed down the corridor.

'For Hood's sake!' Quick Ben shouted, dragging at Tarr to get past, then shoving Corabb to one side. 'They're surrendering, damn you! Stop slaughtering everyone!'

And from the Letherii group, a woman's voice called out in Malazan, 'We surrender! Don't kill us!'

That voice was enough to draw everyone up.

Tarr swung round, as did the others, to look at Fiddler.

After a moment, the sergeant nodded. 'Take 'em prisoner, then. They can lead us to the damned throne room.'

Smiles ran up to the body of the old man and started pulling at all his gaudy rings.

A Letherii officer stepped forward, hands raised. 'There's no-one in the Throne Room,' he said. 'The Emperor is dead – his body's in the arena—'

'Take us there, then,' Quick Ben demanded, with a glare at Fiddler. 'I want to see for myself.'

The officer nodded. 'We just came from there, but very well.'

Fiddler waved his squad forward, then scowled over at Smiles. 'Do that later, soldier—'

She bared her teeth like a dog over a kill, then drew out a large knife and, with two savage chops, took the old man's pretty hands.

Trull Sengar stepped out onto the sand of the arena, eyes fixed on the body lying near the far end. The gleam of coins, the head tilted back. He slowly walked forward.

There was chaos in the corridors and chambers of the Eternal Palace. He could search for his parents later, but he suspected he would not find them. They had gone with the rest of the Tiste Edur. Back north. Back to their homeland. And so, in the end, they too had abandoned Rhulad, their youngest son.

Why does he lie unmoving? Why has he not returned?

He came to Rhulad's side and fell to his knees. Set down his spear. A missing arm, a missing sword.

He reached out and lifted his brother's head. Heavy, the face so scarred, so twisted with pain that it was hardly recognizable. He settled it into his lap.

Twice now, I am made to do this. With a brother whose face, there below me, rests too still. Too emptied of life. They look so . . . wrong.

He would have tried, one last time, a final offering of reason to his young brother, an appeal to all that he had once been. Before all this.

Before, in foolish but understandable zeal, he had grasped hold of a sword on a field of ice.

Rhulad would then, in another moment of weakness, pronounce Trull *Shorn*. Dead in the eyes of all Tiste Edur. And chain him to stone to await a slow, wasting death. Or the rise of water.

Trull had come, yes, to forgive him. It was the cry in his heart, a cry he had lived with for what seemed for ever. *You were wounded, brother. So wounded. He had cut you down, laid you low but not dead. He had done what he needed to do, to end your nightmare. But you did not see it that way. You could not.*

Instead, you saw your brothers abandon you.

So now, my brother, as I forgive you, will you now forgive me?

Of course, there would no answer. Not from that ever still, ever empty face. Trull was too late. Too late to forgive and too late to be forgiven.

He wondered if Seren had known, had perhaps guessed what he would find here.

The thought of her made his breath catch in his throat. Oh, he had not known such love could exist. And now, even in the ashes surrounding him here, the future was unfolding like a flower, its scent sweet beyond belief.

This is what love means. I finally see—

The knife thrust went in under his left shoulder blade, tore through into his heart.

Eyes wide in sudden pain, sudden astonishment, Trull felt Rhulad's head tilt to one side on his lap, then slide down from hands that had lost all strength.

Oh, Seren, my love.

Oh, forgive me.

Teeth bared, Sirryn Kanar stepped back, tugging his weapon free. One last Tiste Edur. Now dead, by his own hand. Pure justice still existed in this world. He had cleansed the Lether Empire with this knife, and look, see the thick blood dripping down, welling round the hilt.

A thrust to the heart, the conclusion of his silent stalk across the sands, his breath held overlong for the last three steps. And his blessed shadow, directly beneath his feet – no risk of its advancing ahead to warn the bastard. There was that one moment when a shadow had flitted across the sand – a damned owl, of all things – but the fool had not noticed.

No indeed: the sun stood at its highest point.

And every shadow huddled, trembling beneath that fierce ruler in the sky.

He could taste iron in his mouth, a gift so bitter he exulted in its cold bite. Stepping back, as the body fell to one side, fell right over that pathetic savage's spear.

The barbarian dies. As he must, for mine is the hand of civilization.

He heard a commotion at the far end and spun round.

The quarrel pounded into his left shoulder, flung him back, where he tripped over the two corpses then twisted in his fall, landing on his wounded side.

Pain flared, stunning him.

'*No*,' Hedge moaned, pushing past Koryk who turned with a chagrined expression on his face.

'Damn you, Koryk,' Fiddler started.

'No,' said Quick Ben, 'You don't understand, Fid.'

Koryk shrugged. 'Sorry, Sergeant. Habit.'

Fiddler watched the wizard follow Hedge over to where the three bodies were lying on the sand. But the sapper was paying no attention to the skewered Letherii, instead landing hard on his knees beside one of the Tiste Edur.

'See the coins on that one?' Cuttle asked. 'Burned right in—'

'That was the Emperor,' said the captain who had brought them here. 'Rhulad Sengar. The other Edur . . . I don't know. But,' he then added, 'your friends do.'

Yes, Fiddler could see that, and it seemed all at once that there was nothing but pain in this place. Trapped in the last breaths, given voice by Hedge's alarmingly uncharacteristic, almost animal cries of grief. Shaken, Fiddler turned to his soldiers. 'Take defensive positions, all of you. Captain, you and the other prisoners over there, by that wall, and don't move if you want to stay alive. Koryk, rest easy with that damned crossbow, all right?'

Fiddler then headed over to his friends.

And almost retreated again when he saw Hedge's face, so raw with anguish, so . . . exposed.

Quick Ben turned and glanced back at Fiddler, a warning of some sort, and then the wizard walked over to the fallen Letherii.

Trembling, confused, Fiddler followed Quick Ben. Stood beside him, looking down at the man.

'He'll live,' he said.

Behind them, Hedge rasped, '*No he won't.*'

That voice did not even sound human. Fiddler turned in alarm, and saw Hedge staring up at Quick Ben, as if silent communication was passing between the two men.

Then Hedge asked, 'Can you do it, Quick? Some place with . . . with eternal torment. Can you do that, wizard? *I asked if you can do that!*'

Quick Ben faced Fiddler, a question in his eyes.

Oh no, Quick, this one isn't for me to say—

'Fiddler, help me decide. Please.'

Gods, even Quick Ben's grieving. Who was *this warrior?* 'You're High Mage, Quick Ben. Do what needs doing.'

The wizard turned back to Hedge. 'Hood owes me, Hedge.'

'What kind of answer is that?'

But Quick Ben turned, gestured, and a dark blur rose round the Letherii, closed entirely about the man's body, then shrank, as if down into the sand, until nothing remained. There was a faint scream as whatever awaited the Letherii had reached out to take hold of him.

Then the wizard snapped out a hand and pulled Fiddler close, and his face was pale with rage. *'Don't you pity him, Fid. You understand me? Don't you pity him!'*

Fiddler shook his head. 'I – I won't, Quick. Not for a moment. Let him scream, for all eternity. Let him scream.'

A grim nod, then Quick Ben pushed him back.

Hedge wept over the Tiste Edur, wept like a man for whom all light in the world has been lost, and would never return.

And Fiddler did not know what to do.

Watching from an unseen place, the Errant stepped back, pulled away as if he would hurl himself from a cliff.

He was what he was.

A tipper of balances.

And now, this day – may the Abyss devour him whole – a maker of widows.

Ascending the beach's gentle slope, Karsa Orlong halted. He reached down to the sword impaling his leg, and closed a hand about the blade itself, just above the hilt. Unmindful of how the notched edges sliced into his flesh, he dragged the weapon free.

Blood bloomed from the puncture wounds, but only for a moment. The leg was growing numb, but he would have use of it for a while yet.

Still holding the cursed sword by its blade, he pushed himself forward, limped onto the sward. And saw, a short distance to his right, a small hut from which smoke gusted out.

The Toblakai warrior headed over.

Coming opposite it, he dropped the iron sword, took another step closer, bent down and pushed one hand under the edge of the hut. With an upward heave, he lifted the entire structure clear, sent it toppling onto its back like an upended turtle.

Smoke billowed, caught the breeze, and was swept away.

Before him, seated cross-legged, was an ancient, bent and broken creature.

A man. A god.

Who looked up with narrowed eyes filled with pain. Then those eyes shifted, to behind Karsa, and the warrior turned.

The spirit of the Emperor had arrived, he saw. Young – younger than Karsa had imagined Rhulad Sengar to be – and, with his clear, unmarred flesh, a man not unhandsome. Lying on the ground as if in gentle sleep.

Then his eyes snapped open and he shrieked.

A short-lived cry.

Rhulad pushed himself onto his side, up onto his hands and knees – and saw, lying close by, his sword.

'Take it!' the Crippled God cried. 'My dear young champion, Rhulad Sengar of the Tiste Edur. Take up your sword!'

'Do not,' Karsa said. 'Your spirit is here – it is all you have, all you are. When I kill it, oblivion will take you.'

'Look at his leg! He is almost as crippled as I am! Take the sword, Rhulad, and cut him down!'

But Rhulad still hesitated, there on his hands and knees, his breaths coming in rapid gasps.

The Crippled God wheezed, coughed, then said in a low, crooning voice, 'You can return, Rhulad. To your world. You can make it right. This time, you can make everything right. Listen to me, Rhulad. Trull is alive! Your brother, he is alive, and he walks to the Eternal Domicile! He walks to find you! Kill this Toblakai and you can return to him, you can say all that needs to be said!

'*Rhulad Sengar, you can ask his forgiveness.*'

At that the Tiste Edur's head lifted. Eyes suddenly alight, making him look . . . *so young*.

And Karsa Orlong felt, in his heart, a moment of regret.

Rhulad Sengar reached for the sword.

And the flint sword swung down, decapitating him.

The head rolled, settled atop the sword. The body pitched sideways, legs kicking spasmodically, then growing still as blood poured from the open neck. In a moment, that blood slowed.

Behind Karsa, the Crippled God hacked laughter, then said, 'I have waited a long time for you, Karsa Orlong. I have worked so hard . . . to bring you to this sword. For it is yours, Toblakai. No other can wield it as you can. No other can withstand its curse, can remain sane, can remain its master. This weapon, my Chosen One, is for you.'

Karsa Orlong faced the Crippled God. 'No-one chooses me. I do not give anyone that right. I am Karsa Orlong of the Teblor. All choices belong to me.'

'Then choose, my friend. Fling away that pathetic thing of stone you carry. Choose the weapon made for you above all others.'

Karsa bared his teeth.

The Crippled God's eyes widened briefly, then he leaned forward, over his brazier of smouldering coals. 'With the sword, Karsa Orlong, you will be immortal.' He waved a gnarled hand and a gate blistered open a few paces away. 'There. Go back to your homeland, Karsa. Proclaim yourself Emperor of the Teblor. Guide your people for ever more. Oh, they are sorely beset. Only you can save them, Karsa Orlong. And with the sword, none can stand before you. You will save them, you will lead them to domination – a campaign of slaughtered "children" such as the world has never seen before. Give answer, Toblakai! Give answer to all the wrongs you and your people have suffered! *Let the children witness!*'

Karsa Orlong stared down at the Crippled God.

And his sneer broadened, a moment, before he turned away.

'*Do not leave it here! It is for you! Karsa Orlong, it is for you!*'

Someone was coming up from the sand. A wide, heavily muscled man, and three black-skinned bhokorala.

Karsa limped to meet them.

Withal felt his heart pounding in his chest. He'd not expected . . . well, he'd not known what to expect, only what was expected *of him*.

'You are not welcome,' said the giant with the tattooed face and the wounded leg.

'I'm not surprised. But here I am anyway.' Withal's eyes flicked to the sword lying in the grass. The Tiste Edur's head was resting on it like a gift. The weaponsmith frowned. 'Poor lad, he never understood—'

'I do,' growled the giant.

Withal looked up at the warrior. Then over to where crouched the Crippled God, before returning once more to his regard of the giant. 'You said no?'

'As much.'

'Good.'

'Will you take it now?'

'I will – to break it on the forge where it was made.' And he pointed to the ramshackle smithy in the distance.

The Crippled God hissed, 'You said it could never be broken, Withal!'

The weaponsmith shrugged. 'We're always saying things like that. Pays the bills.'

A horrid cry was loosed from the Crippled God, ending in strangled hacking coughs.

The giant was studying Withal in return, and he now asked, 'You made this cursed weapon?'

'I did.'

The back-handed slap caught Withal by surprise, sent him flying backward. Thumping hard onto his back, staring up at the spinning blue sky – that suddenly filled with the warrior, looking down.

'Don't do it again.'

And after saying that, the giant moved off.

Blinking in the white sunlight, Withal managed to turn onto his side, and saw the giant walk into a portal of fire, then vanish as the Crippled God screamed again. The portal suddenly disappeared with a snarl.

One of the nachts brought its horrid little face close over Withal, like a cat about to steal his breath. It cooed.

'Yes, yes,' Withal said, pushing it away, 'get the sword. Yes. Break the damned thing.'

The world spun round him and he thought he would be sick. 'Sandalath, love, did you empty the bucket? Sure it was piss but it smelled mostly of beer, didn't it? I coulda drunk it all over again, you see.'

He clambered upward, swayed back and forth briefly, then reached down and, after a few tries, collected the sword.

Off to the smithy. Not many ways of breaking a cursed sword. A weapon even nastier would do it, but in this case there wasn't one. So, back to the old smith's secret. *To break an aspected weapon, bring it home, to the forge where it was born.*

Well, he would do just that, and do it now.

Seeing the three nachts peering up at him, he scowled. 'Go bail out the damned boat – I'm not in the mood to drown fifty sweeps from shore.'

The creatures tumbled over each in their haste to rush back to the beach.

Withal walked to the old smithy, to do what needed doing.

Behind him, the Crippled God bawled to the sky.

A terrible, terrible sound, a god's cry. One he never wanted to hear ever again.

At the forge, Withal found an old hammer, and prepared to undo all that he had done. Although, he realized as he set the sword down on the rust-skinned anvil and studied the blood-splashed blade, that was, in all truth, impossible.

After a moment, the weaponsmith raised the hammer.

Then brought it down.

EPILOGUE

She walked through the shrouds of dusk
And came to repast
At the Gates of Madness.

Where the living gamed with death
And crowed triumphant
At the Gates of Madness.

Where the dead mocked the living
And told tales of futility
At the Gates of Madness.

She came to set down her new child
There on the stained altar
At the Gates of Madness.

'This,' said she, 'is what we must do,
In hope and humility
At the Gates of Madness.'

And the child did cry in the night
To announce bold arrival
At the Gates of Madness.

Have we dreamed this enough now?
Our promise of suffering
At the Gates of Madness?

Will you look down upon its new face
And whisper songs of anguish
At the Gates of Madness?

Taking the sawtoothed key in hand
To let loose a broken future
At the Gates of Madness?

Tell then your tale of futility to the child
All your games with death
At the Gates of Madness.

We who stand here have heard it before
On this the other side
Of the Gates of Madness.

Prayer of Child
The Masked Monks of Cabal

DRAGGING HIS SOUL FROM ITS PLACE OF EXHAUSTION AND HORROR, the sound of a spinning chain awoke Nimander Golit. He stared up at the stained ceiling of his small room, his heart thumping hard in his chest, his body slick with sweat beneath damp blankets.

That sound – it had seemed so real—

And now, with eyes widening, he heard it again.

Spinning, then odd *snaps!* Then spinning once more.

He sat up. The squalid town outside slept, drowned in darkness unrelieved by any moon. And yet . . . the sound was coming from the street directly below.

Nimander rose from the bed, made his way to the door, out into the chilly hallway. Grit and dust beneath his bare feet as he padded down the rickety stairs.

Emerging, he rushed out into the street.

Yes, night's deepest pit, and this was not – could not be – a dream.

The hissing chain and soft clack, close, brought him round. To see another Tiste Andii emerge from the gloom. A stranger. Nimander gasped.

The stranger was twirling a chain from one upraised hand, a chain with rings at each end.

'Hello, Nimander Golit.'

'Who – who are you? How do you know my name?'

'I have come a long way, to this Isle of the Shake – they are our kin, did you know that? I suppose you did – but they can wait, for they are not yet ready and perhaps will never be ready. Not just Andii blood, after all. But Edur. Maybe even Liosan, not to mention human. No matter. Leave Twilight her island . . .' he laughed, 'empire.'

'What do you want?'

'You, Nimander Golit. And your kin. Go now, gather them. It is time for us to leave.'

'What? Where?'

'Are you truly a child?' the stranger snapped in frustration. The rings clicked, the chain spiralled tight about his index finger. 'I am here to lead you home, Nimander. All you spawn of Anomander Rake, the Black-Winged Lord.'

'But where is home?'

'Listen to me! *I am taking you to him!*'

Nimander stared, then stepped back. 'He does not want us—'

'It does not matter what he wants. Nor even what I want! Do you understand yet? *I am her Herald!*'

Her?

All at once Nimander cried out, dropped hard down onto his knees on the cobbles, his hands at his face. 'This – this is not a dream?'

The stranger sneered. 'You can keep your nightmares, Nimander. You can stare down at the blood on your hands for all eternity, for all I care. She was, as you say, insane. And dangerous. I tell you this, I would have left her corpse lying here in the street, this night, if she still lived. So, enough of that.

'Go, bring your kin here. Quickly, Nimander, while Darkness still holds this island.'

And Nimander climbed to his feet, then hobbled into the decrepit tenement.

Her Herald. Oh, Mother Dark, you would summon our father, as you now summon us?

But why?

Oh, it must be. Yes. Our exile – Abyss below – our exile is at an end!

Waiting in the street, Clip spun his chain. A pathetic bunch, if this Nimander was the best among them. Well, they would have to do, for he did not lie when he said the Shake were not yet ready.

That was, in fact, the only truth he had told, on this darkest of nights.

And how did you fare in Letheras, Silchas Ruin? Not well, I'd wager.

You're not your brother. You never were.

Oh, Anomander Rake, we will find you. And you will give answer to us. No, not even a god can blithely walk away, can escape the consequences. Of betrayal.

Yes, we will find you. And we will show you. We will show you just how it feels.

Rud Elalle found his father seated atop a weathered boulder at the edge of the small valley near the village. Climbed up and joined Udinaas, settling onto the sun-warmed stone at his side.

A ranag calf had somehow become separated from its mother, and indeed the entire herd, and now wandered the valley floor, bawling.

'We could feast on that one,' Rud said.

'We could,' Udinaas replied. 'If you have no heart.'

'We must live, and to live we must eat—'

'And to live and eat, we must kill. Yes, yes, Rud, I am aware of all that.'

'How long will you stay?' Rud asked, then his breath caught in his throat. The question had just come out – the one he had been dreading to ask for so long.

Udinaas shot him a surprised look, then returned his attention to the lost calf. 'She grieves,' he said. 'She grieves, so deep in her heart that it reaches out to me – as if the distance was nothing. *Nothing*. This is what comes,' he added without a trace of bitterness, 'of rape.'

Rud decided it was too hard to watch his father's face at this moment, so he swung his gaze down to the distant calf.

'I told Onrack,' Udinaas continued. 'I had to. To just . . . get it out, before it devoured me. Now, well, I regret doing that.'

'You need not. Onrack had no greater friend. It was necessary that he know the truth—'

'No, Rud, that is never *necessary*. Expedient, sometimes. Useful, other times. The rest of the time, it just *wounds*.'

'Father, what will you do?'

'Do? Why, nothing. Not for Seren, not for Onrack. I'm nothing but an ex-slave.' A momentary smile, wry. 'Living with the savages.'

'You are more than just that,' Rud said.

'I am?'

'Yes, you are my father. And so I ask again, how long will you stay?'

'Until you toss me out, I suppose.'

Rud came as close to bursting into tears as he had ever been. His throat closed up, so tight that he could say nothing for a long moment, as the tide of feeling rose within him and only slowly subsided. Through blurred eyes, he watched the calf wander in the valley.

Udinaas resumed as if unmindful of the reaction his words had elicited. 'Not that I can teach you much, Rud. Mending nets, maybe.'

'No, father, you can teach me the most important thing of all.'

Udinaas eyed him askance, sceptical and suspicious.

Three adult ranag appeared on a crest, lumbered down towards the calf. Seeing them, the young beast cried out again, even louder this time, and raced to meet them.

Rud sighed. 'Father, you can teach me your greatest skill. How to *survive*.'

Neither said anything then for some time, and Rud held his eyes on

903

the ranag as they ascended the far side of the valley. In this time, it seemed Udinaas had found something wrong with his eyes, for his hands went to his face again and again. Rud did not turn to observe any of that.

Then, eventually, with the valley empty before them, his father rose. 'Looks like we go hungry after all.'

'Never for long,' Rud replied, also rising.

'No, that's true.'

They made their way back to the village.

His hands stained with paint, Onrack tied the rawhide straps about the bundle, then slung it over a shoulder and faced his wife. 'I must go.'

'So you say,' Kilava replied.

'The journey, to where lies the body of my friend, will ease my spirit.'

'Without doubt.'

'And I must speak to Seren Pedac. I must tell her of her husband, of his life since the time he gave her his sword.'

'Yes.'

'And now,' Onrack said, 'I must go and embrace our son.'

'I will join you.'

Onrack smiled. 'That will embarrass him.'

'No, you damned fool. I said I will join you. If you think you're going anywhere without me, you are mad.'

'Kilava—'

'I have decided. I will let the journey ease your heart, husband. I will not chatter until your ears bleed and like a bhederin you look for the nearest cliff-edge.'

He stared at her with love welling in his eyes. 'Chatter? I have never heard you chatter.'

'You never will, either.'

He nodded. 'This is very well, wife. Join me, then. Help me heal with your presence alone—'

'Be very careful now, Onrack.'

Wisely, he said nothing more.

They went to say goodbye to their son.

'This is exhausting!' Emperor Tehol Beddict said, slumping down onto his throne.

Bugg's face soured as he said, 'Why? You haven't done anything yet.'

'Well, it's only been three weeks. I tell you, my list of reforms is so long I'll never get around to any of them.'

'I applaud your embrace of incompetence,' Bugg said. 'You'll make a fine Emperor.'

'Well,' Brys ventured from where he stood leaning against the wall to the right of the dais, 'there is peace in the land.'

Bugg grimaced. 'Yes, leading one to wonder just how long an entire empire can hold its breath.'

'And if anyone has the answer to that one, dear manservant, it would be you.'

'Oh, now I am amused.'

Tehol smiled. 'We can tell. And now, that wasn't the royal "we". Which we admit we cannot get used to in our fledgling innocence.'

Brys said, 'The Adjunct is on her way, and then there is Shurq Elalle who wants to talk to you about something. Aren't there things that need discussing?' He then waited for a reply, any reply, but instead earned nothing but blank stares from his brother and Bugg.

From a side entrance, the new Chancellor entered in a swirl of gaudy robes. Brys hid his wince. Who would have thought she'd plunge right into bad taste like a grub into an apple?

'Ah,' Tehol said, 'doesn't my Chancellor look lovely this morning?'

Janath's expression remained aloof. 'Chancellors are not supposed to look lovely. Competence and elegance will suffice.'

'No wonder you stand out so in here,' Bugg muttered.

'Besides,' Janath continued, 'such descriptions are better suited to the role of First Concubine, which tells me precisely which brain you're thinking with, beloved husband. Again.'

Tehol held up his hands as if in surrender, then he said in his most reasonable tone – one Brys recognized with faint dismay – 'I still see no reason why you can't be First Concubine as well.'

'I keep telling you,' Bugg said. 'Wife to the Emperor means she's Empress.' He then turned to Janath. 'Giving you three legitimate titles.'

'Don't forget scholar,' Tehol observed, 'which most would hold cancels out all the others. Even wife.'

'Why,' said Bugg, 'now your lessons will never end.'

Another moment of silence, as everyone considered all this.

Then Tehol stirred on his throne. 'There's always Rucket! She'd make a fine First Concubine! Goodness, how the blessings flow over.'

Janath said, 'Careful you don't drown, Tehol.'

'Bugg would never let that happen, sweetness. Oh, since we're discussing important matters before the Adjunct arrives to say goodbye, I was thinking that Preda Varat Taun needs an able Finadd to assist his reconstruction efforts and all that.'

Brys straightened. Finally, they were getting to genuine subjects. 'Who did you have in mind?'

'Why, none other than Ublala Pung!'

Bugg said, 'I'm going for a walk.'

*

Using an iron bar as a lever, Seren Pedac struggled with the heavy pavestones at the entrance to her house. Sweat glistened on her bared arms and her hair had come loose from its ties – she would get it cut short soon. As befitted her life now.

But on this morning, this task remained before her, and she set about it with unrelenting diligence, using her body without regard to the consequences. Prying loose the heavy stones, dragging and pushing them to one side with scraped and bleeding hands.

Once done, she would take a shovel to the underfill, as far down as she could manage.

For the moment, however, the centre stone was defeating her, and she feared she would not have the strength to move it.

'Pardon my intrusion,' said a man's voice, 'but it looks as if you need help.'

She looked up from where she leaned on the bar. Squinted sceptically. 'Not sure you want to risk that, sir,' she said to the old man, and then fell silent. He had a mason's wrists, with large, well-worked hands. She wiped sweat from her brow and frowned down at the pavestone. 'I know, this must look . . . unusual. Where everywhere else in the city people are putting things back, here I am . . .'

The old man approached. 'Not in the least, Acquitor – you were an Acquitor, were you not?'

'Uh, yes. I was. Not any more. I'm Seren Pedac.'

'No, not in the least, then, Seren Pedac.'

She gestured at the centre stone. 'This one defeats me, I'm afraid.'

'Not for long, I suspect, no matter what. You seem very determined.'

She smiled, and was startled by how odd it felt. When had she last smiled – no, she would not think back to that.

'But you should be careful,' the old man continued. 'Here, let me try.'

'Thank you,' she said, stepping back to give him room.

The old man promptly bent the bar.

She stared.

Cursing, he set it aside, then crouched down to dig his fingers into one side of the enormous stone block.

And pulled it into its edge, then, hands going out to the sides, he lifted it with a grunt, pivoted, staggered two steps, and laid it down atop the others. He straightened, brushing dust from his hands. 'Hire a couple of young men to put it back when you're done.'

'How – no, well. But. How do you know I intend to put it back?'

He glanced across at her. 'Do not grieve overlong, Seren Pedac. You are needed. Your life is needed.'

And then he bowed to her and left.

She stared after him.

She needed to go inside now, to collect the stone spear and his sword, to bury the weapons beneath the threshold of her home, her terribly empty home.

Yet still she hesitated.

And the old man suddenly returned. 'I found the Errant,' he said. 'We had much to ... discuss. It is how I learned of you, and of what happened.'

What? Is he addled, then? One of the Errant's new zealots? She made to turn away—

'No, wait! Seren Pedac. You have all there is of him, all that's left. Cherish it, please. Seren Pedac, cherish it. And yourself. Please.'

And, as he walked away, it was as if his words had blessed her in some unaccountable way.

'You have all there is of me, all that's left . . .'

Unconsciously, her hand lifted to settle on her stomach.

Before too long, she would be doing a lot of that.

This ends the seventh tale of the
Malazan Book of the Fallen

GLOSSARY

Acquitor: a sanctioned position as guide/factor when dealing with non-Letherii people
Ahkrata: a Barghast tribe
Andara: temple of the cult of the Black Winged Lord
Arapay: the easternmost tribe of Tiste Edur
Artisan Battalion: a military unit in Lether
Atri-Preda: military commander who governs a city, town or territory
Awl: a town in Lether
Awl'dan: grasslands east of Drene
Barahn: a Barghast tribe
Barghast: pastoral nomadic warrior people
Bast Fulmar: battle site
Beneda: a Tiste Edur tribe
Blue Style Steel: a Letherii steel once used for weapons
Bluerose: a subjugated nation in Lether
Bluerose Battalion: a military unit in Lether
Caladara whip: an Awl weapon
Cabil: an archipelago nation south of Perish
Ceda: a High Mage of the Letherii Empire
Cedance: a chamber of tiles representing the Holds, in Letheras
Crimson Rampant Brigade: a military unit in Lether
Den-Ratha: a Tiste Edur tribe
Docks: coin of Lether
Down Markets: a district in Letheras
Drene: a Lether city east of Bluerose
Emlava: a sabre-toothed cat
Eternal Domicile: seat of Lether Emperor
Faraed: a subjugated people of Lether
Fent: a subjugated people of Lether
Finadd: equivalent of captain in the Letherii military
Froth Wolf: Adjunct Tavore's command ship

Gilani: tribe in Seven Cities
Gilk: a Barghast tribe
Harridict Brigade: a Lether military unit
Hiroth: a Tiste Edur tribe
Ilgres: a Barghast tribe
Jheck: a northern tribe
Just Wars: mythical conflict between the Tiste Liosan and the Forkrul Assail
K'risnan: Tiste Edur sorcerers
Kenryll'ah: demon nobility
Liberty Consign: a loose consortium of businesses in Lether
Lupe fish: a large carnivorous fish of Lether River
Meckros: a seafaring people
Merchants' Battalion: a Lether military unit
Merude: a Tiste Edur tribe
Nerek: a subjugated people of Lether
Nith'rithal: a Barghast tribe
Obsidian Throne: traditional throne of Bluerose
Onyx Wizards: Andii wizards ruling the Andara of Bluerose
Patriotists: Lether Empire's secret police
Pamby Doughty: comic poem
Preda: equivalent of a general or commander in Letherii military
Quillas Canal: a main canal in Letheras
Rat Catchers' Guild: a now outlawed guild in Lether
Refugium: a magical realm surrounded by Omtose Phellack
Rhinazan: a winged lizard
Rise (The): Shake title
Rygtha: Awl crescent axe
Scale House: centre of Rat Catchers' Guild in Letheras
Senan: a Barghast tribe
Settle Lake: a decrepit lake in the centre of Letheras
Second Maiden Fort: a penal island now independent
Shake: a subjugated people in the Lether Empire
Shore (The): religion of the Shake
Sollanta: a Tiste Edur tribe
Thrones of War: Perish ships
Twilight: Shake title
Watch (The): Shake title
Verdith'anath: the Jaghut Bridge of Death
Zorala Snicker: comic poem